ANTHONY TROLLOPE
The Complete Shorter Fiction

ANTHONY TROLLOPE

The Complete Shorter Fiction

Edited by Julian Thompson

Carroll & Graf Publishers, Inc.
New York

First published in Great Britain 1992
First Carroll & Graf Edition 1992

Carroll & Graf Publishers, Inc.
260 Fifth Ave
New York
NY 10001

ISBN 0-88184-854-9

Typeset by Hewer Text Composition Services, Edinburgh

Other Major Works by Anthony Trollope:

The Macdermots of Ballycloran (1847).
The Kellys and the O'Kellys (1848).
La Vendée (1850).
The Warden (1855).
Barchester Towers (1857).
The Three Clerks (1858).
Doctor Thorne (1858).
The Bertrams (1859).
The West Indies and the Spanish Main (1859).
Castle Richmond (1860).
Framley Parsonage (1860).
Orley Farm (1862).
North America (1862).
Rachel Ray (1863).
The Small House at Allington (1864).
Can You Forgive Her? (1864).
Miss Mackenzie (1864).
The Belton Estate (1866).
Nina Balatka (1867).
The Last Chronicle of Barset (1867).
The Claverings (1867).
Linda Tressel (1868).
Phineas Finn (1869).
He Knew He Was Right (1869).
The Vicar of Bullhampton (1870).
The Struggles of Brown, Jones and Robinson (1870).
Sir Harry Hotspur of Humblethwaite (1871).
Ralph the Heir (1871).
The Golden Lion of Granpère (1872).
The Eustace Diamonds (1873).
Australia and New Zealand (1873).
Phineas Redux (1874).
Lady Anna (1874).
Harry Heathcote of Gangoil (1874).
The Way We Live Now (1875).
The Prime Minister (1876).
The American Senator (1877).
South Africa (1878).
Is He Popenjoy? (1878).
An Eye for an Eye (1879).
Thackeray (1879).
John Caldigate (1879).
Cousin Henry (1879).
The Duke's Children (1880).
The Life of Cicero (1880).
Dr Wortle's School (1881).
Ayala's Angel (1881).
Lord Palmerston (1882).
Kept in the Dark (1882).
Marion Fay (1882).
The Fixed Period (1882).
Mr Scarborough's Family (1883).
The Landleaguers (1883).
An Autobiography (1883).
An Old Man's Love (1884).
The Letters of Anthony Trollope, edited by N. John Hall (Stanford, 1983).

CONTENTS

Introduction

TROLLOPE WROTE short stories from 1859 (just before the publication of *Framley Parsonage* in the *Cornhill Magazine* made his name) until the last year of his life, producing them rapidly and apparently without effort—eighteen stories, for instance, between 1859 and 1861. In all, Trollope's 'pile' comprises forty-two stories, the bulk of them assembled into five book-length collections. Nearly all of them remain eminently readable today. They are the work of a craftsman, rarely suggesting that their materials might have been better treated at novel-length, or that their origins lie in otherwise unusable fragments rescued from the novelist's workshop floor. If they are the by-products of Trollope's creative life, they are by no means its waste products. The average quality of the stories is surprisingly high—only the clanking pre-Raphaelite trappings of Trollope's 'fairy-tale', 'The Gentle Euphemia', seem to me to lie beyond critical defence—and the range of themes and subjects treated is considerable.

Trollope explains that each of his first stories is 'intended to be redolent of some different country—but they apply only to localities with which I myself am conversant.'[1] These *Tales of All Countries* (many of them first published in New York) remind us what a 'tireless traveller' Trollope was in his prime. Some of them dramatise the vicissitudes of Victorian tourist-life: the hazard of picking up harridan spinsters whom etiquette will not permit to travel alone ('An Unprotected Female at the Pyramids'); problems with the luggage on Lake Como ('The Man Who Kept His Money in a Box'); an Indian Civil Service widow seduced by a debonair French tailor ('The Château of Prince Polignac'); a would-be Mrs. Leo Hunter coming in for some unexpected Love Among the Artists when she sets up Bohemian open-house in Rome ('Mrs. General Talboys'). There are also plenty of complaints about the ill-maintained and often over-hyped sights the mid-Victorians scrambled to see. In 'The Chateau of Prince Polignac', the celebrated chateau turns out to be no more than a ruined wall and 'an enormous kitchen chimney'; in 'An Unprotected Female', mixed company is obliged to crawl into the dirty, smelly, stuffy interior of a pyramid. Nor are the locals particularly prepossessing: in 'A Ride Across Palestine' the way into the Tomb of the Virgin is blocked by a crowd of 'dirty, fierce-looking, uncouth' orthodox Christians. Throughout these stories there are echoes of Trollope the business-like tourist, who once advised a Post Office colleague: 'Hear the howling dervishes of Cairo at one on Friday. They howl but once a week'[2]; and of Trollope the crusty xenophobe who refused to believe until he got there 'that in these days there should be a living village called Minneapolis by living men.'[3]

Trollope's stories of foreign parts are apt to feature this undertow of grumble and consumer-guide. But they offer much more: canny dramatic meditations on foreign customs and far-off happenings, underpinned by the novelist's solid knowledge of the human heart. Background materials are thoroughly assimilated, and settings squarely convincing, regardless of whether the stories derive from the Trollope family's persistent sorties to continental Europe (his mother and brother settled in Tuscany), one of Anthony's four extended visits to the United States, or his more exotic sojourns in the Middle East, Central America and the Caribbean. Among Trollope's less Anglocentric European narratives (barely a tourist in sight in these), he depicts the Austrian occupation of Venice, the love-life of two Viennese shop-girls, and the eccentricities of an ultramontane Tyrolean landlady who will not put up her prices despite the changing times (one of the sketches of uncompromising Toryism Trollope delighted in throughout his career). The stories with an American setting are just as varied. Here Trollope strays over Jamesian territory to dramatise an array of topics and effects. In two works from the early 1860s Trollope previews James's beloved 'International Theme'. The first of these, 'The Widow's Mite', features a transatlantic marriage; the second, 'Miss Ophelia Gledd', centres upon a breezy Boston sleigh-girl who, like James's Daisy Miller, may or may not 'pass muster' in comparatively strait-laced European society. 'The Two Generals', the tragedy of two brothers who ride away to fight on opposite sides in the American Civil War, matches James's early short stories; whereas the reader of 'The Courtship of Susan Bell', with its institutionally repressed passions, is likely to recall *The Europeans*.

Rich and varied as these records of Trollope's globe-trotting (from Suez to South Island, New Zealand) are, theoretically even more compelling are his stories of literary life. Many of these were written during Trollope's period as editor of *St. Paul's Magazine*, and they deal with what Thackeray termed the 'thorns' in an editor's otherwise cushioned existence. It requires tact and fortitude to deal with madmen ('The Turkish Bath'), pushy thickskinned talentless ladies ('Mrs. Brumby') who won't take 'no' for an answer, and pretty deserving girls with families to support ('Mary Gresley') whose manuscripts are almost equally hopeless. Trollope is in an altogether tougher mood in an earlier tale for *Argosy* magazine, 'The Adventures of Fred Pickering', where an obstinately ambitious (and again talentless) young writer brings himself and his family to the edge of starvation before returning to a steady day-job as an attorney's clerk. The story seems designed to reinforce the passages in *An Autobiography* that emphasise the precariousness of living by one's pen.

Courtship and marriage (Trollope liked to surprise his guests with a tally of the fictional proposals of marriage he had written up) form another staple theme of the short stories. Outwardly crusty relations hiding hearts of gold put temporary obstacles in the way of the juvenile leads in a variety of settings, from Patmore-like Somersetshire mansions to Hawthornian Saratoga Springs, from trim Munich counting-houses to desiccated Spanish Town, Jamaica. Trollope even returns to the 'dear forty-first' county, Barsetshire, to bring off the double wedding of his 'Two Heroines of Plumplington'. Closer to home in a different way, Trollope the ex-Post Office Official returns to St. Martin's Le Grand to investigate the love-lives of the young women at the London Telegraph Office in 'The Telegraph Girl'.

Indeed in some ways Trollope's short stories represent this rather private author's closest approaches to autobiographical fiction. There are wry Wodehousian (or perhaps more accurately Charles Lever-ish) adventures from his earliest days in Ireland, featuring misplaced dancing-pumps ('The O'Conors of Castle Conor') and squeaky-clean bedroom farce (Trollope in bed with a Catholic priest in 'Father Giles of Ballymoy'). In *An Autobiography* Trollope refuses to 'swear to every detail' in these stories, but confesses that 'the main purport' of them 'is true'.[4] From a later period 'John Bull on the Guadalquivir' offers an interesting glimpse of, in Sadleir's words, Trollope 'laughing a little heavily at his own heaviness'.[5] Here the central character (who stands for the author) mistakes a Spanish nobleman for a bullfighter and vulgarly patronises him for what he takes to be his gimcrack attire. But perhaps the most charming and revealing of these 'autobiographical fragments' is 'The Panjandrum', a glimpse of Trollope the would-be novelist as he might have been in his 'Hobbledehoy' days in the Post Office, getting together with a bunch of greenhorn Bohemians to found the 'best' literary magazine 'ever done'. This is a longer story, full of the vaulting ambition and the looking-over-the-shoulder pretentiousness of youth.

Some of the stories are unashamed comic anecdotes which may, like the humour of some of the sub-plots of Trollope's novels, be judged broad and coarse by modern taste, and perhaps brought a blush in Victorian times to the cheek of Mr. Podsnap's 'young person': the hero of 'Relics of General Chassé' is forced to creep home in his long-johns under cover of darkness, when a group of predatory women tourists mistakenly cut up his trousers for souvenirs, while 'A Ride Across Palestine' features a dishy principal 'boy' not all that keen to hide her disguised femininity from a rather obtuse leading man. Other tales show Trollope in more familiar light as an agreeable farceur, for instance the painful domestic slapstick of the misapplied mustard-plaster in 'Christmas at Thompson Hall'. This is one of the more memorable of Trollope's Christmas Stories—like all Victorian novelists, he felt honour bound to supply them occasionally, delivering his copy months in advance, and ringing the changes on the theme of the young man who develops Scrooge-like scruples about the commercialism of the Victorian Christmas, or decides to be unseasonably bad-tempered among the seasonal trimmings, until shown the error of his ways by a bright-eyed fiancée or loving sister. 'Christmas Day at Kirkby Cottage' and 'Not If I Know It' will still pass a few minutes agreeably on Boxing Day afternoon.

But the most memorable of Trollope's short stories are those with a frisson of Gothicism and grimness, much as the most striking character-studies in his novels are often of the psychologically disturbed. Some present lean balladic tragedies, reminiscent of short spare novels such as *Sir Harry Hotspur of Humblethwaite* or *An Eye for an Eye*. 'La Mère Bauche' demonstrates how easily a domineering mother persuades her cagey son to give up the 'charity girl' who loves him. The girl slips away to the summit of a high rock, and at the end of the story the villagers pick up her broken body. 'Returning Home' is almost equally stark. An exiled Englishman who has had enough of his bleak Costa Rican farmstead loses wife and family in a canoeing accident soon after he begins his long trip home. Other stories, though less lugubriously eventful, fix elementary passions in an elemental landscape. 'Aaron Trow' is a gaunt melodrama about an escaped Bermudan convict. 'Malachi's Cove', probably Trollope's best-known short story, is a taut tale of love and selflessness by the angry Cornish Atlantic, where the young and beautiful Mahala Tringlos gathers seaweed to claw a precarious living. The spare vernacular passion and churning ocean winds of 'Malachi's Cove' have put one critic in mind of D.H. Lawrence.[6] Though the average Trollope love-story is more domesticated, its emotional complexities may nevertheless be thrown into relief by the roughness of the chosen setting. Bare Lakeland hills, for instance, frame the scruples of crossgrained Elizabeth Garrow in 'The Mistletoe Bough'. 'The Parson's Daughter of Oxney Colne' is set on the broken edges of Dartmoor—a striking objective correlative for the imposing inner life of its heroine, whose determination to 'succumb forever' to her conventional suitor thoroughly unnerves him before the match is mercifully broken off.

Trollope handles the central situation in 'The Parson's Daughter of Oxney Colne' much as he handles comparable relationships in his great novels (for instance, Adolphus Crosbie's inability to come to terms with Lily Dale's self-contained passion in *The Small House at Allington* (1864)). But at a length of a few thousand words Trollope is denied his habitual elbow-room. Some of the most memorable stories in the present collection seem for this reason 'courageously "unfinished"' (Michael Sadleir's phrase)[7], as they dwindle into agonising ellipses. 'Catherine Carmichael', a bitter study of the solitude of a female heart that seems destined to 'go with the property' in underpopulated New Zealand, teases in this way, as does 'The Journey to Panama'. Here Miss Viner's case-hardened integrity, her powerful but unfocussed hatred of her prospective husband Mr. Gorloch and the mounting impetuosity of the hero Forrest's devotion to her as the voyage draws to its close all deserve more space, and perhaps a sequel, beyond the irresponsible glamour of shipboard romance. But Miss Viner goes her way, and Mr. Forrest his, and the story simply stops—refusing to embellish the bare (if evocative) details of the autobiographical anecdote on which it is based.

This is not to say that Trollope is incapable of cutting short story material to length. Most of the time he does so with notable skill.

Yet he remains a distance-runner among great English writers, and it is no accident, therefore, that one of the most penetrating of his tales should be among his longest (and simplest). This is 'The Spotted Dog', the study of the decline of a feckless freelance author and his alcoholic wife. Here the plot amounts to nothing more than a sequence of vignettes of progressive human dereliction; the setting is nothing more than the interior of a homely London pub. But Trollope has time to get to work on the bitter baffled courage of his anti-hero, and the result is an evocation of vibrant grimness and quiet despair more than a little reminiscent of Gissing.

Trollope is not a great short story writer. The form had not fully evolved—at least in England—in Trollope's hey-day. Occasionally it seems to cramp him. Moreover Trollope's writing, though often highly evocative, lacks the poetic infusion that comes in the mid 1880s with Stevenson and Kipling. And yet Trollope's short stories are fit to be compared with those of the array of great English novelists born between 1810 and 1819. He took the form more seriously than Thackeray, out-produced Mrs. Gaskell and (by a huge margin) George Eliot, and if he failed (even in his best story, 'The Spotted Dog') to rival Dickens's best (perhaps 'The Signal Man'), his average quality of production was higher than Dickens's. Only occasionally does one feel in the presence of a novelist deliberately cramping his hand to work on a smaller canvas. Otherwise Trollope's short stories are lucid, sinewy exercises in their chosen form: professional miniatures, worthy of a place on any bookshelf that features a cross-section of his novels.

Julian Thompson
Brackley 1992

1 Anthony Trollope to W.M. Thackeray, 23 October 1859. See *The Letters of Anthony Trollope*, ed. N. John Hall (Stanford, California: Stanford University Press, 1983), I, p. 89

2 Anthony Trollope to Edmund Yates, 11 March 1858. See *Letters*, I, p. 70.

3 Anthony Trollope, *North America*, ch. 10.

4 Anthony Trollope, *An Autobiography*, ch. 4.

5 Michael Sadleir, *Trollope: A Commentary* (1927; London: Oxford University Press, 1961), p. 185

6 N. John Hall, *Anthony Trollope: A Biography* (Oxford: Oxford University Press, 1991), p. 254.

7 Sadleir, p. 185.

A Note on the Texts

There is no full scholarly edition of Trollope's writings, but the Trollope Society of London hopes to have all the novels and short stories back in print by 2000. The present collection includes all the fiction under novella length published by Trollope in his lifetime, with the exception of a brief skit on the plot of *The Small House at Allington* which Trollope dashed off in December 1875 to raise funds for the Massachusetts Infant Asylum. This *jeu d'esprit* is entitled *Never, Never—Never, Never. A Condensed Novel, in Three Volumes, after the Manner of Bret Harte*. It was privately reprinted in 1971, with a preface by Lance O. Tingay. The short story 'Katchen's Caprices', sometimes included in Trollope bibliographies, is now no longer seriously considered to be by him.

In this collection the stories are arranged, as far as can be established, in order of composition; failing that, in order of first publication. The texts are reproduced from the first edition in book form, except in the case of the uncollected stories, where the original magazine text has been used.

Most of the stories made their first appearance in periodicals, Trollope later gathering them into one or other of five omnibus collections (an account of the publishing history of each story is given in its headnote). Stories which remained uncollected are as follows:

'The Gentle Euphemia.'
'Christmas Day at Kirkby Cottage.'
'Catherine Carmichael.'
'Not If I Know It.'
'The Two Heroines of Plumplington.'

Relics of General Chassé, A Tale of Antwerp

Originally appeared in *Harper's New Monthly Magazine*, February 1860. Reprinted in *Tales of All Countries* [First Series] (1861). Written and submitted to Fletcher Harper in July 1859. Trollope is fond of portraying glossy complacent Prebendaries like the Rev. Augustus Horne. Compare Rev. Mark Robarts in *Framley Parsonage* and Rev. Henry Fitzackerlay Chamberlaine in *The Vicar of Bullhampton*.

THAT BELGIUM is now one of the European kingdoms, living by its own laws, resting on its own bottom, with a king and court, palaces and parliament of its own, is known to all the world. And a very nice little kingdom it is; full of old towns, fine Flemish pictures, and interesting Gothic churches. But in the memory of very many of us who do not think ourselves old men, Belgium, as it is now called—in those days it used to be Flanders and Brabant—was a part of Holland; and it obtained its own independence by a revolution. In that revolution the most important military step was the siege of Antwerp, which was defended on the part of the Dutch by General Chassé, with the utmost gallantry, but nevertheless ineffectually.

After the siege Antwerp became quite a show place; and among the visitors who flocked there to talk of the gallant general, and to see what remained of the great effort which he had made to defend the place, were two Englishmen. One was the hero of this little history; and the other was a young man of considerably less weight in the world. The less I say of the latter the better; but it is necessary that I should give some description of the former.

The Rev. Augustus Horne was, at the time of my narrative, a beneficed clergyman of the Church of England. The profession which he had graced sat easily on him. Its external marks and signs were as pleasing to his friends as were its internal comforts to himself. He was a man of much quiet mirth, full of polished wit, and on some rare occasions he could descend to the more noisy hilarity of a joke. Loved by his friends he loved all the world. He had known no care and seen no sorrow. Always intended for holy orders he had entered them without a scruple, and remained within their pale without a regret. At twenty-four he had been a deacon, at twenty-seven a priest, at thirty a rector, and at thirty-five a prebendary; and as his rectory was rich and his prebendal stall well paid, the Rev. Augustus Horne was called by all, and called himself, a happy man. His stature was about six feet two, and his corpulence exceeded even those bounds which symmetry would have preferred as being most perfectly compatible even with such a height. But nevertheless Mr. Horne was a well-made man; his hands and feet were small; his face was handsome, frank, and full of expression; his bright eyes twinkled with humour; his finely-cut mouth disclosed two marvellous rows of well-preserved ivory; and his slightly aquiline nose was just such a projection as one would wish to see on the face of a well-fed, good-natured dignitary of the Church of England. When I add to all this that the reverend gentleman was as generous as he was rich—and the kind mother in whose arms he had been nurtured had taken care that he should never want—I need hardly say that I was blessed with a very pleasant travelling companion.

I must mention one more interesting particular. Mr. Horne was rather inclined to dandyism, in an innocent way. His clerical starched neckcloth was always of the whitest, his cambric handkerchief of the finest, his bands adorned with the broadest border; his sable suit never degenerated to a rusty brown; it not only gave on all occasions glossy evidence of freshness, but also of the talent which the artisan had displayed in turning out a well-dressed clergyman of the Church of England. His hair was ever brushed with scrupulous attention, and showed in its regular waves the guardian care of each separate bristle. And all this was done with that ease and grace which should be the characteristics of a dignitary of the established English Church.

I had accompanied Mr. Horne to the Rhine; and we had reached Brussels on our return, just at the close of that revolution which ended in affording a throne to the son-in-law of George the Fourth. At that moment General Chassé's name and fame were in every man's mouth, and, like other curious admirers of the brave, Mr. Horne determined to devote two days to the scene of the late events at Antwerp. Antwerp, moreover, possesses perhaps the finest spire, and certainly one of the three or four finest pictures, in the world. Of General Chassé, of the cathedral, and of the Rubens, I had heard much, and was therefore well pleased that such should be his resolution. This accomplished we were to return to Brussels; and thence, *viâ* Ghent, Ostend, and Dover, I to complete my legal studies in London, and Mr. Horne to enjoy once more the peaceful retirement of Ollerton rectory. As we were to be absent from Brussels but one night we were enabled to indulge in the gratification of travelling without our luggage. A small *sac-de-nuit* was prepared; brushes, combs, razors, strops, a change of linen, etc., etc., were carefully put up; but our heavy baggage, our coats, waistcoats, and other wearing apparel were unnecessary. It was delightful to feel oneself so light-handed. The reverend gentleman, with my humble self by his side, left the portal of the Hôtel de Belle Vue at 7 A. M., in good humour with all the world. There were no railroads in those days; but a cabriolet, big enough to hold six persons, with rope traces and corresponding appendages, deposited us at the Golden Fleece in something less than six hours. The inward man was duly fortified, and we started for the castle.

It boots not here to describe the effects which gunpowder and grape-shot had had on the walls of Antwerp. Let the curious in these matters read the horrors of the siege of Troy, or the history of Jerusalem taken by Titus. The one may be found in Homer, and the other in Josephus. Or if they prefer doings of a later date there is the taking of Sebastopol, as narrated in the columns of the *Times* newspaper. The accounts are equally true, instructive, and intelligible. In the mean time allow the Rev. Augustus Horne and myself to enter the private chambers of the renowned though defeated general.

We rambled for a while through the covered way, over the glacis and along the counterscarp, and listened to the guide as he detailed to us, in already accustomed words, how the siege had gone. Then we got into the private apartments of the general, and, having dexterously shaken off our attendant, wandered at large among the deserted rooms.

"It is clear that no one ever comes here," said I.

"No," said the Rev. Augustus; "it seems not: and to tell the truth, I don't know why any one should come. The chambers in themselves are not attractive."

What he said was true. They were plain, ugly, square, unfurnished rooms, here a big one and there a little one, as is usual in most houses;—unfurnished, that is, for the most part. In one place we did find a table and a few chairs, in another a bedstead, and so on. But to me it was pleasant to indulge in those ruminations which any traces of the great or unfortunate create in softly sympathizing minds. For a time we communicated our thoughts to each other as we roamed free as air through the apartments; and then I lingered for a few moments behind, while Mr. Horne moved on with a quicker step.

At last I entered the bedchamber of the general, and there I overtook my friend. He was inspecting, with much attention, an article of the great man's wardrobe which he held in his hand. It was precisely that virile habiliment to which a well-known gallant captain alludes in his conversation with the posthumous appearance of Miss Bailey, as containing a Bank of England 5*l.* note.

"The general must have been a large man, George, or he would hardly have filled these," said Mr. Horne, holding up to the light the respectable leathern articles in question. "He must have been a very large man,—the largest man in Antwerp, I should think; or else his tailor has done him more than justice."

They were certainly large, and had about them a charming regimental military appearance. They were made of white leather, with bright metal buttons at the knees and bright metal buttons at the top. They owned no pockets, and were, with the exception of the legitimate outlet, continuous in the circumference of the waistband. No dangling strings gave them an appearance of senile imbecility. Were it not for a certain rigidity, sternness, and mental inflexibility,—we will call it military ardour,—with which they were imbued, they would have created envy in the bosom of a fox-hunter.

Mr. Horne was no fox-hunter, but still he seemed to be irresistibly taken with the lady-like propensity of wishing to wear them. "Surely, George," he said, "the general must have been a stouter man than I am"—and he contemplated his own proportions with complacency—"these what's-the-names are quite big enough for me."

I differed in opinion, and was obliged to explain that I thought he did the good living of Ollerton insufficient justice.

"I am sure they are large enough for me," he repeated, with considerable obstinacy. I smiled incredulously; and then to settle the matter he resolved that he would try them on. Nobody had been in these rooms for the last hour, and it appeared as though they were never visited. Even the guide had not come on with us, but was employed in showing other parties about the fortifications. It was clear that this portion of the building was left desolate, and that the experiment might be safely made. So the sportive rector declared that he would for a short time wear the regimentals which had once contained the valorous heart of General Chassé.

With all decorum the Rev. Mr. Horne divested himself of the work of the London artist's needle, and, carefully placing his own garments beyond the reach of dust, essayed to fit himself in military garb.

At that important moment—at the critical instant of the attempt—the clatter of female voices was heard approaching the chamber. They must have suddenly come round some passage corner, for it was evident by the sound that they were close upon us before we had any warning of their advent. At this very minute Mr. Horne was somewhat embarrassed in his attempts, and was not fully in possession of his usual active powers of movement, nor of his usual presence of mind. He only looked for escape; and seeing a door partly open he with difficulty retreated through it, and I followed him. We found that we were in a small dressing-room; and as by good luck the door was defended by an inner bolt, my friend was able to protect himself.

"There shall be another siege, at any rate as stout as the last, before I surrender," said he.

As the ladies seemed inclined to linger in the room it became a matter of importance that the above-named articles should fit, not only for ornament but for use. It was very cold, and Mr. Horne was altogether unused to move in a Highland sphere of life. But alas, alas! General Chassé had not been nurtured in the classical retirement of Ollerton. The ungiving leather would stretch no point to accommodate the divine, though it had been willing to minister to the convenience of the soldier. Mr. Horne was vexed and chilled; and throwing the now hateful garments into a corner, and protecting himself from the cold as best he might by standing with his knees together and his body somewhat bent so as to give the skirts of his coat an opportunity of doing extra duty, he begged me to see if those jabbering females were not going to leave him in peace to recover his own property. I accordingly went to the door, and opening it to a small extent I peeped through.

Who shall describe my horror at the sight which I then saw? The scene, which had hitherto been tinted with comic effect, was now becoming so decidedly tragic that I did not dare at once to acquaint my worthy pastor with that which was occurring,—and, alas! had already occurred.

Five country-women of our own—it was easy to know them by their dress and general aspect—were standing in the middle of the room; and one of them, the centre of the group, the senior harpy of the lot, a maiden lady—I could have sworn to that—with a red nose, held in one hand a huge pair of scissors and in the other—the already devoted goods of my most unfortunate companion! Down from the waistband, through that goodly expanse, a fell gash had already gone through and through; and in useless, unbecoming disorder the broadcloth fell pendant from her arm on this side and on that. At that moment I confess that I had not the courage to speak to Mr. Horne,—not even to look at him.

I must describe that group. Of the figure next to me I could only see the back. It was a broad back done up in black silk not of the newest. The whole figure, one may say, was dumpy. The black silk was not long, as dresses now are worn, nor wide in its skirts. In every way it was skimpy, considering the breadth it had to cover; and below the silk I saw the heels of two thick shoes, and enough to swear by of two woollen stockings. Above the silk was a red-and-blue shawl; and above that a ponderous, elaborate brown bonnet, as to the materials of which I should not wish to undergo an examination. Over and beyond this I could only see the backs of her two hands. They were held up as though in wonder at that which the red-nosed holder of the scissors had dared to do.

Opposite to this lady, and with her face fully turned to me, was a kindly-looking, fat motherly woman, with light-coloured hair, not in the best order. She was hot and scarlet with exercise, being perhaps too stout for the steep steps of the fortress; and in one hand she held a handkerchief, with which from time to time she wiped her brow. In the other hand she held one of the extremities of my friend's property, feeling—good, careful soul!—what was the texture of the cloth. As she did so, I could see a glance of approbation pass across her warm features. I liked that lady's face, in spite of her untidy hair, and felt that had she been alone my friend would not have been injured.

On either side of her there stood a flaxen-haired maiden, with long curls, large blue eyes, fresh red cheeks, an undefined lumpy nose, and large good-humoured mouth. They were as like as two peas, only that one was half an inch taller than the other; and there was no difficulty in discovering, at a moment's glance, that they were the children of that overheated matron who was feeling the web of my friend's cloth.

But the principal figure was she who held the centre place in the group. She was tall and thin, with fierce-looking eyes, rendered more fierce by the spectacles which she wore; with a red nose as I said before; and about her an undescribable something which quite convinced me that she had never known—could never know—aught of the comforts of married life. It was she who held the scissors and the black garments. It was she who had given that unkind cut. As I looked at her she whisked herself quickly round from one companion to the other, triumphing in what she had done, and ready to triumph further in what she was about to do. I immediately conceived a deep hatred for that Queen of the Harpies.

"Well, I suppose they can't be wanted again," said the mother, rubbing her forehead.

"Oh dear no!" said she of the red nose. "They are relics!"

I thought to leap forth; but for what purpose should I have leaped? The accursed scissors had already done their work; and the symmetry, nay, even the utility of the vestment was destroyed.

"General Chassé wore a very good article;—I will say that for him," continued the mother.

"Of course he did!" said the Queen Harpy. "Why should he not, seeing that the country paid for it for him? Well, ladies, who's for having a bit?"

"Oh my! you won't go for to cut them up," said the stout back.

"Won't I?" said the scissors; and she immediately made another incision. "Who's for having a bit? Don't all speak at once."

"I should like a morsel for a pincushion," said flaxen haired Miss No. 1, a young lady about nineteen, actuated by a general affection for all sword-bearing, fire-eating heroes. "I should like to have something to make me think of the poor general!"

Snip, snip went the scissors with professional rapidity, and a round piece was extracted from the back of the calf of the left leg. I shuddered with horror; and so did the Rev. Augustus Horne with cold.

"I hardly think it's proper to cut them up," said Miss No. 2.

"Oh isn't it?" said the harpy. "Then I'll do what's improper!" And she got her finger and thumb well through the holes in the scissors' handles. As she spoke resolution was plainly marked on her brow.

"Well; if they are to be cut up, I should certainly like a bit for a pen-wiper," said No. 2. No. 2 was a literary young lady with a periodical correspondence, a journal, and an album. Snip, snip went the scissors again, and the broad part of the upper right division afforded ample materials for a pen-wiper.

Then the lady with the back, seeing that the desecration of the article had been completed, plucked up heart of courage and put in her little request: "I think I might have a needle-case out of it," said she, "just as a *suvneer* of the poor general"—and a long fragment cut rapidly out of the waistband afforded her unqualified delight.

Mamma, with the hot face and untidy hair, came next. "Well, girls," she said, "as you are all served, I don't see why I'm to be left out. Perhaps, Miss Grogram"—she was an old maid, you see—"perhaps, Miss Grogram, you could get me as much as would make a decent-sized reticule."

There was not the slightest difficulty in doing this. The harpy in the centre again went to work, snip, snip, and extracting from that portion of the affairs which usually sustained the greater portion of Mr. Horne's weight two large round pieces of cloth, presented them to the well-pleased matron. "The general knew well where to get a bit of good broadcloth, certainly," said she, again feeling the pieces.

"And now for No. 1," said she whom I so absolutely hated; "I think there is still enough for a pair of slippers. There's nothing so nice for the house as good black cloth slippers that are warm to the feet and don't show the dirt." And so saying, she spread out on the floor the lacerated remainders.

"There's a nice bit there," said young lady No. 2, poking at one of the pockets with the end of her parasol.

"Yes," said the harpy, contemplating her plunder. "But I'm thinking whether I couldn't get leggings as well. I always wear leggings in the thick of the winter." And so she concluded her operations, and there was nothing left but a melancholy skeleton of seams and buttons.

All this having been achieved, they pocketed their plunder and prepared to depart. There are people who have a wonderful appetite for relics. A stone with which Washington had broken a window when a boy—with which he had done so or had not, for there is little difference; a button that was on a coat of Napoleon's, or on that of one of his lackeys; a bullet said to have been picked up at Waterloo or Bunker's Hill; these, and suchlike things are great treasures. And their most desirable characteristic is the ease with which they are attained.

Any bullet or any button does the work. Faith alone is necessary. And now these ladies had made themselves happy and glorious with "Relics" of General Chassé cut from the ill-used habiliments of an elderly English gentleman!

They departed at last, and Mr. Horne, for once in an ill humour, followed me into the bedroom. Here I must be excused if I draw a veil over his manly sorrow at discovering what fate had done for him. Remember what was his position, unclothed in the castle of Antwerp! The nearest suitable change for those which had been destroyed was locked up in his portmanteau at the Hôtel de Belle Vue in Brussels! He had nothing left to him—literally nothing, in that Antwerp world. There was no other wretched being wandering then in that Dutch town so utterly denuded of the goods of life. For what is a man fit,—for what can he be fit,—when left in such a position? There are some evils which seem utterly to crush a man; and if there be any misfortune to which a man may be allowed to succumb without imputation on his manliness, surely it is such as this. How was Mr. Horne to return to his hotel without incurring the displeasure of the municipality? That was my first thought.

He had a cloak, but it was at the inn; and I found that my friend was oppressed with a great horror at the idea of being left alone; so that I could not go in search of it. There is an old saying, that no man is a hero to his *valet de chambre*,—the reason doubtless being this, that it is customary for his valet to see the hero divested of those trappings in which so much of the heroic consists. Who reverences a clergyman without his gown, or a warrior without his sword and sabre-tasche? What would even Minerva be without her helmet?

I do not wish it to be understood that I no longer reverenced Mr. Horne because he was in an undress; but he himself certainly lost much of his composed, well-sustained dignity of demeanour. He was fearful and querulous, cold, and rather cross. When, forgetting his size, I offered him my own he thought that I was laughing at him. He began to be afraid that the story would get abroad, and he then and there exacted a promise that I would never tell it during his lifetime. I have kept my word; but now my old friend has been gathered to his fathers, full of years.

At last I got him to the hotel. It was long before he would leave the castle, cloaked thought he was;—not, indeed, till the shades of evening had dimmed the outlines of men and things, and made indistinct the outward garniture of those who passed to and fro in the streets. Then, wrapped in his cloak, Mr. Horne followed me along the quays and through the narrowest of the streets; and at length, without venturing to return the gaze of any one in the hotel court, he made his way up to his own bedroom.

Dinnerless and supperless he went to his couch. But when there he did consent to receive some consolation in the shape of mutton cutlets and fried potatoes, a savory omelet, and a bottle of claret. The mutton cutlets and fried potatoes at the Golden Fleece at Antwerp are—or were then, for I am speaking now of wellnigh thirty years since—remarkably good; the claret, also, was of the best; and so, by degrees, the look of despairing dismay passed from his face, and some scintillations of the old fire returned to his eyes.

"I wonder whether they find themselves much happier for what they have got?" said he.

"A great deal happier," said I. "They'll boast of those things to all their friends at home, and we shall doubtless see some account of their success in the newspapers."

"It would be delightful to expose their blunder,—to show them up. Would it not, George? To turn the tables on them?"

"Yes," said I, "I should like to have the laugh against them."

"So would I, only that I should compromise myself by telling the story. It wouldn't do at all to have it told at Oxford with my name attached to it."

To this also I assented. To what would I not have assented in my anxiety to make him happy after his misery?

But all was not over yet. He was in bed now, but it was necessary that he should rise again on the morrow. At home, in England, what was required might perhaps have been made during the night; but here, among the slow Flemings, any such exertion would have been impossible. Mr. Horne, moreover, had no desire to be troubled in his retirement by a tailor.

Now the landlord of the Golden Fleece was a very stout man,—a very stout man indeed. Looking at him as he stood with his hands in his pockets at the portal of his own establishment, I could not but think that he was stouter even than Mr. Horne. But then he was certainly much shorter, and the want of due proportion probably added to his unwieldy appearance. I walked round him once or twice wishfully, measuring him in my eye, and thinking of what texture might be the Sunday best of such a man. The clothes which he then had on were certainly not exactly suited to Mr. Horne's tastes.

He saw that I was observing him, and appeared uneasy and offended. I had already ascertained that he spoke a little English. Of Flemish I knew literally nothing, and in French, with which probably he was also acquainted, I was by no means voluble. The business which I had to transact was intricate, and I required the use of my mother-tongue.

It was intricate and delicate, and difficult withal. I began by remarking on the weather, but he did not take my remarks kindly. I am inclined to fancy that he thought I was desirous of borrowing money from him. At any rate he gave me no encouragement in my first advances.

"Vat misfortune?" at last he asked, when I had succeeded in making him understand that a gentleman up stairs required his assistance.

"He has lost these things," and I took hold of my own garments. "It's a long story, or I'd tell you how; but he has not a pair in the world till he gets back to Brussels,—unless you can lend him one."

"Lost hees br— ?" and he opened his eyes wide, and looked at me with astonishment.

"Yes, yes, exactly so," said I, interrupting him. "Most astonishing thing, isn't it? But it's quite true."

"Vas hees money in de pocket?" asked my suspicious landlord.

"No, no, no. It's not so bad as that. His money is all right. I had the money, luckily."

"Ah! dat is better. But he have lost hees b— ?"

"Yes, yes;" I was now getting rather impatient. "There is no mistake about it. He has lost them as sure as you stand there." And then I proceeded to explain that as the gentleman in question was very stout, and as he, the landlord, was stout also, he might assist us in this great calamity by a loan from his own wardrobe.

When he found that the money was not in the pocket, and that his bill therefore would be paid, he was not indisposed to be gracious. He would, he said, desire his servant to take up what was required to Mr. Horne's chamber. I endeavoured to make him understand that a sombre colour would be preferable; but he only answered that he would put the best that he had at the gentleman's disposal. He could not think of offering anything less than his best on such an occasion. And then he turned his back and went his way, muttering as he went something in Flemish, which I believed to be an exclamation of astonishment that any man should, under any circumstances, lose such an article.

It was now getting late; so when I had taken a short stroll by myself, I went to bed without disturbing Mr. Horne again that night. On the following morning I thought it best not to go to him unless he sent for me; so I desired the boots to let him know that I had ordered breakfast in a private room, and that I would await him there unless he wished to see me. He sent me word back to say that he would be with me very shortly.

He did not keep me waiting above half an hour, but I confess that that half-hour was not pleasantly spent. I feared that his temper would be tried in dressing, and that he would not able to eat his breakfast in a happy state of mind. So that when I heard his heavy footstep advancing along the passage my heart did misgive me, and I felt that I was trembling.

That step was certainly slower and more ponderous than usual. There was always a certain dignity in the very sound of his movements, but now this seemed to have been enhanced. To judge merely by the step one would have said that a bishop was coming that way instead of a prebendary.

And then he entered. In the upper half of his august person no alteration was perceptible. The hair was as regular and as graceful as ever, the handkerchief as white, the coat as immaculate; but below his well-filled waistcoat a pair of red plush began to shine in unmitigated splendour, and continued from thence down to within an inch above his knee; nor, as it appeared, could any pulling induce them to descend lower. Mr. Horne always wore black silk stockings,—at least so the world supposed,—but it was now apparent that the world had been wrong in presuming him to be guilty of such extravagance. Those, at any rate, which he exhibited on the present occasion were more economical. They were silk to the calf, but thence upwards they continued their career in white cotton. These then followed the plush; first two snowy, full-sized pillars of white, and then two jet columns of flossy silk. Such was the appearance, on that well-remembered morning, of the Reverend Augustus Horne, as he entered the room in which his breakfast was prepared.

I could see at a glance that a dark frown contracted his eyebrows, and that the compressed muscles of his upper lip gave a strange degree of austerity to his open face. He carried his head proudly on high, determined to be dignified in spite of his misfortunes, and advanced two steps into the room without a remark, as though he were able to show that neither red plush nor black cloth could disarrange the equal poise of his mighty mind!

And after all what are a man's garments but the outward husks in which the fruit is kept, duly tempered from the wind?

"The rank is but the guinea stamp,
The man's the gowd for a' that."

And is not the tailor's art as little worthy, as insignificant as that of the king who makes

"A marquis, duke and a' that?"

Who would be content to think that his manly dignity depended on his coat and waistcoat, or his hold on the world's esteem on any other garment of usual wear? That no such weakness soiled his mind Mr. Horne was determined to prove; and thus he entered the room with measured tread, and stern dignified demeanour.

Having advanced two steps his eye caught mine. I do not know whether he was moved by some unconscious smile on my part;—for in truth I endeavoured to seem as indifferent as himself to the nature of his dress;—or whether he was invincibly tickled by some inward fancy of his own, but suddenly his advancing step ceased, a broad flash of comic humour spread itself over his features, he retreated with his back against the wall, and then burst out into an immoderate roar of loud laughter.

And I—what else could I then do but laugh? He laughed, and I laughed. He roared, and I roared. He lifted up his vast legs to view till the rays of the morning sun shone through the window on the bright hues which he displayed; and he did not sit down to his breakfast till he had in every fantastic attitude shown off to the best advantage the red plush of which he had so recently become proud.

An Antwerp private cabriolet on that day reached the yard of the Hôtel de Belle Vue at about 4 P.M., and four waiters, in a frenzy of astonishment, saw the Reverend Augustus Horne descend from the vehicle and seek his chamber dressed in the garments which I have described. But I am inclined to think that he never again favoured any of his friends with such a sight.

It was on the next evening after this that I went out to drink tea with two maiden ladies, relatives of mine, who kept a seminary for English girls at Brussels. The Misses Macmanus were very worthy women, and earned their bread in an upright, painstaking manner. I would not for worlds have passed through Brussels without paying them this compliment. They were, however, perhaps a little dull, and I was aware that I should not probably meet in their drawing-room many of the fashionable inhabitants of the city. Mr. Horne had declined to accompany me; but in doing so he was good enough to express a warm admiration for the character of my worthy cousins.

The elder Miss Macmanus, in her little note, had informed me that she would have the pleasure of introducing me to a few of my "compatriots." I presumed she meant Englishmen; and as I was in the habit of meeting such every day of my life at home, I cannot say that I was peculiarly elevated by the promise. When, however, I entered the room, there was no Englishman there;—there was no man of any kind. There were twelve ladies collected together with the view of making the evening pass agreeably to me, the single virile being among them all. I felt as though I were a sort of Mohammed in Paradise; but I certainly felt also that the Paradise was none of my own choosing.

In the centre of the amphitheatre which the ladies formed sat the two Misses Macmanus;—there, at least, they sat when they had completed the process of shaking hands with me. To the left of them, making one wing of the semicircle, were arranged the five pupils by attending to whom the Misses Macmanus earned their living; and the other wing consisted of the five ladies who had furnished themselves with relics of General Chassé. They were my "compatriots."

I was introduced to them all, one after the other; but their names did not abide in my memory one moment. I was thinking too much of the singularity of the adventure, and could not attend to such minutiæ. That the red-nosed harpy was Miss Grogram, that I remembered;—that, I may say, I shall never forget. But whether the motherly lady with the somewhat blowsy hair was Mrs. Jones or Mrs. Green, or Mrs. Walker, I cannot now say. The dumpy female with the broad back was always called Aunt Sally by the young ladies.

Too much sugar spoils one's tea; I think I have heard that even prosperity will cloy when it comes in overdoses; and a schoolboy has been known to be overdone with jam. I myself have always been peculiarly attached to ladies' society, and have avoided bachelor parties as things execrable in their very nature. But on this special occasion I felt myself to be that schoolboy;—I was literally overdone with jam. My tea was all sugar, so that I could not drink it. I was one among twelve. What could I do or say? The proportion of alloy was too small to have any effect in changing the nature of the virgin silver, and the conversation became absolutely feminine.

I must confess also that my previous experience as to these compatriots of mine had not prejudiced me in their favour. I regarded them with,—I am ashamed to say so, seeing that they were ladies,—but almost with loathing. When last I had seen them their occupation had reminded me of some obscene feast of harpies, or almost of ghouls. They had brought down to the verge of desperation the man whom of all men I most venerated. On these accounts I was inclined to be taciturn with reference to them;—and then what could I have to say to the Misses Macmanus's five pupils?

My cousin at first made an effort or two in my favour, but these efforts were fruitless. I soon died away into utter unrecognized insignificance, and the conversation, as I have before said, became feminine. And indeed that horrid Miss Grogram, who was, as it were, the princess of the ghouls, nearly monopolized the whole of it. Mamma Jones—we will call her Jones for the occasion—put in a word now and then, as did also the elder and more energetic Miss Macmanus. The dumpy lady with the broad back ate tea-cake incessantly; the two daughters looked scornful, as though they were above their company with reference to the five pupils; and the five pupils themselves sat in a row with the utmost propriety, each with her hands crossed on her lap before her.

Of what they were talking at last I became utterly oblivious. They had ignored me, going into realms of muslin, questions of maid-servants, female rights, and cheap under-clothing; and I therefore had ignored them. My mind had gone back to Mr. Horne and his garments. While they spoke of their rights, I was thinking of his wrongs; when they mentioned the price of flannel I thought of that of broadcloth.

But of a sudden my attention was arrested. Miss Macmanus had said something of the black silks of Antwerp, when Miss Grogram replied that she had just returned from that city and had there enjoyed a great success. My cousin had again asked something about the black silks, thinking, no doubt, that Miss Grogram had achieved some bargain; but that lady had soon undeceived her.

"Oh no," said Miss Grogram, "it was at the castle. We got such beautiful relics of General Chassé! Didn't we, Mrs. Jones?"

"Indeed we did," said Mrs. Jones, bringing out from beneath the skirts of her dress and ostensibly displaying a large black bag.

"And I've got such a beautiful needle-case," said the broad-back, displaying her prize. "I've been making it up all the morning." And she handed over the article to Miss Macmanus.

"And only look at this duck of a pen-wiper," simpered flaxen-hair No. 2. "Only think of wiping one's pens with relics of General Chassé!" and she handed it over to the other Miss Macmanus.

"And mine's a pin-cushion," said No. 1, exhibiting the trophy.

"But that's nothing to what I've got," said Miss Grogram. "In the first place, there's a pair of slippers,—a beautiful pair;—they're not made up yet, of course; and then— "

The two Misses Macmanus and their five pupils were sitting open-eared, open-eyed, and open-mouthed. How all these sombre-looking articles could be relics of General Chassé did not at first appear clear to them.

"What are they, Miss Grogram?" said the elder Miss Macmanus, holding the needle-case in one hand and Mrs. Jones's bag in the other. Miss Macmanus was a strong-minded female, and I reverenced my cousin when I saw the decided way in which she intended to put down the greedy arrogance of Miss Grogram.

"They are relics."

"But where do they come from, Miss Grogram?"

"Why, from the castle, to be sure;—from General Chassé's own rooms."

"Did anybody sell them to you?"

"No."

"Or give them to you?"

"Why, no;—at least not exactly give."

"There they were, and she took 'em," said the broad-back.

Oh, what a look Miss Grogram gave her! "Took them! of course I took them. That is, you took them as much as I did. They were things that we found lying about."

"What things?" asked Miss Macmanus, in a peculiarly strong-minded tone.

Miss Grogram seemed to be for a moment silenced. I had been ignored, as I have said, and my existence forgotten; but now I observed that the eyes of the culprits were turned towards me,—the eyes, that is, of four of them. Mrs. Jones looked at me from beneath her fan; the two girls glanced at me furtively, and then their eyes fell to the lowest flounces of their frocks. Miss Grogram turned her spectacles right upon me, and I fancied that she nodded her head at me as a sort of answer to Miss Macmanus. The five pupils opened their mouths and eyes wider; but she of the broad-back was nothing abashed. It would have been nothing to her had there been a dozen gentlemen in the room. "We just found a pair of black—." The whole truth was told in the plainest possible language.

"Oh, Aunt Sally!" "Aunt Sally, how can you?" "Hold your tongue, Aunt Sally!"

"And then Miss Grogram just cut them up with her scissors," continued Aunt Sally, not a whit abashed, "and gave us each a bit, only she took more than half for herself." It was clear to me that there had been some quarrel, some delicious quarrel, between Aunt Sally and Miss Grogram. Through the whole adventure I had rather respected Aunt Sally. "She took more than half for herself," continued Aunt Sally. "She kept all the—."

"Jemima," said the elder Miss Macmanus, interrupting the speaker and addressing her sister, "it is time, I think, for the young ladies to retire. Will you be kind enough to see them to their rooms?" The five pupils thereupon rose from their seats and courtesied. They then left the room in file, the younger Miss Macmanus showing them the way.

"But we haven't done any harm, have we?" asked Mrs. Jones, with some tremulousness in her voice.

"Well, I don't know," said Miss Macmanus. "What I'm thinking of now is this;—to whom, I wonder, did the garments properly belong? Who had been the owner and wearer of them?"

"Why General Chassé, of course," said Miss Grogram.

"They were the general's," repeated the two young ladies; blushing, however, as they alluded to the subject.

"Well, we thought they were the general's, certainly; and a very excellent article they were," said Mrs. Jones.

"Perhaps they were the butler's?" said Aunt Sally. I certainly had not given her credit for so much sarcasm.

"Butler's!" exclaimed Miss Grogram, with a toss of her head.

"Oh! Aunt Sally, Aunt Sally! how can you?" shrieked the two young ladies.

"Oh laws!" ejaculated Mrs. Jones.

"I don't think that they could have belonged to the butler," said Miss Macmanus, with much authority, "seeing that domestics in this country are never clad in garments of that description; so far my own observation enables me to speak with certainty. But it is equally sure that they were never the property of the general lately in command at Antwerp. Generals, when they are in full dress, wear ornamental lace upon their—their regimentals; and when— " So much she said, and something more, which it may be unnecessary that I should repeat; but such were her eloquence and logic that no doubt would have been left on the mind of any impartial hearer. If an argumentative speaker ever proved anything, Miss Macmanus proved that General Chassé had never been the wearer of the article in question.

"But I know very well they were his!" said Miss Grogram, who was not an impartial hearer. "Of course they were; whose else's should they be?"

"I'm sure I hope they were his," said one of the young ladies, almost crying.

"I wish I'd never taken it," said the other.

"Dear, dear, dear!" said Mrs. Jones.

"I'll give you my needle-case, Miss Grogram," said Aunt Sally.

I had sat hitherto silent during the whole scene, meditating how best I might confound the red-nosed harpy. Now, I thought, was the time for me to strike in.

"I really think, ladies, that there has been some mistake," said I.

"There has been no mistake at all, sir!" said Miss Grogram.

"Perhaps not," I answered, very mildly; "very likely not. But some affair of a similar nature was very much talked about in Antwerp yesterday."

"Oh laws!" again ejaculated Mrs. Jones.

"The affair I allude to has been talked about a good deal, certainly," I continued. "But perhaps it may be altogether a different circumstance."

"And what may be the circumstance to which you allude?" asked Miss Macmanus, in the same authoritative tone.

"I dare say it has nothing to do with these ladies," said I; "but an article of dress, of the nature they have described, was cut up in the Castle of Antwerp on the day before yesterday. It belonged to a gentleman who was visiting the place; and I was given to understand that he is determined to punish the people who have wronged him."

"It can't be the same," said Miss Grogram; but I could see that she was trembling.

"Oh laws! what will become of us?" said Mrs. Jones.

"You can all prove that I didn't touch them, and that I warned her not," said Aunt Sally. In the mean time the two young ladies had almost fainted behind their fans.

"But how had it come to pass," asked Miss Macmanus, "that the gentleman had— "

"I know nothing more about it, cousin," said I; "only it does seem that there is an odd coincidence."

Immediately after this I took my leave. I saw that I had avenged my friend, and spread dismay in the hearts of those who had injured him. I had learned in the course of the evening at what hotel the five ladies were staying; and in the course of the next morning I sauntered into the hall, and finding one of the porters alone, asked if they were still there. The man told me that they had started by the earliest diligence. "And," said he, "if you are a friend of theirs, perhaps you will take charge of these things, which they have left behind them?" So saying, he pointed to a table at the back of the hall, on which were lying the black bag, the black needle-case, the black pin-cushion, and the black pen-wiper. There was also a heap of fragments of cloth which I well knew had been intended by Miss Grogram for the comfort of her feet and ankles.

I declined the commission, however. "They were no special friends of mine," I said; and I left all the relics still lying on the little table in the back hall.

"Upon the whole, I am satisfied!" said the Rev. Augustus Horne, when I told him the finale of the story.

The Courtship of Susan Bell

Originally appeared in *Harper's New Monthly Magazine*, August 1860. Reprinted in *Tales of All Countries* [First Series] (1861). Written and submitted to Fletcher Harper in July 1859. Trollope had visited Albany on his way to Niagara at the end of his first transatlantic visit (June 1859), and Saratoga Springs on his way back from Niagara to New York to take ship for Liverpool. On the crossing home he became good friends with an American widow, Mrs. Harriet Knower, and her 20-year-old daughter Mary. In *Trollope: A Biography* (1991) N. John Hall writes, 'It seems likely that Mary was the original for the heroine, the daughter of a widow in Albany, New York (the Knowers were an old Albany family), in . . . "The Courtship of Susan Bell"'. In their *Guide to Trollope* (1948), Gerould and Gerould note similarities of characterisation with *Rachel Ray*, which Trollope was to write in 1863. The story has 'the same weak mother, the fanatically religious older sister and, as heroine, the younger sister who knew what she wanted.' The treatment of the American Baptist minister Phineas Beckard in 'Susan Bell' is, however, a good deal more sympathetic than the portrait of the evangelical clergyman Mr. Prong in *Rachel Ray*.

JOHN MUNROE BELL had been a lawyer in Albany, State of New York, and as such had thriven well. He had thriven well as long as thrift and thriving on this earth had been allowed to him. But the Almighty had seen fit to shorten his span.

Early in life he had married a timid, anxious, pretty good little wife, whose whole heart and mind had been given up to do his bidding and deserve his love. She had not only deserved it but had possessed it, and as long as John Munroe Bell had lived, Henrietta Bell—Hetta as he called her—had been a woman rich in blessings. After twelve years of such blessings he had left her, and had left with her two daughters, a second Hetta, and the heroine of our little story, Susan Bell.

A lawyer in Albany may thrive passing well for eight or ten years, and yet not leave behind him any very large sum of money if he dies at the end of that time. Some small modicum, some few thousand dollars, John Bell had amassed, so that his widow and daughters were not absolutely driven to look for work or bread.

In those happy days when cash had begun to flow in plenteously to the young father of the family he had taken it into his head to build for himself, or rather for his young female brood, a small neat house in the outskirts of Saratoga Springs. In doing so he was instigated as much by the excellence of the investment for his pocket as by the salubrity of the place for his girls. He furnished the house well, and then during some summer weeks his wife lived there, and sometimes he let it.

How the widow grieved when the lord of her heart and master of her mind was laid in the grave, I need not tell. She had already counted ten years of widowhood, and her children had grown to be young women beside her at the time of which I am now about to speak. Since that sad day on which they had left Albany they had lived together at the cottage at the Springs. In winter their life had been lonely enough; but as soon as the hot weather began to drive the fainting citizens out from New York, they had always received two or three boarders—old ladies generally, and occasionally an old gentleman—persons of very steady habits, with whose pockets the widow's moderate demands agreed better than the hotel charges. And so the Bells lived for ten years.

That Saratoga is a gay place in July, August, and September the world knows well enough. To girls who go there with trunks full of muslin and crinoline, for whom a carriage and pair of horses is always waiting immediately after dinner, whose fathers' pockets are bursting with dollars, it is a very gay place. Dancing and flirtations come as a matter of course, and matrimony follows after with only too great rapidity. But the place was not very gay for Hetta or Susan Bell.

In the first place the widow was a timid woman, and among other fears feared greatly that she should be thought guilty of setting traps for husbands. Poor mothers! how often are they charged with this sin when their honest desires go no further than that their bairns may be "respectit like the lave." And then she feared flirtations; flirtations that should be that and nothing more, flirtations that are so destructive of the heart's sweetest essence. She feared love also, though she longed for that as well as feared it;—for her girls, I mean; all such feelings for herself were long laid under ground;—and then, like a timid creature as she was, she had other indefinite fears, and among them a great fear that those girls of hers would be left husbandless,—a phase of life which after her twelve years of bliss she regarded as anything but desirable. But the upshot was,—the upshot of so many fears and such small means,—that Hetta and Susan Bell had but a dull life of it.

Were it not that I am somewhat closely restricted in the number of my pages, I would describe at full the merits and beauties of Hetta and Susan Bell. As it is I can but say a few words. At our period of their lives Hetta was nearly one-and-twenty, and Susan was just nineteen. Hetta was a short, plump, demure young woman, with the softest smoothed hair, and the brownest brightest eyes. She was very useful in the house, good at corn cakes, and thought much, particularly in these latter months, of her religious duties. Her sister in the privacy of their own little room would sometimes twit her with the admiring patience with which she would listen to the lengthened eloquence of Mr. Phineas Beckard, the Baptist minister. Now Mr. Phineas Beckard was a bachelor.

Susan was not so good a girl in the kitchen or about the house as was her sister; but she was bright in the parlour, and if that motherly heart could have been made to give out its inmost secret—which, however, it could not have been made to give out in any way painful to dear Hetta—perhaps it might have been found that Susan was loved with the closest love. She was taller than her sister, and lighter; her eyes were blue as were her mother's; her hair was brighter than Hetta's, but not always so singularly neat. She had a dimple on her chin, whereas Hetta had none; dimples on her cheeks too, when she smiled; and, oh, such a mouth! There; my allowance of pages permits no more.

One piercing cold winter's day there came knocking at the widow's door—a young man. Winter days, when the ice of January is refrozen by the wind of February, are very cold at Saratoga Springs. In these days there was not often much to disturb the serenity of Mrs. Bell's house; but on the day in question there came knocking at the door—a young man.

Mrs. Bell kept an old domestic, who had lived with them in those happy Albany days. Her name was Kate O'Brien, but though picturesque in name she was hardly so in person. She was a thick-set, noisy, good-natured old Irishwoman, who had joined her lot to that of Mrs. Bell when the latter first began housekeeping, and knowing when she was well off, had remained in the same place from that day forth. She had known Hetta as a baby, and, so to say, had seen Susan's birth.

"And what might you be wanting, sir?" said Kate O'Brien, apparently not quite pleased as she opened the door and let in all the cold air.

"I wish to see Mrs. Bell. Is not this Mrs. Bell's house?" said the young man, shaking the snow from out of the breast of his coat.

He did see Mrs. Bell, and we will now tell who he was, and why he had come, and how it came to pass that his carpet-bag was brought down to the widow's house and one of the front bedrooms was prepared for him, and that he drank tea that night in the widow's parlour.

His name was Aaron Dunn, and by profession he was an engineer. What peculiar misfortune in those days of frost and snow had befallen the line of rails which runs from Schenectady to Lake Champlain, I never quite understood. Banks and bridges had in some way come to grief, and on Aaron Dunn's shoulders was thrown the burden of seeing that they were duly repaired. Saratoga Springs was the centre of these mishaps, and therefore at Saratoga Springs it was necessary that he should take up his temporary abode.

Now there was at that time in New York city a Mr. Bell, great in railway matters—an uncle of the once thriving but now departed Albany lawyer. He was a rich man, but he liked his riches himself; or at any rate had not found himself called upon to share them with the widow and daughters of his nephew. But when it chanced to come to pass that he had a hand in despatching Aaron Dunn to Saratoga, he took the young man aside and recommended him to lodge with the widow. "There," said he, "show her my card." So much the rich uncle thought he might vouchsafe to do for the nephew's widow.

Mrs. Bell and both her daughters were in the parlour when Aaron Dunn was shown in, snow and all. He told his story in a rough, shaky voice, for his teeth chattered; and he gave the card, almost wishing that he had gone to the empty big hotel, for the widow's welcome was not at first quite warm.

The widow listened to him as he gave his message, and then she took the card and looked at it. Hetta, who was sitting on the side of the fireplace facing the door, went on demurely with her work. Susan gave one glance round—her back was to the stranger—and then another; and then she moved her chair a little nearer to the wall, so as to give the young man room to come to the fire, if he would. He did not come, but his eyes glanced upon Susan Bell; and he thought that the old man in New York was right, and that the big hotel would be cold and dull. It was a pretty face to look on that cold evening as she turned it up from the stocking she was mending.

"Perhaps you don't wish to take winter boarders, ma'am?" said Aaron Dunn.

"We never have done so yet, sir," said Mrs. Bell timidly. "Could she let this young wolf in among her lamb-fold? He might be a wolf;—who could tell?"

"Mr. Bell seemed to think it would suit," said Aaron.

Had he acquiesced in her timidity and not pressed the point, it would have been all up with him. But the widow did not like to go against the big uncle; and so she said, "Perhaps it may, sir."

"I guess it will, finely," said Aaron. And then the widow seeing that the matter was so far settled, put down her work and came round into the passage. Hetta followed her, for there would be house-work to do. Aaron gave himself another shake, settled the weekly number of dollars—with very little difficulty on his part, for he had caught another glance at Susan's face; and then went after his bag. 'Twas thus that Aaron Dunn obtained an entrance into Mrs. Bell's house. "But what if he be a wolf?" she said to herself over and over again that night, though not exactly in those words. Ay, but there is another side to that question. What if he be a stalwart man, honest-minded, with clever eye, cunning hand, ready brain, broad back, and warm heart; in want of a wife mayhap; a man that can earn his own bread and another's;—half a dozen others, when the half-dozen come? Would not that be a good sort of lodger? Such a question as that too did flit, just flit, across the widow's sleepless mind. But then she thought so much more of the wolf! Wolves, she had taught herself to think, were more common than stalwart, honest-minded, wife-desirous men.

"I wonder mother consented to take him," said Hetta when they were in the little room together.

"And why shouldn't she?" said Susan. "It will be a help."

"Yes, it will be a little help," said Hetta. "But we have done very well hitherto without winter lodgers."

"But uncle Bell said she was to."

"What is uncle Bell to us?" said Hetta, who had a spirit of her own. And she began to surmise within herself whether Aaron Dunn would join the Baptist congregation, and whether Phineas Beckard would approve of this new move.

He is a very well-behaved young man, at any rate," said Susan, "and he draws beautifully. Did you see those things he was doing?"

"He draws very well, I dare say," said Hetta, who regarded this as but a poor warranty for good behaviour. Hetta also had some fear of wolves—not for herself, perhaps; but for her sister.

Aaron Dunn's work—the commencement of his work—lay at some distance from the Springs, and he left every morning with a lot of workmen by an early train—almost before daylight. And every morning, cold and wintry as the mornings were, the widow got him his breakfast with her own hands. She took his dollars and would not leave him altogether to the awkward mercies of Kate O'Brien; nor would she trust her girls to attend upon the young man. Hetta she might have trusted; but then Susan would have asked why she was spared her share of such hardship.

In the evening, leaving his work when it was dark, Aaron always returned, and then the evening was passed together. But they were passed with the most demure propriety. These women would make the tea, cut the bread and butter, and then sew; while Aaron Dunn, when the cups were removed, would always go to his plans and drawings.

On Sundays they were more together; but even on this day there was cause of separation, for Aaron went to the Episcopalian church, rather to the disgust of Hetta. In the afternoon however they were together; and then Phineas Beckard came in to tea on Sundays, and he and Aaron got to talking on religion; and though they disagreed pretty much, and would not give an inch either one or the other, nevertheless the minister told the widow, and Hetta too probably, that the lad had good stuff in him, though he was so stiff-necked.

"But he should be more modest in talking on such matters with a minister," said Hetta.

The Rev. Phineas acknowledged that perhaps he should; but he was honest enough to repeat that the lad had stuff in him. "Perhaps after all he is not a wolf," said the widow to herself.

Things went on in this way for above a month. Aaron had declared to himself over and over again that that face was sweet to look upon, and had unconsciously promised to himself certain delights in talking and perhaps walking with the owner of it. But the walkings had not been achieved—nor even the talkings as yet. The truth was that Dunn was bashful with young women, though he could be so stiff-necked with the minister.

And then he felt angry with himself, inasmuch as he had advanced no further; and as he lay in his bed—which perhaps those pretty hands had helped to make—he resolved that he would be a thought bolder in his bearing. He had no idea of making love to Susan Bell; of course not. But why should he not amuse himself by talking to a pretty girl when she sat so near him, evening after evening?

"What a very quiet young man he is," said Susan to her sister.

"He has his bread to earn, and sticks to his work," said Hetta. "No doubt he has his amusement when he is in the city," added the elder sister, not wishing to leave too strong an impression of the young man's virtue.

They had all now their settled places in the parlour. Hetta sat on one side of the fire, close to the table, having that side to herself. There she sat always busy. She must have made every dress and bit of linen worn in the house, and hemmed every sheet and towel, so busy was she always. Sometimes, once in a week or so, Phineas Beckard would come in, and then place was made for him between Hetta's usual seat and the table. For when there he would read out loud. On the other side, close also to the table, sat the widow, busy, but not savagely busy as her elder daughter. Between Mrs. Bell and the wall, with her feet ever on the fender, Susan used to sit; not absolutely idle, but doing work of some slender pretty sort, and talking ever and anon to her mother. Opposite to them all, at the other side of the table, far away from the fire, would Aaron Dunn place himself with his plans and drawings before him.

"Are you a judge of bridges, ma'am?" said Aaron, the evening after he had made his resolution. 'Twas thus he began his courtship.

"Of bridges!" said Mrs. Bell—"oh dear, no, sir." But she put out her hand to take the little drawing which Aaron handed to her.

"Because that's one I've planned for our bit of a new branch from Moreau up to Lake George. I guess Miss Susan knows something about bridges."

"I guess I don't," said Susan—"only that they oughtn't to tumble down when the frost comes."

"Ha, ha, ha; no more they ought. I'll tell McEvoy that." McEvoy had been a former engineer on the line. "Well, that won't burst with any frost, I guess."

"Oh, my! how pretty!" said the widow, and then Susan of course jumped up to look over her mother's shoulder.

The artful dodger! He had drawn and coloured a beautiful little sketch of a bridge; not an engineer's plan with sections and measurements, vexatious to a woman's eye, but a graceful little bridge with a string of cars running under it. You could almost hear the bell going.

"Well; that is a pretty bridge," said Susan. "Isn't it, Hetta?"

"I don't know anything about bridges," said Hetta, to whose clever eyes the dodge was quite apparent. But in spite of her cleverness Mrs. Bell and Susan had soon moved their chairs round to the table, and were looking through the contents of Aaron's portfolio. "But yet he may be a wolf," thought the poor widow, just as she was kneeling down to say her prayers.

That evening certainly made a commencement. Though Hetta went on pertinaciously with the body of a new dress, the other two ladies did not put in another stitch that night. From his drawings Aaron got to his instruments, and before bedtime was teaching Susan how to draw parallel lines. Susan found that she had quite an aptitude for parallel lines, and altogether had a good time of it that evening. It is dull to go on week after week, and month after month talking only to one's mother and sister. It is dull though one does not oneself recognize it to be so. A little change in such matters is so very pleasant. Susan had not the slightest idea of regarding Aaron as even a possible lover. But young ladies do like the conversation of young gentlemen. Oh, my exceedingly proper, prim, old lady, you who are so shocked at this as a general doctrine, has it never occurred to you that the Creator has so intended it?

Susan, understanding little of the how and why, knew that she had had a good time, and was rather in spirits as she went to bed. But Hetta had been frightened by the dodge.

"Oh, Hetta, you should have looked at those drawings. He is so clever!" said Susan.

"I don't know that they would have done me much good," replied Hetta.

"Good! Well, they'd do me more good than a long sermon, I know," said Susan; "except on a Sunday, of course," she added apologetically. This was an ill-tempered attack both on Hetta and Hetta's admirer. But then why had Hetta been so snappish?

"I'm sure he's a wolf," thought Hetta as she went to bed.

"What a very clever young man he is!" thought Susan to herself as she pulled the warm clothes round about her shoulders and ears.

"Well; that certainly was an improvement," thought Aaron as he went through the same operation, with a stronger feeling of self-approbation than he had enjoyed for some time past.

In the course of the next fortnight the family arrangements all altered themselves. Unless when Beckard was there Aaron would sit in the widow's place, the widow would take Susan's chair, and the two girls would be opposite. And then Dunn would read to them; not sermons, but passages from Shakspeare, and Byron, and Longfellow. "He reads much better than Mr. Beckard," Susan had said one night. "Of course you're a competent judge!" had been Hetta's retort. "I mean that I like it better," said Susan. "It's well that all people don't think alike," replied Hetta.

And then there was a deal of talking. The widow herself, as unconscious in this respect as her youngest daughter, certainly did find that a little variety was agreeable on those long winter nights; and talked herself with unaccustomed freedom. And Beckard came there oftener and talked very much. When he was there the two young men did all the talking, and they pounded each other immensely. But still there grew up a sort of friendship between them.

"Mr. Beckard seems quite to take to him," said Mrs. Bell to her eldest daughter.

"It is his great good nature, mother," replied Hetta.

It was at the end of the second month when Aaron took another step in advance—a perilous step. Sometimes on evenings he still went on with his drawing for an hour or so; but during three or four evenings he never asked any one to look at what he was doing. On one Friday he sat over his work till late, without any reading or talking at all; so late that at last Mrs. Bell said, "If you're going to sit much longer, Mr. Dunn, I'll get you to put out the candles." Thereby showing, had he known it or had she, that the mother's confidence in the young man was growing fast. Hetta knew all about it, and dreaded that the growth was too quick.

"I've finished now," said Aaron; and he looked carefully at the card-board on which he had been washing in his water-colours. "I've finished now." He then hesitated a moment; but ultimately he put the card into his portfolio and carried it up to his bedroom. Who does not perceive that it was intended as a present to Susan Bell?

The question which Aaron asked himself that night, and which he hardly knew how to answer was this. Should he offer the drawing to Susan in the presence of her mother and sister, or on some occasion when they two might be alone together? No such occasion had ever yet occurred, but Aaron thought that it might probably be brought about. But then he wanted to make no fuss about it. His first intention had been to chuck the drawing lightly across the table when it was completed, and so make nothing of it. But he had finished it with more care than he had at first intended; and then he had hesitated when he had finished it. It was too late now for that plan of chucking it over the table.

On the Saturday evening when he came down from his room, Mr. Beckard was there, and there was no opportunity that night. On the Sunday, in conformity with a previous engagement, he went to hear Mr. Beckard preach, and walked to and from meeting with the family. This pleased Mrs. Bell, and they were all very gracious that afternoon. But Sunday was no day for the picture.

On Monday the thing had become of importance to him. Things always do when they are kept over. Before tea that evening when he came down Mrs. Bell and Susan only were in the room. He knew Hetta for his foe, and therefore determined to use this occasion.

"Miss Susan," he said, stammering somewhat, and blushing too, poor fool! "I have done a little drawing which I want you to accept," and he put his portfolio down on the table.

"Oh! I don't know," said Susan who had seen the blush.

Mrs. Bell had seen the blush also, and pursed her mouth up, and looked grave. Had there been no stammering and no blush, she might have thought nothing of it.

Aaron saw at once that his little gift was not to go down smoothly. He was however in for it now, so he picked it out from among the other papers in the case and brought it over to Susan. He endeavoured to hand it to her with an air of indifference, but I cannot say that he succeeded.

It was a very pretty well-finished, water-coloured drawing, representing still the same bridge, but with more adjuncts. In Susan's eyes it was a work of high art. Of pictures probably she had seen but little, and her liking for the artist no doubt added to her admiration. But the more she admired it and wished for it, the stronger was her feeling that she ought not to take it.

Poor Susan! she stood for a minute looking at the drawing, but she said nothing; not even a word of praise. She felt that she was red in the face, and uncourteous to their lodger; but her mother was looking at her and she did not know how to behave herself.

Mrs. Bell put out her hand for the sketch, trying to bethink herself as she did so in what least uncivil way she could refuse the present. She took a moment to look at it collecting her thoughts, and as she did so her woman's wit came to her aid.

"Oh dear, Mr. Dunn, it is very pretty; quite a beautiful picture. I cannot let Susan rob you of that. You must keep that for some of your own particular friends."

"But I did it for her," said Aaron innocently.

Susan looked down at the ground, half pleased at the declaration. The drawing would look very pretty in a small gilt frame put over her dressing-table. But the matter now was altogether in her mother's hands.

"I am afraid it is too valuable, sir, for Susan to accept."

"It is not valuable at all," said Aaron, declining to take it back from the widow's hand.

"Oh, I am quite sure it is. It is worth ten dollars at least—or twenty," said poor Mrs. Bell, not in the very best taste. But she was perplexed and did not know how to get out of the scrape. The article in question now lay upon the table-cloth, appropriated by no one, and at this moment Hetta came into the room.

"It is not worth ten cents," said Aaron, with something like a frown on his brow. "But as we had been talking about the bridge, I thought Miss Susan would accept it."

"Accept what?" said Hetta. And then her eye fell upon the drawing and she took it up.

"It is beautifully done," said Mrs. Bell, wishing much to soften the matter; perhaps the more so, that Hetta the demure was now present. "I am telling Mr. Dunn that we can't take a present of anything so valuable."

"Oh dear, no," said Hetta. "It wouldn't be right."

It was a cold frosty evening in March, and the fire was burning brightly on the hearth. Aaron Dunn took up the drawing quietly—very quietly—and rolling it up, as such drawings are rolled, put it between the blazing logs. It was the work of four evenings, and his chef-d'œuvre in the way of art.

Susan, when she saw what he had done, burst out into tears. The widow could very readily have done so also, but she was able to refrain herself, and merely exclaimed—"Oh, Mr. Dunn!"

Aaron immediately felt ashamed of what he had done; and he also could have cried, but for his manliness. He walked away to one of the parlour-windows, and looked out upon the frosty night. It was dark, but the stars were bright, and he thought that he should like to be walking fast by himself along the line of rails towards Balston. There he stood, perhaps for three minutes. He thought it would be proper to give Susan time to recover from her tears.

"Will you please to come to your tea, sir?" said the soft voice of Mrs. Bell.

He turned round to do so, and found that Susan was gone. It was not quite in her power to recover from her tears in three minutes. And then the drawing had been so beautiful! It had been done expressly for her too! And there had been something, she knew not what, in his eye as he had so declared. She had watched him intently over those four evenings' work, wondering why he did not show it, till her feminine curiosity had become rather strong. It was something very particular, she was sure, and she had learned that all that precious work had been for her. Now all that precious work was destroyed. How was it possible that she should not cry for more than three minutes?

The others took their meal in perfect silence, and when it was over the two women sat down to their work. Aaron had a book which he pretended to read, but instead of reading he was bethinking himself that he had behaved badly. What right had he to throw them all into such confusion by indulging in his passion? He was ashamed of what he had done, and fancied that Susan would hate him. Fancying that, he began to find at the same time that he by no means hated her.

At last Hetta got up and left the room. She knew that her sister was sitting alone in the cold, and Hetta was affectionate. Susan had not been in fault, and therefore Hetta went up to console her.

"Mrs. Bell," said Aaron, as soon as the door was closed, "I beg your pardon for what I did just now."

"Oh, sir, I'm sorry that the picture is burnt," said poor Mrs. Bell.

"The picture does not matter a straw," said Aaron. "But I see that I have disturbed you all,—and I am afraid I have made Miss Susan unhappy."

"She was grieved because your picture was burnt," said Mrs. Bell, putting some emphasis on the 'your,' intending to show that her daughter had not regarded the drawing as her own. But the emphasis bore another meaning; and so the widow perceived as soon as she had spoken.

"Oh, I can do twenty more of the same if anybody wanted them," said Aaron. "If I do another like it, will you let her take it, Mrs. Bell?—just to show that you have forgiven me, and that we are friends as we were before?"

Was he, or was he not a wolf? That was the question which Mrs. Bell scarcely knew how to answer. Hetta had given her voice, saying he was lupine. Mr. Beckard's opinion she had not liked to ask directly. Mr. Beckard she thought would probably propose to Hetta; but as yet he had not done so. And, as he was still a stranger in the family, she did not like in any way to compromise Susan's name. Indirectly she had asked the question, and, indirectly also, Mr. Beckard's answer had been favourable.

"But it mustn't mean anything, sir," was the widow's weak answer, when she had paused on the question for a moment.

"Oh no, of course not," said Aaron, joyously, and his face became radiant and happy. "And I do beg your pardon too." And then he rapidly got out his card-board, and set himself to work about another bridge. The widow meditating many things in her heart, commenced the hemming of a handkerchief.

In about an hour the two girls came back to the room and silently took their accustomed places. Aaron hardly looked up, but went on diligently with his drawing. This bridge should be a better bridge than that other. Its acceptance was now assured. Of course it was to mean nothing. That was a matter of course. So he worked away diligently, and said nothing to anybody.

When they went off to bed the two girls went into the mother's room. "Oh, mother, I hope he is not very angry," said Susan.

"Angry!" said Hetta, "if anybody should be angry, it is mother. He ought to have known that Susan could not accept it. He should never have offered it."

"But he's doing another," said Mrs. Bell.

"Not for her," said Hetta.

"Yes he is," said Mrs. Bell, "and I have promised that she shall take it." Susan as she heard this sank gently into the chair behind her, and her eyes became full of tears. The intimation was almost too much for her.

"Oh mother!" said Hetta.

"But I particularly said that it was to mean nothing."

"Oh mother, that makes it worse."

Why should Hetta interfere in this way, thought Susan to herself. Had she interfered when Mr. Beckard gave Hetta a testament bound in morocco? Had not she smiled, and looked gratified, and kissed her sister, and declared that Phineas Beckard was a nice dear man, and by far the most elegant preacher at the Springs? Why should Hetta be so cruel?

"I don't see that, my dear," said the mother. Hetta would not explain before her sister, so they all went to bed.

On the Thursday evening the drawing was finished. Not a word had been said about it, at any rate in his presence, and he had gone on working in silence. "There," said he, late on the Thursday evening, "I don't know that it will be any better if I go on daubing for another hour. There, Miss Susan; there's another bridge. I hope that will neither burst with the frost, nor yet be destroyed by fire," and he gave it a light flip with his fingers and sent it skimming over the table.

Susan blushed and smiled, and took it up. "Oh, it is beautiful," she said. "Isn't it beautifully done, mother?" and then all the three got up to look at it, and all confessed that it was excellently done.

"And I am sure we are very much obliged to you," said Susan after a pause, remembering that she had not yet thanked him.

"Oh, it's nothing," said he, not quite liking the word "we."

On the following day he returned from his work to Saratoga about noon. This he had never done before, and therefore no one expected that he would be seen in the house before the evening. On this occasion however he went straight thither, and as chance would have it, both the widow and her elder daughter were out. Susan was there alone in charge of the house.

He walked in and opened the parlour door. There she sat, with her feet on the fender, with her work unheeded on the table behind her, and the picture, Aaron's drawing, lying on her knees. She was gazing at it intently as he entered, thinking in her young heart that it possessed all the beauties which a picture could possess.

"Oh, Mr. Dunn," she said getting up and holding the tell-tale sketch behind the skirt of her dress.

"Miss Susan, I have come here to tell your mother that I must start for New York this afternoon and be there for six weeks, or perhaps longer."

"Mother is out," said she; "I'm so sorry."

"Is she?" said Aaron.

"And Hetta too. Dear me. And you'll be wanting dinner. I'll go and see about it."

Aaron began to swear that he could not possibly eat any dinner. He had dined once, and was going to dine again;—anything to keep her from going.

"But you must have something, Mr. Dunn," and she walked towards the door.

But he put his back to it. "Miss Susan," said he, "I guess I've been here nearly two months."

"Yes, sir, I believe you have," she replied, shaking in her shoes and not knowing which way to look.

"And I hope we have been good friends."

"Yes, sir," said Susan, almost beside herself as to what she was saying.

"I'm going away now, and it seems to be such a time before I'll be back."

"Will it, sir?"

"Six weeks, Miss Susan!" and then he paused, looking into her eyes, to see what he could read there. She leant against the table, pulling to pieces a morsel of half ravelled muslin which she held in her hand; but her eyes were turned to the ground, and he could hardly see them.

"Miss Susan," he continued, "I may as well speak out now as at another time." He too was looking towards the ground, and clearly did not know what to do with his hands. "The truth is just this. I—I love you dearly, with all my heart. I never saw anyone I ever thought so beautiful, so nice, and so good;—and what's more, I never shall. I'm not very good at this sort of thing, I know; but I couldn't go away from Saratoga for six weeks and not tell you." And then he ceased. He did not ask for any love in return. His presumption had not got so far as that yet. He merely declared his passion, leaning against the door, and there he stood twiddling his thumbs.

Susan had not the slightest conception of the way in which she ought to receive such a declaration. She had never had a lover before; nor had she ever thought of Aaron absolutely as a lover, though something very like love for him had been crossing over her spirit. Now, at this moment, she felt that he was the beau-idéal of manhood, though his boots were covered with the railway mud, and though his pantaloons were tucked up in rolls round his ankles. He was a fine, well-grown, open-faced fellow, whose eye was bold and yet tender, whose brow was full and broad, and all his bearing manly. Love him! Of course she loved him. Why else had her heart melted with pleasure when her mother said that that second picture was to be accepted?

But what was she to say? Anything but the open truth; she well knew that. The open truth would not do at all. What would her mother say and Hetta if she were rashly to say that? Hetta, she knew, would be dead against such a lover, and of her mother's approbation she had hardly more hope. Why they should disapprove of Aaron as a lover she had never asked herself. There are many nice things that seem to be wrong only because they are so nice. Maybe that Susan regarded a lover as one of them. "Oh, Mr. Dunn, you shouldn't." That in fact was all that she could say.

"Should not I?" said he. "Well, perhaps not; but there's the truth, and no harm ever comes of that. Perhaps I'd better not ask you for an answer now, but I thought it better you should know it all. And remember this—I only care for one thing now in the world, and that is for your love." And then he paused, thinking possibly that in spite of what he had said he might perhaps get some sort of an answer, some inkling of the state of her heart's disposition towards him.

But Susan had at once resolved to take him at his word when he suggested that an immediate reply was not necessary. To say that she loved him was of course impossible, and to say that she did not was equally so. She determined therefore to close at once with the offer of silence.

When he ceased speaking there was a moment's pause, during which he strove hard to read what might be written on her down-turned face. But he was not good at such reading. "Well, I guess I'll go and get my things ready now," he said, and then turned round to open the door.

"Mother will be in before you are gone, I suppose," said Susan.

"I have only got twenty minutes," said he, looking at his watch. "But, Susan, tell her what I have said to you. Good-bye." And he put out his hand. He knew he should see her again, but this had been his plan to get her hand in his.

"Good-bye, Mr. Dunn," and she gave him her hand.

He held it tight for a moment, so that she could not draw it away,—could not if she would. "Will you tell your mother?" he asked.

"Yes," she answered, quite in a whisper. "I guess I'd better tell her." And then she gave a long sigh. He pressed her hand again and got it up to his lips.

"Mr. Dunn, don't," she said. But he did kiss it. "God bless you, my own dearest, dearest girl! I'll just open the door as I come down. Perhaps Mrs. Bell will be here." And then he rushed up stairs.

But Mrs. Bell did not come in. She and Hetta were at a weekly service at Mr. Beckard's meeting-house, and Mr. Beckard it seemed had much to say. Susan, when left alone, sat down and tried to think. But she could not think; she could only love. She could use her mind only in recounting to herself the perfections of that demigod whose heavy steps were so audible overhead, as he walked to and fro collecting his things and putting them into his bag.

And then, just when he had finished, she bethought herself that he must be hungry. She flew to the kitchen, but she was too late. Before she could even reach at the loaf of bread he descended the stairs with a clattering noise, and heard her voice as she spoke quickly to Kate O'Brien.

"Miss Susan," he said, "don't get anything for me, for I'm off."

"Oh, Mr. Dunn, I am so sorry. You'll be so hungry on your journey," and she came out to him in the passage.

"I shall want nothing on the journey, dearest, if you'll say one kind word to me."

Again her eyes went to the ground. "What do you want me to say, Mr. Dunn?"

"Say, God bless you, Aaron."

"God bless you, Aaron," said she; and yet she was sure that she had not declared her love. He however thought otherwise, and went up to New York with a happy heart.

Things happened in the next fortnight rather quickly. Susan at once resolved to tell her mother, but she resolved also not to tell Hetta. That afternoon she got her mother to herself in Mrs. Bell's own room, and then she made a clean breast of it.

"And what did you say to him, Susan?"

"I said nothing, mother."

"Nothing, dear!"

"No, mother; not a word. He told me he didn't want it." She forgot how she had used his Christian name in bidding God bless him.

"Oh, dear!" said the widow.

"Was it very wrong?" asked Susan.

"But what do you think yourself, my child?" asked Mrs. Bell after a while. "What are your own feelings?"

Mrs. Bell was sitting on a chair, and Susan was standing opposite to her against the post of the bed. She made no answer, but moving from her place, she threw herself into her mother's arms, and hid her face on her mother's shoulder. It was easy enough to guess what were her feelings.

"But, my darling," said her mother, "you must not think that it is an engagement."

"No," said Susan, sorrowfully.

"Young men say those things to amuse themselves." Wolves, she would have said, had she spoken out her mind freely.

"Oh, mother, he is not like that."

The daughter contrived to extract a promise from the mother that Hetta should not be told just at present. Mrs. Bell calculated that she had six weeks before her; as yet Mr. Beckard had not spoken out, but there was reason to suppose that he would do so before those six weeks would be over, and then she would be able to seek counsel from him.

Mr. Beckard spoke out at the end of six days, and Hetta frankly accepted him. "I hope you'll love your brother-in-law," said she to Susan.

"Oh, I will indeed," said Susan; and in the softness of her heart at the moment she almost made up her mind to tell; but Hetta was full of her own affairs, and thus it passed off.

It was then arranged that Hetta should go and spend a week with Mr. Beckard's parents. Old Mr. Beckard was a farmer living near Utica, and now that the match was declared and approved, it was thought well that Hetta should know her future husband's family. So she went for a week, and Mr. Beckard went with her. "He will be back in plenty of time for me to speak to him before Aaron Dunn's six weeks are over," said Mrs. Bell to herself.

But things did not go exactly as she expected. On the very morning after the departure of the engaged couple, there came a letter from Aaron, saying that he would be at Saratoga that very evening. The railway people had ordered him down again for some days' special work; then he was to go elsewhere, and not to return to Saratoga till June. "But he hoped," so said the letter, "that Mrs. Bell would not turn him into the street even then, though the summer might have come, and her regular lodgers might be expected."

"Oh dear, oh dear!" said Mrs. Bell to herself, reflecting that she had no one of whom she could ask advice, and that she must decide that very day. Why had she let Mr. Beckard go without telling him? Then she told Susan, and Susan spent the day trembling. Perhaps, thought Mrs. Bell, he will say nothing about it. In such case, however, would it not be her duty to say something? Poor mother! She trembled nearly as much as Susan.

It was dark when the fatal knock came at the door. The tea-things were already laid, and the tea-cake was already baked; for it would at any rate be necessary to give Mr. Dunn his tea. Susan, when she heard the knock, rushed from her chair and took refuge up stairs. The widow gave a long sigh, and settled her dress. Kate O'Brien with willing step opened the door, and bade her old friend welcome.

"How are the ladies?" asked Aaron, trying to gather something from the face and voice of the domestic.

"Miss Hetta and Mr. Beckard be gone off to Utica, just man-and-wife like; and so they are, more power to them."

"Oh indeed; I'm very glad," said Aaron—and so he was; very glad to have Hetta the demure out of the way. And then he made his way into the parlour, doubting much, and hoping much.

Mrs. Bell rose from her chair, and tried to look grave. Aaron glancing round the room saw that Susan was not there. He walked straight up to the widow, and offered her his hand, which she took. It might be that Susan had not thought fit to tell, and in such case it would not be right for him to compromise her; so he said never a word.

But the subject was too important to the mother to allow of her being silent when the young man stood before her. "Oh, Mr. Dunn," said she, "what is this you have been saying to Susan?"

"I have asked her to be my wife," said he, drawing himself up and looking her full in the face. Mrs. Bell's heart was almost as soft as her daughter's, and it was nearly gone; but at the moment she had nothing to say but, "oh dear, oh dear!"

"May I not call you mother?" said he, taking both her hands in his.

"Oh dear—oh dear! But will you be good to her? Oh, Aaron Dunn, if you deceive my child!"

In another quarter of an hour, Susan was kneeling at her mother's knee, with her face on her mother's lap; the mother was wiping tears out of her eyes; and Aaron was standing by holding one of the widow's hands.

"You are my mother too, now," said he. What would Hetta and Mr. Beckard say, when they came back? But then he surely was not a wolf!

There were four or five days left for courtship before Hetta and Mr. Beckard would return; four or five days during which Susan might be happy, Aaron triumphant, and Mrs. Bell nervous. Days I have said, but after all it was only the evenings that were so left. Every morning Susan got up to give Aaron his breakfast, but Mrs. Bell got up also. Susan boldly declared her right to do so, and Mrs. Bell found no objection which she could urge. But after that Aaron was always absent till seven or eight in the evening, when he would return to his tea. Then came the hour or two of lovers' intercourse.

But they were very tame, those hours. The widow still felt an undefined fear that she was wrong, and though her heart yearned to know that her daughter was happy in the sweet happiness of accepted love, yet she dreaded to be too confident. Not a word had been said about money matters; not a word of Aaron Dunn's relatives. So she did not leave them by themselves, but waited with what patience she could for the return of her wise counsellors.

And then Susan hardly knew how to behave herself with her accepted suitor. She felt that she was very happy; but perhaps she was most happy when she was thinking about him through the long day, assisting in fixing little things for his comfort, and waiting for his evening return. And as he sat there in the parlour, she could be happy then too, if she were but allowed to sit still and look at him,—not stare at him but raise her eyes every now and again to his face for the shortest possible glance, as she had been used to do ever since he came there.

But he, unconscionable lover, wanted to hear her speak, was desirous of being talked to, and perhaps thought that he should by rights be allowed to sit by her, and hold her hand. No such privileges were accorded to him. If they had been alone together, walking side by side on the green turf, as lovers should walk, she would soon have found the use of her tongue,—have talked fast enough no doubt. Under such circumstances, when a girl's shyness has given way to real intimacy, there is in general no end to her power of chatting. But though there was much love between Aaron and Susan, there was as yet but little intimacy. And then, let a mother be ever so motherly—and no mother could have more of a mother's tenderness than Mrs. Bell—still her presence must be a restraint. Aaron was very fond of Mrs. Bell; but nevertheless he did sometimes wish that some domestic duty would take her out of the parlour for a few happy minutes. Susan went out very often, but Mrs. Bell seemed to be a fixture.

Once for a moment he did find his love alone, immediately as he came into the house. "My own Susan, you do love me? do say so to me once." And he contrived to slip his arm round her waist. "Yes," she whispered; but she slipped, like an eel, from his hands, and left him only preparing himself for a kiss. And then when she got to her room, half frightened, she clasped her hands together, and bethought herself that she did really love him with a strength and depth of love which filled her whole existence. Why could she not have told him something of all this?

And so the few days of his second sojourn at Saratoga passed away, not altogether satisfactorily. It was settled that he should return to New York on Saturday night, leaving Saratoga on that evening; and as the Beckards—Hetta was already regarded quite as a Beckard—were to be back to dinner on that day, Mrs. Bell would have an opportunity of telling her wondrous tale. It might be well that Mr. Beckard should see Aaron before his departure.

On that Saturday the Beckards did arrive just in time for dinner. It may be imagined that Susan's appetite was not very keen, nor her manner very collected. But all this passed by unobserved in the importance attached to the various Beckard arrangements which came under discussion. Ladies and gentlemen circumstanced as were Hetta and Mr. Beckard are perhaps a little too apt to think that their own affairs are paramount. But after dinner Susan vanished at once, and when Hetta prepared to follow her, desirous of further talk about matrimonial arrangements, her mother stopped her, and the disclosure was made.

"Proposed to her!" said Hetta, who perhaps thought that one marriage in a family was enough at a time.

"Yes, my love—and he did it, I must say, in a very honourable way, telling her not to make any answer till she had spoken to me;—now that was very nice; was it not, Phineas?" Mrs. Bell had become very anxious that Aaron should not be voted a wolf.

"And what has been said to him since?" asked the discreet Phineas.

"Why—nothing absolutely decisive." Oh, Mrs. Bell! "You see I know nothing as to his means."

"Nothing at all," said Hetta.

"He is a man that will always earn his bread," said Mr. Beckard; and Mrs. Bell blessed him in her heart for saying it.

"But has he been encouraged?" asked Hetta.

"Well; yes, he has," said the widow.

"Then Susan I suppose likes him?" asked Phineas.

"Well; yes, she does," said the widow. And the conference ended in a resolution that Phineas Beckard should have a conversation with Aaron Dunn, as to his worldly means and position; and that he, Phineas, should decide whether Aaron might, or might not be at once accepted as a lover, according to the tenor of that conversation. Poor Susan was not told anything of all this. "Better not," said Hetta the demure. "It will only flurry her the more." How would she have liked it, if without consulting her, they had left it to Aaron to decide whether or no she might marry Phineas?

They knew where on the works Aaron was to be found, and thither Mr. Beckard rode after dinner. We need not narrate at length the conference between the young men. Aaron at once declared that he had nothing but what he made as an engineer, and explained that he held no permanent situation on the line. He was well paid at that present moment, but at the end of summer he would have to look for employment.

"Then you can hardly marry quite at present," said the discreet minister.

"Perhaps not quite immediately."

"And long engagements are never wise," said the other.

"Three or four months," suggested Aaron. But Mr. Beckard shook his head.

The afternoon at Mrs. Bell's house was melancholy. The final decision of the three judges was as follows. There was to be no engagement; of course no correspondence. Aaron was to be told that it would be better that he should get lodgings elsewhere when he returned; but that he would be allowed to visit at Mrs. Bell's house,—and at Mrs. Beckard's, which was very considerate. If he should succeed in getting a permanent appointment, and if he and

Susan still held the same mind, why then—&c. &c. Such was Susan's fate, as communicated to her by Mrs. Bell and Hetta. She sat still and wept when she heard it; but she did not complain. She had always felt that Hetta would be against her.

"Mayn't I see him, then?" she said through her tears.

Hetta thought she had better not. Mrs. Bell thought she might. Phineas decided that they might shake hands, but only in full conclave. There was to be no lovers' farewell. Aaron was to leave the house at half-past five; but before he went Susan should be called down. Poor Susan! She sat down and bemoaned herself; uncomplaining, but very sad.

Susan was soft, feminine, and manageable. But Aaron Dunn was not very soft, was especially masculine, and in some matters not easily manageable. When Mr. Beckard in the widow's presence—Hetta had retired in obedience to her lover—informed him of the court's decision, there came over his face the look which he had worn when he burned the picture. "Mrs. Bell," he said, "had encouraged his engagement; and he did not understand why other people should now come and disturb it."

"Not an engagement, Aaron," said Mrs. Bell piteously.

"He was able and willing to work," he said, "and knew his profession. What young man of his age had done better than he had?" and he glanced round at them with perhaps more pride than was quite becoming.

Then Mr. Beckard spoke out, very wisely no doubt, but perhaps a little too much at length. Sons and daughters as well as fathers and mothers will know very well what he said; so I need not repeat his words. I cannot say that Aaron listened with much attention, but he understood perfectly what the upshot of it was. Many a man understands the purport of many a sermon without listening to one word in ten. Mr. Beckard meant to be kind in his manner; indeed was so, only that Aaron could not accept as kindness any interference on his part.

"I'll tell you what, Mrs. Bell," said he. "I look upon myself as engaged to her. And I look on her as engaged to me. I tell you so fairly; and I believe that's her mind as well as mine."

"But, Aaron, you won't try to see her—or to write to her,—not in secret; will you?

"When I try to see her, I'll come and knock at this door; and if I write to her, I'll write to her full address by the post. I never did and never will do anything in secret."

"I know you're good and honest," said the widow with her handkerchief to her eyes.

"Then why do you separate us?" asked he, almost roughly. "I suppose I may see her at any rate before I go. My time's nearly up now, I guess."

And then Susan was called for, and she and Hetta came down together. Susan crept in behind her sister. Her eyes were red with weeping, and her appearance was altogether disconsolate. She had had a lover for a week, and now she was to be robbed of him.

"Good-bye, Susan," said Aaron, and he walked up to her without bashfulness or embarrassment. Had they all been compliant and gracious to him he would have been as bashful as his love; but now his temper was hot. "Good-bye, Susan," and she took his hand, and he held hers till he had finished. "And remember this, I look upon you as my promised wife, and I don't fear that you'll deceive me. At any rate I sha'n't deceive you."

"Good-bye, Aaron," she sobbed.

"Good-bye, and God bless you, my own darling!" And then without saying a word to any one else, he turned his back upon them and went his way.

There had been something very consolatory, very sweet, to the poor girl in her lover's last words. And yet they had almost made her tremble. He had been so bold, and stern, and confident. He had seemed so utterly to defy the impregnable discretion of Mr. Beckard, so to despise the demure propriety of Hetta. But of this she felt sure, when she came to question her heart, that she could never, never, never cease to love him better than all the world beside. She would wait—patiently if she could find patience—and then, if he deserted her, she would die.

In another month Hetta became Mrs. Beckard. Susan brisked up a little for the occasion, and looked very pretty as bridesmaid. She was serviceable too in arranging household matters, hemming linen and sewing table-cloths; though of course in these matters she did not do a tenth of what Hetta did.

Then the summer came, the Saratoga summer of July, August, and September, during which the widow's house was full; and Susan's hands saved the pain of her heart, for she was forced into occupation. Now that Hetta was gone to her own duties, it was necessary that Susan's part in the household should be more prominent.

Aaron did not come back to his work at Saratoga. Why he did not, they could not then learn. During the whole long summer they heard not a word of him nor from him; and then when the cold winter months came and their boarders had left them, Mrs. Beckard congratulated her sister in that she had given no further encouragement to a lover who cared so little for her. This was very hard to bear. But Susan did bear it.

That winter was very sad. They learned nothing of Aaron Dunn till about January; and then they heard that he was doing very well. He was engaged on the Erie trunk line, was paid highly, and was much esteemed. And yet he neither came nor sent! "He has an excellent situation," their informant told them. "And a permanent one?" asked the widow. "Oh, yes, no doubt," said the gentleman, "for I happen to know that they count greatly on him." And yet he sent no word of love.

After that the winter became very sad indeed. Mrs. Bell thought it to be her duty now to teach her daughter that in all probability she would see Aaron Dunn no more. It was open to him to leave her without being absolutely a wolf. He had been driven from the house when he was poor, and they had no right to expect that he would return, now that he had made some rise in the world. "Men do amuse themselves in that way," the widow tried to teach her.

"He is not like that, mother," she said again.

"But they do not think so much of these things as we do," urged the mother.

"Don't they?" said Susan, oh, so sorrowfully; and so through the whole long winter months she became paler and paler, and thinner and thinner.

And then Hetta tried to console her with religion, and that perhaps did not make things any better. Religious consolation is the best cure for all griefs; but it must not be looked for specially with regard to any individual sorrow. A religious man, should he become bankrupt through the misfortunes of the world, will find true consolation in his religion even for that sorrow. But a bankrupt, who has not thought much of such things, will hardly find solace by taking up religion for that special occasion.

And Hetta perhaps was hardly prudent in her attempts. She thought that it was wicked in Susan to grow thin and pale for love of Aaron Dunn, and she hardly hid her thoughts. Susan was not sure but that it might be wicked, but this doubt in no way tended to make her plump or rosy. So that in those days she found no comfort in her sister.

But her mother's pity and soft love did ease her sufferings, though it could not make them cease. Her mother did not tell her that she was wicked, or bid her read long sermons, or force her to go oftener to the meeting-house.

"He will never come again, I think," she said one day, as with a shawl wrapped around her shoulders, she leant with her head upon her mother's bosom.

"My own darling," said the mother, pressing her child closely to her side.

"You think he never will, eh, mother?" What could Mrs. Bell say? In her heart of hearts she did not think he ever would come again.

"No, my child. I do not think he will." And then the hot tears ran down, and the sobs came thick and frequent.

"My darling, my darling!" exclaimed the mother; and they wept together.

"Was I wicked to love him at the first?" she asked that night.

"No, my child; you were not wicked at all. At least I think not."

"Then why— " Why was he sent away? It was on her tongue to ask that question; but she paused and spared her mother. This was as they were going to bed. The next morning Susan did not get up. She was not ill, she said; but weak and weary. Would her mother let her lie that day? And then Mrs. Bell went down alone to her room, and sorrowed with all her heart for the sorrow of her child. Why, oh why, had she driven away from her door-sill the love of an honest man?

On the next morning Susan again did not get up;—nor did she hear, or if she heard she did not recognize, the step of the postman who brought a letter to the door. Early, before the widow's breakfast the postman came, and the letter which he brought was as follows:-

"MY DEAR MRS. BELL,
"I have now got a permanent situation on the Erie line, and the salary is enough for myself and a wife. At least I think so, and I hope you will too. I shall be down at Saratoga to-morrow evening, and I hope neither Susan nor you will refuse to receive me.

"Yours affectionately,
"AARON DUNN."

That was all. It was very short, and did not contain one word of love; but it made the widow's heart leap for joy. She was rather afraid that Aaron was angry, he wrote so curtly and with such a brusque business-like attention to mere facts; but surely he could have but one object in coming there. And then be alluded specially to a wife. So the widow's heart leapt with joy.

But how was she to tell Susan? She ran up stairs almost breathless with haste, to the bedroom door: but then she stopped: too much joy she had heard was as dangerous as too much sorrow; she must think it over for a while, and so she crept back again.

But after breakfast—that is, when she had sat for a while over her teacup—she returned to the room, and this time she entered it. The letter was in her hand, but held so as to be hidden;—in her left hand as she sat down with her right arm towards the invalid.

"Susan dear," she said, and smiled at her child, "you'll be able to get up this morning? eh, dear?"

"Yes, mother," said Susan, thinking that her mother objected to this idleness of her lying in bed. And so she began to bestir herself.

"I don't mean this very moment, love. Indeed, I want to sit with you for a little while," and she put her right arm affectionately round her daughter's waist.

"Dearest mother," said Susan.

"Ah! there's one dearer than me, I guess," and Mrs. Bell smiled sweetly, as she made the maternal charge against her daughter.

Susan raised herself quickly in the bed, and looked straight into her mother's face. "Mother, mother," she said, "What is it? You've something to tell. Oh, mother!" And stretching herself over, she struck her hand against the corner of Aaron's letter. "Mother, you've a letter. Is he coming, mother?" and with eager eyes and open lips, she sat up, holding tight to her mother's arm.

"Yes, love. I have got a letter."

"Is he—is he coming?"

How the mother answered, I can hardly tell; but she did answer, and they were soon lying in each other's arms, warm with each other's tears. It was almost hard to say which was the happier.

Aaron was to be there that evening—that very evening. "Oh, mother, let me get up," said Susan.

But Mrs. Bell said no, not yet; her darling was pale and thin, and she almost wished that Aaron was not coming for another week. What if he should come and look at her, and finding her beauty gone, vanish again and seek a wife elsewhere!

So Susan lay in bed, thinking of her happiness, dozing now and again, and fearing as she waked that it was a dream, looking constantly at that drawing of his, which she kept outside upon the bed, nursing her love and thinking of it, and endeavouring, vainly endeavouring, to arrange what she would say to him.

"Mother," she said, when Mrs. Bell once went up to her, "you won't tell Hetta and Phineas, will you? Not to-day, I mean?" Mrs. Bell agreed that it would be better not to tell them. Perhaps she thought that she had already depended too much on Hetta and Phineas in the matter.

Susan's finery in the way of dress had never been extensive, and now lately, in these last sad winter days, she had thought but little of the fashion of her clothes. But when she began to dress herself for the evening, she did ask her mother with some anxiety what she had better wear. "If he loves you he will hardly see what you have on," said the mother. But not the less was she careful to smooth her daughter's hair, and make the most that might be made of those faded roses.

How Susan's heart beat,—how both their hearts beat as the hands of the clock came round to seven! And then, sharp at seven, came the knock; that same short bold ringing knock which Susan had so soon learned to know as belonging to Aaron Dunn. "Oh mother, I had better go up stairs," she cried, starting from her chair.

"No dear; you would only be more nervous."

"I will, mother."

"No, no dear; you have not time;" and then Aaron Dunn was in the room.

She had thought much what she would say to him, but had not yet quite made up her mind. It mattered however but very little. On whatever she might have resolved, her resolution would have vanished to the wind. Aaron Dunn came into the room, and in one second she found herself in the centre of a whirlwind, and his arms were the storms that enveloped her on every side.

"My own, own darling girl," he said over and over again, as he pressed her to his heart, quite regardless of Mrs. Bell, who stood by, sobbing with joy. "My own Susan."

"Aaron, dear Aaron," she whispered. But she had already recognized the fact that for the present meeting a passive part would become her well, and save her a deal of trouble. She had her lover there quite safe, safe beyond anything that Mr. or Mrs. Beckard might have to say to the contrary. She was quite happy; only that there were symptoms now and again that the whirlwind was about to engulf her yet once more.

"Dear Aaron, I am so glad you are come," said the innocent-minded widow, as she went up stairs with him, to show him his room; and then he embraced her also. "Dear, dear mother," he said.

On the next day there was, as a matter of course, a family conclave. Hetta and Phineas came down, and discussed the whole subject of the coming marriage with Mrs. Bell. Hetta at first was not quite certain;—ought they not to inquire whether the situation was permanent?

"I won't inquire at all," said Mrs. Bell, with an energy that startled both the daughter and son-in-law. "I would not part them now; no, not if— " and the widow shuddered as she thought of her daughter's sunken eyes, and pale cheeks.

"He is a good lad," said Phineas, "and I trust she will make him a sober steady wife;" and so the matter was settled.

During this time, Susan and Aaron were walking along the Balston road; and they also had settled the matter—quite as satisfactorily.

Such was the courtship of Susan Dunn.

The O'Conors of Castle Conor, County Mayo

Originally appeared in *Harper's New Monthly Magazine*, May 1860. Reprinted in *Tales of All Countries* [First Series] (1861). Written in the Pyrenees between 1 September and 29 October 1859, during the composition of *Castle Richmond*. Like 'Father Giles of Ballymoy', a farcical (but according to *An Autobiography*, substantially true) anecdote dating from Trollope's earliest days in Ireland. Trollope took up hunting soon after he took up his post as a Postal Surveyor's Clerk for the Central District of Ireland in 1841 and remained a lifelong devotee. The broadness of the humour in 'The O'Conors' recalls some of the colourful digressive episodes in Trollope's first novel *The Macdermots of Ballycloran* (1847). One reviewer compared the story to *Pickwick*. In common with 'Miss Ophelia Gledd' and 'Father Giles of Ballymoy', this story features Archibald Green as an authorial persona.

I SHALL NEVER forget my first introduction to country life in Ireland, my first day's hunting there, or the manner in which I passed the evening afterwards. Nor shall I ever cease to be grateful for the hospitality which I received from the O'Conors of Castle Conor. My acquaintance with the family was first made in the following manner. But before I begin my story, let me inform my reader, that my name is Archibald Green.

I had been for a fortnight in Dublin, and was about to proceed into county Mayo on business which would occupy me there for some weeks. My head-quarters would, I found, be at the town of Ballyglass; and I soon learned that Ballyglass was not a place in which I should find hotel accommodation of a luxurious kind, or much congenial society indigenous to the place itself.

"But you are a hunting man, you say," said old Sir P—C—; "and in that case you will soon know Tom O'Conor. Tom won't let you be dull. I'd write you a letter to Tom, only he'll certainly make you out without my taking the trouble."

I did think at the time that the old baronet might have written the letter for me, as he had been a friend of my father's in former days; but he did not, and I started for Ballyglass with no other introduction to any one in the county than that contained in Sir P—'s promise that I should soon know Mr. Thomas O'Conor.

I had already provided myself with a horse, groom, saddle and bridle, and these I sent down, en avant, that the Ballyglassians might know that I was somebody. Perhaps, before I arrived, Tom O'Conor might learn that a hunting man was coming into the neighbourhood, and I might find at the inn a polite note intimating that a bed was at my service at Castle Conor. I had heard so much of the free hospitality of the Irish gentry as to imagine that such a thing might be possible.

But I found nothing of the kind. Hunting gentlemen in those days were very common in county Mayo, and one horse was no great evidence of a man's standing in the world. Men there, as I learnt afterwards, are sought for themselves quite as much as they are elsewhere; and though my groom's top-boots were neat, and my horse a very tidy animal, my entry into Ballyglass created no sensation whatever.

In about four days after my arrival, when I was already infinitely disgusted with the little pot-house in which I was forced to stay, and had made up my mind that the people in county Mayo were a churlish set, I sent my horse on to a meet of the fox-hounds, and followed after myself on an open car.

No one but an erratic fox hunter such as I am—a fox-hunter, I mean, whose lot it has been to wander about from one pack of hounds to another—can understand the melancholy feeling which a man has when he first intrudes himself, unknown by any one, among an entirely new set of sportsmen. When a stranger falls thus, as it were out of the moon into a hunt, it is impossible that men should not stare at him and ask who he is. And it is so disagreeable to be stared at, and to have such questions asked! This feeling does not come upon a man in

Leicestershire or Gloucestershire, where the numbers are large, and a stranger or two will always be overlooked, but in small hunting fields it is so painful that a man has to pluck up much courage before he encounters it.

We met on the morning in question at Bingham's Grove. There were not above twelve or fifteen men out, all of whom, or nearly all, were cousins to each other. They seemed to be all Toms, and Pats, and Larrys, and Micks. I was done up very knowingly in pink, and thought that I looked quite the thing; but for two or three hours nobody noticed me.

I had my eyes about me, however, and soon found out which of them was Tom O'Conor. He was a fine-looking fellow, thin and tall, but not largely made, with a piercing gray eye, and a beautiful voice for speaking to a hound. He had two sons there also, short, slight fellows, but exquisite horsemen. I already felt that I had a kind of acquaintance with the father, but I hardly knew on what ground to put in my claim.

We had no sport early in the morning. It was a cold bleak February day, with occasional storms of sleet. We rode from cover to cover, but all in vain. "I am sorry, sir, that we are to have such a bad day, as you are a stranger here," said one gentleman to me. This was Jack O'Conor, Tom's eldest son, my bosom friend for many a year after. Poor Jack! I fear that the Encumbered Estates Court sent him altogether adrift upon the world.

"We may still have a run from Poulnaroe, if the gentleman chooses to come on," said a voice coming from behind with a sharp trot. It was Tom O'Conor.

"Wherever the hounds go, I'll follow," said I.

"Then come on to Poulnaroe," said Mr. O'Conor. I trotted on quickly by his side, and before we reached the cover, had managed to slip in something about Sir P. C.

"What the deuce!" said he. "What! a friend of Sir P—'s? Why the deuce didn't you tell me so? What are you doing down here? Where are you staying," &c., &c., &c.

At Poulnaroe we found a fox, but before we did so Mr. O'Conor had asked me over to Castle Conor. And this he did in such a way that there was no possibility of refusing him—or, I should rather say, of disobeying him. For his invitation came quite in the tone of a command.

"You'll come to us of course when the day is over—and let me see; we're near Ballyglass now, but the run will be right away in our direction. Just send word for them to send your things to Castle Conor."

"But they're all about, and unpacked," said I.

"Never mind. Write a note and say what you want now, and go and get the rest to-morrow yourself. Here, Patsey!—Patsey! run into Ballyglass for this gentleman at once. Now don't be long, for the chances are we shall find here." And then, after giving some further hurried instructions he left me to write a line in pencil to the innkeeper's wife on the bank of a ditch.

This I accordingly did. "Send my small portmanteau," I said, "and all my black dress clothes, and shirts, and socks, and all that, and above all my dressing things which are on the little table, and the satin neck-handkerchief, and whatever you do, mind you send my *pumps*;" and I underscored the latter word; for Jack O'Conor, when his father left me, went on pressing the invitation. "My sisters are going to get up a dance," said he; "and if you are fond of that kind of things perhaps we can amuse you." Now in those days I was very fond of dancing—and very fond of young ladies too, and therefore glad enough to learn that Tom O'Conor had daughters as well as sons. On this account I was very particular in underscoring the word pumps.

"And hurry, you young divil," he said to Patsey.

"I have told him to take the portmanteau over on a car," said I.

"All right; then you'll find it there on our arrival."

We had an excellent run in which I may make bold to say that I did not acquit myself badly. I stuck very close to the hounds, as did the whole of the O'Conor brood; and when the fellow contrived to earth himself, as he did, I received those compliments on my horse, which is the most approved praise which one fox-hunter ever gives to another.

We'll buy that fellow of you before we let you go," said Peter, the youngest son.

"I advise you to look sharp after your money if you sell him to my brother," said Jack.

And then we trotted slowly off to Castle Conor, which, however, was by no means near to us. "We have ten miles to go;—good Irish miles," said the father. "I don't know that I ever remember a fox from Poulnaroe taking that line before."

"He wasn't a Poulnaroe fox," said Peter.

"I don't know that," said Jack; and then they debated that question hotly.

Our horses were very tired, and it was late before we reached Mr. O'Conor's house. That getting home from hunting with a thoroughly weary animal, who has no longer sympathy or example to carry him on, is very tedious work. In the present instance I had company with me; but when a man is alone, when his horse toes at every ten steps, when the night is dark and the rain pouring, and there are yet eight miles of road to be conquered,—at such times a man is almost apt to swear that he will give up hunting.

At last we were in the Castle Conor stable yard;—for we had approached the house by some back way; and as we entered the house by a door leading through a wilderness of back passages, Mr. O'Conor said out loud, "Now, boys, remember I sit down to dinner in twenty minutes." And then turning expressly to me, he laid his hand kindly upon my shoulder and said, "I hope you will make yourself quite at home at Castle Conor,—and whatever you do, don't keep us waiting for dinner. You can dress in twenty minutes, I suppose?"

"In ten!" said I, glibly.

"That's well. Jack and Peter will show you your room," and so he turned away and left us.

My two young friends made their way into the great hall, and thence into the drawing-room, and I followed them. We were all dressed in pink, and had waded deep through bog and mud. I did not exactly know whither I was being led in this guise, but I soon found myself in the presence of two young ladies, and of a girl about thirteen years of age.

"My sisters," said Jack, introducing me very laconically; "Miss O'Conor, Miss Kate O'Conor, Miss Tizzy O'Conor."

"My name is not Tizzy," said the younger; "it's Eliza. How do you do, sir? I hope you had a fine hunt! Was papa well up, Jack?"

Jack did not condescend to answer this question, but asked one of the elder girls whether anything had come, and whether a room had been made ready for me.

"Oh yes!" said Miss O'Conor; "they came, I know, for I saw them brought into the house; and I hope Mr. Green will find everything comfortable." As she said this I thought I saw a slight smile steal across her remarkably pretty mouth.

They were both exceedingly pretty girls. Fanny the elder wore long glossy curls,—for I write, oh reader, of bygone days, as long ago as that, when ladies wore curls if it pleased them so to do, and gentlemen danced in pumps, with black handkerchiefs round their necks—yes, long black, or nearly black silken curls; and then she had such eyes;—I never knew whether they were most wicked or most bright; and her face was all dimples, and each dimple was laden with laughter and laden with love. Kate was probably the prettier girl of the two, but on the whole not so attractive. She was fairer than her sister, and wore her hair in braids; and was also somewhat more demure in her manner.

In spite of the special injunctions of Mr. O'Conor senior, it was impossible not to loiter for five minutes over the drawing-room fire talking to these houris—more especially as I seemed to know them intimately by intuition before half of the five minutes was over. They were so easy, so pretty, so graceful, so kind, they seemed to take it so much as a matter of course that I should stand there talking in my red coat and muddy boots.

"Well; do go and dress yourselves," at last said Fanny, pretending to speak to her brothers but looking more especially at me. "You know how mad papa will be. And remember, Mr. Green, we expect great things from your dancing to-night. Your coming just at this time is such a Godsend." And again that soupçon of a smile passed over her face.

I hurried up to my room, Peter and Jack coming with me to the door. "Is everything right?" said Peter, looking among the towels and water-jugs. "They've given you a decent fire for a wonder," said Jack stirring up the red hot turf which blazed in the grate. "All right as a trivet," said I. "And look alive like a good fellow," said Jack. We had scowled at each other in the morning as very young men do when they are strangers; and now, after a few hours, we were intimate friends.

I immediately turned to my work, and was gratified to find that all my things were laid out ready for dressing; my portmanteau had of course come open, as my keys were in my pocket, and therefore some of the excellent servants of the house had been able to save me all the trouble of unpacking. There was my shirt hanging before the fire; my black clothes were spread upon the bed, my socks and collar and handkerchief beside them; my brushes were on the toilet table, and everything prepared exactly as though my own man had been there. How nice.

I immediately went to work at getting off my spurs and boots, and then proceeded to loosen the buttons at my knees. In doing this I sat down in the arm-chair which had been drawn up for me, opposite the fire. But what was the object on which my eyes then fell;—the objects I should rather say!

Immediately in front of my chair was placed, just ready for my feet, an enormous pair of shooting-boots—half-boots, made to lace up round the ankles, with thick double leather soles, and each bearing half a stone of iron in the shape of nails and heel-pieces. I had superintended the making of these shoes in Burlington Arcade with the greatest diligence. I was never a good shot; and, like some other sportsmen, intended to make up for my deficiency in performance by the excellence of my shooting apparel. "Those nails are not large enough," I had said; "nor nearly large enough." But when the boots came home they struck even me as being too heavy, too metalsome. "He, he, he," laughed the boot boy as he turned them up for me to look at. It may therefore be imagined of what nature were the articles which were thus set out for the evening's dancing.

And then the way in which they were placed! When I saw this the conviction flew across my mind like a flash of lightning that the preparation had been made under other eyes than those of the servant. The heavy big boots were placed so prettily before the chair, and the strings of each were made to dangle down at the sides, as though just ready for tying! They seemed to say, the boots did, "Now, make haste. We at any rate are ready—you cannot say that you were kept waiting for us." No mere servant's hand had ever enabled a pair of boots to laugh at one so completely.

But what was I to do? I rushed at the small portmanteau, thinking that my pumps also might be there. The woman surely could not have been such a fool as to send me those tons of iron for my evening wear! But alas, alas! no pumps were there. There was nothing else in the way of covering for my feet; not even a pair of slippers.

And now what was I to do? The absolute magnitude of my misfortune only loomed upon me by degrees. The twenty minutes allowed by that stern old paterfamilias were already gone and I had done nothing towards dressing. And indeed it was impossible that I should do anything that would be of avail. I could not go down to dinner in my stocking feet, nor could I put on my black dress trousers over a pair of mud painted top-boots. As for those iron-soled horrors—; and then I gave one of them a kick with the side of my bare foot which sent it half way under the bed.

But what was I to do? I began washing myself and brushing my hair with this horrid weight upon my mind. My first plan was to go to bed, and send down word that I had been taken suddenly ill in the stomach; then to rise early in the morning and get away unobserved. But by such a course of action I should lose all chance of any further acquaintance with those pretty girls! That they were already aware of the extent of my predicament, and were now enjoying it—of that I was quite sure.

What if I boldly put on the shooting-boots, and clattered down to dinner in them? What if I took the bull by the horns, and made myself the most of the joke? This might be very well for the dinner, but it would be a bad joke for me when the hour for dancing came. And, alas! I felt that I lacked the courage. It is not every man that can walk down to dinner, in a strange house full of ladies, wearing such boots as those I have described.

Should I not attempt to borrow a pair? This, all the world will say, should have been my first idea. But I have not yet mentioned that I am myself a large-boned man, and that my feet are especially well developed. I had never for a moment entertained a hope that I should find any one in that house whose boot I could wear. But at last I rang the bell. I would send for Jack, and if everything failed, I would communicate my grief to him.

I had to ring twice before anybody came. The servants, I well knew, were putting the dinner on the table. At last a man entered the room, dressed in rather shabby black, whom I afterwards learned to be the butler.

"What is your name, my friend," said I, determined to make an ally of the man.

"My name? Why Larry sure, yer honor. And the masther is out of his sinses in a hurry, becase yer honer don't come down."

"Is he though? Well, now Larry; tell me this; which of all the gentlemen in the house has got the largest foot?"

"Is it the largest foot, yer honer?" said Larry, altogether surprised by my question.

Yes; the largest foot," and then I proceeded to explain to him my misfortune. He took up first my top-boot, and then the shooting-boot—in looking at which he gazed with wonder at the nails;—and then he glanced at my feet, measuring them with his eye; and after this he pronounced his opinion.

"Yer honer couldn't wear a morsel of leather belonging to ere a one of 'em, young or ould. There niver was a foot like that yet among the O'Conors."

"But are there no strangers staying here?"

"There's three or four on 'em come in to dinner; but they'll be wanting their own boots I'm thinking. And there's young Misther Dillon; he's come to stay. But Lord love you—" and he again looked at the enormous extent which lay between the heel and the toe of the shooting apparatus which he still held in his hand. "I niver see such a foot as that in the whole barony," he said, "barring my own."

Now Larry was a large man, much larger altogether than myself, and as he said this I looked down involuntarily at his feet; or rather at his foot, for as he stood I could only see one. And then a sudden hope filled my heart. On that foot there glittered a shoe—not indeed such as were my own which were now resting ingloriously at Ballyglass while they were so sorely needed at Castle Conor; but one which I could wear before ladies, without shame—and in my present frame of mind with infinite contentment.

"Let me look at that one of your own," said I to the man, as though it were merely a subject for experimental inquiry. Larry, accustomed to obedience, took off the shoe and handed it to me. My own foot was immediately in it, and I found that it fitted me like a glove.

"And now the other," said I—not smiling, for a smile would have put him on his guard; but somewhat sternly, so that that habit of obedience should not desert him at this perilous moment. And then I stretched out my hand.

"But yer honer can't keep 'em you know," said he. "I haven't the ghost of another shoe to my feet." But I only looked more sternly than before, and still held out my hand. Custom prevailed. Larry stooped down slowly, looking at me the while, and pulling off the other slipper handed it to me with much hesitation. Alas! as I put it to my foot I found that it was old, and worn, and irredeemably down at heel;—that it was in fact no counterpart at all to that other one which was to do duty as its fellow. But nevertheless I put my foot into it, and felt that a descent to the drawing-room was now possible.

"But yer honer will give 'em back to a poor man?" said Larry almost crying. "The masther's mad this minute becase the dinner's not up. Glory to God, only listhen to that." And as he spoke a tremendous peal rang out from some bell down stairs that had evidently been shaken by an angry hand.

"Larry," said I—and I endeavoured to assume a look of very grave importance as I spoke—"I look to you to assist me in this matter."

"Och—wirra sthrue then, and will you let me go? just listhen to that," and another angry peal rang out, loud and repeated.

"If you do as I ask you," I continued, "you shall be well rewarded. Look here; look at these boots," and I held up the shooting-shoes new from Burlington Arcade. "They cost thirty shillings—thirty shillings! and I will give them to you for the loan of this pair of slippers."

"They'd be no use at all to me, yer honer; not the laist use in life."

"You could do with them very well for to-night, and then you could sell them. And here are ten shillings besides," and I held out half a sovereign which the poor fellow took into his hand.

I waited no further parley but immediately walked out of the room. With one foot I was sufficiently pleased. As regarded that I felt that I had overcome my difficulty. But the other was not so satisfactory. Whenever I attempted to lift it from the ground the horrid slipper would fall off, or only just hang by the toe. As for dancing, that would be out of the question.

"Och, murther, murther," sang out Larry, as he heard me going down stairs. "What will I do at all? 'Tare and 'ounds; there, he's at it agin, as mad as blazes." This last exclamation had reference to another peal which was evidently the work of the master's hand.

I confess I was not quite comfortable as I walked down stairs. In the first place I was nearly half an hour late, and I knew from the vigour of the peals that had sounded that my slowness had already been made the subject of strong remarks. And then my left shoe went flop, flop on every alternate step of the stairs; by no exertion of my foot in the drawing up of my toe could I induce it to remain permanently fixed upon my foot. But over and above and worse than all this was the conviction strong upon my mind that I should become a subject of merriment to the girls as soon as I entered the room. They would understand the cause of my distress, and probably at this moment were expecting to hear me clatter through the stone hall with those odious metal boots.

However, I hurried down and entered the drawing-room, determined to keep my position near the door, so that I might have as little as possible to do on entering and as little as possible in going out. But I had other difficulties in store for me. I had not as yet been introduced to Mrs. O'Conor; nor to Miss O'Conor, the squire's unmarried sister.

"Upon my word I thought you were never coming," said Mr. O'Conor as soon as he saw me. "It is just one hour since we entered the house. Jack, I wish you would find out what has come to that fellow Larry," and again he rang the bell. He was too angry, or it might be too impatient to go through the ceremony of introducing me to anybody.

I saw that the two girls looked at me very sharply, but I stood at the back of an arm-chair so that no one could see my feet. But that little imp Tizzy walked round deliberately, looked at my heels, and then walked back again. It was clear that she was in the secret.

There were eight or ten people in the room, but I was too much fluttered to notice well who they were.

"Mamma," said Miss O'Conor, "let me introduce Mr. Green to you."

It luckily happened that Mrs. O'Conor was on the same side of the fire as myself, and I was able to take the hand which she offered me without coming round into the middle of the circle. Mrs. O'Conor was a little woman, apparently not of much importance in the world, but if one might judge from first appearance, very good-natured.

"And my aunt Die, Mr. Green," said Kate, pointing to a very straight-backed, grim-looking lady, who occupied a corner of a sofa, on the opposite side of the hearth. I knew that politeness required that I should walk across the room and make acquaintance with her. But under the existing circumstances how was I to obey the dictates of politeness? I was determined therefore to stand my ground, and merely bowed across the room at Miss O'Conor. In so doing I made an enemy who never deserted me during the whole of my intercourse with the family. But for her, who knows who might have been sitting opposite to me as I now write?

"Upon my word, Mr. Green, the ladies will expect much from an Adonis who takes so long over his toilet," said Tom O'Conor in that cruel tone of banter which he knew so well how to use.

"You forget, father, that men in London can't jump in and out of their clothes as quick as we wild Irish-men," said Jack.

"Mr. Green knows that we expect a great deal from him this evening. I hope you polk well, Mr. Green," said Kate.

I muttered something about never dancing, but I knew that that which I said was inaudible.

"I don't think Mr. Green will dance," said Tizzy; "at least not much." The impudence of that child was, I think, unparalleled by any that I have ever witnessed.

"But in the name of all that's holy, why don't we have dinner?" And Mr. O'Conor thundered at the door. "Larry, Larry, Larry!" he screamed.

"Yes, yer honer, it'll be all right in two seconds," answered Larry, from some bottomless abyss. "Tare an' ages; what'll I do at all," I heard him continuing, as he made his way into the hall. Oh what a clatter he made upon the pavement,—for it was all stone! And how the drops of perspiration stood upon my brow as I listened to him!

And then there was a pause, for the man had gone into the dining-room. I could see now that Mr. O'Conor was becoming very angry, and Jack the eldest son—oh, how often he and I have laughed over all this since—left the drawing-room for the second time. Immediately afterwards, Larry's footsteps were again heard, hurrying across the hall, and then there was a great slither, and an exclamation, and the noise of a fall—and I could plainly hear poor Larry's head strike against the stone floor.

"Ochone, ochone!" he cried at the top of his voice—"I'm murthered with 'em now intirely; and d— 'em for boots—St. Peter be good to me."

There was a general rush into the hall, and I was carried with the stream. The poor fellow who had broken his head would be sure to tell how I had robbed him of his shoes. The coachman was already helping him up, and Peter good-naturedly lent a hand.

"What on earth is the matter?" said Mr. O'Conor.

"He must be tipsy," whispered Miss O'Conor, the maiden sister.

"I aint tipsy at all thin," said Larry, getting up and rubbing the back of his head, and sundry other parts of his body. "Tipsy indeed!" And then he added when he was quite upright, "The dinner is served—at last."

And he bore it all without telling. "I'll give that fellow a guinea to-morrow morning," said I to myself—"if it's the last that I have in the world."

I shall never forget the countenance of the Miss O'Conors as Larry scrambled up cursing the unfortunate boots—"What on earth has he got on," said Mr. O'Conor.

"Sorrow take 'em for shoes," ejaculated Larry. But his spirit was good and he said not a word to betray me.

We all then went in to dinner how we best could. It was useless for us to go back into the drawing-room, that each might seek his own partner. Mr. O'Conor "the masther," not caring much for the girls who were around him, and being already half beside himself with the confusion and delay, led the way by himself. I as a stranger should have given my arm to Mrs. O'Conor; but as it was I took her eldest daughter instead, and contrived to shuffle along into the dining-room without exciting much attention, and when there I found myself happily placed between Kate and Fanny.

"I never knew anything so awkward," said Fanny; "I declare I can't conceive what has come to our old servant Larry. He's generally the most precise person in the world, and now he is nearly an hour late—and then he tumbles down in the hall."

"I am afraid I am responsible for the delay," said I.

"But not for the tumble I suppose," said Kate from the other side. I felt that I blushed up to the eyes, but I did not dare to enter into explanations.

"Tom," said Tizzy, addressing her father across the table, "I hope you had a good run to-day." It did seem odd to me that a young lady should call her father Tom, but such was the fact.

"Well; pretty well," said Mr. O'Conor.

"And I hope you were up with the hounds."

"You may ask Mr. Green that. He at any rate was with them, and therefore he can tell you."

"Oh, he wasn't before you, I know. No Englishman could get before you—I am quite sure of that."

"Don't you be impertinent, miss," said Kate. "You can easily see, Mr. Green, that papa spoils my sister Eliza."

"Do you hunt in top-boots, Mr. Green?" said Tizzy.

To this I made no answer. She would have drawn me into a conversation about my feet in half a minute, and the slightest allusion to the subject threw me into a fit of perspiration.

"Are you fond of hunting, Miss O'Conor?" asked I, blindly hurrying into any other subject of conversation.

Miss O'Conor owned that she was fond of hunting—just a little; only papa would not allow it. When the hounds met anywhere within reach of Castle Conor, she and Kate would ride out to look at them; and if papa was not there that day—an omission of rare occurrence—they would ride a few fields with the hounds.

"But he lets Tizzy keep with them the whole day," said she, whispering.

"And has Tizzy a pony of her own?"

"Oh yes, Tizzy has everything. She's papa's pet, you know."

"And whose pet are you?" I asked.

"Oh—I am nobody's pet, unless sometimes Jack makes a pet of

me when he's in a good humour. Do you make pets of your sisters, Mr. Green?"

"I have none. But if I had I should not make pets of them."

"Not of your own sisters?"

"No. As for myself I'd sooner make a pet of my friend's sister; a great deal."

"How very unnatural," said Miss O'Conor with the prettiest look of surprise imaginable.

"Not at all unnatural I think," said I, looking tenderly and lovingly into her face. Where does one find girls so pretty, so easy, so sweet, so talkative as the Irish girls? And then with all their talking and all their ease, who ever hears of their misbehaving? They certainly love flirting as they also love dancing. But they flirt without mischief and without malice.

I had now quite forgotten my misfortune, and was beginning to think how well I should like to have Fanny O'Conor for my wife. In this frame of mind I was bending over towards her as a servant took away a plate from the other side, when a sepulchral note sounded in my ear. It was like the memento mori of the old Roman;—as though some one pointed in the midst of my bliss to the sword hung over my head by a thread. It was the voice of Larry, whispering in his agony just above my head—

"They's disthroying my poor feet intirely, intirely; so they is! I can't bear it much longer, yer honer." I had committed murder like Macbeth; and now my Banquo had come to disturb me at my feast.

"What is it he says to you?" asked Fanny.

"Oh nothing," I answered, once more in my misery.

"There seems to be some point of confidence between you and our Larry," she remarked.

"Oh no," said I, quite confused; "not at all."

"You need not be ashamed of it. Half the gentlemen in the county have their confidences with Larry;—and some of the ladies too, I can tell you. He was born in this house, and never lived anywhere else; and I am sure he has a larger circle of acquaintance than any one else in it."

I could not recover my self-possession for the next ten minutes. Whenever Larry was on our side of the table I was afraid he was coming to me with another agonized whisper. When he was opposite I could not but watch him as he hobbled in his misery. It was evident that the boots were too tight for him, and had they been made throughout of iron they could not have been less capable of yielding to the feet. I pitied him from the bottom of my heart. And I pitied myself also, wishing that I was well in bed upstairs with some feigned malady, so that Larry might have had his own again.

And then for a moment I missed him from the room. He had doubtless gone to relieve his tortured feet in the servants-hall, and as he did so was cursing my cruelty. But what mattered it? Let him curse. If he would only stay away and do that I would appease his wrath when we were alone together with pecuniary satisfaction.

But there was no such rest in store for me. "Larry, Larry," shouted Mr. O'Conor, "where on earth has the fellow gone to?" They were all cousins at the table except myself, and Mr. O'Conor was not therefore restrained by any feeling of ceremony. "There is something wrong with that fellow to-day; what is it, Jack?"

"Upon my word, sir, I don't know," said Jack.

"I think he must be tipsy," whispered Miss O'Conor, the maiden sister, who always sat at her brother's left hand. But a whisper though it was, it was audible all down the table.

"No, ma'am; it aint dhrink at all," said the coachman. "It is his feet as does it."

"His feet!" shouted Tom O'Conor.

"Yes; I know it's his feet," said that horrid Tizzy. "He's got on great thick nailed shoes. It was that that made him tumble down in the hall."

I glanced at each side of me, and could see that there was a certain consciousness expressed in the face of each of my two neighbours;—on Kate's mouth there was decidedly a smile, or rather perhaps the slightest possible inclination that way; whereas on Fanny's part I thought I saw something like a rising sorrow at my distress. So at least I flattered myself.

"Send him back into the room immediately," said Tom, who looked at me as though he had some consciousness that I had introduced all this confusion into his household. What should I do? Would it not be best for me to make a clean breast of it before them all? But alas! I lacked the courage.

The coachman went out, and we were left for five minutes without any servant, and Mr. O'Conor the while became more and more savage. I attempted to say a word to Fanny, but failed—Vox faucibus hæsit.

"I don't think he has got any others," said Tizzy—"at least none others left."

On the whole I am glad I did not marry into the family, as I could not have endured that girl to stay in my house as a sister-in-law.

"Where the d—has that other fellow gone to?" said Tom. "Jack, do go out and see what is the matter. If anybody is drunk send for me."

"Oh, there is nobody drunk," said Tizzy.

Jack went out, and the coachman returned; but what was done and said I hardly remember. The whole room seemed to swim round and round, and as far as I can recollect the company sat mute, neither eating nor drinking. Presently Jack returned.

"It's all right," said he. I always liked Jack. At the present moment he just looked towards me and laughed slightly.

"All right?" said Tom. "But is the fellow coming?"

"We can do with Richard, I suppose," said Jack.

"No—I can't do with Richard," said the father. "And I will know what it all means. Where is that fellow Larry?"

Larry had been standing just outside the door, and now he entered gently as a mouse. No sound came from his footfall, nor was there in his face that look of pain which it had worn for the last fifteen minutes. But he was not the less abashed, frightened, and unhappy.

"What is all this about, Larry?" said his master, turning to him. "I insist upon knowing."

"Och thin, Mr. Green, yer honer, I wouldn't be afther telling agin yer honer; indeed I wouldn't thin, av' the masther would only let me hould my tongue." And he looked across at me, deprecating my anger.

"Mr. Green! said Mr. O'Conor.

"Yes, yer honer. It's all along of his honer's thick shoes," and Larry stepping backwards towards the door, lifted them up from some corner, and coming well forward, exposed them with the soles uppermost to the whole table.

"And that's not all, yer honer; but they've squoze the very toes of me into a jelly."

There was now a loud laugh, in which Jack and Peter and Fanny and Kate and Tizzy all joined; as too did Mr. O'Conor—and I also myself after a while.

"Whose boots are they?" demanded Miss O'Conor senior, with her severest tone and grimmest accent.

"'Deed then and the divil may have them for me, Miss," answered Larry. "They war Mr. Green's, but the likes of him won't wear them agin afther the likes of me—barring he wanted them very particular," added he, remembering his own pumps.

I began muttering something, feeling that the time had come when I must tell the tale. But Jack with great good nature, took up the story and told it so well, that I hardly suffered in the telling.

"And that's it," said Tom O'Conor, laughing till I thought he would have fallen from his chair. "So you've got Larry's shoes on— "

"And very well he fills them," said Jack.

"And it's his honer that's welcome to 'em," said Larry, grinning from ear to ear now that he saw that "the masther" was once more in a good humour.

"I hope they'll be nice shoes for dancing," said Kate.

"Only there's one down at the heel I know," said Tizzy.

"The servant's shoes!" This was an exclamation made by the maiden lady, and intended apparently only for her brother's ear. But it was clearly audible by all the party.

"Better that than no dinner," said Peter.

"But what are you to do about the dancing?" said Fanny, with an air of dismay on her face which flattered me with an idea that she did care whether I danced or no.

In the mean time Larry, now as happy as an emperor, was tripping round the room without any shoes to encumber him as he withdrew the plates from the table.

"And it's his honer that's welcome to 'em," said he again, as he pulled off the table-cloth with a flourish. "And why wouldn't he, and he able to folly the hounds betther nor any Englishman that iver war in these parts before,—anyways so Mick says!"

Now Mick was the huntsman, and this little tale of eulogy from Larry went far towards easing my grief. I had ridden well to the hounds that day, and I knew it.

There was nothing more said about the shoes, and I was soon again at my ease, although Miss O'Conor did say something about the impropriety of Larry walking about in his stocking feet. The ladies however soon withdrew,—to my sorrow, for I was getting on swimmingly with Fanny; and then we gentlemen gathered round the fire and filled our glasses.

In about ten minutes a very light tap was heard, the door was opened to the extent of three inches, and a female voice which I readily recognized called to Jack.

Jack went out, and in a second or two put his head back into the room and called to me—"Green," he said, "just step here a moment, there's a good fellow." I went out, and there I found Fanny standing with her brother.

"Here are the girls at their wits' ends," said he, "about your dancing. So Fanny has put a boy upon one of the horses, and proposes that you should send another line to Mrs. Meehan at Ballyglass. It's only ten miles, and he'll be back in two hours."

I need hardly say that I acted in conformity with this advice. I went into Mr. O'Conor's book room, with Jack and his sister, and there scribbled a note. It was delightful to feel how intimate I was with them, and how anxious they were to make me happy.

"And we won't begin till they come," said Fanny.

"Oh, Miss O'Conor, pray don't wait," said I.

"Oh, but we will," she answered. "You have your wine to drink, and then there's the tea; and then we'll have a song or two. I'll spin it out; see if I don't." And so we went to the front door where the boy was already on his horse—her own nag as I afterwards found.

"And Patsey," said she, "ride for your life now; and Patsey, whatever you do, don't come back without Mr. Green's pumps—his dancing-shoes you know."

And in about two hours the pumps did arrive; and I don't think I ever spent a pleasanter evening or got more satisfaction out of a pair of shoes. They had not been two minutes on my feet before Larry was carrying a tray of negus across the room in those which I had worn at dinner.

"The Dillon girls are going to stay here," said Fanny as I wished her good night at two o'clock. "And we'll have dancing every evening as long as you remain."

"But I shall leave to-morrow," said I.

"Indeed you won't. Papa will take care of that."

And so he did. "You had better go over to Ballyglass yourself to-morrow," said he, "and collect your own things. There's no knowing else what you may have to borrow of Larry."

I stayed there three weeks, and in the middle of the third I thought that everything would be arranged between me and Fanny. But the aunt interfered; and in about a twelvemonth after my adventures she consented to make a more fortunate man happy for his life.

La Mère Bauche

Originally appeared in *Tales of All Countries* [First Series] (1861). Though sold to *Harper's New Monthly Magazine* they did not use it until 1868. Written in the Pyrenees between 1 September and 29 October 1859, during the composition of *Castle Richmond*. This trip also obviously supplied the setting: Rose Trollope's itinerary confirms a stop at Vernet-les-Bains. The hotel-setting and theme of parental interference in marital affairs looks forward to *The Golden Lion of Granpère* (1872); the tragic conclusion may be compared with that of *An Eye For An Eye* (1879).

THE PYRENEEAN valley in which the baths of Vernet are situated is not much known to English, or indeed to any travellers. Tourists in search of good hotels and picturesque beauty combined, do not generally extend their journeys to the Eastern Pyrenees. They rarely get beyond Luchon; and in this they are right, as they thus end their peregrinations at the most lovely spot among these mountains; and are as a rule so deceived, imposed on, and bewildered by guides, inn-keepers, and horse-owners at this otherwise delightful place as to become undesirous of further travel. Nor do invalids from distant parts frequent Vernet. People of fashion go to the Eaux Bonnes and to Luchon, and people who are really ill to Baréges and Cauterets. It is at these places that one meets crowds of Parisians, and the daughters and wives of rich merchants from Bordeaux, with an admixture, now by no means inconsiderable, of Englishmen and Englishwomen. But the Eastern Pyrenees are still unfrequented. And probably they will remain so; for though there are among them lovely valleys—and of all such the valley of Vernet is perhaps the most lovely—they cannot compete with the mountain scenery of other tourists-loved regions in Europe. At the Port de Venasquez and the Brèche de Roland in the Western Pyrenees, or rather, to speak more truly, at spots in the close vicinity of these famous mountain entrances from France into Spain, one can make comparisons with Switzerland, Northern Italy, the Tyrol, and Ireland, which will not be injurious to the scenes then under view. But among the eastern mountains this can rarely be done. The hills do not stand thickly together so as to group themselves; the passes from one valley to another, though not wanting in altitude, are not close pressed together with over-hanging rocks, and are deficient in grandeur as well as loveliness. And then, as a natural consequence of all this, the hotels—are not quite as good as they should be.

But there is one mountain among them which can claim to rank with the Pic Du Midi or the Maledetta. No one can pooh-pooh the stern old Canigou, standing high and solitary, solemn and grand, between the two roads which run from Perpignan into Spain, the one by Prades and the other by Le Boulon. Under the Canigou, towards the west, lie the hot baths of Vernet, in a close secluded valley, which, as I have said before, is, as far as I know, the sweetest spot in these Eastern Pyrenees.

The frequenters of these baths were a few years back gathered almost entirely from towns not very far distant, from Perpignan, Narbonne, Carcassonne, and Bézières, and were not therefore famous, expensive, or luxurious; but those who believed in them believed with great faith; and it was certainly the fact that men and women who went thither worn with toil, sick with excesses, and nervous through over-care, came back fresh and strong, fit once more to attack the world with all its woes. Their character in latter days does not seem to have changed, though their circle of admirers may perhaps be somewhat extended.

In those days, by far the most noted and illustrious person in the village of Vernet was La Mère Bauche. That there had once been a Père Bauche was known to the world, for there was a Fils Bauche who lived with his mother; but no one seemed to remember more of him than that he had once existed. At Vernet he had never been known. La Mère Bauche was a native of the village, but her married life had been passed away from it, and she had returned in her early widowhood to become proprietress and manager, or, as one may say, the heart and soul of the Hôtel Bauche at Vernet.

This hotel was a large and somewhat rough establishment, intended for the accommodation of invalids who came to Vernet for their health. It was built immediately over one of the thermal springs, so that the water flowed from the bowels of the earth directly into the baths. There was accommodation for seventy people, and during the summer and autumn months the place was always full. Not a few also were to be found there during the winter and spring, for the charges of Madame Bauche were low, and the accommodation reasonably good.

And in this respect, as indeed in all others, Madame Bauche had the reputation of being an honest woman. She had a certain price, from which no earthly consideration would induce her to depart; and certain returns for this price in the shape of déjeuners and dinners, baths and beds, which she never failed to give in accordance with the dictates of a strict conscience. These were traits in the character of an hotel-keeper which cannot be praised too highly, and which had met their due reward in the custom of the public. But nevertheless there were those who thought that there was occasionally ground for complaint in the conduct even of Madame Bauche.

In the first place she was deficient in that pleasant smiling softness which should belong to any keeper of a house of public entertainment. In her general mode of life she was stern and silent with her guests, autocratic, authoritative, and sometimes contradictory in her house, and altogether irrational and unconciliatory when any change even for a day was proposed to her, or when any shadow of a complaint reached her ears.

Indeed of complaint, as made against the establishment, she was altogether intolerant. To such she had but one answer. He or she who complained might leave the place at a moment's notice if it so pleased them. There were always others ready to take their places. The power of making this answer came to her from the lowness of her prices; and it was a power which was very dear to her.

The baths were taken at different hours according to medical advice, but the usual time was from five to seven in the morning. The déjeuner or early meal was at nine o'clock, the dinner was at four. After that, no eating or drinking was allowed in the Hôtel Bauche. There was a café in the village, at which ladies and gentlemen could get a cup of coffee or a glass of eau sucré; but no such accommodation was to be had in the establishment. Not by any possible bribery or persuasion could any meal be procured at any other than the authorized hours. A visitor who should enter the salle à manger more than ten minutes after the last bell would be looked at very sourly by Madame Bauche, who on all occasions sat at the top of her own table. Should any one appear as much as half an hour late, he would receive only his share of what had been handed round. But after the last dish had been so handed, it was utterly useless for any one to enter the room at all.

Her appearance at the period of our tale was perhaps not altogether in her favour. She was about sixty years of age and was very stout and short in the neck. She wore her own gray hair, which at dinner was always tidy enough; but during the whole day previous to that hour she might be seen with it escaping from under her cap in extreme disorder. Her eyebrows were large and bushy, but those alone would not have given to her face that look of indomitable sternness which it possessed. Her eyebrows were serious in their effect, but not so serious as the pair of green spectacles which she always wore under them. It was thought by those who had analyzed the subject that the great secret of Madame Bauche's power lay in her green spectacles.

Her custom was to move about and through the whole establishment every day from breakfast till the period came for her to dress for dinner. She would visit every chamber and every bath, walk once or twice round the salle à manger, and very repeatedly round the kitchen; she would go into every hole and corner, and peer into everything through her green spectacles: and in these walks it was not always thought pleasant to meet her. Her custom was to move very slowly, with her hands generally clasped behind her back: she rarely spoke to the guests unless she was spoken to, and on such occasions she would not often diverge into general conversation. If any one had aught to say connected with the business of the establishment, she would listen, and then she would make her answers,—often not pleasant in the hearing.

And thus she walked her path through the world, a stern, hard, solemn old woman, not without gusts of passionate explosion; but honest withal, and not without some inward benevolence and true tenderness of heart. Children she had had many, some seven or eight. One or two had died, others had been married; she had sons settled far away from home, and at the time of which we are now speaking but one was left in any way subject to parental authority.

Adolphe Bauche was the only one of her children of whom much was remembered by the present denizens and hangers-on of the hotel. He was the youngest of the number, and having been born only very shortly before the return of Madame Bauche to Vernet, had been altogether reared there. It was thought by the world of those parts, and rightly thought, that he was his mother's darling—more so than had been any of his brothers and sisters,—the very apple of her eye, and gem of her life. At this time he was about twenty-five years of age, and for the last two years had been absent from Vernet—for reasons which will shortly be made to appear. He had been sent to Paris to see something of the world, and learn to talk French instead of the patois of his valley; and having left Paris had come down south into Languedoc, and remained there picking up some agricultural lore which it was thought might prove useful in the valley farms of Vernet. He was now expected home again very speedily, much to his mother's delight.

That she was kind and gracious to her favourite child does not perhaps give much proof of her benevolence; but she had also been kind and gracious to the orphan child of a neighbour; nay, to the orphan child of a rival innkeeper. At Vernet there had been more than one water establishment, but the proprietor of the second had died some few years after Madame Bauche had settled herself at the place. His house had not thrived, and his only child, a little girl, was left altogether without provision.

This little girl, Marie Clavert, La Mère Bauche had taken into her own house immediately after the father's death, although she had most cordially hated that father. Marie was then an infant, and Madame Bauche had accepted the charge without much thought, perhaps, as to what might be the child's ultimate destiny. But since then she had thoroughly done the duty of a mother by the little girl, who had become the pet of the whole establishment, the favourite plaything of Adolphe Bauche,—and at last of course his early sweetheart.

And then and therefore there had come troubles at Vernet. Of course all the world of the valley had seen what was taking place and what was likely to take place, long before Madame Bauche knew anything about it. But at last it broke upon her senses that her son, Adolphe Bauche, the heir to all her virtues and all her riches, the first young man in that or any neighbouring valley, was absolutely contemplating the idea of marrying that poor little orphan, Marie Clavert!

That any one should ever fall in love with Marie Clavert had never occurred to Madame Bauche. She had always regarded the child as a child, as the object of her charity, and as a little thing to be looked on as poor Marie by all the world. She, looking through her green spectacles, had never seen that Marie Clavert was a beautiful creature, full of ripening charms, such as young men love to look on. Marie was of infinite daily use to Madame Bauche in a hundred little things about the house, and the old lady thoroughly recognized and appreciated her ability. But for this very reason she had never taught herself to regard Marie otherwise than as a useful drudge. She was very fond of her protégée—so much so that she would listen to her in affairs about the house when she would listen to no one else;—but Marie's prettiness and grace and sweetness as a girl had all been thrown away upon Maman Bauche, as Marie used to call her.

But unluckily it had not been thrown away upon Adolphe. He had appreciated, as it was natural that he should do, all that had been so utterly indifferent to his mother; and consequently had fallen in love. Consequently also he had told his love; and consequently also, Marie had returned his love. Adolphe had been hitherto contradicted but in few things, and thought that all difficulty would be prevented by his informing his mother that he wished to marry Marie Clavert. But Marie, with a woman's instinct, had known better. She had trembled and almost crouched with fear when she confessed her love; and had absolutely hid herself from sight when Adolphe went forth, prepared to ask his mother's consent to his marriage.

The indignation and passionate wrath of Madame Bauche were past and gone two years before the date of this story, and I need not therefore much enlarge upon that subject. She was at first abusive and bitter, which was bad for Marie; and afterwards bitter and silent, which was worse. It was of course determined that poor Marie should be sent away to some asylum for orphans or penniless paupers—in short anywhere out of the way. What mattered her outlook into the world, her happiness, or indeed her very existence? The outlook and happiness of Adolphe Bauche,—was not that to be considered as everything at Vernet?

But this terrible sharp aspect of affairs did not last very long. In the first place La Mère Bauche had under those green spectacles a heart that in truth was tender and affectionate, and after the first two days of anger she admitted that something must be done for Marie Clavert; and after the fourth day she acknowledged that the world of the hotel, her world, would not go as well without Marie Clavert as it would with her. And in the next place Madame Bauche had a friend whose advice in grave matters she would sometimes take. This friend had told her that it would be much better to send away Adolphe, since it was so necessary that there should be a sending away of some one; that he would be much benefited by passing some months of his life away from his native valley; and that an absence of a year or two would teach him to forget Marie, even if it did not teach Marie to forget him.

And we must say a word or two about this friend. At Vernet he was usually called M. le Capitaine, though in fact he had never reached that rank. He had been in the army, and having been wounded in the leg while still a sous-lieutenant, had been pensioned, and had thus been interdicted from treading any further the thorny path that leads to glory. For the last fifteen years he had resided under the roof of Madame Bauche, at first as a casual visitor, going and coming, but now for many years as constant there as she was herself.

He was so constantly called Le Capitaine that his real name was seldom heard. It may however as well be known to us that this was Theodore Campan. He was a tall, well-looking man; always dressed in black garments, of a coarse description certainly, but scrupulously clean and well brushed; of perhaps fifty years of age, and conspicuous for the rigid uprightness of his back—and for a black wooden leg.

This wooden leg was perhaps the most remarkable trait in his character. It was always jet black, being painted, or polished, or japanned, as occasion might require, by the hands of the capitaine himself. It was longer than ordinary wooden legs, as indeed the capitaine was longer than ordinary men; but nevertheless it never seemed in any way to impede the rigid punctilious propriety of his movements. It was never in his way as wooden legs usually are in the way of their wearers. And then to render it more illustrious it had round its middle, round the calf of the leg we may so say, a band of bright brass which shone like burnished gold.

It had been the capitaine's custom, now for some years past, to retire every evening at about seven o'clock into the sanctum sanctorum of Madame Bauche's habitation, the dark little private sitting-room in which she made out her bills and calculated her profits, and there regale himself in her presence—and indeed at her expense,—for the items never appeared in the bill, with coffee, and cognac. I have said that there was neither eating nor drinking at the establishment after the regular dinner-hours; but in so saying I spoke of the world at large. Nothing further was allowed in the way of trade; but in the way of friendship so much was now-a-days always allowed to the capitaine.

It was at these moments that Madame Bauche discussed her private affairs, and asked for and received advice. For even Madame Bauche was mortal; nor could her green spectacles without other aid carry her through all the troubles of life. It was now five years since the world of Vernet discovered that La Mère Bauche was going to marry the capitaine; and for eighteen months the world of Vernet had been full of this matter: but any amount of patience is at last exhausted, and as no further steps in that direction were ever taken beyond the daily cup of coffee, that subject died away—very much unheeded by La Mère Bauche.

But she, though she thought of no matrimony for herself, thought much of matrimony for other people; and over most of those cups of evening coffee and cognac a matrimonial project was discussed in these latter days. It has been seen that the capitaine pleaded in Marie's favour when the fury of Madame Bauche's indignation broke forth; and that ultimately Marie was kept at home, and Adolphe sent away by his advice.

"But Adolphe cannot always stay away," Madame Bauche had pleaded in her difficulty. The truth of this the capitaine had admitted; but Marie, he said, might be married to some one else before two years were over. And so the matter had commenced.

But to whom should she be married? To this question the capitaine had answered in perfect innocence of heart, that La Mère Bauche would be much better able to make such a choice than himself. He did not know how Marie might stand with regard to money. If madame would give some little "dot," the affair, the capitaine thought, would be more easily arranged.

All these things took months to say, during which period Marie went on with her work in melancholy listlessness. One comfort she had. Adolphe, before he went, had promised to her, holding in his hand as he did so a little cross which she had given him, that no earthly consideration should sever them;—that sooner or later he would certainly be her husband. Marie felt that her limbs could not work nor her tongue speak were it not for this one drop of water in her cup.

And then, deeply meditating, La Mère Bauche hit upon a plan, and herself communicated it to the capitaine over a second cup of coffee into which she poured a full teaspoonful more than the usual allowance of cognac. Why should not he, the capitaine himself, be the man to marry Marie Clavert?

It was a very startling proposal, the idea of matrimony for himself never having as yet entered into the capitaine's head at any period of his life; but La Mère Bauche did contrive to make it not altogether unacceptable. As to that matter of dowry she was prepared to be more than generous. She did love Marie well, and could find it in her heart to give her anything—anything except her son, her own Adolphe. What she proposed was this. Adolphe, himself, would never keep the baths. If the capitaine would take Marie for his wife, Marie, Madame Bauche declared, should be the mistress after her death; subject of course to certain settlements as to Adolphe's pecuniary interests.

The plan was discussed a thousand times, and at last so far brought to bear that Marie was made acquainted with it—having been called in to sit in presence with La Mère Bauche and her future proposed husband. The poor girl manifested no disgust to the stiff ungainly lover whom they assigned to her,—who through his whole frame was in appearance almost as wooden as his own leg. On the whole, indeed, Marie liked the capitaine, and felt that he was her friend; and in her country such marriages were not uncommon. The capitaine was perhaps a little beyond the age at which a man might usually be thought justified in demanding the services of a young girl as his nurse and wife, but then Marie of herself had so little to give—except her youth, and beauty, and goodness.

But yet she could not absolutely consent; for was she not absolutely pledged to her own Adolphe? And therefore, when the great pecuniary advantages were, one by one, displayed before her, and when La Mère Bauche, as a last argument, informed her that as wife of the capitaine she would be regarded as a second mistress in the establishment and not as a servant,—she could only burst out into tears, and say that she did not know.

"I will be very kind to you," said the capitaine; "as kind as a man can be."

Marie took his hard withered hand and kissed it; and then looked up into his face with beseeching eyes which were not without avail upon his heart.

"We will not press her now," said the capitaine. "There is time enough."

But let his heart be touched ever so much, one thing was certain. It could not be permitted that she should marry Adolphe. To that view of the matter he had given in his unrestricted adhesion; nor could he by any means withdraw it without losing altogether his position in the establishment of Madame Bauche. Nor indeed did his conscience tell him that such a marriage should be permitted. That would be too much. If every pretty girl were allowed to marry the first young man that might fall in love with her, what would the world come to?

And it soon appeared that there was not time enough—that the time was growing very scant. In three months Adolphe would be back. And if everything was not arranged by that time, matters might still go astray.

And then Madame Bauche asked her final question: "You do not think, do you, that you can ever marry Adolphe?" And as she asked it the accustomed terror of her green spectacles magnified itself tenfold. Marie could only answer by another burst of tears.

The affair was at last settled among them. Marie said that she would consent to marry the capitaine when she should hear from Adolphe's own mouth that he, Adolphe, loved her no longer. She declared with many tears that her vows and pledges prevented her from promising more than this. It was not her fault, at any rate not now, that she loved her lover. It was not her fault,—not now at least—that she was bound by these pledges. When she heard from his own mouth that he had discarded her, then she would marry the capitaine—or indeed sacrifice herself in any other way that La Mère Bauche might desire. What would anything signify then?

Madame Bauche's spectacles remained unmoved; but not her heart. Marie, she told the capitaine, should be equal to herself in the establishment, when once she was entitled to be called Madame Campan, and she should be to her quite as a daughter. She should have her cup of coffee every evening, and dine at the big table, and wear a silk gown at church, and the servants should all call her Madame; a great career should be open to her, if she would only give up her foolish girlish childish love for Adolphe. And all these great promises were repeated to Marie by the capitaine.

But nevertheless there was but one thing in the whole world which in Marie's eye was of any value; and that one thing was the heart of Adolphe Bauche. Without that she would be nothing; with that,—with that assured, she could wait patiently till doomsday.

Letters were written to Adolphe during all these eventful doings; and a letter came from him saying that he greatly valued Marie's love, but that as it had been clearly proved to him that their marriage would be neither for her advantage, nor for his, he was willing to give it up. He consented to her marriage with the capitaine, and expressed his gratitude to his mother for the immediate pecuniary advantages which she had held out to him. Oh, Adolphe, Adolphe! But, alas, alas! is not such the way of most men's hearts—and of the hearts of some women?

This letter was read to Marie, but it had no more effect upon her than would have had some dry legal document. In those days and in those places men and women did not depend much upon letters; nor when they were written, was there expressed in them much of heart or of feeling. Marie would understand, as she was well aware, the glance of Adolphe's eye and the tone of Adolphe's voice; she would perceive at once from them what her lover really meant, what he wished, what in the innermost corner of his heart he really desired that she should do. But from that stiff constrained written document she could understand nothing.

It was agreed therefore that Adolphe should return, and that she would accept her fate from his mouth. The capitaine, who knew more of human nature than did poor Marie, felt tolerably sure of his bride. Adolphe, who had seen something of the world, would not care very much for the girl of his own valley. Money and pleasure, and some little position in the world would soon wean him from his love; and then Marie would accept her destiny—as other girls in the same position had done since the French world began.

And now it was the evening before Adolphe's expected arrival. La Mère Bauche was discussing the matter with the capitaine over the usual cup of coffee. Madame Bauche had of late become rather nervous on the matter, thinking that they had been somewhat rash in acceding so much to Marie. It seemed to her that it was absolutely now left to the two young lovers to say whether or no they would have each other or not. Now nothing on earth could be further from Madame Bauche's intention than this. Her decree and resolve was to heap down blessings on all persons concerned—provided always that she could have her own way; but, provided she did not have her own way, to heap down,—anything but blessings. She had her code of morality in this matter. She would do good if possible to everybody around her. But she would not on any score be induced to consent that Adolphe should marry Marie Clavert. Should that be in the wind she would rid the house of Marie, of the capitaine, and even of Adolphe himself.

She had become therefore somewhat querulous, and self-opinionated in her discussions with her friend.

"I don't know," she said on the evening in question; "I don't know. It may be all right; but if Adolphe turns against me, what are we to do then?"

"Mère Bauche," said the capitaine, sipping his coffee and puffing out the smoke of his cigar, "Adolphe will not turn against us." It had been somewhat remarked by many that the capitaine was more at home in the house, and somewhat freer in his manner of talking with Madame Bauche, since this matrimonial alliance had been on the tapis than he had ever been before. La Mère herself observed it, and did not quite like it; but how could she prevent it now? When the capitaine was once married she would make him know his place, in spite of all her promises to Marie.

"But if he says he likes the girl?" continued Madame Bauche.

"My friend, you may be sure that he will say nothing of the kind. He has not been away two years without seeing girls as pretty as Marie. And then you have his letter."

"That is nothing, capitaine; he would eat his letter as quick as you would eat an omelet aux fines herbes." Now the capitaine was especially quick over an omelet aux fines herbes.

"And, Mère Bauche, you also have the purse; he will know that he cannot eat that, except with your good will."

"Ah!" exclaimed Madame Bauche, "poor lad! He has not a sous in the world unless I give it to him." But it did not seem that this reflection was in itself displeasing to her.

"Adolphe will now be a man of the world," continued the capitaine. "He will know that it does not do to throw away everything for a pair of red lips. That is the folly of a boy, and Adolphe will be no longer a boy. Believe me, Mère Bauche, things will be right enough."

"And then we shall have Marie sick and ill and half dying on our hands," said Madame Bauche.

This was not flattering to the capitaine, and so he felt it. "Perhaps so, perhaps not," he said. "But at any rate she will get over it. It is a malady which rarely kills young women—especially when another alliance awaits them."

"Bah!" said Madame Bauche; and in saying that word she avenged herself for the too great liberty which the capitaine had lately taken. He shrugged his shoulders, took a pinch of snuff, and uninvited helped himself to a teaspoonful of cognac. Then the conference ended, and on the next morning before breakfast Adolphe Bauche arrived.

On that morning poor Marie hardly knew how to bear herself. A month or two back, and even up to the last day or two, she had felt a sort of confidence that Adolphe would be true to her; but the nearer came that fatal day the less strong was the confidence of the poor girl. She knew that those two long-headed, aged counsellors were plotting against her happiness, and she felt that she could hardly dare hope for success with such terrible foes opposed to her. On the evening before the day Madame Bauche had met her in the passages, and kissed her as she wished her good night. Marie knew little about sacrifices, but she felt that it was a sacrificial kiss.

In those days a sort of diligence with the mails for Olette passed through Prades early in the morning, and a conveyance was sent from Vernet to bring Adolphe to the baths. Never was prince or princess expected with more anxiety. Madame Bauche was up and dressed long before the hour, and was heard to say five several times that she was sure he would not come. The capitaine was out and on the high road, moving about with his wooden leg, as perpendicular as a lamppost and almost as black. Marie also was up, but nobody had seen her. She was up and had been out about the place before any of them were stirring; but now that the world was on the move she lay hidden like a hare in its form.

And then the old char-à-banc clattered up to the door, and Adolphe jumped out of it into his mother's arms. He was fatter and fairer than she had last seen him, had a larger beard, was more fashionably clothed, and certainly looked more like a man. Marie also saw him out of her little window, and she thought that he looked like a god. Was it probable, she said to herself, that one so godlike would still care for her?

The mother was delighted with her son, who rattled away quite at his ease. He shook hands very cordially with the capitaine—of whose intended alliance with his own sweetheart he had been informed, and then as he entered the house with his hand under his mother's arm, he asked one question about her. "And where is Marie?" said he. "Marie! oh upstairs; you shall see her after breakfast," said La Mère Bauche. And so they entered the house, and went in to breakfast among the guests. Everybody had heard something of the story, and they were all on the alert to see the young man whose love or want of love was considered to be of so much importance.

"You will see that it will be all right," said the capitaine, carrying his head very high.

"I think so, I think so," said La Mère Bauche, who, now that the capitaine was right, no longer desired to contradict him.

"I know that it will be all right," said the capitaine. "I told you that Adolphe would return a man; and he is a man. Look at him; he does not care this for Marie Clavert;" and the capitaine, with much eloquence in his motion, pitched over a neighbouring wall a small stone which he held in his hand.

And then they all went to breakfast with many signs of outward joy. And not without some inward joy; for Madame Bauche thought she saw that her son was cured of his love. In the mean time Marie sat up stairs still afraid to show herself.

"He has come," said a young girl, a servant in the house, running up to the door of Marie's room.

"Yes," said Marie; "I could see that he has come."

"And, oh, how beautiful he is!" said the girl, putting her hands together and looking up to the ceiling. Marie in her heart of hearts wished that he was not half so beautiful, as then her chance of having him might be greater.

"And the company are all talking to him as though he were the préfet," said the girl.

"Never mind who is talking to him," said Marie; "go away, and leave me—you are wanted for your work." Why before this was he not talking to her? Why not, if he were really true to her? Alas, it began to fall upon her mind that he would be false! And what then? What should she do then? She sat still gloomily, thinking of that other spouse that had been promised to her.

As speedily after breakfast as was possible Adolphe was invited to a conference in his mother's private room. She had much debated in her own mind whether the capitaine should be invited to this conference or no. For many reasons she would have wished to exclude him. She did not like to teach her son that she was unable to manage her own affairs, and she would have been well pleased to make the capitaine understand that his assistance was not absolutely necessary to her. But then she had an inward fear that her green spectacles would not now be as efficacious on Adolphe, as they had once been, in old days, before he had seen the world and become a man. It might be necessary that her son, being a man, should be opposed by a man. So the capitaine was invited to the conference.

What took place there need not be described at length. The three were closeted for two hours, at the end of which time they came forth together. The countenance of Madame Bauche was serene and comfortable; her hopes of ultimate success ran higher than ever. The face of the capitaine was masked, as are always the faces of great diplomatists; he walked placid and upright, raising his wooden leg with an ease and skill that was absolutely marvellous. But poor Adolphe's brow was clouded. Yes, poor Adolphe! for he was poor in spirit. He had pledged himself to give up Marie, and to accept the liberal allowance which his mother tendered him; but it remained for him now to communicate these tidings to Marie herself.

"Could not you tell her?" he had said to his mother, with very little of that manliness in his face on which his mother now so prided herself. But La Mère Bauche explained to him that it was a part of the general agreement that Marie was to hear his decision from his own mouth.

"But you need not regard it," said the capitaine, with the most indifferent air in the world. "The girl expects it. Only she has some childish idea that she is bound till you yourself release her. I don't think she will be troublesome." Adolphe at that moment did feel that he should have liked to kick the capitaine out of his mother's house.

And where should the meeting take place? In the hall of the bath-house, suggested Madame Bauche; because, as she observed, they could walk round and round, and nobody ever went there at that time of day. But to this Adolphe objected; it would be so cold and dismal and melancholy.

The capitaine thought that Mère Bauche's little parlour was the place; but La Mère herself did not like this. They might be overheard, as she well knew; and she guessed that the meeting would not conclude without some sobs that would certainly be bitter and might perhaps be loud.

"Send her up to the grotto, and I will follow her," said Adolphe. On this therefore they agreed. Now the grotto was a natural excavation in a high rock, which stood precipitously upright over the establishment of the baths. A steep zigzag path with almost never-ending steps had been made along the face of the rock from a little flower garden attached to the house which lay immediately under the mountain. Close along the front of the hotel ran a little brawling river, leaving barely room for a road between it and the door; over this there was a wooden bridge leading to the garden, and some two or three hundred yards from the bridge began the steps by which the ascent was made to the grotto.

When the season was full and the weather perfectly warm the place was much frequented. There was a green table in it, and four or five deal chairs; a green garden seat also was there, which however had been removed into the innermost back corner of the excavation, as its hinder legs were somewhat at fault. A wall about two feet high ran along the face of it, guarding its occupants from the precipice. In fact it was no grotto, but a little chasm in the rock, such as we often see up above our heads in rocky valleys, and which by means of these steep steps had been turned into a source of exercise and amusement for the visitors at the hotel.

Standing at the wall one could look down into the garden, and down also upon the shining slate roof of Madame Bauche's house; and to the left might be seen the sombre silent snow-capped top of stern old Canigou, king of mountains among those Eastern Pyrenees.

And so Madame Bauche undertook to send Marie up to the grotto, and Adolphe undertook to follow her thither. It was now spring; and though the winds had fallen and the snow was no longer lying on the lower peaks, still the air was fresh and cold, and there was no danger that any of the few guests at the establishment would visit the place.

"Make her put on her cloak, Mère Bauche," said the capitaine, who did not wish that his bride should have a cold in her head on their wedding-day. La Mère Bauche pished and pshawed, as though she were not minded to pay any attention to recommendations on such subjects from the capitaine. But nevertheless when Marie was seen slowly to creep across the little bridge about fifteen minutes after this time, she had a handkerchief on her head, and was closely wrapped in a dark brown cloak.

Poor Marie herself little heeded the cold fresh air, but she was glad to avail herself of any means by which she might hide her face. When Madame Bauche sought her out in her own little room, and with a smiling face and kind kiss bade her go to the grotto, she knew, or fancied that she knew that it was all over.

"He will tell you all the truth,—how it all is," said La Mère. "We will do all we can, you know, to make you happy, Marie. But you must remember what Monsieur le Curé told us the other day. In this vale of tears we cannot have everything; as we shall have some day, when our poor wicked souls have been purged of all their wickedness. Now go, dear, and take your cloak."

"Yes, maman."

"And Adolphe will come to you. And try and behave well, like a sensible girl."

"Yes, maman,"—and so she went, bearing on her brow another sacrificial kiss—and bearing in her heart such an unutterable load of woe!

Adolphe had gone out of the house before her; but standing in the stable yard, well within the gate so that she should not see him, he watched her slowly crossing the bridge and mounting the first flight of the steps. He had often seen her tripping up those stairs, and had, almost as often, followed her with his quicker feet. And she, when she would hear him, would run; and then he would catch her breathless at the top, and steal kisses from her when all power of refusing them had been robbed from her by her efforts at escape. There was no such running now, no such following, no thought of such kisses.

As for him, he would fain have skulked off and shirked the interview had he dared. But he did not dare; so he waited there, out of heart, for some ten minutes, speaking a word now and then to the bath-man, who was standing by, just to show that he was at his ease. But the bath-man knew that he was not at his ease. Such would-be lies as those rarely achieve deception;—are rarely believed. And then, at the end of the ten minutes, with steps as slow as Marie's had been, he also ascended to the grotto.

Marie had watched him from the top, but so that she herself should not be seen. He however had not once lifted up his head to look for her; but, with eyes turned to the ground had plodded his way up to the cave. When he entered she was standing in the middle, with her eyes downcast, and her hands clasped before her. She had retired some way from the wall, so that no eyes might possibly see her but those of her false lover. There she stood when he entered, striving to stand motionless, but trembling like a leaf in every limb.

It was only when he reached the top step that he made up his mind how he would behave. Perhaps after all, the capitaine was right; perhaps she would not mind it.

"Marie," said he, with a voice that attempted to be cheerful; "this is an odd place to meet in after such a long absence," and he held out his hand to her. But only his hand! He offered her no salute. He did not even kiss her cheek as a brother would have done! Of the rules of the outside world it must be remembered that poor Marie knew but little. He had been a brother to her, before he had become her lover.

But Marie took his hand saying, "Yes, it has been very long."

"And now that I have come back," he went on to say, "it seems that we are all in a confusion together. I never knew such a piece of work. However, it is all for the best, I suppose."

"Perhaps so," said Marie still trembling violently, and still looking down upon the ground. And then there was silence between them for a minute or so.

"I tell you what it is, Marie," said Adolphe at last, dropping her hand and making a great effort to get through the work before him. "I am afraid we two have been very foolish. Don't you think we have now? It seems quite clear that we can never get ourselves married. Don't you see it in that light?"

Marie's head turned round and round with her, but she was not of the fainting order. She took three steps backwards and leant against the wall of the cave. She also was trying to think how she might best fight her battle. Was there no chance for her? Could no eloquence, no love prevail? On her own beauty she counted but little; but might not prayers do something, and a reference to those old vows which had been so frequent, so eager, so solemnly pledged between them?

"Never get ourselves married!" she said, repeating his words. "Never, Adolphe? Can we never be married?"

"Upon my word, my dear girl, I fear not. You see my mother is so dead against it."

"But we could wait; could we not?"

"Ah, but that's just it, Marie. We cannot wait. We must decide now,—to-day. You see I can do nothing without money from her—and as for you, you see she won't even let you stay in the house unless you marry old Campan at once. He's a very good sort of fellow though, old as he is. And if you do marry him, why you see you'll stay here, and have it all your own way in everything. As for me, I shall come and see you all from time to time, and shall be able to push my way as I ought to do."

"Then, Adolphe, you wish me to marry the capitaine?"

"Upon my honour I think it is the best thing you can do; I do indeed."

"Oh, Adolphe!"

"What can I do for you, you know? Suppose I was to go down to my mother and tell her that I had decided to keep you myself, what would come of it? Look at it in that light, Marie."

"She could not turn you out—you her own son!"

"But she would turn you out; and deuced quick, too, I can assure you of that; I can, upon my honour."

"I should not care that," and she made a motion with her hand to show how indifferent she would be to such treatment as regarded herself. "Not that—; if I still had the promise of your love."

"But what would you do?"

"I would work. There are other houses besides that one," and she pointed to the slate roof of the Bauche establishment.

"And for me—I should not have a penny in the world," said the young man.

She came up to him and took his right hand between both of hers and pressed it warmly, oh, so warmly. "You would have my love," said she; "my deepest, warmest, best heart's love. I should want nothing more, nothing on earth, if I could still have yours." And she leaned against his shoulder and looked with all her eyes into his face.

"But, Marie; that's nonsense, you know."

"No, Adolphe; it is not nonsense. Do not let them teach you so. What does love mean, if it does not mean that? Oh, Adolphe, you do love me, you do love me; you do love me?"

"Yes;—I love you," he said slowly;—as though he would not have said it, if he could have helped it. And then his arm crept slowly round her waist, as though in that also he could not help himself.

"And do not I love you?" said the passionate girl. "Oh I do, so dearly; with all my heart, with all my soul. Adolphe, I so love you, that I cannot give you up. Have I not sworn to be yours; sworn, sworn a thousand times? How can I marry that man! Oh Adolphe, how can you wish that I should marry him?" And she clung to him, and looked at him, and besought him with her eyes.

"I shouldn't wish it;—only— " and then he paused. It was hard to tell her that he was willing to sacrifice her to the old man because he wanted money from his mother.

"Only what! But, Adolphe, do not wish it at all! Have you not sworn that I should be your wife? Look here, look at this;" and she brought out from her bosom a little charm that he had given her in return for that cross. "Did you not kiss that when you swore before the figure of the virgin that I should be your wife? And do you not remember that I feared to swear too, because your mother was so angry; and then you made me? After that, Adolphe! Oh, Adolphe! Tell me that I may have some hope. I will wait; oh, I will wait so patiently."

He turned himself away from her and walked backwards and forwards uneasily through the grotto. He did love her;—love her as such men do love sweet, pretty girls. The warmth of her hand, the affection of her touch, the pure bright passion of her tear-laden eye had reawakened what power of love there was within him. But what was he to do? Even if he were willing to give up the immediate golden hopes which his mother held out to him, how was he to begin, and then how carry out this work of self-devotion? Marie would be turned away, and he would be left a victim in the hands of his mother, and of that stiff, wooden-legged militaire;—a penniless victim, left to mope about the place without a grain of influence or a morsel of pleasure.

"But what can we do?" he exclaimed again, as he once more met Marie's searching eye.

"We can be true and honest, and we can wait," she said, coming close up to him and taking hold of his arm. "I do not fear it; and she is not my mother, Adolphe. You need not fear your own mother."

"Fear; no, of course I don't fear. But I don't see how the very devil we can manage it."

"Will you let me tell her that I will not marry the capitaine; that I will not give up your promises; and then I am ready to leave the house?"

"It would do no good."

"It would do every good, Adolphe, if I had your promised word once more; if I could hear from your own voice one more tone of love. Do you not remember this place? It was here that you forced me to say that I loved you. It is here also that you will tell me that I have been deceived."

"It is not I that would deceive you," he said. "I wonder that you should be so hard upon me. God knows that I have trouble enough."

"Well; if I am a trouble to you, be it so. Be it as you wish," and she leaned back against the wall of the rock, and crossing her arms upon her breast looked away from him and fixed her eyes upon the sharp granite peaks of Canigou.

He again betook himself to walk backwards and forwards through the cave. He had quite enough of love for her to make him wish to marry her; quite enough, now, at this moment, to make the idea of her marriage with the capitaine very distasteful to him; enough probably to make him become a decently good husband to her, should fate enable him to marry her; but not enough to enable him to support all the punishment which would be the sure effects of his mother's displeasure. Besides, he had promised his mother that he would give up Marie;—had entirely given in his adhesion to that plan of the marriage with the capitaine. He had owned that the path of life as marked out for him by his mother was the one which it behoved him, as a man, to follow. It was this view of his duties as a man which had been specially urged on him with all the capitaine's eloquence. And old Campan had entirely succeeded. It is so easy to get the assent of such young men, so weak in mind and so weak in pocket, when the arguments are backed by a promise of two thousand francs a year.

"I'll tell you what I'll do," at last he said. "I'll get my mother by herself, and will ask her to let the matter remain as it is for the present."

"Not if it be a trouble, M. Adolphe;" and the proud girl still held her hands upon her bosom, and still looked towards the mountain.

"You know what I mean, Marie. You can understand how she and the capitaine are worrying me."

"But tell me, Adolphe, do you love me?"

"You know I love you, only— "

"And you will not give me up?"

"I will ask my mother. I will try and make her yield."

Marie could not feel that she received much confidence from her lover's promise; but still, even that, weak and unsteady as it was, even that was better than absolute fixed rejection. So she thanked him, promised him with tears in her eyes that she would always, always be faithful to him, and then bade him go down to the house. She would follow, she said, as soon as his passing had ceased to be observed.

Then she looked at him as though she expected some sign of renewed love. But no sign was vouchsafed to her. Now that she thirsted for the touch of his lip upon her cheek, it was denied to her. He did as she bade him; he went down, slowly loitering, by himself; and in about half an hour she followed him and unobserved crept to her chamber.

Again we will pass over what took place between the mother and the son; but late in that evening, after the guests had gone to bed, Marie received a message, desiring her to wait on Madame Bauche in a small salon which looked out from one end of the house. It was intended as a private sitting-room should any special stranger arrive who required such accommodation, and therefore was but seldom used. Here she found La Mère Bauche sitting in an arm-chair behind a small table on which stood two candles; and on a sofa against the wall sat Adolphe. The capitaine was not in the room.

"Shut the door, Marie, and come in and sit down," said Madame Bauche. It was easy to understand from the tone of her voice that she was angry and stern, in an unbending mood, and resolved to carry out to the very letter all the threats conveyed by those terrible spectacles.

Marie did as she was bid. She closed the door and sat down on the chair that was nearest to her.

"Marie," said La Mère Bauche—and the voice sounded fierce in the poor girl's ears, and an angry fire glimmered through the green glasses—"What is all this about that I hear? Do you dare to say that you hold my son bound to marry you?" And then the august mother paused for an answer.

But Marie had no answer to give. She looked suppliantly towards her lover, as though beseeching him to carry on the fight for her. But if she could not do battle for herself, certainly he could not do it for her. What little amount of fighting he had had in him, had been thoroughly vanquished before her arrival.

"I will have an answer, and that immediately," said Madame Bauche. "I am not going to be betrayed into ignominy and disgrace by the object of my own charity. Who picked you out of the gutter, miss, and brought you up and fed you, when you would otherwise have gone to the foundling? And is this your gratitude for it all? You are not satisfied with being fed and clothed and cherished by me, but you must rob me of my son! Know this then, Adolphe shall never marry a child of charity such as you are."

Marie sat still, stunned by the harshness of these words. La Mère

Bauche had often scolded her; indeed, she was given to much scolding; but she had scolded her as a mother may scold a child. And when this story of Marie's love first reached her ears, she had been very angry; but her anger had never brought her to such a pass as this. Indeed, Marie had not hitherto been taught to look at the matter in this light. No one had heretofore twitted her with eating the bread of charity. It had not occurred to her that on this account she was unfit to be Adolphe's wife. There, in that valley, they were all so nearly equal, that no idea of her own inferiority had ever pressed itself upon her mind. But now—!

When the voice ceased she again looked at him; but it was no longer with a beseeching look. Did he also altogether scorn her? That was now the inquiry which her eyes were called upon to make. No; she could not say that he did. It seemed to her that his energies were chiefly occupied in pulling to pieces the tassel of the sofa cushion.

"And now, miss, let me know at once whether this nonsense is to be over or not," continued La Mère Bauche; "and I will tell you at once, I am not going to maintain you here, in my house, to plot against our welfare and happiness. As Marie Clavert you shall not stay here. Capitaine Campan is willing to marry you; and as his wife I will keep my word to you, though you little deserve it. If you refuse to marry him, you must go. As to my son, he is there; and he will tell you now, in my presence, that he altogether declines the honour you propose for him."

And then she ceased, waiting for an answer, drumming the table with a wafer stamp which happened to be ready to her hand; but Marie said nothing. Adolphe had been appealed to; but Adolphe had not yet spoken.

"Well, miss?" said La Mère Bauche.

Then Marie rose from her seat, and walking round she touched Adolphe lightly on the shoulder. "Adolphe," she said, "it is for you to speak now. I will do as you bid me."

He gave a long sigh, looked first at Marie and then at his mother, shook himself slightly, and then spoke: "Upon my word, Marie, I think mother is right. It would never do for us to marry; it would not indeed."

"Then it is decided," said Marie, returning to her chair.

"And you will marry the capitaine?" said La Mère Bauche.

Marie merely bowed her head in token of acquiescence.

"Then we are friends again. Come here, Marie, and kiss me. You must know that it is my duty to take care of my own son. But I don't want to be angry with you if I can help it; I don't indeed. When once you are Madame Campan, you shall be my own child; and you shall have any room in the house you like to choose—there!" And she once more imprinted a kiss on Marie's cold forehead.

How they all got out of the room, and off to their own chambers, I can hardly tell. But in five minutes from the time of this last kiss they were divided. La Mère Bauche had patted Marie, and smiled on her, and called her her dear good little Madame Campan, her young little mistress of the Hôtel Bauche; and had then got herself into her own room, satisfied with her own victory.

Nor must my readers be too severe on Madame Bauche. She had already done much for Marie Clavert; and when she found herself once more by her own bedside, she prayed to be forgiven for the cruelty which she felt that she had shown to the orphan. But in making this prayer, with her favourite crucifix in her hand and the little image of the Virgin before her, she pleaded her duty to her son. Was it not right, she asked the Virgin, that she should save her son from a bad marriage? And then she promised ever so much of recompense, both to the Virgin and to Marie; a new trousseau for each, with candles to the Virgin, with a gold watch and chain for Marie, as soon as she should be Marie Campan. She had been cruel; she acknowledged it. But at such a crisis was it not defensible? And then the recompense should be so full!

But there was one other meeting that night, very short indeed, but not the less significant. Not long after they had all separated, just so long as to allow of the house being quiet, Adolphe, still sitting in his room, meditating on what the day had done for him, heard a low tap at his door. "Come in," he said, as men always do say; and Marie opening the door, stood just within the verge of his chamber. She had on her countenance neither the soft look of entreating love which she had worn up there in the grotto, nor did she appear crushed and subdued as she had done before his mother. She carried her head somewhat more erect than usual, and looked boldly out at him from under her soft eyelashes. There might still be love there but it was love proudly resolving to quell itself. Adolphe as he looked at her, felt that he was afraid of her.

"It is all over then between us, M. Adolphe?" she said.

"Well, yes. Don't you think it had better be so, eh, Marie?"

"And this is the meaning of oaths and vows, sworn to each other so sacredly?"

"But, Marie, you heard what my mother said."

"Oh, sir! I have not come to ask you again to love me. Oh, no! I am not thinking of that. But this, this would be a lie if I kept it now; it would choke me if I wore it as that man's wife. Take it back;" and she tendered to him the little charm which she had always worn round her neck since he had given it to her. He took it abstractedly, without thinking what he did, and placed it on his dressing-table.

"And you," she continued, "can you still keep that cross? Oh, no! you must give me back that. It would remind you too often of vows that were untrue."

"Marie," he said, "do not be so harsh to me."

"Harsh!" said she, "no; there has been enough of harshness. I would not be harsh to you, Adolphe. But give me the cross; it would prove a curse to you if you kept it."

He then opened a little box which stood upon the table, and taking out the cross gave it to her.

"And now good-bye," she said. "We shall have but little more to say to each other. I know this now, that I was wrong ever to have loved you. I should have been to you as one of the other poor girls in the house. But, oh! how was I to help it?" To this he made no answer, and she, closing the door softly, went back to her chamber. And thus ended the first day of Adolphe Bauche's return to his own house.

On the next morning the capitaine and Marie were formally betrothed. This was done with some little ceremony, in the presence of all the guests who were staying at the establishment, and with all manner of gracious acknowledgements of Marie's virtues. It seemed as though La Mère Bauche could not be courteous enough to her. There was no more talk of her being a child of charity; no more allusion now to the gutter. La Mère Bauche with her own hand brought her cake with a glass of wine after her betrothal was over, and patted her on the cheek, and called her her dear little Marie Campan. And then the capitaine was made up of infinite politeness, and the guests all wished her joy, and the servants of the house began to perceive that she was a person entitled to respect. How different was all this from that harsh attack that was made on her the preceding evening! Only Adolphe,—he alone kept aloof. Though he was present there he said nothing. He, and he only, offered no congratulations.

In the midst of all these gala doings Marie herself said little or nothing. La Mère Bauche perceived this, but she forgave it. Angrily as she had expressed herself at the idea of Marie's daring to love her son, she had still acknowledged within her own heart that such love had been natural. She could feel no pity for Marie as long as Adolphe was in danger; but now she knew how to pity her. So Marie was still petted and still encouraged, though she went through the day's work sullenly and in silence.

As to the capitaine it was all one to him. He was a man of the world. He did not expect that he should really be preferred, con amore, to a young fellow like Adolphe. But he did expect that Marie, like other girls, would do as she was bid; and that in a few days she would regain her temper and be reconciled to her life.

And then the marriage was fixed for a very early day; for as La Mère said, "What was the use of waiting? All their minds were made up now, and therefore the sooner the two were married the better. Did not the capitaine think so?"

The capitaine said that he did think so.

And then Marie was asked. It was all one to her, she said. Whatever Maman Bauche liked, that she would do; only she would not name a day herself. Indeed she would neither do nor say anything herself which tended in any way to a furtherance of these matrimonials. But then she acquiesced, quietly enough if not readily, in what other people did and said; and so the marriage was fixed for the day week after Adolphe's return.

The whole of that week passed much in the same way. The servants about the place spoke among themselves of Marie's perverseness, obstinacy, and ingratitude, because she would not look pleased, or answer Madame Bauche's courtesies with gratitude; but La Mère herself showed no signs of anger. Marie had yielded to her, and she required no more. And she remembered also the harsh words she had used to gain her purpose; and she reflected on all that Marie had lost. On these accounts she was forbearing and exacted nothing—nothing but that one sacrifice which was to be made in accordance to her wishes.

And it was made. They were married in the great salon, the dining-room, immediately after breakfast. Madame Bauche was dressed in a new puce silk dress and looked very magnificent on the occasion. She simpered and smiled, and looked gay even in spite of her spectacles; and as the ceremony was being performed, she held fast clutched in her hand the gold watch and chain which were intended for Marie as soon as ever the marriage should be completed.

The capitaine was dressed exactly as usual, only that all his clothes were new. Madame Bauche had endeavoured to persuade him to wear a blue coat; but he answered that such a change would not, he was sure, be to Marie's taste. To tell the truth, Marie would hardly have known the difference had he presented himself in scarlet vestments.

Adolphe, however, was dressed very finely, but he did not make himself prominent on the occasion. Marie watched him closely, though none saw that she did so; and of his garments she could have given an account with much accuracy—of his garments, ay! and of every look. "Is he a man," she said at last to herself, "that he can stand by and see all this?"

She too was dressed in silk. They had put on her what they pleased, and she bore the burden of her wedding finery without complaint and without pride. There was no blush on her face as she walked up to the table at which the priest stood, nor hesitation in her low voice as she made the necessary answers. She put her hand into that of the capitaine when required to do so; and when the ring was put on her finger she shuddered, but ever so slightly. No one observed it but La Mère Bauche. "In one week she will be used to it, and then we shall all be happy," said La Mère to herself. "And I,—I will be so kind to her!"

And so the marriage was completed, and the watch was at once given to Marie. "Thank you, maman," said she, as the trinket was fastened to her girdle. Had it been a pincushion that had cost three sous, it would have affected her as much.

And then there was cake, and wine, and sweetmeats; and after a few minutes Marie disappeared. For an hour or so the capitaine was taken up with the congratulations of his friends, and with the efforts necessary to the wearing of his new honours with an air of ease; but after that time he began to be uneasy because his wife did not come to him. At two or three in the afternoon he went to La Mère Bauche to complain. "This lackadaisical nonsense is no good," he said. "At any rate it is too late now. Marie had better come down among us and show herself satisfied with her husband."

But Madame Bauche took Marie's part. "You must not be too hard on Marie," she said. "She has gone through a good deal this week past, and is very young; whereas, capitaine, you are not very young."

The capitaine merely shrugged his shoulders. In the mean time Mère Bauche went up to visit her protégée in her own room, and came down with a report that she was suffering from a headache. She could not appear at dinner, Madame Bauche said; but would make one at the little party which was to be given in the evening. With this the capitaine was forced to be content.

The dinner therefore went on quietly without her, much as it did on other ordinary days. And then there was a little time of vacancy, during which the gentlemen drank their coffee and smoked their cigars at the café, talking over the event that had taken place that morning, and the ladies brushed their hair and added some ribbon or some brooch to their usual apparel. Twice during this time did Madame Bauche go up to Marie's room with offers to assist her. "Not yet, maman; not quite yet," said Marie piteously through her tears, and then twice did the green spectacles leave the room, covering eyes which also were not dry. Ah! What had she done? What had she dared to take upon herself to do? She could not undo it now.

And then it became quite dark in the passages and out of doors, and the guests assembled in the salon. La Mère came in and out three or four times, uneasy in her gait and unpleasant in her aspect, and everybody began to see that things were wrong. "She is ill, I am afraid," said one. "The excitement has been too much," said a second; "and he is so old," whispered a third. And the capitaine stalked about erect on his wooden leg, taking snuff, and striving to look indifferent; but he also was uneasy in his mind.

Presently La Mère came in again, with a quicker step than before, and whispered something, first to Adolphe and then to the capitaine, whereupon they both followed her out of the room.

"Not in her chamber?" said Adolphe.

"Then she must be in yours," said the capitaine.

"She is in neither," said La Mère Bauche, with her sternest voice; "nor is she in the house."

And now there was no longer an affectation of indifference on the part of any of them. They were anything but indifferent. The capitaine was eager in his demands that the matter should still be kept secret from the guests. She had always been romantic, he said, and had now gone out to walk by the river-side. They three and the old bath-man would go out and look for her.

"But it is pitch dark," said La Mère Bauche.

"We will take lanterns," said the capitaine. And so they sallied forth with creeping steps over the gravel, so that they might not be heard by those within, and proceeded to search for the young wife.

"Marie! Marie!" said La Mère Bauche, in piteous accents; "do come to me; pray do!"

"Hush!" said the capitaine. "They'll hear you if you call." He could not endure that the world should learn that a marriage with him had been so distasteful to Marie Clavert.

"Marie, dear Marie!" called Madame Bauche, louder than before, quite regardless of the capitaine's feelings; but no Marie answered. In her innermost heart now did La Mère Bauche wish that this cruel marriage had been left undone.

Adolphe was foremost with his lamp, but he hardly dared to look in the spot where he felt that it was most likely that she should have taken refuge. How could he meet her again, alone, in that grotto? Yet he alone of the four was young. It was clearly for him to ascend. "Marie!" he shouted, "are you there?" as he slowly began the long ascent of the steps.

But he had hardly begun to mount when a whirring sound struck his ear, and he felt that the air near him was moved; and then there was a crash upon the lower platform of rock, and a moan, repeated twice but so faintly, and a rustle of silk, and a slight struggle somewhere as he knew within twenty paces of him; and then all was again quiet and still in the night air.

"What was that?" asked the capitaine in a harsh voice. He made his way half across the little garden, and he also was within forty or fifty yards of thc flat rock. But Adolphe was unable to answer him. He had fainted and the lamp had fallen from his hands, and rolled to the bottom of the steps.

But the capitaine, though even his heart was all but quenched within him, had still strength enough to make his way up to the rock; and there, holding the lantern above his eyes, he saw all that was left for him to see of his bride.

As for La Mère Bauche, she never again sat at the head of that table—never again dictated to guests—never again laid down laws for the management of any one. A poor bedridden old woman, she lay there in her house at Vernet for some seven tedious years, and then was gathered to her fathers.

As for the capitaine—but what matters? He was made of sterner stuff. What matters either the fate of such a one as Adolphe Bauche?

An Unprotected Female at the Pyramids

Originally appeared in *Cassell's Illustrated Family Paper*, 6 and 13 October 1860. Reprinted in *Tales of All Countries* [First Series] (1861). Written in the Pyrenees between 1 September and 29 October 1859, during the composition of *Castle Richmond*. The story was inspired by Trollope's visit to Egypt (February–April 1858) to negotiate a new postal treaty, though the American traveller, Jefferson Ingram, probably owes something to Trollope's first brief visit to the United States in the summer of 1859.

IN THE happy days when we were young, no description conveyed to us so complete an idea of mysterious reality as that of an Oriental city. We knew it was actually there, but had such vague notions of its ways and looks! Let any one remember his early impressions as to Bagdad or Grand Cairo, and then say if this was not so. It was probably taken from the "Arabian Nights," and the picture produced was one of strange, fantastic, luxurious houses; of women who were either very young and very beautiful, or else very old and very cunning; but in either state exercising much more influence in life than women in the East do now; of good-natured, capricious, though sometimes tyrannical monarchs; and of life full of quaint mysteries, quite unintelligible in every phasis, and on that account the more picturesque.

And perhaps Grand Cairo has thus filled us with more wonder even than Bagdad. We have been in a certain manner at home at Bagdad, but have only visited Grand Cairo occasionally. I know no place which was to me, in early years, so delightfully mysterious as Grand Cairo.

But the route to India and Australia has changed all this. Men from all countries going to the East, now pass through Cairo, and its streets and costumes are no longer strange to us. It has become also a resort for invalids, or rather for those who fear that they may become invalids if they remain in a cold climate during the winter months. And thus at Cairo there is always to be found a considerable population of French, Americans, and of English. Oriental life is brought home to us, dreadfully diluted by western customs, and the delights of the "Arabian Nights" are shorn of half their value. When we have seen a thing it is never so magnificent to us as when it was half unknown.

It is not much that we deign to learn from these Orientals,—we who glory in our civilization. We do not copy their silence or their abstemiousness, nor that invariable mindfulness of his own personal dignity which always adheres to a Turk or to an Arab. We chatter as much at Cairo as elsewhere, and eat as much and drink as much, and dress ourselves generally in the same old, ugly costume. But we do usually take upon ourselves to wear red caps, and we do ride on donkeys.

Nor are the visitors from the West to Cairo by any means confined to the male sex. Ladies are to be seen in the streets, quite regardless of the Mahommedan custom which presumes a veil to be necessary for an appearance in public; and, to tell the truth, the Mahommedans in general do not appear to be much shocked by their effrontery.

A quarter of the town has in this way become inhabited by men wearing coats and waistcoats, and by women who are without veils; but the English tongue in Egypt finds its centre at Shepheard's Hotel. It is here that people congregate who are looking out for parties to visit with them the Upper Nile, and who are generally all smiles and courtesy; and here also are to be found they who have just returned from this journey, and who are often in a frame of mind towards their companions that is much less amiable. From hence, during the winter, a *cortége* proceeds almost daily to the Pyramids, or to Memphis, or to the petrified forest, or to the City of the Sun. And then, again, four or five times a month the house is filled with young aspirants going out to India, male and female, full of valour and bloom; or with others coming home, no longer young, no longer aspiring, but laden with children and grievances.

The party with whom we are at present concerned is not about to proceed further than the Pyramids, and we shall be able to go with them and return in one and the same day.

It consisted chiefly of an English family, Mr. and Mrs. Damer, their daughter, and two young sons;—of these chiefly, because they were the nucleus to which the others had attached themselves as adherents; they had originated the journey, and in the whole management of it Mr. Damer regarded himself as the master.

The adherents were, firstly, M. Delabordeau, a Frenchman, now resident in Cairo, who had given out that he was in some way concerned in the canal about to be made between the Mediterranean and the Red Sea. In discussion on this subject he had become acquainted with Mr. Damer; and although the latter gentleman, true to English interests, perpetually declared that the canal would never be made, and thus irritated M. Delabordeau not a little—nevertheless, some measure of friendship had grown up between them.

There was also an American gentleman, Mr. Jefferson Ingram, who was comprising all countries and all nations in one grand tour, as American gentlemen so often do. He was young and good-looking, and had made himself especially agreeable to Mr. Damer, who had declared, more than once, that Mr. Ingram was by far the most rational American he had ever met. Mr. Ingram would listen to Mr. Damer by the half-hour as to the virtue of the British Constitution, and had even sat by almost with patience when Mr. Damer had expressed a doubt as to the good working of the United States' scheme of policy,—which, in an American, was most wonderful. But some of the sojourners at Shepheard's had observed that Mr. Ingram was in the habit of talking with Miss Damer almost as much as with her father, and argued from that, that fond as the young man was of politics, he did sometimes turn his mind to other things also.

And then there was Miss Dawkins. Now Miss Dawkins was an important person, both as to herself and as to her line of life, and she must be described. She was, in the first place, an unprotected female of about thirty years of age. As this is becoming an established profession, setting itself up as it were in opposition to the old-world idea that women, like green peas, cannot come to perfection without supporting-sticks, it will be understood at once what were Miss Dawkins' sentiments. She considered—or at any rate so expressed herself—that peas could grow very well without sticks, and could not only grow thus unsupported, but could also make their way about the world without any incumbrance of sticks whatsoever. She did not intend, she said, to rival Ida Pfeiffer, seeing that she was attached in a moderate way to bed and board, and was attached to society in a manner almost more than moderate; but she had no idea of being prevented from seeing anything she wished to see because she had neither father, nor husband, nor brother available for the purpose of escort. She was a human creature, with arms and legs, she said; and she intended to use them. And this was all very well; but nevertheless she had a strong inclination to use the arms and legs of other people when she could make them serviceable.

In person Miss Dawkins was not without attraction. I should exaggerate if I were to say that she was beautiful and elegant; but she was good looking, and not usually ill mannered. She was tall, and gifted with features rather sharp and with eyes very bright. Her hair was of the darkest shade of brown, and was always worn in *bandeaux*, very neatly. She appeared generally in black, though other circumstances did not lead one to suppose that she was in mourning; and then, no other travelling costume is so convenient! She always wore a dark broad-brimmed straw hat, as to the ribbons on which she was rather particular. She was very neat about her gloves and boots; and though it cannot be said that her dress was got up without reference to expense, there can be no doubt that it was not effected without considerable outlay,—and more considerable thought.

Miss Dawkins—Sabrina Dawkins was her name, but she seldom had friends about her intimate enough to use the word Sabrina,—was certainly a clever young woman. She could talk on most subjects, if not well, at least well enough to amuse. If she had not read much, she never showed any lamentable deficiency; she was good-humoured, as a rule, and could on occasions be very soft and winning. People who had known her long would sometimes say that she was selfish; but with new acquaintance she was forbearing and self-denying.

With what income Miss Dawkins was blessed no one seemed to know. She lived like a gentlewoman, as far as outward appearance went, and never seemed to be in want; but some people would say that she knew very well how many sides there were to a shilling, and some enemy had once declared that she was an "old soldier." Such was Miss Dawkins.

She also, as well as Mr. Ingram and M. Delabordeau, had laid herself out to find the weak side of Mr. Damer. Mr. Damer, with all his family, was going up the Nile, and it was known that he had room for two in his boat over and above his own family. Miss Dawkins had told him that she had not quite made up her mind to undergo so great a fatigue, but that, nevertheless, she had a longing of the soul to see something of Nubia. To this Mr. Damer had answered nothing but "Oh!" which Miss Dawkins had not found to be encouraging.

But she had not on that account despaired. To a married man there are always two sides, and in this instance there was Mrs. Damer as well as Mr. Damer. When Mr. Damer said "Oh!" Miss Dawkins sighed, and said, "Yes, indeed!" then smiled, and betook herself to Mrs. Damer.

Now Mrs. Damer was soft-hearted, and also somewhat old-fashioned. She did not conceive any violent affection for Miss Dawkins, but she told her daughter that "the single lady by herself was a very nice young woman, and that it was a thousand pities she should have to go about so much alone like"

Miss Damer had turned up her pretty nose, thinking, perhaps, how small was the chance that it ever should be her own lot to be an unprotected female. But Miss Dawkins carried her point at any rate as regarded the expedition to the Pyramids.

Miss Damer, I have said, had a pretty nose. I may also say that she had pretty eyes, mouth, and chin, with other necessary appendages, all pretty. As to the two Master Damers, who were respectively of the ages of fifteen and sixteen, it may be sufficient to say that they were conspicuous for red caps and for the constancy with which they raced their donkeys.

And now the donkeys, and the donkey-boys, and the dragomen were all standing at the steps of Shepheard's Hotel. To each donkey there was a donkey-boy, and to each gentleman there was a dragoman, so that a goodly *cortége* was assembled, and a goodly noise was made. It may here be remarked, perhaps with some little pride, that not half the noise is given in Egypt to persons speaking any other language that is bestowed on those whose vocabulary is English.

This lasted for half an hour. Had the party been French the donkeys would have arrived only fifteen minutes before the appointed time. And then out came Damer père and Damer mère, Damer fille and Damer fils. Damer mère was leaning on her husband, as was her wont. She was not an unprotected female, and had no desire to make any attempts in that line. Damer fille was attended sedulously by Mr. Ingram, for whose demolishment, however, Mr. Damer still brought up, in a loud voice, the fag ends of certain political arguments which he would fain have poured direct into the ears of his opponent, had not his wife been so persistent in claiming her privileges. Mr. Delabordeau should have followed with Miss Dawkins, but his French politeness, or else his fear of the unprotected female, taught him to walk on the other side of the mistress of the party.

Miss Dawkins left the house with an eager young Damer yelling on each side of her; but nevertheless, though thus neglected by the gentlemen of the party, she was all smiles and prettiness, and looked so sweetly on Mr. Ingram when that gentleman stayed a moment to help her on to her donkey, that his heart almost misgave him for leaving her as soon as she was in her seat.

And then they were off. In going from the hotel to the Pyramids our party had not to pass through any of the queer old narrow streets of the true Cairo—Cairo the Oriental. They all lay behind them as they went down by the back of the hotel, by the barracks of the Pasha and the College of the Dervishes, to the village of old Cairo and the banks of the Nile.

Here they were kept half an hour while their dragomans made a bargain with the ferryman, a stately reis, or captain of a boat, who declared with much dignity that he could not carry them over for a sum less than six times the amount to which he was justly entitled; while the dragomans, with great energy on behalf of their masters, offered him only five times that sum. As far as the reis was concerned, the contest might soon have been at an end, for the man was not without a conscience; and would have been content with five times and a half; but then the three dragomans quarrelled among themselves as to which should have the paying of the money, and the affair became very tedious.

"What horrid, odious men!" said Miss Dawkins, appealing to Mr. Damer. "Do you think they will let us go over at all?"

"Well, I suppose they will; people do get over generally, I believe. Abdallah! Abdallah! why don't you pay the man? That fellow is always striving to save half a piastre for me."

"I wish he wasn't quite so particular," said Mrs. Damer, who was already becoming rather tired; "but I'm sure he's a very honest man in trying to protect us from being robbed."

"That he is," said Miss Dawkins. "What a delightful trait of national character it is to see these men so faithful to their employers!" And then at last they got over the ferry, Mr. Ingram having descended among the combatants, and settled the matter in dispute by threats and shouts, and an uplifted stick.

They crossed the broad Nile exactly at the spot where the nilometer, or river gauge, measures from day to day, and from year to year, the increasing or decreasing treasures of the stream, and landed at a village where thousands of eggs are made into chickens by the process of artificial incubation.

Mrs. Damer thought that it was very hard upon the maternal hens—the hens which should have been maternal—that they should be thus robbed of the delights of motherhood.

"So unnatural, you know," said Miss Dawkins; "so opposed to the fostering principles of creation. Don't you think so, Mr. Ingram?"

Mr. Ingram said he didn't know. He was again seating Miss Damer on her donkey, and it must be presumed that he performed this feat clumsily; for Fanny Damer could jump on and off the animal with hardly a finger to help her, when her brother or her father was her escort; but now, under the hands of Mr. Ingram, this work of mounting was one which required considerable time and care. All which Miss Dawkins observed with precision.

"It's all very well talking," said Mr. Damer, bringing up his donkey nearly alongside of that of Mr. Ingram, and ignoring his daughter's presence, just as he would have done that of his dog; "but you must admit that political power is more equally distributed in England than it is in America."

"Perhaps it is," said Mr. Ingram; "equally distributed among, we will say, three dozen families," and he made a feint as though to hold in his impetuous donkey, using the spur, however, at the same time on the side that was unseen by Mr. Damer. As he did so, Fanny's donkey became equally impetuous, and the two cantered on in advance of the whole party. It was quite in vain that Mr.Damer, at the top of his voice, shouted out something about "three dozen corruptible demagogues." Mr. Ingram found it quite impossible to restrain his donkey so as to listen to the sarcasm.

"I do believe papa would talk politics," said Fanny, "if he were at the top of Mont Blanc, or under the Falls of Niagara. I do hate politics, Mr. Ingram."

"I am sorry for that, very," said Mr. Ingram, almost sadly.

"Sorry, why? You don't want me to talk politics, do you?"

"In America we are all politicians, more or less; and, therefore, I suppose you will hate us all."

"Well, I rather think I should," said Fanny; "you would be such bores." But there was something in her eye, as she spoke, which atoned for the harshness of her words.

"A very nice young man is Mr. Ingram; don't you think so?" said Miss Dawkins to Mrs. Damer. Mrs. Damer was going along upon her donkey, not altogether comfortably. She much wished to have her lord and legitimate protector by her side, but he had left her to the care of a dragoman whose English was not intelligible to her, and she was rather cross.

"Indeed, Miss Dawkins, I don't know who are nice and who are not. This nasty donkey stumbles at every step. There! I know I shall be down directly."

"You need not be at all afraid of that; they are perfectly safe, I believe, always," said Miss Dawkins rising in her stirrup, and handling her reins quite triumphantly. "A very little practice will make you quite at home."

"I don't know what you mean by a very little practice. I have been here six weeks. Why did you put me on such a bad donkey as this?" and she turned to Abdallah, the dragoman.

"Him berry good donkey, my lady; berry good,—best of all. Call him Jack in Cairo. Him go to Pyramid and back, and mind noting."

"What does he say, Miss Dawkins?"

"He says that that donkey is one called Jack. If so I've had him myself many times, and Jack is a very good donkey."

"I wish you had him now with all my heart," said Mrs. Damer. Upon which Miss Dawkins offered to change; but those perils of mounting and dismounting were to Mrs. Damer a great deal too severe to admit of this.

"Seven miles of canal to be carried out into the sea, at a minimum depth of twenty-three feet, and the stone to be fetched from Heaven knows where! All the money in France wouldn't do it." This was addressed by Mr. Damer to M. Delabordeau, whom he had caught after the abrupt flight of Mr. Ingram.

"Den we will borrow a leetle from England," said M. Delabordeau.

"Precious little, I can tell you. Such stock would not hold its price in our markets for twenty-four hours. If it were made, the freights would be too heavy to allow of merchandise passing through. The heavy goods would all go round; and as for passengers and mails, you don't expect to get them, I suppose, while there is a railroad ready made to their hand?"

"Ve vill carry all your ships through vidout any transportation. Think of that, my friend."

"Pshaw! You are worse than Ingram. Of all the plans I ever heard of it is the most monstrous, the most impracticable, the most— " But here he was interrupted by the entreaties of his wife, who had, in absolute deed and fact, slipped from her donkey, and was now calling lustily for her husband's aid. Whereupon Miss Dawkins allied herself to the Frenchman, and listened with an air of strong conviction to those arguments which were so weak in the ears of Mr. Damer. M. Delabordeau was about to ride across the Great Desert to Jerusalem, and it might perhaps be quite as well to do that with him, as to go up the Nile as far as the second cataract with the Damers.

"And so, M. Delabordeau, you intend really to start for Mount Sinai?"

"Yes, mees; ve intend to make one start on Monday week."

"And so on to Jerusalem. You are quite right. It would be a thousand pities to be in these countries, and to return without going over such ground as that. I shall certainly go to Jerusalem myself by that route."

"Vot, mees! you? Vould you not find it too much fatigante?"

"I care nothing for fatigue, if I like the party I am with,—nothing at all, literally. You will hardly understand me, perhaps, M. Delabordeau; but I do not see any reason why I, as a young woman, should not make any journey that is practicable for a young man."

"Ah! dat is great resolution for you, mees."

"I mean as far as fatigue is concerned. You are a Frenchman, and belong to the nation that is at the head of all human civilization— "

M. Delabordeau took off his hat and bowed low, to the peak of his donkey saddle. He dearly loved to hear his country praised, as Miss Dawkins was aware.

"And I am sure you must agree with me," continued Miss Dawkins, "that the time is gone by for women to consider themselves helpless animals, or to be so considered by others."

"Mees Dawkins vould never be considered, not in any times at all, to be one helpless animal," said M. Delabordeau, civilly.

"I do not, at any rate, intend to be so regarded," said she. "It suits me to travel alone; not that I am averse to society; quite the contrary; if I meet pleasant people I am always ready to join them. But it suits me to travel without any permanent party, and I do not see why false shame should prevent my seeing the world as thoroughly as though I belonged to the other sex. Why should it, M. Delabordeau?"

M. Delabordeau declared that he did not see any reason why it should.

"I am passionately anxious to stand upon Mount Sinai," continued Miss Dawkins; "to press with my feet the earliest spot in sacred history, of the identity of which we are certain; to feel within me the awe-inspiring thrill of that thrice sacred hour!"

The Frenchman looked as though he did not quite understand her, but he said that it would be magnifique.

"You have already made up your party, I suppose, M. Delabordeau?"

M. Delabordeau gave the names of two Frenchmen and one Englishman who were going with him.

"Upon my word it is a great temptation to join you," said Miss Dawkins, "only for that horrid Englishman."

"Vat, Mr. Stanley?"

"Oh, I don't mean any disrespect to Mr. Stanley. The horridness I speak of does not attach to him personally, but to his stiff, respectable, ungainly, well-behaved, irrational, and uncivilized country. You see I am not very patriotic."

"Not quite so moch as my dear friend Mr. Damer."

"Ha! ha! ha! an excellent creature, isn't he? And so they all are; dear creatures. But then they are so backward. They are most anxious that I should join them up the Nile, but—," and then Miss Dawkins shrugged her shoulders gracefully, and, as she flattered herself, like a Frenchwoman. After that they rode on in silence for a few moments.

"Yes, I must see Mount Sinai," said Miss Dawkins, and then sighed deeply. M. Delabordeau, notwithstanding that his country does stand at the head of all human civilization, was not courteous enough to declare that if Miss Dawkins would join his party across the desert, nothing would be wanting to make his beatitude in this world perfect.

Their road from the village of the chicken-hatching ovens lay up along the left bank of the Nile, through an immense grove of lofty palm-trees, looking out from among which our visitors could ever and anon see the heads of the two great pyramids;—that is, such of them could see it as felt any solicitude in the matter.

It is astonishing how such things lose their great charm as men find themselves in their close neighbourhood. To one living in New York or London, how ecstatic is the interest inspired by these huge structures. One feels that no price would be too high to pay for seeing them as long as time and distance, and the world's inexorable task-work forbid such a visit. How intense would be the delight of climbing over the wondrous handiwork of those wondrous architects so long since dead; how thrilling the awe with which one would penetrate down into their interior caves—those caves in which lay buried the bones of ancient kings, whose very names seem to have come to us almost from another world!

But all these feelings become strangely dim, their acute edges wonderfully worn, as the subjects which inspired them are brought near to us. "Ah! so those are the Pyramids, are they?" says the traveller, when the first glimpse of them is shown to him from the window of a railway carriage. "Dear me; they don't look so very high, do they? For Heaven's sake put the blind down, or we shall be destroyed by the dust." And then the ecstasy and keen delight of the Pyramids has vanished, and for ever.

Our friends, therefore, who for weeks past had seen them from a distance, though they had not yet visited them, did not seem to have any strong feeling on the subject as they trotted through the grove of palm-trees. Mr. Damer had not yet escaped from his wife, who was still fretful from the result of her little accident.

"It was all the chattering of that Miss Dawkins," said Mrs. Damer. "She would not let me attend to what I was doing."

"Miss Dawkins is an ass," said her husband.

"It is a pity she has no one to look after her," said Mrs. Damer.

M. Delabordeau was still listening to Miss Dawkins's raptures about Mount Sinai. "I wonder whether she has got any money," said M. Delabordeau to himself. "It can't be much," he went on thinking, "or she would not be left in this way by herself." And the result of his thoughts was that Miss Dawkins, if undertaken, might probably become more plague than profit. As to Miss Dawkins herself, though she was ecstatic about Mount Sinai—which was not present—she seemed to have forgotten the poor Pyramids, which were then before her nose.

The two lads were riding races along the dusty path, much to the disgust of their donkey-boys. Their time for enjoyment was to come. There were hampers to be opened; and then the absolute climbing of the Pyramids would actually be a delight to them.

As for Miss Damer and Mr. Ingram, it was clear that they had forgotten palm-trees, Pyramids, the Nile, and all Egypt. They had escaped to a much fairer paradise.

"Could I bear to live among Republicans?" said Fanny, repeating the last words of her American lover, and looking down from her donkey to the ground as she did so. "I hardly know what Republicans are, Mr. Ingram."

"Let me teach you," said he.

"You do talk such nonsense. I declare there is that Miss Dawkins looking at us as though she had twenty eyes. Could you not teach her, Mr. Ingram?"

And so they emerged from the palm-tree grove, through a village crowded with dirty, straggling Arab children, on to the cultivated plain, beyond which the Pyramids stood, now full before them; the two large Pyramids, a smaller one, and the huge sphinx's head all in a group together.

"Fanny," said Bob Damer, riding up to her, "mamma wants you; so toddle back."

"Mamma wants me! What can she want me for now?" said Fanny, with a look of anything but filial duty in her face.

"To protect her from Miss Dawkins, I think. She wants you to ride at her side, so that Dawkins mayn't get at her. Now, Mr. Ingram, I'll bet you half a crown I'm at the top of the big Pyramid before you."

Poor Fanny! She obeyed, however; doubtless feeling that it would not do as yet to show too plainly that she preferred Mr. Ingram to her mother. She arrested her donkey, therefore, till Mrs. Damer overtook her; and Mr. Ingram, as he paused for a moment with her while she did so, fell into the hands of Miss Dawkins.

"I cannot think, Fanny, how you get on so quick," said Mrs. Damer.

"I'm always last; but then my donkey is such a very nasty one. Look there, now; he's always trying to get me off."

"We shall soon be at the Pyramids now, mamma."

"How on earth I am ever to get back again I cannot think. I am so tired now that I can hardly sit."

"You'll be better, mamma, when you get your luncheon and a glass of wine."

"How on earth we are to eat and drink with those nasty Arab people around us, I can't conceive. They tell me we shall be eaten up by them. But, Fanny, what has Mr. Ingram been saying to you all the day?"

"What has he been saying, mamma? Oh! I don't know;—a hundred things, I dare say. But he has not been talking to me all the time."

"I think he has, Fanny, nearly, since we crossed the river. Oh, dear! oh, dear! this animal does hurt me so! Every time he moves he flings his head about, and that gives me such a bump." And then Fanny commiserated her mother's sufferings, and in her commiseration contrived to elude any further questionings as to Mr. Ingram's conversation.

"Majestic piles, are they not?" said Miss Dawkins, who, having changed her companion, allowed her mind to revert from Mount Sinai to the Pyramids. They were now riding through cultivated ground, with the vast extent of the sands of Libya before them. The two Pyramids were standing on the margin of the sand, with the head of the recumbent sphynx plainly visible between them. But no idea can be formed of the size of this immense figure till it is visited much more closely. The body is covered with sand, and the head and neck alone stand above the surface of the ground. They were still two miles distant, and the sphynx as yet was but an obscure mound between the two vast Pyramids.

"Immense piles!" said Miss Dawkins, repeating her own words.

"Yes, they are large," said Mr. Ingram, who did not choose to indulge in enthusiasm in the presence of Miss Dawkins.

"Enormous! What a grand idea!—eh, Mr. Ingram? The human race does not create such things as those nowadays!"

"No, indeed," he answered; "but perhaps we create better things."

"Better! You do not mean to say, Mr. Ingram, that you are an utilitarian. I do, in truth, hope better things of you than that. Yes! steam mills are better, no doubt, and mechanics' institutes, and penny newspapers. But is nothing to be valued but what is useful?" And Miss Dawkins, in the height of her enthusiasm, switched her donkey severely over the shoulder.

"I might, perhaps, have said also that we create more beautiful things," said Mr. Ingram.

"But we cannot create older things."

"No, certainly; we cannot do that."

"Nor can we imbue what we do create with the grand associations which environ those piles with so intense an interest. Think of the mighty dead, Mr. Ingram, and of their great homes when living. Think of the hands which it took to raise those huge blocks— "

"And of the lives which it cost."

"Doubtless. The tyranny and invincible power of the royal architects add to the grandeur of the idea. One would not wish to have back the kings of Egypt."

"Well, no; they would be neither useful nor beautiful."

"Perhaps not; and I do not wish to be picturesque at the expense of my fellow-creatures."

"I doubt, even, whether they would be picturesque."

"You know what I mean, Mr. Ingram. But the associations of such names, and the presence of the stupendous works with which they are connected, fill the soul with awe. Such, at least, is the effect with mine."

"I fear that my tendencies, Miss Dawkins, are more realistic than your own."

"You belong to a young country, Mr. Ingram, and are naturally prone to think of material life. The necessity of living looms large before you."

"Very large, indeed, Miss Dawkins."

"Whereas with us, with some of us at least, the material aspect has given place to one in which poetry and enthusiasm prevail. To such among us the associations of past times are very dear. Cheops, to me, is more than Napoleon Bonaparte."

"That is more than most of your countrymen can say, at any rate, just at present."

"I am a woman," continued Miss Dawkins.

Mr. Ingram took off his hat in acknowledgment both of the announcement and of the fact.

"And to us it is not given—not given as yet—to share in the great deeds of the present. The envy of your sex has driven us from the paths which lead to honour. But the deeds of the past are as much ours as yours."

"Oh, quite as much."

"'Tis to your country that we look for enfranchisement from this thraldom. Yes, Mr. Ingram, the women of America have that strength of mind which has been wanting to those of Europe. In the United States woman will at last learn to exercise her proper mission."

Mr. Ingram expressed a sincere wish that such might be the case; and then wondering at the ingenuity with which Miss Dawkins had travelled round from Cheops and his Pyramid to the rights of women in America, he contrived to fall back, under the pretence of asking after ailments of Mrs. Damer.

And now at last they were on the sand, in the absolute desert, making their way up to the very foot of the most northern of the two Pyramids. They were by this time surrounded by a crowd of Arab guides, or Arabs professing to be guides, who had already ascertained that Mr. Damer was the chief of the party, and were accordingly driving him almost to madness by the offers of their services, and their assurance that he could not possibly see the outside or the inside of either structure, or even remain alive upon the ground, unless he at once accepted their offers made at their own prices.

"Get away, will you?" said he. "I don't want any of you, and I won't have you! If you take hold of me I'll shoot you!" This was said to one specially energetic Arab, who, in his efforts to secure his prey, had caught hold of Mr. Damer by the leg.

"Yes, yes, I say! Englishmen always take me;—me—me, and then no break him leg. Yes—yes—yes;—I go. Master say, yes. Only one leetle ten shilling!"

"Abdallah!" shouted Mr. Damer, "why don't you take this man away? Why don't you make him understand that if all the Pyramids depended on it, I would not give him sixpence!"

And then Abdallah, thus invoked, came up, and explained to the man in Arabic that he would gain his object more surely if he would behave himself a little more quietly; a hint which the man took for one minute, and for one minute only.

And then poor Mrs. Damer replied to an application for backsheish by the gift of a sixpence. Unfortunate woman! The word backsheish means, I believe, a gift; but it has come in Egypt to signify money, and is eternally dinned into the ears of strangers by Arab suppliants. Mrs. Damer ought to have known better, as, during the last six weeks she had never shown her face out of Shepheard's Hotel without being pestered for backsheish; but she was tired and weak, and foolishly thought to rid herself of the man who was annoying her.

No sooner had the coin dropped from her hand into that of the Arab, than she was surrounded by a cluster of beggars, who loudly made their petitions as though they would, each of them, individually be injured if treated with less liberality than that first comer. They took hold of her donkey, her bridle, her saddle, her legs, and at last her arms and hands, screaming for backsheish in voices that were neither sweet nor mild.

In her dismay she did give away sundry small coins—all, probably, that she had about her; but this only made the matter worse. Money was going, and each man, by sufficient energy, might hope to get some of it. They were very energetic, and so frightened the poor lady that she would certainly have fallen, had she not been kept on her seat by their pressure around her.

"Oh, dear! oh, dear! get away," she cried. "I haven't got any more; indeed, I haven't. Go away, I tell you! Mr. Damer! oh, Mr. Damer!" and then, in the excess of her agony, she uttered one loud, long, and continuous shriek.

Up came Mr. Damer; up came Abdallah; up came M. Delabordeau; up came Mr. Ingram, and at last she was rescued. "You shouldn't go away, and leave me to the mercy of these nasty people. As to that Abdallah, he is of no use to anybody."

"Why you bodder de good lady, you dem black-guard?" said Abdallah, raising his stick, as though he were going to lay them all low with a blow. "Now you get noting, you tief!

The Arabs for a moment retired to a little distance, like flies driven from a sugar-bowl; but it was easy to see that, like the flies, they would return at the first vacant moment.

And now they had reached the very foot of the Pyramids and

proceeded to dismount from their donkeys. Their intention was first to ascend to the top, then to come down to their banquet, and after that to penetrate into the interior. And all this would seem to be easy of performance. The Pyramid is undoubtedly high, but it is so constructed as to admit of climbing without difficulty. A lady mounting it would undoubtedly need some assistance, but any man possessed of moderate activity would require no aid at all.

But our friends were at once imbued with the tremendous nature of the task before them. A sheikh of the Arabs came forth, who communicated with them through Abdallah. The work could be done, no doubt, he said; but a great many men would be wanted to assist. Each lady must have four Arabs, and each gentleman three; and then, seeing that the work would be peculiarly severe on this special day, each of these numerous Arabs must be remunerated by some very large number of piastres.

Mr. Damer, who was by no means a close man in his money dealings, opened his eyes with surprise, and mildly expostulated; M. Delabordeau, who was rather a close man in his reckonings, immediately buttoned up his breeches-pocket and declared that he should decline to mount the Pyramid at all at that price; and then Mr. Ingram descended to the combat.

The protestations of the men were fearful. They declared, with loud voices, eager actions, and manifold English oaths, that an attempt was being made to rob them. They had a right to demand the sums which they were charging, and it was a shame that English gentlemen should come and take the bread out of their mouths. And so they screeched, gesticulated, and swore, and frightened poor Mrs. Damer almost into fits.

But at last it was settled and away they started, the sheikh declaring that the bargain had been made at so low a rate as to leave him not one piastre for himself. Each man had an Arab on each side of him, and Miss Dawkins and Miss Damer had each, in addition, one behind. Mrs. Damer was so frightened as altogether to have lost all ambition to ascend. She sat below on a fragment of stone, with the three dragomans standing around her as guards; but even with the three dragomans the attacks on her were so frequent, and as she declared afterwards she was so bewildered, that she never had time to remember that she had come there from England to see the Pyramids, and that she was now immediately under them.

The boys, utterly ignoring their guides, scrambled up quicker than the Arabs could follow them. Mr. Damer started off at a pace which soon brought him to the end of his tether, and from that point was dragged up by the sheer strength of his assistants; thereby accomplishing the wishes of the men, who induce their victims to start as rapidly as possible, in order that they may soon find themselves helpless from want of wind. Mr. Ingram endeavoured to attach himself to Fanny, and she would have been nothing loth to have him at her right hand instead of the hideous brown, shrieking, one-eyed Arab who took hold of her. But it was soon found that any such arrangement was impossible. Each guide felt that if he lost his own peculiar hold he would lose his prey, and held on, therefore, with invincible tenacity. Miss Dawkins looked, too, as though she had thought to be attended to by some Christian cavalier, but no Christian cavalier was forthcoming. M. Delabordeau was the wisest, for he took the matter quietly, did as he was bid, and allowed the guides nearly to carry him to the top of the edifice.

"Ha! So this is the top of the Pyramid, is it?" said Mr. Damer, bringing out his words one by one, being terribly out of breath. "Very wonderful, very wonderful indeed!"

"It is wonderful," said Miss Dawkins, whose breath had not failed her in the least, "very wonderful indeed! Only think, Mr. Damer, you might travel on for days and days, till days became months, through those interminable sands, and yet you would never come to the end of them. Is it not quite stupendous?"

"Ah, yes, quite,—puff, puff"—said Mr. Damer, striving to regain his breath.

Mr. Damer was now at her disposal; weak and worn with toil and travel, out of breath, and with half his manhood gone; if ever she might prevail over him so as to procure from his mouth an assent to that Nile proposition, it would be now. And after all, that Nile proposition was the best one now before her. She did not quite like the idea of starting off across the Great Desert without any lady, and was not sure that she was prepared to be fallen in love with by M. Delabordeau, even if there should ultimately be any readiness on the part of that gentleman to perform the role of lover. With Mr. Ingram the matter was different, nor was she so diffident of her own charms as to think it altogether impossible that she might succeed, in the teeth of that little chit, Fanny Damer. That Mr. Ingram would join the party up the Nile she had very little doubt; and then there would be one place left for her. She would thus, at any rate, become commingled with a most respectable family, who might be of material service to her.

Thus actuated she commenced an earnest attack upon Mr. Damer.

"Stupendous!" she said again, for she was fond of repeating favourite words. "What a wondrous race must have been those Egyptian kings of old!"

"I dare say they were," said Mr. Damer, wiping his brow as he sat upon a large loose stone, a fragment lying on the flat top of the Pyramid, one of those stones with which the complete apex was once made, or was once about to be made.

"A magnificent race! so gigantic in their conceptions! Their ideas altogether overwhelm us poor, insignificant, latter-day mortals. They built these vast Pyramids; but for us, it is task enough to climb to their top."

"Quite enough," ejaculated Mr. Damer.

But Mr. Damer would not always remain weak and out of breath, and it was absolutely necessary for Miss Dawkins to hurry away from Cheops and his tomb, to Thebes and Karnac.

"After seeing this it is impossible for any one with a spark of imagination to leave Egypt without going further a-field."

Mr. Damer merely wiped his brow and grunted. This Miss Dawkins took as a signal of weakness, and went on with her task perseveringly.

"For myself, I have resolved to go up, at any rate as far as Asouan and the first cataract. I had thought of acceding to the wishes of a party who are going across the Great Desert by Mount Sinai to Jerusalem; but the kindness of yourself and Mrs. Damer is so great, and the prospect of joining in your boat is so pleasurable, that I have made up my mind to accept your very kind offer."

This, it will be acknowledged, was bold on the part of Miss Dawkins; but what will not audacity effect? To use the slang of modern language, cheek carries everything nowadays. And whatever may have been Miss Dawkins's deficiencies, in this virtue she was not deficient.

"I have made up my mind to accept your very kind offer," she said, shining on Mr. Damer with her blandest smile.

What was a stout, breathless, perspiring, middle-aged gentleman to do under such circumstances? Mr. Damer was a man who, in most matters, had his own way. That his wife should have given such an invitation without consulting him, was, he knew, quite impossible. She would as soon have thought of asking all those Arab guides to accompany them. Nor was it to be thought of that he should allow himself to be kidnapped into such an arrangement by the impudence of any Miss Dawkins. But there was, he felt, a difficulty in answering such a proposition from a young lady with a direct negative, especially while he was so scant of breath. So he wiped his brow again, and looked at her.

"But I can only agree to this on one understanding," continued Miss Dawkins, "and that is, that I am allowed to defray my own full share of the expense of the journey."

Upon hearing this Mr. Damer thought that he saw his way out of the wood. "Wherever I go, Miss Dawkins, I am always the paymaster myself," and this he contrived to say with some sternness, palpitating though he still was; and the sternness which was deficient in his voice he endeavoured to put into his countenance.

But he did not know Miss Dawkins. "Oh, Mr. Damer," she said, and as she spoke her smile became almost blander than it was before; "oh, Mr. Damer, I could not think of suffering you to be so liberal; I could not, indeed. But I shall be quite content that you should pay everything, and let me settle with you in one sum afterwards."

Mr. Damer's breath was now rather more under his own command. "I am afraid, Miss Dawkins," he said, "that Mrs. Damer's weak state of health will not admit of such an arrangement."

"What, about the paying?"

"Not only as to that, but we are a family party, Miss Dawkins; and great as would be the benefit of your society to all of us, in Mrs. Damer's present state of health, I am afraid—in short, you would not find it agreeable.—And therefore— " this he added, seeing that she was still about to persevere—"I fear that we must forego the advantage you offer."

And then, looking into his face, Miss Dawkins did perceive that even her audacity would not prevail.

"Oh, very well," she said, and moving from the stone on which she had been sitting, she walked off, carrying her head very high, to a corner of the Pyramid from which she could look forth alone towards the sands of Libya.

In the mean time another little overture was being made on the top of the same Pyramid,—an overture which was not received quite in the same spirit. While Mr. Damer was recovering his breath for the sake of answering Miss Dawkins, Miss Damer had walked to the further corner of the square platform on which they were placed, and there sat herself down with her face turned towards Cairo. Perhaps it was not singular that Mr. Ingram should have followed her.

This would have been very well if a dozen Arabs had not also followed them. But as this was the case, Mr. Ingram had to play his game under some difficulty. He had no sooner seated himself beside her than they came and stood directly in front of the seat, shutting out the view, and by no means improving the fragrance of the air around them.

"And this, then, Miss Damer, will be our last excursion together," he said, in his tenderest, softest tone.

"De good Englishman will gib de poor Arab one little backsheish," said an Arab, putting out his hand and shaking Mr. Ingram's shoulder.

"Yes, yes, yes; him gib backsheish," said another.

"Him berry good man," said a third, putting up his filthy hand, and touching Mr. Ingram's face.

"And young lady berry good, too; she give backsheish to poor Arab."

"Yes," said a fourth, preparing to take a similar liberty with Miss Damer.

This was too much for Mr. Ingram. He had already used very positive language in his endeavour to assure his tormentors that they would not get a piastre from him. But this only changed their soft persuasions into threats. Upon hearing which, and upon seeing what the man attempted to do in his endeavour to get money from Miss Damer, he raised his stick, and struck first one and then the other as violently as he could upon their heads.

Any ordinary civilized men would have been stunned by such blows, for they fell on the bare foreheads of the Arabs; but the objects of the American's wrath merely skulked away; and the others, convinced by the only arguments which they understood, followed in pursuit of victims who might be less pugnacious.

It is hard for a man to be at once tender and pugnacious—to be sentimental, while he is putting forth his physical strength with all the violence in his power. It is difficult, also, for him to be gentle instantly after having been in a rage. So he changed his tactics at the moment, and came to the point at once in a manner befitting his present state of mind.

"Those vile wretches have put me in such a heat," he said, "that I hardly know what I am saying. But the fact is this, Miss Damer, I cannot leave Cairo without knowing—. You understand what I mean, Miss Damer."

"Indeed I do not, Mr. Ingram; except that I am afraid you mean nonsense."

"Yes, you do; you know that I love you. I am sure you must know it. At any rate you know it now."

"Mr. Ingram, you should not talk in such a way."

"Why should I not? But the truth is, Fanny, I can talk in no other way. I do love you dearly. Can you love me well enough to go and be my wife in a country far away from your own?"

Before she left the top of the Pyramid Fanny Damer had said that she would try.

Mr. Ingram was now a proud and happy man, and seemed to think the steps of the Pyramid too small for his elastic energy. But Fanny feared that her troubles were to come. There was papa—that terrible bugbear on all such occasions. What would papa say? She was sure her papa would not allow her to marry and go so far away from her own family and country. For herself, she liked the Americans—always had liked them; so she said;—would desire nothing better than to live among them. But papa! And Fanny sighed as she felt that all the recognized miseries of a young lady in love were about to fall upon her.

Nevertheless, at her lover's instance, she promised, and declared, in twenty different loving phrases, that nothing on earth should ever make her false to her love or to her lover.

"Fanny, where are you? Why are you not ready to come down?" shouted Mr. Damer, not in the best of tempers. He felt that he had almost been unkind to an unprotected female, and his heart misgave him. And yet it would have misgiven him more had he allowed himself to be entrapped by Miss Dawkins.

"I am quite ready, papa," said Fanny, running up to him—for it may be understood that there is quite room enough for a young lady to run on the top of the Pyramid.

"I am sure I don't know where you have been all the time," said Mr. Damer; "and where are those two boys?"

Fanny pointed to the top of the other Pyramid, and there they were, conspicuous with their red caps.

"And M. Delabordeau?"

"Oh! he has gone down, I think;—no, he is there with Miss Dawkins." And in truth Miss Dawkins was leaning on his arm most affectionately, as she stooped over and looked down upon the ruins below her.

"And where is that fellow, Ingram?" said Mr. Damer, looking about him. "He is always out of the way when he's wanted."

To this Fanny said nothing. Why should she? She was not Mr. Ingram's keeper.

And then they all descended, each again with his proper number of

Arabs to hurry and embarrass him; and they found Mrs. Damer at the bottom, like a piece of sugar covered with flies. She was heard to declare afterwards that she would not go to the Pyramids again, not if they were to be given to her for herself, as ornaments for her garden.

The picnic lunch among the big stones at the foot of the Pyramid was not a very gay affair. Miss Dawkins talked more than any one else, being determined to show that she bore her defeat gallantly. Her conversation, however, was chiefly addressed to M. Delabordeau, and he seemed to think more of his cold chicken and ham than he did of her wit and attention.

Fanny hardly spoke a word. There was her father before her, and she could not eat, much less talk, as she thought of all that she would have to go through. What would he say to the idea of having an American for a son-in-law?

Nor was Mr. Ingram very lively. A young man when he has been just accepted, never is so. His happiness under the present circumstances was, no doubt, intense, but it was of a silent nature.

And then the interior of the building had to be visited. To tell the truth none of the party would have cared to perform this feat had it not been for the honour of the thing. To have come from Paris, New York, or London, to the Pyramids, and then not to have visited the very tomb of Cheops, would have shown on the part of all of them an indifference to subjects of interest which would have been altogether fatal to their character as travellers. And so a party for the interior was made up.

Miss Damer when she saw the aperture through which it was expected that she should descend, at once declared for staying with her mother. Miss Dawkins, however, was enthusiastic for the journey. "Persons with so very little command over their nerves might really as well stay at home," she said to Mr. Ingram, who glowered at her dreadfully for expressing such an opinion about his Fanny.

This entrance into the Pyramids is a terrible task, which should be undertaken by no lady. Those who perform it have to creep down, and then to be dragged up, through infinite dirt, foul smells, and bad air; and when they have done it, they see nothing. But they do earn the gratification of saying that they have been inside a Pyramid.

"Well, I've done that once," said Mr. Damer, coming out, "and I do not think that any one will catch me doing it again. I never was in such a filthy place in my life."

"Oh, Fanny! I am so glad you did not go; I am sure it is not fit for ladies," said poor Mrs. Damer, forgetful of her friend Miss Dawkins.

"I should have been ashamed of myself," said Miss Dawkins, bristling up, and throwing back her head as she stood, "if I had allowed any consideration to have prevented my visiting such a spot. If it be not improper for men to go there, how can it be improper for women?"

"I did not say improper, my dear," said Mrs. Damer, apologetically.

"And as for the fatigue, what can a woman be worth who is afraid to encounter as much as I have now gone through for the sake of visiting the last resting-place of such a king as Cheops?" And Miss Dawkins, as she pronounced the last words, looked round her with disdain upon poor Fanny Damer.

"But I meant the dirt," said Mrs. Damer.

"Dirt!" ejaculated Miss Dawkins, and then walked away. Why should she now submit her high tone of feeling to the Damers, or why care longer for their good opinion? Therefore she scattered contempt around her as she ejaculated the last word, "dirt."

And then the return home! "I know I shall never get there," said Mrs. Damer, looking piteously up into her husband's face.

"Nonsense, my dear; nonsense; you must get there." Mrs. Damer groaned, and acknowledged in her heart that she must,—either dead or alive.

"And, Jefferson," said Fanny, whispering—for there had been a moment since their descent in which she had been instructed to call him by his Christian name—"never mind talking to me going home. I will ride by mamma. Do you go with papa and put him in good humour; and if he says anything about the lords and the bishops, don't you contradict him, you know."

What will not a man do for love? Mr. Ingram promised. And in this way they started; the two boys led the van; then came Mr. Damer and Mr. Ingram, unusually and unpatriotically acquiescent as to England's aristocratic propensities; then Miss Dawkins riding, alas! alone; after her, M. Delabordeau, also alone,—the ungallant Frenchman! And the rear was brought up by Mrs. Damer and her daughter, flanked on each side by a dragoman, with a third dragoman behind them.

And in this order they went back to Cairo, riding their donkeys, and crossing the ferry solemnly, and, for the most part, silently. Mr. Ingram did talk, as he had an important object in view,—that of putting Mr. Damer into a good humour.

In this he succeeded so well that by the time they had remounted, after crossing the Nile, Mr. Damer opened his heart to his companion on the subject that was troubling him, and told him all about Miss Dawkins.

"I don't see why we should have a companion that we don't like for eight or ten weeks, merely because it seems rude to refuse a lady."

"Indeed, I agree with you," said Mr. Ingram; "I should call it weak-minded to give way in such a case."

"My daughter does not like her at all," continued Mr. Damer.

"Nor would she be a nice companion for Miss Damer; not according to my way of thinking," said Mr. Ingram.

"And as to my having asked her, or Mrs. Damer having asked her! Why God bless my soul, it is pure invention on the woman's part!"

"Ha! ha! ha!" laughed Mr. Ingram; "I must say she plays her game well; but then she is an old soldier, and has the benefit of experience." What would Miss Dawkins have said had she known that Mr. Ingram called her an old soldier?

"I don't like the kind of thing at all," said Mr. Damer, who was very serious upon the subject. "You see the position in which I am placed. I am forced to be very rude, or— "

"I don't call it rude at all."

"Disobliging, then; or else I must have all my comfort invaded and pleasure destroyed by, by, by— " And Mr. Damer paused, being at a loss for an appropriate name for Miss Dawkins.

"By an unprotected female," suggested Mr. Ingram.

"Yes; just so. I am as fond of pleasant company as anybody; but then I like to choose it myself."

"So do I," said Mr. Ingram, thinking of his own choice.

"Now, Ingram, if you would join us, we should be delighted."

"Upon my word, sir, the offer is too flattering," said Ingram, hesitatingly; for he felt that he could not undertake such a journey until Mr. Damer knew on what terms he stood with Fanny.

"You are a terrible democrat," said Mr. Damer, laughing; "but then, on that matter, you know, we could agree to differ."

"Exactly so," said Mr. Ingram, who had not collected his thoughts or made up his mind as to what he had better say and do, on the spur of the moment.

"Well what do you say to it?" said Mr. Damer, encouragingly. But Ingram paused before he answered.

"For Heaven's sake, my dear fellow, don't have the slightest hesitation in refusing, if you don't like the plan."

"The fact is, Mr. Damer, I should like too well."

"Like it too well?"

"Yes, sir, and I may as well tell you now as later. I had intended this evening to have asked for your permission to address your daughter."

"God bless my soul!" said Mr. Damer, looking as though a totally new idea had now been opened to him.

"And under these circumstances, I will now wait and see whether or no you will renew your offer."

"God bless my soul!" said Mr. Damer again. It often does strike an old gentleman as very odd that any man should fall in love with his daughter, whom he has not ceased to look upon as a child. The case is generally quite different with mothers. They seem to think that every young man must fall in love with their girls.

"And have you said anything to Fanny about this?" asked Mr. Damer.

"Yes, sir, I have her permission to speak to you."

"God bless my soul!" said Mr. Damer; and by this time they had arrived at Shepheard's Hotel.

"Oh, mamma," said Fanny, as soon as she found herself alone with her mother that evening, "I have something that I must tell you."

"Oh, Fanny, don't tell me anything to-night, for I am a great deal too tired to listen."

"But oh, mamma, pray;—you must listen to this; indeed you must." And Fanny knelt down at her mother's knee, and looked beseechingly up into her face.

"What is it, Fanny? You know that all my bones are sore, and that I am so tired that I am almost dead."

"Mamma, Mr. Ingram has— "

"Has what, my dear? has he done anything wrong?"

"No, mamma: but he has;—he has proposed to me." And Fanny bursting into tears hid her face in her mother's lap.

And thus the story was told on both sides of the house. On the next day, as a matter of course, all the difficulties and dangers of such a marriage as that which was now projected were insisted on by both father and mother. It was improper; it would cause a severing of the family not to be thought of; it would be an alliance of a dangerous nature, and not at all calculated to insure happiness; and, in short, it was impossible. On that day, therefore, they all went to bed very unhappy. But on the next day, as was also a matter of course, seeing that there were no pecuniary difficulties, the mother and father were talked over, and Mr. Ingram was accepted as a son-in-law. It need hardly be said that the offer of a place in Mr. Damer's boat was again made, and that on this occasion it was accepted without hesitation.

There was an American Protestant clergyman resident in Cairo, with whom, among other persons, Miss Dawkins had become acquainted. Upon this gentleman or upon his wife Miss Dawkins called a few days after the journey to the Pyramid, and finding him in his study, thus performed her duty to her neighbour:

"You know your countryman Mr. Ingram, I think?" said she.

"Oh, yes; very intimately."

"If you have any regard for him, Mr. Burton," such was the gentleman's name, "I think you should put him on his guard."

"On his guard against what?" said Mr. Burton with a serious air, for there was something serious in the threat of impending misfortune as conveyed by Miss Dawkins.

"Why," said she, "those Damers, I fear, are dangerous people."

"Do you mean that they will borrow money of him?"

"Oh, no; not that exactly; but they are clearly setting their cap at him."

"Setting their cap at him?"

"Yes; there is a daughter, you know; a little chit of a thing; and I fear Mr. Ingram may be caught before he knows where he is. It would be such a pity, you know. He is going up the river with them, I hear. That, in his place, is very foolish. They asked me, but I positively refused."

Mr. Burton remarked that "in such a matter as that Mr. Ingram would be perfectly able to take care of himself."

"Well, perhaps so; but seeing what was going on, I thought it my duty to tell you." And so Miss Dawkins took her leave.

Mr. Ingram did go up the Nile with the Damers, as did an old friend of the Damers who arrived from England. And a very pleasant trip they had of it. And, as far as the present historian knows, the two lovers were shortly afterwards married in England.

Poor Miss Dawkins was left in Cairo for some time on her beam ends. But she was one of those who are not easily vanquished. After an interval of ten days she made acquaintance with an Irish family—having utterly failed in moving the hard heart of M. Delabordeau—and with these she proceeded to Constantinople. They consisted of two brothers and a sister, and were, therefore, very convenient for matrimonial purposes. But nevertheless, when I last heard of Miss Dawkins, she was still an unprotected female.

The Château of Prince Polignac

Originally appeared in *Cassell's Illustrated Family Paper*, 20 and 27 October 1860. Reprinted in *Tales of All Countries* [First Series] (1861). Written in the Pyrenees between 1 September and 29 October 1859, during the composition of *Castle Richmond*. This trip also obviously supplied the setting: Rose Trollope's itinerary confirms a stop at Le Puy (in South-Central France).

FEW ENGLISHMEN or Englishwomen are intimately acquainted with the little town of Le Puy. It is the capital of the old province of Le Velay, which also is now but little known, even to French ears, for it is in these days called by the imperial name of the Department of the Haute Loire. It is to the south-east of Auvergne, and is nearly in the centre of the southern half of France.

But few towns, merely as towns, can be better worth visiting. In the first place, the volcanic formation of the ground on which it stands is not only singular in the extreme, so as to be interesting to the geologist but it is so picturesque as to be equally gratifying to the general tourist. Within a narrow valley there stand several rocks, rising up from the ground with absolute abruptness. Round two of these the town clusters, and a third stands but a mile distant, forming the centre of a faubourg, or suburb. These rocks appear to be, and I believe are, the harder particles of volcanic matter, which have not been carried away through successive ages by the joint agency of water and air. When the tide of lava ran down between the hills the surface left was no doubt on a level with the heads of these rocks; but here and there the deposit became harder than elsewherc, and these harder points have remained, lifting up their steep heads in a line through the valley.

The highest of these is called the Rocher de Corneille. Round this and up its steep sides the town stands. On its highest summit there was an old castle; and there now is, or will be before these pages are printed, a colossal figure in bronze of the Virgin Mary, made from the cannon taken at Sebastopol. Half-way down the hill the cathedral is built, a singularly gloomy edifice,—Romanesque, as it is called, in its style, but extremely similar in its mode of architecture to what we know of Byzantine structures. But there has been no surface on the rock side large enough to form a resting-place for the church, which has therefore been built out on huge supporting piles, which form a porch below the west front; so that the approach is by numerous steps laid along the side of the wall below the church, forming a wondrous flight of stairs. Let all men who may find themselves stopping at Le Puy visit the top of these stairs at the time of the setting sun, and look down from thence through the framework of the porch on the town beneath, and at the hill-side beyond.

Behind the church is the seminary of the priests, with its beautiful walks stretching round the Rocher de Corneille, and overlooking the town and valley below.

Next to this rock, and within a quarter of a mile of it, is the second peak, called the Rock of the Needle. It rises narrow, sharp, and abrupt from the valley, allowing of no buildings on its sides. But on its very point has been erected a church sacred to St. Michael, that lover of rock summits, accessible by stairs cut from the stone. This, perhaps—this rock, I mean—is the most wonderful of the wonders which Nature has formed at Le Puy.

Above this, at a mile's distance, is the rock of Espailly, formed in the same way, and almost equally precipitous. On its summit is a castle, having its own legend, and professing to have been the residence of

Charles VII., when little of France belonged to its kings but the provinces of Berry, Auvergne, and Le Velay. Some three miles further up there is another volcanic rock, larger, indeed, but equally sudden in its spring,—equally remarkable as rising abruptly from the valley—on which stands the castle and old family residence of the house of Polignac. It was lost by them at the time of the Revolution, but was repurchased by the minister of Charles X., and is still the property of the head of the race.

Le Puy itself is a small, moderate, pleasant French town, in which the language of the people has not the pure Parisian aroma, nor is the glory of the boulevards of the capital emulated in its streets. These are crooked, narrow, steep, and intricate, forming here and there excellent sketches for a lover of street picturesque beauty; but hurtful to the feet with their small round-topped paving stones, and not always as clean as pedestrian ladies might desire.

And now I would ask my readers to join me at the morning table d'hôte at the Hôtel des Ambassadeurs. It will of course be understood that this does not mean a breakfast in the ordinary fashion of England, consisting of tea or coffee, bread and butter, and perhaps a boiled egg. It comprises all the requisites for a composite dinner, excepting soup; and as one gets further south in France, this meal is called dinner. It is, however, eaten without any prejudice to another similar and somewhat longer meal at six or seven o'clock, which, when the above name is taken up by the earlier enterprise, is styled supper.

The *déjeuner*, or dinner, at the Hôtel des Ambassadeurs, on the morning in question, though very elaborate, was not a very gay affair. There were some fourteen persons present, of whom half were residents in the town, men employed in some official capacity, who found this to be the cheapest, the most luxurious, and to them the most comfortable mode of living. They clustered together at the head of the table, and as they were customary guests at the house they talked their little talk together—it was very little—and made the most of the good things before them. Then there were two or three *commis-voyageurs*, a chance traveller or two, and an English lady with a young daughter. The English lady sat next to one of the accustomed guests; but he, unlike the others, held converse with her rather than with them. Our story at present has reference only to that lady and to that gentleman.

Place aux dames. We will speak first of the lady, whose name was Mrs. Thompson. She was, shall I say, a young woman, of about thirty-six. In so saying, I am perhaps creating a prejudice against her in the minds of some readers, as they will, not unnaturally, suppose her, after such an announcement, to be in truth over forty. Any such prejudice will be unjust. I would have it believed that thirty-six was the outside, not the inside of her age. She was good-looking, lady-like, and considering that she was an English-woman, fairly well dressed. She was inclined to be rather full in her person, but perhaps not more so than is becoming to ladies at her time of life. She had rings on her fingers and a brooch on her bosom which were of some value, and on the back of her head she wore a jaunty small lace cap, which seemed to tell, in conjunction with her other appointments, that her circumstances were comfortable.

The little girl who sat next to her was the youngest of her two daughters, and might be about thirteen years of age. Her name was Matilda, but infantine circumstances had invested her with the nickname of Mimmy, by which her mother always called her. A nice, pretty, playful little girl was Mimmy Thompson, wearing two long tails of plaited hair hanging behind her head, and inclined occasionally to be rather loud in her sport.

Mrs. Thompson had another and an elder daughter, now some fifteen years old, who was at school in Le Puy; and it was with reference to her tuition that Mrs. Thompson had taken up a temporary residence at the Hôtel des Ambassadeurs in that town. Lilian Thompson was occasionally invited down to dine or breakfast at the inn, and was visited daily at her school by her mother.

"When I'm sure that she'll do, I shall leave her there and go back to England," Mrs. Thompson had said, not in the purest French, to the neighbour who always sat next to her at the table d'hôte, the gentleman, namely, to whom we have above alluded. But still she had remained at Le Puy a month, and did not go; a circumstance which was considered singular, but by no means unpleasant, both by the innkeeper and by the gentleman in question.

The facts, as regarded Mrs. Thompson, were as follows:—She was the widow of a gentleman who had served for many years in the civil service of the East Indies, and who, on dying, had left her a comfortable income of—it matters not how many pounds, but constituting quite a sufficiency to enable her to live at her ease and educate her daughters.

Her children had been sent home to England before her husband's death, and after that event she had followed them; but there, though she was possessed of moderate wealth, she had no friends and few acquaintances, and after a little while she had found life to be rather dull. Her customs were not those of England, nor were her propensities English; therefore she had gone abroad, and having received some recommendation of this school at Le Puy, had made her way thither. As it appeared to her that she really enjoyed more consideration at Le Puy than had been accorded to her either at Torquay or Leamington, there she remained from day to day. The total payment required at the Hôtel des Ambassadeurs was but six francs daily for herself and three and a half for her little girl; and where else could she live with a better junction of economy and comfort? And then the gentleman who always sat next to her was so exceedingly civil!

The gentleman's name was M. Lacordaire. So much she knew, and had learned to call him by his name very frequently. Mimmy, too, was quite intimate with M. Lacordaire; but nothing more than his name was known of him. But M. Lacordaire carried a general letter of recommendation in his face, manner, gait, dress, and tone of voice. In all these respects there was nothing left to be desired; and, in addition to this, he was decorated, and wore the little red ribbon of the Legion of Honour, ingeniously twisted into the shape of a small flower.

M. Lacordaire might be senior in age to Mrs. Thompson by about ten years, nor had he about him any of the airs and graces of a would-be young man. His hair, which he wore very short, was grizzled, as was also the small pretence of a whisker which came down about as far as the middle of his ear; but the tuft on his chin was still brown, without a gray hair. His eyes were bright and tender, his voice was low and soft, his hands were very white, his clothes were always new and well-fitting, and a better-brushed hat could not be seen out of Paris, nor perhaps in it.

Now, during the weeks which Mrs. Thompson had passed at Le Puy, the acquaintance which she had formed with M. Lacordaire had progressed beyond the prolonged meals in the salle à manger. He had occasionally sat beside her evening table as she took her English cup of tea in her own room, her bed being duly screened off in its distinct niche by becoming curtains; and then he had occasionally walked beside her, as he civilly escorted her to the lions of the place; and he had once accompanied her, sitting on the back seat of a French voiture, when she had gone forth to see something of the surrounding country.

On all such occasions she had been accompanied by one of her daughters, and the world of Le Puy had had nothing material to say against her. But still the world of Le Puy had whispered a little, suggesting that M. Lacordaire knew very well what he was about. But might not Mrs. Thompson also know as well what she was about? At any rate, everything had gone on very pleasantly since the acquaintance had been made; and now, so much having been explained, we will go back to the elaborate breakfast at the Hôtel des Ambassadeurs.

Mrs. Thompson, holding Mimmy by the hand, walked into the room some few minutes after the last bell had been rung, and took the place which was now hers by custom. The gentlemen who constantly frequented the house all bowed to her, but M. Lacordaire rose from his seat and offered her his hand.

"And how is Mees Meemy this morning?" said he; for 'twas thus he always pronounced her name.

Miss Mimmy, answering for herself, declared that she was very well, and suggested that M. Lacordaire should give her a fig from off a dish that was placed immediately before him on the table. This M. Lacordaire did, presenting it very elegantly between his two fingers, and making a little bow to the little lady as he did so.

"Fie, Mimmy!" said her mother; "why do you ask for the things before the waiter brings them round?"

"But, mamma," said Mimmy, speaking English, "M. Lacordaire always gives me a fig every morning."

"M. Lacordaire always spoils you, I think," answered Mrs. Thompson, in French. And then they went thoroughly to work at their breakfast. During the whole meal M. Lacordaire attended assiduously to his neighbour; and did so without any evil result, except that one Frenchman with a black moustache, at the head of the table trod on the toe of another Frenchman with another black moustache—winking as he made the sign—just as M. Lacordaire, having selected a bunch of grapes, put it on Mrs. Thompson's place with infinite grace. But who among us all is free from such impertinences as these?

"But madame really must see the château of Prince Polignac before she leaves Le Puy," said M. Lacordaire.

"The château of who?" asked Mimmy, to whose young ears the French words were already becoming familiar.

"Prince Polignac, my dear. Well I really don't know, M. Lacordaire; —I have seen a great deal of the place already, and I shall be going now very soon; probably in a day or two," said Mrs. Thompson.

"But madame must positively see the château," said M. Lacordaire, very impressively; and then after a pause he added, "if madame will have the complaisance to commission me to procure a carriage for this afternoon, and will allow me the honour to be her guide, I shall consider myself one of the most fortunate of men."

"Oh, yes, mamma, do go," said Mimmy, clapping her hands. "And it is Thursday, and Lilian can go with us."

"Be quiet, Mimmy, do. Thank you, no, M. Lacordaire. I could not go to-day; but I am extremely obliged by your politeness."

M. Lacordaire still pressed the matter, and Mrs. Thompson still declined, till it was time to rise from the table. She then declared that she did not think it possible that she should visit the château before she left Le Puy; but that she would give him an answer at dinner.

The most tedious time in the day to Mrs. Thompson were the two hours after breakfast. At one o'clock she daily went to the school, taking Mimmy, who for an hour or two shared her sister's lessons. This and her little excursions about the place, and her shopping, managed to make away with her afternoon. Then in the evening, she generally saw something of M. Lacordaire. But those two hours after breakfast were hard of killing.

On this occasion, when she gained her own room, she as usual placed Mimmy on the sofa with a needle. Her custom then was to take up a novel; but on this morning she sat herself down in her arm-chair, and resting her head upon her hand and elbow, began to turn over certain circumstances in her mind.

"Mamma," said Mimmy, "why won't you go with M. Lacordaire to that place belonging to the prince? Prince—Polly something, wasn't it?"

"Mind your work, my dear," said Mrs. Thompson.

"But I do so wish you'd go, mamma. What was the prince's name?"

"Polignac."

"Mamma, ain't princes very great people?"

"Yes, my dear; sometimes."

"Is Prince Polly-nac like our Prince Alfred?"

"No, my dear; not at all. At least, I suppose not."

"Is his mother a queen?"

"No, my dear."

"Then his father must be a king?"

"No, my dear. It is quite a different thing here. Here in France they have a great many princes."

"Well, at any rate I should like to see a prince's château; so I do hope you'll go." And then there was a pause. "Mamma, could it come to pass, here in France, that M. Lacordaire should ever be a prince?"

"M. Lacordaire a prince! No; don't talk such nonsense, but mind your work."

"Isn't M. Lacordaire a very nice man? Ain't you very fond of him?"

To this question Mrs. Thompson made no answer.

"Mamma," continued Mimmy, after a moment's pause, "won't you tell me whether you are fond of M. Lacordaire? I'm quite sure of this,—that he's very fond of you."

"What makes you think that?" asked Mrs. Thompson, who could not bring herself to refrain from the question.

"Because he looks at you in that way, mamma, and squeezes your hand."

"Nonsense, child," said Mrs. Thompson; "hold your tongue. I don't know what can have put such stuff into your head."

"But he does, mamma," said Mimmy, who rarely allowed her mother to put her down.

Mrs. Thompson made no further answer, but again sat with her head resting on her hand. She also, if the truth must be told, was thinking of M. Lacordaire and his fondness for herself. He had squeezed her hand and he had looked into her face. However much it may have been nonsense on Mimmy's part to talk of such things, they had not the less absolutely occurred. Was it really the fact that M. Lacordaire was in love with her?

And if so, what return should she, or could she make to such a passion? He had looked at her yesterday, and squeezed her hand to-day. Might it not be probable that he would advance a step further to-morrow? If so, what answer would she be prepared to make to him?

She did not think—so she said to herself—that she had any particular objection to marrying again. Thompson had been dead now for four years, and neither his friends, nor her friends, nor the world could say she was wrong on that score. And as to marrying a Frenchman, she could not say that she felt within herself any absolute repugnance to doing that. Of her own country, speaking of England as such, she, in truth, knew but little—and perhaps cared less. She had gone to India almost as a child, and England had not been specially kind to her on her return. She had found it dull and cold, stiff, and almost ill-natured. People there had not smiled on her and been civil as M. Lacordaire had done. As far as England and Englishmen were considered she saw no reason why she should not marry M. Lacordaire.

And then, as regarded the man; could she in her heart say that she was prepared to love, honour, and obey M. Lacordaire? She certainly knew no reason why she should not do so. She did not know much of him, she said to herself at first; but she knew as much, she said afterwards, as she had known personally of Mr. Thompson before their marriage. She had known, to be sure, what was Mr. Thompson's profession and what his income; or, if not, some one else had known for her. As to both these points she was quite in the dark as regarded M. Lacordaire.

Personally, she certainly did like him, as she said to herself more than once. There was a courtesy and softness about him which were very gratifying to her; and then, his appearance was so much in his favour. He was not very young, she acknowledged; but neither was she young herself. It was quite evident that he was fond of her children, and that he would be a kind and affectionate father to them. Indeed, there was kindness in all that he did.

Should she marry again,—and she put it to herself quite hypothetically,—she would look for no romance in such a second marriage. She would be content to sit down in a quiet home, to the tame dull realities of life, satisfied with the companionship of a man who would be kind and gentle to her, and whom she could respect and esteem. Where could she find a companion with whom this could be more safely anticipated than with M. Lacordaire?

And so she argued the question within her own breast in a manner not unfriendly to that gentleman. That there was as yet one great hindrance she at once saw; but then that might be remedied by a word. She did not know what was his income or his profession. The chambermaid, whom she had interrogated, had told her that he was a "marchand." To merchants, generally, she felt that she had no objection. The Barings and the Rothschilds were merchants, as was also that wonderful man at Bombay, Sir Hommajee Bommajee, who was worth she did not know how many thousand lacs of rupees.

That it would behove her, on her own account and that of her daughters, to take care of her own little fortune in contracting any such connection, that she felt strongly. She would never so commit herself as to put security in that respect out of her power. But then she did not think that M. Lacordaire would ever ask her to do so; at any rate, she was determined on this, that there should never be any doubt on that matter; and as she firmly resolved on this, she again took up her book, and for a minute or two made an attempt to read.

"Mamma," said Mimmy, "will M. Lacordaire go up to the school to see Lilian when you go away from this?"

"Indeed, I cannot say, my dear. If Lilian is a good girl, perhaps he may do so now and then."

"And will he write to you and tell you how she is?"

"Lilian can write for herself; can she not?"

"Oh! yes; I suppose she can; but I hope M. Lacordaire will write too. We shall come back here some day; sha'n't we, mamma?"

"I cannot say, my dear."

"I do so hope we shall see M. Lacordaire again. Do you know what I was thinking, mamma?"

"Little girls like you ought not to think," said Mrs. Thompson, walking slowly out of the room to the top of the stairs and back again; for she had felt the necessity of preventing Mimmy from disclosing any more of her thoughts. "And now, my dear, get yourself ready, and we will go up to the school."

Mrs. Thompson always dressed herself with care, though not in especially fine clothes, before she went down to dinner at the table d'hôte; but on this occasion she was more than usually particular. She hardly explained to herself why she did this; but, nevertheless, as she stood before the glass, she did in a certain manner feel that the circumstances of her future life might perhaps depend on what might be said and done that evening. She had not absolutely decided whether or no she would go to the Prince's château; but if she did go—. Well, if she did; what then? She had sense enough, as she assured herself more than once, to regulate her own conduct with propriety in any such emergency.

During the dinner, M. Lacordaire conversed in his usual manner, but said nothing whatever about the visit to Polignac. He was very kind to Mimmy, and very courteous to her mother, but did not appear to be at all more particular than usual. Indeed, it might be a question whether he was not less so. As she had entered the room Mrs. Thompson had said to herself that, perhaps, after all, it would be better that there should be nothing more thought about it; but before the four or five courses were over, she was beginning to feel a little disappointed.

And now the fruit was on the table, after the consumption of which it was her practice to retire. It was certainly open to her to ask M. Lacordaire to take tea with her that evening, as she had done on former occasions; but she felt that she must not do this now, considering the immediate circumstances of the case. If any further steps were to be taken, they must be taken by him, and not by her;—or else by Mimmy, who, just as her mother was slowly consuming her last grapes, ran round to the back of M. Lacordaire's chair, and whispered something into his ear. It may be presumed that Mrs. Thompson did not see the intention of the movement in time to arrest it, for she did nothing till the whispering had been whispered; and then she rebuked the child, bade her not to be troublesome, and with more than usual austerity in her voice, desired her to get herself ready to go up stairs to their chamber.

As she spoke she herself rose from her chair, and made her final little bow to the table, and her other final little bow and smile to M. Lacordaire; but this was certain to all who saw it, that the smile was not as gracious as usual.

As she walked forth, M. Lacordaire rose from his chair—such being his constant practice when she left the table; but on this occasion he accompanied her to the door.

"And has madame decided," he asked, "whether she will permit me to accompany her to the château?"

"Well, I really don't know," said Mrs. Thompson.

"Mees Meemy," continued M. Lacordaire, "is very anxious to see the rock, and I may perhaps hope that Mees Leelian would be pleased with such a little excursion. As for myself— " and then M. Lacordaire put his hand upon his heart in a manner that seemed to speak more plainly than he had ever spoken.

"Well, if the children would really like it, and—as you are so very kind," said Mrs. Thompson; and so the matter was conceded.

"To-morrow afternoon?" suggested M. Lacordaire. But Mrs. Thompson fixed on Saturday, thereby showing that she herself was in no hurry for the expedition.

"Oh, I am so glad!" said Mimmy, when they had re-entered their own room. "Mamma, do let me tell Lilian myself when I go up to the school to-morrow!"

But Mamma was in no humour to say much to her child on this subject at the present moment. She threw herself back on her sofa in perfect silence, and began to reflect whether she would like to sign her name in future as Fanny Lacordaire, instead of Fanny Thompson. It certainly seemed as though things were verging towards such a necessity. A marchand! But a marchand of what? She had an instinctive feeling that the people in the hotel were talking about her and M. Lacordaire, and was therefore more than ever averse to asking any one a question.

As she went up to the school the next afternoon, she walked through more of the streets of Le Puy than was necessary, and in every street she looked at the names which she saw over the doors of the more respectable houses of business. But she looked in vain. It might be that M. Lacordaire was a marchand of so specially high a quality as to be under no necessity to put up his name at all. Sir Hommajee Bommajee's name did not appear over any door in Bombay;—at least, she thought not.

And then came the Saturday morning. "We shall be ready at two," she said, as she left the breakfast-table; "and perhaps you would not mind calling for Lilian on the way."

M. Lacordaire would be delighted to call anywhere for anybody on behalf of Mrs. Thompson; and then, as he got to the door of the salon, he offered her his hand. He did so with so much French courtesy that she could not refuse it, and then she felt that his purpose was more tender than ever it had been. And why not, if this was the destiny which Fate had prepared for her?

Mrs. Thompson would rather have got into the carriage at any other spot in Le Puy than at that at which she was forced to do so—the chief entrance, namely, of the Hôtel des Ambassadeurs. And what made it worse was this, that an appearance of a special fête was given to the occasion. M. Lacordaire was dressed in more than his Sunday best. He had on new yellow kid gloves. His coat, if not new, was newer than any Mrs. Thompson had yet observed, and was lined with silk up to the very collar. He had on patent leather boots, which glittered, as Mrs. Thompson thought, much too conspicuously. And as for his hat, it was quite evident that it was fresh that morning from the maker's block.

In this costume, with his hat in his hand, he stood under the great gateway of the hotel, ready to hand Mrs. Thompson into the carriage. This would have been nothing if the landlord and landlady had not been there also, as well as the man-cook, and the four waiters, and the fille de chambre. Two or three other pair of eyes Mrs. Thompson also saw, as she glanced round, and then Mimmy walked across the yard in her best clothes with a fête-day air about her for which her mother would have liked to have whipped her.

But what did it matter? If it was written in the book that she should become Madame Lacordaire, of course the world would know that there must have been some preparatory love-making. Let them have their laugh; a good husband would not be dearly purchased at so trifling an expense. And so they sallied forth with already half the ceremony of a wedding.

Mimmy seated herself opposite to her mother, and M. Lacordaire also sat with his back to the horses, leaving the second place of honour for Lilian. "Pray make yourself comfortable, M. Lacordaire, and don't mind her," said Mrs. Thompson. But he was firm in his purpose of civility, perhaps making up his mind that when he should in truth stand in the place of papa to the young lady, then would be his time for having the back seat in the carriage.

Lilian, also in her best frock, came down the school steps, and three of the school teachers came with her. It would have added to Mrs. Thompson's happiness at that moment if M. Lacordaire would have kept his polished boots out of sight, and put his yellow gloves into his pocket.

And then they started. The road from Le Puy to Polignac is nearly all up hill; and a very steep hill it is, so that there was plenty of time for conversation. But the girls had it nearly all to themselves. Mimmy thought that she had never found M. Lacordaire so stupid; and Lilian told her sister on the first safe opportunity that occurred, that it seemed very much as though they were all going to church.

"And do any of the Polignac people ever live at this place?" asked Mrs. Thompson, by way of making conversation; in answer to which M. Lacordaire informed madame that the place was at present only a ruin; and then there was again silence till they found themselves under the rock, and were informed by the driver that the rest of the ascent must be made on foot.

The rock now stood abrupt and precipitous above their heads. It was larger in its circumference and with much larger space on its summit than those other volcanic rocks in and close to the town; but then at the same time it was higher from the ground, and quite as inaccessible except by the single path which led up to the château.

M. Lacordaire, with conspicuous gallantry, first assisted Mrs. Thompson from the carriage, and then handed down the two young ladies. No lady could have been so difficult to please as to complain of him, and yet Mrs. Thompson thought that he was not as agreeable as usual. Those horrid boots and those horrid gloves gave him such an air of holiday finery that neither could he be at his ease wearing them, nor could she, in seeing them worn.

They were soon taken in hand by the poor woman whose privilege it was to show the ruins. For a little distance they walked up the path in single file; not that it was too narrow to accommodate two, but M. Lacordaire's courage had not yet been screwed to a point which admitted of his offering his arm to the widow. For in France, it must be remembered, that this means more than it does in some other countries.

Mrs. Thompson felt that all this was silly and useless. If they were not to be dear friends this coming out fêteing together, those boots and gloves and new hat were all very foolish; and if they were, the sooner that they understood each other the better. So Mrs. Thompson, finding that the path was steep and the weather warm, stood still for a while leaning against the wall, with a look of considerable fatigue in her face.

"Will madame permit me the honour of offering her my arm?" said M. Lacordaire. "The road is so extraordinarily steep for madame to climb."

Mrs. Thompson did permit him the honour, and so they went on till they reached the top.

The view from the summit was both extensive and grand, but neither Lilian nor Mimmy were much pleased with the place. The elder sister, who had talked over the matter with her school companions, expected a fine castle with turrets, battlements, and romance; and the other expected a pretty smiling house, such as princes, in her mind, ought to inhabit.

Instead of this they found an old turret, with steps so broken that M. Lacordaire did not care to ascend them, and the ruined walls of a mansion, in which nothing was to be seen but the remains of an enormous kitchen chimney.

"It was the kitchen of the family," said the guide.

"Oh," said Mrs. Thompson.

"And this," said the woman, taking them into the next ruined compartment, "was the kitchen of *monsieur et madame*."

"What! two kitchens?" exclaimed Lilian, upon which M. Lacordaire explained that the ancestors of the Prince de Polignac had been very great people, and had therefore required culinary performances on a great scale.

And then the woman began to chatter something about an oracle of Apollo. There was, she said, a hole in the rock, from which in past times, perhaps more than a hundred years ago, the oracle used to speak forth mysterious words.

"There," she said, pointing to a part of the rock at some distance, "was the hole. And if the ladies would follow her to a little outhouse which was just beyond, she would show them the huge stone mouth out of which the oracle used to speak."

Lilian and Mimmy both declared at once for seeing the oracle, but Mrs. Thompson expressed her determination to remain sitting where she was upon the turf. So the guide started off with the young ladies; and will it be thought surprising that M. Lacordaire should have remained alone by the side of Mrs. Thompson?

It must be now or never, Mrs. Thompson felt; and as regarded M. Lacordaire, he probably entertained some idea of the same kind. Mrs. Thompson's inclinations, though they had never been very strong in the matter, were certainly in favour of the "now." M. Lacordaire's inclinations were stronger. He had fully and firmly made up his mind in favour of matrimony; but then he was not so absolutely in favour of the "now." Mrs. Thompson's mind, if one could have read it, would have shown a great objection to shilly-shallying, as she was accustomed to call it. But M. Lacordaire, were it not for the danger which might thence arise, would have seen no objection to some slight further procrastination. His courage was beginning, perhaps, to ooze out from his fingers' ends.

"I declare that those girls have scampered away ever so far," said Mrs. Thompson.

"Would madame wish that I should call them back?" said M. Lacordaire, innocently.

"Oh, no, dear children! let them enjoy themselves; it will be a pleasure to them to run about the rock, and I suppose they will be safe with that woman?"

"Oh, yes, quite safe," said M. Lacordaire; and then there was another little pause.

Mrs. Thompson was sitting on a broken fragment of a stone just outside the entrance to the old family kitchen, and M. Lacordaire was standing immediately before her. He had in his hand a little cane with which he sometimes slapped his boots and sometimes poked about among the rubbish. His hat was not quite straight on his head, having a little jaunty twist to one side, with reference to which, by-the-by, Mrs. Thompson then resolved that she would make a change, should ever the gentleman become her own property. He still wore his gloves, and was very smart; but it was clear to see that he was not at his ease.

"I hope the heat does not incommode you," he said after a few moment's silence. Mrs. Thompson declared that it did not, that she liked a good deal of heat, and that, on the whole, she was very well where she was. She was afraid, however, that she was detaining M. Lacordaire, who might probably wish to be moving about upon the rock. In answer to which M. Lacordaire declared that he never could be so happy anywhere as in her close vicinity.

"You are too good to me," said Mrs. Thompson, almost sighing. "I don't know what my stay here would have been without your great kindness."

"It is madame that has been kind to me," said M. Lacordaire, pressing the handle of his cane against his heart.

There was then another pause, after which Mrs. Thompson said that that was all his French politeness; that she knew that she had been very troublesome to him, but that she would now soon be gone;

and that then, in her own country, she would never forget his great goodness.

"Ah, madame!" said M. Lacordaire; and, as he said it, much more was expressed in his face than in his words. But, then, you can neither accept nor reject a gentleman by what he says in his face. He blushed, too, up to his grizzled hair, and, turning round, walked a step or two away from the widow's seat, and back again.

Mrs. Thompson the while sat quite still. The displaced fragment, lying, as it did, near a corner of the building, made not an uncomfortable chair. She had only to be careful that she did not injure her hat or crush her clothes, and throw in a word here and there to assist the gentleman, should occasion permit it.

"Madame!" said M. Lacordaire, on his return from a second little walk.

"Monsieur!" replied Mrs. Thompson, perceiving that M. Lacordaire paused in his speech.

"Madame," he began again, and then, as he again paused, Mrs. Thompson looked up to him very sweetly; "madame, what I am going to say will, I am afraid, seem to evince by far too great audacity on my part."

Mrs. Thompson may, perhaps, have thought that, at the present moment, audacity was not his fault. She replied, however, that she was quite sure that monsieur would say nothing that was in any way unbecoming either for him to speak or for her to hear.

"Madame, may I have ground to hope that such may be your sentiments after I have spoken! Madame"—and now he went down, absolutely on his knees, on the hard stones; and Mrs. Thompson, looking about into the distance, almost thought that she saw the top of the guide's cap—"Madame, I have looked forward to this opportunity as one in which I may declare for you the greatest passion that I have ever yet felt. Madame, with all my heart and soul I love you. Madame, I offer to you the homage of my heart, my hand, the happiness of my life, and all that I possess in this world;" and then, taking her hand gracefully between his gloves, he pressed his lips against the tips of her fingers.

If the thing was to be done this way of doing it was, perhaps, as good as any other. It was one, at any rate, which left no doubt whatever as to the gentleman's intentions. Mrs. Thompson, could she have had her own way, would not have allowed her lover of fifty to go down upon his knees, and would have spared him much of the romance of his declaration. So also would she have spared him his yellow gloves and his polished boots. But these were a part of the necessity of the situation, and therefore she wisely took them as matters to be passed over with indifference. Seeing, however, that M. Lacordaire still remained on his knees, it was necessary that she should take some step toward raising him, especially as her two children and the guide would infallibly be upon them before long.

"M. Lacordaire," she said, "you surprise me greatly; but pray get up."

"But will madame vouchsafe to give me some small ground for hope?"

"The girls will be here directly, M. Lacordaire; pray get up. I can talk to you much better if you will stand up, or sit down on one of these stones."

M. Lacordaire did as he was bid; he got up, wiped the knees of his pantaloons with his handkerchief, sat down beside her, and then pressed the handle of his cane to his heart.

"You really have so surprised me that I hardly know how to answer you," said Mrs. Thompson. "Indeed, I cannot bring myself to imagine that you are in earnest."

"Ah, madame, do not be so cruel! How can I have lived with you so long, sat beside you for so many days, without having received your image into my heart? I am in earnest! Alas! I fear too much in earnest!" And then he looked at her with all his eyes, and sighed with all his strength.

Mrs. Thompson's prudence told her that it would be well to settle the matter, in one way or the other, as soon as possible. Long periods of love-making were fit for younger people than herself and her future possible husband. Her object would be to make him comfortable if she could, and that he should do the same for her, if that also were possible. As for lookings and sighings and pressings of the hand, she had gone through all that some twenty years since in India, when Thompson had been young, and she was still in her teens.

"But, M. Lacordaire, there are so many things to be considered. There! I hear the children coming! Let us walk this way for a minute." And they turned behind a wall which placed them out of sight, and walked on a few paces till they reached a parapet, which stood on the uttermost edge of the high rock. Leaning upon this they continued their conversation.

"There are so many things to be considered," said Mrs. Thompson again.

"Yes, of course," said M. Lacordaire. "But my one great consideration is this;—that I love madame to distraction."

"I am very much flattered: of course, any lady would so feel. But, M. Lacordaire— "

"Madame, I am all attention. But, if you would deign to make me happy, say that one word, 'I love you!'" M. Lacordaire, as he uttered these words, did not look, as the saying is, at his best. But Mrs. Thompson forgave him. She knew that elderly gentlemen under such circumstances do not look at their best.

"But if I consented to—to—to such an arrangement, I could only do so on seeing that it would be beneficial—or, at any rate, not injurious;—to my children; and that it would offer to ourselves a fair promise of future happiness."

"Ah, madame! it would be the dearest wish of my heart to be a second father to those two young ladies; except, indeed— " and then M. Lacordaire stopped the flow of his speech.

"In such matters it is so much the best to be explicit at once," said Mrs. Thompson.

"Oh, yes; certainly! Nothing can be more wise than madame."

"And the happiness of a household depends so much on money."

"Madame!"

"Let me say a word or two, Monsieur Lacordaire. I have enough for myself and my children; and, should I ever marry again, I should not, I hope, be felt as a burden by my husband; but it would, of course, be my duty to know what were his circumstances, before I accepted him. Of yourself, personally, I have seen nothing that I do not like."

"Oh, madame!"

"But as yet I know nothing of your circumstances."

M. Lacordaire, perhaps, did feel that Mrs. Thompson's prudence was of a strong, masculine description; but he hardly liked her the less on this account. To give him his due he was not desirous of marrying her solely for her money's sake. He also wished for a comfortable home, and proposed to give as much as he got; only he had been anxious to wrap up the solid cake of this business in a casing of sugar of romance. Mrs. Thompson would not have the sugar; but the cake might not be the worse on that account.

"No, madame; not as yet: but they shall all be made open and at your disposal," said M. Lacordaire; and Mrs. Thompson bowed approvingly.

"I am in business," continued M. Lacordaire: "and my business gives me eight thousand francs a year."

"Four times eight are thirty-two," said Mrs. Thompson to herself; putting the francs into pounds sterling, in the manner that she had always found to be the readiest. Well, so far the statement was satisfactory. An income of three hundred and twenty pounds a year from business, joined to her own, might do very well. She did not in the least suspect M. Lacordaire of being false, and so far the matter sounded well.

"And what is the business?" she asked, in a tone of voice intended to be indifferent, but which nevertheless showed that she listened anxiously for an answer to her question.

They were both standing with their arms upon the wall, looking down upon the town of Le Puy; but they had so stood that each could see the other's countenance as they talked. Mrs. Thompson could now perceive that M. Lacordaire became red in the face, as he paused before answering her. She was near to him, and seeing his emotion gently touched his arm with her hand. This she did to reassure him, for she saw that he was ashamed of having to declare that he was a tradesman. As for herself, she had made up her mind to bear with this, if she found, as she felt sure she would find, that the trade was one which would not degrade either him or her. Hitherto, indeed,—in her early days,—she had looked down on trade; but of what benefit had her grand ideas been to her when she had returned to England? She had tried her hand at English genteel society, and no one had seemed to care for her.

Therefore, she touched his arm lightly with her fingers that she might encourage him.

He paused for a moment, as I have said, and became red; and then feeling that he had shown some symptoms of shame—and feeling also, probably, that it was unmanly in him to do so, he shook himself slightly, raised his head up somewhat more proudly than was his wont, looked her full in the face with more strength of character than she had yet seen him assume; and then, declared his business.

"Madame," he said, in a very audible, but not in a loud voice; "madame—*je suis tailleur*." And having so spoken, he turned slightly from her and looked down over the valley towards Le Puy.

There was nothing more said upon the subject as they drove down from the rock of Polignac back to the town. Immediately on receiving the announcement, Mrs. Thompson found that she had no answer to make. She withdrew her hand—and felt at once that she had received a blow. It was not that she was angry with M. Lacordaire for being a tailor; nor was she angry with him in that, being a tailor, he had so addressed her. But she was surprised, disappointed, and altogether put beyond her ease. She had, at any rate, not expected this. She had dreamed of his being a banker; thought that, perhaps, he might have been a wine merchant; but her idea had never gone below a jeweller or watchmaker. When those words broke upon her ear, "Madame, *je suis tailleur*," she had felt herself to be speechless.

But the words had not been a minute spoken when Lilian and Mimmy ran up to their mother. "Oh, mamma," said Lilian, "we thought you were lost; we have searched for you all over the château."

"We have been sitting very quietly here, my dear, looking at the view," said Mrs. Thompson.

"But, mamma, I do wish you'd see the mouth of the oracle. It is so large, and so round, and so ugly. I put my arm into it all the way," said Mimmy.

But at the present moment her mamma felt no interest in the mouth of the oracle; and so they all walked down together to the carriage. And, though the way was steep, Mrs. Thompson managed to pick her steps without the assistance of an arm; nor did M. Lacordaire presume to offer it.

The drive back to town was very silent. Mrs. Thompson did make one or two attempts at conversation, but they were not effectual. M. Lacordaire could not speak at his ease till this matter was settled, and he already had begun to perceive that his business was against him. Why is it that the trade of a tailor should be less honourable than that of an haberdasher, or even a grocer?

They sat next each other at dinner, as usual; and here, as all eyes were upon them, they both made a great struggle to behave in their accustomed way. But even in this they failed. All the world of the Hôtel des Ambassadeurs knew that M. Lacordaire had gone forth to make an offer to Mrs. Thompson, and all that world, therefore, was full of speculation. But all the world could make nothing of it. M. Lacordaire did look like a rejected man, but Mrs. Thompson did not look like the woman who had rejected him. That the offer had been made—in that everybody agreed, from the senior habitué of the house who always sat at the head of the table, down to the junior assistant garçon. But as to reading the riddle, there was no accord among them.

When the dessert was done Mrs. Thompson, as usual, withdrew, and M. Lacordaire, as usual, bowed as he stood behind his own chair. He did not, however, attempt to follow her.

But when she reached the door, she called him. He was at her side in a moment, and then she whispered in his ear—

"And I, also—I will be of the same business."

When M. Lacordaire regained the table the senior habitué, the junior garçon, and all the intermediate ranks of men at the Hôtel des Ambassadeurs knew that they might congratulate him.

Mrs. Thompson had made a great struggle; but, speaking for myself, I am inclined to think that she arrived at last at a wise decision.

Miss Sarah Jack of Spanish Town, Jamaica

Originally appeared in *Cassell's Illustrated Family Paper*, 3 and 10 November 1860. First published in *Tales of All Countries* [First Series] (1861). Written in the Pyrenees between 1 September and 29 October 1859, during the composition of *Castle Richmond*. Trollope spent a month on an official postal mission in Jamaica in the winter of 1858–59, when he also began gathering material for his travel-book *The West Indies and the Spanish Main* (1859). The chapters on 'Jamaica' (chs 2–9) in the latter work furnish many insights into the background of the story, especially into the commercial decline of the colony after the emancipation of the slaves in 1833.

THERE IS nothing so melancholy as a country in its decadence, unless it be a people in their decadence. I am not aware that the latter misfortune can be attributed to the Anglo-Saxon race in any part of the world; but there is reason to fear that it has fallen on an English colony in the island of Jamaica.

Jamaica was one of those spots on which fortune shone with the full warmth of all her noonday splendour. That sun has set;—whether for ever or no none but a prophet can tell; but, as far as a plain man may see, there are at present but few signs of a coming morrow, or of another summer.

It is not just or proper that one should grieve over the misfortunes of Jamaica with a stronger grief because her savannahs are so lovely, her forests so rich, her mountains so green, and her rivers so rapid; but it is so. It is piteous that a land so beautiful should be one which fate has marked for misfortune. Had Guiana, with its flat level unlovely soil, become poverty-stricken, one would hardly sorrow over it as one does sorrow for Jamaica.

As regards scenery she is the gem of the western tropics. It is impossible to conceive spots on the earth's surface more gracious to the eye than those steep green valleys which stretch down to the south-west from the Blue Mountain peak towards the sea; and but little behind these in beauty are the rich wooded hills which in the western part of the island divide the counties of Hanover and Westmoreland. The hero of the tale which I am going to tell was a sugar-grower in the latter district, and the heroine was a girl who lived under that Blue Mountain peak.

The very name of a sugar-grower as connected with Jamaica savours of fruitless struggle, failure, and desolation. And from his earliest growth fruitless struggle, failure, and desolation had been the lot of Maurice Cumming. At eighteen years of age he had been left by his father sole possessor of the Mount Pleasant estate, than which in her palmy days Jamaica had little to boast of that was more pleasant or more palmy. But those days had passed by before Roger Cumming, the father of our friend, had died.

These misfortunes coming on the head of one another, at intervals of a few years, had first stunned and then killed him. His slaves rose against him, as they did against other proprietors around him, and burned down his house and mills, his homestead and offices. Those who know the amount of capital which a sugar-grower must invest in such buildings will understand the extent of his misfortune. Then the slaves were emancipated. It is not perhaps possible that we, nowadays, should regard this as a calamity; but it was quite impossible that a Jamaica proprietor of those days should not have done so. Men will do much for philanthropy, they will work hard, they will give the coat from their back;—nay the very shirt from their body: but few men will endure to look on with satisfaction while their commerce is destroyed.

But even this Mr. Cumming did bear after a while, and kept his shoulder to the wheel. He kept his shoulder to the wheel till that third misfortune came upon him—till the protection duty on Jamaica sugar was abolished. Then he turned his face to the wall and died.

His son at this time was not of age, and the large but lessening property which Mr. Cumming left behind him was for three years in the hands of trustees. But nevertheless Maurice, young as he was, managed the estate. It was he who grew the canes, and made the sugar;—or else failed to make it. He was the "massa" to whom the free negroes looked as the source from whence their wants should be supplied, notwithstanding that being free, they were ill inclined to work for him let his want of work be ever so sore.

Mount Pleasant had been a very large property. In addition to his sugar-canes Mr. Cumming had grown coffee; for his land ran up into the hills of Trelawney to that altitude which in the tropics seems necessary for the perfect growth of the coffee berry. But it soon became evident that labour for the double produce could not be had, and the coffee plantation was abandoned. Wild brush and the thick undergrowth of forest reappeared on the hill-sides which had been rich with produce. And the evil re-created and exaggerated itself. Negroes squatted on the abandoned property; and being able to live with abundance from their stolen gardens, were less willing than ever to work in the cane pieces.

And thus things went from bad to worse. In the good old times Mr. Cumming's sugar produce had spread itself annually over some three hundred acres; but by degrees this dwindled down to half that extent of land. And then in those old golden days they had always taken a full hogshead from the acre;—very often more. The estate had sometimes given four hundred hogsheads in the year. But in the days of which we now speak the crop had fallen below fifty.

At this time Maurice Cumming was eight-and-twenty, and it is hardly too much to say that misfortune had nearly crushed him. But nevertheless it had not crushed him. He, and some few like him, had still hoped against hope;—had still persisted in looking forward to a future for the island which once was so generous with its gifts. When his father died he might still have had enough for the wants of life had he sold his property for what it would fetch. There was money in England, and the remains of large wealth. But he would not sacrifice Mount Pleasant or abandon Jamaica; and now after ten years' struggling he still kept Mount Pleasant, and the mill was still going; but all other property had parted from his hands.

By nature Maurice Cumming would have been gay and lively, a man with a happy spirit and easy temper; but struggling had made him silent if not morose, and had saddened if not soured his temper. He had lived alone at Mount Pleasant, or generally alone. Work or want of money, and the constant difficulty of getting labour for his estate, had left him but little time for a young man's ordinary amusements. Of the charms of ladies' society he had known but little. Very many of the estates around him had been absolutely abandoned, as was the case with his own coffee plantation, and from others men had sent away their wives and daughters. Nay, most of the proprietors had gone themselves, leaving an overseer to extract what little might yet be extracted out of the property. It too often happened that that little was not sufficient to meet the demands of the overseer himself.

The house at Mount Pleasant had been an irregular, low-roofed, picturesque residence, built with only one floor, and surrounded on all sides by large verandahs. In the old days it had always been kept in perfect order, but now this was far from being the case. Few young bachelors can keep a house in order, but no bachelor young or old can do so under such a doom as that of Maurice Cumming. Every shilling that Maurice Cumming could collect was spent in bribing negroes to work for him. But bribe as he would the negroes would not work. "No, massa; me pain here; me no workee to-day," and Sambo would lay his fat hand on his fat stomach.

I have said that he lived generally alone. Occasionally his house at Mount Pleasant was enlivened by visits of an aunt, a maiden sister of his mother, whose usual residence was at Spanish Town. It is or should be known to all men that Spanish Town was and is the seat of the Jamaica legislature.

But Maurice was not overfond of his relative. In this he was both wrong and foolish, for Miss Sarah Jack—such was her name—was in many respects a good woman, and was certainly a rich woman. It is true that she was not a handsome woman, nor a fashionable woman, nor perhaps altogether an agreeable woman. She was tall, thin, ungainly, and yellow. Her voice, which she used freely, was harsh. She was a politician and a patriot. She regarded England as the greatest of countries, and Jamaica as the greatest of colonies. But much as she loved England she was very loud in denouncing what she called the perfidy of the mother to the brightest of her children. And much as she loved Jamaica she was equally severe in her taunts against those of her brother-islanders who would not believe that the island might yet flourish as it had flourished in her father's days.

"It is because you and men like you will not do your duty by your country," she had said some score of times to Maurice—not with much justice considering the laboriousness of his life.

But Maurice knew well what she meant. "What could I do there up at Spanish Town," he would answer, "among such a pack as there are there? Here I may do something."

And then she would reply with the full swing of her eloquence. "It is because you and such as you think only of yourself and not of Jamaica, that Jamaica has come to such a pass as this. Why is there a pack there as you call them in the honourable House of Assembly? Why are not the best men in the island to be found there, as the best men in England are to be found in the British House of Commons? A pack, indeed! My father was proud of a seat in that house, and I remember the day, Maurice Cumming, when your father also thought it no shame to represent his own parish. If men like you, who have a stake in the country, will not go there, of course the house is filled with men who have no stake. If they are a pack, it is you who send them there;—you, and others like you."

All this had its effect, though at the moment Maurice would shrug his shoulders and turn away his head from the torrent of the lady's discourse. But Miss Jack, though she was not greatly liked, was greatly respected. Maurice would not own that she convinced him; but at last he did allow his name to be put up as candidate for his own parish, and in due time he became a member of the honourable House of Assembly in Jamaica.

This honour entails on the holder of it the necessity of living at or within reach of Spanish Town for some ten weeks towards the close of every year. Now on the whole face of the uninhabited globe there is perhaps no spot more dull to look at, more Lethean in its aspect, more corpse-like or more cadaverous than Spanish Town. It is the head-quarters of the government, the seat of the legislature, the residence of the governor;—but nevertheless it is, as it were, a city of the very dead.

Here, as we have said before, lived Miss Jack in a large forlorn ghost-like house in which her father and all her family had lived before her. And as a matter of course Maurice Cumming when he came up to attend to his duties as a member of the legislature took up his abode with her.

Now at the time of which we are specially speaking he had completed the first of these annual visits. He had already benefited his country by sitting out one session of the colonial parliament, and had satisfied himself that he did no other good than that of keeping away some person more objectionable than himself. He was however prepared to repeat this self-sacrifice in a spirit of patriotism for which he received a very meagre meed of eulogy from Miss Jack, and an amount of self-applause which was not much more extensive.

"Down at Mount Pleasant I can do something," he would say over and over again, "but what good can any man do up here?"

"You can do your duty," Miss Jack would answer, "as others did before you when the colony was made to prosper." And then they would run off into a long discussion about free labour and protective duties. But at the present moment Maurice Cumming had another vexation on his mind over and above that arising from his wasted hours at Spanish Town and his fruitless labours at Mount Pleasant. He was in love, and was not altogether satisfied with the conduct of his lady love.

Miss Jack had other nephews besides Maurice Cumming, and nieces also, of whom Marian Leslie was one. The family of the Leslies lived up near Newcastle—in the mountains, that is, which stand over Kingston—at a distance of some eighteen miles from Kingston, but in a climate as different from that of the town as the climate of Naples is from that of Berlin. In Kingston the heat is all but intolerable throughout the year, by day and by night, in the house and out of it. In the mountains round Newcastle, some four thousand feet above the sea, it is merely warm during the day, and cool enough at night to make a blanket desirable.

It is pleasant enough living up among those green mountains. There are no roads there for wheeled carriages, nor are there carriages with or without wheels. All journeys are made on horseback. Every visit paid from house to house is performed in this manner. Ladies old and young live before dinner in their riding-habits. The hospitality is free, easy, and unembarrassed. The scenery is magnificent. The tropical foliage is wild and luxuriant beyond measure. There may be enjoyed all that a southern climate has to offer of enjoyment, without the penalties which such enjoyments usually entail.

Mrs. Leslie was a half-sister of Miss Jack, and Miss Jack had been a half-sister also of Mrs. Cumming; but Mrs. Leslie and Mrs. Cumming had in no way been related. And it had so happened that up to the period of his legislative efforts Maurice Cumming had seen nothing of the Leslies. Soon after his arrival at Spanish Town he had been taken by Miss Jack to Shandy Hall, for so the residence of the Leslies was called, and having remained there for three days, had fallen in love with Marian Leslie. Now in the West Indies all young ladies flirt; it is the first habit of their nature—and few young ladies in the West Indies were more given to flirting, or understood the science better, than Marian Leslie.

Maurice Cumming fell violently in love, and during his first visit at Shandy Hall found that Marian was perfection—for during this first visit her propensities were exerted altogether in his own favour. That little circumstance does make such a difference in a young man's judgment of a girl! He came back full of admiration, not altogether to Miss Jack's dissatisfaction; for Miss Jack was willing enough that both her nephew and her niece should settle down into married life.

But then Maurice met his fair one at a governor's ball—at a ball where red coats abounded, and aides-de-camp dancing in spurs, and narrow-waisted lieutenants with sashes or epaulets! The aides-de-camp and narrow-waisted lieutenants waltzed better than he did; and as one after the other whisked round the ball-room with Marian firmly clasped in his arms, Maurice's feelings were not of the sweetest. Nor was this the worst of it. Had the whisking been divided equally among ten, he might have forgiven it; but there was one specially narrow-waisted lieutenant, who towards the end of the evening kept Marian nearly wholly to himself. Now to a man in love, who has had but little experience of either balls or young ladies, this is intolerable.

He only met her twice after that before his return to Mount Pleasant, and on the first occasion that odious soldier was not there. But a specially devout young clergyman was present, an unmarried evangelical handsome young curate fresh from England; and Marian's piety had been so excited that she had cared for no one else. It appeared moreover that the curate's gifts for conversion were confined, as regarded that opportunity, to Marian's advantage. "I will have nothing more to say to her," said Maurice to himself, scowling. But just as he went away Marian had given him her hand, and called him Maurice—for she pretended that they were cousins—and had looked into his eyes and declared that she did hope that the assembly at Spanish Town would soon be sitting again. Hitherto, she said, she had not cared one straw about it. Then poor Maurice pressed the little fingers which lay within his own, and swore that he would be at Shandy Hall on the day before his return to Mount Pleasant. So he was; and there he found the narrow-waisted lieutenant, not now bedecked with sash and epaulettes, but lolling at his ease on Mrs. Leslie's sofa in a white jacket, while Marian sat at his feet telling his fortune with a book about flowers.

"Oh, a musk rose, Mr. Ewing; you know what a musk rose means!" Then she got up and shook hands with Mr. Cumming; but her eyes still went away to the white jacket and the sofa. Poor Maurice had often been nearly broken-hearted in his efforts to manage his free black labourers; but even that was easier than managing such as Marian Leslie.

Marian Leslie was a Creole—as also were Miss Jack and Maurice Cumming—a child of the tropics; but by no means such a child as tropical children are generally thought to be by us in more northern latitudes. She was black-haired and black-eyed, but her lips were as red and her cheeks as rosy as though she had been born and bred in regions where the snow lies in winter. She was a small, pretty, beautifully made little creature, somewhat idle as regards the work of the world, but active and strong enough when dancing or riding were required from her. Her father was a banker, and was fairly prosperous in spite of the poverty of his country. His house of business was at Kingston, and he usually slept there twice a week; but he always resided at Shandy Hall, and Mrs. Leslie and her children knew but very little of the miseries of Kingston. For be it known to all men, that of all towns Kingston, Jamaica, is the most miserable.

I fear that I shall have set my readers very much against Marian Leslie;—much more so than I would wish to do. As a rule they will not know how thoroughly flirting is an institution in the West Indies—practised by all young ladies, and laid aside by them when they marry, exactly as their young-lady names and young-lady habits of various kinds are laid aside. All I would say of Marian Leslie is this, that she understood the working of the institution more thoroughly than others did. And I must add also in her favour that she did not keep her flirting for sly corners, nor did her admirers keep their distance till mamma was out of the way. It mattered not to her who was present. Had she been called on to make one at a synod of the clergy of the island, she would have flirted with the bishop before all his priests. And there have been bishops in the colony who would not have gainsayed her!

But Maurice Cumming did not rightly calculate all this; nor indeed did Miss Jack do so as thoroughly as she should have done, for Miss Jack knew more about such matters than did poor Maurice. "If you like Marian, why don't you marry her?" Miss Jack had once said to him; and this coming from Miss Jack, who was made of money, was a great deal.

"She wouldn't have me," Maurice had answered.

"That's more than you know or I either," was Miss Jack's reply. "But if you like to try, I'll help you."

With reference to this, Maurice as he left Miss Jack's residence on his return to Mount Pleasant, had declared that Marian Leslie was not worth an honest man's love.

"Psha!" Miss Jack replied; "Marian will do like other girls. When you marry a wife I suppose you mean to be master?"

"At any rate I sha'n't marry her," said Maurice. And so he went his way back to Hanover with a sore heart. And no wonder, for that was the very day on which Lieutenant Ewing had asked the question about the musk rose.

But there was a dogged constancy of feeling about Maurice which could not allow him to disburden himself of his love. When he was again at Mount Pleasant among his sugar-canes and hogsheads he could not help thinking about Marian. It is true he always thought of her as flying round that ball-room in Ewing's arms, or looking up with rapt admiration into that young parson's face; and so he got but little pleasure from his thoughts. But not the less was he in love with her;—not the less, though he would swear to himself three times in the day that for no earthly consideration would he marry Marian Leslie.

The early months of the year from January to May are the busiest with a Jamaica sugar-grower, and in this year they were very busy months with Maurice Cumming. It seemed as though there were actually some truth in Miss Jack's prediction that prosperity would return to him if he attended to his country; for the prices of sugar had risen higher than they had ever been since the duty had been withdrawn, and there was more promise of a crop at Mount Pleasant than he had seen since his reign commenced. But then the question of labour? How he slaved in trying to get work from those free negroes; and alas, how often he slaved in vain! But it was not all in vain; for as things went on it became clear to him that in this year he would, for the first time since he commenced, obtain something like a return from his land. What if the turning-point had come, and things were now about to run the other way?

But then the happiness which might have accrued to him from this source was dashed by his thoughts of Marian Leslie. Why had he thrown himself in the way of that syren? Why had he left Mount Pleasant at all? He knew that on his return to Spanish Town his first work would be to visit Shandy Hall; and yet he felt that of all places in the island, Shandy Hall was the last which he ought to visit.

And then about the beginning of May, when he was hard at work turning the last of his canes into sugar and rum, he received his annual visit from Miss Jack. And whom should Miss Jack bring with her but Mr. Leslie.

"I'll tell you what it is," said Miss Jack; "I have spoken to Mr. Leslie about you and Marian."

"Then you had no business to do anything of the kind," said Maurice, blushing up to his ears.

"Nonsense," replied Miss Jack, "I understand what I am about. Of course Mr. Leslie will want to know something about the estate."

"Then he may go back as wise as he came, for he'll learn nothing from me. Not that I have anything to hide."

"So I told him. Now there are a large family of them, you see; and of course he can't give Marian much."

"I don't care a straw if he doesn't give her a shilling. If she cared for me, or I for her, I shouldn't look after her for her money."

"But a little money is not a bad thing, Maurice," said Miss Jack, who in her time had had a good deal, and had managed to take care of it.

"It is all one to me."

"But what I was going to say is this—hum—ha—. I don't like to pledge myself for fear I should raise hopes which mayn't be fulfilled."

"Don't pledge yourself to anything, aunt, in which Marian Leslie and I are concerned."

"But what I was going to say is this; my money, what little I have, you know, must go some day either to you or to the Leslies."

"You may give all to them if you please."

"Of course I may, and I dare say I shall," said Miss Jack, who was beginning to be irritated. "But at any rate you might have the civility to listen to me when I am endeavouring to put you on your legs. I am sure I think about nothing else, morning, noon, and night, and yet I never get a decent word from you. Marian is too good for you; that's the truth."

But at length Miss Jack was allowed to open her budget, and to make her proposition; which amounted to this—that she had already told Mr. Leslie that she would settle the bulk of her property conjointly on Maurice and Marian if they would make a match of it. Now as Mr. Leslie had long been casting a hankering eye after Miss Jack's money, with a strong conviction however that Maurice Cumming was her favourite nephew and probable heir, this proposition was not unpalatable. So he agreed to go down to Mount Pleasant and look about him.

"But you may live for the next thirty years, my dear Miss Jack," Mr. Leslie had said.

"Yes, I may," Miss Jack replied, looking very dry.

"And I am sure I hope you will," continued Mr. Leslie. And then the subject was allowed to drop; for Mr. Leslie knew that it was not always easy to talk to Miss Jack on such matters.

Miss Jack was a person in whom I think we may say that the good predominated over the bad. She was often morose, crabbed, and self-opinionated; but then she knew her own imperfections, and forgave those she loved for evincing their dislike of them. Maurice Cumming was often inattentive to her, plainly showing that he was worried by her importunities and ill at ease in her company. But she loved her nephew with all her heart; and though she dearly liked to tyrannize over him, never allowed herself to be really angry with him, though he so frequently refused to bow to her dictation. And she loved Marian Leslie also, though Marian was so sweet and lovely and she herself so harsh and ill-favoured. She loved Marian, though Marian would often be impertinent. She forgave the flirting, the light-heartedness, the love of amusement. Marian, she said to herself, was young and pretty. She, Miss Jack, had never known Marian's temptation. And so she resolved in her own mind that Marian should be made a good and happy woman;—but always as the wife of Maurice Cumming.

But Maurice turned a deaf ear to all these good tidings—or rather he turned to them an ear that seemed to be deaf. He dearly, ardently loved that little flirt; but seeing that she was a flirt, that she had flirted so grossly when he was by, he would not confess his love to a human being. He would not have it known that he was wasting his heart for a worthless little chit, to whom every man was the same—except that those were most eligible whose toes were the lightest and their outside trappings the brightest. That he did love her he could not help, but he would not disgrace himself by acknowledging it.

He was very civil to Mr. Leslie, but he would not speak a word that could be taken as a proposal for Marian. It had been part of Miss Jack's plan that the engagement should absolutely be made down there at Mount Pleasant, without any reference to the young lady; but Maurice could not be induced to break the ice. So he took Mr. Leslie through his mills and over his cane-pieces, talked to him about the laziness of the "niggers," while the "niggers" themselves stood by tittering, and rode with him away to the high grounds where the coffee plantation had been in the good old days; but not a word was said between them about Marian. And yet Marian was never out of his heart.

And then came the day on which Mr. Leslie was to go back to Kingston. "And you won't have her then?" said Miss Jack to her nephew early that morning. "You won't be said by me?"

"Not in this matter, aunt."

"Then you will live and die a poor man; you mean that, I suppose?"

"It's likely enough that I shall. There's this comfort, at any rate, I'm used to it." And then Miss Jack was silent again for a while.

"Very well, sir; that's enough," she said angrily. And then she began again. "But, Maurice, you wouldn't have to wait for my death, you know." And she put out her hand and touched his arm, entreating him as it were to yield to her. "Oh, Maurice," she said, "I do so want to make you comfortable. Let us speak to Mr. Leslie."

But Maurice would not. He took her hand and thanked her, but said that on this matter he must be his own master. "Very well, sir," she exclaimed, "I have done. In future you may manage for yourself. As for me, I shall go back with Mr. Leslie to Kingston." And so she did. Mr. Leslie returned that day, taking her with him. When he took his leave, his invitation to Maurice to come to Shandy Hall was not very pressing. "Mrs. Leslie and the children will always be glad to see you," said he.

"Remember me very kindly to Mrs. Leslie and the children," said Maurice. And so they parted.

"You have brought me down here on a regular fool's errand," said Mr. Leslie, on their journey back to town.

"It will all come right yet," replied Miss Jack. "Take my word for it, he loves her."

"Fudge," said Mr. Leslie. But he could not afford to quarrel with his rich connection.

In spite of all that he had said and thought to the contrary, Maurice did look forward during the remainder of the summer to his return to Spanish Town with something like impatience. It was very dull work, being there alone at Mount Pleasant; and let him do what he would to prevent it, his very dreams took him to Shandy Hall. But at last the slow time made itself away, and he found himself once more in his aunt's house.

A couple of days passed and no word was said about the Leslies. On the morning of the third day he determined to go to Shandy Hall. Hitherto he had never been there without staying for the night; but on this occasion he made up his mind to return the same day. "It would not be civil of me not to go there," he said to his aunt.

"Certainly not," she replied, forbearing to press the matter further. "But why make such a terrible hard day's work of it?"

"Oh, I shall go down in the cool, before breakfast; and then I need not have the bother of taking a bag."

And in this way he started. Miss Jack said nothing further; but she longed in her heart that she might be at Marian's elbow unseen during the visit.

He found them all at breakfast, and the first to welcome him at the hall door was Marian. "Oh, Mr. Cumming, we are so glad to see you;" and she looked into his eyes with a way she had, that was enough to make a man's heart wild. But she did not call him Maurice now.

Miss Jack had spoken to her sister Mrs. Leslie, as well as to Mr. Leslie about this marriage scheme. "Just let them alone," was Mrs. Leslie's advice. "You can't alter Marian by lecturing her. If they really love each other they'll come together; and if they don't, why then they'd better not."

"And you really mean that you're going back to Spanish Town to-day?" said Mrs. Leslie to her visitor.

"I'm afraid I must. Indeed I haven't brought my things with me." And then he again caught Marian's eye, and began to wish that his resolution had not been so sternly made.

"I suppose you are so fond of that house of assembly," said Marian, "that you cannot tear yourself away for more than one day. You'll not be able, I suppose, to find time to come to our picnic next week?"

Maurice said he feared that he should not have time to go to a picnic.

"Oh, nonsense," said Fanny—one of the younger girls—"you must come. We can't do without him, can we?"

"Marian has got your name down the first on the list of the gentlemen," said another.

"Yes; and Captain Ewing's second," said Bell, the youngest.

"I'm afraid I must induce your sister to alter her list," said Maurice, in his sternest manner. "I cannot manage to go, and I'm sure she will not miss me."

Marian looked at the little girl who had so unfortunately mentioned the warrior's name, and the little girl knew that she had sinned.

"Oh, we cannot possibly do without you; can we Marian?" said Fanny. "It's to be at Bingley's dell, and we've got a bed for you at Newcastle; quite near, you know."

"And another for—," began Bell, but she stopped herself.

"Go away to your lessons, Bell," said Marian. "You know how angry mamma will be at your staying here all the morning;" and poor Bell with a sorrowful look left the room.

"We are all certainly very anxious that you should come; very anxious for a great many reasons," said Marian, in a voice that was rather solemn, and as though the matter were one of considerable import. "But if you really cannot, why of course there is no more to be said."

"There will be plenty without me, I am sure."

"As regards numbers, I dare say there will; for we shall have pretty nearly the whole of the two regiments;" and Marian as she alluded to the officers spoke in a tone which might lead one to think that she would much rather be without them; "but we counted on you as being one of ourselves; and as you had been away so long, we thought—we thought—," and then she turned away her face, and did not finish her speech. Before he could make up his mind as to his answer she had risen from her chair, and walked out of the room. Maurice almost thought that he saw a tear in her eye as she went.

He did ride back to Spanish Town that afternoon, after an early dinner; but before he went Marian spoke to him alone for one minute.

"I hope you are not offended with me," she said.

"Offended! oh no; how could I be offended with you?"

"Because you seem so stern. I am sure I would do anything I could to oblige you, if I knew how. It would be so shocking not to be good friends with a cousin like you."

"But there are so many different sorts of friends," said Maurice.

"Of course there are. There are a great many friends that one does not care a bit for,—people that one meets at balls and places like that—."

"And at picnics," said Maurice.

"Well, some of them there too; but we are not like that; are we?"

What could Maurice do but say, "no," and declare that their friendship was of a warmer description? And how could he resist promising to go to the picnic, though as he made the promise he knew that misery would be in store for him? He did promise, and then she gave him her hand and called him Maurice.

"Oh! I am so glad," she said. "It seemed so shocking that you should refuse to join us. And mind and be early, Maurice; for I shall want to explain it all. We are to meet, you know, at Clifton Gate at one o'clock, but do you be a little before that, and we shall be there."

Maurice Cumming resolved within his own breast as he rode back to Spanish Town, that if Marian behaved to him all that day at the picnic as she had done this day at Shandy Hall, he would ask her to be his wife before he left her.

And Miss Jack also was to be at the picnic.

"There is no need of going early," said she, when her nephew made a fuss about the starting. "People are never very punctual at such affairs as that; and then they are always quite long enough." But Maurice explained that he was anxious to be early, and on this occasion he carried his point.

When they reached Clifton Gate the ladies were already there; not in carriages, as people go to picnics in other and tamer countries, but each on her own horse or her own pony. But they were not alone. Beside Miss Leslie was a gentleman, whom Maurice knew as Lieutenant Graham, of the flag ship at Port Royal; and at a little distance which quite enabled him to join in the conversation was Captain Ewing, the lieutenant with the narrow waist of the previous year.

"We shall have a delightful day, Miss Leslie," said the lieutenant.

"Oh, charming, isn't it?" said Marian.

"But now to choose a place for dinner, Captain Ewing;—what do you say?"

"Will you commission me to select? You know I'm very well up in geometry, and all that."

"But that won't teach you what sort of a place does for a picnic dinner;—will it, Mr. Cumming?" And then she shook hands with Maurice, but did not take any further special notice of him. "We'll all go together, if you please. The commission is too important to be left to one." And then Marian rode off, and the lieutenant and the captain rode with her.

It was open for Maurice to join them if he chose, but he did not choose. He had come there ever so much earlier than he need have done, dragging his aunt with him, because Marian had told him that his services would be specially required by her. And now as soon as she saw him she went away with those two officers!—went away without vouchsafing him a word. He made up his mind, there on the spot, that he would never think of her again—never speak to her otherwise than he might speak to the most indifferent of mortals.

And yet he was a man that could struggle right manfully with the world's troubles; one who had struggled with them from his boyhood, and had never been overcome. Now he was unable to conceal the bitterness of his wrath because a little girl had ridden off to look for a green spot for her tablecloth without asking his assistance!

Picnics are, I think, in general, rather tedious for the elderly people who accompany them. When the joints become a little stiff dinners are eaten most comfortably with the accompaniment of chairs and tables, and a roof overhead is an agrément de plus. But, nevertheless, picnics cannot exist without a certain allowance of elderly people. The Miss Marians and Captains Ewing cannot go out to dine on the grass without some one to look after them. So the elderly people go to picnics, in a dull tame way, doing their duty, and wishing the day over. Now on the morning in question, when Marian rode off with Captain Ewing and Lieutenant Graham, Maurice Cumming remained among the elderly people.

A certain Mr. Pomken, a great Jamaica agriculturist, one of the Council, a man who had known the good old times, got him by the button and held him fast, discoursing wisely of sugar and rum, of Gadsden pans and recreant negroes, on all of which subjects Maurice Cumming was known to have an opinion of his own. But as Mr. Pomken's words sounded into one ear, into the other fell notes, listened to from afar,—the shrill laughing voice of Marian Leslie as she gave her happy order to her satellites around her, and ever and anon the bass haw-haw of Captain Ewing, who was made welcome as the chief of her attendants. That evening in a whisper to a brother councillor Mr. Pomken communicated his opinion that after all there was not so much in that young Cumming as some people said. But Mr. Pomken had no idea that that young Cumming was in love.

And then the dinner came, spread over half an acre. Maurice was among the last who seated himself; and when he did so it was in an awkward comfortless corner, behind Mr. Pomken's back, and far away from the laughter and mirth of the day. But yet from his comfortless corner he could see Marian as she sat in her pride of power, with her friend Julia Davis near her, a flirt as bad as herself, and her satellites around her, obedient to her nod, and happy in her smiles.

"Now I won't allow any more champagne," said Marian; "or who will there be steady enough to help me over the rocks to the grotto?"

"Oh, you have promised me!" cried the captain.

"Indeed, I have not; have I, Julia?"

"Miss Davis has certainly promised me," said the lieutenant.

"I have made no promise, and don't think I shall go at all," said Julia, who was sometimes inclined to imagine that Captain Ewing should be her own property.

All which and much more of the kind Maurice Cumming could not hear; but he could see—and imagine, which was worse. How innocent and inane are, after all, the flirtings of most young ladies, if all their words and doings in that line could be brought to paper! I do not know whether there be as a rule more vocal expression of the sentiment of love between a man and woman than there is between two thrushes! They whistle and call to each other, guided by instinct rather than by reason.

"You are going home with the ladies to-night, I believe," said Maurice to Miss Jack, immediately after dinner. Miss Jack acknowledged that such was her destination for the night.

"Then my going back to Spanish Town at once won't hurt any one—for, to tell the truth, I have had enough of this work."

"Why, Maurice, you were in such a hurry to come."

"The more fool I; and so now I am in a hurry to go away. Don't notice it to anybody."

Miss Jack looked in his face and saw that he was really wretched; and she knew the cause of his wretchedness.

"Don't go yet, Maurice," she said; and then added, with a tenderness that was quite uncommon with her, "Go to her, Maurice, and speak to her openly and freely, once for all; you will find that she will listen then. Dear Maurice, do, for my sake."

He made no answer, but walked away, roaming sadly by himself among the trees. "Listen!" he exclaimed to himself. "Yes, she will alter a dozen times in as many hours. Who can care for a creature that can change as she changes?" And yet he could not help caring for her.

As he went on, climbing among rocks, he again came upon the sound of voices, and heard especially that of Captain Ewing. "Now, Miss Leslie, if you will take my hand you will soon be over all the difficulty." And then a party of seven or eight, scrambling over some stones, came nearly on the level on which he stood, in full view of him; and leading the others were Captain Ewing and Miss Leslie.

He turned on his heel to go away, when he caught the sound of a step following him, and a voice saying, "Oh, there is Mr. Cumming, and I want to speak to him;" and in a minute a light hand was on his arm.

"Why are you running away from us?" said Marian.

"Because—oh, I don't know. I am not running away. You have your party made up, and I am not going to intrude on it."

"What nonsense! Do come now; we are going to this wonderful grotto. I thought it so ill-natured of you, not joining us at dinner. Indeed you know you had promised."

He did not answer her, but he looked at her—full in the face, with his sad eyes laden with love. She half understood his countenance, but only half understood it.

"What is the matter, Maurice?" she said. "Are you angry with me? Will you come and join us?"

"No, Marian, I cannot do that. But if you can leave them and come with me for half an hour, I will not keep you longer."

She stood hesitating a moment, while her companion remained on the spot where she had left him. "Come Miss Leslie," called Captain Ewing. "You will have it dark before we can get down."

"I will come with you," whispered she to Maurice, "but wait a moment." And she tripped back, and in some five minutes returned after an eager argument with her friends. "There," she said, "I don't care about the grotto, one bit, and I will walk with you now;—only they will think it so odd." And so they started off together.

Before the tropical darkness had fallen upon them Maurice had told the tale of his love,—and had told it in a manner differing much from that of Marian's usual admirers. He spoke with passion and almost with violence; he declared that his heart was so full of her image that he could not rid himself of it for one minute; "nor would he wish to do so," he said, "if she would be his Marian, his own Marian, his very own. But if not— " and then he explained to her, with all a lover's warmth, and with almost more than a lover's liberty, what was his idea of her being "his own, his very own," and in doing so inveighed against her usual lightheartedness in terms which at any rate were strong enough.

But Marian bore it all well. Perhaps she knew that the lesson was somewhat deserved; and perhaps she appreciated at its value the love of such a man as Maurice Cumming, weighing in her judgment the difference between him and the Ewings and the Grahams.

And then she answered him well and prudently, with words which startled him by their prudent seriousness as coming from her. She begged his pardon heartily, she said, for any grief which she had caused him: but yet how was she to be blamed, seeing that she had known nothing of his feelings? Her father and mother had said something to her of this proposed marriage; something, but very little; and she had answered by saying that she did not think Maurice had any warmer regard for her than of a cousin. After this answer neither father nor mother had pressed the matter further. As to her own feelings she could then say nothing, for she then knew nothing;—nothing but this, that she loved no one better than him, or rather that she loved no one else. She would ask herself if she could love him; but he must give her some little time for that. In the mean time—and she smiled sweetly at him as she made the promise—she would endeavour to do nothing that would offend him; and then she added that on that evening she would dance with him any dances that he liked. Maurice, with a self-denial that was not very wise, contented himself with engaging her for the first quadrille.

They were to dance that night in the mess-room of the officers at Newcastle. This scheme had been added on as an adjunct to the picnic, and it therefore became necessary that the ladies should retire to their own or their friends' houses at Newcastle to adjust their dresses. Marian Leslie and Julia Davis were there accommodated with the loan of a small room by the major's wife, and as they were brushing their hair, and putting on their dancing-shoes, something was said between them about Maurice Cumming.

"And so you are to be Mrs. C. of Mount Pleasant," said Julia. "Well; I didn't think it would come to that at last."

"But it has not come to that, and if it did why should I not be Mrs. C., as you call it?"

"The knight of the rueful countenance, I call him."

"I tell you what then, he is an excellent young man, and the fact is you don't know him."

"I don't like excellent young men with long faces. I suppose you won't be let to dance quick dances at all now."

"I shall dance whatever dances I like, as I have always done," said Marian, with some little asperity in her tone.

"Not you; or if you do, you'll lose your promotion. You'll never live to be my Lady Rue. And what will Graham say? You know you've given him half a promise."

"That's not true, Julia;—I never gave him the tenth part of a promise."

"Well, he says so;" and then the words between the young ladies became a little more angry. But, nevertheless, in due time they came forth with faces smiling as usual, with their hair properly brushed, and without any signs of warfare.

But Marian had to stand another attack before the business of the evening commenced, and this was from no less doughty an antagonist than her aunt, Miss Jack. Miss Jack soon found that Maurice had not kept his threat of going home; and though she did not absolutely learn from him that he had gone so far towards perfecting her dearest hopes as to make a formal offer to Marian, nevertheless she did gather that things were fast that way tending. If only this dancing were over! she said to herself, dreading the unnumbered waltzes with Ewing, and the violent polkas with Graham. So Miss Jack resolved to say one word to Marian—"A wise word in good season," said Miss Jack to herself, "how sweet a thing it is."

"Marian," said she. "Step here a moment, I want to say a word to you."

"Yes, aunt Sarah," said Marian, following her aunt into a corner, not quite in the best humour in the world; for she had a dread of some further interference.

"Are you going to dance with Maurice to-night?"

"Yes, I believe so,—the first quadrille."

"Well, what I was going to say is this. I don't want you to dance many quick dances to-night, for a reason I have:—that is, not a great many."

"Why, aunt, what nonsense!"

"Now my dearest, dearest girl, it is all for your own sake. Well, then, it must out. He does not like it, you know."

"What he?"

"Maurice."

"Well, aunt, I don't know that I'm bound to dance or not to dance just as Mr. Cumming may like. Papa does not mind my dancing. The people have come here to dance, and you can hardly want to make me ridiculous by sitting still." And so that wise word did not appear to be very sweet.

And then the amusement of the evening commenced, and Marian stood up for a quadrille with her lover. She however was not in the very best humour. She had, as she thought, said and done enough for one day in Maurice's favour. And she had no idea, as she declared to herself, of being lectured by aunt Sarah.

"Dearest Marian," he said to her, as the quadrille came to a close, "it is in your power to make me so happy,—so perfectly happy."

"But then people have such different ideas of happiness," she replied. "They can't all see with the same eyes, you know." And so they parted.

But during the early part of the evening she was sufficiently discreet; she did waltz with Lieutenant Graham, and polk with Captain Ewing, but she did so in a tamer manner than was usual with her, and she made no emulous attempts to dance down other couples. When she had done she would sit down, and then she consented to stand up for two quadrilles with two very tame gentlemen, to whom no lover could object.

"And so, Marian, your wings are regularly clipped at last," said Julia Davis coming up to her.

"No more clipped than your own," said Marian.

"If Sir Rue won't let you waltz now, what will he require of you when you're married to him?"

"I am just as well able to waltz with whom I like as you are, Julia; and if you say so in that way, I shall think it's envy."

"Ha—ha—ha; I may have envied you some of your beaux before now; I dare say I have. But I certainly do not envy you Sir Rue." And then she went off to her partner.

All this was too much for Marian's weak strength, and before long she was again whirling round with Captain Ewing. "Come, Miss Leslie," said he, "let us see what we can do. Graham and Julia Davis have been saying that your waltzing days are over, but I think we can put them down."

Marian as she got up, and raised her arm in order that Ewing might put his round her waist, caught Maurice's eye as he leaned against a wall, and read in it a stern rebuke. "This is too bad," she said to herself. "He shall not make a slave of me, at any rate as yet." And away she went as madly, more madly than ever, and for the rest of the evening she danced with Captain Ewing and with him alone.

There is an intoxication quite distinct from that which comes from strong drink. When the judgment is altogether overcome by the spirits this species of drunkenness comes on, and in this way Marian Leslie was drunk that night. For two hours she danced with Captain Ewing, and ever and anon she kept saying to herself that she would teach the world to know—and of all the world Mr. Cumming especially—that she might be led but not driven.

Then about four o'clock she went home, and as she attempted to undress herself in her own room she burst into violent tears and opened her heart to her sister—"Oh, Fanny, I do love him, I do love him so dearly! and now he will never come to me again!"

Maurice stood still with his back against the wall, for the full two hours of Marian's exhibition, and then he said to his aunt before he left—"I hope you have now seen enough; you will hardly mention her name to me again." Miss Jack groaned from the bottom of her heart but she said nothing. She said nothing that night to any one; but she lay awake in her bed, thinking, till it was time to rise and dress herself. "Ask Miss Marian to come to me," she said to the black girl who came to assist her. But it was not till she had sent three times, that Miss Marian obeyed the summons.

At three o'clock on the following day Miss Jack arrived at her own hall door in Spanish Town. Long as the distance was she ordinarily rode it all, but on this occasion she had provided a carriage to bring her over as much of the journey as it was practicable for her to perform on wheels. As soon as she reached her own hall door she asked if Mr. Cumming was at home. "Yes," the servant said. "He was in the small book room, at the back of the house, up stairs." Silently, as if afraid of being heard, she stepped up her own stairs into her own drawing-room; and very silently she was followed by a pair of feet lighter and smaller than her own.

Miss Jack was usually somewhat of a despot in her own house, but there was nothing despotic about her now as she peered into the book-room. This she did with her bonnet still on, looking round the half-opened door as though she were afraid to disturb her nephew. He sat at the window looking out into the verandah which ran behind the house, so intent on his thoughts that he did not hear her.

"Maurice," she said, "can I come in?"

"Come in? oh yes, of course;" and he turned round sharply at her. "I tell you what, aunt; I am not well here, and I cannot stay out the session. I shall go back to Mount Pleasant."

"Maurice," and she walked close up to him as she spoke, "Maurice, I have brought some one with me to ask your pardon."

His face became red up to the roots of his hair as he stood looking at her without answering. "You would grant it certainly," she continued, "if you knew how much it would be valued."

"Whom do you mean? who is it?" he asked at last.

"One who loves you as well as you love her—and she cannot love you better. Come in, Marian." The poor girl crept in at the door, ashamed of what she was induced to do, but yet looking anxiously into her lover's face. "You asked her yesterday to be your wife," said Miss Jack, "and she did not then know her own mind. Now she has had a lesson. You will ask her once again; will you not, Maurice?"

What was he to say? How was he to refuse, when that soft little hand was held out to him; when those eyes laden with tears just ventured to look into his face?

"I beg your pardon if I angered you last night," she said.

In half a minute Miss Jack had left the room, and in the space of another thirty seconds Maurice had forgiven her. "I am your own now, you know," she whispered to him in the course of that long evening. "Yesterday, you know—," but the sentence was never finished.

It was in vain that Julia Davis was ill natured and sarcastic, in vain that Ewing and Graham made joint attempt upon her constancy. From that night to the morning of her marriage—and the interval was only three months—Marian Leslie was never known to flirt.

John Bull on the Guadalquivir

Originally appeared in *Cassell's Illustrated Family Paper*, 17 and 24 November 1860. This is the 'Spanish Story' listed in Trollope's working-diary for *Framley Parsonage*, and was therefore written between 1 and 7 June 1860. Reprinted in *Tales of All Countries* [First Series] (1861). Trollope took a six-day holiday in Spain in April 1858, at the end of his Postal Mission to Egypt. In *An Autobiography* he reveals that the 'chief incident' in 'John Bull on the Guadalquivir' 'occurred to me and a friend of mine on our way up that river to Seville. We both of us handled the gold ornaments of a man whom we believed to be a bull-fighter, but who turned out to be a duke,—and a duke, too, who could speak English! How gracious he was to us, yet how thoroughly he covered us with ridicule!' The rowdy male group the narrator encounters in Seville Cathedral are similar to 'The United Englishmen Who Travel For Fun' described by Trollope in *Travelling Sketches* (1865). 'Englishmen of the class in question,' he writes in this essay, 'are boys for a more protracted period of their life, and remain longer in a state of hobbledehoyhood, than the youths of probably any other nation.'

I AM an Englishman living, as all Englishmen should do, in England, and my wife would not, I think, be well pleased were any one to insinuate that she were other than an Englishwoman, but in the circumstances of my marriage I became connected with the south of Spain, and the narrative which I am to tell requires that I should refer to some of those details.

The Pomfrets and Daguilars have long been in trade together in this country, and one of the partners has usually resided at Seville for the sake of the works which the firm there possesses. My father, James Pomfret, lived there for ten years before his marriage; and since that, and up to the present period, old Mr. Daguilar has been always on the spot. He was, I believe, born in Spain, but he came very early to England; he married an English wife, and his sons have been educated exclusively in England. His only daughter, Maria Daguilar, did not pass so large a proportion of her early life in this country, but she came to us for a visit at the age of seventeen, and when she returned I made up my mind that I most assuredly would go after her. So I did, and she is now sitting on the other side of the fireplace with a legion of small linen habiliments in a huge basket by her side.

I felt, at the first, that there was something lacking to make my cup of love perfectly delightful. It was very sweet, but there was wanting that flower of romance which is generally added to the heavenly draught by a slight admixture of opposition. I feared that the path of my true love would run too smooth. When Maria came to our house my mother and elder sister seemed to be quite willing that I should be continually alone with her; and she had not been there ten days before my father, by chance, remarked that there was nothing old Mr. Daguilar valued so highly as a thorough feeling of intimate alliance between the two families which had been so long connected in trade. I was never told that Maria was to be my wife, but I felt that the same thing was done without words; and when, after six weeks of somewhat elaborate attendance upon her, I asked her to be Mrs. John Pomfret, I had no more fear of a refusal, or even of hesitation on her part, than I now have when I suggest to my partner some commercial transaction of undoubted advantage.

But Maria, even at that age, had about her a quiet sustained decision of character quite unlike anything I had seen in English girls. I used to hear, and do still hear, how much more flippant is the education of girls in France and Spain than in England; and I know that this is shown to be the result of many causes—the Roman Catholic religion being, perhaps, the chief offender; but, nevertheless, I rarely see in one of our own young women the same power of a self-sustained demeanour as I meet on the Continent. It goes no deeper than the demeanour, people say. I can only answer that I have not found that shallowness in my own wife.

Miss Daguilar replied to me that she was not prepared with an answer; she had only known me six weeks, and wanted more time to think about it; besides, there was one in her own country with whom she would wish to consult. I knew she had no mother; and as for consulting old Mr. Daguilar on such a subject, that idea, I knew, could not have troubled her. Besides, as I afterwards learned, Mr. Daguilar had already proposed the marriage to his partner exactly as he would have proposed a division of assets. My mother declared that Maria was a foolish chit—in which, by-the-by, she showed her entire ignorance of Miss Daguilar's character; my eldest sister begged that no constraint might be put on the young lady's inclinations—which provoked me to assert that the young lady's inclinations were by no means opposed to my own; and my father, in the coolest manner, suggested that the matter might stand over for twelve months, and that I might then go to Seville, and see about it! Stand over for twelve months! Would not Maria, long before that time, have been snapped up and carried off by one of those inordinately rich Spanish grandees who are still to be met with occasionally in Andalucia?

My father's dictum, however, had gone forth; and Maria, in the calmest voice, protested that she thought it very wise. I should be less of a boy by that time, she said, smiling on me, but driving wedges between every fibre of my body as she spoke. "Be it so," I said, proudly. "At any rate, I am not so much of a boy that I shall forget you." "And, John, you still have the trade to learn," she added, with her deliciously foreign intonation—speaking very slowly, but with perfect pronunciation. The trade to learn! However, I said not a word, but stalked out of the room, meaning to see her no more before she went. But I could not resist attending on her in the hall as she started; and, when she took leave of us, she put her face up to be kissed by me, as she did by my father, and seemed to receive as much emotion from one embrace as from the other. "He'll go out by the packet of the 1st April," said my father, speaking of me as though I were a bale of goods. "Ah! that will be so nice," said Maria, settling her dress in the carriage; "the oranges will be ripe for him then!"

On the 17th April I did sail, and felt still very like a bale of goods. I had received one letter from her, in which she merely stated that her papa would have a room ready for me on my arrival; and, in answer to that, I had sent an epistle somewhat longer, and, as I then thought, a little more to the purpose. Her turn of mind was more practical than mine, and I must confess my belief that she did not appreciate my poetry.

I landed at Cadiz and was there joined by an old family friend, one of the very best fellows that ever lived. He was to accompany me up as far as Seville; and, as he had lived for a year or two at Xeres, was supposed to be more Spanish almost than a Spaniard. His name was Johnson, and he was in the wine trade; and whether for travelling or whether for staying at home—whether for paying you a visit in your own house, or whether for entertaining you in his—there never was (and I am prepared to maintain there never will be) a stancher friend, a choicer companion, or a safer guide than Thomas Johnson. Words cannot produce a eulogium sufficient for his merits. But, as I have since learned, he was not quite so Spanish as I had imagined. Three years among the *bodegas* of Xeres had taught him, no doubt, to appreciate the exact twang of a good, dry sherry; but not, as I now conceive, the exactest flavour of the true Spanish character. I was very lucky, however, in meeting such a friend, and now reckon him as one of the stanchest allies of the house of Pomfret, Daguilar, and Pomfret.

He met me at Cadiz, took me about the town which appeared to me to be of no very great interest;—though the young ladies were all very well. But, in this respect, I was then a Stoic, till such time as I might be able to throw myself at the feet of her whom I was ready to proclaim the most lovely of all the Dulcineas of Andalucia. He carried me up by boat and railway to Xeres; gave me a most terrific headache, by dragging me out into the glare of the sun, after I had tasted some half a dozen different wines, and went through all the ordinary hospitalities. On the next day we returned to Puerto, and from thence getting across to St. Lucar and Bonanza, found ourselves on the banks of the Guadalquivir, and took our places in the boat for Seville. I need say but little to my readers respecting that far-famed river. Thirty years ago we in England generally believed that on its banks was to be found a pure elysium of pastoral beauty; that picturesque shepherds and lovely maidens here fed their flocks in fields of asphodel; that the limpid stream ran cool and crystal over bright stones and beneath perennial shade; and that everything on the Guadalquivir was as lovely and as poetical as its name. Now, it is pretty widely known that no uglier river oozes down to its bourn in the sea through unwholesome banks of low mud. It is brown and dirty; ungifted by any scenic advantage; margined for miles upon miles by huge, flat, expansive fields, in which cattle are reared—the bulls wanted for the bull-fights among other—and birds of prey sit constant on the shore, watching for the carcasses of such as die. Such are the charms of the golden Guadalquivir.

At first we were very dull on board that steamer. I never found myself in a position in which there was less to do. There was a nasty smell about the little boat which made me almost ill; every turn in the river was so exactly like the last, that we might have been standing still; there was no amusement except eating, and that, when once done, was not of a kind to make an early repetition desirable. Even Johnson was becoming dull, and I began to doubt whether I was so desirous as I once had been to travel the length and breadth of all Spain. But about noon a little incident occurred which did for a time remove some of our tedium. The boat had stopped to take in passengers on the river; and, among others, a man had come on board dressed in a fashion that, to my eyes, was equally strange and picturesque. Indeed, his appearance was so singular, that I could not but regard him with care, though I felt at first averse to stare at a fellow-passenger on account of his clothes. He was a man of about fifty, but as active apparently as though not more than twenty-five; he was of low stature, but of admirable make; his hair was just becoming grizzled, but was short and crisp and well cared for; his face was prepossessing, having a look of good humour added to courtesy, and there was a pleasant, soft smile round his mouth which ingratiated one at the first sight. But it was his dress rather than his person which attracted attention. He wore the ordinary Andalucian cap—of which such hideous parodies are now making themselves common in England—but was not contented with the usual ornament of the double tuft. The cap was small, and jaunty; trimmed with silk velvet—as is common here with men careful to adorn their persons; but this man's cap was finished off with a jewelled button and golden filigree work. He was dressed in a short jacket with a stand-up collar; and that also was covered with golden buttons and with golden button-holes. It was all gilt down the front, and all lace down the back. The rows of buttons were double; and those of the more backward row hung down in heavy pendules. His waistcoat was of coloured silk—very pretty to look at; and ornamented with a small sash, through which gold threads were worked. All the buttons of his breeches also were of gold; and there were gold tags to all the button-holes. His stockings were of the finest silk, and clocked with gold from the knee to the ankle.

Dress any Englishman in such a garb and he will at once give you the idea of a hog in armour. In the first place he will lack the proper spirit to carry it off, and in the next place the motion of his limbs will disgrace the ornaments they bear. "And so best," most Englishmen will say. Very likely; and, therefore, let no Englishman try it. But my Spaniard did not look at all like a hog in armour. He walked slowly down the plank into the boat, whistling lowly but very clearly, a few bars from an opera tune. It was plain to see that he was master of himself, of his ornaments, and of his limbs. He had no appearance of thinking that men were looking at him, or of feeling that he was beauteous in his attire;—nothing could be more natural than his foot-fall, or the quiet glance of his cheery gray eye. He walked up to the captain, who held the helm, and lightly raised his hand to his cap. The captain, taking one hand from the wheel, did the same, and then the stranger, turning his back to the stern of the vessel, and fronting down the river with his face, continued to whistle slowly, clearly, and in excellent time. Grand as were his clothes they were no burthen on his mind.

"What is he?" said I, going up to my friend Johnson, with a whisper.

"Well, I've been looking at him," said Johnson—which was true enough; "he's a—an uncommonly good-looking fellow, isn't he?"

"Particularly so," said I; "and got up quite irrespective of expense. Is he a—a—a gentleman, now, do you think?"

"Well, those things are so different in Spain, that it's almost impossible to make an Englishman understand them. One learns to know all this sort of people by being with them in the country, but one can't explain."

"No; exactly. Are they real gold?"

"Yes, yes; I dare say they are. They sometimes have them silver gilt."

"It is quite a common thing, then, isn't it?" asked I.

"Well, not exactly; that—Ah! yes; I see! of course. He is a torero."

"A what?"

"A mayo. I will explain it all to you. You will see them about in all places, and will get used to them."

"But I haven't seen one other as yet."

"No, and they are not all so gay as this, nor so new in their finery, you know."

"And what is a torero?"

"Well, a torero is a man engaged in bull-fighting."

"Oh! he is a matador, is he?" said I, looking at him with more than all my eyes.

"No, not exactly that;—not of necessity. He is probably a mayo. A fellow that dresses himself smart for fairs, and will be seen hanging about with the bull-fighters. What would be a sporting fellow in England—only he won't drink and curse like a low man on the turf there. Come, shall we go and speak to him?"

"I can't talk to him," said I, diffident of my Spanish. I had received lessons in England from Maria Daguilar; but six weeks is little enough for making love, let alone the learning of a foreign language.

"Oh! I'll do the talking. You'll find the language easy enough before long. It soon becomes the same as English to you, when you live among them." And then Johnson, walking up to the stranger, accosted him with that good-natured familiarity with which a thoroughly nice fellow always opens a conversation with his inferior. Of course I could not understand the words which were exchanged; but it was clear enough that the "mayo" took the address in good part, and was inclined to be communicative and social.

"They are all of pure gold," said Johnson, turning to me after a minute, making as he spoke a motion with his head to show the importance of the information.

"Are they indeed?" said I. "Where on earth did a fellow like that get them?" Whereupon Johnson again returned to his conversation with the man. After another minute he raised his hand, and began to finger the button on the shoulder; and to aid him in doing so, the man of the bull-ring turned a little on one side.

"They are wonderfully well made," said Johnson, talking to me, and still fingering the button. "They are manufactured, he says, at Osuna, and he tells me that they make them better there than anywhere else."

"I wonder what the whole set would cost?" said I. "An enormous deal of money for a fellow like him, I should think!"

"Over twelve ounces," said Johnson, having asked the question; "and that will be more than forty pounds."

"What an uncommon ass he must be!" said I.

As Johnson by this time was very closely scrutinizing the whole set of ornaments I thought I might do so also, and going up close to our friend, I too began to handle the buttons and tags on the other side. Nothing could have been more good-humoured than he was—so much so that I was emboldened to hold up his arm that I might see the cut of his coat, to take off his cap and examine the make, to stuff my finger in beneath his sash, and at last to kneel down while I persuaded him to hold up his legs that I might look to the clocking. The fellow was thoroughly good-natured, and why should I not indulge my curiosity?

"You'll upset him if you don't take care," said Johnson; for I had got fast hold of him by one ankle, and was determined to finish the survey completely.

"Oh, no, I sha'n't," said I; "a bull-fighting chap can surely stand on one leg. But what I wonder at is, how on earth he can afford it!" Whereupon Johnson again began to interrogate him in Spanish.

"He says he had got no children," said Johnson, having received a reply, "and that as he has nobody but himself to look after, he is able to allow himself such little luxuries."

"Tell him that I say he would be better with a wife and couple of babies," said I—and Johnson interpreted.

"He says that he'll think of it some of these days, when he finds that the supply of fools in the world is becoming short," said Johnson.

We had nearly done with him now; but after regaining my feet, I addressed myself once more to the heavy pendules, which hung down almost under his arm. I lifted one of these, meaning to feel its weight between my fingers; but unfortunately I gave a lurch, probably through the motion of the boat, and still holding by the button, tore it almost off from our friend's coat.

"Oh, I am so sorry!" I said, in broad English.

"It do not matter at all," he said, bowing, and speaking with equal plainness. And then, taking a knife from his pocket, he cut the pendule off, leaving a bit of torn cloth on the side of his jacket.

"Upon my word, I am quite unhappy," said I; "but I always am so awkward." Whereupon he bowed low.

"Couldn't I make it right!" said I, bringing out my purse.

He lifted his hand, and I saw that it was small and white; he lifted it, and gently put it upon my purse, smiling sweetly as he did so. "Thank you, no, senor; thank you, no." And then, bowing to us both, he walked away down into the cabin.

"Upon my word, he is a deuced well-mannered fellow," said I.

"You shouldn't have offered him money," said Johnson; "a Spaniard does not like it."

"Why, I thought you could do nothing without money in this country. Doesn't every one take bribes?"

"Ah! yes; that is a different thing; but not the price of a button. By Jove! he understood English, too. Did you see that?"

"Yes; and I called him an ass! I hope he doesn't mind it."

"Oh! no; he won't think anything about it," said Johnson. "That sort of fellows don't. I dare say we shall see him in the bull-ring next Sunday, and then we'll make all right with a glass of lemonade."

And so our adventure ended with the man of the gold ornaments. I was sorry that I had spoken English before him so heedlessly, and resolved that I would never be guilty of such *gaucherie* again. But, then, who would think that a Spanish bull-fighter would talk a foreign language? I was sorry, also, that I had torn his coat;—it had looked so awkward; and sorry again that I had offered the man money. Altogether I was a little ashamed of myself; but I had too much to look forward to at Seville to allow any heaviness to remain long at my heart; and before I had arrived at the marvellous city I had forgotten both him and his buttons.

Nothing could be nicer than the way in which I was welcomed at Mr. Daguilar's house, or more kind—I may almost say affectionate—than Maria's manner to me. But it was too affectionate; and I am not sure that I should not have liked my reception better had she been more diffident in her tone, and less inclined to greet me with open warmth. As it was, she again gave me her cheek to kiss, in her father's presence, and called me dear John, and asked me specially after some rabbits which I had kept at home merely for a younger sister; and then it seemed as though she were in no way embarrassed by the peculiar circumstances of our position. Twelve months since I had asked her to be my wife, and now she was to give me an answer; and yet she was as assured in her gait, and as serenely joyous in her tone, as though I were a brother just returned from college. It could not be that she meant to refuse me, or she would not smile on me and be so loving; but I could almost have found it in my heart to wish that she would. "It is quite possible," said I to myself, "that I may not be found so ready for this family bargain. A love that is to be had like a bale of goods is not exactly the love to suit my taste." But then, when I met her again in the morning, I could no more have quarrelled with her than I could have flown.

I was inexpressibly charmed with the whole city, and especially with the house in which Mr. Daguilar lived. It opened from the corner of a narrow, unfrequented street—a corner like an elbow—and, as seen from the exterior, there was nothing prepossessing to recommend it; but the outer door led by a short hall or passage to an inner door or *grille*, made of open ornamental iron-work, and through that we entered a court, or patio, as they called it. Nothing could be more lovely or deliciously cool than was this small court. The building on each side was covered by trellis-work; and beautiful creepers, vines, and parasite flowers, now in the full magnificence of the early summer, grew up and clustered round the window. Every inch of wall was covered, so that none of the glaring whitewash wounded the eye. In the four corners of the patio were four large orange-trees, covered with fruit. I would not say a word in special praise of these, remembering that childish promise she had made on my behalf. In the middle of the court there was a fountain, and round about on the marble floor there were chairs, and here and there a small table, as though the space were really a portion of the house. It was here that we used to take our cup of coffee and smoke our cigarettes, I and old Mr. Daguilar, while Maria sat by, not only approving, but occasionally rolling for me the thin paper round the fragrant weed with her taper fingers. Beyond the patio was an open passage or gallery, filled also with flowers in pots; and then, beyond this, one entered the drawing-room of the house. It was by no means a princely palace or mansion, fit for the owner of untold wealth. The rooms were not over large nor very numerous; but the most had been made of a small space, and everything had been done to relieve the heat of an almost tropical sun.

"It is pretty, is it not?" she said, as she took me through it.

"Very pretty," I said. "I wish we could live in such houses."

"Oh, they would not do at all for dear old fat, cold, cozy England. You are quite different, you know, in everything from us in the south; more phlegmatic, but then so much steadier. The men and the houses are all the same."

I can hardly tell why, but even this wounded me. It seemed to me as though she were inclined to put into one and the same category things English, dull, useful, and solid; and that she was disposed to show a sufficient appreciation for such necessaries of life, though she herself had another and inner sense—a sense keenly alive to the poetry of her own southern clime; and that I, as being English, was to have no participation in this latter charm. An English husband might do very well, the interests of the firm might make such an arrangement desirable, such a *mariage de convenance*—so I argued to myself—might be quite compatible with—with heaven only knows what delights of super-terrestrial romance, from which I, as being an English thick-headed lump of useful coarse mortality, was to be altogether debarred. She had spoken to me of oranges, and having finished the survey of the house, she offered me some sweet little cakes. It could not be that of such things were the thoughts which lay undivulged beneath the clear waters of those deep black eyes—undivulged to me, though no one else could have so good a right to read those thoughts! It could not be that that noble brow gave index of a mind intent on the trade of which she spoke so often! Words of other sort than any that had been vouchsafed to me must fall at times from the rich curves of that perfect mouth.

So felt I then, pining for something to make me unhappy. Ah, me! I know all about it now, and am content. But I wish that some learned pundit would give us a good definition of romance, would describe in words that feeling with which our hearts are so pestered when we are young, which makes us sigh for we know not what, and forbids us to be contented with what God sends us. We invest female beauty with impossible attributes, and are angry because our women have not the spiritualized souls of angels, anxious as we are that they should also be human in the flesh. A man looks at her he would love as at a distant landscape in a mountainous land. The peaks are glorious with more than the beauty of earth and rock and vegetation. He dreams of some mysterious grandeur of design which tempts him on under the hot sun, and over the sharp rock, till he has reached the mountain goal which he had set before him. But when there, he finds that the beauty is well-nigh gone, and as for that delicious mystery on which his soul had fed, it has vanished for ever.

I know all about it now, and am, as I said, content. Beneath those deep black eyes there lay a well of love, good, honest, homely love,

love of father and husband and children that were to come—of that love which loves to see the loved one prospering in honesty. That noble brow—for it is noble; I am unchanged in that opinion, and will go unchanged to my grave—covers thoughts as to the welfare of many, and an intellect fitted to the management of a household, of servants, namely, and children and perchance a husband. That mouth can speak words of wisdom, of very useful wisdom—though of poetry it has latterly uttered little that was original. Poetry and romance! They are splendid mountain views seen in the distance. So let men be content to see them, and not attempt to tread upon the fallacious heather of the mystic hills.

In the first week of my sojourn in Seville I spoke no word of overt love to Maria, thinking, as I confess, to induce her thereby to alter her mode of conduct to myself. "She knows that I have come here to make love to her—to repeat my offer; and she will at any rate be chagrined if I am slow to do so." But it had no effect. At home my mother was rather particular about her table, and Maria's greatest efforts seemed to be used in giving me as nice dinners as we gave her. In those days I did not care a straw about my dinner, and so I took an opportunity of telling her. "Dear me," said she, looking at me almost with grief, "do you not? What a pity! And do you not like music either?" "Oh, yes, I adore it," I replied. I felt sure at the time that had I been born in her own sunny clime, she would never have talked to me about eating. But that was my mistake.

I used to walk out with her about the city, seeing all that is there of beauty and magnificence. And in what city is there more that is worth the seeing? At first this was very delightful to me, for I felt that I was blessed with a privilege that would not be granted to any other man. But its value soon fell in my eyes, for others would accost her, and walk on the other side, talking to her in Spanish, as though I hardly existed, or were a servant there for her protection. And I was not allowed to take her arm, and thus to appropriate her, as I should have done in England. "No, John," she said, with the sweetest, prettiest smile, "we don't do that here; only when people are married." And she made this allusion to married life out, openly, with no slightest tremor on her tongue.

"Oh, I beg pardon," said I, drawing back my hand, and feeling angry with myself for not being fully acquainted with all the customs of a foreign country.

"You need not beg pardon," said she, "when we were in England we always walked so. It is just a custom, you know." And then I saw her drop her large dark eyes to the ground, and bow gracefully in answer to some salute.

I looked round, and saw that we had been joined by a young cavalier,—a Spanish nobleman, as I saw at once; a man with jet black hair, and a straight nose, and a black moustache, and patent leather boots, very slim and very tall, and—though I would not confess it then—uncommonly handsome. I myself am inclined to be stout, my hair is light, my nose broad, I have no hair on my upper lip, and my whiskers are rough and uneven. "I could punch your head though, my fine fellow," said I to myself, when I saw that he placed himself at Maria's side, "and think very little of the achievement."

The wretch went on with us round the plaza for some quarter of an hour, talking Spanish with the greatest fluency, and she was every whit as fluent. Of course, I could not understand a word that they said. Of all positions that a man can occupy, I think that that is about the most uncomfortable; and I cannot say that, even up to this day, I have quite forgiven her for that quarter of an hour.

"I shall go in," said I, unable to bear my feelings, and preparing to leave her. "The heat is unendurable."

"Oh dear, John, why did you not speak before?" she answered. "You cannot leave me here, you know, as I am in your charge; but I will go with you almost directly." And then she finished her conversation with the Spaniard, speaking with an animation she had never displayed in her conversations with me.

It had been agreed between us for two or three days before this, that we were to rise early on the following morning for the sake of ascending the tower of the cathedral, and visiting the Giralda, as the iron figure is called, which turns upon a pivot on the extreme summit. We had often wandered together up and down the long dark gloomy aisle of the stupendous building, and had, together, seen its treasury of art; but as yet we had not performed the task which has to be achieved by all visitors to Seville; and in order that we might have a clear view over the surrounding country, and not be tormented by the heat of an advanced sun, we had settled that we would ascend the Giralda before breakfast.

And now, as I walked away from the plaza towards Mr. Daguilar's house, with Maria by my side, I made up my mind that I would settle my business during this visit to the cathedral. Yes, and I would so manage the settlement that there should be no doubt left as to my intentions and my own ideas. I would not be guilty of shilly-shally conduct; I would tell her frankly what I felt and what I thought, and would make her understand that I did not desire her hand if I could not have her heart. I did not value the kindness of her manner, seeing that that kindness sprung from indifference rather than passion; and so I would declare to her. And I would ask her, also, who was this young man with whom she was intimate—for whom all her volubility and energy of tone seemed to be employed? She had told me once that it behoved her to consult a friend in Seville as to the expediency of her marriage with me. Was this the friend whom she had wished to consult? If so, she need not trouble herself. Under such circumstances I should decline the connection! And I resolved that I would find out how this might be. A man who proposes to take a woman to his bosom as his wife, has a right to ask for information—ay, and to receive it too. If flashed upon my mind at this moment that Donna Maria was well enough inclined to come to me as my wife, but—. I could hardly define the "buts" to myself, for there were three or four of them. Why did she always speak to me in a tone of childish affection, as though I were a schoolboy home for the holidays? I would have all this out with her on the tower on the following morning, standing under the Giralda.

On that morning we met together in the patio, soon after five o'clock, and started for the cathedral. She looked beautiful, with her black mantilla over her head, and with black gloves on, and her black morning silk dress—beautiful, composed, and at her ease, as though she were well satisfied to undertake this early morning walk from feelings of good nature—sustained, probably, by some under-current of a deeper sentiment. Well; I would know all about it before I returned to her father's house.

There hardly stands, as I think, on the earth a building more remarkable than the cathedral of Seville, and hardly one more grand. Its enormous size; its gloom and darkness; the richness of ornamentation in the details, contrasted with the severe simplicity of the larger outlines; the variety of its architecture; the glory of its paintings; and the wonderous splendour of its metallic decoration, its altar-friezes, screens, rails, gates, and the like, render it, to my mind, the first in interest among churches. It has not the coloured glass of Chartres, or the marble glory of Milan, or such a forest of aisles as Antwerp, or so perfect a hue in stone as Westminster, nor in mixed beauty of form and colour does it possess anything equal to the choir of Cologne; but, for combined magnificence and awe-compelling grandeur, I regard it as superior to all other ecclesiastical edifices.

It is its deep gloom with which the stranger is so greatly struck on his first entrance. In a region so hot as the south of Spain, a cool interior is a main object with the architect, and this it has been necessary to effect by the exclusion of light; consequently the church is dark, mysterious, and almost cold. On the morning in question, as we entered, it seemed to be filled with gloom, and the distant sound of a slow footstep here and there beyond the transept inspired one almost with awe. Maria, when she first met me, had begun to talk with her usual smile, offering me coffee and a biscuit before I started. "I never eat biscuit," I said, with almost a severe tone, as I turned from her. That dark, horrid man of the plaza—would she have offered him a cake had she been going to walk with him in the gloom of the morning? After that little had been spoken between us. She walked by my side with her accustomed smile; but she had, as I flattered myself, begun to learn that I was not to be won by a meaningless good nature. "We are lucky in our morning for the view;" that was all she said, speaking with that peculiarly clear, but slow, pronunciation which she had assumed in learning our language.

We entered the cathedral, and, walking the whole length of the aisle, left it again at the porter's porch at the further end. Here we passed through a low door on to the stone flight of steps, and at once began to ascend. "There are a party of your countrymen up before us," said Maria; "the porter says that they went through the lodge half an hour since." "I hope they will return before we are on the top," said I, bethinking myself of the task that was before me. And indeed my heart was hardly at ease within me, for that which I had to say would require all the spirit of which I was master.

The ascent to the Giralda is very long and very fatiguing; and we had to pause on the various landings and in the singular belfry in order that Miss Daguilar might recruit her strength and breath. As we rested on one of these occasions, in a gallery which runs round the tower below the belfry, we heard a great noise of shouting, and a clattering of sticks among the balls. "It is the party of your countrymen who went up before us," said she. "What a pity that Englishmen should always make so much noise!" And then she spoke in Spanish to the custodian of the bells, who is usually to be found in a little cabin up there within the tower. "He says that they went up shouting like demons," continued Maria; and it seemed to me that she looked as though I ought to be ashamed of the name of an Englishman. "They may not be so solemn in their demeanour as Spaniards," I answered; "but, for all that, there may be quite as much in them."

We then again began to mount, and before we had ascended much further we passed my three countrymen. They were young men, with gray coats and gray trousers, with slouched hats, and without gloves. They had fair faces and fair hair, and swung big sticks in their hands, with crooked handles. They laughed and talked loud, and when we met them, seemed to be racing with each other; but nevertheless they were gentlemen. No one who knows by sight what an English gentleman is, could have doubted that; but I did acknowledge to myself that they should have remembered that the edifice they were treading was a church, and that the silence they were invading was the cherished property of a courteous people.

"They are all just the same as big boys," said Maria. The colour instantly flew into my face, and I felt that it was my duty to speak up for my own countrymen. The word "boys" especially wounded my ears. It was as a boy that she treated me; but, on looking at that befringed young Spanish Don—who was not, apparently, my elder in age—she had recognized a man. However, I said nothing further till I reached the summit. One cannot speak with manly dignity while one is out of breath on a staircase.

"There, John," she said, stretching her hands away over the fair plain of the Guadalquivir, as soon as we stood against the parapet; "is not that lovely?"

I would not deign to notice this. "Maria," I said, "I think that you are too hard upon my countrymen!"

"Too hard! No; for I love them. They are so good and industrious; and they come home to their wives, and take care of their children. But why do they make themselves so—so—what the French call *gauche*?"

"Good and industrious, and come home to their wives!" thought I. "I believe you hardly understand us as yet," I answered. "Our domestic virtues are not always so very prominent; but, I believe, we know how to conduct ourselves as gentlemen: at any rate, as well as Spaniards." I was very angry—not at the faults, but at the good qualities imputed to us.

"In affairs of business, yes," said Maria, with a look of firm confidence in her own opinion—that look of confidence she has never lost, and I pray that she may never lose it while I remain with her—"but in the little intercourses of the world, no! A Spaniard never forgets what is personally due either to himself or his neighbours. If he is eating an onion, he eats it as an onion should be eaten."

"In such matters as that he is very grand, no doubt," said I, angrily.

"And why should you not eat an onion properly, John? Now, I heard a story yesterday from Don——about two Englishmen, which annoyed me very much." I did not exactly catch the name of the Don in question, but I felt through every nerve in my body that it was the man who had been talking to her on the plaza.

"And what have they done?" said I. "But it is the same everywhere. We are always abused; but, nevertheless, no people are so welcome. At any rate, we pay for the mischief we do." I was angry with myself the moment the words were out of my mouth, for, after all, there is no feeling more mean than that pocket-confidence with which an Englishman sometimes swaggers.

"There was no mischief done in this case," she answered. "It was simply that two men have made themselves ridiculous for ever. The story is all about Seville, and, of course, it annoys me that they should be Englishmen."

"And what did they do?"

"The Marquis D'Almavivas was coming up to Seville in the boat, and they behaved to him in the most outrageous manner. He is here now, and is going to give a series of *fêtes*. Of course he will not ask a single Englishman."

"We shall manage to live, even though the Marquis D'Almavivas may frown upon us," said I, proudly.

"He is the richest, and also the best of our noblemen," continued Maria; "and I never heard of anything so absurd as what they did to him. It made me blush when Don——told me." Don Tomas, I thought she said.

"If he be the best of your noblemen, how comes it that he is angry because he has met two vulgar men? It is not to be supposed that every Englishman is a gentleman."

"Angry! Oh, no! he was not angry; he enjoyed the joke too much for that. He got completely the best of them, though they did not know it; poor fools! How would your Lord John Russell behave if two Spaniards in an English railway carriage were to pull him about and tear his clothes?"

"He would give them in charge to a policeman, of course," said I, speaking of such a matter with the contempt it deserved.

"If that were done here your ambassador would be demanding national explanations. But Almavivas did much better;—he laughed at them without letting them know it."

"But do you mean that they took hold of him violently, without any provocation? They must have been drunk."

"Oh, no, they were sober enough. I did not see it, so I do not quite know exactly how it was, but I understand that they committed themselves most absurdly, absolutely took hold of his coat and tore it, and—; but they did such ridiculous things that I cannot tell you." And yet Don Tomàs, if that was the man's name, had been able to tell her, and she had been able to listen to him.

"What made them take hold of the marquis?" said I.

"Curiosity, I suppose," she answered. "He dresses somewhat fancifully, and they could not understand that any one should wear garments different from their own." But even then the blow did not strike home upon me.

"Is it not pretty to look down upon the quiet town?" she said, coming close up to me, so that the skirt of her dress pressed me, and her elbow touched my arm. Now was the moment I should have asked her how her heart stood towards me; but I was sore and uncomfortable, and my destiny was before me. She was willing enough to let these English faults pass by without further notice, but I would not allow the subject to drop.

"I will find out who these men were," said I, "and learn the truth of it. When did it occur?"

"Last Thursday, I think he said."

"Why, that was the day we came up in the boat, Johnson and myself. There was no marquis there then, and we were the only Englishmen on board."

"It was on Thursday, certainly, because it was well known in Seville that he arrived on that day. You must have remarked him because he talks English perfectly—though, by-the-by, these men would go on chattering before him about himself as though it were impossible that a Spaniard should know their language. They are ignorant of Spanish, and they cannot bring themselves to believe that any one should be better educated than themselves."

Now the blow had fallen, and I straightway appreciated the necessity of returning immediately to Clapham, where my family resided, and giving up for ever all idea of Spanish connections. I had resolved to assert the full strength of my manhood on that tower, and now words had been spoken which left me weak as a child. I felt that I was shivering, and did not dare to pronounce the truth which must be made known. As to speaking of love, and signifying my pleasure that Don Tomas should for the future be kept at a distance, any such effort was quite beyond me. Had Don Tomas been there, he might have walked off with her from before my face without a struggle on my part. "Now I remember about it," she continued, "I think he must have been in the boat on Thursday."

"And now that I remember," I replied, turning away to hide my embarrassment, "he was there. Your friend down below in the plaza seems to have made out a grand story. No doubt he is not fond of the English. There was such a man there, and I did take hold— "

"O, John, was it you?"

"Yes, Donna Maria, it was I; and if Lord John Russell were to dress himself in the same way— " But I had no time to complete my description of what might occur under so extravagantly impossible a combination of circumstances, for as I was yet speaking, the little door leading out on to the leads of the tower was opened, and my friend, the mayo of the boat, still bearing all his gewgaws on his back, stepped up on to the platform. My eye instantly perceived that the one pendule was still missing from his jacket. He did not come alone, but three other gentlemen followed him, who, however, had no peculiarities in their dress. He saw me at once, and bowed and smiled; and then observing Donna Maria, he lifted his cap from his head, and addressing himself to her in Spanish, began to converse with her as though she were an old friend.

"Señor," said Maria, after the first words of greeting had been spoken between them; "you must permit me to present to you my father's most particular friend, and my own,—Mr. Pomfret; John, this is the Marquis D'Almavivas."

I cannot now describe the grace with which this introduction was effected, or the beauty of her face as she uttered the word. There was a boldness about her as though she had said, "I know it all—the whole story. But, in spite of that, you must take him on my representation, and be gracious to him in spite of what he has done. You must be content to do that; or in quarrelling with him you must quarrel with me also." And it was done at the spur of the moment—without delay. She, who not five minutes since had been loudly condemning the unknown Englishman for his rudeness, had already pardoned him, now that he was known to be her friend; and had determined that he should be pardoned by others also or that she would share his disgrace. I recognized the nobleness of this at the moment; but, nevertheless, I was so sore that I would almost have preferred that she should have disowned me.

The marquis immediately lifted his cap with his left hand while he gave me his right. "I have already had the pleasure of meeting this gentleman," he said; "we had some conversation in the boat together."

"Yes," said I, pointing to his rent, "and you still bear the marks of our encounter."

"Was it not delightful, Donna Maria," he continued, turning to her; "your friend's friend took me for a torero?"

"And it served you properly, señor," said Donna Maria, laughing; "you have no right to go about with all those rich ornaments upon you."

"Oh! quite properly; indeed, I make no complaint; and I must beg your friend to understand, and his friend also, how grateful I am for their solicitude as to my pecuniary welfare. They were inclined to be severe on me for being so extravagant in such trifles. I was obliged to explain that I had no wife at home kept without her proper allowance of dresses, in order that I might be gay."

"They are foreigners, and you should forgive their error," said she.

"And in token that I do so," said the marquis, "I shall beg your friend to accept the little ornament which attracted his attention." And so saying, he pulled the identical button out of his pocket, and gracefully proffered it to me.

"I shall carry it about with me always," said I, accepting it, "as a memento of humiliation. When I look at it, I shall ever remember the folly of an Englishman and the courtesy of a Spaniard;" and as I made the speech I could not but reflect whether it might, under any circumstances, be possible that Lord John Russell should be induced to give a button off his coat to a Spaniard.

There were other civil speeches made, and before we left the tower the marquis had asked me to his parties, and exacted from me an unwilling promise that I would attend them. "The señora," he said, bowing again to Maria, "would, he was sure, grace them. She had done so on the previous year; and as I had accepted his little present I was bound to acknowledge him as my friend." All this was very pretty, and of course I said that I would go, but I had not at that time the slightest intention of doing so. Maria had behaved admirably; she had covered my confusion, and shown herself not ashamed to own me, delinquent as I was; but, not the less, had she expressed her opinion, in language terribly strong, of the awkwardness of which I had been guilty, and had shown almost an aversion to my English character. I should leave Seville as quickly as I could, and should certainly not again put myself in the way of the Marquis D'Almavivas. Indeed, I dreaded the moment that I should be first alone with her, and should find myself forced to say something indicative of my feelings—to hear something also indicative of her feelings. I had come out this morning resolved to demand my rights and to exercise them—and now my only wish was to run away. I hated the marquis, and longed to be alone that I might cast his button from me. To think that a man should be so ruined by such a trifle!

We descended that prodigious flight without a word upon the subject, and almost without a word at all. She had carried herself well in the presence of Almavivas, and had been too proud to seem ashamed of her companion; but now, as I could well see, her feelings of disgust and contempt had returned. When I begged her not to hurry herself, she would hardly answer me; and when she did speak, her voice was constrained and unlike herself. And yet how beautiful she was! Well, my dream of Spanish love must be over. But I was sure of this: that having known her, and given her my heart, I could never afterwards share it with another.

We came out at last on the dark, gloomy aisle of the cathedral, and walked together without a word up along the side of the choir, till we came to the transept. There was not a soul near us, and not a sound was to be heard but the distant, low pattering of a mass, then in course of celebration at some far-off chapel in the cathedral. When we got to the transept Maria turned a little, as though she was going to the transept door, and then stopped herself. She stood still; and when I stood also, she made two steps towards me, and put her hand on my arm. "Oh, John!" she said.

"Well," said I; "after all it does not signify. You can make a joke of it when my back is turned."

"Dearest John!"—she had never spoken to me in that way before—"you must not be angry with me. It is better that we should explain to each other, is it not?"

"Oh, much better. I am very glad you heard of it at once. I do not look at it quite in the same light that you do; but nevertheless— "

"What do you mean? But I know you are angry with me. And yet you cannot think that I intended those words for you. Of course I know now that there was nothing rude in what passed."

"Oh, but there was."

"No, I am sure there was not. You could not be rude though you are so free hearted. I see it all now, and so does the marquis. You will like him so much when you come to know him. Tell me that you won't be cross with me for what I have said. Sometimes I think that I have displeased you, and yet my whole wish has been to welcome you to Seville, and to make you comfortable as an old friend. Promise me that you will not be cross with me."

Cross with her! I certainly had no intention of being cross, but I had begun to think that she would not care what my humour might be. "Maria," I said, taking hold of her hand.

"No, John, do not do that. It is in the church, you know."

"Maria, will you answer me a question?"

"Yes," she said, very slowly, looking down upon the stone slabs beneath our feet.

"Do you love me?"

"Love you!"

"Yes, do you love me? You were to give me an answer here, in Seville, and now I ask for it. I have almost taught myself to think that it is needless to ask; and now this horrid mischance— "

"What do you mean?" said she, speaking very quickly.

"Why this miserable blunder about the marquis's button! After that I suppose— "

"The marquis! Oh, John, is that to make a difference between you and me?—a little joke like that?"

"But does it not?"

"Make a change between us!—such a thing as that! Oh, John!"

"But tell me, Maria, what am I to hope? If you will say that you can love me, I shall care nothing for the marquis. In that case I can bear to be laughed at."

"Who will dare to laugh at you? Not the marquis, whom I am sure you will like."

"Your friend in the plaza, who told you of all this."

"What, poor Tomàs!"

"I do not know about his being poor. I mean the gentleman who was with you last night."

"Yes, Tomàs. You do not know who he is?"

"Not in the least."

"How droll! He is your own clerk—partly your own, now that you are one of the firm. And, John, I mean to make you do something for him; he is such a good fellow; and last year he married a young girl whom I love—oh, almost like a sister."

Do something for him! Of course I would. I promised, then and there, that I would raise his salary to any conceivable amount that a Spanish clerk could desire; which promise I have since kept, if not absolutely to the letter, at any rate, to an extent which has been considered satisfactory by the gentleman's wife.

"But, Maria—dearest Maria— "

"Remember, John, we are in the church; and poor papa will be waiting breakfast."

I need hardly continue the story further. It will be known to all that my love-suit throve in spite of my unfortunate raid on the button of the Marquis D'Almavivas, at whose series of *fêtes* through that month I was, I may boast, an honoured guest. I have since that had the pleasure of entertaining him in my own poor house in England, and one of our boys bears his Christian name.

From that day in which I ascended the Giralda to this present day in which I write, I have never once had occasion to complain of a deficiency of romance either in Maria Daguilar or in Maria Pomfret.

A Ride Across Palestine

Originally appeared in *The London Review*, 5, 12 and 19 January 1861, under the title 'The Banks of the Jordan.' Reprinted in *Tales of All Countries* [Second Series] (1863). A letter of 29 July 1860 states that the story was written 'within the last ten days.' The Holy Land setting (cf. *The Bertrams*) obviously derives from Trollope's 1858–59 postal mission to the Middle East. Trollope offered 'A Ride Across Palestine' to George Smith at the newly-formed *Cornhill Magazine*, who rejected it on grounds of indelicacy, but suggested alterations and cuts. Smith seems to have been particularly disturbed by the scene where the hero takes hold of his androgynous travelling companion's 'leg' to show where a Turkish saddle might chafe it. Trollope reckoned he might tone this down, but on the subject of a general trimming of the story he was adamant: 'One cannot shorten a story,' he wrote. 'Little passages are sure to hang on to what is taken out.' The story was eventually published by *The London Review* (together with 'Mrs. General Talboys'), whereupon Smith's worst fears were realised. A 'mild' complaint from the magazine's readership (among many stronger ones which have not survived) suggested that Trollope was writing for 'persons of morbid imagination and a low tone of morals.'

CIRCUMSTANCES TOOK me to the Holy Land without a companion, and compelled me to visit Bethany, the Mount of Olives, and the Church of the Sepulchre alone. I acknowledge myself to be a gregarious animal, or, perhaps, rather one of those which Nature has intended to go in pairs. At any rate I dislike solitude, and especially travelling solitude, and was, therefore, rather sad at heart as I sat one night at Z—'s hotel, in Jerusalem, thinking over my proposed wanderings for the next few days. Early on the following morning I intended to start, of course on horseback, for the Dead Sea, the banks of Jordan, Jericho, and those mountains of the wilderness through which it is supposed that Our Saviour wandered for the forty days when the Devil tempted him. I would then return to the Holy City, and remaining only long enough to refresh my horse and wipe the dust from my hands and feet, I would start again for Jaffa, and there catch a certain Austrian steamer which would take me to Egypt. Such was my programme, and I confess that I was but ill contented with it, seeing that I was to be alone during the time.

I had already made all my arrangements, and though I had no reason for any doubt as to my personal security during the trip, I did not feel altogether satisfied with them. I intended to take a French guide, or dragoman, who had been with me for some days, and to put myself under the peculiar guardianship of two Bedouin Arabs, who were to accompany me as long as I should remain east of Jerusalem. This travelling through the desert under the protection of Bedouins was, in idea, pleasant enough; and I must here declare that I did not at all begrudge the forty shillings which I was told by our British consul that I must pay them for their trouble, in accordance with the established tariff. But I did begrudge the fact of the tariff. I would rather have fallen in with my friendly Arabs, as it were, by chance, and have rewarded their fidelity at the end of our joint journeyings by a donation of piastres to be settled by myself, and which, under such circumstances, would certainly have been as agreeable to them as the stipulated sum. In the same way I dislike having waiters put down in my bill. I find that I pay them twice over, and thus lose money; and as they do not expect to be so treated, I never have the advantage of their civility. The world, I fear, is becoming too fond of tariffs.

"A tariff!" said I to the consul, feeling that the whole romance of my expedition would be dissipated by such an arrangement. "Then I'll go alone; I'll take a revolver with me."

"You can't do it, sir," said the consul, in a dry and somewhat angry tone. "You have no more right to ride through that country without paying the regular price for protection, than you have to stop in Z—'s hotel without settling the bill."

I could not contest the point, so I ordered my Bedouins for the appointed day, exactly as I would send for a ticket-porter at home, and determined to make the best of it. The wild unlimited sands, the desolation of the Dead Sea, the rushing waters of Jordan, the outlines of the mountains of Moab;—those things the consular tariff could not alter, nor deprive them of the glories of their association.

I had submitted, and the arrangements had been made. Joseph, my dragoman, was to come to me with the horses and an Arab groom at five in the morning, and we were to encounter our Bedouins outside the gate of St. Stephen, down the hill, where the road turns, close to the tomb of the Virgin.

I was sitting alone in the public room at the hotel, filling my flask with brandy,—for matters of primary importance I never leave to servant, dragoman, or guide,—when the waiter entered, and said that a gentleman wished to speak with me. The gentleman had not sent in his card or name; but any gentleman was welcome to me in my solitude, and I requested that the gentleman might enter. In appearance the gentleman certainly was a gentleman, for I thought that I had never before seen a young man whose looks were more in his favour, or whose face and gait and outward bearing seemed to betoken better breeding. He might be some twenty or twenty-one years of age, was slight and well made, with very black hair, which he wore rather long, very dark long bright eyes, a straight nose, and teeth that were perfectly white. He was dressed throughout in grey tweed clothing, having coat, waistcoat, and trousers of the same; and in his hand he carried a very broad-brimmed straw hat.

"Mr. Jones, I believe," he said, as he bowed to me. Jones is a good travelling name, and, if the reader will allow me, I will call myself Jones on the present occasion.

"Yes," I said, pausing with the brandy-bottle in one hand and the flask in the other. "That's my name; I'm Jones. Can I do anything for you, sir?"

"Why, yes, you can," said he. "My name is Smith,—John Smith."

"Pray sit down, Mr. Smith," I said, pointing to a chair. "Will you do anything in this way?" and I proposed to hand the bottle to him. "As far as I can judge from a short stay, you won't find much like that in Jerusalem."

He declined the Cognac, however, and immediately began his story. "I hear, Mr. Jones," said he, "that you are going to Moab to-morrow."

"Well," I replied; "I don't know whether I shall cross the water. It's not very easy, I take it, at all times; but I shall certainly get as far as Jordan. Can I do anything for you in those parts?"

And then he explained to me what was the object of his visit. He was quite alone in Jerusalem, as I was myself, and was staying at H—'s hotel. He had heard that I was starting for the Dead Sea, and had called to ask if I objected to his joining me. He had found himself, he said, very lonely; and as he had heard that I also was alone, he had ventured to call and make his proposition. He seemed to be very bashful, and half ashamed of what he was doing; and when he had done speaking he declared himself conscious that he was intruding, and expressed a hope that I would not hesitate to say so if his suggestion were from any cause disagreeable to me.

As a rule I am rather shy of chance travelling English friends. It has so frequently happened to me that I have had to blush for the acquaintances whom I have selected, that I seldom indulge in any close intimacies of this kind. But, nevertheless, I was taken with John Smith, in spite of his name. There was so much about him that was pleasant, both to the eye and to the understanding! One meets constantly with men from contact with whom one revolts without knowing the cause of such dislike. The cut of their beard is displeasing, or the mode in which they walk or speak. But, on the other hand, there are men who are attractive, and I must confess that I was attracted by John Smith at first sight. I hesitated, however, for a minute; for there are sundry things of which it behoves a traveller to think before he can join a companion for such a journey as that which I was about to make. Could the young man rise early, and remain in the saddle for ten hours together? Could he live upon hard-boiled eggs and brandy-and-water? Could he take his chance of a tent under which to sleep, and make himself happy with the bare fact of being in the desert? He saw my hesitation, and attributed it to a cause which was not present in my mind at the moment, though the subject is one of the greatest importance when strangers consent to join themselves together for a time, and agree to become no strangers on the spur of the moment.

"Of course I will take half the expense," said he, absolutely blushing as he mentioned the matter.

"As to that there will be very little. You have your own horse, of course?"

"Oh, yes."

"My dragoman and groom-boy will do for both. But you'll have to pay forty shillings to the Arabs! There's no getting over that. The consul won't even look after your dead body, if you get murdered, without going through that ceremony."

Mr. Smith immediately produced his purse, which he tendered to me. "If you will manage it all," said he, "it will make it so much the easier, and I shall be infinitely obliged to you." This of course I declined to do. I had no business with his purse, and explained to him that if we went together we could settle that on our return to Jerusalem. "But could he go through really hard work?" I asked. He answered me with an assurance that he would and could do anything in that way that it was possible for man to perform. As for eating and drinking he cared nothing about it, and would undertake to be astir at any hour of the morning that might be named. As for sleeping accommodation, he did not care if he kept his clothes on for a week together. He looked slight and weak; but he spoke so well, and that without boasting, that I ultimately agreed to his proposal, and in a few minutes he took his leave of me, promising to be at Z—'s door with his horse at five o'clock on the following morning.

"I wish you'd allow me to leave my purse with you," he said again.

"I cannot think of it. There is no possible occasion for it," I said again. "If there is anything to pay, I'll ask you for it when the journey is over. That forty shillings you must fork out. It's a law of the Medes and Persians."

"I'd better give it to you at once," he said, again offering me money. But I would not have it. It would be quite time enough for that when the Arabs were leaving us.

"Because," he added, "strangers, I know, are sometimes suspicious about money; and I would not, for worlds, have you think that I would put you to expense." I assured him that I did not think so, and then the subject was dropped.

He was, at any rate, up to his time, for when I came down on the following morning I found him in the narrow street, the first on horseback. Joseph, the Frenchman, was strapping on to a rough pony our belongings, and was staring at Mr. Smith. My new friend, unfortunately, could not speak a word of French, and therefore I had to explain to the dragoman how it had come to pass that our party was to be enlarged.

"But the Bedouins will expect full pay for both," said he, alarmed. Men in that class, and especially Orientals, always think that every arrangement of life, let it be made in what way it will, is made with the intention of saving some expense, or cheating somebody out of some amount of money. They do not understand that men can have any other object, and are ever on their guard lest the saving should be made at their cost, or lest they should be the victims of the fraud.

"All right," said I.

"I shall be responsible, Monsieur," said the dragoman, piteously.

"It shall be all right," said I, again. "If that does not satisfy you, you may remain behind."

"If Monsieur says it is all right, of course it is so;" and then he completed his strapping. We took blankets with us, of which I had to borrow two out of the hotel for my friend Smith, a small hamper of provisions, a sack containing forage for the horses, and a large empty jar, so that we might supply ourselves with water when leaving the neighbourhood of wells for any considerable time.

"I ought to have brought these things for myself," said Smith, quite unhappy at finding that he had thrown on me the necessity of catering for him. But I laughed at him, saying that it was nothing; he should do as much for me another time. I am prepared to own that I do not willingly rush up-stairs and load myself with blankets out of strange rooms for men whom I do not know; nor, as a rule, do I make all the Smiths of the world free of my canteen. But, with reference to this fellow I did feel more than ordinarily good-natured and unselfish. There was something in the tone of his voice which was satisfactory; and I should really have felt vexed had anything occurred at the last moment to prevent his going with me.

Let it be a rule with every man to carry an English saddle with him when travelling in the East. Of what material is formed the nether man of a Turk I have never been informed, but I am sure that it is not flesh and blood. No flesh and blood,—simply flesh and blood,—could withstand the wear and tear of a Turkish saddle. This being the case, and the consequences being well known to me, I was grieved to find that Smith was not properly provided. He was seated in one of those hard, red, high-pointed machines, to which the shovels intended to act as stirrups are attached in such a manner, and hang at such an angle, as to be absolutely destructive to the leg of a Christian. There is no part of the Christian body with which the Turkish saddle comes in contact that does not become more or less macerated. I have sat in one for days, but I left it a flayed man; and, therefore, I was sorry for Smith.

I explained this to him, taking hold of his leg by the calf to show how the leather would chafe him; but it seemed to me that he did not quite like my interference. "Never mind," said he, twitching his leg away, "I have ridden in this way before."

"Then you must have suffered the very mischief?"

"Only a little, and I shall be used to it now. You will not hear me complain."

"By heavens, you might have heard me complain a mile off when I came to the end of a journey I once took. I roared like a bull when I began to cool. Joseph, could you not get a European saddle for Mr. Smith?" But Joseph did not seem to like Mr. Smith, and declared such a thing to be impossible. No European in Jerusalem would think of lending so precious an article, except to a very dear friend. Joseph himself was on an English saddle, and I made up my mind that after the first stage, we would bribe him to make an exchange. And then we started. The Bedouins were not with us, but we were to meet them, as I have said before, outside St. Stephen's gate. "And if they are not there," said Joseph, "we shall be sure to come across them on the road."

"Not there!" said I. "How about the consul's tariff, if they don't keep their part of the engagement?" But Joseph explained to me that their part of the engagement really amounted to this,—that we should ride into their country without molestation, provided that such and such payments were made.

It was the period of Easter, and Jerusalem was full of pilgrims. Even at that early hour of the morning we could hardly make our way through the narrow streets. It must be understood that there is no accommodation in the town for the fourteen or fifteen thousand strangers who flock to the Holy Sepulchre at this period of the year. Many of them sleep out in the open air, lying on low benches which run along the outside walls of the houses, or even on the ground, wrapped in their thick hoods and cloaks. Slumberers such as these are easily disturbed, nor are they detained long at their toilets. They shake themselves like dogs, and growl and stretch themselves, and then they are ready for the day.

We rode out of the town in a long file. First went the groom-boy; I forget his proper Syrian appellation, but we used to call him Mucherry, that sound being in some sort like the name. Then followed the horse with the forage and blankets, and next to him my friend Smith in the Turkish saddle. I was behind him and Joseph brought up the rear. We moved slowly down the Via Dolorosa, noting the spot at which our Saviour is said to have fallen while bearing his cross; we passed by Pilate's house, and paused at the gate of the Temple,—the gate which once was beautiful,—looking down into the hole of the pool in which the maimed and halt were healed whenever the waters moved. What names they are! And yet there at Jerusalem they are bandied to and fro with as little reverence as are the fanciful appellations given by guides to rocks and stones and little lakes in all countries overrun by tourists.

"For those who would still fain believe,—let them stay at home," said my friend Smith.

"For those who cannot divide the wheat from the chaff, let *them* stay at home," I answered. And then we rode out through St. Stephen's gate, having the mountain of the men of Galilee directly before us, and the Mount of Olives a little to our right, and the Valley of Jehoshaphat lying between us and it. "Of course you know all these places now?" said Smith. I answered that I did know them well. "And was it not better for you when you knew them only in Holy Writ?" he asked.

"No, by Jove," said I. "The mountains stand where they ever stood. The same valleys are still green with the morning dew, and the water-courses are unchanged. The children of Mahomet may build their tawdry temple on the threshing-floor which David bought that there might stand the Lord's house. Man may undo what man did, even though the doer was Solomon. But here we have God's handiwork and his own evidences."

At the bottom of the steep descent from the city gate we came to the tomb of the Virgin; and by special agreement made with Joseph we left our horses here for a few moments, in order that we might descend into the subterranean chapel under the tomb, in which mass was at this moment being said. There is something awful in that chapel, when, as at the present moment, it is crowded with Eastern worshippers from the very altar up to the top of the dark steps by which the descent is made. It must be remembered that Eastern worshippers are not like the churchgoers of London, or even of Rome or Cologne. They are wild men of various nations and races,—Maronites from Lebanon, Roumelians, Candiotes, Copts from Upper Egypt, Russians from the Crimea, Armenians and Abyssinians. They savour strongly of Oriental life and of Oriental dirt. They are clad in skins or hairy cloaks with huge hoods. Their heads are shaved, and their faces covered with short, grisly, fierce beards. They are silent mostly, looking out of their eyes ferociously, as though murder were in their thoughts, and rapine. But they never slouch, or cringe in their bodies, or shuffle in their gait. Dirty, fierce-looking, uncouth, repellent as they are, there is always about them a something of personal dignity which is not compatible with an Englishman's ordinary hat and pantaloons.

As we were about to descend, preparing to make our way through the crowd, Smith took hold of my arm. "That will never do, my dear fellow," said I, "the job will be tough enough for a single file, but we should never cut our way two and two. I'm broad-shouldered and will go first." So I did, and gradually we worked our way into the body of the chapel. How is it that Englishmen can push themselves anywhere? These men were fierce-looking, and had murder and rapine, as I have said, almost in their eyes. One would have supposed that they were not lambs or doves, capable of being thrust here or there without anger on their part; and they, too, were all anxious to descend and approach the altar. Yet we did win our way through them, and apparently no man was angry with us. I doubt, after all, whether a ferocious eye and a strong smell and dirt are so efficacious in creating awe and obedience in others, as an open brow and traces of soap and water. I know this, at least,—that a dirty Maronite would make very little progress, if he attempted to shove his way unfairly through a crowd of Englishmen at the door of a London theatre. We did shove unfairly, and we did make progress, till we found ourselves in the centre of the dense crowd collected in the body of the chapel.

Having got so far, our next object was to get out again. The place was dark, mysterious, and full of strange odours; but darkness, mystery, and strange odours soon lose their charms when men have much work before them. Joseph had made a point of being allowed to attend mass before the altar of the Virgin, but a very few minutes sufficed for his prayers. So we again turned round and pushed our way back again, Smith still following in my wake. The men who had let us pass once let us pass again without opposition or show of anger. To them the occasion was very holy. They were stretching out their hands in every direction, with long tapers, in order that they might obtain a spark of the sacred fire which was burning on one of the altars. As we made our way out we passed many who, with dumb motions, begged us to assist them in their object. And we did assist them, getting lights for their tapers, handing them to and fro, and using the authority with which we seemed to be invested. But Smith, I observed, was much more courteous in this way to the women than to the men, as I did not forget to remind him when we were afterwards on our road together.

Remounting our horses we rode slowly up the winding ascent of the Mount of Olives, turning round at the brow of the hill to look back over Jerusalem. Sometimes I think that of all spots in the world this one should be the spot most cherished in the memory of Christians. It was there that He stood when He wept over the city. So much we do know, though we are ignorant, and ever shall be so, of the site of His cross and of the tomb. And then we descended on the eastern side of the hill, passing through Bethany, the town of Lazarus and his sisters, and turned our faces steadily towards the mountains of Moab.

Hitherto we had met no Bedouins, and I interrogated my dragoman about them more than once; but he always told me that it did not signify; we should meet them, he said, before any danger could arise. "As for danger," said I, "I think more of this than I do of the Arabs," and I put my hand on my revolver. "But as they agreed to be here, here they ought to be. Don't you carry a revolver, Smith?"

Smith said that he never had done so, but that he would take the charge of mine if I liked. To this, however, I demurred. "I never part with my pistol to any one," I said, rather drily. But he explained that he only intended to signify that if there were danger to be encountered, he would be glad to encounter it; and I fully believed him. "We shan't have much fighting," I replied; "but if there be any, the tool will come readiest to the hand of its master. But if you mean to remain here long I would advise you to get one. These Orientals are a people with whom appearances go a long way, and, as a rule, fear and respect mean the same thing with them. A pistol hanging over your loins is no great trouble to you, and looks as though you could bite. Many a dog goes through the world well by merely showing his teeth."

And then my companion began to talk of himself. "He did not," he said, "mean to remain in Syria very long."

"Nor I either," said I. "I have done with this part of the world for the present, and shall take the next steamer from Jaffa for Alexandria. I shall only have one night in Jerusalem on my return."

After this he remained silent for a few moments, and then declared that that also had been his intention. He was almost ashamed to say so, however, because it looked as though he had resolved to hook himself on to me. So he answered, expressing almost regret at the circumstance.

"Don't let that trouble you," said I; "I shall be delighted to have your company. When you know me better, as I hope you will do, you will find that if such were not the case I should tell you so as frankly. I shall remain in Cairo some little time; so that beyond our arrival in Egypt, I can answer for nothing."

He said that he expected letters at Alexandria which would govern his future movements. I thought he seemed sad as he said so, and imagined, from his manner, that he did not expect very happy tidings. Indeed I had made up my mind that he was by no means free from care or sorrow. He had not the air of a man who could say of himself that he was "totus teres atque rotundus." But I had no wish to inquire, and the matter would have dropped had he not himself added—"I fear that I shall meet acquaintances in Egypt whom it will give me no pleasure to see."

"Then," said I, "if I were you, I would go to Constantinople instead;—indeed, anywhere rather than fall among friends who are not friendly. And the nearer the friend is, the more one feels that sort of thing. To my way of thinking, there is nothing on earth so pleasant as a pleasant wife; but then, what is there so damnable as one that is unpleasant?"

"Are you a married man?" he inquired. All his questions were put in a low tone of voice which seemed to give to them an air of special interest, and made one almost feel that they were asked with some special view to one's individual welfare. Now the fact is, that I am a married man with a family; but I am not much given to talk to strangers about my domestic concerns, and, therefore, though I had no particular object in view, I denied my obligations in this respect. "No," said I; "I have not come to that promotion yet. I am too frequently on the move to write myself down as Paterfamilias."

"Then you know nothing about that pleasantness of which you spoke just now?"

"Nor of the unpleasantness, thank God; my personal experiences are all to come,—as also are yours, I presume?"

It was possible that he had hampered himself with some woman, and that she was to meet him at Alexandria. Poor fellow! thought I. But his unhappiness was not of that kind. "No," said he; "I am not married; I am all alone in the world."

"Then I certainly would not allow myself to be troubled by unpleasant acquaintances."

It was now four hours since we had left Jerusalem, and we had arrived at the place at which it was proposed that we should breakfast. There was a large well there, and shade afforded by a rock under which the water sprung; and the Arabs had constructed a tank out of which the horses could drink, so that the place was ordinarily known as the first stage out of Jerusalem.

Smith had said not a word about his saddle, or complained in any way of discomfort, so that I had in truth forgotten the subject. Other matters had continually presented themselves, and I had never even asked him how he had fared. I now jumped from my horse, but I perceived at once that he was unable to do so. He smile faintly, as his eye caught mine, but I knew that he wanted assistance. "Ah," said I, "that confounded Turkish saddle has already galled your skin. I see how it is; I shall have to doctor you with a little brandy,—externally applied, my friend." But I lent him my shoulder, and with that assistance he got down, very gently and slowly.

We ate our breakfast with a good will; bread and cold fowl and brandy-and-water, with a hard boiled egg by way of a final delicacy; and then I began to bargain with Joseph for the loan of his English saddle. I saw that Smith could not get through the journey with that monstrous Turkish affair, and that he would go on without complaining till he fainted or came to some other signal grief. But the Frenchman, seeing the plight in which we were, was disposed to drive a very hard bargain. He wanted forty shillings, the price of a pair of live Bedouins, for the accommodation, and declared that, even then, he should make the sacrifice only out of consideration to me.

"Very well," said I. "I'm tolerably tough myself, and I'll change with the gentleman. The chances are, that I shall not be in a very liberal humour when I reach Jaffa with stiff limbs and a sore skin. I have a very good memory, Joseph."

"I'll take thirty shillings, Mr. Jones; though I shall have to groan all the way like a condemned devil."

I struck a bargain with him at last for five-and-twenty, and set him to work to make the necessary change on the horses. "It will be just the same thing to him," I said to Smith. "I find that he is as much used to one as to the other."

"But how much money are you to pay him?" he asked. "Oh, nothing," I replied. "Give him a few piastres when you part with him at Jaffa." I do not know why I should have felt thus inclined to pay money out of my pocket for this Smith,—a man whom I had only seen for the first time on the preceding evening, and whose temperament was so essentially different from my own; but so I did. I would have done almost anything in reason for his comfort; and yet he was a melancholy fellow, with good inward pluck as I believed, but without that outward show of dash and hardihood which I confess I love to see. "Pray tell him that I'll pay him for it," said he. "We'll make that all right," I answered; and then we remounted,—not without some difficulty on his part. "You should have let me rub in that brandy," I said. "You can't conceive how efficaciously I would have done it." But he made me no answer.

At noon we met a caravan of pilgrims coming up from Jordan. There might be some three or four hundred, but the number seemed to be treble that, from the loose and straggling line in which they journeyed. It was a very singular sight, as they moved slowly along the narrow path through the sand, coming out of a defile among the hills which was perhaps a quarter of a mile in front of us, passing us as we stood still by the wayside, and then winding again out of sight on the track over which we had come. Some rode on camels,—a whole family, in many cases, being perched on the same animal. I observed a very old man and a very old woman slung in panniers over a camel's back,—not such panniers as might be befitting such a purpose, but square baskets, so that the heads and heels of each of the old couple hung out of the rear and front. "Surely the journey will be their death," I said to Joseph. "Yes, it will," he replied, quite coolly; "but what matter how soon they die now that they have bathed in Jordan?" Very many rode on donkeys; two, generally, on each donkey; others, who had command of money, on horses; but the greater number walked, toiling painfully from Jerusalem to Jericho on the first day, sleeping there in tents and going to bathe in Jordan on the second day, and then returning from Jericho to Jerusalem on the third. The pilgrimage is made throughout in accordance with fixed rules, and there is a tariff for the tent accommodation at Jericho,—so much per head per night, including the use of hot water.

Standing there, close by the wayside, we could see not only the garments and faces of these strange people, but we could watch their gestures and form some opinion of what was going on within their thoughts. They were much quieter,—tamer, as it were,—than Englishmen would be under such circumstances. Those who were carried seemed to sit on their beasts in passive tranquillity, neither enjoying anything nor suffering anything. Their object had been to wash in Jordan,—to do that once in their lives;—and they had washed in Jordan. The benefit expected was not to be immediately spiritual. No earnest prayerfulness was considered necessary after the ceremony. To these members of the Greek Christian Church it had been handed down from father to son that washing in Jordan once during life was efficacious towards salvation. And therefore the journey had been made at terrible cost and terrible risk; for these people had come from afar, and were from their habits but little capable of long journeys. Many die under the toil; but this matters not if they do not die before they have reached Jordan. Some few there are, undoubtedly, more ecstatic in this great deed of their religion. One man I especially noticed on this day. He had bound himself to make the pilgrimage from Jerusalem to the river with one foot bare. He was of a better class, and was even nobly dressed, as though it were a part of his vow to show to all men that he did this deed, wealthy and great though he was. He was a fine man, perhaps thirty years of age, with a well-grown beard descending on his breast, and at his girdle he carried a brace of pistols. But never in my life had I seen bodily pain so plainly written in a man's face. The sweat was falling from his brow, and his eyes were strained and bloodshot with agony. He had no stick, his vow, I presume, debarring him from such assistance, and he limped along, putting to the ground the heel of the unprotected foot. I could see it, and it was a mass of blood, and sores, and broken skin. An Irish girl would walk from Jerusalem to Jericho without shoes, and be not a penny the worse for it. This poor fellow clearly suffered so much that I was almost inclined to think that in the performance of his penance he had done something to aggravate his pain. Those around him paid no attention to him, and the dragoman seemed to think nothing of the affair whatever. "Those fools of Greeks do not understand the Christian religion," he said, being himself a Latin or Roman Catholic.

At the tail of the line we encountered two Bedouins, who were in charge of the caravan, and Joseph at once addressed them. The men were mounted, one on a very sorry-looking jade, but the other on a good stout Arab barb. They had guns slung behind their backs, coloured handkerchiefs on their heads, and they wore the striped bernouse. The parley went on for about ten minutes, during which the procession of pilgrims wound out of sight; and it ended in our being accompanied by the two Arabs, who thus left their greater charge to take care of itself back to the city. I understood afterwards that they had endeavoured to persuade Joseph that we might just as well go on alone, merely satisfying the demand of the tariff. But he had pointed out that I was a particular man, and that under such circumstances the final settlement might be doubtful. So they turned and accompanied us; but, as a matter of fact, we should have been as well without them.

The sun was beginning to fall in the heavens when we reached the actual margin of the Dead Sea. We had seen the glitter of its still waters for a long time previously, shining under the sun as though it were not real. We have often heard, and some of us have seen, how effects of light and shade together will produce so vivid an appearance of water where there is no water, as to deceive the most experienced. But the reverse was the case here. There was the lake, and there it had been before our eyes for the last two hours; and yet it looked, then and now, as though it were an image of a lake, and not real water. I had long since made up my mind to bathe in it, feeling well convinced that I could do so without harm to myself, and I had been endeavouring to persuade Smith to accompany me; but he positively refused. He would bathe, he said, neither in the Dead Sea nor in the river Jordan. He did not like bathing, and preferred to do his washing in his own room. Of course I had nothing further to say, and begged that, under these circumstances, he would take charge of my purse and pistols while I was in the water. This he agreed to do; but even in this he was strange and almost uncivil. I was to bathe from the furthest point of a little island, into which there was a rough causeway from the land made of stones and broken pieces of wood, and I exhorted him to go with me thither; but he insisted on remaining with his horse on the mainland at some little distance from the island. He did not feel inclined to go down to the water's edge, he said.

I confess that at this I almost suspected that he was going to play me foul, and I hesitated. He saw in an instant what was passing through my mind. "You had better take your pistol and money with you; they will be quite safe on your clothes." But to have kept the things now would have shown suspicion too plainly, and as I could not bring myself to do that, I gave them up. I have sometimes thought that I was a fool to do so.

I went away by myself to the end of the island, and then I did bathe. It is impossible to conceive anything more desolate than the appearance of the place. The land shelves very gradually away to the water, and the whole margin, to the breadth of some twenty or thirty feet, is strewn with the débris of rushes, bits of timber, and old white withered reeds. Whence these bits of timber have come it seems difficult to say. The appearance is as though the water had receded and left them there. I have heard it said that there is no vegetation near the Dead Sea; but such is not the case, for these rushes do grow on the bank. I found it difficult enough to get into the water, for the ground shelves down very slowly, and is rough with stones and large pieces of half-rotten wood; moreover, when I was in nearly up to my hips, the water knocked me down; indeed, it did so when I had gone as far as my knees, but I recovered myself, and by perseverance did proceed somewhat further. It must not be imagined that this knocking down was effected by the movement of the water. There is no such movement. Everything is perfectly still, and the fluid seems hardly to be displaced by the entrance of the body; but the effect is that one's feet are tripped up, and that one falls prostrate on to the surface. The water is so strong and buoyant, that, when above a foot in depth has to be encountered, the strength and weight of the bather are not sufficient to keep down his feet and legs. I then essayed to swim; but I could not do this in the ordinary way, as I was unable to keep enough of my body below the surface; so that my head and face seemed to be propelled down upon it. I turned round and floated, but the glare of the sun was so powerful that I could not remain long in that position. However, I had bathed in the Dead Sea, and was so far satisfied.

Anything more abominable to the palate than this water, if it be water, I never had inside my mouth. I expected it to be extremely salt, and no doubt, if it were analyzed, such would be the result; but there is a flavour in it which kills the salt. No attempt can be made at describing this taste. It may be imagined that I did not drink heartily, merely taking up a drop or two with my tongue from the palm of my hand; but it seemed to me as though I had been drenched with it. Even brandy would not relieve me from it. And then my whole body was in a mess, and I felt as though I had been rubbed with pitch. Looking at my limbs, I saw no sign on them of the fluid. They seemed to dry from this as they usually do from any other water; but still the feeling remained. However, I was to ride from hence to a spot on the banks of Jordan, which I should reach in an hour, and at which I would wash; so I clothed myself, and prepared for my departure.

Seated in my position in the island I was unable to see what was going on among the remainder of the party, and therefore could not tell whether my pistols and money were safe. I dressed, therefore, rather hurriedly, and on getting again to the shore, found that Mr. John Smith had not levanted. He was seated on his horse at some distance from Joseph and the Arabs, and had no appearance of being in league with those, no doubt, worthy guides. I certainly had suspected a ruse, and now was angry with myself that I had done so; and yet, in London, one would not trust one's money to a stranger whom one had met twenty-four hours since in a coffee-room! Why, then, do it with a stranger whom one chanced to meet in a desert?

"Thanks," I said, as he handed me my belongings. "I wish I could have induced you to come in also. The Dead Sea is now at your elbow, and, therefore, you think nothing of it; but in ten or fifteen years' time, you would be glad to be able to tell your children that you had bathed in it."

"I shall never have any children to care for such tidings," he replied.

The river Jordan, for some miles above the point at which it joins the Dead Sea, runs through very steep banks,—banks which are almost precipitous,—and is, as it were, guarded by the thick trees and bushes which grow upon its sides. This is so much the case, that one may ride, as we did, for a considerable distance along the margin, and not be able even to approach the water. I had a fancy for bathing in some spot of my own selection, instead of going to the open shore frequented by all the pilgrims; but I was baffled in this. When I did force my way down to the river side, I found that the water ran so rapidly, and that the bushes and boughs of trees grew so far over and into the stream, as to make it impossible for me to bathe. I could not have got in without my clothes, and having got in, I could not have got out again. I was, therefore, obliged to put up with the open muddy shore to which the bathers descend, and at which we may presume that Joshua passed when he came over as one of the twelve spies to spy out the land. And even here I could not go full into the stream as I would fain have done, lest I should be carried down, and so have assisted to whiten the shores of the Dead Sea with my bones. As to getting over to the Moabitish side of the river, that was plainly impossible; and, indeed, it seemed to be the prevailing opinion that the passage of the river was not practicable without going up as far as Samaria. And yet we know that there, or thereabouts, the Israelites did cross it.

I jumped from my horse the moment I got to the place, and once more gave my purse and pistols to my friend. "You are going to bathe again?" he said. "Certainly," said I; "you don't suppose that I would come to Jordan and not wash there, even if I were not foul with the foulness of the Dead Sea!" "You'll kill yourself, in your present state of heat;" he said, remonstrating just as one's mother or wife might do. But even had it been my mother or wife I could not have attended to such remonstrance then; and before he had done looking at me with those big eyes of his, my coat and waist-coat and cravat were on the ground, and I was at work at my braces; whereupon he turned from me slowly, and strolled away into the wood. On this occasion I had no base fears about my money.

And then I did bathe,—very uncomfortably. The shore was muddy with the feet of the pilgrims, and the river so rapid that I hardly dared to get beyond the mud. I did manage to take a plunge in, head-foremost, but I was forced to wade out through the dirt and slush, so that I found it difficult to make my feet and legs clean enough for my shoes and stockings; and then, moreover, the flies plagued me most unmercifully. I should have thought that the filthy flavour from the Dead Sea would have saved me from that nuisance; but the mosquitoes thereabouts are probably used to it. Finding this process of bathing to be so difficult, I inquired as to the practice of the pilgrims. I found that with them, bathing in Jordan has come to be much the same as baptism has with us. It does not mean immersion. No doubt they do take off their shoes and stockings; but they do not strip, and go bodily into the water.

As soon as I was dressed I found that Smith was again at my side with purse and pistols. We then went up a little above the wood, and sat down together on the long sandy grass. It was now quite evening, so that the short Syrian twilight had commenced, and the sun was no longer hot in the heavens. It would be night as we rode on to the tents at Jericho; but there was no difficulty as to the way, and therefore we did not hurry the horses, who were feeding on the grass. We sat down together on a spot from which we could see the stream,—close together, so that when I stretched myself out in my weariness, as I did before we started, my head rested on his legs. Ah, me! one does not take such liberties with new friends in England. It was a place which led one on to some special thoughts. The mountains of Moab were before us, very plain in their outline. "Moab is my wash-pot, and over Edom will I cast out my shoe!" There they were before us, very visible to the eye, and we began naturally to ask questions of each other. Why was Moab the wash-pot, and Edom thus cursed with indignity? Why had the right bank of the river been selected for such great purposes, whereas the left was thus condemned? Was there, at that time, any special fertility in this land of promise which has since departed from it? We are told of a bunch of grapes which took two men to carry it; but now there is not a vine in the whole country side. Now-a-days the sandy plain round Jericho is as dry and arid as are any of the valleys of Moab. The Jordan was running beneath our feet,—the Jordan in which the leprous king had washed, though the bright rivers of his own Damascus were so much nearer to his hand. It was but a humble stream to which he was sent; but the spot, probably, was higher up, above the Sea of Galilee, where the river is narrow. But another also had come down to this river, perhaps to this very spot on its shores, and submitted himself to its waters;—as to whom, perhaps, it will better that I should not speak much in this light story.

The Dead Sea was on our right, still glittering in the distance, and behind us lay the plains of Jericho and the wretched collection of huts which still bears the name of the ancient city. Beyond that, but still seemingly within easy distance of us, were the mountains of the wilderness. The wilderness! In truth, the spot was one which did lead to many thoughts.

We talked of these things, as to many of which I found that my friend was much more free in his doubts and questionings than myself; and then our words came back to ourselves, the natural centre of all men's thoughts and words. "From what you say," I said, "I gather that you have had enough of this land?"

"Quite enough," he said. "Why seek such spots as these, if they only dispel the associations and veneration of one's childhood?"

"But with me such associations and veneration are riveted the stronger by seeing the places, and putting my hand upon the spots. I do not speak of that fictitious marble slab up there; but here, among the sandhills by this river, and at the Mount of Olives over which we passed, I do believe."

He paused a moment, and then replied: "To me it is all nothing,—absolutely nothing. But then do we not know that our thoughts are formed, and our beliefs modelled, not on the outward signs or intrinsic evidences of things,—as would be the case were we always rational,—but by the inner workings of the mind itself? At the present turn of my life I can believe in nothing that is gracious."

"Ah, you mean that you are unhappy. You have come to grief in some of your doings or belongings, and therefore find that all things are bitter to the taste. I have had my palate out of order too; but the proper appreciation of flavours has come back to me. Bah,—how noisome was that Dead Sea water!"

"The Dead Sea waters are noisome," he said; "and I have been drinking of them by long draughts."

"Long draughts!" I answered, thinking to console him. "Draughts have not been long which can have been swallowed in your years. Your disease may be acute, but it cannot yet have become chronic. A man always thinks at the moment of each misfortune that that special misery will last his lifetime; but God is too good for that. I do not know what ails you; but this day twelvemonth will see you again as sound as a roach."

We then sat silent for a while, during which I was puffing at a cigar. Smith, among his accomplishments, did not reckon that of smoking,—which was a grief to me; for a man enjoys the tobacco doubly when another is enjoying it with him.

"No, you do not know what ails me," he said at last, "and, therefore, cannot judge."

"Perhaps not, my dear fellow. But my experience tells me that early wounds are generally capable of cure; and, therefore, I surmise that yours may be so. The heart at your time of life is not worn out, and has strength and soundness left wherewith to throw off its maladies. I hope it may be so with you."

"God knows. I do not mean to say that there are none more to be pitied than I am; but at the present moment, I am not—not light-hearted."

"I wish I could ease your burden, my dear fellow."

"It is most preposterous in me thus to force myself upon you, and then trouble you with my cares. But I had been alone so long, and I was so weary of it!"

"By Jove, and so had I. Make no apology. And let me tell you this,—though perhaps you will not credit me;—that I would sooner laugh with a comrade than cry with him is true enough; but, if occasion demands, I can do the latter also." He then put out his hand to me, and I pressed it in token of my friendship. My own hand was hot and rough with the heat and sand; but his was soft and cool almost as a woman's. I thoroughly hate an effeminate man; but, in spite of a certain womanly softness about this fellow, I could not hate him. "Yes," I continued, "though somewhat unused to the melting mood, I also sometimes give forth my medicinal gums. I don't want to ask you any questions, and, as a rule, I hate to be told secrets, but if I can be of any service to you in any matter I will do my best. I don't say this with reference to the present moment, but think of it before we part."

I looked round at him and saw that he was in tears. "I know that you will think that I am a weak fool," he said, pressing his handkerchief to his eyes.

"By no means. There are moments in a man's life when it becomes him to weep like a woman; but the older he grows the more seldom those moments come to him. As far as I can see of men, they never cry at that which disgraces them."

"It is left for women to do that," he answered.

"Oh, women! A woman cries for everything and for nothing. It is the sharpest arrow she has in her quiver,—the best card in her hand. When a woman cries, what can you do but give her all she asks for?"

"Do you—dislike women?"

"No, by Jove! I am never really happy unless one is near me,—or more than one. A man, as a rule, has an amount of energy within him which he cannot turn to profit on himself alone. It is good for him to have a woman by him that he may work for her, and thus have exercise for his limbs and faculties. I am very fond of women. But I always like those best who are most helpless."

We were silent again for a while, and it was during this time that I found myself lying with my head in his lap. I had slept, but it could have been but for a few minutes, and when I woke I found his hand upon my brow. As I started up he said that the flies had been annoying me, and that he had not chosen to waken me as I seemed weary. "It has been that double bathing," I said, apologetically; for I always feel ashamed when I am detected sleeping in the day. "In hot weather the water does make one drowsy. By Jove, it's getting dark; we had better have the horses."

"Stay half a moment," he said, speaking very softly, and laying his hand upon my arm, "I will not detain you a minute."

"There is no hurry in life," I said.

"You promised me just now you would assist me."

"If it be in my power, I will."

"Before we part at Alexandria I will endeavour to tell you the story of my troubles, and then, if you can aid me— " It struck me as he paused that I had made a rash promise, but nevertheless I must stand by it now—with one or two provisoes. The chances were that the young man was short of money, or else that he had got into a scrape about a girl. In either case I might give him some slight assistance; but, then, it behoved me to make him understand that I would not consent to become a participator in mischief. I was too old to get my head willingly into a scrape, and this I must endeavour to make him understand.

"I will, if it be in my power," I said. "I will ask no questions now; but if your trouble be about some lady— "

"It is not," said he.

"Well; so be it. Of all troubles those are the most troublesome. If you are short of cash— "

"No, I am not short of cash."

"You are not. That's well too; for want of money is a sore trouble also." And then I paused before I came to the point. "I do not suspect anything bad of you, Smith. Had I done so, I should not have spoken as I have done. And if there be nothing bad— "

"There is nothing disgraceful," he said.

"That is just what I mean; and in that case I will do anything for you that may be within my power. Now let us look for Joseph and the mucherry-boy, for it is time that we were at Jericho."

I cannot describe at length the whole of our journey from thence to our tents at Jericho, nor back to Jerusalem, nor even from Jerusalem to Jaffa. At Jericho we did sleep in tents, paying so much per night, according to the tariff. We wandered out at night, and drank coffee with a family of Arabs in the desert, sitting in a ring round their coffee-kettle. And we saw a Turkish soldier punished with the bastinado,—a sight which did not do me any good, and which made Smith very sick. Indeed after the first blow he walked away. Jericho is a remarkable spot in that pilgrim week, and I wish I had space to describe it. But I have not, for I must hurry on, back to Jerusalem and thence to Jaffa. I had much to tell also of those Bedouins; how they were essentially true to us, but teased us almost to frenzy by their continual begging. They begged for our food and our drink, for our cigars and our gunpowder, for the clothes off our backs, and the handkerchiefs out of our pockets. As to gunpowder I had none to give them, for my charges were all made up in cartridges; and I learned that the guns behind their backs were a mere pretence, for they had not a grain of powder among them.

We slept one night in Jerusalem, and started early on the following morning. Smith came to my hotel so that we might be ready together for the move. We still carried with us Joseph and the mucherry-boy; but for our Bedouins, who had duly received their forty shillings a piece, we had no further use. On our road down to Jerusalem we had much chat together, but only one adventure. Those pilgrims, of whom I have spoken, journey to Jerusalem in the greatest number by the route which we were now taking from it, and they come in long droves, reaching Jaffa in crowds by the French and Austrian steamers from Smyrna, Damascus, and Constantinople. As their number confers security in that somewhat insecure country, many travellers from the west of Europe make arrangements to travel with them. On our way down we met the last of these caravans for the year, and we were passing it for more than two hours. On this occasion I rode first, and Smith was immediately behind me; but of a sudden I observed him to wheel his horse round, and to clamber downwards among bushes and stones towards a river that ran below us. "Hallo, Smith," I cried, "you will destroy your horse, and yourself too." But he would not answer me, and all I could do was to draw up in the path and wait. My confusion was made the worse, as at that moment a long string of pilgrims was passing by. "Good morning, sir," said an old man to me in good English. I looked up as I answered him, and saw a grey-haired gentleman, of very solemn and sad aspect. He might be seventy years of age, and I could see that he was attended by three or four servants. I shall never forget the severe and sorrowful expression of his eyes, over which his heavy eyebrows hung low. "Are there many English in Jerusalem?" he asked. "A good many," I replied; "there always are at Easter." "Can you tell me anything of any of them?" he asked. "Not a word," said I, for I knew no one; "but our consul can." And then we bowed to each other and he passed on.

I got off my horse and scrambled down on foot after Smith. I found him gathering berries and bushes as though his very soul were mad with botany; but as I had seen nothing of this in him before, I asked what strange freak had taken him.

"You were talking to that old man," he said.

"Well, yes, I was."

"That is the relation of whom I have spoken to you."

"The d——he is!"

"And I would avoid him, if it be possible."

I then learned that the old gentleman was his uncle. He had no living father or mother, and he now supposed that his relative was going to Jerusalem in quest of him. "If so," said I, "you will undoubtedly give him leg bail, unless the Austrian boat is more than ordinarily late. It is as much as we shall do to catch it, and you may be half over Africa, or far gone on your way to India, before he can be on your track again."

"I will tell you all about it at Alexandria," he replied; and then he scrambled up again with his horse, and we went on. That night we slept at the Armenian convent at Ramlath, or Ramath. This place is supposed to stand on the site of Arimathea, and is marked as such in many of the maps. The monks at this time of the year are very busy, as the pilgrims all stay here for one night on their routes backwards and forwards, and the place on such occasions is terribly crowded. On the night of our visit it was nearly empty, as a caravan had left it that morning; and thus we were indulged with separate cells, a point on which my companion seemed to lay considerable stress.

On the following day, at about noon, we entered Jaffa, and put up at an inn there which is kept by a Pole. The boat from Beyrout, which touches at Jaffa on its way to Alexandria, was not yet in, nor even sighted; we were therefore amply in time. "Shall we sail to-night?" I asked of the agent. "Yes, in all probability," he replied. "If the signal be seen before three we shall do so. If not, then not;" and so I returned to the hotel.

Smith had involuntarily shown signs of fatigue during the journey, but yet he had borne up well against it. I had never felt called on to grant any extra indulgence as to time because the work was too much for him. But now he was a good deal knocked up, and I was a little frightened, fearing that I had over-driven him under the heat of the sun. I was alarmed lest he should have fever, and proposed to send for the Jaffa doctor. But this he utterly refused. He would shut himself for an hour or two in his room, he said, and by that time he trusted the boat would be in sight. It was clear to me that he was very anxious on the subject, fearing that his uncle would be back upon his heels before he had started.

I ordered a serious breakfast for myself, for with me, on such occasions, my appetite demands more immediate attention than my limbs. I also acknowledge that I become fatigued, and can lay myself at length during such idle days and sleep from hour to hour; but the desire to do so never comes till I have well eaten and drunken. A bottle of French wine, three or four cutlets of goats' flesh, an omelet made not of the freshest eggs, and an enormous dish of oranges, was the banquet set before me; and though I might have found fault with it in Paris or London, I thought that it did well enough in Jaffa. My poor friend could not join me, but had a cup of coffee in his room. "At any rate take a little brandy in it," I said to him, as I stood over his bed. "I could not swallow it," said he, looking at me with almost beseeching eyes. "Beshrew the fellow," I said to myself as I left him, carefully closing the door, so that the sound should not shake him; "He is little better than a woman, and yet I have become as fond of him as though he were my brother."

I went out at three, but up to that time the boat had not been signalled. "And we shall not get out to-night?" "No, not to-night," said the agent. "And at what time to-morrow?" "If she comes in this evening, you will start by daylight. But they so manage her departure from Beyrout, that she seldom is here in the evening." "It will be noon to-morrow then?" "Yes," the man said, "noon to-morrow." I calculated, however, that the old gentleman could not possibly be on our track by that time. He would not have reached Jerusalem till late in the day on which we saw him, and it would take him some time to obtain tidings of his nephew. But it might be possible that messengers sent by him should reach Jaffa by four or five on the day after his arrival. That would be this very day which we were now wasting at Jaffa. Having thus made my calculations, I returned to Smith to give him such consolation as it might be in my power to afford.

He seemed to be dreadfully afflicted by all this. "He will have traced me to Jerusalem, and then again away; and will follow me immediately."

"That is all very well," I said; "but let even a young man do the best he can, and he will not get from Jerusalem to Jaffa in less than twelve hours. Your uncle is not a young man, and could not possibly do the journey under two days."

"But he will send. He will not mind what money he spends."

"And if he does send, take off your hat to his messengers, and bid them carry your compliments back. You are not a felon whom he can arrest."

"No, he cannot arrest me; but, ah! you do not understand;" and then he sat up on the bed, and seemed as though he were going to wring his hands in despair.

I waited for some half hour in his room, thinking that he would tell me this story of his. If he required that I should give him my aid in the presence either of his uncle or of his uncle's myrmidons, I must at any rate know what was likely to be the dispute between them. But as he said nothing I suggested that he should stroll out with me among the orange-groves by which the town is surrounded. In answer to this he looked up piteously into my face as though begging me to be merciful to him. "You are strong," said he, "and cannot understand what it is to feel fatigue as I do." And yet he had declared on commencing his journey that he would not be found to complain? Nor had he complained by a single word till after that encounter with his uncle. Nay he had borne up well till this news had reached us of the boat being late. I felt convinced that if the boat were at this moment lying in the harbour all that appearance of excessive weakness would soon vanish. What it was that he feared I could not guess; but it was manifest to me that some great terror almost overwhelmed him.

"My idea is," said I,—and I suppose that I spoke with something less of good-nature in my tone than I had assumed for the last day or two, "that no man should, under any circumstances, be so afraid of another man, as to tremble at his presence,—either at his presence or his expected presence."

"Ah, now you are angry with me; now you despise me!"

"Neither the one nor the other. But if I may take the liberty of a friend with you, I would advise you to combat this feeling of horror. If you do not, it will unman you. After all, what can your uncle do to you? He cannot rob you of your heart or soul. He cannot touch your inner self."

"You do not know," he said.

"Ah but, Smith, I do know that. Whatever may be this quarrel between you and him, you should not tremble at the thought of him; unless indeed— "

"Unless what?"

"Unless you had done aught that should make you tremble before every honest man." I own I had begun to have my doubts of him, and to fear that he had absolutely disgraced himself. Even in such case I,—I individually,—did not wish to be severe on him; but I should be annoyed to find that I had opened my heart to a swindler or a practised knave.

"I will tell you all to-morrow," said he; "but I have been guilty of nothing of that sort."

In the evening he did come out, and sat with me as I smoked my cigar. The boat, he was told, would almost undoubtedly come in by daybreak on the following morning, and be off at nine; whereas it was very improbable that any arrival from Jerusalem would be so early as that. "Beside," I reminded him, "your uncle will hardly hurry down to Jaffa, because he will have no reason to think but what you have already started. There are no telegraphs here, you know."

In the evening he was still very sad, though the paroxysm of his terror seemed to have passed away. I would not bother him, as he had himself chosen the following morning for the telling of his story. So I sat and smoked, and talked to him about our past journey, and by degrees the power of speech came back to him, and I again felt that I loved him. Yes, loved him! I have not taken many such fancies into my head, at so short a notice; but I did love him, as though he were a younger brother. I felt a delight in serving him, and though I was almost old enough to be his father, I ministered to him as though he had been an old man, or a woman.

On the following morning we were stirring at day-break, and found that the vessel was in sight. She would be in the roads off the town in two hours' time, they said, and would start at eleven or twelve. And then we walked round by the gate of the town, and sauntered a quarter of a mile or so along the way that leads towards Jerusalem. I could see that his eye was anxiously turned down the road, but he said nothing. We saw no cloud of dust, and then we returned to breakfast.

"The steamer has come to anchor," said our dirty Polish host to us in execrable English. "And we may be off on board," said Smith. "Not yet," he said; "they must put their cargo out first." I saw, however, that Smith was uneasy, and I made up my mind to go off to the vessel at once. When they should see an English portmanteau making an offer to come up the gangway, the Austrian sailors would not stop it. So I called for the bill, and ordered that the things should be taken down to the wretched broken heap of rotten timber which they called a quay. Smith had not told me his story, but no doubt he would as soon as he was on board.

I was in the very act of squabbling with the Pole over the last demand for piastres, when we heard a noise in the gateway of the inn, and I saw Smith's countenance become pale. It was an Englishman's voice asking if there were any strangers there; so I went into the courtyard, closing the door behind me, and turning the key upon the landlord and Smith. "Smith," said I to myself, "will keep the Pole quiet if he have any wit left."

The man who had asked the question had the air of an upper English servant, and I thought that I recognised one of those whom I had seen with the old gentleman on the road; but the matter was soon put at rest by the appearance of that gentleman himself. He walked up into the courtyard, looked hard at me from under those bushy eyebrows, just raised his hat, and then said, "I believe I am speaking to Mr. Jones."

"Yes," said I, "I am Mr. Jones. Can I have the honour of serving you?"

There was something peculiarly unpleasant about this man's face. At the present moment I examined it closely, and could understand the great aversion which his nephew felt towards him. He looked like a gentleman and like a man of talent, nor was there anything of meanness in his face; neither was he ill-looking, in the usual acceptation of the word; but one could see that he was solemn, austere, and overbearing; that he would be incapable of any light enjoyment, and unforgiving towards all offences. I took him to be a man who, being old himself, could never remember that he had been young, and who, therefore, hated the levities of youth. To me such a character is specially odious; for I would fain, if it be possible, be young even to my grave. Smith, if he were clever, might escape from the window of the room, which opened out upon a terrace, and still get down to the steamer. I would keep the old man in play for some time; and, even though I lost my passage, would be true to my friend. There lay our joint luggage at my feet in the yard. If Smith would venture away without his portion of it, all might yet be right.

"My name, sir, is Sir William Weston," he began. I had heard of the name before, and knew him to be a man of wealth, and family, and note. I took off my hat, and said that I had much honour in meeting Sir William Weston.

"And I presume you know the object with which I am now here," he continued.

"Not exactly," said I. "Nor do I understand how I possibly should know it, seeing that, up to this moment, I did not even know your name, and have heard nothing concerning either your movements or your affairs."

"Sir," said he, "I have hitherto believed that I might at any rate expect from you the truth."

"Sir," said I, "I am bold to think that you will not dare to tell me, either now, or at any other time, that you have received, or expect to receive, from me anything that is not true."

He then stood still, looking at me for a moment or two, and I beg to assert that I looked as fully at him. There was, at any rate, no cause why I should tremble before him. I was not his nephew, nor was I responsible for his nephew's doings towards him. Two of his servants were behind him, and on my side there stood a boy and girl belonging to the inn. They, however, could not understand a word of English. I saw that he was hesitating, but at last he spoke out. I confess, now, that his words, when they were spoken, did, at the first moment, make me tremble.

"I have to charge you," said he, "with eloping with my niece, and I demand of you to inform me where she is. You are perfectly aware that I am her guardian by law."

I did tremble;—not that I cared much for Sir William's guardianship, but I saw before me so terrible an embarrassment! And then I felt so thoroughly abashed in that I had allowed myself to be so deceived! It all came back upon me in a moment, and covered me with a shame that even made me blush. I had travelled through the desert with a woman for days, and had not discovered her, though she had given me a thousand signs. All those signs I remembered now, and I blushed painfully. When her hand was on my forehead I still thought that she was a man! I declare that at this moment I felt a stronger disinclination to face my late companion than I did to encounter her angry uncle.

"Your niece!" I said, speaking with a sheepish bewilderment which should have convinced him at once of my innocence. She had asked me, too, whether I was a married man, and I had denied it. How was I to escape from such a mess of misfortunes? I declare that I began to forget her troubles in my own.

"Yes, my niece,—Miss Julia Weston. The disgrace which you have brought upon me must be wiped out; but my first duty is to save that unfortunate young woman from further misery."

"If it be as you say," I exclaimed, "by the honour of a gentleman— "

"I care nothing for the honour of a gentleman till I see it proved. Be good enough to inform me, sir, whether Miss Weston is in this house."

For a moment I hesitated; but I saw at once that I should make myself responsible for certain mischief, of which I was at any rate hitherto in truth innocent, if I allowed myself to become a party to concealing a young lady. Up to this period I could at any rate defend myself, whether my defence were believed or not believed. I still had a hope that the charming Julia might have escaped through the window, and a feeling that if she had done so I was not responsible. When I turned the lock I turned it on Smith.

For a moment I hesitated, and then walked slowly across the yard and opened the door. "Sir William," I said, as I did so, "I travelled here with a companion dressed as a man; and I believed him to be what he seemed till this minute."

"Sir!" said Sir William, with a look of scorn in his face which gave me the lie in my teeth as plainly as any words could do. And then he entered the room. The Pole was standing in one corner, apparently amazed at what was going on, and Smith,—I may as well call her Miss Weston at once, for the baronet's statement was true,—was sitting on a sort of divan in the corner of the chamber, hiding her face in her hands. She had made no attempt at an escape, and a full explanation was therefore indispensable. For myself I own that I felt ashamed of my part in the play,—ashamed even of my own innocency. Had I been less innocent I should certainly have contrived to appear much less guilty. Had it occurred to me on the banks of the Jordan that Smith was a lady, I should not have travelled with her in her gentleman's habiliments from Jerusalem to Jaffa. Had she consented to remain under my protection, she must have done so without a masquerade.

The uncle stood still and looked at his niece. He probably understood how thoroughly stern and disagreeable was his own face, and considered that he could punish the crime of his relative in no severer way than by looking at her. In this I think he was right. But at last there was a necessity for speaking. "Unfortunate young woman!" he said, and then paused.

"We had better get rid of the landlord," I said, "before we come to any explanation." And I motioned to the man to leave the room. This he did very unwillingly, but at last he was gone.

"I fear that it is needless to care on her account who may hear the story of her shame," said Sir William. I looked at Miss Weston, but she still sat hiding her face. However, if she did not defend herself, it was necessary that I should defend both her and me.

"I do not know how far I may be at liberty to speak with reference to the private matters of yourself or of your—your niece, Sir William Weston. I would not willingly interfere— "

"Sir," said he, "your interference has already taken place. Will you have the goodness to explain to me what are your intentions with regard to that lady?"

My intentions! Heaven help me! My intentions, of course, were to leave her in her uncle's hands. Indeed, I could hardly be said to have formed any intention since I had learned that I had been honoured by a lady's presence. At this moment I deeply regretted that I had thoughtlessly stated to her that I was an unmarried man. In doing so I had had no object. But at that time "Smith" had been quite a stranger to me, and I had not thought it necessary to declare my own private concerns. Since that I had talked so little of myself that the fact of my family at home had not been mentioned. "Will you have the goodness to explain what are your intentions with regard to that lady?" said the baronet.

"Oh, Uncle William!" exclaimed Miss Weston, now at length raising her head from her hands.

"Hold your peace, madam," said he. "When called upon to speak, you will find your words with difficulty enough. Sir, I am waiting for an answer from you."

"But, uncle, he is nothing to me;—the gentleman is nothing to me!"

"By the heavens above us, he shall be something, or I will know the reason why! What! he has gone off with you; he has travelled through the country with you, hiding you from your only natural friend; he has been your companion for weeks— "

"Six days, sir," said I.

"Sir!" said the baronet, again giving me the lie. "And now," he continued, addressing his niece, "you tell me that he is nothing to you. He shall give me his promise that he will make you his wife at the consulate at Alexandria, or I will destroy him. I know who he is."

"If you know who I am," said I, "you must know— "

But he would not listen to me. "And as for you, madam, unless he makes me that promise— " And then he paused in his threat, and, turning round, looked me in the face. I saw that she also was looking at me, though not openly as he did; and some flattering devil that was at work round my heart, would have persuaded that she also would have heard a certain answer given without dismay,—would even have received comfort in her agony from such answer. But the reader knows how completely that answer was out of my power.

"I have not the slightest ground for supposing," said I, "that the lady would accede to such an arrangement,—if it were possible. My acquaintance with her has been altogether confined to—. To tell the truth, I have not been in Miss Weston's confidence, and have taken her to be only that which she has seemed to be."

"Sir!" said the baronet, again looking at me as though he would wither me on the spot for my falsehood.

"It is true!" said Julia, getting up from her seat, and appealing with clasped hands to her uncle—"as true as Heaven."

"Madam!" said he, "do you both take me for a fool?"

"That you should take me for one," said I, "would be very natural. The facts are as we state to you. Miss Weston,—as I now learn that she is,—did me the honour of calling at my hotel, having heard— " And then it seemed to me as though I were attempting to screen myself by telling the story against her, so I was again silent. Never in my life had I been in a position of such extraordinary difficulty. The duty which I owed to Julia as a woman, and to Sir William as a guardian, and to myself as the father of a family, all clashed with each other. I was anxious to be generous, honest, and prudent, but it was impossible; so I made up my mind to say nothing further.

"Mr. Jones," said the baronet, "I have explained to you the only arrangement which under the present circumstances I can permit to pass without open exposure and condign punishment. That you are a gentleman by birth, education, and position I am aware,"—whereupon I raised my hat, and then he continued: "That lady has three hundred a year of her own— "

"And attractions, personal and mental, which are worth ten times the money," said I, and I bowed to my fair friend, who looked at me the while with sad beseeching eyes. I confess that the mistress of my bosom, had she known my thoughts at that one moment, might have had cause for anger.

"Very well," continued he. "Then the proposal which I name cannot, I imagine, but be satisfactory. If you will make to her and to me the only amends which it is in your power as a gentleman to afford, I will forgive all. Tell me that you will make her your wife on your arrival in Egypt."

I would have given anything not to have looked at Miss Weston at this moment, but I could not help it. I did turn my face half round to her before I answered, and then felt that I had been cruel in doing so. "Sir William," said I, "I have at home already a wife and family of my own."

"It is not true!" said he, retreating a step, and staring at me with amazement.

"There is something, sir," I replied, "in the unprecedented circumstances of this meeting, and in your position with regard to that lady, which, joined to your advanced age, will enable me to regard that useless insult as unspoken. I am a married man. There is the signature of my wife's last letter," and I handed him one which I had received as I was leaving Jerusalem.

But the coarse violent contradiction which Sir William had given me was as nothing compared with the reproach conveyed in Miss Weston's countenance. She looked at me as though all her anger were now turned against me. And yet, methought, there was more of sorrow than of resentment in her countenance. But what cause was there for either? Why should I be reproached, even by her look? She did not remember at the moment that when I answered her chance question as to my domestic affairs, I had answered it as to a man who was a stranger to me, and not as to a beautiful woman, with whom I was about to pass certain days in close and intimate society. To her, at the moment, it seemed as though I had cruelly deceived her. In truth the one person really deceived had been myself.

And here I must explain, on behalf of the lady, that when she first joined me she had no other view than that of seeing the banks of the Jordan in that guise which she had chosen to assume, in order to escape from the solemnity and austerity of a disagreeable relative. She had been very foolish, and that was all. I take it that she had first left her uncle at Constantinople, but on this point I never got certain information. Afterwards, while we were travelling together, the idea had come upon her, that she might go on as far as Alexandria with me. And then—. I know nothing further of the lady's intentions, but I am certain that her wishes were good and pure. Her uncle had been intolerable to her, and she had fled from him. Such had been her offence, and no more.

"Then, sir," said the baronet, giving me back my letter, "you must be a double-dyed villain."

"And you, sir," said I— " But here Julia Weston interrupted me.

"Uncle, you altogether wrong this gentleman," she said. "He has been kind to me beyond my power of words to express; but, till told by you, he knew nothing of my secret. Nor would he have known it," she added, looking down upon the ground. As to that latter assertion, I was at liberty to believe as much as I pleased.

The Pole now came to the door, informing us that any who wished to start by the packet must go on board, and therefore, as the unreasonable old gentleman perceived, it was necessary that we should all make our arrangements. I cannot say that they were such as enable me to look back on them with satisfaction. He did seem now at last to believe that I had been an unconscious agent in his niece's stratagem, but he hardly on that account became civil to me. "It was absolutely necessary," he said, "that he and that unfortunate young woman," as he would call her, "should depart at once,—by this ship now going." To this proposition of course I made no opposition. "And you, Mr. Jones," he continued, "will at once perceive that you, as a gentleman, should allow us to proceed on our journey without the honour of your company."

This was very dreadful, but what could I say; or, indeed, what could I do? My most earnest desire in the matter was to save Miss Weston from annoyance; and under existing circumstances my presence on board could not but be a burden to her. And then, if I went,—if I did go, in opposition to the wishes of the baronet, could I trust my own prudence? It was better for all parties that I should remain.

"Sir William," said I, after a minute's consideration, "if you will apologise to me for the gross insults you have offered me, it shall be as you say."

"Mr. Jones," said Sir William, "I do apologise for the words which I used to you while I was labouring under a very natural misconception of the circumstances." I do not know that I was much the better for the apology, but at the moment I regarded it sufficient.

Their things were then hurried down to the strand, and I accompanied them to the ruined quay. I took off my hat to Sir William as he was first let down into the boat. He descended first, so that he might receive his niece,—for all Jaffa now knew that it was a lady,—and then I gave her my hand for the last time. "God bless you, Miss Weston," I said, pressing it closely. "God bless you, Mr. Jones," she replied. And from that day to this I have neither spoken to her nor seen her.

I waited a fortnight at Jaffa for the French boat, eating cutlets of goats' flesh, and wandering among the orange groves. I certainly look back on that fortnight as the most miserable period of my life. I had been deceived, and had failed to discover the deceit, even though the deceiver had perhaps wished that I should do so. For that blindness I have never forgiven myself.

Mrs. General Talboys

Originally appeared in *The London Review*, 2 February 1861. Reprinted in *Tales of All Countries* [Second Series] (1863). Probably written 6–10 November, 1860, during the composition of *Orley Farm*, and perhaps inspired by two weeks Trollope spent in Italy in October with his brother Tom. 'Mrs. General Talboys' was rejected by the *Cornhill Magazine* on grounds of indelicacy, and it attracted adverse criticism when it appeared in the *London Review*, probably because of its references to illegitimate children. Rose Trollope, in one of her few recorded literary comments, thought it 'ill-natured.' On 15 November 1860 Trollope wrote a long and important letter to Thackeray (then editor of the *Cornhill*) on the subject of the story, arguing that a good deal of 'delicacy' on the part of the Victorian novel-reading public was in reality only 'squeamishness.'

WHY MRS. General Talboys first made up her mind to pass the winter of 1859 at Rome I never clearly understood. To myself she explained her purposes, soon after her arrival at the Eternal City, by declaring, in her own enthusiastic manner, that she was inspired by a burning desire to drink fresh at the still living fountains of classical poetry and sentiment. But I always thought that there was something more than this in it. Classical poetry and sentiment were doubtless very dear to her; but so also, I imagine, were the substantial comforts of Hardover Lodge, the General's house in Berkshire; and I do not think that she would have emigrated for the winter had there not been some slight domestic misunderstanding. Let this, however, be fully made clear,—that such misunderstanding, if it existed, must have been simply an affair of temper. No impropriety of conduct has, I am very sure, ever been imputed to the lady. The General, as all the world knows, is hot; and Mrs. Talboys, when the sweet rivers of her enthusiasm are unfed by congenial waters, can, I believe, make herself disagreeable.

But be this as it may, in November, 1859, Mrs. Talboys came among us English at Rome, and soon succeeded in obtaining for herself a comfortable footing in our society. We all thought her more remarkable for her mental attributes than for physical perfection; but, nevertheless, she was, in her own way, a sightly woman. She had no special brilliance, either of eye or complexion, such as would produce sudden flames in susceptible hearts; nor did she seem to demand instant homage by the form and step of a goddess; but we found her to be a good-looking woman of some thirty or thirty-three years of age, with soft peach-like cheeks,—rather too like those of a cherub, with sparkling eyes which were hardly large enough, with good teeth, a white forehead, a dimpled chin and a full bust. Such, outwardly, was Mrs. General Talboys. The description of the inward woman is the purport to which these few pages will be devoted.

There are two qualities to which the best of mankind are much subject, which are nearly related to each other, and as to which the world has not yet decided whether they are to be classed among the good or evil attributes of our nature. Men and women are under the influence of them both, but men oftenest undergo the former, and women the latter. They are ambition and enthusiasm. Now Mrs. Talboys was an enthusiastic woman.

As to ambition, generally as the world agrees with Mark Antony in stigmatising it as a grievous fault, I am myself clear that it is a virtue; but with ambition at present we have no concern. Enthusiasm also, as I think, leans to virtue's side; or, at least, if it be a fault, of all faults it is the prettiest. But then, to partake at all of virtue, or even to be in any degree pretty, the enthusiasm must be true.

Bad coin is known from good by the ring of it; and so is bad enthusiasm. Let the coiner be ever so clever at his art, in the coining of enthusiasm the sound of true gold can never be imparted to the false metal. And I doubt whether the cleverest she in the world can make false enthusiasm palatable to the taste of man. To the taste of any woman the enthusiasm of another woman is never very palatable.

We understood at Rome that Mrs. Talboys had a considerable family,—four or five children, we were told; but she brought with her only one daughter, a little girl about twelve years of age. She had torn herself asunder, as she told me, from the younger nurslings of her heart, and had left them to the care of a devoted female attendant, whose love was all but maternal. And then she said a word or two about the General, in terms which made me almost think that this quasi-maternal love extended itself beyond the children. The idea, however, was a mistaken one, arising from the strength of her language, to which I was then unaccustomed. I have since become aware that nothing can be more decorous than old Mrs. Upton, the excellent head-nurse at Hardover Lodge; and no gentleman more discreet in his conduct than General Talboys.

And I may as well here declare, also, that there could be no more virtuous woman than the General's wife. Her marriage vow was to her paramount to all other vows and bonds whatever. The General's honour was quite safe when he sent her off to Rome by herself; and he no doubt knew that it was so. *Illi robur et æs triplex*, of which I believe no weapons of any assailant could get the better. But, nevertheless, we used to fancy that she had no repugnance to impropriety in other women,—to what the world generally calls impropriety. Invincibly attached herself to the marriage tie, she would constantly speak of it as by no means necessarily binding on others; and, virtuous herself as any griffin of propriety, she constantly patronised, at any rate, the theory of infidelity in her neighbours. She was very eager in denouncing the prejudices of the English world, declaring that she had found existence among them to be no longer possible for herself. She was hot against the stern unforgiveness of British matrons, and equally eager in reprobating the stiff conventionalities of a religion in which she said that none of its votaries had faith, though they all allowed themselves to be enslaved.

We had at that time a small set at Rome, consisting chiefly of English and Americans, who habitually met at each other's rooms, and spent many of our evening hours in discussing Italian politics. We were, most of us, painters, poets, novelists, or sculptors;—perhaps I should say would-be painters, poets, novelists, and sculptors,—aspirants, hoping to become some day recognised; and among us Mrs. Talboys took her place, naturally enough, on account of a very pretty taste she had for painting. I do not know that she ever originated anything that was grand; but she made some nice copies, and was fond, at any rate, of art conversation. She wrote essays, too, which she showed in confidence to various gentlemen, and had some idea of taking lessons in modelling.

In all our circle Conrad Mackinnon, an American, was, perhaps, the person most qualified to be styled its leader. He was one who absolutely did gain his living, and an ample living too, by his pen, and was regarded on all sides as a literary lion, justified by success in roaring at any tone he might please. His usual roar was not exactly that of a sucking-dove or a nightingale; but it was a good-humoured roar, not very offensive to any man, and apparently acceptable enough to some ladies. He was a big burly man, near to fifty as I suppose, somewhat awkward in his gait, and somewhat loud in his laugh. But though nigh to fifty, and thus ungainly, he liked to be smiled on by pretty women, and liked, as some said, to be flattered by them also. If so, he should have been happy, for the ladies at Rome at that time made much of Conrad Mackinnon.

Of Mrs. Mackinnon no one did make very much, and yet she was one of the sweetest, dearest, quietest, little creatures that ever made glad a man's fireside. She was exquisitely pretty, always in good humour, never stupid, self-denying to a fault, and yet she was generally in the background. She would seldom come forward of her own will, but was contented to sit behind her teapot and hear Mackinnon do his roaring. He was certainly much given to what the world at Rome called flirting, but this did not in the least annoy her. She was twenty years his junior, and yet she never flirted with any one. Women would tell her—good-natured friends—how Mackinnon went on; but she received such tidings as an excellent joke, observing that he had always done the same, and no doubt always would till he was ninety. I do believe that she was a happy woman; and yet I used to think that she should have been happier. There is, however, no knowing the inside of another man's house, or reading the riddles of another man's joy and sorrow.

We had also there another lion,—a lion cub,—entitled to roar a little, and of him also I must say something. Charles O'Brien was a young man, about twenty-five years of age, who had sent out from his studio in the preceding year a certain bust, supposed by his admirers to be unsurpassed by any effort of ancient or modern genius. I am no judge of sculpture, and will not, therefore, pronounce an opinion; but many who considered themselves to be judges, declared that it was a "goodish head and shoulders," and nothing more. I merely mention the fact, as it was on the strength of that head and shoulders that O'Brien separated himself from a throng of others such as himself in Rome, walked solitary during the days, and threw himself at the feet of various ladies when the days were over. He had ridden on the shoulders of his bust into a prominent place in our circle, and there encountered much feminine admiration—from Mrs. General Talboys and others.

Some eighteen or twenty of us used to meet every Sunday evening in Mrs. Mackinnon's drawing-room. Many of us, indeed, were in the habit of seeing each other daily, and of visiting together the haunts in Rome which are best loved by art-loving strangers; but here, in this drawing-room, we were sure to come together, and here before the end of November Mrs. Talboys might always be found, not in any accustomed seat, but moving about the room as the different male mental attractions of our society might chance to move themselves. She was at first greatly taken by Mackinnon,—who also was, I think, a little stirred by her admiration, though he stoutly denied the charge. She became, however, very dear to us all before she left us, and certainly we owed to her our love, for she added infinitely to the joys of our winter.

"I have come here to refresh myself," she said to Mackinnon one evening,—to Mackinnon and myself, for we were standing together.

"Shall I get you tea?" said I.

"And will you have something to eat?" Mackinnon asked.

"No, no, no;" she answered. "Tea, yes; but for heaven's sake let nothing solid dispel the associations of such a meeting as this."

"I thought you might have dined early," said Mackinnon. Now Mackinnon was a man whose own dinner was very dear to him. I have seen him become hasty and unpleasant, even under the pillars of the Forum, when he thought that the party were placing his fish in jeopardy by their desire to linger there too long.

"Early! Yes: No; I know not when it was. One dines and sleeps in obedience to that dull clay which weighs down so generally the particle of our spirit. But the clay may sometimes be forgotten. Here I can always forget it."

"I thought you asked for refreshment," I said. She only looked at me, whose small attempts at prose composition had, up to that time, been altogether unsuccessful, and then addressed herself in reply to Mackinnon.

"It is the air which we breathe that fills our lungs and gives us life and light. It is that which refreshes us if pure, or sinks us into stagnation if it be foul. Let me for a while inhale the breath of an invigorating literature. Sit down, Mr. Mackinnon; I have a question that I must put to you." And then she succeeded in carrying him off into a corner. As far as I could see he went willingly enough at that time, though he soon became averse to any long retirement in company with Mrs. Talboys.

We none of us quite understood what were her exact ideas on the subject of revealed religion. Somebody, I think, had told her that there were among us one or two whose opinions were not exactly orthodox according to the doctrines of the established English church. If so, she was determined to show us that she also was advanced beyond the prejudices of an old and dry school of theology. "I have thrown down all the barriers of religion," she said to poor Mrs. Mackinnon, "and am looking for the sentiments of a pure Christianity."

"Thrown down all the barriers of religion!" said Mrs. Mackinnon, in a tone of horror which was not appreciated.

"Indeed, yes," said Mrs. Talboys, with an exulting voice. "Are not the days for such trammels gone by?"

"But yet you hold by Christianity?"

"A pure Christianity, unstained by blood and perjury, by hypocrisy and verbose genuflection. Can I not worship and say my prayers among the clouds?" And she pointed to the lofty ceiling and the handsome chandelier.

"But Ida goes to church," said Mrs. Mackinnon. Ida Talboys was her daughter. Now, it may be observed that many who throw down the barriers of religion, so far as those barriers may affect themselves, still maintain them on behalf of their children. "Yes," said Mrs. Talboys; "dear Ida! her soft spirit is not yet adapted to receive the perfect truth.

We are obliged to govern children by the strength of their prejudices." And then she moved away, for it was seldom that Mrs. Talboys remained long in conversation with any lady.

Mackinnon, I believe, soon became tired of her. He liked her flattery, and at first declared that she was clever and nice; but her niceness was too purely celestial to satisfy his mundane tastes. Mackinnon himself can revel among the clouds in his own writings, and can leave us sometimes in doubt whether he ever means to come back to earth; but when his foot is on *terra firma*, he loves to feel the earthly substratum which supports his weight. With women he likes a hand that can remain an unnecessary moment within his own, an eye that can glisten with the sparkle of champagne, a heart weak enough to make its owner's arm tremble within his own beneath the moonlight gloom of the Coliseum arches. A dash of sentiment the while makes all these things the sweeter; but the sentiment alone will not suffice for him. Mrs. Talboys did, I believe, drink her glass of champagne, as do other ladies; but with her it had no such pleasing effect. It loosened only her tongue, but never her eye. Her arm, I think, never trembled, and her hand never lingered. The General was always safe, and happy, perhaps, in his solitary safety.

It so happened that we had unfortunately among us two artists who had quarrelled with their wives. O'Brien, whom I have before mentioned, was one of them. In his case, I believe him to have been almost as free from blame as a man can be, whose marriage was in itself a fault. However, he had a wife in Ireland, some ten years older than himself; and though he might sometimes almost forget the fact, his friends and neighbours were well aware of it. In the other case the whole fault probably was with the husband. He was an ill-tempered, bad-hearted man, clever enough, but without principle; and he was continually guilty of the great sin of speaking evil of the woman whose name he should have been anxious to protect. In both cases our friend Mrs. Talboys took a warm interest, and in each of them she sympathised with the present husband against the absent wife.

Of the consolation which she offered in the latter instance we used to hear something from Mackinnon. He would repeat to his wife, and to me and my wife, the conversations which she had with him. "Poor Brown;" she would say, "I pity him, with my very heart's blood."

"You are aware that he has comforted himself in his desolation," Mackinnon replied.

"I know very well to what you allude. I think I may say that I am conversant with all the circumstances of this heart-blighting sacrifice." Mrs. Talboys was apt to boast of the thorough confidence reposed in her by all those in whom she took an interest. "Yes, he has sought such comfort in another love as the hard cruel world would allow him."

"Or perhaps something more than that," said Mackinnon. "He has a family here in Rome, you know; two little babies."

"I know it, I know it," she said. "Cherub angels!" and as she spoke, she looked up into the ugly face of Marcus Aurelius; for they were standing at the moment under the figure of the great horseman on the Campidoglio. "I have seen them, and they are the children of innocence. If all the blood of all the Howards ran in their veins it could not make their birth more noble!"

"Not if the father and mother of all the Howards had never been married," said Mackinnon.

"What; that from you, Mr. Mackinnon!" said Mrs. Talboys, turning her back with energy upon the equestrian statue, and looking up into the faces, first of Pollux and then of Castor, as though from them she might gain some inspiration on the subject which Marcus Aurelius in his coldness had denied to her. "From you, who have so nobly claimed for mankind the divine attributes of free action! From you, who have taught my mind to soar above the petty bonds which one man in his littleness contrives for the subjection of his brother. Mackinnon! you who are so great!" And she now looked up into his face. "Mackinnon, unsay those words."

"They *are* illegitimate," said he; "and if there was any landed property— "

"Landed property! and that from an American!"

"The children are English, you know."

"Landed property! The time will shortly come—ay, and I see it coming—when that hateful word shall be expunged from the calendar; when landed property shall be no more. What! shall the free soul of a God-born man submit itself for ever to such trammels as that? Shall we never escape from the clay which so long has manacled the subtler particles of the divine spirit? Ay, yes, Mackinnon;" and then she took him by the arm, and led him to the top of the huge steps which lead down from the Campidoglio into the streets of modern Rome. "Look down upon that countless multitude." Mackinnon looked down, and saw three groups of French soldiers, with three or four little men in each group; he saw, also, a couple of dirty friars, and three priests very slowly beginning the side ascent to the church of the Ara Cœli. "Look down upon that countless multitude," said Mrs. Talboys, and she stretched her arms out over the half-deserted city. "They are escaping now from these trammels,—now, now,—now that I am speaking."

"They have escaped long ago from all such trammels as that of landed property," said Mackinnon.

"Ay, and from all terrestrial bonds," she continued, not exactly remarking the pith of his last observation; "from bonds quasi-terrestrial and quasi-celestial. The full-formed limbs of the present age, running with quick streams of generous blood, will no longer bear the ligatures which past times have woven for the decrepit. Look down upon that multitude, Mackinnon; they shall all be free." And then, still clutching him by the arm, and still standing at the top of those stairs, she gave forth her prophecy with the fury of a Sibyl.

"They shall all be free. Oh, Rome, thou eternal one, thou who hast bowed thy neck to imperial pride and priestly craft; thou who hast suffered sorely, even to this hour, from Nero down to Pio Nono,—the days of thine oppression are over. Gone from thy enfranchised ways for ever is the clang of Prætorian cohorts, and the more odious drone of meddling monks!" And yet, as Mackinnon observed, there still stood the dirty friars and the small French soldiers; and there still toiled the slow priests, wending their tedious way up to the church of the Ara Cœli. But that was the mundane view of the matter,—a view not regarded by Mrs. Talboys in her ecstasy. "O Italia," she continued, "O Italia una, one and indivisible in thy rights, and indivisible also in thy wrongs! to us is it given to see the accomplishment of thy glory. A people shall arise around thine altars greater in the annals of the world than thy Scipios, thy Gracchi, or thy Cæsars. Not in torrents of blood, or with screams of bereaved mothers, shall thy new triumphs be stained. But mind shall dominate over matter; and doomed, together with Popes and Bourbons, with cardinals, diplomatists, and police spies, ignorance and prejudice shall be driven from thy smiling terraces. And then Rome shall again become the fair capital of the fairest region of Europe. Hither shall flock the artisans of the world, crowding into thy marts all that God and man can give. Wealth, beauty, and innocence shall meet in thy streets— "

"There will be a considerable change before that takes place," said Mackinnon.

"There shall be a considerable change," she answered. "Mackinnon, to thee it is given to read the signs of the time; and hast thou not read? Why have the fields of Magenta and Solferino been piled with the corpses of dying heroes? Why have the waters of the Mincio ran red with the blood of martyrs? That Italy might be united and Rome immortal. Here, standing on the Capitolium of the ancient city, I say that it shall be so; and thou, Mackinnon, who hearest me, knowest that my words are true."

There was not then in Rome,—I may almost say there was not in Italy, an Englishman or an American who did not wish well to the cause for which Italy was and is still contending; as also there is hardly one who does not now regard that cause as well nigh triumphant; but, nevertheless, it was almost impossible to sympathise with Mrs. Talboys. As Mackinnon said, she flew so high that there was no comfort in flying with her.

"Well," said he, "Brown and the rest of them are down below. Shall we go and join them?"

"Poor Brown! How was it that, in speaking of his troubles, we were led on to this heart-stirring theme? Yes, I have seen them, the sweet angels; and I tell you also that I have seen their mother. I insisted on going to her when I heard her history from him."

"And what is she like, Mrs. Talboys?"

"Well; education has done more for some of us than for others; and there are those from whose morals and sentiments we might thankfully draw a lesson, whose manners and outward gestures are not such as custom has made agreeable to us. You, I know, can understand that. I have seen her, and feel sure that she is pure in heart and high in principle. Has she not sacrificed herself, and is not self-sacrifice the surest guarantee for true nobility of character? Would Mrs. Mackinnon object to my bringing them together?"

Mackinnon was obliged to declare that he thought his wife would object; and from that time forth he and Mrs. Talboys ceased to be very close in their friendship. She still came to the house every Sunday evening, still refreshed herself at the fountains of his literary rills; but her special prophecies from henceforth were poured into other ears. And it so happened that O'Brien now became her chief ally. I do not remember that she troubled herself much further with the cherub angels or with their mother; and I am inclined to think that, taking up warmly, as she did, the story of O'Brien's matrimonial wrongs, she forgot the little history of the Browns. Be that as it may, Mrs. Talboys and O'Brien now became strictly confidential, and she would enlarge by the half-hour together on the miseries of her friend's position, to any one whom she could get to hear her.

"I'll tell you what, Fanny," Mackinnon said to his wife one day,—to his wife and to mine, for we were all together; "we shall have a row in the house if we don't take care. O'Brien will be making love to Mrs. Talboys."

"Nonsense," said Mrs. Mackinnon. "You are always thinking that somebody is going to make love to some one."

"Somebody always is," said he.

"She's old enough to be his mother," said Mrs. Mackinnon.

"What does that matter to an Irishman?" said Mackinnon. "Besides, I doubt if there is more than five years' difference between them."

"There must be more than that," said my wife. "Ida Talboys is twelve, I know, and I am not quite sure that Ida is the eldest."

"If she had a son in the Guards, it would make no difference," said Mackinnon. "There are men who consider themselves bound to make love to a woman under certain circumstances, let the age of the lady be what it may. O'Brien is such a one; and if she sympathises with him much oftener, he will mistake the matter, and go down on his knees. You ought to put him on his guard," he said, addressing himself to his wife.

"Indeed I shall do no such thing," said she; "if they are two fools, they must, like other fools, pay the price of their folly." As a rule there could be no softer creature than Mrs. Mackinnon; but it seemed to me that her tenderness never extended itself in the direction of Mrs. Talboys.

Just at this time, towards the end, that is, of November, we made a party to visit the tombs which lie along the Appian Way, beyond that most beautiful of all sepulchres, the tomb of Cecilia Metella. It was a delicious day, and we had driven along this road for a couple of miles beyond the walls of the city, enjoying the most lovely view which the neighbourhood of Rome affords,—looking over the wondrous ruins of the old aqueducts, up towards Tivoli and Palestrina. Of all the environs of Rome this is, on a fair clear day, the most enchanting; and here perhaps, among a world of tombs, thoughts and almost memories of the old, old days come upon one with the greatest force. The grandeur of Rome is best seen and understood from beneath the walls of the Coliseum, and its beauty among the pillars of the Forum and the arches of the Sacred Way; but its history and fall become more palpable to the mind, and more clearly realised, out here among the tombs, where the eyes rest upon the mountains whose shades were cool to the old Romans as to us,—than anywhere within the walls of the city. Here we look out at the same Tivoli and the same Præneste, glittering in the sunshine, embowered among the far-off valleys, which were dear to them; and the blue mountains have not crumbled away into ruins. Within Rome itself we can see nothing as they saw it.

Our party consisted of some dozen or fifteen persons, and as a hamper with luncheon in it had been left on the grassy slope at the base of the tomb of Cecilia Metella, the expedition had in it something of the nature of a picnic. Mrs. Talboys was of course with us, and Ida Talboys. O'Brien also was there. The hamper had been prepared in Mrs. Mackinnon's room, under the immediate eye of Mackinnon himself, and they therefore were regarded as the dominant spirits of the party. My wife was leagued with Mrs. Mackinnon, as was usually the case; and there seemed to be a general opinion among those who were closely in confidence together, that something would happen in the O'Brien-Talboys matter. The two had been inseparable on the previous evening, for Mrs. Talboys had been urging on the young Irishman her counsels respecting his domestic troubles. Sir Cresswell Cresswell, she had told him, was his refuge. "Why should his soul submit to bonds which the world had now declared to be intolerable? Divorce was not now the privilege of the dissolute rich. Spirits which were incompatible need no longer be compelled to fret beneath the same couples." In short she had recommended him to go to England and get rid of his wife, as she would, with a little encouragement, have recommended any man to get rid of anything. I am sure that, had she been skilfully brought on to the subject, she might have been induced to pronounce a verdict against such ligatures for the body as coats, waistcoats, and trowsers. Her aspirations for freedom ignored all bounds, and, in theory, there were no barriers which she was not willing to demolish.

Poor O'Brien, as we all now began to see, had taken the matter amiss. He had offered to make a bust of Mrs. Talboys, and she had consented, expressing a wish that it might find a place among those who had devoted themselves to the enfranchisement of their fellow-creatures. I really think she had but little of a woman's customary personal vanity. I know she had an idea that her eye was lighted up in her warmer moments by some special fire, that sparks of liberty shone round her brow, and that her bosom heaved with glorious aspirations; but all these feelings had reference to her inner genius, not to any outward beauty. But O'Brien misunderstood the woman, and thought it necessary to gaze into her face, and sigh as though his heart were breaking. Indeed he declared to a young friend that Mrs. Talboys was perfect in her style of beauty, and began the bust with this idea. It was gradually becoming clear to us all that he would bring himself to grief; but in such a matter who can caution a man?

Mrs. Mackinnon had contrived to separate them in making the carriage arrangements on this day, but this only added fuel to the fire which was now burning within O'Brien's bosom. I believe that he really did love her, in his easy, eager, susceptible Irish way. That he would get over the little episode without any serious injury to his heart no one doubted; but then, what would occur when the declaration was made? How would Mrs. Talboys bear it?

"She deserves it," said Mrs. Mackinnon.

"And twice as much," my wife added. Why is it that women are so spiteful to each other?

Early in the day Mrs. Talboys clambered up to the top of a tomb, and made a little speech, holding a parasol over her head. Beneath her feet, she said, reposed the ashes of some bloated senator, some glutton of the empire, who had swallowed into his maw the provision necessary for a tribe. Old Rome had fallen through such selfishness as that; but new Rome would not forget the lesson. All this was very well, and then O'Brien helped her down; but after this there was no separating them. For her own part she would sooner have had Mackinnon at her elbow. But Mackinnon now had found some other elbow. "Enough of that was as good as a feast," he had said to his wife. And therefore Mrs. Talboys, quite unconscious of evil, allowed herself to be engrossed by O'Brien.

And then, about three o'clock, we returned to the hamper. Luncheon under such circumstances always means dinner, and we arranged ourselves for a very comfortable meal. To those who know the tomb of Cecilia Metella no description of the scene is necessary, and to those who do not, no description will convey a fair idea of its reality. It is itself a large low tower of great diameter, but of beautiful proportion, standing far outside the city, close on to the side of the old Roman way. It has been embattled on the top by some latter-day baron, in order that it might be used for protection to the castle, which has been built on and attached to it. If I remember rightly, this was done by one of the Frangipani, and a very lovely ruin he has made of it. I know no castellated old tumble-down residence in Italy more picturesque than this baronial adjunct to the old Roman tomb, or which better tallies with the ideas engendered within our minds by Mrs. Radcliffe and the Mysteries of Udolpho. It lies along the road, protected on the side of the city by the proud sepulchre of the Roman matron, and up to the long ruined walls of the back of the building stretches a grassy slope, at the bottom of which are the remains of an old Roman circus. Beyond that is the long, thin, graceful line of the Claudian aqueduct, with Soracte in the distance to the left, and Tivoli, Palestrina, and Frascati lying among the hills which bound the view. That Frangipani baron was in the right of it, and I hope he got the value of his money out of the residence which he built for himself. I doubt, however, that he did but little good to those who lived in his close neighbourhood.

We had a very comfortable little banquet seated on the broken lumps of stone which lie about under the walls of the tomb. I wonder whether the shade of Cecilia Metella was looking down upon us. We have heard much of her in these latter days, and yet we know nothing about her, nor can conceive why she was honoured with a bigger tomb than any other Roman matron. There were those then among our party who believed that she might still come back among us, and with due assistance from some cognate susceptible spirit, explain to us the cause of her widowed husband's liberality. Alas, alas! if we may judge of the Romans by ourselves, the true reason for such sepulchral grandeur would redound little to the credit of the lady Cecilia Metella herself, or to that of Crassus, her bereaved and desolate lord.

She did not come among us on the occasion of this banquet, possibly because we had no tables there to turn in preparation for her presence; but, had she done so, she could not have been more eloquent of things of the other world than was Mrs. Talboys. I have said that Mrs. Talboys' eye never glanced more brightly after a glass of champagne, but I am inclined to think that on this occasion it may have done so. O'Brien enacted Ganymede, and was, perhaps, more liberal than other latter-day Ganymedes, to whose services Mrs. Talboys had been accustomed. Let it not, however, be suspected by any one that she exceeded the limits of a discreet joyousness. By no means! The generous wine penetrated, perhaps, to some inner cells of her heart, and brought forth thoughts in sparkling words, which otherwise might have remained concealed; but there was nothing in what she thought or spoke calculated to give umbrage either to an anchorite or to a vestal. A word or two she said or sung about the flowing bowl, and once she called for Falernian; but beyond this her converse was chiefly of the rights of man and the weakness of women; of the iron ages that were past, and of the golden time that was to come.

She called a toast and drank to the hopes of the latter historians of the nineteenth century. Then it was that she bade O'Brien "Fill high the bowl with Samian wine." The Irishman took her at her word, and she raised the bumper, and waved it over her head before she put it to her lips. I am bound to declare that she did not spill a drop. "The true 'Falernian grape,'" she said, as she deposited the empty beaker on the grass beneath her elbow. Viler champagne I do not think I ever swallowed; but it was the theory of the wine, not its palpable body present there, as it were, in the flesh, which inspired her. There was really something grand about her on that occasion, and her enthusiasm almost amounted to reality.

Mackinnon was amused, and encouraged her, as, I must confess, did I also. Mrs. Mackinnon made useless little signs to her husband, really fearing that the Falernian would do its good offices too thoroughly. My wife, getting me apart as I walked round the circle distributing viands, remarked that "the woman was a fool, and would disgrace herself." But I observed that after the disposal of that bumper she worshipped the rosy god in theory only, and therefore saw no occasion to interfere. "Come, Bacchus," she said; "and come, Silenus, if thou wilt; I know that ye are hovering round the graves of you departed favourites. And ye, too, nymphs of Egeria," and she pointed to the classic grove which was all but close to us as we sat there. "In olden days ye did not always despise the abodes of men. But why should we invoke the presence of the gods,—we, who can become godlike ourselves! We ourselves are the deities of the present age. For us shall the tables be spread with ambrosia; for us shall the nectar flow."

Upon the whole it was very good fooling,—for awhile; and as soon as we were tired of it we arose from our seats, and began to stroll about the place. It was beginning to be a little dusk, and somewhat cool, but the evening air was pleasant, and the ladies, putting on their shawls, did not seem inclined at once to get into the carriages. At any rate, Mrs. Talboys was not so inclined, for she started down the hill towards the long low wall of the old Roman circus at the bottom; and O'Brien, close at her elbow, started with her.

"Ida, my dear, you had better remain here," she said to her daughter; "you will be tired if you come as far as we are going."

"Oh, no, mamma, I shall not," said Ida. "You get tired much quicker than I do."

"Oh, yes, you will; besides, I do not wish you to come." There was an end of it for Ida, and Mrs. Talboys and O'Brien walked off together, while we all looked into each other's faces.

"It would be a charity to go with them," said Mackinnon.

"Do you be charitable, then," said his wife.

"It should be a lady," said he.

"It is a pity that the mother of the spotless cherubim is not here for the occasion," said she. "I hardly think that any one less gifted will undertake such a self-sacrifice." Any attempt of the kind would, however, now have been too late, for they were already at the bottom of the hill. O'Brien certainly had drunk freely of the pernicious contents of those long-necked bottles; and though no one could fairly accuse him of being tipsy, nevertheless that which might have made others drunk had made him bold, and he dared to do—perhaps more than might become a man. If under any circumstances he could be fool enough to make an avowal of love to Mrs. Talboys, he might be expected, as we all felt, to do it now.

We watched them as they made for a gap in the wall which led through into the large enclosed space of the old circus. It had been an arena for chariot games, and they had gone down with the avowed purpose of searching where might have been the meta, and ascertaining how the drivers could have turned when at their full speed. For awhile we had heard their voices,—or rather her voice especially. "The heart of a man, O'Brien, should suffice for all emergencies," we had heard her say. She had assumed a strange habit of calling men by their simple names, as men address each other. When she did this to Mackinnon, who was much older than herself, we had been all amused by it, and other ladies of our party had taken to call him "Mackinnon" when Mrs. Talboys was not by; but we had felt the comedy to be less safe with O'Brien, especially when, on one occasion, we heard him address her as Arabella. She did not seem to be in any way struck by his doing so, and we supposed, therefore, that it had become frequent between them. What reply he made at the moment about the heart of a man I do not know;—and then in a few minutes they disappeared through the gap in the wall.

None of us followed them, though it would have seemed the most natural thing in the world to do so had nothing out of the way been expected. As it was we remained there round the tomb quizzing the little foibles of our dear friend, and hoping that O'Brien would be quick in what he was doing. That he would undoubtedly get a slap in the face—metaphorically—we all felt certain, for none of us doubted the rigid propriety of the lady's intentions. Some of us strolled into the buildings, and some of us got out on the road; but we all of us were thinking that O'Brien was very slow a considerable time before we saw Mrs. Talboys reappear through the gap.

At last, however, she was there, and we at once saw that she was alone. She came on, breasting the hill with quick steps, and when she drew near we could see that there was a frown as of injured majesty on her brow. Mackinnon and his wife went forward to meet her. If she were really in trouble it would be fitting in some way to assist her; and of all women Mrs. Mackinnon was the last to see another woman suffer from ill usage without attempting to aid her. "I certainly never liked her," Mrs. Mackinnon said afterwards; "but I was bound to go and hear her tale, when she really had a tale to tell."

And Mrs. Talboys now had a tale to tell,—if she chose to tell it. The ladies of our party declared afterwards that she would have acted more wisely had she kept to herself both O'Brien's words to her and her answer. "She was well able to take care of herself," Mrs. Mackinnon said; "and, after all, the silly man had taken an answer when he got it." Not, however, that O'Brien had taken his answer quite immediately, as far as I could understand from what we heard of the matter afterwards.

At the present moment Mrs. Talboys came up the rising ground all alone, and at a quick pace. "The man has insulted me," she said aloud, as well as her panting breath would allow her, and as soon as she was near enough to Mrs. Mackinnon to speak to her.

"I am sorry for that," said Mrs. Mackinnon. "I suppose he has taken a little too much wine."

"No; it was a premeditated insult. The base-hearted churl has failed to understand the meaning of true, honest sympathy."

"He will forget all about it when he is sober," said Mackinnon, meaning to comfort her.

"What care I what he remembers or what he forgets!" she said, turning upon poor Mackinnon indignantly. "You men grovel so in your ideas— " "And yet," as Mackinnon said afterwards, "she had been telling me that I was a fool for the last three weeks."—"You men grovel so in your ideas, that you cannot understand the feelings of a true-hearted woman. What can his forgetfulness or his remembrance be to me? Must not I remember this insult? Is it possible that I should forget it?"

Mr. and Mrs. Mackinnon only had gone forward to meet her; but, nevertheless, she spoke so loud that all heard her who were still clustered round the spot on which we had dined.

"What has become of Mr. O'Brien?" a lady whispered to me.

I had a field-glass with me, and, looking round, I saw his hat as he was walking inside the walls of the circus in the direction towards the city. "And very foolish he must feel," said the lady.

"No doubt he's used to it," said another.

"But considering her age, you know," said the first, who might have been perhaps three years younger than Mrs. Talboys, and who was not herself averse to the excitement of a moderate flirtation. But then why should she have been averse, seeing that she had not as yet become subject to the will of any imperial lord?

"He would have felt much more foolish," said the third, "if she had listened to what he said to her."

"Well I don't know," said the second; "nobody would have known anything about it then, and in a few weeks they would have gradually become tired of each other in the ordinary way."

But in the meantime Mrs. Talboys was among us. There had been no attempt at secresy, and she was still loudly inveighing against the grovelling propensities of men. "That's quite true, Mrs. Talboys," said one of the elder ladies; "but then women are not always so careful as they should be. Of course I do not mean to say that there has been any fault on your part."

"Fault on my part! Of course there has been fault on my part. No one can make any mistake without fault to some extent. I took him to be a man of sense, and he is a fool. Go to Naples indeed!"

"Did he want you to go to Naples?" asked Mrs. Mackinnon.

"Yes; that was what he suggested. We were to leave by the train for Civita Vecchia at six to-morrow morning, and catch the steamer which leaves Leghorn to-night. Don't tell me of wine. He was prepared for it!" And she looked round about on us with an air of injured majesty in her face which was almost insupportable.

"I wonder whether he took the tickets over-night," said Mackinnon.

"Naples!" she said, as though now speaking exclusively to herself, "the only ground in Italy which has as yet made no struggle on behalf of freedom;—a fitting residence for such a dastard!"

"You would have found it very pleasant at this season," said the unmarried lady, who was three years her junior.

My wife had taken Ida out of the way when the first complaining note from Mrs. Talboys had been heard ascending the hill. But now, when matters began gradually to become quiescent, she brought her back, suggesting, as she did so, that they might begin to think of returning.

"It is getting very cold, Ida, dear, is it not?" said she. "But where is Mr. O'Brien?" said Ida.

"He has fled,—as poltroons always fly," said Mrs. Talboys. I believe in my heart that she would have been glad to have had him there in the middle of the circle, and to have triumphed over him publicly among us all. No feeling of shame would have kept her silent for a moment.

"Fled!" said Ida, looking up into her mother's face.

"Yes, fled, my child." And she seized her daughter in her arms, and pressed her closely to her bosom. "Cowards always fly."

"Is Mr. O'Brien a coward?" Ida asked.

"Yes, a coward, a very coward! And he has fled before the glance of an honest woman's eye. Come, Mrs. Mackinnon, shall we go back to the city? I am sorry that the amusement of the day should have received this check." And she walked forward to the carriage and took her place in it with an air that showed that she was proud of the manner in which she had conducted herself.

"She is a little conceited about it after all," said that unmarried lady. "If poor Mr. O'Brien had not shown so much premature energy with reference to that little journey to Naples, things might have gone quietly after all."

But the unmarried lady was wrong in her judgment. Mrs. Talboys was proud and conceited in the matter,—but not proud of having excited the admiration of her Irish lover. She was proud of her own subsequent conduct, and gave herself credit for coming out strongly as a noble-minded matron. "I believe she thinks," said Mrs. Mackinnon, "that her virtue is quite Spartan and unique; and if she remains in Rome she'll boast of it through the whole winter."

"If she does, she may be certain that O'Brien will do the same," said Mackinnon. "And in spite of his having fled from the field, it is upon the cards that he may get the best of it. Mrs. Talboys is a very excellent woman. She has proved her excellence beyond a doubt. But, nevertheless, she is susceptible of ridicule."

We all felt a little anxiety to hear O'Brien's account of the matter, and after having deposited the ladies at their homes, Mackinnon and I went off to his lodgings. At first he was denied to us, but after awhile we got his servant to acknowledge that he was at home, and then we made our way up to his studio. We found him seated behind a half-formed model, or rather a mere lump of clay punched into something resembling the shape of a head, with a pipe in his mouth and a bit of stick in his hand. He was pretending to work, though we both knew that it was out of the question that he should do anything in his present frame of mind.

"I think I heard my servant tell you that I was not at home," said he.

"Yes, he did," said Mackinnon, "and would have sworn to it too if we would have let him. Come, don't pretend to be surly."

"I am very busy, Mr. Mackinnon."

"Completing your head of Mrs. Talboys, I suppose, before you start for Naples."

"You don't mean to say that she has told you all about it," and he turned away from his work, and looked up into our faces with a comical expression, half of fun and half of despair.

"Every word of it," said I. "When you want a lady to travel with you, never ask her to get up so early in winter."

"But, O'Brien, how could you be such an ass?" said Mackinnon. "As it has turned out, there is no very great harm done. You have insulted a respectable middle-aged woman, the mother of a family, and the wife of a general officer, and there is an end of it;—unless, indeed, the general officer should come out from England to call you to account."

"He is welcome," said O'Brien, haughtily.

"No doubt, my dear fellow," said Mackinnon; "that would be a dignified and pleasant ending to the affair. But what I want to know is this,—what would you have done if she had agreed to go?"

"He never calculated on the possibility of such a contingency," said I.

"By heavens, then, I thought she would like it," said he.

"And to oblige her you were content to sacrifice yourself," said Mackinnon.

"Well, that was just it. What the deuce is a fellow to do when a woman goes on in that way. She told me down there, upon the old race course you know, that matrimonial bonds were made for fools and slaves. What was I to suppose that she meant by that? But to make all sure, I asked her what sort of a fellow the General was. 'Dear old man,' she said, clasping her hands together. 'He might, you know, have been my father.' 'I wish he were,' said I, 'because then you'd be free.' 'I am free,' said she, stamping on the ground, and looking up at me as much as to say that she cared for no one. 'Then,' said I, 'accept all that is left of the heart of Wenceslaus O'Brien,' and I threw myself before her in her path. 'Hand,' said I, 'I have none to give, but the blood which runs red through my veins is descended from a double line of kings.' I said that because she is always fond of riding a high horse. I had gotten close under the wall, so that none of you should see me from the tower."

"And what answer did she make?" said Mackinnon.

"Why she was pleased as Punch;—gave me both her hands, and declared that we would be friends for ever. It is my belief, Mackinnon, that that woman never heard anything of the kind before. The General, no doubt, did it by letter."

"And how was it that she changed her mind."

"Why; I got up, put my arm round her waist, and told her that we would be off to Naples. I'm blest if she didn't give me a knock in the ribs that nearly sent me backwards. She took my breath away, so that I couldn't speak to her."

"And then— "

"Oh, there was nothing more. Of course I saw how it was. So she walked off one way and I the other. On the whole I consider that I am well out of it."

"And so do I," said Mackinnon, very gravely. "But if you will allow me to give you my advice, I would suggest that it would be well to avoid such mistakes in future."

"Upon my word," said O'Brien, excusing himself, "I don't know what a man is to do under such circumstances. I give you my honour that I did it all to oblige her."

We then decided that Mackinnon should convey to the injured lady the humble apology of her late admirer. It was settled that no detailed excuses should be made. It should be left to her to consider whether the deed which had been done might have been occasioned by wine, or by the folly of a moment,—or by her own indiscreet enthusiasm. No one but the two were present when the message was given, and therefore we were obliged to trust to Mackinnon's accuracy for an account of it.

She stood on very high ground indeed, he said, at first refusing to hear anything that he had to say on the matter. "The foolish young man," she declared, "was below her anger, and below her contempt."

"He is not the first Irishman that has been made indiscreet by beauty," said Mackinnon.

"A truce to that," she replied, waving her hand with an air of assumed majesty. "The incident, contemptible as it is, has been unpleasant to me. It will necessitate my withdrawal from Rome."

"Oh, no, Mrs. Talboys; that will be making too much of him."

"The greatest hero that lives," she answered, "may have his house made uninhabitable by a very small insect." Mackinnon swore that those were her own words. Consequently a *sobriquet* was attached to O'Brien of which he by no means approved. And from that day we always called Mrs. Talboys "the hero."

Mackinnon prevailed at last with her, and she did not leave Rome. She was even induced to send a message to O'Brien, conveying her forgiveness. They shook hands together with great *éclat* in Mrs. Mackinnon's drawing-room; but I do not suppose that she ever again offered to him sympathy on the score of his matrimonial troubles.

The Parson's Daughter of Oxney Colne

Originally appeared in *The London Review*, 2 March 1861. Reprinted in *Tales of All Countries* [Second Series] (1863). Written 13–19 January 1861, during the composition of *Orley Farm*. This was the last Trollope short story to be printed in *The London Review*. Probably because 'A Ride Across Palestine' and 'Mrs. General Talboys' had offended the magazine's readers, five other Trollope manuscripts were sold on to a newly-founded weekly, *Public Opinion*.

THE PRETTIEST scenery in all England—and if I am contradicted in that assertion, I will say in all Europe—is in Devonshire, on the southern and south-eastern skirts of Dartmoor, where the rivers Dart, and Avon, and Teign form themselves, and where the broken moor is half cultivated, and the wild-looking upland fields are half moor. In making this assertion I am often met with much doubt, but it is by persons who do not really know the locality. Men and women talk to me on the matter, who have travelled down the line of railway from Exeter to Plymouth, who have spent a fortnight at Torquay, and perhaps made an excursion from Tavistock to the convict prison on Dartmoor. But who knows the glories of Chagford? Who has walked through the parish of Manaton? Who is conversant with Lustleigh Cleeves and Withycombe in the moor? Who has explored Holne Chase? Gentle reader, believe me that you will be rash in contradicting me, unless you have done these things.

There or thereabouts—I will not say by the waters of which little river it is washed—is the parish of Oxney Colne. And for those who would wish to see all the beauties of this lovely country, a sojourn in Oxney Colne would be most desirable, seeing that the sojourner would then be brought nearer to all that he would wish to visit, than at any other spot in the country. But there is an objection to any such arrangement. There are only two decent houses in the whole parish, and these are—or were when I knew the locality—small and fully occupied by their possessors. The larger and better is the parsonage, in which lived the parson and his daughter; and the smaller is the freehold residence of a certain Miss Le Smyrger, who owned a farm of a hundred acres, which was rented by one Farmer Cloysey, and who also possessed some thirty acres round her own house, which she managed herself, regarding herself to be quite as great in cream as Mr. Cloysey, and altogether superior to him in the article of cider. "But yeu has to pay no rent, Miss," Farmer Cloysey would say, when Miss Le Smyrger expressed this opinion of her art in a manner too defiant. "Yeu pays no rent, or yeu couldn't do it." Miss Le Smyrger was an old maid, with a pedigree and blood of her own, a hundred and thirty acres of fee-simple land on the borders of Dartmoor, fifty years of age, a constitution of iron, and an opinion of her own on every subject under the sun.

And now for the parson and his daughter. The parson's name was Woolsworthy—or Woolathy as it was pronounced by all those who lived around him—the Rev. Saul Woolsworthy; and his daughter was Patience Woolsworthy, or Miss Patty, as she was known to the Devonshire world of those parts. That name of Patience had not been well chosen for her, for she was a hot-tempered damsel, warm in her convictions, and inclined to express them freely. She had but two closely intimate friends in the world, and by both of them this freedom of expression had now been fully permitted to her since she was a child. Miss Le Smyrger and her father were well accustomed to her ways, and on the whole well satisfied with them. The former was equally free and equally warm-tempered as herself, and as Mr. Woolsworthy was allowed by his daughter to be quite paramount on his own subject—for he had a subject—he did not object to his daughter being paramount on all others. A pretty girl was Patience Woolsworthy at the time of which I am writing, and one who possessed much that was worthy of remark and admiration, had she lived where beauty meets with admiration, or where force of character is remarked. But at Oxney Colne, on the borders of Dartmoor, there were few to appreciate her, and it seemed as though she herself had but little idea of carrying her talent further afield, so that it might not remain for ever wrapped in a blanket.

She was a pretty girl, tall and slender, with dark eyes and black hair. Her eyes were perhaps too round for regular beauty, and her hair was perhaps too crisp; her mouth was large and expressive; her nose was finely formed, though a critic in female form might have declared it to be somewhat broad. But her countenance altogether was wonderfully attractive—if only it might be seen without that resolution for dominion which occasionally marred it, though sometimes it even added to her attractions.

It must be confessed on behalf of Patience Woolsworthy, that the circumstances of her life had peremptorily called upon her to exercise dominion. She had lost her mother when she was sixteen, and had had neither brother nor sister. She had no neighbours near her fit either from education or rank to interfere in the conduct of her life, excepting always Miss Le Smyrger. Miss Le Smyrger would have done anything for her, including the whole management of her morals and of the parsonage household, had Patience been content with such an arrangement. But much as Patience had ever loved Miss Le Smyrger, she was not content with this, and therefore she had been called on to put forth a strong hand of her own. She had put forth this strong hand early, and hence had come the character which I am attempting to describe. But I must say on behalf of this girl, that it was not only over others that she thus exercised dominion. In acquiring that power she had also acquired the much greater power of exercising rule over herself.

But why should her father have been ignored in these family arrangements? Perhaps it may almost suffice to say, that of all living men her father was the man best conversant with the antiquities of the county in which he lived. He was the Jonathan Oldbuck of Devonshire, and especially of Dartmoor, without that decision of character which enabled Oldbuck to keep his womenkind in some kind of subjection, and probably enabled him also to see that his weekly bills did not pass their proper limits. Our Mr. Oldbuck, of Oxney Colne, was sadly deficient in these. As a parish pastor with but a small cure, he did his duty with sufficient energy to keep him, at any rate, from reproach. He was kind and charitable to the poor, punctual in his services, forbearing with the farmers around him, mild with his brother clergymen, and indifferent to aught that bishop or archdeacon might think or say of him. I do not name this latter attribute as a virtue, but as a fact. But all these points were as nothing in the known character of Mr. Woolsworthy, of Oxney Colne. He was the antiquarian of Dartmoor. That was his line of life. It was in that capacity that he was known to the Devonshire world; it was as such that he journeyed about with his humble carpet-bag, staying away from his parsonage a night or two at a time; it was in that character that he received now and again stray visitors in the single spare bedroom—not friends asked to see him and his girl because of their friendship—but men who knew something as to this buried stone, or that old land-mark. In all these things his daughter let him have his own way, assisting and encouraging him. That was his line of life, and therefore she respected it. But in all other matters she chose to be paramount at the parsonage.

Mr. Woolsworthy was a little man, who always wore, except on Sundays, grey clothes—clothes of so light a grey that they would hardly have been regarded as clerical in a district less remote. He had now reached a goodly age, being full seventy years old; but still he was wiry and active, and shewed but few symptoms of decay. His head was bald, and the few remaining locks that surrounded it were nearly white. But there was a look of energy about his mouth, and a humour in his light grey eye, which forbade those who knew him to regard him altogether as an old man. As it was, he could walk from Oxney Colne to Priestown, fifteen long Devonshire miles across the moor; and he who could do that could hardly be regarded as too old for work.

But our present story will have more to do with his daughter than with him. A pretty girl, I have said, was Patience Woolsworthy; and one, too, in many ways remarkable. She had taken her outlook into life, weighing the things which she had and those which she had not, in a manner very unusual, and, as a rule, not always desirable for a young lady. The things which she had not were very many. She had not society; she had not a fortune; she had not any assurance of future means of livelihood; she had not high hope of procuring for herself a position in life by marriage; she had not that excitement and pleasure in life which she read of in such books as found their way down to Oxney Colne Parsonage. It would be easy to add to the list of the things which she had not; and this list against herself she made out with the utmost vigour. The things which she had, or those rather which she assured herself of having, were much more easily counted. She had the birth and education of a lady, the strength of a healthy woman, and a will of her own. Such was the list as she made it out for herself, and I protest that I assert no more than the truth in saying that she never added to it either beauty, wit, or talent.

I began these descriptions by saying that Oxney Colne would, of all places, be the best spot from which a tourist could visit those parts of Devonshire, but for the fact that he could obtain there none of the accommodation which tourists require. A brother antiquarian might, perhaps, in those days have done so, seeing that there was, as I have said, a spare bedroom at the parsonage. Any intimate friend of Miss Le Smyrger's might be as fortunate, for she was equally well provided at Oxney Combe, by which name her house was known. But Miss Le

Smyrger was not given to extensive hospitality, and it was only to those who were bound to her, either by ties of blood or of very old friendship, that she delighted to open her doors. As her old friends were very few in number, as those few lived at a distance, and as her nearest relations were higher in the world than she was, and were said by herself to look down upon her, the visits made to Oxney Combe were few and far between.

But now, at the period of which I am writing, such a visit was about to be made. Miss Le Smyrger had a younger sister, who had inherited a property in the parish of Oxney Colne equal to that of the lady who now lived there; but this the younger sister had inherited beauty also, and she therefore, in early life, had found sundry lovers, one of whom became her husband. She had married a man even then well to do in the world, but now rich and almost mighty; a Member of Parliament, a Lord of this and that board, a man who had a house in Eaton-square, and a park in the north of England; and in this way her course of life had been very much divided from that of our Miss Le Smyrger. But the Lord of the Government board had been blessed with various children; and perhaps it was now thought expedient to look after Aunt Penelope's Devonshire acres. Aunt Penelope was empowered to leave them to whom she pleased; and though it was thought in Eaton-square that she must, as a matter of course, leave them to one of the family, nevertheless a little cousinly intercourse might make the thing more certain. I will not say that this was the sole cause for such a visit, but in these days a visit was to be made by Captain Broughton to his aunt. Now Captain John Broughton was the second son of Alfonso Broughton, of Clapham Park and Eaton-square, Member of Parliament, and Lord of the aforesaid Government Board.

"And what do you mean to do with him?" Patience Woolsworthy asked of Miss Le Smyrger when that lady walked over from the Combe to say that her nephew John was to arrive on the following morning.

"Do with him? Why, I shall bring him over here to talk to your father."

"He'll be too fashionable for that, and papa won't trouble his head about him if he finds that he doesn't care for Dartmoor."

"Then he may fall in love with you, my dear."

"Well, yes; there's that resource at any rate, and for your sake I dare say I should be more civil to him than papa. But he'll soon get tired of making love, and what you'll do then I cannot imagine."

That Miss Woolsworthy felt no interest in the coming of the Captain I will not pretend to say. The advent of any stranger with whom she would be called on to associate must be matter of interest to her in that secluded place; and she was not so absolutely unlike other young ladies that the arrival of an unmarried young man would be the same to her as the advent of some patriarchal paterfamilias. In taking that outlook into life of which I have spoken she had never said to herself that she despised those things from which other girls received the excitement, the joys, and the disappointment of their lives. She had simply given herself to understand that very little of such things would come her way, and that it behoved her to live—to live happily if such might be possible—without experiencing the need of them. She had heard, when there was no thought of any such visit to Oxney Colne, that John Broughton was a handsome, clever man—one who thought much of himself, and was thought much of by others—that there had been some talk of his marrying a great heiress, which marriage, however, had not taken place through unwillingness on his part, and that he was on the whole a man of more mark in the world than the ordinary captain of ordinary regiments.

Captain Broughton came to Oxney Combe, stayed there a fortnight,—the intended period for his projected visit having been fixed at three or four days—and then went his way. He went his way back to his London haunts, the time of the year then being the close of the Easter holydays; but as he did so he told his aunt that he should assuredly return to her in the autumn.

"And assuredly I shall be happy to see you, John—if you come with a certain purpose. If you have no such purpose, you had better remain away."

"I shall assuredly come," the Captain had replied, and then he had gone on his journey.

The summer passed rapidly by, and very little was said between Miss Le Smyrger and Miss Woolsworthy about Captain Broughton. In many respects—nay, I may say, as to all ordinary matters, no two women could well be more intimate with each other than they were,—and more than that, they had the courage each to talk to the other with absolute truth as to things concerning themselves—a courage in which dear friends often fail. But, nevertheless, very little was said between them about Captain John Broughton. All that was said may be here repeated.

"John says that he shall return here in August," Miss Le Smyrger said, as Patience was sitting with her in the parlour at Oxney Combe, on the morning after that gentleman's departure.

"He told me so himself," said Patience; and as she spoke her round dark eyes assumed a look of more than ordinary self-will. If Miss Le Smyrger had intended to carry the conversation any further, she changed her mind as she looked at her companion. Then, as I said, the summer ran by, and towards the close of the warm days of July, Miss Le Smyrger, sitting in the same chair in the same room, again took up the conversation.

"I got a letter from John this morning. He says that he shall be here on the third."

"Does he?"

"He is very punctual to the time he named."

"Yes; I fancy that he is a punctual man," said Patience.

"I hope that you will be glad to see him," said Miss Le Smyrger.

"Very glad to see him," said Patience, with a bold clear voice; and then the conversation was again dropped, and nothing further was said till after Captain Broughton's second arrival in the parish.

Four months had then passed since his departure, and during that time Miss Woolsworthy had performed all her usual daily duties in their accustomed course. No one could discover that she had been less careful in her household matters than had been her wont, less willing to go among her poor neighbours, or less assiduous in her attentions to her father. But not the less was there a feeling in the minds of those around her that some great change had come upon her. She would sit during the long summer evenings on a certain spot outside the parsonage orchard, at the top of a small sloping field in which their solitary cow was always pastured, with a book on her knees before her, but rarely reading. There she would sit, with the beautiful view down to the winding river below her, watching the setting sun, and thinking, thinking, thinking—thinking of something of which she had never spoken. Often would Miss Le Smyrger come upon her there, and sometimes would pass by her even without a word; but never—never once did she dare to ask her of the matter of her thoughts. But she knew the matter well enough. No confession was necessary to inform her that Patience Woolsworthy was in love with John Broughton—ay, in love, to the full and entire loss of her whole heart.

On one evening she was so sitting till the July sun had fallen and hidden himself for the night, when her father came upon her as he returned from one of his rambles on the moor. "Patty," he said, "you are always sitting there now. Is it not late? Will you not be cold?"

"No, papa," she said, "I shall not be cold."

"But won't you come to the house? I miss you when you come in so late that there's no time to say a word before we go to bed."

She got up and followed him into the parsonage, and when they were in the sitting-room together, and the door was closed, she came up to him and kissed him. "Papa," she said, "would it make you very unhappy if I were to leave you?"

"Leave me!" he said, startled by the serious and almost solemn tone of her voice. "Do you mean for always?"

"If I were to marry, papa?"

"Oh, marry! No; that would not make me unhappy. It would make me very happy, Patty, to see you married to a man you would love—very, very happy; though my days would be desolate without you."

"That is it, papa. What would you do if I went from you?"

"What would it matter, Patty? I should be free, at any rate, from a load which often presses heavy on me now. What will you do when I shall leave you? A few more years and all will be over with me. But who is it, love? Has anybody said anything to you?"

"It was only an idea, papa. I don't often think of such a thing; but I did think of it then." And so the subject was allowed to pass by. This had happened before the day of the second arrival had been absolutely fixed and made known to Miss Woolsworthy.

And then that second arrival took place. The reader may have understood from the words with which Miss Le Smyrger authorised her nephew to make his second visit to Oxney Combe that Miss Woolsworthy's passion was not altogether unauthorised. Captain

Broughton had been told that he was not to come unless he came with a certain purpose; and having been so told, he still persisted in coming. There can be no doubt but that he well understood the purport to which his aunt alluded. "I shall assuredly come," he had said. And true to his word, he was now there.

Patience knew exactly the hour at which he must arrive at the station at Newton Abbot, and the time also which it would take to travel over those twelve uphill miles from the station to Oxney. It need hardly be said that she paid no visit to Miss Le Smyrger's house on that afternoon; but she might have known something of Captain Broughton's approach without going thither. His road to the Combe passed by the parsonage-gate, and had Patience sat even at her bedroom window she must have seen him. But on such a morning she would not sit at her bedroom window—she would do nothing which would force her to accuse herself of a restless longing for her lover's coming. It was for him to seek her. If he chose to do so, he knew the way to the parsonage.

Miss Le Smyrger—good, dear, honest, hearty Miss Le Smyrger, was in a fever of anxiety on behalf of her friend. It was not that she wished her nephew to marry Patience—or rather that she had entertained any such wish when he first came among them. She was not given to match-making, and moreover thought, or had thought within herself, that they of Oxney Colne could do very well without any admixture from Eaton-square. Her plan of life had been that, when old Mr. Woolsworthy was taken away from Dartmoor, Patience should live with her; and that when she also shuffled off her coil, then Patience Woolsworthy should be the maiden mistress of Oxney Combe—of Oxney Combe and Mr. Cloysey's farm—to the utter detriment of all the Broughtons. Such had been her plan before nephew John had come among them—a plan not to be spoken of till the coming of that dark day which should make Patience an orphan. But now her nephew had been there, and all was to be altered. Miss Le Smyrger's plan would have provided a companion for her old age; but that had not been her chief object. She had thought more of Patience than of herself, and now it seemed that a prospect of a higher happiness was opening for her friend.

"John," she said, as soon as the first greetings were over, "do you remember the last words that I said to you before you went away?" Now, for myself, I much admire Miss Le Smyrger's heartiness, but I do not think much of her discretion. It would have been better, perhaps, had she allowed things to take their course.

"I can't say that I do," said the Captain. At the same time the Captain did remember very well what those last words had been.

"I am so glad to see you, so delighted to see you, if—if—if—," and then she paused, for with all her courage she hardly dared to ask her nephew whether he had come there with the express purpose of asking Miss Woolsworthy to marry him.

To tell the truth—for there is no room for mystery within the limits of this short story,—to tell, I say, at a word the plain and simple truth, Captain Broughton had already asked that question. On the day before he left Oxney Colne, he had in set terms proposed to the parson's daughter, and indeed the words, the hot and frequent words, which previously to that had fallen like sweetest honey into the ears of Patience Woolsworthy, had made it imperative on him to do so. When a man in such a place as that has talked to a girl of love day after day, must not he talk of it to some definite purpose on the day on which he leaves her? Or if he do not, must he not submit to be regarded as false, selfish, and almost fraudulent? Captain Broughton, however, had asked the question honestly and truly. He had done so honestly and truly, but in words, or, perhaps, simply with a tone, that had hardly sufficed to satisfy the proud spirit of the girl he loved. She by that time had confessed to herself that she loved him with all her heart; but she had made no such confession to him. To him she had spoken no word, granted no favour, that any lover might rightfully regard as a token of love returned. She had listened to him as he spoke, and bade him keep such sayings for the drawing-rooms of his fashionable friends. Then he had spoken out and had asked for that hand,—not, perhaps, as a suitor tremulous with hope,—but as a rich man who knows that he can command that which he desires to purchase.

"You should think more of this," she had said to him at last. "If you would really have me for your wife, it will not be much to you to return here again when time for thinking of it shall have passed by." With these words she had dismissed him, and now he had again come back to Oxney Colne. But still she would not place herself at the window to look for him, nor dress herself in other than her simple morning country dress, nor omit one item of her daily work. If he wished to take her at all, he should wish to take her as she really was, in her plain country life, but he should take her also with full observance of all those privileges which maidens are allowed to claim from their lovers. He should contract no ceremonious observance because she was the daughter of a poor country parson who would come to him without a shilling, whereas he stood high in the world's books. He had asked her to give him all that she had, and that all she was ready to give, without stint. But the gift must be valued before it could be given or received. He also was to give her as much, and she would accept it as being beyond all price. But she would not allow that that which was offered to her was in any degree the more precious because of his outward worldly standing.

She would not pretend to herself that she thought he would come to her that day, and therefore she busied herself in the kitchen and about the house, giving directions to her two maids as though the afternoon would pass as all other days did pass in that household. They usually dined at four, and she rarely, in these summer months, went far from the house before that hour. At four precisely she sat down with her father, and then said that she was going up as far as Helpholme after dinner. Helpholme was a solitary farmhouse in another parish, on the border of the moor, and Mr. Woolsworthy asked her whether he should accompany her.

"Do, papa," she said, "if you are not too tired." And yet she had thought how probable it might be that she should meet John Broughton on her walk. And so it was arranged; but, just as dinner was over, Mr. Woolsworthy remembered himself.

"Gracious me," he said, "how my memory is going. Gribbles, from Ivybridge, and old John Poulter, from Bovey, are coming to meet here by appointment. You can't put Helpholme off till to-morrow?"

Patience, however, never put off anything, and therefore at six o'clock, when her father had finished his slender modicum of toddy, she tied on her hat and went on her walk. She started forth with a quick step, and left no word to say by which route she would go. As she passed up along the little lane which led towards Oxney Combe, she would not even look to see if he was coming towards her; and when she left the road, passing over a stone stile into a little path which ran first through the upland fields, and then across the moor ground towards Helpholme, she did not look back once, or listen for his coming step.

She paid her visit, remaining upwards of an hour with the old bedridden mother of the tenant of Helpholme. "God bless you, my darling!" said the old woman as she left her; "and send you some one to make your own path bright and happy through the world." These words were still ringing in her ears with all their significance as she saw John Broughton waiting for her at the first stile which she had to pass after leaving the farmer's haggard.

"Patty," he said, as he took her hand, and held it close within both his own, "what a chase I have had after you!"

"And who asked you, Captain Broughton?" she answered, smiling. "If the journey was too much for your poor London strength, could you not have waited till to-morrow morning, when you would have found me at the parsonage?" But she did not draw her hand away from him, or in any way pretend that he had not a right to accost her as a lover.

"No, I could not wait. I am more eager to see those I love than you seem to be."

"How do you know whom I love, or how eager I might be to see them? There is an old woman there whom I love, and I have thought nothing of this walk with the object of seeing her." And now, slowly drawing her hand away from him, she pointed to the farmhouse which she had left.

"Patty," he said, after a minute's pause, during which she had looked full into his face with all the force of her bright eyes; "I have come from London to-day, straight down here to Oxney, and from my aunt's house close upon your footsteps after you, to ask you that one question. Do you love me?"

"What a Hercules!" she said, again laughing. "Do you really mean that you left London only this morning? Why, you must have been five hours in a railway carriage and two in a postchaise, not to talk of the walk afterwards. You ought to take more care of yourself, Captain Broughton!"

He would have been angry with her—for he did not like to be quizzed—had she not put her hand on his arm as she spoke, and the softness of her touch had redeemed the offence of her words.

"All that have I done," said he, "that I may hear one word from you."

"That any word of mine should have such potency! But let us walk on, or my father will take us for some of the standing stones of the moor. How have you found your aunt? If you only knew the cares that have sat on her dear shoulders for the last week past, in order that your high mightiness might have a sufficiency to eat and drink in these desolate half-starved regions."

"She might have saved herself such anxiety. No one can care less for such things than I do."

"And yet I think I have heard you boast of the cook of your club." And then again there was silence for a minute or two.

"Patty," said he, stopping again in the path; "answer my question. I have a right to demand an answer. Do you love me?"

"And what if I do? What if I have been so silly as to allow your perfections to be too many for my weak heart? What then, Captain Broughton?"

"It cannot be that you love me, or you would not joke now."

"Perhaps not, indeed," she said. It seemed as though she were resolved not to yield an inch in her own humour. And then again they walked on.

"Patty," he said once more, "I shall get an answer from you to-night,—this evening; now, during this walk, or I shall return to-morrow, and never revisit this spot again."

"Oh, Captain Broughton, how should we ever manage to live without you?"

"Very well," he said; "up to the end of this walk I can bear it all;—and one word spoken then will mend it all."

During the whole of this time she felt that she was ill-using him. She knew that she loved him with all her heart; that it would nearly kill her to part with him; that she had heard his renewed offer with an ecstacy of joy. She acknowledged to herself that he was giving proof of his devotion as strong as any which a girl could receive from her lover. And yet she could hardly bring herself to say the word he longed to hear. That word once said, and then she knew that she must succumb to her love for ever! That word once said, and there would be nothing for her but to spoil him with her idolatry! That word once said, and she must continue to repeat it into his ears, till perhaps he might be tired of hearing it! And now he had threatened her, and how could she speak it after that? She certainly would not speak it unless he asked her again without such threat. And so they walked on again in silence.

"Patty," he said at last. "By the heavens above us you shall answer me. Do you love me?"

She now stood still, and almost trembled as she looked up into his face. She stood opposite to him for a moment, and then placing her two hands on his shoulders, she answered him. "I do, I do, I do," she said, "with all my heart; with all my heart—with all my heart and strength." And then her head fell upon his breast.

Captain Broughton was almost as much surprised as delighted by the warmth of the acknowledgment made by the eager-hearted passionate girl whom he now held within his arms. She had said it now; the words had been spoken; and there was nothing for her but to swear to him over and over again with her sweetest oaths, that those words were true—true as her soul. And very sweet was the walk down from thence to the parsonage gate. He spoke no more of the distance of the ground, or the length of his day's journey. But he stopped her at every turn that he might press her arm the closer to his own, that he might look into the brightness of her eyes, and prolong his hour of delight. There were no more gibes now on her tongue, no raillery at his London finery, no laughing comments on his coming and going. With downright honesty she told him everything: how she had loved him before her heart was warranted in such a passion; how, with much thinking, she had resolved that it would be unwise to take him at his first word, and had thought it better that he should return to London, and then think over it; how she had almost repented of her courage when she had feared, during those long summer days, that he would forget her; and how her heart had leapt for joy when her old friend had told her that he was coming.

"And yet," said he, "you were not glad to see me!"

"Oh, was I not glad? You cannot understand the feelings of a girl who has lived secluded as I have done. Glad is no word for the joy I felt. But it was not seeing you that I cared for so much. It was the knowledge that you were near me once again. I almost wish now that I had not seen you till to-morrow." But as she spoke she pressed his arm, and this caress gave the lie to her last words.

"No, do not come in to-night," she said, when she reached the little wicket that led up to the parsonage. "Indeed, you shall not. I could not behave myself properly if you did."

"But I don't want you to behave properly."

"Oh! I am to keep that for London, am I? But, nevertheless, Captain Broughton, I will not invite you either to tea or to supper to-night."

"Surely I may shake hands with your father."

"Not to-night—not till—. John, I may tell him, may I not? I must tell him at once."

"Certainly," said he.

"And then you shall see him to-morrow. Let me see—at what hour shall I bid you come?"

"To breakfast."

"No, indeed. What on earth would your aunt do with her broiled turkey and the cold pie? I have got no cold pie for you."

"I hate cold pie."

"What a pity! But, John, I should be forced to have you directly after breakfast. Come down—come down at two, or three; and then I will go back with you to Aunt Penelope. I must see her to-morrow;" and so at last the matter was settled, and the happy Captain, as he left her, was hardly resisted in his attempt to press her lips to his own.

When she entered the parlour in which her father was sitting, there still were Gribbles and Poulter discussing some knotty point of Devon lore. So Patience took off her hat, and sat herself down, waiting till they should go. For full an hour she had to wait, and then Gribbles and Poulter did go. But it was not in such matters as this that Patience Woolsworthy was impatient. She could wait, and wait, and wait, curbing herself for weeks and months, while the thing waited for was in her eyes good; but she could not curb her hot thoughts or her hot words when things came to be discussed which she did not think to be good.

"Papa," she said, when Gribbles' long-drawn last word had been spoken at the door. "Do you remember how I asked you the other day what you would say if I were to leave you?"

"Yes, surely," he replied, looking up at her in astonishment.

"I am going to leave you now," she said. "Dear, dearest father, how am I to go from you?"

"Going to leave me," said he, thinking of her visit to Helpholme, and thinking of nothing else.

Now, there had been a story about Helpholme. That bed-ridden old lady there had a stalwart son, who was now the owner of the Helpholme pastures. But though owner in fee of all those wild acres, and of the cattle which they supported, he was not much above the farmers around him, either in manners or education. He had his merits, however; for he was honest, well-to-do in the world, and modest withal. How strong love had grown up, springing from neighbourly kindness, between our Patience and his mother, it needs not here to tell; but rising from it had come another love—or an ambition which might have grown to love. The young man, after much thought, had not dared to speak to Miss Woolsworthy, but he had sent a message by Miss Le Smyrger. If there could be any hope for him, he would present himself as a suitor—on trial. He did not owe a shilling in the world, and had money by him—saved. He wouldn't ask the parson for a shilling of fortune. Such had been the tenor of his message, and Miss Le Smyrger had delivered it faithfully. "He does not mean it," Patience had said with her stern voice. "Indeed he does, my dear. You may be sure he is in earnest," Miss Le Smyrger had replied; "and there is not an honester man in these parts."

"Tell him," said Patience, not attending to the latter portion of her friend's last speech, "that it cannot be—make him understand, you know—and tell him also that the matter shall be thought of no more." The matter had, at any rate, been spoken of no more, but the young farmer still remained a bachelor, and Helpholme still wanted a mistress. But all this came back upon the parson's mind when his daughter told him that she was about to leave him.

"Yes, dearest," she said; and as she spoke she now knelt at his knees. "I have been asked in marriage, and I have given myself away."

"Well, my love, if you will be happy— "

"I hope I shall; I think I shall. But you, papa?"

"You will not be far from us."

"Oh, yes; in London."

"In London?"

"Captain Broughton lives in London generally."

"And has Captain Broughton asked you to marry him?"

"Yes, papa—who else? Is he not good? Will you not love him? Oh, papa, do not say that I am wrong to love him?"

He never told her his mistake, or explained to her that he had not thought it possible that the high-placed son of the London great man should have fallen in love with his undowered daughter; but he embraced her, and told her, with all his enthusiasm, that he rejoiced in her joy, and would be happy in her happiness. "My own Patty," he said, "I have ever known that you were too good for this life of ours here." And then the evening wore away into the night, with many tears, but still with much happiness.

Captain Broughton, as he walked back to Oxney Combe, made up his mind that he would say nothing on the matter to his aunt till the next morning. He wanted to think over it all, and to think it over, if possible, by himself. He had taken a step in life, the most important that a man is ever called on to take, and he had to reflect whether or no he had taken it with wisdom.

"Have you seen her?" said Miss Le Smyrger, very anxiously, when he came into the drawing-room.

"Miss Woolsworthy you mean," said he. "Yes, I've seen her. As I found her out, I took a long walk, and happened to meet her. Do you know, aunt, I think I'll go to bed; I was up at five this morning, and have been on the move ever since."

Miss Le Smyrger perceived that she was to hear nothing that evening, so she handed him his candle-stick and allowed him to go to his room.

But Captain Broughton did not immediately retire to bed, nor when he did so was he able to sleep at once. Had this step that he had taken been a wise one? He was not a man who, in worldly matters, had allowed things to arrange themselves for him, as is the case with so many men. He had formed views for himself, and had a theory of life. Money for money's sake he had declared to himself to be bad. Money, as a concomitant to things which were in themselves good, he had declared to himself to be good also. That concomitant in this affair of his marriage, he had now missed. Well; he had made up his mind to that, and would put up with the loss. He had means of living of his own, the means not so extensive as might have been desirable. That it would be well for him to become a married man, looking merely to that state of life as opposed to his present state, he had fully resolved. On that point, therefore, there was nothing to repent. That Patty Woolsworthy was good, affectionate, clever, and beautiful he was sufficiently satisfied. It would be odd indeed if he were not so satisfied now, seeing that for the last four months he had so declared to himself daily with many inward asseverations. And yet though, he repeated, now again that he was satisfied, I do not think that he was so fully satisfied of it as he had been throughout the whole of those four months. It is sad to say so, but I fear—I fear that such was the case. When you have your plaything, how much of the anticipated pleasure vanishes, especially if it be won easily.

He had told none of his family what were his intentions in this second visit to Devonshire, and now he had to bethink himself whether they would be satisfied. What would his sister say, she who had married the Honourable Augustus Gumbleton, gold-stick-in-waiting to Her Majesty's Privy Council? Would she receive Patience with open arms, and make much of her about London? And then how far would London suit Patience, or would Patience suit London? There would be much for him to do in teaching her, and it would be well for him to set about the lesson without loss of time. So far he got that night, but when the morning came he went a step further, and began mentally to criticise her manner to himself. It had been very sweet, that warm, that full, that ready declaration of love. Yes; it had been very sweet; but—but—; when, after her little jokes, she did confess her love, had she not been a little too free for feminine excellence? A man likes to be told that he is loved, but he hardly wishes that the girl he is to marry should fling herself at his head!

Ah me! yes; it was thus he argued to himself as on that morning he went through the arrangements of his toilet. "Then he was a brute," you say, my pretty reader. I have never said that he was not a brute. But this I remark, that many such brutes are to be met with in the beaten paths of the world's high highway. When Patience Woolsworthy had answered him coldly, bidding him go back to London and think over his love; while it seemed from her manner that at any rate as yet she did not care for him; while he was absent from her, and, therefore, longing for her, the possession of her charms, her talent and bright honesty of purpose had seemed to him a thing most desirable. Now they were his own. They had, in fact, been his own from the first. The heart of this country-bred girl had fallen at the first word from his mouth. Had she not so confessed to him? She was very nice—very nice indeed. He loved her dearly. But had he not sold himself too cheaply?

I by no means say that he was not a brute. But whether brute or no he was an honest man, and had no remotest dream, either then, on that morning, or during the following days on which such thoughts pressed more thickly on his mind—of breaking away from his pledged word. At breakfast on that morning he told all to Miss Le Smyrger, and that lady, with warm and gracious intentions, confided to him her purpose regarding her property. "I have always regarded Patience as my heir," she said, "and shall do so still."

"Oh, indeed," said Captain Broughton.

"But it is a great, great pleasure to me to think that she will give back the little property to my sister's child. You will have your mother's, and thus it will all come together again."

"Ah!" said Captain Broughton. He had his own ideas about property, and did not, even under existing circumstances, like to hear that his aunt considered herself at liberty to leave the acres away to one who was by blood quite a stranger to the family.

"Does Patience know of this?" he asked.

"Not a word," said Miss Le Smyrger. And then nothing more was said upon the subject.

On that afternoon he went down and received the parson's benediction and congratulations with a good grace. Patience said very little on the occasion, and indeed was absent during the greater part of the interview. The two lovers then walked up to Oxney Combe, and there were more benedictions and more congratulations. "All went merry as a marriage bell," at any rate as far as Patience was concerned. Not a word had yet fallen from that dear mouth, not a look had yet come over that handsome face, which tended in any way to mar her bliss. Her first day of acknowledged love was a day altogether happy, and when she prayed for him as she knelt beside her bed there was no feeling in her mind that any fear need disturb her joy.

I will pass over the next three or four days very quickly, merely saying that Patience did not find them so pleasant as that first day after her engagement. There was something in her lover's manner—something which at first she could not define—which by degrees seemed to grate against her feelings. He was sufficiently affectionate, that being a matter on which she did not require much demonstration; but joined to his affection there seemed to be—; she hardly liked to suggest to herself a harsh word, but could it be possible that he was beginning to think that she was not good enough for him? And then she asked herself the question—was she good enough for him? If there were doubt about that, the match should be broken off, though she tore her own heart out in the struggle. The truth, however, was this—that he had begun that teaching which he had already found to be so necessary. Now, had any one essayed to teach Patience German or mathematics, with that young lady's free consent, I believe that she would have been found a meek scholar. But it was not probable that she would be meek when she found a self-appointed tutor teaching her manners and conduct without her consent.

So matters went on for four or five days, and on the evening of the fifth day, Captain Broughton and his aunt drank tea at the parsonage. Nothing very especial occurred; but as the parson and Miss Le Smyrger insisted on playing backgammon with devoted perseverance during the whole evening, Broughton had a good opportunity of saying a word or two about those changes in his lady-love which a life in London would require—and some word he said also—some single slight word as to the higher station in life to which he would exalt his bride. Patience bore it—for her father and Miss Le Smyrger were in the room—she bore it well, speaking no syllable of anger, and enduring, for the moment, the implied scorn of the old parsonage. Then the evening broke up, and Captain Broughton walked back to Oxney Combe with his aunt. "Patty," her father said to her before they went to bed, "he seems to me to be a most excellent young man." "Dear papa," she answered, kissing him. "And terribly deep in love," said Mr. Woolsworthy. "Oh, I don't know about that," she answered, as she left him with her sweetest smile. But though she could thus smile at her father's joke, she had already made up her mind that there was still something to be learned as to her promised husband before she could place herself altogether in his hands. She would ask him whether he thought himself liable to injury from this proposed marriage; and though he should deny any such thought, she would know from the manner of his denial what his true feelings were.

And he, too, on that night, during his silent walk with Miss Le Smyrger, had entertained some similar thoughts. "I fear she is obstinate," he had said to himself, and then he had half accused her of being sullen also. "If that be her temper, what a life of misery I have before me!"

"Have you fixed a day yet?" his aunt asked him as they came near to her house.

"No, not yet: I don't know whether it will suit me to fix it before I leave."

"Why, it was but the other day you were in such a hurry."

"Ah—yes—I have thought more about it since then."

"I should have imagined that this would depend on what Patty thinks," said Miss Le Smyrger, stand-up for the privileges of her sex. "It is presumed that the gentleman is always ready as soon the lady will consent."

"Yes, in ordinary cases it is so; but when a girl is taken out of her own sphere— "

"Her own sphere! Let me caution you, Master John, not to talk to Patty about her own sphere."

"Aunt Penelope, as Patience is to be my wife and not yours, I must claim permission to speak to her on such subjects as may seem suitable to me." And then they parted—not in the best humour with each other.

On the following day Captain Broughton and Miss Woolsworthy did not meet till the evening. She had said, before those few ill-omened words had passed her lover's lips, that she would probably be at Miss Le Smyrger's house on the following morning. Those ill-omened words did pass her lover's lips, and then she remained at home. This did not come from sullenness, nor even from anger, but from a conviction that it would be well that she should think much before she met him again. Nor was he anxious to hurry a meeting. His thought—his base thought—was this; that she would be sure to come up to the Combe after him; but she did not come, and therefore in the evening he went down to her, and asked her to walk with him.

They went away by the path that led to Helpholme, and little was said between them till they had walked some mile together. Patience, as she went along the path, remembered almost to the letter the sweet words which had greeted her ears as she came down that way with him on the night of his arrival; but he remembered nothing of that sweetness then. Had he not made an ass of himself during these last six months? That was the thought which very much had possession of his mind.

"Patience," he said at last, having hitherto spoken only an indifferent word now and again since they had left the parsonage, "Patience, I hope you realise the importance of the step which you and I are about to take?"

"Of course I do," she answered: "what an odd question that is for you to ask!"

"Because," said he, "sometimes I almost doubt it. It seems to me as though you thought you could remove yourself from here to your new home with no more trouble than when you go from home up to the Combe."

"Is that meant for a reproach, John?"

"No, not for a reproach, but for advice. Certainly not for a reproach."

"I am glad of that."

"But I should wish to make you think how great is the leap in the world which you are about to take." Then again they walked on for many steps before she answered him.

"Tell me then, John," she said, when she had sufficiently considered what words she would speak; and as she spoke a bright colour suffused her face, and her eyes flashed almost with anger. "What leap do you mean? Do you mean a leap upwards?"

"Well, yes; I hope it will be so."

"In one sense, certainly, it would be a leap upwards. To be the wife of the man I loved; to have the privilege of holding his happiness in my hand; to know that I was his own—the companion whom he had chosen out of all the world—that would, indeed, be a leap upwards; a leap almost to heaven, if all that were so. But if you mean upwards in any other sense— "

"I was thinking of the social scale."

"Then, Captain Broughton, your thoughts were doing me dishonour."

"Doing you dishonour!"

"Yes, doing me dishonour. That your father is, in the world's esteem, a greater man than mine is doubtless true enough. That you, as a man, are richer than I am as a woman, is doubtless also true. But you dishonour me, and yourself also, if these things can weigh with you now."

"Patience,—I think you can hardly know what words you are saying to me."

"Pardon me, but I think I do. Nothing that you can give me—no gifts of that description—can weigh aught against that which I am giving you. If you had all the wealth and rank of the greatest lord in the land, it would count as nothing in such a scale. If—as I have not doubted—if in return for my heart you have given me yours, then—then—then you have paid me fully. But when gifts such as those are going, nothing else can count even as a make-weight."

"I do not quite understand you," he answered, after a pause. "I fear you are a little high-flown." And then, while the evening was still early, they walked back to the parsonage almost without another word.

Captain Broughton at this time had only one full day more to remain at Oxney Colne. On the afternoon following that he was to go as far as Exeter, and thence return to London. Of course, it was to be expected that the wedding day would be fixed before he went, and much had been said about it during the first day or two of his engagement. Then he had pressed for an early time, and Patience, with a girl's usual diffidence, had asked for some little delay. But now nothing was said on the subject; and how was it probable that such a matter could be settled after such a conversation as that which I have related? That evening, Miss Le Smyrger asked whether the day had been fixed. "No," said Captain Broughton harshly; "nothing has been fixed." "But it will be arranged before you go." "Probably not," he said; and then the subject was dropped for the time.

"John," she said, just before she went to bed, "if there be anything wrong between you and Patience, I conjure you to tell me."

"You had better ask her," he replied. "I can tell you nothing."

On the following morning he was much surprised by seeing Patience on the gravel path before Miss Le Smyrger's gate immediately after breakfast. He went to the door to open it for her, and she, as she gave him her hand, told him that she came up to speak to him. There was no hesitation in her manner, nor any look of anger in her face. But there was in her gait and form, in her voice and countenance, a fixedness of purpose which he had never seen before, or at any rate had never acknowledged.

"Certainly," said he. "Shall I come out with you, or will you come up stairs?"

"We can sit down in the summer-house," she said; and thither they both went.

"Captain Broughton," she said—and she began her task the moment that they were both seated—"You and I have engaged ourselves as man and wife, but perhaps we have been over rash."

"How so?" said he.

"It may be—and indeed I will say more—it is the case that we have made this engagement without knowing enough of each other's character."

"I have not thought so."

"The time will perhaps come when you will so think, but for the sake of all that we most value, let it come before it is too late. What would be our fate—how terrible would be our misery—if such a thought should come to either of us after we have linked our lots together."

There was a solemnity about her as she thus spoke which almost repressed him,—which for a time did prevent him from taking that tone of authority which on such a subject he would choose to adopt. But he recovered himself. "I hardly think that this comes well from you," he said.

"From whom else should it come? Who else can fight my battle for me; and, John, who else can fight that same battle on your behalf? I tell you this, that with your mind standing towards me as it does stand at present, you could not give me your hand at the altar with true words and a happy conscience. Am I not true? You have half repented of your bargain already. Is it not so?"

He did not answer her; but getting up from his seat walked to the front of the summer-house, and stood there with his back turned upon her. It was not that he meant to be ungracious, but in truth he did not know how to answer her. He had half repented of his bargain.

"John," she said, getting up and following him, so that she could put her hand upon his arm, "I have been very angry with you."

"Angry with me!" he said, turning sharp upon her.

"Yes, angry with you. You would have treated me like a child. But that feeling has gone now. I am not angry now. There is my hand;—the hand of a friend. Let the words that have been spoken between us be as though they had not been spoken. Let us both be free."

"Do you mean it?" he asked.

"Certainly I mean it." As she spoke these words her eyes were filled with tears, in spite of all the efforts she could make; but he was not looking at her, and her efforts had sufficed to prevent any sob from being audible.

"With all my heart," he said; and it was manifest from his tone that he had no thought of her happiness as he spoke. It was true that she had been angry with him—angry, as she had herself declared; but nevertheless, in what she had said and what she had done, she had thought more of his happiness than of her own. Now she was angry once again.

"With all your heart, Captain Broughton! Well, so be it. If with all your heart, then is the necessity so much the greater. You go to-morrow. Shall we say farewell now?"

"Patience, I am not going to be lectured."

"Certainly not by me. Shall we say farewell now?"

"Yes, if you are determined."

"I am determined. Farewell, Captain Broughton. You have all my wishes for your happiness." And she held out her hand to him.

"Patience!" he said. And he looked at her with a dark frown, as though he would strive to frighten her into submission. If so, he might have saved himself any such attempt.

"Farewell, Captain Broughton. Give me your hand, for I cannot stay." He gave her his hand, hardly knowing why he did so. She lifted it to her lips and kissed it, and then, leaving him, passed from the summer-house down through the wicket-gate, and straight home to the parsonage.

During the whole of that day she said no word to anyone of what had occurred. When she was once more at home she went about her household affairs as she had done on that day of his arrival. When she sat down to dinner with her father he observed nothing to make him think that she was unhappy; nor during the evening was there any expression in her face, or any tone in her voice, which excited his attention. On the following morning Captain Broughton called at the parsonage, and the servant-girl brought word to her mistress that he was in the parlour. But she would not see him. "Laws, miss, you ain't a quarrelled with your beau?" the poor girl said. "No, not quarrelled," she said; "but give him that." It was a scrap of paper, containing a word or two in pencil. "It is better that we should not meet again. God bless you." And from that day to this, now more than ten years, they never have met.

"Papa," she said to her father that afternoon, "dear papa, do not be angry with me. It is all over between me and John Broughton. Dearest, you and I will not be separated."

It would be useless here to tell how great was the old man's surprise and how true his sorrow. As the tale was told to him no cause was given for anger with anyone. Not a word was spoken against the suitor who had on that day returned to London with a full conviction that now at least he was relieved from his engagement. "Patty, my darling child," he said, "may God grant that it be for the best!"

"It is for the best," she answered stoutly. "For this place I am fit; and I much doubt whether I am fit for any other."

On that day she did not see Miss Le Smyrger, but on the following morning, knowing that Captain Broughton had gone off, having heard the wheels of the carriage as they passed by the parsonage gate on his way to the station,—she walked up to the Combe.

"He has told you, I suppose?" said she.

"Yes," said Miss Le Smyrger. "And I will never see him again unless he asks your pardon on his knees. I have told him so. I would not even give him my hand as he went."

"But why so, thou kindest one? The fault was mine more than his."

"I understand. I have eyes in my head," said the old maid. "I have watched him for the last four or five days. If you could have kept the truth to yourself and bade him keep off from you, he would have been at your feet now, licking the dust from your shoes."

"But, dear friend, I do not want a man to lick dust from my shoes."

"Ah, you are a fool. You do not know the value of your own wealth."

"True; I have been a fool. I was a fool to think that one coming from such a life as he has led could be happy with such as I am. I know the truth now. I have bought the lesson dearly,—but perhaps not too dearly, seeing that it will never be forgotten."

There was but little more said about the matter between our three friends at Oxney Colne. What, indeed, could be said? Miss Le Smyrger for a year or two still expected that her nephew would return and claim his bride; but he has never done so, nor has there been any correspondence between them. Patience Woolsworthy had learned her lesson dearly. She had given her whole heart to the man; and, though she so bore herself that no one was aware of the violence of the struggle, nevertheless the struggle within her bosom was very violent. She never told herself that she had done wrong; she never regretted her loss; but yet—yet!—the loss was very hard to bear. He also had loved her, but he was not capable of a love which could much injure his daily peace. Her daily peace was gone for many a day to come.

Her father is still living; but there is a curate now in the parish. In conjunction with him and with Miss Le Smyrger she spends her time in the concerns of the parish. In her own eyes she is a confirmed old maid; and such is my opinion also. The romance of her life was played out in that summer. She never sits now lonely on the hill-side thinking how much she might do for one whom she really loved. But with a large heart she loves many, and, with no romance, she works hard to lighten the burdens of those she loves.

As for Captain Broughton, all the world know that he did marry that great heiress with whom his name was once before connected, and that he is now a useful member of Parliament, working on committees three or four days a week with a zeal that is indefatigable. Sometimes, not often, as he thinks of Patience Woolsworthy, a gratified smile comes across his face.

Returning Home

Originally appeared in *Public Opinion*, 30 November and 7 December 1861. Reprinted in *Tales of All Countries* [Second Series] (1863). Written 20–26 January 1861, during the composition of *Orley Farm*. The story is closely based on fact. Trollope visited Costa Rica in the spring of 1859, and himself followed the route described in the story. From San José to the Serapiqui River the first stage was on muleback, the next by canoe down to its confluence with the San Juan River, and finally down that river to Greytown. Not long before Trollope reached San José, an Englishman and his wife had started their journey the same way, coming to grief much as is described in 'Returning Home.' A further account of their ordeal will be found in Trollope's first travel-book, *The West Indies and the Spanish Main* (1859), ch. 20.

It is generally supposed that people who live at home,—good domestic people, who love tea and their arm-chairs, and who keep the parlour hearth-rug ever warm,—it is generally supposed that these are the people who value home the most, and best appreciate all the comforts of that cherished institution. I am inclined to doubt this. It is, I think, to those who live farthest away from home, to those who find the greatest difficulty in visiting home, that the word conveys the sweetest idea. In some distant parts of the world it may be that an Englishman acknowledges his permanent resting place; but there are many others in which he will not call his daily house, his home. He would, in his own idea, desecrate the word by doing so. His Home is across the blue waters, in the little northern island, which perhaps he may visit no more; which he has left, at any rate, for half his life; from which circumstances, and the necessity of living, have banished him. His home is still in England, and when he speaks of home his thoughts are there.

No one can understand the intensity of this feeling who has not seen or felt the absence of interest in life which falls to the lot of many who have to eat their bread on distant soils. We are all apt to think that a life in strange countries will be a life of excitement, of stirring enterprise, and varied scenes;—that in abandoning the comforts of home, we shall receive in exchange more of movement and of adventure than would come in our way in our own tame country; and this feeling has, I am sure, sent many a young man roaming. Take any spirited fellow of twenty, and ask him whether he would like to go to Mexico for the next ten years! Prudence and his father may ultimately save him from such banishment, but he will not refuse without a pang of regret.

Alas; it is a mistake, Bread may be earned, and fortunes, perhaps, made in such countries; and as it is the destiny of our race to spread itself over the wide face of the globe, it is well that there should be something to gild and paint the outward face of that lot which so many are called upon to choose. But for a life of daily excitement, there is no life like life in England; and the farther that one goes from England the more stagnant, I think, do the waters of existence become.

But if it be so for men, it is ten times more so for women. An Englishman, if he be at Guatemala or Belize, must work for his bread, and that work will find him in thought and excitement. But what of his wife? Where will she find excitement? By what pursuit will she repay herself for all that she has left behind her at her mother's fireside? She will love her husband. Yes; that at least! If there be not that, there will be a hell, indeed. Then she will nurse her children, and talk of her—home. When the time shall come that her promised return thither is within a year or two of its accomplishment, her thoughts will all be fixed on that coming pleasure, as are the thoughts of a young girl on her first ball for the fortnight before that event comes off.

On the central plain of that portion of Central America which is called Costa Rica stands the city of San José. It is the capital of the Republic,—for Costa Rica is a Republic,—and, for Central America, is a town of some importance. It is in the middle of the coffee district, surrounded by rich soil on which the sugar-cane is produced, is blessed with a climate only moderately hot, and the native inhabitants are neither cut-throats nor cannibals. It may be said, therefore, that by comparison with some other spots to which Englishmen and others are congregated for the gathering together of money, San José may be considered as a happy region; but, nevertheless, a life there is not in every way desirable. It is a dull place, with little to interest either the eye or the ear. Although the heat of the tropics is but little felt there on account of its altitude, men and women become too lifeless for much enterprise. There is no society. There are a few Germans and a few Englishmen in the place, who see each other on matters of business during the day; but, sombre as life generally is, they seem to care little for each other's company on any other footing. I know not to what point the aspirations of the Germans may stretch themselves, but to the English the one idea that gives salt to life is the idea of home. On some day, however distant it may be, they will once more turn their faces towards the little northern island, and then all will be well with them.

To a certain Englishman there, and to his dear little wife, this prospect came some few years since somewhat suddenly. Events and tidings, it matters not which or what, brought it about that they resolved between themselves that they would start immediately;—almost immediately. They would pack up and leave San José within four months of the day on which their purpose was first formed. At San José a period of only four months for such a purpose was immediately. It creates a feeling of instant excitement, a necessity for instant doing, a consciousness that there was in those few weeks ample work both for the hands and thoughts,—work almost more than ample. The dear little wife, who for the last two years had been so listless, felt herself flurried.

"Harry," she said to her husband, "How shall we ever be ready?" And her pretty face was lighted up with unusual brightness at the happy thought of so much haste with such an object. "And baby's things too," she said, as she thought of all the various little articles of dress that would be needed. A journey from San José to Southampton cannot in truth be made as easily as one from London to Liverpool. Let us think of a month to be passed without any aid from the washerwoman, and the greatest part of that month amidst the sweltering heats of the West Indian tropics!

In the first month of her hurry and flurry Mrs. Arkwright was a happy woman. She would see her mother again and her sisters. It was now four years since she had left them on the quay at Southampton, while all their hearts were broken at the parting. She was a young bride then going forth with her new lord to meet the stern world. He had then been home to look for a wife, and he had found what he looked for in the younger sister of his partner. For he, Henry Arkwright, and his wife's brother, Abel Ring, had established themselves together in San José. And now, she thought, how there would be another meeting on those quays at which there should be no broken hearts; at which there should be love without sorrow, and kisses, sweet with the sweetness of welcome, not bitter with the bitterness of parting. And people told her,—the few neighbours around her,—how happy, how fortunate she was to get home thus early in her life. They had been out some ten,—some twenty years, and still the day of their return was distant. And then she pressed her living baby to her breast, and wiped away a tear as she thought of the other darling whom she would leave beneath that distant sod.

And then came the question as to the route home. San José stands in the middle of the high plain of Costa Rica, half way between the Pacific and the Atlantic. The journey thence down to the Pacific is, by comparison, easy. There is a road, and the mules on which the travellers must ride go steadily and easily down to Punta Arenas, the port on that ocean. There are inns too on the way,—places of public entertainment at which refreshment may be obtained, and beds, or fair substitutes for beds. But then by this route the traveller must take a long additional sea voyage. He must convey himself and his weary baggage down to that wretched place on the Pacific, there wait for a steamer to take him to Panamá, cross the isthmus, and reship himself in the other waters for his long journey home. That terrible unshipping and reshipping is a sore burden to the unaccustomed traveller. When it is absolutely necessary,—then indeed it is done without much thought; but in the case of the Arkwrights it was not absolutely necessary. And there was another reason which turned Mrs. Arkwright's heart against that journey by Punt' Arenas. The place is unhealthy, having at certain seasons a very bad name;—and here on their outward journey her husband had been taken ill. She had never ceased to think of the fortnight she had spent there among uncouth strangers during a portion of which his life had trembled in the balance. Early, therefore, in those four months she begged that she might not be taken round by Punt' Arenas. There was another route. "Harry, if you love me, let me go by the Serapiqui." As to Harry's loving her, there was no doubt about that, as she well knew.

There was this other route by the Serapiqui river, and by Greytown. Greytown, it is true, is quite as unhealthy as Punt' Arenas, and by that route one's baggage must be shipped and unshipped into small boats. There are all manner of difficulties attached to it. Perhaps no direct road to and from any city on the world's surface is subject to sharper fatigue while it lasts. Journeying by this route also, the traveller leaves San José mounted on his mule, and so mounted he makes his way through the vast primeval forests down to the banks of the Serapiqui river. That there is a track for him is of course true; but it is simply a track, and during nine months of the twelve is so deep in mud that the mules sink in it to their bellies. Then, when the river has been reached, the traveller seats him in his canoe, and for two days is paddled down,—down along the Serapiqui, into the San Juan river, and down along the San Juan till he reaches Greytown, passing one night at some hut on the river side. At Greytown he waits for the steamer which will carry him his first stage on his road towards Southampton. He must be a connoisseur in disagreeables of every kind who can say with any precision whether Greytown or Punt' Arenas is the better place for a week's sojourn.

For a full month Mr. Arkwright would not give way to his wife. At first he all but conquered her by declaring that the Serapiqui journey would be dangerous for the baby; but she heard from some one that it could be made less fatiguing for the baby than the other route. A baby had been carried down in a litter strapped on to a mule's back. A guide at the mule's head would be necessary, and that was all. When once in her boat the baby would be as well as in her cradle. What purpose cannot a woman gain by perseverance? Her purpose in this instance Mrs. Arkwright did at last gain by persevering.

And then their preparations for the journey went on with much flurrying and hot haste. To us at home, who live and feel our life everyday, the manufacture of endless baby-linen and the packing of mountains of clothes does not give an idea of much pleasurable excitement; but at San José, where there was scarcely motion enough in existence to prevent its waters from becoming foul with stagnation, this packing of baby-linen was delightful, and for a month or so the days went by with happy wings.

But by degrees reports began to reach both Arkwright and his wife as to this new route, which made them uneasy. The wet season had been prolonged, and even though they might not be deluged by rain themselves, the path would be in such a state of mud as to render the labour incessant. One or two people declared that the road was unfit at any time for a woman,—and then the river would be much swollen. These tidings did not reach Arkwright and his wife together, or at any rate not till late amidst their preparations, or a change might still have been made. As it was, after all her entreaties, Mrs. Arkwright did not like to ask him again to alter his plans; and he, having altered them once, was averse to change them again. So things went on till the mules and the boats had been hired, and things had gone so far that no change could then be made without much cost and trouble.

During the last ten days of their sojourn at San José Mrs. Arkwright had lost all that appearance of joy which had cheered up her sweet face during the last few months. Terror at that terrible journey obliterated in her mind all the happiness which had arisen from the hope of being soon at home. She was thoroughly cowed by the danger to be encountered, and would gladly have gone down to Punt' Arenas, had it been now possible that she could so arrange it. It rained, and rained, and still rained, when there was now only a week from the time before they started. Oh! if they could only wait for another month! But this she said to no one. After what had passed between her and her husband, she had not the heart to say such words to him. Arkwright himself was a man not given to much talking, a silent thoughtful man, stern withall in his outward bearing, but tender hearted and loving in his nature. The sweet young wife who had left all and come with him out to that dull distant place, was very dear to him,—dearer than she herself was aware, and in these days he was thinking much of her coming troubles. Why had he given way to her foolish prayers? Ah, why indeed?

And thus the last few days of their sojourn in San José passed away from them. Once or twice during these days she did speak out, expressing her fears. Her feelings were too much for her, and she could not restrain herself. "Poor mamma," she said, "I shall never see her!" And then again, "Harry, I know I shall never reach home alive."

"Fanny, my darling, that is nonsense." But in order that his spoken word might not sound stern to her, he took her in his arms and kissed her.

"You must behave well, Fanny," he said to her the day before they started. Though her heart was then very low within her, she promised him that she would do her best, and then she made a great resolution. Though she should be dying on the road, she would not complain beyond the absolute necessity of her nature. She fully recognised his thoughtful tender kindness, for though he thus cautioned her, he never told her that the dangers which she feared were the result of her own choice. He never threw in her teeth those prayers which she had made, in yielding to which he knew that he had been weak.

Then came the morning of their departure. The party of travellers consisted of four besides the baby. There was Mr. Arkwright, his wife, and an English nurse, who was going to England with them, and her brother Abel Ring, who was to accompany them as far as the Serapiqui river. When they had reached that, the real labour of the journey would be over. They had eight mules: four for the four travellers, one for the baby, a spare mule laden simply with blankets, so that Mrs. Arkwright might change in order that she should not be fatigued by the fatigue of her beast, and two for their luggage. The heavier portion of their baggage had already been sent off by Punt' Arenas, and would meet them at the other side of the Isthmus of Panama.

For the last four days the rain had ceased,—had ceased at any rate at San José. Those who knew the country well, would know that it might still be raining over those vast forests; but now, as the matter was settled, they would hope for the best. On that morning on which they started the sun shone fairly, and they accepted this as an omen of good. Baby seemed to lay comfortably on her pile of blankets on the mule's back, and the face of the tall Indian guide who took his place at that mule's head pleased the anxious mother.

"Not leave him ever," he said in Spanish, laying his hand on the cord which was fastened to the beast's head; and not for one moment did he leave his charge, though the labour of sticking close to him was very great.

They had four attendants or guides, all of whom made the journey on foot. That they were all men of mixed race was probable; but three of them would have been called Spaniards, Spaniards, that is, of Costa Rica, and the other would be called an Indian. One of the Spaniards was the leader, or chief man of the party, but the others seemed to stand on an equal footing with each other; and indeed the place of greatest care had been given to the Indian.

For the first four or five miles their route lay along the high road which leads from San José to Punt' Arenas, and so far a group of acquaintances followed them, all mounted on mules. Here, where the ways forked, their road leading through the great forests to the Atlantic, they separated, and many tears were shed on each side. What might be the future life of the Arkwrights had not been absolutely fixed, but there was a strong hope on their part that they might never be forced to return to Costa Rica. Those from whom they now parted had not seemed to be dear to them in any especial degree while they all lived together in the same small town, seeing each other day by day; but now,—now that they might never meet again, a certain love sprang up for the old familiar faces, and women kissed each other who hitherto had hardly cared to enter each other's houses.

And then the party of the Arkwrights again started, and its steady work began. In the whole of the first day the way beneath their feet was tolerably good, and the weather continued fine. It was one long gradual ascent from the plain where the roads parted, but there was no real labour in travelling. Mrs. Arkwright rode beside her baby's mule, at the head of which the Indian always walked, and the two men went together in front. The husband had found that his wife would prefer this, as long as the road allowed of such an arrangement. Her heart was too full to admit of much speaking, and so they went on in silence.

The first night was passed in a hut by the roadside, which seemed to have been deserted,—a hut or rancho, as it is called in that country. Their food they had, of course, brought with them; and here, by common consent, they endeavoured in some sort to make themselves merry.

"Fanny," Arkwright said to her, "it is not so bad after all; eh, my darling?"

"No," she answered; "only that the mule tires one so. Will all the days be as long as that?"

He had not the heart to tell her that, as regarded hours of work, that first day must of necessity be the shortest. They had risen to a considerable altitude, and the night was very cold; but baby was enveloped among a pile of coloured blankets, and things did not go very badly with them; only this, that when Fanny Arkwright rose from her hard bed, her limbs were more weary and much more stiff than they had been when Arkwright had lifted her from her mule.

On the second morning they mounted before the day had quite broken, in order that they might breakfast on the summit of the ridge which separates the two oceans. At this spot the good road comes to an end, and the forest track begins; and here, also, they would, in truth, enter the forest, though their path had for some time been among straggling trees and bushes. And now, again, they rode two and two, up to this place of halting, Arkwright and Ring well knowing that from hence their labours would in truth commence.

Poor Mrs. Arkwright, when she reached this resting-place, would fain have remained there for the rest of the day. One word, in her low, plaintive voice, she said, asking whether they might not sleep in the large shed which stands there. But this was manifestly impossible. At such a pace they would never reach Greytown; and she spoke no further word when he told her that they must go on.

At about noon that day the file of travellers formed itself into the line which it afterwards kept during the whole of the journey, and then started by the narrow path into the forest. First walked the leader of the guides, then another man following him; Abel Ring came next, and behind him the maid-servant; then the baby's mule, with the Indian ever at its head; close at his heels followed Mrs. Arkwright, so that the mother's eye might be always on her child; and after her her husband; then another guide on foot completed the number of the travellers. In this way they went on and on, day after day, till they reached the banks of the Serapiqui, never once varying their places in the procession. As they started in the morning, so they went on till their noon-day's rest, and so again they made their evening march. In that journey there was no idea of variety, no searching after the pleasures of scenery, no attempts at conversation with any object of interest or amusement. What words were spoken were those simply needful, or produced by sympathy for suffering. So they journeyed, always in the same places, with one exception. They began their work with two guides leading them, but before the first day was over one of them had fallen back to the side of Mrs. Arkwright, for she was unable to sit on her mule without support.

Their daily work was divided into two stages, so as to give some hours for rest in the middle of the day. It had been arranged that the distance for each day should not be long,—should be very short as was thought by them all when they talked it over up at San José; but now the hours which they passed in the saddle seemed to be endless. Their descent began from that ridge of which I have spoken, and they had no sooner turned their faces down upon the mountain slopes looking towards the Atlantic, than that passage of mud began to which there was no cessation till they found themselves on the banks of the Serapiqui river. I doubt whether it be possible to convey in words an adequate idea of the labour of riding over such a path. It is not that any active exertion is necessary,—that there is anything which requires doing. The traveller had before him the simple task of sitting on his mule from hour to hour, and of seeing that his knees do not get themselves jammed against the trees; but at every step the beast he rides has to drag his legs out from the deep clinging mud, and the body of the rider never knows one moment of ease. Why the mules do not die on the road, I cannot say. They live through it, and do not appear to suffer. They have their own way in everything, for no exertion on the rider's part will make them walk either faster or slower than is their wont.

On the day on which they entered the forest,—that being the second of their journey,—Mrs. Arkwright had asked for mercy, for permission to escape that second stage. On the next she allowed herself to be lifted into her saddle after her mid-day rest without a word. She had tried to sleep, but in vain; and had sat within a little hut, looking out upon the desolate scene before her, with her baby in her lap. She had this one comfort, that of all the travellers, she, the baby, suffered the least.

They had now left the high grounds, and the heat was becoming great, though not as yet intense. And then, the Indian guide, looking out slowly over the forest, saw that the rain was not yet over. He spoke a word or two to one of his companions in a low voice and in a patois which Mrs. Arkwright did not understand, and then going after the husband, told him that the heavens were threatening.

"We have only two leagues," said Arkwright, "and it may perhaps hold up."

"It will begin in an hour," said the Indian, "and the two leagues are four hours."

"And to-morrow?" asked Arkwright.

"To-morrow, and to-morrow, and to-morrow it will still rain," said the guide, looking as he spoke up over the huge primeval forest.

"Then we had better start at once," said Arkwright, "before the first falling drops frighten the women." So the mules were brought out, and he lifted his uncomplaining wife on to the blankets which formed her pillion. The file again formed itself, and slowly they wound their way out from the small enclosure by which the hut was surrounded;—out from the enclosure on to a rough scrap of undrained pasture ground from which the trees had been cleared. In a few minutes they were once more struggling through the mud.

The name of the spot which our travellers had just left is Carablanco. There they had found a woman living all alone. Her husband was away, she told them, at San José, but would be back to her when the dry weather came, to look up the young cattle which were straying in the forest. What a life for a woman! Nevertheless, in talking with Mrs. Arkwright she made no complaint of her own lot, but had done what little she could to comfort the poor lady who was so little able to bear the fatigues of her journey.

"Is the road very bad?" Mrs. Arkwright asked her in a whisper.

"Ah, yes; it is a bad road."

"And when shall we be at the river?"

"It took me four days," said the woman.

"Then I shall never see my mother again," and as she spoke Mrs. Arkwright pressed her baby to her bosom. Immediately after that her husband came in, and they started.

Their path now led away across the slope of a mountain which seemed to fall from the very top of that central ridge in an unbroken descent down to the valley at its foot. Hitherto, since they had entered the forest, they had had nothing before their eyes but the trees and bushes which grew close around them. But now a prospect of unrivalled grandeur was opened before them, if only they had been able to enjoy it. At the bottom of the valley ran a river, which, so great was the depth, looked like a moving silver cord; and on the other side of this there arose another mountain, steep but unbroken, so that the eye could stretch from the river up to the very summit. Not a spot on that mountain side or on their side either was left uncovered by thick forest, which had stood there untouched by man since nature first produced it.

But all this was nothing to our travellers, nor was the clang of the macaws anything, or the roaring of the little congo ape. Nothing was gained by them from beautiful scenery, nor was there any fear from the beasts of prey. The immediate pain of each step of the journey drove all other feelings from them, and their thoughts were bounded by an intense desire for the evening halt.

And then, as the guide had prophesied, the rain began. At first it came in such small soft drops that it was found to be refreshing, but the clouds soon gathered and poured forth their collected waters as though it had not rained for months among those mountains. Not that it came in big drops, or with the violence which wind can give it, beating hither and thither, breaking branches from the trees, and rising up again as it pattered against the ground. There was no violence in the rain. It fell softly in a long, continuous, noiseless stream, sinking into everything that it touched, converting the deep rich earth on all sides into mud.

Not a word was said by any of them as it came on. The Indian covered the baby with her blanket, closer than she was covered before, and the guide who walked by Mrs. Arkwright's side drew her cloak around her knees. But such efforts were in vain. There is a rain that will penetrate everything, and such was the rain which fell upon them now. Nevertheless, as I have said, hardly a word was spoken. The poor woman, finding that the heat of her cloak increased her sufferings, threw it open again.

"Fanny," said her husband, "you had better let him protect you as well as he can."

She answered him merely by an impatient wave of her hand, intending to signify that she could not speak, but that in this matter she must have her way.

After that her husband made no further attempt to control her. He could see, however, that ever and again she would have slipped forward from her mule and fallen, had not the man by her side steadied her with his hand. At every tree he protected her knees and feet, though there was hardly room for him to move between the beast and the bank against which he was thrust.

And then, at last, that day's work was also over, and Fanny Arkwright slipped from her pillion down into her husband's arms at the door of another rancho in the forest. Here there lived a large family adding from year to year to the patch of ground which they had rescued from the wood, and valiantly doing their part in the extension of civilisation. Our party was but a few steps from the door when they left their mules, but Mrs. Arkwright did not now as heretofore hasten to receive her baby in her arms. When placed upon the ground, she still leaned against the mule, and her husband saw that he must carry her into the hut. This he did, and then wet, mud-laden, dishevelled as she was, she laid herself down upon the planks that were to form her bed, and there stretched out her arms for her infant. On that evening they undressed and tended her like a child; and then, when she was alone with her husband, she repeated to him her sad foreboding.

"Harry," she said, "I shall never see my mother again."

"Oh, yes, Fanny, you will see her and talk over all these troubles with pleasure. It is very bad, I know; but we shall live through it yet."

"You will, of course; and you will take baby home to her."

"And face her without you! No, my darling, Three more days' riding, or rather two and a half will bring us to the river, and then your trouble will be over. All will be easy after that."

"Ah, Harry, you do not know."

"I do know that it is very bad, my girl, but you must cheer up. We shall be laughing at all this in a month's time."

On the following morning she allowed herself to be lifted up, speaking no word of remonstrance. Indeed she was like a child in their hands, having dropped all the dignity and authority of a woman's demeanour. It rained again during the whole of this day, and the heat was becoming oppressive as every hour they were descending nearer and nearer to the sea level. During this first stage hardly a word was spoken by any one; but when she was again taken from her mule she was in tears. The poor servant-girl, too, was almost prostrate with fatigue, and absolutely unable to wait upon her mistress, or even to do anything for herself. Nevertheless they did make the second stage, seeing that their mid-day resting place had been under the trees of the forest. Had there been any hut there, they would have remained for the night.

On the following day they rested altogether, though the place at which they remained had but few attractions. It was another forest hut inhabited by an old Spanish couple who were by no means willing to give them room, although they paid for their accommodation at exorbitant rates. It is one singularity of places strange and out of the way like such forest tracks as these, that money in small sums is hardly valued. Dollars there were not appreciated as six-pences are in this rich country. But there they stayed for a day, and the guides employed themselves in making a litter with long poles so that they might carry Mrs. Arkwright over a portion of the ground. Poor fellows! When once she had thus changed her mode of conveyance, she never again was lifted on to the mule.

There was strong reason against this day's delay. They were to go down the Serapiqui along with the post, which would overtake them on its banks. But if the post should pass them before they got there, it could not wait; and then they would be deprived of the best canoe on the water. Then also it was possible, if they encountered further delay, that the steamer might sail from Greytown without them, and a month's residence at that frightful place be thus made necessary.

The day's rest apparently did little to relieve Mrs. Arkwright's sufferings. On the following day she allowed herself to be put upon the mule, but after the first hour the beasts were stopped and she was taken off it. During that hour they had travelled hardly over half a league. At that time she so sobbed and moaned that Arkwright absolutely feared that she would perish in the forest, and he implored the guides to use the poles which they had prepared. She had declared to him over and over again that she felt sure that she should die, and half delirious with weariness and suffering, had begged him to leave her at the last hut. They had not yet come to the flat ground over which a litter might be carried with comparative ease; but nevertheless the men yielded, and she was placed in a recumbent position upon blankets supported by boughs of trees. In this way she went through that day with somewhat less of suffering than before, and without that necessity for self-exertion which had been worse to her than any suffering.

There were places between that and the river at which one would have said that it was impossible that a litter should be carried, or even impossible that a mule should walk with a load on his back. But still they went on, and the men carried their burden without complaining. Not a word was said about money, or extra pay;—not a word at least by them; and when Arkwright was profuse in his offer, their leader told him that they would not have done it for money. But for the poor suffering Señora they would make exertions which no money would have bought from them.

On the next day about noon the post did pass them, consisting of three strong men carrying great weights on their backs, suspended by bands from their foreheads. They travelled much quicker than our friends, and would reach the banks of the river that evening. In their ordinary course they would start down the river close upon daybreak on the following day; but, after some consultation with the guides, they agreed to wait till noon. Poor Mrs. Arkwright knew nothing of hours or of any such arrangements now, but her husband greatly doubted their power of catching this mail despatch. However, it did not much depend on their exertions that afternoon. Their resting place was marked out for them, and they could not go beyond it, unless indeed they could make the whole journey, which was impossible.

But towards evening matters seemed to improve with them. They had now got on to ground which was more open, and the men who carried the litter could walk with greater ease. Mrs. Arkwright also complained less, and when they reached their resting place on that night, said nothing of a wish to be left there to her fate. This was a place called Padregal, a cacao plantation, which had been cleared in the forest with much labour. There was a house here containing three rooms, and some forty or fifty acres round it had been stripped of the forest trees. But nevertheless the adventure had not been a prosperous one, for the place was at that time deserted. There were the cacao plants, but there was no one to pick the cacao. There was a certain melancholy beauty about the place. A few grand trees had been left standing near the house, and the grass around was rich and park-like. But it was deserted, and nothing was heard but the roaring of the congos. Ah me! Indeed it was a melancholy place as it was seen by some of that party afterwards.

On the following morning they were astir very early, and Mrs. Arkwright was so much better that she offered to sit again upon her mule. The men however declared that they would finish their task, and she was placed again upon the litter. And then with slow and weary step they did make their way to the river bank. It was not yet noon when they saw the mud fort which stands there, and as they drew into the enclosure round a small house which stands close by the river side, they saw the three postmen still busy about their packages.

"Thank God," said Arkwright.

"Thank God, indeed," said his brother. "All will be right with you now."

"Well, Fanny," said her husband, as he took her very gently from the litter and seated her on a bench which stood outside the door, "It is all over now,—is it not?"

She answered him by a shower of tears, but they were tears which brought her relief. He was aware of this, and therefore stood by her, still holding her by both her hands while her head rested against his side. "You will find the motion of the boat very gentle," he said; "indeed there will be no motion, and you and baby will sleep all the way down to Greytown." She did not answer him in words, but she looked up into his face, and he could see that her spirit was recovering itself.

There was almost a crowd of people collected on the spot, preparatory to the departure of the canoes. In the first place there was the commandant of the fort, to whom the small house belonged. He was looking to the passports of our friends, and with due diligence endeavouring to make something of the occasion, by discovering fatal legal impediments to the further prosecution of their voyage, which impediments would disappear on the payment of certain dollars. And then there were half a dozen Costa Rican soldiers, men with coloured caps and old muskets, ready to support the dignity and authority of the commandant. There were the guides taking payment from Abel Ring for their past work, and the postmen preparing their boats for the further journey. And then there was a certain German there, with a German servant, to whom the boats belonged. He also was very busy preparing for the river voyage. He was not going down with them, but it was his business to see them well started. A singular looking man was he, with a huge shaggy beard, and shaggy uncombed hair, but with bright blue eyes, which gave to his face a remarkable look of sweetness. He was an uncouth man to the eye, and yet a child would have trusted herself with him in a forest.

At this place they remained some two hours. Coffee was prepared here, and Mrs. Arkwright refreshed herself and her child. They washed and arranged their clothes, and when she stepped down the steep bank, clinging to her husband's arm as she made her way towards the boat, she smiled upon him as he looked at her.

"It is all over now,—is it not, my girl?"—he said, encouraging her.

"Oh Harry, do not talk about it," she answered, shuddering.

"But I want you to say a word to me to let me know that you are better."

"I am better,—much better."

"And you will see your mother again; will you not; and give baby to her yourself?"

To this she made no immediate answer, for she was on a level with the river, and the canoe was close at her feet. And then she had to bid farewell to her brother. He was now the unfortunate one of the party, for his destiny required that he should go back to San José alone,—go back and remain there perhaps some ten years longer before he might look for the happiness of home.

"God bless you, dearest Abel," she said, kissing him and sobbing as she spoke.

"Good-bye, Fanny," he said, "and do not let them forget me in England. It is a great comfort to think that the worst of your troubles are over."

"Oh,—she's all right now," said Arkwright. "Good-bye, old boy,"—and the two brothers-in-law grasped each other's hands heartily. "Keep up your spirits, and we'll have you home before long."

"Oh, I am all right," said the other. But from the tone of the voices, it was clear that poor Ring was despondent at the thoughts of his coming solitude, and that Arkwright was already triumphing in his emancipation.

And then, with much care, Fanny Arkwright was stowed away in the boat. There was a great contest about the baby, but at last it was arranged, that at any rate for the first few hours, she should be placed in the boat with the servant. The mother was told that by this plan she would feel herself at liberty to sleep during the heat of the day, and then she might hope to have strength to look to the child when they should be on shore during the night. In this way therefore they prepared to start, while Abel Ring stood on the bank looking at them with wishful eyes. In the first boat were two Indians paddling, and a third man steering with another paddle. In the middle there was much luggage, and near the luggage so as to be under shade, was the baby's soft bed. If nothing evil happened to the boat, the child could not be more safe in the best cradle that was ever rocked. With her was the maid servant and some stranger who was also going down to Greytown.

In the second boat were the same number of men to paddle, the Indian guide being one of them, and there were the mails placed. Then there was a seat arranged with blankets, cloaks, and cushions, for Mrs. Arkwright, so that she might lean back and sleep without fatigue, and immediately opposite to her her husband placed himself. "You all look very comfortable," said poor Abel from the bank.

"We shall do very well now," said Arkwright.

"And I do think I shall see mamma again," said his wife.

"That's right, old girl;—of course you will see her. Now then,—we are all ready." And with some little assistance from the German on the bank, the first boat was pushed off into the stream.

The river in this place is rapid, because the full course of the water is somewhat impeded by a bank of earth jutting out from the opposite side of the river into the stream; but it is not so rapid as to make any recognised danger in the embarkation. Below this bank, which is opposite to the spot at which the boats were entered, there were four or five broken trees in the water, some of the shattered boughs of which showed themselves above the surface. These are called snags, and are very dangerous if they are met with in the course of the stream; but in this instance no danger was apprehended from them, as they lay considerably to the left of the passage which the boats would take. The first canoe was pushed off by the German, and went rapidly away. The waters were strong with the rain, and it was pretty to see with what velocity the boat was carried on some hundred of yards in advance of the other by the force of the first effort of the paddle. The German however from the bank holloaed to the first men in Spanish, bidding them relax their efforts for a while; and then he said a word or two of caution to those who were now on the point of starting.

The boat then was pushed steadily forward, the man at the stern keeping it with his paddle a little further away from the bank at which they had embarked. It was close under the land that the stream ran the fastest, and in obedience to the directions given to him he made his course somewhat nearer to the sunken trees. It was but one turn of his hand that gave the light boat its direction, but that turn of the hand was too strong. Had the anxious master of the canoes been but a thought less anxious, all might have been well; but, as it was, the prow of the boat was caught by some slight hidden branch which impeded its course and turned it round in the rapid river. The whole length of the canoe was thus brought against the sunken tree, and in half a minute the five occupants of the boat were struggling in the stream.

Abel Ring and the German were both standing on the bank close to the water when this happened, and each for a moment looked into the other's face. "Stand where you are," shouted the German, "so that you may assist them from the shore. I will go in." And then, throwing from him his boots and coat, he plunged into the river.

The canoe had been swept round so as to be brought by the force of the waters absolutely in among the upturned roots and broken stumps of the trees which impeded the river, and thus, when the party was upset, they were at first to be seen scrambling among the branches. But unfortunately there was much more wood below the water than above it, and the force of the stream was so great, that those who caught hold of the timber were not able to support themselves by it above the surface. Arkwright was soon to be seen some forty yards down, having been carried clear of the trees, and here he got out of the river on the further bank. The distance to him was not above forty yards, but from the nature of the ground he could not get up towards his wife, unless he could have forced his way against the stream.

The Indian who had had charge of the baby rose quickly to the surface, was carried once round in the eddy, with his head high above the water, and then was seen to throw himself among the broken wood. He had seen the dress of the poor woman, and made his effort to save her. The other two men were so caught by the fragments of the boughs, that they could not extricate themselves so as to make any exertions; ultimately, however, they also got out on the further bank.

Mrs. Arkwright had sunk at once on being precipitated into the water, but the buoyancy of her clothes had brought her for a moment again to the surface. She had risen for a moment, and then had again gone down, immediately below the forked trunk of a huge tree;—had gone down, alas, alas! never to rise again with life within her bosom. The poor Indian made two attempts to save her, and then came up himself, incapable of further effort.

It was then that the German, the owner of the canoes, who had fought his way with great efforts across the violence of the waters, and indeed up against the stream for some few yards, made his effort to save the life of that poor frail creature. He had watched the spot at which she had gone down, and even while struggling across the river, had seen how the Indian had followed her and had failed. It was now his turn. His life was in his hand, and he was prepared to throw it away in that attempt. Having succeeded in placing himself a little above the large tree, he turned his face towards the bottom of the river, and dived down among the branches. And he also, after that, was never again seen with the life-blood flowing round his heart.

When the sun set that night, the two swollen corpses were lying in the Commandant's hut, and Abel Ring and Arkwright were sitting beside them. Arkwright had his baby sleeping in his arms, but he sat there for hours,—into the middle of the long night,—without speaking a word to any one.

"Harry," said his brother at last, "come away and lay down. It will be good for you to sleep."

"Nothing ever will be good again for me," said he.

"You must bear up against your sorrow as other men do," said Ring.

"Why am I not sleeping with her as the poor German sleeps? Why did I let another man take my place in dying for her?" And then he walked away that the other might not see the tears on his face.

It was a sad sight,—that at the Commandant's hut, and a sad morning followed upon it. It must be remembered that they had there none of those appurtenances which are so necessary to make woe decent and misfortune comfortable. They sat through the night in the small hut, and in the morning they came forth with their clothes still wet and dirty, with their haggard faces, and weary stiff limbs, encumbered with the horrid task of burying that loved body among the forest trees. And then, to keep life in them till it was done, the brandy flask passed from hand to hand; and after that, with slow but resolute efforts, they reformed the litter on which the living woman had been carried thither, and took her body back to the wild plantation at Padregal. There they dug for her her grave, and repeating over her some portion of the service for the dead, left her to sleep the sleep of death. But before they left her, they erected a pallisade of timber round the grave, so that the beasts of the forest should not tear the body from its resting-place.

When that was done Arkwright and his brother made their slow journey back to San José. The widowed husband could not face his darling's mother with such a tale upon his tongue as that.

The Man Who Kept His Money in a Box

Originally appeared in *Public Opinion*, 2 and 9 November 1861. Reprinted in *Tales of All Countries* [Second Series] (1863). Written 27 January-1 February 1861, during the composition of *Orley Farm*. Trollope visited Lake Como, where the story is set, in the autumn of 1857. It is a familiar place of exile in the novels: Canon Vesey Stanhope collects butterflies there in *Barchester Towers* (1857), and the Marquis of Brotherton hides away there for many years in *Is He Popenjoy*? (1878).

I first saw the man who kept his money in a box in the midst of the ravine of the Via Mala. I interchanged a few words with him or with his wife at the hospice, at the top of the Splugen; and I became acquainted with him in the court-yard of Conradi's hotel at Chiavenna. It was, however, afterwards at Bellaggio, on the lake of Como, that that acquaintance ripened into intimacy. A good many years have rolled by since then, and I believe this little episode in his life may be told without pain to the feelings of any one.

His name was—; let us for the present say that his name was Greene. How he learned that my name was Robinson I do not know, but I remember well that he addressed me by my name at Chiavenna. To go back, however, for a moment to the Via Mala;—I had been staying for a few days at the Golden Eagle at Tusis,—which, by the bye, I hold to be the best small inn in all Switzerland, and its hostess to be, or to have been, certainly the prettiest landlady,—and on the day of my departure southwards, I had walked on, into the Via Mala, so that the diligence might pick me up in the gorge. This pass I regard as one of the grandest spots to which my wandering steps have ever carried me, and though I had already lingered about it for many hours, I now walked thither again to take my last farewell of its dark towering rocks, its narrow causeway and roaring river, trusting to my friend the landlady to see that my luggage was duly packed upon the diligence. I need hardly say that my friend did not betray her trust.

As one goes out from Switzerland towards Italy, the road through the Via Mala ascends somewhat steeply, and passengers by the diligence may walk from the inn at Tusis into the gorge, and make their way through the greater part of the ravine before the vehicle will overtake them. This, however, Mr. Greene with his wife and daughter had omitted to do. When the diligence passed me in the defile, the horses trotting for a few yards over some level portion of the road, I saw a man's nose pressed close against the glass of the coupé window. I saw more of his nose than of any other part of his face, but yet I could perceive that his neck was twisted and his eye upturned, and that he was making a painful effort to look upwards to the summit of the rocks from his position inside the carriage.

There was such a roar of wind and waters at the spot that it was not practicable to speak to him, but I beckoned with my finger and then pointed to the road, indicating that he should have walked. He understood me, though I did not at the moment understand his answering gesture. It was subsequently, when I knew somewhat of his habits, that he explained to me that on pointing to his open mouth, he had intended to signify that he would be afraid of sore throat in exposing himself to the air of that damp and narrow passage.

I got up into the conductor's covered seat at the back of the diligence, and in this position encountered the drifting snow of the Splugen. I think it is coldest of all the passes. Near the top of the pass the diligence stops for awhile, and it is here, if I remember, that the Austrian officials demand the travellers' passports. At least in those days they did so. These officials have now retreated behind the Quadrilatère,—soon, as we hope, to make a further retreat,—and the district belongs to the kingdom of United Italy. There is a place of refreshment or hospice here, into which we all went for a few moments, and I then saw that my friend with the weak throat was accompanied by two ladies.

"You should not have missed the Via Mala," I said to him, as he stood warming his toes at the huge covered stove.

"We miss everything," said the elder of the two ladies, who, however, was very much younger than the gentleman, and not very much older than her companion.

"I saw it beautifully, mamma," said the younger one; whereupon mamma gave her head a toss, and made up her mind, as I thought, to take some little vengeance before long upon her step-daughter. I observed that Miss Greene always called her stepmother mamma on the first approach of any stranger, so that the nature of the connection between them might be understood. And I observed also that the elder lady always gave her head a toss when she was so addressed.

"We don't mean to enjoy ourselves till we get down to the Lake of Como," said Mr. Greene. As I looked at him cowering over the stove, and saw how oppressed he was with great coats and warm wrappings for his throat, I quite agreed with him that he had not begun to enjoy himself as yet. Then we all got into our places again, and I saw no more of the Greenes till we were standing huddled together in the large court-yard of Conradi's hotel at Chiavenna.

Chiavenna is the first Italian town which the tourist reaches by this route, and I know no town in the North of Italy which is so closely surrounded by beautiful scenery. The traveller as he falls down to it from the Splugen road is bewildered by the loveliness of the valleys,—that is to say, if he so arranges that he can see them without pressing his nose against the glass of a coach window. And then from the town itself there are walks of two, three, and four hours, which I think are unsurpassed for wild and sometimes startling beauties. One gets into little valleys, green as emeralds, and surrounded on all sides by grey broken rocks, in which Italian Rasselases might have lived in perfect bliss; and then again one comes upon distant views up the river courses, bounded far away by the spurs of the Alps, which are perfect,—to which the fancy can add no additional charm. Conradi's hotel also is by no means bad; or was not in those days. For my part I am inclined to think that Italian hotels have received a worse name than they deserve; and I must profess that, looking merely to creature comforts, I would much sooner stay a week at the Golden Key at Chiavenna, than with mine host of the King's Head in the thriving commercial town of Muddleboro, on the borders of Yorkshire and Lancashire.

I am always rather keen about my room in travelling, and having secured a chamber looking out upon the mountains, had returned to the court-yard to collect my baggage before Mr. Greene had succeeded in realising his position, or understanding that he had to take upon himself the duties of settling his family for the night in the hotel by which he was surrounded. When I descended he was stripping off the outermost of three great coats, and four waiters around him were beseeching him to tell them what accommodation he would require. Mr. Greene was giving sundry very urgent instructions to the conductor respecting his boxes; but as these were given in English, I was not surprised to find that they were not accurately followed. The man, however, was much too courteous to say in any language that he did not understand every word that was said to him. Miss Greene was standing apart, doing nothing. As she was only eighteen years of age, it was of course her business to do nothing; and a very pretty little girl she was, by no means ignorant of her own beauty, and possessed of quite sufficient wit to enable her to make the most of it.

Mr. Greene was very leisurely in his proceedings, and the four waiters were almost reduced to despair.

"I want two bed-rooms, a dressing-room, and some dinner," he said at last, speaking very slowly, and in his own vernacular. I could not in the least assist him by translating it into Italian, for I did not speak a word of the language myself; but I suggested that the man would understand French. The waiter, however, had understood English. Waiters do understand all languages with a facility that is marvellous; and this one now suggested that Mrs. Greene should follow him up-stairs. Mrs. Greene, however, would not move till she had seen that her boxes were all right; and as Mrs. Greene was also a pretty woman, I found myself bound to apply myself to her assistance.

"Oh, thank you," said she. "The people are so stupid that one can really do nothing with them. And as for Mr. Greene, he is of no use at all. You see that box, the smaller one. I have four hundred pounds' worth of jewellery in that, and therefore I am obliged to look after it."

"Indeed," said I, rather startled at this amount of confidence on rather a short acquaintance. "In that case I do not wonder at your being careful. But is it not rather rash, perhaps— "

"I know what you are going to say. Well, perhaps it is rash. But when you are going to foreign courts, what are you to do? If you have got those sort of things you must wear them."

As I was not myself possessed of any thing of that sort, and had no intention of going to any foreign court, I could not argue the matter with her. But I assisted her in getting together an enormous pile of luggage, among which there were seven large boxes covered with canvas, such as ladies not uncommonly carry with them when travelling. That one which she represented as being smaller than the others, and as holding jewellery might be about a yard long by a foot and a half deep. Being ignorant in those matters, I should have thought it sufficient to carry all a lady's wardrobe for twelve months. When the boxes were collected together, she sat down upon the jewel-case and looked up into my face. She was a pretty woman, perhaps thirty years of age, with long light yellow hair, which she allowed to escape from her bonnet, knowing, perhaps, that it was not unbecoming to her when thus dishevelled. Her skin was very delicate, and her complexion good. Indeed her face would have been altogether prepossessing had there not been a want of gentleness in her eyes. Her hands, too, were soft and small, and on the whole she may be said to have been possessed of a strong battery of feminine attractions. She also well knew how to use them.

"Whisper," she said to me, with a peculiar but very proper aspiration on the h—"Wh-hisper," and both by the aspiration and the use of the word I knew at once from what island she had come. "Mr. Greene keeps all his money in this box also; so I never let it go out of my sight for a moment. But whatever you do, don't tell him that I told you so."

I laid my hand on my heart, and made a solemn asseveration that I would not divulge her secret. I need not, however, have troubled myself much on that head, for as I walked up stairs, keeping my eye upon the precious trunk, Mr. Greene addressed me.

"You are an Englishman, Mr. Robinson," said he. I acknowledged that I was.

"I am another. My wife, however, is Irish. My daughter,—by a former marriage,—is English also. You see that box there."

"Oh, yes," said I, "I see it." I began to be so fascinated by the box that I could not keep my eyes off it.

"I don't know whether or no it is prudent, but I keep all my money there; my money for travelling, I mean."

"If I were you, then," I answered, "I would not say anything about it to any one."

"Oh, no, of course not," said he; "I should not think of mentioning it. But those brigands in Italy always take away what you have about your person, but they don't meddle with the heavy luggage."

"Bills of exchange, or circular notes," I suggested.

"Ah, yes; and if you can't identify yourself, or happen to have a headache, you can't get them changed. I asked an old friend of mine, who has been connected with the Bank of England for the last fifty years, and he assured me that there was nothing like sovereigns."

"But you never get the value for them."

"Well, not quite. One loses a franc, or a franc and a half. But still, there's the certainty, and that's the great matter. An English sovereign will go anywhere," and he spoke these words with considerable triumph.

"Undoubtedly, if you consent to lose a shilling on each sovereign."

"At any rate, I have got three hundred and fifty in that box," he said. "I have them done up in rolls of twenty-five pounds each."

"I again recommended him to keep this arrangement of his as private possible,—a piece of counsel which I confess seemed to me to be much needed,—and then I went away to my own room, having first accepted an invitation from Mrs. Greene to join their party at dinner. "Do," said she; "we have been so dull, and it will be so pleasant."

I did not require to be much pressed to join myself to a party in which there was so pretty a girl as Miss Greene, and so attractive a woman as Mrs. Greene. I therefore accepted the invitation readily, and went away to make my toilet. As I did so I passed the door of

Mr. Greene's room, and saw the long file of boxes being borne into the centre of it.

I spent a pleasant evening, with, however, one or two slight drawbacks. As to old Greene himself, he was all that was amiable; but then he was nervous, full of cares, and somewhat apt to be a bore. He wanted information on a thousand points, and did not seem to understand that a young man might prefer the conversation of his daughter to his own. Not that he showed any solicitude to prevent conversation on the part of his daughter. I should have been perfectly at liberty to talk to either of the ladies had he not wished to engross all my attention to himself. He also had found it dull to be alone with his wife and daughter for the last six weeks.

He was a small spare man, probably over fifty years of age, who gave me to understand that he had lived in London all his life, and had made his own fortune in the city. What he had done in the city to make his fortune he did not say. Had I come across him there I should no doubt have found him to be a sharp man of business, quite competent to teach me many a useful lesson of which I was as ignorant as an infant. Had he caught me on the Exchange, or at Lloyd's, or in the big room of the Bank of England, I should have been compelled to ask him everything. Now, in this little town under the Alps, he was as much lost as I should have been in Lombard Street, and was ready enough to look to me for information. I was by no means chary in giving him my counsel, and imparting to him my ideas on things in general in that part of the world;—only I should have preferred to be allowed to make myself civil to his daughter.

In the course of conversation it was mentioned by him that they intended to stay a few days at Bellaggio, which, as all the world knows, is a central spot on the lake of Como, and a favourite resting-place for travellers. There are three lakes which all meet here, and to all of which we give the name of Como. They are properly called the lakes of Como, Colico, and Lecco; and Bellaggio is the spot at which their waters join each other. I had half made up my mind to sleep there one night on my road into Italy, and now, on hearing their purpose, I declared that such was my intention.

"How very pleasant," said Mrs. Greene. "It will be quite delightful to have some one to show us how to settle ourselves, for really— "

"My dear, I'm sure you can't say that you ever have much trouble."

"And who does then, Mr. Green? I am sure Sophonisba does not do much to help me."

"You won't let me," said Sophonisba, whose name I had not before heard. Her papa had called her Sophy in the yard of the inn. Sophonisba Greene! Sophonisba Robinson did not sound so badly in my ears, and I confess that I had tried the names together. Her papa had mentioned to me that he had no other child, and had mentioned also that he had made his fortune.

And then there was a little family contest as to the amount of travelling labour which fell to the lot of each of the party, during which I retired to one of the windows of the big front room in which we were sitting. And how much of this labour there is incidental to a tourist's pursuits! And how often these little contests do arise upon a journey! Who has ever travelled and not known them? I had taken up such a position at the window as might, I thought, have removed me out of hearing; but nevertheless from time to time a word would catch my ear about that precious box. "I have never taken my eyes off it since I left England," said Mrs. Greene, speaking quick, and with a considerable brogue superinduced by her energy. "Where would it have been at Basle if I had not been looking afther it?" "Quite safe," said Sophonisba; "those large things always are safe." "Are they, Miss? That's all you know about it. I suppose your bonnet-box was quite safe when I found it on the platform at—at—I forget the name of the place?"

"Freidrichshafen," said Sophonisba, with almost an unnecessary amount of Teutonic skill in her pronunciation. "Well, mamma, you have told me of that at least twenty times." Soon after that, the ladies took them to their own rooms, weary with the travelling of two days and a night, and Mr. Greene went fast asleep in the very comfortless chair in which he was seated.

At four o'clock on the next morning we started on our journey.

> "Early to bed, and early to rise,
> Is the way to be healthy and wealthy and wise."

We all know that lesson, and many of us believe in it; but if the lesson be true, the Italians ought to be the healthiest and wealthiest and wisest of all men and women. Three or four o'clock seems to them quite a natural hour for commencing the day's work. Why we should have started from Chiavenna at four o'clock in order that we might be kept waiting for the boat an hour and a half on the little quay at Colico, I don't know; but such was our destiny. There we remained an hour and a half, Mrs. Greene sitting pertinaciously on the one important box. She had designated it as being smaller than the others, and as all the seven were now ranged in a row, I had an opportunity of comparing them. It was something smaller,—perhaps an inch less high, and an inch and a half shorter. She was a sharp woman, and observed my scrutiny. "I always know it," she said in a loud whisper, "by this little hole in the canvas," and she put her finger on a slight rent on one of the ends. "As for Greene, if one of those Italian brigands were to walk off with it on his shoulders, before his eyes, he wouldn't be the wiser. How helpless you men are, Mr. Robinson!"

"It is well for us that we have women to look after us."

"But you have got no one to look after you;—or perhaps you have left her behind?"

"No, indeed. I'm all alone in the world as yet. But it's not my own fault. I have asked half a dozen."

"Now, Mr. Robinson!" And in this way the time passed on the quay at Colico, till the boat came and took us away. I should have preferred to pass my time in making myself agreeable to the younger lady; but the younger lady stood aloof, turning up her nose, as I thought, at her mamma.

I will not attempt to describe the scenery about Colico. The little town itself is one of the vilest places under the sun, having no accommodation for travellers, and being excessively unhealthy; but there is very little either north or south of the Alps,—and, perhaps I may add, very little elsewhere,—to beat the beauty of the mountains which cluster round the head of the lake. When we had sat upon those boxes that hour and a half, we were taken on board the steamer, which had been lying off a little way from the shore, and then we commenced our journey. Of course there was a good deal of exertion and care necessary in getting the packages off from the shore on to the boat, and I observed that any one with half an eye in his head might have seen that the mental anxiety expended on that one box which was marked by the small hole in the canvas far exceeded that which was extended to all the other six boxes. "They deserve that it should be stolen," I said to myself, "for being such fools." And then we went down to breakfast in the cabin.

"I suppose it must be safe," said Mrs. Greene to me, ignoring the fact that the cabin waiter understood English, although she had just ordered some veal cutlets in that language.

"As safe as a church," I replied, not wishing to give much apparent importance to the subject.

"They can't carry it off here," said Mr. Greene. But he was innocent of any attempt at a joke, and was looking at me with all his eyes.

"They might throw it overboard," said Sophonisba. I at once made up my mind that she could not be a good-natured girl. The moment that breakfast was over, Mrs. Greene returned again up-stairs, and I found her seated on one of the benches near the funnel, from which she could keep her eyes fixed upon the box. "When one is obliged to carry about one's jewels with one, one must be careful, Mr. Robinson," she said to me apologetically. But I was becoming tired of the box, and the funnel was hot and unpleasant, therefore I left her.

I had made up my mind that Sophonisba was ill-natured; but, nevertheless, she was pretty, and I now went through some little manoeuvres with the object of getting into conversation with her. This I soon did, and was surprised by her frankness. "How tired you must be of mamma and her box," she said to me. To this I made some answer, declaring that I was rather interested than otherwise, in the safety of the precious trunk. "It makes me sick," said Sophonisba, "to hear her go on in that way to a perfect stranger. I heard what she said about her jewellery."

"It is natural she should be anxious," I said, "seeing that it contains so much that is valuable."

"Why did she bring them?" said Sophonisba. "She managed to live very well without jewels till papa married her, about a year since; and now she can't travel about for a month without lugging them with her everywhere. I should be so glad if some one would steal them."

"But all Mr. Greene's money is there also."

"I don't want papa to be bothered, but I declare I wish the box might be lost for a day or so. She is such a fool; don't you think so, Mr. Robinson?"

At this time it was just fourteen hours since I first had made their acquaintance in the yard of Conradi's hotel, and of those fourteen hours more than half had been passed in bed. I must confess that I looked upon Sophonisba as being almost more indiscreet than her mother-in-law. Nevertheless, she was not stupid, and I continued my conversation with her the greatest part of the way down the lake towards Bellaggio.

These steamers, which run up and down the lake of Como and the Lago Maggiore, put out their passengers at the towns on the banks of the water by means of small rowing-boats, and the persons who are about to disembark generally have their own articles ready to their hands when their turn comes for leaving the steamer. As we came near to Bellaggio, I looked up my own portmanteau, and, pointing to the beautiful wood-covered hill that stands at the fork of the waters, told my friend Greene that he was near his destination. "I am very glad to hear it," said he, complacently, but he did not at the moment busy himself about the boxes. Then the small boat ran up alongside the steamer, and the passengers for Como and Milan crowded up the side.

"We have to go in that boat," I said to Greene.

"Nonsense!" he exclaimed.

"Oh, but we have."

"What! put our boxes into that boat," said Mrs. Greene. "Oh dear! Here, boatman! there are seven of these boxes, all in white like this," and she pointed to the one that had the hole in the canvas. "Make haste. And there are two bags, and my dressing-case, and Mr. Greene's portmanteau. Mr. Greene, where is your portmanteau?"

The boatman whom she addressed, no doubt did not understand a word of English, but nevertheless he knew what she meant, and, being well accustomed to the work, got all the luggage together in an incredibly small number of moments.

"If you will get down into the boat," I said, "I will see that the luggage follows you before I leave the deck."

"I won't stir," she said, "till I see that box lifted down. Take care; you'll let it fall into the lake. I know you will."

"I wish they would," Sophonisba whispered into my ear.

Mr. Greene said nothing, but I could see that his eyes were as anxiously fixed on what was going on, as were those of his wife. At last, however, the three Greenes were in the boat, as also were all the packages. Then I followed them, my portmanteau having gone down before me, and we pushed off for Bellaggio. Up to this period most of the attendants around us had understood a word or two of English, but now it would be well if we could find some one to whose ears French would not be unfamiliar. As regarded Mr. Greene and his wife, they, I found, must give up all conversation, as they knew nothing of any language but their own. Sophonisba could make herself understood in French, and was quite at home, as she assured me, in German. And then the boat was beached on the shore at Bellaggio, and we all had to go again to work with the object of getting ourselves lodged at the hotel which overlooks the water.

I had learned before that the Greenes were quite free from any trouble in this respect, for their rooms had been taken for them before they left England. Trusting to this, Mrs. Greene gave herself no inconsiderable airs the moment her foot was on the shore, and ordered the people about as though she were the Lady Paramount of Bellaggio. Italians, however, are used to this from travellers of a certain description. They never resent such conduct, but simply put it down in the bill with the other articles. Mrs. Greene's words on this occasion were innocent enough, seeing that they were English; but had I been that head waiter who came down to the beach with his nice black shiny hair, and his napkin under his arm, I should have thought her manner very insolent.

Indeed, as it was, I did think so, and was inclined to be angry with her. She was to remain for some time at Bellaggio, and therefore it behoved her, as she thought, to assume the character of the grand lady at once. Hitherto she had been willing enough to do the work, but now she began to order about Mr. Greene and Sophonisba; and, as it appeared to me, to order me about also. I did not quite enjoy this; so leaving her still among her luggage and satellites, I walked up to the hotel to see about my own bedroom. I had some seltzer water, stood at the window for three or four minutes, and then walked up and down the room. But still the Greenes were not there. As I had put in at Bellaggio solely with the object of seeing something more of Sophonisba, it would not do for me to quarrel with them, or to allow them so to settle themselves in their private sitting-room, that I should be excluded. Therefore I returned again to the road by which they must come up, and met the procession near the house.

Mrs. Greene was leading it with great majesty, the waiter with the shiny hair walking by her side to point out to her the way. Then came all the luggage,—each porter carrying a white canvas-covered box. That which was so valuable no doubt was carried next to Mrs. Greene, so that she might at a moment's notice put her eye upon the well-known valuable rent. I confess that I did not observe the hole as the train passed by me, nor did I count the number of the boxes. Seven boxes, all alike, are very many; and then they were followed by three other men with the inferior articles,—Mr. Greene's portmanteau, the carpet-bag, &c., &c. At the tail of the line, I found Mr. Greene, and behind him Sophonisba. "All your fatigues will be over now," I said to the gentleman, thinking it well not to be too particular in my attentions to his daughter. He was panting beneath a terrible great-coat, having forgotten that the shores of an Italian lake are not so cold as the summits of the Alps, and did not answer me. "I'm sure I hope so," said Sophonisba. "And I shall advise papa not to go any further unless he can persuade Mrs. Greene to send her jewels home." "Sophy, my dear," he said, "for Heaven's sake let us have a little peace since we are here." From all which I gathered that Mr. Greene had not been fortunate in his second matrimonial adventure. We then made our way slowly up to the hotel, having been altogether distanced by the porters, and when we reached the house we found that the different packages were already being carried away through the house, some this way and some that. Mrs. Greene, the meanwhile, was talking loudly at the door of her own sitting-room.

"Mr. Greene," she said, as soon as she saw her heavily oppressed spouse,—for the noonday sun was up,—"Mr. Greene, where are you?"

"Here, my dear," and Mr. Greene threw himself panting into the corner of a sofa.

"A little seltzer water and brandy," I suggested. Mr. Greene's inmost heart leaped at the hint, and nothing that his remonstrant wife could say would induce him to move, until he had enjoyed the delicious draught. In the mean time the box with the hole in the canvas had been lost.

Yes; when we came to look into matters, to count the packages, and to find out where we were, the box with the hole in the canvas was not there. Or, at at any rate, Mrs. Greene said it was not there. I worked hard to look it up, and even went into Sophonisba's bed-room in my search. In Sophonisba's bed-room there was but one canvas-covered box. "That is my own," said she, "and it is all that I have, except this bag."

"Where on earth can it be?" said I, sitting down on the trunk in question. At the moment I almost thought that she had been instrumental in hiding it.

"How am I to know?" she answered; and I fancied that even she was dismayed. "What a fool that woman is!"

"The box must be in the house," I said.

"Do find it, for papa's sake; there's a good fellow. He will be so wretched without his money. I heard him say that he had only two pounds in his purse."

"Oh, I can let him have money to go on with," I answered grandly. And then I went off to prove that I was a good fellow, and searched throughout the house. Two white boxes had by order been left downstairs, as they would not be needed; and these two were in a large cupboard off the hall, which was used expressly for stowing away luggage. And then there were three in Mrs. Greene's bed-room, which had been taken there as containing the wardrobe which she would require while remaining at Bellaggio. I searched every one of these myself to see if I could find the hole in the canvas. But the hole in the canvas was not there. And, let me count as I would, I could make out only six. Now there certainly had been seven on board the steamer, though I could not swear that I had seen the seven put into the small boat.

"Mr. Greene," said the lady, standing in the middle of her remaining treasures, all of which were now open, "you are worth nothing when travelling. Were you not behind?" But Mr. Greene's mind was full, and he did not answer.

"It has been stolen before your very eyes," she continued.

"Nonsense, mamma," said Sophonisba. "If ever it came out of the steamer it certainly came into the house."

"I saw it out of the steamer," said Mrs. Greene, "and it certainly is not in the house. Mr. Robinson, may I trouble you to send for the police?—at once, if you please, sir."

I had been at Bellaggio twice before, but nevertheless I was ignorant of their system of police. And then, again, I did not know what was the Italian for the word.

"I will speak to the landlord," I said.

"If you will have the goodness to send for the police at once, I will be obliged to you." And as she thus reiterated her command, she stamped with her foot upon the floor.

"There are no police at Bellaggio," said Sophonisba.

"What on earth shall I do for money to go on with?" said Mr. Greene, looking piteously up to the ceiling, and shaking both his hands.

And now the whole house was in an uproar, including not only the landlord, his wife and daughters, and all the servants, but also every other visitor at the hotel. Mrs. Greene was not a lady who hid either her glories or her griefs under a bushel, and, though she spoke only in English, she soon made her protestations sufficiently audible. She protested loudly that she had been robbed, and that she had been robbed since she left the steamer. The box had come on shore; of that she was quite certain. If the landlord had any regard either for his own character or for that of his house, he would ascertain before an hour was over where it was, and who had been the thief. She would give him an hour. And then she sat herself down; but in two minutes she was up again, vociferating her wrongs as loudly as ever. All this was filtered through me and Sophonisba to the waiter in French, and from the waiter to the landlord; but the lady's gestures required no translation to make them intelligible, and the state of her mind on the matter was, I believe, perfectly well understood.

Mr. Greene I really did pity. His feelings of dismay seemed to be quite as deep, but his sorrow and solicitude were repressed into more decorum. "What am I to do for money?" he said. "I have not a shilling to go on with!" And he still looked up at the ceiling.

"You must send to England," said Sophonisba.

"It will take a month," he replied.

"Mr. Robinson will let you have what you want at present," added Sophonisba. Now I certainly had said so, and had meant it at the time. But my whole travelling store did not exceed forty or fifty pounds, with which I was going on to Venice, and then back to England through the Tyrol. Waiting a month for Mr. Greene's money from England might be even more inconvenient to me than to him. Then it occurred to me that the wants of the Greene family would be numerous and expensive, and that my small stock would go but a little way among so many. And what also if there had been no money and no jewels in that accursed box! I confess that at the moment such an idea did strike my mind. One hears of sharpers on every side committing depredations by means of most singular intrigues and contrivances. Might it not be possible that the whole batch of Greenes belonged to this order of society. It was a base idea, I own; but I confess that I entertained it for a moment.

I retired to my own room for a while that I might think over all the circumstances. There certainly had been seven boxes, and one had had a hole in the canvas. All the seven had certainly been on board the steamer. To so much I felt that I might safely swear. I had not counted the seven into the small boat, but on leaving the larger vessel I had looked about the deck to see that none of the Greene trappings were forgotten. If left on the steamer, it had been so left through an intent on the part of some one there employed. It was quite possible that the contents of the box had been ascertained through the imprudence of Mrs. Greene, and that it had been conveyed away so that it might be rifled at Como. As to Mrs. Greene's assertion that all the boxes had been put into the small boat, I thought nothing of it. The people at Bellaggio could not have known which box to steal, nor had there been time to concoct the plan in carrying the boxes up to the hotel. I came at last to this conclusion, that the missing trunk had either been purloined and carried on to Como,—in which case it would be necessary to lose no time in going after it; or that it had been put out of sight in some uncommonly clever way, by the Greenes themselves, as an excuse for borrowing as much money as they could raise and living without payment of their bills. With reference to the latter hypothesis, I declared to myself that Greene did not look like a swindler; but as to Mrs. Greene—! I confess that I did not feel so confident in regard to her.

Charity begins at home, so I proceeded to make myself comfortable in my room, feeling almost certain that I should not be able to leave Bellaggio on the following morning. I had opened my portmanteau when I first arrived, leaving it open on the floor, as is my wont. Some people are always being robbed, and are always locking up everything; while others wander safe over the world and never lock up anything. For myself, I never turn a key anywhere, and no one ever purloins from me even a handkerchief. Cantabit vacuus—, and I am always sufficiently vacuus. Perhaps it is that I have not a handkerchief worth the stealing. It is your heavy-laden, suspicious, mal-adroit Greenes that the thieves attack. I now found that the accommodating Boots, who already knew my ways, had taken my travelling gear into a dark recess which was intended to do for a dressing-room, and had there spread my portmanteau open upon some table or stool in the corner. It was a convenient arrangement, and there I left it during the whole period of my sojourn.

Mrs. Greene had given the landlord an hour to find the box, and during that time the landlord, the landlady, their three daughters, and all the servants in the house certainly did exert themselves to the utmost. Half a dozen times they came to my door, but I was luxuriating in a washing-tub, making up for that four-o'clock start from Chiavenna. I assured them, however, that the box was not there, and so the search passed by. At the end of the hour I went back to the Greenes according to promise, having resolved that some one must be sent on to Como to look after the missing article.

There was no necessity to knock at their sitting-room door, for it was wide open. I walked in, and found Mrs. Greene still engaged in attacking the landlord, while all the porters who had carried the luggage up to the house were standing round. Her voice was loud above the others, but, luckily for them all, she was speaking English. The landlord, I saw, was becoming sulky. He spoke in Italian, and we none of us understood him, but I gathered that he was declining to do anything further. The box, he was certain, had never come out of the steamer. The Boots stood by interpreting into French, and, acting as second interpreter, I put it into English.

"Mr. Greene," said the lady, turning to her husband, "you must go at once to Como."

Mr. Greene, who was seated on the sofa, groaned audibly, but said nothing. Sophonisba, who was sitting by him, beat upon the floor with both her feet.

"Do you hear, Mr. Greene?" said she, turning to him. "Do you mean to allow that vast amount of property to be lost without an effort? Are you prepared to replace my jewels?"

"Her jewels!" said Sophonisba, looking up into my face. "Papa had to pay the bill for every stitch she had when he married her." These last words were so spoken as to be audible only by me, but her first exclamation was loud enough. Were they people for whom it would be worth my while to delay my journey, and put myself to serious inconvenience with reference to money?

A few minutes afterwards I found myself with Greene on the terrace before the house. "What ought I to do?" said he.

"Go to Como," said I, "and look after your box. I will remain here and go on board the return steamer. It may perhaps be there."

"But I can't speak a word of Italian," said he.

"Take the Boots," said I.

"But I can't speak a word of French." And then it ended in my undertaking to go to Como. I swear that the thought struck me that I might as well take my portmanteau with me, and cut and run when I got there. The Greenes were nothing to me.

I did not, however, do this. I made the poor man a promise, and I kept it. I took merely a dressing-bag, for I knew that I must sleep at Como; and, thus resolving to disarrange all my plans, I started. I was in the midst of beautiful scenery, but I found it quite impossible to draw any enjoyment from it;—from that or from anything around me. My whole mind was given up to anathemas against this odious box, as to which I had undoubtedly heavy cause of complaint. What was the box to me? I went to Como by the afternoon steamer, and spent a long dreary evening down on the steamboat quays searching everywhere, and searching in vain. The boat by which we had left

Colico had gone back to Colico, but the people swore that nothing had been left on board it. It was just possible that such a box might have gone on to Milan with the luggage of other passengers.

I slept at Como, and on the following morning I went on to Milan. There was no trace of the box to be found in that city. I went round to every hotel and travelling office, but could hear nothing of it. Parties had gone to Venice, and Florence, and Bologna, and any of them might have taken the box. No one, however, remembered it; and I returned back to Como, and thence to Bellaggio, reaching the latter place at nine in the evening, disappointed, weary, and cross.

"Has Monsieur found the accursed trunk?" said the Bellaggio Boots, meeting me on the quay.

"In the name of the—, no. Has it not turned up here?"

"Monsieur," said the Boots, "we shall all be mad soon. The poor master, he is mad already." And then I went up to the house.

"My jewels!" shouted Mrs. Greene, rushing to me with her arms stretched out as soon as she heard my step in the corridor. I am sure that she would have embraced me had I found the box. I had not, however, earned any such reward. "I can hear nothing of the box either at Como or Milan," I said.

"Then what on earth am I to do for my money?" said Mr. Greene.

I had had neither dinner nor supper, but the elder Greenes did not care for that. Mr. Greene sat silent in despair, and Mrs. Greene stormed about the room in her anger. "I am afraid you are very tired," said Sophonisba.

"I am tired, and hungry, and thirsty," said I. I was beginning to get angry, and to think myself ill used. And that idea as to a family of swindlers became strong again. Greene had borrowed ten napoleons from me before I started for Como, and I had spent above four in my fruitless journey to that place and Milan. I was beginning to fear that my whole purpose as to Venice and the Tyrol would be destroyed; and I had promised to meet friends at Innspruck, who,—who were very much preferable to the Greenes. As events turned out, I did meet them. Had I failed in this, the present Mrs. Robinson would not have been sitting opposite to me.

I went to my room and dressed myself, and then Sophonisba presided over the tea-table for me. "What are we to do?" she asked me in a confidential whisper.

"Wait for money from England."

"But they will think we are all sharpers," she said; "and upon my word I do not wonder at it from the way in which that woman goes on." She then leaned forward, resting her elbow on the table and her face on her hand, and told me a long history of all their family discomforts. Her papa was a very good sort of man, only he had been made a fool of by that intriguing woman, who had been left without a sixpence with which to bless herself. And now they had nothing but quarrels and misery. Papa did not always get the worst of it;—papa could rouse himself sometimes; only now he was beaten down and cowed by the loss of his money. This whispering confidence was very nice in its way, seeing that Sophonisba was a pretty girl; but the whole matter seemed to be full of suspicion.

"If they did not want to take you in one way, they did in another," said the present Mrs. Robinson, when I told the story to her at Innspruck. I beg that it may be understood that at the time of my meeting the Greenes I was not engaged to the present Mrs. Robinson, and was open to make any matrimonial engagement that might have been pleasing to me.

On the next morning, after breakfast, we held a council of war. I had been informed that Mr. Greene had made a fortune, and was justified in presuming him to be a rich man. It seemed to me, therefore, that his course was easy. Let him wait at Bellaggio for more money, and when he returned home, let him buy Mrs. Greene more jewels. A poor man always presumes that a rich man is indifferent about his money. But in truth a rich man never is indifferent about his money, and poor Greene looked very blank at my proposition.

"Do you mean to say that it's gone for ever?" he asked.

"I'll not leave the country without knowing more about it," said Mrs. Greene.

"It certainly is very odd," said Sophonisba. Even Sophonisba seemed to think that I was too off-hand.

"It will be a month before I can get money, and my bill here will be something tremendous," said Greene.

"I wouldn't pay them a farthing till I got my box," said Mrs. Greene.

"That's nonsense," said Sophonisba. And so it was.

"Hold your tongue, Miss!" said the step-mother.

"Indeed, I shall not hold my tongue," said the step-daughter.

Poor Greene! He had lost more than his box within the last twelve months; for, as I had learned in that whispered conversation over the tea-table with Sophonisba, this was in reality her papa's marriage trip.

Another day was now gone, and we all went to bed. Had I not been very foolish I should have had myself called at five in the morning, and have gone away by the early boat, leaving my ten napoleons behind me. But, unfortunately, Sophonisba had exacted a promise from me that I would not do this, and thus all chance of spending a day or two in Venice was lost to me. Moreover, I was thoroughly fatigued, and almost glad of any excuse which would allow me to lie in bed on the following morning. I did lie in bed till nine o'clock, and then found the Greenes at breakfast.

"Let us go and look at the Serbelloni Gardens," said I, as soon as the silent meal was over; "or take a boat over to the Sommariva Villa."

"I should like it so much," said Sophonisba.

"We will do nothing of the kind till I have found my property," said Mrs. Greene. "Mr. Robinson, what arrangement did you make yesterday with the police at Como?"

"The police at Como?" I said. "I did not go to the police."

"Not go to the police? And do you mean to say that I am to be robbed of my jewels and no efforts made for redress? Is there no such thing as a constable in this wretched country? Mr. Greene, I do insist upon it that you at once go to the nearest British consul."

"I suppose I had better write home for money," said he.

"And do you mean to say that you haven't written yet?" said I, probably with some acrimony in my voice.

"You needn't scold papa," said Sophonisba.

"I don't know what I am to do," said Mr. Greene, and he began walking up and down the room; but still he did not call for pen and ink, and I began again to feel that he was a swindler. Was it possible that a man of business, who had made his fortune in London, should allow his wife to keep all her jewels in a box, and carry about his own money in the same?

"I don't see why you need be so very unhappy, papa," said Sophonisba. "Mr. Robinson, I'm sure, will let you have whatever money you may want at present." This was pleasant!

"And will Mr. Robinson return me my jewels, which were lost, I must say, in a great measure through his carelessness," said Mrs. Greene. This was pleasanter!

"Upon my word, Mrs. Greene, I must deny that," said I, jumping up. "What on earth could I have done more than I did do? I have been to Milan and nearly fagged myself to death."

"Why didn't you bring a policeman back with you?"

"You would tell everybody on board the boat what there was in it," said I.

"I told nobody but you," she answered.

"I suppose you mean to imply that I've taken the box," I rejoined. So that on this, the third or fourth day of our acquaintance, we did not go on together quite pleasantly.

But what annoyed me, perhaps, the most, was the confidence with which it seemed to be Mr. Greene's intention to lean upon my resources. He certainly had not written home yet, and had taken my ten napoleons, as one friend may take a few shillings from another when he finds that he has left his own silver on his dressing-table. What could he have wanted of ten napoleons? He had alleged the necessity of paying the porters, but the few francs he had had in his pocket would have been enough for that. And now Sophonisba was ever and again prompt in her assurances that he need not annoy himself about money, because I was at his right hand. I went up-stairs into my own room, and counting all my treasures, found that thirty-six pounds and some odd silver was the extent of my wealth. With that I had to go, at any rate, as far as Innspruck, and from thence back to London. It was quite impossible that I should make myself responsible for the Greenes' bill at Bellaggio.

We dined early, and after dinner, according to a promise made in the morning, Sophonisba ascended with me into the Serbelloni Gardens, and walked round the terraces on that beautiful hill which commands the view of the three lakes. When we started I confess that I would sooner have gone alone, for I was sick of the Greenes in my very soul. We had had a terrible day. The landlord had been sent for so often, that he refused to show himself again. The landlady—though Italians of that class are always courteous—had been so driven that she snapped her finger in Mrs. Greene's face. The three girls would not show themselves. The waiters kept out of the way as much as possible; and the Boots, in confidence, abused them to me behind their back. "Monsieur," said the Boots, "do you think there ever was such a box?" "Perhaps not," said I; and yet I knew that I had seen it.

I would, therefore, have preferred to walk without Sophonisba; but that now was impossible. So I determined that I would utilise the occasion by telling her of my present purpose. I had resolved to start on the following day, and it was now necessary to make my friends understand that it was not in my power to extend to them any further pecuniary assistance.

Sophonisba, when we were on the hill, seemed to have forgotten the box, and to be willing that I should forget it also. But this was impossible. When, therefore, she told me how sweet it was to escape from that terrible woman, and leaned on my arm with all the freedom of old acquaintance, I was obliged to cut short the pleasure of the moment.

"I hope your father has written that letter," said I.

"He means to write it from Milan. We know you want to get on, so we purpose to leave here the day after to-morrow."

"Oh!" said I, thinking of the bill immediately, and remembering that Mrs. Greene had insisted on having champagne for dinner.

"And if anything more is to be done about the nasty box, it may be done there," continued Sophonisba.

"But I must go to-morrow," said I, "at 5 A.M."

"Nonsense," said Sophonisba. "Go to-morrow, when I,—I mean we,—are going on the next day!"

"And I might as well explain," said I, gently dropping the hand that was on my arm, "that I find,—I find it will be impossible for me—to—to— "

"To what?"

"To advance Mr. Greene any more money just at present." Then Sophonisba's arm dropped all at once, and she exclaimed, "Oh, Mr. Robinson!"

After all, there was a certain hard good sense about Miss Greene which would have protected her from my evil thoughts had I known all the truth. I found out afterwards that she was a considerable heiress, and, in spite of the opinion expressed by the present Mrs. Robinson when Miss Walker, I do not for a moment think she would have accepted me had I offered to her.

"You are quite right not to embarrass yourself," she said, when I explained to her my immediate circumstances; "but why did you make papa an offer which you cannot perform? He must remain here now till he hears from England. Had you explained it all at first, the ten napoleons would have carried us to Milan." This was all true, and yet I thought it hard upon me.

It was evident to me now, that Sophonisba was prepared to join her step-mother in thinking that I had ill-treated them, and I had not much doubt that I should find Mr. Greene to be of the same opinion. There was very little more said between us during the walk, and when we reached the hotel at seven or half-past seven o'clock, I merely remarked that I would go in and wish her father and mother good bye. "I suppose you will drink tea with us," said Sophonisba, and to this I assented.

I went into my own room, and put all my things into my portmanteau, for according to the custom, which is invariable in Italy when an early start is premeditated, the Boots was imperative in his demand that the luggage should be ready over night. I then went to the Greenes' sitting-room, and found that the whole party was now aware of my intentions.

"So you are going to desert us," said Mrs. Greene.

"I must go on upon my journey," I pleaded in a weak apologetic voice.

"Go on upon your journey, Sir!" said Mrs. Greene. "I would not for a moment have you put yourself to inconvenience on our account." And yet I had already lost fourteen napoleons, and given up all prospect of going to Venice!

"Mr. Robinson is certainly right not to break his engagement with Miss Walker," said Sophonisba. Now I had said not a word about an engagement with Miss Walker, having only mentioned incidentally that she would be one of the party at Innspruck. "But," continued she, "I think he should not have misled us." And in this way we enjoyed our evening meal.

I was just about to shake hands with them all, previous to my final departure from their presence, when the Boots came into the room.

"I'll leave the portmanteau till to-morrow morning," said he.

"All right," said I.

"Because," said he, "there will be such a crowd of things in the hall. The big trunk I will take away now."

"Big trunk,—what big trunk?"

"The trunk with your rug over it, on which your portmanteau stood."

I looked round at Mr., Mrs., and Miss Greene, and saw that they were all looking at me. I looked round at them, and as their eyes met mine I felt that I turned as red as fire. I immediately jumped up, and rushed away to my own room, hearing as I went that all their steps were following me. I rushed to the inner recess, pulled down the portmanteau, which still remained in its old place, tore away my own carpet rug which covered the support beneath it, and there saw—a white canvas-covered box, with a hole in the canvas on the side next to me!

"It is my box," said Mrs. Greene, pushing me away, as she hurried up and put her finger within the rent.

"It certainly does look like it," said Mr. Greene, peering over his wife's shoulder.

"There's no doubt about the box," said Sophonisba.

"Not the least in life," said I, trying to assume an indifferent look.

"Mon Dieu!" said the Boots.

"Corpo di Baccho!" exclaimed the landlord, who had now joined the party.

"Oh—h—h—h—!" screamed Mrs. Greene, and then she threw herself back on to my bed, and shrieked hysterically.

There was no doubt whatsoever about the fact. There was the lost box, and there it had been during all those tedious hours of unavailing search. While I was suffering all that fatigue in Milan, spending my precious zwanzigers in driving about from one hotel to another, the box had been safe, standing in my own room at Bellaggio, hidden by my own rug. And now that it was found everybody looked at me as though it were all my fault. Mrs. Greene's eyes, when she had done being hysterical, were terrible, and Sophonisba looked at me as though I were a convicted thief.

"Who put the box here?" I said, turning fiercely upon the Boots.

"I did," said the Boots, "by Monsieur's express order."

"By my order?" I exclaimed.

"Certainly," said the Boots.

"Corpo di Baccho!" said the landlord, and he also looked at me as though I were a thief. In the meantime the landlady and the three daughters had clustered round Mrs. Greene, administering to her all manner of Italian consolation. The box, and the money, and the jewels were after all a reality; and much incivility can be forgiven to a lady who has really lost her jewels, and has really found them again.

There and then there arose a hurly-burly among us as to the manner in which the odious trunk found its way into my room. Had anybody been just enough to consider the matter coolly, it must have been quite clear that I could not have ordered it there. When I entered the hotel, the boxes were already being lugged about, and I had spoken a word to no one concerning them. That traitorous Boots had done it,—no doubt without malice prepense; but he had done it; and now that the Greenes were once more known as moneyed people, he turned upon me, and told me to my face, that I had desired that box to be taken to my own room as part of my own luggage!

"My dear," said Mr. Greene, turning to his wife, "you should never mention the contents of your luggage to any one."

"I never will again," said Mrs. Greene, with a mock repentant air, "but I really thought— "

"One never can be sure of sharpers," said Mr. Greene.

"That's true," said Mrs. Greene.

"After all, it may have been accidental," said Sophonisba, on hearing which good-natured surmise both papa and mamma Greene shook their suspicious heads.

I was resolved to say nothing then. It was all but impossible that they should really think that I had intended to steal their box; nor, if they did think so, would it have become me to vindicate myself before the landlord and all his servants. I stood by therefore in silence, while two of the men raised the trunk, and joined the procession which followed it as it was carried out of my room into that of the legitimate owner.

Everybody in the house was there by that time, and Mrs. Greene, enjoying her triumph, by no means grudged them the entrance into her sitting-room. She had felt that she was suspected, and now she was determined that the world of Bellaggio should know how much she was above suspicion. The box was put down upon two chairs, the supporters who had borne it retiring a pace each. Mrs. Greene then advanced proudly with the selected key, and Mr. Greene stood by at her right shoulder, ready to receive his portion of the hidden treasure. Sophonisba was now indifferent, and threw herself on the sofa, while I walked up and down the room thoughtfully,—meditating what words I should say when I took my last farewell of the Greenes.

But as I walked I could see what occurred. Mrs. Greene opened the box, and displayed to view the ample folds of a huge yellow woollen dressing-gown. I could fancy that she would not willingly have exhibited this article of her toilet, had she not felt that its existence would speedily be merged in the presence of the glories which were to follow. This had merely been the padding at the top of the box. Under that lay a long papier-maché case, and in that were all her treasures. "Ah, they are safe," she said, opening the lid and looking upon her tawdry pearls and carbuncles.

Mr. Greene, in the meantime, well knowing the passage for his hand, had dived down to the very bottom of the box, and seized hold of a small canvas bag. "It is here," said he, dragging it up, "and as far as I can tell, as yet, the knot has not been untied." Whereupon he sat himself down by Sophonisba, and employing her to assist him in holding them, began to count his rolls. "They are all right," said he; and he wiped the perspiration from his brow.

I had not yet made up my mind in what manner I might best utter my last words among them so as to maintain the dignity of my character, and now I was standing over against Mr. Greene with my arms folded on my breast. I had on my face a frown of displeasure, which I am able to assume upon occasions, but I had not yet determined what words I would use. After all, perhaps, it might be as well that I should leave them without any last words.

"Greene, my dear," said the lady, "pay the gentleman his ten napoleons."

"Oh yes, certainly;" whereupon Mr. Greene undid one of the rolls and extracted eight sovereigns. "I believe that will make it right, Sir," said he, handing them to me.

I took the gold, slipped it with an indifferent air into my waistcoat pocket, and then refolded my arms across my breast.

"Papa," said Sophonisba, in a very audible whisper, "Mr. Robinson went for you to Como. Indeed, I believe he says he went to Milan."

"Do not let that be mentioned," said I.

"By all means pay him his expenses," said Mrs. Greene; "I would not owe him anything for worlds."

"He should be paid," said Sophonisba.

"Oh, certainly," said Mr. Greene. And he at once extracted another sovereign, and tendered it to me in the face of the assembled multitude.

This was too much! "Mr. Greene," said I, "I intended to be of service to you when I went to Milan, and you are very welcome to the benefit of my intentions. The expense of that journey, whatever may be its amount, is my own affair." And I remained standing with my closed arms.

"We will be under no obligation to him," said Mrs. Greene; "and I shall insist on his taking the money."

"The servant will put it on his dressing-table," said Sophonisba. And she handed the sovereign to the Boots, giving him instructions.

"Keep it yourself, Antonio," I said. Whereupon the man chucked it to the ceiling with his thumb, caught it as it fell, and with a well-satisfied air, dropped it into the recesses of his pocket. The air of the Greenes was also well satisfied, for they felt that they had paid me in full for all my services.

And now, with many obsequious bows and assurances of deep respect, the landlord and his family withdrew from the room. "Was there anything else they could do for Mrs. Greene?" Mrs. Greene was all affability. She had shown her jewels to the girls, and allowed them to express their admiration in pretty Italian superlatives. There was nothing else she wanted to-night. She was very happy and liked Bellagio. She would stay yet a week, and would make herself quite happy. And, though none of them understood a word that the other said, each understood that things were now rose-coloured, and so with scrapings, bows, and grinning smiles, the landlord and all his myrmidons withdrew. Mr. Greene was still counting his money, sovereign by sovereign, and I was still standing with my folded arms upon my bosom.

"I believe I may now go," said I.

"Good night," said Mrs. Greene.

"Adieu," said Sophonisba.

"I have the pleasure of wishing you good bye," said Mr. Greene.

And then I walked out of the room. After all, what was the use of saying anything? And what could I say that would have done me any service? If they were capable of thinking me a thief,—which they certainly did,—nothing that I could say would remove the impression. Nor, as I thought, was it suitable that I should defend myself from such an imputation. What were the Greenes to me? So I walked slowly out of the room, and never again saw one of the family from that day to this.

As I stood upon the beach the next morning, while my portmanteau was being handed into the boat, I gave the Boots five zwanzigers. I was determined to show him that I did not condescend to feel anger against him.

He took the money, looked into my face, and then whispered to me, "Why did you not give me a word of notice beforehand?" he said, and winked his eye. He was evidently a thief, and took me to be another;—but what did it matter?

I went thence to Milan, in which city I had no heart to look at anything; thence to Verona, and so over the pass of the Brenner to

Innspruck. When I once found myself near to my dear friends the Walkers I was again a happy man; and I may safely declare that, though a portion of my journey was so troublesome and unfortunate, I look back upon that tour as the happiest and the luckiest epoch of my life.

Aaron Trow

Originally appeared in *Public Opinion*, 14 and 21 December 1861. Reprinted in *Tales of All Countries* [Second Series] (1863). Written 3–12 February 1861, during the composition of *Orley Farm*. Trollope visited Bermuda, where the story is set, in May 1859, at the end of his Caribbean tour. For a full account of this trip, *see The West Indies and the Spanish Main* (1859), ch. 22.

I WOULD wish to declare, at the beginning of this story, that I shall never regard that cluster of islets which we call Bermuda as the Fortunate Islands of the Ancients. Do not let professional geographers take me up, and say that no one has so accounted them, and that the ancients have never been supposed to have gotten themselves so far westwards. What I mean to assert is this—that, had any ancient been carried thither by enterprise or stress of weather, he would not have given those islands so good a name. That the Neapolitan sailors of King Alonzo should have been wrecked here, I consider to be more likely. The vexed Bermoothes is a good name for them. There is no getting in or out of them without the greatest difficulty, and a patient, slow navigation, which is very heart-rending. That Caliban should have lived here I can imagine; that Ariel would have been sick of the place is certain; and that Governor Prospero should have been willing to abandon his governorship, I conceive to have been only natural. When one regards the present state of the place, one is tempted to doubt whether any of the governors have been conjurors since his days.

Bermuda, as all the world knows, is a British colony at which we maintain a convict establishment. Most of our outlying convict establishments have been sent back upon our hands from our colonies, but here one is still maintained. There is also in the islands a strong military fortress, though not a fortress looking magnificent to the eyes of civilians as do Malta and Gibraltar. There are also here some six thousand white people and some six thousand black people, eating, drinking, sleeping, and dying.

The convict establishment is the most notable feature of Bermuda to a stranger, but it does not seem to attract much attention from the regular inhabitants of the place. There is no intercourse between the prisoners and the Bermudians. The convicts are rarely seen by them, and the convict islands are rarely visited. As to the prisoners themselves, of course it is not open to them—or should not be open to them—to have intercourse with any but the prison authorities.

There have, however, been instances in which convicts have escaped from their confinement, and made their way out among the islands. Poor wretches! As a rule, there is but little chance for any that can so escape. The whole length of the cluster is but twenty miles, and the breadth is under four. The prisoners are, of course, white men, and the lower orders of Bermuda, among whom alone could a runagate have any chance of hiding himself, are all negroes; so that such a one would be known at once. Their clothes are all marked. Their only chance of a permanent escape would be in the hold of an American ship; but what captain of an American or other ship would willingly encumber himself with an escaped convict? But, nevertheless, men have escaped; and in one instance, I believe, a convict got away, so that of him no further tidings were ever heard.

For the truth of the following tale I will not by any means vouch. If one were to inquire on the spot one might probably find that the ladies all believe it, and the old men; that all the young men know exactly how much of it is false and how much true; and that the steady, middle-aged, well-to-do islanders are quite convinced that it is romance from beginning to end. My readers may range themselves with the ladies, the young men, or the steady, well-to do, middle-aged islanders, as they please.

Some years ago, soon after the prison was first established on its present footing, three men did escape from it, and among them a certain notorious prisoner named Aaron Trow. Trow's antecedents in England had not been so villanously bad as those of many of his fellow-convicts, though the one offence for which he was punished had been of a deep dye: he had shed man's blood. At a period of great distress in a manufacturing town he had led men on to riot, and with his own hand had slain the first constable who had endeavoured to do his duty against him. There had been courage in the doing of the deed, and probably no malice; but the deed, let its moral blackness have been what it might, had sent him to Bermuda, with a sentence against him of penal servitude for life. Had he been then amenable to prison discipline,—even then, with such a sentence against him as that,—he might have won his way back, after the lapse of years, to the children, and, perhaps, to the wife, that he had left behind him; but he was amenable to no rules—to no discipline. His heart was sore to death with an idea of injury, and he lashed himself against the bars of his cage with a feeling that it would be well if he could so lash himself till he might perish in his fury.

And then a day came in which an attempt was made by a large body of convicts, under his leadership, to get the better of the officers of the prison. It is hardly necessary to say that the attempt failed. Such attempts always fail. It failed on this occasion signally, and Trow, with two other men, were condemned to be scourged terribly, and then kept in solitary confinement for some lengthened term of months. Before, however, the day of scourging came, Trow and his two associates had escaped.

I have not the space to tell how this was effected, nor the power to describe the manner. They did escape from the establishment into the islands, and though two of them were taken after a single day's run at liberty, Aaron Trow had not been yet retaken even when a week was over. When a month was over he had not been retaken, and the officers of the prison began to say that he had got away from them in a vessel to the States. It was impossible, they said, that he should have remained in the islands and not been discovered. It was not impossible that he might have destroyed himself, leaving his body where it had not yet been found. But he could not have lived on in Bermuda during that month's search. So, at least, said the officers of the prison. There was, however, a report through the islands that he had been seen from time to time; that he had gotten bread from the negroes at night, threatening them with death if they told of his whereabouts; and that all the clothes of the mate of a vessel had been stolen while the man was bathing, including a suit of dark blue cloth, in which suit of clothes, or in one of such a nature, a stranger had been seen skulking about the rocks near St. George. All this the governor of the prison affected to disbelieve, but the opinion was becoming very rife in the islands that Aaron Trow was still there.

A vigilant search, however, is a task of great labour, and cannot be kept up for ever. By degrees it was relaxed. The warders and gaolers ceased to patrol the island roads by night, and it was agreed that Aaron Trow was gone, or that he would be starved to death, or that he would in time be driven to leave such traces of his whereabouts as must lead to his discovery; and this at last did turn out to be the fact.

There is a sort of prettiness about these islands which, though it never rises to the loveliness of romantic scenery, is nevertheless attractive in its way. The land breaks itself into little knolls, and the sea runs up, hither and thither, in a thousand creeks and inlets; and then, too, when the oleanders are in bloom, they give a wonderfully bright colour to the landscape. Oleanders seem to be the roses of Bermuda, and are cultivated round all the villages of the better class through the islands. There are two towns, St. George and Hamilton, and one main high road, which connects them; but even this high road is broken by a ferry, over which every vehicle going from St. George to Hamilton must be conveyed. Most of the locomotion in these parts is done by boats, and the residents look to the sea with its narrow creeks, as their best highway from their farms to their best market. In those days—and those days were not very long since—the building of small ships was their chief trade, and they valued their land mostly for the small scrubby cedar-trees with which this trade was carried on.

As one goes from St. George to Hamilton the road runs between two seas; that to the right is the ocean; that on the left is an inland creek, which runs up through a large portion of the islands, so that the land on the other side of it is near to the traveller. For a considerable portion of the way there are no houses lying near the road, and there is one residence, some way from the road, so secluded that no other house lies within a mile of it by land. By water it might probably be reached within half a mile. This place was called Crump Island, and here lived, and had lived for many years, an old gentleman, a native of Bermuda, whose business it had been to buy up cedar wood and sell it to the ship-builders at Hamilton. In our story we shall not have very much to do with old Mr. Bergen, but it will be necessary to say a word or two about his house.

It stood on what would have been an island in the creek, had not a narrow causeway, barely broad enough for a road, joined it to that larger island on which stands the town of St. George. As the main road approaches the ferry it runs through some rough, hilly, open ground, which on the right side towards the ocean has never been cultivated. The distance from the ocean here may, perhaps, be a quarter of a mile, and the ground is for the most part covered with low furze. On the left of the road the land is cultivated in patches, and here, some half mile or more from the ferry, a path turns away to Crump Island. The house cannot be seen from the road, and, indeed, can hardly be seen at all, except from the sea. It lies, perhaps, three furlongs from the high road, and the path to it is but little used, as the passage to and from it is chiefly made by water.

Here, at the time of our story, lived Mr. Bergen, and here lived Mr. Bergen's daughter. Miss Bergen was well known at St. George as a steady, good girl, who spent her time in looking after her father's household matters, in managing his two black maid-servants and the black gardener, and who did her duty in that sphere of life to which she had been called. She was a comely, well-shaped young woman, with a sweet countenance, rather large in size, and very quiet in demeanour. In her earlier years, when young girls usually first bud forth into womanly beauty, the neighbours had not thought much of Anastasia Bergen, nor had the young men of St. George been wont to stay their boats under the window of Crump Cottage in order that they might listen to her voice or feel the light of her eye; but slowly, as years went by, Anastasia Bergen became a woman that a man might well love; and a man learned to love her who was well worthy of a woman's heart. This was Caleb Morton, the Presbyterian minister of St. George; and Caleb Morton had been engaged to marry Miss Bergen for the last two years past, at the period of Aaron Trow's escape from prison.

Caleb Morton was not a native of Bermuda, but had been sent thither by the synod of his church from Nova Scotia. He was a tall, handsome man, at this time of some thirty years of age, of a presence which might almost have been called commanding. He was very strong, but of a temperament which did not often give him opportunity to put forth his strength; and his life had been such that neither he nor others knew of what nature might be his courage. The greater part of his life was spent in preaching to some few of the white people around him, and in teaching as many of the blacks as he could get to hear him. His days were very quiet, and had been altogether without excitement until he had met with Anastasia Bergen. It will suffice for us to say that he did meet her, and that now, for two years past, they had been engaged as man and wife.

Old Mr. Bergen, when he heard of the engagement, was not well pleased at the information. In the first place, his daughter was very necessary to him, and the idea of her marrying and going away had hardly as yet occurred to him; and then he was by no means inclined to part with any of his money. It must not be presumed that he had amassed a fortune by his trade in cedar wood. Few tradesmen in Bermuda do, as I imagine, amass fortunes. Of some few hundred pounds he was possessed, and these, in the course of nature, would go to his daughter when he died; but he had no inclination to hand any portion of them over to his daughter before they did go to her in the course of nature. Now, the income which Caleb Morton earned as a Presbyterian clergyman was not large, and, therefore, no day had been fixed as yet for his marriage with Anastasia.

But, though the old man had been from the first averse to the match, his hostility had not been active. He had not forbidden Mr. Morton his house, or affected to be in any degree angry because his daughter had a lover. He had merely grumbled forth an intimation that those who marry in haste repent at leisure,—that love kept nobody warm if the pot did not boil; and that, as for him, it was as much as he could do to keep his own pot boiling at Crump Cottage. In answer to this Anastasia said nothing. She asked him for no money, but still kept his accounts, managed his household, and looked patiently forward for better days.

Old Mr. Bergen himself spent much of his time at Hamilton, where he had a woodyard with a couple of rooms attached to it. It was his custom to remain here three nights of the week, during which Anastasia was left alone at the cottage; and it happened by no means seldom that she was altogether alone, for the negro whom they called the gardener would go to her father's place at Hamilton, and the two black girls would crawl away up to the road, tired with the monotony of the sea at the cottage. Caleb had more than once told her that she was too much alone, but she had laughed at him, saying that solitude in Bermuda was not dangerous. Nor, indeed, was it; for the people are quiet and well-mannered, lacking much energy, but being, in the same degree, free from any propensity to violence.

"So you are going," she said to her lover, one evening, as he rose from the chair on which he had been swinging himself at the door of the cottage which looks down over the creek of the sea. He had sat there for an hour talking to her as she worked, or watching her as she moved about the place. It was a beautiful evening, and the sun had been falling to rest with almost tropical glory before his feet. The bright oleanders were red with their blossoms all around him, and he had thoroughly enjoyed his hour of easy rest. "So you are going," she said to him, not putting her work out of her hand as he rose to depart.

"Yes; and it is time for me to go. I have still work to do before I can get to bed. Ah, well; I suppose the day will come at last when I need not leave you as soon as my hour of rest is over."

"Come; of course it will come. That is, if your reverence should choose to wait for it another ten years or so."

"I believe you would not mind waiting twenty years."

"Not if a certain friend of mine would come down and see me of evenings when I'm alone after the day. It seems to me that I shouldn't mind waiting as long as I had that to look for."

"You are right not to be impatient," he said to her, after a pause, as he held her hand before he went. "Quite right. I only wish I could school myself to be as easy about it."

"I did not say I was easy," said Anastasia. "People are seldom easy in this world, I take it. I said I could be patient. Do not look in that way, as though you pretended that you were dissatisfied with me. You know that I am true to you, and you ought to be very proud of me."

"I am proud of you, Anastasia— " on hearing which she got up and curtseyed to him. "I am proud of you; so proud of you that I feel you should not be left here all alone, with no one to help you if you were in trouble."

"Women don't get into trouble as men do, and do not want any one to help them. If you were alone in the house you would have to go to bed without your supper, because you could not make a basin of boiled milk ready for your own meal. Now, when your reverence has gone, I shall go to work and have my tea comfortably." And then he did go, bidding God bless her as he left her. Three hours after that he was disturbed in his own lodgings by one of the negro girls from the cottage rushing to his door, and begging him in Heaven's name to come down to the assistance of her mistress.

When Morton left her, Anastasia did not proceed to do as she had said, and seemed to have forgotten her evening meal. She had been working sedulously with her needle during all that last conversation; but when her lover was gone, she allowed the work to fall from her hands, and sat motionless for awhile, gazing at the last streak of colour left by the setting sun; but there was no longer a sign of its glory to be traced in the heavens around her. The twilight in Bermuda is not long and enduring as it is with us, though the daylight does not depart suddenly, leaving the darkness of night behind it without any intermediate time of warning, as is the case farther south, down among the islands of the tropics. But the soft, sweet light of the evening had waned and gone, and night had absolutely come upon her, while Anastasia was still seated before the cottage with her eyes fixed upon the white streak of motionless sea which was still visible through the gloom. She was thinking of him, of his ways of life, of his happiness, and of her duty towards him. She had told him, with her pretty feminine falseness, that she could wait without impatience; but now she said to herself that it would not be good for him to wait longer. He lived alone and without comfort, working very hard for his poor pittance, and she could see and feel and understand that a companion in his life was to him almost a necessity. She would tell her father that all this must be brought to an end. She would not ask him for money, but she would make him understand that her services must, at any rate in part, be transferred. Why should not she and Morton still live at the cottage when they were married? And so thinking, and at last resolving, she sat there till the dark night fell upon her.

She was at last disturbed by feeling a man's hand upon her shoulder. She jumped from her chair and faced him,—not screaming, for it was especially within her power to control herself, and to make no utterance except with forethought. Perhaps it might have been better for her had she screamed, and sent a shrill shriek down the shore of that inland sea. She was silent, however, and with awe-struck face and outstretched hands gazed into the face of him who still held her by the shoulder. The night was dark; but her eyes were now accustomed to the darkness, and she could see indistinctly something of his features. He was a low-sized man, dressed in a suit of sailor's blue clothing, with a rough cap of hair on his head, and a beard that had not been clipped for many weeks. His eyes were large, and hollow, and frightfully bright, so that she seemed to see nothing else of him; but she felt the strength of his fingers as he grasped her tighter and more tightly by the arm.

"Who are you?" she said, after a moment's pause.

"Do you know me?" he asked.

"Know you! No." But the words were hardly out of her mouth before it struck her that the man was Aaron Trow, of whom every one in Bermuda had been talking.

"Come into the house," he said, "and give me food." And he still held her with his hand as though he would compel her to follow him.

She stood for a moment thinking what she would say to him; for even then, with that terrible man standing close to her in the darkness, her presence of mind did not desert her, "Surely," she said, "I will give you food if you are hungry. But take your hand from me. No man would lay his hands on a woman."

"A woman!" said the stranger. "What does the starved wolf care for that? A woman's blood is as sweet to him as that of a man. Come into the house, I tell you." And then she preceded him through the open door into the narrow passage, and thence to the kitchen. There she saw that the back door, leading out on the other side of the house, was open, and she knew that he had come down from the road and entered on that side. She threw her eyes round, looking for the negro girls; but they were away, and she remembered that there was no human being within sound of her voice but this man who had told her that he was as a wolf thirsty after her blood!

"Give me food at once," he said.

"And will you go if I give it you?" she asked.

"I will knock out your brains if you do not," he replied, lifting from the grate a short, thick poker which lay there. "Do as I bid you at once. You also would be like a tiger if you had fasted for two days, as I have done."

She could see, as she moved across the kitchen, that he had already searched there for something that he might eat, but that he had searched in vain. With the close economy common among his class in the islands, all comestibles were kept under close lock and key in the house of Mr. Bergen. Their daily allowance was given day by day to the negro servants, and even the fragments were then gathered up and locked away in safety. She moved across the kitchen to the accustomed cupboard, taking the keys from her pocket, and he followed close upon her. There was a small oil lamp hanging from the low ceiling which just gave them light to see each other. She lifted her hand to this to take it from its hook, but he prevented her. "No, by Heaven!" he said, "you don't touch that till I've done with it. There's light enough for you to drag out your scraps."

She did drag out her scraps and a bowl of milk, which might hold perhaps a quart. There was a fragment of bread, a morsel of cold potato-cake, and the bone of a leg of kid. "And is that all?" said he. But as he spoke he fleshed his teeth against the bone as a dog would have done.

"It is the best I have," she said; "I wish it were better, and you should have had it without violence, as you have suffered so long from hunger."

"Bah! Better; yes! You would give the best no doubt, and set the hell hounds on my track the moment I am gone. I know how much I might expect from your charity."

"I would have fed you for pity's sake," she answered.

"Pity! Who are you, that you should dare to pity me! By——my young woman, it is I that pity you. I must cut your throat unless you give me money. Do you know that?"

"Money! I have got no money."

"I'll make you have some before I go. Come; don't move till I have done." And as he spoke to her he went on tugging at the bone, and swallowing the lumps of stale bread. He had already finished the bowl of milk. "And, now," said he, "tell me who I am."

"I suppose you are Aaron Trow," she answered, very slowly.

He said nothing on hearing this, but continued his meal, standing close to her so that she might not possibly escape from him out into the darkness. Twice or thrice in those few minutes she made up her mind to make such an attempt, feeling that it would be better to leave him in possession of the house, and make sure, if possible, of her own life. There was no money there; not a dollar! What money her father kept in his possession was locked up in his safe at Hamilton. And might he not keep to his threat, and murder her, when he found that she could give him nothing? She did not tremble outwardly, as she stood there watching him as he ate, but she thought how probable it might be that her last moments were very near. And yet she could scrutinise his features, form, and garments, so as to carry away in her mind a perfect picture of them. Aaron Trow,—for of course it was the escaped convict,—was not a man of frightful, hideous aspect. Had the world used him well, giving him when he was young ample wages and separating him from turbulent spirits, he also might have used the world well; and then women would have praised the brightness of his eye and the manly vigour of his brow. But things had not gone well with him. He had been separated from the wife he had loved, and the children who had been raised at his knee,—separated by his own violence; and now, as he had said of himself, he was a wolf rather than a man. As he stood there satisfying the craving of his appetite, breaking up the large morsels of food, he was an object very sad to be seen. Hunger had made him gaunt and yellow, he was squalid with the dirt of his hidden lair, and he had the look of a beast;—that look to which men fall when they live like the brutes of prey, as outcasts from their brethren. But still there was that about his brow which might have redeemed him,—which might have turned her horror into pity, had he been willing that it should be so.

"And now give me some brandy," he said.

There was brandy in the house,—in the sitting-room which was close at their hand, and the key of the little press which held it was in her pocket. It was useless, she thought, to refuse him; and so she told him that there was a bottle partly full, but that she must go to the next room to fetch it him.

"We'll go together, my darling," he said. "There's nothing like good company." And he again put his hand upon her arm as they passed into the family sitting-room.

"I must take the light," she said. But he unhooked it himself, and carried it in his own hand.

Again she went to work without trembling. She found the key of the side cupboard, and unlocking the door, handed him a bottle which might contain about half-a-pint of spirits. "And is that all?" he said.

"There is a full bottle here," she answered, handing him another; "but if you drink it, you will be drunk, and they will catch you."

"By Heavens, yes; and you would be the first to help them; would you not?"

"Look here," she answered. "If you will go now, I will not say a word to any one of your coming, nor set them on your track to follow you. There, take the full bottle with you. If you will go, you shall be safe from me."

"What, and go without money!"

"I have none to give you. You may believe me when I say so. I have not a dollar in the house."

Before he spoke again he raised the half empty bottle to his mouth, and drank as long as there was a drop to drink. "There," said he, putting the bottle down, "I am better after that. As to the other you are right, and I will take it with me. And now, young woman, about the money?"

"I tell you that I have not a dollar."

"Look here," said he, and he spoke now in a softer voice, as though he would be on friendly terms with her. "Give me ten sovereigns, and I will go. I know you have it, and with ten sovereigns it is possible that I may save my life. You are good, and would not wish that a man should die so horrid a death. I know you are good. Come, give me the money." And he put his hands up, beseeching her, and looked into her face with imploring eyes.

"On the word of a Christian woman I have not got money to give you," she replied.

"Nonsense!" And as he spoke he took her by the arm and shook her. He shook her violently so that he hurt her, and her breath for a moment was all but gone from her. "I tell you you must make dollars before I leave you, or I will so handle you that it would have been better for you to coin your very blood."

"May God help me at my need," she said, "as I have not above a few penny pieces in the house."

"And you expect me to believe that! Look here! I will shake the teeth out of your head, but I will have it from you." And he did shake her again, using both his hands and striking her against the wall.

"Would you—murder me?" she said, hardly able now to utter the words.

"Murder you, yes; why not? I cannot be worse than I am, were I to murder you ten times over. But with money I may possibly be better."

"I have it not."

"Then I will do worse than murder you. I will make you such an object that all the world shall loathe to look on you." And so saying he took her by the arm and dragged her forth from the wall against which she had stood.

Then there came from her a shriek that was heard far down the shore of that silent sea, and away across to the solitary houses of those living on the other side,—a shriek very sad, sharp, and prolonged,—which told plainly to those who heard it of woman's woe when in her extremest peril. That sound was spoken of in Bermuda for many a day after that, as something which had been terrible to hear. But then, at that moment, as it came wailing through the dark, it sounded as though it were not human. Of those who heard it, not one guessed from whence it came, nor was the hand of any brother put forward to help that woman at her need.

"Did you hear that?" said the young wife to her husband, from the far side of the arm of the sea.

"Hear it! Oh Heaven, yes! Whence did it come?" The young wife could not say from whence it came, but clung close to her husband's breast, comforting herself with the knowledge that that terrible sorrow was not hers.

But aid did come at last, or rather that which seemed as aid. Long and terrible was the fight between that human beast of prey and the poor victim which had fallen into his talons. Anastasia Bergen was a strong, well-built woman, and now that the time had come to her when a struggle was necessary, a struggle for life, for honour, for the happiness of him who was more to her than herself, she fought like a tigress attacked in her own lair. At such a moment as this she also could become wild and savage as the beast of the forest. When he pinioned her arms with one of his, as he pressed her down upon the floor, she caught the first joint of the forefinger of his other hand between her teeth till he yelled in agony, and another sound was heard across the silent water. And then, when one hand was loosed in the struggle, she twisted it through his long hair, and dragged back his head till his eyes were nearly starting from their sockets. Anastasia Bergen had hitherto been a sheer woman, all feminine in her nature. But now the foam came to her mouth, and fire sprang from her eyes, and the muscles of her body worked as though she had been trained to deeds of violence. Of violence, Aaron Trow had known much in his rough life, but never had he combated with harder antagonist than her whom he now held beneath his breast.

"By——I will put an end to you," he exclaimed, in his wrath, as he struck her violently across the face with his elbow. His hand was occupied, and he could not use it for a blow, but, nevertheless, the violence was so great that the blood gushed from her nostrils, while the back of her head was driven with violence against the floor. But yet she did not lose her hold of him. Her hand was still twined closely through his thick hair, and in every move he made she clung to him with all her might. "Leave go my hair," he shouted at her, but she still kept her hold, though he again dashed her head against the floor.

There was still light in the room, for when he first grasped her with both his hands, he had put the lamp down on a small table. Now they were rolling on the floor together, and twice he had essayed to kneel on her that he might thus crush the breath from her body, and deprive her altogether of her strength; but she had been too active for him, moving herself along the ground, though in doing so she dragged him with her. But by degrees he got one hand at liberty, and with that he pulled a clasp knife out of his pocket and opened it. "I will cut your head off, if you do not let go my hair," he said. But still she held fast by him. He then stabbed at her arm, using his left hand and making short ineffectual blows. Her dress partly saved her, and partly also the continual movement of all her limbs; but, nevertheless, the knife wounded her. It wounded her in several places about the arm, covering them both with blood;—but still she hung on. So close was her grasp in her agony, that, as she afterwards found, she cut the skin of her own hand with her own nails. Had the man's hair been less thick or strong, or her own tenacity less steadfast, he would have murdered her before any interruption could have saved her.

And yet he had not purposed to murder her, or even, in the first instance, to inflict on her any bodily harm. But he had been determined to get money. With such a sum of money as he had named, it might, he thought, be possible for him to win his way across to America. He might bribe men to hide him in the hold of a ship, and thus there might be for him, at any rate, a possibility of escape. That there must be money in the house, he had still thought when first he laid hands on the poor woman; and then, when the struggle had once begun, when he had felt her muscles contending with his, the passion of the beast was aroused within him, and he strove against her as he would have striven against a dog. But yet, when the knife was in his hand, he had not driven it against her heart.

Then suddenly, while they were yet rolling on the floor, there was a sound of footsteps in the passage. Aaron Trow instantly leaped to his feet, leaving his victim on the ground, with huge lumps of his thick clotted hair in her hand. Thus, and thus only, could he have liberated himself from her grasp. He rushed at the door with the open knife still in his hand, and there he came against the two negro servant-girls who had returned down to their kitchen from the road on which they had been straying. Trow, as he half saw them in the dark, not knowing how many there might be, or whether there was a man among them, rushed through them, upsetting one scared girl in his passage. With the instinct and with the timidity of a beast, his impulse now was to escape, and he hurried away back to the road and to his lair, leaving the three women together in the cottage. Poor wretch! As he crossed the road, not skulking in his impotent haste, but running at his best, another pair of eyes saw him, and when the search became hot after him, it was known that his hiding-place was not distant.

It was some time before any of the women were able to act, and when some step was taken, Anastasia was the first to take it. She had not absolutely swooned, but the reaction, after the violence of her efforts, was so great, that for some minutes she had been unable to speak. She had risen from the floor when Trow left her, and had even followed him to the door; but since that she had fallen back into her father's old armchair, and there she sat gasping not only for words, but for breath also. At last she bade one of the girls to run into St. George, and beg Mr. Morton to come to her aid. The girl would not stir without her companion; and even then, Anastasia, covered as she was with blood, with dishevelled hair and her clothes half torn from her body, accompanied them as far as the road. There they found a negro lad still hanging about the place, and he told them that he had seen the man cross the road, and run down over the open ground towards the rocks of the sea-coast. "He must be there," said the lad, pointing in the direction of a corner of the rocks; "unless he swim across the mouth of the ferry." But the mouth of that ferry is an arm of the sea, and it was not probable that a man would do that when he might have taken the narrow water by keeping on the other side of the road.

At about one that night Caleb Morton reached the cottage breathless with running, and before a word was spoken between them, Anastasia had fallen on his shoulder and had fainted. As soon as she was in the arms of her lover, all her power had gone from her. The spirit and passion of the tiger had gone, and she was again a weak woman shuddering at the thought of what she had suffered. She remembered that she had had the man's hand between her teeth, and by degrees she found his hair still clinging to her fingers; but even then she could hardly call to mind the nature of the struggle she had undergone. His hot breath close to her own cheek she did remember, and his glaring eyes, and even the roughness of his beard as he pressed his face against her own; but she could not say whence had come the blood, nor till her arm became stiff and motionless did she know that she had been wounded.

It was all joy with her now, as she sat motionless without speaking, while he administered to her wants and spoke words of love into her ears. She remembered the man's horrid threat, and knew that by God's mercy she had been saved. And *he* was there caressing her, loving her, comforting her! As she thought of the fate that had threatened her, of the evil that had been so imminent, she fell forward on her knees, and with incoherent sobs uttered her thanksgivings, while her head was still supported on his arms.

It was almost morning before she could induce herself to leave him and lie down. With him she seemed to be so perfectly safe; but the moment he was away she could see Aaron Trow's eyes gleaming at her across the room. At last, however, she slept; and when he saw that she was at rest, he told himself that his work must then begin. Hitherto Caleb Morton had lived in all respects the life of a man of peace; but now, asking himself no questions as to the propriety of what he would do, using no inward arguments as to this or that line of conduct, he girded the sword on his loins, and prepared himself for war. The wretch who had thus treated the woman whom he loved should be hunted down like a wild beast, as long as he had arms and legs with which to carry on the hunt. He would pursue the miscreant with any weapons that might come to his hands; and might Heaven help him at his need, as he dealt forth punishment to that man, if he caught him within his grasp. Those who had hitherto known Morton in the island, could not recognise the man as he came forth on that day, thirsty after blood, and desirous to thrust himself into personal conflict with the wild ruffian who had injured him. The meek Presbyterian minister had been a preacher, preaching ways of peace, and living in accordance with his own doctrines. The world had been very quiet for him, and he had walked quietly in his appointed path. But now the world was quiet no longer, nor was there any preaching of peace. His cry was for blood; for the blood of the untamed savage brute who had come upon his young doe in her solitude, and striven with such brutal violence to tear her heart from her bosom.

He got to his assistance early in the morning some of the constables from St. George, and before the day was over, he was joined by two or three of the warders from the convict establishment. There was with him also a friend or two, and thus a party was formed, numbering together ten or twelve persons. They were of course all armed, and therefore it might be thought that there would be but small chance for the wretched man if they should come upon his track. At first they all searched together, thinking, from the tidings which had reached them, that he must be near to them; but gradually they spread themselves along the rocks between St. George and the ferry, keeping watchmen on the road, so that he should not escape unnoticed into the island.

Ten times during the day did Anastasia send from the cottage up to Morton, begging him to leave the search to others, and come down to her. But not for a moment would he lose the scent of his prey. What! should it be said that she had been so treated, and that others had avenged her? He sent back to say that her father was with her now, and that he would come when his work was over. And in that job of work the life-blood of Aaron Trow was counted up.

Towards evening they were all congregated on the road near to the spot at which the path turns off towards the cottage, when a voice was heard hallooing to them from the summit of a little hill which lies between the road and the sea on the side towards the ferry, and presently a boy came running down to them full of news. "Danny Lund has seen him," said the boy, "he has seen him plainly in among the rocks." And then came Danny Lund himself, a small negro lad about fourteen years of age, who was known in those parts as the idlest, most dishonest, and most useless of his race. On this occasion, however, Danny Lund became important, and every one listened to him. He had seen, he said, a pair of eyes moving down in a cave of the rocks which he well knew. He had been in the cave often, he said, and could get there again. But not now; not while that pair of eyes was moving at the bottom of it. And so they all went up over the hill, Morton leading the way with hot haste. In his waistband he held a pistol, and his hand grasped a short iron bar with which he had armed himself. They ascended the top of the hill, and when there, the open sea was before them on two sides, and on the third was the narrow creek over which the ferry passed. Immediately beneath their feet were the broken rocks; for on that side, towards the sea, the earth and grass of the hill descended but a little way towards the water. Down among the rocks they all went, silently, Caleb Morton leading the way, and Danny Lund directing him from behind.

"Mr. Morton," said an elderly man from St. George, "had you not better let the warders of the gaol go first; he is a desperate man, and they will best understand his ways?"

In answer to this Morton said nothing, but he would let no one put a foot before him. He still pressed forward among the rocks, and at last came to a spot from whence he might have sprung at one leap into the ocean. It was a broken cranny on the sea-shore into which the sea beat, and surrounded on every side but the one by huge broken fragments of stone, which at first sight seemed as though they would have admitted of a path down among them to the water's edge; but which, when scanned more closely, were seen to be so large in size, that no man could climb from one to another. It was a singularly romantic spot, but now well known to them all there, for they had visited it over and over again that morning.

"In there," said Danny Lund, keeping well behind Morton's body, and pointing at the same time to a cavern high up among the rocks, but quite on the opposite side of the little inlet of the sea. The mouth of the cavern was not twenty yards from them where they stood, but at the first sight it seemed as though it must be impossible to reach it. The precipice on the brink of which they all now stood, ran down sheer into the sea, and the fall from the mouth of the cavern on the other side was as steep. But Danny solved the mystery by pointing upwards, and showing them how he had been used to climb to a projecting rock over their heads, and from thence creep round by certain vantages of the stone till he was able to let himself down into the aperture. But now, at the present moment, he was unwilling to make essay of his prowess as a cragsman. He had, he said, been up on that projecting rock thrice, and there had seen the eyes moving in the cavern. He was quite sure of that fact of the pair of eyes, and declined to ascend the rock again.

Traces soon became visible to them by which they knew that some one had passed in and out of the cavern recently. The stone, when examined, bore those marks of friction which passage and repassage over it will always give. At the spot from whence the climber left the platform and commenced his ascent, the side of the stone had been rubbed by the close friction of a man's body. A light boy like Danny Lund might find his way in and out without leaving such marks behind him, but no heavy man could do so. Thus before long they all were satisfied that Aaron Trow was in the cavern before them.

Then there was a long consultation as to what they would do to carry on the hunt, and how they would drive the tiger from his lair. That he should not again come out, except to fall into their hands, was to all of them a matter of course. They would keep watch and ward there, though it might be for days and nights. But that was a process which did not satisfy Morton, and did not indeed well satisfy any of them. It was not only that they desired to inflict punishment on the miscreant in accordance with the law, but also that they did not desire that the miserable man should die in a hole like a starved dog, and that then they should go after him to take out his wretched skeleton. There was something in that idea so horrid in every way, that all agreed that active steps must be taken. The warders of the prison felt that they would all be disgraced if they could not take their prisoner alive. Yet who would get round that perilous ledge in the face of such an adversary? A touch to any man while climbing there would send him headlong down among the waves! And then his fancy told to each what might be the nature of an embrace with such an animal as that, driven to despair, hopeless of life, armed, as they knew, at any rate, with a knife! If the first adventurous spirit should succeed in crawling round that ledge, what would be the reception which he might expect in the terrible depth of that cavern?

They called to their prisoner, bidding him come out, and telling him that they would fire in upon him if he did not show himself; but not a sound was heard. It was indeed possible that they should send their bullets to, perhaps, every corner of the cavern; and if so, in that way they might slaughter him; but even of this they were not sure. Who could tell that there might not be some protected nook in which he could lay secure? And who could tell when the man was struck, or whether he were wounded?

"I will get to him," said Morton, speaking with a low dogged voice, and so saying he clambered up to the rock to which Danny Lund had pointed. Many voices at once attempted to restrain him, and one or two put their hands upon him to keep him back, but he was too quick for them, and now stood upon the ledge of rock. "Can you see him?" they asked below.

"I can see nothing within the cavern," said Morton.

"Look down very hard, Massa," said Danny, "very hard indeed, down in deep dark hole, and then see him big eyes moving!"

Morton now crept along the ledge, or rather he was beginning to do so, having put forward his shoulders and arms to make a first step in advance from the spot on which he was resting, when a hand was put forth from one corner of the cavern's mouth,—a hand armed with a pistol;—and a shot was fired. There could be no doubt now but that Danny Lund was right, and no doubt now as to the whereabouts of Aaron Trow.

A hand was put forth, a pistol was fired, and Caleb Morton still clinging to a corner of the rock with both his arms, was seen to falter. "He is wounded," said one of the voices from below; and then they all expected to see him fall into the sea. But he did not fall, and after a moment or two, he proceeded carefully to pick his steps along the ledge. The ball had touched him, grazing his cheek and cutting through the light whiskers that he wore; but he had not felt it, though the blow had nearly knocked him from his perch. And then four or five shots were fired from the rocks into the mouth of the cavern. The man's arm had been seen, and indeed one or two declared that they had traced the dim outline of his figure. But no sound was heard to come from the cavern, except the sharp crack of the bullets against the rock, and the echo of the gunpowder. There had been no groan as of a man wounded, no sound of a body falling, no voice wailing in despair. For a few seconds all was dark with the smoke of the gunpowder, and then the empty mouth of the cave was again yawning before their eyes. Morton was now near it, still cautiously creeping. The first danger to which he was exposed was this; that his enemy within the recess might push him down from the rocks with a touch. But on the other hand, there were three or four men ready to fire, the moment that a hand should be put forth; and then Morton could swim,—was known to be a strong swimmer;—whereas of Aaron Trow it was already declared by the prison gaolers that he could not swim. Two of the warders had now followed Morton on the rocks, so that in the event of his making good his entrance into the cavern, and holding his enemy at bay for a minute, he would be joined by aid.

It was strange to see how those different men conducted themselves as they stood on the opposite platform watching the attack. The officers from the prison had no other thought but of their prisoner, and were intent on taking him alive or dead. To them it was little or nothing what became of Morton. It was their business to encounter peril, and they were ready to do so;—feeling, however, by no means sorry to have such a man as Morton in advance of them. Very little was said by them. They had their wits about them, and remembered that every word spoken for the guidance of their ally would be heard also by the escaped convict. Their prey was sure, sooner or later, and had not Morton been so eager in his pursuit, they would have waited till some plan had been devised of trapping him without danger. But the townsmen from St. George, of whom some dozen were now standing there, were quick and eager and loud in their counsels. "Stay where you are, Mr. Morton,—stay awhile for the love of God,—or he'll have you down." "Now's your time, Caleb; in on him now, and you'll have him." "Close with him, Morton, close with him at once; it's your only chance." "There's four of us here; we'll fire on him if he as much as shows a limb." All of which words as they were heard by that poor wretch within, must have sounded to him as the barking of a pack of hounds thirsting for his blood. For him at any rate there was no longer any hope in this world.

My reader, when chance has taken you into the hunting-field, has it ever been your lot to sit by on horseback, and watch the digging out of a fox? The operation is not an uncommon one, and in some countries it is held to be accordance with the rules of fair sport. For myself, I think that when the brute has so far saved himself, he should be entitled to the benefit of his cunning; but I will not now discuss the propriety or impropriety of that practice in venery. I can never, however, watch the doing of that work without thinking much of the agonising struggles of the poor beast whose last refuge is being torn from over his head. There he lies within a few yards of his arch enemy, the huntsman. The thick breath of the hounds make hot the air within his hole. The sound of their voices is close upon his ears. His breast is nearly bursting with the violence of that effort which at last has brought him to his retreat. And then pickaxe and mattock are plied above his head, and nearer and more near to him press his foes,—his double foes, human and canine,—till at last a huge hand grasps him, and he is dragged forth among his enemies. Almost as soon as his eyes have seen the light the eager noses of a dozen hounds have moistened themselves in his entrails. Ah me! I know that he is vermin, the vermin after whom I have been risking my neck, with a bold ambition that I might ultimately witness his death-struggles; but, nevertheless, I would fain have saved him that last half hour of gradually diminished hope.

And Aaron Trow was now like a hunted fox, doomed to be dug out from his last refuge, with this addition to his misery, that these hounds when they caught their prey, would not put him at once out of his misery. When first he saw that throng of men coming down from the hill top and resting on the platform, he knew that his fate was come. When they called to him to surrender himself he was silent, but he knew that his silence was of no avail. To them who were so eager to be his captors the matter seemed to be still one of considerable difficulty; but, to his thinking, there was no difficulty. There were there some score of men, fully armed, within twenty yards of him. If he but showed a trace of his limbs he would become a mark for their bullets. And then if he were wounded, and no one would come to him! If they allowed him to lie there without food till he perished! Would it not be well for him to yield himself? Then they called again and he was still silent. That idea of yielding is very terrible to the heart of a man. And when the worst had come to the worst, did not the ocean run deep beneath his cavern's mouth?

But as they yelled at him and halloa-ed, making their preparations for his death, his presence of mind deserted the poor wretch. He had stolen an old pistol on one of his marauding expeditions, of which one barrel had been loaded. That in his mad despair he had fired; and now, as he lay near the mouth of the cavern, under the cover of the projecting stone, he had no weapon with him but his hands. He had had a knife, but that had dropped from him during the struggle on the floor of the cottage. He had now nothing but his hands, and was considering how he might best use them in ridding himself of the first of his pursuers. The man was near him, armed, with all the power and majesty of right on his side; whereas on his side, Aaron Trow had nothing,—not a hope. He raised his head that he might look forth, and a dozen voices shouted as his face appeared above the aperture. A dozen weapons were levelled at him, and he could see the gleaming of the muzzles of the guns. And then the foot of his pursuer was already on the corner stone at the cavern's mouth. "Now, Caleb, on him at once!" shouted a voice. Ah me! it was a moment in which to pity even such a man as Aaron Trow.

"Now, Caleb, at him at once!" shouted the voice. No, by heavens; not so, even yet! The sound of triumph in those words roused the last burst of energy in the breast of that wretched man; and he sprang forth, head foremost, from his prison house. Forth he came, manifest enough before the eyes of them all, and with head well down, and hands outstretched, but with his wide glaring eyes still turned towards his pursuers as he fell, he plunged down into the waves beneath him. Two of those who stood by, almost unconscious of what they did, fired at his body as it made its rapid way to the water; but, as they afterwards found, neither of the bullets struck him. Morton, when his prey thus leaped forth, escaping him for awhile, was already on the verge of the cavern,—had even then prepared his foot for that onward spring which should bring him to the throat of his foe. But he arrested himself, and for a moment stood there watching the body as it struck the water, and hid itself at once beneath the ripple. He stood there for a moment watching the deed and its effect, and then, leaving his hold upon the rock, he once again followed his quarry. Down he went, head foremost, right on to the track in the waves which the other had made; and when the two rose to the surface together, each was struggling in the grasp of the other.

It was a foolish, nay, a mad deed to do. The poor wretch who had first fallen could not have escaped. He could not even swim, and had therefore flung himself to certain destruction when he took that leap from out of the cavern's mouth. It would have been sad to see him perish beneath the waves,—to watch him as he rose gasping for breath, and then to see him sinking again, to rise again and then to go for ever. But his life had been fairly forfeit,—and why should one so much more precious have been flung after it? It was surely with no view of saving that pitiful life that Caleb Morton had leaped after his enemy. But the hound, hot with the chace, will follow the stag over the precipice and dash himself to pieces against the rocks. The beast thirsting for blood, will rush in even among the weapons of men. Morton in his fury had felt but one desire, burned with but one passion. If the Fates would but grant him to fix his clutches in the throat of the man who had ill-used his love;—for the rest it might all go as it would!

In the earlier part of the morning, while they were all searching for their victim, they had brought a boat up into this very inlet among the rocks; and the same boat had been at hand during the whole day. Unluckily, before they had come hither, it had been taken round the headland to a place among the rocks at which a government skiff is always moored. The sea was still so quiet that there was hardly a ripple on it, and the boat had been again sent for when first it was supposed that they had at last traced Aaron Trow to his hiding-place. Anxiously now were all eyes turned to the headland, but as yet no boat was there.

The two men rose to the surface, each struggling in the arms of the other. Trow, though he was in an element to which he was not used, though he had sprung thither as another suicide might spring to certain death beneath a railway engine, did not altogether lose his presence of mind. Prompted by a double instinct, he had clutched hold of Morton's body when he encountered it beneath the waters. He held on to it, as to his only protection, and he held on to him also as to his only enemy. If there was a chance for a life struggle, they would share that chance together; and if not, then together would they meet that other fate.

Caleb Morton was a very strong man, and though one of his arms was altogether encumbered by his antagonist, his other arm and his legs were free. With these he seemed to succeed in keeping his head above the water, weighted as he was with the body of his foe. But Trow's efforts were also used with the view of keeping himself above the water. Though he had purposed to destroy himself in taking that leap, and now hoped for nothing better than that they might both perish together, he yet struggled to keep his head above the waves. Bodily power he had none left to him, except that of holding on to Morton's arm and plunging with his legs; but he did hold on, and thus both their heads remained above the surface.

But this could not last long. It was easy to see that Trow's strength was nearly spent, and that when he went down Morton must go with him. If indeed they could be separated,—if Morton could once make himself free from that embrace into which he had been so anxious to leap,—then indeed there might be a hope. All round that little inlet the rock fell sheer down into the deep sea, so that there was no resting place for a foot; but round the headlands on either side, even within forty or fifty yards of that spot, Morton might rest on the rocks, till a boat should come to his assistance. To him that distance would have been nothing, if only his limbs had been at liberty.

Upon the platform of rock they were all at their wit's ends. Many were anxious to fire at Trow; but even if they hit him, would Morton's position have been better? Would not the wounded man have still clung to him who was not wounded? And then there could be no certainty that any one of them would hit the right man. The ripple of the waves, though it was very slight, nevertheless sufficed to keep the bodies in motion; and then, too, there was not among them any marksman peculiar for his skill.

Morton's efforts in the water were too severe to admit of his speaking, but he could hear and understand the words which were addressed to him. "Shake him off, Caleb." "Strike him from you with your foot." "Swim to the right shore; swim for it, even if you take him with you." Yes; he could hear them all; but hearing and obeying were very different. It was not easy to shake off that dying man; and as for swimming with him, that was clearly impossible. It was as much as he could do to keep his head above water, let alone any attempt to move in one settled direction.

For some four or five minutes they lay thus battling on the waves before the head of either of them went down. Trow had been twice below the surface, but it was before he had succeeded in supporting himself by Morton's arm. Now it seemed as though he must sink again,—as though both must sink. His mouth was barely kept above the water, and as Morton shook him with his arm, the tide would pass over him. It was horrid to watch from the shore the glaring upturned eyes of the dying wretch, as his long streaming hair lay back upon the wave. "Now, Caleb, hold him down. Hold him under," was shouted in the voice of some eager friend. Rising up on the water, Morton made a last effort to do as he was bid. He did press the man's head down,—well down below the surface,—but still the hand clung to him, and as he struck out against the water, he was powerless against that grasp.

Then there came a loud shout along the shore, and all those on the platform, whose eyes had been fixed so closely on that terrible struggle beneath them, rushed towards the rocks on the other coast. The sound of oars was heard close to them,—an eager pressing stroke, as of men who knew well that they were rowing for the salvation of a life. On they came, close under the rocks, obeying with every muscle of their bodies the behests of those who called to them from the shore. The boat came with such rapidity,—was so recklessly urged,—that it was driven somewhat beyond the inlet; but in passing, a blow was struck which made Caleb Morton once more the master of his own life. The two men had been carried out in their struggle towards the open sea; and as the boat curved in, so as to be as close as the rocks would allow, the bodies of the men were brought within the sweep of the oars. He in the bow—for there were four pulling in the boat—had raised his oar as he neared the rocks,—had raised it high above the water; and now, as they passed close by the struggling men, he let it fall with all its force on the upturned face of the wretched convict. It was a terrible, frightful thing to do,—thus striking one who was so stricken; but who shall say that the blow was not good and just? Methinks, however, that the eyes and face of that dying man will haunt for ever the dreams of him who carried that oar!

Trow never rose again to the surface. Three days afterwards his body was found at the ferry, and then they carried him to the convict island and buried him. Morton was picked up and taken into the boat. His life was saved; but it may be a question how the battle might have gone had not that friendly oar been raised in his behalf. As it was, he lay at the cottage for days before he was able to be moved, so as to receive the congratulations of those who had watched that terrible conflict from the shore. Nor did he feel that there had been anything in that day's work of which he could be proud;—much rather of which it behoved him to be thoroughly ashamed. Some six months after that he obtained the hand of Anastasia Bergen, but they did not remain long in Bermuda. "He went away, back to his own country," my informant told me; "because he could not endure to meet the ghost of Aaron Trow, at that point of the road which passes near the cottage." That the ghost of Aaron Trow may be seen there and round the little rocky inlet of the sea, is part of the creed of every young woman in Bermuda.

The House of Heine Brothers in Munich

Originally appeared in *Public Opinion*, 16 and 23 November 1861. Reprinted in *Tales of All Countries* [Second Series] (1863). Written c. 7–10 April 1861, during the composition of *Orley Farm*. Trollope passed through Munich on his 1855 Continental tour.

THE HOUSE of Heine Brothers, in Munich, was of good repute at the time of which I am about to tell,—a time not long ago; and is so still, I trust. It was of good repute in its own way, seeing that no man doubted the word or solvency of Heine Brothers; but they did not possess, as bankers, what would in England be considered a large or profitable business. The operations of English bankers are bewildering in their magnitude. Legions of clerks are employed. The senior book-keepers, though only salaried servants, are themselves great men; while the real partners are inscrutable, mysterious, opulent beyond measure, and altogether unknown to their customers. Take any firm at random,—Brown, Jones, and Cox, let us say;—the probability is that Jones has been dead these fifty years, that Brown is a Cabinet Minister, and that Cox is master of a pack of hounds in Leicestershire. But it was by no means so with the house of Heine Brothers, of Munich. There they were, the two elderly men, daily to be seen at their dingy office in the Schrannen Platz; and if any business was to be transacted requiring the interchange of more than a word or two, it was the younger brother with whom the customer was, as a matter of course, brought into contact. There were three clerks in the establishment; an old man, namely, who sat with the elder brother and had no personal dealings with the public; a young Englishman, of whom we shall anon hear more; and a boy who ran messages, put the wood on to the stoves, and swept out the bank. Truly the house of Heine Brothers was of no great importance; but nevertheless it was of good repute.

The office, I have said, was in the Schrannen Platz, or old Market-place. Munich, as every one knows, is chiefly to be noted as a new town,—so new that many of the streets and most of the palaces look as though they had been sent home last night from the builders, and had only just been taken out of their bandboxes. It is angular, methodical, unfinished, and palatial. But there is an old town; and, though the old town be not of surpassing interest, it is as dingy, crooked, intricate, and dark as other old towns in Germany. Here, in the old Market-place, up one long broad staircase, were situated the two rooms in which was held the bank of Heine Brothers.

Of the elder member of the firm we shall have something to say before this story be completed. He was an old bachelor, and was possessed of a bachelor's dwelling somewhere out in the suburbs of the city. The junior brother was a married man, with a wife some twenty years younger than himself, with two daughters, the elder of whom was now one-and-twenty, and one son. His name was Ernest Heine, whereas the senior brother was known as Uncle Hatto. Ernest Heine and his wife inhabited a portion of one of those new palatial residences at the further end of the Ludwigs Strasse; but not because they thus lived must it be considered that they were palatial people. By no means let it be so thought, as such an idea would altogether militate against whatever truth of character painting there may be in this tale. They were not palatial people, but the very reverse, living in homely guise, pursuing homely duties, and satisfied with homely pleasures. Up two pairs of stairs, however, in that street of palaces, they lived, having there a commodious suite of large rooms, furnished, after the manner of the Germans, somewhat gaudily as regarded their best salon, and with somewhat meagre comfort as regarded their other rooms. But, whether in respect of that which was meagre, or whether in respect of that which was gaudy, they were as well off as their neighbours; and this, as I take it, is the point of excellence which is desirable.

Ernest Heine was at this time over sixty; his wife was past forty; and his eldest daughter, as I have said, was twenty-one years of age. His second child, also a girl, was six years younger; and their third child, a boy, had not been born till another similar interval had elapsed. He was named Hatto after his uncle, and the two girls had been christened Isa and Agnes. Such, in number and mode of life, was the family of the Heines.

We English folk are apt to imagine that we are nearer akin to Germans than to our other continental neighbours. This may be so in blood, but, nevertheless, the difference in manners is so striking, that it could hardly be enhanced. An Englishman moving himself off to a city in the middle of Central America will find the customs to which he must adapt himself less strange to him there, than he would in many a German town. But in no degree of life is the difference more remarkable than among unmarried but marriagable young women. It is not my purpose at the present moment to attribute a superiority in this matter to either nationality. Each has its own charm, its own excellence, its own Heaven-given grace, whereby men are led up to purer thoughts and sweet desires; and each may possibly have its own defect. I will not here describe the excellence or defect of either; but will, if it be in my power, say a word as to this difference. The German girl of one-and-twenty,—our Isa's age,—is more sedate, more womanly, more meditative than her English sister. The world's work is more in her thoughts, and the world's amusements less so. She probably knows less of those things which women learn than the English girl, but that which she does know is nearer to her hand for use. She is not so much accustomed to society, but nevertheless she is more mistress of her own manner. She is not taught to think so much of those things which flurry and disturb the mind, and therefore she is seldom flurried and disturbed. To both of them, love,—the idea of love,—must be the thought of all the most absorbing; for is it not fated for them that the joys and sorrows of their future life must depend upon it? But the idea of the German girl is the more realistic, and the less romantic. Poetry and fiction she may have read, though of the latter sparingly; but they will not have imbued her with that hope for some transcendental Paradise of affection which so often fills and exalts the hearts of our daughters here at home. She is moderate in her aspirations, requiring less excitement than an English girl; and never forgetting the solid necessities of life,—as they are so often forgotten here in England. In associating with young men, an English girl will always remember that in each one she so meets she may find an admirer whom she may possibly love, or an admirer whom she may probably be called on to repel. She is ever conscious of the fact of this position; and a romance is thus engendered which, if it may at times be dangerous, is at any rate always charming. But the German girl, in her simplicity, has no such consciousness. As you and I, my reader, might probably become dear friends were we to meet and know each other, so may the German girl learn to love the fair-haired youth with whom chance has for a time associated her; but to her mind there occurs no suggestive reason why it should be so,—no probability that the youth may regard her in such light, because that chance has come to pass. She can therefore give him her hand without trepidation, and talk with him for half an hour, when called on to do so, as calmly as she might do with his sister.

Such a one was Isa Heine at the time of which I am writing. We English, in our passion for daily excitement, might call her phlegmatic, but we should call her so unjustly. Life to her was a serious matter, of which the daily duties and daily wants were sufficient to occupy her thoughts. She was her mother's companion, the instructress of both her brother and her sister, and the charm of her father's vacant hours. With such calls upon her time, and so many realities around her, her imagination did not teach her to look for joys beyond those of her present life and home. When love and marriage should come to her, as come they probably might, she would endeavour to attune herself to a new happiness and a new sphere of duties. In the meantime she was contented to keep her mother's accounts, and look after her brother and sister up two pair of stairs in the Ludwigs Strasse. But change would certainly come, we may prophesy; for Isa Heine was a beautiful girl, tall and graceful, comely to the eye, and fit in every way to be loved and cherished as the partner of a man's home.

I have said that an English clerk made a part of that small establishment in the dingy banking-office in the Schrannen Platz, and I must say a word or two of Herbert Onslow. In his early career he had not been fortunate. His father, with means sufficiently moderate, and with a family more than sufficiently large, had sent him to a public school at which he had been very idle, and then to one of the universities, at which he had run into debt, and had therefore left without a degree. When this occurred, a family council of war had been held among the Onslows, and it was decided that Herbert should be sent off to the banking-house of Heines, at Munich, there being a cousinship between the families, and some existing connections of business. It was, therefore, so settled; and Herbert, willing enough to see the world,—as he considered he should do by going to Munich,—started for his German home, with injuctions, very tender from his mother, and very solemn from his aggrieved father. But there was nothing bad at the heart about young Onslow, and if the solemn father had well considered it, he might perhaps have felt that those debts at Cambridge reflected more fault on him than on his son. When Herbert arrived at Munich, his cousins, the Heines,—far-away cousins though they were,—behaved kindly to him. They established him at first in lodgings, where he was boarded with many others, having heard somewhat of his early youth. But when Madame Heine, at the end of twelve months, perceived that he was punctual at the bank, and that his allowances, which, though moderate in England, were handsome in Munich, carried him on without debt, she opened her motherly arms and suggested to his mother and to himself, that he should live with them. In this way he also was domiciled up two pairs of stairs in the palatial residence in the Ludwigs Strasse.

But all this happened long ago. Isa Heine had been only seventeen when her cousin had first come to Munich, and had made acquaintance with him rather as a child than as a woman. And when, as she ripened into womanhood, this young man came more closely among them, it did not strike her that the change would affect her more powerfully than it would the others. Her uncle and father, she knew, had approved of Herbert at the bank; and Herbert had shown that he could be steady; therefore he was to be taken into their family, paying his annual subsidy, instead of being left with strangers at the boarding-house. All this was very simple to her. She assisted in mending his linen, as she did her father's; she visited his room daily, as she visited all the others; she took notice of his likings and dislikings as touching their table arrangements,—but by no means such notice as she did of her father's; and without any flutter, inwardly in her imagination or outwardly as regarded the world, she made him one of the family. So things went on for a year,—nay, so things went on for two years with her, after Herbert Onslow had come to the Ludwigs Strasse.

But the matter had been regarded in a very different light by Herbert himself. When the proposition had been made to him, his first idea had been that so close a connection with a girl so very pretty would be delightful. He had blushed as he had given in his adhesion; but Madame Heine, when she saw the blush, had attributed it to anything but the true cause. When Isa had asked him as to his wants and wishes, he had blushed again, but she had been as ignorant as her mother. The father had merely stipulated that, as the young Englishman paid for his board, he should have the full value of his money, so that Isa and Agnes gave up their pretty front room, going into one that was inferior, and Hatto was put to sleep in the little closet that had been papa's own peculiar property. But nobody complained of this, for it was understood that the money was of service.

For the first year Herbert found that nothing especial happened. He always fancied that he was in love with Isa, and wrote some poetry about her. But the poetry was in English, and Isa could not read it, even had he dared to show it to her. During the second year he went home to England for three months, and by confessing a passion to one of his sisters, really brought himself to feel one. He returned to Munich resolved to tell Isa that the possibility of his remaining there depended upon her acceptance of his heart; but for months he did not find himself able to put his resolution in force. She was so sedate, so womanly, so attentive as regarded cousinly friendship, and so cold as regarded everything else, that he did not know how to speak to her. With an English girl whom he had met three times at a ball, he might have been much more able to make progress. He was alone with Isa frequently, for neither father, mother, nor Isa herself objected to such communion; but yet things so went between them that he could not take her by the hand and tell her that he loved her. And thus the third year of his life in Munich, and the second of his residence in the Ludwigs Strasse, went by him. So the years went by, and Isa was now past twenty. To Herbert, in his reveries, it seemed as though life, and the joys of life, were slipping away from him. But no such feeling disturbed any of the Heines. Life, of course, was slipping away; but then is it not the destiny of man that life should slip away? Their wants were all satisfied, and for them, that, together with their close family affection, was happiness enough.

At last, however, Herbert so spoke, or so looked, that both Isa and her mother knew that his heart was touched. He still declared to himself that he had made no sign, and that he was an oaf, an ass, a coward, in that he had not done so. But he had made some sign, and the sign had been read. There was no secret,—no necessity for a secret on the subject between the mother and daughter, but yet it was not spoken of all at once. There was some little increase of caution between them as Herbert's name was mentioned, so that gradually each knew what the other thought; but for weeks, that was all. Then at last the mother spoke out.

"Isa," she said, "I think that Herbert Onslow is becoming attached to you."

"He has never said so, mamma."

"No; I am sure he has not. Had he done so, you would have told me. Nevertheless, is it not true?"

"Well, mamma, I cannot say. It may be so. Such an idea has occured to me, but I have abandoned it as needless. If he has anything to say he will say it."

"And if he were to speak, how should you answer him?"

"I should take time to think. I do not at all know what means he has for a separate establishment." Then the subject was dropped between them for that time, and Isa, in her communications with her cousin, was somewhat more reserved than she had been.

"Isa, are you in love with Herbert?" Agnes asked her, as they were together in their room one night.

"In love with him? No; why should I be in love with him?"

"I think he is in love with you," said Agnes.

"That is quite another thing," said Isa, laughing. But if so, he has not taken me into his confidence. Perhaps he has you."

"Oh no. He would not do that, I think. Not but what we are great friends, and I love him dearly. Would it not be nice for you and him to be betrothed?"

"That depends on many things, my dear."

"Oh yes, I know. Perhaps he has not got money enough. But you could live here, you know, and he has got some money, because he so often rides on horseback." And then the matter was dropped between the two sisters.

Herbert had given English lessons to the two girls, but the lessons had been found tedious, and had dwindled away. Isa, nevertheless, had kept up her exercises, duly translating German into English, and English into German; and occasionally she had shown them to her cousin. Now, however, she altogether gave over such showing of them, but, nevertheless, worked at the task with more energy than before.

"Isa," he said to her one day,—having with some difficulty found her alone in the parlour,—"Isa, why should not we go on with our English?"

"Because it is troublesome,—to you I mean."

"Troublesome. Well; yes; it is troublesome. Nothing good is to be had without trouble. But I should like it if you would not mind."

"You know how sick you were of it before;—besides, I shall never be able to speak it."

"I shall not get sick of it now, Isa."

"Oh yes you would;—in two days."

"And I want you to speak it. I desire it especially."

"Why especially?" asked Isa. And even she, with all her tranquillity of demeanour, could hardly preserve her even tone and quiet look, as she asked the necessary question.

"I will tell you why," said Herbert; and as he spoke, he got up from his seat, and took a step or two over towards her, where she was sitting near the window. Isa, as she saw him, still continued her work, and strove hard to give to the stitches all that attention which they required. "I will tell you why I would wish you to talk my language. Because I love you, Isa, and would have you for my wife,—if that be possible."

She still continued her work, and the stitches, if not quite as perfect as usual, sufficed for their purpose.

"That is why I wish it. Now will you consent to learn from me again?"

"If I did, Herbert, that consent would include another."

"Yes; certainly it would. That is what I intend. And now will you learn from me again?"

"That is,—you mean to ask, will I marry you?"

"Will you love me? Can you learn to love me? Oh, Isa, I have thought of this so long! But you have seemed so cold that I have not dared to speak. Isa, can you love me?" And he sat himself close beside her. Now that the ice was broken, he was quite prepared to become an ardent lover,—if she would allow of such ardour. But as he sat down she rose.

"I cannot answer such a question on the sudden," she said. "Give me till to-morrow, Herbert, and then I will make you a reply;" whereupon she left him, and he stood alone in the room, having done the deed on which he had been meditating for the last two years. About half an hour afterwards he met her on the stairs as he was going to his chamber. "May I speak to your father about this," he said, hardly stopping her as he asked the question. "Oh yes; surely," she answered; and then again they parted. To him this last-accorded permission sounded as though it carried with it more weight than it in truth possessed. In his own country a reference to the lady's father is taken as indicating a full consent on the lady's part, should the stern paterfamilias raise no objection. But Isa had no such meaning. She had told him that she could not give her answer till the morrow. If, however, he chose to consult her father on the subject, she had no objection. It would probably be necessary that she should discuss the whole matter in family conclave, before she could bring herself to give any reply.

On that night, before he went to bed, he did speak to her father; and Isa also, before she went to rest, spoke to her mother. It was singular to him that there should appear to be so little privacy on the subject; that there should be held to be so little necessity for a secret. Had he made a suggestion that an extra room should be allotted to him at so much per annum, the proposition could not have been discussed with simpler ease. At last, after a three days' debate, the matter ended thus,—with by no means a sufficiency of romance for his taste. Isa had agreed to become his betrothed if certain pecuniary conditions should or could be fulfilled. It appeared now that Herbert's father had promised that some small modicum of capital should be forthcoming after a term of years, and that Heine Brothers had agreed that the Englishman should have a proportionate share in the bank when that promise should be brought to bear. Let it not be supposed that Herbert would thus become a millionnaire. If all went well, the best would be that some three hundred a year would accrue to him from the bank, instead of the quarter of that income which he at present received. But three hundred a year goes a long way at Munich, and Isa's parents were willing that she should be Herbert's wife if such an income should be forthcoming.

But even of this there was much doubt. Application to Herbert's father could not be judiciously made for some months. The earliest period at which, in accordance with old Hatto Heine's agreement, young Onslow might be admitted to the bank, was still distant by four years; and the present moment was thought to be inopportune for applying to him for any act of grace. Let them wait, said papa and mamma Heine,—at any rate till New Year's Day, then ten months distant. Isa quietly said that she would wait till New Year's Day. Herbert fretted, fumed, and declared that he was ill treated. But in the end he also agreed to wait. What else could he do?

"But we shall see each other daily, and be close to each other," he said to Isa, looking tenderly into her eyes. "Yes," she replied, "we shall see each other daily—of course. But Herbert— "

Herbert looked up at her and paused for her to go on.

"I have promised mamma that there shall be no change between us,—in our manner to each other, I mean. We are not betrothed as yet, you know, and perhaps we may never be so."

"Isa!"

"It may not be possible, you know. And therefore we will go on as before. Of course we shall see each other, and of course we shall be friends."

Herbert Onslow again fretted and again fumed, but he did not have his way. He had looked forward to the ecstasies of a lover's life, but very few of those ecstasies were awarded to him. He rarely found himself alone with Isa, and when he did do so, her coldness overawed him. He could dare to scold her, and sometimes did do so, but he could not dare to take the slightest liberty. Once, on that night when the qualified consent of papa and mamma Heine had first been given, he had been allowed to touch her lips with his own; but since that day there had been for him no such delight as that. She would not even allow her hand to remain in his. When they all passed their evenings together in the beer-garden, she would studiously manage that his chair should not be close to her own. Occasionally she would walk with him, but not more frequently now than of yore. Very few, indeed, of a lover's privileges did he enjoy. And in this way the long year wore itself out, and Isa Heine was one-and-twenty.

All those family details which had made it inexpedient to apply either to old Hatto or to Herbert's father before the end of the year need not be specially explained. Old Hatto, who had by far the greater share in the business, was a tyrant somewhat feared both by his brother and sister-in-law; and the elder Onslow, as was known to them all, was a man straitened in circumstances. But soon after New Year's Day the proposition was made in the Schrannen Platz, and the letter was written. On this occasion Madame Heine went down to the bank, and, together with her husband, was closeted for an hour with old Hatto. Uncle Hatto's verdict was not favourable. As to the young people's marriage, that was his brother's affair, not his. But as to the partnership, that was a serious matter. Who ever heard of a partnership being given away merely because a man wanted to marry? He would keep to his promise, and if the stipulated moneys were forthcoming, Herbert Onslow should become a partner,—in four years. Nor was the reply from England more favourable. The alliance was regarded by all the Onslows very favourably. Nothing could be nicer than such a marriage! They already knew dear Isa so well by description! But as for the money,—that could not in any way be forthcoming till the end of the stipulated period.

"And what shall we do?" said Herbert, to Papa Heine.

"You must wait," said he.

"For four years!" asked Herbert.

"You must wait,—as I did," said Papa Heine. "I was forty before I could marry." Papa Heine, however, should not have forgotten to say that his bride was only twenty, and that if he had waited, she had not.

"Isa," Herbert said to her when all this had been fully explained to her, "what do you say now?"

"Of course it is all over," said she, very calmly.

"Oh Isa, is that your love?"

"No, Herbert, that is not my love; that is my discretion;" and she even laughed with her mild low laughter, as she answered him. "You know you are too impatient to wait four years, and what else therefore can I say?"

"I wonder whether you love me?" said Herbert, with a grand look of injured sentiment.

"Well; in your sense of the word I do not think I do. I do not love you so that I need make every one around us unhappy because circumstances forbid me to marry you. That sort of love would be baneful."

"Ah no, you do not know what love means!"

"Not your boisterous, heartbreaking English love, Herbert. And, Herbert, sometimes I think you had better go home and look for a bride there. Though you fancy that you love me, in your heart you hardly approve of me."

"Fancy that I love you! Do you think, Isa, that a man can carry his heart round to one customer after another as the huckster carries his wares?"

"Yes; I think he can. I know that men do. What did your hero Waverley do with his heart in that grand English novel which you gave me to read? I am not Flora Mac Ivor, but you may find a Rose Bradwardine."

"And you really wish me to do so?"

"Look here, Herbert. It is bad to boast, but I will make this boast. I am so little selfish, that I desire above all that you should do that which may make you most happy and contented. I will be quite frank with you. I love you well enough to wait these four years with the hope of becoming your wife when they are over. But you will think but little of my love when I tell you that this waiting would not make me unhappy. I should go on as I do now, and be contented."

"Oh heavens!" sighed Herbert.

"But as I know that this would not suit you,—as I feel sure that such delay would gall you every day, as I doubt whether it would not make you sick of me long before the four years be over,—my advice is, that we should let this matter drop."

He now walked up to her and took her hand, and as he did so there was something in his gait and look and tone of voice that stirred her heart more sharply than it had yet been stirred. "And even that would not make you unhappy," he said.

She paused before she replied, leaving her hand in his, for he was contented to hold it without peculiar pressure. "I will not say so," she replied. "But, Herbert, I think that you press me too hard. Is it not enough that I leave you to be the arbiter of my destiny?"

"I would learn the very truth of your heart," he replied.

"I cannot tell you that truth more plainly. Methinks I have told it too plainly already. If you wish it, I will hold myself as engaged to you,—to be married to you when those four years are past. But, remember, I do not advise it. If you wish it, you shall have back your troth. And that I think will be the wiser course."

But neither alternative contented Herbert Onslow, and at the time he did not resolve on either. He had some little present income from home, some fifty pounds a year or so, and he would be satisfied to marry on that and on his salary as a clerk; but to this papa and mamma Heine would not consent;—neither would Isa.

"You are not a saving, close man," she said to him, when he boasted of his economies. "No Englishmen are. You could not live comfortably in two small rooms, and with bad dinners."

"I do not care a straw about my dinners."

"Not now that you are a lover, but you would do when you were a husband. And you change your linen almost every day."

"Bah!"

"Yes; bah, if you please. But I know what these things cost. You had better go to England and fetch a rich wife. Then you will become a partner at once, and Uncle Hatto won't snub you. And you will be a grand man, and have a horse to ride on." Whereupon Herbert went away in disgust. Nothing in all this made him so unhappy as the feeling that Isa, under all their joint privations, would not be unhappy herself. As far as he could see, all this made no difference in Isa.

But, in truth, he had not yet read Isa's character very thoroughly. She had spoken truly in saying that she knew nothing of that boisterous love which was now tormenting him and making him gloomy; but nevertheless she loved him. She, in her short life, had learnt many lessons of self-denial; and now with reference to this half-promised husband she would again have practised such a lesson. Had he agreed at once to go from her, she would have balanced her own account within her own breast, and have kept to herself all her sufferings. There would have been no outward show of baffled love,—none even in the colour of her cheeks; for such was the nature of her temperament. But she did suffer for him. Day by day she began to think that his love, though boisterous as she had at first called it, was more deep-seated than she had believed. He made no slightest sign that he would accept any of those proffers which she had made him of release. Though he said so loudly that this waiting for four years was an impossibility, he spoke of no course that would be more possible,—except that evidently impossible course of an early marriage. And thus, while he with redoubled vehemence charged her with coldness and want of love, her love waxed warmer and warmer, and his happiness became the chief object of her thoughts. What could she do that he might no longer suffer?

And then he took a step which was very strange to them all. He banished himself altogether from the house, going away again into lodgings, "No," he said, on the morning of his departure, "I do not release you. I will never release you. You are mine, and I have a right so to call you. If you choose to release yourself, I cannot help it; but in doing so you will be forsworn."

"Nay, but, Herbert, I have sworn to nothing," said she, meaning that she had not been formally betrothed to him.

"You can do as you please; it is a matter of conscience; but I tell you what are my feelings. Here I cannot stay, for I should go mad; but I shall see you occasionally;—perhaps on Sundays."

"Oh, Herbert!"

"Well, what would you have? If you really cared to see me it would not be thus. All I ask of you now is this, that if you decide,—absolutely decide on throwing me over, you will tell me at once. Then I shall leave Munich."

"Herbert, I will never throw you over." So they parted, and Onslow went forth to his new lodgings.

Her promise that she would never throw him over was the warmest word of love that she had ever spoken, but even that was said in her own quiet, unimpassioned way. There was in it but very little show of love, though there might be an assurance of constancy. But her constancy he did not, in truth, much doubt. Four years,—fourteen,—or twenty-four, would be the same to her, he said, as he seated himself in the dull, cold room which he had chosen. While living in the Ludwigs Strasse he did not know how much had been daily done for his comfort by that hand which he had been so seldom allowed to press; but he knew that he was now cold and comfortless, and he wished himself back in the Ludwigs Strasse.

"Mamma," said Isa, when they were alone. "Is not Uncle Hatto rather hard on us? Papa said that he would ask this as a favour from his brother."

"So he did, my dear; and offered to give up more of his own time. But your Uncle Hatto is hard."

"He is rich, is he not?"

"Well; your father says not. Your father says that he spends all his income. Though he is hard and obstinate, he is not selfish. He is very good to the poor, but I believe he thinks that early marriages are very foolish."

"Mamma," said Isa again, when they had sat for some minutes in silence over their work.

"Well, my love?"

"Have you spoken to Uncle Hatto about this?"

"No, dear; not since that day when your papa and I first went to him. To tell the truth, I am almost afraid to speak to him; but, if you wish it, I will do so."

"I do wish it, mamma. But you must not think that I am discontented or impatient. I do not know that I have any right to ask my uncle for his money;—for it comes to that."

"I suppose it does, my dear."

"And as for myself, I am happy here with you and papa. I do not think so much of these four years."

"You would still be young, Isa;—quite young enough."

"And what if I were not young? What does it matter? But, mamma, there has been that between Herbert and me which makes me feel myself bound to think of him. As you and papa have sanctioned it, you are bound to think of him also. I know that he is unhappy, living there all alone."

"But why did he go, dear?"

"I think he was right to go. I could understand his doing that. He is not like us, and would have been fretful here, wanting that which I could not give him. He became worse from day to day, and was silent and morose. I am glad he went. But, mamma, for his sake I wish that this could be shortened."

Madame Heine again told her daughter that she would, if Isa wished it, herself go to the Schrannen Platz, and see what could be done by talking to Uncle Hatto. "But," she added, "I fear that no good will come of it."

"Can harm come, mamma?"

"No, I do not think harm can come."

"I'll tell you what, mamma, I will go to Uncle Hatto myself, if you will let me. He is cross I know; but I shall not be afraid of him. I feel that I ought to do something." And so the matter was settled, Madame Heine being by no means averse to escape a further personal visit to the Head of the banking establishment.

Madame Heine well understood what her daughter meant, when she said she ought to do something, though Isa feared that she had imperfectly expressed her meaning. When he, Herbert, was willing to do so much to prove his love,—when he was ready to sacrifice all the little comforts of comparative wealth to which he had been accustomed, in order that she might be his companion and wife,—did it not behove her to give some proof of her love also? She could not be demonstrative as he was. Such exhibition of feeling would be quite contrary to her ideas of female delicacy, and to her very nature. But if called on to work for him, that she could do as long as strength remained to her. But there was no sacrifice which would be of service, nor any work which would avail. Therefore she was driven to think what she might do on his behalf, and at last she resolved to make her personal appeal to Uncle Hatto.

"Shall I tell papa?" Isa asked of her mother.

"I will do so," said Madame Heine. And then the younger member of the firm was informed as to the step which was to be taken; and he, though he said nothing to forbid the attempt, held out no hope that it would be successful.

Uncle Hatto was a little snuffy man, now full seventy years of age, who passed seven hours of every week-day of his life in the dark back chamber behind the banking-room of the firm, and he had so passed every week-day of his life for more years than any of the family could now remember. He had made the house what it was, and had taken his brother into partnership when that brother married. All the family were somewhat afraid of him, including even his partner. He rarely came to the apartments in the Ludwigs Strasse, as he himself lived in one of the older and shabbier suburbs on the other side of the town. Thither he always walked, starting punctually from the bank at four o'clock, and from thence he always walked in the morning, reaching the bank punctually at nine. His two nieces knew him well; for on certain stated days they were wont to attend on him at his lodgings, where they would be regaled with cakes, and afterwards go with him to some old-fashioned beer-garden in his neighbourhood. But these festivities were of a sombre kind; and if, on any occasion, circumstances prevented the fulfilment of the ceremony, neither of the girls would be loud in their lamentations.

In London, a visit paid by a niece to her uncle would, in all probability, be made at the uncle's private residence; but at Munich private and public matters were not so effectually divided. Isa therefore, having put on her hat and shawl, walked off by herself to the Schrannen Platz.

"Is Uncle Hatto inside?" she asked; and the answer was given to her by her own lover. Yes, he was within; but the old clerk was with him. Isa, however, signified her wish to see her uncle alone, and in a few minutes the ancient grey-haired servant of the house came out into the larger room.

"You can go in now, Miss Isa," he said. And Isa found herself in the presence of her uncle before she had been two minutes under the roof. In the mean time Ernest Heine, her father, had said not a word, and Herbert knew that something very special must be about to occur.

"Well, my bonny bird," said Uncle Hatto, "and what do you want at the bank?" Cheery words, such as these, were by no means uncommon with Uncle Hatto; but Isa knew very well that no presage could be drawn from them of any special good nature or temporary weakness on his part.

"Uncle Hatto," she began, rushing at once into the middle of her affair, "you know, I believe, that I am engaged to marry Herbert Onslow?"

"I know no such thing," said he. "I thought I understood your father specially to say that there had been no betrothal."

"No, Uncle Hatto, there has been no betrothal; that certainly is true; but, nevertheless, we are engaged to each other."

"Well," said Uncle Hatto, very sourly; and now there was no longer any cheery tone, or any calling of pretty names.

"Perhaps you may think all this very foolish," said Isa, who, in spite of her resolves to do so, was hardly able to look up gallantly into her uncle's face as she thus talked of her own love affairs.

"Yes, I do," said Uncle Hatto. "I do think it foolish for young people to hold themselves betrothed before they have got anything to live on, and so I have told your father. He answered me by saying that you were not betrothed."

"Nor are we. Papa is quite right in that."

"Then, my dear, I would advise you to tell the young man that, as neither of you have means of your own, the thing must be at an end. It is the only step for you to take. If you agreed to wait, one of you might die, or his money might never be forthcoming, or you might see somebody else that you liked better."

"I don't think I shall do that."

"You can't tell. And if you don't, the chances are ten to one that he will."

This little blow, which was intended to be severe, did not hit Isa at all hard. That plan of a Rose Bradwardine she herself had proposed in good faith, thinking that she could endure such a termination to the affair without flinching. She was probably wrong in this estimate of her power; but, nevertheless, her present object was his release from unhappiness and doubt, not her own.

"It might be so," she said.

"Take my word for it, it would. Look all around. There was Adelaide Schropner,—but that was before your time, and you won't remember." Considering that Adelaide Schropner had been for many years a grandmother, it was probable that Isa would not remember.

"But, Uncle Hatto, you have not heard me. I want to say something to you, if it will not take too much of your time." In answer to which, uncle Hatto muttered something which was unheeded, to signify that Isa might speak.

"I also think that a long engagement is a foolish thing, and so does Herbert."

"But he wants to marry at once."

"Yes, he wants to marry—perhaps not at once, but soon."

"And I suppose you have come to say that you want the same thing."

Isa blushed ever so faintly as she commenced her answer. "Yes, uncle, I do wish the same thing. What he wishes, I wish."

"Very likely,—very likely."

"Don't be scornful to me, uncle. When two people love each other, it is natural that each should wish that which the other earnestly desires."

"Oh, very natural, my dear, that you should wish to get married!"

"Uncle Hatto, I did not think that you would be unkind to me, though I knew that you would be stern."

"Well, go on. What have you to say? I am not stern; but I have no doubt you will think me unkind. People are always unkind who do not do what they are asked."

"Papa says that Herbert Onslow is some day to become a partner in the bank."

"That depends on certain circumstances. Neither I nor your papa can say whether he will or no."

But Isa went on as though she had not heard the last reply. "I have come to ask you to admit him as a partner at once."

"Ah, I supposed so;—just as you might ask me to give you a new ribbon."

"But, uncle, I never did ask you to give me a new ribbon. I never asked you to give me anything for myself; nor do I ask this for myself."

"Do you think that if I could do it,—which of course I can't,—I would not sooner do it for you, who are my own flesh and blood, than for him, who is a stranger?"

"Nay; he is no stranger. He has sat at your desk and obeyed your orders for nearly four years. Papa says that he has done well in the bank."

"Humph! If every clerk that does well,—pretty well, that is,—wanted a partnership, where should we be, my dear? No, my dear, go home and tell him when you see him in the evening that all this must be at an end. Men's places in the world are not given away so easily as that. They must either be earned or purchased. Herbert Onslow has as yet done neither, and therefore he is not entitled to take a wife. I should have been glad to have had a wife at his age,—at least I suppose I should, but at any rate I could not afford it."

But Isa had by means as yet done. So far the interview had progressed exactly as she had anticipated. She had never supposed it possible that her uncle would grant her so important a request as soon as she opened her mouth to ask it. She had not for a moment expected that things would go so easily with her. Indeed she had never expected that any success would attend her efforts; but, if any success were possible, the work which must achieve that success must now commence. It was necessary that she should first state her request plainly before she began to urge it with such eloquence as she had at her command.

"I can understand what you say, Uncle Hatto."

"I am glad of that, at any rate."

"And I know that I have no right to ask you for anything."

"I do not say that. Anything in reason, that a girl like you should ask of her old uncle, I would give you."

"I have no such reasonable request to make, uncle. I have never wanted new ribbons from you or gay toys. Even from my own mother I have not wanted them;—not wanted them faster than they seemed to come without any asking."

"No, no; you have been a good girl."

"I have been a happy girl; and quite happy with those I loved, and with what Providence had given me. I had nothing to ask for. But now I am no longer happy, nor can I be unless you do for me this which I ask of you. I have wanted nothing till now, and now in my need I come to you."

"And now you want a husband with a fortune!"

"No!" and that single word she spoke, not loudly, for her voice was low and soft, but with an accent which carried it sharply to his ear and to his brain. And then she rose from her seat as she went on. "Your scorn, uncle, is unjust,—unjust and untrue. I have ever acted maidenly, as has become my mother's daughter."

"Yes, yes, yes;—I believe that."

"And I can say more than that for myself. My thoughts have been the same, nor have my wishes even, ever gone beyond them. And when this young man came to me, telling me of his feelings, I gave him no answer till I had consulted my mother."

"She should have bade you not to think of him."

"Ah, you are not a mother, and cannot know. Why should I not think of him when he was good and kind, honest and hard-working? And then he had thought of me first. Why should I not think of him? Did not mamma listen to my father when he came to her?"

"But your father was forty years old, and had a business."

"You gave it him, Uncle Hatto. I have heard him say so."

"And therefore I am to do as much for you. And then next year Agnes will come to me; and so before I die I shall see you all in want, with large families. No, Isa; I will not scorn you, but this thing I cannot do."

"But I have not told you all yet. You say that I want a husband."

"Well, well; I did not mean to say it harshly."

"I do want—to be married." And here her courage failed her a little, and for a moment her eye fell to the ground. "It is true, uncle. He has asked me whether I could love him, and I have told him I could. He has asked me whether I would be his wife, and I have given him a promise. After that, must not his happiness be my happiness, and his misery my misery? Am I not his wife already before God?"

"No, no," said Uncle Hatto loudly.

"Ah, but I am. None feel the strength of the bonds but those who are themselves bound. I know my duty to my father and mother, and with God's help I will do it, but I am not the less bound to him. Without their approval I will not stand with him at the altar; but not the less is my lot joined to his for this world. Nothing could release me from that but his wish."

"And he will wish it in a month or two."

"Excuse me, Uncle Hatto, but in that I can only judge for myself as best I may. He has loved me now for two years— "

"Psha!"

"And, whether it be wise or foolish, I have sanctioned it. I cannot now go back with honour, even if my own heart would let me. His welfare must be my welfare, and his sorrow my sorrow. Therefore I am bound to do for him anything that a girl may do for the man she loves; and, as I knew of no other resource, I come to you to help me."

"And he, sitting out there, knows what you are saying."

"Most certainly not. He knows no more than that he has seen me enter this room."

"I am glad of that, because I would not wish that he should be disappointed. In this matter, my dear, I cannot do anything for you."

"And that is your last answer, uncle?"

"Yes, indeed. When you come to think over this some twenty years hence, you will know then that I am right, and that your request was unreasonable.

"It may be so," she replied, "but I do not think it."

"It will be so. Such favours as you now ask are not granted in this world for light reasons."

"Light reasons! Well, uncle, I have had my say, and will not take up your time longer."

"Good by, my dear. I am sorry that I cannot oblige you;—that it is quite out of my power to oblige you."

Then she went, giving him her hand as she parted from him; and he, as she left the room, looked anxiously at her, watching her countenance and her gait, and listening to the very fall of her footstep. "Ah!" he said to himself, when he was alone, "the young people have the best of it. The sun shines for them; but why should they have all? Poor as he is, he is a happy dog,—a happy dog. But she is twice too good for him. Why did she not take to one of her own country?"

Isa, as she passed through the bank, smiled sweetly on her father, and then smiled sweetly at her lover, nodding to him with a pleasant kindly nod. If he could have heard all that had passed at that interview, how much more he would have known of her than he now knew, and how proud he would have been of her love. No word was spoken as she went out, and then she walked home with even step, as she had walked thither. It can hardly be said that she was disappointed, as she had expected nothing. But people hope who do not expect, and though her step was even and her face calm, yet her heart was sad.

"Mamma," she said, "there is no hope from uncle Hatto."

"So I feared, my dear."

"But I thought it right to try—for Herbert's sake."

"I hope it will not do him an injury in the bank."

"Oh, mamma, do not put that into my head. If that were added to it all, I should indeed be wretched."

"No; he is too just for that. Poor young man! Sometimes I almost think it would be better that he should go back to England."

"Mamma, if he did, I should—break my heart."

"Isa!"

"Well, mamma! But do not suppose that I mean to complain, whatever happens."

"But I had been so sure that you had constrained your feelings!"

"So I had,—till I knew myself. Mamma, I could wait for years, if he were contented to wait by my side. If I could see him happy, I could watch him and love him, and be happy also. I do not want to have him kneeling to me, and making sweet speeches; but it has gone too far now,—and I could not bear to lose him." And thus to her mother she confessed the truth.

There was nothing more said between Isa and her mother on the subject, and for two days the matter remained as it then stood. Madame Heine had been deeply grieved at hearing those last words which her daughter had spoken. To her also that state of quiescence which Isa had so long affected seemed to be the proper state to which a maiden's heart should stand till after her marriage vows had been pronounced. She had watched her Isa, and had approved of everything,—of everything till this last avowal had been made. But now, though she could not approve, she expressed no disapproval in words. She pressed her daughter's hand and sighed, and then the two said no more upon the matter. In this way, for two days, there was silence in the apartments in the Ludwigs Strasse; for even when the father returned from his work, the whole circle felt that their old family mirth was for the present necessarily laid aside.

On the morning of the third day, about noon, Madame Heine returned home from the market with Isa, and as they reached the landing, Agnes met them with a packet. "Fritz brought it from the bank," said Agnes. Now Fritz was the boy who ran messages and swept out the office, and Madame Heine put out her hand for the parcel, thinking, not unnaturally, that it was for her. But Agnes would not give it to her mother. "It is for you, Isa," she said. Then Isa, looking at the address, recognised the handwriting of her uncle. "Mamma," she said, "I will come to you directly;" and then she passed quickly away into her own room.

The parcel was soon opened, and contained a note from her uncle, and a stiff, large document, looking as though it had come from the hands of a lawyer. Isa glanced at the document, and read some few of the words on the outer fold, but they did not carry home to her mind any clear perception of their meaning. She was flurried at the moment, and the words, perhaps, were not very plain. Then she took up her note, and that was plain enough. It was very short, and ran as follows:—

> "My dear Niece,
>
> "You told me on Monday that I was stern, and harsh, and unjust. Perhaps I was. If so, I hope the enclosed will make amends, and that you will not think me such an old fool as I think myself.
>
> "Your affectionate uncle,
>
> "HATTO HEINE.
>
> "I have told nobody yet, and the enclosed will require my brother's signature; but I suppose he will not object."

"But he does not know it, mamma," said Isa. "Who is to tell him? Oh mamma, you must tell him."

"Nay, my dear; but it must be your own present to him."

"I could not give it him. It is uncle Hatto's present. Mamma, when I left him I thought that his eye was kind to me."

"His heart, at any rate, has been very kind." And then again they looked over the document, and talked of the wedding which must now be near at hand. But still they had not as yet decided how Herbert should be informed.

At last Isa resolved that she herself would write to him. She did write, and this was her letter:—

> "Dear Herbert,
>
> "Mamma and I wish to see you, and beg that you will come up to us this evening. We have tidings for you which we hope you will receive with joy. I may as well tell you at once, as I do not wish to flurry you. Uncle Hatto has sent to us a document which admits you as a partner into the bank. If, therefore, you wish to go on with our engagement, I suppose there is nothing now to cause any very great delay.
>
> ISA."

The letter was very simple, and Isa, when she had written it, subsided into all her customary quiescence. Indeed, when Herbert came to the Ludwigs Strasse, not in the evening as he was bidden to do, but instantly, leaving his own dinner uneaten, and coming upon the Heines in the midst of their dinner, she was more than usually tranquil. But his love was, as she had told him, boisterous. He could not contain himself, and embraced them all, and then scolded Isa because she was so calm.

"Why should I not be calm," said she, "now that I know you are happy?"

The house in the Schrannen Platz still goes by the name of Heine Brothers, but the mercantile world in Bavaria, and in some cities out of Bavaria, is well aware that the real pith and marrow of the business is derived from the energy of the young English partner.

George Walker at Suez

Originally appeared in *Public Opinion*, 28 December 1861. Reprinted in *Tales of All Countries* [Second Series] (1863). Written c. 12–15 April 1861, during the composition of *Orley Farm*, and obviously inspired by Trollope's 1858 postal mission to Egypt.

OF ALL the spots on the world's surface that I, George Walker, of Friday Street, London, have ever visited, Suez in Egypt at the head of the Red Sea is by far the vilest, the most unpleasant, and the least interesting. There are no women there, no water, and no vegetation. It is surrounded, and indeed often filled, by a world of sand. A scorching sun is always overhead; and one is domiciled in a huge cavernous hotel, which seems to have been made purposely destitute of all the comforts of civilised life. Nevertheless, in looking back upon the week of my life which I spent there I always enjoy a certain sort of triumph;—or rather, upon one day of that week, which lends a sort of halo not only to my sojourn at Suez, but to the whole period of my residence in Egypt.

I am free to confess that I am not a great man, and that, at any rate in the earlier part of my career, I had a hankering after the homage which is paid to greatness. I would fain have been a popular orator, feeding myself on the incense tendered to me by thousands; or failing that, a man born to power, whom those around him were compelled to respect, and perhaps to fear. I am not ashamed to acknowledge this, and I believe that most of my neighbours in Friday Street would own as much were they as candid and open hearted as myself.

It is now some time since I was recommended to pass the first four months of the year in Cairo because I had a sore-throat. The doctor may have been right, but I shall never divest myself of the idea that my partners wished to be rid of me while they made certain changes in the management of the firm. They would not otherwise have shown such interest every time I blew my nose or relieved my huskiness by a slight cough;—they would not have been so intimate with that surgeon from St. Bartholomew's who dined with them twice at the Albion; nor would they have gone to work directly that my back was turned, and have done those very things which they could not have done had I remained at home. Be that as it may, I was frightened and went to Cairo, and while there I made a trip to Suez for a week.

I was not happy at Cairo, for I knew nobody there and the people at the hotel were as I thought uncivil. It seemed to me as though I were allowed to go in and out merely by sufferance; and yet I paid my bill regularly every week. The house was full of company, but the company was made up of parties of twos and threes, and they all seemed to have their own friends. I did make attempts to overcome that terrible British exclusiveness, that *noli me tangere* with which an Englishman arms himself, and in which he thinks it necessary to envelop his wife; but it was in vain, and I found myself sitting down to breakfast and dinner, day after day, as much alone as I should do if I called for a chop at a separate table in the Cathedral Coffee-house. And yet at breakfast and dinner I made one of an assemblage of thirty or forty people. That I thought dull.

But as I stood one morning on the steps before the hotel, bethinking myself that my throat was as well as ever I remembered it to be, I was suddenly slapped on the back. Never in my life did I feel a more pleasant sensation, or turn round with more unaffected delight to return a friend's greeting. It was as though a cup of water had been handed to me in the desert. I knew that a cargo of passengers for Australia had reached Cairo that morning, and were to be passed on to Suez as soon as the railway would take them, and did not therefore expect that the greeting had come from any sojourner in Egypt. I should perhaps have explained that the even tenor of our life at the hotel was disturbed some four times a month by a flight through Cairo of a flock of travellers, who like locusts eat up all that there was eatable at the Inn for the day. They sat down at the same tables with us, never mixing with us, having their separate interests and hopes, and being often, as I thought, somewhat loud and almost selfish in the expression of them. These flocks consisted of passengers passing and repassing by the overland route to and from India and Australia; and had I nothing else to tell, I should delight to describe all that I watched of their habits and manners—the outward bound being so different in their traits from their brethren on their return. But I have to tell of my own triumph at Suez, and must therefore hasten on to say that on turning round quickly with my outstretched hand, I found it clasped by John Robinson.

"Well, Robinson, is this you?" "Holloa, Walker, what are you doing here?" That of course was the style of greeting. Elsewhere I should not have cared much to meet John Robinson, for he was a man who had never done well in the world. He had been in business and connected with a fairly good house in Size Lane, but he had married early, and things had not exactly gone well with him. I don't think the house broke, but he did; and so he was driven to take himself and five children off to Australia. Elsewhere I should not have cared to come across him, but I was positively glad to be slapped on the back by anybody on that landing-place in front of Shepperd's Hotel at Cairo.

I soon learned that Robinson with his wife and children, and indeed with all the rest of the Australian cargo, were to be passed on to Suez that afternoon, and after awhile I agreed to accompany their party. I had made up my mind, on coming out from England, that I would see all the wonders of Egypt, and hitherto I had seen nothing. I did ride on one day some fifteen miles on a donkey to see the petrified forest; but the guide, who called himself a dragoman, took me wrong or cheated me in some way. We rode half the day over a stony, sandy plain, seeing nothing, with a terrible wind that filled my mouth with grit, and at last the dragoman got off. "Dere," said he, picking up a small bit of stone, "Dis is de forest made of stone. Carry that home." Then we turned round and rode back to Cairo. My chief observation as to the country was this—that whichever way we went, the wind blew into our teeth. The day's work cost me five-and-twenty shillings, and since that I had not as yet made any other expedition. I was therefore glad of an opportunity of going to Suez, and of making the journey in company with an acquaintance.

At that time the railway was open, as far as I remember, nearly half the way from Cairo to Suez. It did not run four or five times a day, as railways do in other countries, but four or five times a month. In fact, it only carried passengers on the arrival of these flocks passing between England and her Eastern possessions. There were trains passing backwards and forwards constantly, as I perceived in walking to and from the station; but, as I learned, they carried nothing but the labourers working on the line, and the water sent into the Desert for their use. It struck me forcibly at the time that I should not have liked to have money in that investment.

Well; I went with Robinson to Suez. The journey, like everything else in Egypt, was sandy, hot, and unpleasant. The railway carriages were pretty fair, and we had room enough; but even in them the dust was a great nuisance. We travelled about ten miles an hour, and stopped about an hour at every ten miles. This was tedious, but we had cigars with us and a trifle of brandy and water; and in this manner the railway journey wore itself away. In the middle of the night, however, we were moved from the railway carriages into omnibuses, as they were called, and then I was not comfortable. These omnibuses were wooden boxes, placed each upon a pair of wheels, and supposed to be capable of carrying six passengers. I was thrust into one with Robinson, his wife and five children, and immediately began to repent of my good-nature in accompanying them. To each vehicle were attached four horses or mules, and I must acknowledge that as on the railway they went as slow as possible, so now in these conveyances, dragged through the sand, they went as fast as the beasts could be made to gallop. I remember the Fox Tally-ho coach on the Birmingham road when Boyce drove it, but as regards pace the Fox Tally-ho was nothing to these machines in Egypt. On the first going off I was jolted right on to Mrs. R. and her infant; and for a long time that lady thought that the child had been squeezed out of its proper shape; but at last we arrived at Suez, and the baby seemed to me to be all right when it was handed down into the boat at Suez.

The Robinsons were allowed time to breakfast at that cavernous hotel—which looked to me like a scheme to save the expense of the passengers' meal on board the ship—and then they were off. I shook hands with him heartily as I parted with him at the quay, and wished him well through all his troubles. A man who takes a wife and five young children out into a colony, and that with his pockets but indifferently lined, certainly has his troubles before him. So he has at home, no doubt; but, judging for myself, I should always prefer sticking to the old ship as long as there is a bag of biscuits in the locker. Poor Robinson! I have never heard a word of him or his since that day, and sincerely trust that the baby was none the worse for the little accident in the box.

And now I had the prospect of a week before me at Suez, and the Robinsons had not been gone half an hour before I began to feel that I should have been better off even at Cairo. I secured a bedroom at the hotel—I might have secured sixty bedrooms had I wanted them—and then went out and stood at the front door, or gate. It is a large house, built round a quadrangle, looking with one front towards the head of the Red Sea, and with the other into and on a sandy, dead-looking, open square. There I stood for ten minutes, and finding that it was too hot to go forth, returned to the long cavernous room in which we had breakfasted. In that long cavernous room I was destined to eat all my meals for the next six days. Now at Cairo I could, at any rate, see my fellow-creatures at their food. So I lit a cigar, and began to wonder whether I could survive the week. It was now clear to me that I had done a very rash thing in coming to Suez with the Robinsons.

Somebody about the place had asked me my name, and I had told it plainly—George Walker. I never was ashamed of my name yet, and never had cause to be. I believe at this day it will go as far in Friday Street as any other. A man may be popular, or he may not. That depends mostly on circumstances which are in themselves trifling. But the value of his name depends on the way in which he is known at his bank. I have never dealt in tea spoons or gravy spoons, but my name will go as far as another name. "George Walker," I answered, therefore, in a tone of some little authority, to the man who asked me, and who sat inside the gate of the hotel in an old dressing gown and slippers.

That was a melancholy day with me, and twenty times before dinner did I wish myself back at Cairo. I had been travelling all night, and therefore hoped that I might get through some little time in sleeping, but the mosquitoes attacked me the moment I laid myself down. In other places mosquitoes torment you only at night, but at Suez they buzz around you, without ceasing, at all hours. A scorching sun was blazing overhead, and absolutely forbade me to leave the house. I stood for awhile in the verandah, looking down at the few small vessels which were moored to the quay, but there was no life in them; not a sail was set, not a boatman or a sailor was to be seen, and the very water looked as though it were hot. I could fancy the glare of the sun was cracking the paint on the gunwales of the boats. I was the only visitor in the house, and during all the long hours of the morning it seemed as though the servants had deserted it.

I dined at four; not that I chose that hour, but because no choice was given to me. At the hotels in Egypt one has to dine at an hour fixed by the landlord, and no entreaties will suffice to obtain a meal at any other. So at four I dined, and after dinner was again reduced to despair.

I was sitting in the cavernous chamber almost mad at the prospect of the week before me, when I heard a noise as of various feet in the passage leading from the quadrangle. Was it possible that other human beings were coming into the hotel—Christian human beings at whom I could look, whose voices I could hear, whose words I could understand, and with whom I might possibly associate? I did not move, however, for I was still hot, and I knew that my chances might be better, if I did not show myself over-eager for companionship at the first moment. The door, however, was soon opened, and I saw that at least in one respect I was destined to be disappointed. The strangers who were entering the room were not Christians—if I might judge by the nature of the garments in which they were clothed.

The door had been opened by the man in an old dressing gown and slippers, whom I had seen sitting inside the gate. He was the Arab porter of the hotel, and as he marshalled the new visitors into the room, I heard him pronounce some sound similar to my own name, and perceived that he pointed me out to the most prominent person of those who then entered the apartment. This was a stout, portly man, dressed from head to foot in Eastern costume of the brightest colours. He wore, not only the red fez cap which everybody wears—even I had accustomed myself to a fez cap—but a turban round it, of which the voluminous folds were snowy white. His face was fat, but not the less grave, and the lower part of it was enveloped in a magnificent beard, which projected round it on all sides, and touched his breast as he walked. It was a grand grizzled beard, and I acknowledged at a moment that it added a singular dignity to the appearance of the stranger. His flowing robe was of bright colours, and the under garment which fitted close round his breast, and then descended, becoming beneath his sash a pair of the loosest pantaloons—I might, perhaps, better describe them as bags—was a rich tawny silk. These loose pantaloons were tied close round his legs, above the ankle, and over a pair of scrupulously white stockings, and on his feet he wore a pair of yellow slippers. It was manifest to me at a glance that the Arab gentleman was got up in his best raiment, and that no expense had been spared on the suit.

And here I cannot but make a remark on the personal bearing of these Arabs. Whether they be Arabs, or Turks, or Copts, it is always the same. They are a mean, false, cowardly race, I believe. They will bear blows, and respect the man who gives them. Fear goes further with them than love, and between man and man they understand nothing of forbearance. He who does not exact from them all that he can exact is simply a fool in their estimation, to the extent of that which he loses. In all this, they are immeasurably inferior to us who have had Christian teaching. But in one thing they beat us. They always know how to maintain their personal dignity.

Look at my friend and partner Judkins, as he stands with his hands in his trousers pockets at the door of our house in Friday Street. What can be meaner than his appearance? He is a stumpy, short, podgy man; but then so also was my Arab friend at Suez. Judkins is always dressed from head to foot in a decent black cloth suit; his coat is ever a dress coat, and is neither old nor shabby. On his head he carries a shining new silk hat, such as fashion in our metropolis demands. Judkins is rather a dandy than otherwise, piquing himself somewhat on his apparel. And yet how mean is his appearance, as compared with the appearance of that Arab;—how mean also is his gait, how ignoble his step! Judkins could buy that Arab out four times over, and hardly feel the loss; and yet were they to enter a room together, Judkins would know and acknowledge by his look that he was the inferior personage. Not the less, should a personal quarrel arise between them, would Judkins punch the Arab's head; ay, and reduce him to utter ignominy at his feet. Judkins would break his heart in despair, rather than not return a blow; whereas the Arab would put up with any indignity of that sort. Nevertheless Judkins is altogether deficient in personal dignity.

I often thought, as the hours hung in Egypt, whether it might not be practicable to introduce an oriental costume into Friday Street.

At this moment, as the Arab gentleman entered the cavernous coffee-room, I felt that I was greatly the inferior personage. He was followed by four or five others, dressed somewhat as himself, though by no means in such magnificent colours, and by one gentleman in a coat and trowsers. The gentleman in the coat and trowsers came last, and I could see that he was one of the least of the number. As for myself, I felt almost overawed by the dignity of the stout party in the turban, and seeing that he came directly across the room to the place where I was seated, I got upon my legs and made him some sign of Christian obeisance. I am a little man, and not podgy, as is Judkins, and I flatter myself that I showed more deportment, at any rate, than he would have exhibited.

I made, as I have said, some Christian obeisance. I bobbed my head, that is, rubbing my hands together the while, and expressed an opinion that it was a fine day. But if I was civil, as I hope I was, the Arab was much more so. He advanced till he was about six paces from me, then placed his right hand open upon his silken breast, and inclining forward with his whole body, made to me a bow which Judkins never could accomplish. The turban and flowing robe might be possible in Friday Street, but of what avail would be the outer garments and mere symbols, if the inner sentiment of personal dignity were wanting? I have often since tried it when alone, but I could never accomplish anything like that bow. The Arab with the flowing robe bowed, and then the other Arabs all bowed also; and after that the Christian gentleman with the coat and trowsers made a leg. I made a leg also, rubbing my hands again, and added to my former remarks that it was rather hot.

"Dat berry true," said the porter in the dirty dressing gown, who stood by. I could see at a glance that the manner of that porter towards me was greatly altered, and I began to feel comforted in my wretchedness. Perhaps a Christian from Friday Street, with plenty of money in his pockets, would stand in higher esteem at Suez than at Cairo. If so, that alone would go far to atone for the apparent wretchedness of the place. At Cairo I had not received that attention which had certainly been due to me as the second partner in the flourishing Manchester house of Grimes, Walker, and Judkins.

But now, as my friend with the beard again bowed to me, I felt that this deficiency was to be made up. It was clear, however, that this new acquaintance, though I liked the manner of it, would be attended with considerable inconvenience, for the Arab gentleman commenced an address to me in French. It has always been to me a source of sorrow that my parents did not teach me the French language, and this deficiency on my part has given rise to an incredible amount of supercilious overbearing pretension on the part of Judkins—who after all can hardly do more than translate a correspondent's letter. I do not believe that he could have understood a word of that Arab's oration, but at any rate I did not. He went on to the end, however, speaking for some three or four minutes, and then again he bowed. If I could only have learned that bow, I might still have been greater than Judkins with all his French.

"I am very sorry," said I, "but I don't exactly follow the French language—when it is spoken."

"Ah! no French!" said the Arab in very broken English, "dat is one sorrow." How is it that these fellows learn all languages under the sun? I afterwards found that this man could talk Italian and Turkish and Armenian fluently, and say a few words in German, as he could also in English. I could not ask for my dinner in any other language than English, if it were to save me from starvation. Then he called to the Christian gentleman in the pantaloons, and, as far as I could understand, made over to him the duty of interpreting between us. There seemed, however, to be one difficulty in the way of this being carried on with efficiency. The Christian gentleman could not speak English himself. He knew of it, perhaps, something more than did the Arab, but by no means enough to enable us to have a fluent conversation.

And had the interpreter—who turned out to be an Italian from Trieste, attached to the Austrian Consulate at Alexandria—had the interpreter spoken English with the greatest ease, I should have had considerable difficulty in understanding, and digesting in all its bearings, the proposition made to me. But before I proceed to the proposition, I must describe a ceremony which took place previous to its discussion. I had hardly observed, when first the procession entered the room, that one of my friend's followers—my friend's name, as I learned afterwards, was Mahmoud al Ackbar, and I will therefore call him Mahmoud—that one of Mahmoud's followers bore in his arms a bundle of long sticks, and that another carried an iron pot and a tray. Such was the case, and these two followers came forward to perform their services, while I, having been literally pressed down on to the sofa by Mahmoud, watched them in their progress. Mahmoud also sat down, and not a word was spoken while the ceremony went on. The man with the sticks first placed on the ground two little pans—one at my feet, and then one at the feet of his master. After that he loosed an ornamented bag which he carried round his neck, and producing from it tobacco, proceeded to fill two pipes. This he did with the utmost gravity, and apparently with very peculiar care. The pipes had been already fixed at one end of the stick, and to the other end the man had fastened two large yellow balls. These, as I afterwards perceived, were mouthpieces made of amber. Then he lit the pipes, drawing up the difficult smoke by long painful suckings at the mouthpiece, and then, when the work had become apparently easy, he handed one pipe to me, and the other to his master. The bowls he had first placed in the little pans on the ground.

During all this time no word was spoken, and I was left altogether in the dark as to the cause which had produced this extraordinary courtesy. There was a stationary sofa—they called it there a divan—which was fixed into the corner of the room, and on one side of the angle sat

Mahmoud al Ackbar, with his feet tucked under him, while I sat on the other. The remainder of the party stood around, and I felt so little master of the occasion, that I did not know whether it would become me to bid them be seated. I was not master of the entertainment. They were not my pipes. Nor was it my coffee, which I saw one of the followers preparing in a distant part of the room. And, indeed, I was much confused as to the management of the stick and amber mouth-piece with which I had been presented. With a cigar I am as much at home as any man in the city. I can nibble off the end of it, and smoke it to the last ash, when I am three parts asleep. But I had never before been invited to regale myself with such an instrument as this. What was I to do with that huge yellow ball? So I watched my new friend closely.

It had manifestly been a part of his urbanity not to commence till I had done so, but seeing my difficulty he at last raised the ball to his mouth and sucked at it. I looked at him, and envied the gravity of his countenance, and the dignity of his demeanour. I sucked also, but I made a sputtering noise, and must confess that I did not enjoy it. The smoke curled gracefully from his mouth and nostrils as he sat there in mute composure. I was mute as regarded speech, but I coughed as the smoke came from me in convulsive puffs. And then the attendant brought us coffee in little tin cups—black coffee, without sugar and full of grit, of which the berries had been only bruised, not ground. I took the cup and swallowed the mixture, for I could not refuse, but I wish that I might have asked for some milk and sugar. Nevertheless there was something very pleasing in the whole ceremony, and at last I began to find myself more at home with my pipe.

When Mahmoud had exhausted his tobacco, and perceived that I also had ceased to puff forth smoke, he spoke in Italian to the interpreter, and the interpreter forthwith proceeded to explain to me the purport of this visit. This was done with much difficulty, for the interpreter's stock of English was very scanty—but after awhile I understood, or thought I understood, as follows:—At some previous period of my existence I had done some deed which had given infinite satisfaction to Mahmoud al Ackbar. Whether, however, I had done it myself, or whether my father had done it, was not quite clear to me. My father, then some time deceased, had been a wharfinger at Liverpool, and it was quite possible that Mahmoud might have found himself at that port. Mahmoud had heard of my arrival in Egypt, and had been given to understand that I was coming to Suez—to carry myself away in the ship, as the interpreter phrased it. This I could not understand, but I let it pass. Having heard these agreeable tidings—and Mahmoud, sitting in the corner, bowed low to me as this was said—he had prepared for my acceptance a slight refection for the morrow, hoping that I would not carry myself away in the ship till this had been eaten. On this subject I soon made him quite at ease, and he then proceeded to explain that as there was a point of interest at Suez, Mahmoud was anxious that I should partake of the refection somewhat in the guise of a picnic, at the Well of Moses, over in Asia, on the other side of the head of the

Red Sea. Mahmoud would provide a boat to take across the party in the morning, and camels on which we would return after sunset. Or else we would go and return on camels, or go on camels and return in the boat. Indeed any arrangement would be made that I preferred. If I was afraid of the heat, and disliked the open boat, I could be carried round in a litter. The provisions had already been sent over to the Well of Moses in the anticipation that I would not refuse this little request.

I did not refuse it. Nothing could have been more agreeable to me than this plan of seeing something of the sights and wonders of this land,—and of this seeing them in good company. I had not heard of the Well of Moses before, but now that I learned that it was in Asia,—in another quarter of the globe, to be reached by a transit of the Red Sea, to be returned from by a journey on camels' backs,—I burned with anxiety to visit its waters. What a story would this be for Judkins! This was, no doubt, the point at which the Israelites had passed. Of those waters had they drunk. I almost felt that I had already found one of Pharaoh's chariot wheels. I readily gave my assent, and then, with much ceremony and many low salaams, Mahmoud and his attendant left me. "I am very glad that I came to Suez," said I to myself.

I did not sleep much that night, for the mosquitoes of Suez are very persevering; but I was saved from the agonising despair which these animals so frequently produce, by my agreeable thoughts as to Mahmoud al Ackbar. I will put it to any of my readers who have travelled, whether it is not a painful thing to find one's-self regarded among strangers without any kindness or ceremonious courtesy. I had on this account been wretched at Cairo, but all this was to be made up to me at Suez. Nothing could be more pleasant than the whole conduct of Mahmoud al Ackbar, and I determined to take full advantage of it, not caring overmuch what might be the nature of those previous favours to which he had alluded. That was his look-out, and if he was satisfied, why should not I be so also?

On the following morning I was dressed at six, and, looking out of my bed-room, I saw the boat in which we were to be wafted into Asia being brought up to the quay close under my window. It had been arranged that we should start early, so as to avoid the mid-day sun, breakfast in the boat,—Mahmoud in this way engaged to provide me with two refections,—take our rest at noon in a pavilion which had been built close upon the well of the patriarch, and then eat our dinner, and return riding upon camels in the cool of the evening. Nothing could sound more pleasant than such a plan; and, knowing as I did that the hampers of provisions had already been sent over, I did not doubt that the table arrangements would be excellent. Even now, standing at my window, I could see a basket laden with long-necked bottles going into the boat, and became aware that we should not depend altogether for our morning repast on that gritty coffee which my friend Mahmoud's followers prepared.

I had promised to be ready at six, and having carefully completed my toilet, and put a clean collar and comb into my pocket ready for dinner, I descended to the great gateway and walked slowly round to the quay. As I passed out, the porter greeted me with a low obeisance, and walking on, I felt that I stepped the ground with a sort of dignity of which I had before been ignorant. It is not, as a rule, the man who gives grace and honour to the position, but the position which confers the grace and honour upon the man. I have often envied the solemn gravity and grand demeanour of the Lord Chancellor, as I have seen him on the bench; but I almost think that even Judkins would look grave and dignified under such a wig. Mahmoud al Ackbar had called upon me and done me honour, and I felt myself personally capable of sustaining before the people of Suez the honour which he had done me.

As I walked forth with a proud step from beneath the portal, I perceived, looking down from the square along the street, that there was already some commotion in the town. I saw the flowing robes of many Arabs, with their backs turned towards me, and I thought that I observed the identical gown and turban of my friend Mahmoud on the back and head of a stout short man, who was hurrying round a corner in the distance. I felt sure that it was Mahmoud. Some of his servants had failed in their preparations, I said to myself, as I made my way round to the water's edge. This was only another testimony how anxious he was to do me honour.

I stood for awhile on the edge of the quay looking into the boat, and admiring the comfortable cushions which were luxuriously arranged around the seats. The men who were at work did not know me, and I was unnoticed, but I should soon take my place upon the softest of those cushions. I walked slowly backwards and forwards on the quay, listening to a hum of voices that came to me from a distance. There was clearly something stirring in the town, and I felt certain that all the movement and all those distant voices were connected in some way with my expedition to the Well of Moses. At last there came a lad upon the walk dressed in Frank costume, and I asked him what was in the wind. He was a clerk attached to an English warehouse, and he told me that there had been an arrival from Cairo. He knew no more than that, but he had heard that the omnibuses had just come in. Could it be possible that Mahmoud al Ackbar had heard of another old acquaintance, and had gone to welcome him also?

At first my ideas on the subject were altogether pleasant. I by no means wished to monopolise the delights of all those cushions, nor would it be to me a cause of sorrow that there should be some one to share with me the conversational powers of that interpreter. Should another guest be found, he might also be an Englishman, and I might thus form an acquaintance which would be desirable. Thinking of these things, I walked the quay for some minutes in a happy state of mind; but by degrees I became impatient, and by degrees also disturbed in my spirit. I observed that one of the Arab boatmen walked round from the vessel to the front of the hotel, and that on his return he looked at me—as I thought, not with courteous eyes. Then also I saw, or rather heard, some one in the verandah of the hotel above me, and was conscious that I was being viewed from thence. I walked and walked, and nobody came to me, and I perceived by my watch that it was seven o'clock. The noise, too, had come nearer and nearer, and I was now aware that wheels had been drawn up before the front door of the hotel, and that many voices were speaking there. It might be that Mahmoud should wait for some other friend, but why did he not send some one to inform me? And then, as I made a sudden turn at the end of the quay, I caught sight of the retreating legs of the Austrian interpreter, and I became aware that he had been sent down, and had gone away, afraid to speak to me. "What can I do?" said I to myself, "I can but keep my ground." I own that I feared to go round to the front of the hotel. So I still walked slowly up and down the length of the quay, and began to whistle to show that I was not uneasy. The Arab sailors looked at me uncomfortably, and from time to time some one peered at me round the corner. It was now fully half-past seven, and the sun was becoming hot in the heavens. Why did we not hasten to place ourselves beneath the awning in that boat?

I had just made up my mind that I would go round to the front and penetrate this mystery, when, on turning, I saw approaching to me a man dressed at any rate like an English gentleman. As he came near to me, he raised his hat, and accosted me in our own language. "Mr. George Walker, I believe?" said he. "Yes," said I, with some little attempt at a high demeanour, "of the firm of Grimes, Walker, and Judkins, Friday Street, London."

"A most respectable house, I am sure," said he. "I'm afraid there has been a little mistake here."

"No mistake as to the respectability of that house," said I. I felt that I was again alone in the world, and that it was necessary that I should support myself. Mahmoud al Ackbar had separated himself from me for ever. Of that I had no longer a doubt.

"Oh, none at all," said he. "But about this little expedition over the water;" and he pointed contemptuously to the boat. "There has been a mistake about that, Mr. Walker; I happen to be the English Vice-Consul here."

I took off my hat and bowed. It was the first time I had ever been addressed civilly by any English consular authority.

"And they have made me get out of bed to come down here and explain all this to you."

"All what?" said I.

"You are a man of the world, I know, and I'll just tell it you plainly. My old friend, Mahmoud al Ackbar, has mistaken you for Sir George Walker, the new Lieutenant-Governor of Pegu. Sir George Walker is here now; he has come this morning; and Mahmoud is ashamed to face you after what has occurred. If you won't object to withdraw with me into the hotel, I'll explain it all."

I felt as though a thunderbolt had fallen; and I must say, that even up to this day I think that the Consul might have been a little less abrupt. "We can get in here," said he, evidently in a hurry, and pointing to a small door which opened out from one corner of the house to the quay. What could I do but follow him? I did follow him, and in a few words learned the remainder of the story. When he had once withdrawn me from the public walk he seemed but little anxious about the rest, and soon left me again alone. The facts, as far as I could learn them, were simply these.

Sir George Walker, who was now going out to Pegu as Governor, had been in India before, commanding an army there. I had never heard of him before, and had made no attempt to pass myself off as his relative. Nobody could have been more innocent than I was—or have received worse usage. I have as much right to the name as he has. Well; when he was in India before, he had taken the city of Begum after a terrible siege—Begum, I think the Consul called it; and Mahmoud had been there, having been, it seems, a great man at Begum, and Sir George had spared him and his money; and in this way the whole thing had come to pass. There was no further explanation than that. The rest of it was all transparent. Mahmoud, having heard my name from the porter, had hurried down to invite me to his party. So far so good. But why had he been afraid to face me in the morning? And, seeing that the fault had all been his, why had he not asked me to join the expedition? Sir George and I may, after all, be cousins. But, coward as he was, he had been afraid of me. When they found that I was on the quay, they had been afraid of me, not knowing how to get rid of me. I wish that I had kept the quay all day, and stared them down one by one as they entered the boat. But I was down in the mouth, and when the Consul left me, I crept wearily back to my bed-room.

And the Consul did leave me almost immediately. A faint hope had, at one time, come upon me that he would have asked me to breakfast. Had he done so, I should have felt it as a full compensation for all that I had suffered. I am not an exacting man, but I own that I like civility. In Friday Street I can command it, and in Friday Street for the rest of my life will I remain. From this Consul I received no civility. As soon as he had got me out of the way and spoken the few words which he had to say, he again raised his hat and left me. I also again raised mine, and then crept up to my bed-room.

From my window, standing a little behind the white curtain, I could see the whole embarkation. There was Mahmoud al Ackbar, looking indeed a little hot, but still going through his work with all that excellence of deportment which had graced him on the preceding evening. Had his foot slipped, and had he fallen backwards into that shallow water, my spirit would, I confess, have been relieved. But, on the contrary, everything went well with him. There was the real Sir George, my namesake and perhaps my cousin, as fresh as paint, cool from the bath which he had been taking while I had been walking on that terrace. How is it that these governors and commanders-in-chief go through such a deal of work without fagging? It was not yet two hours since he was jolting about in that omnibus-box, and there he had been all night. I could not have gone off to the Well of Moses immediately on my arrival. It's the dignity of the position that does it. I have long known that the head of a firm must never count on a mere clerk to get through as much work as he could do himself. It's the interest in the matter that supports the man.

There they went, and Sir George, as I was well assured, had never heard a word about me. Had he done so, is it not probable that he would have requested my attendance?

But Mahmoud and his followers no doubt kept their own counsel as to that little mistake. There they went, and the gentle rippling breeze filled their sail pleasantly, as the boat moved away into the bay. I felt no spite against any of them but Mahmoud. Why had he avoided me with such cowardice? I could still see them when the morning tchibouk was handed to Sir George; and, though I wished him no harm, I did envy him as he lay there reclining luxuriously upon the cushions.

A more wretched day than that, I never spent in my life. As I went in and out, the porter at the gate absolutely scoffed at me. Once I made up my mind to complain within the house. But what could I have said of the dirty Arab? They would have told me that it was his religion, or a national observance, or meant for a courtesy. What can a man do, in a strange country, when he is told that a native spits in his face by way of civility? I bore it, I bore it—like a man; and sighed for the comforts of Friday Street.

As to one matter, I made up my mind on that day, and I fully carried out my purpose on the next: I would go across to the Well of Moses in a boat. I would visit the coasts of Asia. And I would ride back into Africa on a camel. Though I did it alone, I would have my day's pleasuring. I had money in my pocket, and, though it might cost me £20, I would see all that my namesake had seen. It did cost me the best part of £20; and as for the pleasuring, I cannot say much for it.

I went to bed early that night, having concluded my bargain for the morrow with a rapacious Arab who spoke English. I went to bed early in order to escape the returning party, and was again on the quay at six the next morning. On this occasion, I stepped boldly into the boat the very moment that I came along the shore. There is nothing in the world like paying for what you use. I saw myself to the bottle of brandy and the cold meat, and acknowledged that a cigar out of my case would suit me better than that long stick. The long stick might do very well for a Governor of Pegu, but would be highly inconvenient in Friday Street.

Well, I am not going to give an account of my day's journey here, though perhaps I may do so some day. I did go to the Well of Moses—if a small dirty pool of salt water, lying high above the sands, can be called a well; I did eat my dinner in the miserable ruined cottage which they graced by the name of a pavilion; and, alas for my poor bones! I did ride home upon a camel. If Sir George did so early, and started for Pegu the next morning—and I was informed such was the fact—he must have been made of iron. I laid in bed the whole day suffering grievously; but I was told that on such a journey I should have slakened my throat with oranges, and not with brandy.

I survived those four terrible days which remained to me at Suez, and after another month was once again in Friday Street. I suffered greatly on the occasion; but it is some consolation to me to reflect that I smoked a pipe of peace with Mahmoud al

Ackbar; that I saw the hero of Begum while journeying out to new triumphs at Pegu; that I sailed into Asia in my own yacht—-hired for the occasion; and that I rode back into Africa on a camel. Nor can Judkins, with all his ill-nature, rob me of these remembrances.

The Mistletoe Bough

Originally appeared in *The Illustrated London News*, Christmas Supplement, 21 December 1861. Reprinted in *Tales of All Countries* [Second Series] (1863). Written by 15 August 1861, when the MS was sent to *The Illustrated London News*. Lakeland settings are not uncommon in Trollope's fiction: see, among other novels, *Can You Forgive Her*? (1864), *Sir Harry Hotspur of Humblethwaite* (1871) and *Lady Anna* (1874). Trollope's mother and brother Tom rented a house at Carlton Hill near Penrith, Cumberland in 1842–43, and Trollope's sister Cecilia (d. 1849) lived nearby.

"LET THE boys have it if they like it," said Mrs. Garrow, pleading to her only daughter on behalf of her two sons.

"Pray don't, mamma," said Elizabeth Garrow. "It only means romping. To me all that is detestable, and I am sure it is not the sort of thing that Miss Holmes would like."

"We always had it at Christmas when we were young."

"But, mamma, the world is so changed."

The point in dispute was one very delicate in its nature, hardly to be discussed in all its bearings, even in fiction, and the very mention of which between a mother and daughter showed a great amount of close confidence between them. It was no less than this. Should that branch of mistletoe which Frank Garrow had brought home with him out of the Lowther woods be hung up on Christmas Eve in the dining-room at Thwaite Hall, according to his wishes; or should permission for such hanging be positively refused? It was clearly a thing not to be done after such a discussion, and therefore the decision given by Mrs. Garrow was against it.

I am inclined to think that Miss Garrow was right in saying that the world is changed as touching mistletoe boughs. Kissing, I fear, is less innocent now than it used to be when our grandmothers were alive, and we have become more fastidious in our amusements. Nevertheless, I think that she made herself fairly open to the raillery with which her brothers attacked her.

"Honi soit qui mal y pense," said Frank, who was eighteen.

"Nobody will want to kiss you, my lady Fineairs," said Harry, who was just a year younger.

"Because you choose to be a Puritan, there are to be no more cakes and ale in the house," said Frank.

"Still waters run deep; we all know that," said Harry.

The boys had not been present when the matter was decided between Mrs. Garrow and her daughter, nor had the mother been present when these little amenities had passed between the brothers and sister.

"Only that mamma has said it, and I wouldn't seem to go against her," said Frank, "I'd ask my father. He wouldn't give way to such nonsense, I know."

Elizabeth turned away without answering, and left the room. Her eyes were full of tears, but she would not let them see that they had vexed her. They were only two days home from school, and for the last week before their coming, all her thoughts had been to prepare for their Christmas pleasures. She had arranged their rooms, making everything warm and pretty. Out of her own pocket she had bought a shot-belt for one, and skates for the other. She had told the old groom that her pony was to belong exclusively to Master Harry for the holidays, and now Harry told her that still waters ran deep. She had been driven to the use of all her eloquence in inducing her father to purchase that gun for Frank, and now Frank called her a Puritan. And why? She did not choose that a mistletoe bough should be hung in her father's hall, when Godfrey Holmes was coming to visit him. She could not explain this to Frank, but Frank might have had the wit to understand it. But Frank was thinking only of Patty Coverdale, a blue-eyed little romp of sixteen, who, with her sister Kate, was coming from Penrith to spend the Christmas at Thwaite Hall. Elizabeth left the room with her slow, graceful step, hiding her tears,—hiding all emotion, as latterly she had taught herself that it was feminine to do. "There goes my lady Fineairs," said Harry, sending his shrill voice after her.

Thwaite Hall was not a place of much pretension. It was a moderate-sized house, surrounded by pretty gardens and shrubberies, close down upon the river Eamont, on the Westmoreland side of the river, looking over to a lovely wooded bank in Cumberland. All the world knows that the Eamont runs out of Ulleswater, dividing the two counties, passing under Penrith Bridge and by the old ruins of Brougham Castle, below which it joins the Eden. Thwaite Hall nestled down close upon the clear rocky stream about half way between Ulleswater and Penrith, and had been built just at a bend of the river. The windows of the dining-parlour and of the drawing-room stood at right angles to each other, and yet each commanded a reach of the stream. Immediately from a side door of the house steps were cut down through the red rock to the water's edge, and here a small boat was always moored to a chain. The chain was stretched across the river, fixed to the staples driven into the rock on either side, and the boat was pulled backwards and forwards over the stream without aid from oars or paddles. From the opposite side a path led through the woods and across the fields to Penrith, and this was the route commonly used between Thwaite Hall and the town.

Major Garrow was a retired officer of Engineers, who had seen service in all parts of the world, and who was now spending the evening of his days on a small property which had come to him from his father. He held in his own hands about twenty acres of land, and he was the owner of one small farm close by, which was let to a tenant. That, together with his half-pay, and the interest of his wife's thousand pounds, sufficed to educate his children and keep the wolf at a comfortable distance from his door. He himself was a spare thin man, with quiet, lazy, literary habits. He had done the work of life, but had so done it as to permit of his enjoying that which was left to him. His sole remaining care was the establishment of his children; and, as far as he could see, he had no ground for anticipating disappointment. They were clever, good-looking, well-disposed young people, and upon the whole it may be said that the sun shone brightly on Thwaite Hall. Of Mrs. Garrow it may suffice to say that she always deserved such sunshine.

For years past it had been the practice of the family to have some sort of gathering at Thwaite Hall during Christmas. Godfrey Holmes had been left under the guardianship of Major Garrow, and, as he had always spent his Christmas holidays with his guardian, this, perhaps, had given rise to the practice. Then the Coverdales were cousins of the Garrows, and they had usually been there as children. At the Christmas last past the custom had been broken, for young Holmes had been abroad. Previous to that, they had all been children, excepting him. But now that they were to meet again, they were no longer children.

Elizabeth, at any rate, was not so, for she had already counted nineteen winters. And Isabella Holmes was coming. Now Isabella was two years older than Elizabeth, and had been educated in Brussels; moreover she was comparatively a stranger at Thwaite Hall, never having been at those early Christmas meetings.

And now I must take permission to begin my story by telling a lady's secret. Elizabeth Garrow had already been in love with Godfrey Holmes, or perhaps it might be more becoming to say that Godfrey Holmes had already been in love with her. They had already been engaged; and, alas! they had already agreed that that engagement should be broken off!

Young Holmes was now twenty-seven years of age, and was employed in a bank at Liverpool, not as a clerk, but as assistant manager, with a large salary. He was a man well to do in the world, who had money also of his own, and who might well afford to marry. Some two years since, on the eve of leaving Thwaite Hall, he had with low doubting whisper told Elizabeth that he loved her, and she had flown trembling to her mother. "Godfrey, my boy," the father said to him, as he parted with him the next morning, "Bessy is only a child, and too young to think of this yet." At the next Christmas Godfrey was in Italy, and the thing was gone by,—so at least the father and mother said to each other. But the young people had met in the summer, and one joyful letter had come from the girl home to her mother. "I have accepted him. Dearest, dearest mamma, I do love him. But don't tell papa yet, for I have not quite accepted him. I think I am sure, but I am not quite sure. I am not quite sure about him."

And then, two days after that, there had come a letter that was not at all joyful. "Dearest Mamma,—It is not to be. It is not written in the book. We have both agreed that it will not do. I am so glad that you have not told dear papa, for I could never make him understand. You will understand, for I shall tell you everything, down to his very words. But we have agreed that there shall be no quarrel. It shall be exactly as it was, and he will come at Christmas all the same. It would never do that he and papa should be separated, nor could we now put off Isabella. It is better so in every way, for there is and need be no quarrel. We still like each other. I am sure I like him, but I know that I should not make him happy as his wife. He says it is my fault. I, at any rate, have never told him that I thought it his." From all which it will be seen that the confidence between the mother and daughter was very close.

Elizabeth Garrow was a very good girl, but it might almost be a question whether she was not too good. She had learned, or thought that she had learned, that most girls are vapid, silly, and useless,—given chiefly to pleasure-seeking and a hankering after lovers; and she had resolved that she would not be such a one. Industry, self-denial, and a religious purpose in life, were the tasks which she set herself; and she went about the performance of them with much courage. But such tasks, though they are excellently well adapted to fit a young lady for the work of living, may also be carried too far, and thus have the effect of unfitting her for that work. When Elizabeth Garrow made up her mind that the finding of a husband was not the only purpose of life, she did very well. It is very well that a young lady should feel herself capable of going through the world happily without one. But in teaching herself this she also taught herself to think that there was a certain merit in refusing herself the natural delight of a lover, even though the possession of the lover were compatible with all her duties to herself, her father and mother, and the world at large. It was not that she had determined to have no lover. She made no such resolve, and when the proper lover came he was admitted to her heart. But she declared to herself unconsciously that she must put a guard upon herself, lest she should be betrayed into weakness by her own happiness. She had resolved that in loving her lord she would not worship him, and that in giving her heart she would only so give it as it should be given to a human creature like herself. She had acted on these high resolves, and hence it had come to pass,—not unnaturally,—that Mr. Godfrey Holmes had told her that it was "her fault."

She was a pretty, fair girl, with soft dark-brown hair, and soft long dark eyelashes. Her grey eyes, though quiet in their tone, were tender and lustrous. Her face was oval, and the lines of her cheek and chin perfect in their symmetry. She was generally quiet in her demeanour, but when moved she could rouse herself to great energy, and speak with feeling and almost with fire. Her fault was a reverence for martyrdom in general, and a feeling, of which she was unconscious, that it became a young woman to be unhappy in secret;—that it became a young woman I might rather say, to have a source of unhappiness hidden from the world in general, and endured without any detriment to her outward cheerfulness. We know the story of the Spartan boy who held the fox under his tunic. The fox was biting into him,—into the very entrails; but the young hero spake never a word. Now Bessy Garrow was inclined to think that it was a good thing to have a fox always biting, so that the torment caused no ruffling to her outward smiles. Now at this moment the fox within her bosom was biting her sore enough, but she bore it without flinching.

"If you would rather that he should not come I will have it arranged," her mother had said to her.

"Not for worlds," she had answered. "I should never think well of myself again."

Her mother had changed her own mind more than once as to the conduct in this matter which might be best for her to follow, thinking solely of her daughter's welfare. "If he comes they will be reconciled, and she will be happy," had been her first idea. But then there was a stern fixedness of purpose in Bessy's words when she spoke of Mr. Holmes, which had expelled this hope, and Mrs. Garrow had for awhile thought it better that the young man should not come. But Bessy would not permit this. It would vex her father, put out of course the arrangements of other people, and display weakness on her own part. He should come, and she would endure without flinching while the fox gnawed at her.

That battle of the mistletoe had been fought on the morning before Christmas-day, and the Holmes's came on Christmas-eve. Isabella was comparatively a stranger, and therefore received at first the greater share of attention. She and Elizabeth had once seen each other, and for the last year or two had corresponded, but personally they had never been intimate. Unfortunately for the latter, that story of Godfrey's offer and acceptance had been communicated to Isabella, as had of course the immediately subsequent story of their separation. But now it would be almost impossible to avoid the subject in conversation. "Dearest Isabella, let it be as though it had never been," she had said in one of her letters. But sometimes it is very difficult to let things be as though they had never been.

The first evening passed over very well. The two Coverdale girls were there, and there had been much talking and merry laughter, rather juvenile in its nature, but on the whole none the worse for that. Isabella Holmes was a fine, tall, handsome girl; good-humoured, and well disposed to be pleased; rather Frenchified in her manners, and quite able to take care of herself. But she was not above round games, and did not turn up her nose at the boys. Godfrey behaved himself excellently, talking much to the Major, but by no means avoiding Miss Garrow. Mrs. Garrow, though she had known him since he was a boy, had taken an aversion to him since he had quarrelled with her daughter; but there was no room on this first night for showing such aversion, and everything went off well.

"Godfrey is very much improved," the Major said to his wife that night.

"Do you think so?"

"Indeed I do. He has filled out and become a fine man."

"In personal appearance, you mean. Yes, he is well-looking enough."

"And in his manner too. He is doing uncommonly well in Liverpool, I can tell you; and if he should think of Bessy— "

"There is nothing of that sort," said Mrs. Garrow.

"He did speak to me, you know,—two years ago. Bessy was too young then, and so indeed was he. But if she likes him— "

"I don't think she does."

"Then there's and end of it." And so they went to bed.

"Frank," said the sister to her elder brother, knocking at his door when they had all gone up stairs, "may I come in,—if you are not in bed?"

"In bed," said he, looking up with some little pride from his Greek book; "I've one hundred and fifty lines to do before I can get to bed. It'll be two, I suppose. I've got to mug uncommon hard these holidays. I have only one more half, you know, and then— "

"Don't overdo it, Frank."

"No; I won't overdo it. I mean to take one day a week, and work eight hours a day on the other five. That will be forty hours a week, and will give me just two hundred hours for the holidays. I have got it all down here on a table. That will be a hundred and five for Greek play, forty for Algebra— " and so he explained to her the exact destiny of all his long hours of proposed labour. He had as yet been home a day and a half, and had succeeded in drawing out with red lines and blue figures the table which he showed her. "If I can do that, it will be pretty well; won't it?"

"But, Frank, you have come home for your holidays,—to enjoy yourself?"

"But a fellow must work now-a-days."

"Don't overdo it, dear; that's all. But, Frank, I could not rest if I went to bed without speaking to you. You made me unhappy to-day."

"Did I, Bessy?"

"You called me a Puritan, and then you quoted that ill-natured French proverb at me. Do you really believe your sister thinks evil, Frank?" and as she spoke she put her arm caressingly round his neck.

"Of course I don't."

"Then why say so? Harry is so much younger and so thoughtless that I can bear what he says without so much suffering. But if you and I are not friends I shall be very wretched. If you knew how I have looked forward to your coming home!"

"I did not mean to vex you, and I won't say such things again."

"That's my own Frank. What I said to mamma, I said because I thought it right; but you must not say that I am a Puritan. I would do anything in my power to make your holidays bright and pleasant. I know that boys require so much more to amuse them than girls do. Good night, dearest; pray don't overdo yourself with work, and do take care of your eyes." So saying she kissed him and went her way. In twenty minutes after that, he had gone to sleep over his book; and when he woke up to find the candle guttering down, he resolved that he would not begin his measured hours till Christmas-day was fairly over.

The morning of Christmas-day passed very quietly. They all went to church, and then sat round the fire chatting until the four-o'clock dinner was ready. The Coverdale girls thought it was rather more dull than former Thwaite Hall festivities, and Frank was seen to yawn. But then everybody knows that the real fun of Christmas never begins till the day itself be passed. The beef and pudding are ponderous, and unless there be absolute children in the party, there is a difficulty in grafting any special afternoon amusements on the Sunday pursuits of the morning. In the evening they were to have a dance;—that had been distinctly promised to Patty Coverdale; but the dance would not commence till eight. The beef and pudding were ponderous, but with due efforts they were overcome and disappeared. The glass of port was sipped, the almonds and raisins were nibbled, and then the ladies left the room. Ten minutes after that Elizabeth found herself seated with Isabella Holmes over the fire in her father's little book-room. It was not by her that this meeting was arranged, for she dreaded such a constrained confidence; but of course it could not be avoided, and perhaps it might be as well now as hereafter.

"Bessy," said the elder girl, "I am dying to be alone with you for a moment."

"Well, you shall not die; that is, if being alone with me will save you."

"I have so much to say to you. And if you have any true friendship in you, you also will have so much to say to me." Miss Garrow perhaps had no true friendship in her at that moment, for she would gladly have avoided saying anything, had that been possible. But, in order to prove that she was not deficient in friendship, she gave her friend her hand.

"And now tell me everything about Godfrey," said Isabella.

"Dear Bella, I have nothing to tell;—literally nothing."

"That is nonsense. Stop a moment, dear, and understand that I do not mean to offend you. It cannot be that you have nothing to tell, if you choose to tell it. You are not the girl to have accepted Godfrey without loving him, nor is he the man to have asked you without loving you. When you write me word that you have changed your mind, as you might about a dress, of course I know you have not told me all. Now I insist upon knowing it,—that is, if we are to be friends. I would not speak a word to Godfrey till I had seen you, in order that I might hear your story first."

"Indeed, Bella, there is no story to tell."

"Then I must ask him."

"If you wish to play the part of a true friend to me, you will let the matter pass by and say nothing. You must understand that, circumstanced as we are, your brother's visit here,—what I mean is, that it is very difficult for me to act and speak exactly as I should do, and a few unfortunate words spoken may make my position unendurable."

"Will you answer me one question?"

"I cannot tell. I think I will."

"Do you love him?" For a moment or two Bessy remained silent, striving to arrange her words so that they should contain no falsehood, and yet betray no truth. "Ah, I see you do," continued Miss Holmes. "But of course you do. Why else did you accept him?"

"I fancied that I did, as young ladies do sometimes fancy."

"And will you say that you do not, now?" Again Bessy was silent, and then her friend rose from her seat. "I see it all," she said. "What a pity it was that you both had not some friend like me by you at the time! But perhaps it may not be too late."

I need not repeat at length all the protestations which upon this were poured forth with hot energy by poor Bessy. She endeavoured to explain how great had been the difficulty of her position. This Christmas visit had been arranged before that unhappy affair at Liverpool had occurred. Isabella's visit had been partly one of business, it being necessary that certain money affairs should be arranged between her, her brother, and the Major. "I determined," said Bessy, "not to let my feelings stand in the way; and hoped that things might settle down to their former friendly footing. I already fear that I have been wrong, but it will be ungenerous in you to punish me." Then she went on to say that if anybody attempted to interfere with her, she should at once go away to her mother's sister, who lived at Hexham, in Northumberland.

Then came the dance, and the hearts of Kate and Patty Coverdale were at last happy. But here again poor Bessy was made to understand how terribly difficult was this experiment of entertaining on a footing of friendship a lover with whom she had quarrelled only a month or two before. That she must as a necessity become the partner of Godfrey Holmes she had already calculated, and so much she was prepared to endure. Her brothers would of course dance with the Coverdale girls, and her father would of course stand up with Isabella. There was no other possible arrangement, at any rate as a beginning. She had schooled herself too as to the way in which she would speak to him on the occasion, and how she would remain mistress of herself and of her thoughts. But when the time came the difficulty was almost too much for her.

"You do not care much for dancing, if I remember?" said he.

"Oh yes, I do. Not as Patty Coverdale does. It's a passion with her. But then I am older than Patty Coverdale." After that he was silent for a minute or two.

"It seems so odd to me to be here again," he said. It was odd;—she felt that it was odd. But he ought not to have said so.

"Two years make a great difference. The boys have grown so much."

"Yes, and there are other things," said he.

"Bella was never here before; at least not with you."

"No. But I did not exactly mean that. All that would not make the place so strange. But your mother seems altered to me. She used to be almost like my own mother."

"I suppose she finds that you are a more formidable person as you grow older. It was all very well scolding you when you were a clerk in the bank, but it does not do to scold the manager. These are the penalties men pay for becoming great."

"It is not my greatness that stands in my way, but— "

"Then I'm sure I cannot say what it is. But Patty will scold you if you do not mind the figure, though you were the whole Board of Directors packed into one. She won't respect you if you neglect your present work."

When Bessy went to bed that night she began to feel that she had attempted too much. "Mamma," she said, "could I not make some excuse and go away to Aunt Mary?"

"What, now?"

"Yes, mamma; now; to-morrow. I need not say that it will make me very unhappy to be away at such a time, but I begin to think that it will be better."

"What will papa say?"

"You must tell him all."

"And Aunt Mary must be told also. You would not like that. Has he said anything?"

"No, nothing;—very little, that is. But Bella has spoken to me. Oh, mamma, I think we have been very wrong in this. That is, I have been wrong. I feel as though I should disgrace myself, and turn the whole party here into a misfortune."

It would be dreadful, that telling of the story to her father and to her aunt, and such a necessity must, if possible, be avoided. Should such a necessity actually come, the former task would, no doubt, be done by her mother, but that would not lighten the load materially. After a fortnight she would again meet her father, and would be forced to discuss it. "I will remain if it be possible," she said; "but, mamma, if I wish to go, you will not stop me?" Her mother promised that she would not stop her, but strongly advised her to stand her ground.

On the following morning, when she came down stairs before breakfast, she found Frank standing in the hall with his gun of which he was trying the lock. "It is not loaded, is it, Frank?" said she.

"Oh dear, no; no one thinks of loading now-a-days till he has got out of the house. Directly after breakfast I am going across with Godfrey to the back of Greystock, to see after some moor-fowl. He asked me to go, and I couldn't well refuse."

"Of course not. Why should you?"

"It will be deuced hard work to make up the time. I was to have been up at four this morning, but that alarum went off and never woke me. However, I shall be able to do something to-night."

"Don't make a slavery of your holidays, Frank. What's the good of having a new gun if you're not to use it?"

"It's not the new gun. I'm not such a child as that comes to. But, you see, Godfrey is here, and one ought to be civil to him. I'll tell you what I want you girls to do, Bessy. You must come and meet us on our way home. Come over in the boat and along the path to the Patterdale road. We'll be there under the hill at about five."

"And if you are not, we are to wait in the snow?"

"Don't make difficulties, Bessy. I tell you we will be there. We are to go in the cart, and so shall have plenty of time."

"And how do you know the other girls will go?"

"Why, to tell you the truth, Patty Coverdale has promised. As for Miss Holmes, if she won't, why you must leave her at home with mamma. But Kate and Patty can't come without you."

"Your discretion has found that out, has it?"

"They say so. But you will come; won't you Bessy? As for waiting, it's all nonsense. Of course you can walk on. But we'll be at the stile by five. I've got my watch, you know." And then Bessy promised him. What would she not have done for him that was in her power to do?

"Go! Of course I'll go," said Miss Holmes. "I'm up to anything. I'd have gone with them this morning, and have taken a gun if they'd asked me. But, by the bye, I'd better not."

"Why not?" said Patty, who was hardly yet without fear lest something should mar the expedition.

"What will three gentlemen do with four ladies?"

"Oh, I forgot," said Patty innocently.

"I'm sure I don't care," said Kate; "you may have Harry if you like."

"Thank you for nothing," said Miss Holmes. "I want one for myself. It's all very well for you to make the offer, but what should I do if Harry wouldn't have me? There are two sides, you know, to every bargain."

"I'm sure he isn't anything to me," said Kate. "Why, he's not quite seventeen years old yet!"

"Poor boy! What a shame to dispose of him so soon. We'll let him off for a year or two; won't we, Miss Coverdale? But as there seems by acknowledgement to be one beau with unappropriated services— "

"I'm sure I have appropriated nobody," said Patty, "and didn't intend."

"Godfrey, then, is the only knight whose services are claimed," said Miss Holmes, looking at Bessy. Bessy made no immediate answer with either her eyes or tongue; but when the Coverdales were gone, she took her new friend to task.

"How can you fill those young girls' heads with such nonsense?"

"Nature has done that, my dear."

"But nature should be trained; should it not? You will make them think that those foolish boys are in love with them."

"The foolish boys, as you call them, will look after that themselves. It seems to me that the foolish boys know what they are about better than some of their elders." And then, after a moment's pause, she added, "As for my brother, I have no patience with him."

"Pray do not discuss your brother," said Bessy. "And, Bella, unless you wish to drive me away, pray do not speak of him and me together as you did just now."

"Are you so bad as that,—that the slightest commonplace joke upsets you? Would not his services be due to you as a matter of course? If you are so sore about it, you will betray your own secret."

"I have no secret,—none at least from you, or from mamma; and, indeed, none from him. We were both very foolish, thinking that we knew each other and our own hearts, when we knew neither."

"I hate to hear people talk of knowing their hearts. My idea is, that if you like a young man, and he asks you to marry him, you ought to have him. That is, if there is enough to live on. I don't know what more is wanted. But girls are getting to talk and think as though they were to send their hearts through some fiery furnace of trial before they may give them up to a husband's keeping. I'm not at all sure that the French fashion is not the best, and that these things shouldn't be managed by the fathers and mothers, or perhaps by the family lawyers. Girls who are so intent upon knowing their own hearts generally end by knowing nobody's heart but their own; and then they die old maids."

"Better that than give themselves to the keeping of those they don't know and cannot esteem."

"That's a matter of taste. I mean to take the first that comes, so long as he looks like a gentleman, and has not less than eight hundred a year. Now Godfrey does look like a gentleman, and has double that. If I had such a chance I shouldn't think twice about it."

"But I have no such chance. And if you have not, you would not think of it at all. That's the way the wind blows; is it?"

"No, no. Oh, Bella, pray, pray leave me alone. Pray do not interfere. There is no wind blowing in any way. All that I want is your silence and your sympathy."

"Very well. I will be silent and sympathetic as the grave. Only don't imagine that I am cold as the grave also. I don't exactly appreciate your ideas; but if I can do no good, I will at any rate endeavour to do no harm."

After lunch, at about three, they started on their walk, and managed to ferry themselves over the river. "Oh, do let me, Bessy," said Kate Coverdale. "I understand all about it. Look here, Miss Holmes. You pull the chain through your hands— "

"And inevitably tear your gloves to pieces," said Miss Holmes. Kate certainly had done so, and did not seem to be particularly well pleased with the accident. "There's a nasty nail in the chain," she said. "I wonder those stupid boys did not tell us."

Of course they reached the trysting-place much too soon, and were very tired of walking up and down to keep their feet warm, before the sportsmen came up. But this was their own fault, seeing that they had reached the stile half an hour before the time fixed.

"I never will go anywhere to meet gentlemen again," said Miss Holmes. "It is most preposterous that ladies should be left in the snow for an hour. Well, young men, what sport have you had?"

"I shot the big black cock," said Harry.

"Did you indeed?" said Kate Coverdale.

"And here are the feathers out of his tail for you. He dropped them in the water, and I had to go in after them up to my middle. But I told you that I would, so I was determined to get them."

"Oh you silly, silly boy," said Kate. "But I'll keep them for ever. I will indeed." This was said a little apart, for Harry had managed to draw the young lady aside before he presented the feathers.

Frank had also his trophies for Patty, and the tale to tell of his own prowess. In that he was a year older than his brother, he was by a year's growth less ready to tender his present to his lady-love, openly in the presence of them all. But he found his opportunity, and then he and Patty went on a little in advance. Kate also was deep in her consolations to Harry for his ducking; and therefore the four disposed of themselves in the manner previously suggested by Miss Holmes. Miss Holmes, therefore, and her brother, and Bessy Garrow, were left together in the path, and discussed the performances of the day in a manner that elicited no very ecstatic interest. So they walked for a mile, and by degrees the conversation between them dwindled down almost to nothing.

"There is nothing I dislike so much as coming out with people younger than myself," said Miss Holmes. "One always feels so old and dull. Listen to those children there; they make me feel as though I were an old maiden aunt, brought out with them to do propriety."

"Patty won't at all approve if she hears you call her a child."

"Nor shall I approve, if she treats me like an old woman," and then she stepped on and joined the children. "I wouldn't spoil even their sport if I could help it," she said to herself. "But with them I shall only be a temporary nuisance; if I remain behind I shall become a permanent evil." And thus Bessy and her old lover were left by themselves.

"I hope you will get on well with Bella," said Godfrey, when they had remained silent for a minute or two.

"Oh, yes. She is so good-natured and light-spirited that everybody must like her. She has been used to so much amusement and active life, that I know she must find it very dull here."

"She is never dull anywhere,—even at Liverpool, which, for a young lady, I sometimes think the dullest place on earth. I know it is for a man."

"A man who has work to do can never be dull; can he?"

"Indeed he can; as dull as death. I am so often enough. I have never been very bright there, Bessy, since you left us." There was nothing in his calling her Bessy, for it had become a habit with him since they were children; and they had formerly agreed that everything between them should be as it had been before that foolish whisper of love had been spoken and received. Indeed, provision had been made by them specially on this point, so that there need be no awkwardness in this mode of addressing each other. Such provision had seemed to be very prudent, but it hardly had the desired effect on the present occasion.

"I hardly know what you mean by brightness," she said, after a pause. "Perhaps it is not intended that people's lives should be what you call bright."

"Life ought to be as bright as we can make it."

"It all depends on the meaning of the word. I suppose we are not very bright here at Thwaite Hall, but yet we think ourselves very happy."

"I am sure you are," said Godfrey. "I very often think of you here."

"We always think of places where we have been when we were young," said Bessy; and then again they walked on for some way in silence, and Bessy began to increase her pace with the view of catching the children. The present walk to her was anything but bright, and she bethought herself with dismay that there were still two miles before she reached the Ferry.

"Bessy," Godfrey said at last. And then he stopped as though he were doubtful how to proceed. She, however, did not say a word, but walked on quickly, as though her only hope was in catching the party before her. But they also were walking quickly, for Bella had determined that she would not be caught.

"Bessy, I must speak to you once of what passed between us at Liverpool."

"Must you?" said she.

"Unless you positively forbid it."

"Stop, Godfrey," she said. And they did stop in the path, for now she no longer thought of putting an end to her embarrassment by overtaking her companions. "If any such words are necessary for your comfort, it would hardly become me to forbid them. Were I to speak so harshly you would accuse me afterwards in your own heart. It must be for you to judge whether it is well to re-open a wound that is nearly healed."

"But with me it is not nearly healed. The wound is open always."

"There are some hurts," she said, "which do not admit of an absolute and perfect cure, unless after long years." As she said so, she could not but think how much better was his chance of such perfect cure than her own. With her,—so she said to herself,—such curing was all but impossible; whereas with him, it was as impossible that the injury should last.

"Bessy," he said, and he again stopped her on the narrow path, standing immediately before her on the way, "you remember all the circumstances that made us part?"

"Yes; I think I remember them."

"And you still think that we were right to part?"

She paused for a moment before she answered him; but it was only for a moment, and then she spoke quite firmly. "Yes, Godfrey, I do; I have thought about it much since then. I have thought, I fear, to no good purpose about aught else. But I have never thought that we had been unwise in that."

"And yet I think you loved me."

"I am bound to confess I did so, as otherwise I must confess myself a liar. I told you at the time that I loved you, and I told you so truly. But it is better, ten times better, that those who love should part, even though they still should love, than that two should be joined together who are incapable of making each other happy. Remember what you told me."

"I do remember."

"You found yourself unhappy in your engagement, and you said it was my fault."

"Bessy, there is my hand. If you have ceased to love me, there is an end of it. But if you love me still, let all that be forgotten."

"Forgotten, Godfrey! How can it be forgotten? You were unhappy, and it was my fault. My fault, as it would be if I tried to solace a sick child with arithmetic, or feed a dog with grass. I had no right to love you, knowing you as I did; and knowing also that my ways would not be your ways. My punishment I understand, and it is not more than I can bear; but I had hoped that your punishment would have been soon over."

"You are too proud, Bessy."

"That is very likely. Frank says that I am a Puritan, and pride was the worst of their sins."

"Too proud and unbending. In marriage should not the man and woman adapt themselves to each other?"

"When they are married, yes. And every girl who thinks of marrying should know that in very much she must adapt herself to her husband. But I do not think that a woman should be the ivy, to take the direction of every branch of the tree to which she clings. If she does so, what can be her own character? But we must go on, or we shall be too late."

"And you will give me no other answer?"

"None other, Godfrey. Have you not just now, at this very moment, told me that I was too proud? Can it be possible that you should wish to tie yourself for life to female pride? And if you tell me that now, at such a moment as this, what would you tell me in the close intimacy of married life, when the trifles of every day would have worn away the courtesies of guest and lover?"

There was a sharpness of rebuke in this which Godfrey Holmes could not at the moment overcome. Nevertheless he knew the girl, and understood the workings of her heart and mind. Now, in her present state, she could be unbending, proud, and almost rough. In that she had much to lose in declining the renewed offer which he made her, she would, as it were, continually prompt herself to be harsh and inflexible. Had he been poor, had she not loved him, had not all good things seemed to have attended the promise of such a marriage, she would have been less suspicious of herself in receiving the offer, and more gracious in replying to it. Had he lost all his money before he came back to her, she would have taken him at once; or had he been deprived of an eye, or become crippled in his legs, she would have done so. But, circumstanced as he was, she had no motive to tenderness. There was an organic defect in her character, which no doubt was plainly marked by its own bump in her cranium,—the bump of philomartyrdom, it might properly be called. She had shipwrecked her own happiness in rejecting Godfrey Holmes; but it seemed to her to be the proper thing that a well-behaved young lady should shipwreck her own happiness. For the last month or two she had been tossed about by the waters and was nearly drowned. Now there was beautiful land again close to her, and a strong pleasant hand stretched out to save her. But though she had suffered terribly among the waves, she still thought it wrong to be saved. It would be so pleasant to take that hand, so sweet, so joyous, that it surely must be wrong. That was her doctrine; and Godfrey Holmes, though he hardly analyzed the matter, partly understood that it was so. And yet, if once she were landed on that green island, she would be so happy. She spoke with scorn of a woman clinging to a tree like ivy; and yet, were she once married, no woman would cling to her husband with sweeter feminine tenacity than Bessy Garrow. He spoke no further word to her as he walked home, but in handing her down to the ferry-boat he pressed her hand. For a second it seemed as though she had returned this pressure. If so, the action was involuntary, and her hand instantly resumed its stiffness to his touch.

It was late that night when Major Garrow went to his bedroom, but his wife was still up, waiting for him. "Well," said she, "what has he said to you? He has been with you above an hour."

"Such stories are not very quickly told; and in this case it was necessary to understand him very accurately. At length I think I do understand him."

It is not necessary to repeat at length all that was said on that night between Major and Mrs. Garrow, as to the offer which had now for a third time been made to their daughter. On that evening after the ladies had gone, and when the two boys had taken themselves off, Godfrey Holmes told his tale to his host, and had honestly explained to him what he believed to be the state of his daughter's feelings. "Now you know all," said he. "I do believe that she loves me, and if she does, perhaps she may still listen to you." Major Garrow did not feel sure that he "knew it all." But when he had fully discussed the matter that night with his wife, then he thought that perhaps he had arrived at that knowledge.

On the following morning Bessy learned from the maid, at an early hour, that Godfrey Holmes had left Thwaite Hall and gone back to Liverpool. To the girl she said nothing on the subject, but she felt obliged to say a word or two to Bella. "It is his coming that I regret," she said;—"that he should have had the trouble and annoyance for nothing. I acknowledge that it was my fault, and I am very sorry."

"It cannot be helped," said Miss Holmes, somewhat gravely. "As to his misfortunes, I presume that his journeys between here and Liverpool are not the worst of them."

After breakfast on that day Bessy was summoned into her father's book-room, and found him there, and her mother also. "Bessy," said he, "sit down, my dear. You know why Godfrey has left us this morning?"

Bessy walked round the room, so that in sitting she might be close to her mother and take her mother's hand in her own. "I suppose I do, papa," she said.

"He was with me late last night, Bessy; and when he told me what had passed between you I agreed with him that he had better go."

"It was better that he should go, papa."

"But he has left a message for you."

"A message, papa?"

"Yes, Bessy. And your mother agrees with me that it had better be given to you. It is this,—that if you will send him word to come again, he will be here by Twelfth-night. He came before on my invitation, but if he returns it must be on yours."

"Oh, papa, I cannot."

"I do not say that you can, but think of it calmly before you altogether refuse. You shall give me your answer on New Year's morning."

"Mamma knows that it would be impossible," said Bessy.

"Not impossible, dearest.

"In such a matter you should do what you believe to be right," said her father.

"If I were to ask him here again, it would be telling him that I would— "

"Exactly, Bessy. It would be telling him that you would be his wife.

He would understand it so, and so would your mother and I. It must be so understood altogether."

"But, papa, when we were at Liverpool— "

"I have told him everything, dearest," said Mrs. Garrow.

"I think I understand the whole," said the Major; "and in such a matter as this I will not give you counsel on either side. But you must remember that in making up your mind, you must think of him as well as of yourself. If you do not love him;—if you feel that as his wife you should not love him, there is not another word to be said. I need not explain to my daughter that under such circumstances she would be wrong to encourage the visits of a suitor. But your mother says you do love him."

"Oh, mamma!"

"I will not ask you. But if you do;—if you have so told him, and allowed him to build up an idea of his life-happiness on such telling, you will, I think, sin greatly against him by allowing a false feminine pride to mar his happiness. When once a girl has confessed to a man that she loves him, the confession and the love together put upon her the burden of a duty towards him, which she cannot with impunity throw aside." Then he kissed her, and bidding her give him a reply on the morning of the new year, left her with her mother.

She had four days for consideration, and they went past her by no means easily. Could she have been alone with her mother, the struggle would not have been so painful; but there was the necessity that she should talk to Isabella Holmes, and the necessity also that she should not neglect the Coverdales. Nothing could have been kinder than Bella. She did not speak on the subject till the morning of the last day, and then only in a very few words. "Bessy," she said, "as you are great, be merciful."

"But I am not great, and it would not be mercy."

"As to that," said Bella "he has surely a right to his own opinion."

On that evening she was sitting alone in her room when her mother came to her, and her eyes were red with weeping. Pen and paper were before her, as though she were resolved to write, but hitherto no word had been written.

"Well, Bessy," said her mother, sitting down close beside her; "is the deed done?"

"What deed, mamma? Who says that I am to do it?"

"The deed is not the writing, but the resolution to write. Five words will be sufficient,—if only those five words may be written."

"It is for one's whole life, mamma. For his life, as well as my own."

"True, Bessy;—that is quite true. But equally true whether you bid him come or allow him to remain away. That task of making up one's mind for life, must at last be done in some special moment of that life."

"Mamma, mamma; tell me what I should do."

But this Mrs. Garrow would not do. "I will write the words for you if you like," she said, "but it is you who must resolve that they shall be written. I cannot bid my darling go away and leave me for another home;—I can only say that in my heart I do believe that home would be a happy one."

It was morning before the note was written, but when the morning came Bessy had written it and brought it to her mother. "You must take it to papa," she said. Then she went and hid herself from all eyes till the noon had passed. "Dear Godfrey," the letter ran, "Papa says that you will return on Wednesday if I write to ask you. Do come back to us,—if you wish it. Yours always, Bessy."

"It is as good as though she had filled the sheet," said the Major. But in sending it to Godfrey Holmes, he did not omit a few accompanying remarks of his own.

An answer came from Godfrey by return of post; and on the afternoon of the sixth of January, Frank Garrow drove over to the station at Penrith to meet him. On their way back to Thwaite Hall there grew up a very close confidence between the two future brothers-in-law, and Frank explained with great perspicuity a little plan which he had arranged himself. "As soon as it is dark, so that she won't see it, Harry will hang it up in the dining-room," he said, "and mind you go in there before you go anywhere else."

"I am very glad you have come back, Godfrey," said the Major, meeting him in the hall.

"God bless you, dear Godfrey," said Mrs. Garrow, "you will find Bessy in the dining-room," she whispered; but in so whispering she was quite unconscious of the mistletoe bough.

And so also was Bessy, nor do I think that she was much more conscious when that introduction was over. Godfrey had made all manner of promises to Frank, but when the moment arrived, he had found the moment too important for any special reference to the little bough above his head. Not so, however, Patty Coverdale. "It's a shame," she said, bursting out of the room, "and if I'd known what you had done, nothing on earth should have induced me to go in. I won't enter the room till I know that you have taken it out." Nevertheless her sister Kate was bold enough to solve the mystery before the evening was over.

The Journey to Panama

Originally appeared in *The Victoria Regia: Original Contributions in Poetry and Prose*, edited by Adelaide A. Proctor (London: Emily Faithfull and Co. at the Victoria Press, 1861). Emily Faithfull's press employed female compositors and, according to Michael Sadleir in *Trollope: A Bibliography* (1928), was 'designed to show that printing and its allied trades offered new opportunities for the remunerative employment of women and girls, which would not conflict with existing wage conditions or raise social or trade prejudices.' Contributions to *Victoria Regia* were made gratuitously, and Trollope's fellow-benefactors included Tennyson, Mrs. Oliphant, Harriet Martineau, Patmore and Arnold. As Richard Mullen has pointed out, the theme of the story, 'the plight of a woman without money, forced to seek a refuge in an arranged marriage, was an appropriate one for Emily Faithful.' The story was written by November 1861, when *Victoria Regia* appeared, and reprinted in *Lotta Schmidt and Other Stories* (1867). It was inspired by Trollope's 1858–9 Caribbean trip. For further accounts of the various settings, see *The West Indies and the Spanish Main* (1859). St. Thomas is discussed in chs. 1 and 15, and Aspinwall/Colon in ch. 26. The romances and acquaintances of shipboard life also feature in Trollope's novel *The Bertrams* (1859). In an 1867 letter, Trollope revealed the story's factual basis: 'It fell to my lot once to tell a lady who was going out to be married, (she and I being in the same ship,)—that news had met us that her intended husband was dead. I left her seated on the floor of a small ladies' cabin, &

she at once asked to have a large trunk brought to her. In the course of an hour I found her packing & unpacking the trunk, putting the new wedding clothes at the bottom & bringing the old things, now suitable for her use, to the top. And so she employed herself during the entire day.'

THERE IS perhaps no form of life in which men and women of the present day frequently find themselves for a time existing, so unlike their customary conventional life, as that experienced on board the large ocean steamers. On the voyages so made, separate friendships are formed and separate enmities are endured. Certain lines of temporary politics are originated by the energetic, and intrigues, generally innocent in their conclusions, are carried on with the keenest spirit by those to whom excitement is necessary; whereas the idle and torpid sink into insignificance and general contempt,—as it is their lot to do on board ship as in other places. But the enjoyments and activity of such a life do not display themselves till the third or fourth day of the voyage. The men and women at first regard each with distrust and ill-concealed dislike. They by no means anticipate the strong feelings which are to arise, and look forward to ten, fifteen, or twenty days of gloom or sea-sickness. Sea-sickness disappears, as a general condition, on the evening of the second day, and the gloom about noon on the fourth. Then the men begin to think that the women are not so ugly, vulgar, and insipid; and the women drop their monosyllables, discontinue the close adherence to their own niches, which they first observed, and become affable, perhaps even beyond their wont on shore. And alliances spring up among the men themselves. On their first entrance to this new world, they generally regard each other with marked aversion, each thinking that those nearest to him are low fellows, or perhaps worse; but by the fourth day, if not sooner, every man has his two or three intimate friends with whom he talks and smokes, and to whom he communicates those peculiar politics, and perhaps intrigues, of his own voyage. The female friendships are slower in their growth, for the suspicion of women is perhaps stronger than that of men; but when grown they also are stronger, and exhibit themselves sometimes in instances of feminine affection.

But the most remarkable alliances are those made between gentlemen and ladies. This is a matter of course on board ship quite as much as on shore, and it is of such an alliance that the present tale purports to tell the story. Such friendships, though they may be very dear, can seldom be very lasting. Though they may be full of sweet romance,—for people become very romantic among the discomforts of a sea voyage—such romance is generally short-lived and delusive, and occasionally is dangerous.

There are several of these great ocean routes, of which by the common consent, as it seems, of the world England is the centre. There is the Great Eastern line, running from Southampton across the Bay of Biscay and up the Mediterranean. It crosses the Isthmus of Suez, and branches away to Australia, to India, to Ceylon, and to China. There is the great American line, traversing the Atlantic to New York and Boston with the regularity of clockwork. The voyage here is so much a matter of every-day routine, that romance has become scarce upon the route. There are one or two other North American lines, perhaps open to the same objection. Then there is the line of packets to the African coast,—very romantic as I am given to understand; and there is the great West-Indian route, to which the present little history is attached,—great, not on account of our poor West Indian Islands, which cannot at the present moment make anything great, but because it spreads itself out from thence to Mexico and Cuba, to Guiana and the republics of Grenada and Venezuela, to Central America, the Isthmus of Panama, and from thence to California, Vancouver's Island, Peru and Chili.

It may be imagined how various are the tribes which leave the shores of Great Britain by this route. There are Frenchmen for the French sugar islands, as a rule not very romantic; there are old Spaniards, Spaniards of Spain, seeking to renew their fortunes amidst the ruins of their former empire; and new Spaniards—Spaniards, that is, of the American republics, who speak Spanish, but are unlike the Don both in manners and physiognomy,—men and women with a touch perhaps of Indian blood, very keen after dollars, and not much given to the graces of life. There are Dutchmen too, and Danes, going out to their own islands. There are citizens of the stars and stripes, who find their way everywhere—and, alas! perhaps, now also citizens of the new Southern flag, with the palmetto leaf. And there are Englishmen of every shade and class, and Englishwomen also.

It is constantly the case that women are doomed to make the long voyage alone. Some are going out to join their husbands, some to find a husband, some few peradventure to leave a husband. Girls who have been educated at home in England, return to their distant homes across the Atlantic, and others follow their relatives who have gone before them as pioneers into a strange land. It must not be supposed that these females absolutely embark in solitude, putting their feet upon the deck without the aid of any friendly arm. They are generally consigned to some prudent elder, and appear as they first show themselves on the ship to belong to a party. But as often as not their real loneliness shows itself after a while. The prudent elder is not, perhaps, congenial; and by the evening of the fourth day a new friendship is created.

Not a long time since such a friendship was formed under the circumstances which I am now about to tell. A young man—not very young, for he had turned his thirtieth year, but still a young man—left Southampton by one of the large West Indian steam-boats, purposing to pass over the Isthmus of Panama, and thence up to California and Vancouver's Island. It would be too long to tell the cause which led to these distant voyagings. Suffice to say, it was not the accursed hunger after gold—*auri sacra fames*—which so took him; nor had he any purpose of permanently settling himself in those distant colonies of Great Britain. He was at the time a widower, and perhaps his home was bitter to him without the young wife whom he had early lost. As he stepped on board he was accompanied by a gentleman some fifteen years his senior, who was to be the companion of his sleeping apartment as far as St. Thomas. The two had been introduced to each other, and therefore appeared as friends on board the "Serrapiqui;" but their acquaintance had commenced in Southampton, and my hero, Ralph Forrest by name, was alone in the world as he stood looking over the side of the ship at the retreating shores of Hampshire.

"I say, old fellow, we'd better see about our places," said his new friend, slapping him on his back. Mr. Matthew Morris was an old traveller, and knew how to become intimate with his temporary allies at a very short notice. A long course of travelling had knocked all bashfulness out of him and when he had a mind to do so he could make any man his brother in half-an-hour, and any woman his sister in ten minutes.

"Places? what places?" said Forrest.

"A pretty fellow you are to go to California. If you don't look sharper than that you'll get little to drink and nothing to eat till you come back again. Don't you know the ship's as full as ever she can hold?"

Forrest acknowledged that she was full.

"There are places at table for about a hundred, and we have a hundred and thirty on board. As a matter of course those who don't look sharp will have to scramble. However I've put cards on the plates and taken the seats. We had better go down and see that none of these Spanish fellows oust us." So Forrest descended after his friend, and found that the long tables were already nearly full of expectant dinner-eaters. When he took his place a future neighbour informed him, not in the most gracious voice, that he was encroaching on a lady's seat; and when he immediately attempted to leave that which he held, Mr. Matthew Morris forbade him to do so. Thus a little contest arose, which, however, happily was brought to a close without bloodshed. The lady was not present at the moment, and the grumpy gentleman agreed to secure for himself a vacant seat on the other side.

For the first three days the lady did not show herself. The grumpy gentleman, who, as Forrest afterwards understood, was the owner of stores in Bridgetown, Barbadoes, had other ladies with him also. First came forth his daughter, creeping down to dinner on the second day, declaring that she would be unable to eat a morsel, and prophesying that she would be forced to retire in five minutes. On this occasion, however, she agreeably surprised herself and her friends. Then came the grumpy gentleman's wife, and the grumpy gentleman's wife's brother—on whose constitution the sea seemed to have an effect quite as violent as on that of the ladies; and lastly, at breakfast on the fourth day, appeared Miss Viner, and took her place as Mr. Forrest's neighbour at his right hand.

He had seen her before on deck, as she lay on one of the benches, vainly endeavouring to make herself comfortable, and had remarked to his companion that she was very unattractive and almost ugly. Dear young ladies, it is thus that men always speak of you when they first see you on board ship! She was disconsolate, sick at heart, and ill at ease in body also. She did not like the sea. She did not in the least like the grumpy gentleman, in whose hands she was placed. She did not especially like the grumpy gentleman's wife; and she altogether hated the grumpy gentleman's daughter, who was the partner of her berth.

That young lady had been very sick and very selfish; and Miss Viner had been very sick also, and perhaps equally selfish. They might have been angels, and yet have hated each other under such circumstances. It was no wonder that Mr. Forrest thought her ugly as she twisted herself about on the broad bench, vainly striving to be comfortable.

"She'll brighten up wonderfully before we're in the tropics," said Mr. Morris. "And you won't find her so bad then. It's she that is to sit next you."

"Heaven forbid!" said Forrest. But, nevertheless, he was very civil to her when she did come down on the fourth morning. On board the West Indian Packets, the world goes down to its meals. In crossing between Liverpool and the States, the world goes up to them.

Miss Viner was by no means a very young lady. She also was nearly thirty. In guessing her age on board the ship the ladies said that she was thirty-six, but the ladies were wrong. She was an Irish woman, and when seen on shore, in her natural state, and with all her wits about her, was by no means without attraction. She was bright-eyed, with a clear dark skin, and good teeth; her hair was of a dark brown and glossy, and there was a touch of feeling and also of humour about her mouth, which would have saved her from Mr. Forrest's ill-considered criticism, had he first met her under more favourable circumstances.

"You'll see a good deal of her," Mr. Morris said to him, as they began to prepare themselves for luncheon, by a cigar immediately after breakfast. "She's going across the Isthmus and down to Peru."

"How on earth do you know?"

"I pretty well know where they're all going by this time. Old Grumpy told me so. He has her in tow as far as St. Thomas, but knows nothing about her. He gives her up there to the captain. You'll have a chance of making yourself very agreeable as you run across with her to the Spanish main."

Mr. Forrest replied that he did not suppose he should know her much better than he did now; but he made no further remark as to her ugliness. She had spoken a word or two to him at table, and he had seen that her eyes were bright, and had found that her tone was sweet.

"I also am going to Panama," he said to her, on the morning of the fifth day. The weather at that time was very fine, and the October sun as it shone on them, while hour by hour they made more towards the South, was pleasant and genial. The big ship lay almost without motion on the bosom of the Atlantic, as she was driven through the waters at the rate of twelve miles per hour. All was as pleasant now as things can be on board a ship, and Forrest had forgotten that Miss Viner had seemed so ugly to him when he first saw her. At this moment, as he spoke to her, they were running through the Azores, and he had been assisting her with his field-glass to look for orange-groves on their sloping shores, orange-groves they had not succeeded in seeing, but their failure had not disturbed their peace.

"I also am going to Panama."

"Are you, indeed?" said she. "Then I shall not feel so terribly alone and disconsolate. I have been looking forward with such fear to that journey on from St. Thomas."

"You shall not be disconsolate, if I can help it," he said. "I am not much of a traveller myself, but what I can do I will."

"Oh, thank you!"

"It is a pity Mr. Morris is not going on with you. He's at home everywhere, and knows the way across the Isthmus as well as he does down Regent Street."

"Your friend, you mean?"

"My friend, if you call him so; and indeed I hope he is, for I like him. But I don't know more of him than I do of you. I also am as much alone as you are. Perhaps more so."

"But," she said, "a man never suffers in being alone."

"Oh! does he not? Don't think me uncivil, Miss Viner, if I say that you may be mistaken in that. You feel your own shoe when it pinches, but do not realise the tight boot of your neighbour."

"Perhaps not," said she. And then there was a pause, during which she pretended to look again for the orange-groves. "But there are worse things, Mr. Forrest, than being alone in the world. It is often a woman's lot to wish that she were let alone." Then she left him and retreated to the side of the grumpy gentleman's wife, feeling perhaps that it might be prudent to discontinue a conversation, which, seeing that Mr. Forrest was quite a stranger to her, was becoming particular.

"You're getting on famously, my dear," said the lady, from Barbadoes.

"Pretty well, thank you, ma'am," said Miss Viner.

"Mr. Forrest seems to be making himself quite agreeable. I tell Amelia,"—Amelia was the young lady to whom in their joint cabin Miss Viner could not reconcile herself,—"I tell Amelia that she is wrong not to receive attentions from gentlemen on board ship. If it is not carried too far," and she put great emphasis on the "too far,"—"I see no harm in it."

"Nor I, either," said Miss Viner.

"But then Amelia is so particular."

"The best way is to take such things as they come," said Miss Viner,—perhaps meaning that such things never did come in the way of Amelia. "If a lady knows what she is about she need not fear a gentleman's attentions."

"That's just what I tell Amelia; but then, my dear, she has not had so much experience as you and I."

Such being the amenities which passed between Miss Viner and the prudent lady who had her in charge, it was not wonderful that the former should feel ill at ease with her own "party," as the family of the Grumpy Barbadian was generally considered to be by those on board.

"You're getting along like a house on fire with Miss Viner," said Matthew Morris, to his young friend.

"Not much fire I can assure you," said Forrest.

"She ain't so ugly as you thought her?"

"Ugly!—no; she's not ugly. I don't think I ever said she was. But she is nothing particular as regards beauty."

"No; she won't be lovely for the next three days to come, I dare say. By the time you reach Panama, she'll be all that is perfect in woman. I know how these things go."

"Those sort of things don't go at all quickly with me," said Forrest, gravely. "Miss Viner is a very interesting young woman, and as it seems that her route and mine will be together for some time, it is well that we should be civil to each other. And the more so, seeing that the people she is with are not congenial to her."

"No; they are not. There is no young man with them. I generally observe that on board ship no one is congenial to unmarried ladies except unmarried men. It is a recognised nautical rule. Uncommon hot, isn't it? We are beginning to feel the tropical air. I shall go and cool myself with a cigar in the fiddle." The "fiddle" is a certain part of the ship devoted to smoking, and thither Mr. Morris betook himself. Forrest, however, did not accompany him, but going forward into the bow of the vessel, threw himself along upon the sail, and meditated on the loneliness of his life.

On board the Serrapiqui, the upper tier of cabins opened on to a long gallery, which ran round that part of the ship, immediately over the saloon, so that from thence a pleasant inspection could be made of the viands as they were being placed on the tables. The custom on board these ships is for two bells to ring preparatory to dinner, at an interval of half-an-hour. At the sound of the first, ladies would go to their cabins to adjust their toilets; but as dressing for dinner is not carried to an extreme at sea, these operations are generally over before the second bell, and the lady passengers would generally assemble in the balcony for some fifteen minutes before dinner. At first they would stand here alone, but by degrees they were joined by some of the more enterprising of the men, and so at last a kind of little drawing-room was formed. The cabins of Miss Viner's party opened to one side of this gallery, and that of Mr. Morris and Forrest on the other. Hitherto Forrest had been contented to remain on his own side, occasionally throwing a word across to the ladies on the other; but on this day he boldly went over as soon as he had washed his hands and took his place between Amelia and Miss Viner.

"We are dreadfully crowded here, ma'am," said Amelia.

"Yes, my dear, we are," said her mother. "But what can one do?"

"There's plenty of room in the ladies' cabin," said Miss Viner. Now if there be one place on board aship more distasteful to ladies than another, it is the ladies' cabin. Mr. Forrest stood his ground, but it may be doubted whether he would have done so had he fully understood all that Amelia had intended.

Then the last bell rang. Mr. Grumpy gave his arm to Miss Grumpy. The brother-in-law gave his arm to Amelia, and Forrest did the same to Miss Viner. She hesitated for a moment, and then took it, and by so doing transferred herself mentally and bodily from the charge of the prudent and married Mr. Grumpy to that of the perhaps imprudent, and certainly unmarried Mr. Forrest. She was wrong. A kind-hearted, motherly, old lady from Jamaica, who had seen it all knew that she was wrong, and wished that she could tell her so. But there are things of this sort which kind-hearted old ladies cannot find it in their hearts to say. After all, it was only for the voyage. Perhaps Miss Viner was imprudent, but who in Peru would be the wiser? Perhaps, indeed, it was the world that was wrong, and not Miss Viner. "*Honi soit qui mal y pense*," she said to herself, as she took his arm, and leaning on it, felt that she was no longer so lonely as she had been. On that day she allowed him to give her a glass of wine out of his decanter. "Hadn't you better take mine, Miss Viner?" asked Mr. Grumpy, in a loud voice, but before he could be answered, the deed had been done.

"Don't go too fast, old fellow," Morris said to our hero that night, as they were walking the deck together before they turned in. "One gets into a hobble in such matters before one knows where one is."

"I don't think I have anything particular to fear," said Forrest.

"I dare say not, only keep your eyes open. Such haridans as Mrs. Grumpy allow any latitude to their tongues out in these diggings. You'll find that unpleasant tidings will be put on board the ship going down to Panama, and everybody's eye will be upon you." So warned, Mr. Forrest did put himself on his guard, and the next day and a half his intimacy with Miss Viner progressed but little. These were, probably, the dullest hours that he had on the whole voyage.

Miss Viner saw this and drew back. On the afternoon of that second day she walked a turn or two on deck with the weak brother-in-law, and when Mr. Forrest came near her, she applied herself to her book. She meant no harm; but if she were not afraid of what people might say, why should he be so? So she turned her shoulder towards him at dinner, and would not drink of his cup.

"Have some of mine, Miss Viner," said Mr. Grumpy, very loudly. But on that day Miss Viner drank no wine.

The sun sets quickly as one draws near to the tropics, and the day was already gone, and the dusk had come on, when Mr. Forrest walked out upon the deck that evening a little after six. But the night was beautiful and mild, and there was a hum of many voices from the benches. He was already uncomfortable, and sore with a sense of being deserted. There was but one person on board the ship that he liked, and why should he avoid her and be avoided? He soon perceived where she was standing. The Grumpy family had a bench to themselves, and she was opposite to it, on her feet, leaning against the side of the vessel. "Will you walk this evening, Miss Viner?" he asked.

"I think not," she answered.

"Then I shall persevere in asking till you are sure. It will do you good, for I have not seen you walking all day."

"Have you not? Then I will take a turn. Oh, Mr. Forrest, if you knew what it was to have to live with such people as those." And then, out of that, on that evening, there grew up between them something like the confidence of real friendship. Things were told such as none but friends do tell to one another, and warm answering words were spoken such as the sympathy of friendship produces. Alas, they were both foolish; for friendship and sympathy should have deeper roots.

She told him all her story. She was going out to Peru to be married to a man who was nearly twenty years her senior. It was a long engagement, of ten years' standing. When first made, it was made as being contingent on certain circumstances. An option of escaping from it had then been given to her, but now there was no longer an option. He was rich, and she was pennyless. He had even paid her passage-money and her outfit. She had not at last given way and taken these irrevocable steps till her only means of support in England had been taken from her. She had lived the last two years with a relative who was now dead. "And he also is my cousin,—a distant cousin—you understand that."

"And do you love him?"

"Love him! What; as you loved her whom you have lost?—as she loved you when she clung to you before she went? No; certainly not. I shall never know anything of that love."

"And is he good?"

"He is a hard man. Men become hard when they deal in money as he has done. He was home five years since, and then I swore to myself that I would not marry him. But his letters to me are kind."

Forrest sat silent for a minute or two, for they were up in the bow again, seated on the sail that was bound round the bowsprit, and then he answered her, "A woman should never marry a man unless she loves him."

"Ah," says she, "of course you will condemn me. That is the way in which women are always treated. They have no choice given them, and are then scolded for choosing wrongly."

"But you might have refused him."

"No; I could not. I cannot make you understand the whole,—how it first came about that the marriage was proposed, and agreed to by me under certain conditions. Those conditions have come about, and I am now bound to him. I have taken his money and have no escape. It is easy to say that a woman should not marry without love, as easy as it is to say that a man should not starve. But there are men who starve,—starve although they work hard."

"I did not mean to judge you, Miss Viner."

"But I judge myself, and condemn myself so often. Where should I be in half-an-hour from this if I were to throw myself forward into the sea? I often long to do it. Don't you feel tempted sometimes to put an end to it all?"

"The waters look cool and sweet, but I own I am afraid of the bourne beyond."

"So am I, and that fear will keep me from it."

"We are bound to bear our burden of sorrow. Mine, I know, is heavy enough."

"Yours, Mr. Forrest! Have you not all the pleasures of memory to fall back on, and every hope for the future? What can I remember, or what can I hope? But, however, it is near eight o'clock, and they have all been at tea this hour past. What will my Cerberus say to me? I do not mind the male mouth, if only the two feminine mouths could be stopped." Then she rose and went back to the stern of the vessel; but as she slid into a seat, she saw that Mrs. Grumpy was standing over her.

From thence to St. Thomas the voyage went on in the customary manner. The sun became very powerful, and the passengers in the lower part of the ship complained loudly of having their portholes closed. The Spaniards sat gambling in the cabin all day, and the ladies prepared for the general move which was to be made at St. Thomas. The alliance between Forrest and Miss Viner went on much the same as ever, and Mrs. Grumpy said very ill-natured things. On one occasion she ventured to lecture Miss Viner; but that lady knew how to take her own part, and Mrs. Grumpy did not get the best of it. The dangerous alliance, I have said, went on the same as ever; but it must not be supposed that either person in any way committed aught that was wrong. They sat together and talked together, each now knowing the other's circumstances; but had it not been for the prudish caution of some of the ladies there would have been nothing amiss. As it was there was not much amiss. Few of the passengers really cared whether or no Miss Viner had found an admirer. Those who were going down to Panama were mostly Spaniards, and as the great separation became nearer, people had somewhat else of which to think.

And then the separation came. They rode into that pretty harbour of St. Thomas early in the morning, and were ignorant, the most of them, that they were lying in the very worst centre of yellow fever among all those plague-spotted islands. St. Thomas is very pretty as seen from the ships; and when that has been said, all has been said that can be said in its favour. There was a busy, bustling time of it then. One vessel after another was brought up alongside of the big ship that had come from England, and each took its separate freight of passengers and luggage. First started the boat that ran down the Leeward Islands to Demerara, taking with her Mr. Grumpy and all his family.

"Good-bye, Miss Viner," said Mrs. Grumpy. "I hope you'll get quite safely to the end of your voyage; but do take care."

"I'm sure I hope everything will be right," said Amelia, as she absolutely kissed her enemy. It is astonishing how well young women can hate each other, and yet kiss at parting.

"As to everything being right," said Miss Viner, "that is too much to hope. But I do not know that anything is going especially wrong.—Good-bye, Sir," and then she put out her hand to Mr. Grumpy. He was at the moment leaving the ship laden with umbrellas, sticks, and coats, and was forced to put them down in order to free his hand.

"Well, good-bye," he said. "I hope you'll do, till you meet your friends at the Isthmus."

"I hope I shall, sir," she replied; and so they parted.

Then the Jamaica packet started.

"I dare say we shall never see each other again," said Morris, as he shook his friend's hand heartily. "One never does. Don't interfere with the rights of that gentleman in Peru, or he might run a knife into you."

"I feel no inclination to injure him on that point."

"That's well; and now good-bye." And thus they also were parted. On the following morning the branch ship was despatched to Mexico; and then, on the afternoon of the third day that for Colon—as we Englishmen call the town on this side of the Isthmus of Panama. Into that vessel Miss Viner and Mr. Forrest moved themselves and their effects; and now that the three-headed Cerberus was gone, she had no longer hesitated in allowing him to do for her all those little things which it is well that men should do for women when they are travelling. A woman without assistance under such circumstances is very forlorn, very apt to go to the wall, very ill able to assert her rights as to accommodation; and I think that few can blame Miss Viner for putting herself and her belongings under the care of the only person who was disposed to be kind to her.

Late in the evening the vessel steamed out of St. Thomas' harbour, and as she went Ralph Forrest and Emily Viner were standing together at the stern of the boat looking at the retreating lights of the Danish town. If there be a place on the earth's surface odious to me, it is that little Danish isle to which so many of our young seamen are sent to die,—there being no good cause whatever for such sending. But the question is one which cannot well be argued here.

"I have five more days of self and liberty left me," said Miss Viner. "That is my life's allowance."

"For heaven's sake do not say words that are so horrible."

"But am I to lie for heaven's sake, and say words that are false; or shall I be silent for heaven's sake, and say nothing during these last hours that are allowed to me for speaking? It is so. To you I can say that it is so, and why should you begrudge me the speech?"

"I would begrudge you nothing that I could do for you."

"No, you should not. Now that my incubus has gone to Barbadoes, let me be free for a day or two. What chance is there, I wonder, that the ship's machinery should all go wrong, and that we should be tossed about in the seas here for the next six months? I suppose it would be very wicked to wish it?"

"We should all be starved; that's all."

"What, with a cow on board, and a dozen live sheep, and thousands of cocks and hens! But we are to touch at Santa Martha and Cartagena. What would happen to me if I were to run away at Santa Martha?"

"I suppose I should be bound to run with you."

"Oh, of course. And therefore, as I would not wish to destroy you, I won't do it. But it would not hurt you much to be shipwrecked, and wait for the next packet."

"Miss Viner," he said after a pause,—and in the meantime he had drawn nearer to her, too near to her considering all things—"in the name of all that is good, and true, and womanly, go back to England.

With your feelings, if I may judge of them by words which are spoken half in jest— "

"Mr. Forrest, there is no jest."

"With your feelings a poorhouse in England would be better than a palace in Peru."

"An English workhouse would be better, but an English poorhouse is not open to me. You do not know what it is to have friends—no, not friends, but people belonging to you—just so near as to make your respectability a matter of interest to them, but not so near that they should care for your happiness. Emily Viner married to Mr. Gorloch in Peru is put out of the way respectably. She will cause no further trouble, but her name may be mentioned in family circles without annoyance. The fact is, Mr. Forrest, that there are people who have no business to live at all."

"I would go back to England," he added, after another pause. "When you talk to me with such bitterness of five more days of living liberty you scare my very soul. Return, Miss Viner, and brave the worst. He is to meet you at Panama. Remain on this side of the Isthmus, and send him word that you must return. I will be the bearer of the message."

"And shall I walk back to England?" said Miss Viner.

"I had not quite forgotten all that," he replied, very gently. "There are moments when a man may venture to propose that which under ordinary circumstances would be a liberty. Money, in a small moderate way, is not greatly an object to me. As a return for my valiant defence of you against your West Indian Cerberus, you shall allow me to arrange that with the agent at Colon."

"I do so love plain English, Mr. Forrest. You are proposing I think, to give me something about fifty guineas."

"Well, call it so if you will," said he, "if you will have plain English that is what I mean."

"So that by my journey out here, I should rob and deceive the man I do know, and also rob the man I don't know. I am afraid of that bourne beyond the waters of which we spoke; but I would rather face that than act as you suggest."

"Of the feelings between him and you, I can of course be no judge."

"No, no; you cannot. But what a beast I am not to thank you! I do thank you. That which it would be mean in me to take, it is noble, very noble, in you to offer. It is a pleasure to me—I cannot tell why—but it is a pleasure to me to have had the offer. But think of me as a sister, and you will feel that it would not be accepted;—could not be accepted, I mean, even if I could bring myself to betray that other man."

Thus they ran across the Caribbean Sea, renewing very often such conversations as that just given. They touched at Santa Martha and Cartagena on the coast of the Spanish main, and at both places he went with her on shore. He found that she was fairly well educated, and anxious to see and to learn all that might be seen and learned in the course of her travels. On the last day, as they neared the Isthmus, she became more tranquil and quiet in the expression of her feelings than before, and spoke with less of gloom than she had done.

"After all ought I not to love him?" she said. "He is coming all the way up from Callao merely to meet me. What man would go from London to Moscow to pick up a wife?"

"I would—and thence round the world to Moscow again—if she were the wife I wanted."

"Yes; but a wife who has never said that she loved you! It is purely a matter of convenience. Well; I have locked my big box, and I shall give the key to him before it is ever again unlocked. He has a right to it, for he has paid for nearly all that it holds."

"You look at things from such a mundane point of view."

"A woman should, or she will always be getting into difficulty. Mind, I shall introduce you to him, and tell him all that you have done for me. How you braved Cerberus and the rest of it."

"I shall certainly be glad to meet him."

"But I shall not tell him of your offer;—not yet at least. If he be good and gentle with me, I shall tell him that too after a time. I am very bad at keeping secrets,—as no doubt you have perceived. We go across the Isthmus at once; do we not?"

"So the Captain says."

"Look!"—and she handed him back his own field-glass. "I can see the men on the wooden platform. Yes; and I can see the smoke of an engine." And then, in little more than an hour from that time the ship had swung round on her anchor.

Colon, or Aspinwall as it should be called, is a place in itself as detestable as St. Thomas. It is not so odious to an Englishman, for it is not used by Englishmen more than is necessary. We have no great depôt of traffic there, which we might with advantage move elsewhere. Taken, however, on its own merits, Aspinwall is not a detestable place. Luckily, however, travellers across the Isthmus to the Pacific are never doomed to remain there long. If they arrive early in the day, the railway thence to Panama takes them on at once. If it be not so, they remain on board ship till the next morning. Of course it will be understood that the transit line chiefly affects Americans, as it is the highroad from New York to California.

In less than an hour from their landing, their baggage had been examined by the Custom House officers of New Grenada, and they were on the railway cars, crossing the Isthmus. The officials in those out-of-the-way places always seem like apes imitating the doings of men. The officers at Aspinwall open and look at the trunks just as monkeys might do, having clearly no idea of any duty to be performed, nor any conception that goods of this or that class should not be allowed to pass. It is the thing in Europe to examine luggage going into a new country; and why should not they be as good as Europeans?

"I wonder whether he will be at the station?" she said, when the three hours of the journey had nearly passed. Forrest could perceive that her voice trembled as she spoke, and that she was becoming nervous.

"If he has already reached Panama, he will be there. As far as I could learn the arrival up from Peru had not been telegraphed."

"Then I have another day,—perhaps two. We cannot say how many. I wish he were there. Nothing is so intolerable as suspense."

"And the box must be opened again."

When they reached the station at Panama they found that the vessel from the South American coast was in the roads, but that the passengers were not yet on shore. Forrest, therefore, took Miss Viner down to the hotel, and there remained with her, sitting next to her in the common drawing-room of the house, when she had come back from her own bed-room. It would be necessary that they should remain there four or five days, and Forrest had been quick in securing a room for her. He had assisted in taking up her luggage, had helped her in placing her big box, and had thus been recognised by the crowd in the hotel as her friend. Then came the tidings that the passengers were landing, and he became nervous as she was. "I will go down and meet him," said he, "and tell him that you are here. I shall soon find him by his name." And so he went out.

Everybody knows the scrambling manner in which passengers arrive at an hotel out of a big ship. First came two or three energetic, heated men, who, by dint of screeching and bullying, have gotten themselves first disposed. They always get the worst rooms at the inns, the housekeepers having a notion that the richest people, those with the most luggage, must be more tardy in their movements. Four or five of this nature passed by Forrest in the hall, but he was not tempted to ask questions of them. One, from his age, might have been Mr. Gorloch, but he instantly declared himself to be Count Sapparello. Then came an elderly man alone, with a small bag in his hand. He was one of those who pride themselves on going from pole to pole without encumbrance, and who will be behoved to no one for the carriage of their luggage. To him, as he was alone in the street, Forrest addressed himself. "Gorloch," said he. "Gorloch: are you a friend of his?"

"A friend of mine is so," said Forrest.

"Ah, indeed; yes," said the other. And then he hesitated. "Sir," he then said, "Mr. Gorloch died at Callao, just seven days before the ship sailed. You had better see Mr. Cox." And then the elderly man passed in with his little bag.

Mr. Gorloch was dead. "Dead!" said Forrest, to himself, as he leaned back against the wall of the hotel still standing on the street pavement. "She has come out here; and now he is gone!" And then a thousand thoughts crowded on him. Who should tell her? And how would she bear it? Would it in truth be a relief to her to find that that liberty for which she had sighed had come to her? Or now that the testing of her feelings had come to her, would she regret the loss of home and wealth, and such position as life in Peru would give her? And above all would this sudden death of one who was to have been so near to her, strike her to the heart?

But what was he to do? How was he now to show his friendship? He was returning slowly in at the hotel door, where crowds of men and women were now thronging, when he was addressed by a middle-aged, good-looking gentleman, who asked him whether his name was Forrest. "I am told," said the gentleman, when Forrest had answered him, "that you are a friend of Miss Viner's. Have you heard the sad tidings from Callao?" It then appeared that this gentleman had been a stranger to Mr. Gorloch, but had undertaken to bring a letter up to Miss Viner. This letter was handed to Mr. Forrest, and he found himself burdened with the task of breaking the news to his poor friend. Whatever he did do, he must do at once, for all those who had come up by the Pacific steamer knew the story, and it was incumbent on him that Miss Viner should not hear the tidings in a sudden manner and from a stranger's mouth.

He went up into the drawing-room, and found Miss Viner seated there in the midst of a crew of women. He went up to her, and taking her hand, asked her in a whisper whether she would come out with him for a moment.

"Where is he?" said she. "I know that something is the matter. What is it?"

"There is such a crowd here. Step out for a moment." And he led her away to her own room.

"Where is he?" said she. "What is the matter? He has sent to say that he no longer wants me. Tell me; am I free from him?"

"Miss Viner, you are free."

Though she had asked the question herself, she was astounded by the answer; but, nevertheless, no idea of the truth had yet come upon her. "It is so," she said. "Well, what else? Has he written? He has bought me, as he would a beast of burden, and has, I suppose, a right to treat me as he pleases."

"I have a letter; but, dear Miss Viner— "

"Well, tell me all,—out at once. Tell me everything."

"You are free, Miss Viner; but you will be cut to the heart when you learn the meaning of your freedom."

"He has lost everything in trade. He is ruined."

"Miss Viner, he is dead!"

She stood staring at him for a moment or two, as though she could not realise the information which he gave her. Then gradually she retreated to the bed, and sat upon it. "Dead, Mr. Forrest!" she said. He did not answer her, but handed her the letter, which she took and read as though it were mechanically. The letter was from Mr. Gorloch's partner, and told her everything which it was necessary that she should know.

"Shall I leave you now?" he said, when he saw that she had finished reading it.

"Leave me; yes,—no. But you had better leave me, and let me think about it. Alas me, that I should have so spoken of him!"

"But you have said nothing unkind."

"Yes; much that was unkind. But spoken words cannot be recalled. Let me be alone now, but come to me soon. There is no one else here that I can speak to."

He went out, and finding that the hotel dinner was ready, he went in and dined. Then he strolled into the town, among the hot, narrow, dilapidated streets; and then, after two hours' absence, returned to Miss Viner's room. When he knocked, she came and opened the door, and he found that the floor was strewed with clothes. "I am preparing, you see, for my return. The vessel starts back for St. Thomas the day after to-morrow."

"You are quite right to go,—to go at once. Oh, Miss Viner! Emily, now at least you must let me help you."

He had been thinking of her most during those last two hours, and her voice had become pleasant to his ears, and her eyes very bright to his sight.

"You shall help me," she said. "Are you not helping me when at such a time you come to speak to me?"

"And you will let me think that I have a right to act as your protector?"

"My protector! I do know that I want such aid as that. During the days that we are here together you shall be my friend."

"You shall not return alone. My journeys are nothing to me. Emily, I will return with you to England."

Then she rose up from her seat and spoke to him.

"Not for the world," she said. "Putting out of question the folly of your forgetting your own objects, do you think it possible that I should go with you, now that he is dead? To you I have spoken of him harshly; and now that it is my duty to mourn for him, could I do so heartily if you were with me? While he lived, it seemed to me that in those last days I had a right to speak my thoughts plainly. You and I were to part and meet no more, and I regarded us both as people apart, who for a while might drop the common usages of the world. It is so no longer. Instead of going with you farther, I must ask you to forget that we were ever together."

"Emily, I shall never forget you."

"Let your tongue forget me. I have given you no cause to speak good of me, and you will be too kind to speak evil."

After that she explained to him all that the letter had contained. The arrangements for her journey had all been made; money also had been sent to her; and Mr. Gorloch in his will had provided for her, not liberally, seeing that he was rich, but still sufficiently.

And so they parted at Panama. She would not allow him even to cross the Isthmus with her, but pressed his hand warmly as he left her at the station. "God bless you!" he said. "And may God bless you, my friend!" she answered.

Thus alone she took her departure for England, and he went on his way to California.

The Widow's Mite

Originally appeared in *Good Words*, January 1863. Reprinted in *Lotta Schmidt and Other Stories* (1867). Written at some time between 18 November and 8 December 1862. The parabolic quality of this story is in keeping with the taste of *Good Words* magazine, an organ of liberal evangelical churchmanship. Its concentration on a major issue (the Lancashire cotton famine) from a sympathetic upper-class viewpoint recalls the presentation of the Irish famine in *Castle Richmond* (1860). Norman Macleod, the editor of *Good Words*, wished Trollope to write a tale of an even more topical cast called 'Out of Work', but Trollope felt that he was not up to examining the issue from the perspective of an 'operative'.

But I'm not a widow, and I haven't got two mites."

"My dear, you are a widow, and you have got two mites."

"I'll tell both of you something that will astonish you. I've made a calculation, and I find that if everybody in England would give up their Christmas dinner—that is, in Scotland, and Ireland too— "

"They never have any in Ireland, Bob."

"Hold your tongue till I've done, Charley. They do have Christmas dinners in Ireland. It's pretty nearly the only day that they do, and I don't count much upon them either. But if everybody gave up his special Christmas dinner, and dined as he does on other days, the saving would amount to two millions and a half."

Charley whistled.

"Two millions and a half is a large sum of money," said Mrs. Granger, the elder lady of the party.

"Those calculations never do any good," said the younger lady, who had declared herself not to be a widow.

"Those calculations do a great deal of good," continued Bob, carrying on his argument with continued warmth. "They show us what a great national effort would do."

"A little national effort, I should call that," said Mrs. Granger. "But I should doubt the two millions and a half."

"Half-a-crown a-head on thirty million people would do it. You are to include all the beer, wine, and whisky. But suppose you take off one-fifth for the babies and young girls, who don't drink."

"Thank you, Bob," said the younger lady—Nora Field by name.

"And two more fifths for the poor, who haven't got the half-crown a-head," said the elder lady.

"And you'd ruin the grocer and butcher," said Charley.

"And never get your half-crown, after all," said Nora.

It need hardly be said that the subject under discussion was the best mode of abstracting from the pockets of the non-suffering British public a sufficiency of money to sustain the suffering portion during the period of the cotton famine.

Mr. Granger was the rector of Plumstock, a parish in Cheshire, sufficiently near to the manufacturing districts to give to every incident of life at that time a colouring taken from the distress of the neighbourhood; which had not, however, itself ever depended on cotton,—for Plumstock boasted that it was purely agricultural. Mr. Granger was the chairman of a branch relief committee, which had its centre in Liverpool; and the subject of the destitution, with the different modes by which it might be, should be, or should not be relieved, were constantly under discussion in the rectory. Mr. Granger himself was a practical man, somewhat hard in his manners, but by no means hard in his heart, who had in these times taken upon himself the business of alms-begging on a large scale. He declined to look at the matter in a political, statistical, or economical point of view, and answered all questions as to rates, rates in aid, loans, and the Consolidated Fund, with a touch of sarcasm, which showed the bent of his own mind.

"I've no doubt you'll have settled all that in the wisest possible way by the time that the war is over, and the river full of cotton again."

"Father," Bob replied, pointing across the Cheshire flats to the Mersey, "that river will never again be full of American cotton."

"It will be all the same for the present purpose, if it comes from India," said the rector declining all present argument on the great American question.

To collect alms was his immediate work, and he would do nothing else. Five-pound notes, sovereigns, half-crowns, shillings, and pence! In search of these he was urgent, we may almost say day and night, begging with a pertinacity which was disagreeable, but irresistible. The man who gave him five sovereigns instantly became the mark for another petition.

"When you have got your dinner, you have not done with the butcher for ever," he would say in answer to reproaches. "Of course, we must go on as long as this thing lasts."

Then his friends and neighbours buttoned up their pockets; but Mr. Granger would extract coin from them even when buttoned.

The two young men who had taken part in the above argument were his sons. The elder, Charles, was at Oxford, but now in these Christmas days—for Christmas was close at hand—had come home. Bob, the second son, was in a merchant's house in Liverpool, intending to become, in the fulness of time, a British merchant prince. It had been hinted to him, however, more than once, that if he would talk a little less and work a little harder, the path to his princedom would be quicker found than if his present habits were maintained. Nora Field was Mrs. Granger's niece. She was Miss Field, and certainly not a widow in the literal sense of the word; but she was about to become a bride a few weeks after Christmas.

"It is spoil from the Amalekites," Mr. Granger had said, when she had paid in some contribution from her slender private stores to his treasury:—"spoil from the Amalekites, and therefore the more precious." He had called Nora Field's two sovereigns spoil from the Amalekites, because she was about to marry an American.

Frederic Frew, or Frederic F. Frew, as he delighted to hear himself called, for he had been christened Franklin as well as Frederic,—and to an American it is always a point of honour that, at any rate, the initial of his second Christian name should be remembered by all men,—was a Pennsylvanian from Philadelphia; a strong Democrat, according to the politics of his own country, hating the Republicans, as the Tories used to hate the Whigs among us before political feeling had become extinct; speaking against Lincoln the President, and Seward his minister, and the Fremonts, and Summers, and Philipses, and Beechers of the Republican party, fine hard racy words of powerful condemnation, such as used to be spoken against Earl Grey and his followers, but nevertheless as steady for the war as Lincoln, or Seward, or any Republican of them all;—as steady for the war, and as keen in his bitterness against England.

His father had been a partner in a house of business, of which the chief station had been in Liverpool. That house had now closed its transactions, and young Frew was living and intended to live an easy idle life on the moderate fortune which had been left to him; but the circumstances of his family affairs had made it necessary for him to pass many months in Liverpool, and during that sojourn he had become engaged to Nora Field. He had travelled much, going everywhere with his eyes open, as Americans do. He knew many things, had read many books, and was decided in his opinion on most subjects. He was good-looking too, and well-mannered; was kindly-hearted, and capable of much generosity. But he was hard, keen in his intelligence, but not broad in genius, thin and meagre in his aspirations,—not looking to or even desirous of anything great, but indulging a profound contempt for all that is very small. He was a well-instructed, but by no means learned man, who greatly despised those who were ignorant. I fear that he hated England in his heart; but he did not hate Nora Field, and was about to make her his wife in three or four weeks from the present time.

When Nora declared to her aunt that she was not a widow, and that she possessed no two mites, and when her aunt flatly contradicted her, stating that she was a widow, and did possess two mites, they had not intended to be understood by each other literally. It was an old dispute between them.

"What the widow gave," said Nora, "she gave off her own poor back, and therefore was very cold. She gave it out of her own poor mouth, and was very hungry afterwards in consequence. I have given my two pounds, but I shall not be cold or hungry. I wish I was a widow with two mites; only, the question is whether I should not keep them for my own back after all, and thus gain nothing by the move."

"As to that," replied her aunt, "I cannot speak. But the widowhood and the two mites are there for us all, if we choose to make use of them."

"In these days," said Bob, "the widows with two mites should not be troubled at all. We can do it all without them, if we go to work properly."

"If you had read your Bible properly, sir," said Mrs. Granger, "you would understand that the widows would not thank you for the exemption."

"I don't want the widows to thank me. I only want to live, and allow others to live according to the existing circumstances of the world." It was manifest from Bob's tone that he regarded his mother as little better than an old fogey.

In January, Nora was to become Mrs. Frederic F. Frew, and be at once taken away to new worlds, new politics, and new loves and hatreds. Like a true, honest-hearted girl as she was, she had already become half an American in spirit. She was an old Union American, and as such was strong against the South; and in return for her fervour in that matter, her future husband consented to abstain from any present loud abuse of things English, and generously allowed her to defend her own country when it was abused. This was much as coming from an American. Let us hope that the same privilege may be accorded to her in her future home in Philadelphia. But in the meantime, during these last weeks of her girlhood, these cold, cruel weeks of desperate want, she strove vigorously to do what little might be in her power for the poor of the country she was leaving. All this want had been occasioned by the wretched rebels of the South.

This was her theory. And she was right in much of this. Whether the Americans of the South are wretched or are rebels we will not say here; but of this there can be no doubt, that they created all the misery which we then endured.

"But I have no way of making myself a widow," she said again. "Uncle Robert would not let me give away the cloak he gave me the other day."

"He would have to give you another," said Mrs. Granger.

"Exactly. It is not so easy, after all, to be a widow with two mites!"

Nora Field had no fortune of her own, nor was her uncle in a position to give her any. He was not a poor man; but like many men who are not poor, he had hardly a pound of his own in the shape of ready money.

To Nora and to her cousins, and to certain other first cousins of the same family, had been left, some eighteen months since, by a grand-aunt, a hundred pounds a-piece, and with this hundred pounds Nora was providing for herself her wedding trousseau.

A hundred pounds do not go far in such provision, as some young married women who may read this will perhaps acknowledge; but Mr. Frederic F. Frew had been told all about it, and he was contented. Miss Field was fond of nice clothes, and had been tempted more than once to wish that her great-aunt had left them all two hundred pounds a-piece instead of one.

"If I were to cast in my wedding veil?" said Nora.

"That will be your husband's property," said her aunt.

"Ah, but before I'm married."

"Then why have it at all?"

"It is ordered, you know."

"Couldn't you bedizen yourself with one made of false lace?" said her uncle. "Frew would never find it out, and that would be a most satisfactory spoiling of the Amalekite."

"He isn't an Amalekite, uncle Robert. Or if he is, I'm another."

"Just so; and therefore false lace will be quite good enough for you. Molly,"—Mrs. Granger's name was Molly,—"I've promised to let them have the use of the great boiler in the back kitchen once a-week, and you are to furnish them with fuel."

"Oh, dear!" said Mrs. Granger, upon whose active charity this loan of her own kitchen boiler made a strain that was almost too severe. But she recovered herself in half a minute. "Very well, my dear; but you won't expect any dinner on that day."

"No; I shall expect no dinner; only some food in the rough. You may boil that in the copper too if you like it."

"You know, my dear, you don't like anything boiled."

"As for that, Molly, I don't suppose any of them like it. They'd all prefer roast mutton."

"The copper will be your two mites," whispered the niece.

"Only I have not thrown them in of my own accord," said Mrs. Granger.

Mr. Frew, who was living in Liverpool, always came over to Plumstock on Friday evening, and spent Saturday and Sunday with the rector and his family. For him those Saturdays were happy days, for Frederick F. Frew was a good lover. He liked to be with Nora, to walk with her, and to talk with her. He liked to show her that he loved her, and make himself gracious and pleasant. I am not so sure that his coming was equally agreeable to Mr. Granger. Mr. Frew would talk about American politics, praising the feeling and spirit of his countrymen in the North; whereas Mr. Granger, when driven into the subject, was constrained to make a battle for the South. All his prejudices, and what he would have called his judgment, went with the South, and he was not ashamed of his opinion; but he disliked arguing with Frederic F. Frew. I fear it must be confessed that Frederic F. Frew was too strong for him in such arguments. Why it should be so I cannot say; but an American argues more closely on politics than does an Englishman. His convictions are not the truer on that account; very often the less true, as are the conclusions of a logician, because he trusts to syllogisms which are often false, instead of to the experience of his life and daily workings of his mind. But though not more true in his political convictions than an Englishman, he is more unanswerable, and therefore Mr. Granger did not care to discuss the subject of the American war with Frederic F. Frew.

"It riles me," Frew said, as he sat after dinner the Plumstock drawing-room on the Friday evening before Christmas Day, "to hear your folks talking of our elections. They think the war will come to an end, and the rebels of the South have their own way, because the Democrats have carried their ticket."

"It will have that tendency," said the parson.

"Not an inch; any more than your carrying the Reform Bill or repealing the Corn Laws had a tendency to put down the throne. It's the same sort of argument. Your two parties were at daggers drawn about the Reform Bill; but that did not cause you to split on all other matters."

"But the throne wasn't in question," said the parson.

"Nor is the war in question; not in that way. The most popular Democrat in the States at this moment is M'Clellan."

"And they say no one is so anxious to see the war ended."

"Whoever says so slanders him. If you don't trust his deeds, look at his words."

"I believe in neither," said the parson.

"Then put him aside as a nobody. But you can't do that, for he is the man whom the largest party in the Northern States trusts most implicitly. The fact is, sir," and Frederic F. Frew gave the proper twang to the last letter of the last word, "you, none of you here, understand our politics. You can't realise the blessing of a— "

"Molly, give me some tea," said the rector, in a loud voice. When matters went as far as this he did not care by what means he stopped the voice of his future relative.

"All I say is this," continued Frew, "you will find out your mistake if you trust to the Democratic elections to put an end to the war, and bring cotton back to Liverpool."

"And what is to put an end to the war?" asked Nora.

"Victory and union," said Frederic F. Frew.

"Exhaustion," said Charley, from Oxford.

"Compromise," said Bobby, from Liverpool.

"The Lord Almighty, when He shall have done His work," said the parson. "And, in the meantime, Molly, do you keep plenty of fire under the kitchen boiler."

That was clearly the business of the present hour, for all in Mr. Granger's part of the country;—we may say, indeed, for all on Mr. Granger's side of the water. It mattered little, then, in Lancashire, whether New York might have a Democratic or a Republican governor. The old cotton had been burned; the present crop could not be garnered; the future crop—the crop which never would be future, could not get itself sown.

Mr. Granger might be a slow politician, but he was a practical man, understanding the things immediately around him; and they all were aware, Frederic F. Frew with the rest of them, that he was right when he bade his wife keep the fire well hot beneath the kitchen boiler.

"Isn't it almost wicked to be married in such a time as this?" It was much later in the evening when Nora, still troubled in her mind about her widow's mite, whispered these words into her lover's ears. If she were to give up her lover for twelve months, would not that be a throwing in of something to the treasury from off her own back and out of her own mouth? But then this matter of her marriage had been so fully settled that she feared to think of disturbing it. He would never consent to such a postponement. And then the offering, to be of avail for her, must be taken from her own back, not from his; and Nora had an idea that in the making of such an offering as that suggested, Mr. Frederic F. Frew would conceive that he had contributed by far the greater part. Her uncle called him an Amalekite, and she doubted whether it would be just to spoil an Amalekite after such a fashion as that. Nevertheless, into his ears she whispered her little proposition.

"Wicked to get married!" said Frederic; "not according to my idea of the Christian religion."

"Oh! but you know what I mean," and she gave his arm a slight caressing pinch.

At this time her uncle had gone to his own room; her cousins had gone to their studies, by which I believe they intended to signify the proper smoking of a pipe of tobacco in the rectory kitchen; and Mrs. Granger, seated in her easy chair, had gone to her slumbers, dreaming of the amount of fuel with which that kitchen boiler must be supplied.

"I shall bring a breach of promise against you," said Frederic, "if you don't appear in church with bridal array on Monday, the 12th of January, and pay the penalty into the war-treasury. That would be a spoiling of the Amalekite."

Then he got hold of the fingers which had pinched him.

"Of course I shan't put it off, unless you agree."

"Of course you won't."

"But, dear Fred, don't you think we ought?"

"No; certainly not. If I thought you were in earnest I would scold you."

"I am in earnest, quite. You need not look in that way, for you know very well how truly I love you. You know I want to be your wife above all things."

"Do you?"

And then he began to insinuate his arm round her waist; but she got up and moved away, not as in anger at his caress, but as showing that the present moment was unfit for it.

"I do," she said, "above all things. I love you so well that I could hardly bear to see you go away again without taking me with you. I could hardly bear it,—but I could bear it."

"Could you? Then I couldn't. I'm a weaker vessel than you, and your strength must give way to my weakness."

"I know I've no right to tax you, if you really care about it."

Frederic F. Frew made no answer to this in words, but pursued her in her retreat from the sofa on which they had sat.

"Don't, Fred. I am so much in earnest! I wish I knew what I ought to do to throw in my two mites."

"Not throw me over certainly, and break all the promises you have made for the last twelve months. You can't be in earnest. It's out of the question, you know."

"Oh! I am in earnest."

"I never heard of such a thing in my life. What good would it do? It wouldn't bring the cotton in. It wouldn't feed the poor. It wouldn't keep your aunt's boiler hot."

"No; that it wouldn't," said Mrs. Granger, starting up; "and coals are such a terrible price."

Then she went to sleep again, and ordered in large supplies in her dreams.

"But I should have done as much as the widow did. Indeed I should, Fred. Oh, dear! to have to give you up! But I only meant for a year."

"As you are so very fond of me— "

"Of course I'm fond of you. Should I let you do like that if I was not?"

At the moment of her speaking he had again got his arm round her waist.

"Then I'm too charitable to allow you to postpone your happiness for a day. We'll look at it in that way."

"You won't understand me, or rather you do understand me, and pretend that you don't, which is very wrong."

"I always was very wicked."

"Then why don't you make yourself better? Do not you too wish to be a widow? You ought to wish it."

"I should like to have an opportunity of trying married life first."

"I won't stay any longer with you, sir, because you are scoffing. Aunt, I'm going to bed." Then she returned again across the room, and whispered to her lover, "I'll tell you what, sir, I'll marry you on Monday, the 12th of January, if you'll take me just as I am now; with a bonnet on, and a shawl over my dress, exactly as I walked out with you before dinner. When I made the promise, I never said anything about fine clothes."

"You may come in an old red cloak, if you like it."

"Very well; now mind I've got your consent. Good night, sir. After all it will only be half a mite."

She had turned towards the door, and had her hand upon the lock, but she came back into the room, close up to him.

"It will not be a quarter of a mite," she said. "How can it be anything if I get you?" Then she kissed him, and hurried away out of the room, before he could again speak to her.

"What, what, what!" said Mrs. Granger, waking up. "So Nora has gone, has she?"

"Gone; yes, just this minute," said Frew, who had turned his face to the fire, so that the tear in his eyes might not be seen. As he took himself off to his bed, he swore to himself that Nora Field was a trump, and that he had done well in securing for himself such a wife; but it never occurred to him that she was in any way in earnest about her wedding dress. She was a trump because she was so expressive in her love to himself, and because her eyes shone so brightly when she spoke eagerly on any matter; but as to her appearing at the altar in a red cloak, or, as was more probable, in her own customary thick woollen shawl, he never thought about it. Of course she would be married as other girls are married.

Nor had Nora thought of it till that moment in which she made the proposition to her lover. As she had said before, her veil was ordered, and so was her white silk dress. Her bonnet also had been ordered, with its bridal wreath, and the other things assorting therewith. A vast hole was to be made in her grand-aunt's legacy for the payment of all this finery; but, as Mrs. Granger had said to her, in so spending it, she would best please her future husband. He had enough of his own, and would not care that she should provide herself with articles which he could afterwards give her, at the expense of that little smartness at his wedding which an American likes, at any rate, as well as an Englishman. Nora, with an honesty which some ladies may not admire, had asked her lover the question in the plainest language.

"You will have to buy my things so much the sooner," she had said.

"I'd buy them all to-morrow, only you'll not let me."

"I should rather think not, Master Fred."

Then she had gone off with her aunt, and ordered her wedding-clothes. But now as she prepared for bed, after the conversation which has just been recorded, she began to think in earnest whether it would not be well to dispense with white silk and orange-wreaths while so many were dispensing with—were forced to dispense with bread and fuel. Could she bedizen herself with finery from Liverpool, while her uncle was, as she well knew, refusing himself a set of new shirts which he wanted sorely, in order that he might send to the fund at Liverpool the money which they would cost him. He was throwing in his two mites daily, as was her aunt, who toiled unceasingly at woollen shawls and woollen stockings, so that she went on knitting even in her sleep. But she, Nora, since the earnestness of these bad days began, had done little or nothing. Her needle, indeed, had been very busy, but it had been busy in preparation for Mr. Frederic F. Frew's nuptials. Even Bob and Charley worked for the Relief Committee; but she had done nothing,—nothing but given her two pounds. She had offered four, but her uncle, with a self-restraint never before or afterwards practised by him, had chucked her back two, saying that he would not be too hard even upon an Amalekite. As she thought of the word, she asked herself whether it was not more incumbent on her, than on any one else, to do something in the way of self-sacrifice. She was now a Briton, but would shortly be an American. Should it be said of her that the distress of her own countrywomen,—the countrywomen whom she was leaving, did not wring her heart? It was not without a pang that she prepared to give up that nationality, which all its owners rank as the first in the world, and most of those who do not own it, rank, if not as the first, then as the second. Now it seemed to her as though she were deserting her own family in its distress, deserting her own ship in the time of its storm, and she was going over to those from whom this distress and this storm had come! Was it not needful that she should do something,—that she should satisfy herself that she had been willing to suffer in the cause?

She would throw in her two mites if she did but know where to find them.

"I could only do it, in truth!," she said to herself, as she rose from her prayers, "by throwing in him. I have got one very great treasure, but I have not got anything else that I care about. After all, it isn't so easy to be a widow with two mites."

Then she sat down and thought about it. As to postponing her marriage, that she knew to be in truth quite out of the question. Even if she could bring herself to do it, everybody about her would say that she was mad, and Mr. Frederic F. Frew might not impossibly destroy himself with one of those pretty revolvers which he sometimes brought out from Liverpool for her to play with. But was it not practicable for her to give up her wedding-clothes? There would be considerable difficulty even in this. As to their having been ordered, that might be overcome by the sacrifice of some portion of the price. But then her aunt, and even her uncle, would oppose her; her cousins would cover her with ridicule; in the latter matter she might, however, achieve something of her widowhood;—and, after all, the loss would fall more upon F. F. Frew than upon herself. She really did not care, for herself, in what clothes she was married, so that she was made his wife. But as regarded him, might it not be disagreeable to him to stand before the altar with a dowdy creature in an old gown? And then there was one other consideration. Would it not seem that she was throwing in her two mites publicly, before the eyes of all men, as a Pharisee might do it? Would there not be an ostentation in her widowhood? But as she continued to reflect, she cast this last thought behind her. It might be so said of her, but if such saying were untrue, if the offering were made in a widow's spirit, and not in the spirit of a Pharisee, would it not be cowardly to regard what men might say? Such false accusation would make some part of the two mites.

"I'll go into Liverpool about it on Monday," she said to herself as she finally tucked the clothes around her.

Early in the following morning she was up and out of her room, with the view of seeing her aunt before she came down to breakfast; but the first person she met was her uncle. He accosted her in one of the passages.

"What, Nora, this is early for you! Are you going to have a morning lovers' walk with Frederic Franklin?"

"Frederic Franklin, as you choose to call him, uncle," said Nora, "never comes out of his room much before breakfast time. And it's raining hard."

"Such a lover as he is ought not to mind rain."

"But I should mind it, very much. But, uncle, I want to speak to you, very seriously. I have been making up my mind about something."

"There's nothing wrong; is there, my dear?"

"No; there's nothing very wrong. It is not exactly about anything being wrong. I hardly know how to tell you what it is."

And then she paused, and he could see by the light of the candle in his hand that she blushed.

"Hadn't you better speak to your aunt?" said Mr. Granger.

"That's what I meant to do when I got up," said Nora; "but as I have met you, if you don't mind— "

He assured her that he did not mind, and putting his hand upon her shoulder caressingly, promised her any assistance in his power.

"I'm not afraid that you will ask anything I ought not to do for you."

Then she revealed to him her scheme, turning her face away from him as she spoke. "It will be so horrid," she said, "to have a great box of finery coming home when you are all giving up everything for the poor people. And if you don't think it would be wrong— "

"It can't be wrong," said her uncle. "It may be a question whether it would be wise."

"I mean wrong to him. If it was to be any other clergyman, I should be ashamed of it. But as you are to marry us— "

"I don't think you need mind about the clergyman."

"And of course I should tell the Foster girls."

"The Foster girls?"

"Yes; they are to be my bridesmaids, and I am nearly sure they have not bought anything new yet. Of course they would think it all very dowdy, but I don't care a bit about that. I should just tell them that we had all made up our minds that we couldn't afford wedding-clothes. That would be true; wouldn't it?"

"But the question is about that wild American?"

"He isn't a wild American."

"Well, then, about that tamed American. What will he say?"

"He said I might come in an old cloak."

"You have told him, then?"

"But I am afraid he thought I was only joking. But, uncle, if you'll help me, I think I can bring him round."

"I daresay you can—to anything, just at present."

"I didn't at all mean that. Indeed, I'm sure I couldn't bring him round to putting off the marriage."

"No, no, no; not to that; to anything else."

"I know you are laughing at me, but I don't much mind being laughed at. I should save very nearly fifteen pounds, if not quite. Think of that!"

"And you'd give it all to the soup-kitchen?"

"I'd give it all to you for the distress."

Then her uncle spoke to her somewhat gravely.

"You're a good girl, Nora,—a dear good girl. I think I understand your thoughts on this matter, and I love you for them. But I doubt whether there be any necessity for you to make this sacrifice. A marriage should be a gala festival according to the means of the people married, and the bridegroom has a right to expect that his bride shall come to him fairly arrayed, and bright with wedding trappings. I think we can do, my pet, without robbing you of your little braveries."

"Oh, as for that, of course you can do without me."

There was a little soreness in her tone; not because she was feeling herself to be misunderstood, but because she knew that she could not explain herself further. She could not tell her uncle that the poor among the Jews might have been relieved without the contribution of those two mites, but that the widow would have lost all had she not so contributed. She had hardly arranged her thoughts as to the double blessing of charity, and certainly could not express them with reference to her own case; but she felt the need of giving in this time of trouble something that she herself valued. She was right when she had said that it was hard to be a widow. How many among us, when we give, give from off our own backs, and from out of our own mouths? Who can say that he has sacrificed a want of his own; that he has abandoned a comfort; that he has worn a thread-bare coat, when coats with their gloss on have been his customary wear; that he has fared roughly on cold scraps, whereas a well-spread board has been his usual daily practice? He who has done so has thrown in his two mites, and for him will Charity produce her double blessing.

Nora thought that it was not well in her uncle to tell her that he could do without her wedding-clothes. Of course he could do without them. But she soon threw those words behind her, and went back upon the words which had preceded them. "The bridegroom has a right to expect that the bride shall come to him fairly arrayed." After all, that must depend upon circumstances. Suppose the bride had no means of arraying herself fairly without getting into debt; what would the bridegroom expect in that case?

"If he'll consent, you will?" she said, as she prepared to leave her uncle.

"You'll drive him to offer to pay for the thing himself."

"I daresay he will, and then he'll drive me to refuse. You may be quite sure of this, uncle, that whatever clothes I do wear, he will never see the bill of them;" and then that conference was ended.

"I've made that calculation again," said Bob at breakfast, "and I feel convinced that if an Act of Parliament could be passed restricting the consumption of food in Christmas week,—the entire week, mind,—to that of ordinary weeks, we should get two millions of money, and that those two millions would tide us over till the Indian cotton comes in. Of course I mean by food, butchers' meat, groceries, spirits, and wines. Only think, that by one measure, which would not entail any real disappointment on any one, the whole thing would be done."

"But the Act of Parliament wouldn't give us the money," said his father.

"Of course I don't really mean an Act of Parliament; that would be absurd. But the people might give up their Christmas dinners."

"A great many will, no doubt. Many of those most in earnest are pretty nearly giving up their daily dinners. Those who are indifferent will go on feasting the same as ever. You can't make a sacrifice obligatory."

"It would be no sacrifice if you did," said Nora, still thinking of her wedding-clothes.

"I doubt whether sacrifices ever do any real good," said Frederic F. Frew.

"Oh, Fred!" said Nora.

"We have rather high authority as to the benefit of self-denial," said the parson.

"A man who can't sacrifice himself must be selfish," said Bobby; "and we are all agreed to hate selfish people."

"And what about the widow's mite?" said Mrs. Granger.

"That's all very well, and you may knock me down with the Bible if you like, as you might do also if I talked about pre-Adamite formations. I believe every word of the Bible, but I do not believe that I understand it all thoroughly."

"You might understand it better if you studied it more," said the parson.

"Very likely. I won't be so uncourteous as to say the same thing of my elders. But now, about these sacrifices. You wouldn't wish to keep people in distress that you might benefit yourself by releasing them?"

"But the people in distress are there," said Nora.

"They oughtn't to be there; and as your self-sacrifices, after all, are very insufficient to prevent distress, there certainly seems to be a question open whether some other mode should not be tried. Give me the country in which the humanitarian principle is so exercised that no one shall be degraded by the receipt of charity. It seems to me that you like poor people here in England that you may gratify yourselves by giving them, not as much to eat as they want, but just enough to keep their skins from falling off their bones. Charity may have its double blessing, but it may also have its double curse."

"Not charity, Mr. Frew," said Mrs. Granger.

"Look at your Lady Bountifuls."

"Of course it depends on the heart," continued the lady; "but charity, if it be charity— "

"I'll tell you what," said Frederic F. Frew, interrupting her. "In Philadelphia, which in some matters is the best organised city I know— "

"I'm going down to the village," said the parson, jumping up. "Who is to come with me?" and he escaped out of the room before Frew had had an opportunity of saying a word further about Philadelphia.

"That's the way with your uncle always," said he, turning to Nora, almost in anger. "It certainly is the most conclusive argument I know—that of running away."

"Mr. Granger meant it to be conclusive," said the elder lady.

"But the pity is that it never convinces."

"Mr. Granger probably had no desire of convincing."

"Ah! Well, it does not signify," said Frew. "When a man has a pulpit of his own, why should he trouble himself to argue in any place where counter arguments must be met and sustained?"

Nora was almost angry with her lover, whom she regarded as stronger and more clever than any of her uncle's family, but tyrannical and sometimes overbearing in the use of his strength. One by one her aunt and cousin left the room, and she was left alone with him. He had taken up a newspaper as a refuge in his wrath, for in truth he did not like the manner in which his allusions to his own country were generally treated at the Parsonage. There are Englishmen who think that every man differing with them is bound to bet with them on any point in dispute. "Then you decline to back your opinion," such men say when the bet is refused. The feeling of an American is the same as to those who are unwilling to argue with him. He considers that every intelligent being is bound to argue whenever matter of argument is offered to him; nor can he understand that any subject may be too sacred for argument. Frederic F. Frew, on the present occasion, was as a dog from whose very mouth a bone had been taken. He had given one or two loud, open growls, and now sat with his newspaper, showing his teeth as far as the spirit of the thing went. And it was in this humour that Nora found herself called upon to attack him on the question of her own proposed charity. She knew well that he could bark, even at her, if things went wrong with him. "But then he never bites," she said to herself. He had told her that she might come to her wedding in an old cloak if she pleased, but she had understood that there was nothing serious in this permission. Now, at this very moment, it was incumbent on her to open his eyes to the reality of her intention.

"Fred," she said, "are you reading that newspaper because you are angry with me?"

"I am reading the newspaper because I want to know what there is in it."

"You know all that now, just as well as if you had written it. Put it down, sir!" And she put her hand on to the top of the sheet. "If we are to be married in three weeks' time, I expect that you will be a little attentive to me now. You'll read as many papers as you like after that, no doubt."

"Upon my word, Nora, I think your uncle is the most unfair man I ever met in my life."

"Perhaps he thinks the same of you, and that will make it equal."

"He can't think the same of me. I defy him to think that I'm unfair. There's nothing so unfair as hitting a blow, and then running away when the time comes for receiving the counterblow. It's what your Lord Chatham did, and he never ought to have been listened to in Parliament again."

"That's a long time ago," said Nora, who probably felt that her lover should not talk to her about Lord Chatham just three weeks before their marriage.

"I don't know that the time makes any difference."

"Ah! but I have got something else that I want to speak about. And, Fred, you mustn't turn up your nose at what we are all doing here,—as to giving away things, I mean."

"I don't turn up my nose at it. Haven't I been begging of every American in Liverpool till I'm ashamed of myself?"

"I know you have been very good, and now you must be more good still,—good to me specially, I mean. That isn't being good. That's only being foolish." What little ceremony had led to this last assertion I need not perhaps explain. "Fred, I'm an Englishwoman to-day, but in a month's time I shall be an American."

"I hope so, Nora,—heart and soul."

"Yes; that is what I mean. Whatever is my husband's country must be mine. And you know how well I love your country; do you not? I never run away when you talk to me about Philadelphia,—do I? And you know how I admire all your institutions,—my institutions, as they will be."

"Now I know you're going to ask some very great favour."

"Yes, I am; and I don't mean to be refused, Master Fred. I'm to be an American almost to-morrow, but as yet I am an Englishwoman, and I am bound to do what little I can before I leave my country. Don't you think so?"

"I don't quite understand."

"Well, it's about my wedding-clothes. It does seem stupid talking about them, I know. But I want you to let me do without them altogether. Now you've got the plain truth. I want to give uncle Robert the money for his soup-kitchen, and to be married just as I am now. I do not care one straw what any other creature in the world may say about it, so long as I do not displease you."

"I think it's nonsense, Nora."

"Oh, Fred, don't say so. I have set my heart upon it. I'll do anything for you afterwards. Indeed, for the matter of that, I'd do anything on earth for you, whether you agree or whether you do not. You know that."

"But, Nora, you wouldn't wish to make yourself appear foolish? How much money will you save?"

"Very nearly twenty pounds altogether."

"Let me give you twenty pounds, so that you may leave it with your uncle by way of your two mites, as you call it."

"No, no, certainly not. I might just as well send you the milliner's bill, might I not?"

"I don't see why you shouldn't do that."

"Ah, but I do. You wouldn't wish me to be guilty of the pretence of giving a thing away, and then doing it out of your pocket. I have no doubt that what you were saying about the evil of promiscuous charity is quite true." And then, as she flattered him with this wicked flattery, she looked up with her bright eyes into his face.

"But now, as the things are, we must be charitable, or the people will die. I feel almost like a rat leaving a falling house, in going away at this time; and if you would postpone it— "

"Nora!"

"Then I must be like a rat; but I won't be a rat in a white silk gown. Come now, say that you agree. I never asked you for anything before."

"Everybody will think that you're mad, and that I'm mad, and that we are all mad together."

"Because I go to church in a merino dress? Well; if that makes madness, let us be mad. Oh, Fred, do not refuse me the first thing I've asked you! What difference will it make? Nobody will know it over in Philadelphia!"

"Then you are ashamed of it?"

No, not ashamed. Why should I be ashamed? But one does not wish to have that sort of thing talked about by everybody."

"And you are so strong-minded, Nora, that you do not care about finery yourself?"

"Fred, that's ill-natured. You know very well what my feelings are. You are sharp enough to understand them without any further explanation. I do like finery, quite well enough, as you'll find out to your cost some day. And if ever you scold me for extravagance, I shall tell you about this."

"It's downright Quixotism."

"Quixotism leads to nothing, but this will lead to twenty pounds' worth of soup,—and to something else too."

When he pressed her to explain what that something else was, she declined to speak further on the subject. She could not tell him that the satisfaction she desired was that of giving up something,—of having made a sacrifice,—of having thrown into the treasury her two mites,—two mites off her own back, as she had said to her aunt, and out of her own mouth. He had taxed her with indifference to a woman's usual delight in gay plumage, and had taxed her most unjustly. "He ought to know," she said to herself, "that I should not take all this trouble about it, unless I did care for it." But, in truth, he did understand her motives thoroughly, and half approved them. He approved the spirit of self-abandonment, but disapproved the false political economy by which, according to his light, that spirit was accompanied. "After all," said he, "the widow would have done better to have invested her small capital in some useful trade."

"Oh, Fred;—but never mind now. I have your consent, and now I've only got to talk over my aunt." So saying, she left her lover to turn over in his mind the first principles of that large question of charity.

"The giving of pence and halfpence, of scraps of bread and sups of soup, is, after all, but the charity of a barbarous, half-civilised race. A dog would let another dog starve before he gave him a bone, and would see his starved fellow-dog die without a pang. We have just got beyond that, only beyond that, as long as we dole out sups of soup. But Charity, when it shall have made itself perfect, will have destroyed this little trade of giving, which makes the giver vain and the receiver humble. The Charity of the large-hearted is that which opens to every man the profit of his own industry; to every man and to every woman." Then having gratified himself with the enunciation of this fine theory, he allowed his mind to run away to a smaller subject, and began to think of his own wedding garments. If Nora insisted on carrying out this project of hers, in what guise must he appear on the occasion? He also had ordered new clothes. "It's just the sort of thing that they'll make a story of in Chestnut Street." Chestnut Street, as we all know, is the West End of Philadelphia.

When the morning came of the twelfth of January,—the morning that was to make Nora Field a married woman, she had carried her point; but she was not allowed to feel that she had carried it triumphantly. Her uncle had not forbidden her scheme, but had never encouraged it. Her lover had hardly spoken to her on the subject since the day on which she had explained to him her intention. "After all, it's a mere bagatelle," he had said; "I am not going to marry your clothes." One of her cousins, Bob, had approved; but he had coupled his approval with an intimation that something should be done to prevent any other woman from wearing bridal wreaths for the next three months. Charley had condemned her altogether, pointing out that it was bad policy to feed the cotton-spinners at the expense of the milliners. But the strongest opposition had come from her aunt and the Miss Fosters. Mrs. Granger, though her heart was in the battle which her husband was fighting, could not endure to think that all the time-honoured ceremonies of her life should be abandoned. In spite of all that was going on around her, she had insisted on having mince-pies on the table on Christmas Day. True, there were not many of them, and they were small and flavourless. But the mince-pies were there, with whisky to burn with them instead of brandy, if any of the party chose to go through the ceremony. And to her the idea of a wedding without wedding-clothes was very grievous. It was she who had told Nora that she was a widow with two mites, or might make herself one, if she chose to encounter self-sacrifice. But in so saying she had by no means anticipated such a widowhood as this.

"I really think, Nora, you might have one of those thinner silks, and you might do without a wreath; but you should have a veil;—indeed you should."

But Nora was obstinate. Having overcome her future lord, and quieted her uncle, she was not at all prepared to yield to the mild remonstrances of her aunt. The two Miss Fosters were very much shocked, and for three days there was a disagreeable coolness between them and the Plumstock family. A friend's bridal is always an occasion for a new dress, and the Miss Fosters naturally felt that they were being robbed of their rights.

"Sensible girl," said old Foster, when he heard of it. "When you're married, if ever you are, I hope you'll do the same."

"Indeed we won't, papa," said the two Miss Fosters. But the coolness gradually subsided, and the two Miss Fosters consented to attend in their ordinary Sunday bonnets.

It had been decided that they should be married early, at eight o'clock; that they should then go to the parsonage for breakfast, and that the married couple should start for London immediately afterwards. They were to remain there for a week, and then return to Liverpool for one other remaining week before their final departure for America.

"I should only have had them on for about an hour if I'd got them, and then it would have been almost dark," she said to her aunt.

"Perhaps it won't signify very much," her aunt replied. Then when the morning came, it seemed that the sacrifice had dwindled down to a very little thing. The two Miss Fosters had come to the Parsonage over night, and as they sat up with the bride over a bed-room fire, had been good-natured enough to declare that they thought it would be very good fun.

"You won't have to get up in the cold to dress me," said Nora, "because I can do it all myself; that will be one comfort."

"Oh, we shouldn't have minded that; and as it is, of course, we'll turn you out nice. You'll wear one of your other new dresses; won't you?"

"Oh, I don't know; just what I'm to travel in. It isn't very old. Do you know, after all, I'm not sure that it isn't a great deal better."

"I suppose it will be the same thing in the end," said the younger Miss Foster.

"Of course it will," said the elder.

"And there won't be all that bother of changing my dress," said Nora.

Frederic F. Frew came out to Plumstock by an early train from Liverpool, bringing with him a countryman of his own as his friend on the occasion. It had been explained to the friend that he was to come in his usual habiliments.

"Oh, nonsense!" said the friend, "I guess I'll see you turned off in a new waistcoat." But Frederic F. Frew had made it understood that an old waistcoat was imperative.

"It's something about the cotton, you know. They're all beside themselves here, as though there was never going to be a bit more in the country to eat. That's England all over. Never mind; do you come just as if you were going into your counting-house. Brown cotton gloves, with a hole in the thumbs, will be the thing, I should say."

There were candles on the table when they were all assembled in the Parsonage drawing-room previous to the marriage. The two gentlemen were there first. Then came Mrs. Granger, who rather frightened Mr. Frew by kissing him, and telling him that she should always regard him as a son-in-law.

"Nora has always been like one of ourselves, you know," she said, apologisingly.

"And let me tell you, Master Frew," said the parson, "that you're a very lucky fellow to get her."

"I say, isn't it cold?" said Bob, coming in—"where are the girls?"

"Here are the girls," said Miss Foster, heading the procession of three which now entered the room, Nora, of course, being the last. Then Nora was kissed by everybody, including the strange American gentleman, who seemed to have made some mistake as to his privilege in the matter. But it all passed off very well, and I doubt if Nora knew who kissed her. It was very cold, and they were all wrapped close in their brown shawls and greatcoats, and the women looked very snug and comfortable in their ordinary winter bonnets.

"Come," said the parson, "we mustn't wait for Charley; he'll follow us to church." So the uncle took his niece on his arm, and the two Americans took the two bridesmaids, and Bob took his mother, and went along the beaten path over the snow to the church, and, as they got to the door, Charley rushed after them quite out of breath.

"I haven't even got a pair of gloves at all," he whispered to his mother.

"It doesn't matter; nobody's to know," said Mrs. Granger.

Nora by this time had forgotten the subject of her dress altogether, and it may be doubted if even the Misses Foster were as keenly alive to it as they thought they would have been. For myself, I think they all looked more comfortable on that cold winter morning without the finery which would have been customary than they could have done with it. It had seemed to them all beforehand that a marriage without veils and wreaths, without white gloves and new gay dresses, would be but a triste affair; but the idea passed away altogether when the occasion came. Mr. Granger and his wife and the two lads clustered round Nora as they made themselves ready for the ceremony, uttering words of warm love, and it seemed as though even the clerk and the servants took nothing amiss. Frederic F. Frew had met with a rebuff in the hall of the Parsonage, in being forbidden to take his own bride under his own arm; but when the time for action came, he bore no malice, but went through his work manfully. On the whole, it was a pleasant wedding, homely, affectionate, full of much loving greeting; not without many sobs on the part of the bride and of Mrs. Granger, and some slight suspicion of an eagerly-removed tear in the parson's eye; but this, at any rate, was certain, that the wedding-clothes were not missed. When they all sat down to their breakfast in the Parsonage dining-room, that little matter had come to be clean forgotten. No one knew, not even the Misses Foster, that there was anything extraordinary in their garb. Indeed, as to all gay apparel, we may say that we only miss it by comparison. It is very sad to be the wearer of the only frock-coat in company, to carry the one solitary black silk handerchief at a dinner-party. But I do not know but that a dozen men so arrayed do not seem to be as well dressed as though they had obeyed the latest rules of fashion as to their garments. One thing, however, had been made secure. That sum of twenty pounds, saved from the milliners, had been duly paid over into Mr. Granger's hands. "It has been all very nice," said Mrs. Granger, still sobbing, when Nora went upstairs to tie on her bonnet before she started. "Only you are going!"

"Yes, I'm going now, aunt. Dear aunt! But, aunt, I have failed in one thing—absolutely failed."

"Failed in what, my darling?"

"There has been no widow's mite. It is not easy to be a widow with two mites."

"What you have given will be blessed to you, and blessed to those who will receive it."

"I hope it may; but I almost feel that I have been wrong in thinking of it so much. It has cost me nothing. I tell you, aunt, that it is not easy to be a widow with two mites."

When Mrs. Granger was alone with her husband after this, the two Miss Fosters having returned to Liverpool under the discreet protection of the two young Grangers, for they had positively refused to travel with no other companion than the strange American,—she told him all that Nora had said.

"And who can tell us," he replied, "that it was not the same with the widow herself? She threw in all that she had, but who can say that she suffered aught in consequence? It is my belief that all that is given in a right spirit comes back instantly, in this world, with interest."

"I wish my coals would come back," said Mrs. Granger.

"Perhaps you have not given them in a right spirit, my dear."

The Two Generals

Originally appeared in *Good Words*, December 1863. Reprinted in *Lotta Schmidt and Other Stories* (1867). Written c. 29 October–8 November 1863, during the composition of *Can You Forgive Her*? The germ of the story may have been Trollope's meeting at Washington with Senator John Crittenden (1862). Crittenden's two sons fought as generals on opposite sides in the American Civil War. For a discussion of the causes and early course of the war, see Trollope's travel-book *North America* (1862); for a discussion of the closing stages of the war see the series of articles Trollope contributed to the *Pall Mall Gazette* in 1865. He visited Kentucky, where 'The Two Generals' is set, in January–February 1862, and in *North America* offers a comment on the heart-rending internal politics of the border states at this time: 'Fathers were divided from sons, and mothers from daughters. Terrible tales were told of threats uttered by one member of a family against another. Old ties of friendship were broken up. Society had so divided itself, that one side could hold no terms of courtesy with the other.'

CHRISTMAS OF 1860 is now three years past, and the civil war which was then being commenced in America is still raging without any apparent sign of an end. The prophets of that time who prophesied the worst never foretold anything so black as this. On that Christmas day, Major Anderson, who then held the command of the forts in Charleston harbour on the part of the United States Government, removed his men and stores from Fort Moultrie to Fort Sumter, thinking that he might hold the one, though not both, against any attack from the people of Charleston, whose state, that of South Carolina, had seceded five days previously. That was in truth the beginning of the war, though at that time Mr. Lincoln was not yet President. He became so on the 4th of March, 1861, and on the 15th of April following Fort Sumter was evacuated by Major Anderson, on the part of the United States Government, under fire from the people of Charleston. So little bloody, however, was that affair, that no one was killed in the assault; though one poor fellow perished in the saluting fire with which the retreating officer was complimented as he retired with the so-called honours of war. During the three years that have since passed, the combatants have better learned the use of their weapons of war. No one can now laugh at them for their bloodless battles. Never have the shores of any stream been so bathed in blood, as have the shores of those Virginian rivers whose names have lately become familiar to us. None of those old death-dooming generals of Europe, whom we have learned to hate for the cold-blooded energy of their trade,—Tilly, Gustavus Adolphus, Frederic, or Napoleon,—none of these ever left so many carcases to the kites as have the Johnsons, Jacksons, and Hookers of the American armies, who come and go so fast that they are almost forgotten before the armies they have led have melted into clay.

Of all the states of the old Union, Virginia has probably suffered the most, but Kentucky has least deserved the suffering which has fallen to her lot. In Kentucky the war has raged hither and thither, every town having been subject to inroads from either army. But she would have been loyal to the Union if she could;—nay, on the whole she has been loyal. She would have thrown off the plague chain of slavery if the prurient virtue of New England would have allowed her to do so by her own means. But virtuous New England was too proud of her own virtue to be content that the work of abolition should thus pass from her hands. Kentucky, when the war was beginning, desired nothing but to go on in her own course. She wished for no sudden change. She grew no cotton. She produced corn and meat, and was a land flowing with milk and honey. Her slaves were not as the slaves of the Southern States. They were few in number; tolerated for a time because their manumission was understood to be of all questions the most difficult,—rarely or never sold from the estates to which they belonged. When the war broke out Kentucky said that she would be neutral. Neutral, and she lying on the front lines of the contest! Such neutrality was impossible to her,—impossible to any of her children!

Near to the little State capital of Frankfort, there lived at that

Christmas time of 1860 an old man, Major Reckenthorpe by name, whose life had been marked by many circumstances which had made him well known throughout Kentucky. He had sat for nearly thirty years in the Congress of the United States at Washington, representing his own State sometimes as Senator and sometimes in the lower house. Though called a major he was by profession a lawyer, and as such had lived successfully. Time had been when friends had thought it possible that he might fill the President's chair; but his name had been too much and too long in men's mouths for that. Who had heard of Lincoln, Pierce, or Polk, two years before they were named as candidates for the Presidency? But Major Reckenthorpe had been known and talked of in Washington longer perhaps than any other living politician.

Upon the whole he had been a good man, serving his country as best he knew how, and adhering honestly to his own political convictions. He had been, and now was, a slave-owner, but had voted in the Congress of his own State for the abolition of slavery in Kentucky. He had been a passionate man, and had lived not without the stain of blood on his hands; for duels had been familiar to him. But he had lived in a time and in a country in which it had been hardly possible for a leading public man not to be familiar with a pistol. He had been known as one whom no man could attack with impunity; but he had also been known as one who would not willingly attack any one. Now, at the time of which I am writing, he was old,—almost on the shelf,—past his duellings and his strong short invectives on the floors of Congress; but he was a man whom no age could tame, and still he was ever talking, thinking, and planning for the political well-being of his State.

In person he was tall, still upright, stiff, and almost ungainly in his gait, with eager grey eyes that the waters of age could not dim, with short, thick, grizzled hair which age had hardly thinned, but which ever looked rough and uncombed, with large hands, which he stretched out with extended fingers when he spoke vehemently;—and of the Major it may be said that he always spoke with vehemence. But now he was slow in his steps, and infirm on his legs. He suffered from rheumatism, sciatica, and other maladies of the old, which no energy of his own could repress. In these days he was a stern, unhappy, all but broken-hearted old man; for he saw that the work of his life had been wasted.

And he had another grief, which at this Christmas of 1860 had already become terrible to him, and which afterwards bowed him with sorrow to the ground. He had two sons, both of whom were then at home with him, having come together under the family roof-tree that they might discuss with their father the political position of their country, and especially the position of Kentucky. South Carolina had already seceded, and other Slave States were talking of secession. What should Kentucky do? So the Major's sons, young men of eight-and-twenty and five-and-twenty, met together at their father's house;—they met and quarrelled deeply, as their father had well known would be the case.

The eldest of these sons was at that time the owner of the slaves and land which his father had formerly possessed and farmed. He was a Southern gentleman, living on the produce of slave labour, and as such had learned to vindicate, if not love, that social system which has produced as its result the war which is still raging at this Christmas of 1863. To him this matter of secession or non-secession was of vital import. He was prepared to declare that the wealth of the South was derived from its agriculture, and that its agriculture could only be supported by its slaves. He went further than this, and declared also, that no further league was possible between a Southern gentleman and a Puritan from New England. His father, he said, was an old man, and might be excused by reason of his age from any active part in the contest that was coming. But for himself there could be but one duty,—that of supporting the new Confederacy, to which he would belong, with all his strength and with whatever wealth was his own.

The second son had been educated at Westpoint, the great military school of the old United States, and was now an officer in the national army. Not on that account need it be supposed that he would, as a matter of course, join himself to the Northern side in the war,—to the side which, as being in possession of the capital and the old Government establishments, might claim to possess a right to his military services. A large proportion of the officers in the pay of the United States leagued themselves with Secession,—and it is difficult to see why such an act would be more disgraceful in them than in others. But with Frank Reckenthorpe such was not the case. He declared that he would be loyal to the Government which he served, and in saying so, seemed to imply that the want of such loyalty in any other person, soldier or non-soldier, would be disgraceful, as in his opinion it would have been disgraceful in himself.

"I can understand your feeling," said his brother, who was known as Tom Reckenthorpe, "on the assumption that you think more of being a soldier than of being a man; but not otherwise."

"Even if I were no soldier, I would not be a rebel," said Frank.

"How a man can be a rebel for sticking to his own country, I cannot understand," said Tom.

"Your own country!" said Frank. "Is it to be Kentucky or South Carolina? And is it to be a republic or a monarchy? Or shall we hear of Emperor Davis? You already belong to the greatest nation on the earth, and you are preparing yourself to belong to the least;—that is, if you should be successful. Luckily for yourself, you have no chance of success."

"At any rate, I will do my best to fight for it."

"Nonsense, Tom," said the old man, who was sitting by.

"It is no nonsense, sir. A man can fight without having been at Westpoint. Whether he can do so after having his spirit drilled and drummed out of him there, I don't know."

"Tom!" said the old man.

"Don't mind him, father," said the younger. "His appetite for fighting will soon be over. Even yet I doubt whether we shall ever see a regiment in arms sent from the Southern States against the Union."

"Do you?" said Tom. "If you stick to your colours, as you say you will, your doubts will be soon set at rest. And I'll tell you what, if your regiment is brought into the field, I trust that I may find myself opposite to it. You have chosen to forget that we are brothers, and you shall find that I can forget it also."

"Tom!" said the father, "you should not say such words as that; at any rate, in my presence."

"It is true, sir," said he. "A man who speaks as he speaks does not belong to Kentucky, and can be no brother of mine. If I were to meet him face to face, I would as soon shoot him as another;—sooner, because he is a renegade."

"You are very wicked,—very wicked," said the old man, rising from his chair,—"very wicked." And then, leaning on his stick, he left the room.

"Indeed, what he says is true," said a sweet, soft voice from a sofa in the far corner of the room. "Tom, you are very wicked to speak to your brother thus. Would you take on yourself the part of Cain?"

"He is more silly than wicked, Ada," said the soldier. "He will have no chance of shooting me, or of seeing me shot. He may succeed in getting himself locked up as a rebel; but I doubt whether he'll ever go beyond that."

"If I ever find myself opposite to you with a pistol in my grasp," said the elder brother, "may my right hand— "

But his voice was stopped, and the imprecation remained unuttered. The girl who had spoken rushed from her seat, and put her hand before his mouth.

"Tom," she said, "I will never speak to you again if you utter such an oath,—never!"

And her eyes flashed fire at his and made him dumb.

Ada Forster called Mrs. Reckenthorpe her aunt, but the connexion between them was not so near as that of aunt and niece. Ada nevertheless lived with the Reckenthorpes, and had done so for the last two years. She was an orphan, and on the death of her father had followed her father's sister-in-law from Maine down to Kentucky;—for Mrs. Reckenthorpe had come from that farthest and most strait-laced State of the Union, in which people bind themselves by law to drink neither beer, wine, nor spirits, and all go to bed at nine o'clock. But Ada Forster was an heiress, and therefore it was thought well by the elder Reckenthorpes that she should marry one of their sons. Ada Forster was also a beauty, with slim, tall form, very pleasant to the eye; with bright, speaking eyes and glossy hair; with ivory teeth of the whitest,—only to be seen now and then when a smile could be won from her; and therefore such a match was thought desirable also by the younger Reckenthorpes. But unfortunately it had been thought desirable by each of them whereas the father and mother had intended Ada for the soldier.

I have not space in this short story to tell how progress had been made in the troubles of this love affair. So it was now, that Ada had consented to become the wife of the elder brother,—of Tom Reckenthorpe, with his home among the slaves,—although she, with all her New England feelings strong about her, hated slavery and all its adjuncts. But when has Love stayed to be guided by any such consideration as that? Tom Reckenthorpe was a handsome, high-spirited, intelligent man. So was his brother Frank. But Tom Reckenthorpe could be soft to a woman, and in that, I think, had he found the means of his success. Frank Reckenthorpe was never soft.

Frank had gone angrily from home when, some three months since, Ada had told him her determination. His brother had been then absent, and they had not met till this their Christmas meeting. Now it had been understood between them, by the intervention of their mother, that they would say nothing to each other as to Ada Forster. The elder had, of course, no cause for saying aught, and Frank was too proud to wish to speak on such a matter before his successful rival. But Frank had not given up the battle. When Ada had made her speech to him, he had told her that he would not take it as conclusive.

"The whole tenor of Tom's life," he had said to her, "must be distasteful to you. It is impossible that you should live as the wife of a slave-owner."

"In a few years there will be no slaves in Kentucky," she had answered.

"Wait till then," he had answered; "and I also will wait."

And so he had left her, resolving that he would bide his time. He thought that the right still remained to him of seeking Ada's hand, although she had told him that she loved his brother.

"I know that such a marriage would make each of them miserable," he said to himself over and over again. And now that these terrible times had come upon them, and that he was going one way with the Union, while his brother was going the other way with Secession, he felt more strongly than ever that he might still be successful. The political predilections of American women are as strong as those of American men. And Frank Reckenthorpe knew that all Ada's feelings were as strongly in favour of the Union as his own. Had not she been born and bred in Maine? Was she not ever keen for total abolition, till even the old Major, with all his gallantry for womanhood and all his love for the young girl who had come to his house in his old age, would be driven occasionally by stress of feeling to rebuke her? Frank Reckenthorpe was patient, hopeful, and firm. The time must come when Ada would learn that she could not be a fit wife for his brother. The time had, he thought, perhaps come already; and so he spoke to her a word or two on the evening of that day on which she had laid her hand upon his brother's mouth.

"Ada," he had said, "there are bad times coming to us."

"Good times, I hope," she had answered. "No one could expect that the thing could be done without some struggle. When the struggle has passed we shall say that good times have come." The thing of which she spoke was that little thing of which she was ever thinking—the enfranchisement of four millions of slaves.

"I fear that there will be bad times first. Of course I am thinking of you now."

"Bad or good, they will not be worse to me than to others."

"They would be very bad to you if this State were to secede, and if you were to join your lot to my brother's. In the first place, all your fortune would be lost to him and to you."

"I do not see that; but of course I will caution him that it may be so. If it alters his views, I shall hold him free to act as he chooses."

"But, Ada, should it not alter yours?"

"What,—because of my money?—or because Tom could not afford to marry a girl without a fortune?"

"I did not mean that. He might decide that for himself. But your marriage with him under such circumstances as those which he now contemplates, would be as though you married a Spaniard or a Greek adventurer. You would be without country, without home, without fortune, and without standing-ground in the world. Look you, Ada, before you answer. I frankly own that I tell you this because I want you to be my wife, and not his."

"Never, Frank; I shall never be your wife, whether I marry him or no."

"All I ask of you now is to pause. This is no time for marrying or for giving in marriage."

"There I agree with you; but as my word is pledged to him, I shall let him be my adviser in that."

Late on that same night Ada saw her betrothed and bade him adieu. She bade him adieu with many tears, for he came to tell her that he intended to leave Frankfort very early on the following morning.

"My staying here now is out of the question," said he. "I am resolved to secede, whatever the State may do. My father is resolved against secession. It is necessary, therefore, that we should part. I have already left my father and mother, and now I have come to say good-bye to you."

"And your brother, Tom?"

"I shall not see my brother again."

"And is that well after such words as you have spoken to each other? Perhaps it may be that you will never see him again. Do you remember what you threatened?"

"I do remember what I threatened."

"And did you mean it?"

"No; of course I did not mean it. You, Ada, have heard me speak many angry words, but I do not think that you have known me do many angry things."

"Never one, Tom:—never. See him then before you go, and tell him so."

"No,—he is hard as iron, and would take any such telling from me amiss. He must go his way, and I mine."

"But though you differ as men, Tom, you need not hate each other as brothers."

"It will be better that we should not meet again. The truth is, Ada, that he always despises any one who does not think as he does. If I offered him my hand he would take it, but while doing so he would let me know that he thought me a fool. Then I should be angry, and threaten him again, and things would be worse. You must not quarrel with me, Ada, if I say that he has all the faults of a Yankee."

"And the virtues too, sir, while you have all the faults of a Southern—But, Tom, as you are going from us, I will not scold you. I have, too, a word of business to say to you."

"And what's the word of business, dear?" said Tom, getting nearer to her, as a lover should do, and taking her hand in his.

"It is this. You and those who think like you are dividing yourselves from your country. As to whether that be right or wrong, I will say nothing now,—nor will I say anything as to your chance of success. But I am told that those who go with the South will not be able to hold property in the North."

"Did Frank tell you that?"

"Never mind who told me, Tom."

"And is that to make a difference between you and me?"

"That is just the question that I am asking you. Only you ask me with a reproach in your tone, and I ask you with none in mine. Till we have mutually agreed to break our engagement you shall be my adviser. If you think it better that it should be broken,—better for your own interests, be man enough to say so."

But Tom Reckenthorpe either did not think so, or else he was not man enough to speak his thoughts. Instead of doing so, he took the girl in his arms and kissed her, and swore that, whether with fortune or no fortune, she should be his, and his only. But still he had to go,—to go now, within an hour or two of the very moment at which they were speaking. They must part, and before parting must make some mutual promise as to their future meeting. Marriage now, as things stood at this Christmas time, could not be thought of even by Tom Reckenthorpe. At last he promised that if he were then alive he would be with her again, at the old family-house at Frankfort, on the next coming Christmas day. So he went, and as he let himself out of the old house, Ada, with her eyes full of tears, took herself up to her bedroom.

During the year that followed,—the year 1861,—the American war progressed only as a school for fighting. The most memorable action was that of Bull's Run, in which both sides ran away, not from individual cowardice in either set of men, but from that feeling of panic which is engendered by ignorance and inexperience. Men saw wagons rushing hither and thither, and thought that all was lost. After that the year was passed in drilling and in camp-making,—in the making of soldiers, of gun-powder, and of cannons. But of all the articles of war made in that year, the article that seemed easiest of fabrication was a general officer. Generals were made with the greatest rapidity, owing their promotion much more frequently to local interest than to military success. Such a State sent such and such regiments, and therefore must be rewarded by having such and such generals nominated from among its citizens. The wonder, perhaps, is that with armies so formed battles should have been fought so well.

Before the end of 1861, both Major Reckenthorpe's sons had become general officers. That Frank, the soldier, should have been so promoted was, at such a period as this, nothing strange. Though a young man he had been a soldier, or learning the trade of a soldier, for more than ten years, and such service as that might well be counted for much in the sudden construction of an army intended to number seven hundred thousand troops, and which at one time did contain all those soldiers. Frank, too, was a clever fellow, who knew his business, and there were many generals made in those days who understood less of their work than he did. As much could not be said for Tom's quick military advancement. But this could be said for them in the South,—that unless they did make their generals in this way, they would hardly have any generals at all, and General Reckenthorpe, as he so quickly became,—General Tom as they used to call him in Kentucky,—recommended himself specially to the Confederate leaders by the warmth and eagerness with which he had come among them. The name of the old man so well known throughout the Union, who had ever loved the South without hating the North, would have been a tower of strength to them. Having him they would have thought that they might have carried the State of Kentucky into open secession. He was now worn-out and old, and could not be expected to take upon his shoulders the crushing burden of a new contest. But his eldest son had come among them eagerly, with his whole heart; and so they made him a general.

The poor old man was in part proud of this and in part grieved.

"I have a son a general in each army," he said to a stranger who came to his house in those days; "but what strength is there in a fagot when it is separated? Of what use is a house that is divided against itself? The boys would kill each other if they met."

"It is very sad," said the stranger.

"Sad!" said the old man. "It is as though the devil were let loose upon the earth;—and so he is; so he is."

The family came to understand that General Tom was with the Confederate army which was confronting the Federal army of the Potomac and defending Richmond; whereas it was well known that Frank was in Kentucky with the army on the Green River, which was hoping to make its way into Tennessee, and which did so early in the following year. It must be understood that Kentucky, though a slave state, had never seceded, and that therefore it was divided off from the Southern States, such as Tennessee and that part of Virginia which had seceded, by a cordon of pickets; so that there was no coming up from the Confederate army to Frankfort, in Kentucky. There could, at any rate, be no easy or safe coming up for such a one as General Tom, seeing that being a soldier he would be regarded as a spy, and certainly treated as a prisoner if found within the northern lines. Nevertheless, General as he was, he kept his engagement with Ada, and made his way into the gardens of his father's house on the night of Christmas-eve. And Ada was the first who knew that he was there. Her ear first caught the sound of his footsteps, and her hand raised for him the latch of the garden door.

"Oh, Tom, it is not you?"

"But it is though, Ada, my darling!" Then there was a little pause in his speech. "Did I not tell you that I should see you to-day?"

"Hush. Do you know who is here? Your brother came across to us from the Green River yesterday."

"The mischief he did! Then I shall never find my way back again. If you knew what I have gone through for this!"

Ada immediately stepped out through the door and on to the snow, standing close up against him as she whispered to him, "I don't think Frank would betray you," she said. "I don't think he would."

"I doubt him,—doubt him hugely. But I suppose I must trust him. I got through the pickets close to Cumberland Gap, and I left my horse at Stoneley's half way between this and Lexington. I cannot go back to-night now that I have come so far!"

"Wait, Tom; wait a minute, and I will go in and tell your mother. But you must be hungry. Shall I bring you food?"

"Hungry enough, but I will not eat my father's victuals out here in the snow."

"Wait a moment, dearest, till I speak to my aunt."

Then Ada slipped back into the house and soon managed to get Mrs. Reckenthorpe away from the room in which the Major and his second son were sitting.

"Tom is here," she said, "in the garden. He has encountered all this danger to pay us a visit because it is Christmas. Oh, aunt, what are we to do? He says that Frank would certainly give him up!"

Mrs. Reckenthorpe was nearly twenty years younger than her husband, but even with this advantage on her side Ada's tidings were almost too much for her. She, however, at last managed to consult the Major, and he resolved upon appealing to the generosity of his younger son. By this time the Confederate General was warming himself in the kitchen, having declared that his brother might do as he pleased;—he would not skulk away from his father's house in the night.

"Frank," said the father, as his younger son sat silently thinking of what had been told him, "it cannot be your duty to be false to your father in his own house."

"It is not always easy, sir, for a man to see what is his duty. I wish that either he or I had not come here."

"But he is here; and you, his brother, would not take advantage of his coming to his father's house?" said the old man.

"Do you remember, sir, how he told me last year that if ever he met me on the field he would shoot me like a dog?"

"But, Frank, you know that he is the last man in the world

to carry out such a threat. Now he has come here with great danger."

"And I have come with none; but I do not see that that makes any difference."

"He has put up with it all that he may see the girl he loves."

"Psha!" said Frank, rising up from his chair. "When a man has work to do, he is a fool to give way to play. The girl he loves! Does he not know that it is impossible that she should ever marry him? Father, I ought to insist that he should leave this house as a prisoner. I know that that would be my duty."

"You would have, sir, to bear my curse."

"I should not the less have done my duty. But, father, independently of your threat, I will neglect that duty. I cannot bring myself to break your heart and my mother's. But I will not see him. Good-bye, sir. I will go up to the hotel, and will leave the place before daybreak to-morrow."

After some few further words Frank Reckenthorpe left the house without encountering his brother. He also had not seen Ada Forster since that former Christmas when they had all been together, and he had now left his camp and come across from the army much more with the view of inducing her to acknowledge the hopelessness of her engagement with his brother, than from any domestic idea of passing his Christmas at home. He was a man who would not have interfered with his brother's prospects, as regarded either love or money, if he had thought that in doing so he would in truth have injured his brother. He was a hard man, but one not wilfully unjust. He had satisfied himself that a marriage between Ada and his brother must, if it were practicable, be ruinous to both of them. If this were so, would not it be better for all parties that there should be another arrangement made? North and South were as far divided now as the two poles. All Ada's hopes and feelings were with the North. Could he allow her to be taken as a bride among perishing slaves and ruined whites?

But when the moment for his sudden departure came he knew that it would be better that he should go without seeing her. His brother Tom had made his way to her through cold, and wet, and hunger, and through infinite perils of a kind sterner even than these. Her heart now would be full of softness towards him. So Frank Reckenthorpe left the house without seeing any one but his mother. Ada, as the front door closed behind him, was still standing close by her lover over the kitchen fire, while the slaves of the family with whom Master Tom had always been the favourite, were administering to his little comforts.

Of course General Tom was a hero in the house for the few days that he remained there, and of course the step he had taken was the very one to strengthen for him the affection of the girl whom he had come to see.

North and South were even more bitterly divided now than they had been when the former parting had taken place. There were fewer hopes of reconciliation; more positive certainty of war to the knife; and they who adhered strongly to either side—and those who did not adhere strongly to either side were very few,—held their opinions now with more acrimony than they had then done. The peculiar bitterness of civil war, which adds personal hatred to national enmity, had come upon the minds of the people. And here, in Kentucky, on the borders of the contest, members of the same household were, in many cases, at war with each other.

Ada Forster and her aunt were passionately Northern, while the feelings of the old man had gradually turned themselves to that division in the nation to which he naturally belonged. For months past the matter on which they were all thinking,—the subject which filled their minds morning, noon, and night,—was banished from their lips because it could not be discussed without the bitterness of hostility. But, nevertheless, there was no word of bitterness between Tom Reckenthorpe and Ada Forster. While these few short days lasted it was all love. Where is the woman whom one touch of romance will not soften, though she be ever so impervious to argument? Tom could sit up-stairs with his mother and his betrothed, and tell them stories of the gallantry of the South,—of the sacrifices women were making, and of the deeds men were doing,—and they would listen and smile and caress his hand, and all for a while would be pleasant; while the old Major did not dare to speak before them of his Southern hopes. But down in the parlour, during the two or three long nights which General Tom passed in Frankfort, open secession was discussed between the two men. The old man now had given away altogether. The Yankees, he said, were too bitter for him.

"I wish I had died first; that is all," he said. "I wish I had died first. Life is wretched now to a man who can do nothing."

His son tried to comfort him, saying that secession would certainly be accomplished in twelve months, and that every Slave State would certainly be included in the Southern confederacy. But the Major shook his head. Though he hated the political bitterness of the men whom he called Puritans and Yankees, he knew their strength and acknowledged their power.

"Nothing good can come in my time," he said; "not in my time,—not in my time."

In the middle of the fourth night General Tom took his departure. An old slave arrived with his horse a little before midnight, and he started on his journey.

"Whatever turns up, Ada," he said, "you will be true to me."

"I will; though you are a rebel all the same for that."

"So was Washington."

"We are making another, dear; that's all. But I won't talk secesh to you out here in the cold. Go in, and be good to my father; and remember this, Ada, I'll be here again next Christmas-eve, if I'm alive."

So he went, and made his journey back to his own camp in safety. He slept at a friend's house during the following day, and on the next night again made his way through the Northern lines back into Virginia. Even at that time there was considerable danger in doing this, although the frontier to be guarded was so extensive. This arose chiefly from the paucity of roads, and the impossibility of getting across the country where no roads existed. But General Tom got safely back to Richmond, and no doubt found that the tedium of his military life had been greatly relieved by his excursion.

Then, after that, came a year of fighting,—and there has since come another year of fighting; of such fighting that we, hearing the accounts from day to day, have hitherto failed to recognise its extent and import. Every now and then we have even spoken of the inaction of this side or of that, as though the drawn battles which have lasted for days, in which men have perished by tens of thousands, could be renewed as might the old German battles, in which an Austrian general would be ever retreating with infinite skill and military efficacy. For constancy, for blood, for hard determination to win at any cost of life or material, history has known no such battles as these. That the South have fought the best as regards skill no man can doubt. As regards pluck and resolution there has not been a pin's choice between them. They have both fought as Englishmen fight when they are equally in earnest. As regards result, it has been almost altogether in favour of the North, because they have so vast a superiority in numbers and material.

General Tom Reckenthorpe remained during the year in Virginia, and was attached to that corps of General Lee's army which was commanded by Stonewall Jackson. It was not probable, therefore, that he would be left without active employment. During the whole year he was fighting, assisting in the wonderful raids that were made by that man whose loss was worse to the Confederates than the loss of Vicksburg or of New Orleans. And General Tom gained for himself mark, name, and glory,—but it was the glory of a soldier rather than of a general. No one looked upon him as the future commander of an army; but men said that if there was a rapid stroke to be stricken, under orders from some more thoughtful head, General Tom was the hand to strike it. Thus he went on making wonderful rides by night, appearing like a warrior ghost leading warrior ghosts in some quiet valley of the Federals, seizing supplies and cutting off cattle, till his name came to be great in the State of Kentucky, and Ada Forster, Yankee though she was, was proud of her rebel lover.

And Frank Reckenthorpe, the other general, made progress also, though it was progress of a different kind. Men did not talk of him so much as they did of Tom; but the War Office at Washington knew that he was useful,—and used him. He remained for a long time attached to the Western army, having been removed from Kentucky to St. Louis, in Missouri, and was there when his brother last heard of him.

"I am fighting day and night," he once said to one who was with him from his own State, "and, as far as I can learn, Frank is writing day and night. Upon my word, I think that I have the best of it."

It was but a couple of days after this, the time then being about the latter end of September, that Tom Reckenthorpe found himself on horseback at the head of three regiments of cavalry, near the foot of one of those valleys which lead up into the Blue Mountain ridge of

Virginia. He was about six miles in advance of Jackson's army, and had pushed forward with the view of intercepting certain Federal supplies which he and others had hoped might be within his reach. He had expected that there would be fighting, but he had hardly expected so much fighting as came that day in his way. He got no supplies. Indeed, he got nothing but blows, and though on that day the Confederates would not admit that they had been worsted, neither could they claim to have done more than hold their own. But General Tom's fighting was on that day brought to an end.

It must be understood that there was no great battle fought on this occasion. General Reckenthorpe, with about 1500 troopers, had found himself suddenly compelled to attack about double that number of Federal infantry. He did so once, and then a second time, but on each occasion without breaking the lines to which he was opposed; and towards the close of the day he found himself unhorsed, but still unwounded, with no weapon in his hand but his pistol, immediately surrounded by about a dozen of his own men, but so far in advance of the body of his troops as to make it almost impossible that he should find his way back to them.

As the smoke cleared away and he could look about him, he saw that he was close to an uneven, irregular line of Federal soldiers. But there was still a chance, and he had turned for a rush, with his pistol ready for use in his hand, when he found himself confronted by a Federal officer. The pistol was already raised, and his finger was on the trigger, when he saw that the man before him was his brother.

"Your time is come," said Frank, standing his ground very calmly. He was quite unarmed, and had been separated from his men and ridden over; but hitherto had not been hurt.

"Frank!" said Tom, dropping his pistol arm, "is that you?"

"And you are not going to do it then?" said Frank.

"Do what?" said Tom, whose calmness was altogether gone. But he had forgotten that threat as soon as it had been uttered, and did not even know to what his brother was alluding.

But Tom Reckenthorpe, in his confusion at meeting his brother, had lost whatever chance there remained to him of escaping. He stood for a moment or two, looking at Frank, and wondering at the coincidence which had brought them together, before he turned to run. Then it was too late. In the hurry and scurry of the affair all but two of his own men had left him, and he saw that a rush of Federal soldiers was coming up around him.

Nevertheless he resolved to start for a run.

"Give me a chance, Frank," he said, and prepared to run. But as he went,—or rather before he had left the ground on which he was standing before his brother, a shot struck him, and he was disabled. In a minute he was as though he were stunned; then he smiled faintly, and slowly sunk upon the ground.

"It's all up, Frank," he said, "and you are in at the death."

Frank Reckenthorpe was soon kneeling beside his brother, amidst a crowd of his own men.

"Spurrell," he said to a young officer who was close to him, "it is my own brother."

"What, General Tom?" said Spurrell. "Not dangerously, I hope?"

By this time the wounded man had been able, as it were, to feel himself and to ascertain the amount of the damage done him.

"It's my right leg," he said; "just on the knee. If you'll believe me, Frank, I thought it was my heart at first. I don't think much of the wound, but I suppose you won't let me go."

Of course they wouldn't let him go, and indeed if they had been minded so to do, he could not have gone. The wound was not fatal, as he had at first thought; but neither was it a matter of little consequence as he afterwards asserted. His fighting was over, unless he could fight with a leg amputated between the knee and the hip.

Before nightfall General Tom found himself in his brother's quarters, a prisoner on parole, with his leg all but condemned by the surgeon. The third day after that saw the leg amputated. For three weeks the two brothers remained together, and after that the elder was taken to Washington,—or rather to Alexandria, on the other side of the Potomac, as a prisoner, there to await his chance of exchange. At first the intercourse between the two brothers was cold, guarded, and uncomfortable; but after a while it became more kindly than it had been for many a day. Whether it were cold or kindly, its nature, we may be sure, was such as the younger brother made it. Tom was ready enough to forget all personal animosity as soon as his brother would himself be willing to do so; though he was willing enough also to quarrel,—to quarrel bitterly as ever,—if Frank should give him occasion. As to that threat of the pistol, it had passed away from Tom Reckenthorpe, as all his angry words passed from him. It was clean forgotten. It was not simply that he had not wished to kill his brother, but that such a deed was impossible to him. The threat had been like a curse that means nothing,—which is used by passion as its readiest weapon when passion is impotent. But with Frank Reckenthorpe words meant what they were intended to mean. The threat had rankled in his bosom from the time of its utterance, to that moment when a strange coincidence had given the threatener the power of executing it. The remembrance of it was then strong upon him, and he had expected that his brother would have been as bad as his word. But his brother had spared him; and now, slowly, by degrees, he began to remember that also.

"What are your plans, Tom?" he said, as he sat one day by his brother's bed before the removal of the prisoner to Alexandria.

"Plans?" said Tom. "How should a poor fellow like me have plans? To eat bread and water in prison at Alexandria, I suppose?"

"They'll let you up to Washington on your parole, I should think. Of course, I can say a word for you."

"Well, then, do say it. I'd have done as much for you, though I don't like your Yankee politics."

"Never mind my politics now, Tom."

"I never did mind them. But at any rate, you see I can't run away."

It should have been mentioned a little way back in this story that the poor old Major had been gathered to his fathers during the past year. As he had said himself, it would be better for him that he should die. He had lived to see the glory of his country, and had gloried in it. If further glory, or even further gain, were to come out of this terrible war,—as great gains to men and nations do come from contests which are very terrible while they last,—he at least would not live to see it. So when he was left by his sons, he turned his face to the wall and died. There had of course been much said on this subject between the two brothers when they were together, and Frank had declared how special orders had been given to protect the house of the widow, if the waves of the war in Kentucky should surge up around Frankfort. Land very near to Frankfort had become debateable between the two armies, and the question of flying from their house had more than once been mooted between the aunt and her niece; but, so far, that evil day had been staved off, and as yet Frankfort, the little capital of the State, was Northern territory.

"I suppose you will get home," said Frank, after musing awhile, "and look after my mother and Ada?"

"If I can I shall, of course. What else can I do with one leg?"

"Nothing in this war, Tom, of course."

Then there was another pause between them.

"And what will Ada do?" said Frank.

"What will Ada do? Stay at home with my mother."

"Ay,—yes. But she will not remain always as Ada Forster."

"Do you mean to ask whether I shall marry her;—because of my one leg? If she will have me, I certainly shall."

"And will she? Ought you to ask her?"

"If I found her seamed all over with small-pox, with her limbs broken, blind, disfigured by any misfortune which could have visited her, I would take her as my wife all the same. If she were penniless it would make no difference. She shall judge for herself; but I shall expect her to act by me as I would have acted by her." Then there was another pause. "Look here, Frank," continued General Tom, "if you mean that I am to give her up as a reward to you for being sent home, I will have nothing to do with the bargain."

"I had intended no such bargain," said Frank, gloomily.

"Very well; then you can do as you please. If Ada will take me, I shall marry her as soon as she will let me. If my being sent home depends upon that, you will know how to act now."

Nevertheless he was sent home. There was not another word spoken between the two brothers about Ada Forster. Whether Frank thought that he might still have a chance through want of firmness on the part of the girl; or whether he considered that in keeping his brother away from home he could at least do himself no good; or whether, again, he resolved that he would act by his brother as a brother should act, without reference to Ada Forster, I will not attempt to say. For a day or two after the above conversation he was somewhat sullen, and did not talk freely with his brother. After that he brightened up once more, and before long the two parted on friendly terms. General Frank remained with his command, and General Tom was sent to the hospital at Alexandria,—or to such hospitalities as he might be able to enjoy at Washington in his mutilated state,—till that affair of his exchange had been arranged.

In spite of his brother's influence at head-quarters this could not be done in a day; nor could permission be obtained for him to go home to Kentucky till such exchange had been effected. In this way he was kept in terrible suspense for something over two months, and mid-winter was upon him before the joyful news arrived that he was free to go where he liked. The officials in Washington would have sent him back to Richmond had he so pleased, seeing that a Federal general officer, supposed to be of equal weight with himself, had been sent back from some Southern prison in his place; but he declined any such favour, declaring his intention of going home to Kentucky. He was simply warned that no pass South could after this be granted to him, and then he went his way.

Disturbed as was the state of the country, nevertheless railways ran from Washington to Baltimore, from Baltimore to Pittsburgh, from Pittsburgh to Cincinnati, and from Cincinnati to Frankfort. So that General Tom's journey home, though with but one leg, was made much faster, and with less difficulty, than that last journey by which he reached the old family house. And again he presented himself on Christmas Eve. Ada declared that he remained purposely at Washington, so that he might make good his last promise to the letter; but I am inclined to think that he allowed no such romantic idea as that to detain him among the amenities of Washington.

He arrived again after dark, but on this occasion did not come knocking at the back door. He had fought his fight, had done his share of the battle, and now had reason to be afraid of no one. But again it was Ada who opened the door for him. "Oh, Tom; oh, my own one!" There never was a word of question between them as to whether that unseemly crutch and still unhealed wound was to make any difference between them. General Tom found before three hours were over that he lacked the courage to suggest that he might not be acceptable to her as a lover with one leg. There are times in which girls throw off all their coyness, and are as bold in their loves as men. Such a time was this with Ada Forster. In the course of another month the elder general simply sent word to the younger that they intended to be married in May, if the war did not prevent them; and the younger general simply sent back word that his duties at head-quarters would prevent his being present at the ceremony.

And they were married in May, though the din of war was going on around them on every side. And from that time to this the din of war is still going on, and they are in the thick of it. The carnage of their battles, and the hatreds of their civil contests, are terrible to us when we think of them; but may it not be that the beneficent power of Heaven, which they acknowledge as we do, is thus cleansing their land from that stain of slavery, to abolish which no human power seemed to be sufficient?

Miss Ophelia Gledd

Originally appeared in *A Welcome: Original Contributions in Poetry and Prose Addressed to Alexandra, Princess of Wales* (London: Emily Faithfull and Co., 1863). This volume, similar in format to *Victoria Regia* (see 'The Journey to Panama'), was issued in celebration of the marriage of the Prince of Wales with the Princess Alexandra. Trollope's fellow contributors included the Rossettis (Dante Gabriel and Christina), George Macdonald, Charles Kingsley and F.D. Maurice. 'Miss Ophelia Gledd' was reprinted in *Lotta Schmidt and Other Stories* (1867). Trollope himself had a go at sleighing when he returned to Boston in March 1862, and the results are recorded in *North America*: 'There was a lady with me on the sleigh whom, for a while, I felt I was doomed to consign to a snowy grave,—whom I would willingly have overturned into a drift of snow, so as to avoid worse consequences, had I only known how to do so.' A slightly sentimental tradition suggests that Ophelia Gledd owes something to the author's close Boston friend Kate Field. Like 'The O'Conors of Castle Conor' and 'Father Giles of Ballymoy', this story features Archibald Green as an authorial persona.

WHO CAN say what is a lady? My intelligent and well-bred reader of either sex will at once declare that he and she knows very well who is a lady. So, I hope, do I. But the present question goes further than that. What is it, and whence does it come? Education does not give it, nor intelligence, nor birth, not even the highest. The thing, which in its presence or absence is so well known and understood, may be wanting to the most polished manners, to the sweetest disposition, to the truest heart. There are thousands among us who know it at a glance, and can recognise its presence from the sound of a dozen words, but there is not one among us who can tell us what it is.

Miss Ophelia Gledd was a young lady of Boston, Massachussetts, and I should be glad to know whether in the estimation of my countrymen and countrywomen she is to be esteemed a lady.

An Englishman, even of the best class, is often at a loss to judge of the "ladyship" of a foreigner, unless he has really lived in foreign cities and foreign society; but I do not know that he is ever so much puzzled in this matter by any nationality as he is by the American.

American women speak his own language, read his own literature, and in many respects think his own thoughts; but there have crept into American society so many little social ways at variance with our social ways, there have been wafted thither so many social atoms which there fit into their places, but which with us would clog the wheels, that the words, and habits, and social carriage, of an American woman, of the best class, too often offend the taste of an Englishman; as do, quite as strongly, those of the Englishwoman offend the American.

There are those who declare that there are no American ladies; but these are people who would probably declare the same of the French and the Italians, if the languages of France and Italy were as familiar to their ears as is the language of the States. They mean that American women do not grow up to be English ladies,—not bethinking themselves that such a growth was hardly to be expected. Now I will tell my story, and ask my readers to answer this question,—Was Miss Ophelia Gledd a lady?

When I knew her she was at any rate great in the society of Boston, Massachussetts, in which city she had been as well known for the last four or five years as the yellow dome of the State House. She was as pure and perfect a specimen of a Yankee girl as ever it was my fortune to know.

Standing about five feet eight, she seemed to be very tall, because she always carried herself at her full height. She was thin too, and rather narrower at the shoulders than the strictest rules of symmetry would have made her. Her waist was very slight; so much so, that to the eye it would seem that some unjust and injurious force had created its slender compass; but I have fair ground for stating my belief that no such force had been employed. But yet, though she was slight and thin, and even narrow, there was a vivacity and quickness about all her movements, and an easiness in her mode of moving which made it impossible to deny to her the merit of a pleasing figure.

No man would, I think, at first sight, declare her to be pretty, and certainly no woman would do so; and yet I have seldom known a face in the close presence of which it was more gratifying to sit, and talk, and listen. Her brown hair was always brushed close off from her forehead. Her brow was high, and her face narrow and thin; but that face was ever bright with motion, and her clear, deep, grey eyes, full of life and light, were always ready for some combat or some enterprise. Her nose and mouth were the best features in her face, and her teeth were perfect,—miracles of perfection; but her lips were too thin for feminine beauty; and indeed such personal charms as she had were not the charms which men love most,—sweet changing colour, soft full flowing lines of grace, and womanly gentleness in every movement. Ophelia Gledd had none of these. She was hard and sharp in shape, of a good brown steady colour, hard and sharp also in her gait; with no full flowing lines, with no softness; but she was bright as burnished steel.

And yet she was the belle of Boston. I do not know that any man of Boston,—or any stranger knowing Boston would have ever declared that she was the prettiest girl in the city; but this was certain almost to all,—that she received more of that admiration which is generally given to beauty than did any other lady there; and that the upper social world of Boston had become so used to her appearance, such as it was, that no one ever seemed to question the fact of her being a beauty. She had been passed as a beauty by examiners whose certificate in that matter was held to be good, and had received high rank as a beauty in the drawing-rooms at Boston.

The fact was never questioned now, unless by some passing stranger who would be told in flat terms that he was wrong.

"Yes, sir; you'll find you're wrong; you'll find you aire, if you'll bide here awhile."

I did bide there awhile, and did find that I was wrong. Before I left I was prepared to allow that Miss Ophelia Gledd was a beauty. And moreover, which was more singular, all the women allowed it.

Ophelia Gledd, though the belle of Boston, was not hated by the other belles. The female feeling with regard to her was, I think this, that the time had arrived in which she should choose her husband, and settle down, so as to leave room for others less attractive than herself.

When I knew her she was very fond of men's society; but I doubt if any one could fairly say that Miss Gledd ever flirted. In the proper sense of the word she certainly never flirted. Interesting conversations with interesting young men at which none but themselves were present she had by the dozen. It was as common for her to walk up and down Beacon Street,—the parade of Boston,—with young Jones, or Smith, or more probably with young Mr. Optimus M. Opie, or young Mr. Hannibal H. Hoskins, as it is for our young Joneses, and young Smiths, and young Hoskinses, to saunter out together.

That is the way of the country, and no one took wider advantage of the ways of her own country than did Miss Ophelia Gledd. She told young men also when to call upon her, if she liked them; and in seeking or in avoiding their society, did very much as she pleased.

But these practices are right or wrong, not in accordance with a fixed rule of morality prevailing over all the earth,—such a rule, for instance, as that which orders men not to steal; but they are right or wrong according to the usages of the country in which they are practised.

In Boston it is right that Miss Ophelia Gledd should walk up Beacon Street with Hannibal Hoskins the morning after she has met him at a ball, and that she should invite him to call upon her at twelve o'clock on the following day.

She had certainly a nasal twang in speaking. Before my intercourse with her was over, her voice had become pleasant in my ears, and it may be that that nasal twang which had at first been so detestable to me, had recommended itself to my sense of hearing. At different periods of my life I have learned to love an Irish brogue and a northern burr.

Be that as it may, I must acknowledge that Miss Ophelia Gledd spoke with a certain nasal twang. But then such is the manner of speech at Boston; and she only did that which the Joneses and Smiths, the Opies and Hoskinses, were doing around her.

Ophelia Gledd's mother was, for a living being, the nearest thing to a nonentity that I ever met. Whether within her own house in Chesnut Street she exerted herself in her domestic duties and held authority over her maidens I cannot say, but neither in her dining parlour nor in her drawing-room did she hold any authority. Indeed, throughout the house, Ophelia was paramount, and it seemed as though her mother could not venture on a hint in opposition to her daughter's behests.

Mrs. Gledd never went out, but her daughter frequented all balls, dinners, and assemblies, which she chose to honour. To all these she went alone, and had done since she was eighteen years of age. She went also to lectures, to meetings of wise men, for which the Western Athens is much noted, to political debates, and wherever her enterprising heart and inquiring head chose to carry her. But her mother never went anywhere; and it always seemed to me that Mrs. Gledd's intercourse with her domestics must have been nearer, closer, and almost dearer to her, than any that she could have with her daughter.

Mr. Gledd had been a merchant all his life. When Ophelia Gledd first came before the Boston world he had been a rich merchant; and as she was an only child she had opened her campaign with all the advantages which attach to an heiress. But now, in these days, Mr. Gledd was known to be a merchant without riches. He still kept the same house, and lived apparently as he had always lived; but the world knew that he had been a broken merchant and was now again struggling. That Miss Gledd felt the disadvantage of this no one can, I suppose, doubt. But she never showed that she felt it. She spoke openly of her father's poverty as of a thing that was known, and of her own. Where she had been exigeant before, she was exigeant now. Those she disliked when rich she disliked now that she was poor. Where she had been patronising before, she patronised now. Where she had loved, she still loved. In former days she had a carriage, and now she had none. Where she had worn silk, she now wore cotton. In her gloves, her laces, her little belongings, there was all the difference which money makes or the want of money; but in her manner there was none.

Nor was there any difference in the manner of others to her. The loss of wealth seemed to entail on Miss Gledd no other discomfort than the actual want of those things which hard money buys. To go in a coach might have been a luxury to her, and that she had lost; but she had lost none of her ascendancy, none of her position, none of her sovereignty.

I remember well where, when, and how, I first met Miss Gledd. At that time her father's fortune was probably already gone, but if so, she did not then know that it was gone.

It was in winter,—towards the end of winter,—when the passion for sleighing became ecstatic. I expect all my readers to know that sleighing is the grand winter amusement of Boston. And indeed it is not bad fun. There is the fashionable course for sleighing,—the Brighton Road, and along that you drive, seated among furs, with a young lady beside you if you can get one to trust you; your horse or horses carry little bells, which add to the charms; the motion is rapid and pleasant, and, which is the great thing, you see and are seen by everybody. Of course it is expedient that the frost should be sound and perfect, so that the sleigh should run over a dry, smooth surface. But as the season draws to an end, and when sleighing intimacies have become close and warm, the horses are made to travel through slush and wet, and the scene becomes one of peril and discomfort, though one also of excitement, and not unfrequently of love.

Sleighing was fairly over at the time of which I now speak, so that the Brighton Road was deserted in its slush and sloppiness. Nevertheless, there was a possibility of sleighing; and as I was a stranger newly arrived, a young friend of mine, took me, or rather allowed me to take him out, so that the glory of the charioteer might be mine.

"I guess we're not alone," said he, after we had passed the bridge out of the town. "There's young Hoskins with Pheely Gledd just a-head of us."

That was the first I had ever heard of Ophelia, and then as I pushed along after her, instigated by a foolish Briton's ambition to pass the Yankee whip, I did hear a good deal about her; and in addition to what has already been told, I then heard that this Mr. Hannibal Hoskins, to pass whom on the road was now my only earthly desire, was Miss Gledd's professed admirer; in point of fact, that it was known to all Boston that he had offered his hand to her more than once already.

"She has accepted him now, at any rate," said I, looking at their close contiguity on the sleigh before me. But my friend explained to me that such was by no means probable; that Miss Gledd had twenty hangers-on of the same description, with any one of whom she might be seen sleighing, walking, or dancing; but that no argument as to any further purpose on her part was to be deduced from any such practice. "Our girls," said my friend, "don't go about tied to their mother's aprons, as girls do in the old country. Our free institutions," &c., &c. I confessed my blunder, and acknowledged that a wide and perhaps salutary latitude was allowed to the feminine creation on his side of the Atlantic. But, do what I would, I couldn't pass Hannibal Hoskins.

Whether he guessed that I was an ambitious Englishman, or whether he had a general dislike to be passed on the road, I don't know; but he raised his whip to his horses and went away from us suddenly and very quickly through the slush. The snow was half gone, and hard ridges of it remained across the road, so that his sleigh was bumped about most uncomfortably. I soon saw that his horses were running away, and that Hannibal Hoskins was in a fix. He was standing up, pulling at them with all his strength and weight, and the carriage was yawing about and across the road in a manner that made us fear it would go to pieces. Miss Ophelia Gledd, however, kept her seat, and there was no shrieking. In about five minutes they were well planted into a ditch, and we were alongside of them.

"You fixed that pretty straight, Hoskins," said my friend.

"Darn them for horses," said Hoskins, as he wiped the perspiration from his brow and looked down upon the fiercest of the quadrupeds, sprawling up to his withers in the snow. Then he turned to Miss Gledd, who was endeavouring to unroll herself from her furs.

"Oh, Miss Gledd, I am so sorry. What am I to say?"

"You'd better say that the horses ran away, I think," said Miss Gledd. Then she stepped carefully out, on to a buffalo-robe, and moved across from that, quite dry-footed, on to our sleigh. As my friend and Hoskins were very intimate, and could, as I thought, get on very well by themselves with the debris in the ditch, I offered to drive Miss Gledd back to town. She looked at me with eyes which gave me, as I thought, no peculiar thanks, and then remarked that she had come out with Mr. Hoskins, and that she would go back with him.

"Oh, don't mind me," said Hoskins, who was at that time up to his middle in snow.

"Ah, but I do mind you," said Ophelia. "Don't you think we could go back and send some people to help these gentlemen?"

It was the coolest proposition that I had ever heard, but in two minutes Miss Gledd was putting it into execution. Hannibal Hoskins was driving her back in the sledge which I had hired, and I was left with my friend to extricate those other two brutes from the ditch.

"That's so like Pheely Gledd," said my friend. "She always has her own way."

Then it was that I questioned Miss Gledd's beauty, and was told that before long I should find myself to be wrong. I had almost acknowledged myself to be wrong before that night was over.

I was at a tea-party that same evening at which Miss Gledd was present;—it was called a tea-party though I saw no tea. I did, however, see a large hot supper, and a very large assortment of long-necked bottles. I was standing rather listlessly near the door, being short of acquaintance, when a young Yankee dandy, with a very stiff neck, informed me that Miss Gledd wanted to speak to me. Having given me this intimation he took himself off, with an air of disgust, among the long-necked bottles.

"Mr. Green," she said,—I had just been introduced to her as she was being whisked away by Hoskins in my sleigh—"Mr. Green, I believe I owe you an apology. When I took your sleigh from you I didn't know you were a Britisher,—I didn't, indeed."

I was a little nettled, and endeavoured to explain to her that an Englishman would be just as ready to give up his carriage to a lady as any American.

"Oh, dear, yes; of course," she said. "I didn't mean that; and now I've put my foot into it worse than ever; I thought you were at home here, and knew our ways, and if so you wouldn't mind being left with a broken sleigh."

I told her that I didn't mind it. That what I had minded was the being robbed of the privilege of driving her home, which I had thought to be justly mine.

"Yes," said she, "and I was to leave my friend in the ditch! That's what I never do. You didn't suffer any disgrace by remaining there till the men came."

"I didn't remain there till any men came. I got it out and drove it home."

"What a wonderful man! But then you're English. However, you can understand that if I had left my driver he would have been disgraced. If ever I go out anywhere with you, Mr. Green, I'll come home with you. At any rate it shan't be my fault if I don't." After that I couldn't be angry with her, and so we became great friends.

Shortly afterwards the crash came; but Miss Gledd seemed to disregard the crash altogether, and held her own in Boston. As far as I could see there were just as many men desirous of marrying her as ever, and among the number Hannibal H. Hoskins was certainly no defaulter.

My acquaintance with Boston had become intimate; but, after a while, I went away for twelve months, and when I returned, Miss Gledd was still Miss Gledd. "And what of Hoskins?" I said to my friend,—the same friend who had been with me in the sleighing expedition.

"He's just on the old tack. I believe he proposes once a-year regularly. But they say now that she's going to marry an Englishman."

It was not long before I had an opportunity of renewing my friendship with Miss Gledd,—for our acquaintance had latterly amounted to a friendship,—and of seeing the Englishman with her. As it happened, he also was a friend of my own,—an old friend, and the last man in the world whom I should have picked out as a husband for Ophelia. He was a literary man of some mark, fifteen years her senior, very sedate in his habits, not much given to love-making, and possessed of a small fortune sufficient for his own wants, but not sufficient to enable him to marry with what he would consider comfort. Such was Mr. Pryor, and I was given to understand that Mr. Pryor was a suppliant at the feet of Ophelia. He was a suppliant, too, with so much hope, that Hannibal Hoskins and the other suitors were up in arms against him. I saw them together at some evening assembly, and on the next morning I chanced to be in Miss Gledd's drawing-room. On my entrance there were others there, but the first moment that we were alone, she turned round sharp upon me with a question,—

"You know your countryman, Mr. Pryor; what sort of a man is he?"

"But you know him also," I answered. "If the rumours in Boston are true, he is already a favourite in Chesnut Street."

"Well, then, for once in a way the rumours in Boston are true, for he is a favourite. But that is no reason you shouldn't tell me what sort of a man he is. You've known him these ten years."

"Pretty nearly twenty," I said,—I had known him ten or twelve.

"Ah," said she, "you want to make him out to be older than he is. I knew his age today."

"And does he know yours?"

"He may if he wishes it. Everybody in Boston knows it,—including yourself. Now tell me; what sort of man is Mr. Pryor?"

"He is a man highly esteemed in his own country."

"So much I knew before; and he is highly esteemed here also. But I hardly understand what high estimation means in your country."

"It is much the same thing in all countries, as I take it," said I.

"There you are absolutely wrong. Here in the States, if a man be highly esteemed it amounts almost to everything; such estimation will carry him everywhere,—and will carry his wife everywhere too, so as to give her a chance of making standing ground for herself."

"But Mr. Pryor has not got a wife."

"Don't be stupid. Of course he hasn't got a wife, and of course you know what I mean."

But I did not know what she meant. I knew that she was meditating whether or no it would be good for her to become Mrs. Pryor, and that she was endeavouring to get from me some information which might assist her in coming to a decision on that matter; but I did not understand the exact gist and point of her inquiry.

"You have so many prejudices of which we know nothing," she continued. "Now don't put your back up and fight for that blessed old country of yours, as though I were attacking it."

"It is a blessed old country," said I, patriotically.

"Quite so; very blessed, and very old,—and nice too, I'm sure. But you must admit that you have prejudices. You are very much the better, perhaps, for having them. I often wish that we had a few." Then she stopped her tongue, and asked no further question about Mr. Pryor; but it seemed to me that she wanted me to go on with the conversation.

"I hate discussing the relative merits of the two countries," said I; "and I especially hate to discuss them with you. You always begin as though you meant to be fair, and end by an amount of unfairness, that—that— "

"Which would be insolent if I were not a woman, and which is pert as I am one. That is what you mean."

"Something like it."

"And yet I love your country so dearly, that I would sooner live there than in any other land in the world, if only I thought that I could be accepted. You English people," she continued, "are certainly wanting in intelligence, or you would read in the anxiety of all we say about England how much we all think of you. What will England say of us? what will England think of us? what will England do in this or that matter as it concerns us? that is our first thought as to every matter that is of importance to us. We abuse you, and admire you. You abuse us, and despise us. That is the difference. So you won't tell me anything about Mr. Pryor? Well, I shan't ask you again. I never again ask a favour that has been refused." Then she turned away to some old gentleman that was talking to her mother, and the conversation was at an end.

I must confess, that as I walked away from Chesnut Street into Beacon Street, and across the Common, my anxiety was more keen with regard to Mr. Pryor than as concerned Miss Gledd. He was an Englishman and an old friend, and being also a man not much younger than myself, he was one regarding whom I might, perhaps, form some correct judgment as to what would and what would not suit him. Would he do well in taking Ophelia Gledd home to England with him as his wife? Would she be accepted there, as she herself had phrased it,—accepted in such fashion as to make him contented? She was intelligent,—so intelligent that few women whom she would meet in her proposed new country could beat her there; she was pleasant, good-humoured, true, as I believed; but would she be accepted in London? There was a freedom and easiness about her, a readiness to say anything that came into her mind, an absence of all reticence, which would go very hard with her in London. But I never had heard her say anything that she should not have said. Perhaps, after all, we have got our prejudices in England. When next I met Pryor, I spoke to him about Miss Gledd.

"The long and the short of it is," I said; "that people say that you are going to marry her."

"What sort of people?"

"They were backing you against Hannibal Hoskins the other night at the club, and it seemed clear that you were the favourite."

"The vulgarity of these people surpasses anything that I ever dreamed of," said Pryor. "That is, of some of them. It's all very well for you to talk, but could such a bet as that be proposed in the open room of any club in London?"

"The clubs in London are too big, but I dare say it might down in the country. It would be just the thing for Little Pedlington."

"But Boston is not Little Pedlington. Boston assumes to be the Athens of the States. I shall go home by the first boat next month." He had said nothing to me about Miss Gledd, but it was clear that if he went home by the first boat next month, he would go home without a wife; and as I certainly thought that the suggested marriage was undesirable, I said nothing to persuade him to remain at Boston.

It was again sleighing time, and some few days after my meeting with Pryor I was out upon the Brighton Road in the thick of the crowd. Presently I saw the hat and back of Hannibal Hoskins, and by his side was Ophelia Gledd. Now, it must be understood that Hannibal Hoskins, though he was in many respects most unlike an English gentleman, was neither a fool nor a bad fellow. A fool he certainly was not. He had read much. He could speak glibly, as is the case with all Americans. He was scientific, classical, and poetical,—probably not to any great depth. And he knew how to earn a large income with the full approbation of his fellow-citizens. I had always hated him since the day on which he had driven Miss Gledd home: but I had generally attributed my hatred to the manner in which he wore his hat on one side. I confess I had often felt amazed that Miss Gledd should have so far encouraged him. I think I may at any rate declare that he would not have been accepted in London,—not accepted for much! And yet Hannibal Hoskins was not a bad fellow. His true devotion to Ophelia Gledd proved that.

"Miss Gledd," said I, speaking to her from my sleigh, "do you remember your calamity? There is the very ditch not a hundred yards ahead of you."

"And here is the very knight that took me home in your sleigh," said she, laughing.

Hoskins sat bolt upright and took off his hat. Why he took off his hat I don't know, unless that thereby he got an opportunity of putting it on again a little more on one side.

"Mr. Hoskins would not have the goodness to upset you again, I suppose?" said I.

"No, sir," said Hoskins; and he raised the reins and squared up his elbows, meaning to look like a knowing charioteer. "I guess we'll go back; eh, Miss Gledd?"

"I guess we will," said she. "But, Mr. Green, don't you remember that I once told you if you'd take me out, I'd be sure to come home with you? You never tried me, and I take it bad of you." So encouraged I made an engagement with her, and in two or three days' time from that I had her beside me in my sleigh on the same road.

By this time I had quite become a convert to the general opinion, and was ready to confess in any presence, that Miss Gledd was a beauty. As I started with her out of the city warmly enveloped in buffalo furs, I could not but think how nice it would be to drive on and on, so that nobody should ever catch us. There was a sense of companionship about her in which no woman that I have ever known excelled her. She had a way of adapting herself to the friend of the moment which was beyond anything winning. Her voice was decidedly very pleasant; and as to that nasal twang I am not sure that I was ever right about it. I wasn't in love with her myself, and didn't want to fall in love with her. But I felt that I should have liked to cross the Rocky Mountains with her, over to the Pacific, and to have come home round by California, Peru, and the Pampas. And for such a journey I should not at all have desired to hamper the party with the society either of Hannibal Hoskins or of Mr. Pryor! "I hope you feel that you're having your revenge," said she.

"But I don't mean to upset you."

"I almost wish you would, so as to make it even. And my poor friend

Mr. Hoskins would feel himself so satisfied. He says you Englishmen are conceited about your driving."

"No doubt, he thinks we are conceited about everything."

"So you are, and so you should be. Poor Hannibal! He is wild with despair because— "

"Because what?"

"Oh, never mind. He is an excellent fellow, but I know you hate him."

"Indeed, I don't."

"Yes, you do; and so does Mr. Pryor. But he is so good! You can't either understand or appreciate the kind of goodness which our young men have. Because he pulls his hat about, and can't wear his gloves without looking stiff, you won't remember that out of his hard earnings he gives his mother and sisters everything that they want."

"I didn't know anything of his mother and sisters."

"No, of course you didn't. But you know a great deal about his hat and gloves. You are too hard, and polished, and well-mannered in England to know anything about anybody's mother or sisters, or indeed to know anything about anybody's anything. It is nothing to you whether a man be moral, or affectionate, or industrious, or good-tempered. As long as he can wear his hat properly, and speak as though nothing on the earth, or over the earth, or under the earth, could ever move him, that is sufficient."

"And yet I thought you were so fond of England?"

"So I am. I too like,—nay, love that ease of manner which you all possess and which I cannot reach."

Then there was silence between us for perhaps half a mile, and yet I was driving slow, as I did not wish to bring our journey to an end. I had fully made up my mind that it would be in every way better for my friend Pryor that he should give up all thoughts of this Western Aspasia, and yet I was anxious to talk to her about him as though such a marriage were still on the cards. It had seemed that lately she had thrown herself much into an intimacy with myself, and that she was anxious to speak openly to me if I would only allow it. But she had already declared, on a former occasion, that she would ask me no further question about Mr. Pryor. At last I plucked up courage, and put to her a direct proposition about the future tenour of her life. "After all that you have said about Mr. Hoskins, I suppose I may expect to hear that you have at last accepted him?" I could not have asked such a question of any English girl that I ever knew,—not even of my own sister in these plain terms. And yet she took it not only without anger, but even without surprise. And she answered it, as though I had asked her the most ordinary question in the world.

"I wish I had," she said. "That is, I think I wish I had. It is certainly what I ought to do."

"Then why do you not do it?"

"Ah! why do I not? Why do we not all do just what we ought to do? But why am I to be cross-questioned by you? You would not answer me a question when I asked you the other day."

"You tell me that you wish you had accepted Mr. Hoskins. Why do you not do so?" said I, continuing my cross-examination.

"Because I have a vain ambition,—a foolish ambition,—a silly, moth-like ambition,—by which, if I indulge it, I shall only burn my wings. Because I am such an utter ass that I would fain make myself an Englishwoman."

"I don't see that you need burn your wings!"

"Yes; should I go there I shall find myself to be nobody, whereas here I am in good repute. Here I could make my husband a man of mark by dint of my own power. There I doubt whether even his esteem would so shield and cover me as to make me endurable. Do you think that I do not know the difference; that I am not aware of what makes social excellence there? And yet, though I know it all, and covet it, I despise it. Social distinction with us is given on sounder terms than it is with you, and is more frequently the deserved reward of merit. Tell me; if I go to London they will ask who was my grandfather?"

"Indeed, no; they will not ask even of your father unless you speak of him."

"No; their manners are too good. But they will speak of their fathers, and how shall I talk with them? Not but what my grandfather was a good man; and you are not to suppose that I am ashamed of him because he stood in a store and sold leather with his own hands. Or rather I am ashamed of it. I should tell my husband's old friends and my new acquaintances that it was so because I am not a coward; and yet as I told them I should be ashamed. His brother is what you call a baronet."

"Just so!"

"And what would the baronet's wife say to me with all my sharp Boston notions? Can't you see her looking at me over the length of the drawing-room? And can't you fancy how pert I should be, and what snappish words I should say to the she baronet? Upon the whole, don't you think I should do better with Mr. Hoskins?"

Again I sat silent for some time. She had now asked me a question to which I was bound to give her a true answer,—an answer that should be true as to herself without reference to Pryor. She was sitting back in the sleigh, tamed as it were by her own thoughts, and she had looked at me as though she had really wanted counsel. "If I am to answer you in truth— " I said.

"You are to answer me in truth."

"Then," said I, "I can only bid you take him of the two whom you love; that is, if it be the case that you love either."

"Love!" she said.

"And if it be the case," I continued, "that you love neither, then leave them both as they are."

"I am not then to think of the man's happiness?"

"Certainly not by marrying him without affection."

"Ah! but I may regret him,—with affection."

"And for which of them do you feel affection?" I asked. And as I asked, we were already within the streets of Boston.

She again remained silent, almost till I had placed her at her own door; then she looked at me with eyes full, not only of meaning, but of love also;—with that in her eyes for which I had not hitherto given her credit.

"You know the two men," she said, "and do you ask me that?" When these words were spoken, she jumped from the sleigh, and hurried up the steps to her father's door. In very truth, the hat and gloves of Hannibal Hoskins had influenced her as they had influenced me, and they had done so although she knew how devoted he was as a son and a brother.

For a full month after that I had no further conversation with Miss Gledd or with Mr. Pryor on the subject. At this time I was living in habits of daily intimacy with Pryor, but as he did not speak to me about Ophelia, I did not often mention her name to him. I was aware that he was often with her,—or at any rate often in her company. But I did not believe that he had any daily habit of going to the house, as he would have done had he been her accepted suitor. And indeed I believed him to be a man who would be very persevering in offering his love; but who, if persistently refused, would not probably tender it again. He still talked of returning to England, though he had fixed no day. I myself purposed doing so early in May, and used such influence as I had in endeavouring to keep him at Boston till that time. Miss Gledd, also, I constantly saw. Indeed, one could not live in the society of Boston without seeing her almost daily, and I was aware that Mr. Hoskins was frequently with her. But, as regarded her, this betokened nothing, as I have before endeavoured to explain. She never deserted a friend, and had no idea of being reserved in her manners with a man because it was reported that such man was her lover. She would be very gracious to Hannibal in Mr. Pryor's presence; and yet it was evident, at any rate to me, that in doing so, she had no thought of grieving her English admirer.

I was one day seated in my room at the hotel when a servant brought me up a card. "Misther Hoskins; he's a waiting below, and wants to see yer honour very partickler," said the raw Irishman. Mr. Hoskins had never done me the honour of calling on me before, nor had I ever become intimate with him even at the club; but, nevertheless, as he had come to me, of course I was willing to see him, and so he was shown up into my room. When he entered, his hat was, I suppose, in his hand; but it looked as though it had been on one side of his head the moment before, and as though it would be on one side again the moment he left me.

"I beg your pardon, Mr. Green," said he. "Perhaps I ought not to intrude upon you here."

"No intrusion at all. Won't you take a chair, and put your hat down?" He did take a chair, but he wouldn't put his hat down. I confess that I had been actuated by a foolish desire to see it placed for a few minutes in a properly perpendicular position.

"I've just come,—I'll tell you why I've come. There are some things, Mr. Green, in which a man doesn't like to be interfered with." I could not but agree with this, but in doing so I expressed a hope that Mr. Hoskins had not been interfered with to any very disagreeable extent. "Well!" I scorn to say that the Boston dandy said "wa'all," but if this story were written by any Englishman less conscientious than myself, that latter form of letters is the one which he would adopt in his endeavour to convey the sound as uttered by Mr. Hoskins. "Well, I don't quite know about that. Now, Mr. Green, I'm not a quarrelsome man. I don't go about with six- shooters in my pocket, and I don't want to fight, nohow, if I can help it."

In answer to this I was obliged to tell him that I sincerely hoped that he would not have to fight; but that if fighting became necessary to him, I trusted that his fighting propensities would not be directed against any friend of mine.

"We don't do much in that way on our side of the water," said I.

"I am well aware of that," said he. "I don't want any one to teach me what are usages of genteel life in England. I was there the whole fall, two years ago."

"As regards myself," said I, "I don't think much good was ever done by duelling."

"That depends, sir, on how things eventuate. But, Mr. Green, satisfaction of that description is not what I desiderate on the present occasion. I wish to know whether Mr. Pryor is, or is not, engaged to marry Miss Ophelia Gledd."

"If he is, Mr. Hoskins, I don't know it."

"But, sir, you are his friend."

This I admitted, but again assured Mr. Hoskins that I knew nothing of any such engagement. He pleaded also that I was her friend as well as his. This, too, I admitted, but again declared that from neither side had I been made aware of the fact of any such engagement.

"Then, Mr. Green," said he, "may I ask you for your own private opinion?"

Upon the whole I was inclined to think that he might not, and so I told him in what most courteous words I could find for the occasion. His bust at first grew very long and stiff, and his hat became more and still more sloped as he held it. I began to fear that, though he might not have a six-shooter in his pocket, he had nevertheless some kind of pistol in his thoughts. At last he started up on his feet and confronted me, as I thought, with a look of great anger. But his words when they came were no longer angry.

"Mr. Green," said he, "if you knew all that I've done to get that girl!"

My heart was instantly softened to him.

"For aught that I know," said I, "you may have her this moment for asking."

"No," said he, "no." His voice was very melancholy, and as he spoke he looked into his sloping hat. "No; I've just come from Chesnut Street, and I think she's rather more turned against me than ever."

He was a tall man, good-looking after a fashion, dark, with thick black shiny hair, and huge bold moustachioes. I myself do not like his style of appearance, but he certainly had a manly bearing. And in the society of Boston generally he was regarded as a stout fellow, well able to hold his own; as a man, by no means soft, or green, or feminine. And yet now, in the presence of me, a stranger to him, he was almost crying about his lady love. In England no man tells another that he has been rejected; but then in England so few men tell to others anything of their real feeling. As Ophelia had said to me, we are hard and polished, and nobody knows anything about anybody's anything. What could I say to him? I did say something. I went so far as to assure him that I had heard Miss Gledd speak of him in the highest language; and at last perhaps I hinted,—though I don't think I did quite hint it,—that if Pryor were out of the way, Hoskins might find the lady more kind. He soon became quite confidential, as though I were his bosom friend. He perceived, I think, that I was not anxious that Pryor should carry off the prize, and he wished me to teach Pryor that the prize was not such a prize as would suit him.

"She's the very girl for Boston," he said, in his energy; "but, I put it to you, Mr. Green, she hasn't the gait of going that would suit London."

Whether her gait of going would or would not suit our metropolis, I did not undertake to say in the presence of Mr. Hoskins, but I did at last say that I would speak to Pryor, so that the field might be left open for others if he had no intention of running for the cup himself.

I could not but be taken, and indeed charmed, by the honest strength of affection which Hannibal Hoskins felt for the object of his adoration. He had come into my room determined to display himself as a man of will, of courage, and of fashion. But he had broken down in all that, under his extreme desire to obtain assistance in getting the one thing which he wanted. When he parted with me he shook hands almost boisterously, while he offered me most exuberant thanks. And yet I had not suggested that I could do anything for him. I did think that Ophelia Gledd would accept his offer as soon as Pryor was gone; but I had not told him that I thought so.

About two days afterwards I had a very long and a very serious conversation with Pryor, and at that time I do not think that he had made up his mind as to what he intended to do. He was the very opposite to Hoskins in all his ways and all his moods. There was not only no swagger with him, but a propriety and quiescence of demeanour the very opposite to swagger. In conversation his most violent opposition was conveyed by a smile. He displayed no other energy than what might be shown in the slight curl of his upper lip. If he reproved you he did it by silence. There could be no greater contrast than that between him and Hoskins, and there could be no doubt which man would recommend himself most to our English world by his gait and demeanour. But I think there may be a doubt as to which was the best man, and a doubt also as to which would make the best husband. That my friend was not then engaged to Miss Gledd I did learn,—but I learned nothing further,—except this, that he would take his departure with me the first week in May, unless anything special occurred to keep him in Boston.

It was some time early in April that I got a note from Miss Gledd, asking me to call on her.

"Come at once," she said, "as I want your advice above all things." And she signed herself, "Yours in all truth, O. G."

I had had many notes from her, but none written in this strain; and therefore, feeling that there was some circumstance to justify such instant notice, I got up and went to her then, at ten o'clock in the morning. She jumped up to meet me, giving me both her hands.

"Oh, Mr. Green," she said to me, "I am so glad you have come to me. It is all over."

"What is over?" said I.

"My chance of escape from the she baronet. I gave in last night. Pray tell me that I was right. Yet I want you to tell me the truth. And yet, above all things, you must not tell me that I have been wrong."

"Then you have accepted Mr. Pryor?"

"I could not help it," she said. "The temptation was too much for me. I love the very cut of his coat, the turn of his lip, the tone of his voice. The very sound which he makes as he closes the door behind him is too much for me. I believe that I ought to have let him go,—but I could not do it."

"And what will Mr. Hoskins do?"

"I wrote to him immediately and told him everything. Of course I had John's leave for doing so."

This calling of my sedate friend by the name of John was, to my feeling, a most wonderful breaking down of all proprieties.

"I told him the exact truth. This morning I got an answer from him saying that he should visit Russia. I am so sorry because of his mother and sisters."

"And when is it to be?"

"Oh, at once, immediately. So John says. When we resolve on doing these things here, on taking the plunge, we never stand shilly-shallying on the brink as your girls do in England. And that is one reason why I have sent for you. You must promise to go over with us. Do you know I am half afraid of him,—much more afraid of him than I am of you."

They were to be married very early in May, and of course I promised to put off my return for a week or two to suit them.

"And then for the she baronet," she said, "and for all the terrible grandeur of London!"

When I endeavoured to explain to her that she would encounter no great grandeur, she very quickly corrected me.

"It is not grandeur of that sort, but the grandeur of coldness that I mean. I fear that I shall not do for them. But, Mr. Green, I must tell you one thing. I have not cut off from myself all means of retreat."

"Why, what do you mean? You have resolved to marry him."

"Yes, I have promised to do so; but I did not promise till he had said that if I could not be made to suit his people in Old England, he would return here with me and teach himself to suit my people in New England. The task will be very much easier."

They were married in Boston, not without some considerable splendour of ceremony,—as far as the splendour of Boston went. She was so unusual a favourite that every one wished to be at her wedding, and she had no idea of giving herself airs and denying her friends a favour. She was married with much *éclat*, and, as far as I could judge, seemed to enjoy the marriage herself.

Now comes the question; will she or will she not be received in London as a lady,—as such a lady as my friend Pryor might have been expected to take for his wife?

Malachi's Cove

Originally appeared in *Good Words*, December 1864. Reprinted in *Lotta Schmidt and Other Stories* (1867). Written c. 6–9 September 1864, during the composition of *The Claverings*. In 1876 Trollope disclaimed any special knowledge of Cornwall or its coast. Cornish settings and materials are also to be found in *The Three Clerks* (1858), *The Duke's Children* (1880) and *Ayala's Angel* (1881). Richard Mullen suggests in *Malachi's Cove and Other Stories* (1985) that the details of Mally's churchgoing were calculated to appeal to the readership of the evangelical magazine *Good Words*.

On the northern coast of Cornwall, between Tintagel and Bossiney, down on the very margin of the sea, there lived not long since an old man who got his living by saving seaweed from the waves, and selling it for manure. The cliffs there are bold and fine, and the sea beats in upon them from the north with a grand violence. I doubt whether it be not the finest morsel of cliff scenery in England, though it is beaten by many portions of the west coast of Ireland, and perhaps also by spots in Wales and Scotland. Cliffs should be nearly precipitous, they should be broken in their outlines, and should barely admit here and there of an insecure passage from their summit to the sand at their feet. The sea should come, if not up to them, at least very near to them, and then, above all things, the water below them should be blue, and not of that dead leaden colour which is so familiar to us in England. At Tintagel all these requisites are there, except that bright blue colour which is so lovely. But the cliffs themselves are bold and well broken, and the margin of sand at high water is very narrow,—so narrow that at spring-tides there is barely a footing there.

Close upon this margin was the cottage or hovel of Malachi Trenglos, the old man of whom I have spoken. But Malachi, or old Glos, as he was commonly called by the people around him, had not built his house absolutely upon the sand. There was a fissure in the rock so great that at the top it formed a narrow ravine, and so complete from the summit to the base that it afforded an opening for a steep and rugged track from the top of the rock to the bottom. This fissure was so wide at the bottom that it had afforded space for Trenglos to fix his habitation on a foundation of rock, and here he had lived for many years. It was told of him that in the early days of his trade he had always carried the weed in a basket on his back to the top, but latterly he had been possessed of a donkey, which had been trained to go up and down the steep track with a single pannier over his loins, for the rocks would not admit of panniers hanging by his side; and for this assistant he had built a shed adjoining his own, and almost as large as that in which he himself resided.

But, as years went on, old Glos procured other assistance than that of the donkey, or, as I should rather say, Providence supplied him with other help; and, indeed, had it not been so, the old man must have given up his cabin and his independence and gone into the workhouse at Camelford. For rheumatism had afflicted him, old age had bowed him till he was nearly double, and by degrees he became unable to attend the donkey on its upward passage to the world above, or even to assist in rescuing the coveted weed from the waves.

At the time to which our story refers Trenglos had not been up the cliff for twelve months, and for the last six months he had done nothing towards the furtherance of his trade, except to take the money and keep it, if any of it was kept, and occasionally to shake down a bundle of fodder for the donkey. The real work of the business was done altogether by Mahala Trenglos, his granddaughter.

Mally Trenglos was known to all the farmers round the coast, and to all the small tradespeople in Camelford. She was a wild-looking, almost unearthly creature, with wild-flowing, black, uncombed hair, small in stature, with small hands and bright black eyes; but people said that she was very strong, and the children around declared that she worked day and night and knew nothing of fatigue. As to her age there were many doubts. Some said she was ten, and others five-and-twenty, but the reader may be allowed to know that at this time she had in truth passed her twentieth birthday. The old people spoke well of Mally, because she was so good to her grandfather; and it was said of her that though she carried to him a little gin and tobacco almost daily, she bought nothing for herself;—and as to the gin, no one who looked at her would accuse her of meddling with that. But she had no friends and but few acquaintances among people of her own age. They said that she was fierce and ill-natured, that she had not a good word for any one, and that she was, complete at all points, a thorough little vixen. The young men did not care for her; for, as regarded dress, all days were alike with her. She never made herself smart on Sundays. She was generally without stockings, and seemed to care not at all to exercise any of those feminine attractions which might have been hers had she studied to attain them. All days were the same to her in regard to dress; and, indeed, till lately, all days had, I fear, been the same to her in other respects. Old Malachi had never been seen inside a place of worship since he had taken to live under the cliff.

But within the last two years Mally had submitted herself to the teaching of the clergyman at Tintagel, and had appeared at church on Sundays, if not absolutely with punctuality, at any rate so often that no one who knew the peculiarity of her residence was disposed to quarrel with her on that subject. But she made no difference in her dress on these occasions. She took her place on a low stone seat just inside the church door, clothed as usual in her thick red serge petticoat and loose brown serge jacket, such being the apparel which she had found to be best adapted for her hard and perilous work among the waters. She had pleaded to the clergyman when he attacked her on the subject of church attendance with vigour that she had got no church-going clothes. He had explained to her that she would be received there without distinction to her clothing. Mally had taken him at his word, and had gone, with a courage which certainly deserved admiration, though I doubt whether there was not mingled with it an obstinacy which was less admirable.

For people said that old Glos was rich, and that Mally might have proper clothes if she chose to buy them. Mr. Polwarth, the clergyman, who, as the old man could not come to him, went down the rocks to the old man, did make some hint on the matter in Mally's absence. But old Glos, who had been patient with him on other matters, turned upon him so angrily when he made an allusion to money, that Mr. Polwarth found himself obliged to give that matter up, and Mally continued to sit upon the stone bench in her short serge petticoat, with her long hair streaming down her face. She did so far sacrifice to decency as on such occasions to tie up her black hair with an old shoestring. So tied it would remain through the Monday and Tuesday, but by Wednesday afternoon Mally's hair had generally managed to escape.

As to Mally's indefatigable industry there could be no manner of doubt, for the quantity of sea-weed which she and the donkey amassed between them was very surprising. Old Glos, it was declared, had never collected half what Mally gathered together; but then the article was becoming cheaper, and it was necessary that the exertion should be greater. So Mally and the donkey toiled and toiled, and the seaweed came up in heaps which surprised those who looked at her little hands and light form. Was there not some one who helped her at nights, some fairy, or demon, or the like? Mally was so snappish in her answers to people that she had no right to be surprised if ill-natured things were said of her.

No one ever heard Mally Trenglos complain of her work, but about this time she was heard to make great and loud complaints of the treatment she received from some of her neighbours. It was known that she went with her plaints to Mr. Polwarth; and when he could not help her, or did not give her such instant help as she needed, she went—ah, so foolishly! to the office of a certain attorney at Camelford, who was not likely to prove himself a better friend than Mr. Polwarth.

Now the nature of her injury was as follows. The place in which she collected her seaweed was a little cove;—the people had come to call it Malachi's Cove from the name of the old man who lived there;—which was so formed, that the margin of the sea therein could only be reached by the passage from the top down to Trenglos's hut. The breadth of the cove when the sea was out might perhaps be two hundred yards, and on each side the rocks ran out in such a way that both from north and south the domain of Trenglos was guarded from intruders. And this locality had been well chosen for its intended purpose.

There was a rush of the sea into the cove, which carried there large, drifting masses of seaweed, leaving them among the rocks when the tide was out. During the equinoctial winds of the spring and autumn the supply would never fail; and even when the sea was calm, the long, soft, salt-bedewed, trailing masses of the weed, could be gathered there when they could not be found elsewhere for miles along the coast. The task of getting the weed from the breakers was often difficult and dangerous,—so difficult that much of it was left to be carried away by the next incoming tide.

Mally doubtless did not gather half the crop that was there at her feet. What was taken by the returning waves she did not regret; but when interlopers came upon her cove, and gathered her wealth,—her grandfather's wealth, beneath her eyes, then her heart was broken. It was this interloping, this intrusion, that drove poor Mally to the Camelford attorney. But, alas, though the Camelford attorney took Mally's money, he could do nothing for her, and her heart was broken!

She had an idea, in which no doubt her grandfather shared, that the path to the cove was, at any rate, their property. When she was told that the cove, and sea running into the cove, were not the freeholds of her grandfather, she understood that the statement might be true. But what then as to the use of the path? Who had made the path what it was? Had she not painfully, wearily, with exceeding toil, carried up bits of rock with her own little hands, that her grandfather's donkey might have footing for his feet? Had she not scraped together crumbs of earth along the face of the cliff that she might make easier to the animal the track of that rugged way? And now, when she saw big farmer's lads coming down with other donkeys,—and, indeed, there was one who came with a pony; no boy, but a young man, old enough to know better than rob a poor old man and a young girl,—she reviled the whole human race, and swore that the Camelford attorney was a fool.

Any attempt to explain to her that there was still weed enough for her was worse than useless. Was it not all hers and his, or, at any rate, was not the sole way to it his and hers? And was not her trade stopped and impeded? Had she not been forced to back her laden donkey down, twenty yards she said, but it had, in truth, been five, because Farmer Gunliffe's son had been in the way with his thieving pony? Farmer Gunliffe had wanted to buy her weed at his own price, and because she had refused he had set on his thieving son to destroy her in this wicked way.

"I'll hamstring the beast the next time as he's down here!" said Mally to old Glos, while the angry fire literally streamed from her eyes.

Farmer Gunliffe's small homestead,—he held about fifty acres of land, was close by the village of Tintagel, and not a mile from the cliff. The sea-wrack, as they call it, was pretty well the only manure within his reach, and no doubt he thought it hard that he should be kept from using it by Mally Trenglos and her obstinacy.

"There's heaps of other coves, Barty," said Mally to Barty Gunliffe, the farmer's son.

"But none so nigh, Mally, nor yet none that fills 'emselves as this place."

Then he explained to her that he would not take the weed that came up close to hand. He was bigger than she was, and stronger, and would get it from the outer rocks, with which she never meddled. Then, with scorn in her eye, she swore that she could get it where he durst not venture, and repeated her threat of hamstringing the pony. Barty laughed at her wrath, jeered her because of her wild hair, and called her a mermaid.

"I'll mermaid you!" she cried. "Mermaid, indeed! I wouldn't be a man to come and rob a poor girl and an old cripple. But you're no man, Barty Gunliffe! You're not half a man."

Nevertheless, Bartholomew Gunliffe was a very fine young fellow as far as the eye went. He was about five feet eight inches high, with strong arms and legs, with light curly brown hair and blue eyes. His father was but in a small way as a farmer, but, nevertheless, Barty Gunliffe was well thought of among the girls around. Everybody liked Barty,—excepting only Mally Trenglos, and she hated him like poison.

Barty, when he was asked why so good-natured a lad as he persecuted a poor girl and an old man, threw himself upon the justice of the thing. It wouldn't do at all, according to his view, that any single person should take upon himself to own that which God Almighty sent as the common property of all. He would do Mally no harm, and so he had told her. But Mally was a vixen,—a wicked little vixen; and she must be taught to have a civil tongue in her head. When once Mally would speak him civil as he went for weed, he would get his father to pay the old man some sort of toll for the use of the path.

"Speak him civil?" said Mally. "Never; not while I have a tongue in my mouth!" And I fear old Glos encouraged her rather than otherwise in her view of the matter.

But her grandfather did not encourage her to hamstring the pony. Hamstringing a pony would be a serious thing, and old Glos thought it might be very awkward for both of them if Mally were put into prison. He suggested, therefore, that all manner of impediments should be put in the way of the pony's feet, surmising that the well-trained donkey might be able to work in spite of them. And Barty Gunliffe, on his next descent, did find the passage very awkward when he came near to Malachi's hut, but he made his way down, and poor Mally saw the lumps of rock at which she had laboured so hard pushed on one side or rolled out of the way with a steady persistency of injury towards herself that almost drove her frantic.

"Well, Barty, you're a nice boy," said old Glos, sitting in the doorway of the hut, as he watched the intruder.

"I ain't a doing no harm to none as doesn't harm me," said Barty. "The sea's free to all, Malachi."

"And the sky's free to all, but I musn't get up on the top of your big barn to look at it," said Mally, who was standing among the rocks with a long hook in her hand. The long hook was the tool with which she worked in dragging the weed from the waves. "But you ain't got no justice, nor yet no sperrit, or you wouldn't come here to vex an old man like he."

"I didn't want to vex him, nor yet to vex you, Mally. You let me be for a while, and we'll be friends yet."

"Friends!" exclaimed Mally. "Who'd have the likes of you for a friend? What are you moving them stones for? Them stones belongs to grandfather." And in her wrath she made a movement as though she were going to fly at him.

"Let him be, Mally," said the old man; "let him be. He'll get his punishment. He'll come to be drowned some day if he comes down here when the wind is in shore."

"That he may be drowned then!" said Mally, in her anger. "If he was in the big hole there among the rocks, and the sea running in at half-tide, I wouldn't lift a hand to help him out."

"Yes, you would, Mally; you'd fish me up with your hook like a big stick of sea-weed."

She turned from him with scorn as he said this, and went into the hut. It was time for her to get ready for her work, and one of the great injuries done her lay in this,—that such a one as Barty

Gunliffe should come and look at her during her toil among the breakers.

It was an afternoon in April, and the hour was something after four o'clock. There had been a heavy wind from the north-west all the morning, with gusts of rain, and the sea-gulls had been in and out of the cove all the day, which was a sure sign to Mally that the incoming tide would cover the rocks with weed.

The quick waves were now returning with wonderful celerity over the low reefs, and the time had come at which the treasure must be seized, if it was to be garnered on that day. By seven o'clock it would be growing dark, at nine it would be high water, and before daylight the crop would be carried out again if not collected. All this Mally understood very well, and some of this Barty was beginning to understand also.

As Mally came down with her bare feet, bearing her long hook in her hand, she saw Barty's pony standing patiently on the sand, and in her heart she longed to attack the brute. Barty at this moment, with a common three-pronged fork in his hand, was standing down on a large rock, gazing forth towards the waters. He had declared that he would gather the weed only at places which were inaccessible to Mally, and he was looking out that he might settle where he would begin.

"Let 'un be, let 'un be," shouted the old man to Mally, as he saw her take a step towards the beast, which she hated almost as much as she hated the man.

Hearing her grandfather's voice through the wind, she desisted from her purpose, if any purpose she had had, and went forth to her work. As she passed down the cove, and scrambled in among the rocks, she saw Barty still standing on his perch; out beyond, the white-curling waves were cresting and breaking themselves with violence, and the wind was howling among the caverns and abutments of the cliff.

Every now and then there came a squall of rain, and though there was sufficient light, the heavens were black with clouds. A scene more beautiful might hardly be found by those who love the glories of the coast. The light for such objects was perfect. Nothing could exceed the grandeur of the colours,—the blue of the open sea, the white of the breaking waves, the yellow sands, or the streaks of red and brown which gave such richness to the cliff.

But neither Mally nor Barty were thinking of such things as these. Indeed they were hardly thinking of their trade after its ordinary forms. Barty was meditating how he might best accomplish his purpose of working beyond the reach of Mally's feminine powers, and Mally was resolving that wherever Barty went she would go farther.

And, in many respects, Mally had the advantage. She knew every rock in the spot, and was sure of those which gave a good foothold, and sure also of those which did not. And then her activity had been made perfect by practice for the purpose to which it was to be devoted. Barty, no doubt, was stronger than she, and quite as active. But Barty could not jump among the waves from one stone to another as she could do, nor was he as yet able to get aid in his work from the very force of the water as she could get it. She had been hunting seaweed in that cove since she had been an urchin of six years old, and she knew every hole and corner and every spot of vantage. The waves were her friends, and she could use them. She could measure their strength, and knew when and where it would cease.

Mally was great down in the salt pools of her own cove,—great, and very fearless. As she watched Barty make his way forward from rock to rock, she told herself, gleefully, that he was going astray. The curl of the wind as it blew into the cove would not carry the weed up to the northern buttresses of the cove; and then there was the great hole just there,—the great hole of which she had spoken when she wished him evil.

And now she went to work, hooking up the dishevelled hairs of the ocean, and landing many a cargo on the extreme margin of the sand, from whence she would be able in the evening to drag it back before the invading waters would return to reclaim the spoil.

And on his side also Barty made his heap up against the northern buttresses of which I have spoken. Barty's heap became big and still bigger, so that he knew, let the pony work as he might, he could not take it all up that evening. But still it was not as large as Mally's heap. Mally's hook was better than his fork, and Mally's skill was better than his strength. And when he failed in some haul Mally would jeer him with a wild, weird laughter, and shriek to him through the wind that he was not half a man. At first he answered her with laughing words, but before long, as she boasted of her success and pointed to his failure, he became angry, and then he answered her no more. He became angry with himself, in that he missed so much of the plunder before him.

The broken sea was full of the long straggling growth which the waves had torn up from the bottom of the ocean, but the masses were carried past him, away from him,—nay, once or twice over him; and then Mally's weird voice would sound in his ear, jeering him. The gloom among the rocks was now becoming thicker and thicker, the tide was beating in with increased strength, and the gusts of wind came with quicker and greater violence. But still he worked on. While Mally worked he would work, and he would work for some time after she was driven in. He would not be beaten by a girl.

The great hole was now full of water, but of water which seemed to be boiling as though in a pot. And the pot was full of floating masses,—large treasures of sea-weed which were thrown to and fro upon its surface, but lying there so thick that one would seem almost able to rest upon it without sinking.

Mally knew well how useless it was to attempt to rescue aught from the fury of that boiling caldron. The hole went in under the rocks, and the side of it towards the shore lay high, slippery, and steep. The hole, even at low water, was never empty; and Mally believed that there was no bottom to it. Fish thrown in there could escape out to the ocean, miles away,—so Mally in her softer moods would tell the visitors to the cove. She knew the hole well. Poulnadioul she was accustomed to call it; which was supposed, when translated, to mean that this was the hole of the Evil One. Never did Mally attempt to make her own of weed which had found its way into that pot.

But Barty Gunliffe knew no better, and she watched him as he endeavoured to steady himself on the treacherously slippery edge of the pool. He fixed himself there and made a haul, with some small success. How he managed it she hardly knew, but she stood still for a while watching him anxiously, and then she saw him slip. He slipped, and recovered himself;—slipped again, and again recovered himself.

"Barty, you fool!" she screamed, "if you get yourself pitched in there, you'll never come out no more."

Whether she simply wished to frighten him, or whether her heart relented and she had thought of his danger with dismay, who shall say? She could not have told herself. She hated him as much as ever,—but she could hardly have wished to see him drowned before her eyes.

"You go on, and don't mind me," said he, speaking in a hoarse, angry tone.

"Mind you!—who minds you?" retorted the girl. And then she again prepared herself for her work.

But as she went down over the rocks with her long hook balanced in her hands, she suddenly heard a splash, and, turning quickly round, saw the body of her enemy tumbling amidst the eddying waves in the pool. The tide had now come up so far that every succeeding wave washed into it and over it from the side nearest to the sea, and then ran down again back from the rocks, as the rolling wave receded, with a noise like the fall of a cataract. And then, when the surplus water had retreated for a moment, the surface of the pool would be partly calm, though the fretting bubbles would still boil up and down, and there was ever a simmer on the surface, as though, in truth, the caldron were heated. But this time of comparative rest was but a moment, for the succeeding breaker would come up almost as soon as the foam of the preceding one had gone, and then again the waters would be dashed upon the rocks, and the sides would echo with the roar of the angry wave.

Instantly Mally hurried across to the edge of the pool, crouching down upon her hands and knees for security as she did so. As a wave receded, Barty's head and face was carried round near to her, and she could see that his forehead was covered with blood. Whether he were alive or dead she did not know. She had seen nothing but his blood, and the light-coloured hair of his head lying amidst the foam. Then his body was drawn along by the suction of the retreating wave; but the mass of water that escaped was not on this occasion large enough to carry the man out with it.

Instantly Mally was at work with her hook, and getting it fixed into his coat, dragged him towards the spot on which she was kneeling. During the half minute of repose she got him so close that she could touch his shoulder. Straining herself down, laying herself over the long bending handle of the hook, she strove to grasp him with her right hand. But she could not do it; she could only touch him.

Then came the next breaker, forcing itself on with a roar, looking to

Mally as though it must certainly knock her from her resting-place, and destroy them both. But she had nothing for it but to kneel, and hold by her hook.

What prayer passed through her mind at that moment for herself or for him, or for that old man who was sitting unconsciously up at the cabin, who can say? The great wave came and rushed over her as she lay almost prostrate, and when the water was gone from her eyes, and the tumult of the foam, and the violence of the roaring breaker had passed by her, she found herself at her length upon the rock, while his body had been lifted up, free from her hook, and was lying upon the slippery ledge, half in the water and half out of it. As she looked at him, in that instant, she could see that his eyes were open and that he was struggling with his hands.

"Hold by the hook, Barty," she cried, pushing the stick of it before him, while she seized the collar of his coat in her hands.

Had he been her brother, her lover, her father she could not have clung to him with more of the energy of despair. He did contrive to hold by the stick which she had given him, and when the succeeding wave had passed by, he was still on the ledge. In the next moment she was seated a yard or two above the hole, in comparative safety, while Barty lay upon the rocks with his still bleeding head resting upon her lap.

What could she do now? She could not carry him; and in fifteen minutes the sea would be up where she was sitting. He was quite insensible, and very pale, and the blood was coming slowly,—very slowly,—from the wound on his forehead. Ever so gently she put her hand upon his hair to move it back from his face; and then she bent over his mouth to see if he breathed, and as she looked at him she knew that he was beautiful.

What would she not give that he might live? Nothing now was so precious to her as his life,—as this life which she had so far rescued from the waters. But what could she do? Her grandfather could scarcely get himself down over the rocks, if indeed he could succeed in doing so much as that. Could she drag the wounded man backwards, if it were only a few feet, so that he might lie above the reach of the waves till further assistance could be procured?

She set herself to work and she moved him, almost lifting him. As she did so she wondered at her own strength, but she was very strong at that moment. Slowly, tenderly, falling on the rocks herself so that he might fall on her, she got him back to the margin of the sand, to a spot which the waters would not reach for the next two hours.

Here her grandfather met them, having seen at last what had happened from the door.

"Dada," she said, "he fell into the pool yonder, and was battered against the rocks. See there at his forehead."

"Mally, I'm thinking that he's dead already," said old Glos, peering down over the body.

"No, dada; he is not dead; but mayhap he's dying. But I'll go at once up to the farm."

"Mally," said the old man, "look at his head. They'll say we murdered him."

"Who'll say so? Who'll lie like that? Didn't I pull him out of the hole?"

"What matters that? His father'll say we killed him."

It was manifest to Mally that whatever any one might say hereafter, her present course was plain before her. She must run up the path to Gunliffe's farm and get necessary assistance. If the world were as bad as her grandfather said, it would be so bad that she would not care to live longer in it. But be that as it might, there was no doubt as to what she must do now.

So away she went as fast as her naked feet could carry her up the cliff. When at the top she looked round to see if any person might be within ken, but she saw no one. So she ran with all her speed along the headland of the corn-field which led in the direction of old Gunliffe's house, and as she drew near to the homestead she saw that Barty's mother was leaning on the gate. As she approached she attempted to call, but her breath failed her for any purpose of loud speech, so she ran on till she was able to grasp Mrs. Gunliffe by the arm.

"Where's himself?" she said, holding her hand upon her beating heart that she might husband her breath.

"Who is it you mean?" said Mrs. Gunliffe, who participated in the family feud against Trenglos and his granddaughter. "What does the girl clutch me for in that way?"

"He's dying then, that's all."

"Who is dying? Is it old Malachi? If the old man's bad, we'll send some one down."

"It ain't dada; it's Barty! Where's himself? where's the master?" But by this time Mrs. Gunliffe was in an agony of despair, and was calling out for assistance lustily. Happily Gunliffe, the father, was at hand, and with him a man from the neighbouring village.

"Will you not send for the doctor?" said Mally. "Oh, man, you should send for the doctor!"

Whether any orders were given for the doctor she did not know, but in a very few minutes she was hurrying across the field again towards the path to the cove, and Gunliffe with the other man and his wife were following her.

As Mally went along she recovered her voice, for their step was not so quick as hers, and that which to them was a hurried movement, allowed her to get her breath again. And as she went she tried to explain to the father what had happened, saying but little, however, of her own doings in the matter. The wife hung behind listening, exclaiming every now and again that her boy was killed, and then asking wild questions as to his being yet alive. The father, as he went, said little. He was known as a silent, sober man, well spoken of for diligence and general conduct, but supposed to be stern and very hard when angered.

As they drew near to the top of the path the other man whispered something to him, and then he turned round upon Mally and stopped her.

"If he has come by his death between you, your blood shall be taken for his," said he.

Then the wife shrieked out that her child had been murdered, and Mally, looking round into the faces of the three, saw that her grandfather's words had come true. They suspected her of having taken the life, in saving which she had nearly lost her own.

She looked round at them with awe in her face, and then, without saying a word, preceded them down the path. What had she to answer when such a charge as that was made against her? If they chose to say that she pushed him into the pool and hit him with her hook as he lay amidst the waters, how could she show that it was not so?

Poor Mally knew little of the law of evidence, and it seemed to her that she was in their hands. But as she went down the steep track with a hurried step,—a step so quick that they could not keep up with her,—her heart was very full,—very full and very high. She had striven for the man's life as though he had been her brother. The blood was yet not dry on her own legs and arms, where she had torn them in his service. At one moment she had felt sure that she would die with him in that pool. And now they said that she had murdered him! It may be that he was not dead, and what would he say if ever he should speak again? Then she thought of that moment when his eyes had opened, and he had seemed to see her. She had no fear for herself, for her heart was very high. But it was full also,—full of scorn, disdain, and wrath.

When she had reached the bottom, she stood close to the door of the hut waiting for them, so that they might precede her to the other group, which was there in front of them, at a little distance on the sand.

"He is there, and dada is with him. Go and look at him," said Mally.

The father and mother ran on stumbling over the stones, but Mally remained behind by the door of the hut.

Barty Gunliffe was lying on the sand where Mally had left him, and old Malachi Trenglos was standing over him, resting himself with difficulty upon a stick.

"Not a move he's moved since she left him," said he; "not a move. I put his head on the old rug as you see, and I tried 'un with a drop of gin, but he wouldn't take it,—he wouldn't take it."

"Oh, my boy! my boy!" said the mother, throwing herself beside her son upon the sand.

"Haud your tongue, woman," said the father, kneeling down slowly by the lad's head, "whimpering that way will do 'un no good."

Then having gazed for a minute or two upon the pale face beneath him, he looked up sternly into that of Malachi Trenglos.

The old man hardly knew how to bear this terrible inquisition.

"He would come," said Malachi; "he brought it all upon hisself."

"Who was it struck him?" said the father.

"Sure he struck hisself, as he fell among the breakers."

"Liar!" said the father, looking up at the old man.

"They have murdered him!—they have murdered him!" shrieked the mother.

"Haud your peace, woman!" said the husband again. "They shall give us blood for blood."

Mally, leaning against the corner of the hovel, heard it all, but did not stir. They might say what they liked. They might make it out to be murder. They might drag her and her grandfather to Camelford gaol, and then to Bodmin, and the gallows; but they could not take from her the conscious feeling that was her own. She had done her best to save him,—her very best. And she had saved him!

She remembered her threat to him before they had gone down on the rocks together, and her evil wish. Those words had been very wicked; but since that she had risked her life to save his. They might say what they pleased of her, and do what they pleased. She knew what she knew.

Then the father raised his son's head and shoulders in his arms, and called on the others to assist him in carrying Barty towards the path. They raised him between them carefully and tenderly, and lifted their burden on towards the spot at which Mally was standing. She never moved, but watched them at their work; and the old man followed them, hobbling after them with his crutch.

When they had reached the end of the hut she looked upon Barty's face, and saw that it was very pale. There was no longer blood upon the forehead, but the great gash was to be seen there plainly, with its jagged cut, and the skin livid and blue round the orifice. His light brown hair was hanging back, as she had made it to hang when she had gathered it with her hand after the big wave had passed over them. Ah, how beautiful he was in Mally's eyes with that pale face, and the sad scar upon his brow! She turned her face away, that they might not see her tears; but she did not move, nor did she speak.

But now, when they had passed the end of the hut, shuffling along with their burden, she heard a sound which stirred her. She roused herself quickly from her leaning posture, and stretched forth her head as though to listen; then she moved to follow them. Yes, they had stopped at the bottom of the path, and had again laid the body on the rocks. She heard that sound again, as of a long, long sigh, and then, regardless of any of them, she ran to the wounded man's head.

"He is not dead," she said. "There; he is not dead."

As she spoke Barty's eyes opened, and he looked about him.

"Barty, my boy, speak to me," said the mother.

Barty turned his face upon his mother, smiled, and then stared about him wildly.

"How is it with thee, lad?" said his father. Then Barty turned his face again to the latter voice, and as he did so his eyes fell upon Mally.

"Mally!" he said, "Mally!"

It could have wanted nothing further to any of those present to teach them that, according to Barty's own view of the case, Mally had not been his enemy; and, in truth, Mally herself wanted no further triumph. That word had vindicated her, and she withdrew back to the hut.

"Dada," she said, "Barty is not dead, and I'm thinking they won't say anything more about our hurting him."

Old Glos shook his head. He was glad the lad hadn't met his death there; he didn't want the young man's blood, but he knew what folk would say. The poorer he was the more sure the world would be to trample on him. Mally said what she could to comfort him, being full of comfort herself.

She would have crept up to the farm if she dared, to ask how Barty was. But her courage failed her when she thought of that, so she went to work again, dragging back the weed she had saved to the spot at which on the morrow she would load the donkey. As she did this she saw Barty's pony still standing patiently under the rock; so she got a lock of fodder and threw it down before the beast.

It had become dark down in the cove, but she was still dragging back the sea-weed, when she saw the glimmer of a lantern coming down the pathway. It was a most unusual sight, for lanterns were not common down in Malachi's Cove. Down came the lantern rather slowly,—much more slowly than she was in the habit of descending, and then through the gloom she saw the figure of a man standing at the bottom of the path. She went up to him, and saw that it was Mr. Gunliffe, the father.

"Is that Mally?" said Gunliffe.

"Yes, it is Mally; and how is Barty, Mr. Gunliffe?"

"You must come to 'un yourself, now at once," said the farmer. "He won't sleep a wink till he's seed you. You must not say but you'll come."

"Sure I'll come if I'm wanted," said Mally.

Gunliffe waited a moment, thinking that Mally might have to prepare herself, but Mally needed no preparation. She was dripping with salt water from the weed which she had been dragging, and her elfin locks were streaming wildly from her head; but, such as she was, she was ready.

"Dada's in bed," she said, "and I can go now if you please."

Then Gunliffe turned round and followed her up the path, wondering at the life which this girl led so far away from all her sex. It was now dark night, and he had found her working at the very edge of the rolling waves by herself, in the darkness, while the only human being who might seem to be her protector had already gone to his bed.

When they were at the top of the cliff Gunliffe took her by her hand, and led her along. She did not comprehend this, but she made no attempt to take her hand from his. Something he said about falling on the cliffs, but it was muttered so lowly that Mally hardly understood him. But in truth the man knew that she had saved his boy's life, and that he had injured her instead of thanking her. He was now taking her to his heart, and as words were wanting to him, he was showing his love after this silent fashion. He held her by the hand as though she were a child, and Mally tripped along at his side asking him no questions.

When they were at the farm-yard gate he stopped there for a moment.

"Mally, my girl," he said, "he'll not be content till he sees thee, but thou must not stay long wi' him, lass. Doctor says he's weak like, and wants sleep badly."

Mally merely nodded her head, and then they entered the house. Mally had never been within it before, and looked about with wondering eyes at the furniture of the big kitchen. Did any idea of her future destiny flash upon her then, I wonder? But she did not pause here a moment, but was led up to the bedroom above stairs, where Barty was lying on his mother's bed.

"Is it Mally herself?" said the voice of the weak youth.

"It's Mally herself," said the mother, "so now you can say what you please."

"Mally," said he, "Mally, it's along of you that I'm alive this moment."

"I'll not forget it on her," said the father, with his eyes turned away from her. "I'll never forget it on her."

"We hadn't a one but only him," said the mother, with her apron up to her face.

"Mally, you'll be friends with me now?" said Barty.

To have been made lady of the manor of the cove for ever, Mally couldn't have spoken a word now. It was not only that the words and presence of the people there cowed her and made her speechless, but the big bed, and the looking-glass, and the unheard-of wonders of the chamber, made her feel her own insignificance. But she crept up to Barty's side, and put her hand upon his.

"I'll come and get the weed, Mally; but it shall all be for you," said Barty.

"Indeed, you won't then, Barty dear," said the mother; "you'll never go near the awsome place again. What would we do if you were took from us?"

"He mustn't go near the hole if he does," said Mally, speaking at last in a solemn voice, and imparting the knowledge which she had kept to herself while Barty was her enemy; "'specially not if the wind's any way from the nor'rard."

"She'd better go down now," said the father.

Barty kissed the hand which he held, and Mally, looking at him as he did so, thought that he was like an angel.

"You'll come and see us to-morrow, Mally?" said he.

To this she made no answer, but followed Mrs. Gunliffe out of the room. When they were down in the kitchen the mother had tea for her, and thick milk, and a hot cake,—all the delicacies which the farm could afford. I don't know that Mally cared much for the eating and drinking that night, but she began to think that the Gunliffes were good people,—very good people. It was better thus, at any rate, than being accused of murder and carried off to Camelford prison.

"I'll never forget it on her—never," the father had said.

Those words stuck to her from that moment, and seemed to sound in her ears all the night. How glad she was that Barty had come down to the cove,—oh, yes, how glad! There was no question of his dying now, and as for the blow on his forehead, what harm was that to a lad like him?

"But father shall go with you," said Mrs. Gunliffe, when Mally prepared to start for the cove by herself. Mally, however, would not hear of this. She could find her way to the cove whether it was light or dark.

"Mally, thou art my child now, and I shall think of thee so," said the mother, as the girl went off by herself.

Mally thought of this, too, as she walked home. How could she become Mrs. Gunliffe's child; ah, how?

I need not, I think, tell the tale any further. That Mally did become Mrs. Gunliffe's child, and how she became so the reader will understand; and in process of time the big kitchen and all the wonders of the farm-house were her own. The people said that Barty Gunliffe had married a mermaid out of the sea; but when it was said in Mally's hearing I doubt whether she liked it; and when Barty himself would call her a mermaid she would frown at him, and throw about her black hair, and pretend to cuff him with her little hand.

Old Glos was brought up to the top of the cliff, and lived his few remaining days under the roof of Mr. Gunliffe's house; and as for the cove and the right of sea-weed, from that time forth all that has been supposed to attach itself to Gunliffe's farm, and I do not know that any of the neighbours are prepared to dispute the right.

Father Giles of Ballymoy

Originally appeared in *The Argosy*, May 1866. Reprinted in *Lotta Schmidt and Other Stories* (1867). Like 'The O'Conors of Castle Conor', a farcical (but according to *An Autobiography*, substantially true) anecdote dating from Trollope's earliest days in Ireland. Another version, differing in some particulars, is given in W.R. LeFanu, *Seventy Years of Irish Life* (London: Edward Arnold, 1893), pp. 190–92. The broadness of the story's humour recalls some of the colourful digressive episodes in *The Macdermots of Ballycloran* (1847). In common with 'The O'Conors of Castle Conor' and 'Miss Ophelia Gledd', this story features Archibald Green as an authorial persona.

IT IS nearly thirty years since I, Archibald Green, first entered the little town of Ballymoy, in the west of Ireland, and became acquainted with one of the honestest fellows and best Christians whom it has ever been my good fortune to know. For twenty years he and I were fast friends, though he was much my elder. As he has now been ten years beneath the sod, I may tell the story of our first meeting.

Ballymoy is a so-called town,—or was in the days of which I am speaking,—lying close to the shores of Lough Corrib, in the county of Galway. It is on the road to no place, and, as the end of a road, has in itself nothing to attract a traveller. The scenery of Lough Corrib is grand; but the lake is very large, and the fine scenery is on the side opposite to Ballymoy, and hardly to be reached, or even seen, from that place. There is fishing,—but it is lake fishing. The salmon fishing of Lough Corrib is far away from Ballymoy, where the little river runs away from the lake down to the town of Galway. There was then in Ballymoy one single street, of which the characteristic at first sight most striking to a stranger was its general appearance of being thoroughly wet through. It was not simply that the rain water was generally running down its unguttered streets in muddy, random rivulets, hurrying towards the lake with true Irish impetuosity, but that each separate house looked as though the walls were reeking with wet; and the alternated roofs of thatch and slate,—the slated houses being just double the height of those that were thatched,—assisted the eye and mind of the spectator in forming this opinion. The lines were broken everywhere, and at every break it seemed as though there was a free entrance for the waters of heaven. The population of Ballymoy was its second wonder. There had been no famine then; no rot among the potatoes; and land round Ballymoy had been let for nine, ten, and even eleven pounds an acre. At all hours of the day, and at nearly all hours of the night, able-bodied men were to be seen standing in the streets, with knee-breeches unbuttoned, with stockings rolled down over their brogues, and with swallow-tailed frieze coats. Nor, though thus idle, did they seem to suffer any of the distress of poverty. There were plenty of beggars, no doubt, in Ballymoy, but it never struck me that there was much distress in those days. The earth gave forth its potatoes freely, and neither man nor pig wanted more.

It was to be my destiny to stay a week at Ballymoy, on business, as to the nature of which I need not trouble the present reader. I was not, at that time, so well acquainted with the manners of the people of Connaught as I became afterwards, and I had certain misgivings as I was driven into the village on a jaunting-car from Tuam. I had just come down from Dublin, and had been informed there that there were two "hotels" in Ballymoy, but that one of the "hotels" might, perhaps, be found deficient in some of those comforts which I, as an Englishman, might require. I was therefore to ask for the "hotel" kept by Pat Kirwan. The other hotel was kept by Larry Kirwan; so that it behoved me to be particular. I had made the journey down from Dublin in a night and a day, travelling, as we then did travel in Ireland, by canal boats and by Bianconi's long cars; and I had dined at Tuam, and been driven over, after dinner on an April evening; and when I reached Ballymoy I was tired to death and very cold.

"Pat Kirwan's hotel," I said to the driver, almost angrily. "Mind you don't go to the other."

"Shure, yer honour, and why not to Larry's? You'd be getting better enthertainment at Larry's, because of Father Giles."

I understood nothing about Father Giles, and wished to understand nothing. But I did understand that I was to go to Pat Kirwan's "hotel," and thither I insisted on being taken.

It was quite dusk at this time, and the wind was blowing down the street of Ballymoy, carrying before it wild gusts of rain. In the west of Ireland March weather comes in April, and it comes with a violence of its own, though not with the cruelty of the English east wind. At this moment my neck was ricked by my futile endeavours to keep my head straight on the side car, and the water had got under me upon the seat, and the horse had come to a stand-still half-a-dozen times in the last two minutes, and my apron had been trailed in the mud, and I was very unhappy. For the last ten minutes I had been thinking evil of everything Irish, and especially of Connaught.

I was driven up to a queerly-shaped, three-cornered house, that stood at the bottom of the street, and which seemed to possess none of the outside appurtenances of an inn.

"Is this Pat Kirwan's hotel?" said I.

"Faix, and it is then, yer honour," said the driver. "And barring only that Father Giles— "

But I had rung the bell, and as the door was now opened by a barefooted girl, I entered the little passage without hearing anything further about Father Giles.

"Could I have a bedroom immediately, with a fire in it?"

Not answering me directly, the girl led me into a sitting-room, in which my nose was at once greeted by that peculiar perfume which is given out by the relics of hot whisky-punch mixed with a great deal of sugar, and there she left me.

"Where is Pat Kirwan himself?" said I, coming to the door, and blustering somewhat. For, let it be remembered, I was very tired; and it may be a fair question whether in the far west of Ireland a little bluster may not sometimes be of service. "If you have not a room ready, I will go to Larry Kirwan's," said I, showing that I understood the bearings of the place.

"It's right away at the furder end then, yer honour," said the driver, putting in his word, "and we comed by it ever so long since. But shure yer honour wouldn't think of leaving this house for that?"

This he said because Pat Kirwan's wife was close behind him.

Then Mrs. Kirwan assured me that I could and should be accommodated. The house, to be sure, was crowded, but she had already made arrangements, and had a bed ready. As for a fire in my bed-room, she could not recommend that, "becase the wind blew so mortial sthrong down the chimney since the pot had blown off,—bad cess to it; and that loon, Mick Hackett, wouldn't lend a hand to put it up again, because there were jobs going on at the big house,—bad luck to every joint of his body, thin," said Mrs. Kirwan, with great energy. Nevertheless, she and Mick Hackett the mason were excellent friends.

I professed myself ready to go at once to the bedroom without the fire, and was led away up stairs. I asked where I was to eat my breakfast and dine on the next day, and was assured that I should have the room so strongly perfumed with whisky all to myself. I had been rather cross before, but on hearing this, I became decidedly sulky. It was not that I could not eat my breakfast in the chamber in question, but that I saw before me seven days of absolute misery, if I could have no other place of refuge for myself than a room in which, as was too plain, all Ballymoy came to drink and smoke. But there was no alternative, at any rate for that night and the following morning, and I therefore gulped down my anger without further spoken complaint, and followed the barefooted maiden upstairs, seeing my portmanteau carried up before me.

Ireland is not very well known now to all Englishmen, but it is much better known than it was in those days. On this my first visit into Connaught, I own that I was somewhat scared lest I should be made a victim to the wild lawlessness and general savagery of the people; and I fancied, as in the wet, windy gloom of the night, I could see the crowd of natives standing round the doors of the inn, and just discern their naked legs and old battered hats, that Ballymoy was probably one of those places so far removed from civilisation and law, as to be an unsafe residence for an English Protestant. I had undertaken the service on which I was employed, with my eyes more or less open, and was determined to go through with it;—but I confess that I was by this time alive to its dangers. It was an early resolution with me that I would not allow my portmanteau to be out of my sight. To that I would cling; with that ever close to me would I live; on that, if needful, would I die. I therefore required that it should be carried up the narrow stairs before me, and I saw it deposited safely in the bedroom.

The stairs were very narrow and very steep. Ascending them was like climbing into a loft. The whole house was built in a barbarous, uncivilised manner, and as fit to be an hotel as it was to be a church. It was triangular and all corners,—the most uncomfortably arranged building I had ever seen. From the top of the stairs I was called upon to turn abruptly into the room destined for me; but there was a side step which I had not noticed under the glimmer of the small tallow candle, and I stumbled headlong into the chamber, uttering imprecations against Pat Kirwan, Ballymoy, and all Connaught.

I hope the reader will remember that I had travelled for thirty consecutive hours, had passed sixteen in a small comfortless canal boat without the power of stretching my legs, and that the wind had been at work upon me sideways for the last three hours. I was terribly tired, and I spoke very uncivilly to the young woman.

"Shure, yer honour, it's as clane as clane, and as dhry as dhry, and has been slept in every night since the big storm," said the girl, good humouredly. Then she went on to tell me something more about Father Giles, of which, however I could catch nothing, as she was bending over the bed, folding down the bedclothes. "Feel of 'em," said she, "they's dhry as dhry."

I did feel them, and the sheets were dry and clean, and the bed, though very small, looked as if it would be comfortable. So I somewhat softened my tone to her, and bade her call me the next morning at eight.

"Shure, yer honour, and Father Giles will call yer hisself," said the girl.

I begged that Father Giles might be instructed to do no such thing. The girl, however, insisted that he would, and then left me. Could it be that in this savage place, it was considered to be the duty of the parish priest to go round, with matins perhaps, or some other abominable papist ceremony, to the beds of all the strangers? My mother, who was a strict woman, had warned me vehemently against the machinations of the Irish priests, and I, in truth, had been disposed to ridicule her. Could it be that there were such machinations? Was it possible that my trousers might be refused me till I had taken mass? Or that force would be put upon me in some other shape, perhaps equally disagreeable?

Regardless of that and other horrors, or rather, I should perhaps say, determined to face manfully whatever horrors the night or morning might bring upon me, I began to prepare for bed. There was something pleasant in the romance of sleeping at Pat Kirwan's house in Ballymoy, instead of in my own room in Keppel Street, Russell Square. So I chuckled inwardly at Pat Kirwan's idea of an hotel, and unpacked my things.

There was a little table covered with a clean cloth, on which I espied a small comb. I moved the comb carefully without touching it, and brought the table up to my bedside. I put out my brushes and clean linen for the morning, said my prayers, defying Father Giles and his machinations, and jumped into bed. The bed certainly was good, and the sheets were very pleasant. In five minutes I was fast asleep.

How long I had slept when I was awakened, I never knew. But it was at some hour in the dead of night, when I was disturbed by footsteps in my room, and on jumping up, I saw a tall, stout, elderly man standing with his back towards me, in the middle of the room, brushing his clothes with the utmost care. His coat was still on his back, and his pantaloons on his legs; but he was most assiduous in his attention to every part of his body which he could reach.

I sat upright, gazing at him, as I thought then, for ten minutes,—we will say that I did so perhaps for forty seconds,—and of one thing I became perfectly certain,—namely, that the clothes-brush was my own! Whether, according to Irish hotel law, a gentleman would be justified in entering a stranger's room at midnight for the sake of brushing his clothes, I could not say; but I felt quite sure that in such a case, he would be bound at least to use the hotel brush or his own. There was a manifest trespass in regard to my property.

"Sir," said I, speaking very sharply, with the idea of startling him, "what are you doing here in this chamber?"

"Deed, then, and I'm sorry I've waked ye, my boy," said the stout gentleman.

"Will you have the goodness, sir, to tell me what you are doing here?"

"Bedad, then, just at this moment it's brushing my clothes, I am. It was badly they wanted it."

"I daresay they did. And you were doing it with my clothes-brush."

"And that's thrue too. And if a man hasn't a clothes-brush of his own, what else can he do but use somebody else's?"

"I think it's a great liberty, sir," said I.

"And I think it's a little one. It's only in the size of it we differ. But I beg your pardon. There is your brush. I hope it will be none the worse."

Then he put down the brush, seated himself on one of the two chairs which the room contained, and slowly proceeded to pull off his shoes, looking me full in the face all the while.

"What are you going to do, sir?" said I, getting a little further out from under the clothes, and leaning over the table.

"I am going to bed," said the gentleman.

"Going to bed—where?"

"Here," said the gentleman; and he still went on untying the knot of his shoe-string.

It had always been a theory with me, in regard not only to my own country, but to all others, that civilisation displays itself never more clearly than when it ordains that every man shall have a bed for himself. In older days Englishmen of good position,—men supposed to be gentlemen,—would sleep together and think nothing of it, as ladies, I am told, will still do. And in outlandish regions, up to this time, the same practice prevails. In parts of Spain you will be told that one bed offers sufficient accommodation for two men, and in Spanish America the traveller is considered to be fastidious who thinks that one on each side of him is oppressive. Among the poorer classes with ourselves this grand touchstone of civilisation has not yet made itself felt. For aught I know there might be no such touchstone in Connaught at all. There clearly seemed to be none such at Ballymoy.

"You can't go to bed here," said I, sitting bolt upright on the couch.

"You'll find you are wrong there, my friend," said the elderly gentleman. "But make yourself aisy, I won't do you the least harm in life, and I sleep as quiet as a mouse."

It was quite clear to me that time had come for action. I certainly would not let this gentleman get into my bed. I had been the first comer, and was for the night, at least, the proprietor of this room. Whatever might be the custom of this country in these wild regions, there could be no special law in the land justifying the landlord in such treatment of me as this.

"You won't sleep here, sir," said I, jumping out of the bed, over the table, on to the floor, and confronting the stranger just as he had succeeded in divesting himself of his second shoe. "You won't sleep here to-night, and so you may as well go away."

With that I picked up his two shoes, took them to the door, and chucked them out. I heard them go rattling down the stairs, and I was glad that they made so much noise. He would see that I was quite in earnest.

"You must follow your shoes," said I, "and the sooner the better."

I had not even yet seen the man very plainly, and even now, at this time, I hardly did so, though I went close up to him and put my hand upon his shoulder. The light was very imperfect, coming from one small farthing candle, which was nearly burnt out in the socket. And I, myself, was confused, ill at ease, and for the moment unobservant. I knew that the man was older than myself, but I had not recognised him as being old enough to demand or enjoy personal protection by reason of his age. He was tall, and big, and burly,—as he appeared to me then. Hitherto, till his shoes had been chucked away, he had maintained imperturbable good-humour. When he heard the shoes clattering down-stairs, it seemed that he did not like it, and he began to talk fast and in an angry voice. I would not argue with him, and I did not understand him, but still keeping my hand on the collar of his coat, I insisted that he should not sleep there. Go away out of that chamber he should.

"But it's my own," he said, shouting the words a dozen times. "It's my own room. It's my own room."

So this was Pat Kirwan himself,—drunk probably, or mad.

"It may be your own," said I; "but you've let it to me for to-night, and you sha'n't sleep here;" so saying I backed him towards the door, and in so doing I trod upon his unguarded toe.

"Bother you, thin, for a pig-headed Englishman!" said he. "You've kilt me entirely now. So take your hands off my neck, will ye, before you have me throttled outright?"

I was sorry to have trod on his toe, but I stuck to him all the same. I had him near the door now, and I was determined to put him out into the passage. His face was very round and very red, and I thought that he must be drunk; and since I had found out that it was Pat Kirwan the landlord, I was more angry with the man than ever.

"You sha'n't sleep here, so you might as well go," I said, as I backed him away towards the door. This had not been closed since the shoes had been thrown out, and with something of a struggle between the doorposts, I got him out. I remembered nothing whatever as to the suddenness of the stairs. I had been fast asleep since I came up them, and hardly even as yet knew exactly where I was. So, when I got him through the aperture of the door, I gave him a push, as was most natural, I think, for me to do. Down he went backwards,—down the stairs, all in a heap, and I could hear that in his fall he had stumbled against Mrs. Kirwan, who was coming up, doubtless to ascertain the cause of all the trouble above her head.

A hope crossed my mind that the wife might be of assistance to her husband in this time of his trouble. The man had fallen very heavily, I knew, and had fallen backwards. And I remembered then how steep the stairs were. Heaven and earth! Suppose that he were killed,—or even seriously injured in his own house. What, in such case as that, would my life be worth in that wild country? Then I began to regret that I had been so hot. It might be that I had murdered a man on my first entrance into Connaught!

For a moment or two I could not make up my mind what I would first do. I was aware that both the landlady and the servant were occupied with the body of the ejected occupier of my chamber, and I was aware also that I had nothing on but my night-shirt. I returned, therefore, within the door, but could not bring myself to shut myself in and return to bed without making some inquiry as to the man's fate. I put my head out, therefore, and did make inquiry.

"I hope he is not much hurt by his fall," I said.

"Ochone, ochone! murdher, murdher! Spake, Father Giles, dear, for the love of God!" Such and many such exclamations I heard from the women at the bottom of the stairs.

"I hope he is not much hurt," I said again, putting my head out from the doorway; "but he shouldn't have forced himself into my room."

"His room, the omadhaun!—the born idiot!" said the landlady.

"Faix, ma'am, and Father Giles is a dead man," said the girl, who was kneeling over the prostrate body in the passage below.

I heard her say Father Giles as plain as possible, and then I became aware that the man whom I had thrust out was not the landlord, but the priest of the parish! My heart became sick within me as I thought of the troubles around me. And I was sick also with fear lest the man who had fallen should be seriously hurt. But why—why—why had he forced his way into my room? How was it to be expected that I should have remembered that the stairs of the accursed house came flush up to the door of the chamber?

"He shall be hanged if there's law in Ireland," said a voice down below; and as far as I could see it might be that I should be hung. When I heard that last voice I began to think that I had in truth killed a man, and a cold sweat broke out all over me, and I stood for a while shivering where I was. Then I remembered that it behoved me as a man to go down among my enemies below, and to see what had really happened, to learn whom I had hurt,—let the consequences to myself be what they might. So I quickly put on some of my clothes,—a pair of trousers, a loose coat, and a pair of slippers, and I descended the stairs. By this time they had taken the priest into the whisky-perfumed chamber below, and although the hour was late, there were already six or seven persons with him. Among them was the real Pat Kirwan himself, who had not been so particular about his costume as I had.

Father Giles,—for indeed it was Father Giles, the priest of the parish,—had been placed in an old armchair, and his head was resting against Mrs. Kirwan's body. I could tell from the moans which he emitted that there was still, at any rate, hope of life.

Pat Kirwan, who did not quite understand what had happened, and who was still half asleep, and as I afterwards learned, half tipsy, was standing over him wagging his head. The girl was also standing by, with an old woman and two men who had made their way in through the kitchen.

"Have you sent for a doctor?" said I.

"Oh, you born blagghuard!" said the woman. "You thief of the world! That the like of you should ever have darkened my door!"

"You can't repent it more than I do, Mrs. Kirwan; but hadn't you better send for the doctor?"

"Faix, and for the police too, you may be shure of that, young man. To go and chuck him out of the room like that—his own room too, and he a priest and an ould man—he that had given up the half of it, though I axed him not to do so, for a stranger as nobody knowed nothing about."

The truth was coming out by degrees. Not only was the man I had put out Father Giles, but he was also the proper occupier of the room. At any rate somebody ought to have told me all this before they put me to sleep in the same bed with the priest.

I made my way round to the injured man, and put my hand upon his shoulder, thinking that perhaps I might be able to ascertain the extent of the injury. But the angry woman, together with the girl, drove me away, heaping on me terms of reproach, and threatening me with the gallows at Galway.

I was very anxious that a doctor should be brought as soon as possible; and as it seemed that nothing was being done, I offered to go and search for one. But I was given to understand that I should not be allowed to leave the house until the police had come. I had therefore to remain there for half-an-hour, or nearly so, till a sergeant, with two other policemen, really did come. During this time I was in a most wretched frame of mind. I knew no one at Ballymoy or in the neighbourhood. From the manner in which I was addressed, and also threatened by Mrs. Kirwan and by those who came in and out of the room, I was aware that I should encounter the most intense hostility. I had heard of Irish murders, and heard also of the love of the people for their priests, and I really began to doubt whether my life might not be in danger.

During this time, while I was thus waiting, Father Giles himself recovered his consciousness. He had been stunned by the fall, but his mind came back to him, though by no means all at once; and while I was left in the room with him he hardly seemed to remember all the events of the past hour.

I was able to discover from what was said that he had been for some days past, or, as it afterwards turned out for the last month, the tenant of the room, and that when I arrived he had been drinking tea with Mrs. Kirwan. The only other public bedroom in the hotel was occupied, and he had with great kindness given the landlady permission to put the Saxon stranger into his chamber. All this came out by degrees, and I could see how the idea of my base and cruel ingratitude rankled in the heart of Mrs. Kirwan. It was in vain that I expostulated and explained, and submitted myself humbly to everything that was said around me.

"But, ma'am," I said, "if I had only been told that it was the reverend gentleman's bed!"

"Bed, indeed! To hear the blagghuard talk you'd think it was axing Father Giles to sleep along with the likes of him we were. And there's two beds in the room as dacent as any Christian iver stretched in."

It was a new light to me. And yet I had known over night, before I undressed, that there were two bedsteads in the room! I had seen them, and had quite forgotten the fact in my confusion when I was woken. I had been very stupid, certainly. I felt that now. But I had truly believed that that big man was going to get into my little bed. It was terrible as I thought of it now. The good-natured priest, for the sake of accommodating a stranger, had consented to give up half of his room, and had been repaid for his kindness by being—perhaps murdered! And yet, though just then I hated myself cordially, I could not quite bring myself to look at the matter as they looked at it. There were excuses to be made, if only I could get any one to listen to them.

"He was using my brush—my clothes-brush—indeed he was," I said. "Not but what he'd be welcome; but it made me think he was an intruder."

"And wasn't it too much honour for the likes of ye?" said one of the women, with infinite scorn in the tone of her voice.

"I did use the gentleman's clothes-brush, certainly," said the priest. They were the first collected words he had spoken, and I felt very grateful to him for them. It seemed to me that a man who could condescend to remember that he had used a clothes-brush, could not really be hurt to death, even though he had been pushed down such very steep stairs as those belonging to Pat Kirwan's hotel.

"And I'm sure you were very welcome, sir," said I. "It wasn't that I minded the clothes-brush. It wasn't, indeed; only I thought,—indeed, I did think that there was only one bed. And they had put me into the room, and had not said anything about anybody else. And what was I to think when I woke up in the middle of the night?"

"Faix, and you'll have enough to think of in Galway gaol, for that's where you're going to," said one of the bystanders.

I can hardly explain the bitterness that was displayed against me. No violence was absolutely shown to me, but I could not move without eliciting a manifest determination that I was not to be allowed to stir out of the room. Red, angry eyes were glowering at me, and every word I spoke called down some expression of scorn and ill-will. I was beginning to feel glad that the police were coming, thinking that I needed protection. I was thoroughly ashamed of what I had done, and yet I could not discover that I had been very wrong at any particular moment. Let any man ask himself the question, what he would do, if he supposed that a stout old gentleman had entered his room at an inn and insisted on getting into his bed? It was not my fault that there had been no proper landing-place at the top of the stairs.

Two sub-constables had been in the room for some time before the sergeant came, and with the sergeant arrived also the doctor, and another priest,—Father Columb he was called,—who, as I afterwards learned, was curate or coadjutor to Father Giles. By this time there was quite a crowd in the house, although it was past one o'clock, and it seemed that all Ballymoy knew that its priest had been foully misused. It was manifest to me that there was something in the Roman Catholic religion which made the priests very dear to the people; for I doubt whether in any village in England, had such an accident happened to the rector, all the people would have roused themselves at midnight to wreak their vengeance on the assailant. For vengeance they were now beginning to clamour, and even before the sergeant of police had come, the two sub-constables were standing over me; and I felt that they were protecting me from the people in order that they might give me up—to the gallows!

I did not like the Ballymoy doctor at all,—then, or even at a later period of my visit to that town. On his arrival he made his way up to the priest through the crowd, and would not satisfy their affection or my anxiety by declaring at once that there was no danger. Instead of doing so he insisted on the terrible nature of the outrage and the brutality shown by the assailant. And at every hard word he said, Mrs. Kirwan would urge him on.

"That's thrue for you, doctor!" "'Deed, and you may say that, doctor; two as good beds as ever Christian stretched in!" "'Deed, and it was just Father Giles's own room, as you may say, since the big storm fetched the roof off his riverence's house below there."

Thus gradually I was learning the whole history. The roof had been blown off Father Giles's own house, and therefore he had gone to lodge at the inn! He had been willing to share his lodging with a stranger, and this had been his reward!

"I hope, doctor, that the gentleman is not much hurt," said I, very meekly.

"Do you suppose a gentleman like that, sir, can be thrown down a long flight of stairs without being hurt?" said the doctor, in an angry voice. "It is no thanks to you, sir, that his neck has not been sacrificed."

Then there arose a hum of indignation, and the two policemen standing over me bustled about a little, coming very close to me, as though they thought they should have something to do to protect me from being torn to pieces.

I bethought me that it was my special duty in such a crisis to show a spirit, if it were only for the honour of my Saxon blood among the Celts. So I spoke up again, as loud as I could well speak.

"No one in this room is more distressed at what has occurred than I am. I am most anxious to know, for the gentleman's sake, whether he has been seriously hurt?"

"Very seriously hurt indeed," said the doctor; "very seriously hurt. The vertebræ may have been injured for aught I know at present."

"Arrah, blazes, man," said a voice, which I learned afterwards had belonged to an officer of the revenue corps of men which was then stationed at Ballymoy, a gentleman with whom I became afterwards familiarly acquainted; Tom Macdermot was his name, Captain Tom Macdermot, and he came from the county of Leitrim,—"Arrah, blazes, man; do ye think a gentleman's to fall sthrait headlong backwards down such a ladder as that, and not find it inconvanient? Only that he's the priest, and has had his own luck, sorrow a neck belonging to him there would be this minute."

"Be aisy, Tom," said Father Giles himself; and I was delighted to hear him speak. Then there was a pause for a moment. "Tell the gentleman I ain't so bad at all," said the priest; and from that moment I felt an affection to him which never afterwards waned.

They got him upstairs back into the room from which he had been evicted, and I was carried off to the police-station, where I positively spent the night. What a night it was! I had come direct from London, sleeping on my road but once in Dublin, and now I found myself accommodated with a stretcher in the police barracks at Ballymoy! And the worst of it was that I had business to do at Ballymoy which required that I should hold up my head and make much of myself. The few words which had been spoken by the priest had comforted me, and had enabled me to think again of my own position. Why was I locked up? No magistrate had committed me. It was really a question whether I had done anything illegal. As that man whom Father Giles called Tom had very properly explained, if people will have ladders instead of staircases in their houses, how is anybody to put an intruder out of the room without risk of breaking the intruder's neck? And as to the fact,—now an undoubted fact,—that Father Giles was no intruder, the fault in that lay with the Kirwans, who had told me nothing of the truth. The boards of the stretcher in the police-station were very hard, in spite of the blankets with which I had been furnished; and as I lay there I began to remind myself that there certainly must be law in county Galway. So I called to the attendant policeman and asked him by whose authority I was locked up.

"Ah, thin, don't bother," said the policeman; "shure, and you've given throuble enough this night!" The dawn was at that moment breaking so I turned myself on the stretcher, and resolved that I would put a bold face on it all when the day should come.

The first person I saw in the morning was Captain Tom, who came into the room where I was lying, followed by a little boy with my portmanteau. The sub-inspector of police who ruled over the men at Ballymoy lived, as I afterwards learned, at Oranmore, so that I had not, at this conjuncture, the honour of seeing him. Captain Tom assured me that he was an excellent fellow, and rode to hounds like a bird. As in those days I rode to hounds myself,—as nearly like a bird as I was able,—I was glad to have such an account of my head-gaoler. The sub-constables seemed to do just what Captain Tom told them, and there was, no doubt, a very good understanding between the police force and the revenue officer.

"Well, now, I'll tell you what you must do, Mr. Green," said the Captain.

"In the first place," said I, "I must protest that I'm now locked up here illegally."

"Oh, bother; now don't make yourself unaisy."

"That's all very well, Captain—. I beg your pardon, sir, but I didn't catch any name plainly except the Christian name."

"My name is Macdermot—Tom Macdermot. They call me Captain—but that's neither here nor there."

"I suppose, Captain Macdermot, the police here cannot lock up anybody they please, without a warrant?"

"And where would you have been if they hadn't locked you up? I'm blessed if they wouldn't have had you into the Lough before this time."

There might be something in that, and I therefore resolved to forgive the personal indignity which I had suffered, if I could secure something like just treatment for the future. Captain Tom had already told me that Father Giles was doing pretty well.

"He's as sthrong as a horse, you see, or, sorrow a doubt, he'd be a dead man this minute. The back of his neck is as black as your hat with the bruises, and it's the same way with him all down his loins. A man like that, you know, not just as young as he was once, falls mortial heavy. But he's as jolly as a four-year old," said Captain Tom, "and you're to go and ate your breakfast with him, in his bedroom, so that you may see with your own eyes that there are two beds there."

"I remembered it afterwards quite well," said I.

"'Deed, and Father Giles got such a kick of laughter this morning, when he came to understand that you thought he was going to get into bed alongside of you, that he strained himself all over again, and I thought he'd have frightened the house, yelling with the pain. But anyway you've to go over and see him. So now you'd better get yourself dressed."

This announcement was certainly very pleasant. Against Father Giles, of course, I had no feeling of bitterness. He had behaved well throughout, and I was quite alive to the fact that the light of his countenance would afford me a better aegis against the ill-will of the people of Ballymoy, than anything the law would do for me. So I dressed myself in the barrack-room, while Captain Tom waited without; and then I sallied out under his guidance to make a second visit to Pat Kirwan's hotel. I was amused to see that the police, though by no means subject to Captain Tom's orders, let me go without the least difficulty, and that the boy was allowed to carry my portmanteau away with him.

"Oh, it's all right," said Captain Tom when I alluded to this. "You're not down in the sheet. You were only there for protection, you know."

Nevertheless, I had been taken there by force, and had been locked up by force. If, however, they were disposed to forget all that, so was I. I did not return to the barracks again; and when, after that, the policemen whom I had known met me in the street, they always accosted me as though I were an old friend; hoping my honour had found a better bed than when they last saw me. They had not looked at me with any friendship in their eyes when they had stood over me in Pat Kirwan's parlour.

This was my first view of Ballymoy, and of the "hotel" by daylight. I now saw that Mrs. Pat Kirwan kept a grocery establishment, and that the three-cornered house which had so astonished me was very small. Had I seen it before I entered it, I should hardly have dared to look there for a night's lodging. As it was, I stayed there for a fortnight, and was by no means uncomfortable. Knots of men and women were now standing in groups round the door, and, indeed, the lower end of the street was almost crowded.

"They're all here," whispered Captain Tom, "because they've heard how Father Giles has been murdered during the night by a terrible Saxon; and there isn't a man or woman among them who doesn't know that you are the man who did it."

"But they know also, I suppose," said I, "that Father Giles is alive."

"Bedad, yes, they know that, or I wouldn't be in your skin, my boy. But come along. We mustn't keep the priest waiting for his breakfast."

I could see that they all looked at me, and there were some of them, especially among the women, whose looks I did not even yet like. They spoke among each other in Gaelic, and I could perceive that they were talking of me.

"Can't you understand, then," said Captain Tom, speaking to them aloud, just as he entered the house, "that Father Giles, the Lord be praised, is as well as ever he was in his life? Shure it was only an accident."

"An accident done on purpose, Captain Tom," said one person.

"What is it to you how it was done, Mick Healy? If Father Giles is satisfied, isn't that enough for the likes of you? Get out of that, and let the gentleman pass." Then Captain Tom pushed Mick away roughly, and the others let us enter the house. "Only they wouldn't do it unless somebody gave them the wink, they'd pull you in pieces this moment for a dandy of punch—they would, indeed."

Perhaps Captain Tom exaggerated the prevailing feeling, thinking thereby to raise the value of his own service in protecting me; but I was quite alive to the fact that I had done a most dangerous deed, and had a most narrow escape.

I found Father Giles sitting up in his bed, while Mrs. Kirwan was rubbing his shoulder diligently with an embrocation of arnica. The girl was standing by with a basin half full of the same, and I could see that the priest's neck and shoulders were as red as a raw beefsteak. He winced grievously under the rubbing, but he bore it like a man.

"And here comes the hero," said Father Giles. "Now stop a minute or two, Mrs. Kirwan, while we have a mouthful of breakfast, for I'll go bail that Mr. Green is hungry after his night's rest. I hope you got a better bed, Mr. Green, than the one I found you in when I was unfortunate enough to waken you last night. There it is, all ready for you still," said he; "and if you accept of it to-night, take my advice and don't let a trifle stand in the way of your dhraims."

"I hope, thin, the gintleman will contrive to suit hisself elsewhere," said Mrs. Kirwan.

"He'll be very welcome to take up his quarters here if he likes," said the priest. "And why not? But, bedad, sir, you'd better be a little more careful the next time you see a stranger using your clothes-brush. They are not so strict here in their ideas of meum and tuum as they are perhaps in England; and if you had broken my neck for so small an offence, I don't know but what they'd have stretched your own."

We then had breakfast together, Father Giles, Captain Tom, and I; and a very good breakfast we had. By degrees even Mrs. Kirwan was induced to look favourably at me, and before the day was over I found myself to be regarded as a friend in the establishment. And as a friend I certainly was regarded by Father Giles—then, and for many a long day afterwards. And many times when he has, in years since that, but years nevertheless which are now long back, come over and visited me in my English home, he has told the story of the manner in which we first became acquainted. "When you find a gentleman asleep," he would say, "always ask his leave before you take a liberty with his clothes-brush."

The Gentle Euphemia

Originally appeared in *The Fortnightly Review*, 1 May 1866. This burlesque was not reprinted in Trollope's lifetime, and is his only contribution to the mid-Victorian cult of sham medievalism. It might be compared with the squib 'Crinoline and Macassar' in *The Three Clerks* (1858), which Charley Tudor is supposed to have written for *The Daily Delight*.

"Lo, I must tell a tale of chivalry,
For large white plumes are dancing in mine eye."

KEATS.

Chapter I

"—Knowledge, so my daughter held,
Was all in all."—TENNYSON.

THE GENTLE Euphemia lived in a castle, and her father was the Count Grandnostrel. The wise Alasco, who had dwelt for fifty years in the mullioned chamber of the North Tower, was her tutor, and he taught her poetry, arithmetic and philosophy, to love virtue, and the use of the globes.

And there came the lord of Mountfidget to her father's halls to drink the blood-red wine, and make exchange of the beeves and swine of Mountfidget against the olives and dried fruits which grow upon the slopes of Grandnostrel. For the pastures of Mountfidget are very rich, and its beeves and swine are fat.

"And peradventure I shall see the fair Euphemia," said the young lord to Lieutenant Hossbach, of the Marines, who sojourned oft at Grange of Mountfidget, and delighted more in the racket-court, the billiard-table, and the game of cards, than in guiding the manoeuvres of his trusty men-at-arms. "Peradventure," said the young lord, "I shall see the fair Euphemia,—for the poets of Grandnostrel sing of her peerless beauty, and declare her to be the pearl of pearls."

"Nay, my lord," said the lieutenant, "but an you behold the girl once in that spirit, thou art but a lost man, a kestrel with a broken wing, a spavined steed, a noseless hound, a fish out of water; for credit me, the fair Euphemia wants but a husband;—and therefore do the poets sing so loudly." For Lieutenant Hossbach knew that were there a lady at the Grange the spigot would not turn so freely.

"By my halidome," said the young lord, "I will know whether the poets sing sooth or not."

So the lord of Mountfidget departed for the Castle of Grandnostrel, and his beeves and his swine were driven before him.

Alasco the Wise sat in the mullioned chamber, with the globes before him and Aristotle's volume under his arm, and the gentle Euphemia sat lowly on a stool at his feet. And she asked him as to the lore of the ancient schools. "Teach me," she said, "as Plato taught, and the learned Esculapius and Aristides the Just; for I would fain walk in the paths of knowledge, and be guided by the rules of virtue." But he answered her not at all, nor did he open the books of wisdom. "Nay, my father," she said; "but the winged hours pass by, and my soul is athirst!"

Then he answered her and said; "My daughter, there cometh hither this day the young lord of Mountfidget, whose beeves and swine are as the stars of heaven in number, and whose ready money in many banks brings in rich harvest of interest. He cometh hither to drink the blood-red wine with your father, and to exchange his beeves and swine for the olives and the dried fruits which grow upon the slopes of Grandnostrel; and peradventure he will ask to see thy father's daughter. Then wilt thou no longer desire to hear what Plato teaches, or how the just man did according to justice."

But Euphemia replied; "Nay, my father. Am I no better than other girls that I should care for the glance of the young man's eye? Have I not sat at your feet since I was but as high as your knee? Teach me still as Plato taught."

But Alasco said; "Love will still be lord of all."

"He shall never be lord of me," said Euphemia.

Chapter II

"And from the platform spare ye not
To fire a noble salvo shot—
Lord Marmion waits below."—Scott.

And in those days there was the rinderpest in the land among the cattle, and the swine were plagued with a sore disease, and there had gone forth an edict and a command from the Queen's Councillors that no beeves or swine should be driven on the Queen's highways. So there came upon the lord of Mountfidget men armed with authority from the Queen, and they slew his beeves and his swine, and buried their carcases twenty fathom deep beneath the ground.

And the young lord was angered much, for he loved his beeves and his swine, and he said to himself, "What will my lord, the Count Grandnostrel, say unto me, if I visit him with empty hands? Will the blood-red wine be poured, or shall I see the gentle Euphemia?" For the Count Grandnostrel was a hard man, and loved a bargain well. "But I have much money in many banks," said the lord of Mountfidget, in council with himself. "And though my beeves and my swine are slain and buried, yet will he receive me; for the rich are ever welcome, though their hands be empty." So he went up the slopes which led to the Castle of Grandnostrel.

And at the portal, within the safeguard of the drawbridge, there were huge heaps of dried fruits, and mountains of olives. And there came out to him the Count Grandnostrel, and demanded of him where were his beeves and his swine. And the lord told the count how men in authority from the Queen had come upon him on the road, and had slain the beasts, and buried them twenty fathom beneath the earth,—because of the rinderpest which raged in the land, and because of the disease among the swine. Then said the Count Grandnostrel: "And art thou come empty-handed to drink the blood-red wine; and hast thou never a horn or a tusk? If my butler draw but a sorry pint for thee, I'll butler him with a bastinado! No;—not a cork! Get thee gone to thy Grange." So he drew up the drawbridge, and the sweet scent of the olives and of the dried fruits were borne aloft by the zephyrs, and struck upon the envious senses of the young lord.

"And shall I not see thy daughter, the gentle Euphemia?" said he.

Then the Count Grandnostrel called to his archers and bade them twang their bows; and the archers twanged their bows, and seven arrows struck the Lord Mountfidget full upon his breast. But their points availed nought against his steel cuirass; so he smiled and turned away.

"Nay, my lord, Count Grandnostrel," said he, "thou shalt rue the day when thou treated thus one who has ready money in many banks; I will set the lawyers at thee, and ruin thee with many costs."

Then, as he walked away, the archers twanged again, and struck him on the back. The good steel turned the points, and the arrows of Grandnostrel fell blunted to the ground. But I fear there was one arrow which entered just above the joint of the knight's harness, and galled the neck of the young lord.

But as he went down the slopes there waved a kerchief from the oriel window over the eastern parapet.

Chapter III

"Oh coz, coz, coz, coz, my pretty little coz,
Dost know how many fathom deep I am in love?"—SHAKSPEARE.

'TWAS MIDNIGHT, and there came a soft knock at the door of Alasco the Wise. But Alasco heard it not, for he was drinking in the wisdom of the ancients with all his senses, and his ears were deaf to all earthly sounds.

"Sleepest thou, my father?" said the gentle Euphemia, as she opened the door, "or is thy soul buried amidst thy books?"

"Daughter," said Alasco the Wise, "my soul is buried among my books. The hour is short, and the night cometh, and he who maketh not his hay while the sun of life shineth, shall hardly garner his crop beneath the cold, damp hand of death. But for thee, my child, and thy needs, all other things shall give way." Then he wiped his pen, and put a mark in his book, and closed his lexicon.

"My father," said the girl, "didst thou hear my father's archers, how their bows twanged this morn?"

"I heard a rattling as of dried peas against a window-pane," said the sage.

"It was the noise, father, of the arrows as they fell upon the breast of the Lord Mountfidget. And they fell upon his back, also, and alack! one has struck him on the nape of his neck! And then he rode away. Oh, father!"

"And is it thus with thee, my child?" said Alasco.

"Thus, father," said Euphemia. And she hid her face upon the serge of his mantle.

"Did I not say that love should still be lord of all?" said the sage.

"Spare me, father," said the damsel. "Spare the child that has stood at thy footstool since she was as high as thy knee. Spare me, and aid me to save my lord!"

Then they sallied forth from the small wicket which opens into the forest from beneath the west barbican.

Chapter IV

"Come back! come back! he cried in grief,
My daughter, oh, my daughter!"—CAMPBELL.

"When he found she'd levanted, the Count of Alsace
At first turned remarkably red in the face."—BARHAM.

AND IN the morning the Count of Grandnostrel called for his daughter. And his eyes were red with drinking, and his breath was thick, and he sat with his head between his hands. For he had drunk the blood-red wine sitting all alone through the night, laughing, as he quaffed down goblet after goblet, at the discomfiture of the lord of Mountfidget. "Rinderpest, indeed!" he had said. "He that cometh hither empty-handed is likely to return a-dry. Ho! there, butler! another stoup of Malvoisie, and let it be that with the yellow seal." But in the morning he had called for a cool tankard, and now he demanded his daughter's presence, that she might pour for him the cup which cheers but not inebriates. "Where is the Lady Euphemia? Why tarries the Lady Euphemia?" But the attendants answered him never a word. Then he called again. "Why cometh not my child to pour for her father the beverage which he loves? Now, by cock and pie, an that old greybeard detain her, he shall hence from the mullioned chamber,—and that with a flea in each ear." But still they answered him not a word. Then he up with the tankard from which he had taken his morning's brewst, and flung it at the menial's head. "Thou churl, thou sot, thou knave, thou clod! why answerest thou not thy liege and lord?" But the menial put his hands to his bruised head, and still answered he never a word.

Then there entered Dame Ulrica, a poor and aged cousin of the house, who went abroad to dances and to tea-parties with the gentle Euphemia. "An please you, my lord count" said dame Ulrica, "Euphemia has fled this morning by the small wicket which leads from beneath the west barbican into the forest, and Alasco the Wise has gone with her."

Then the Count Grandnostrel stood up in his wrath, and sat down in his wrath, and stood up in his wrath once again. "That tankard full of gold pieces," said he, "to him who shall bring me the grey-beard's head!"

Then the archers twanged their bows, and the men-at-arms sharpened their sabres, and the volunteers looked to their rifles, and the drummers drummed, and the fifers fifed, and they let down the drawbridge, and they went forth in pursuit of the wise Alasco and the gentle Euphemia.

"By cock and pie," said the Count Grandnostrel, "an it be as I expect, and that sorry knave from Mountfidget is at the bottom of this— "

"In that case it will be meetest, my lord, that she should be his wife," said the Dame Ulrica, who was riding on a palfrey at his right hand. And when she spoke the ancient virtue of the old race was to be seen in her eye, and might be heard in her voice.

"Thou sayest well, dame," answered the count.

"And the lord of Mountfidget has beeves and swine numerous as the stars, and ready money in many banks," said Dame Ulrica. For Dame Ulrica was not virtuous only, but prudent also.

"By cock and pie thou sayest sooth," said the Count Grandnostrel. And as they had now reached the Fiery Nostril, a hostel that standeth on the hill overlooking the olive gardens of the castle, the count called loudly for the landlord's ale. "By cock and pie this is dry work," said the Count Grandnostrel. "But we will squeeze Mountfidget drier before we have done with him."

Then the menials laughed, and the pot-bellied landlord swayed his huge paunch hither and thither, as he shook his sides with merriment. "Faix, and it is my lord the count is ever ready with his joke," said the landlord.

So they paid for the beer and rode on.

Chapter V

> "A breathing but devoted warrior lay.
> T'was Lara bleeding fast from life away."—BYRON.

IN THE upper chamber of a small cottage, covered with ivy and vines, lay the lord of Mountfidget, hurt unto death. For one of the arrows had touched him on the nape of the neck, and the point had been dipped in the oil of strychnine. And there leaned over his couch a widow, watching him from moment to moment, touching his lips ever and anon with orange juice mixed with brandy, and wiping the clammy dew from his cold brow. "Lord of Mountfidget," she said, "when my dear husband was torn from my widowed arms, thy father gave unto the poor widow this cottage. Would I could repay the debt with my heart's blood."

"Aha! alas! alack! and well-a-day," said the young lord. "Nought can repay me now,—either interest or principal. All my money at all the banks cannot prolong my life one hour. No, nor my beeves and swine, though they outnumber the stars of heaven, and are fatter than a butter-tub. It is all up with poor Mountfidget."

"Nay; say not so, my lord. If only I could reach the wise man that liveth in the mullioned chamber of the north tower, he hath a medicine that might yet be of avail."

Then Mountfidget demanded who was the wise man, and where was the mullioned chamber of the north tower; and when he learned that aid could be had only from the Castle of Grandnostrel, he sighed amain, and sighed again, and then thus he addressed the widow; "Ay, help from Grandnostrel;—yes; but not such aid as that. I want no grey-bearded senior to rack my dying brains with wise saws; but, if it might be given me to let my eyes rest but once on the form of the gentle Euphemia, methinks I could die contented."

Then the door of the chamber was opened, and there entered a young page, whose slashed doublet and silken hose were foul with the mud of many lanes, and the dirt of the forest clung to his short cloak, and his hair was wet with the dropping of the leaves, and his cap was crushed and his jacket was torn. "He is here! he is here!" said the page. "I have followed him by his blood through the forest." Then the page fell at the bed-foot, and there he fainted.

Chapter VI

"Meanwhile war arose."—MILTON.

BUT AS the page sank upon the floor, a small bottle fell from his breast coat-pocket, and the widow saw that it was labelled "antidote for the oil of strychnine." Then the widow's heart leaped for joy, and as she poured the precious drops into the gaping wound, she said a prayer that the page might recover also.

But what noise is this of horses and of men around the humble vineyard of that poor widow? "Tiraloo, Tiraloo, Tiraloo-ooh," "Ha!" said the Mountfidget, raising himself on his elbow, "'tis the war-cry of the Grandnostrel!" "Rowdadow, Rowdadow, Rowdadow-dow," then greeted his ears. "Ha! ha!" he cried. "Rowdadow, a Rowdadow, Rowdadow-dow; 'tis the war-cry of the Mountfidget!" And he grasped the sword which lay beneath his pillow. "Mountfidget to the rescue! Shall a man lie still and perish beneath the bedclothes? Ho, a Hossbach! Ho, a Walker!" For Walker was the captain of the men-at-arms at Mountfidget, and the lord knew the voice of his trusty clansman.

Then the widow looked through the lattice-window, and told him how the fight went. But no one thought of the page upon whose brow the clammy hand of death was falling as he lay at the bed-foot.

Chapter VII

"Close against her heaving breast
Something in her hand is pressed."—LONGFELLOW.

Alasco the Wise had been left in the forest, and was unable to stir another step. "'Tis the blood of the Mountfidget," he had said, when he saw the gouts upon the path. "I know it by its purple hue, and by its violet-scented perfume. Follow it on, but take that bottle with thee. And stay, lest thy sex betray thee to ill-usage from the boors, take this page's raiment which I carry in my wallet, and put the bottle in thy breast coat-pocket. If thou find, as is too likely, a gaping wound in the nape of the neck, naught can restore him but this. Pour it in freely, and he shall live. But if he shall first have heard the war-cry of thy father to disturb him, then he shall surely die." So the gentle Euphemia had gone through the forest, and had reached the chamber of the widow in which lay the lord of Mountfidget.

And as she lay at the foot of the bed, slowly there came back upon her mind a knowledge that she was there. She put her hand to her bosom in haste, and found that the bottle was gone. Then a terrible sound greeted her ears, and she heard the war-cry of her father. Tiraloo, Tiraloo, Tiraloo-ooh! "He is dead," she cried, springing to her feet. "He is dead, and I will die also."

Then the widow knew that it was the gentle Euphemia. "No, thou gentlest one," she said; "he shall not die. He shall live to count the fat beeves and the many swine of Mountfidget, and shall be the possessor of much money in many banks; and thou, thou gentlest one, shall share his blessings. For love shall still be lord of all."

"I do confess," said the gentle Euphemia in a silvern whisper,—in a silvern whisper that was heard by him beneath the bedclothes,—"I do confess that love is lord of me." Then she sank upon the floor.

Chapter VIII

"I charge you be his faithful and true wife,
Keep warm his hearth and clean his board; and when
He speaks, be quick in your obedience."—Eliz. B. Browning.

And then they all returned to the Castle of Grandnostrel, and on their way they took up the wise Alasco, who had remained in the forest.

"Nay, father," said the damsel smiling, "but thou hast been right in all things, and hast taught me better than Plato ever taught."

"And was not I young once myself!" said the sage. So when the blood-red wine had warmed his old veins, and made supple the joints of his aged legs, he tripped a measure in the castle hall, and was very jocund.

So the lord of Mountfidget was married to the gentle Euphemia. But when three months were passed and gone, Lieutenant Hossbach had returned to his regimental duties.

And love shall still be lord of all.

Lotta Schmidt

Originally appeared in *The Argosy*, July 1866. Reprinted in *Lotta Schmidt and Other Stories* (1867). Trollope took in Vienna during his Central European tour of 1865—the trip which also inspired the 1867 novels *Nina Balatka* (set in Prague), and *Linda Tressel* (set in Nuremberg).

As all the world knows, the old fortifications of Vienna have been pulled down,—the fortifications which used to surround the centre or kernel of the city; and the vast spaces thus thrown open and forming a broad ring in the middle of the town have not as yet been completely filled up with those new buildings and gardens which are to be there, and which, when there, will join the outside city and the inside city together, so as to make them into one homogeneous whole.

The work, however, is going on, and if the war which has come and passed has not swallowed everything appertaining to Austria into its maw, the ugly remnants of destruction will be soon carted away, and the old glacis will be made bright with broad pavements, and gilded railings, and well-built lofty mansions, and gardens beautiful with shrubs,—and beautiful with turf also, if Austrian patience can make turf to grow beneath an Austrian sky.

On an evening of September, when there was still something left of daylight, at eight o'clock, two girls were walking together in the Burgplatz, or large open space which lies between the city palace of the Emperor and the gate which passes thence from the old town out to the new town. Here at present stand two bronze equestrian statues, one of the Archduke Charles, and the other of Prince Eugene. And they were standing there also, both of them, when these two girls were walking round them; but that of the Prince had not as yet been uncovered for the public.

There was coming a great gala day in the city. Emperors and empresses, archdukes and grand-dukes, with their archduchesses and grand-duchesses, and princes and ministers, were to be there, and the new statue of Prince Eugene was to be submitted to the art-critics of the world. There was very much thought at Vienna of the statue in those days. Well; since that, the statue has been submitted to the art-critics, and henceforward it will be thought of as little as any other huge bronze figure of a prince on horseback. A very ponderous prince is poised in an impossible position, on an enormous dray horse. But yet the thing is grand, and Vienna is so far a finer city in that it possesses the new equestrian statue of Prince Eugene.

"There will be such a crowd, Lotta," said the elder of the two girls, "that I will not attempt it. Besides, we shall have plenty of time for seeing it afterwards."

"Oh, yes," said the younger girl, whose name was Lotta Schmidt; "of course we shall all have enough of the old prince for the rest of our lives; but I should like to see the grand people sitting up there on the benches; and there will be something nice in seeing the canopy drawn up. I think I will come. Herr Crippel has said that he would bring me, and get me a place."

"I thought, Lotta, you had determined to have nothing more to say to Herr Crippel."

"I don't know what you mean by that. I like Herr Crippel very much, and he plays beautifully. Surely a girl may know a man old enough to be her father without having him thrown in her teeth as her lover."

"Not when the man old enough to be her father has asked her to be his wife twenty times, as Herr Crippel has asked you. Herr Crippel would not give up his holiday afternoon to you if he thought it was to be for nothing."

"There I think you are wrong, Marie. I believe Herr Crippel likes to have me with him simply because every gentleman likes to have a lady on such a day as that. Of course it is better than being alone. I don't suppose he will say a word to me except to tell me who the people are, and to give me a glass of beer when it is over."

It may be as well to explain at once, before we go any further, that Herr Crippel was a player on the violin, and that he led the musicians in the orchestra of the great beer-hall in the Volksgarten. Let it not be thought that because Herr Crippel exercised his art in a beer-hall therefore he was a musician of no account. No one will think so who has once gone to a Vienna beer-hall, and listened to such music as is there provided for the visitors.

The two girls, Marie Weber and Lotta Schmidt, belonged to an establishment in which gloves were sold in the Graben, and now, having completed their work for the day,—and indeed their work for the week, for it was Saturday evening,—had come out for such recreation as the evening might afford them. And on behalf of these two girls, as to one of whom at least I am much interested, I must beg my English readers to remember that manners and customs differ much in Vienna from those which prevail in London.

Were I to tell of two London shop girls going out into the streets after their day's work, to see what friends and what amusement the fortune of the evening might send to them, I should be supposed to be speaking of young women as to whom it would be better that I should be silent; but these girls in Vienna were doing simply that which all their friends would expect and wish them to do. That they should have some amusement to soften the rigours of long days of work was recognised to be necessary; and music, beer, dancing, with the conversation of young men, are thought in Vienna to be the natural amusements of young women, and in Vienna are believed to be innocent.

The Viennese girls are almost always attractive in their appearance, without often coming up to our English ideas of prettiness. Sometimes they do fully come up to our English idea of beauty. They are generally dark, tall, light in figure, with bright eyes, which are however very unlike the bright eyes of Italy, and which constantly remind the traveller that his feet are carrying him eastward in Europe. But perhaps the peculiar characteristic in their faces which most strikes a stranger is a certain look of almost fierce independence, as though they had recognised the necessity, and also acquired the power, of standing alone, and of protecting themselves. I know no young women by whom the assistance of a man's arm seems to be so seldom required as the young women of Vienna. They almost invariably dress well, generally preferring black, or colours that are very dark; and they wear hats that are, I believe, of Hungarian origin, very graceful in form, but which are peculiarly calculated to add something to that assumed savageness of independence of which I have spoken.

Both the girls who were walking in the Burgplatz were of the kind that I have attempted to describe. Marie Weber was older, and not so tall, and less attractive than her friend; but as her position in life was fixed, and as she was engaged to marry a cutter of diamonds, I will not endeavour to interest the reader specially in her personal appearance. Lotta Schmidt was essentially a Viennese pretty girl of the special Viennese type. She was tall and slender, but still had none of that appearance of feminine weakness which is so common among us with girls who are tall and slim. She walked as though she had plenty both of strength and courage for all purposes of life without the assistance of any extraneous aid. Her hair was jet-black, and very plentiful, and was worn in long curls which were brought round from the back of her head over her shoulders. Her eyes were blue,—dark blue,—and were clear and deep rather than bright. Her nose was well formed, but somewhat prominent, and made you think at the first glance of the tribes of Israel. But yet no observer of the physiognomy of races would believe for half a moment that Lotta Schmidt was a Jewess. Indeed, the type of form which I am endeavouring to describe is in truth as far removed from the Jewish type as it is from the Italian; and it has no connexion whatever with that which we ordinarily conceive to be the German type. But, overriding everything in her personal appearance, in her form, countenance, and gait, was that singular fierceness of independence, as though she were constantly asserting that she would never submit herself to the inconvenience of feminine softness. And yet Lotta Schmidt was a simple girl, with a girl's heart, looking forward to find all that she was to have of human happiness in the love of some man, and expecting and hoping to do her duty as a married woman and the mother of a family. Nor would she have been at all coy in saying as much had the subject of her life's prospects become matter of conversation in any company; no more than one lad would be coy in saying that he hoped to be a doctor, or another in declaring a wish for the army.

When the two girls had walked twice round the hoarding within which stood all those tons of bronze which were intended to represent Prince Eugene, they crossed over the centre of the Burgplatz, passed under the other equestrian statue, and came to the gate leading into the Volksgarten. There, just at the entrance, they were overtaken by a man with a fiddle-case under his arm, who raised his hat to them, and then shook hands with both of them.

"Ladies," he said, "are you coming in to hear a little music? We will do our best."

"Herr Crippel always does well," said Marie Weber. "There is never any doubt when one comes to hear him."

"Marie, why do you flatter him?" said Lotta.

"I do not say half to his face that you said just now behind his back," said Marie.

"And what did she say of me behind my back?" said Herr Crippel.

He smiled as he asked the question, or attempted to smile, but it was easy to see that he was too much in earnest. He blushed up to his eyes, and there was a slight trembling motion in his hands as he stood with one of them pressed upon the other.

As Marie did not answer at the moment, Lotta replied for her.

"I will tell you what I said behind your back. I said that Herr Crippel had the firmest hand upon a bow, and the surest fingers among the strings, in all Vienna,—when his mind was not wool-gathering. Marie, is not that true?"

"I do not remember anything about the wool-gathering," said Marie.

"I hope I shall not be wool-gathering to-night; but I shall doubtless;—I shall doubtless,—for I shall be thinking of your judgement. Shall I get you seats at once? There; you are just before me. You see I am not coward enough to fly from my critics." And he placed them to sit at a little marble table, not far from the front of the low orchestra in the foremost place in which he would have to take his stand.

"Many thanks, Herr Crippel," said Lotta. "I will make sure of a third chair, as a friend is coming."

"Oh, a friend!" said he; and he looked sad, and all his sprightliness was gone.

"Marie's friend," said Lotta, laughing. "Do not you know Carl Stobel?"

Then the musician became bright and happy again. "I would have got two more chairs if you would have let me; one for the fraulein's sake, and one for his own. And I will come down presently, and you shall present me, if you will be so very kind."

Marie Weber smiled and thanked him, and declared that she should be very proud;—and the leader of the band went up into his place.

"I wish he had not placed us here," said Lotta.

"And why not?"

"Because Fritz is coming."

"No!"

"But he is."

"And why did you not tell me?"

"Because I did not wish to be speaking of him. Of course you understand why I did not tell you. I would rather it should seem that he came of his own account,—with Carl. Ha, ha!" Carl Stobel was the diamond-cutter to whom Marie Weber was betrothed. "I should not have told you now,—only that I am disarranged by what Herr Crippel has done."

"Had we not better go,—or at least move our seats? We can make any excuse afterwards."

"No," said Lotta. "I will not seem to run away from him. I have nothing to be ashamed of. If I choose to keep company with Fritz Planken, that should be nothing to Herr Crippel."

"But you might have told him."

"No; I could not tell him. And I am not sure Fritz is coming either. He said he would come with Carl if he had time. Never mind; let us be happy now. If a bad time comes by-and-bye, we must make the best of it."

Then the music began, and, suddenly, as the first note of a fiddle was heard, every voice in the great beer-hall of the Volksgarten became silent. Men sat smoking, with their long beer-glasses before them, and women sat knitting, with their long beer-glasses also before them, but not a word was spoken. The waiters went about with silent feet, but even orders for beer were not given, and money was not received. Herr Crippel did his best, working with his wand as carefully,—and I may say as accurately,—as a leader in a fashionable opera-house in London or Paris. But every now and then, in the course of the piece, he would place his fiddle to his shoulder and join in the performance. There was hardly one there in the hall, man or woman, boy or girl, who did not know, from personal knowledge and judgment, that Herr Crippel was doing his work very well.

"Excellent, was it not?" said Marie.

"Yes; he is a musician. Is it not a pity he should be so bald?" said Lotta.

"He is not so very bald," said Marie.

"I should not mind his being bald so much, if he did not try to cover his old head with the side hairs. If he would cut off those loose straggling locks, and declare himself to be bald at once, he would be ever so much better. He would look to be fifty then. He looks sixty now."

"What matters his age? He is forty-five, just; for I know. And he is a good man."

"What has his goodness to do with it?"

"A great deal. His old mother wants for nothing, and he makes two hundred florins a month. He has two shares in the summer theatre. I know it."

"Bah! what is all that when he will plaster his hair over his old bald head?"

"Lotta, I am ashamed of you." But at this moment the further expression of Marie's anger was stopped by the entrance of the diamond-cutter; and as he was alone, both the girls received him very pleasantly. We must give Lotta her due, and declare that, as things had gone, she would much prefer now that Fritz should stay away, though Fritz Planken was as handsome a young fellow as there was in Vienna, and one who dressed with the best taste, and danced so that no one could surpass him, and could speak French, and was confidential clerk at one of the largest hotels in Vienna, and was a young man acknowledged to be of much general importance,—and had, moreover, in plain language declared his love for Lotta Schmidt. But Lotta would not willingly give unnecessary pain to Herr Crippel, and she was generously glad when Carl Stobel, the diamond-cutter, came by himself. Then there was a second and third piece played, and after that Herr Crippel came down, according to promise, and was presented to Marie's lover.

"Ladies," said he, "I hope I have not gathered wool."

"You have surpassed yourself," said Lotta.

"At wool gathering?" said Herr Crippel.

"At sending us out of this world into another," said Lotta.

"Ah! go into no other world but this," said Herr Crippel, "lest I should not be able to follow you." And then he went away again to his post.

Before another piece had been commenced, Lotta saw Fritz Planken enter the door. He stood for a moment gazing round the hall, with his cane in his hand and his hat on his head, looking for the party which he intended to join. Lotta did not say a word, nor would she turn her eyes towards him. She would not recognise him if it were possible to avoid it. But he soon saw her, and came up to the table at which they were sitting. When Lotta was getting the third chair for Marie's lover, Herr Crippel, in his gallantry, had brought a fourth, and now Fritz occupied the chair which the musician had placed there. Lotta, as she perceived this, was sorry that it should be so. She could not even dare to look up to see what effect this new arrival would have upon the leader of the band.

The new comer was certainly a handsome young man,—such a one as inflicts unutterable agonies on the hearts of the Herr Crippels of the world. His boots shone like mirrors, and fitted his feet like gloves. There was something in the make and set of his trousers which Herr Crippel, looking at them, as he could not help looking at them, was quite unable to understand. Even twenty years ago, Herr Crippel's trousers, as Herr Crippel very well knew, had never looked like that. And Fritz Planken wore a blue frock coat with silk lining to the breast, which seemed to have come from some tailor among the gods. And he had on primrose gloves, and round his neck a bright pink satin handkerchief, joined by a ring, which gave a richness of colouring to the whole thing which nearly killed Herr Crippel, because he could not but acknowledge that the colouring was good. And then the hat! And when the hat was taken off for a moment, then the hair—perfectly black, and silky as a raven's wing, just waving with one curl! And when Fritz put up his hand, and ran his fingers through his locks, their richness and plenty and beauty were conspicious to all beholders. Herr Crippel, as he saw it, involuntarily dashed his hand up to his own pate, and scratched his straggling, lanky hairs from off his head.

"You are coming to Sperl's to-morrow, of course?" said Fritz to Lotta. Now Sperl's is a great establishment for dancing in the Leopoldstadt, which is always open of a Sunday evening, and which Lotta Schmidt was in the habit of attending with much regularity. It was here she had become acquianted with Fritz. And certainly to dance with Fritz was to dance indeed! Lotta, too, was a beautiful dancer. To a Viennese such as Lotta Schmidt, dancing is a thing of serious importance. It was a misfortune to her to have to dance with a bad dancer, as it is to a great whist-player among us to sit down with a bad partner. Oh, what she had suffered more than once when Herr Crippel had induced her to stand up with him!

"Yes; I shall go. Marie, you will go?"

"I do not know," said Marie.

"You will make her go, Carl; will you not?" said Lotta.

"She promised me yesterday, as I understood," said Carl.

"Of course we will all be there," said Fritz, somewhat grandly; "and I will give a supper for four."

Then the music began again, and the eyes of all of them became fixed upon Herr Crippel. It was unfortunate that they should have been placed so fully before him, as it was impossible that he should avoid seeing them. As he stood up with his violin to his shoulder, his eyes were fixed on Fritz Planken and Fritz Planken's boots, and coat, and hat, and hair. And as he drew his bow over the strings he was thinking of his own boots and of his own hair. Fritz was sitting, leaning forward in his chair, so that he could look up into Lotta's face, and he was playing with a little amber-headed cane, and every now and then he whispered a word. Herr Crippel could hardly play a note. In very truth he was wool-gathering. His hand became unsteady, and every instrument was more or less astray.

"Your old friend is making a mess of it tonight," said Fritz to Lotta. "I hope he has not taken a glass too much of schnapps."

"He never does anything of the kind," said Lotta, angrily. "He never did such a thing in his life."

"He is playing awfully bad," said Fritz.

"I never heard him play better in my life than he has played to-night," said Lotta.

"His hand is tired. He is getting old," said Fritz. Then Lotta moved her chair and drew herself back, and was determined that Marie and Carl should see that she was angry with her young lover. In the meantime the piece of music had been finished, and the audience had shown their sense of the performers' inferiority by withdrawing those plaudits which they were so ready to give when they were pleased.

After this some other musician led for a while, and then Herr Crippel had to come forward to play a solo. And on this occasion the violin was not to be his instrument. He was a great favourite among the lovers of music in Vienna, not only because he was good at the fiddle and because with his bow in his hand he could keep a band of musicians together, but also as a player on the zither. It was not often now-a-days that he would take his zither to the music-hall in the Volksgarten; for he would say that he had given up that instrument; that he now played it only in private; that it was not fit for a large hall, as a single voice, the scraping of a foot, would destroy its music. And Herr Crippel was a man who had his fancies and his fantasies, and would not always yield to entreaty. But occasionally he would send his zither down to the public hall; and in the programme for this evening there had been put forth that Herr Crippel's zither would be there and that Herr Crippel would perform. And now the zither was brought forward, and a chair was put for the zitherist, and Herr Crippel stood for a moment behind his chair and bowed. Lotta glanced up at him, and could see that he was he was very pale. She could even see that the perspiration stood upon his brow. She knew that he was trembling, and that he would have given almost his zither itself to be quit of his promised performance for that night. But she knew also that he would make the attempt.

"What! the zither?" said Fritz. "He will break down as sure as he is a living man."

"Let us hope not," said Carl Stobel.

"I love to hear him play the zither better than anything," said Lotta.

"It used to be very good," said Fritz; "but everybody says he has lost his touch. When a man has the slightest feeling of nervousness he is done for the zither."

"H—sh; let him have his chance at any rate," said Marie.

Reader, did you ever hear the zither? When played, as it is sometimes played in Vienna, it combines all the softest notes of the human voice. It sings to you of love, and then wails to you of disappointed love, till it fills you with a melancholy from which there is no escaping,—from which you never wish to escape. It speaks to you as no other instrument ever speaks, and reveals to you with wonderful eloquence the sadness in which it delights. It produces a luxury of anguish, a fulness of the satisfaction of imaginary woe, a realization of the mysterious delights of romance, which no words can ever thoroughly supply. While the notes are living, while the music is still in the air, the ear comes to covet greedily every atom of tone which the instrument will produce, so that the slightest extraneous sound becomes an offence. The notes sink and sink so low and low, with their soft sad wail of delicious woe, that the listener dreads that something will be lost in the struggle of listening. There seems to come some lethargy on his sense of hearing, which he fears will shut out from his brain the last, lowest, sweetest strain, the very pearl of the music, for which he has been watching with all the intensity of prolonged desire. And then the zither is silent, and there remains a fond memory together with a deep regret.

Herr Crippel seated himself on his stool and looked once or twice round about upon the room almost with dismay. Then he struck his zither, uncertainly, weakly, and commenced the prelude of his piece. But Lotta thought that she had never heard so sweet a sound. When he paused after a few strokes there was a noise of applause in the room,—of applause intended to encourage by commemorating past triumphs. The musician looked again away from his music to his audience, and his eyes caught the eyes of the girl he loved; and his gaze fell also upon the face of the handsome, well-dressed, young Adonis who was by her side.

He, Herr Crippel the musician, could never make himself look like that; he could make no slightest approach to that outward triumph. But then, he could play the zither, and Fritz Planken could only play with his cane! He would do what he could! He would play his best! He had once almost resolved to get up and declare that he was too tired that evening to do justice to his instrument. But there was an insolence of success about his rival's hat and trousers which spirited him on to the fight. He struck his zither again, and they who understood him and his zither knew that he was in earnest.

The old men who had listened to him for the last twenty years declared that he had never played as he played on that night. At first he was somewhat bolder, somewhat louder than was his wont; as though he were resolved to go out of his accustomed track; but, after a while, he gave that up; that was simply the effect of nervousness, and was continued only while the timidity remained present with him. But he soon forgot everything but his zither and his desire to do it justice. The attention of all present soon became so close that you might have heard a pin fall. Even Fritz sat perfectly still, with his mouth open, and forgot to play with his cane. Lotta's eyes were quickly full of tears, and before long they were rolling down her cheeks. Herr Crippel, though he did not know that he looked at her, was aware that it was so. Then came upon them all there an ecstasy of delicious sadness. As I have said before, every ear was struggling that no softest sound might escape unheard. And then at last the zither was silent, and no one could have marked the moment when it had ceased to sing.

For a few moments there was perfect silence in the room, and the musician still kept his seat with his face turned upon his instrument. He knew well that he had succeeded, that his triumph had been complete, and every moment that the applause was suspended was an added jewel to his crown. But it soon came, the loud shouts of praise, the ringing bravos, the striking of glasses, his own name repeated from all parts of the hall, the clapping of hands, the sweet sound of women's voices, and the waving of white handkerchiefs. Herr Crippel stood up, bowed thrice, wiped his face with a handkerchief, and then sat down on a stool in the corner of the orchestra.

"I don't know much about his being too old," said Carl Stobel.

"Nor I either," said Lotta.

"That is what I call music," said Marie Weber.

"He can play the zither, certainly," said Fritz; "but as to the violin, it is more doubtful."

"He is excellent with both,—with both," said Lotta, angrily.

Soon after that the party got up to leave the hall, and as they went out they encountered Herr Crippel.

"You have gone beyond yourself to-night," said Marie, "and we wish you joy."

"Oh, no. It was pretty good, was it? With the zither it depends mostly on the atmosphere; whether it is hot, or cold, or wet, or dry, or on I know not what. It is an accident if one plays well. Good-night to you. Good-night, Lotta. Good-night, sir." And he took off his hat, and bowed,—bowed, as it were, expressly to Fritz Planken.

"Herr Crippel," said Lotta, "one word with you." And she dropped behind from Fritz, and returned to the musician. "Herr Crippel, will you meet me at Sperl's to-morrow night?"

"At Sperl's? No. I do not go to Sperl's any longer, Lotta. You told me that Marie's friend was coming to-night, but you did not tell me of your own."

"Never mind what I told you, or did not tell you. Herr Crippel, will you come to Sperl's to-morrow?"

"No; you would not dance with me, and I should not care to see you dance with any one else."

"But I will dance with you."

"And Planken will be there?"

"Yes, Fritz will be there. He is always there; I cannot help that."

"No, Lotta; I will not go to Sperl's. I will tell you a little secret. At forty-five one is too old for Sperl's."

"There are men there every Sunday over fifty,—over sixty, I am sure."

"They are men different in their ways of life from me, my dear. No, I will not go to Sperl's. When will you come and see my mother?"

Lotta promised that she would go and see the Frau Crippel before long, and then tripped off and joined her party.

Stobel and Marie had walked on, while Fritz remained a little behind for Lotta.

"Did you ask him to come to Sperl's to-morrow?" he said.

"To be sure I did."

"Was that nice of you, Lotta?"

"Why not nice? Nice or not, I did it. Why should not I ask him, if I please?"

"Because I thought I was to have the pleasure of entertaining you; that it was a little party of my own."

"Very well, Herr Planken," said Lotta, drawing herself a little away from him; "if a friend of mine is not welcome at your little party, I certainly shall not join it myself."

"But, Lotta, does not every one know what it is that Crippel wishes of you?"

"There is no harm in his wishing. My friends tell me that I am very foolish not to give him what he wishes. But I still have the chance."

"O yes, no doubt you still have the chance."

"Herr Crippel is a very good man. He is the best son in the world, and he makes two hundred florins a month."

"Oh, if that is to count!"

"Of course it is to count. Why should it not count? Would the Princess Theresa have married the other day if the young Prince had had no income to support her?"

"You can do as you please, Lotta."

"Yes, I can do as I please, certainly. I suppose Adela Bruhl will be at Sperl's to-morrow?"

"I should say so, certainly. I hardly ever knew her to miss her Sunday evening."

"Nor I. I, too, am fond of dancing,—very. I delight in dancing. But I am not a slave to Sperl's, and then I do not care to dance with every one."

"Adela Bruhl dances very well," said Fritz.

"That is as one may think. She ought to; for she begins at ten, and goes on till two, always. If there is no one nice for dancing she puts up with some one that is not nice. But all that is nothing to me."

"Nothing, I should say, Lotta."

"Nothing in the world. But this is something; last Sunday you danced three times with Adela."

"Did I? I did not count."

"I counted. It is my business to watch those things, if you are to be ever anything to me, Fritz. I will not pretend that I am indifferent. I am not indifferent. I care very much about it. Fritz, if you dance to-morrow with Adela you will not dance with me again,—either then or ever." And having uttered this threat she ran on and found Marie, who had just reached the door of the house in which they both lived.

Fritz, as he walked home by himself, was in doubt as to the course which it would be his duty as a man to pursue in reference to the lady whom he loved. He had distinctly heard that lady ask an old admirer of hers to go to Sperl's and dance with her; and yet, within ten minutes afterwards, she had peremptorily commanded him not to dance with another girl! Now, Fritz Planken had a very good opinion of himself, as he was well entitled to have, and was quite aware that other pretty girls besides Lotta Schmidt were within his reach. He did not receive two hundred florins a month, as did Herr Crippel, but then he was five-and-twenty instead of five-and-forty; and, in the matter of money, too, he was doing pretty well. He did love Lotta Schmidt. It would not be easy for him to part with her. But she, too, loved him, as he told himself, and she would hardly push matters to extremities. At any rate, he would not submit to a threat. He would dance with Adela Bruhl, at Sperl's. He thought, at least, that when the time should come he would find it well to dance with her.

Sperl's dancing saloon, in the Tabor Strasse, is a great institution at Vienna. It is open always of a Sunday evening, and dancing there commences at ten, and is continued till two or three o'clock in the morning. There are two large rooms, in one of which the dancers dance, and in the other the dancers and visitors who do not dance, eat, and drink, and smoke continually. But the most wonderful part of Sperl's establishment is this, that there is nothing there to offend any one. Girls dance and men smoke, and there is eating and drinking, and everybody is as well behaved as though there was a protecting phalanx of dowagers sitting round the walls of the saloon. There are no dowagers, though there may probably be a policeman somewhere about the place. To a stranger it is very remarkable that there is so little of what we call flirting;—almost none of it. It would seem that to the girls dancing is so much a matter of business, that here at Sperl's they can think of nothing else. To mind their steps, and at the same time their dresses, lest they should be trod upon, to keep full pace with the music, to make all the proper turns at every proper time, and to have the foot fall on the floor at the exact instant; all this is enough, without further excitement. You will see a girl dancing with a man as though the man were a chair, or a stick, or some necessary piece of furniture. She condescends to use his services, but as soon as the dance is over she sends him away. She hardly speaks a word to him, if a word! She has come there to dance, and not to talk; unless, indeed, like Marie Weber and Lotta Schmidt, she has a recognised lover there of her very own.

At about half-past ten Marie and Lotta entered the saloon, and paid their kreutzers and sat themselves down on seats in the further saloon, from which through open archways they could see the dancers. Neither Carl nor Fritz had come as yet, and the girls were quite content to wait. It was to be presumed that they would be there before the men, and they both understood that the real dancing was not commenced early in the evening. It might be all very well for such as Adela Bruhl to dance with any one who came at ten o'clock, but Lotta Schmidt would not care to amuse herself after that fashion. As to Marie, she was to be married after another week, and of course she would dance with no one but Carl Stobel.

"Look at her," said Lotta, pointing with her foot to a fair girl, very pretty, but with hair somewhat untidy, who at this moment was waltzing in the other room. "That lad is a waiter from the Minden hotel. I know him. She would dance with any one."

"I suppose she likes dancing, and there is no harm in the boy," said Marie.

"No, there is no harm, and if she likes it I do not begrudge it her. See what red hands she has."

"She is of that complexion," said Marie.

"Yes, she is of that complexion all over; look at her face. At any rate she might have better shoes on. Did you ever see anybody so untidy?"

"She is very pretty," said Marie.

"Yes, she is pretty. There is no doubt she is pretty. She is not a native here. Her people are from Munich. Do you know, Marie, I think girls are always thought more of in other countries than in their own."

Soon after this Carl and Fritz came in together, and Fritz, as he passed across the end of the first saloon, spoke a word or two to Adela. Lotta saw this, but determined that she would take no offence at so small a matter. Fritz need not have stopped to speak, but his doing so might be all very well. At any rate, if she did quarrel with him she would quarrel on a plain, intelligible ground. Within two minutes Carl and Marie were dancing, and Fritz had asked Lotta to stand up. "I will wait a little," said she, "I never like to begin much before eleven."

"As you please," said Fritz; and he sat down in the chair which Marie had occupied. Then he played with his cane, and as he did so his eyes followed the steps of Adela Bruhl.

"She dances very well," said Lotta.

"H—m—m, yes." Fritz did not choose to bestow any strong praise on Adela's dancing.

"Yes, Fritz, she does dance well,—very well, indeed. And she is never tired. If you ask me whether I like her style, I cannot quite say that I do. It is not what we do here,—not exactly."

"She has lived in Vienna since she was a child."

"It is in the blood then, I suppose. Look at her fair hair, all blowing about. She is not like one of us."

"Oh no, she is not."

"That she is very pretty, I quite admit," said Lotta. "Those soft grey eyes are delicious. Is it not a pity she has no eyebrows?"

"But she has eyebrows."

"Ah! you have been closer than I, and you have seen them. I have never danced with her, and I cannot see them. Of course they are there,—more or less."

After a while the dancing ceased, and Adela Bruhl came up into the supper-room, passing the seats on which Fritz and Lotta were sitting.

"Are you not going to dance, Fritz?" she said, with a smile, as she passed them.

"Go, go," said Lotta; "why do you not go? She has invited you."

"No; she has not invited me. She spoke to us both."

"She did not speak to me, for my name is not Fritz. I do not see how you can help going, when she asked you so prettily."

"I shall be in plenty of time presently. Will you dance now, Lotta? They are going to begin a waltz, and we will have a quadrille afterwards."

"No, Herr Planken, I will not dance just now."

"I do not want to be one of two. I will not be one of two. Adela Bruhl is very pretty, and I advise you to go to her. I was told only yesterday her father can give her fifteen hundred florins of fortune! For me,—I have no father."

"But you may have a husband to-morrow."

"Yes, that is true, and a good one. Oh, such a good one!"

"What do you mean by that?"

"You go and dance with Adela Bruhl, and you shall see what I mean."

Fritz had some idea in his own mind, more or less clearly developed, that his fate, as regarded Lotta Schmidt, now lay in his own hands. He undoubtedly desired to have Lotta for his own. He would have married her there and then,—at that moment, had it been possible. He had quite made up his mind that he preferred her much to Adela Bruhl, though Adela Bruhl had fifteen hundred florins. But he did not like to endure tyranny, even from Lotta, and he did not know how to escape the tyranny otherwise than by dancing with Adela. He paused a moment, swinging his cane, endeavouring to think how he might best assert his manhood and yet not offend the girl he loved. But he found that to assert his manhood was now his first duty.

"Well, Lotta," he said, "since you are so cross with me, I will ask Adela to dance." And in two minutes he was spinning round the room with Adela Bruhl in his arms.

"Certainly she dances very well," said Lotta, smiling, to Marie, who had now come back to her seat.

"Very well," said Marie, who was out of breath.

"And so does he."

"Beautifully," said Marie.

"Is it not a pity that I should have lost such a partner for ever?"

"Lotta!"

"It is true. Look here, Marie, there is my hand upon it. I will never dance with him again—never—never—never. Why was he so hard upon Herr Crippel last night?"

"Was he hard upon Herr Crippel?"

"He said that Herr Crippel was too old to play the zither; too old! Some people are too young to understand. I shall go home, I shall not stay to sup with you to-night."

"Lotta, you must stay for supper."

"I will not sup at his table. I have quarrelled with him. It is all over. Fritz Planken is as free as the air for me."

"Lotta, do not say anything in a hurry. At any rate do not do anything in a hurry."

"I do not mean to do anything at all. It is simply this,—I do not care very much for Fritz, after all. I don't think I ever did. It is all very well to wear your clothes nicely, but if that is all, what does it come to? If he could play the zither, now!"

"There are other things except playing the zither. They say he is a good book-keeper."

"I don't like book-keeping. He has to be at his hotel from eight in the morning till eleven at night."

"You know best."

"I am not so sure of that. I wish I did know best. But I never saw such a girl as you are. How you change! It was only yesterday you scolded me because I did not wish to be the wife of your dear friend Crippel."

"Herr Crippel is a very good man."

"You go away with your good man! You have got a good man of your own. He is standing there waiting for you, like a gander on one leg. He wants you to dance; go away." Then Marie did go away, and Lotta was left alone by herself. She certainly had behaved badly to Fritz, and she was aware of it. She excused herself to herself by remembering that she had never yet given Fritz a promise. She was her own mistress, and had, as yet, a right to do what she pleased with herself. He had asked her for her love, and she had not told him that he should not have it. That was all. Herr Crippel had asked her a dozen times, and she had at last told him definitely, positively, that there was no hope for him. Herr Crippel, of course, would not ask her again;—so she told herself. But if there was no such person as Herr Crippel in all the world, she would have nothing more to do with Fritz Planken,—nothing more to do with him as a lover. He had given her fair ground for a quarrel, and she would take advantage of it. Then as she sat still while they were dancing, she closed her eyes and thought of the zither and of the zitherist. She remained alone for a long time. The musicians in Vienna will play a waltz for twenty minutes, and the same dancers will continue to dance almost without a pause; and then, almost immediately afterwards, there was a quadrille. Fritz, who was resolved to put down tyranny, stood up with Adela for the quadrille also. "I am so glad," said Lotta to herself. "I will wait till this is over, and then I will say good-night to Marie, and will go home." Three or four men had asked her to dance, but she had refused. She would not dance to-night at all. She was inclined, she thought, to be a little serious, and would go home. At last Fritz returned to her, and bade her come to supper. He was resolved to see how far his mode of casting off tyranny might be successful, so he approached her with a smile, and offered to take her to his table as though nothing had happened.

"My friend," she said, "your table is laid for four, and the places will all be filled."

"The table is laid for five," said Fritz.

"It is one too many. I shall sup with my friend, Herr Crippel."

"Herr Crippel is not here."

"Is he not? Ah me! then I shall be alone, and I must go to bed supperless. Thank you, no, Herr Planken."

"And what will Marie say?"

"I hope she will enjoy the nice dainties you will give her. Marie is all right. Marie's fortune is made. Woe is me! my fortune is to seek. There is one thing certain, it is not to be found here in this room."

Then Fritz turned on his heel and went away; and as he went Lotta saw the figure of a man, as he made his way slowly and hesitatingly into the saloon from the outer passage. He was dressed in a close frock-coat, and had on a hat of which she knew the shape as well as she did the make of her own gloves. "If he has not come after all!" she said to herself. Then she turned herself a little round, and drew her chair somewhat into an archway, so that Herr Crippel should not see her readily.

The other four had settled themselves at their table, Marie having said a word of reproach to Lotta as she passed. Now, on a sudden, she got up from her seat and crossed to her friend.

"Herr Crippel is here," she said.

"Of course he is here," said Lotta.

"But you did not expect him?"

"Ask Fritz if I did not say I would sup with Herr Crippel. You ask him. But I shall not, all the same. Do not say a word. I shall steal away when nobody is looking."

The musician came wandering up the room, and had looked into every corner before he had even found the supper-table at which the four were sitting. And then he did not see Lotta. He took off his hat as he addressed Marie, and asked some questions as to the absent one.

"She is waiting for you somewhere, Herr Crippel," said Fritz, as he filled Adela's glass with wine.

"For me?" said Herr Crippel as he looked round. "No, she does not expect me." And in the meantime Lotta had left her seat, and was hurrying away to the door.

"There! there!" said Marie; "you will be too late if you do not run."

Then Herr Crippel did run, and caught Lotta as she was taking her hat from the old woman, who had the girls' hats and shawls in charge near the door.

"What! Herr Crippel, you at Sperl's? When you told me expressly, in so many words, that you would not come! That is not behaving well to me, certainly."

"What, my coming? Is that behaving bad?"

"No; but why did you say you would not come when I asked you? You have come to meet some one. Who is it?"

"You, Lotta; you."

"And yet you refused me when I asked you! Well, and now you are here, what are you going to do? You will not dance."

"I will dance with you, if you will put up with me."

"No, I will not dance. I am too old. I have given it up. I shall come to Sperl's no more after this. Dancing is a folly."

"Lotta, you are laughing at me now."

"Very well; if you like, you may have it so." By this time he had brought her back into the room, and was walking up and down the length of the saloon with her. "But it is no use our walking about here," she said. "I was just going home, and now, if you please, I will go."

"Not yet, Lotta."

"Yes; now, if you please."

"But why are you not supping with them?"

"Because it did not suit me. You see there are four. Five is a foolish number for a supper party."

"Will you sup with me, Lotta?" She did not answer him at once. "Lotta," he said, "if you sup with me now you must sup with me always. How shall it be?"

"Always? No. I am very hungry now, but I do not want supper always. I cannot sup with you always, Herr Crippel."

"But you will to-night?"

"Yes, to-night."

"Then it shall be always."

And the musician marched up to a table, and threw his hat down, and ordered such a supper that Lotta Schmidt was frightened. And when presently Carl Stobel and Marie Weber came up to their table,—for Fritz Planken did not come near them again that evening,—Herr Crippel bowed courteously to the diamond-cutter, and asked him when he was to be married. "Marie says it shall be next Sunday," said Carl.

"And I will be married the Sunday afterwards," said Herr Crippel. "Yes; and there is my wife."

And he pointed across the table with both his hands to Lotta Schmidt.

"Herr Crippel, how can you say that?" said Lotta.

"Is it not true, my dear?"

"In fourteen days! No, certainly not. It is out of the question."

But, nevertheless, what Herr Crippel said came true, and on the next Sunday but one he took Lotta Schmidt home to his house as his wife.

"It was all because of the zither," Lotta said to her old mother-in-law. "If he had not played the zither that night I should not have been here now."

The Adventures of Fred Pickering

Originally appeared in *The Argosy*, September 1866, under the title 'The Misfortunes of Fred Pickering'. Reprinted in *Lotta Schmidt and Other Stories* (1867). Fred's vision of himself as Milton's Samson at the mercy of the Philistines resembles Mr Crawley's similar fantasy in *The Last Chronicle of Barset* (1867). R.H. Super in *The Chronicler of Barsetshire* (1988) suggests Trollope may have encountered cases like Fred's in the course of his work at the Royal Literary Fund.

THERE WAS something almost grand in the rash courage with which Fred Pickering married his young wife, and something quite grand in her devotion in marrying him. She had not a penny in the world, and he, when he married her, had two hundred and fifty pounds, and no profession. She was the daughter of parents whom she had never seen, and had been brought up by the kindness of an aunt, who died when she was eighteen. Distant friends then told her that it was her duty to become a governess; but Fred Pickering intervened, and Mary Crofts became Mary Pickering when she was nineteen years old. Fred himself, our hero, was six years older, and should have known better and have conducted his affairs with more wisdom. His father had given him a good education, and had articled him to an attorney at Manchester. While at Manchester he had written three or four papers in different newspapers, and had succeeded in obtaining admission for a poem in the "Free Trader," a Manchester monthly magazine, which was expected to do great things as the literary production of Lancashire. These successes, joined, no doubt, to the natural bent of his disposition, turned him against the law; and when he was a little more than twenty-five, having then been four years in the office of the Manchester attorney, he told his father that he did not like the profession chosen for him, and that he must give it up. At that time he was engaged to marry Mary Crofts; but of this fact he did not tell his father. Mr. Pickering, who was a stern man,—one not given at any time to softnesses with his children,—when so informed by his son, simply asked him what were his plans. Fred replied that he looked forward to a literary career,—that he hoped to make literature his profession. His father assured him that he was a silly fool. Fred replied that on that subject he had an opinion of his own by which he intended to be guided. Old Pickering then declared that in such circumstances he should withdraw all pecuniary assistance; and young Pickering upon this wrote an ungracious epistle, in which he expressed himself quite ready to take upon himself the burden of his own maintenance. There was one, and only one, further letter from his father, in which he told his son that the allowance made to him would be henceforth stopped. Then the correspondence between Fred and the ex-governor, as Mary used to call him, was brought to a close.

Most unfortunately there died at this time an old maiden aunt, who left four hundred pounds a-piece to twenty nephews and nieces, of whom Fred Pickering was one. The possession of this sum of money strengthened him in his rebellion against his father. Had he had nothing on which to begin, he might probably even yet have gone to the old house at home, and have had something of a fatted calf killed for him, in spite of the ungraciousness of his letter. As it was he was reliant on the resources which Fortune had sent to him, thinking that they would suffice till he had made his way to a beginning of earning money. He thought it all over for full half-an-hour, and then came to a decision. He would go to Mary,—his Mary,—to Mary who was about to enter the family of a very vulgar tradesman as governess to six young children with a salary of twenty-five pounds per annum, and ask her to join him in throwing all prudence to the wind. He did go to Mary; and Mary at last consented to be as imprudent as himself, and she consented without any of that confidence which animated him. She consented simply because he asked her to do so, knowing that she was doing a thing so rash that no father or mother would have permitted it.

"Fred," she had said, half laughing as she spoke, "I am afraid we shall starve if we do."

"Starving is bad," said Fred; "I quite admit that; but there are worse things than starving. For you to be a governess at Mrs. Boullem's is worse. For me to write lawyer's letters all full of lies is worse. Of course we may come to grief. I dare say we shall come to grief. Perhaps we shall suffer awfully,—be very hungry and very cold. I am quite willing to make the worst of it. Suppose that we die in the street! Even that,—the chance of that with the chance of success on the other side, is better than Mrs. Boullem's. It always seems to me that people are too much afraid of being starved."

"Something to eat and drink is comfortable," said Mary. "I don't say that it is essential."

"If you will dare the consequences with me, I will gladly dare them with you," said Fred, with a whole rhapsody of love in his eyes. Mary had not been proof against this. She had returned the rhapsody of his eyes with a glance of her own, and then, within six weeks of that time, they were married. There were some few things to be bought, some little bills to be paid, and then there was the fortnight of honeymooning among the Lakes in June. "You shall have that, though there were not another shot in the locker," Fred had said, when his bride that was to be had urged upon him the prudence of settling down into a small lodging the very day after their marriage. The fortnight of honeymooning among the Lakes was thoroughly enjoyed, almost without one fearful look into the future. Indeed Fred, as he would sit in the late evening on the side of a mountain, looking down upon the lakes, and watching the fleeting brightness of the clouds, with his arm round his loving wife's waist and her head upon his shoulder, would declare that he was glad that he had nothing on which to depend except his own intellect and his own industry. "To make the score off his own bat; that should be a man's ambition, and it is that which nature must have intended for a man. She could never have meant that we should be bolstered up, one by another, from generation to generation." "You shall make the score off your own bat," Mary had said to him. Though her own heart might give way a little as she thought, when alone, of the danger of the future, she was always brave before him. So she enjoyed the fortnight of her honeymooning, and when that was over set herself to her task with infinite courage. They went up to London in a third-class carriage, and, on their arrival there went at once to lodgings which had been taken for them by a friend in Museum Street. Museum Street is not cheering by any special merits of its own; but lodgings there were found to be cheap, and it was near to the great library by means of which, and the treasures there to be found, young Pickering meant to make himself a famous man.

He had had his literary successes at Manchester, as has been already stated, but they had not been of a remunerative nature. He had never yet been paid for what he had written. He reaped, however, this reward, that the sub-editor of a Manchester newspaper gave him a letter to a gentleman connected with a London periodical, which might probably be of great service to him. It is at any rate a comfort to a man to know that he can do something towards the commencement of the work that he has in hand,—that there is a step forward which he can take. When Fred and Mary sat down to their tea and broiled ham on the first night, the letter of introduction was a great comfort to them, and much was said about it. The letter was addressed to Roderick Billings, Esq., office of the Lady Bird, 99 Catherine Street, Strand. By ten o'clock on the following morning Fred Pickering was at the office of the Lady Bird, and there learned that Mr. Billings never came to the office, or almost never. He was on the staff of the paper, and the letter should be sent to him. So Fred Pickering returned to his wife; and as he was resolved that no time should be lost, he began a critical reading of Paradise Lost, with a note-book and pencil beside him, on that very day.

They were four months in London, during which they never saw Mr. Billings or any one else connected with the publishing world, and these four months were very trying to Mrs. Pickering. The study of Milton did not go on with unremitting ardour. Fred was not exactly idle, but he changed from one pursuit to another, and did nothing worthy of note except a little account of his honeymooning tour in verse. In this poem the early loves of a young married couple were handled with much delicacy and some pathos of expression, so that Mary thought that her husband would assuredly drive Tennyson out of the field. But no real good had come from the poem by the end of the four months, and Fred Pickering had sometimes been very cross. Then he had insisted more than once or twice, more than four times or five times, on going to the theatre; and now at last his wife had felt compelled to say that she would not go there with him again. They had not means, she said, for such pleasures. He did not go without her, but sometimes of an evening he was very cross. The poem had been sent to Mr. Billings, with a letter, and had not as yet been sent back. Three or four letters had been written to Mr. Billings, and one or two very short answers had been received. Mr. Billings had been out of town. "Of course all the world is out of town in September," said Fred; "what fools we were to think of beginning just at this time of the year!" Nevertheless he had urged plenty of reasons why the marriage should not be postponed till after June. On the first of November, however, they found that they had still a hundred and eighty pounds left. They looked their affairs in the face cheerfully, and Fred, taking upon his own shoulders all the blame of their discomfiture up to the present moment, swore that he would never be cross with his darling Molly again. After that he went out with a letter of introduction from Mr. Billings to the sub-editor of a penny newspaper. He had never seen

Mr. Billings; but Mr. Billings thus passed him on to another literary personage. Mr. Billings in his final very short note communicated to Fred his opinion that he would find "work on the penny daily press easier got."

For months Fred Pickering hung about the office of the Morning Comet. November went, and December, and January, and he was still hanging about the office of the Morning Comet. He did make his way to some acquaintance with certain persons on the staff of the Comet, who earned their bread, if not absolutely by literature, at least by some work cognate to literature. And when he was asked to sup with one Tom Wood on a night in January, he thought that he had really got his foot upon the threshold. When he returned home that night, or I should more properly say on the following morning, his wife hoped that many more such preliminary suppers might not be necessary for his success.

At last he did get employment at the office of the Morning Comet. He attended there six nights a-week, from ten at night till three in the morning, and for this he received twenty shillings a-week. His work was almost altogether mechanical, and after three nights disgusted him greatly. But he stuck to it, telling himself that as the day was still left to him for work he might put up with drudgery during the night. That idea, however, of working day and night soon found itself to be a false one. Twelve o'clock usually found him still in bed. After his late breakfast he walked out with his wife, and then;—well, then he would either write a few verses or read a volume of an old novel.

"I must learn shorthand-writing," he said to his wife, one morning when he came home.

"Well, dear, I have no doubt you would learn it very quickly."

"I don't know that; I should have begun younger. It's a thousand pities that we are not taught anything useful when we are at school. Of what use is Latin and Greek to me?"

"I heard you say once that it would be of great use to you some day."

"Ah, that was when I was dreaming of what will never come to pass; when I was thinking of literature as a high vocation." It had already come to him to make such acknowledgments as this. "I must think about mere bread now. If I could report I might, at any rate, gain a living. And there have been reporters who have risen high in the profession. Dickens was a reporter. I must learn, though I suppose it will cost me twenty pounds."

He paid his twenty pounds and did learn shorthand-writing. And while he was so doing he found he might have learned just as well by teaching himself out of a book. During the period of his tuition in this art he quarrelled with his employers at the Morning Comet, who, as he declared, treated him with an indignity which he could not bear. "They want me to fetch and carry, and be a menial," he said to his wife. He thereupon threw up his employment at the Comet office. "But now you will get an engagement as a reporter," his wife said. He hoped that he might get an engagement as a reporter; but, as he himself acknowledged, the world was all to begin again. He was at last employed, and made his first appearance at a meeting of discontented tidewaiters, who were anxious to petition Parliament for some improvement in their position. He worked very hard in his efforts to take down the words of the eloquent leading tidewaiter; whereas he could see that two other reporters near him did not work at all. And yet he failed. He struggled at this work for a month, and failed at last. "My hand is not made for it," he said to his wife, almost in an agony of despair. "It seems to me as though nothing would come within my reach." "My dear," she said, "a man who can write the Braes of Birken"—the Braes of Birken was the name of his poem on the joys of honeymooning—"must not be ashamed of himself because he cannot acquire a small mechanical skill." "I am ashamed of myself all the same," said Fred.

Early in April they looked their affairs in the face again, and found that they had still in hand something just over a hundred pounds. They had been in London nine months, and when they had first come up they had expressed to each other their joint conviction that they could live very comfortably on forty shillings a-week. They had spent nearly double that over and beyond what he had earned, and after all they had not lived comfortably. They had a hundred pounds left on which they might exist for a year, putting aside all idea of comfort; and then—and then would come that starving of which Fred had once spoken so gallantly, unless some employment could in the meantime be found for him. And, by the end of the year, the starving would have to be done by three,—a development of events on which he had not seemed to calculate when he told his dearest Mary that after all there were worse things in the world than starving.

But before the end of the month there came upon them a gleam of comfort, which might be cherished and fostered till it should become a whole midday sun of nourishing heat. His friend of the Manchester Free Trader had become the editor of the Salford Reformer, a new weekly paper which had been established with the view of satisfying certain literary and political wants which the public of Salford had long experienced, and among these wants was an adequate knowledge of what was going on in London. Fred Pickering was asked whether he would write the London letter, once a-week, at twenty shillings a-week. Write it! Ay, that he would. There was a whole heaven of joy in the idea. This was literary work. This was the sort of thing that he could do with absolute delight. To guide the public by his own wit and discernment, as it were from behind a mask,—to be the motive power and yet unseen,—this had ever been his ambition. For three days he was in an ecstasy, and Mary was ecstatic with him. For the first time it was a joy to him that the baby was coming. A pound a-week earned would of itself prolong their means of support for two years, and a pound a-week so earned would surely bring other pounds. "I knew it was to be done," he said, in triumph, to his wife, "if one only had the courage to make the attempt." The morning of the fourth day somewhat damped his joy, for there came a long letter of instruction from the Salford editor, in which there were hints of certain difficulties. He was told in this letter that it would be well that he should belong to a London Club. Such work as was now expected from him could hardly be done under favourable circumstances unless he did belong to a club. "But as everybody now-a-days does belong to a club, you will soon get over that difficulty." So said the editor. And then the editor in his instructions greatly curtailed that liberty of the pen which Fred specially wished to enjoy. He had anticipated that in his London letter he might give free reins to his own political convictions, which were of a very liberal nature, and therefore suitable to the Salford Reformer. And he had a theological bias of his own, by the putting forward of which, in strong language, among the youth of Salford, he had intended to do much towards the clearing away of prejudice and the emancipation of truth. But the editor told him that he should hardly touch politics at all in his London letter, and never lay a finger on religion. He was to tell the people of Salford what was coming out at the different theatres, how the Prince and Princess looked on horseback, whether the Thames Embankment made proper progress, and he was to keep his ears especially open for matters of social interest, private or general. His style was to be easy and colloquial, and above all things he was to avoid being heavy, didactic, and profound. Then there was sent to him, as a model, a column and a half cut out from a certain well-known newspaper, in which the names of people were mentioned very freely. "If you can do that sort of thing," said the editor, "we shall get on together like a house on fire."

"It is a farrago of ill-natured gossip," he said, as he chucked the fragment over to his wife.

"But you are so clever, Fred," said his wife. "You can do it without the ill-nature."

"I will do my best," he said; "but as for telling them about this woman and that, I cannot do it. In the first place, where am I to learn it all?" Nevertheless, the London letter to the Salford Reformer was not abandoned. Four or five such letters were written, and four or five sovereigns were paid into his little exchequer in return for so much work. Alas! after the four or five there came a kindly-worded message from the editor to say that the articles did not suit. Nothing could be better than Pickering's language, and his ideas were manly and for the most part good. But the Salford Reformer did not want that sort of thing. The Salford Reformer felt that Fred Pickering was too good for the work required. Fred for twenty-four hours was broken-hearted. After that he was able to resolve that he would take the thing up in the right spirit. He wrote to the editor, saying that he thought that the editor was right. The London letter required was not exactly within the compass of his ability. Then he enclosed a copy of the Braes of Birken, and expressed an opinion that perhaps that might suit a column in the Salford Reformer,—one of those columns which were furthest removed from the corner devoted to the London letter. The editor replied that he would publish the Braes of Birken if Pickering wished; but that they never paid for poetry. Anything being better than silence, Pickering permitted the editor to publish the Braes of Birken in the gratuitous manner suggested.

At the end of June, when they had just been twelve months in London, Fred was altogether idle as far as any employment was concerned. There was no going to the theatre now; and it had come to that with him, in fear of his approaching privations, that he would discuss within his own heart the expediency of taking this or that walk with reference to the effect it would have upon his shoes. In those days he strove to work hard, going on with his Milton and his note-book, and sitting for two or three hours a-day over heavy volumes in the reading-room at the Museum. When he first resolved upon doing this there had come a difficulty as to the entrance. It was necessary that he should have permission to use the library, and for a while he had not known how to obtain it. Then he had written a letter to a certain gentleman well known in the literary world, an absolute stranger to him, but of whom he had heard a word or two among his newspaper acquaintances, and had asked this gentleman to give him, or to get for him, the permission needed. The gentleman having made certain inquiry, having sent for Pickering and seen him, had done as he was asked, and Fred was free of the library.

"What sort of a man is Mr. Wickham Webb?" Mary asked him, when he returned from the club at which, by Mr. Webb's appointment, the meeting had taken place.

"According to my ideas he is the only gentleman whom I have met since I have been in London," said Fred, who in these days was very bitter.

"Was he civil to you?"

"Very civil. He asked me what I was doing up in London, and I told him. He said that literature is the hardest profession in the world. I told him that I thought it was, but at the same time the most noble."

"What did he say to that?"

"He said that the nobler the task it was always the more difficult; and that, as a rule, it was not well that men should attempt work too difficult for their hands because of its nobility."

"What did he mean by that, Fred?"

"I knew what he meant very well. He meant to tell me that I had better go and measure ribbons behind a counter; and I don't know but what he was right."

"But yet you liked him?"

"Why should I have disliked him for giving me good advice? I liked him because his manner was kind, and because he strove hard to say an unpleasant thing in the pleasantest words that he could use. Besides, it did me good to speak to a gentleman once again."

Throughout July not a shilling was earned, nor was there any prospect of the earning of a shilling. People were then still in town, but in another fortnight London would have emptied itself of the rich and prosperous. So much Pickering had learned, little as he was qualified to write the London letter for the Salford Reformer. In the last autumn he had complained to his wife that circumstances had compelled him to begin at the wrong period of the year,—in the dull months when there was nobody in London who could help him. Now the dull months were coming round again, and he was as far as ever from any help. What was he to do? "You said that Mr. Webb was very civil," suggested his wife: "could you not write to him and ask him to help us?"

"He is a rich man, and that would be begging," said Fred.

"I would not ask him for money," said Mary; "but perhaps he can tell you how you can get employment."

The letter to Mr. Webb was written with many throes and the destruction of much paper. Fred found it very difficult to choose words which should describe with sufficient force the extreme urgency of his position, but which should have no appearance of absolute begging.

"I hope you will understand," he said, in his last paragraph, "that what I want is simply work for which I may be paid, and that I do not care how hard I work, or how little I am paid, so that I and my wife may live. If I have taken an undue liberty in writing to you, I can only beg you to pardon my ignorance."

This letter led to another interview between our hero and Mr. Wickham Webb. Mr. Webb sent his compliments and asked Mr. Pickering to come and breakfast with him. This kindness, though it produced some immediate pleasure, created fresh troubles. Mr. Wickham Webb lived in a grand house near Hyde Park, and poor Fred was badly off for good clothes.

"Your coat does not look at all amiss," his wife said to him, comforting him; "and as for a hat, why don't you buy a new one?"

"I shan't breakfast in my hat," said Fred; "but look here;" and Fred exhibited his shoes.

"Get a new pair," said Mary.

"No," said he; "I've sworn to have nothing new till I've earned the money. Mr. Webb won't expect to see me very bright, I dare say. When a man writes to beg for employment, it must naturally be supposed that he will be rather seedy about his clothes." His wife did the best she could for him, and he went out to his breakfast.

Mrs. Webb was not there. Mr. Webb explained that she had already left town. There was no third person at the table, and before his first lamb-chop was eaten, Fred had told the pith of his story. He had a little money left, just enough to pay the doctor who must attend upon his wife, and carry him through the winter; and then he would be absolutely bare. Upon this Mr. Webb asked as to his relatives. "My father has chosen to quarrel with me," said Fred. "I did not wish to be an attorney, and therefore he has cast me out." Mr. Webb suggested that a reconciliation might be possible; but when Fred said at once that it was impossible, he did not recur to the subject.

When the host had finished his own breakfast, he got up from his chair, and standing on the rug spoke such words of wisdom as were in him. It should be explained that Pickering, in his letter to Mr. Webb, had enclosed a copy of the Braes of Birken, another little poem in verse, and two of the London letters which he had written for the Salford

Reformer. "Upon my word, Mr. Pickering, I do not know how to help you. I do not, indeed."

"I am sorry for that, sir."

"I have read what you sent me, and am quite ready to acknowledge that there is enough, both in the prose and verse, to justify you in supposing it to be possible that you might hereafter live by literature as a profession; but all who make literature a profession should begin with independent means."

"That seems to be hard on the profession as well as on the beginner."

"It is not the less true; and is, indeed, true of most other professions as well. If you had stuck to the law your father would have provided you with the means of living till your profession had become profitable."

"Is it not true that many hundreds in London live on literature?" said our hero.

"Many hundreds do so, no doubt. They are of two sorts, and you can tell yourself whether you belong to either. There are they who have learned to work in accordance with the directions of others. The great bulk of what comes out to us almost hourly in the shape of newspapers is done by them. Some are very highly paid, many are paid liberally, and a great many are paid scantily. There is that side of the profession, and you say that you have tried it and do not like it. Then there are those who do their work independently; who write either books or articles which find acceptance in magazines."

"It is that which I would try if the opportunity were given me."

"But you have to make your own opportunity," said Mr. Wickham Webb. "It is the necessity of the position that it should be so. What can I do for you?"

"You know the editors of magazines?"

"Granted that I do, can I ask a man to buy what he does not want because he is my friend?"

"You could get your friend to read what I write."

It ended in Mr. Webb strongly advising Fred Pickering to go back to his father, and in his writing two letters of introduction for him, one to the editor of the International, a weekly gazette of mixed literature, and the other to Messrs. Brook and Boothby, publishers in St. James's Street. Mr. Webb, though he gave the letters open to Fred, read them to him with the view of explaining to him how little and how much they meant. "I do not know that they can do you the slightest service," said he; "but I give them to you because you ask me. I strongly advise you to go back to your father; but if you are still in town next spring, come and see me again." Then the interview was over, and Fred returned to his wife, glad to have the letters; but still with a sense of bitterness against Mr. Webb. When one word of encouragement would have made him so happy, might not Mr. Webb have spoken it? Mr. Webb had thought that he had better not speak any such word. And Fred, when he read the letters of introduction over to his wife, found them to be very cold.

"I don't think I'll take them," he said.

But he did take them, of course, on the very next day, and saw Mr. Boothby, the publisher, after waiting for half-an-hour in the shop. He swore to himself that the time was an hour and a half, and became sternly angry at being so treated. It did not occur to him that Mr. Boothby was obliged to attend to his own business, and that he could not put his other visitors under the counter, or into the cupboards, in order to make way for Mr. Pickering. The consequence was that poor Fred was seen at his worst, and that the Boothbyan heart was not much softened towards him. "There are so many men of this kind who want work," said Mr. Boothby, "and so very little work to give them!"

"It seems to me," said Pickering, "that the demand for the work is almost unlimited." As he spoke, he looked at a hole in his boot, and tried to speak in a tone that should show that he was above his boots.

"It may be so," said Boothby; "but if so, the demands do not run in my way. I will, however, keep Mr. Webb's note by me, and if I find I can do anything for you, I will. Good morning."

Then Mr. Boothby got up from his chair, and Fred Pickering understood that he was told to go away. He was furious in his abuse of Boothby as he described the interview to his wife that evening.

The editor of the International he could not get to see; but he got a note from him. The editor sent his compliments, and would be glad to read the article to which Mr. W. W—had alluded. As Mr. W. W—had alluded to no article, Fred saw that the editor was not inclined to take much trouble on his behalf. Nevertheless, an article should be sent. An article was written to which Fred gave six weeks of hard work, and which contained an elaborate criticism on the Samson Agonistes. Fred's object was to prove that Milton had felt himself to be a superior Samson—blind, indeed, in the flesh, as Samson was blind, but not blind in the spirit, as was Samson when he crushed the Philistines. The poet had crushed his Philistines with all his intellectual eyes about him. Then there was a good deal said about the Philistines of those days as compared with the other Philistines, in all of which Fred thought that he took much higher ground than certain other writers in magazines on the same subject. The editor sent back his compliments, and said that the International never admitted reviews of old books.

"Insensate idiot!" said Fred, tearing the note asunder, and then tearing his own hair, on both sides of his head. "And these are the men who make the world of letters! Idiot!—thick-headed idiot!"

"I suppose he has not read it," said Mary.

"Then why hasn't he read it? Why doesn't he do the work for which he is paid? If he has not read it, he is a thief as well as an idiot."

Poor Fred had not thought much of his chance from the International when he first got the editor's note; but as he had worked at his Samson he had become very fond of it, and golden dreams had fallen on him, and he had dared to whisper to himself words of wondrous praise which might be forthcoming, and to tell himself of inquiries after the unknown author of the great article about the Philistines. As he had thought of this, and as the dreams and the whispers had come to him, he had rewritten his essay from the beginning, making it grander, bigger, more eloquent than before. He became very eloquent about the Philistines, and mixed with his eloquence some sarcasm which could not, he thought, be without effect even in dull-brained, heavy-livered London. Yes; he had dared to hope. And then his essay,—such an essay as this,—was sent back to him with a notice that the International did not insert reviews of old books. Hideous, brainless, meaningless idiot! Fred in his fury tore his article into a hundred fragments; and poor Mary was employed, during the whole of the next week, in making another copy of it from the original blotted sheets, which had luckily been preserved.

"Pearls before swine!" Fred said to himself, as he slowly made his way up to the library of the Museum on the last day of that week.

That was in the end of October. He had not then earned a single shilling for many months, and the nearer prospect of that starvation of which he had once spoken so cheerily was becoming awfully frightful to him. He had said that there were worse fates than to starve. Now, as he looked at his wife, and thought of the baby that was to be added to them, and counted the warning heap of sovereigns, he began to doubt whether there was in truth anything worse than to starve. And now, too, idleness made his life more wretched to him than it had ever been. He could not bring himself to work when it seemed to him that his work was to have no result; literally none.

"Had you not better write to your father?" said Mary.

He made no reply, but went out and walked up and down Museum Street.

He had been much disgusted by the treatment he had received from Mr. Boothby, the publisher; but in November he brought himself to write to Mr. Boothby, and ask him whether some employment could not be found.

"You will perhaps remember Mr. Wickham Webb's letter," wrote Fred, "and the interview which I had with you last July."

His wife had wished him to speak more civilly, and to refer to the pleasure of the interview. But Fred had declined to condescend so far. There were still left to them some thirty pounds.

A fortnight afterwards, when December had come, he got a reply from Mr. Boothby, in which he was asked to call at a certain hour at the shop in St. James's Street. This he did, and saw the great man again. The great man asked him whether he could make an index to an historical work. Fred of course replied that he could do that,—that or anything else. He could make the index; or, if need was, write the historical work itself. That, no doubt, was his feeling. Ten pounds would be paid for the index if it was approved. Fred was made to understand that payment was to depend altogether on approval of the work. Fred took away the sheets confided to him without any doubt as to the ultimate approval. It would be odd indeed if he could not make an index.

"That young man will never do any good," said Mr. Boothby,

to his foreman, as Fred took his departure. "He thinks he can do everything, and I doubt very much whether he can do anything as it should be done."

Fred worked very hard at the index, and the baby was born to him as he was doing it. A fortnight, however, finished the index, and if he could earn money at the rate of ten pounds a fortnight he might still live. So he took his index to St. James's Street, and left it for approval. He was told by the foreman that if he would call again in a week's time he should hear the result. Of course he called on that day week. The work had not yet been examined, and he must call again after three days. He did call again; and Mr. Boothby told him that his index was utterly useless,—that, in fact, it was not an index at all.

"You couldn't have looked at any other index, I think," said Mr. Boothby.

"Of course you need not take it," said Fred; "but I believe it to be as good an index as was ever made."

Mr. Boothby, getting up from his chair, declared that there was nothing more to be said. The gentleman for whom the work had been done begged that Mr. Pickering should receive five pounds for his labour,—which unfortunately had been thus thrown away. And in saying this Mr. Boothby tendered a five-pound note to Fred. Fred pushed the note away from him, and left the room with a tear in his eye. Mr. Boothby saw the tear, and ten pounds was sent to Fred on the next day, with the gentleman's compliments. Fred sent the ten pounds back. There was still a shot in the locker, and he could not as yet take money for work that he had not done.

By the end of January Fred had retreated with his wife and child to the shelter of a single small bedroom. Hitherto there had been a sitting-room and a bedroom; but now there were but five pounds between him and that starvation which he had once almost coveted, and every shilling must be strained to the utmost. His wife's confinement had cost him much of his money, and she was still ill. Things were going very badly with him, and among all the things that were bad with him, his own idleness was probably the worst. When starvation was so near to him, he could not seat himself in the Museum library and read to any good purpose. And, indeed, he had no purpose. Milton was nothing to him now, as his lingering shillings became few, and still fewer. He could only sit brooding over his misfortunes, and cursing his fate. And every day, as he sat eating his scraps of food over the morsel of fire in his wife's bedroom, she would implore him to pocket his pride and write to his father.

"He would do something for us, so that baby should not die," Mary said to him. Then he went into Museum Street, and bethought himself whether it would not be a manly thing for him to cut his throat. At any rate there would be much relief in such a proceeding.

One day as he was sitting over the fire while his wife still lay in bed, the servant of the house brought up word that a gentleman wanted to see him. "A gentleman! what gentleman?" The girl could not say who was the gentleman, so Fred went down to receive his visitor at the door of the house. He met an old man of perhaps seventy years of age, dressed in black, who with much politeness asked him whether he was Mr. Frederick Pickering. Fred declared himself to be that unfortunate man, and explained that he had no apartment in which to be seen. "My wife is in bed upstairs, ill; and there is not a room in the house to which I can ask you." So the old gentleman and Fred walked up Museum Street and had their conversation on the pavement. "I am Mr. Burnaby, for whose book you made an index," said the old man.

Mr. Burnaby was an author well known in those days, and Fred, in the midst of his misfortunes, felt that he was honoured by the visit.

"I was sorry that my index did not suit you," said Fred.

"It did not suit at all," said Mr. Burnaby. "Indeed it was no index. An index should comprise no more than words and figures. Your index conveyed opinions, and almost criticism."

"If you suffered inconvenience, I regret it much," said Fred. "I was punished at any rate by my lost labour."

"I do not wish you to be punished at all," said Mr. Burnaby, "and therefore I have come to you with the price in my hand. I am quite sure that you worked hard to do your best." Then Mr. Burnaby's fingers went into his waistcoat pocket, and returned with a crumpled note.

"Certainly not, Mr. Burnaby," said Fred. "I can take nothing that I have not earned."

"Now, my dear young friend, listen to me. I know that you are poor."

"I am very poor."

"And I am rich."

"That has nothing to do with it. Can you put me in the way of earning anything by literature? I will accept any such kindness as that at your hand; but nothing else."

"I cannot. I have no means of doing so."

"You know so many authors;—and so many publishers."

"Though I knew all the authors and all the publishers, what can I do? Excuse me if I say that you have not served the apprenticeship that is necessary."

"And do all authors serve apprenticeships?"

"Certainly not. And it may be that you will rise to wealth and fame without apprenticeship;—but if so, you must do it without help."

After that they walked silently together half the length of the street before Fred spoke again. "You mean," said he, "that a man must be either a genius or a journeyman."

"Yes, Mr. Pickering; that, or something like it, is what I mean."

Fred told Mr. Burnaby his whole story, walking up and down Museum Street,—even to that early assurance given to his young bride that there were worse things in the world than starvation. And then Mr. Burnaby asked him what were his present intentions. "I suppose we shall try it," said Pickering, with a forced laugh.

"Try what?" said Mr. Burnaby.

"Starvation," said Fred.

"What! with your baby,—with your wife and baby? Come; you

must take my ten-pound note at any rate. And while you are spending it, write home to your father. Heaven and earth! is a man to be ashamed to tell his father that he has been wrong?" When Fred said that his father was a stern man, and one whose heart would not be melted into softness at the tale of a baby's sufferings, Mr. Burnaby went on to say that the attempt should at any rate be made. "There can be no doubt what duty requires of you, Mr. Pickering. And, upon my word, I do not see what other step you can take. You are not, I suppose, prepared to send your wife and child to the poor-house." Then Fred Pickering burst into tears, and Mr. Burnaby left him at the corner of Great Russell Street, after cramming the ten-pound note into his hand.

To send his wife and child to the poor-house! In all his misery that idea had never before presented itself to Fred Pickering. He had thought of starvation, or rather of some high-toned extremity of destitution, which might be borne with an admirable and perhaps sublime magnanimity. But how was a man to bear with magnanimity a poor-house jacket, and the union mode of hair-cutting? It is not easy for a man with a wife and baby to starve in this country, unless he be one to whom starvation has come very gradually. Fred saw it all now. The police would come to him, and take his wife and baby away into the workhouse, and he would follow them. It might be that this was worse than starvation, but it lacked all that melodramatic grandeur to which he had looked forward almost with satisfaction.

"Well," said Mary to him, when he returned to her bedside, "who was it? Has he told you of anything? Has he brought you anything to do?"

"He has given me that," said Fred, throwing the bank-note on to the bed, "—out of charity! I may as well go out into the streets and beg now. All the pride has gone out of me." Then he sat over the fire crying, and there he sat for hours.

"Fred," said his wife to him, "if you do not write to your father to-morrow I will write."

He went again to every person connected in the slightest degree with literature of whom he had the smallest knowledge; to Mr. Roderick Billings, to the teacher who had instructed him in shorthand-writing, to all those whom he had ever seen among the newspapers, to the editor of the International, and to Mr. Boothby. Four different visits he made to Mr. Boothby, in spite of his previous anger, but it was all to no purpose. No one could find him employment for which he was suited. He wrote to Mr. Wickham Webb, and Mr. Wickham Webb sent him a five-pound note. His heart was, I think, more broken by his inability to refuse charity than by anything else that had occurred to him.

His wife had threatened to write to his father, but she had not carried her threat into execution. It is not by such means that a young wife overcomes her husband. He had looked sternly at her when she had so spoken, and she had known that she could not bring herself to do such a thing without his permission. But when she fell ill, wanting the means of nourishment for her child, and in her illness begged of him to implore succour from his father for her baby when she should be gone, then his pride gave way, and he sat down and wrote his letter. When he went to his ink-bottle it was dry. It was nearly two months since he had made any attempt at working in that profession to which he had intended to devote himself.

He wrote to his father, drinking to the dregs the bitter cup of broken pride. It always seems to me that the prodigal son who returned to his father after feeding with the swine suffered but little mortification in his repentant submission. He does, indeed, own his unworthiness, but the calf is killed so speedily that the pathos of the young man's position is lost in the hilarity of the festival. Had he been compelled to announce his coming by post; had he been driven to beg permission to return, and been forced to wait for a reply, his punishment, I think, would have been more severe. To Fred Pickering the punishment was very severe, and indeed for him no fatted calf was killed at last. He received without delay a very cold letter from his father, in which he was told that his father would consider the matter. In the meanwhile thirty shillings a-week should be allowed him. At the end of a fortnight he received a further letter, in which he was informed that if he would return to Manchester he would be taken in at the attorney's office which he had left. He must not, however, hope to become himself an attorney; he must look forward to be a paid attorney's clerk, and in the meantime his father would continue to allow him thirty shillings a-week. "In the present position of affairs," said his father, "I do not feel that anything would be gained by our seeing each other." The calf which was thus killed for poor Fred Pickering was certainly by no means a fatted calf.

Of course he had to do as he was directed. He took his wife and baby back to Manchester, and returned with sad eyes and weary feet to the old office which he had in former days not only hated but despised. Then he had been gallant and gay among the other young men, thinking himself to be too good for the society of those around him; now he was the lowest of the low, if not the humblest of the humble.

He told his whole story by letters to Mr. Burnaby, and received some comfort from the kindness of that gentleman's replies. "I still mean," he said, in one of those letters, "to return some day to my old aspirations; but I will endeavour first to learn my trade as a journeyman of literature."

The Last Austrian Who Left Venice

Originally appeared in *Good Words*, January 1867. Reprinted in *Lotta Schmidt and Other Stories* (1867). Written 8–14 December 1866, during the composition of *Phineas Finn*. Trollope visited Venice in the summer of 1855.

IN THE spring and early summer of the year last past,—the year 1866,—the hatred felt by Venetians towards the Austrian soldiers who held their city in thraldom, had reached its culminating point. For years this hatred had been very strong; how strong can hardly be understood by those who never recognise the fact that there had been, so to say, no mingling of the conquered and the conquerors, no process of assimilation between the Italian vassals and their German masters.

Venice as a city was as purely Italian as though its barracks were filled with no Hungarian long-legged soldiers, and its cafés crowded with no white-coated Austrian officers. And the regiments which held the town, lived as completely after their own fashion as though they were quartered in Pesth, or Prague, or Vienna,—with this exception, that in Venice they were enabled, and, indeed, from circumstances were compelled,—to exercise a palpable ascendancy which belonged to them nowhere else. They were masters, daily visible as such to the eye of every one who merely walked the narrow ways of the city or strolled through the open squares; and, as masters, they were as separate as the gaoler is separate from the prisoner.

The Austrian officers sat together in the chief theatre,—having the best part of it to themselves. Few among them spoke Italian. None of the common soldiers did so. The Venetians seldom spoke German; and could hold no intercourse whatever with the Croats, Hungarians, and Bohemians, of whom the garrison was chiefly composed. It could not be otherwise than that there should be intense hatred in a city so ruled. But the hatred which had been intense for years had reached its boiling point in the May preceding the outbreak of the war.

Whatever other nations might desire to do, Italy, at any rate, was at this time resolved to fight. It was not that the King and the Government were so resolved. What was the purpose just then of the powers of the state, if any purpose had then been definitely formed by them, no one now knows. History, perhaps, may some day tell us. But the nation was determined to fight. Hitherto all had been done for the Italians by outside allies, and now the time had come in which Italians would do something for themselves.

The people hated the French aid by which they had been allowed to live, and burned with a desire to prove that they could do something great without aid. There was an enormous army, and that army should be utilised for the enfranchisement of Venetia and to the great glory of Italy. The King and the ministers appreciated the fact that the fervour of the people was too strong to be repressed, and were probably guided to such resolutions as they did make by that appreciation.

The feeling was as strong in Venice as it was in Florence or in Milan; but in Venice only,—or rather in Venetia only—all outward signs of such feeling were repressible, and were repressed. All through Lombardy and Tuscany any young man who pleased might volunteer with Garibaldi; but to volunteer with Garibaldi was not, at first, so easy for young men in Verona or in Venice. The more complete was this repression, the greater was this difficulty, the stronger, of course, arose the hatred of the Venetians for the Austrian soldiery. I have never heard that the Austrians were cruel in what they did; but they were determined; and, as long as they had any intention of holding the province, it was necessary that they should be so.

During the past winter there had been living in Venice a certain Captain von Vincke,—Hubert von Vincke,—an Austrian officer of artillery, who had spent the last four or five years among the fortifications of Verona, and who had come to Venice, originally, on account of ill health. Some military employment had kept him in Venice, and he remained there till the outbreak of the war; going backwards and forwards, occasionally, to Verona, but still having Venice as his head-quarters.

Now Captain von Vincke had shown so much consideration for the country which he assisted in holding under subjection as to learn its language, and to study its manners; and had, by these means, found his way more or less, into Italian society. He was a thorough soldier, good-looking, perhaps eight-and-twenty or thirty years of age, well educated, ambitious, very free from the common vice of thinking that the class of mankind to which he belonged was the only class in which it would be worth a man's while to live; but nevertheless imbued with a strong feeling that Austria ought to hold her own, that an Austrian army was indomitable, and that the quadrilateral fortresses, bound together as they were now bound by Austrian strategy, were impregnable. So much Captain von Vincke thought and believed on the part of his country; but in thinking and believing this, he was still desirous that much should be done to relieve Austrian-Italy from the grief of foreign rule. That Italy should think of succeeding in repelling Austria from Venice was to him an absurdity.

He had become intimate at the house of a widow lady, who lived in the Campo San Luca, one Signora Pepé, whose son had first become acquainted with Captain von Vincke at Verona.

Carlo Pepé was a young advocate, living and earning his bread at Venice, but business had taken him for a time to Verona; and when leaving that city he had asked his Austrian friend to come and see him in his mother's house.

Both Madame Pepé and her daughter Nina, Carlo's only sister, had somewhat found fault with the young advocate's rashness in thus seeking the close intimacy of home-life with one whom, whatever might be his own peculiar virtues, they could not but recognise as an enemy of their country.

"That would be all very fine if it were put into a book," said the Signora to her son, who had been striving to show that an Austrian, if good in himself, might be as worthy a friend as an Italian; "but it is always well to live on the safe side of the wall. It is not convenient that the sheep and the wolves should drink at the same stream."

This she said with all that caution which everywhere forms so marked a trait in the Italian character. "Who goes softly goes soundly." Half of the Italian nature is told in that proverb, though it is not the half which was becoming most apparent in the doings of the nation in these days. And the Signorina was quite of one mind with her mother.

"Carlo," she said, "how is it that one never sees one of these Austrians in the house of any friend? Why is it that I have never yet found myself in a room with one of them?"

"Because men and women are generally so pigheaded and unreasonable," Carlo had replied. "How am I, for instance, ever to learn what a German is at the core, or a Frenchman, or an Englishman, if I refuse to speak to one?"

It ended by Captain von Vincke being brought to the house in the Campo San Luca, and there becoming as intimate with the Signora and the Signorina as he was with the advocate.

Our story must be necessarily too short to permit us to see how the affair grew in all its soft and delicate growth; but by the beginning of April Nina Pepé had confessed her love to Hubert von Vincke, and both the captain and Nina had had a few words with the Signora on the subject of their projected marriage.

"Carlo will never allow it," the old lady had said, trembling as she thought of the danger that was coming upon the family.

"He should not have brought Captain von Vincke to the house, unless he was prepared to regard such a thing as possible," said Nina proudly.

"I think he is too good a fellow to object to anything that you will ask him," said the captain, holding by the hand the lady whom he hoped to call his mother-in-law.

Throughout January and February Captain von Vincke had been an invalid. In March he had been hardly more than convalescent, and had then had time and all that opportunity which convalescence gives for the sweet business of love-making.

During this time, through March and in the first weeks of April, Carlo Pepé had been backwards and forwards to Verona, and had in truth had more business on hand than that which simply belonged to him as a lawyer. Those were the days in which the Italians were beginning to prepare for the great attack which was to be made, and in which correspondence was busily carried on between Italy and Venetia as to the enrolment of Venetian Volunteers.

It will be understood that no Venetian was allowed to go into Italy without an Austrian passport, and that at this time the Austrians were becoming doubly strict in seeing that the order was not evaded. Of course it was evaded daily, and twice in that April did young Pepé travel between Verona and Bologna in spite of all that Austria could say to the contrary.

When at Venice he and von Vincke discussed very freely the position of the country, nothing of course being said as to those journeys to Bologna. Indeed, of them no one in the Campo San Luca knew aught. They were such journeys that a man says nothing of them to his mother or his sister, or even to his wife, unless he has as much confidence in her courage as he has in her love. But of politics he would talk freely, as would also the German; and though each of them would speak of the cause as though they two were simply philosophical lookers-on, and were not and could not become actors, and though each had in his mind a settled resolve to bear with the political opinion of the other, yet it came to pass that they now and again were on the verge of quarrelling.

The fault, I think, was wholly with Carlo Pepé, whose enthusiasm of course was growing as those journeys to Bologna were made successfully, and who was beginning to feel assured that Italy at last would certainly do something for herself. But there had not come any open quarrel,—not as yet, when Nina, in her lover's presence, was arguing as to the impropriety of bringing Captain von Vincke to the house, if Captain von Vincke was to be regarded as altogether unfit for matrimonial purposes. At that moment Carlo was absent at Verona, but was to return on the following morning. It was decided at this conference between the two ladies and the lover, that Carlo should be told on his return of Captain von Vincke's intentions. Captain von Vincke himself would tell him.

There is a certain hotel or coffee-house, or place of general public entertainment in Venice, kept by a German, and called the Hotel Bauer, probably from the name of the German who keeps it. It stands near the church of St. Moses, behind the grand piazza, between that and the great canal, in a narrow intricate throng of little streets, and is approached by a close dark water-way which robs it of any attempt at hotel grandeur. Nevertheless it is a large and commodious house, at which good dinners may be eaten at prices somewhat lower than are compatible with the grandeur of the Grand Canal. It used to be much affected by Germans, and had, perhaps, acquired among Venetians a character of being attached to Austrian interests.

There was not much in this, or Carlo Pepé would not have frequented the house, even in company with his friend Von Vincke. He did so frequent it, and now, on this occasion of his return home, Von Vincke left word for him that he would breakfast at the hotel at eleven o'clock. Pepé by that time would have gone home after his journey, and would have visited his office. Von Vincke also would have done the greatest part of his day's work. Each understood the habits of the other, and they met at Bauer's for breakfast.

It was the end of April, and Carlo Pepé had returned to Venice full of schemes for that revolution which he now regarded as imminent. The alliance between Italy and Prussia was already discussed. Those Italians who were most eager said that it was a thing done, and no Italian was more eager than Carlo Pepé. And it was believed at this time, and more thoroughly believed in Italy than elsewhere, that Austria and Prussia would certainly go to war. Now, if ever, Italy must do something for herself.

Carlo Pepé was in this mood, full of these things, when he sat down to breakfast at Bauer's with his friend Captain von Vincke.

"Von Vincke," he said, "in three months' time you will be out of Venice."

"Shall I?" said the other; "and where shall I be?"

"In Vienna, as I hope; or at Berlin if you can get there. But you will not be here, or in the Quadrilatere, unless you are left behind as a prisoner."

The captain went on for a while cutting his meat and drinking his wine, before he made any reply to this. And Pepé said more of the same kind, expressing strongly his opinion that the empire of the Austrians in Venice was at an end. Then the captain wiped his moustaches carefully with his napkin, and did speak.

"Carlo, my friend," he said, "you are rash to say all this."

"Why rash?" said Carlo; "you and I understand each other."

"Just so, my friend; but we do not know how far that long-eared waiter may understand either of us."

"The waiter has heard nothing, and I do not care if he did."

"And beyond that," continued the captain, "you make a difficulty for me. What am I to say when you tell me these things? That you should have one political opinion and I another is natural. The question between us, in an abstract point of view, I can discuss with you willingly. The possibility of Venice contending with Austria I could discuss, if no such rebellion were imminent. But when you tell me that it is imminent, that it is already here, I cannot discuss it."

"It is imminent," said Carlo.

"So be it," said Von Vincke.

And then they finished their breakfast in silence. All this was very unfortunate for our friend the captain, who had come to Bauer's with the intention of speaking on quite another subject. His friend Pepé had evidently taken what he had said in a bad spirit, and was angry with him. Nevertheless, as he had told Nina and her mother that he would declare his purpose to Carlo on this morning, he must do it. He was not a man to be frightened out of his purpose by his friend's ill-humour.

"Will you come into the piazza, and smoke a cigar?" said Von Vincke, feeling that he could begin upon the other subject better as soon as the scene should be changed.

"Why not let me have my cigar and coffee here?" said Carlo.

"Because I have something to say which I can say better walking than sitting. Come along."

Then they paid the bill and left the house, and walked in silence through the narrow ways to the piazza. Von Vincke said no word till he found himself in the broad passage leading into the great square. Then he put his hand through the other's arm and told his tale at once.

"Carlo," said he, "I love your sister, and would have her for my wife. Will you consent?"

"By the body of Bacchus, what is this you say?" said the other, drawing his arm away, and looking up into the German's face.

"Simply that she has consented and your mother. Are you willing that I should be your brother?"

"This is madness," said Carlo Pepé.

"On their part, you mean?"

"Yes, and on yours. Were there nothing else to prevent it, how could there be marriage between us when this war is coming?"

"I do not believe in the war; that is, I do not believe in war between us and Italy. No war can affect you here in Venice. If there is to be a war in which I shall be concerned, I am quite willing to wait till it be over."

"You understand nothing about it," said Carlo, after a pause; "nothing! You are in the dark altogether. How should it not be so, when those who are over you never tell you anything? No, I will not consent. It is a thing out of the question."

"Do you think that I am personally unfit to be your sister's husband?"

"Not personally, but politically and nationally. You are not one of us; and now, at this moment, any attempt at close union between an Austrian and a Venetian must be ruinous. Von Vincke, I am heartily sorry for this. I blame the women, and not you."

Then Carlo Pepé went home, and there was a rough scene between him and his mother, and a scene still rougher between him and his sister.

And in these interviews he told something, though not the whole of the truth as to the engagements into which he had entered. That he was to be the officer second in command in a regiment of Venetian volunteers, of those volunteers whom it was hoped that Garibaldi would lead to victory in the coming war, he did not tell them; but he did make them understand that when the struggle came he would be away from Venice, and would take a part in it. "And how am I to do this," he said, "if you here are joined hand and heart to an Austrian? A house divided against itself must fall."

Let the reader understand that Nina Pepé, in spite of her love and of her lover, was as good an Italian as her brother, and that their mother was equally firm in her political desires and national antipathies. Where would you have found the Venetian, man or woman, who did not detest Austrian rule, and look forward to the good day coming when Venice should be a city of Italia?

The Signora and Nina had indeed, some six months before this, been much stronger in their hatred of all things German, than had the son and brother. It had been his liberal feeling, his declaration that even a German might be good, which had induced them to allow this Austrian to come among them.

Then the man and the soldier had been two; and Von Vincke had himself shown tendencies so strongly at variance with those of his comrades that he had disarmed their fears. He had read Italian, and condescended to speak it; he knew the old history of their once great city, and would listen to them when they talked of their old Doges. He loved their churches, and their palaces, and their pictures. Gradually he had come to love Nina Pepé with all his heart, and Nina loved him too with all her heart.

But when her brother spoke to her and to her mother with more than his customary vehemence of what was due from them to their country, of the debt which certainly should be paid by him, of obligations to him from which they could not free themselves; and told them also, that by that time six months not an Austrian would be found in Venice, they trembled and believed him, and Nina felt that her love would not run smooth.

"You must be with us or against us," said Carlo.

"Why then did you bring him here?" Nina replied.

"Am I to suppose that you cannot see a man without falling in love with him?"

"Carlo, that is unkind, almost unbrotherly. Was he not your friend, and were not you the first to tell us how good he is? And he is good; no man can be better."

"He is a honest young man," said the Signora.

"He is Austrian to the backbone," said Carlo.

"Of course he is," said Nina. "What should he be?"

"And will you be Austrian?" her brother asked.

"Not if I must be an enemy of Italy," Nina said. "If an Austrian may be a friend to Italy, then I will be an Austrian. I wish to be Hubert's wife. Of course I shall be an Austrian if he is my husband."

"Then I trust that you may never be his wife," said Carlo.

By the middle of May Carlo Pepé and Captain von Vincke had absolutely quarrelled. They did not speak, and Von Vincke had been ordered by the brother not to show himself at the house in the Campo San Luca.

Every German in Venice had now become more Austrian than before, and every Venetian more Italian. Even our friend the captain had come to believe in the war.

Not only Venice but Italy was in earnest, and Captain von Vincke foresaw, or thought that he foresaw, that a time of wretched misery was coming upon that devoted town. He would never give up Nina, but perhaps it might be well that he should cease to press his suit till he might be enabled to do so with something of the éclat of Austrian success.

And now at last it became necessary that the two women should be told of Carlo's plans, for Carlo was going to leave Venice till the war should be over and he could re-enter the city as an Italian should enter a city of his own.

"Oh! my son, my son," said the mother; "why should it be you?"

"Many must go, mother. Why not I as well as another?"

"In other houses there are fathers; and in other families more sons than one."

"The time has come, mother, in which no woman should grudge either husband or son to the cause. But the thing is settled. I am already second colonel in a regiment which will serve with Garibaldi. You would not ask me to desert my colours?"

There was nothing further to be said. The Signora threw herself on her son's neck and wept, and both mother and sister felt that their Carlo was already a second Garibaldi. When a man is a hero to women, they will always obey him. What could Nina do at such a time, but promise that she would not see Hubert von Vincke during his absence. Then there was a compact made between the brother and sister.

During three weeks past, that is, since the breakfast at Bauer's, Nina had seen Hubert von Vincke but once, and had then seen him in the presence of her mother and brother. He had come in one evening in the old way, before the quarrel, to take his coffee, and had been received, as heretofore, as a friend, Nina sitting very silent during the evening, but with a gracious silence; and after that the mother had signified to the lover that he had better come no more for the present. He therefore came no more.

I think it is the fact that love, though no doubt it may run as strong with an Italian or with an Austrian as it does with us English, is not allowed to run with so uncontrollable a stream. Young lovers, and especially young women, are more subject to control, and are less inclined to imagine that all things should go as they would have them. Nina, when she was made to understand that the war was come, that her brother was leaving her and her mother and Venice, that he might fight for them, that an Austrian soldier must for the time be regarded as an enemy in that house, resolved with a slow, melancholy firmness that she would accept the circumstances of her destiny.

"If I fall," said Carlo, "you must then manage for yourself. I would not wish to bind you after my death."

"Do not talk like that, Carlo."

"Nay, my child, but I must talk like that; and it is at least well that we should understand each other. I know that you will keep your promise to me."

"Yes," said Nina; "I will keep my promise."

"Till I come back, or till I be dead, you will not again see Captain von Vincke; or till the cause be gained."

"I will not see him, Carlo, till you come back, or till the cause be gained."

"Or till I be dead. Say it after me."

"Or till you be dead, if I must say it."

But there was a clause in the contract that she was to see her lover once before her brother left them. She had acknowledged the propriety of her brother's behests, backed as they came to be at last by their mother; but she declared through it all that she had done no wrong, and that she would not be treated as though she were an offender. She would see her lover and tell him what she pleased. She would obey her brother, but she would see her lover first. Indeed, she would make no promise of obedience at all, would promise disobedience instead, unless she were allowed to see him. She would herself write to him and bid him come.

This privilege was at last acceded to her, and Captain von Vincke was summoned to the Campo San Luca. The morning sitting-room of the Signora Pepé was up two pairs of stairs, and the stairs were not paved as are the stairs of the palaces in Venice. But the room was large and lofty, and seemed to be larger than its size from the very small amount of furniture which it contained. The floor was of hard, polished cement, which looked like variegated marble, and the amount of carpet upon it was about four yards long, and was extended simply beneath the two chairs in which sat habitually the Signora and her daughter. There were two large mirrors and a large gold clock, and a large table and a small table, a small sofa and six chairs, and that was all. In England the room would have received ten times as much furniture, or it would not have been furnished at all. And there were in it no more than two small books, belonging both to Nina, for the Signora read but little. In England, in such a sitting-room, tables, various tables, would have been strewed with books; but then, perhaps, Nina Pepé's eye required the comfort of no other volumes than those she was actually using.

Nina was alone in the room when her lover came to her. There had been a question whether her mother should or should not be present; but Nina had been imperative, and she received him alone.

"It is to bid you good-bye, Hubert," she said, as she got up and touched his hand,—just touched his hand.

"Not for long, my Nina."

"Who can say for how long, now that the war is upon us? As far as I can see, it will be for very long. It is better that you should know it all. For myself, I think, I fear that it will be for ever."

"For ever! why for ever?"

"Because I cannot marry an enemy of Italy. I do not think that we can ever succeed."

"You can never succeed."

"Then I can never be your wife. It is so, Hubert; I see that it must be so. The loss is to me, not to you."

"No, no—no. The loss is to me,—to me."

"You have your profession. You are a soldier. I am nothing."

"You are all in all to me."

"I can be nothing, I shall be nothing, unless I am your wife. Think how I must long for that which you say is so impossible. I do long for it; I shall long for it. Oh, Hubert! go and lose your cause; let our men have their Venice. Then come to me, and your country shall be my country, and your people my people."

As she said this she gently laid her hand upon his arm, and the touch of her fingers thrilled through his whole frame. He put out his arms as though his whole frame. He put out his arms as though to grasp her in his embrace.

"No, Hubert—no; that must not be till Venice is our own."

"I wish it were," he said; "but it will never be so. You may make me a traitor in heart, but that will not drive out fifty thousand troops from the fortresses."

"I do not understand these things, Hubert, and I have felt your country's power to be so strong, that I cannot now doubt it."

"It is absurd to doubt it."

"But yet they say that we shall succeed."

"It is impossible. Even though Prussia should be able to stand against us, we should not leave Venetia. We shall never leave the fortresses."

"Then, my love, we may say farewell for ever. I will not forget you. I will never be false to you. But we must part."

He stood there arguing with her, and she argued with him, but they always came round to the same point. There was to be the war, and she would not become the wife of her brother's enemy. She had sworn, she said, and she would keep her word. When his arguments became stronger than hers, she threw herself back upon her plighted word.

"I have said it, and I must not depart from it. I have told him that my love for you should be eternal, and I tell you the same. I told him that I would see you no more, and I can only tell you so also."

He could ask her no questions as to the cause of her resolution, because he could not make inquiries as to her brother's purpose. He knew that Carlo was at work for the Venetian cause; or, at least, he thought that he knew it. But it was essential for his comfort that he should really know as little of this as might be possible. That Carlo Pepé was coming and going in the service of the cause he could not but surmise: but should authenticated information reach him as to whither Carlo went, and how he came, it might become his duty to put a stop to Carlo's comings and Carlo's goings. On this matter, therefore, he said nothing, but merely shook his head, and smiled with a melancholy smile when she spoke of the future struggle. "And now, Hubert, you must go. I was determined that I would see you, that I might tell you that I would be true to you."

"What good will be such truth?"

"Nay; it is for you to say that. I ask you for no pledge."

"I shall love no other woman. I would if I could. I would if I could—to-morrow."

"Let us have our own, and then come and love me. Or you need not come. I will go to you, though it be to the furthest end of Galicia. Do not look like that at me. You should be proud when I tell you that I love you. No, you shall not kiss me. No man shall ever kiss me till Venice is our own. There,—I have sworn it. Should that time come, and should a certain Austrian gentleman care for Italian kisses then, he will know where to seek for them. God bless you now, and go."

She made her way to the door and opened it, and there was nothing for him but that he must go. He touched her hand once more as he went, but there was no other word spoken between them.

"Mother," she said, when she found herself again with the Signora, "my little dream of life is over. It has been very short."

"Nay, my child, life is long for you yet. There will be many dreams, and much of reality."

"I do not complain of Carlo," Nina continued. "He is sacrificing much, perhaps everything, for Venice. And why should his sacrifice be greater than mine? But I feel it to be severe,—very severe. Why did he bring him here if he felt thus?"

June came, that month of June that was to be so fatal to Italian glory, and so fraught with success for the Italian cause, and Carlo Pepé was again away.

Those who knew nothing of his doings, knew only that he had gone to Verona—on matters of law. Those who were really acquainted with the circumstances of his present life were aware that he had made his way out of Verona, and that he was already with his volunteers near the lakes waiting for Garibaldi, who was then expected from Caprera. For some weeks to come, for some months probably, during the war perhaps, the two women in the Campo San Luca would know nothing of the whereabouts or of the fate of him whom they loved. He had gone to risk all for the cause, and they too must be content to risk all in remaining desolate at home without the comfort of his presence;—and she also, without the sweeter comfort of that other presence.

It is thus that women fight their battles. In these days men by hundreds were making their way out of Venice, and by thousands out of the province of Venetia, and the Austrians were endeavouring in vain to stop the emigration. Some few were caught, and kept in prison; and many Austrian threats were uttered against those who should prove themselves to be insubordinate. But it is difficult for a garrison to watch a whole people, and very difficult indeed when there is a war on hand.

It at last became a fact, that any man from the province could go and become a volunteer under Garibaldi if he pleased, and very many did go. History will say that they were successful,—but their success certainly was not glorious.

It was in the month of June that all the battles of that short war were fought. Nothing will ever be said or sung in story to the honour of the volunteers who served in that campaign with Garibaldi, amidst the mountains of the Southern Tyrol; but nowhere, probably, during the war was there so much continued fighting, or an equal amount endured of the hardships of military life.

The task they had before them, of driving the Austrians from the fortresses amidst their own mountains, was an impossible one, impossible even had Garibaldi been supplied with ordinary military equipments,—but ridiculously impossible for him in all the nakedness in which he was sent. Nothing was done to enable him to succeed. That he should be successful was neither intended nor desired. He was, in fact,—then, as he has been always, since the days in which he gave Naples to Italy,—simply a stumbling-block in the way of the king, of the king's ministers, and of the king's generals. "There is that Garibaldi again,—with volunteers flocking to him by thousands:—what shall we do to rid ourselves of Garibaldi and his volunteers? How shall we dispose of them?" That has been the feeling of those in power in Italy,—and not unnaturally their feeling,—with regard to Garibaldi. A man so honest, so brave, so patriotic, so popular, and so impracticable, cannot but have been a trouble to them. And here he was with twenty-five thousand volunteers, all armed after a fashion, all supplied, at least, with a red shirt. What should be done with Garibaldi and his army? So they sent him away up into the mountains, where his game of play might at any rate detain him for some weeks; and in the meantime everything might get itself arranged by the benevolent and omnipotent interference of the emperor.

Things did get themselves arranged while Garibaldi was up among the mountains, kicking with unarmed toes against Austrian pricks—with sad detriment to his feet. Things did get themselves arranged very much to the advantage of Venetia, but not exactly by the interference of the emperor.

The facts of the war became known more slowly in Venice than they did in Florence, in Paris, or in London. That the battle of Custozza had been fought and lost by the Italian troops was known. And then it was known that the battle of Lissa also had been fought and lost by Italian ships. But it was not known, till the autumn was near at hand that Venetia had, in fact, been surrendered. There were rumours; and women, who knew that their husbands had been beaten, could not believe that success was to be the result of such calamities.

There were weeks in which came no news from Carlo Pepé to the women in the Campo San Luca, and then came simply tidings that he had been wounded.

"I shall see my son never again," said the widow in her ecstasy of misery.

And Nina was able to talk to her mother only of Carlo. Of Hubert von Vincke she spoke not then a word. But she repeated to herself over and over again the last promise she had given him. She had sent him away from her, and now she knew nothing of his whereabouts. That he would be fighting she presumed. She had heard that most of the soldiers from Venice had gone to the fortresses. He, too, might be wounded,—might be dead. If alive at the end of the war, he would hardly return to her after what had passed between them. But if he did not come back no lover should ever take a kiss from her lips.

Then there was the long truce, and a letter from Carlo reached Venice. His wound had been slight, but he had been very hungry. He wrote in great anger, abusing, not the Austrians, but the Italians. There had been treachery, and the Italian general-in-chief had been the head of the traitors. The king was a traitor! The emperor was a traitor! All concerned were traitors, but yet Venetia was to be surrendered to Italy.

I think that the two ladies in the Campo San Luca never really believed that this would be so until they received that angry letter from Carlo.

"When I may get home, I cannot tell," he said. "I hardly care to return, and I shall remain with the General as long as he may wish to have any one remaining with him. But you may be sure that I shall never go soldiering again. Venetia, may, perhaps, prosper, and become a part of Italy; but there will be no glory for us. Italy has been allowed to do nothing for herself." The mother and sister endeavoured to feel some sympathy for the young soldier who spoke so sadly of his own career, but they could hardly be unhappy because his fighting was over and the cause was won.

The cause was won. Gradually there came to be no doubt about that.

It was now September, and as yet it had not come to pass

that shop-windows were filled with wonderful portraits of Victor Emmanuel and Garibaldi, cheek by jowl—they being the two men who at that moment were perhaps, in all Italy, the most antagonistic to each other; nor were there as yet fifty different new journals cried day and night under the arcades of the Grand Piazza, all advocating the cause of Italy, one and indivisible, as there came to be a month afterwards; but still it was known that Austria was to cede Venetia, and that Venice would henceforth be a city of Italy. This was known; and it was also known in the Campo San Luca that Carlo Pepé, though very hungry up among the mountains, was still safe.

Then Nina thought that the time had come in which it would become her to speak of her lover. "Mother," she said, "I must know something of Hubert."

"But how, Nina? how will you learn? Will you not wait till Carlo comes back?"

"No," she said. "I cannot wait longer. I have kept my promise. Venice is no longer Austrian, and I will seek him. I have kept my word to Carlo, and now I will keep my word to Hubert."

But how to seek him? The widow, urged by her daughter, went out and asked at barrack doors; but new regiments had come and gone, and everything was in confusion. It was supposed that any officer of artillery who had been in Venice and had left it during the war must be in one of the four fortresses.

"Mother," she said, "I shall go to Verona."

And to Verona she went, all alone, in search of her lover. At that time the Austrians still maintained a sort of rule in the province; and there were still current orders against private travelling, orders that passports should be investigated, orders that the communication with the four fortresses should be specially guarded; but there was an intense desire on the part of the Austrians themselves that the orders should be regarded as little as possible. They had to go, and the more quietly they went the better. Why should they care now who passed hither and thither? It must be confessed on their behalf that in their surrender of Venetia they gave as little trouble as it was possible in them to cause.

The chief obstruction to Nina's journey she experienced in the Campo San Luca itself. But in spite of her mother, in spite of the not yet defunct Austrian mandates, she did make her way to Verona. "As I was true in giving him up," she said to herself, "so will I be true in clinging to him."

Even in Verona her task was not easy, but she did at last find all that she sought. Captain von Vincke had been in command of a battery at Custozza, and was now lying wounded in an Austrian hospital. Nina contrived to see an old grey-haired surgeon before she saw Hubert himself. Captain von Vincke had been terribly mauled; so the surgeon told her; his left arm had been amputated, and—and—and—

It seemed as though wounds had been showered on him. The surgeon did not think that his patient would die; but he did think that he must be left in Verona when the Austrians were marched out of the fortress. "Can he not be taken to Venice?" said Nina Pepé.

At last she found herself by her lover's bedside; but with her there were two hospital attendants, both of them worn-out Austrian soldiers,—and there was also there the grey-haired surgeon. How was she to tell her love, all that she had in her heart before such witnesses? The surgeon was the first to speak. "Here is your friend, Captain," he said; but as he spoke in German, Nina did not understand him.

"Is it really you, Nina?" said her lover. "I could hardly believe that you should be in Verona."

"Of course it is I. Who could have so much business to be in Verona as I have? Of course I am here."

"But,—but—what has brought you here, Nina?"

"If you do not know I cannot tell you."

"And Carlo?"

"Carlo is still with the General; but he is well."

"And the Signora?"

"She also is well; well, but not easy in mind while I am here."

"And when do you return?"

"Nay; I cannot tell you that. It may be to-day. It may be to-morrow. It depends not on myself at all."

He spoke not a word of love to her then, nor she to him, unless there was love in such greeting as has been here repeated. Indeed, it was not till after that first interview that he fully understood that she had made her journey to Verona, solely in quest of him. The words between them for the first day or two were very tame, as though neither had full confidence in the other; and she had taken her place as nurse by his side, as a sister might have done by a brother, and was established in her work,—nay, had nearly completed her work, before there came to be any full understanding between them. More than once she had told herself that she would go back to Venice and let there be an end of it. "The great work of the war," she said to herself, "has so filled his mind, that the idleness of his days in Venice and all that he did then, are forgotten. If so, my presence here is surely a sore burden to him, and I will go." But she could not now leave him without a word of farewell. "Hubert," she said, for she had called him Hubert when she first came to his bedside, as though she had been his sister, "I think I must return now to Venice. My mother will be lonely without me."

At that moment it appeared almost miraculous to her that she should be sitting there by his bedside, that she should have loved him, that she should have had the courage to leave her home and seek him after the war, that she should have found him, and that she should now be about to leave him, almost without a word between them.

"She must be very lonely," said the wounded man.

"And you, I think, are stronger than you were?"

"For me, I am strong enough. I have lost my arm, and I shall carry this gaping scar athwart my face to the grave, as my cross of honour won in the Italian war; but otherwise I shall soon be well."

"It is a fair cross of honour."

"Yes; they cannot rob us of our wounds when our service is over. And so you will go, Signorina?"

"Yes; I will go. Why should I remain here? I will go, and Carlo will return, and I will tend upon him. Carlo also was wounded."

"But you have told me that he is well again."

"Nevertheless, he will value the comfort of a woman's care after his sufferings. May I say farewell to you now, my friend?" And she put her hand down upon the bed so that he might reach it. She had been with him for days, and there had been no word of love. It had seemed as though he had understood nothing of what she had done in coming to him; that he had failed altogether in feeling that she had come as a wife goes to a husband. She had made a mistake in this journey, and must now rectify her error with as much of dignity as might be left to her.

He took her hand in his, and held it for a moment before he answered her. "Nina," he said, "why did you come hither?"

"Why did I come?"

"Why are you here in Verona, while your mother is alone in Venice?"

"I had business here; a matter of some moment. It is finished now, and I shall return."

"Was it other business than to sit at my bedside?"

She paused a moment before she answered him.

"Yes," she said; "it was other business than that."

"And you have succeeded?"

"No; I have failed."

He still held her hand; and she, though she was thus fencing with him, answering him with equivoques, felt that at last there was coming from him some word which would at least leave her no longer in doubt.

"And I too, have I failed?" he said. "When I left Venice I told myself heartily that I had failed."

"You told yourself, then!" said she, "that Venetia never would be ceded. You know that I would not triumph over you, now that your cause has been lost. We Italians have not much cause for triumphing."

"You will admit always that the fortresses have not been taken from us," said the sore-hearted soldier.

"Certainly we shall admit that?"

"And my own fortress,—the stronghold that I thought I had made altogether mine,—is that, too, lost for ever to the poor German?"

"You speak in riddles, Captain von Vincke," she said.

She had now taken back her hand; but she was sitting quietly by his bedside, and made no sign of leaving him.

"Nina," he said, "Nina,—my own Nina. In losing a single share of Venice,—one soldier's share of the province,—shall I have gained all the world for myself? Nina, tell me truly, what brought you to Verona?"

She knelt slowly down by his bedside, and again taking his one hand in hers, pressed it first to her lips and then to her bosom.

"It was an unmaidenly purpose," she said. "I came to find the man I loved."

"But you said you had failed?"

"And I now say that I have succeeded. Do you not know that success in great matters always trembles in the balance before it turns the beam, thinking, fearing, all but knowing that failure has weighed down the scale?"

"But now—?"

"Now I am sure that—Venice has been won."

It was three months after this, and half of December had passed away, and all Venetia had in truth been ceded, and Victor Emmanuel had made his entry into Venice and exit out of it, with as little of real triumph as ever attended a king's progress through a new province, and the Austrian army had moved itself off very quietly, and the city had become as thoroughly Italian as Florence itself, and was in a way to be equally discontented, when a party of four, two ladies and two gentlemen, sat down to breakfast in the Hôtel Bauer.

The ladies were the Signora Pepé and her daughter, and the men were Carlo Pepé and his brother-in-law, Hubert von Vincke. It was but a poor fête, this family breakfast at an obscure inn, but it was intended as a gala feast to mark the last day of Nina's Italian life.

To-morrow, very early in the morning, she was to leave Venice for Trieste,—so early that it would be necessary that she should be on board this very night.

"My child," said the Signora, "do not say so; you will never cease to be Italian. Surely, Hubert, she may still call herself Venetian?"

"Mother," she said, "I love a losing cause. I will be Austrian now. I told him that he could not have both. If he kept his Venice, he could not have me; but as he has lost his province, he shall have his wife entirely."

"I told him that it was fated that he should lose Venetia," said Carlo, "but he would never believe me."

"Because I knew how true were our soldiers," said Hubert, "and could not understand how false were our statesmen."

"See how he regrets it," said Nina; "what he has lost, and what he has won, will, together, break his heart for him."

"Nina," he said, "I learned this morning in the city, that I shall be the last Austrian soldier to leave Venice, and I hold that of all who have entered it, and all who have left it, I am the most successful and the most triumphant."

The Turkish Bath

Originally appeared in *Saint Paul's Magazine*, October 1869. Reprinted in *An Editor's Tales* (1870). In *An Autobiography* Trollope admits that this story of 'how an ingenious gentleman got into a conversation with me, I knowing that he knew me to be an editor, and pressed his little article on my notice' was closely based on fact.

It was in the month of August. The world had gone to the moors and the Rhine, but we were still kept in town by the exigencies of our position. We had been worked hard during the preceding year, and were not quite as well as our best friends might have wished us;—and we resolved upon taking a Turkish bath. This little story records the experience of one individual man; but our readers, we hope, will, without a grudge, allow us the use of the editorial we. We doubt whether the story could be told at all in any other form. We resolved upon taking a Turkish bath, and at about three o'clock in the day we strutted from the outer to the inner room of the establishment in that light costume and with that air of Arab dignity which are peculiar to the place.

As everybody has not taken a Turkish Bath in Jermyn Street, we will give the shortest possible description of the position. We had entered of course in the usual way, leaving our hat and our boots and our "valuables" among the numerous respectable assistants who throng the approaches; and as we had entered we had observed a stout, middle-aged gentleman on the other side of the street, clad in vestments somewhat the worse for wear, and to our eyes particularly noticeable by reason of the tattered condition of his gloves. A well-to-do man may have no gloves, or may simply carry in his hands those which appertain to him rather as a thing of custom than for any use for which he requires them. But a tattered glove, worn on the hand, is to our eyes the surest sign of a futile attempt at outer respectability. It is melancholy to us beyond expression. Our brother editors, we do not doubt, are acquainted with the tattered glove, and have known the sadness which it produces. If there be an editor whose heart has not been softened by the feminine tattered glove, that editor is not our brother. In this instance the tattered glove was worn by a man; and though the usual indication of poor circumstances was conveyed, there was nevertheless something jaunty in the gentleman's step which preserved him from the desecration of pity. We barely saw him, but still were thinking of him as we passed into the building with the oriental letters on it, and took off our boots, and pulled out our watch and purse.

We were of course accommodated with two checked towels; and, having in vain attempted to show that we were to the manner born by fastening the larger of them satisfactorily round our own otherwise naked person, had obtained the assistance of one of those very skilful eastern boys who glide about the place and create envy by their familiarity with its mysteries. With an absence of all bashfulness which soon grows upon one, we had divested ourselves of our ordinary trappings beneath the gaze of five or six young men lying on surrounding sofas,—among whom we recognised young Walker of the Treasury, and hereby testify on his behalf that he looks almost as fine a fellow without his clothes as he does with them,—and had strutted through the doorway into the bath-room, trailing our second towel behind us. Having observed the matter closely in the course of perhaps half-a-dozen visits, we are prepared to recommend that mode of entry to our young friends as being at the same time easy and oriental. There are those who wear the second towel as a shawl, thereby no doubt achieving a certain decency of garb; but this is done to the utter loss of all dignity; and a feminine appearance is produced,—such as is sometimes that of a lady of fifty looking after her maidservants at seven o'clock in the morning and intending to dress again before breakfast. And some there are who carry it under the arm,—simply as a towel; but these are they who, from English perversity, wilfully rob the institution of that picturesque orientalism which should be its greatest charm. A few are able to wear the article as a turban, and that no doubt should be done by all who are competent to achieve the position. We have observed that men who can do so enter the bath-room with an air and are received there with a respect which no other arrangement of the towel will produce. We have tried this; but as the turban gets over our eyes, and then falls altogether off our brow, we have abandoned it. In regard to personal deportment, depending partly on the step, somewhat on the eye, but chiefly on the costume, it must be acknowledged that "the attempt and not the deed confounds us." It is not every man who can carry a blue towel as a turban, and look like an Arab in the streets of Cairo, as he walks slowly down the room in Jermyn Street with his arms crossed on his naked breast. The attempt and not the deed does confound one shockingly. We, therefore, recommend that the second towel should be trailed. The effect is good, and there is no difficulty in the trailing which may not be overcome.

We had trailed our way into the bath-room, and had slowly walked to one of those arm-chairs in which it is our custom on such occasions to seat ourselves and to await sudation. There are marble couches; and if a man be able to lie on stone for half an hour without a movement beyond that of clapping his hands, or a sound beyond a hollow-voiced demand for water, the effect is not bad. But he loses everything if he tosses himself uneasily on his hard couch, and we acknowledge that our own elbows are always in the way of our own comfort, and that our bones become sore. We think that the marble sofas must be intended for the younger Turks. If a man can stretch himself on stone without suffering for the best part of an hour,—or, more bravely perhaps, without appearing to suffer, let him remember that all is not done even then. Very much will depend on the manner in which he claps his hands, and the hollowness of the voice in which he calls for water. There should, we think, be two blows of the palms. One is very weak and proclaims its own futility. Even to dull London ears it seems at once to want the eastern tone. We have heard three given effectively, but we think that it requires much practice; and even when it is perfect, the result is that of western impatience rather than of eastern gravity. No word should be pronounced, beyond that one word,—Water. The effect should be as though the whole mind were so devoted to the sudorific process as to admit of no extraneous idea. There should seem to be almost an agony in the effort,—as though the man enduring it, conscious that with success he would come forth a god, was aware that being as yet but mortal he may perish in the attempt. Two claps of the hand and a call for water, and that repeated with an interval of ten minutes, are all the external signs of life that the young Turkish bather may allow to himself while he is stretched upon his marble couch.

We had taken a chair,—well aware that nothing god-like could be thus achieved, and contented to obtain the larger amount of human comfort. The chairs are placed two and two, and a custom has grown up,—of which we scarcely think that the origin has been eastern,—in accordance with which friends occupying these chairs will spend their time in conversation. The true devotee to the Turkish bath will, we think, never speak at all; but when the speaking is low in tone, just something between a whisper and an articulate sound, the slight murmuring hum produced is not disagreeable. We cannot quite make up our mind whether this use of the human voice be or be not oriental; but we think that it adds to the mystery, and upon the whole it gratifies. Let it be understood, however, that harsh, resonant, clearly-expressed speech is damnable. The man who talks aloud to his friend about the trivial affairs of life is selfish, ignorant, unpoetical,—and English in the very worst sense of the word. Who but an ass proud of his own capacity for braying would venture to dispel the illusions of a score of bathers by observing aloud that the House sat till three o'clock that morning?

But though friends may talk in low voices, a man without a friend will hardly fall into conversation at the Turkish Bath. It is said that our countrymen are unapt to speak to each other without introduction, and this inaptitude is certainly not decreased by the fact that two men meet each other with nothing on but a towel apiece. Finding yourself next to a man in such a garb you hardly know where to begin. And then there lies upon you the weight of that necessity of maintaining a certain dignity of deportment which has undoubtedly grown upon you since you succeeded in freeing yourself from your socks and trousers. For ourselves, we have to admit that the difficulty is much increased by the fact that we are short-sighted, and are obligated by the sudorific processes and by the shampooing and washing that are to come, to leave our spectacles behind us. The delicious wonder of the place is no doubt increased to us, but our incapability of discerning aught of those around us in that low gloomy light is complete. Jones from Friday Street, or even Walker from the Treasury, is the same to us as one of those Asiatic slaves who administer to our comfort, and flit about the place with admirable decorum and self-respect. On this occasion we had barely seated ourselves, when another bather, with slow, majestic step, came to the other chair; and, with a manner admirably adapted to the place, stretching out his naked legs, and throwing back his naked shoulders, seated himself beside us. We are much given to speculations on the characters and probable circumstances of those with whom we are brought in contact. Our editorial duties require that it should be so. How should we cater for the public did we not observe the public in all its moods? We thought that we could see at once that this was no ordinary man, and we may as well aver here, at the beginning of our story, that subsequent circumstances proved our first conceptions to be correct. The absolute features of the gentleman we did not, indeed, see plainly. The gloom of the place and our own deficiency of sight forbade it. But we could discern the thorough man of the world, the traveller who had seen many climes, the cosmopolitan to whom East and West were alike, in every motion that he made. We confess that we were anxious for conversation, and that we struggled within ourselves for an apt subject, thinking how we might begin. But the apt subject did not occur to us, and we should have passed that half-hour of repose in silence had not our companion been more ready than ourselves. "Sir," said he, turning round in his seat with a peculiar and captivating grace, "I shall not, I hope, offend or transgress any rule of politeness by speaking to a stranger." There was ease and dignity in his manner, and at the same time some slight touch of humour which was very charming. I thought that I detected just a hint of an Irish accent in his tone; but if so the dear brogue of his country, which is always delightful to me, had been so nearly banished by intercourse with other tongues as to leave the matter still a suspicion,—a suspicion, or rather a hope.

"By no means," we answered, turning round on our left shoulder, but missing the grace with which he had made his movement.

"There is nothing," said he, "to my mind so absurd as that two men should be seated together for an hour without venturing to open their mouths because they do not know each other. And what matter does it make whether a man has his breeches on or is without them?"

My hope had now become an assurance. As he named the article of clothing which peculiarly denotes a man he gave a picturesque emphasis to the word which was certainly Hibernian. Who does not know the dear sound? And, as a chance companion for a few idle minutes, is there any one so likely to prove himself agreeable as a well-informed, travelled Irishman?

"And yet," said we, "men do depend much on their outward paraphernalia."

"Indeed and they do," said our friend. "And why? Because they can trust their tailors when they can't trust themselves. Give me the man who can make a speech without any of the accessories of the pulpit, who can preach what sermon there is in him without a pulpit." His words were energetic, but his voice was just suited to the place. Had he spoken aloud, so that others might have heard him, we should have left our chair, and have retreated to one of the inner and hotter rooms at the moment. His words were perfectly audible, but he spoke in a fitting whisper. "It is a part of my creed," he continued, "that we should never lose even a quarter of an hour. What a strange mass of human beings one finds in this city of London!"

"A mighty maze, but not without a plan," we replied.

"Bedad,—and it's hard enough to find the plan," said he. It struck me that after that he rose into a somewhat higher flight of speech, as though he had remembered and was desirous of dropping his country. It is the customary and perhaps the only fault of an Irishman. "Whether it be there or not, we can expatiate free, as the poet says. How unintelligible is London! New York or Constantinople one can understand,—or even Paris. One knows what the world is doing in these cities, and what men desire."

"What men desire is nearly the same in all cities," we remarked,—and not without truth, as we think.

"Is it money you mane?" he said, again relapsing. "Yes; money, no doubt, is the grand desideratum,—the 'to prepon,' the 'to kalon,' the 'to pan!'" Plato and Pope were evidently at his fingers' ends. We did not conclude from this slight evidence that he was thoroughly imbued with the works either of the poet or the philosopher; but we hold that for the ordinary purposes of conversation a superficial knowledge of many things goes further than an intimacy with one or two. "Money," continued he, "is everything, no doubt; rem,—rem; rem, si possis recte, si non,—; you know the rest. I don't complain of that. I like money myself. I know its value. I've had it, and,—I'm not ashamed to say it, sir,—I've been without it."

"Our sympathies are completely with you in reference to the latter position," we said,—remembering, with a humility which we hope is natural to us, that we were not always editors.

"What I complain of is," said our new friend still whispering, as he passed his hand over his arms and legs, to learn whether the temperature of the room was producing its proper effect, "that if a man here in London have a diamond, or a pair of boots, or any special skill at his command, he cannot take his article to the proper mart, and obtain for it the proper price."

"Can he do that in Constantinople?" we inquired.

"Much better and more accurately than he can in London. And so he can in Paris!" We did not believe this; but as we were thinking after what fashion we would express our doubts, he branched off so quickly to a matter of supply and demand with which we were specially interested, that we lost the opportunity of arguing the general question. "A man of letters," he said, "a capable and an instructed man of letters, can always get a market for his wares in Paris."

"A capable and instructed man of letters will do so in London," we said, "as soon as he has proved his claims. He must prove them in Paris before they can be allowed."

"Yes;—he must prove them. By-the-bye, will you have a cheroot?" So saying, he stretched out his hand, and took from the marble slab beside him two cheroots which he had placed there. He then proceeded to explain that he did not bring in his case because of the heat, but that he was always "muni,"—that was his phrase,—with a couple, in the hope that he might meet an acquaintance with whom to share them. I accepted his offer, and when we had walked round the chamber to a light provided for the purpose, we reseated ourselves. His manner of moving about the place was so good that I felt it to be a pity that he should ever have a rag on more than he wore at present. His tobacco, I must own, did not appear to me to be of the first class; but then I am not in the habit of smoking cheroots, and am no judge of the merits of the weed as grown in the East. "Yes;—a man in Paris must prove his capability; but then how easily he can do it, if the fact to be proved be there! And how certain is the mart, if he have the thing to sell!"

We immediately denied that in this respect there was any difference between the two capitals, pointing out what we believe to be a fact,—that in one capital as in the other, there exists, and must ever exist, extreme difficulty in proving the possession of an art so difficult to define as capability of writing for the press. "Nothing but success can prove it," we said, as we slapped our thigh with an energy altogether unbecoming our position as a Turkish bather.

"A man may have a talent then, and he cannot use it till he have used it! He may possess a diamond, and cannot sell it till he have sold it! What is a man to do who wishes to engage himself in any of the multifarious duties of the English press? How is he to begin? In New York I can tell such a one where to go at once. Let him show in conversation that he is an educated man, and they will give him a trial on the staff of any newspaper;—they will let him run his venture for the pages of any magazine. He may write his fingers off here, and not an editor of them all will read a word that he writes."

Here he touched us, and we were indignant. When he spoke of the magazines we knew that he was wrong. "With newspapers," we said, "we imagine it to be impossible that contributions from the outside world should be looked at; but papers sent to the magazines,—at any rate to some of them,—are read."

"I believe," said he, "that a little farce is kept up. They keep a boy to look at a line or two and then return the manuscript. The pages are filled by the old stock writers, who are sure of the market let them send what they will,—padding-mongers who work eight hours a day, and hardly know what they write about." We again loudly expressed our opinion that he was wrong, and that there did exist magazines, the managers of which were sedulously anxious to obtain the assistance of what he called literary capacity, wherever they could find it. Sitting there at the Turkish bath with nothing but a towel round us, we could not declare ourselves to a perfect stranger, and we think that as a rule editors should be impalpable;—but we did express our opinion very strongly.

"And you believe," said he, with something of scorn in his voice, "that if a man who had been writing English for the press in other countries,—in New York say, or in Doblin,—a man of undoubted capacity, mind you, were to make the attempt here, in London, he would get a hearing."

"Certainly he would," said we.

"And would any editor see him unless he came with an introduction from some special friend?"

We paused a moment before we answered this, because the question was to us one having a very special meaning. Let an editor do his duty with ever so pure a conscience, let him spend all his days and half his nights reading manuscripts and holding the balance fairly between the public and those who wish to feed the public, let his industry be never so unwearied and his impartiality never so unflinching, still he will, if possible, avoid the pain of personally repelling those to whom he is obliged to give an unfavourable answer. But we at the Turkish bath were quite unknown to the outer world, and might hazard an opinion, as any stranger might have done. And we have seen very many such visitors as those to whom our friend alluded; and may, perhaps, see many more.

"Yes," said we. "An editor might or might not see such a gentleman; but, if pressed, no doubt he would. An English editor would be quite as likely to do so as a French editor." This we declared with energy, having felt ourselves to be ruffled by the assertion that these things are managed better in Paris or in New York than in London.

"Then, Mr.——, would you give me an interview, if I call with a little manuscript which I have to-morrow morning?" said my Irish friend, addressing us with a beseeching tone, and calling us by the very name by which we are known among our neighbours and tradesmen. We felt that everything was changed between us, and that the man had plunged a dagger into us.

Yes; he had plunged a dagger into us. Had we had our clothes on, had we felt ourselves to possess at the moment our usual form of life, we think that we could have rebuked him. As it was we could only rise from our chair, throw away the fag end of the filthy cheroot which he had given us, and clap our hands half-a-dozen times for the Asiatic to come and shampoo us. But the Irishman was at our elbow. "You will let me see you tomorrow?" he said. "My name is Molloy,—Michael Molloy. I have not a card about me, because my things are outside there."

"A card would do no good at all," we said, again clapping our hands for the shampooer.

"I may call, then?" said Mr. Michael Molloy.

"Certainly;—yes, you can call if you please." Then, having thus ungraciously acceded to the request made to us, we sat down on the marble bench and submitted ourselves to the black attendant. During the whole of the following operation, while the man was pummelling our breast and poking our ribs, and pinching our toes,—while he was washing us down afterwards, and reducing us gradually from the warm water to the cold,—we were thinking of Mr. Michael Molloy, and the manner in which he had entrapped us into a confidential conversation. The scoundrel must have plotted it from the very first, must have followed us into the bath, and taken his seat beside us with a deliberately premeditated scheme. He was, too, just the man whom we should not have chosen to see with a worthless magazine article in his hand. We think that we can be efficacious by letter, but we often feel ourselves to be weak when brought face to face with our enemies. At that moment our anger was hot against Mr. Molloy. And yet we were conscious of a something of pride which mingled with our feelings. It was clear to us that Mr. Molloy was no ordinary person; and it did in some degree gratify our feelings that such a one should have taken so much trouble to encounter us. We had found him to be a well-informed, pleasant gentleman; and the fact that he was called Molloy and desired to write for the magazine over which we presided, could not really be taken as detracting from his merits. There had doubtless been a fraud committed on us,—a palpable fraud. The man had extracted assurances from us by a false pretence that he did not know us. But then the idea, on his part, that anything could be gained by his doing so, was in itself a compliment to us. That such a man should take so much trouble to approach us,—one who could quote Horace and talk about the "to kalon,"—was an acknowledgment of our power. As we returned to the outer chamber we looked round to see Mr. Molloy in his usual garments, but he was not as yet there. We waited while we smoked one of our own cigars, but he came not. He had, so far, gained his aim; and, as we presumed, preferred to run the risk of too long a course of hot air to risking his object by seeing us again on that afternoon. At last we left the building, and are bound to confess that our mind dwelt much on Mr. Michael Molloy during the remainder of that evening.

It might be that after all we should gain much by the singular mode of introduction which the man had adopted. He was certainly clever, and if he could write as well as he could talk his services might be of value. Punctually at the hour named he was announced, and we did not now for one moment think of declining the interview. Mr. Molloy had so far succeeded in his stratagem that we could not now resort to the certainly not unusual practice of declaring ourselves to be too closely engaged to see any one, and of sending him word that he should confide to writing whatever he might have to say to us. It had, too, occurred to us that, as Mr. Molloy had paid his three shillings and sixpence for the Turkish Bath, he would not prove to be one of that class of visitors whose appeals to tender-hearted editors are so peculiarly painful. "I am willing to work day and night for my wife and children; and if you will use this short paper in your next number it will save us from starvation for a month! Yes, sir, from,—starvation!" Who is to resist such an appeal as that, or to resent it? But the editor knows that he is bound in honesty to resist it altogether,—so to steel himself against it that it shall have no effect upon him, at least, as regards the magazine which is in his hands. And yet if the short thing be only decently written, if it be not absurdly bad, what harm will its publication do to any one? If the waste,—let us call it waste,—of half-a-dozen pages will save a family from hunger for a month, will they not be well wasted? But yet, again, such tenderness is absolutely incompatible with common honesty,—and equally so with common prudence. We think that our readers will see the difficulty, and understand how an editor may wish to avoid those interviews with tattered gloves. But my friend, Mr. Michael Molloy, had had three and sixpence to spend on a Turkish Bath, had had money wherewith to buy,—certainly, the very vilest of cigars. We thought of all this as Mr. Michael Molloy was ushered into our room.

The first thing we saw was the tattered glove; and then we immediately recognised the stout middle-aged gentleman whom we had seen on the other side of Jermyn Street as we entered the bathing establishment. It had never before occurred to us that the two persons were the same,—not though the impression made by the poverty-stricken appearance of the man in the street had remained distinct upon our mind. The features of the gentleman we had hardly even yet seen at all. Nevertheless we had known and distinctly recognised his outward gait and mien, both with and without his clothes. One tattered glove he now wore, and the other he carried in his gloved hand. As we saw this we were aware at once that all our preconception had been wrong, that that too common appeal would be made, and that we must resist it as best we might. There was still a certain jauntiness in his air as he addressed us. "I hope thin," said he as we shook hands with him, "ye'll not take amiss the little ruse by which we caught ye."

"It was a ruse then, Mr. Molloy?"

"Divil a doubt o' that, Mr. Editor."

"But you were coming to the Turkish Bath independently of our visit there?"

"Sorrow a bath I'd 've cum to at all, only I saw you go into the place. I'd just three and ninepence in my pocket, and says I to myself, Mick, me boy, it's a good investment. There was three and sixpence for them savages to rub me down, and threepence for the two cheroots from the little shop round the corner. I wish they'd been better for your sake."

It had been a plant from beginning to end, and the "to kalon" and the half-dozen words from Horace had all been parts of Mr. Molloy's little game! And how well he had played it! The outward trappings of the man as we now saw them were poor and mean, and he was meanlooking too, because of his trappings. But there had been nothing mean about him as he strutted along with a blue-checked towel round his body. How well the fellow had understood it all, and had known his own capacity! "And now that you are here, Mr. Molloy, what can we do for you?" we said with as pleasant a smile as we were able to assume. Of course we knew what was to follow. Out came the roll of paper of which we had already seen the end projecting from his breast pocket, and we were assured that we should find the contents of it exactly the thing for our magazine. There is no longer any diffidence in such matters,—no reticence in preferring claims and singing one's own praises. All that has gone by since competitive examination has become the order of the day. No man, no woman, no girl, no boy, hesitates now to declare his or her own excellence and capability. "It's just a short thing on social manners," said Mr. Molloy, "and if ye'll be so good as to cast ye'r eye over it, I think ye'll find I've hit the nail on the head. 'The Five-o'clock Tay-table' is what I've called it."

"Oh;—'The Five-o'clock Tea-table.'"

"Don't ye like the name?"

"About social manners, is it?"

"Just a rap on the knuckles for some of 'em. Sharp, short, and decisive! I don't doubt but what ye'll like it."

To declare, as though by instinct, that that was not the kind of thing we wanted, was as much a matter of course as it is for a man buying a horse to say that he does not like the brute's legs or that he falls away in his quarters. And Mr. Molloy treated our objection just as does the horse-dealer those of his customers. He assured us with a smile,—with a smile behind which we could see the craving eagerness of his heart,—that his little article was just the thing for us. Our immediate answer was of course ready. If he would leave the paper with us, we would look at it and return it if it did not seem to suit us. There is a half-promise about this reply which too often produces a false satisfaction in the breast of a beginner. With such a one it is the second interview which is to be dreaded. But my friend Mr. Molloy was not new to the work, and was aware that if possible he should make further use of the occasion which he had earned for himself at so considerable a cost. "Ye'll read it;—will ye?" he said.

"Oh, certainly. We'll read it certainly."

"And ye'll use it if ye can?"

"As to that, Mr. Molloy, we can say nothing. We've got to look solely to the interest of the periodical."

"And, sure, what can ye do better for the periodical than print a paper like that, which there is not a lady at the West End of the town won't be certain to read?"

"At any rate we'll look at it, Mr. Molloy," said we, standing up from our chair.

But still he hesitated in his going,—and did not go. "I'm a married man, Mr.—," he said. We simply bowed our head at the announcement. "I wish you could see Mrs. Molloy," he added. We murmured something as to the pleasure it would give us to make the acquaintance of so estimable a lady. "There isn't a better woman than herself this side of heaven, though I say it that oughtn't," said he. "And we've three young ones." We knew the argument that was coming;—knew it so well, and yet were so unable to accept it as any argument! "Sit down one moment, Mr.—," he continued, "till I tell you a short story." We pleaded our engagements, averring that they were peculiarly heavy at that moment. "Sure, and we know what that manes," said Mr. Molloy. "It's just,—walk out of this as quick as you came in. It's that what it manes." And yet as he spoke there was a twinkle of humour in his eye that was almost irresistible; and we ourselves,—we could not forbear to smile. When we smiled we knew that we were lost. "Come, now, Mr. Editor; when you think how much it cost me to get the introduction, you'll listen to me for five minutes any way."

"We will listen to you," we said, resuming our chair,—remembering as we did so the three-and-sixpence, the two cigars, the "to kalon," the line from Pope, and the half line from Horace. The man had taken much trouble with the view of placing himself where he now was. When we had been all but naked together I had taken him to be the superior of the two, and what were we that we should refuse him an interview simply because he had wares to sell which we should only be too willing to buy at his price if they were fit for our use?

Then he told his tale. As for Paris, Constantinople, and New York, he frankly admitted that he knew nothing of those capitals. When we reminded him, with some ill-nature as we thought afterwards, that he had assumed an intimacy with the current literature of the three cities, he told us that such remarks were "just the sparkling gims of conversation in which a man shouldn't expect to find rale diamonds." Of "Doblin" he knew every street, every lane, every newspaper, every editor; but the poverty, dependence, and general poorness of a provincial press had crushed him, and he had boldly resolved to try a fight in the "methropolis of litherature." He referred us to the managers of the "Boyne Bouncer," the "Clontarf Chronicle," the "Donnybrook Debater," and the "Echoes of Erin," assuring us that we should find him to be as well esteemed as known in the offices of those widely-circulated publications. His reading he told us was unbounded, and the pen was as ready to his hand as is the plough to the hand of the husbandman. Did we not think it a noble ambition in him thus to throw himself into the great "areanay," as he called it, and try his fortune in the "methropolis of litherature?" He paused for a reply, and we were driven to acknowledge that whatever might be said of our friend's prudence, his courage was undoubted. "I've got it here," said he. "I've got it all here." And he touched his right breast with the fingers of his left hand, which still wore the tattered glove.

He had succeeded in moving us. "Mr. Molloy," we said, "we'll read your paper, and we'll then do the best we can for you. We must tell you fairly that we hardly like your subject, but if the writing be good you can try your hand at something else."

"Sure there's nothing under the sun I won't write about at your bidding."

"If we can be of service to you, Mr. Molloy, we will." Then the editor broke down, and the man spoke to the man. "I need not tell you, Mr. Molloy, that the heart of one man of letters always warms to another."

"It was because I knew ye was of that sort that I followed ye in yonder," he said, with a tear in his eye.

The butter-boat of benevolence was in our hand, and we proceeded to pour out its contents freely. It is a vessel which an editor should lock up carefully; and, should he lose the key, he will not be the worse for the loss. We need not repeat here all the pretty things that we said to him, explaining to him from a full heart with how much agony we were often compelled to resist the entreaties of literary suppliants, declaring to him how we had longed to publish tons of manuscript,—simply in order that we might give pleasure to those who brought them to us. We told him how accessible we were to a woman's tear, to a man's struggle, to a girl's face, and assured him of the daily wounds which were inflicted on ourselves by the impossibility of reconciling our duties with our sympathies. "Bedad, thin," said Mr. Molloy, grasping our hand, "you'll find none of that difficulty wid me. If you'll sympathise like a man, I'll work for you like a horse." We assured him that we would, really thinking it probable that he might do some useful work for the magazine; and then we again stood up waiting for his departure.

"Now I'll tell ye a plain truth," said he, "and ye may do just as ye plaise about it. There isn't an ounce of tay or a pound of mait along with Mrs. Molloy this moment; and, what's more, there isn't a shilling between us to buy it. I never begged in my life;—not yet. But if you can advance me a sovereign on that manuscript, it will save me from taking the coat on my back to a pawnbroker's shop for whatever it'll fetch there." We paused a moment as we thought of it all, and then we handed him the coin for which he asked us. If the manuscript should be worthless the loss would be our own. We would not grudge a slice from the wholesome home-made loaf after we had used the butter-boat of benevolence. "It don't become me," said Mr. Molloy, "to thank you for such a thrifle as a loan of twenty shillings; but I'll never forget the feeling that has made you listen to me, and that too after I had been rather down on you at thim baths." We gave him a kindly nod of the head, and then he took his departure. "Ye'll see me again anyways?" he said, and we promised that we would.

We were anxious enough about the manuscript, but we could not examine it at that moment. When our office work was done we walked home with the roll in our pocket, speculating as we went on the probable character of Mr. Molloy. We still believed in him,—still believed in him in spite of the manner in which he had descended in his language, and had fallen into a natural flow of words which alone would not have given much promise of him as a man of letters. But a human being, in regard to his power of production, is the reverse of a rope. He is as strong as his strongest part, and remembering the effect which Molloy's words had had upon us at the Turkish Bath, we still thought that there must be something in him. If so, how pleasant would it be to us to place such a man on his legs,—modestly on his legs, so that he might earn for his wife and bairns that meat and tea which he had told us that they were now lacking. An editor is always striving to place some one modestly on his legs in literature,—on his or her,—striving, and alas! so often failing. Here had come a man in regard to whom, as I walked home with his manuscript in my pocket, I did feel rather sanguine.

Of all the rubbish that I ever read in my life, that paper on the Five-o'clock Tea-table was, I think, the worst. It was not only vulgar, foolish, unconnected, and meaningless; but it was also ungrammatical and unintelligible even in regard to the wording of it. The very spelling was defective. The paper was one with which no editor, sub-editor, or reader would have found it necessary to go beyond the first ten lines before he would have known that to print it would have been quite out of the question. We went through with it because of our interest in the man; but as it was in the beginning, so it was to the end,—a farrago of wretched nonsense, so bad that no one, without experience in such matters, would believe it possible that even the writer should desire the publication of it! It seemed to us to be impossible that Mr. Molloy should ever have written a word for those Hibernian periodicals which he had named to us. He had got our sovereign; and with that, as far as we were concerned, there must be an end of Mr. Molloy. We doubted even whether he would come for his own manuscript.

But he came. He came exactly at the hour appointed, and when we looked at his face we felt convinced that he did not doubt his own success. There was an air of expectant triumph about him which dismayed us. It was clear enough that he was confident that he should take away with him the full price of his article, after deducting the sovereign which he had borrowed. "You like it thin," he said, before we had been able to compose our features to a proper form for the necessary announcement.

"Mr. Molloy," we said, "it will not do. You must believe us that it will not do."

"Not do?"

"No, indeed. We need not explain further;—but,—but,—you had really better turn your hand to some other occupation."

"Some other occupa-ation!" he exclaimed, opening wide his eyes, and holding up both his hands.

"Indeed we think so, Mr. Molloy."

"And you've read it?"

"Every word of it;—on our honour."

"And you won't have it?"

"Well;—no, Mr. Molloy, certainly we cannot take it."

"Ye reject my article on the Five-o'clock Tay-table!" Looking into his face as he spoke, we could not but be certain that its rejection was to him as astonishing as would have been its acceptance to the readers of the magazine. He put his hand up to his head and stood wondering. "I suppose ye'd better choose your own subject for yourself," he said, as though by this great surrender on his own part he was getting rid of all the difficulty on ours.

"Mr. Molloy," we began, "we may as well be candid with you— "

"I'll tell you what it is," said he, "I've taken such a liking to you there's nothing I won't do to plaise ye. I'll just put it in my pocket, and begin another for ye as soon as the children have had their bit of dinner." At last we did succeed, or thought that we succeeded, in making him understand that we regarded the case as being altogether hopeless, and were convinced that it was beyond his powers to serve us. "And I'm to be turned off like that," he said, bursting into open tears as he threw himself into a chair and hid his face upon the table. "Ah! wirra, wirra, what'll I do at all? Sure, and didn't I think it was fixed as firm between us as the Nelson monument? When ye handselled me with the money, didn't I think it was as good as done and done?" I begged him not to regard the money, assuring him that he was welcome to the sovereign. "There's my wife'll be brought to bed any day," he went on to say, "and not a ha'porth of anything ready for it! 'Deed, thin, and the world's hard. The world's very hard!" And this was he who had talked to me about Constantinople and New York at the Baths, and had made me believe that he was a well-informed, well-to-do man of the world!

Even now we did not suspect that he was lying to us. Why he should be such as he seemed to be was a mystery; but even yet we believed in him after a fashion. That he was sorely disappointed and broken-hearted because of his wife, was so evident to us, that we offered him another sovereign, regarding it as the proper price of that butter-boat of benevolence which we had permitted ourselves to use. But he repudiated our offer. "I've never begged," said he, "and, for myself, I'd sooner starve. And Mary Jane would sooner starve than I should beg. It will be best for us both to put an end to ourselves and to have done with it." This was very melancholy; and as he lay with his head upon the table, we did not see how we were to induce him to leave us.

"You'd better take the sovereign,—just for the present," we said.

"Niver!" said he, looking up for a moment, "niver!" And still he continued to sob. About this period of the interview, which before it was ended was a very long interview, we ourselves made a suggestion the imprudence of which we afterwards acknowledged to ourselves. We offered to go to his lodgings and see his wife and children. Though the man could not write a good magazine article, yet he might be a very fitting object for our own personal kindness. And the more we saw of the man, the more we liked him,—in spite of his incapacity. "The place is so poor," he said, objecting to our offer. After what had passed between us, we felt that that could be no reason against our visit, and we began for a moment to fear that he was deceiving us. "Not yet," he cried, "not quite yet. I will try once again;—once again. You will let me see you once more?"

"And you will take the other sovereign," we said,—trying him. He should have had the other sovereign if he would have taken it; but we confess that had he done so then we should have regarded him as an impostor. But he did not take it, and left us in utter ignorance as to his true character.

After an interval of three days he came again, and there was exactly the same appearance. He wore the same tattered gloves. He had not pawned his coat. There was the same hat,—shabby when observed closely, but still carrying a decent appearance when not minutely examined. In his face there was no sign of want, and at moments there was cheeriness about him which was almost refreshing. "I've got a something this time that I think ye must like,—unless you're harder to plaise than Rhadhamanthus." So saying, he tendered me another roll of paper, which I at once opened, intending to read the first page of it. The essay was entitled the "Church of England;—a Question for the People." It was handed to me as having been written within the last three days; and, from its bulk, might have afforded fair work for a fortnight to a writer accustomed to treat of subjects of such weight. As we had expected, the first page was unintelligible, absurd, and farcical. We began to be angry with ourselves for having placed ourselves in such a connection with a man so utterly unable to do that which he pretended to do. "I think I've hit it off now," said he, watching our face as we were reading.

The reader need not be troubled with a minute narrative of the circumstances as they occurred during the remainder of the interview. What had happened before was repeated very closely. He wondered, he remonstrated, he complained, and he wept. He talked of his wife and family, and talked as though up to this last moment he had felt confident of success. Judging from his face as he entered the room, we did not doubt but that he had been confident. His subsequent despair was unbounded, and we then renewed our offer to call on his wife. After some hesitation he gave us an address in Hoxton, begging us to come after seven in the evening if it were possible. He again declined the offer of money, and left us, understanding that we would visit his wife on the following evening. "You are quite sure about the manuscript?" he said as he left us. We replied that we were quite sure.

On the following day we dined early at our club and walked in the evening to the address which Mr. Molloy had given us in Hoxton. It was a fine evening in August, and our walk made us very warm. The street named was a decent little street, decent as far as cleanliness and newness could make it; but there was a melancholy sameness about it, and an apparent absence of object which would have been very depressing to our own spirits. It led no whither, and had been erected solely with the view of accommodating decent people with small incomes. We at once priced the houses in our mind at ten and sixpence a week, and believed them to be inhabited by pianoforte-tuners, coach-builders, firemen, and public-office messengers. There was no squalor about the place, but it was melancholy, light-coloured, and depressive. We made our way to No. 14, and finding the door open entered the passage. "Come in," cried the voice of our friend; and in the little front parlour we found him seated with a child on each knee, while a winning little girl of about twelve was sitting in a corner of the room, mending her stockings. The room itself and the appearance of all around us were the very opposite of what we had expected. Everything no doubt was plain,—was, in a certain sense, poor; but nothing was poverty-stricken. The children were decently clothed, and apparently were well fed. Mr. Molloy himself, when he saw me, had that twinkle of humour in his eye which I had before observed, and seemed to be afflicted at the moment with none of that extreme agony which he had exhibited more than once in our presence. "Please, sir, mother ain't in from the hospital,—not yet," said the little girl, rising up from her chair; "but it's past seven and she won't be long." This announcement created some surprise. We had indeed heard that of Mrs. Molloy which might make it very expedient that she should seek the accommodation of an hospital, but we could not understand that in such circumstances she should be able to come home regularly at seven o'clock in the evening. Then there was a twinkle in our friend Molloy's eye which almost made us think for the moment that we had been made the subject of some, hitherto unintelligible, hoax. And yet there had been the man at the Baths in Jermyn Street, and the two manuscripts had been in our hands, and the man had wept as no man weeps for a joke. "You would come, you know," said Mr. Molloy, who had now put down the two bairns and had risen from his seat to greet us.

"We are glad to see you so comfortable," we replied.

"Father is quite comfortable, sir," said the little girl. We looked into Mr. Molloy's face and saw nothing but the twinkle in the eye. We had certainly been "done" by the most elaborate hoax that had ever been perpetrated. We did not regret the sovereign so much as those outpourings from the butter-boat of benevolence of which we felt that we had been cheated. "Here's mother," said the girl, running to the door. Mr. Molloy stood grinning in the middle of the room with the youngest child again in his arms. He did not seem to be in the least ashamed of what he had done, and even at that moment conveyed to us more of liking for his affection for the little boy than of anger for the abominable prank that he had played us.

That he had lied throughout was evident as soon as we saw Mrs. Molloy. Whatever ailment might have made it necessary that she should visit the hospital, it was not one which could interfere at all with her power of going and returning. She was a strong hearty-looking woman of about forty, with that mixture in her face of practical kindness with severity in details which we often see in strong-minded women who are forced to take upon themselves the management and government of those around them. She curtseyed, and took off her bonnet and shawl, and put a bottle into a cupboard, as she addressed us. "Mick said as you was coming, sir, and I'm sure we is glad to see you;—only sorry for the trouble, sir."

We were so completely in the dark that we hardly knew how to be civil to her,—hardly knew whether we ought to be civil to her or not. "We don't quite understand why we've been brought here," we said, endeavouring to maintain, at any rate, a tone of good-humour. He was still embracing the little boy, but there had now come a gleam of fun across his whole countenance, and he seemed to be almost shaking his sides with laughter. "Your husband represented himself as being in distress," we said gravely. We were restrained by a certain delicacy from informing the woman of the kind of distress to which Mr. Molloy had especially alluded,—most falsely.

"Lord love you, sir," said the woman, "just step in here." Then she led us into a little back-room in which there was a bedstead, and an old writing-desk or escritoire, covered with papers. Her story was soon told. Her husband was a madman.

"Mad!" we said, preparing for escape from what might be to us most serious peril.

"He wouldn't hurt a mouse," said Mrs. Molloy. "As for the children, he's that good to them, there ain't a young woman in all London that'd be better at handling 'em." Then we heard her story, in which it appeared to us that downright affection for the man was the predominant characteristic. She herself was, as she told us, head day nurse at Saint Patrick's Hospital, going there every morning at eight, and remaining till six or seven. For these services she received thirty shillings a week and her board, and she spoke of herself and her husband as being altogether removed from pecuniary distress. Indeed, while the money part of the question was being discussed, she opened a little drawer in the desk and handed us back our sovereign,—almost without an observation. Molloy himself had "come of decent people." On this point she insisted very often, and gave us to understand that he was at this moment in receipt of a pension of a hundred a year from his family. He had been well educated, she said, having been at Trinity College, Dublin, till he had been forced to leave his university for some slight, but repeated irregularity. Early in life he had proclaimed his passion for the press, and when he and she were married absolutely was earning a living in Dublin by some use of the scissors and paste-pot. The whole tenor of his career I could not learn, though Mrs. Molloy would have told us everything had time allowed. Even during the years of his sanity in Dublin he had only been half-sane, treating all the world around him with the effusions of his terribly fertile pen. "He'll write all night if I'll let him have a candle," said Mrs. Molloy. We asked her why she did let him have a candle, and made some inquiry as to the family expenditure in paper. The paper, she said, was given to him from the office of a newspaper which she would not name, and which Molloy visited regularly every day. "There ain't a man in all London works harder," said Mrs. Molloy. "He is mad. I don't say nothing against it. But there is some of it so beautiful, I wonder they don't print it." This was the only word she spoke with which we could not agree. "Ah, sir," said she; "you haven't seen his poetry!" We were obliged to tell her that seeing poetry was the bane of our existence.

There was an easy absence of sham about this woman, and an acceptance of life as it had come to her, which delighted us. She complained of nothing, and was only anxious to explain the little eccentricities of her husband. When we alluded to some of his marvellously untrue assertions, she stopped us at once. "He do lie," she said. "Certainly he do. How he makes 'em all out is wonderful. But he wouldn't hurt a fly." It was evident to us that she not only loved her husband, but admired him. She showed us heaps of manuscript with which the old drawers were crammed; and yet that paper on the Church of England had been new work, done expressly for us.

When the story had been told we went back to him, and he received us with a smile. "Good-bye, Molloy," we said. "Good-bye to you, sir," he replied, shaking hands with us. We looked at him closely, and could hardly believe that it was the man who had sat by us at the Turkish Bath.

He never troubled us again or came to our office, but we have often called on him, and have found that others of our class do the same. We have even helped to supply him with the paper which he continues to use,—we presume for the benefit of other editors.

Mary Gresley

Originally appeared in *Saint Paul's Magazine*, November 1869. Reprinted in *An Editor's Tales* (1870). In *An Autobiography* Trollope confirms that this story of 'how I was appealed to by the dearest of little women whom here I have called Mary Gresley' was closely based on fact. Incidentally, Mary Gresley was the name of Trollope's maternal grandmother.

We have known many prettier girls than Mary Gresley, and many handsomer women,—but we never knew girl or woman gifted with a face which in supplication was more suasive, in grief more sad, in mirth more merry. It was a face that compelled sympathy, and it did so with the conviction on the mind of the sympathiser that the girl was altogether unconscious of her own power. In her intercourse with us there was, alas! much more of sorrow than of mirth, and we may truly say that in her sufferings we suffered; but still there came to us from our intercourse with her much of delight mingled with the sorrow; and that delight arose, partly no doubt from her woman's charms, from the bright eye, the beseeching mouth, the soft little hand, and the feminine grace of her unpretending garments; but chiefly, we think, from the extreme humanity of the girl. She had little, indeed none, of that which the world calls society, but yet she was pre-eminently social. Her troubles were very heavy, but she was making ever an unconscious effort to throw them aside, and to be jocund in spite of their weight. She would even laugh at them, and at herself as bearing them. She was a little fair-haired creature, with broad brow and small nose and dimpled chin, with no brightness of complexion, no luxuriance of hair, no swelling glory of bust and shoulders; but with a pair of eyes which, as they looked at you, would be gemmed always either with a tear or with some spark of laughter, and with a mouth in the corners of which was ever lurking some little spark of humour, unless when some unspoken prayer seemed to be hanging on her lips. Of woman's vanity she had absolutely none. Of her corporeal self, as having charms to rivet man's love, she thought no more than does a dog. It was a fault with her that she lacked that quality of womanhood. To be loved was to her all the world; unconscious desire for the admiration of men was as strong in her as in other women; and her instinct taught her, as such instincts do teach all women, that such love and admiration was to be the fruit of what feminine gifts she possessed; but the gifts on which she depended,—depending on them without thinking on the matter,—were her softness, her trust, her woman's weakness, and that power of supplicating by her eye without putting her petition into words which was absolutely irresistible. Where is the man of fifty, who in the course of his life has not learned to love some woman simply because it has come in his way to help her, and to be good to her in her struggles? And if added to that source of affection there be brightness, some spark of humour, social gifts, and a strong flavour of that which we have ventured to call humanity, such love may become almost a passion without the addition of much real beauty.

But in thus talking of love we must guard ourselves somewhat from miscomprehension. In love with Mary Gresley, after the common sense of the word, we never were, nor would it have become us to be so. Had such a state of being unfortunately befallen us, we certainly should be silent on the subject. We were married and old; she was very young, and engaged to be married, always talking to us of her engagement as a thing fixed as the stars. She looked upon us, no doubt,—after she had ceased to regard us simply in our editorial capacity,—as a subsidiary old uncle whom Providence had supplied to her, in order that if it were possible, the troubles of her life might be somewhat eased by assistance to her from that special quarter. We regarded her first almost as a child, and then as a young woman to whom we owed that sort of protecting care which a greybeard should ever be ready to give to the weakness of feminine adolescence. Nevertheless we were in love with her, and we think such a state of love to be a wholesome and natural condition. We might, indeed, have loved her grandmother,—but the love would have been very different. Had circumstances brought us into connection with her grandmother, we hope we should have done our duty, and had that old lady been our friend we should, we trust, have done it with alacrity. But in our intercourse with Mary Gresley there was more than that. She charmed us. We learned to love the hue of that dark grey stuff frock which she seemed always to wear. When she would sit in the low arm-chair opposite to us, looking up into our eyes as we spoke to her words which must often have stabbed her little heart, we were wont to caress her with that inward undemonstrative embrace that one spirit is able to confer upon another. We thought of her constantly, perplexing our mind for her succour. We forgave all her faults. We exaggerated her virtues. We exerted ourselves for her with a zeal that was perhaps fatuous. Though we attempted sometimes to look black at her, telling her that our time was too precious to be wasted in conversation with her, she soon learned to know how welcome she was to us. Her glove,—which, by-the-bye, was never tattered, though she was very poor,—was an object of regard to us. Her grandmother's gloves would have been as unacceptable to us as any other morsel of old kid or cotton. Our heart bled for her. Now the heart may suffer much for the sorrows of a male friend, but it may hardly for such be said to bleed. We loved her, in short, as we should not have loved her, but that she was young and gentle, and could smile,—and, above all, but that she looked at us with those, bright, beseeching, tear-laden eyes.

Sterne, in his latter days, when very near his end, wrote passionate love-letters to various women, and has been called hard names by Thackeray,—not for writing them, but because he thus showed himself to be incapable of that sincerity which should have bound him to one love. We do not ourselves much admire the sentimentalism of Sterne, finding the expression of it to be mawkish, and thinking that too often he misses the pathos for which he strives from a want of appreciation on his own part of that which is really vigorous in language and touching in sentiment. But we think that Thackeray has been somewhat wrong in throwing that blame on Sterne's heart which should have been attributed to his taste. The love which he declared when he was old and sick and dying,—a worn-out wreck of a man,—disgusts us, not because it was felt, or not felt, but because it was told;—and told as though the teller meant to offer more than that warmth of sympathy which woman's strength and woman's weakness combined will ever produce in the hearts of certain men. This is a sympathy with which neither age, nor crutches, nor matrimony, nor position of any sort need consider itself to be incompatible. It is unreasoning, and perhaps irrational. It gives to outward form and grace that which only inward merit can deserve. It is very dangerous because, unless watched, it leads to words which express that which is not intended. But, though it may be controlled, it cannot be killed. He, who is of his nature open to such impression, will feel it while breath remains to him. It was that which destroyed the character and happiness of Swift, and which made Sterne contemptible. We do not doubt that such unreasoning sympathy, exacted by feminine attraction, was always strong in Johnson's heart;—but Johnson was strong all over, and could guard himself equally from misconduct and from ridicule. Such sympathy with women, such incapability of withstanding the feminine magnet was very strong with Goethe,—who could guard himself from ridicule, but not from misconduct. To us the child of whom we are speaking,—for she was so then,—was ever a child. But she bore in her hand the power of that magnet, and we admit that the needle within our bosom was swayed by it. Her story,—such as we have to tell it,—was as follows.

Mary Gresley, at the time when we first knew her, was eighteen years old, and was the daughter of a medical practitioner, who had lived and died in a small town in one of the northern counties. For facility in telling our story we will call that town Cornboro. Dr. Gresley, as he seemed to have been called though without proper claim to the title, had been a diligent man, and fairly successful,—except in this, that he died before he had been able to provide for those whom he left behind him. The widow still had her own modest fortune, amounting to some eighty pounds a year; and that, with the furniture of her house, was her whole wealth, when she found herself thus left with the weight of the world upon her shoulders. There was one other daughter older than Mary, whom we never saw, but who was always mentioned as poor Fanny. There had been no sons, and the family consisted of the mother and the two girls. Mary had been only fifteen when her father died, and up to that time had been regarded quite as a child by all who had known her. Mrs. Gresley, in the hour of her need, did as widows do in such cases. She sought advice from her clergyman and neighbours, and was counselled to take a lodger into her house. No lodger could be found so fitting as the curate, and when Mary was seventeen years old, she and the curate were engaged to be married. The curate paid thirty pounds a year for his lodgings, and on this, with their own little income, the widow and her two daughters had managed to live. The engagement was known to them all as soon as it had been known to Mary. The love-making, indeed, had gone on beneath the eyes of the mother. There had been not only no deceit, no privacy, no separate interests, but, as far as we ever knew, no question as to prudence in the making of the engagement. The two young people had been brought together, had loved each other, as was so natural, and had become engaged as a matter of course. It was an event as easy to be foretold, or at least as easy to be believed, as the pairing of two birds. From what we heard of this curate, the Rev. Arthur Donne,—for we never saw him,—we fancy that he was a simple, pious, commonplace young man, imbued with a strong idea that in being made a priest he had been invested with a nobility and with some special capacity beyond that of other men, slight in body, weak in health, but honest, true, and warm-hearted. Then, the engagement having been completed, there arose the question of matrimony. The salary of the curate was a hundred a year. The whole income of the vicar, an old man, was, after payment made to his curate, two hundred a year. Could the curate, in such circumstances, afford to take to himself a penniless wife of seventeen? Mrs. Gresley was willing that the marriage should take place, and that they should all do as best they might on their joint income. The vicar's wife, who seems to have been a strong-minded, sage, though somewhat hard woman, took Mary aside, and told her that such a thing must not be. There would come, she said, children, and destitution, and ruin. She knew perhaps more than Mary knew when Mary told us her story, sitting opposite to us in the low arm-chair. It was the advice of the vicar's wife that the engagement should be broken off; but that, if the breaking-off of the engagement were impossible, there should be an indefinite period of waiting. Such engagements cannot be broken off. Young hearts will not consent to be thus torn asunder. The vicar's wife was too strong for them to get themselves married in her teeth, and the period of indefinite waiting was commenced.

And now for a moment we will go further back among Mary's youthful days. Child as she seemed to be, she had in very early years taken a pen in her hand. The reader need hardly be told that had not such been the case there would not have arisen any cause for friendship between her and us. We are telling an Editor's tale, and it was in our editorial capacity that Mary first came to us. Well;—in her earliest attempts, in her very young days, she wrote,—heaven knows what; poetry first, no doubt; then, God help her, a tragedy; after that, when the curate-influence first commenced, tales for the conversion of the ungodly;—and at last, before her engagement was a fact, having tried her wing at fiction, in the form of those false little dialogues between Tom the Saint and Bob the Sinner, she had completed a novel in one volume. She was then seventeen, was engaged to be married, and had completed her novel! Passing her in the street you would almost have taken her for a child to whom you might give an orange.

Hitherto her work had come from ambition,—or from a feeling of restless piety inspired by the curate. Now there arose in her young mind the question whether such talent as she possessed might not be turned to account for ways and means, and used to shorten, perhaps absolutely to annihilate, that uncertain period of waiting. The first novel was seen by "a man of letters" in her neighbourhood, who pronounced it to be very clever;—not indeed fit as yet for publication, faulty in grammar, faulty even in spelling,—how I loved the tear that shone in her eye as she confessed this delinquency!—faulty of course in construction, and faulty in character;—but still clever. The man of letters had told her that she must begin again.

Unfortunate man of letters in having thrust upon him so terrible a task! In such circumstances what is the candid, honest, soft-hearted man of letters to do? "Go, girl, and mend your stockings. Learn to make a pie. If you work hard, it may be that some day your intellect will suffice to you to read a book and understand it. For the writing of a book that shall either interest or instruct a brother human being many gifts are required. Have you just reason to believe that they have been given to you?" That is what the candid, honest man of letters says who is not soft-hearted;—and in ninety-nine cases out of a hundred it will probably be the truth. The soft hearted man of letters remembers that this special case submitted to him may be the hundredth; and, unless the blotted manuscript is conclusive against such possibility, he reconciles it to his conscience to tune his counsel to that hope. Who can say that he is wrong? Unless such evidence be conclusive, who can venture to declare that this aspirant may not be the one who shall succeed? Who in such emergency does not remember the day in which he also was one of the hundred of whom the ninety-and-nine must fail;—and will not remember also the many convictions on his own mind that he certainly would not be the one appointed? The man of letters in the neighbourhood of Cornboro to whom poor Mary's manuscript was shown was not sufficiently hard-hearted to make any strong attempt to deter her. He made no reference to the easy stockings, or the wholesome pie,—pointed out the manifest faults which he saw, and added, we do not doubt with much more energy than he threw into his words of censure,—his comfortable assurance that there was great promise in the work. Mary Gresley that evening burned the manuscript, and began another, with the dictionary close at her elbow.

Then, during her work, there occurred two circumstances which brought upon her,—and, indeed, upon the household to which she belonged,—intense sorrow and greatly-increased trouble. The first of these applied more especially to herself. The Rev. Arthur Donne did not approve of novels,—of other novels than those dialogues between Tom and Bob, of the falsehood of which he was unconscious,—and expressed a desire that the writing of them should be abandoned. How far the lover went in his attempt to enforce obedience we, of course, could not know; but he pronounced the edict, and the edict, though not obeyed, created tribulation. Then there came forth another edict which had to be obeyed,—an edict from the probable successor of the late Dr. Gresley,—ordering the poor curate to seek employment in some clime more congenial to his state of health than that in which he was then living. He was told that his throat and lungs and general apparatus for living and preaching were not strong enough for those hyperborean regions, and that he must seek a southern climate. He did do so, and, before I became acquainted with Mary, had transferred his services to a small town in Dorsetshire. The engagement, of course, was to be as valid as ever, though matrimony must be postponed, more indefinitely even than heretofore. But if Mary could write novels and sell them, then how glorious would it be to follow her lover into Dorsetshire! The Rev. Arthur Donne went, and the curate who came in his place was a married man, wanting a house, and not lodgings. So Mary Gresley persevered with her second novel, and completed it before she was eighteen.

The literary friend in the neighbourhood,—to the chance of whose acquaintance I was indebted for my subsequent friendship with Mary Gresley,—found this work to be a great improvement on the first. He was an elderly man who had been engaged nearly all his life in the conduct of a scientific and agricultural periodical, and was the last man whom I should have taken as a sound critic on works of fiction;—but with spelling, grammatical construction, and the composition of sentences he was acquainted; and he assured Mary that her progress had been great. Should she burn that second story? she asked him. She would if he so recommended, and begin another the next day. Such was not his advice. "I have a friend in London," said he, "who has to do with such things, and you shall go to him. I will give you a letter." He gave her the fatal letter, and she came to us.

She came up to town with her novel; but not only with her novel, for she brought her mother with her. So great was her eloquence, so excellent her suasive power either with her tongue or by that look of supplication in her face, that she induced her mother to abandon her home in Cornboro, and trust herself to London lodgings. The house was let furnished to the new curate, and when I first heard of the Gresleys they were living on the second floor in a small street near to the Euston Square station. Poor Fanny, as she was called, was left in some humble home at Cornboro, and Mary travelled up to try her fortune in the great city. When we came to know her well we expressed our doubts as to the wisdom of such a step. Yes; the vicar's wife had been strong against the move. Mary confessed as much. That lady had spoken most forcible words, had uttered terrible predictions, had told sundry truths. But Mary had prevailed, and the journey was made, and the lodgings were taken.

We can now come to the day on which we first saw her. She did not write, but came direct to us with her manuscript in her hand. "A young woman, sir, wants to see you," said the clerk, in that tone to which we were so well accustomed, and which indicated the dislike which he had learned from us to the reception of unknown visitors.

"Young woman! What young woman?"

"Well, sir; she is a very young woman;—quite a girl like."

"I suppose she has got a name. Who sent her? I cannot see any young woman without knowing why. What does she want?"

"Got a manuscript in her hand, sir."

"I've no doubt she has, and a ton of manuscripts in drawers and cupboards. Tell her to write. I won't see any woman, young or old, without knowing who she is." The man retired, and soon returned with an envelope belonging to the office, on which was written, "Miss Mary Gresley, late of Cornboro." He also brought me a note from "the man of letters" down in Yorkshire. "Of what sort is she?" I asked, looking at the introduction.

"She ain't amiss as to looks," said the clerk; "and she's modest-like." Now certainly it is the fact that all female literary aspirants are not "modest-like." We read our friend's letter through, while poor Mary was standing at the counter below. How eagerly should we have run to greet her, to save her from the gaze of the public, to welcome her at least with a chair and the warmth of our editorial fire, had we guessed then what were her qualities! It was not long before she knew the way up to our sanctum without any clerk to show her, and not long before we knew well the sound of that low but not timid knock at our door made always with the handle of the parasol, with which her advent was heralded. We will confess that there was always music to our ears in that light tap from the little round wooden knob. The man of letters in Yorkshire, whom we had known well for many years, had been never known to us with intimacy. We had bought with him and sold with him, had talked with him, and, perhaps, walked with him; but he was not one with whom we had eaten, or drunk, or prayed. A dull, well-instructed, honest man he was, fond of his money, and, as we had thought, as unlikely as any man to be waked to enthusiasm by the ambitious dreams of a young girl. But Mary had been potent even over him, and he had written to me, saying that Miss Gresley was a young lady of exceeding promise, in respect of whom he had a strong presentiment that she would rise, if not to eminence, at least to a good position as a writer. "But she is very young," he added. Having read this letter, we at last desired our clerk to send the lady up.

We remember her step as she came to the door, timid enough then,—hesitating, but yet with an assumed lightness as though she was determined to show us that she was not ashamed of what she was doing. She had on her head a light straw hat, such as then was very unusual in London,—and is not now, we believe, commonly worn in the streets of the metropolis by ladies who believe themselves to know what they are about. But it was a hat, worn upon her head, and not a straw plate done up with ribbons, and reaching down the incline of the forehead as far as the top of the nose. And she was dressed in a grey stuff frock, with a little black band round her waist. As far as our memory goes, we never saw her in any other dress, or with other hat or bonnet on her head. "And what can we do for you,—Miss Gresley?" we said, standing up and holding the literary gentleman's letter in our hand. We had almost said, "my dear," seeing her youth and remembering our own age. We were afterwards glad that we had not so addressed her; though it came before long that we did call her "my dear,"—in quite another spirit.

She recoiled a little from the tone of our voice, but recovered herself at once. "Mr.——thinks that you can do something for me. I have written a novel, and I have brought it to you."

"You are very young, are you not, to have written a novel?"

"I am young," she said, "but perhaps older than you think. I am eighteen." Then for the first time there came into her eye that gleam of a merry humour which never was allowed to dwell there long, but which was so alluring when it showed itself.

"That is a ripe age," we said laughing, and then we bade her seat herself. At once we began to pour forth that long and dull and ugly lesson which is so common to our life, in which we tried to explain to our unwilling pupil that of all respectable professions for young women literature is the most uncertain, the most heart-breaking, and the most dangerous. "You hear of the few who are remunerated," we said; "but you hear nothing of the thousands that fail."

"It is so noble!" she replied.

"But so hopeless."

"There are those who succeed."

"Yes, indeed. Even in a lottery one must gain the prize; but they who trust to lotteries break their hearts."

"But literature is not a lottery. If I am fit, I shall succeed. Mr.——thinks I may succeed." Many more words of wisdom we spoke to her, and well do we remember her reply when we had run all our line off the reel, and had completed our sermon. "I shall go on all the same," she said. "I shall try, and try again,—and again."

Her power over us, to a certain extent, was soon established. Of course we promised to read the MS., and turned it over, no doubt with an anxious countenance, to see of what kind was the writing. There is a feminine scrawl of a nature so terrible that the task of reading it becomes worse than the treadmill. "I know I can write well,—though I am not quite sure about the spelling," said Mary, as she observed the glance of our eyes. She spoke truly. The writing was good, though the erasures and alterations were very numerous. And then the story was intended to fill only one volume. "I will copy it for you if you wish it," said Mary. "Though there are so many scratchings out, it has been copied once." We would not for worlds have given her such labour, and then we promised to read the tale. We forget how it was brought about, but she told us at that interview that her mother had obtained leave from the pastrycook round the corner to sit there waiting till Mary should rejoin her. "I thought it would be trouble enough for you to have one of us here," she said with her little laugh when I asked her why she had not brought her mother on with her. I own that I felt that she had been wise; and when I told her that if she would call on me again that day week I would then have read at any rate so much of her work as would enable me to give her my opinion, I did not invite her to bring her mother with her. I knew that I could talk more freely to the girl without the mother's presence. Even when you are past fifty, and intend only to preach a sermon, you do not wish to have a mother present.

When she was gone we took up the roll of paper and examined it. We looked at the division into chapters, at the various mottoes the poor child had chosen, pronounced to ourselves the name of the story,—it was simply the name of the heroine, an easy-going, unaffected, well-chosen name,—and read the last page of it. On such occasions the reader of the work begins his task almost with a conviction that the labour which he is about to undertake will be utterly thrown away. He feel all but sure that the matter will be bad, that it will be better for all parties, writer, intended readers, and intended publisher, that the written words should not be conveyed into type,—that it will be his duty after some fashion to convey that unwelcome opinion to the writer, and that the writer will go away incredulous, and accusing mentally the Mentor of the moment of all manner of literary sins, among which ignorance, jealousy, and falsehood, will, in the poor author's imagination, be most prominent. And yet when the writer was asking for that opinion, declaring his especial desire that the opinion should be candid, protesting that his present wish is to have some gauge of his own capability, and that he has come to you believing you to be above others able to give him that gauge,—while his petition to you was being made, he was in every respect sincere. He had come desirous to measure himself, and had believed that you could measure him. When coming he did not think that you would declare him to be an Apollo. He had told himself, no doubt, how probable it was that you would point out to him that he was a dwarf. You find him to be an ordinary man, measuring perhaps five feet seven, and unable to reach the standard of the particular regiment in which he is ambitious of serving. You tell him so in what civillest words you know, and you are at once convicted in his mind of jealousy, ignorance, and falsehood! And yet he is perhaps a most excellent fellow, and capable of performing the best of service,—only in some other regiment! As we looked at Miss Gresley's manuscript, tumbling it through our hands, we expected even from her some such result. She had gained two things from us already by her outward and inward gifts, such as they were,—first that we would read her story, and secondly that we would read it quickly; but she had not as yet gained from us any belief that by reading it we could serve it.

We did read it,—the most of it before we left our editorial chair on that afternoon, so that we lost altogether the daily walk so essential to our editorial health, and were put to the expense of a cab on our return home. And we incurred some minimum of domestic discomfort from the fact that we did not reach our own door till twenty minutes after our appointed dinner hour. "I have this moment come from the office as hard as a cab could bring me," we said in answer to the mildest of reproaches, explaining nothing as to the nature of the cause which had kept us so long at our work.

We must not allow our readers to suppose that the intensity of our application had arisen from the overwhelming interest of the story. It was not that the story entranced us, but that our feeling for the writer grew as we read the story. It was simple, unaffected, and almost painfully unsensational. It contained, as I came to perceive afterwards, little more than a recital of what her imagination told her might too probably be the result of her own engagement. It was the story of two young people who became engaged and could not be married. After a course of years the man, with many true arguments, asked to be absolved. The woman yields with an expressed conviction that her lover is right, settles herself down for maiden life, then breaks her heart and dies. The character of the man was utterly untrue to nature. That of the woman was true, but commonplace. Other interest, or other character there was none. The dialogues between the lovers were many and tedious, and hardly a word was spoken between them which two lovers really would have uttered. It was clearly not a work as to which I could tell my little friend that she might depend upon it for fame or fortune. When I had finished it I was obliged to tell myself that I could not advise her even to publish it. But yet I could not say that she had mistaken her own powers or applied herself to a profession beyond her reach. There were a grace and delicacy in her work which were charming. Occasionally she escaped from the trammels of grammar, but only so far that it would be a pleasure to point out to her her errors. There was not a word that a young lady should not have written; and there were throughout the whole evident signs of honest work. We had six days to think it over between our completion of the task and her second visit.

She came exactly at the hour appointed, and seated herself at once in the arm-chair before us as soon as the young man had closed the door behind him. There had been no great occasion for nervousness at her first visit, and she had then, by an evident effort, overcome the diffidence incidental to a meeting with a stranger. But now she did not attempt to conceal her anxiety. "Well," she said, leaning forward, and looking up into our face, with her two hands folded together.

Even though Truth, standing full panoplied at our elbow, had positively demanded it, we could not have told her then to mend her stockings and bake her pies and desert the calling that she had chosen. She was simply irresistible, and would, we fear, have constrained us into falsehood had the question been between falsehood and absolute reprobation of her work. To have spoken hard, heart-breaking words to her, would have been like striking a child when it comes to kiss you. We fear that we were not absolutely true at first, and that by that absence of truth we made subsequent pain more painful. "Well," she said, looking up into our face. "Have you read it?" We told her that we had read every word of it. "And it is no good?"

We fear that we began by telling her that it certainly was good,—after a fashion, very good,—considering her youth and necessary inexperience, very good indeed. As we said this she shook her head, and sent out a spark or two from her eyes, intimating her conviction that excuses or quasi praise founded on her youth would avail her nothing. "Would anybody buy it from me?" she asked. No;—we did not think that any publisher would pay her money for it. "Would they print it for me without costing me anything?" Then we told her the truth as nearly as we could. She lacked experience; and if, as she had declared to us before, she was determined to persevere, she must try again, and must learn more of that lesson of the world's ways which was so necessary to those who attempted to teach that lesson to others. "But I shall try again at once," she said. We shook our head, endeavouring to shake it kindly. "Currer Bell was only a young girl when she succeeded," she added. The injury which Currer Bill did after this fashion was almost equal to that perpetrated by Jack Sheppard, and yet Currer Bell was not very young when she wrote.

She remained with us then for above an hour;—for more than two probably, though the time was not specially marked by us; and before her visit was brought to a close she had told us of her engagement with the curate. Indeed, we believe that the greater part of her little history as hitherto narrated was made known to us on that occasion. We asked after her mother early in the interview, and learned that she was not on this occasion kept waiting at the pastrycook's shop. Mary had come alone, making use of some friendly omnibus, of which she had learned the route. When she told us that she and her mother had come up to London solely with the view of forwarding her views in her intended profession, we ventured to ask whether it would not be wiser for them to return to Cornboro, seeing how improbable it was that she would have matter fit for the press within any short period. Then she explained that they had calculated that they would be able to live in London for twelve months, if they spent nothing except on absolute necessaries. The poor girl seemed to keep back nothing from us. "We have clothes that will carry us through, and we shall be very careful. I came in an omnibus;—but I shall walk if you will let me come again." Then she asked me for advice. How was she to set about further work with the best chance of turning it to account?

It had been altogether the fault of that retired literary gentleman down in the north, who had obtained what standing he had in the world of letters by writing about guano and the cattle plague! Divested of all responsibility, and fearing no further trouble to himself, he had ventured to tell this girl that her work was full of promise. Promise means probability, and in this case there was nothing beyond a remote chance. That she and her mother should have left their little household gods, and come up to London on such a chance, was a thing terrible to the mind. But we felt before these two hours were over that we could not throw her off now. We had become old friends, and there had been that between us which gave her a positive claim upon our time. She had sat in our arm-chair, leaning forward with her elbows on her knees and her hands stretched out, till we, caught by the charm of her unstudied intimacy, had wheeled round our chair, and had placed ourselves, as nearly as the circumstances would admit, in the same position. The magnetism had already begun to act upon us. We soon found ourselves taking it for granted that she was to remain in London and begin another book. It was impossible to resist her. Before the interview was over, we, who had been conversant with all these matters before she was born; we, who had latterly come to regard our own editorial fault as being chiefly that of personal harshness; we, who had repulsed aspirant novelists by the score,—we had consented to be a party to the creation, if not to the actual writing, of this new book!

It was to be done after this fashion. She was to fabricate a plot, and to bring it to us, written on two sides of a sheet of letter paper. On the reverse sides we were to criticise this plot, and prepare emendations. Then she was to make out skeletons of the men and women who were afterwards to be clothed with flesh and made alive with blood, and covered with cuticles. After that she was to arrange her proportions;

and at last, before she began to write the story, she was to describe in detail such part of it as was to be told in each chapter. On every advancing wavelet of the work we were to give her our written remarks. All this we promised to do because of the quiver in her lip, and the alternate tear and sparkle in her eye. "Now that I have found a friend, I feel sure that I can do it," she said, as she held our hand tightly before she left us.

In about a month, during which she had twice written to us and twice been answered, she came with her plot. It was the old story, with some additions and some change. There was matrimony instead of death at the end, and an old aunt was brought in for the purpose of relenting and producing an income. We added a few details, feeling as we did so that we were the very worst of botchers. We doubt now whether the old, sad, simple story was not the better of the two. Then, after another lengthened interview, we sent our pupil back to create her skeletons. When she came with the skeletons we were dear friends and learned to call her Mary. Then it was that she first sat at our editorial table, and wrote a love-letter to the curate. It was then mid-winter, wanting but a few days to Christmas, and Arthur, as she called him, did not like the cold weather. "He does not say so," she said, "but I fear he is ill. Don't you think there are some people with whom everything is unfortunate?" She wrote her letter, and had recovered her spirits before she took her leave.

We then proposed to her to bring her mother to dine with us on Christmas Day. We had made a clean breast of it at home in regard to our heart-flutterings, and had been met with a suggestion that some kindness might with propriety be shown to the old lady as well as to the young one. We had felt grateful to the old lady for not coming to our office with her daughter, and had at once assented. When we made the suggestion to Mary there came first a blush over all her face, and then there followed the well-known smile before the blush was gone. "You'll all be dressed fine," she said. We protested that not a garment would be changed by any of the family after the decent church-going in the morning. "Just as I am?" she asked. "Just as you are," we said, looking at the dear grey frock, adding some mocking assertion that no possible combination of millinery could improve her. "And mamma will be just the same? Then we will come," she said. We told her an absolute falsehood, as to some necessity which would take us in a cab to Euston Square on the afternoon of that Christmas Day, so that we could call and bring them both to our house without trouble or expense. "You shan't do anything of the kind," she said. However, we swore to our falsehood,—perceiving, as we did so, that she did not believe a word of it; but in the matter of the cab we had our own way.

We found the mother to be what we had expected,—a weak, ladylike, lachrymose old lady, endowed with a profound admiration for her daughter, and so bashful that she could not at all enjoy her plum-pudding. We think that Mary did enjoy hers thoroughly. She made a little speech to the mistress of the house, praising ourselves with warm words and tearful eyes, and immediately won the heart of a new friend. She allied herself warmly to our daughters, put up with the schoolboy pleasantries of our sons, and before the evening was over was dressed up as a ghost for the amusement of some neighbouring children who were brought in to play snapdragon. Mrs. Gresley, as she drank her tea and crumbled her bit of cake, seated on a distant sofa, was not so happy, partly because she remembered her old gown, and partly because our wife was a stranger to her. Mary had forgotten both circumstances before the dinner was half over. She was the sweetest ghost that ever was seen. How pleasant would be our ideas of departed spirits if such ghosts would visit us frequently!

They repeated their visits to us not unfrequently during the twelve months; but as the whole interest attaching to our intercourse had reference to circumstances which took place in that editorial room of ours, it will not be necessary to refer further to the hours, very pleasant to ourselves, which she spent with us in our domestic life. She was ever made welcome when she came, and was known by us as a dear, well-bred, modest, clever little girl. The novel went on. That catalogue of the skeletons gave us more trouble than all the rest, and many were the tears which she shed over it, and sad were the misgivings by which she was afflicted, though never vanquished! How was it to be expected that a girl of eighteen should portray characters such as she had never known? In her intercourse with the curate all the intellect had been on her side. She had loved him because it was requisite to her to love some one; and now, as she had loved him, she was as true as steel to him. But there had been almost nothing for her to learn from him. The plan of the novel went on, and as it did so we became more and more despondent as to its success. And through it all we knew how contrary it was to our own judgment to expect, even to dream of, anything but failure. Though we went on working with her, finding it to be quite impossible to resist her entreaties, we did tell her from day to day that, even presuming she were entitled to hope for ultimate success, she must go through an apprenticeship of ten years before she could reach it. Then she would sit silent, repressing her tears, and searching for arguments with which to support her cause.

"Working hard is apprenticeship," she said to us once.

"Yes, Mary; but the work will be more useful, and the apprenticeship more wholesome, if you will take them for what they are worth."

"I shall be dead in ten years," she said.

"If you thought so you would not intend to marry Mr. Donne. But even were it certain that such would be your fate, how can that alter the state of things? The world would know nothing of that; and if it did, would the world buy your book out of pity?"

"I want no one to pity me," she said; "but I want you to help me." So we went on helping her. At the end of four months she had not put pen to paper on the absolute body of her projected novel; and yet she had worked daily at it, arranging its future construction.

During the next month, when we were in the middle of March, a gleam of real success came to her. We had told her frankly that we would publish nothing of hers in the periodical which we were ourselves conducting. She had become too dear to us for us not to feel that were we to do so, we should be doing it rather for her sake than for that of our readers. But we did procure for her the publication of two short stories elsewhere. For these she received twelve guineas, and it seemed to her that she had found an El Dorado of literary wealth. I shall never forget her ecstasy when she knew that her work would be printed, or her renewed triumph when the first humble cheque was given into her hands. There are those who will think that such a triumph, as connected with literature, must be sordid. For ourselves, we are ready to acknowledge that money payment for work done is the best and most honest test of success. We are sure that it is so felt by young barristers and young doctors, and we do not see why rejoicing on such realisation of long-cherished hope should be more vile with the literary aspirant than with them. "What do you think I'll do first with it?" she said. We thought she meant to send something to her lover, and we told her so. "I'll buy mamma a bonnet to go to church in. I didn't tell you before, but she hasn't been these three Sundays because she hasn't one fit to be seen." I changed the cheque for her, and she went off and bought the bonnet.

Though I was successful for her in regard to the two stories, I could not go beyond that. We could have filled pages of periodicals with her writing had we been willing that she should work without remuneration. She herself was anxious for such work, thinking that it would lead to something better. But we opposed it, and, indeed, would not permit it, believing that work so done can be serviceable to none but those who accept it that pages may be filled without cost.

During the whole winter, while she was thus working, she was in a state of alarm about her lover. Her hope was ever that when warm weather came he would again be well and strong. We know nothing sadder than such hope founded on such source. For does not the winter follow the summer, and then again comes the killing spring? At this time she used to read us passages from his letters, in which he seemed to speak of little but his own health. In her literary ambition he never seemed to have taken part since she had declared her intention of writing profane novels. As regarded him, his sole merit to us seemed to be in his truth to her. He told her that in his opinion they two were as much joined together as though the service of the Church had bound them; but even in saying that he spoke ever of himself and not of her. Well;—May came, dangerous, doubtful, deceitful May, and he was worse. Then, for the first time, the dread word, Consumption, passed her lips. It had already passed ours, mentally, a score of times. We asked her what she herself would wish to do. Would she desire to go down to Dorsetshire and see him? She thought awhile, and said that she would wait a little longer.

The novel went on, and at length, in June, she was writing the actual words on which, as she thought, so much depended. She had really brought the story into some shape in the arrangement of her chapters; and sometimes even I began to hope. There were moments in which with her hope was almost certainty. Towards the end of June

Mr. Donne declared himself to be better. He was to have a holiday in August, and then he intended to run up to London and see his betrothed. He still gave details, which were distressing to us, of his own symptoms; but it was manifest that he himself was not desponding, and she was governed in her trust or in her despair altogether by him. But when August came the period of his visit was postponed. The heat had made him weak, and he was to come in September.

Early in August we ourselves went away for our annual recreation;—not that we shoot grouse, or that we have any strong opinion that August and September are the best months in the year for holiday-making,—but that everybody does go in August. We ourselves are not specially fond of August. In many places to which one goes a-touring mosquitoes bite in that month. The heat, too, prevents one from walking. The inns are all full, and the railways crowded. April and May are twice pleasanter months in which to see the world and the country. But fashion is everything, and no man or woman will stay in town in August for whom there exists any practicability of leaving it. We went on the 10th,—just as though we had a moor, and one of the last things we did before our departure was to read and revise the last-written chapter of Mary's story.

About the end of September we returned, and up to that time the lover had not come to London. Immediately on our return we wrote to Mary, and the next morning she was with us. She had seated herself on her usual chair before she spoke, and we had taken her hand and asked after herself and her mother. Then, with something of mirth in our tone, we demanded the work which she had done since our departure. "He is dying," she replied.

She did not weep as she spoke. It was not on such occasions as this that the tears filled her eyes. But there was in her face a look of fixed and settled misery which convinced us that she at least did not doubt the truth of her own assertion. We muttered something as to our hope that she was mistaken. "The doctor, there, has written to tell mamma that it is so. Here is his letter." The doctor's letter was a good letter, written with more of assurance than doctors can generally allow themselves to express. "I fear that I am justified in telling you," said the doctor, "that it can only be a question of weeks." We got up and took her hand. There was not a word to be uttered.

"I must go to him," she said, after a pause.

"Well;—yes. It will be better."

"But we have no money." It must be explained now that offers of slight, very slight, pecuniary aid had been made by us both to Mary and to her mother on more than one occasion. These had been refused with adamantine firmness, but always with something of mirth, or at least of humour, attached to the refusal. The mother would simply refer to the daughter, and Mary would declare that they could manage to see the twelvemonth through and go back to Cornboro, without becoming absolute beggars. She would allude to their joint wardrobe, and would confess that there would not have been a pair of boots between them but for that twelve guineas; and indeed she seemed to have stretched that modest incoming so as to cover a legion of purchases. And of these things she was never ashamed to speak. We think there must have been at least two grey frocks, because the frock was always clean, and never absolutely shabby. Our girls at home declared that they had seen three. Of her frock, as it happened, she never spoke to us, but the new boots and the new gloves, "and ever so many things that I can't tell you about, which we really couldn't have gone without," all came out of the twelve guineas. That she had taken, not only with delight, but with triumph. But pecuniary assistance from ourselves she had always refused. "It would be a gift," she would say.

"Have it as you like."

"But people don't give other people money."

"Don't they? That's all you know about the world."

"Yes; to beggars. We hope we needn't come to that." It was thus that she always answered us,—but always with something of laughter in her eye, as though their poverty was a joke. Now, when the demand upon her was for that which did not concern her personal comfort, which referred to a matter felt by her to be vitally important, she declared, without a minute's hesitation, that she had not money for the journey.

"Of course you can have money," we said. "I suppose you will go at once?"

"Oh yes;—at once. That is, in a day or two,—after he shall have received my letter. Why should I wait?" We sat down to write a cheque, and she, seeing what we were doing, asked how much it was to be. "No;—half that will do," she said. "Mamma will not go. We have talked it over and decided it. Yes; I know all about that. I am going to see my lover,—my dying lover; and I have to beg for the money to take me to him. Of course I am a young girl; but in such a condition am I to stand upon the ceremony of being taken care of? A housemaid wouldn't want to be taken care of at eighteen." We did exactly as she bade us, and then attempted to comfort her while the young man went to get money for the cheque. What consolation was possible? It was simply necessary to admit with frankness that sorrow had come from which there could be no present release. "Yes," she said. "Time will cure it,—in a way. One dies in time, and then of course it is all cured." "One hears of this kind of thing often," she said afterwards, still leaning forward in her chair, still with something of the old expression in her eyes,—something almost of humour in spite of her grief; "but it is the girl who dies. When it is the girl, there isn't, after all, so much harm done. A man goes about the world and can shake it off; and then, there are plenty of girls." We could not tell her how infinitely more important, to our thinking, was her life than that of him whom she was going to see now for the last time; but there did spring up within our mind a feeling, greatly opposed to that conviction which formerly we had endeavoured to impress upon herself,—that she was destined to make for herself a successful career.

She went, and remained by her lover's bed-side for three weeks. She wrote constantly to her mother, and once or twice to ourselves. She never again allowed herself to entertain a gleam of hope, and she spoke of her sorrow as a thing accomplished. In her last interview with us she had hardly alluded to her novel, and in her letters she never mentioned it. But she did say one word which made us guess what was coming. "You will find me greatly changed in one thing," she said; "so much changed that I need never have troubled you." The day for her return to London was twice postponed, but at last she was brought to leave him. Stern necessity was too strong for her. Let her pinch herself as she might, she must live down in Dorsetshire,—and could not live on his means, which were as narrow as her own. She left him; and on the day after her arrival in London she walked across from Euston Square to our office.

"Yes," she said, "it is all over. I shall never see him again on this side of heaven's gates." We do not know that we ever saw a tear in her eyes produced by her own sorrow. She was possessed of some wonderful strength which seemed to suffice for the bearing of any burden. Then she paused, and we could only sit silent, with our eyes fixed upon the rug. "I have made him a promise," she said at last. Of course we asked her what was the promise, though at the moment we thought that we knew. "I will make no more attempt at novel writing."

"Such a promise should not have been asked,—or given," we said vehemently.

"It should have been asked,—because he thought it right," she answered. "And of course it was given. Must he not know better than I do? Is he not one of God's ordained priests? In all the world is there one so bound to obey him as I?" There was nothing to be said for it at such a moment as that. There is no enthusiasm equal to that produced by a death-bed parting. "I grieve greatly," she said, "that you should have had so much vain labour with a poor girl who can never profit by it."

"I don't believe the labour will have been vain," we answered, having altogether changed those views of ours as to the futility of the pursuit which she had adopted.

"I have destroyed it all," she said.

"What;—burned the novel?"

"Every scrap of it. I told him that I would do so, and that he should know that I had done it. Every page was burned after I got home last night, and then I wrote to him before I went to bed."

"Do you mean that you think it wicked that people should write novels?" we asked.

"He thinks it to be a misapplication of God's gifts, and that has been enough for me. He shall judge for me, but I will not judge for others. And what does it matter? I do not want to write a novel now."

They remained in London till the end of the year for which the married curate had taken their house, and then they returned to Cornboro. We saw them frequently while they were still in town, and despatched them by the train to the north just when the winter was beginning. At that time the young clergyman was still living down in Dorsetshire, but he was lying in his grave when Christmas came.

Mary never saw him again, nor did she attend his funeral. She wrote to us frequently then, as she did for years afterwards. "I should have liked to have stood at his grave," she said; "but it was a luxury of sorrow that I wished to enjoy, and they who cannot earn luxuries should not have them. They were going to manage it for me here, but I knew I was right to refuse it." Right, indeed! As far as we knew her, she never moved a single point from what was right.

All these things happened many years ago. Mary Gresley, on her return to Cornboro, apprenticed herself, as it were, to the married curate there, and called herself, I think, a female Scripture reader. I know that she spent her days in working hard for the religious aid of the poor around her. From time to time we endeavoured to instigate her to literary work; and she answered our letters by sending us wonderful little dialogues between Tom the Saint and Bob the Sinner. We are in no humour to criticise them now; but we can assert, that though that mode of religious teaching is most distasteful to us, the literary merit shown even in such works as these was very manifest. And there came to be apparent in them a gleam of humour which would sometimes make us think that she was sitting opposite to us and looking at us, and that she was Tom the Saint, and that we were Bob the Sinner. We said what we could to turn her from her chosen path, throwing into our letters all the eloquence and all the thought of which we were masters; but our eloquence and our thought were equally in vain.

At last, when eight years had passed over her head after the death of Mr. Donne, she married a missionary who was going out to some forlorn country on the confines of African colonisation; and there she died. We saw her on board the ship in which she sailed, and before we parted there had come that tear into her eyes, the old look of supplication on her lips, and gleam of mirth across her face. We kissed her once,—for the first and only time,—as we bade God bless her!

Josephine de Montmorenci

Originally appeared in *Saint Paul's Magazine*, December 1869. Reprinted in *An Editor's Tales* (1870). In *An Autobiography* Trollope confirms that this story of 'how I was addressed by a lady with a becoming pseudonyme and with much equally becoming audacity' was closely based on fact. In *The Chronicler of Barsetshire* (1988), R.H. Super shows that Trollope may have spiked the story with playful hidden references to another (more famous) pseudonymous lady: '["Josephine de Montmorenci's"] name was actually Maryanne, though she was called Polly by her relatives, one of whom, named Charles, worked at the Post Office and smoked incessantly. Now "George Eliot" was a pseudonym designed to disguise a woman named Marian, nicknamed "Polly", who had a metaphysical bent. Her common-law husband George Henry Lewes was constantly buying cigars from Trollope, and indeed had written an article on tobacco smoking for *Saint Paul's*. Moreover his son Charles worked in the Post Office.'

THE LITTLE story which we are about to relate refers to circumstances which occurred some years ago, and we desire, therefore, that all readers may avoid the fault of connecting the personages of the tale,—either the Editor who suffered so much, and who behaved, we think, so well, or the ladies with whom he was concerned,—with any editor or with any ladies known to such readers either personally or by name. For though the story as told is a true story, we who tell it have used such craft in the telling, that we defy the most astute to fix the time or to recognise the characters. It will be sufficient if the curious will accept it as a fact that at some date since magazines became common in the land, a certain editor, sitting in his office, came upon the perusal of the following letter, addressed to him by name;—

"19, King-Charles Street,
"1st May, 18—.

"Dear Sir,

"I think that literature needs no introduction, and, judging of you by the character which you have made for yourself in its paths, I do not doubt but you will feel as I do. I shall therefore write to you without reserve. I am a lady not possessing that modesty which should make me hold a low opinion of my own talents, and equally free from that feeling of self-belittlement which induces so many to speak humbly while they think proudly of their own acquirements. Though I am still young, I have written much for the press, and I believe I may boast that I have sometimes done so successfully. Hitherto I have kept back my name, but I hope soon to be allowed to see it on the title-page of a book which shall not shame me.

"My object in troubling you is to announce the fact, agreeable enough to myself, that I have just completed a novel in three volumes, and to suggest to you that it should make its first appearance to the world in the pages of the magazine under your control. I will frankly tell you that I am not myself fond of this mode of publication; but Messrs. X., Y., Z., of Paternoster Row, with whom you are doubtless acquainted, have assured me that such will be the better course. In these matters one is still terribly subject to the tyranny of the publishers, who surely of all cormorants are the most greedy, and of all tyrants are the most arrogant. Though I have never seen you, I know you too well to suspect for a moment that my words will ever be repeated to my respectable friends in the Row.

"Shall I wait upon you with my MS.,—or will you call for it? Or perhaps it may be better that I should send it to you. Young ladies should not run about,—even after editors; and it might be so probable that I should not find you at home. Messrs. X., Y., and Z. have read the MS.,—or more probably the young man whom they keep for the purpose has done so,—and the nod of approval has been vouchsafed. Perhaps this may suffice; but if a second examination be needful, the work is at your service.

"Yours faithfully, and in hopes of friendly relations,
"JOSEPHINE DE MONTMORENCI.

"I am English, though my unfortunate name will sound French in your ears."

For facility in the telling of our story we will call this especial editor Mr. Brown. Mr. Brown's first feeling on reading the letter was decidedly averse to the writer. But such is always the feeling of editors to would-be contributors, though contributions are the very food on which an editor must live. But Mr. Brown was an unmarried man, who loved the rustle of feminine apparel, who delighted in the brightness of a woman's eye when it would be bright for him, and was not indifferent to the touch of a woman's hand. As editors go, or went then, he knew his business, and was not wont to deluge his pages with weak feminine ware in return for smiles and flattering speeches,—as editors have done before now; but still he liked an adventure, and was perhaps afflicted by some slight flaw of judgment, in consequence of which the words of pretty women found with him something of preponderating favour. Who is there that will think evil of him because it was so?

He read the letter a second time, and did not send that curt, heart-rending answer which is so common to editors,—"The Editor's compliments and thanks, but his stock of novels is at present so great that he cannot hope to find room for the work which has been so kindly suggested."

Of King-Charles Street, Brown could not remember that he had ever heard, and he looked it out at once in the Directory. There was a King-Charles Street in Camden Town, at No. 19 of which street it was stated that a Mr. Puffle resided. But this told him nothing. Josephine de Montmorenci might reside with Mrs. Puffle in Camden Town, and yet write a good novel,—or be a very pretty girl. And there was a something in the tone of the letter which made him think that the writer was no ordinary person. She wrote with confidence. She asked no favour. And then she declared that Messrs. X., Y., Z., with whom Mr. Brown was intimate, had read and approved her novel. Before he answered the note he would call in the Row and ask a question or two.

He did call, and saw Mr. Z. Mr. Z. remembered well that the MS. had been in their house. He rather thought that X., who was out of town, had seen Miss Montmorenci,—perhaps on more than one occasion. The novel had been read, and,—well, Mr. Z. would not quite say approved; but it had been thought that there was a good deal in it. "I think I remember X. telling me that she was an uncommon pretty young woman," said Z.,—"and there is some mystery about her. I didn't see her myself, but I am sure there was a mystery." Mr. Brown made up his mind that he would, at any rate, see the MS.

He felt disposed to go at once to Camden Town, but still had fears that in doing so he might seem to make himself too common. There are so many things of which an editor is required to think! It is almost essential that they who are ambitious of serving under him should believe that he is enveloped in MSS. from morning to night,—that he cannot call an hour his own,—that he is always bringing out that periodical of his in a frenzy of mental exertion,—that he is to be approached only with difficulty,—and that a call from him is a visit from a god. Mr. Brown was a Jupiter willing enough on occasions to go a little out of his way after some literary Leda, or even on behalf of a Danae desirous of a price for her compositions;—but he was obliged to acknowledge to himself that the occasion had not as yet arisen. So he wrote to the young lady as follows:—

"Office of the Olympus Magazine,
"4th May, 18—.

"The Editor presents his compliments to Miss de Montmorenci, and will be very happy to see her MS. Perhaps she will send it to the above address. The Editor has seen Mr. Z., of Paternoster Row, who speaks highly of the work. A novel, however, may be very clever and yet hardly suit a magazine. Should it be accepted by the 'Olympus,' some time must elapse before it appears. The Editor would be very happy to see Miss de Montmorenci if it would suit her to call any Friday between the hours of two and three."

When the note was written Mr. Brown felt that it was cold;—but then it behoves an editor to be cold. A gushing editor would ruin any publication within six months. Young women are very nice; pretty young women are especially nice; and of all pretty young women, clever young women who write novels are perhaps as nice as any;—but to an editor they are dangerous. Mr. Brown was at this time about forty, and had had his experiences. The letter was cold, but he was afraid to make it warmer. It was sent;—and when he received the following answer, it may fairly be said that his editorial hair stood on end.

"Dear Mr. Brown,

"I hate you and your compliments. That sort of communication means nothing, and I won't send you my MS. unless you are more in earnest about it. I know the way in which rolls of paper are shoved into pigeon-holes and left there till they are musty, while the writers' hearts are being broken. My heart may be broken some day, but not in that way.

"I won't come to you between two and three on Friday. It sounds a great deal too like a doctor's appointment, and I don't think much of you if you are only at your work one hour in the week. Indeed, I won't go to you at all. If an interview is necessary you can come here. But I don't know that it will be necessary.

"Old X. is a fool and knows nothing about it. My own approval is to me very much more than his. I don't suppose he'd know the inside of a book if he saw it. I have given the very best that is in me to my work, and I know that it is good. Even should you say that it is not I shall not believe you. But I don't think you will say so, because I believe you to be in truth a clever fellow in spite of your 'compliments' and your 'two and three o'clock on a Friday.'

"If you want to see my MS., say so with some earnestness, and it shall be conveyed to you. And please to say how much I shall be paid for it, for I am as poor as Job. And name a date. I won't be put off with your 'some time must elapse.' It shall see the light, or, at least, a part of it, within six months. That is my intention. And don't talk nonsense to me about clever novels not suiting magazines,—unless you mean that as an excuse for publishing so many stupid ones as you do.

"You will see that I am frank; but I really do mean what I say. I want it to come out in the 'Olympus;' and if we can I shall be so happy to come to terms with you.

"Yours as I find you,
"JOSEPHINE DE MONTMORENCI."

"Thursday.—King-Charles Street."

This was an epistle to startle an editor as coming from a young lady; but yet there was something in it that seemed to imply strength. Before answering it Mr. Brown did a thing which he must be presumed to have done as man and not as editor. He walked off to King-Charles Street in Camden Town, and looked at the house. It was a nice little street, very quiet, quite genteel, completely made up with what we vaguely call gentlemen's houses, with two windows to each drawing-room, and with a balcony to some of them, the prettiest balcony in the street belonging to No. 19, near the Park, and equally removed from poverty and splendour. Brown walked down the street, on the opposite side, towards the Park, and looked up at the house. He intended to walk at once homewards, across the Park, to his own little home in St. John's Wood Road; but when he had passed half a street away from the Puffle residence, he turned to have another look, and retraced his steps. As he passed the door it was opened, and there appeared upon the steps,—one of the prettiest little women he had ever seen in his life. She was dressed for walking, with that jaunty, broad, open bonnet which women then wore, and seemed, as some women do seem, to be an amalgam of softness, prettiness, archness, fun, and tenderness,—and she carried a tiny blue parasol. She was fair, grey-eyed, dimpled, all alive, and dressed so nicely and yet simply, that Mr. Brown was carried away for the moment by a feeling that he would like to publish her novel, let it be what it might. And he heard her speak. "Charles," she said, "you shan't smoke." Our editor could, of course, only pass on, and had not an opportunity of even seeing Charles. At the corner of the street he turned round and saw them walking the other way. Josephine was leaning on Charles's arm. She had, however, distinctly avowed herself to be a young lady,—in other words, an unmarried woman. There was, no doubt, a mystery, and Mr. Brown felt it to be incumbent on him to fathom it. His next letter was as follows:—

"MY DEAR MISS DE MONTMORENCI,

"I am sorry that you should hate me and my compliments. I had intended to be as civil and as nice as possible. I am quite in earnest, and you had better send the MS. As to all the questions you ask, I cannot answer them to any purpose till I have read the story,—which I will promise to do without subjecting it to the pigeon-holes. If you do not like Friday, you shall come on Monday, or Tuesday, or Wednesday, or Thursday, or Saturday, or even on Sunday, if you wish it;—and at any hour, only let it be fixed.

"Yours faithfully,
"JONATHAN BROWN."

"Friday."

In the course of the next week the novel came, with another short note, to which was attached no ordinary beginning or ending. "I send my treasure, and, remember, I will have it back in a week if you do not intend to keep it. I have not £5 left in the world, and I owe my milliner ever so much, and money at the stables where I get a horse. And I am determined to go to Dieppe in July. All must come out of my novel. So do be a good man. If you are I will see you." Herein she declared plainly her own conviction that she had so far moved the editor by her correspondence,—for she knew nothing, of course, of that ramble of his through King-Charles Street,—as to have raised in his bosom a desire to see her. Indeed, she made no secret of such conviction. "Do as I wish," she said plainly, "and I will gratify you by a personal interview." But the interview was not to be granted till the novel had been accepted and the terms fixed,—such terms, too, as it would be very improbable that any editor could accord.

"Not so Black as he's Painted;"—that was the name of the novel which it now became the duty of Mr. Brown to read. When he got it home, he found that the writing was much worse than that of the letters. It was small, and crowded, and carried through without those technical demarcations which are so comfortable to printers, and so essential to readers. The erasures were numerous, and bits of the story were written, as it were, here and there. It was a manuscript to which Mr. Brown would not have given a second glance, had there not been an adventure behind it. The very sending of such a manuscript to any editor would have been an impertinence, if it were sent by any but a pretty woman. Mr. Brown, however, toiled over it, and did read it,—read it, or at least enough of it to make him know what it was. The verdict which Mr. Z. had given was quite true. No one could have called the story stupid. No Mentor experienced in such matters would have ventured on such evidence to tell the aspirant that she had mistaken her walk in life, and had better sit at home and darn her stockings. Out of those heaps of ambitious manuscripts which are daily subjected to professional readers such verdicts may safely be given in regard to four-fifths,—either that the aspirant should darn her stockings, or that he should prune his fruit trees. It is equally so with the works of one sex as with those of the other. The necessity of saying so is very painful, and the actual stocking, or the fruit tree itself, is not often named. The cowardly professional reader indeed, unable to endure those thorns in the flesh of which poor Thackeray spoke so feelingly, when hard-pressed for definite answers, generally lies. He has been asked to be candid, but he cannot bring himself to undertake a duty so onerous, so odious, and one as to which he sees to little reason that he personally should perform it. But in regard to these aspirations,—to which have been given so much labours, which have produced so many hopes, offsprings which are so dear to the poor parents,—the decision at least is easy. And there are others in regard to which a hopeful reader finds no difficulty,—as to which he feels assured that he is about to produce to the world the fruit of some new-found genius. But there are doubtful cases which worry the poor judge till he knows not how to trust his own judgment. At this page he says, "Yes, certainly;" at the next he shakes his head as he sits alone amidst his papers. Then he is dead against the aspirant. Again there is improvement, and he asks himself,—where is he to find anything that is better? As our editor read Josephine's novel,—he had learned to call her Josephine in that silent speech in which most of us indulge, and which is so necessary to an editor,—he was divided between Yes and No throughout the whole story. Once or twice he found himself wiping his eyes, and then it was all "yes" with him. Then he found the pages ran with a cruel heaviness, which seemed to demand decisive editorial severity. A whole novel, too, is so great a piece of business! There would be such difficulty were he to accept it! How much must he cut out! How many of his own hours must he devote to the repairing of mutilated sentences, and the remodelling of indistinct scenes! In regard to a small piece an editor, when moved that way, can afford to be good-natured. He can give to it the hour or so of his own work which it may require. And if after all it be nothing,—or, as will happen sometimes, much worse than nothing,—the evil is of short duration. In admitting such a thing he has done an injury,—but the injury is small. It passes in the crowd, and is forgotten. The best Homer that ever edited must sometimes nod. But a whole novel! A piece of work that would last him perhaps for twelve months! No editor can afford to nod for so long a period.

But then this tale, this novel of "Not so Black as he's Painted," this story of a human devil, for whose crimes no doubt some Byronic apology was made with great elaboration by the sensational Josephine, was not exactly bad. Our editor had wept over it. Some tender-hearted Medora, who on behalf of her hyena-in-love had gone through miseries enough to kill half a regiment of heroines, had dimmed the judge's eyes with tears. What stronger proof of excellence can an editor have? But then there were those long pages of metaphysical twaddle, sure to elicit scorn and neglect from old and young. They, at any rate, must be cut out. But in the cutting of them out a very mincemeat would be made of the story. And yet Josephine de Montmorenci, with her impudent little letters, had already made herself so attractive! What was our editor to do?

He knew well the difficulty that would be before him should he once dare to accept, and then undertake to alter. She would be as a tigress to him,—as a tigress fighting for her young. That work of altering is so ungracious, so precarious, so incapable of success in its performance! The long-winded, far-fetched, high-stilted, unintelligible sentence which you elide with so much confidence in your judgment, has been the very apple of your author's eye. In it she has intended to convey to the world the fruits of her best meditation for the last twelve months. Thinking much over many things in her solitude, she has at last invented a truth, and there it lies. That wise men may adopt it, and candid women admire it, is the hope, the solace, and at last almost the certainty of her existence. She repeats the words to herself, and finds that they will form a choice quotation to be used in coming books. It is for the sake of that one newly invented truth,—so she tells herself, though not quite truly,—that she desires publication. You come,—and with a dash of your pen you annihilate the precious gem! Is it in human nature that you should be forgiven? Mr. Brown had had his experiences, and understood all this well. Nevertheless he loved dearly to please a pretty woman.

And it must be acknowledged that the letters of Josephine were such as to make him sure that there might be an adventure if he chose to risk the pages of his magazine. The novel had taken him four long evenings to read, and at the end of the fourth he sat thinking of it for an hour. Fortune either favoured him or the reverse,—as the reader may choose to regard the question,—in this, that there was room for the story in his periodical if he chose to take it. He wanted a novel;—but then he did not want feminine metaphysics. He sat thinking of it, wondering in his mind how that little smiling, soft creature with the grey eyes, and the dimples, and the pretty walking-dress, could have written those interminable pages as to the questionable criminality of crime; whether a card-sharper might not be a hero; whether a murderer might not sacrifice his all, even the secret of his murder, for the woman he loved; whether devil might not be saint, and saint devil. At the end of the hour he got up from his chair, stretched himself, with his hands in his trousers-pockets, and said aloud, though alone, that he'd be d—if he would. It was an act of great self-denial, a triumph of principle over passion.

But though he had thus decided, he was not minded to throw over altogether either Josephine or her novel. He might still, perhaps, do something for her if he could find her amenable to reason. Thinking kindly of her, very anxious to know her personally, and still desirous of seeing the adventure to the end, he wrote the following note to her that evening;—

"Cross Bank, St. John's Wood,
"Saturday Night.

"My dear Miss de Montmorenci,

"I knew how it would be. I cannot give you an answer about your novel without seeing you. It so often happens that the answer can't be Yes or No. You said something very cruel about dear old X., but after all he was quite right in his verdict about the book. There is a great deal in it; but it evidently was not written to suit the pages of a magazine. Will you come to me, or shall I come to you;—or shall I send the MS. back, and so let there be an end of it? You must decide. If you direct that the latter course be taken, I will obey; but I shall do so with most sincere regret, both on account of your undoubted aptitude for literary work, and because I am very anxious to become acquainted with my fair correspondent. You see I can be as frank as you are yourself.

"Yours most faithfully,
"Jonathan Brown.

"My advice to you would be to give up the idea of publishing this tale in parts, and to make terms with X., Y., and Z.,—in endeavouring to do which I shall be most happy to be of service to you."

This note he posted on the following day, and when he returned home on the next night from his club, he found three replies from the divine, but irritable and energetic, Josephine. We will give them according to their chronology.

No. 1. "Monday Morning.—Let me have my MS. back,—and, pray, without any delay.—J. DE M."

No. 2. "Monday, 2 o'clock.—How can you have been so ill-natured,—and after keeping it twelve days?"

His answer had been written within a week of the receipt of the parcel at his office, and he had acted with a rapidity which nothing but some tender passion would have instigated.—

"What you say about being clever, and yet not fit for a magazine, is rubbish. I know it is rubbish. I do not wish to see you. Why should I see a man who will do nothing to oblige me? If X., Y., Z. choose to buy it, at once, they shall have it. But I mean to be paid for it, and I think you have behaved very ill to me.—JOSEPHINE."

No. 3. "Monday Evening.—My dear Mr. Brown,—Can you wonder that I should have lost my temper and almost my head? I have written twice before to-day, and hardly know what I said. I cannot understand you editing people. You are just like women;—you will and you won't. I am so unhappy. I had allowed myself to feel almost certain that you would take it, and have told that cross man at the stables he should have his money. Of course I can't make you publish it;—but how you can put in such yards of stupid stuff, all about nothing on earth, and then send back a novel which you say yourself is very clever, is what I can't understand. I suppose it all goes by favour, and the people who write are your uncles, and aunts, and grandmothers, and lady-loves. I can't make you do it, and therefore I suppose I must take your advice about those old hugger-muggers in Paternoster Row. But there are ever so many things you must arrange. I must have the money at once. And I won't put up with just a few pounds. I have been at work upon that novel for more than two years, and I know that it is good. I hate to be grumbled at, and complained of, and spoken to as if a publisher were doing me the greatest favour in the world when he is just going to pick my brains to make money of them. I did see old X., or old Z., or old Y., and the stuffy old fellow told me that if I worked hard I might do something some day. I have worked harder than ever he did,—sitting there and squeezing brains, and sucking the juice out of them like an old ghoul. I suppose I had better see you, because of money and all that. I'll come, or else send some one, at about two on Wednesday. I can't put it off till Friday, and I must be home by three. You might as well go to X., Y., Z., in the meantime, and let me know what they say.—J. DE M."

There was an unparalleled impudence in all this which affronted, amazed, and yet in part delighted our editor. Josephine evidently regarded him as her humble slave, who had already received such favours as entitled her to demand from him any service which she might require of him. "You might as well go to X., Y., Z., and let me know what they say!" And then that direct accusation against him,—that all went by favour with him! "I think you have behaved very ill to me!" Why,—had he not gone out of his way, very much out of his way indeed, to do her a service? Was he not taking on her behalf an immense trouble for which he looked for no remuneration,—unless remuneration should come in that adventure of which he had but a dim foreboding? All this was unparalleled impudence. But then impudence from pretty women is only sauciness; and such sauciness is attractive. None but a very pretty woman who openly trusted in her prettiness would dare to write such letters; and the girl whom he had seen on the door-step was very pretty. As to his going to X., Y., Z., before he had seen her, that was out of the question. That very respectable firm in the Row would certainly not give money for a novel without considerable caution, without much talking, and a regular understanding and bargain. As a matter of course, they would take time to consider. X., Y., and Z. were not in a hurry to make money to pay a milliner or to satisfy a stable-keeper, and would have but little sympathy for such troubles;—all which it would be Mr. Brown's unpleasant duty to explain to Josephine de Montmorenci.

But though this would be unpleasant, still there might be pleasure. He could foresee that there would be a storm, with much pouting, some violent complaint, and perhaps a deluge of tears. But it would be for him to dry the tears and allay the storm. The young lady could do him no harm, and must at last be driven to admit that his kindness was disinterested. He waited, therefore, for the Wednesday, and was careful to be at the office of his magazine at two o'clock. In the ordinary way of his business the office would not have seen him on that day, but the matter had now been present in his mind so long, and had been so much considered,—had assumed so large a proportion in his thoughts,—that he regarded not at all this extra trouble. With an air of indifference he told the lad who waited upon him as half clerk and half errand-boy, that he expected a lady; and then he sat down, as though to compose himself to his work. But no work was done. Letters were not even opened. His mind was full of Josephine de Montmorenci. If all the truth is to be told, it must be acknowledged that he did not even wear the clothes that were common to him when he sat in his editorial chair. He had prepared himself somewhat, and a new pair of gloves was in his hat. It might be that circumstances would require him to accompany Josephine at least a part of the way back to Camden Town.

At half-past two the lady was announced,—Miss de Montmorenci; and our editor, with palpitating heart, rose to welcome the very figure, the very same pretty walking-dress, the same little blue parasol, which he had seen upon the steps of the house in King-Charles Street. He could swear to the figure, and to the very step, although he could not as yet see the veiled face. And this was a joy to him; for, though he had not allowed himself to doubt much, he had doubted a little whether that graceful houri might or might not be his Josephine. Now she was there, present to him in his own castle, at his mercy as it were, so that he might dry her tears and bid her hope, or tell her that there was no hope so that she might still weep on, just as he pleased. It was not one of those cases in which want of bread and utter poverty are to be discussed. A horsekeeper's bill and a visit to Dieppe were the melodramatic incidents of the tragedy, if tragedy it must be. Mr. Brown had in his time dealt with cases in which a starving mother or a dying father was the motive to which appeal was made. At worst there could be no more than a rose-water catastrophe; and it might be that triumph, and gratitude, and smiles would come. He rose from his chair, and, giving his hand gracefully to his visitor, led her to a seat.

"I am very glad to see you here, Miss de Montmorenci," he said. Then the veil was raised, and there was the pretty face half blushing, half smiling, wearing over all a mingled look of fun and fear.

"We are so much obliged to you, Mr. Brown, for all the trouble you have taken," she said.

"Don't mention it. It comes in the way of my business to take such trouble. The annoyance is in this, that I can so seldom do what is wanted."

"It is so good of you to do anything!"

"An editor is, of course, bound to think first of the periodical which he produces." This announcement Mr. Brown made, no doubt, with some little air of assumed personal dignity. The fact was one which no heaven-born editor ever forgets.

"Of course, sir. And no doubt there are hundreds who want to get their things taken."

"A good many there are, certainly."

"And everything can't be published," said the sagacious beauty.

"No, indeed; very much comes into our hands which cannot be published," replied the experienced editor. "But this novel of yours, perhaps, may be published."

"You think so?"

"Indeed I do. I cannot say what X., Y., and Z. may say to it. I'm afraid they will not do more than offer half profits."

"And that doesn't mean any money paid at once?" asked the lady plaintively.

"I'm afraid not."

"Ah! if that could be managed!"

"I haven't seen the publishers, and of course I can say nothing myself. You see I'm so busy myself with my uncles, and aunts, and grandmothers, and lady-loves— "

"Ah,—that was very naughty, Mr. Brown."

"And then, you know, I have so many yards of stupid stuff to arrange."

"Oh, Mr. Brown, you should forget all that!"

"So I will. I could not resist the temptation of telling you of it again, because you are so much mistaken in your accusation. And now about your novel."

"It isn't mine, you know."

"Not yours?"

"Not my own, Mr. Brown."

"Then whose is it?" Mr. Brown, as he asked this question, felt that he had a right to be offended. "Are you not Josephine de Montmorenci?"

"Me an author! Oh no, Mr. Brown," said the pretty little woman. And our editor almost thought that he could see a smile on her lips as she spoke.

"Then who are you?" asked Mr. Brown.

"I am her sister;—or rather her sister-in-law. My name is Mrs. Puffle." How could Mrs. Puffle be the sister-in-law of Miss de Montmorenci? Some such thought as this passed through the editor's mind, but it was not followed out to any conclusion. Relationships are complex things, and, as we all know, give rise to most intricate questions. In the half-moment that was allowed to him Mr. Brown reflected that Mrs. Puffle might be the sister-in-law of a Miss de Montmorenci; or, at least, half sister-in-law. It was even possible that Mrs. Puffle, young as she looked, might have been previously married to a De Montmorenci. Of all that, however, he would not now stop to unravel the details, but endeavoured as he went on to take some comfort from the fact that Puffle was no doubt Charles. Josephine might perhaps have no Charles. And then it became evident to him that the little fair, smiling, dimpled thing before him could hardly have written "Not so Black as he's Painted," with all its metaphysics. Josephine must be made of sterner stuff. And, after all, for an adventure, little dimples and a blue parasol are hardly appropriate. There should be more of stature than Mrs. Puffle possessed, with dark hair, and piercing eyes. The colour of the dress should be black, with perhaps yellow trimmings; and the hand should not be of pearly whiteness,—as Mrs. Puffle's no doubt was, though the well-fitting little glove gave no absolute information on this subject. For such an adventure the appropriate colour of the skin would be,—we will not say sallow exactly,—but running a little that way. The beauty should be just toned by sadness; and the blood, as it comes and goes, should show itself, not in blushes, but in the mellow, changing lines of the brunette. All this Mr. Brown understood very well.

"Oh,—you are Mrs. Puffle," said Brown, after a short but perhaps insufficient pause. "You are Charles Puffle's wife?"

"Do you know Charles?" asked the lady, putting up both her little hands. "We don't want him to hear anything about this. You haven't told him?"

"I've told him nothing as yet," said Mr. Brown.

"Pray don't. It's a secret. Of course he'll know it some day. Oh, Mr. Brown, you won't betray us. How very odd that you should know Charles!"

"Does he smoke as much as ever, Mrs. Puffle?"

"How very odd that he never should have mentioned it! Is it at his office that you see him?"

"Well, no; not at his office. How is it that he manages to get away on an afternoon as he does?"

"It's very seldom,—only two or three times in a month,—when he really has a headache from sitting at his work. Dear me, how odd! I thought he told me everything, and he never mentioned your name."

"You needn't mention mine, Mrs. Puffle, and the secret shall be kept. But you haven't told me about the smoking. Is he as inveterate as ever?"

"Of course he smokes. They all smoke. I suppose then he used always to be doing it before he married. I don't think men ever tell the real truth about things, though girls always tell everything."

"And now about your sister's novel?" asked Mr. Brown, who felt that he had mystified the little woman sufficiently about her husband.

"Well, yes. She does want to get some money so badly! And it is clever;—isn't it? I don't think I ever read anything cleverer. Isn't it enough to take your breath away when Orlando defends himself before the lords?" This referred to a very high-flown passage which Mr. Brown had determined to cut out when he was thinking of printing the story for the pages of the "Olympus." "And she will be so broken-hearted! I hope you are not angry with her because she wrote in that way."

"Not in the least. I liked her letters. She wrote what she really thought."

"That is so good of you! I told her that I was sure you were good-natured, because you answered so civilly. It was a kind of experiment of hers, you know."

"Oh,—an experiment!"

"It is so hard to get at people. Isn't it? If she'd just written, 'Dear sir, I send you a manuscript,'—you never would have looked at it;—would you?"

"We read everything, Mrs. Puffle."

"But the turn for all the things comes so slowly; doesn't it? So Polly thought—"

"Polly,—what did Polly think?"

"I mean Josephine. We call her Polly just as a nickname. She was so anxious to get you to read it at once! And now what must we do?" Mr. Brown sat silent awhile, thinking. Why did they call Josephine de Montmorenci, Polly? But there was the fact of the MS., let the name of the author be what it might. On one thing he was determined. He would take no steps till he had himself seen the lady who wrote the novel. "You'll go to the gentlemen in Paternoster Row immediately; won't you?" asked Mrs. Puffle, with a pretty little beseeching look which it was very hard to resist.

"I think I must ask to see the authoress first," said Mr. Brown.

"Won't I do?" asked Mrs. Puffle. "Josephine is so particular. I mean she dislikes so very much to talk about her own writings and her own works." Mr. Brown thought of the tenor of the letters which he had received, and found that he could not reconcile with it this character which was given to him of Miss de Montmorenci. "She has an idea," continued Mrs. Puffle, "that genius should not show itself publicly. Of course she does not say that herself. And she does not think herself to be a genius;—though I think it. And she is a genius. There are things in 'Not so Black as he's Painted' which nobody but Polly could have written."

Nevertheless Mr. Brown was firm. He explained that he could not possibly treat with Messrs. X., Y., and Z.,—if any treating should become possible,—without direct authority from the principal. He must have from Miss de Montmorenci's mouth what might be the arrangements to which she would accede. If this could not be done he must wash his hands of the affair. He did not doubt, he said, but that Miss de Montmorenci might do quite as well with the publishers by herself, as she could with any aid from him. Perhaps it would be better that she should see Mr. X. herself. But if he, Brown, was to be honoured by any delegated authority, he must see the author. In saying this he implied that he had not the slightest desire to interfere further, and that he had no wish to press himself on the lady. Mrs. Puffle, with just a tear, and then a smile, and then a little coaxing twist of her lips, assured him that their only hope was in him. She would carry his message to Josephine, and he should have a further letter from that lady. "And you won't tell Charles that I have been here," said Mrs. Puffle as she took her leave.

"Certainly not. I won't say a word of it."

"It is so odd that you should have known him."

"Don't let him smoke too much, Mrs. Puffle."

"I don't intend. I've brought him down to one cigar and a pipe a day,—unless he smokes at the office."

"They all do that;—nearly the whole day."

"What; at the Post Office!"

"That's why I mention it. I don't think they're allowed at any of the other offices, but they do what they please there. I shall keep the MS. till I hear from Josephine herself." Then Mrs. Puffle took her leave with many thanks, and a grateful pressure from her pretty little hand.

Two days after this there came the promised letter from Josephine.

"Dear Mr. Brown,

"I cannot understand why you should not go to X., Y., and Z. without seeing me. I hardly ever see anybody; but, of course, you must come if you will. I got my sister to go because she is so gentle and nice, that I thought she could persuade anybody to do anything. She says that you know Mr. Puffle quite well, which seems to be so very odd. He doesn't know that I ever write a word, and I didn't think he had an acquaintance in the world whom I don't know the name of. You're quite wrong about one thing. They never smoke at the Post Office, and they wouldn't be let to do it. If you choose to come, you must. I shall be at home any time on Friday morning,—that is, after half-past nine, when Charles goes away.

"Yours truly,

"J. de M.

"We began to talk about Editors after dinner, just for fun; and Charles said that he didn't know that he had ever seen one. Of course we didn't say anything about the 'Olympus;' but I don't know why he should be so mysterious."

Then there was a second postscript, written down in a corner of the sheet of paper. "I know you'll be sorry you came."

Our editor was now quite determined that he would see the adventure to an end. He had at first thought that Josephine was keeping herself in the background merely that she might enhance the favour of a personal meeting when that favour should be accorded. A pretty woman believing herself to be a genius, and thinking that good things should ever be made scarce, might not improbably fall into such a foible. But now he was convinced that she would prefer to keep herself unseen if her doing so might be made compatible with her great object. Mr. Brown was not a man to intrude himself unnecessarily upon any woman unwilling to receive him; but in this case it was, so he thought, his duty to persevere. So he wrote a pretty little note to Miss Josephine saying that he would be with her at eleven o'clock on the day named.

Precisely at eleven o'clock he knocked at the door of the house in King-Charles Street, which was almost instantaneously opened for him by the fair hands of Mrs. Puffle herself. "H—sh," said Mrs. Puffle; "we don't want the servants to know anything about it." Mr. Brown, who cared nothing for the servants of the Puffle establishment, and who was becoming perhaps a little weary of the unravelled mystery of the affair, simply bowed and followed the lady into the parlour. "My sister is up-stairs," said Mrs. Puffle, "and we will go to her immediately." Then she paused, as though she were still struggling with some difficulty;—"I am so sorry to say that Polly is not well.—But she means to see you," Mrs. Puffle added, as she saw that the editor, over whom they had so far prevailed, made some sign as though he was about to retreat. "She never is very well," said Mrs. Puffle, "and her work does tell upon her so much. Do you know, Mr. Brown, I think the mind sometimes eats up the body; that is, when it is called upon for such great efforts." They were now upon the stairs, and Mr. Brown followed the little lady into her drawing-room.

There, almost hidden in the depths of a low arm-chair, sat a little wizened woman, not old indeed,—when Mr. Brown came to know her better, he found that she had as yet only counted five-and-twenty summers,—but with that look of mingled youth and age which is so painful to the beholder. Who has not seen it,—the face in which the eye and the brow are young and bright, but the mouth and the chin are old and haggard? See such a one when she sleeps,—when the brightness of the eye is hidden, and all the countenance is full of pain and decay, and then the difference will be known to you between youth with that health which is generally given to it, and youth accompanied by premature decrepitude. "This is my sister-in-law," said Mrs. Puffle, introducing the two correspondents to each other. The editor looked at the little woman who made some half attempt to rise, and thought that he could see in the brightness of the eye some symptoms of the sauciness which had appeared so very plainly in her letters. And there was a smile too about the mouth, though the lips were thin and the chin poor, which seemed to indicate that the owner of them did in some sort enjoy this unravelling of her riddle,—as though she were saying to herself, "What do you think now of the beautiful young woman who has made you write so many letters, and read so long a manuscript, and come all the way at this hour of the morning to Camden Town?" Mr. Brown shook hands with her, and muttered something to the effect that he was sorry not to see her in better health.

"No," said Josephine de Montmorenci, "I am not very well. I never am. I told you that you had better put up with seeing my sister."

We say no more than the truth of Mr. Brown in declaring that he was now more ready than ever to do whatever might be in his power to forward the views of this young authoress. If he was interested before when he believed her to be beautiful, he was doubly interested for her now when he knew her to be a cripple;—for he had seen when she made that faint attempt to rise that her spine was twisted, and that, when she stood up, her head sank between her shoulders. "I am very glad to make your acquaintance," he said, seating himself near her. "I should never have been satisfied without doing so."

"It is so very good of you to come," said Mrs. Puffle.

"Of course it is good of him," said Josephine; "especially after the way we wrote to him. The truth is, Mr. Brown, we were at our wits' end to catch you."

This was an aspect of the affair which our editor certainly did not like. An attempt to deceive anybody else might have been pardonable; but deceit practised against himself was odious to him. Nevertheless, he did forgive it. The poor little creature before him had worked hard, and had done her best. To teach her to be less metaphysical in her writings, and more straightforward in her own practices, should be his care. There is something to a man inexpressibly sweet in the power of protecting the weak; and no one had ever seemed to be weaker than Josephine. "Miss de Montmorenci," he said, "we will let bygones be bygones, and will say nothing about the letters. It is no doubt the fact that you did write the novel yourself?"

"Every word of it," said Mrs. Puffle energetically.

"Oh, yes; I wrote it," said Josephine.

"And you wish to have it published?"

"Indeed I do."

"And you wish to get money for it?"

"That is the truest of all," said Josephine.

"Oughtn't one to be paid when one has worked so very hard?" said Mrs. Puffle.

"Certainly one ought to be paid if it can be proved that one's work is worth buying," replied the sage Mentor of literature.

"But isn't it worth buying?" demanded Mrs. Puffle.

"I must say that I think that publishers do buy some that are worse," observed Josephine.

Mr. Brown with words of wisdom explained to them as well as he was able the real facts of the case. It might be that that manuscript, over which the poor invalid had laboured for so many painful hours, would prove to be an invaluable treasure of art, destined to give delight to thousands of readers, and to be, when printed, a source of large profits to publishers, booksellers, and author. Or, again, it might be that, with all its undoubted merits,—and that there were such merits Mr. Brown was eager in acknowledging,—the novel would fail to make any way with the public. "A publisher,"—so said Mr. Brown,—"will hardly venture to pay you a sum of money down, when the risk of failure is so great."

"But Polly has written ever so many things before," said Mrs. Puffle.

"That counts for nothing," said Miss de Montmorenci. "They were short pieces, and appeared without a name."

"Were you paid for them?" asked Mr. Brown.

"I have never been paid a halfpenny for anything yet."

"Isn't that cruel," said Mrs. Puffle, "to work, and work, and work, and never get the wages which ought to be paid for it?"

"Perhaps there may be a good time coming," said our editor. "Let us see whether we can get Messrs. X., Y., and Z. to publish this at their own expense, and with your name attached to it. Then, Miss de Montmorenci— "

"I suppose we had better tell him all," said Josephine.

"Oh, yes; tell everything. I am sure he won't be angry; he is so good-natured," said Mrs. Puffle.

Mr. Brown looked first at one, and then at the other, feeling himself to be rather uncomfortable. What was there that remained to be told? He was good-natured, but he did not like being told of that virtue. "The name you have heard is not my name," said the lady who had written the novel.

"Oh, indeed! I have heard Mrs. Puffle call you,—Polly."

"My name is,—Maryanne."

"It is a very good name," said Mr. Brown,—"so good that I cannot quite understand why you should go out of your way to assume another."

"It is Maryanne,—Puffle."

"Oh;—Puffle!" said Mr. Brown.

"And a very good name, too," said Mrs. Puffle.

"I haven't a word to say against it," said Mr. Brown. "I wish I could say quite as much as to that other name,—Josephine de Montmorenci."

"But Maryanne Puffle would be quite unendurable on a title-page," said the owner of the unfortunate appellation.

"I don't see it," said Mr. Brown doggedly.

"Ever so many have done the same," said Mrs. Puffle. "There's Boz."

"Calling yourself Boz isn't like calling yourself Josephine de Montmorenci," said the editor, who could forgive the loss of beauty, but not the assumed grandeur of the name.

"And Currer Bell, and Jacob Omnium, and Barry Cornwall," said poor Polly Puffle, pleading hard for her falsehood.

"And Michael Angelo Titmarsh! That was quite the same sort of thing," said Mrs. Puffle.

Our editor tried to explain to them that the sin of which he now complained did not consist in the intention,—foolish as that had been,—of putting such a name as Josephine de Montmorenci on the title-page, but in having corresponded with him,—with him who had been so willing to be a friend,—under a false name. "I really think you ought to have told me sooner," he said.

"If we had known you had been a friend of Charles's we would have told you at once," said the young wife.

"I never had the pleasure of speaking to Mr. Puffle in my life," said Mr. Brown. Mrs. Puffle opened her little mouth, and held up both her little hands. Polly Puffle stared at her sister-in-law. "And what is more," continued Mr. Brown, "I never said that I had had that pleasure."

"You didn't tell me that Charles smoked at the Post Office," exclaimed Mrs. Puffle,—"which he swears that he never does and that he would be dismissed at once if he attempted it?" Mr. Brown was driven to a smile. "I declare I don't understand you, Mr. Brown."

"It was his little Roland for our little Oliver," said Miss Puffle.

Mr. Brown felt that his Roland had been very small, whereas the Oliver by which he had been taken in was not small at all. But he was forced to accept the bargain. What is a man against a woman in such a matter? What can he be against two women, both young, of whom one was pretty and the other an invalid? Of course he gave way, and of course he undertook the mission to X., Y., and Z. We have not ourselves read "Not so Black as he's Painted," but we can say that it came out in due course under the hands of those enterprising publishers, and that it made what many of the reviews called quite a success.

The Panjandrum

Originally appeared in *Saint Paul's Magazine*, January-February 1870. Reprinted in *An Editor's Tales* (1870). In *An Autobiography* Trollope admits that this story of 'how in my own early days there was a struggle over an abortive periodical which was intended to be the best thing ever done' was closely based on fact. In *Anthony Trollope*: A *Biography* (1991), N. John Hall suggests that *Trollope* might have been involved in such a scheme immediately before his departure for Ireland in 1840–41. 'Panjandrum' is a nonsense word, invented by Samuel Foote, actor and dramatist (1720–77). It is usually taken to mean a self-important local magnate. The account given in the story of how the narrator came to write 'The New Inmate' probably reflects Trollope's own methods of composition.

Part I.—Hope.

WE HARDLY feel certain that we are justified in giving the following little story to the public as an Editor's Tale, because at the time to which it refers, and during the circumstances with which it deals, no editorial power was, in fact, within our grasp. As the reader will perceive, the ambition and the hopes, and something of a promise of the privileges, were there; but the absolute chair was not mounted for us. The great WE was not, in truth, ours to use. And, indeed, the interval between the thing we then so cordially desired, and the thing as it has since come to exist, was one of so many years, that there can be no right on our part to connect the two periods. We shall, therefore, tell our story, as might any ordinary individual, in the first person singular, and speak of such sparks of editorship as did fly up around us as having created but a dim coruscation, and as having been quite insufficient to justify the delicious plural.

It is now just thirty years ago since we determined to establish the "Panjandrum" Magazine. The "we" here spoken of is not an editorial we, but a small set of human beings who shall be personally introduced to the reader. The name was intended to be delightfully meaningless, but we all thought that it was euphonious, graphic, also,—and sententious, even though it conveyed no definite idea. That question of a name had occupied us a good deal, and had almost split us into parties. I,—for I will now speak of myself as I,—I had wished to call it by the name of a very respectable young publisher who was then commencing business, and by whom we intended that the trade part of our enterprise should be undertaken. "Colburn's" was an old affair in those days, and I doubt whether "Bentley's" was not already in existence. "Blackwood's" and "Fraser's" were at the top of the tree, and, as I think, the "Metropolitan" was the only magazine then in much vogue not called by the name of this or that enterprising publisher. But some of our colleagues would not hear of this, and were ambitious of a title that should describe our future energies and excellences. I think we should have been called the "Pandrastic," but that the one lady who joined our party absolutely declined the name. At one moment we had almost carried "Panurge." The "Man's" Magazine was thought of, not as opposed to womanhood, but as intended to trump the "Gentleman's." But a hint was given to us that we might seem to imply that our periodical was not adapted for the perusal of females. We meant the word "man" in the great generic sense;—but the somewhat obtuse outside world would not have so taken it. "The H. B. P." was for a time in the ascendant, and was favoured by the lady, who drew for us a most delightful little circle containing the letters illustrated;—what would now be called a monogram, only that the letters were legible. The fact that nobody would comprehend that "H. B. P." intended to express the general opinion of the shareholders that "Honesty is the Best Policy," was felt to be a recommendation rather than otherwise. I think it was the enterprising young publisher who objected to the initials,—not, I am sure, from any aversion to the spirit of the legend. Many other names were tried, and I shall never forget the look which went round our circle when one young and gallant, but too indiscreet reformer, suggested that were it not for offence, whence offence should not come, the "Purge" was the very name for us;—from all which it will be understood that it was our purpose to put right many things that were wrong. The matter held us in discussion for some months, and then we agreed to call the great future lever of the age,—the "Panjandrum."

When a new magazine is about to be established in these days, the first question raised will probably be one of capital. A very considerable sum of money, running far into four figures,—if not going beyond it,—has to be mentioned, and made familiar to the ambitious promoters of the enterprise. It was not so with us. Nor was it the case that our young friend the publisher agreed to find the money, leaving it to us to find the wit. I think we selected our young friend chiefly because, at that time, he had no great business to speak of, and could devote his time to the interests of the "Panjandrum." As for ourselves we were all poor; and in the way of capital a set of human beings more absurdly inefficient for any purposes of trade could not have been brought together. We found that for a sum of money which we hoped that we might scrape together among us, we could procure paper and print for a couple of thousand copies of our first number;—and, after that, we were to obtain credit for the second number by the reputation of the first. Literary advertising, such as is now common to us, was then unknown. The cost of sticking up "The Panjandrum" at railway stations and on the tops of the omnibuses, certainly would not be incurred. Of railway stations there were but few in the country, and even omnibuses were in the infancy. A few modest announcements in the weekly periodicals of the day were thought to be sufficient; and, indeed, there pervaded us all an assurance that the coming of the "Panjandrum" would be known to all men, even before it had come. I doubt whether our desire was not concealment rather than publicity. We measured the importance of the "Panjandrum" by its significance to ourselves, and by the amount of heart which we intended to throw into it. Ladies and gentlemen who get up magazines in the present day are wiser. It is not heart that is wanted, but very big letters on very big boards, and plenty of them.

We were all heart. It must be admitted now that we did not bestow upon the matter of literary excellence quite so much attention as that branch of the subject deserves. We were to write and edit our magazine and have it published, not because we were good at writing or editing, but because we had ideas which we wished to promulgate. Or it might be the case with some of us that we only thought that we had ideas. But there was certainly present to us all a great wish to do some good. That, and a not altogether unwholesome appetite for a reputation which should not be personal, were our great motives. I do not think that we dreamed of making fortunes; though no doubt there might be present to the mind of each of us an idea that an opening to the profession of literature might be obtained through the pages of the "Panjandrum." In that matter of reputation we were quite agreed that fame was to be sought, not for ourselves, nor for this or that name, but for the "Panjandrum." No man or woman was to declare himself to be the author of this or that article;—nor indeed was any man or woman to declare himself to be connected with the magazine. The only name to be known to a curious public was that of the young publisher. All intercourse between the writers and the printers was to be through him. If contributions should come from the outside world,—as come they would,—they were to be addressed to the Editor of the "Panjandrum," at the publisher's establishment. It was within the scope of our plan to use any such contribution that might please us altogether; but the contents of the magazine were, as a rule, to come from ourselves. A magazine then, as now, was expected to extend itself through something over a hundred and twenty pages; but we had no fear as to our capacity for producing the required amount. We feared rather that we might jostle each other in our requirements for space.

We were six, and, young as I was then, I was to be the editor. But to the functions of the editor was to be attached very little editorial responsibility. What should and what should not appear in each monthly number was to be settled in conclave. Upon one point, however, we were fully agreed,—that no personal jealousy should ever arise among us so as to cause quarrel or even embarrassment. As I had already written some few slight papers for the press, it was considered probable that I might be able to correct proofs, and do the fitting and dovetailing. My editing was not to go beyond that. If by reason of parity of numbers in voting there should arise a difficulty, the lady was to have a double vote. Anything more noble, more chivalrous, more trusting, or, I may add, more philanthropic than our scheme never was invented; and for the persons, I will say that they were noble, chivalrous, trusting, and philanthropic;—only they were so young!

Place aux dames. We will speak of the lady first,—more especially as our meetings were held at her house. I fear that I may, at the very outset of our enterprise, turn the hearts of my readers against her by saying that Mrs. St. Quinten was separated from her husband. I must, however, beg them to believe that this separation had been occasioned by no moral fault or odious misconduct on her part. I will confess that I did at that time believe that Mr. St. Quinten was an ogre, and that I have since learned to think that he simply laboured under a strong and, perhaps, monomaniacal objection to literary pursuits. As Mrs. St. Quinten was devoted to them, harmony was impossible, and the marriage was unfortunate. She was young, being perhaps about thirty; but I think that she was the eldest among us. She was good-looking, with an ample brow, and bright eyes, and large clever mouth; but no woman living was ever further removed from any propensity to flirtation. There resided with her a certain Miss Collins, an elderly, silent lady, who was present at all our meetings, and who was considered to be pledged to secrecy. Once a week we met and drank tea at Mrs. St. Quinten's house. It may be as well to explain that Mrs. St. Quinten really had an available income, which was a condition of life unlike that of her colleagues,—unless as regarded one, who was a fellow of an Oxford college. She could certainly afford to give us tea and muffins once a week;—but, in spite of our general impecuniosity, the expense of commencing the magazine was to be borne equally by us all. I can assure the reader, with reference to more than one of the members, that they occasionally dined on bread and cheese, abstaining from meat and pudding with the view of collecting the sum necessary for the great day.

The idea had originated, I think, between Mrs. St. Quinten and Churchill Smith. Churchill Smith was a man with whom, I must own, I never felt that perfect sympathy which bound me to the others. Perhaps among us all he was the most gifted. Such at least was the opinion of Mrs. St. Quinten and, perhaps, of himself. He was a cousin of the lady's, and had made himself particularly objectionable to the husband by instigating his relative to write philosophical essays. It was his own speciality to be an unbeliever and a German scholar; and we gave him credit for being so deep in both arts that no man could go deeper. It had, however, been decided among us very early in our arrangements,—and so decided, not without great chance of absolute disruption,—that his infidelity was not to bias the magazine. He was to take the line of deep thinking, German poetry, and unintelligible speculation generally. He used to talk of Comte, whose name I had never heard till it fell from his lips, and was prepared to prove that Coleridge was very shallow. He was generally dirty, unshorn, and, as I thought, disagreeable. He called Mrs. St. Quinten, Lydia, because of his cousinship, and no one knew how or where he lived. I believe him to have been a most unselfish, abstemious man,—one able to control all appetites of the flesh. I think that I have since heard that he perished in a Russian prison.

My dearest friend among the number was Patrick Regan, a young Irish barrister, who intended to shine at the English Bar. I think the world would have used him better had his name been John Tomkins. The history of his career shows very plainly that the undoubted brilliance of his intellect, and his irrepressible personal humour and good-humour have been always unfairly weighted by those Irish names. What attorney, with any serious matter in hand, would willingly go to a barrister who called himself Pat Regan? And then, too, there always remained with him just a hint of a brogue,—and his nose was flat in the middle! I do not believe that all the Irishmen with flattened noses have had the bone of the feature broken by a crushing blow in a street row; and yet they certainly look as though that peculiar appearance had been the result of a fight with sticks. Pat has told me a score of times that he was born so, and I believe him. He had a most happy knack of writing verses, which I used to think quite equal to Mr. Barham's, and he could rival the droll Latinity of

Father Prout who was coming out at that time with his "Dulcis Julia Callage," and the like. Pat's father was an attorney at Cork; but not prospering, I think, for poor Pat was always short of money. He had, however, paid the fees, and was entitled to appear in wig and gown wherever common-law barristers do congregate.

He is Attorney-General at one of the Turtle Islands this moment, with a salary of £400 a year. I hear from him occasionally, and the other day he sent me "Captain Crosbie is my name," done into endecasyllabics. I doubt, however, whether he ever made a penny by writing for the press. I cannot say that Pat was our strongest prop. He sometimes laughed at "Lydia,"—and then I was brought into disgrace, as having introduced him to the company.

Jack Hallam, the next I will name, was also intended for the Bar; but, I think, never was called. Of all the men I have encountered in life he was certainly the most impecunious. Now he is a millionaire. He was one as to whom all who knew him,—friends and foes alike,—were decided that under no circumstances would he ever work, or by any possibility earn a penny. Since then he has applied himself to various branches of commerce, first at New York and then at San Francisco; he has laboured for twenty-four years almost without a holiday, and has shown a capability for sustaining toil which few men have equalled. He had been introduced to our set by Walter Watt, of whom I will speak just now; and certainly, when I remember the brightness of his wit and the flow of his words, and his energy when he was earnest, I am bound to acknowledge that in searching for sheer intellect,—for what I may call power,—we did not do wrong to enroll Jack Hallam. He had various crude ideas in his head of what he would do for us,—having a leaning always to the side of bitter mirth. I think he fancied that satire might be his forte. As it is, they say that no man living has a quicker eye to the erection of a block of buildings in a coming city. He made a fortune at Chicago, and is said to have erected Omaha out of his own pocket. I am told that he pays income-tax in the United States on nearly a million dollars per annum. I wonder whether he would lend me five pounds if I asked him? I never knew a man so free as Jack at borrowing half-a-crown or a clean pocket-handkerchief.

Walter Watt was a fellow of——. —— I believe has fellows who do not take orders. It must have had one such in those days, for nothing could have induced our friend, Walter Watt, to go into the Church. How it came to pass that the dons of a college at Oxford should have made a fellow of so wild a creature was always a mystery to us. I have since been told that at——the reward could hardly be refused to a man who had gone out a "first" in classics and had got the "Newdegate." Such had been the career of young Watt. And, though I say that he was wild, his moral conduct was not bad. He simply objected on principle to all authority, and was of opinion that the goods of the world should be in common. I must say of him that in regard to one individual his practice went even beyond his preaching; for Jack Hallam certainly consumed more of the fellowship than did Walter Watt himself. Jack was dark and swarthy. Walter was a fair little man, with long hair falling on the sides of his face, and cut away over his forehead,—as one sees it sometimes cut in a picture. He had round blue eyes, a well-formed nose, and handsome mouth and chin. He was very far gone in his ideas of reform, and was quite in earnest in his hope that by means of the "Panjandrum" something might be done to stay the general wickedness,—or rather ugliness of the world. At that time Carlyle was becoming prominent as a thinker and writer among us, and Watt was never tired of talking to us of the hero of "Sartor Resartus." He was an excellent and most unselfish man,—whose chief fault was an inclination for the making of speeches, which he had picked up at an Oxford debating society. He now lies buried at Kensal Green. I thought to myself, when I saw another literary friend laid there some eight years since, that the place had become very quickly populated since I and Regan had seen poor Watt placed in his last home, almost amidst a desert.

Of myself, I need only say that at that time I was very young, very green, and very ardent as a politician. The Whigs were still in office; but we, who were young then, and warm in our political convictions, thought that the Whigs were doing nothing for us. It must be remembered that things and ideas have advanced so quickly during the last thirty years, that the conservatism of 1870 goes infinitely further in the cause of general reform than did the radicalism of 1840. I was regarded as a democrat because I was loud against the Corn Laws; and was accused of infidelity when I spoke against the Irish Church Endowments. I take some pride to myself that I should have seen these evils to be evils even thirty years ago. But to Household Suffrage I doubt whether even my spirit had ascended. If I remember rightly I was great upon annual parliaments; but I know that I was discriminative, and did not accept all the points of the seven-starred charter. I had an idea in those days,—I can confess it now after thirty years,—that I might be able to indite short political essays which should be terse, argumentative, and convincing, and at the same time full of wit and frolic. I never quite succeeded in pleasing even myself in any such composition. At this time I did a little humble work for the——, but was quite resolved to fly at higher game than that. As I began with the lady, so I must end with her. I had seen and read sheaves of her MS., and must express my conviction at this day, when all illusions are gone, that she wrote with wonderful ease and with some grace. A hard critic might perhaps say that it was slip-slop; but still it was generally readable. I believe that in the recesses of her privacy, and under the dark and secret guidance of Churchill Smith, she did give way to German poetry and abstruse thought. I heard once that there was a paper of hers on the essence of existence, in which she answered that great question, as to personal entity, or as she put it, "What is it, to be?" The paper never appeared before the Committee, though I remember the question to have been once suggested for discussion. Pat Regan answered it at once,—"A drop of something short," said he. I thought then that everything was at an end! Her translation into a rhymed verse of a play of Schiller's did come before us, and nobody could have behaved better than she did, when she was told that it hardly suited our project. What we expected from Mrs. St. Quinten in the way of literary performance I cannot say that we ourselves had exactly realised, but we knew that she was always ready for work. She gave us tea and muffins, and bore with us when we were loud, and devoted her time to our purpose, and believed in us. She had exquisite tact in saving us from wordy quarrelling, and was never angry herself, except when Pat Regan was too hard upon her. What became of her I never knew. When the days of the "Panjandrum" were at an end she vanished from our sight. I always hoped that Mr. St. Quinten reconciled himself to literature, and took her back to his bosom.

While we were only determining that the thing should be, all went smoothly with us. Columns, or the open page, made a little difficulty; but the lady settled it for us in favour of the double column. It is a style of page which certainly has a wiser look about it than the other; and then it has the advantage of being clearly distinguished from the ordinary empty book of the day. The word "padding," as belonging to literature, was then unknown; but the idea existed,—and perhaps the thing. We were quite resolved that there should be no padding in the "Panjandrum." I think our most ecstatic, enthusiastic, and accordant moments were those in which we resolved that it should be all good, all better than anything else,—all best. We were to struggle after excellence with an energy that should know no relaxing,—and the excellence was not to be that which might produce for us the greatest number of half-crowns, but of the sort which would increase truth in the world, and would teach men to labour hard and bear their burdens nobly, and become gods upon earth. I think our chief feeling was one of impatience in having to wait to find to what heaven death would usher us, who unfortunately had to be human before we could put on divinity. We wanted heaven at once,—and were not deterred though Jack Hallam would borrow ninepence and Pat Regan make his paltry little jokes.

We had worked hard for six months before we began to think of writing, or even of apportioning to each contributor what should be written for the first number. I shall never forget the delight there was in having the young publisher in to tea, and in putting him through his figures, and in feeling that it became us for the moment to condescend to matters of trade. We felt him to be an inferior being; but still it was much for us to have progressed so far towards reality as to have a real publisher come to wait upon us. It was at that time clearly understood that I was to be the editor, and I felt myself justified in taking some little lead in arranging matters with our energetic young friend. A remark that I made one evening was very mild,—simply some suggestion as to the necessity of having a more than ordinarily well-educated set of printers;—but I was snubbed infinitely by Churchill Smith. "Mr. X.," said he, "can probably tell us more about printing than we can tell him." I felt so hurt that I was almost tempted to leave the room at once. I knew very well that if I seceded Pat Regan would go with me, and that the whole thing must fall to the ground. Mrs. St. Quinten, however, threw instant oil upon the waters. "Churchill," said she, "let us live and learn. Mr. X., no doubt, knows. Why should we not share his knowledge?" I smothered my feeling in the public cause, but I was conscious of a wish that Mr. Smith might fall among the Philistines of Cursitor Street, and so of necessity be absent from our meetings. There was an idea among us that he crept out of his hiding-place, and came to our conferences by by-ways; which was confirmed when our hostess proposed that our evening should be changed from Thursday, the day first appointed, to Sunday. We all acceded willingly, led away somewhat, I fear, by an idea that it was the proper thing for advanced spirits such as ours to go to work on that day which by ancient law is appointed for rest.

Mrs. St. Quinten would always open our meeting with a little speech. "Gentlemen and partners in this enterprise," she would say, "the tea is made, and the muffins are ready. Our hearts are bound together in the work. We are all in earnest in the good cause of political reform and social regeneration. Let the spirit of harmony prevail among us. Mr. Hallam, perhaps you'll take the cover off." To see Jack Hallam eat muffins was,—I will say "a caution," if the use of the slang phrase may be allowed to me for the occasion. It was presumed among us that on these days he had not dined. Indeed, I doubt whether he often did dine,—supper being his favourite meal. I have supped with him more than once, at his invitation,—when to be without coin in my own pocket was no disgrace,—and have wondered at the equanimity with which the vendors of shell-fish have borne my friend's intimation that he must owe them the little amount due for our evening entertainment. On these occasions his friend Watt was never with him, for Walter's ideas as to the common use of property were theoretical. Jack dashed at once into the more manly course of practice. When he came to Mrs. St. Quinten's one evening in my best,—nay, why dally with the truth?—in my only pair of black dress trousers, which I had lent him ten days before, on the occasion, as I then believed, of real dinner party, I almost denounced him before his colleagues. I think I should have done so had I not felt that he would in some fashion have so turned the tables on me that I should have been the sufferer. There are men with whom one comes by the worst in any contest, let justice on one's own side be ever so strong and ever so manifest.

But this is digression. After the little speech, Jack would begin upon the muffins, and Churchill Smith,—always seated at his cousin's left hand,—would hang his head upon his hand, wearing a look of mingled thought and sorrow on his brow. He never would eat muffins. We fancied that he fed himself with penny hunches of bread as he walked along the streets. As a man he was wild, unsociable, untamable; but, as a philosopher, he had certainly put himself beyond most of those wants to which Jack Hallam and others among us were still subject. "Lydia," he once said, when pressed hard to partake of the good things provided, "man cannot live by muffins alone,—no, nor by tea and muffins. That by which he can live is hard to find. I doubt we have not found it yet."

This, to me, seemed to be rank apostasy,—infidelity to the cause which he was bound to trust as long as he kept his place in that society. How shall you do anything in the world, achieve any success, unless you yourself believe in yourself? And if there be a partnership either in mind or matter, your partner must be the same to you as yourself. Confidence is so essential to the establishment of a magazine! I felt then, at least, that the "Panjandrum" could have no chance without it, and I rebuked Mr. Churchill Smith. "We know what you mean by that," said I;—"because we don't talk German metaphysics, you think we ain't worth our salt."

"So much worth it," said he, "that I trust heartily you may find enough to save you even yet."

I was about to boil over with wrath; but Walter Watt was on his legs, making a speech about the salt of the earth, before I had my words ready. Churchill Smith would put up with Walter when he would endure words from no one else. I used to think him mean enough to respect the Oxford fellowship, but I have since fancied that he believed that he had discovered a congenial spirit. In those days I certainly did despise Watt's fellowship, but in later life I have come to believe that men who get rewards have generally earned them. Watt on this occasion made a speech to which in my passion I hardly attended; but I well remember how, when I was about to rise in my wrath, Mrs. St. Quinten put her hand on my arm, and calmed me. "If you," said she, "to whom we most trust for orderly guidance, are to be the first to throw down the torch of discord, what will become of us?"

"I haven't thrown down any torch," said I.

"Neither take one up," said she, pouring out my tea for me as she spoke.

"As for myself," said Regan, "I like metaphysics,—and I like them German. Is there anything so stupid and pig-headed as that insular feeling which makes us think nothing to be good that is not home-grown?"

"All the same," said Jack, "who ever eat a good muffin out of London?"

"Mr. Hallam, Mary Jane is bringing up some more," said our hostess. She was an open-handed woman, and the supply of these delicacies never ran low as long as the "Panjandrum" was a possibility.

It was, I think, on this evening that we decided finally for columns and for a dark grey wrapper,—with a portrait of the Panjandrum in the centre; a fancy portrait it must necessarily be; but we knew that we could trust for that to the fertile pencil of Mrs. St. Quinten. I had come prepared with a specimen cover, as to which I had in truth consulted an artistic friend, and had taken with it no inconsiderable labour. I am sure, looking back over the long interval of years at my feelings on that occasion,—I am sure, I say, that I bore well the alterations and changes which were made in that design until at last nothing remained of it. But what matters a wrapper? Surely of any printed and published work it is by the interior that you should judge it. It is not that old conjuror's head that has given its success to "Blackwood," nor yet those four agricultural boys that have made the "Cornhill" what it is.

We had now decided on columns, on the cover, and the colour. We had settled on the number of pages, and had thumbed four or five specimens of paper submitted to us by our worthy publisher. In that matter we had taken his advice, and chosen the cheapest; but still we liked the thumbing of the paper. It was business. Paper was paper then, and bore a high duty. I do not think that the system of illustration had commenced in those days, though a series of portraits was being published by one distinguished contemporary. We readily determined that we would attempt nothing of that kind. There then arose a question as to the insertion of a novel. Novels were not then, as now, held to be absolutely essential for the success of a magazine. There were at that time magazines with novels and magazines without them. The discreet young publisher suggested to us that we were not able to pay for such a story as would do us any credit. I myself, who was greedy for work, with bated breath offered to make an attempt. It was received with but faint thanks, and Walter Watt, rising on his legs, with eyes full of fire and arms extended, denounced novels in the general. It was not for such purpose that he was about to devote to the production of the "Panjandrum" any erudition that he might have acquired and all the intellect that God had given him. Let those who wanted novels go for them to the writer who dealt with fiction in the open market. As for him, he at any rate would search for truth. We reminded him of Blumine.* "Tell your novel in three pages," said he, "and tell it as that is told, and I will not object to it." We were enabled, however, to decide that there should be no novel in the "Panjandrum."

Then at length came the meeting at which we were to begin our real work and divide our tasks among us. Hitherto Mr. X. had usually joined us, but a hint had been given to him that on this and a few following meetings we would not trespass on his time. It was quite understood that he, as publisher, was to have nothing to do with the preparation or arrangement of the matter to be published. We were, I think, a little proud of keeping him at a distance when we came to the discussion of that actual essence of our combined intellects which was to be issued to the world under the grotesque name which we had selected. That mind and matter should be kept separated was impressed very strongly upon all of us. Now, we were "mind," and Mr. X. was "matter." He was matter at any rate in reference to this special work, and, therefore, when we had arrived at that vital point we told him,—I had been commissioned to do so,—that we did not require his attendance just at present. I am bound to say that Mr. X. behaved well to the end, but I do not think that he ever warmed to the "Panjandrum" after that. I fancy that he owns two or three periodicals now, and hires his editors quite as easily as he does his butlers,—and with less regard to their characters.

I spent a nervous day in anticipation of that meeting. Pat Regan was

* See "Sartor Resartus."

with me all day, and threatened dissolution. "There isn't a fellow in the world," said he, "that I love better than Walter Watt, and I'd go to Jamaica to serve him;"—when the time came, which it did, oh, so soon! he was asked to go no further than Kensal Green;—"but—!" and then Pat paused.

"You're ready to quarrel with him," said I, "simply because he won't laugh at your jokes."

"There's a good deal in that," said Regan; "and when two men are in a boat together each ought to laugh at the other's jokes. But the question as to our laughing. If we can't make the public laugh sometimes we may as well shut up shop. Walter is so intensely serious that nothing less austere than lay sermons will suit his conscience."

"Let him preach his sermon, and do you crack your jokes. Surely we can't be dull when we have you and Jack Hallam?"

"Jack'll never write a line," said Regan; "he only comes for the muffins. Then think of Churchill Smith, and the sort of stuff he'll expect to force down our readers' throats."

"Smith is sour, but never tedious," said I. Indeed, I expected great things from Smith, and so I told my friend.

"'Lydia' will write," said Pat. We used to call her Lydia behind her back. "And so will Churchill Smith and Watt. I do not doubt that they have quires written already. But no one will read a word of it. Jack, and you, and I will intend to write, but we shall never do anything."

This I felt to be most unjust, because, as I have said before, I was already engaged upon the press. My work was not remunerative, but it was regularly done. "I am afraid of nothing," said I, "but distrust. You can move a mountain if you will only believe that you can move it."

"Just so;—but in order to avoid the confusion consequent on general motion among the mountains, I and other men have been created without that sort of faith." It was always so with my poor friend, and, consequently, he is now Attorney-General at a Turtle Island. Had he believed as I did,—he and Jack,—I still think that the "Panjandrum" might have been a great success. "Don't you look so glum," he went on to say. "I'll stick to it, and do my best. I did put Lord Bateman into rhymed Latin verse for you last night."

Then he repeated to me various stanzas, of which I still remember one;—

> "Tuam duxi, verum est, filiam, sed merum est;
>   Si virgo mihi data fuit, virgo tibi redditur.
> Venit in ephippio mihi, et concipio
>   Satis est si triga pro reditu conceditur."

This cheered me a little, for I thought that Pat was good at these things, and I was especially anxious to take the wind out of the sails of "Fraser" and Father Prout. "Bring it with you," said I to him, giving him great praise. "It will raise our spirits to know that we have something ready." He did bring it; but "Lydia" required to have it all translated to her, word by word. It went off heavily, and was at last objected to by the lady. For the first and last time during our debates Miss Collins ventured to give an opinion on the literary question under discussion. She agreed, she said, with her friend in thinking that Mr. Regan's Latin poem should not be used. The translation was certainly as good as the ballad, and I was angry. Miss Collins, at any rate, need not have interfered.

At last the evening came, and we sat round the table, after the tea-cups had been removed, each anxious for his allotted task. Pat had been so far right in his views as to the diligence of three of our colleagues, that they came furnished with piles of manuscript. Walter Watt, who was afflicted with no false shame, boldly placed before him on the table a heap of blotted paper. Churchill Smith held in his hand a roll; but he did not, in fact, unroll it during the evening. He was a man very fond of his own ideas, of his own modes of thinking and manner of life, but not prone to put himself forward. I do not mind owning that I disliked him; but he had a power of self-abnegation which was, to say the least of it, respectable. As I entered the room, my eyes fell on a mass of dishevelled sheets of paper which lay on the sofa behind the chair on which Mrs. St. Quinten always sat, and I knew that these were her contributions. Pat Regan, as I have said, produced his unfortunate translation, and promised with the greatest good-humour to do another when he was told that his last performance did not quite suit Mrs. St. Quinten's views. Jack had nothing ready; nor, indeed, was anything "ready" ever expected from him. I, however, had my own ideas as to what Jack might do for us. For myself, I confess that I had in my pocket from two to three hundred lines of what I conceived would be a very suitable introduction, in verse, for the first number. It was my duty, I thought, as editor, to provide the magazine with a few initiatory words. I did not, however, produce the rhymes on that evening, having learned to feel that any strong expression of self on the part of one member at that board was not gratifying to the others. I did take some pains in composing those lines, and thought at the time that I had been not unhappy in mixing the useful with the sweet. How many hours shall I say that I devoted to them? Alas, alas, it matters not now! Those words which I did love well never met any eye but my own. Though I had them then by heart, they were never sounded in any ear. It was not personal glory that I desired. They were written that the first number of the "Panjandrum" might appear becomingly before the public, and the first number of the "Panjandrum" never appeared! I looked at them the other day, thinking whether it might be too late for them to serve another turn. I will never look at them again.

But from the first starting of the conception of the "Panjandrum" I had had a great idea, and that idea was discussed at length on the evening of which I am speaking. We must have something that should be sparkling, clever, instructive, amusing, philosophical, remarkable, and new, all at the same time! That such a thing might be achieved in literature I felt convinced. And it must be the work of three or four together. It should be something that should force itself into notice, and compel attention. It should deal with the greatest questions of humanity, and deal with them wisely,—but still should deal with them in a sportive spirit. Philosophy and humour might, I was sure, be combined. Social science might be taught with witty words, and abstract politics made as agreeable as a novel. There had been the "Corn Law Rhymes,"—and the "Noctes." It was, however, essentially necessary that we should be new, and therefore I endeavoured,—vainly endeavoured,—to get those old things out of my head. Fraser's people had done a great stroke of business by calling their Editor Mr. Yorke. If I could get our people to call me Mr. Lancaster, something might come of it. But yet it was so needful that we should be new! The idea had been seething in my brain so constantly that I had hardly eat or slept free from it for the last six weeks. If I could roll Churchill Smith and Jack Hallam into one, throw in a dash of Walter Watt's fine political eagerness, make use of Regan's ready poetical facility, and then control it all by my own literary experience, the thing would be done. But it is so hard to blend the elements!

I had spoken often of it to Pat, and he had assented. "I'll do anything into rhyme," he used to say, "if that's what you mean." It was not quite what I meant. One cannot always convey one's meaning to another; and this difficulty is so infinitely increased when one is not quite clear in one's own mind! And then Pat, who was the kindest fellow in the world, and who bore with the utmost patience a restless energy which must often have troubled him sorely, had not really his heart in it as I had. "If Churchill Smith will send me ever so much of his stuff, I'll put it into Latin or English verse, just as you please,—and I can't say more than that." It was a great offer to make, but it did not exactly reach the point at which I was aiming.

I had spoken to Smith about it also. I knew that if we were to achieve success, we must do so in a great measure by the force of his intellectual energy. I was not seeking pleasure, but success, and was willing therefore to endure the probable discourtesy, or at least want of cordiality, which I might encounter from the man. I must acknowledge that he listened to me with a rapt attention. Attention so rapt is more sometimes than one desires. Could he have helped me with a word or two now and again I should have felt myself to be more comfortable with him. I am inclined to think that two men get on better together in discussing a subject when they each speak a little at random. It creates a confidence, and enables a man to go on to the end. Churchill Smith heard me without a word, and then remarked that he had been too slow quite to catch my idea. Would I explain it again? I did explain it again,—though no doubt I was flustered, and blundered. "Certainly," said Churchill Smith, "if we can all be witty and all wise, and all witty and wise at the same time, and altogether, it will be very fine. But then, you see, I'm never witty, and seldom wise." The man was so uncongenial that there was no getting anything from him. I did not dare to suggest to him that he should submit the prose exposition of his ideas to the metrical talent of our friend Regan.

As soon as we were assembled I rose upon my legs, saying that I proposed to make a few preliminary observations. It certainly was the case that at this moment Mrs. St. Quinten was rinsing the teapot, and

Mary Jane had not yet brought in the muffins. We all know that when men meet together for special dinners, the speeches are not commenced till the meal is over;—and I would have kept my seat till Jack had done his worst with the delicacies, had it not been our practice to discuss our business with our plates and cups and saucers still before us. "You can't drink your tea on your legs," said Jack Hallam. "I have no such intention," said I. "What I have to lay before you will not take a minute." A suggestion, however, came from another quarter that I should not be so formal; and Mrs. St. Quinten, touching my sleeve, whispered to me a precaution against speech-making. I sat down, and remarked in a manner that I felt to be ludicrously inefficient, that I had been going to propose that the magazine should be opened by a short introductory paper. As the reader knows, I had the introduction then in my pocket. "Let us dash into the middle of our work at once," said Walter Watt. "No one reads introductions," said Regan;—my own friend, Pat Regan! "I own I don't think an introduction would do us any particular service," said "Lydia," turning to me with that smile which was so often used to keep us in good-humour. I can safely assert that it was never vainly used on me. I did not even bring the verses out of my pocket, and thus I escaped at least the tortures of that criticism to which I should have been subjected had I been allowed to read them to the company. "So be it," said I. "Let us then dash into the middle of our work at once. It is only necessary to have a point settled. Then we can progress."

After that I was silent for awhile, thinking it well to keep myself in the background. But no one seemed to be ready for speech. Walter Watt fingered his manuscript uneasily, and Mrs. St. Quinten made some remark not distinctly audible as to the sheets on the sofa. "But I must get rid of the tray first," she said. Churchill Smith sat perfectly still with his roll in his pocket. "Mrs. St. Quinten and gentlemen," I said, "I am happy to tell you that I have had a contribution handed to me which will go far to grace our first number. Our friend Regan has done 'Lord Bateman' into Latin verse with a Latinity and a rhythm so excellent that it will go far to make us at any rate equal to anything else in that line." Then I produced the translated ballad, and the little episode took place which I have already described. Mrs. St. Quinten insisted on understanding it in detail, and it was rejected. "Then, upon my word, I don't know what you are to get," said I. "Latin translations are not indispensable," said Walter Watt. "No doubt we can live without them," said Pat, with a fine good humour. He bore the disgrace of having his first contribution rejected with admirable patience. There was nothing, he could not bear. To this day he bears being Attorney-General at the Turtle Islands.

Something must be done. "Perhaps," said I, turning to the lady, "Mrs. St. Quinten will begin by giving us her ideas as to our first number. She will tell us what she intends to do for us herself." She was still embarrassed by the tea-things. And I acknowledge that I was led to appeal to her at that moment because it was so. If I could succeed in extracting ideas they would be of infinitely more use to us than the reading of manuscript. To get the thing "licked into shape" must be our first object. As I had on this evening walked up to the sombre street leading into the New Road in which Mrs. St. Quinten lived I had declared to myself a dozen times that to get the thing "licked into shape" was the great desideratum. In my own imaginings I had licked it into some shape. I had suggested to myself my own little introductory poem as a commencement, and Pat Regan's Latin ballad as a pretty finish to the first number. Then there should be some thirty pages of dialogue,—or trialogue,—or hexalogue if necessary, between the different members of our Board, each giving, under an assumed name, his view of what a perfect magazine should be. This I intended to be the beginning of a conversational element which should be maintained in all subsequent numbers, and which would enable us in that light and airy fashion which becomes a magazine to discuss all subjects of politics, philosophy, manners, literature, social science, and even religion if necessary, without inflicting on our readers the dulness of a long unbroken essay. I was very strong about these conversations, and saw my way to a great success,—if I could only get my friends to act in concert with me. Very much depended on the names to be chosen, and I had my doubts whether Watt and Churchill Smith would consent to this slightly theatrical arrangement. Mrs. St. Quinten had already given in her adhesion, but was doubting whether she would call herself "Charlotte,"—partly after Charlotte Corday and partly after the lady who cut bread and butter, or "Mrs. Freeman,"—that name having, as she observed, been used before as a nom de plume,—or "Sophronie," after Madame de Sévigné, who was pleased so to call herself among the learned ladies of Madame de Rambouillet's bower. I was altogether in favour of Mrs. Freeman, which has the merit of simplicity;—but that was a minor point. Jack Hallam had chosen his appellation. Somewhere in the Lowlands he had seen over a small shop-door the name of John Neverapenny; and "John Neverapenny" he would be. I turned it over on my tongue a score of times, and thought that perhaps it might do. Pat wanted to call himself "The O'Blazes," but was at last persuaded to adopt the quieter name of "Tipperary," in which county his family had been established since Ireland was,—settled I think he said. For myself I was indifferent. They might give me what title they pleased. I had had my own notion, but that had been rejected. They might call me "Jones" or "Walker," if they thought proper. But I was very much wedded to the idea, and I still think that had it been stoutly carried out the results would have been happy.

I was the first to acknowledge that the plan was not new. There had been the "Noctes," and some imitations even of the "Noctes." But then, what is new? The "Noctes" themselves had been imitations from older works. If Socrates and Hippias had not conversed, neither probably would Mr. North and his friends. "You might as well tell me," said I, addressing my colleagues, "that we must invent a new language, find new forms of expression, print our ideas in an unknown type, and impress them on some strange paper. Let our thoughts be new," said I, "and then let us select for their manifestation the most convenient form with which experience provides us." But they didn't see it. Mrs. St. Quinten liked the romance of being "Sophronie," and to Jack and Pat there was some fun in the nicknames; but in the real thing for which I was striving they had no actual faith. "If I could only lick them into shape," I had said to myself at the last moment, as I was knocking at Mrs. St. Quinten's door.

Mrs. St. Quinten was nearer, to my way of thinking, in this respect than the others; and therefore I appealed to her while the tea-things were still before her, thinking that I might obtain from her a suggestion in favour of the conversations. The introductory poem and the Latin balled were gone. For spilt milk what wise man weeps? My verses had not even left my pocket. Not one there knew that they had been written. And I was determined that not one should know. But my conversations might still live. Ah, if I could only blend the elements! "Sophronie," said I, taking courage, and speaking with a voice from which all sense of shame and fear of failure were intended to be banished; "Sophronie will tell us what she intends to do for us herself."

I looked into my friend's face and saw that she liked it. But she turned to her cousin, Churchill Smith, as though for approval,—and met none. "We had better be in earnest," said Churchill Smith, without moving a muscle of his face or giving the slightest return to the glance which had fallen upon him from his cousin.

"No one can be more thoroughly in earnest than myself," I replied.

"Let us have no calling of names," said Churchill Smith. "It is inappropriate, and especially so when a lady is concerned."

"It has been done scores of times," I rejoined; "and that too in the very highest phases of civilisation, and among the most discreet of matrons."

"It seems to me to be twaddle," said Walter Watt.

"To my taste it's abominably vulgar," said Churchill Smith.

"It has answered very well in other magazines," said I.

"That's just the reason we should avoid it," said Walter Watt.

"I think the thing has been about worn out," said Pat Regan.

I was now thrown upon my mettle. Rising again upon my legs,—for the tea-things had now been removed,—I poured out my convictions, my hopes, my fears, my ambitions. If we were thus to disagree on every point, how should we ever blend the elements? If we could not forbear with one another, how could we hope to act together upon the age as one great force? If there was no agreement between us, how could we have the strength of union? Then I adverted with all the eloquence of which I was master to the great objects to be attained by these imaginary conversations. "That we may work together, each using his own words,—that is my desire," I said. And I pointed out to them how willing I was to be the least among them in this contest, to content myself with simply acting as chorus, and pointing to the lessons of wisdom which would fall from out of their mouths. I must say that they listened to me on this occasion with great patience. Churchill Smith sat there, with his great hollow eyes fixed upon me; and it seemed to me, as he looked, that even he was being persuaded. I threw myself into my words, and implored them to allow me on this occasion to put them on the road to success. When I had finished speaking I looked around, and for a moment I thought they were convinced. There was just a whispered word between our Sophronie and her cousin, and then she turned to me and spoke. I was still standing, and I bent down over her to catch the sentence she should pronounce. "Give it up," she said.

And I gave it up. With what a pang this was done few of my readers can probably understand. It had been my dream from my youth upwards. I was still young, no doubt, and looking back now I can see how insignificant were the aspirations which were then in question. But there is no period in a man's life in which it does not seem to him that his ambition is then, at that moment, culminating for him,—till the time comes in which he begins to own to himself that his life is not fit for ambition. I had believed that I might be the means of doing something, and of doing it in this way. Very vague indeed had been my notions;—most crude my ideas. I can see that now. What it was that my interlocutors were to say to each other I had never clearly known. But I had felt that in this way each might speak his own speech without confusion and with delight to the reader. The elements, I had thought, might be so blent. Then there came that little whisper between Churchill Smith and our Sophronie, and I found that I had failed. "Give it up," said she.

"Oh, of course," I said, as I sat down; "only just settle what you mean to do." For some few minutes I hardly heard what matters were being discussed among them, and, indeed, during the remainder of the evening I took no real share in the conversation. I was too deeply wounded even to listen. I was resolute at first to abandon the whole affair. I had already managed to scrape together the sum of money which had been named as the share necessary for each of us to contribute towards the production of the first number, and that should be altogether at their disposal. As for editing a periodical in the management of which I was not allowed to have the slightest voice, that was manifestly out of the question. Nor could I contribute when every contribution which I suggested was rejected before it was seen. My money I could give them, and that no doubt would be welcome. With these gloomy thoughts my mind was so full that I actually did not hear the words with which Walter Watt and Churchill Smith were discussing the papers proposed for the first number.

There was nothing read that evening. No doubt it was visible to them all that I was, as it were, a blighted spirit among them. They could not but know how hard I had worked, how high had been my hopes, how keen was my disappointment;—and they felt for me. Even Churchill Smith, as he shook hands with me at the door, spoke a word of encouragement. "Do not expect to do things too quickly," said he. " I don't expect to do anything," said I. "We may do something even yet," said he, "if we can be humble, and patient, and persevering. We may do something though it be ever so little." I was humble enough certainly, and knew that I had persevered. As for patience;—well; I would endeavour even to be patient.

But, prior to that, Mrs. St. Quinten had explained to me the programme which had now been settled between the party. We were not to meet again till that day fortnight, and then each of us was to come provided with matter that would fill twenty-one printed pages of the magazine. This, with the title-page, would comprise the whole first number. We might all do as we liked with our own pages,—each within his allotted space,—filling the whole with one essay, or dividing it into two or three short papers. In this way there might be scope for Pat Regan's verse, or for any little badinage in which Jack Hallam might wish to express himself. And in order to facilitate our work, and for the sake of general accommodation, a page or two might be lent or borrowed. "Whatever anybody writes then," I asked, "must be admitted?" Mrs. St. Quinten explained to me that this had not been their decision. The whole matter produced was of course to be read,—each contributor's paper by the contributor himself, and it was to be printed and inserted in the first number, if any three would vote for its insertion. On this occasion the author, of course, would have no vote. The votes were to be handed in, written on slips of paper, so that there might be no priority in voting,—so that no one should be required to express himself before or after his neighbour. It was very complex, but I made no objection.

As I walked home alone,—for I had no spirits to join Regan and Jack Hallam, who went in search of supper at the Haymarket,—I turned over Smith's words in my mind, and resolved that I would be humble, patient, and persevering,—so that something might be done, though it were, as he said, ever so little. I would struggle still. Though everything was to be managed in a manner adverse to my own ideas and wishes, I would still struggle. I would still hope that the "Panjandrum" might become a great fact in the literature of my country.

Part II.—Despair.

A FORTNIGHT HAD been given to us to prepare our matter, and during that fortnight I saw none of my colleagues. I purposely kept myself apart from them in order that I might thus give a fairer chance to the scheme which had been adopted. Others might borrow or lend their pages, but I would do the work allotted to me, and would attend the next meeting as anxious for the establishment and maintenance of the Panjandrum as I had been when I had hoped that the great consideration which I had given personally to the matter might have been allowed to have some weight. And gradually, as I devoted the first day of my fortnight to thinking of my work, I taught myself to hope again, and to look forward to a time when, by the sheer weight of my own industry and persistency, I might acquire that influence with my companions of which I had dreamed of becoming the master. After all, could I blame them for not trusting me, when as yet I had given them no ground for such confidence? What had I done that they should be willing to put their thoughts, their aspirations, their very brains and inner selves under my control? But something might be done which would force them to regard me as their leader. So I worked hard at my twenty-one pages, and during the fortnight spoke no word of the "Panjandrum" to any human being.

But my work did not get itself done without very great mental distress. The choice of a subject had been left free to each contributor. For myself I would almost have preferred that some one should have dictated to me the matter to which I should devote myself. How would it be with our first number if each of us were to write a political essay of exactly twenty-one pages, or a poem of that length in blank verse, or a humorous narrative? Good heavens! How were we to expect success with the public if there were no agreement between ourselves as to the nature of our contributions, no editorial power in existence for our mutual support? I went down and saw Mr. X., and found him to be almost indifferent as to the magazine. "You see, sir," said he, "the matter isn't in my hands. If I can give any assistance, I shall be very happy; but it seems to me that you want some one with experience." "I could have put them right if they'd have let me," I replied. He was very civil, but it was quite clear to me that Mr. X.'s interest in the matter was over since the day of his banishment from Mrs. St. Quinten's tea-table. "What do you think is a good sort of subject," I asked him,—as it were cursorily; "with a view, you know, to the eye of the public, just at the present moment?" He declined to suggest any subject, and I was thrown back among the depths of my own feelings and convictions. Now, could we have blended our elements together, and discussed all this in really amicable council, each would have corrected what there might have been of rawness in the other, and in the freedom of conversation our wits would have grown from the warmth of mutual encouragement. Such, at least, was my belief then. Since that I have learned to look at the business with eyes less enthusiastic. Let a man have learned the trick of the pen, let him not smoke too many cigars overnight, and let him get into his chair within half an hour after breakfast, and I can tell you almost to a line how much of a magazine article he will produce in three hours. It does not much matter what the matter be,—only this, that if his task be that of reviewing, he may be expected to supply a double quantity. Three days, three out of the fourteen, passed by, and I could think of no fitting subject on which to begin the task I had appointed myself of teaching the British public. Politics at the moment were rather dull, and no very great question was agitating the minds of men. Lord Melbourne was Prime Minister, and had in the course of the Session been subjected to the usual party attacks. We intended to go a great deal further than Lord Melbourne in advocating liberal measures, and were disposed to regard him and his colleagues as antiquated fogies in State-craft; but, nevertheless, as against Sir Robert Peel, we should have given him the benefit of our defence. I did not, however, feel any special call to write up Lord Melbourne. Lord John was just then our pet minister; but even on his behalf I did not find myself capable of filling twenty-one closely-printed pages with matter which should really stir the public mind. In a first number, to stir the public mind is everything. I didn't think that my colleagues sufficiently realised that fact, though I had indeed endeavoured to explain it to them. In the second, third, or fourth publication you may descend gradually to an ordinary level; you may become,—not exactly dull, for dulness in a magazine should be avoided,—but what I may perhaps call "adagio" as compared with the "con forza" movement with which the publication certainly should be opened. No reader expects to be supplied from month to month with the cayenne pepper and shallot style of literature; but in the preparation of a new literary banquet, the first dish cannot be too highly spiced. I knew all that,—and then turned it over in my mind whether I could not do something about the ballot.

It had never occurred to me before that there could be any difficulty in finding a subject. I had to reject the ballot because at that period of my life I had, in fact, hardly studied the subject. I was liberal, and indeed radical, in all my political ideas. I was ready to "go in" for anything that was undoubtedly liberal and radical. In a general way I was as firm in my politics as any member of the House of Commons, and had thought as much on public subjects as some of them. I was an eager supporter of the ballot. But when I took the pen in my hand there came upon me a feeling that,—that,—that I didn't exactly know how to say anything about it that other people would care to read. The twenty-one pages loomed before me as a wilderness, which, with such a staff, I could never traverse. It had not occurred to me before that it would be so difficult for a man to evoke from his mind ideas on a subject with which he supposed himself to be familiar. And, such thoughts as I had, I could clothe in no fitting words. On the fifth morning, driven to despair, I did write a page or two upon the ballot; and then,—sinking back in my chair, I began to ask myself a question, as to which doubt was terrible to me. Was this the kind of work to which my gifts were applicable? The pages which I had already written were manifestly not adapted to stir the public mind. The sixth and seventh days I passed altogether within my room, never once leaving the house. I drank green tea. I eat meat very slightly cooked. I debarred myself from food for several hours, so that the flesh might be kept well under. I sat up one night, nearly till daybreak, with a wet towel round my head. On the next I got up, and lit my own fire at four o'clock. Thinking that I might be stretching the cord too tight, I took to reading a novel, but could not remember the words as I read them, so painfully anxious was I to produce the work I had undertaken to perform. On the morning of the eighth day I was still without a subject.

I felt like the man who undertook to play the violin at a dance for five shillings and a dinner,—the dinner to be paid in advance; but who, when making his bargain, had forgotten that he had never learned a note of music! I had undertaken even to lead the band, and, as it seemed, could not evoke a sound. A horrid idea came upon me that I was struck, as it were, with a sudden idiotcy. My mind had absolutely fled from me. I sat in my armchair, looking at the wall, counting the pattern on the paper, and hardly making any real effort to think. All the world seemed at once to have become a blank to me. I went on muttering to myself, "No, the ballot won't do;" as though there was nothing else but the ballot with which to stir the public mind. On the eighth morning I made a minute and quite correct calculation of the number of words that were demanded of me,—taking the whole as forty-two pages, because of the necessity of recopying,—and I found that about four hours a day would be required for the mere act of writing. The paper was there, and the pen and ink;—but beyond that there was nothing ready. I had thought to rack my brain, but I began to doubt whether I had a brain to rack. Of all those matters of public interest which had hitherto been to me the very salt of my life, I could not remember one which could possibly be converted into twenty-one pages of type. Unconsciously I kept on muttering words about the ballot. "The ballot be—!" I said, aloud to myself in my agony.

On that Sunday evening I began to consider what excuse I might best make to my colleagues. I might send and say I was very sick. I might face them, and quarrel with them,—because of their ill-treatment of me. Or I might tell only half a lie, keeping within the letter of the truth, and say that I had not yet finished my work. But no. I would not lie at all. Late on that Sunday evening there came upon me a grand idea. I would stand up before them and confess my inability to do the work I had undertaken. I arranged the words of my little speech, and almost took delight in them. "I, who have intended to be a teacher, am now aware that I have hardly as yet become a pupil." In such case the "Panjandrum" would be at an end. The elements had not been happily blended; but without me they could not, I was sure, be kept in any concert. The "Panjandrum,"—which I had already learned to love as a mother loves her first-born,—the dear old "Panjandrum" must perish before its birth. I felt the pity of it! The thing itself,—the idea and theory of it, had been very good. But how shall a man put forth a magazine when he finds himself unable to write a page of it within the compass of a week? The meditations of that Sunday were very bitter, but perhaps they were useful. I had long since perceived that mankind are divided into two classes,—those who shall speak, and those who shall listen to the speech of others. In seeing clearly the existence of such a division I had hitherto always assumed myself to belong to the first class. Might it not be probable that I had made a mistake, and that it would become me modestly to take my allotted place in the second?

On the Monday morning I began to think that I was ill, and resolved that I would take my hat and go out into the Park, and breathe some air,—let the "Panjandrum" live or die. Such another week as the last would, I fancied, send me to Hanwell. It was now November, and at ten o'clock, when I looked out, there was a soft drizzling rain coming down, and the pavement of the street was deserted. It was just the morning for work, were work possible. There still lay on the little table in the corner of the room the square single sheet of paper, with its margin doubled down, all fitted for the printer,—only that the sheet was still blank. I looked at the page, and I rubbed my brow, and I gazed into the street,—and then determined that a two hours' ring round the Regent's Park was the only chance left for me.

As I put on my thick boots and old hat and prepared myself for a thorough wetting, I felt as though at last I had hit upon the right plan. Violent exercise was needed, and then inspiration might come. Inspiration would come the sooner if I could divest myself from all effort in searching for it. I would take my walk and employ my mind, simply, in observing the world around me. For some distance there was but little of the world to observe. I was lodging at this period in a quiet and eligible street not far from Theobald's Road. Thence my way lay through Bloomsbury Square, Russell Square, and Gower Street, and as I went I found the pavement to be almost deserted. The thick soft rain came down, not with a splash and various currents, running off and leaving things washed though wet, but gently insinuating itself everywhere, and covering even the flags with mud. I cared nothing for the mud. I went through it all with a happy scorn for the poor creatures who were endeavouring to defend their clothes with umbrellas. "Let the heavens do their worst to me," I said to myself as I spun along with eager steps; and I was conscious of a feeling that external injuries could avail me nothing if I could only cure the weakness that was within.

The Park too was nearly empty. No place in London is ever empty now, but thirty years ago the population was palpably thinner. I had not come out, however, to find a crowd. A damp boy sweeping a crossing, or an old woman trying to sell an apple, was sufficient to fill my mind with thoughts as to the affairs of my fellow-creatures. Why should it have been allotted to that old woman to sit there, placing all her hopes on the chance sale of a few apples, the cold rain entering her very bones and driving rheumatism into all her joints, while another old woman, of whom I had read a paragraph that morning, was appointed to entertain royalty, and go about the country with five or six carriages and four? Was there injustice in this,—and if so, whence had the injustice come? The reflection was probably not new; but, if properly thought out, might it not suffice for the one-and-twenty pages? "Sally Brown, the barrow-woman, *v.* the Duchess of—!" Would it not be possible to make the two women plead against each other in some imaginary court of justice, beyond the limits of our conventional life,—some court in which the duchess should be forced to argue her own case, and in which the barrow-woman would decidedly get the better of her? If this could be done how happy would have been my walk through the mud and slush!

As I was thinking of this I saw before me on the pathway a stout woman,—apparently middle-aged, but her back was towards me,—leading a girl who perhaps might be ten or eleven years old. They had come up one of the streets from the New Road to the Park, and were hurrying along so fast that the girl, who held the woman by the arm, was almost running. The woman was evidently a servant, but in authority,—an upper nurse perhaps, or a housekeeper. Why she should have brought her charge out in the rain was a mystery; but I could see from the elasticity of the child's step that she was happy and very eager. She was a well-made girl, with long well-rounded legs, which came freely down beneath her frock, with strong firm boots, a straw hat, and a plaid shawl wound carefully round her throat and waist. As I followed them those rapid legs of hers seemed almost to twinkle in their motion as she kept pace with the stout woman who was conducting her. The mud was all over her stockings; but still there was about her an air of well-to-do comfort which made me feel that the mud was no more than a joke to her. Every now and then I caught something of a glimpse of her face as she half turned herself round in talking to the woman. I could see, or at least I could fancy that I saw, that she was fair, with large round eyes and soft light brown hair. Children did not then wear wigs upon their backs, and I was driven to exercise my fancy as to her locks. At last I resolved that I would pass them and have one look at her,—and I did so. It put me to my best pace to do it, but gradually I overtook them and could hear that the girl never ceased talking as she ran. As I went by them I distinctly heard the words, "Oh, Anne, I do so wonder what he's like!" "You'll see, miss," said Anne. I looked back and saw that she was exactly as I had thought,—a fair, strong, healthy girl, with round eyes and large mouth, broad well-formed nose, and light hair. Who was the "he," as to whom her anxiety was so great,—the "he" whom she was tripping along through the rain and mud to see, and kiss, and love, and wonder at? And why hadn't she been taken in a cab? Would she be allowed to take off those very dirty stockings before she was introduced to her new-found brother, or wrapped in the arms of her stranger father?

I saw no more of them, and heard no further word; but I thought a great deal of the girl. Ah, me, if she could have been a young unknown, newly-found sister of my own, how warmly would I have welcomed her! How little should I have cared for the mud on her stockings; how closely would I have folded her in my arms; how anxious would I have been with Anne as to those damp clothes; what delight would I have had in feeding her, coaxing her, caressing her, and playing with her! There had seemed to belong to her a wholesome strong health, which it had made me for the moment happy even to witness. And then the sweet, eloquent anxiety of her voice,—"Oh, Anne, I do so wonder what he's like!" While I heard her voice I had seemed to hear and know so much of her! And then she had passed out of my ken for ever!

I thought no more about the duchess and the applewoman, but devoted my mind entirely to the girl and her brother. I was persuaded that it must be a brother. Had it been a father there would have been more of awe in her tone. It certainly was a brother. Gradually, as the unforced imagination came to play upon the matter, a little picture fashioned itself in my mind. The girl was my own sister,—a sister whom I had never seen till she was thus brought to me for protection and love; but she was older, just budding into womanhood, instead of running beside her nurse with twinkling legs. There, however, was the same broad, honest face, the same round eyes, the same strong nose and mouth. She had come to me for love and protection, having no other friend in the world to trust. But, having me, I proudly declared to myself that she needed nothing further. In two short months I was nothing to her,—or almost nothing. I had a friend, and in two little months my friend had become so much more than I ever could have been!

These wondrous castles in the air never get themselves well built when the mind, with premeditated skill and labour, sets itself to work to build them. It is when they come uncalled for that they stand erect and strong before the mind's eye, with every mullioned window perfect, the rounded walls all there, the embrasures cut, the fosse dug, and the drawbridge down. As I had made this castle for myself, as I had sat with this girl by my side, calling her the sweetest names, as I had seen her blush when my friend came near her, and had known at once, with a mixed agony and joy, how the thing was to be, I swear that I never once thought of the "Panjandrum." I walked the whole round of the Regent's Park, perfecting the building;—and I did perfect it, took the girl to church, gave her away to my friend Walker, and came back and sobbed and sputtered out my speech at the little breakfast, before it occurred to me to suggest to myself that I might use the thing.

Churchill Smith and Walter Watt had been dead against a novel; and, indeed, the matter had been put to the vote, and it had been decided that there should be no novel. But, what is a novel? The purport of that vote had been to negative a long serial tale, running on from number to number, in a manner which has since become well understood by the reading public. I had thought my colleagues wrong, and so thinking, it was clearly my duty to correct their error, if I might do so without infringing that loyalty and general obedience to expressed authority which are so essential to such a society as ours. Before I had got back to Theobald's Road I had persuaded myself that a short tale would be the very thing for the first number. It might not stir the public mind. To do that I would leave to Churchill Smith and Walter Watt. But a well-formed little story, such as that of which I had now the full possession, would fall on the readers of the "Panjandrum" like sweet rain in summer, making things fresh and green and joyous. I was quite sure that it was needed. Walter Watt might say what he pleased, and Churchill Smith might look at me as sternly as he would, sitting there silent with his forehead on his hand; but I knew at least as much about a magazine as they did. At any rate, I would write my tale. That very morning it had seemed to me to be impossible to get anything written. Now, as I hurried up-stairs to get rid of my wet clothes, I felt that I could not take the pen quickly enough into my hand. I had a thing to say, and I would say it. If I could complete my story,—and I did not doubt its completion from the very moment in which I realised its conception,—I should be saved, at any rate, from the disgrace of appearing empty-handed in Mrs. St. Quinten's parlour. Within a quarter of an hour of my arrival at home I had seated myself at my table and written the name of the tale,—"The New Inmate."

I doubt whether any five days in my life were ever happier than those which were devoted to this piece of work. I began it that Monday afternoon, and finished it on the Friday night. While I was at the task all doubt vanished from my mind. I did not care a fig for Watt or Smith, and was quite sure that I should carry Mrs. St. Quinten with me. Each night I copied fairly what I had written in the day, and I came to love the thing with an exceeding love. There was a deal of pathos in it,—at least so I thought,—and I cried over it like a child. I had strained all my means to prepare for the coming of the girl,—I am now going back for a moment to my castle in the air,—and had furnished for her a little sitting-room and as pretty a white-curtained chamber as a girl ever took pleasure in calling her own. There were books for her, and a small piano, and a low sofa, and all little feminine belongings. I had said to myself that everything should be for her, and I had sold my horse,—the horse of my imagination, the reader will understand, for I had never in truth possessed such an animal,—and told my club friends that I should no longer be one of them. Then the girl had come, and had gone away to Walker,—as it seemed to me at once,—to Walker, who still lived in lodgings, and had not even a second sitting-room for her comfort,—to Walker, who was, indeed, a good fellow in his way, but possessed of no particular attractions either in wit, manners, or beauty! I wanted them to change with me, and to take my pretty home. I should have been delighted to go to a garret, leaving them everything. But Walker was proud, and would not have it so; and the girl protested that the piano and the white dimity curtains were nothing to her. Walker was everything;—Walker, of whom she had never heard, when she came but a few weeks since to me as the only friend left to her in the world! I worked myself up to such a pitch of feeling over my story, that I could hardly write it for my tears. I saw myself standing all alone in that pretty sitting-room after they were gone, and I pitied myself with an exceeding pity. "Si vis me flere, dolendum est primum ipsi tibi." If success was to be obtained by obeying that instruction, I might certainly expect success.

The way in which my work went without a pause was delightful. When the pen was not in my hand I was longing for it. While I was walking, eating, or reading, I was still thinking of my story. I dreamt of it. It came to me to be a matter that admitted of no doubt. The girl with the muddy stockings, who had thus provided me in my need, was to me a blessed memory. When I kissed my sister's brow, on her first arrival, she was in my arms,—palpably. All her sweetnesses were present to me, as though I had her there, in the little street turning out of Theobald's Road. To this moment I can distinguish the voice in which she spoke to me that little whispered word, when I asked her whether she cared for Walker. When one thinks of it, the reality of it all is appalling. What need is there of a sister or a friend in the flesh,—a sister or a friend with probably so many faults,—when by a little exercise of the mind they may be there at your elbow, faultless? It came to pass that the tale was more dear to me than the magazine. As I read it through for the third or fourth time on the Sunday morning,

I was chiefly anxious for the "Panjandrum," in order that "The New Inmate" might see the world.

We were to meet that evening at eight o'clock, and it was understood that the sitting would be prolonged to a late hour, because of the readings. It would fall to my lot to take the second reading, as coming next to Mrs. St. Quinten, and I should, at any rate, not be subjected to a weary audience. We had, however, promised each other to be very patient; and I was resolved that, even to the production of Churchill Smith, who would be the last, I would give an undivided and eager attention. I determined also in my joy that I would vote against the insertion of no colleague's contribution. Were we not in a boat together, and would not each do his best? Even though a paper might be dull, better a little dulness than the crushing of a friend's spirit. I fear that I thought that "The New Inmate" might atone for much dulness. I dined early on that day; then took a walk round the Regent's Park, to renew my thoughts on the very spot on which they had first occurred to me, and after that, returning home, gave a last touch to my work. Though it had been written after so hurried a fashion, there was not a word in it which I had not weighed and found to be fitting.

I was the first at Mrs. St. Quinten's house, and found that lady very full of the magazine. She asked, however, no questions as to my contribution. Of her own she at once spoke to me. "What do you think I have done at last?" she said. In my reply to her question I made some slight allusion to "The New Inmate," but I don't think she caught the words. "I have reviewed Bishop Berkeley's whole Theory on Matter," said she. What feeling I expressed by my gesture I cannot say, but I think it must have been one of great awe. "And I have done it exhaustively," she continued; "so that the subject need not be continued. Churchill does not like continuations." Perhaps it did not signify much. If she were heavy, I at any rate was light. If her work should prove difficult of comprehension, mine was easy. If she spoke only to the wise and old, I had addressed myself to babes and sucklings. I said something as to the contrast, again naming my little story. But she was too full of Bishop Berkeley to heed me. If she had worked as I had worked, of course she was full of Bishop Berkeley. To me, "The New Inmate" at that moment was more than all the bishops.

The other men soon came in, clustering together, and our number was complete. Regan whispered to me that Jack Hallam had not written a line. "And you?" I asked. "Oh, I am all right," said he. "I don't suppose they'll let it pass; but that's their affair;—not mine." Watt and Smith took their places almost without speaking, and preparation was made for the preliminary feast of the body. The after-feast was matter of such vital importance to us that we hardly possessed our customary light-hearted elasticity. There was, however, an air of subdued triumph about our "Lydia,"—of triumph subdued by the presence of her cousin. As for myself, I was supremely happy. I said a word to Watt, asking him as to his performance. "I don't suppose you will like it," he replied; "but it is at any rate a fair specimen of that which it has been my ambition to produce." I assured him with enthusiasm that I was thoroughly prepared to approve, and that, too, without carping criticism. "But we must be critics," he observed. Of Churchill Smith I asked no question.

When we had eaten and drunk we began the work of the evening by giving in the names of our papers, and describing the nature of the work we had done. Mrs. St. Quinten was the first, and read her title from a scrap of paper. "A Review of Bishop Berkeley's Theory." Churchill Smith remarked that it was a very dangerous subject. The lady begged him to wait till he should hear the paper read. "Of course I will hear it read," said her cousin. To me it was evident that Smith would object to this essay without any scruple, if he did not in truth approve of it. Then it was my turn, and I explained in the quietest tone which I could assume that I had written a little tale called "The New Inmate." It was very simple, I said, but I trusted it might not be rejected on that score. There was silence for a moment, and I prompted Regan to proceed; but I was interrupted by Walter Watt. "I thought," said he, "that we had positively decided against 'prose fiction.'" I protested that the decision had been given against novels, against long serial stories to be continued from number to number. This was a little thing, completed within my twenty-one allotted pages. "Our vote was taken as to prose fiction," said Watt. I appealed to Hallam, who at once took my part,—as also did Regan. "Walter is quite correct as to the purport of our decision," said Churchill Smith. I turned to Mrs. St. Quinten. "I don't see why we shouldn't have a short story," she said. I then declared that with their permission I would at any rate read it, and again requested Regan to proceed. Upon this Walter Watt rose upon his feet, and made a speech. The vote had been taken, and could not be rescinded. After such a vote it was not open to me to read my story. The story, no doubt, was very good,—he was pleased to say so,—but it was not matter of the sort which they intended to use. Seeing the purpose which they had in view, he thought that the reading of the story would be waste of time. "It will clearly be waste of time," said Churchill Smith. Walter Watt went on to explain to us that if from one meeting to another we did not allow ourselves to be bound by our own decisions, we should never appear before the public.

I will acknowledge that I was enraged. It seemed to me impossible that such folly should be allowed to prevail, or that after all my efforts I should be treated by my own friends after such a fashion. I also got upon my legs and protested loudly that Mr. Watt and Mr. Smith did not even know what had been the subject under discussion, when the vote adverse to novels had been taken. No record was kept of our proceedings; and, as I clearly showed to them, Mr. Regan and Mr. Hallam were quite as likely to hold correct views on this subject as were Mr. Watt and Mr. Smith. All calling of men Pat, and Jack, and Walter, was for the moment over. Watt admitted the truth of this argument, and declared that they must again decide whether my story of "The New Inmate" was or was not a novel in the sense intended when the previous vote was taken. If not,—if the decision on that point should be in my favour,—then the privilege of reading it would at any rate belong to me. I believed so thoroughly in my own work that I desired nothing beyond this. We went to work, therefore, and took the votes on the proposition,—Was or was not the story of "The New Inmate" debarred by the previous resolution against the admission of novels?

The decision manifestly rested with Mrs. St. Quinten. I was master, easily master, of three votes. Hallam and Regan were altogether with me, and in a matter of such import I had no hesitation in voting for myself. Had the question been the acceptance or rejection of the story for the magazine, then, by the nature of our constitution, I should have had no voice in the matter. But this was not the case, and I recorded my own vote in my own favour without a blush. Having done so, I turned to Mrs. St. Quinten with an air of supplication in my face of which I myself was aware, and of which I became at once ashamed. She looked round at me almost furtively, keeping her eyes otherwise fixed upon Churchill Smith's immovable countenance. I did not condescend to speak a word to her. What words I had to say, I had spoken to them all, and was confident in the justice of my cause. I quickly dropped that look of supplication and threw myself back in my chair. The moment was one of intense interest, almost of agony, but I could not allow myself to think that in very truth my work would be rejected by them before it was seen. If such were to be their decision, how would it be possible that the "Panjandrum" should ever be brought into existence? Who could endure such ignominy and still persevere?

There was silence among us, which to me in the intensity of my feelings seemed to last for minutes. Regan was the first to speak. "Now, Mrs. St. Quinten," he said, "it all rests with you." An idea shot across my mind at the moment, of the folly of which we had been guilty in placing our most vital interests in the hands of a woman merely on the score of gallantry. Two votes had been given to her as against one of ours simply because,—she was a woman. It may be that there had been something in the arrangement of compensation for the tea and muffins; but if so, how poor was the cause for so great an effect! She sat there the arbiter of our destinies. "You had better give your vote," said Smith roughly. "You think it is a novel?" she said, appealing to him. "There can be no doubt of it," he replied; "a novel is not a novel because it is long or short. Such is the matter which we intended to declare that we would not put forth in our magazine." "I protest," said I, jumping up,—"I protest against this interference."

Then there was a loud and a very angry discussion whether Churchill Smith was justified in his endeavour to bias Mrs. St. Quinten; and we were nearly brought to a vote upon that. I myself was very anxious to have that question decided,—to have any question decided in which Churchill Smith could be shown to be in the wrong. But no one would back me, and it seemed to me as though even Regan and Jack Hallam were falling off from me,—though Jack had never yet restored to me that article of clothing to which allusion was made in the first chapter of this little history, and I had been almost as anxious for Pat's Latin translation as for my own production. It was decided without a vote that any amount of free questioning as to each other's opinions, and of free anwering, was to be considered fair. "I tell her my opinion. You can tell her yours," said Churchill Smith. "It is my opinion," said I, "that you want to dictate to everybody and to rule the whole thing." "I think we did mean to exclude all story-telling," said Mrs. St. Quinten, and so the decision was given against me.

Looking back at it I know that they were right on the exact point then under discussion. They had intended to exclude all stories. But,—heaven and earth,—was there ever such folly as that of which they had been guilty in coming to such a resolution? I have often suggested to myself since, that had "The New Inmate" been read on that evening, the "Panjandrum" might have become a living reality, and that the fortieth volume of the publication might now have been standing on the shelves of many a well-filled library. The decision, however, had been given against me, and I sat like one stricken dumb, paralysed, or turned to stone. I remember it as though it were yesterday. I did not speak a word, but simply moving my chair an inch or two, I turned my face away from the lady who had thus blasted all my hopes. I fear that my eyes were wet, and that a hot tear trickled down each cheek. No note of triumph was sounded, and I verily believe they all suffered in my too conspicuous sufferings. To both Watt and Smith it had been a matter of pure conscience. Mrs. St. Quinten, woman-like, had obeyed the man in whose strength she trusted. There was silence for a few moments, and then Watt invited Regan to proceed. He had divided his work into three portions, but what they were called, whether they were verse or prose, translations or original, comic or serious, I never knew. I could not listen then. For me to continue my services to the "Panjandrum" was an impossibility. I had been crushed,—so crushed that I had not vitality left me to escape from the room, or I should not have remained there. Pat Regan's papers were nothing to me now. Watt I knew had written an essay called "The Real Aristocrat," which was published elsewhere afterwards. Jack Hallam's work was not ready. There was something said of his delinquency, but I cared not what. I only wished that my work also had been unready. Churchill Smith also had some essay, "On the Basis of Political Right." That, if I remember rightly, was its title. I often talked the matter over in after days with Pat Regan, and I know that from the moment in which my consternation was made apparent to them, the thing went very heavily. At the time, and for some hours after the adverse decision, I was altogether unmanned and unable to collect my thoughts. Before the evening was over there occurred a further episode in our affairs which awakened me.

The names of the papers had been given in, and Mrs. St. Quinten began to read her essay. Nothing more than the drone of her voice reached the tympanum of my ears. I did not look at her, or think of her, or care to hear a word that she uttered. I believe I almost slept in my agony; but sleeping or waking I was turning over in my mind, wearily and incapably, the idea of declining to give any opinion as to the propriety of inserting or rejecting the review of

Bishop Berkeley's theory, on the score that my connection with the "Panjandrum" had been severed. But the sound of the reading went on, and I did not make up my mind. I hardly endeavoured to make it up, but sat dreamily revelling in my own grievance, and pondering over the suicidal folly of the "Panjandrum" Company. The reading went on and on without interruption, without question, and without applause. I know I slept during some portion of the time, for I remember that Regan kicked my shin. And I remember, also, a feeling of compassion for the reader, who was hardly able to rouse herself up to the pitch of spirit necessary for the occasion,—but allowed herself to be quelled by the cold, steady gaze of her cousin Churchill. Watt sat immovable, with his hands in his trousers pockets, leaning back in his chair, the very picture of dispassionate criticism. Jack Hallam amused himself by firing paper pellets at Regan, sundry of which struck me on the head and face. Once Mrs. Quinten burst forth in offence. "Mr. Hallam," she said, "I am sorry to be so tedious." "I like it of all things," said Jack. It was certainly very long. Half comatose, as I was, with my own sufferings I had begun to ask myself before Mrs. St. Quinten had finished her task whether it would be possible to endure three other readings lengthy as this. Ah! if I might have read "My New Inmate," how different would the feeling have been! Of what the lady said about Berkeley, I did not catch a word; but the name of the philosophical bishop seemed to be repeated usque ad nauseam. Of a sudden I was aware that I had snored,—a kick from Pat Regan wounded my shin; a pellet from Jack Hallam fell on my nose; and the essay was completed. I looked up, and could see that drops of perspiration were standing on the lady's brow.

There was a pause, and even I was now aroused to attention. We were to write our verdict on paper,—simply the word, "Insert," or "Reject,"—and what should I write? Instead of doing so, should I declare at once that I was severed from the "Panjandrum" by the treatment I had received? That I was severed, in fact, I was very sure. Could any human flesh and blood have continued its services to any magazine after such humiliation as I had suffered? Nevertheless it might perhaps be more manly were I to accept the responsibility of voting on the present occasion,—and if so, how should I vote? I had not followed a single sentence, and yet I was convinced that matter such as that would never stir the British public mind. But as the thing went, we were not called upon for our formal verdicts. "Lydia," as soon as she had done reading, turned at once to her cousin. She cared for no verdict but his. "Well," said she, "what do you think of it?" At first he did not answer. "I know I read it badly," she continued, "but I hope you caught my meaning."

"It is utter nonsense," he said, without moving his head.

"Oh, Churchill!" she exclaimed.

"It is utter nonsense," he repeated. "It is out of the question that it should be published." She glanced her eyes round the company, but ventured no spoken appeal. Jack Hallam said something about unnecessary severity and want of courtesy. Watt simply shook his head. "I say it is trash," said Smith, rising from his chair. "You shall not disgrace yourself. Give it to me." She put her hand upon the manuscript, as though to save it. "Give it to me," he said sternly, and took it from her unresisting grasp. Then he stalked to the fire, and tearing the sheets in pieces, thrust them between the bars.

Of course there was a great commotion. We were all up in a moment, standing around her as though to console her. Miss Collins came in and absolutely wept over her ill-used friend. For the instant I had forgotten "The New Inmate," as though it had never been written. She was deluged in tears, hiding her face upon the table; but she uttered no word of reproach, and ventured not a syllable in defence of her essay. "I didn't think it was so bad as that," she murmured amidst her sobs. I did not dare to accuse the man of cruelty. I myself had become so small among them that my voice would have had no weight. But I did think him cruel, and hated him on her account as well as on my own. Jack Hallam remarked that for this night, at least, our work must be considered to be over. "It is over altogether," said Churchill Smith. "I have known that for weeks past; and I have known, too, what fools we have been to make the attempt. I hope, at least, that we may have learnt a lesson that will be of service to us. Perhaps you had better go now, and I'll just say a word or two to my cousin before I leave her."

How we got out of the room I hardly remember. There was, no doubt, some leave-taking between us four and the unfortunate Lydia, but it amounted, I think, to no more than mere decency required. To Churchill Smith I know that I did not speak. I never saw either of the cousins again; nor, as has been already told, did I ever distinctly hear what was their fate in life. And yet how intimately connected with them had I been for the last six or eight months! For not calling upon her, so that we might have mingled the tears of our disappointment together, I much blamed myself; but the subject which we must have discussed,—the failure, namely, of the "Panjandrum,"—was one so sore and full of sorrow, that I could not bring myself to face the interview. Churchill Smith, I know, made various efforts to obtain literary employment; but never succeeded, because he would yield no inch in the expression of his own violent opinions. I doubt whether he ever earned as much as £10 by his writings. I heard of his living,—and almost starving,—still in London, and then that he went to fight for Polish freedom. It is believed that he died in a Russian prison, but I could never find any one who knew with accuracy the circumstances of his fate. He was a man who could go forth with his life in his hand, and in meeting death could feel that he encountered only that which he had expected. Mrs. St. Quinten certainly vanished during the next summer from the street in which she had bestowed upon us so many muffins, and what became of her I never heard.

On that evening Pat Regan and I consoled ourselves together as best we might, Jack Hallam and Walter Watt having parted from us under the walls of Marylebone Workhouse. Pat and I walked down to a modest house of refreshment with which we were acquainted in Leicester Square, and there arranged the obsequies of the "Panjandrum" over a pint of stout and a baked potato. Pat's equanimity was marvellous. It had not even yet been ruffled, although the indignities thrown upon him had almost surpassed those inflicted on myself. His "Lord Bateman" had been first rejected; and, after that, his subsequent contributions had been absolutely ignored, merely because Mr. Churchill Smith had not approved his cousin's essay upon Bishop Berkeley! "It was rot; real rot," said Pat, alluding to Lydia's essay, and apologising for Smith. "But why not have gone on and heard yours?" said I. "Mine would have been rot, too," said Pat. "It isn't so easy, after all, to do this kind of thing."

We agreed that the obsequies should be very private. Indeed, as the "Panjandrum" had as yet not had a body of its own, it was hardly necessary to open the earth for the purposes of interment. We agreed simply to say nothing about it to any one. I would go to Mr. X. and tell him that we had abandoned our project, and there would be an end of it. As the night advanced, I offered to read "The New Inmate" to my friend; but he truly remarked that of reading aloud they had surely had enough that night. When he reflected that but for the violence of Mr. Smith's proceedings we might even then, at that moment, have been listening to an essay upon the "Basis of Political Rights," I think that he rejoiced that the "Panjandrum" was no more.

On the following morning I called on Mr. X., and explained to him that portion of the occurrences of the previous evening with which it was necessary that he should be made acquainted. I thought that he was rather brusque; but I cannot complain that he was, upon the whole, unfriendly. "The truth is, sir," he said, "you none of you exactly knew what you wanted to be after. You were very anxious to do something grand, but hadn't got this grand thing clear before your eye. People, you know, may have too much genius, or may have too little." Which of the two was our case he did not say; but he did promise to hear my story of "The New Inmate" read, with reference to its possible insertion in another periodical publication with which he had lately become connected. Perhaps some of my readers may remember its appearance in the first number of the "Marble Arch," where it attracted no little attention, and was supposed to have given assistance, not altogether despicable, towards the establishment of that excellent periodical.

Such was the history of the "Panjandrum."

The Spotted Dog

Originally appeared in *Saint Paul's Magazine*, March–April 1870. Reprinted in *An Editor's Tales* (1870). In *An Autobiography* Trollope admits that this story of 'the tragedy of a poor drunkard, who with infinite learning at his command made one sad final effort to reclaim himself, and perished while he was making it' was closely based on fact. He also reckoned this story the best of the six 'Editor's Tales'.

Part I—The Attempt

Some few years since we received the following letter;—

"Dear Sir,

"I write to you for literary employment, and I implore you to provide me with it if it be within your power to do so. My capacity for such work is not small, and my acquirements are considerable. My need is very great, and my views in regard to remuneration are modest. I was educated at—, and was afterwards a scholar of—College, Cambridge. I left the university without a degree, in consequence of a quarrel with the college tutor. I was rusticated, and not allowed to return. After that I became for awhile a student for the Chancery Bar. I then lived for some years in Paris, and I understand and speak French as though it were my own language. For all purposes of literature I am equally conversant with German. I read Italian. I am, of course, familiar with Latin. In regard to Greek I will only say that I am less ignorant of it than nineteen-twentieths of our national scholars. I am well read in modern and ancient history. I have especially studied political economy. I have not neglected other matters necessary to the education of an enlightened man,—unless it be natural philosophy. I can write English, and can write it with rapidity. I am a poet;—at least, I so esteem myself. I am not a believer. My character will not bear investigation;—in saying which, I mean you to understand, not that I steal or cheat, but that I live in a dirty lodging, spend many of my hours in a public-house, and cannot pay tradesmen's bills where tradesmen have been found to trust me. I have a wife and four children,—which burden forbids me to free myself from all care by a bare bodkin. I am just past forty, and since I quarrelled with my family because I could not understand The Trinity, I have never been the owner of a ten-pound note. My wife was not a lady. I married her because I was determined to take refuge from the conventional thraldom of so-called 'gentlemen' amidst the liberty of the lower orders. My life, of course, has been a mistake. Indeed, to live at all,—is it not a folly?

"I am at present employed on the staff of two or three of the 'Penny Dreadfuls.' Your august highness in literature has perhaps never heard of a 'Penny Dreadful.' I write for them matter, which we among ourselves call 'blood and nastiness,'—and which is copied from one to another. For this I am paid forty-five shillings a week. For thirty shillings a week I will do any work that you may impose upon me for the term of six months. I write this letter as a last effort to rescue myself from the filth of my present position, but I entertain no hope of any success. If you ask it I will come and see you; but do not send for me unless you mean to employ me, as I am ashamed of myself. I live at No. 3, Cucumber Court, Gray's Inn Lane;—but if you write, address to the care of Mr. Grimes, the Spotted Dog, Liquorpond Street. Now I have told you my whole life, and you may help me if you will. I do not expect an answer.

"Yours truly,
"Julius Mackenzie."

Indeed he had told us his whole life, and what a picture of a life he had drawn! There was something in the letter which compelled attention. It was impossible to throw it, half read, into the waste-paper basket, and to think of it not at all. We did read it, probably twice, and then put ourselves to work to consider how much of it might be true and how much false. Had the man been a boy at—, and then a scholar of his college? We concluded that, so far, the narrative was true. Had he abandoned his dependence on wealthy friends from conscientious scruples, as he pretended; or had other and less creditable reasons caused the severance? On that point we did not quite believe him. And then, as to those assertions made by himself in regard to his own capabilities,—how far did they gain credence with us? We think that we believed them all, making some small discount,—with the exception of that one in which he proclaimed himself to be a poet. A man may know whether he understands French, and be quite ignorant whether the rhymed lines which he produces are or are not poetry. When he told us that he was an infidel, and that his character would not bear investigation, we went with him altogether. His allusion to suicide we regarded as a foolish boast. We gave him credit for the four children, but were not certain about the wife. We quite believed the general assertion of his impecuniosity. That stuff about "conventional thraldom" we hope we took at its worth. When he told us that his life had been a mistake he spoke to us Gospel truth.

Of the "Penny Dreadfuls," and of "blood and nastiness," so called, we had never before heard, but we did not think it remarkable that a man so gifted as our correspondent should earn forty-five shillings a week by writing for the cheaper periodicals. It did not, however, appear to us probable that any one so remunerated would be willing to leave that engagement for another which should give him only thirty shillings. When he spoke of the "filth of his present position," our heart began to bleed for him. We know what it is so well, and can fathom so accurately the degradation of the educated man who, having been ambitious in the career of literature, falls into that slough of despond by which the profession of literature is almost surrounded. There we were with him, as brothers together. When we came to Mr. Grimes and the Spotted Dog, in Liquorpond Street, we thought that we had better refrain from answering the letter,—by which decision on our part he would not, according to his own statement, be much disappointed. Mr. Julius Mackenzie! Perhaps at this very time rich uncles and aunts were buttoning up their pockets against the sinner because of his devotion to the Spotted Dog. There are well-to-do people among the Mackenzies. It might be the case that that heterodox want of comprehension in regard to The Trinity was the cause of it; but we have observed that in most families, grievous as are doubts upon such sacred subjects, they are not held to be cause of hostility so invincible as is a thorough-going devotion to a Spotted Dog. If the Spotted Dog had brought about these troubles, any interposition from ourselves would be useless.

For twenty-four hours we had given up all idea of answering

the letter; but it then occurred to us that men who have become disreputable as drunkards do not put forth their own abominations when making appeals for aid. If this man were really given to drink he would hardly have told us of his association with the public-house. Probably he was much at the Spotted Dog, and hated himself for being there. The more we thought of it the more we fancied that the gist of his letter might be true. It seemed that the man had desired to tell the truth as he himself believed it.

It so happened that at that time we had been asked to provide an index to a certain learned manuscript in three volumes. The intended publisher of the work had already procured an index from a professional compiler of such matters; but the thing had been so badly done that it could not be used. Some knowledge of the classics was required, though it was not much more than a familiarity with the names of Latin and Greek authors, to which perhaps should be added some acquaintance, with the names also, of the better-known editors and commentators. The gentleman who had had the task in hand had failed conspicuously, and I had been told by my enterprising friend Mr. X—, the publisher, that £25 would be freely paid on the proper accomplishment of the undertaking. The work, apparently so trifling in its nature, demanded a scholar's acquirements, and could hardly be completed in less than two months. We had snubbed the offer, saying that we should be ashamed to ask an educated man to give his time and labour for so small a remuneration;—but to Mr. Julius Mackenzie £25 for two months' work would manifestly be a godsend. If Mr. Julius Mackenzie did in truth possess the knowledge for which he gave himself credit; if he was, as he said, "familiar with Latin," and was "less ignorant of Greek than nineteen-twentieths of our national scholars," he might perhaps be able to earn this £25. We certainly knew no one else who could and who would do the work properly for that money. We therefore wrote to Mr. Julius Mackenzie, and requested his presence. Our note was short, cautious, and also courteous. We regretted that a man so gifted should be driven by stress of circumstances to such need. We could undertake nothing, but if it would not put him to too much trouble to call upon us, we might perhaps be able to suggest something to him. Precisely at the hour named Mr. Julius Mackenzie came to us.

We well remember his appearance, which was one unutterably painful to behold. He was a tall man, very thin,—thin we might say as a whipping-post, were it not that one's idea of a whipping-post conveys erectness and rigidity, whereas this man, as he stood before us, was full of bends, and curves, and crookedness. His big head seemed to lean forward over his miserably narrow chest. His back was bowed, and his legs were crooked and tottering. He had told us that he was over forty, but we doubted, and doubt now, whether he had not added something to his years, in order partially to excuse the wan, worn weariness of his countenance. He carried an infinity of thick, ragged, wild, dirty hair, dark in colour, though not black, which age had not yet begun to grizzle. He wore a miserable attempt at a beard, stubbly, uneven, and half shorn,—as though it had been cut down within an inch of his chin with blunt scissors. He had two ugly projecting teeth, and his cheeks were hollow. His eyes were deep-set, but very bright, illuminating his whole face; so that it was impossible to look at him and to think him to be one wholly insignificant. His eyebrows were large and shaggy, but well formed, not meeting across the brow, with single, stiffly-projecting hairs,—a pair of eyebrows which added much strength to his countenance. His nose was long and well shaped,—but red as a huge carbuncle. The moment we saw him we connected that nose with the Spotted Dog. It was not a blotched nose, not a nose covered with many carbuncles, but a brightly red, smooth, well-formed nose, one glowing carbuncle in itself. He was dressed in a long brown great-coat, which was buttoned up round his throat, and which came nearly to his feet. The binding of the coat was frayed, the buttons were half uncovered, the button-holes were tattered, the velvet collar had become party-coloured with dirt and usage. It was in the month of December, and a great-coat was needed; but this great-coat looked as though it were worn because other garments were not at his command. Not an inch of linen or even of flannel shirt was visible. Below his coat we could only see his broken boots and the soiled legs of his trousers, which had reached that age which in trousers defies description. When we looked at him we could not but ask ourselves whether this man had been born a gentleman and was still a scholar. And yet there was that in his face which prompted us to believe the account he had given of himself. As we looked at him we felt sure that he possessed keen intellect, and that he was too much of a man to boast of acquirements which he did not believe himself to possess. We shook hands with him, asked him to sit down, and murmured something of our sorrow that he should be in distress.

"I am pretty well used to it," said he. There was nothing mean in his voice;—there was indeed a touch of humour in it, and in his manner there was nothing of the abjectness of supplication. We had his letter in our hands, and we read a portion of it again as he sat opposite to us. We then remarked that we did not understand how he, having a wife and family dependent on him, could offer to give up a third of his income with the mere object of changing the nature of his work. "You don't know what it is," said he, "to write for the 'Penny Dreadfuls.' I'm at it seven hours a day, and hate the very words that I write. I cursed myself afterwards for sending that letter. I know that to hope is to be an ass. But I did send it, and here I am."

We looked at his nose and felt that we must be careful before we suggested to our learned friend Dr.—to put his manuscript into the hands of Mr. Julius Mackenzie. If it had been a printed book the attempt might have been made without much hazard, but our friend's work, which was elaborate, and very learned, had not yet reached the honours of the printing-house. We had had our own doubts whether it might ever assume the form of a real book; but our friend, who was a wealthy as well as a learned man, was, as yet, very determined. He desired, at any rate, that the thing should be perfected, and his publisher had therefore come to us offering £25 for the codification and index. Were anything other than good to befall his manuscript, his lamentations would be loud, not on his own score,—but on behalf of learning in general. It behoved us therefore to be cautious. We pretended to read the letter again, in order that we might gain time for a decision, for we were greatly frightened by that gleaming nose.

Let the reader understand that the nose was by no means Bardolphian. If we have read Shakespeare aright Bardolph's nose was a thing of terror from its size as well as its hue. It was a mighty vat, into which had ascended all the divinest particles distilled from the cellars of the hostelrie in Eastcheap. Such at least is the idea which stage representations have left upon all our minds. But the nose now before us was a well-formed nose, would have been a commanding nose,—for the power of command shows itself much in the nasal organ,—had it not been for its colour. While we were thinking of this, and doubting much as to our friend's manuscript, Mr. Mackenzie interrupted us. "You think I am a drunkard," said he. The man's mother-wit had enabled him to read our inmost thoughts.

As we looked up the man had risen from his chair, and was standing over us. He loomed upon us very tall, although his legs were crooked, and his back bent. Those piercing eyes, and that nose which almost assumed an air of authority as he carried it, were a great way above us. There seemed to be an infinity of that old brown great-coat. He had divined our thoughts, and we did not dare to contradict him. We felt that a weak, vapid, unmanly smile was creeping over our face. We were smiling as a man smiles who intends to imply some contemptuous assent with the self-depreciating comment of his companion. Such a mode of expression is in our estimation most cowardly, and most odious. We had not intended it, but we knew that the smile had pervaded us. "Of course you do," said he. "I was a drunkard, but I am not one now. It doesn't matter;—only I wish you hadn't sent for me. I'll go away at once."

So saying, he was about to depart, but we stopped him. We assured him with much energy that we did not mean to offend him. He protested that there was no offence. He was too well used to that kind of thing to be made "more than wretched by it." Such was his heart-breaking phrase. "As for anger, I've lost all that long ago. Of course you take me for a drunkard, and I should still be a drunkard, only— "

"Only what?" I asked.

"It don't matter," said he. "I need not trouble you with more than I have said already. You haven't got anything for me to do, I suppose?" Then I explained to him that I had something he might do, if I could venture to entrust him with the work. With some trouble I got him to sit down again, and to listen while I explained to him the circumstances. I had been grievously afflicted when he alluded to his former habit of drinking,—a former habit as he himself now stated,—but I entertained no hesitation in raising questions as to his erudition. I felt almost assured that his answers would be satisfactory, and that no discomfiture would arise from such questioning. We were quickly able to perceive that we at any rate could not examine him in classical literature. As soon as we mentioned the name and nature of the work he went off at score, and satisfied us amply that he was familiar at least with the title pages of editions. We began, indeed, to fear whether he might not be too caustic a critic on our own friend's performance. "Dr.—is only an amateur himself," said we, deprecating in advance any such exercise of the red-nosed man's too severe erudition. "We never get much beyond dilettanteism here," said he, "as far as Greek and Latin are concerned." What a terrible man he would have been could he have got upon the staff of the Saturday Review, instead of going to the Spotted Dog!

We endeavoured to bring the interview to an end by telling him that we would consult the learned Doctor from whom the manuscript had emanated; and we hinted that a reference would be of course acceptable. His impudence,—or perhaps we should rather call it his straightforward sincere audacity,—was unbounded. "Mr. Grimes of the Spotted Dog knows me better than any one else," said he. We blew the breath out of our mouth with astonishment. "I'm not asking you to go to him to find out whether I know Latin and Greek," said Mr. Mackenzie. "You must find that out for yourself." We assured him that we thought we had found that out. "But he can tell you that I won't pawn your manuscript." The man was so grim and brave that he almost frightened us. We hinted, however, that literary reference should be given. The gentleman who paid him forty-five shillings a week,—the manager, in short, of the "Penny Dreadful,"—might tell us something of him. Then he wrote for us a name on a scrap of paper, and added to it an address in the close vicinity of Fleet Street, at which we remembered to have seen the title of a periodical which we now knew to be a "Penny Dreadful."

Before he took his leave he made us a speech, again standing up over us, though we also were on our legs. It was that bend in his neck, combined with his natural height, which gave him such an air of superiority in conversation. He seemed to overshadow us, and to have his own way with us, because he was enabled to look down upon us. There was a footstool on our hearth-rug, and we remember to have attempted to stand upon that, in order that we might escape this supervision; but we stumbled, and had to kick it from us, and something was added to our sense of inferiority by this little failure. "I don't expect much from this," he said. "I never do expect much. And I have misfortunes independent of my poverty which make it impossible that I should be other than a miserable wretch."

"Bad health?" we asked.

"No;—nothing absolutely personal;—but never mind. I must not trouble you with more of my history. But if you can do this thing for me, it may be the means of redeeming me from utter degradation." We then assured him that we would do our best, and he left us with a promise that he would call again on that day week.

The first step which we took on his behalf was one the very idea of which had at first almost moved us to ridicule. We made inquiry respecting Mr. Julius Mackenzie, of Mr. Grimes, the landlord of the Spotted Dog. Though Mr. Grimes did keep the Spotted Dog, he might be a man of sense and, possibly, of conscience. At any rate he would tell us something, or confirm our doubts by refusing to tell us anything. We found Mr. Grimes seated in a very neat little back parlour, and were peculiarly taken by the appearance of a lady in a little cap and black silk gown, whom we soon found to be Mrs. Grimes. Had we ventured to employ our intellect in personifying for ourselves an imaginary Mrs. Grimes as the landlady of a Spotted Dog public-house in Liquorpond Street, the figure we should have built up for ourselves would have been the very opposite of that which this lady presented to us. She was slim, and young, and pretty, and had pleasant little tricks of words, in spite of occasional slips in her grammar, which made us almost think that it might be our duty to come very often to the Spotted Dog to inquire about Mr. Julius Mackenzie. Mr. Grimes was a man about forty,—fully ten years the senior of his wife,—with a clear grey eye, and a mouth and chin from which we surmised that he would be competent to clear the Spotted Dog of unruly visitors after twelve o'clock, whenever it might be his wish to do so. We soon made known our request. Mr. Mackenzie had come to us for literary employment. Could they tell us anything about Mr. Mackenzie?

"He's as clever an author, in the way of writing and that kind of thing, as there is in all London," said Mrs. Grimes with energy. Perhaps her opinion ought not to have been taken for much, but it had its weight. We explained, however, that at the present moment we were specially anxious to know something of the gentleman's character and mode of life. Mr. Grimes, whose manner to us was quite courteous, sat silent, thinking how to answer us. His more impulsive and friendly wife was again ready with her assurance. "There ain't an honester gentleman breathing;—and I say he is a gentleman, though he's that poor he hasn't sometimes a shirt to his back."

"I don't think he's ever very well off for shirts," said Mr. Grimes.

"I wouldn't be slow to give him one of yours, John, only I know he wouldn't take it," said Mrs. Grimes. "Well now, look here, sir;—we've that feeling for him that our young woman there would draw anything for him he'd ask,—money or no money. She'd never venture to name money to him if he wanted a glass of anything,—hot or cold, beer or spirits. Isn't that so, John?"

"She's fool enough for anything as far as I know," said Mr. Grimes.

"She ain't no fool at all; and I'd do the same if I was there;—and so'd you, John. There is nothing Mackenzie'd ask as he wouldn't give him," said Mrs. Grimes, pointing with her thumb over her shoulder to her husband, who was standing on the hearth-rug;—"that is, in the way of drawing liquor, and refreshments, and such like. But he never raised a glass to his lips in this house as he didn't pay for, nor yet took a biscuit out of that basket. He's a gentleman all over, is Mackenzie."

It was strong testimony; but still we had not quite got at the bottom of the matter. "Doesn't he raise a great many glasses to his lips?" we asked.

"No he don't," said Mrs. Grimes,—"only in reason."

"He's had misfortunes," said Mr. Grimes.

"Indeed he has," said the lady,—"what I call the very troublesomest of troubles. If you was troubled like him, John, where'd you be?"

"I know where you'd be," said John.

"He's got a bad wife, sir; the worst as ever was," continued Mrs. Grimes. "Talk of drink;—there is nothing that woman wouldn't do for it. She'd pawn the very clothes off her children's back in mid-winter to get it. She'd rob the food out of her husband's mouth for a drop of gin. As for herself,—she ain't no woman's notion left of keeping herself any way. She'd as soon be picked out of the gutter as not;—and as for words out of her mouth or clothes on her back, she hasn't got, sir, not an item of a female's feeling left about her."

Mrs. Grimes had been very eloquent, and had painted the "troublesomest of all troubles" with glowing words. This was what the wretched man had come to by marrying a woman who was not a lady in order that he might escape the "conventional thraldom" of gentility! But still the drunken wife was not all. There was the evidence of his own nose against himself, and the additional fact that he had acknowledged himself to have been formerly a drunkard. "I suppose he has drunk, himself?" we said.

"He has drunk, in course," said Mrs. Grimes.

"The world has been pretty rough with him, sir," said Mr. Grimes.

"But he don't drink now," continued the lady. "At least if he do, we don't see it. As for her, she wouldn't show herself inside our door."

"It ain't often that man and wife draws their milk from the same cow," said Mr. Grimes.

"But Mackenzie is here every day of his life," said Mrs. Grimes. "When he's got a sixpence to pay for it, he'll come in here and have a glass of beer and a bit of something to eat. We does make him a little extra welcome, and that's the truth of it. We knows what he is, and we knows what he was. As for book learning, sir;—it don't matter what language it is, it's all as one to him. He knows 'em all round just as I know my catechism."

"Can't you say fairer than that for him, Polly?" asked Mr. Grimes.

"Don't you talk of catechisms, John; nor yet of nothing else as a man ought to set his mind to;—unless it is keeping the Spotted Dog. But as for Mackenzie;—he knows off by heart whole books full of learning. There was some furreners here as come from,—I don't know where it was they come from, only it wasn't France, nor yet Germany, and he talked to them just as though he hadn't been born in England at all. I don't think there ever was such a man for knowing things. He'll go on with poetry out of his own head till you think it comes from him like web from a spider." We could not help thinking of the wonderful companionship which there must have been in that parlour while the reduced man was spinning his web and Mrs. Grimes, with her needlework lying idle in her lap, was sitting by, listening with rapt admiration. In passing by the Spotted Dog one would not imagine such a scene to have its existence within. But then so many things do have existence of which we imagine nothing!

Mr. Grimes ended the interview. "The fact is, sir, if you can give him employment better than what he has now, you'll be helping a man who has seen better days, and who only wants help to see 'em again. He's got it all there," and Mr. Grimes put his finger up to his head.

"He's got it all here too," said Mrs. Grimes, laying her hand upon her heart. Hereupon we took our leave, suggesting to these excellent friends that if it should come to pass that we had further dealings with Mr. Mackenzie we might perhaps trouble them again. They assured us that we should always be welcome, and Mr. Grimes himself saw us to the door, having made profuse offers of such good cheer as the house afforded. We were upon the whole much taken with the Spotted Dog.

From thence we went to the office of the "Penny Dreadful," in the vicinity of Fleet Street. As we walked thither we could not but think of Mrs. Grimes' words. The troublesomest of troubles! We acknowledged to ourselves that they were true words. Can there be any trouble more troublesome than that of suffering from the shame inflicted by a degraded wife? We had just parted from Mr. Grimes,—not, indeed, having seen very much of him in the course of our interview,—but little as we had seen, we were sure that he was assisted in his position by a buoyant pride in that he called himself the master, and owner, and husband of Mrs. Grimes. In the very step with which he passed in and out of his own door you could see that there was nothing that he was ashamed of about his household. When abroad he could talk of his "missus" with a conviction that the picture which the word would convey to all who heard him would redound to his honour. But what must have been the reflections of Julius Mackenzie when his mind dwelt upon his wife? We remembered the words of his letter. "I have a wife and four children, which burden forbids me to free myself from all care with a bare bodkin." As we thought of them, and of the story which had been told to us at the Spotted Dog, they lost that tone of rhodomontade with which they had invested themselves when we first read them. A wife who is indifferent to being picked out of the gutter, and who will pawn her children's clothes for gin, must be a trouble than which none can be more troublesome.

We did not find that we ingratiated ourselves with the people at the office of the periodical for which Mr. Mackenzie worked; and yet we endeavoured to do so, assuming in our manner and tone something of the familiarity of a common pursuit. After much delay we came upon a gentleman sitting in a dark cupboard, who twisted round his stool to face us while he spoke to us. We believe that he was the editor of more than one "Penny Dreadful," and that as many as a dozen serial novels were being issued to the world at the same time under his supervision. "Oh!" said he, "so you're at that game, are you?" We assured him that we were at no game at all, but were simply influenced by a desire to assist a distressed scholar. "That be blowed," said our brother. "Mackenzie's doing as well here as he'll do anywhere. He's a drunken blackguard, when all's said and done. So you're going to buy him up, are you? You won't keep him long,—and then he'll have to starve." We assured the gentleman that we had no desire to buy up Mr. Mackenzie; we explained our ideas as to the freedom of the literary profession, in accordance with which Mr. Mackenzie could not be wrong in applying to us for work; and we especially deprecated any severity on our brother's part towards the man, more especially begging that nothing might be decided, as we were far from thinking it certain that we could provide Mr. Mackenzie with any literary employment. "That's all right," said our brother, twisting back his stool. "He can't work for both of us;—that's all. He has his bread here regular, week after week; and I don't suppose you'll do as much as that for him." Then we went away, shaking the dust off our feet, and wondering much at the great development of literature which latter years have produced. We had not even known of the existence of these papers;—and yet there they were, going forth into the hands of hundreds of thousands of readers, all of whom were being, more or less, instructed in their modes of life and manner of thinking by the stories which were thus brought before them.

But there might be truth in what our brother had said to us. Should Mr. Mackenzie abandon his present engagement for the sake of the job which we proposed to put in his hands, might he not thereby injure rather than improve his prospects? We were acquainted with only one learned doctor desirous of having his manuscripts codified and indexed at his own expense. As for writing for the periodical with which we were connected, we knew enough of the business to be aware that Mr. Mackenzie's gifts of erudition would very probably not so much assist him in attempting such work as would his late training act against him. A man might be able to read and even talk a dozen languages,—"just as though he hadn't been born in England at all,"—and yet not write the language with which we dealt after the fashion which suited our readers. It might be that he would fly much above our heads, and do work infinitely too big for us. We did not regard our own heads as being very high. But, for such altitude as they held, a certain class of writing was adapted. The gentleman whom we had just left would require, no doubt, altogether another style. It was probable that Mr. Mackenzie had already fitted himself to his present audience. And, even were it not so, we could not promise him forty-five shillings a week, or even that thirty shillings for which he asked. There is nothing more dangerous than the attempt to befriend a man in middle life by transplanting him from one soil to another.

When Mr. Mackenzie came to us again we endeavoured to explain all this to him. We had in the meantime seen our friend the Doctor, whose beneficence of spirit in regard to the unfortunate man of letters was extreme. He was charmed with our account of the man, and saw with his mind's eye the work, for the performance of which he was pining, perfected in a manner that would be a blessing to the scholars of all future ages. He was at first anxious to ask Julius Mackenzie down to his rectory, and, even after we had explained to him that this would not at present be expedient, was full of a dream of future friendship with a man who would be able to discuss the digamma with him, who would have studied Greek metres, and have an opinion of his own as to Porson's canon. We were in possession of the manuscript, and had our friend's authority for handing it over to Mr. Mackenzie.

He came to us according to appointment, and his nose seemed to be redder than ever. We thought that we discovered a discouraging flavour of spirits in his breath. Mrs. Grimes had declared that he drank,—only in reason; but the ideas of the wife of a publican,—even though that wife were Mrs. Grimes,—might be very different from our own as to what was reasonable in that matter. And as we looked at him he seemed to be more rough, more ragged, almost more wretched than before. It might be that, in taking his part with my brother of the "Penny Dreadful," with the Doctor, and even with myself in thinking over his claims, I had endowed him with higher qualities than I had been justified in giving to him. As I considered him and his appearance I certainly could not assure myself that he looked like a man worthy to be trusted. A policeman, seeing him at a street corner, would have had an eye upon him in a moment. He rubbed himself together within his old coat, as men do when they come out of gin-shops. His eye was as bright as before, but we thought that his mouth was meaner, and his nose redder. We were almost disenchanted with him. We said nothing to him at first about the Spotted Dog, but suggested to him our fears that if he undertook work at our hands he would lose the much more permanent employment which he got from the gentleman whom we had seen in the cupboard. We then explained to him that we could promise to him no continuation of employment.

The violence with which he cursed the gentleman who had sat in the cupboard appalled us, and had, we think, some effect in bringing back to us that feeling of respect for him which we had almost lost. It may be difficult to explain why we respected him because he cursed and swore horribly. We do not like cursing and swearing, and were any of our younger contributors to indulge themselves after that fashion in our presence we should, at the very least,—frown upon them. We did not frown upon Julius Mackenzie, but stood up, gazing into his face above us, again feeling that the man was powerful. Perhaps we respected him because he was not in the least afraid of us. He went on to assert that he cared not,—not a straw, we will say,—for the gentleman in the cupboard. He knew the gentleman in the cupboard very well; and the gentleman in the cupboard knew him. As long as he took his work to the gentleman in the cupboard, the gentleman in the cupboard would be only too happy to purchase that work at the rate of sixpence for a page of manuscript containing two hundred and fifty words. That was his rate of payment for prose fiction, and at that rate he could earn forty-five shillings a week. He wasn't afraid of the gentleman in the cupboard. He had had some words with the gentleman in the cupboard before now, and they two understood each other very well. He hinted, moreover, that there were other gentlemen in other cupboards; but with none of them could he advance beyond forty-five shillings a week. For this he had to sit, with his pen in his hand, seven hours seven days a week, and the very paper, pens, and ink came to fifteenpence out of the money. He had struck for wages once, and for a halcyon month or two had carried his point of sevenpence halfpenny a page; but the gentlemen in the cupboards had told him that it could not be. They, too, must live. His matter was no doubt attractive; but any price above sixpence a page unfitted it for their market. All this Mr. Julius Mackenzie explained to us with much violence of expression. When I named Mrs. Grimes to him the tone of his voice was altered. "Yes;" said he,—"I thought they'd say a word for me. They're the best friends I've got now. I don't know that you ought quite to believe her, for I think she'd perhaps tell a lie to do me a service." We assured him that we did believe every word Mrs. Grimes had said to us.

After much pausing over the matter we told him that we were empowered to trust him with our friend's work, and the manuscript was produced upon the table. If he would undertake the work and perform it, he should be paid £8:6*s*.:8*d*. for each of the three volumes as they were completed. And we undertook, moreover, on our own responsibility, to advance him money in small amounts through the hands of Mrs. Grimes, if he really settled himself to the task. At first he was in ecstasies, and as we explained to him the way in which the index should be brought out and the codification performed, he turned over the pages rapidly, and showed us that he understood at any rate the nature of the work to be done. But when we came to details he was less happy. In what workshop was this new work to be performed? There was a moment in which we almost thought of telling him to do the work in our own room; but we hesitated, luckily, remembering that his continual presence with us for two or three months would probably destroy us altogether. It appeared that his present work was done sometimes at the Spotted Dog, and sometimes at home in his lodgings. He said not a word to us about his wife, but we could understand that there would be periods in which to work at home would be impossible to him. He did not pretend to deny that there might be danger on that score, nor did he ask permission to take the entire manuscript at once away to his abode. We knew that if he took part he must take the whole, as the work could not be done in parts. Counter references would be needed. "My circumstances are bad;—very bad indeed," he said. We expressed the great trouble to which we should be subjected if any evil should happen to the manuscript. "I will give it up," he said, towering over us again, and shaking his head. "I cannot expect that I should be trusted." But we were determined that it should not be given up. Sooner than give the matter up we would make some arrangement by hiring a place in which he might work. Even though we were to pay ten shillings a week for a room for him out of the money, the bargain would be a good one for him. At last we determined that we would pay a second visit to the Spotted Dog, and consult Mrs. Grimes. We felt that we should have a pleasure in arranging together with Mrs. Grimes any scheme of benevolence on behalf of this unfortunate and remarkable man. So we told him that we would think over the matter, and send a letter to his address at the Spotted Dog, which he should receive on the following morning. He then gathered himself up, rubbed himself together again inside his coat, and took his departure.

As soon as he was gone we sat looking at the learned Doctor's manuscript, and thinking of what we had done. There lay the work of years, by which our dear and venerable old friend expected that he would take rank among the great commentators of modern times. We, in truth, did not anticipate for him all the glory to which he looked forward. We feared that there might be disappointment. Hot discussion on verbal accuracies or on rules of metre are perhaps not so much in vogue now as they were a hundred years ago. There might be disappointment and great sorrow; but we could not with equanimity anticipate the prevention of this sorrow by the possible loss or destruction of the manuscript which had been entrusted to us. The Doctor himself had seemed to anticipate no such danger. When we told him of Mackenzie's learning and misfortunes, he was eager at once that the thing should be done, merely stipulating that he should have an interview with Mr. Mackenzie before he returned to his rectory.

That same day we went to the Spotted Dog, and found Mrs. Grimes alone. Mackenzie had been there immediately after leaving our room, and had told her what had taken place. She was full of the subject and anxious to give every possible assistance. She confessed at once that the papers would not be safe in the rooms inhabited by Mackenzie and his wife. "He pays five shillings a week," she said, "for a wretched place round in Cucumber Court. They are all huddled together, any way; and how he manages to do a thing at all there,—in the way of author-work,—is a wonder to everybody. Sometimes he can't, and then he'll sit for hours together at the little table in our tap-room." We went into the tap-room and saw the little table. It was a wonder indeed that any one should be able to compose and write tales of imagination in a place so dreary, dark, and ill-omened. The little table was hardly more than a long slab or plank, perhaps eighteen inches wide. When we visited the place there were two brewers' draymen seated there, and three draggled, wretched-looking women. The carters were eating enormous hunches of bread and bacon, which they cut and put into their mouths slowly, solemnly, and in silence. The three women were seated on a bench, and when I saw them had no signs of festivity before them. It must be presumed that they had paid for something, or they would hardly have been allowed to sit there. "It's empty now," said Mrs. Grimes, taking no immediate notice of the men or of the women; "but sometimes he'll sit writing in that corner, when there's such a jabber of voices as you wouldn't hear a cannon go off over at Reid's, and that thick with smoke you'd a'most cut it with a knife. Don't he, Peter?" The man whom she addressed endeavoured to prepare himself for answer by swallowing at the moment three square inches of bread and bacon, which he had just put into his mouth. He made an awful effort, but failed; and, failing, nodded his head three times. "They all know him here, sir," continued Mrs. Grimes. "He'll go on writing, writing, writing, for hours together; and nobody'll say nothing to him. Will they, Peter?" Peter, who was now half-way through the work he had laid out for himself, muttered some inarticulate grunt of assent.

We then went back to the snug little room inside the bar. It was quite clear to me that the man could not manipulate the Doctor's manuscript, of which he would have to spread a dozen sheets before him at the same time, in the place I had just visited. Even could he have occupied the chamber alone, the accommodation would not have been sufficient for the purpose. It was equally clear that he could not be allowed to use Mrs. Grimes' snuggery. "How are we to get a place for him?" said I, appealing to the lady. "He shall have a place," she said, "I'll go bail; he shan't lose the job for want of a workshop." Then she sat down and began to think it over. I was just about to propose the hiring of some decent room in the neighbourhood, when she made a suggestion, which I acknowledge startled me. "I'll have a big table put into my own bed-room," said she, "and he shall do it there. There ain't another hole or corner about the place as 'd suit; and he can lay the gentleman's papers all about on the bed, square and clean and orderly. Can't he now? And I can see after 'em, as he don't lose 'em. Can't I now?"

By this time there had sprung up an intimacy between ourselves and Mrs. Grimes which seemed to justify an expression of the doubt which I then threw on the propriety of such a disarrangement of her most private domestic affairs. "Mr. Grimes will hardly approve of that," we said.

"Oh, John won't mind. What'll it matter to John as long as Mackenzie is out in time for him to go to bed? We ain't early birds, morning or night,—that's true. In our line folks can't be early. But from ten to six there's the room, and he shall have it. Come up and see, sir." So we followed Mrs. Grimes up the narrow staircase to the marital bower. "It ain't large, but there'll be room for the table, and for him to sit at it;—won't there now?"

It was a dark little room, with one small window looking out under the low roof, and facing the heavy high dead wall of the brewery opposite. But it was clean and sweet, and the furniture in it was all solid and good, old-fashioned, and made of mahogany. Two or three of Mrs. Grimes' gowns were laid upon the bed, and other portions of her dress were hung on pegs behind the doors. The only untidy article in the room was a pair of "John's" trousers, which he had failed to put out of sight. She was not a bit abashed, but took them up and folded them and patted them, and laid them in the capacious wardrobe. "We'll have all these things away," she said, "and then he can have all his papers out upon the bed just as he pleases."

We own that there was something in the proposed arrangement which dismayed us. We also were married, and what would our wife have said had we proposed that a contributor,—even a contributor not red-nosed and seething with gin,—that any best-disciplined contributor should be invited to write an article within the precincts of our sanctum? We could not bring ourselves to believe that Mr. Grimes would authorise the proposition. There is something holy about the bed-room of a married couple; and there would be a special desecration in the continued presence of Mr. Julius Mackenzie. We thought it better that we should explain something of all this to her. "Do you know," we said, "this seems to be hardly prudent?"

"Why not prudent?" she asked.

"Up in your bed-room, you know! Mr. Grimes will be sure to dislike it."

"What,—John! Not he. I know what you're a-thinking of, Mr.—," she said. "But we're different in our ways than what you are. Things to us are only just what they are. We haven't time, nor yet money, nor perhaps edication, for seemings and thinkings as you have. If you was travelling out amongst the wild Injeans, you'd ask any one to have a bit in your bed-room as soon as look at 'em, if you'd got a bit for 'em to eat. We're travelling among wild Injeans all our lives, and a bed-room ain't no more to us than any other room. Mackenzie shall come up here, and I'll have the table fixed for him, just there by the window." I hadn't another word to say to her, and I could not keep myself from thinking for many an hour afterwards, whether it may not be a good thing for men, and for women also, to believe that they are always travelling among wild Indians.

When we went down Mr. Grimes himself was in the little parlour. He did not seem at all surprised at seeing his wife enter the room from above accompanied by a stranger. She at once began her story, and told the arrangement which she proposed,—which she did, as I observed, without any actual request for his sanction. Looking at Mr. Grimes' face, I thought that he did not quite like it; but he accepted it, almost without a word, scratching his head and raising his eyebrows. "You know, John, he could no more do it at home than he could fly," said Mrs. Grimes.

"Who said he could do it at home?"

"And he couldn't do it in the tap-room;—could he? If so, there ain't no other place, and so that's settled." John Grimes again scratched his head, and the matter was settled. Before we left the house Mackenzie himself came in, and was told in our presence of the accommodation which was to be prepared for him. "It's just like you, Mrs. Grimes," was all he said in the way of thanks. Then Mrs. Grimes made her bargain with him somewhat sternly. He should have the room for five hours a day,—ten till three, or twelve till five; but he must settle which, and then stick to his hours. "And I won't have nothing up there in the way of drink," said John Grimes.

"Who's asking to have drink there?" said Mackenzie.

"You're not asking now, but maybe you will. I won't have it, that's all."

"That shall be all right, John," said Mrs. Grimes, nodding her head.

"Women are that soft,—in the way of judgment,—that they'll go and do a'most anything, good or bad, when they've got their feelings up." Such was the only rebuke which in our hearing Mr. Grimes administered to his pretty wife. Mackenzie whispered something to the publican, but Grimes only shook his head. We understood it all thoroughly. He did not like the scheme, but he would not contradict his wife in an act of real kindness. We then made an appointment with the scholar for meeting our friend and his future patron at our rooms, and took our leave of the Spotted Dog. Before we went, however, Mrs. Grimes insisted on producing some cherry-bounce, as she called it, which, after sundry refusals on our part, was brought in on a small round shining tray, in a little bottle covered all over with gold sprigs, with four tiny glasses similarly ornamented. Mrs. Grimes poured out the liquor, using a very sparing hand when she came to the glass which was intended for herself. We find it, as a rule, easier to talk with the Grimeses of the world than to eat with them or to drink with them. When the glass was handed to us we did not know whether or no we were expected to say something. We waited, however, till Mr. Grimes and Mackenzie had been provided with their glasses. "Proud to see you at the Spotted Dog, Mr.—," said Grimes. "That we are," said Mrs. Grimes, smiling at us over her almost imperceptible drop of drink. Julius Mackenzie just bobbed his head, and swallowed the cordial at a gulp,—as a dog does a lump of meat, leaving the impression on his friends around him that he has not got from it half the enjoyment which it might have given him had he been a little more patient in the process. I could not but think that had Mackenzie allowed the cherry-bounce to trickle a little in his palate, as I did myself, it would have gratified him more than it did in being chucked down his throat with all the impetus which his elbow could give to the glass. "That's tidy tipple," said Mr. Grimes, winking his eye. We acknowledged that it was tidy. "My mother made it, as used to keep the Pig and Magpie, at Colchester," said Mrs. Grimes. In this way we learned a good deal of Mrs. Grimes' history. Her very earliest years had been passed among wild Indians.

Then came the interview between the Doctor and Mr. Mackenzie. We must confess that we greatly feared the impression which our younger friend might make on the elder. We had of course told the Doctor of the red nose, and he had accepted the information with a smile. But he was a man who would feel the contamination of contact with a drunkard, and who would shrink from an unpleasant association. There are vices of which we habitually take altogether different views in accordance with the manner in which they are brought under our notice. This vice of drunkenness is often a joke in the mouths of those to whom the thing itself is a horror. Even before our boys we talk of it as being rather funny, though to see one of them funny himself would almost break our hearts. The learned commentator had accepted our account of the red nose as though it were simply a part of the undeserved misery of the wretched man; but should he find the wretched man to be actually redolent of gin his feelings might be changed. The Doctor was with us first, and the volumes of the MS. were displayed upon the table. The compiler of them, as he lifted here a page and there a page, handled them with the gentleness of a lover. They had been exquisitely arranged, and were very fair. The pagings, and the margins, and the chapterings, and all the complementary paraphernalia of authorship, were perfect. "A lifetime, my friend; just a lifetime!" the Doctor had said to us, speaking of his own work while we were waiting for the man to whose hands was to be entrusted the result of so much labour and scholarship. We wished at that moment that we had never been called on to interfere in the matter.

Mackenzie came, and the introduction was made. The Doctor was a gentleman of the old school, very neat in his attire,—dressed in perfect black, with knee-breeches and black gaiters, with a closely-shorn chin, and an exquisitely white cravat. Though he was in truth simply the rector of his parish, his parish was one which entitled him to call himself a dean, and he wore a clerical rosette on his hat. He was a well-made, tall, portly gentleman, with whom to take the slightest liberty would have been impossible. His well-formed full face was singularly expressive of benevolence, but there was in it too an air of command which created an involuntary respect. He was a man whose means were ample, and who could afford to keep two curates, so that the appanages of a Church dignitary did in some sort belong to him. We doubt whether he really understood what work meant,—even when he spoke with so much pathos of the labour of his life; but he was a man not at all exacting in regard to the work of others, and who was anxious to make the world as smooth and rosy to those around him as it had been to himself. He came forward, paused a moment, and then shook hands with Mackenzie. Our work had been done, and we remained in the background during the interview. It was now for the Doctor to satisfy himself with the scholarship,—and, if he chose to take cognizance of the matter, with the morals of his proposed assistant.

Mackenzie himself was more subdued in his manner than he had been when talking with ourselves. The Doctor made a little speech, standing at the table with one hand on one volume and the other on another. He told of all his work, with a mixture of modesty as to the thing done, and self-assertion as to his interest in doing it, which was charming. He acknowledged that the sum proposed for the aid which he required was inconsiderable;—but it had been fixed by the proposed publisher. Should Mr. Mackenzie find that the labour was long he would willingly increase it. Then he commenced a conversation respecting the Greek dramatists, which had none of the air or tone of an examination, but which still served the purpose of enabling Mackenzie to show his scholarship. In that respect there was no doubt that the ragged, red-nosed, disreputable man, who stood there longing for his job, was the greater proficient of the two. We never discovered that he had had access to books in later years; but his memory of the old things seemed to be perfect. When it was suggested that references would be required, it seemed that he did know his way into the library of the British Museum. "When I wasn't quite so shabby," he said boldly, "I used to be there." The Doctor instantly produced a ten-pound note, and insisted that it should be taken in advance. Mackenzie hesitated, and we suggested that it was premature; but the Doctor was firm. "If an old scholar mayn't assist one younger than himself," he said, "I don't know when one man may aid another. And this is no alms. It is simply a pledge for work to be done." Mackenzie took the money, muttering something of an assurance that as far as his ability went, the work should be done well. "It would certainly," he said, "be done diligently."

When money had passed, of course the thing was settled; but in truth the bank-note had been given, not from judgment in settling the matter, but from the generous impulse of the moment. There was, however, no receding. The Doctor expressed by no hint a doubt as to the safety of his manuscript. He was by far too fine a gentleman to give the man whom he employed pain in that direction. If there were risk, he would now run the risk. And so the thing was settled.

We did not, however, give the manuscript on that occasion into Mackenzie's hands, but took it down afterwards, locked in an old despatch box of our own, to the Spotted Dog, and left the box with the key of it in the hands of Mrs. Grimes. Again we went up into that lady's bed-room, and saw that the big table had been placed by the window for Mackenzie's accommodation. It so nearly filled the room, that, as we observed, John Grimes could not get round at all to his side of the bed. It was arranged that Mackenzie was to begin on the morrow.

Part II—The Result

DURING THE next month we saw a good deal of Mr. Julius Mackenzie, and made ourselves quite at home in Mrs. Grimes' bed-room. We went in and out of the Spotted Dog as if we had known that establishment all our lives, and spent many a quarter of an hour with the hostess in her little parlour, discussing the prospects of Mr. Mackenzie and his family. He had procured for himself decent, if not exactly new, garments out of the money so liberally provided by my learned friend the Doctor, and spent much of his time in the library of the British Museum. He certainly worked very hard, for he did not altogether abandon his old engagement. Before the end of the first month the index of the first volume, nearly completed, had been sent down for the inspection of the Doctor, and had been returned with ample eulogium and some little criticism. The criticisms Mackenzie answered by letter, with true scholarly spirit, and the Doctor was delighted. Nothing could be more pleasant to him than a correspondence, prolonged almost indefinitely, as to the respective merits of a τὸ or a τοῦ, or on the demand for a spondee or an iamb. When he found that the work was really in industrious hands, he ceased to be clamorous for early publication, and gave us to understand privately that Mr. Mackenzie was not to be limited to the sum named. The matter of remuneration was, indeed, left very much to ourselves, and Mackenzie had certainly found a most efficient friend in the author whose works had been confided to his hands.

All this was very pleasant, and Mackenzie throughout that month worked very hard. According to the statements made to me by Mrs. Grimes he took no more gin than what was necessary for a hard-working man. As to the exact quantity of that cordial which she imagined to be beneficial and needful, we made no close inquiry. He certainly kept himself in a condition for work, and so far all went on happily. Nevertheless, there was a terrible skeleton could not be got to hide itself. A certain portion of his prosperity reached the hands of his wife, and she was behaving herself worse than ever. The four children had been covered with decent garments under Mrs. Grimes' care, and then Mrs. Mackenzie had appeared at the Spotted Dog, loudly demanding a new outfit for herself. She came not only once, but often, and Mr. Grimes was beginning to protest that he saw too much of the family. We had become very intimate with Mrs. Grimes, and she did not hesitate to confide to us her fears lest "John should cut up rough" before the thing was completed. "You see," she said, "it is against the house, no doubt, that woman coming nigh it." But still she was firm, and Mackenzie was not disturbed in the possession of the bed-room. At last Mrs. Mackenzie was provided with some articles of female attire;—and then, on the very next day, she and the four children were again stripped almost naked. The wretched creature must have steeped herself in gin to the shoulders, for in one day she made a sweep of everything. She then came in a state of furious intoxication to the Spotted Dog, and was removed by the police under the express order of the landlord.

We can hardly say which was the most surprising to us, the loyalty of Mrs. Grimes or the patience of John. During that night, as we were told two days afterwards by his wife, he stormed with passion. The papers she had locked up in order that he should not get at them and destroy them. He swore that everything should be cleared out on the following morning. But when the morning came he did not even say a word to Mackenzie, as the wretched, downcast, broken-hearted creature passed up-stairs to his work. "You see I knows him, and how to deal with him," said Mrs. Grimes, speaking of her husband. "There ain't another like himself nowheres;—he's that good. A softer-hearteder man there ain't in the public line. He can speak dreadful when his dander is up, and can look—; oh, laws, he just can look at you! But he could no more put his hands upon a woman, in the way of hurting,—no more than be an archbishop." Where could be the man, thought we to ourselves as this was said to us, who could have put a hand,—in the way of hurting,—upon Mrs. Grimes?

On that occasion, to the best of our belief, the policeman contented himself with depositing Mrs. Mackenzie at her own lodgings. On the next day she was picked up drunk in the street, and carried away to the lock-up house. At the very moment in which the story was being told to us by Mrs. Grimes, Mackenzie had gone to the police office to pay the fine, and to bring his wife home. We asked with dismay and surprise why he should interfere to rescue her,—why he did not leave her in custody as long as the police would keep her? "Who'd there be to look after the children?" asked Mrs. Grimes, as though she were offended at our suggestion. Then she went on to explain that in such a household as that of poor Mackenzie the wife is absolutely a necessity, even though she be an habitual drunkard. Intolerable as she was, her services were necessary to him. "A husband as drinks is bad," said Mrs. Grimes,—with something, we thought, of an apologetic tone for the vice upon which her own prosperity was partly built,—"but when a woman takes to it, it's the—devil." We thought that she was right, as we pictured to ourselves that man of letters satisfying the magistrate's demand for his wife's misconduct, and taking the degraded, half-naked creature once more home to his children.

We saw him about twelve o'clock on that day, and he had then, too evidently, been endeavouring to support his misery by the free use of alcohol. We did not speak of it down in the parlour; but even Mrs. Grimes, we think, would have admitted that he had taken more than was good for him. He was sitting up in the bed-room with his head hanging upon his hand, with a swarm of our learned friend's papers spread on the table before him. Mrs. Grimes, when he entered the house, had gone upstairs to give them out to him; but he had made no attempt to settle himself to his work. "This kind of thing must come to an end," he said to us with a thick, husky voice. We muttered something to him as to the need there was that he should exert a manly courage in his troubles. "Manly!" he said. "Well, yes; manly. A man should be a man, of course. There are some things which a man can't bear. I've borne more than enough, and I'll have an end of it."

We shall never forget that scene. After awhile he got up, and became almost violent. Talk of bearing! Who had borne half as much as he? There were things a man should not bear. As for manliness, he believed that the truly manly thing would be to put an end to the lives of his wife, his children, and himself at one swoop. Of course the judgment of a mealy-mouthed world would be against him, but what would that matter to him when he and they had vanished out of this miserable place into the infinite realms of nothingness? Was he fit to live, or were they? Was there any chance for his children but that of becoming thieves and prostitutes? And for that poor wretch of a woman, from out of whose bosom even her human instincts had been washed by gin,—would not death to her be, indeed, a charity? There was but one drawback to all this. When he should have destroyed them, how would it be with him if he should afterwards fail to make sure work with his own life? In such case it was not hanging that he would fear, but the self-reproach that would come upon him in that he had succeeded in sending others out of their misery, but had flinched when his own turn had come. Though he was drunk when he said these horrid things, or so nearly drunk that he could not perfect the articulation of his words, still there was a marvellous eloquence with him. When we attempted to answer, and told him of that canon which had been set against self-slaughter, he laughed us to scorn. There was something terrible to us in the audacity of the arguments which he used, when he asserted for himself the right to shuffle off from his shoulders a burden which they had not been made broad enough to bear. There was an intensity and a thorough hopelessness of suffering in his case, an openness of acknowledged degradation, which robbed us for the time of all that power which the respectable ones of the earth have over the disreputable. When we came upon him with our wise saws, our wisdom was shattered instantly, and flung back upon us in fragments. What promise could we dare to hold out to him that further patience would produce any result that could be beneficial? What further harm could any such doing on his part bring upon him? Did we think that were he brought out to stand at the gallows' foot with the knowledge that ten minutes would usher him into what folks called eternity, his sense of suffering would be as great as it had been when he conducted that woman out of court and along the streets to his home, amidst the jeering congratulations of his neighbours? "When you have fallen so low," said he, "that you can fall no lower, the ordinary trammels of the world cease to bind you." Though his words were knocked against each other with the dulled utterances of intoxication, his intellect was terribly clear, and his scorn for himself, and for the world that had so treated him, was irrepressible.

We must have been over an hour with him up there in the bed-room, and even then we did not leave him. As it was manifest that he could do no work on that day, we collected the papers together, and proposed that he should take a walk with us. He was patient as we shovelled together the Doctor's pages, and did not object to our suggestion. We found it necessary to call up Mrs. Grimes to assist us in putting away the "Opus magnum," and were astonished to find how much she had come to know about the work. Added to the Doctor's manuscript there were now the pages of Mackenzie's indexes,—and there were other pages of reference, for use in making future indexes,—as to all of which Mrs. Grimes seemed to be quite at home. We have no doubt that she was familiar with the names of Greek tragedians, and could have pointed out to us in print the performances of the chorus. "A little fresh air'll do you a deal of good, Mr. Mackenzie," she said to the unfortunate man,—"only take a biscuit in your pocket." We got him out into the street, but he angrily refused to take the biscuit which she endeavoured to force into his hands.

That was a memorable walk. Turning from the end of Liquorpond Street up Gray's Inn Lane towards Holborn, we at once came upon the entrance into a miserable court. "There," said he; "it is down there that I live. She is sleeping it off now, and the children are hanging about her, wondering whether mother has got money to have another go at it when she rises. I'd take you down to see it all, only it'd sicken you." We did not offer to go down the court, abstaining rather for his sake than for our own. The look of the place was as of a spot squalid, fever-stricken, and utterly degraded. And this man who was our companion had been born and bred a gentleman,—had been nourished with that soft and gentle care which comes of wealth and love combined,—had received the education which the country gives to her most favoured sons, and had taken such advantage of that education as is seldom taken by any of those favoured ones;—and Cucumber Court, with a drunken wife and four half-clothed, half-starved children, was the condition to which he had brought himself! The world knows nothing higher nor brighter than had been his outset in life,—nothing lower nor more debased than the result. And yet he was one whose time and intellect had been employed upon the pursuit of knowledge,—who even up to this day had high ideas of what should be a man's career,—who worked very hard and had always worked,—who as far as we knew had struck upon no rocks in the pursuit of mere pleasure. It had all come to him from that idea of his youth that it would be good for him "to take refuge from the conventional thraldom of so-called gentlemen amidst the liberty of the lower orders." His life, as he had himself owned, had indeed been a mistake.

We passed on from the court, and crossing the road went through the squares of Gray's Inn, down Chancery Lane, through the little iron gate into Lincoln's Inn, round through the old square,—than which we know no place in London more conducive to suicide; and the new square,—which has a gloom of its own, not so potent, and savouring only of madness, till at last we found ourselves in the Temple Gardens. I do not know why we had thus clung to the purlieus of the Law, except it was that he was telling us how in his early days, when he had been sent away from Cambridge,—as on this occasion he acknowledged to us, for an attempt to pull the tutor's nose, in revenge for a supposed insult,—he had intended to push his fortunes as a barrister. He pointed up to a certain window in a dark corner of that suicidal old court, and told us that for one year he had there sat at the feet of a great Gamaliel in Chancery, and had worked with all his energies. Of course we asked him why he had left a prospect so alluring. Though his answers to us were not quite explicit, we think that he did not attempt to conceal the truth. He learned to drink, and that Gamaliel took upon himself to rebuke the failing, and by the end of that year he had quarrelled irreconcilably with his family. There had been great wrath at home when he was sent from Cambridge, greater wrath when he expressed his opinion upon certain questions of religious faith, and wrath to the final severance of all family relations when he told the chosen Gamaliel that he should get drunk as often as he pleased. After that he had "taken refuge among the lower orders," and his life, such as it was, had come of it.

In Fleet Street, as we came out of the Temple, we turned into an eating-house and had some food. By this time the exercise and the air had carried off the fumes of the liquor which he had taken, and I knew that it would be well that he should eat. We had a mutton chop and a hot potato and a pint of beer each, and sat down to table for the first and last time as mutual friends. It was odd to see how in his converse with us on that day he seemed to possess a double identity. Though the hopeless misery of his condition was always present to him, was constantly on his tongue, yet he could talk about his own career and his own character as though they belonged to a third person. He could even laugh at the wretched mistake he had made in life, and speculate as to its consequences. For himself he was well aware that death was the only release that he could expect. We did not dare to tell him that if his wife should die, then things might be better with him. We could only suggest to him that work itself, if he would do honest work, would console him for many sufferings. "You don't know the filth of it," he said to us. Ah, dear; how well we remember the terrible word, and the gesture with which he pronounced it, and the gleam of his eyes as he said it! His manner to us on this occasion was completely changed, and we had a gratification in feeling that a sense had come back upon him of his old associations. "I remember this room so well," he said,—"when I used to have friends and money." And, indeed, the room was one which has been made memorable by Genius. "I did not think ever to have found myself here again." We observed, however, that he could not eat the food that was placed before him. A morsel or two of the meat he swallowed, and struggled to eat the crust of his bread, but he could not make a clean plate of it, as we did,—regretting that the nature of chops did not allow of ampler dimensions. His beer was quickly finished, and we suggested to him a second tankard. With a queer, half-abashed twinkle of the eye, he accepted our offer, and then the second pint disappeared also. We had our doubts on the subject, but at last decided against any further offer. Had he chosen to call for it he must have had a third; but he did not call for it. We left him at the door of the tavern, and he then promised that in spite of all that he had suffered and all that he had said he would make another effort to complete the Doctor's work. "Whether I go or stay," he said, "I'd like to earn the money that I've spent." There was something terrible in that idea of his going! Whither was he to go?

The Doctor heard nothing of the misfortune of these three or four inauspicious days; and the work was again going on prosperously when he came up again to London at the end of the second month. He told us something of his banker, and something of his lawyer, and murmured a word or two as to a new curate whom he needed; but we knew that he had come up to London because he could not bear a longer absence from the great object of his affections. He could not endure to be thus parted from his manuscript, and was again childishly anxious that a portion of it should be in the printer's hands. "At sixty-five, sir," he said to us, "a man has no time to dally with his work." He had been dallying with his work all his life, and we sincerely believed that it would be well with him if he could be contented to dally with it to the end. If all that Mackenzie said of it was true, the Doctor's erudition was not equalled by his originality, or by his judgment. Of that question, however, we could take no cognizance. He was bent upon publishing, and as he was willing and able to pay for his whim and was his own master, nothing that we could do would keep him out of the printer's hands.

He was desirous of seeing Mackenzie, and was anxious even to see him once at his work. Of course he could meet his assistant in our editorial room, and all the papers could easily be brought backwards and forwards in the old despatch-box. But in the interest of all parties we hesitated as to taking our revered and reverend friend to the Spotted Dog. Though we had told him that his work was being done at a public-house, we thought that his mind had conceived the idea of some modest inn, and that he would be shocked at being introduced to a place which he would regard simply as a gin-shop. Mrs. Grimes, or if not Mrs. Grimes, then Mr. Grimes, might object to another visitor to their bed-room; and Mackenzie himself would be thrown out of gear by the appearance of those clerical gaiters upon the humble scene of his labours. We, therefore, gave him such reasons as were available for submitting, at any rate for the present, to having the papers brought up to him at our room. And we ourselves went down to the Spotted Dog to make an appointment with Mackenzie for the following day. We had last seen him about a week before, and then the task was progressing well. He had told us that another fortnight would finish it. We had inquired also of Mrs. Grimes about the man's wife. All she could tell us was that the woman had not again troubled them at the Spotted Dog. She expressed her belief, however, that the drunkard had been more than once in the hands of the police since the day on which Mackenzie had walked with us through the squares of the Inns of Court.

It was late when we reached the public-house on the occasion to which we now allude, and the evening was dark and rainy. It was then the end of January, and it might have been about six o'clock. We knew that we should not find Mackenzie at the public-house; but it was probable that Mrs. Grimes could send for him, or, at least, could make the appointment for us. We went into the little parlour, where she was seated with her husband, and we could immediately see, from the countenance of both of them, that something was amiss. We began by telling Mrs. Grimes that the Doctor had come to town. "Mackenzie ain't here, sir," said Mrs. Grimes, and we almost thought that the very tone of her voice was altered. We explained that we had not expected to find him at that hour, and asked if she could send for him. She only shook her head. Grimes was standing with his back to the fire and his hands in his trousers pockets. Up to this moment he had not spoken a word. We asked if the man was drunk. She again shook her head. Could she bid him to come to us to-morrow, and bring the box and the papers with him? Again she shook her head.

"I've told her that I won't have no more of it," said Grimes; "nor yet I won't. He was drunk this morning,—as drunk as an owl."

"He was sober, John, as you are, when he came for the papers this afternoon at two o'clock." So the box and the papers had all been taken away!

"And she was here yesterday rampaging about the place, without as much clothes on as would cover her nakedness," said Mr. Grimes. "I won't have no more of it. I've done for that man what his own flesh and blood wouldn't do. I know that; and I won't have no more of it. Mary Anne, you'll have that table cleared out after breakfast to-morrow." When a man, to whom his wife is usually Polly, addresses her as Mary Anne, then it may be surmised that that man is in earnest. We knew that he was in earnest, and she knew it also.

"He wasn't drunk, John,—no, nor yet in liquor, when he come and took away that box this afternoon." We understood this reiterated assertion. It was in some sort excusing to us her own breach of trust in having allowed the manuscript to be withdrawn from her own charge, or was assuring us that, at the worst, she had not been guilty of the impropriety of allowing the man to take it away when he was unfit to have it in his charge. As for blaming her, who could have thought of it? Had Mackenzie at any time chosen to pass down-stairs with the box in his hands, it was not to be expected that she should stop him violently. And now that he had done so we could not blame her; but we felt that a great weight had fallen upon our own hearts. If evil should come to the manuscript would not the Doctor's wrath fall upon us with a crushing weight? Something must be done at once. And we suggested that it would be well that somebody should go round to Cucumber Court. "I'd go as soon as look," said Mrs. Grimes, "but he won't let me."

"You don't stir a foot out of this to-night;—not that way," said Mr. Grimes.

"Who wants to stir?" said Mrs. Grimes.

We felt that there was something more to be told than we had yet heard, and a great fear fell upon us. The woman's manner to us was altered, and we were sure that this had come not from altered feelings on her part, but from circumstances which had frightened her. It was not her husband that she feared, but the truth of something that her husband had said to her. "If there is anything more to tell, for God's sake tell it," we said, addressing ourselves rather to the man than to the woman. Then Grimes did tell us his story. On the previous evening Mackenzie had received three or four sovereigns from Mrs. Grimes, being, of course, a portion of the Doctor's payments; and early on that morning all Liquorpond Street had been in a state of excitement with the drunken fury of Mackenzie's wife. She had found her way into the Spotted Dog, and was being actually extruded by the strength of Grimes himself,—of Grimes, who had been brought down, half dressed, from his bedroom by the row,—when Mackenzie himself, equally drunk, appeared upon the scene. "No, John;—not equally drunk," said Mrs. Grimes. "Bother!" exclaimed her husband, going on with his story. The man had struggled to take the woman by the arm, and the two had fallen and rolled in the street together. "I was looking out of the window, and it was awful to see," said Mrs. Grimes. We felt that it was "awful to hear." A man,—and such a man, rolling in the gutter with a drunken woman,—himself drunk,—and that woman his wife! "There ain't to be no more of it at the Spotted Dog; that's all," said John Grimes, as he finished his part of the story.

Then, at last, Mrs. Grimes became voluble. All this had occurred before nine in the morning. "The woman must have been at it all night," she said. "So must the man," said John. "Anyways he came back about dinner, and he was sober then. I asked him not to go up, and offered to make him a cup of tea. It was just as you'd gone out after dinner, John."

"He won't have no more tea here," said John.

"And he didn't have any then. He wouldn't, he said, have any tea, but went up-stairs. What was I to do? I couldn't tell him as he shouldn't. Well;—during the row in the morning John had said something as to Mackenzie not coming about the premises any more."

"Of course I did," said Grimes.

"He was a little cut, then, no doubt," continued the lady; "and I didn't think as he would have noticed what John had said."

"I mean it to be noticed now."

"He had noticed it then, sir, though he wasn't just as he should be at that hour of the morning. Well;—what does he do? He goes up-stairs and packs up all the papers at once. Leastways, that's as I suppose. They ain't there now. You can go and look if you please, sir. Well; when he came down, whether I was in the kitchen,—though it isn't often as my eyes is off the bar, or in the tap-room, or busy drawing, which I do do sometimes, sir, when there are a many calling for liquor, I can't say;—but if I ain't never to stand upright again, I didn't see him pass out with the box. But Miss Wilcox did. You can ask her." Miss Wilcox was the young lady in the bar, whom we did not think ourselves called upon to examine, feeling no doubt whatever as to the fact of the box having been taken away by Mackenzie. In all this Mrs. Grimes seemed to defend herself, as though some serious charge was to be brought against her; whereas all that she had done had been done out of pure charity; and in exercising her charity towards Mackenzie she had shown an almost exaggerated kindness towards ourselves.

"If there's anything wrong, it isn't your fault," we said.

"Nor yet mine," said John Grimes.

"No, indeed," we replied.

"It ain't none of our faults," continued he; "only this;—you can't wash a blackamoor white, nor it ain't no use trying. He don't come here any more, that's all. A man in drink we don't mind. We has to put up with it. And they ain't that tarnation desperate as is a woman. As long as a man can keep his legs he'll try to steady hisself; but there is women who, when they've liquor, gets a fury for rampaging. There ain't a many as can beat this one, sir. She's that strong, it took four of us to hold her; though she can't hardly do a stroke of work, she's that weak when she's sober."

We had now heard the whole story, and, while hearing it, had determined that it was our duty to go round into Cucumber Court and seek the manuscript and the box. We were unwilling to pry into the wretchedness of the man's home; but something was due to the Doctor; and we had to make that appointment for the morrow, if it were still possible that such an appointment should be kept. We asked for the number of the house, remembering well the entrance into the court. Then there was a whisper between John and his wife, and the husband offered to accompany us. "It's a roughish place," he said, "but they know me." "He'd better go along with you," said Mrs. Grimes. We, of course, were glad of such companionship, and glad also to find that the landlord, upon whom we had inflicted so much trouble, was still sufficiently our friend to take this trouble on our behalf.

"It's a dreary place enough," said Grimes, as he led us up the narrow archway. Indeed it was a dreary place. The court spread itself a little in breadth, but very little, when the passage was passed, and there were houses on each side of it. There was neither gutter nor, as far as we saw, drain, but the broken flags were slippery with moist mud, and here and there, strewed about between the houses, there were the remains of cabbages and turnip-tops. The place swarmed with children, over whom one ghastly gas-lamp at the end of the court threw a flickering and uncertain light. There was a clamour of scolding voices, to which it seemed that no heed was paid; and there was a smell of damp, rotting nastiness, amidst which it seemed to us to be almost impossible that life should be continued. Grimes led the way, without further speech, to the middle house on the left hand of the court, and asked a man who was sitting on the low threshold of the door whether Mackenzie was within. "So that be you, Muster Grimes; be it?" said the man, without stirring. "Yes; he's there I guess, but they've been and took her." Then we passed on into the house. "No matter about that," said the man, as we apologised for kicking him in our passage. He had not moved, and it had been impossible to enter without kicking him.

It seemed that Mackenzie held the two rooms on the ground floor, and we entered them at once. There was no light, but we could see the glimmer of a fire in the grate; and presently we became aware of the presence of children. Grimes asked after Mackenzie, and a girl's voice told us that he was in the inner room. The publican then demanded a light, and the girl, with some hesitation, lit the end of a farthing candle, which was fixed in a small bottle. We endeavoured to look round the room by the glimmer which this afforded, but could see nothing but the presence of four children, three of whom seemed to be seated in apathy on the floor. Grimes, taking the candle in his hand, passed at once into the other room, and we followed him. Holding the bottle something over his head, he contrived to throw a gleam of light upon one of the two beds with which the room was fitted, and there we saw the body of Julius Mackenzie stretched in the torpor of dead intoxication. His head lay against the wall, his body was across the bed, and his feet dangled on to the floor. He still wore his dirty boots, and his clothes as he had worn them in the morning. No sight so piteous, so wretched, and at the same time so eloquent had we ever seen before. His eyes were closed, and the light of his face was therefore quenched. His mouth was open, and the slaver had fallen upon his beard. His dark, clotted hair had been pulled over his face by the unconscious movement of his hands. There came from him a stertorous sound of breathing, as though he were being choked by the attitude in which he lay; and even in his drunkenness there was an uneasy twitching as of pain about his face. And there sat, and had been sitting for hours past, the four children in the other room, knowing the condition of the parent whom they most respected, but not even endeavouring to do anything for his comfort. What could they do? They knew, by long training and thorough experience, that a fit of drunkenness had to be got out of by sleep. To them there was nothing shocking in it. It was but a periodical misfortune. "She'll have to own he's been and done it now," said Grimes, looking down upon the man, and alluding to his wife's good-natured obstinacy. He handed the candle to us, and, with a mixture of tenderness and roughness, of which the roughness was only in the manner and the tenderness was real, he raised Mackenzie's head and placed it on the bolster, and lifted the man's legs on to the bed. Then he took off the man's boots, and the old silk handkerchief from the neck, and pulled the trousers straight, and arranged the folds of the coat. It was almost as though he were laying out one that was dead. The eldest girl was now standing by us, and Grimes asked her how long her father had been in that condition. "Jack Hoggart brought him in just afore it was dark," said the girl. Then it was explained to us that Jack Hoggart was the man whom we had seen sitting on the door-step.

"And your mother?" asked Grimes.

"The perlice took her afore dinner."

"And you children;—what have you had to eat?" In answer to this the girl only shook her head. Grimes took no immediate notice of this, but called the drunken man by his name, and shook his shoulder, and looked round to a broken ewer which stood on the little table, for water to dash upon him;—but there was no water in the jug. He called again, and repeated the shaking, and at last Mackenzie opened his eyes, and in a dull, half-conscious manner looked up at us. "Come, my man," said Grimes, "shake this off and have done with it."

"Hadn't you better try to get up?" we asked.

There was a faint attempt at rising, then a smile,—a smile which was terrible to witness, so sad was all which it said; then a look of utter, abject misery, coming, as we thought, from a momentary remembrance of his degradation; and after that he sank back in the dull, brutal, painless, death-like apathy of absolute unconsciousness.

"It'll be morning afore he'll move," said the girl.

"She's about right," said Grimes. "He's got it too heavy for us to do anything but just leave him. We'll take a look for the box and the papers."

And the man upon whom we were looking down had been born a gentleman, and was a finished scholar,—one so well educated, so ripe in literary acquirement, that we knew few whom we could call his equal. Judging of the matter by the light of our reason, we cannot say that the horror of the scene should have been enhanced to us by these recollections. Had the man been a shoemaker or a coalheaver there would have been enough of tragedy in it to make an angel weep,—that sight of the child standing by the bedside of her drunken father, while the other parent was away in custody,—and in no degree shocked at what she saw, because the thing was common to her! But the thought of what the man had been, of what he was, of what he might have been, and the steps by which he had brought himself to the foul degradation which we witnessed, filled us with a dismay which we should hardly have felt had the gifts which he had polluted and the intellect which he had wasted been less capable of noble uses.

Our purpose in coming to the court was to rescue the Doctor's papers from danger, and we turned to accompany Grimes into the other room. As we did so the publican asked the girl if she knew anything of a black box which her father had taken away from the Spotted Dog. "The box is here," said the girl.

"And the papers?" asked Grimes. Thereupon the girl shook her head, and we both hurried into the outer room. I hardly know who first discovered the sight which we encountered, or whether it was shown to us by the child. The whole fire-place was strewn with half-burnt sheets of manuscript. There were scraps of pages of which almost the whole had been destroyed, others which were hardly more than scorched, and heaps of paper-ashes all lying tumbled together about the fender. We went down on our knees to examine them, thinking at the moment that the poor creature might in his despair have burned his own work and have spared that of the Doctor. But it was not so. We found scores of charred pages of the Doctor's elaborate handwriting. By this time Grimes had found the open box, and we perceived that the sheets remaining in it were tumbled and huddled together in absolute confusion. There were pages of the various volumes mixed with those which Mackenzie himself had written, and they were all crushed, and rolled, and twisted, as though they had been thrust thither as waste-paper,—out of way. "'Twas mother as done it," said the girl, "and we put 'em back again when the perlice took her."

There was nothing more to learn,—nothing more by the hearing which any useful clue could be obtained. What had been the exact course of the scenes which had been enacted there that morning it little booted us to inquire. It was enough and more than enough that we knew that the mischief had been done. We went down on our knees before the fire, and rescued from the ashes with our hands every fragment of manuscript that we could find. Then we put the mass all together into the box, and gazed upon the wretched remnants almost in tears. "You'd better go and get a bit of some'at to eat," said Grimes, handing a coin to the elder girl. "It's hard on them to starve 'cause their father's drunk, sir." Then he took the closed box in his hand, and we followed him out into the street. "I'll send or step up and look after him to-morrow," said Grimes, as he put us and the box into a cab. We little thought, when we made to the drunkard that foolish request to arise, that we should never speak to him again.

As we returned to our office in the cab that we might deposit the box there ready for the following day, our mind was chiefly occupied in thinking over the undeserved grievances which had fallen upon ourselves. We had been moved by the charitable desire to do services to two different persons,—to the learned Doctor and to the rednosed drunkard, and this had come of it! There had been nothing for us to gain by assisting either the one or the other. We had taken infinite trouble, attempting to bring together two men who wanted each other's services,—working hard in sheer benevolence;—and what had been the result? We had spent half an hour on our knees in the undignified and almost disreputable work of raking among Mrs. Mackenzie's cinders, and now we had to face the anger, the dismay, the reproach, and,—worse than all,—the agony of the Doctor. As to Mackenzie,—we asserted to ourselves again and again that nothing further could be done for him. He had made his bed, and he must lie upon it; but, oh! why,—why had we attempted to meddle with a being so degraded? We got out of the cab at our office door, thinking of the Doctor's countenance as we should see it on the morrow. Our heart sank within us, and we asked ourselves, if it was so bad with us now, how it would be with us when we returned to the place on the following morning.

But on the following morning we did return. No doubt each individual reader to whom we address ourselves has at some period felt that indescribable load of personal, short-lived care, which causes the heart to sink down into the boots. It is not great grief that does it;—nor is it excessive fear; but the unpleasant operation comes from the mixture of the two. It is the anticipation of some imperfectly-understood evil that does it,—some evil out of which there might perhaps be an escape if we could only see the way. In this case we saw no way out of it. The Doctor was to be with us at one o'clock, and he would come with smiles, expecting to meet his learned colleague. How should we break it to the Doctor? We might indeed send to him, putting off the meeting, but the advantage coming from that would be slight, if any. We must see the injured Grecian sooner or later; and we had resolved, much as we feared, that the evil hour should not be postponed. We spent an hour that morning in arranging the fragments. Of the first volume about a third had been destroyed. Of the second nearly every page had been either burned or mutilated. Of the third but little had been injured. Mackenzie's own work had fared better than the Doctor's; but there was no comfort in that. After what had passed I thought it quite improbable that the Doctor would make any use of Mackenzie's work. So much of the manuscript as could still be placed in continuous pages, we laid out upon the table, volume by volume,—that in the middle sinking down from its original goodly bulk almost to the dimensions of a poor sermon;—and the half-burned bits we left in the box. Then we sat ourselves down at our accustomed table, and pretended to try to work. Our ears were very sharp, and we heard the Doctor's step upon our stairs within a minute or two of the appointed time. Our heart went to the very toes of our boots. We shuffled in our chair, rose from it, and sat down again,—and were conscious that we were not equal to the occasion. Hitherto we had, after some mild literary form, patronised the Doctor,—as a man of letters in town will patronise his literary friend from the country;—but we now feared him as a truant school-boy fears his master. And yet it was necessary that we should wear some air of self-assurance!

In a moment he was with us, wearing that bland smile which we knew so well, and which at the present moment almost overpowered us. We had been sure that he would wear that smile, and had especially feared it. "Ah," said he, grasping us by the hand, "I thought I should have been late. I see that our friend is not here yet."

"Doctor," we replied, "a great misfortune has happened."

"A great misfortune! Mr. Mackenzie is not dead?"

"No;—he is not dead. Perhaps it would have been better that he had died long since. He has destroyed your manuscript." The Doctor's face fell, and his hands at the same time, and he stood looking at us. "I need not tell you, Doctor, what my feelings are, and how great my remorse."

"Destroyed it!" Then we took him by the hand and led him to the table. He turned first upon the appetising and comparatively uninjured third volume, and seemed to think that we had hoaxed him. "This is not destroyed," he said, with a smile. But before I could explain anything, his hands were among the fragments in the box. "As I am a living man, they have burned it!" he exclaimed. "I—I—I— " Then he turned from us, and walked twice the length of the room, backwards and forwards, while we stood still, patiently waiting the explosion of his wrath. "My friend," he said, when his walk was over, "a great man underwent the same sorrow. Newton's manuscript was burned. I will take it home with me, and we will say no more about it." I never thought very much of the Doctor as a divine, but I hold him to have been as good a Christian as I ever met.

But that plan of his of saying no more about it could not quite be carried out. I was endeavouring to explain to him, as I thought it necessary to do, the circumstances of the case, and he was protesting his indifference to any such details, when there came a knock at the door, and the boy who waited on us below ushered Mrs. Grimes into the room. As the reader is aware, we had, during the last two months, become very intimate with the landlady of the Spotted Dog, but we had never hitherto had the pleasure of seeing her outside her own house.

"Oh, Mr.— " she began, and then she paused, seeing the Doctor.

We thought it expedient that there should be some introduction. "Mrs. Grimes," we said, "this is the gentleman whose invaluable manuscript has been destroyed by that unfortunate drunkard."

"Oh, then;—you're the Doctor, sir?" The Doctor bowed and smiled. His heart must have been very heavy, but he bowed politely and smiled sweetly. "Oh, dear," she said, "I don't know how to tell you!"

"To tell us what?" asked the Doctor.

"What has happened since?" we demanded. The woman stood shaking before us, and then sank into a chair. Then arose to us at the moment some idea that the drunken woman, in her mad rage, had done some great damage to the Spotted Dog,—had set fire to the house, or injured Mr. Grimes personally, or perhaps run amuck amidst the jugs and pitchers, window glass, and gas lights. Something had been done which would give the Grimeses a pecuniary claim on me or on the Doctor, and the woman had been sent hither to make the first protest. Oh,—when should I see the last of the results of my imprudence in having attempted to befriend such a one as Julius Mackenzie! "If you have anything to tell, you had better tell it," we said, gravely.

"He's been, and— "

"Not destroyed himself?" asked the Doctor.

"Oh yes, sir. He have indeed,—from ear to ear,—and is now a lying at the Spotted Dog!"

And so, after all, that was the end of Julius Mackenzie! We need hardly say that our feelings, which up to that moment had been very hostile to the man, underwent a sudden revulsion. Poor, overburdened, struggling, ill-used, abandoned creature! The world had been hard upon him, with a severity which almost induced one to make complaint against Omnipotence. The poor wretch had been willing to work, had been industrious in his calling, had had capacity for work; and he had also struggled gallantly against his evil fate, had recognised and endeavoured to perform his duty to his children and to the miserable woman who had brought him to his ruin! And that sin of drunkenness had seemed to us to be in him rather the reflex of her vice than the result of his own vicious tendencies. Still it might be doubtful whether she had not learned the vice from him. They had both in truth been drunkards as long as they had been known in the neighbourhood of the Spotted Dog; but it was stated by all who had known them there that he was never seen to be drunk unless when she had disgraced him by the public exposure of her own abomination. Such as he was he had now come to his end! This was the upshot of his loud claims for liberty from his youth upwards;—liberty as against his father and family; liberty as against his college tutor; liberty as against all pastors, masters, and instructors; liberty as against the conventional thraldom of the world! He was now lying a wretched corpse at the Spotted Dog, with his throat cut from ear to ear, till the coroner's jury should have decided whether or not they would call him a suicide!

Mrs. Grimes had come to tell us that the coroner was to be at the Spotted Dog at four o'clock, and to say that her husband hoped that we would be present. We had seen Mackenzie so lately, and had so much to do with the employment of the last days of his life, that we could not refuse this request, though it came accompanied by no legal summons. Then Mrs. Grimes again became voluble, and poured out to us her biography of Mackenzie as far as she knew it. He had been married to the woman ten years, and certainly had been a drunkard before he married her. "As for her, she'd been well-nigh suckled on gin," said Mrs. Grimes, "though he didn't know it, poor fellow." Whether this was true or not, she had certainly taken to drink soon after her marriage, and then his life had been passed in alternate fits of despondency and of desperate efforts to improve his own condition and that of his children. Mrs. Grimes declared to us that when the fit came on them,—when the woman had begun and the man had followed,—they would expend upon drink in two days what would have kept the family for a fortnight. "They say as how it was nothing for them to swallow forty shillings' worth of gin in forty-eight hours." The Doctor held up his hands in horror. "And it didn't, none of it, come our way," said Mrs. Grimes. "Indeed, John wouldn't let us serve it for 'em."

She sat there for half an hour, and during the whole time she was telling us of the man's life; but the reader will already have heard more than enough of it. By what immediate demon the woman had been instigated to burn the husband's work almost immediately on its production within her own home, we never heard. Doubtless there had been some terrible scene in which the man's sufferings must have been carried almost beyond endurance. "And he had feelings, sir, he had," said Mrs. Grimes; "he knew as a woman should be decent, and a man's wife especial; I'm sure we pitied him so, John and I, that we could have cried over him. John would say a hard word to him at times, but he'd have walked round London to do him a good turn. John ain't to say edicated hisself, but he do respect learning."

When she had told us all, Mrs. Grimes went, and we were left alone with the Doctor. He at once consented to accompany us to the Spotted Dog, and we spent the hour that still remained to us in discussing the fate of the unfortunate man. We doubt whether an allusion was made during the time to the burned manuscript. If so, it was certainly not made by the Doctor himself. The tragedy which had occurred in connection with it had made him feel it to be unfitting even to mention his own loss. That such a one should have gone to his account in such a manner, without hope, without belief, and without fear,—as Burley said to Bothwell, and Bothwell boasted to Burley,—that was the theme of the Doctor's discourse. "The mercy of God is infinite," he said, bowing his head, with closed eyes and folded hands. To threaten while the life is in the man is human. To believe in the execution of those threats when the life has passed away is almost beyond the power of humanity.

At the hour fixed we were at the Spotted Dog, and found there a crowd assembled. The coroner was already seated in Mrs. Grimes' little parlour, and the body as we were told had been laid out in the tap-room. The inquest was soon over. The fact that he had destroyed himself in the low state of physical suffering and mental despondency which followed his intoxication was not doubted. At the very time that he was doing it, his wife was being taken from the lock-up house to the police office in the police van. He was not penniless, for he had sent the children out with money for their breakfasts, giving special caution as to the youngest, a little toddling thing of three years old;—and then he had done it. The eldest girl, returning to the house, had found him lying dead upon the floor. We were called upon for our evidence, and went into the tap-room accompanied by the Doctor. Alas! the very table which had been dragged up-stairs into the landlady's bed-room with the charitable object of assisting Mackenzie in his work,—the table at which we had sat with him conning the Doctor's pages,—had now been dragged down again and was used for another purpose. We had little to say as to the matter, except that we had known the man to be industrious and capable, and that we had, alas! seen him utterly prostrated by drink on the evening before his death.

The saddest sight of all on this occasion was the appearance of Mackenzie's wife,—whom we had never before seen. She had been brought there by a policeman, but whether she was still in custody we did not know. She had been dressed, either by the decency of the police or by the care of her neighbours, in an old black gown, which was a world too large and too long for her. And on her head there was a black bonnet which nearly enveloped her. She was a small woman, and, as far as we could judge from the glance we got of her face, pale, and worn, and wan. She had not such outward marks of a drunkard's career as those which poor Mackenzie always carried with him. She was taken up to the coroner, and what answers she gave to him were spoken in so low a voice that they did not reach us. The policeman, with whom we spoke, told us that she did not feel it much,—that she was callous now and beyond the power of mental suffering. "She's frightened just this minute, sir; but it isn't more than that," said the policeman. We gave one glance along the table at the burden which it bore, but we saw nothing beyond the outward lines of that which had so lately been the figure of a man. We should have liked to see the countenance once more. The morbid curiosity to see such horrid sights is strong with most of us. But we did not wish to be thought to wish to see it,—especially by our friend the Doctor,—and we abstained from pushing our way to the head of the table. The Doctor himself remained quiescent in the corner of the room the farthest from the spectacle. When the matter was submitted to them, the jury lost not a moment in declaring their verdict. They said that the man had destroyed himself while suffering under temporary insanity produced by intoxication. And that was the end of Julius Mackenzie, the scholar.

On the following day the Doctor returned to the country, taking with him our black box, to the continued use of which, as a sarcophagus, he had been made very welcome. For our share in bringing upon him the great catastrophe of his life, he never uttered to us, either by spoken or written word, a single reproach. That idea of suffering as the great philosopher had suffered seemed to comfort him. "If Newton bore it, surely I can," he said to us with his bland smile, when we renewed the expression of our regret. Something passed between us, coming more from us than from him, as to the expediency of finding out some youthful scholar who could go down to the rectory, and reconstruct from its ruins the edifice of our friend's learning. The Doctor had given us some encouragement, and we had begun to make inquiry, when we received the following letter:—

"——Rectory,——, 18——.

"Dear Mr.——,—You were so kind as to say that you would endeavour to find for me an assistant in arranging and reconstructing the fragments of my work on The Metres of the Greek Dramatists. Your promise has been an additional kindness."

Dear, courteous, kind old gentleman! For we knew well that no slightest sting of sarcasm was intended to be conveyed in these words.

"Your promise has been an additional kindness; but looking upon the matter carefully, and giving to it the best consideration in my power, I have determined to relinquish the design. That which has been destroyed cannot be replaced; and it may well be that it was not worth replacing. I am old now, and never could do again that which perhaps I was never fitted to do with any fair prospect of success. I will never turn again to the ashes of my unborn child; but will console myself with the memory of my grievance, knowing well, as I do so, that consolation from the severity of harsh but just criticism might have been more difficult to find. When I think of the end of my efforts as a scholar, my mind reverts to the terrible and fatal catastrophe of one whose scholarship was infinitely more finished and more ripe than mine.

"Whenever it may suit you to come into this part of the country, pray remember that it will give very great pleasure to myself and to my daughter to welcome you at our parsonage.

"Believe me to be,

"My dear Mr.——,

"Yours very sincerely,

"—— ——."

We never have found the time to accept the Doctor's invitation, and our eyes have never again rested on the black box containing the ashes of the unborn child to which the Doctor will never turn again. We can picture him to ourselves standing, full of thought, with his hand upon the lid, but never venturing to turn the lock. Indeed, we do not doubt but that the key of the box is put away among other secret treasures, a lock of his wife's hair, perhaps, and the little shoe of the boy who did not live long enough to stand at his father's knee. For a tender, soft-hearted man was the Doctor, and one who fed much on the memories of the past.

We often called upon Mr. and Mrs. Grimes at the Spotted Dog, and would sit there talking of Mackenzie and his family. Mackenzie's widow soon vanished out of the neighbourhood, and no one there knew what was the fate of her or of her children. And then also Mr. Grimes went and took his wife with him. But they could not be said to vanish. Scratching his head one day, he told me with a dolorous voice that he had—made his fortune. "We've got as snug a little place as ever you see, just two mile out of Colchester," said Mrs. Grimes triumphantly,—"with thirty acres of land just to amuse John. And as for the Spotted Dog, I'm that sick of it, another year'd wear me to a dry bone." We looked at her, and saw no tendency that way. And we looked at John, and thought that he was not triumphant.

Who followed Mr. and Mrs. Grimes at the Spotted Dog we have never visited Liquorpond Street to see.

Mrs Brumby

Originally appeared in *Saint Paul's Magazine*, May 1870. Reprinted in *An Editor's Tales* (1870). In *An Autobiography* Trollope admits that this story of 'how a poor weak editor was driven nearly to madness by threatened litigation from a rejected contributor' was closely based on fact.

WE THINK that we are justified in asserting that of all the persons with whom we have been brought in contact in the course of our editorial experiences, men or women, boys or girls, Mrs. Brumby was the most hateful and the most hated. We are sure of this,—that for some months she was the most feared, during which period she made life a burden to us, and more than once induced us to calculate whether it would not be well that we should abandon our public duties and retire to some private corner into which it would be impossible that Mrs. Brumby should follow us. Years have rolled on since then, and we believe that Mrs. Brumby has gone before the great Judge and been called upon to account for the injuries she did us. We know that she went from these shores to a distant land when her nefarious projects failed at home. She was then by no means a young woman. We never could find that she left relative or friend behind her, and we know of none now, except those close and dearest friends of our own who supported us in our misery, who remember even that she existed. Whether she be alive or whether she be dead, her story shall be told,—not in a spirit of revenge, but with strict justice.

What there was in her of good shall be set down with honesty; and indeed there was much in her that was good. She was energetic, full of resources, very brave, constant, devoted to the interests of the poor creature whose name she bore, and by no means a fool. She was utterly unscrupulous, dishonest, a liar, cruel, hard as a nether mill-stone to all the world except Lieutenant Brumby,—harder to him than to all the world besides when he made any faintest attempt at rebellion,—and as far as we could judge, absolutely without conscience. Had she been a man and had circumstances favoured her, she might have been a prime minister, or an archbishop, or a chiefjustice. We intend no silly satire on present or past holders of the great offices indicated; but we think that they have generally been achieved by such a combination of intellect, perseverance, audacity, and readiness as that which Mrs. Brumby certainly possessed. And that freedom from the weakness of scruple,—which in men who have risen in public life we may perhaps call adaptability to compromise,—was in her so strong, that had she been a man, she would have trimmed her bark to any wind that blew, and certainly have sailed into some port. But she was a woman,—and the ports were not open to her.

Those ports were not open to her which had she been a man would have been within her reach; but,—fortunately for us and for the world at large as to the general question, though so very unfortunately as regarded this special case,—the port of literature is open to women. It seems to be the only really desirable harbour to which a female captain can steer her vessel with much hope of success. There are the Fine Arts, no doubt. There seems to be no reason why a woman should not paint as well as Titian. But they don't. With the pen they hold their own, and certainly run a better race against men on that course than on any other. Mrs. Brumby, who was very desirous of running a race and winning a place, and who had seen all this, put on her cap and jacket, and boots, chose her colours, and entered her name. Why, oh why, did she select the course upon which we, wretched we, were bound by our duties to regulate the running?

We may as well say at once that though Mrs. Brumby might have made a very good prime minister, she could not write a paper for a magazine, or produce literary work of any description that was worth paper and ink. We feel sure that we may declare without hesitation that no perseverance on her part, no labour however unswerving, no training however long, would have enabled her to do in a fitting manner even a review for the "Literary Curricle." There was very much in her, but that was not in her. We find it difficult to describe the special deficiency under which she laboured;—but it existed and was past remedy. As a man suffering from a chronic stiff joint cannot run, and cannot hope to run, so was it with her. She could not combine words so as to make sentences, or sentences so as to make paragraphs. She did not know what style meant. We believe that had she ever read, Johnson, Gibbon, Archdeacon Coxe, Mr. Grote, and Macaulay would have been all the same to her. And yet this woman chose literature as her profession, and clung to it for awhile with a persistence which brought her nearer to the rewards of success than many come who are at all points worthy to receive them.

We have said that she was not a young woman when we knew her. We cannot fancy her to have been ever young. We cannot bring our imagination to picture to ourselves the person of Mrs. Brumby surrounded by the advantages of youth. When we knew her she may probably have been forty or forty-five, and she then possessed a rigidity of demeanour and a sternness of presence which we think must have become her better than any softer guise or more tender phase of manner could ever have done in her earlier years. There was no attempt about her to disguise or modify her sex, such as women have made since those days. She talked much about her husband, the lieutenant, and she wore a double roll of very stiff dark brown curls on each side of her face,—or rather over her brows,—which would not have been worn by a woman meaning to throw off as far as possible her feminity. Whether those curls were or were not artificial we never knew. Our male acquaintances who saw her used to swear that they were false, but a lady who once saw her, assured us that they were real. She told us that there is a kind of hair growing on the heads of some women, thick, short, crisp, and shiny, which will maintain its curl unbroken and unruffled for days. She told us, also, that women blessed with such hair are always pachydermatous and strong-minded. Such certainly was the character of Mrs. Brumby. She was a tall, thin woman, not very tall or very thin. For aught that we can remember, her figure may have been good;—but we do remember well that she never seemed to us to have any charm of womanhood. There was a certain fire in her dark eyes,—eyes which were, we think, quite black,—but it was the fire of contention and not of love. Her features were well formed, her nose somewhat long, and her lips thin, and her face too narrow, perhaps, for beauty. Her chin was long, and the space from her nose to her upper lip was long. She always carried a well-wearing brown complexion;—a complexion with which no man had a right to find fault, but which, to a pondering, speculative man, produced unconsciously a consideration whether, in a matter of kissing, an ordinary mahogany table did not offer a preferable surface. When we saw her she wore, we think always, a dark stuff dress,—a fur tippet in winter and a most ill-arranged shawl in summer,—and a large commanding bonnet, which grew in our eyes till it assumed all the attributes of a helmet,—inspiring that reverence and creating that fear which Minerva's headgear is intended to produce. When we add our conviction that Mrs. Brumby trusted nothing to female charms, that she neither suffered nor enjoyed anything from female vanity, and that the lieutenant was perfectly safe, let her roam the world alone, as she might, in search of editors, we shall have said enough to introduce the lady to our readers.

Of her early life, or their early lives, we know nothing; but the unfortunate circumstances which brought us into contact with Mrs. Brumby, made us also acquainted with the lieutenant. The lieutenant, we think, was younger than his wife;—a good deal younger we used to imagine, though his looks may have been deceptive. He was a confirmed invalid, and there are phases of ill-health which give an appearance of youthfulness rather than of age. What was his special ailing we never heard,—though, as we shall mention further on, we had our own idea on that subject; but he was always spoken of in our hearing as one who always had been ill, who always was ill, who always would be ill, and who never ought to think of getting well. He had been in some regiment called the Duke of Sussex's Own, and his wife used to imagine that her claims upon the public as a woman of literature were enhanced by the royalty of her husband's corps. We never knew her attempt to make any other use whatever of his services. He was not confined to his bed, and could walk at any rate about the house; but she never asked him, or allowed him to do anything. Whether he ever succeeded in getting his face outside the door we do not know. He wore, when we saw him, an old dressing-gown and slippers. He was a pale, slight, light-haired man, and we fancy that he took a delight in novels.

Their settled income consisted of his half-pay and some very small property which belonged to her. Together they might perhaps have possessed £150 per annum. When we knew them they had lodgings in Harpur Street, near Theobald's Road, and she had resolved to push her way in London as a woman of literature. She had been told that she would have to deal with hard people, and that she must herself be hard;—that advantage would be taken of her weakness, and that she must therefore struggle vehemently to equal the strength of those with whom she would be brought in contact;—that editors, publishers, and brother authors would suck her brains and give her nothing for them, and that, therefore, she must get what she could out of them, giving them as little as possible in return. It was an evil lesson that she had learned; but she omitted nothing in the performance of the duties which that lesson imposed upon her.

She first came to us with a pressing introduction from an acquaintance of ours who was connected with a weekly publication called the "Literary Curricle." The "Literary Curricle" was not in our estimation a strong paper, and we will own that we despised it. We did not think very much of the acquaintance by whom the strong introductory letter was written. But Mrs. Brumby forced herself into our presence with the letter in her hand, and before she left us extracted from us a promise that we would read a manuscript which she pulled out of a bag which she carried with her. Of that first interview a short account shall be given, but it must first be explained that the editor of the "Literary Curricle" had received Mrs. Brumby with another letter from another editor, whom she had first taken by storm without any introduction whatever. This first gentleman, whom we had not the pleasure of knowing, had, under what pressure we who knew the lady can imagine, printed three or four short paragraphs from Mrs. Brumby's pen. Whether they reached publication we never could learn, but we saw the printed slips. He, however, passed her on to the "Literary Curricle,"—which dealt almost exclusively in the reviewing of books,—and our friend at the office of that influential "organ" sent her to us with an intimation that her very peculiar and well-developed talents were adapted rather for the creation of tales, or the composition of original treatises, than for reviewing. The letter was very strong, and we learned afterwards that Mrs. Brumby had consented to abandon her connection with the "Literary Curricle" only on the receipt of a letter in her praise that should be very strong indeed. She rejected the two first offered to her, and herself dictated the epithets with which the third was loaded. On no other terms would she leave the office of the "Literary Curricle."

We cannot say that the letter, strong as it was, had much effect upon us; but this effect it had perhaps,—that after reading it we could not speak to the lady with that acerbity which we might have used had she come to us without it. As it was we were not very civil, and began our intercourse by assuring her that we could not avail ourselves of her services. Having said so, and observing that she still kept her seat, we rose from our chair, being well aware how potent a spell that movement is wont to exercise upon visitors who are unwilling to go. She kept her seat and argued the matter out with us. A magazine such as that which we then conducted must, she surmised, require depth of erudition, keenness of intellect, grasp of hand, force of expression, and lightness of touch. That she possessed all these gifts she had, she alleged, brought to us convincing evidence. There was the letter from the editor of the "Literary Curricle," with which she had been long connected, declaring the fact! Did we mean to cast doubt upon the word of our own intimate friend? For the gentleman at the office of the "Literary Curricle" had written to us as "Dear—," though as far as we could remember we had never spoken half-a-dozen words to him in our life. Then she repeated the explanation, given by her godfather, of the abrupt termination of the close connection which had long existed between her and the "Curricle." She could not bring herself to waste her energies in the reviewing of books. At that moment we certainly did believe that she had been long engaged on the "Curricle," though there was certainly not a word in our correspondent's letter absolutely stating that to be the fact. He declared to us her capabilities and excellences, but did not say that he had ever used them himself. Indeed, he told us that great as they were, they were hardly suited for his work. She, before she had left us on that occasion, had committed herself to positive falsehoods. She boasted of the income she had earned from two periodicals, whereas up to that moment she had never received a shilling for what she had written.

We find it difficult, even after so many years,—when the shame of the thing has worn off together with the hairs of our head,—to explain how it was that we allowed her to get, in the first instance, any hold upon us. We did not care a brass farthing for the man who had written from the "Literary Curricle." His letter to us was an impertinence, and we should have stated as much to Mrs. Brumby had we cared to go into such matter with her. And our first feelings with regard to the lady herself were feelings of dislike,—and almost of contempt even, though we did believe that she had been a writer for the press. We disliked her nose, and her lips, and her bonnet, and the colour of her face. We didn't want her. Though we were very much younger then than we are now, we had already learned to set our backs up against strong-minded female intruders. As we said before, we rose from our chair with the idea of banishing her, not absolutely uncivilly, but altogether unceremoniously. It never occurred to us during that meeting that she could be of any possible service to us, or that we should ever be of any slightest service to her. Nevertheless she had extracted from us a great many words, and had made a great many observations herself before she left us.

When a man speaks a great many words it is impossible that he should remember what they all were. That we told Mrs. Brumby on that occasion that we did not doubt but that we would use the manuscript which she left in our hands, we are quite sure was not true. We never went so near making a promise in our lives,—even when pressed by youth and beauty,—and are quite sure that what we did say to Mrs. Brumby was by no means near akin to this. That we undertook to read the manuscript we think probable, and therein lay our first fault,—the unfortunate slip from which our future troubles sprang, and grew to such terrible dimensions. We cannot now remember how the hated parcel, the abominable roll, came into our hands. We do remember the face and form and figure of the woman as she brought it out of the large reticule which she carried, and we remember also how we put our hands behind us to avoid it, as she presented it to us. We told her flatly that we did not want it, and would not have it;—and yet it came into our hands! We think that it must have been placed close to our elbow, and that, being used to such playthings, we took it up. We know that it was in our hands, and that we did not know how to rid ourselves of it when she began to tell us the story of the lieutenant. We were hard-hearted enough to inform her,—as we have, under perhaps lesser compulsion, informed others since,—that the distress of the man or of the woman should never be accepted as a reason for publishing the works of the writer. She answered us gallantly enough that she had never been weak enough or foolish enough so to think. "I base my claim to attention," she said, "on quite another ground. Do not suppose, sir, that I am appealing to your pity. I scorn to do so. But I wish you should know my position as a married woman, and that you should understand that my husband, though unfortunately an invalid, has been long attached to a regiment which is peculiarly the Duke of Sussex's own. You cannot but be aware of the connection which His Royal Highness has long maintained with literature."

Mrs. Brumby could not write, but she could speak. The words she had just uttered were absolutely devoid of sense. The absurdity of them was ludicrous and gross. But they were not without a certain efficacy. They did not fill us with any respect for her literary capacity because of her connection with the Duke of Sussex, but they did make us feel that she was able to speak up for herself. We are told sometimes that the world accords to a man that treatment which he himself boldly demands; and though the statement seems to be monstrous, there is much truth in it. When Mrs. Brumby spoke of her husband's regiment being "peculiarly the Duke of Sussex's own," she used a tone which compelled from us more courtesy than we had hitherto shown her. We knew that the Duke was neither a man of letters nor a warrior, though he had a library, and, as we were now told, a regiment. Had he been both, his being so would have formed no legitimate claim for Mrs. Brumby upon us. But, nevertheless, the royal Duke helped her to win her way. It was not his royalty, but her audacity that was prevailing. She sat with us for more than an hour; and when she left us the manuscript was with us, and we had no doubt undertaken to read it. We are perfectly certain that at that time we had not gone beyond this in the way of promising assistance to Mrs. Brumby.

The would-be author, who cannot make his way either by intellect or favour, can hardly do better, perhaps, than establish a grievance. Let there be anything of a case of ill-usage against editor or publisher, and the aspirant, if he be energetic and unscrupulous, will greatly increase his chance of working his way into print. Mrs. Brumby was both energetic and unscrupulous, and she did establish her grievance. As soon as she brought her first visit to a close, the roll, which was still in our hands, was chucked across our table to a corner commodiously supported by the wall, so that occasionally there was accumulated in it a heap of such unwelcome manuscripts. In the doing of this, in the moment of our so chucking the parcel, it was always our conscientious intention to make a clearance of the whole heap, at the very furthest, by the end of the week. We knew that strong hopes were bound up in those various little packets, that eager thoughts were imprisoned there the owners of which believed that they were endowed with wings fit for aërial soaring, that young hearts,—ay, and old hearts, too,—sore with deferred hope, were waiting to know whether their aspirations might now be realised, whether those azure wings might at last be released from bondage and allowed to try their strength in the broad sunlight of public favour. We think, too, that we had a conscience; and, perhaps, the heap was cleared as frequently as are the heaps of other editors. But there it would grow, in the commodious corner of our big table, too often for our own peace of mind. The aspect of each individual little parcel would be known to us, and we would allow ourselves to fancy that by certain external signs we could tell the nature of the interior. Some of them would promise well,—so well as to create even almost an appetite for their perusal. But there would be others from which we would turn with aversion, which we seemed to abhor, which, when we handled the heap, our fingers would refuse to touch, and which, thus lying there neglected and ill-used, would have the dust of many days added to those other marks which inspired disgust. We confess that as soon as Mrs. Brumby's back was turned her roll was sent in upon this heap with that determined force which a strong feeling of dislike can lend even to a man's little finger. And there it lay for,—perhaps a fortnight. When during that period we extracted first one packet and then another for judgment, we would still leave Mrs. Brumby's roll behind in the corner. On such occasions a pang of conscience will touch the heart; some idea of neglected duty will be present to the mind; a silent promise will perhaps be made that it shall be the next; some momentary sudden resolve will be half formed that for the future a rigid order of succession shall be maintained, which no favour shall be allowed to infringe. But, alas! when the hand is again at work selecting, the odious ugly thing is left behind, till at last it becomes infested with strange terrors, with an absolute power of its own, and the guilty conscience will become afraid. All this happened in regard to Mrs. Brumby's manuscript. "Dear, dear, yes;—Mrs. Brumby!" we would catch ourselves exclaiming with that silent inward voice which occasionally makes itself audible to most of us. And then, quite silently, without even whispered violence, we would devote Mrs. Brumby to the infernal gods. And so the packet remained amidst the heap,—perhaps for a fortnight.

"There's a lady waiting in your room, sir!" This was said to us one morning on our reaching our office by the lad whom we used to call our clerk. He is now managing a red-hot Tory newspaper down in Barsetshire, has a long beard, a flaring eye, a round belly, and is upon the whole the most arrogant personage we know. In the days of Mrs. Brumby he was a little wizened fellow about eighteen years old, but looking three years younger, modest, often almost dumb, and in regard to ourselves not only reverential but timid. We turned upon him in great anger. What business had any woman to be in our room in our absence? Were not our orders on this subject exact and very urgent? Was he not kept at an expense of 14*s.* a week,—we did not actually throw the amount in his teeth, but such was intended to be the effect of our rebuke,—at 14*s.* a week, paid out of our own pocket,—nominally, indeed, as a clerk, but chiefly for the very purpose of keeping female visitors out of our room? And now, in our absence and in his, there was actually a woman among the manuscripts! We felt from the first moment that it was Mrs. Brumby.

With bated breath and downcast eyes the lad explained to us his inability to exclude her. "She walked straight in, right over me," he said; "and as for being alone,—she hasn't been alone. I haven't left her, not a minute."

We walked at once into our own room, feeling how fruitless it was to discuss the matter further with the boy in the passage, and there we found Mrs. Brumby seated in the chair opposite to our own. We had gathered ourselves up, if we may so describe an action which was purely mental, with a view to severity. We thought that her intrusion was altogether unwarrantable, and that it behoved us to let her know that such was the case. We entered the room with a clouded brow, and intended that she should read our displeasure in our eyes. But Mrs. Brumby could,—"gather herself up," quite as well as we could do, and she did so. She also could call clouds to her forehead and could flash anger from her eyes. "Madam," we exclaimed, as we paused for a moment, and looked at her.

But she cared nothing for our "Madam," and condescended to no apology. Rising from her chair, she asked us why we had not kept the promise we had made her to use her article in our next number. We don't know how far our readers will understand all that was included in this accusation. Use her contribution in our next number! It had never occurred to us as probable, or hardly as possible, that we should use it in any number. Our eye glanced at the heap to see whether her fingers had been at work, but we perceived that the heap had not been touched. We have always flattered ourselves that no one can touch our heap without our knowing it. She saw the motion of our eye, and at once understood it. Mrs. Brumby, no doubt, possessed great intelligence, and, moreover, a certain majesty of demeanour. There was always something of the helmet of Minerva in the bonnet which she wore. Her shawl was an old shawl, but she was never ashamed of it; and she could always put herself forward, as though there were nothing behind her to be concealed, the concealing of which was a burden to her. "I cannot suppose," she said, "that my paper has been altogether neglected!"

We picked out the roll with all the audacity we could assume, and proceeded to explain how very much in error she was in supposing that we had ever even hinted at its publication. We had certainly said that we would read it, mentioning no time. We never did mention any time in making any such promise. "You named a week, sir," said Mrs. Brumby, "and now a month has passed by. You assured me that it would be accepted unless returned within seven days. Of course it will be accepted now." We contradicted her flatly. We explained, we protested, we threatened. We endeavoured to put the manuscript into her hand, and made a faint attempt to stick it into her bag. She was indignant, dignified, and very strong. She said nothing on that occasion about legal proceedings, but stuck manfully to her assertion that we had bound ourselves to decide upon her manuscript within a week. "Do you think, sir," said she, "that I would entrust the very essence of my brain to the keeping of a stranger, without some such assurance as that?" We acknowledged that we had undertaken to read the paper, but again disowned the week. "And how long would you be justified in taking?" demanded Mrs. Brumby. "If a month, why not a year? Does it not occur to you, sir, that when the very best of my intellect, my inmost thoughts, lie there at your disposal," and she pointed to the heap, "it may be possible that a property has been confided to you too valuable to justify neglect? Had I given you a ring to keep you would have locked it up, but the best jewels of my mind are left to the tender mercies of your charwoman." What she said was absolutely nonsense,—abominable, villanous trash; but she said it so well that we found ourselves apologising for our own misconduct. There had perhaps been a little undue delay. In our peculiar business such would occasionally occur. When we had got to this, any expression of our wrath at her intrusion was impossible. As we entered the room we had intended almost to fling her manuscript at her head. We now found ourselves handling it almost affectionately while we expressed regret for our want of punctuality. Mrs. Brumby was gracious, and pardoned us, but her forgiveness was not of the kind which denotes the intention of the injured one to forget as well as forgive the trespass. She had suffered from us a great injustice; but she would say no more on that score now, on the condition that we would at once attend to her essay. She thrice repeated the words, "at once," and she did so without rebuke from us. And then she made us a proposition, the like of which never reached us before or since. Would we fix an hour within the next day or two at which we would call upon her in Harpur Street and arrange as to terms! The lieutenant, she said, would be delighted to make our acquaintance. Call upon her;—upon Mrs. Brumby! Travel to Harpur Street, Theobald's Road, on the business of a chance bit of scribbling, which was wholly indifferent to us except in so far as it was a trouble to us! And then we were invited to make arrangements as to terms! Terms!! Had the owner of the most illustrious lips in the land offered to make us known in those days to the partner of her greatness, she could not have done so with more assurance that she was conferring on us an honour, than was assumed by Mrs. Brumby when she proposed to introduce us to the lieutenant.

When many wrongs are concentrated in one short speech, and great injuries inflicted by a few cleverly-combined words, it is generally difficult to reply so that some of the wrongs shall not pass unnoticed. We cannot always be so happy as was Mr. John Robinson, when in saying that he hadn't been "dead at all," he did really say everything that the occasion required. We were so dismayed by the proposition that we should go to Harpur Street, so hurt in our own personal dignity, that we lost ourselves in endeavouring to make it understood that such a journey on our part was quite out of the question. "Were we to do that, Mrs. Brumby, we should live in cabs and spend our entire days in making visits." She smiled at us as we endeavoured to express our indignation, and said something as to circumstances being different in different cases;—something also, if we remember right, she hinted as to the intelligence needed for discovering the differences. She left our office quicker than we had expected, saying that as we could not afford to spend our time in cabs she would call again on the day but one following. Her departure was almost abrupt, but she went apparently in good-humour. It never occurred to us at the moment to suspect that she hurried away before we should have had time to repudiate certain suggestions which she had made.

When we found ourselves alone with the roll of paper in our hands, we were very angry with Mrs. Brumby, but almost more angry with ourselves. We were in no way bound to the woman, and yet she had in some degree substantiated a claim upon us. We piqued ourselves specially on never making any promise beyond the vaguest assurance that this or that proposed contribution should receive consideration at some altogether undefined time; but now we were positively pledged to read Mrs. Brumby's effusion and have our verdict ready by the day after to-morrow. We were wont, too, to keep ourselves much secluded from strangers; and here was Mrs. Brumby, who had already been with us twice, positively entitled to a third audience. We had been scolded, and then forgiven, and then ridiculed by a woman who was old, and ugly, and false! And there was present to us a conviction that though she was old, and ugly, and false, Mrs. Brumby was no ordinary woman. Perhaps it might be that she was really qualified to give us valuable assistance in regard to the magazine, as to which we must own we were sometimes driven to use matter that was not quite so brilliant as, for our readers' sakes, we would have wished it to be. We feel ourselves compelled to admit that old and ugly women, taken on the average, do better literary work than they who are young and pretty. I did not like Mrs. Brumby, but it might be that in her the age would find another De Staël. So thinking, we cut the little string, and had the manuscript open in our own hands. We cannot remember whether she had already indicated to us the subject of the essay, but it was headed, "Costume in 18—." There were perhaps thirty closely-filled pages, of which we read perhaps a third. The hand-writing was unexceptionable, orderly, clean, and legible; but the matter was undeniable twaddle. It proffered advice to women that they should be simple, and to men that they should be cleanly in their attire. Anything of less worth for the purpose of amusement or of instruction could not be imagined. There was, in fact, nothing in it. It has been our fate to look at a great many such essays, and to cause them at once either to be destroyed or returned. There could be no doubt at all as to Mrs. Brumby's essay.

She came punctual as the clock. As she seated herself in our chair and made some remark as to her hope that we were satisfied, we felt something like fear steal across our bosom. We were about to give offence, and dreaded the arguments that would follow. It was, however, quite clear that we could not publish Mrs. Brumby's essay on Costume, and therefore, though she looked more like Minerva now than ever, we must go through our task. We told her in half-a-dozen words that we had read the paper, and that it would not suit our columns.

"Not suit your columns!" she said, looking at us by no means in sorrow, but in great anger. "You do not mean to trifle with me like that after all you have made me suffer?" We protested that we were responsible for none of her sufferings. "Sir," she said, "when I was last here you owned the wrong you had done me." We felt that we must protest against this, and we rose in our wrath. There were two of us angry now.

"Madam," we said, "you have kindly offered us your essay, and we have courteously declined it. You will allow us to say that this must end the matter." There were allusions here to kindness and courtesy, but the reader will understand that the sense of the words was altogether changed by the tone of the voice.

"Indeed, sir, the matter will not be ended so. If you think that your position will enable you to trample upon those who make literature really a profession, you are very much mistaken."

"Mrs. Brumby," we said, "we can give you no other answer, and as our time is valuable— "

"Time valuable!" she exclaimed,—and as she stood up an artist might have taken her for a model of Minerva had she only held a spear in her hand. "And is no time valuable, do you think, but yours? I had, sir, your distinct promise that the paper should be published if it was left in your hands above a week."

"That is untrue, madam."

"Untrue, sir?"

"Absolutely untrue." Mrs. Brumby was undoubtedly a woman, and might be very like a goddess, but we were not going to allow her to palm off upon us without flat contradiction so absolute a falsehood as that. "We never dreamed of publishing your paper."

"Then why, sir, have you troubled yourself to read it,—from the beginning to the end?" We had certainly intimated that we had made ourselves acquainted with the entire essay, but we had in fact skimmed and skipped through about a third of it. "How dare you say, sir, you have never dreamed of publishing it, when you know that you studied it with that view?"

"We didn't read it all," we said, "but we read quite enough."

"And yet but this moment ago you told me that you had perused it carefully." The word peruse we certainly never used in our life. We object to "perusing," as we do to "commencing" and "performing." We "read," and we "begin," and we "do." As to that assurance which the word "carefully" would intend to convey, we believe that we were to that extent guilty. "I think, sir," she continued, "that you had better see the lieutenant."

"With a view to fighting the gentleman?" we asked.

"No, sir. An officer in the Duke of Sussex's Own draws his sword against no enemy so unworthy of his steel." She had told me at a former interview that the lieutenant was so confirmed an invalid as to be barely able, on his best days, to drag himself out of bed. "One fights with one's equal, but the law gives redress from injury, whether it be inflicted by equal, by superior, or by,—INFERIOR." And Mrs. Brumby, as she uttered the last word, wagged her helmet at us in a manner which left no doubt as to the position which she assigned to us.

It became clearly necessary that an end should be put to an intercourse which had become so very unpleasant. We told our Minerva very plainly that we must beg her to leave us. There is, however, nothing more difficult to achieve than the expulsion of a woman who is unwilling to quit the place she occupies. We remember to have seen a lady take possession of a seat in a mail coach to which she was not entitled, and which had been booked and paid for by another person. The agent for the coaching business desired her with many threats to descend, but she simply replied that the journey to her was a matter of such moment that she felt herself called upon to keep her place. The agent sent the coachman to pull her out. The coachman threatened,—with his hands as well as with his words,—and then set the guard at her. The guard attacked her with inflamed visage and fearful words about Her Majesty's mails, and then set the ostlers at her. We thought the ostlers were going to handle her roughly, but it ended by their scratching their heads, and by a declaration on the part of one of them that she was "the rummest go he'd ever seen." She was a woman, and they couldn't touch her. A policeman was called upon for assistance, who offered to lock her up, but he could only do so if allowed to lock up the whole coach as well. It was ended by the production of another coach, by an exchange of the luggage and passengers, by a delay of two hours, and an embarrassing possession of the original vehicle by the lady in the midst of a crowd of jeering boys and girls. We could tell Mrs. Brumby to go, and we could direct our boy to open the door, and we could make motions indicatory of departure with our left hand, but we could not forcibly turn her out of the room. She asked us for the name of our lawyer, and we did write down for her on a slip of paper the address of a most respectable firm, whom we were pleased to regard as our attorneys, but who had never yet earned six and eight-pence from the magazine. Young Sharp, of the firm of Sharp and Butterwell, was our friend, and would no doubt see to the matter for us should it be necessary;—but we could not believe that the woman would be so foolish. She made various assertions to us as to her position in the world of literature, and it was on this occasion that she brought out those printed slips which we have before mentioned. She offered to refer the matter in dispute between us to the arbitration of the editor of the "Curricle;" and when we indignantly declined such interference, protesting that there was no matter in dispute, she again informed us that if we thought to trample upon her we were very much mistaken. Then there occurred a little episode which moved us to laughter in the midst of our wrath. Our boy, in obedience to our pressing commands that he should usher Mrs. Brumby out of our presence, did lightly touch her arm. Feeling the degradation of the assault, Minerva swung round upon the unfortunate lad and gave him a box on the ear which we'll be bound the editor of the "West Barsetshire Gazette" remembers to this day. "Madam," we said, as soon as we had swallowed down the first involuntary attack of laughter, "if you conduct yourself in this manner we must send for the police."

"Do, sir, if you dare," replied Minerva, "and every man of letters in the metropolis shall hear of your conduct." There was nothing in her threat to move us, but we confess that we were uncomfortable. "Before I leave you, sir," she said, "I will give you one more chance. Will you perform your contract with me, and accept my contribution?"

"Certainly not," we replied. She afterwards quoted this answer as admitting a contract.

We are often told that everything must come to an end,—and there was an end at last to Mrs. Brumby's visit. She went from us with an assurance that she should at once return home, pick up the lieutenant,—hinting that the exertion, caused altogether by our wickedness, might be the death of that gallant officer,—and go with him direct to her attorney. The world of literature should hear of the terrible injustice which had been done to her, and the courts of law should hear of it too.

We confess that we were grievously annoyed. By the time that Mrs. Brumby had left the premises, our clerk had gone also. He had rushed off to the nearest police-court to swear an information against her on account of the box on the ear which she had given him, and we were unable to leave our desk till he had returned. We found that for the present the doing of any work in our line of business was quite out of the question. A calm mind is required for the critical reading of manuscripts, and whose mind could be calm after such insults as those we had received? We sat in our chair, idle, reflective indignant, making resolutions that we would never again open our lips to a woman coming to us with a letter of introduction and a contribution, till our lad returned to us. We were forced to give him a sovereign before we could induce him to withdraw his information. We object strongly to all bribery, but in this case we could see the amount of ridicule which would be heaped upon our whole establishment if some low-conditioned lawyer were allowed to cross-examine us as to our intercourse with Mrs. Brumby. It was with difficulty that the clerk arranged the matter the next day at the police-office, and his object was not effected without the further payment by us of £1 2s. 6d. for costs. It was then understood between us and the clerk that on no excuse whatever should Mrs. Brumby be again admitted to my room, and I thought that the matter was over. "She shall have to fight her way through if she does get in," said the lad. "She ain't going to knock me about any more,—woman or no woman." "O, dea, certe," we exclaimed. "It shall be a dear job to her if she touches me again," said the clerk, catching up the sound.

We really thought we had done with Mrs. Brumby, but at the end of four or five days there came to us a letter, which we have still in our possession, and which we will now venture to make public. It was as follows. It was addressed not to ourselves, but to Messrs. X., Y., and

Z., the very respectable proprietors of the periodical which we were managing on their behalf.

"Pluck Court, Gray's Inn, 31st March, 18—.

"Gentlemen,

"We are instructed by our client, Lieutenant Brumby, late of the Duke of Sussex's Own Regiment, to call upon you for payment of the sum of twenty-five guineas due to him for a manuscript essay on Costume, supplied by his wife to the—Magazine, which is, we believe, your property, by special contract with Mr.—, the Editor. We are also directed to require from you and from Mr.—a full apology in writing for the assault committed on Mrs. Brumby in your Editor's room on the 27th instant; and an assurance also that the columns of your periodical shall not be closed against that lady because of this transaction. We request that £1 13s. 8d., our costs, may be forwarded to us, together with the above-named sum of twenty-five guineas.

"We are, Gentlemen,

"Your obedient servants,

"Badger and Blister.

"Messrs. X., Y., Z., Paternoster Row."

We were in the habit of looking in at the shop in Paternoster Row on the first of every month, and on that inauspicious first of April the above letter was handed to us by our friend Mr. X. "I hope you haven't been and put your foot in it," said Mr. X. We protested that we had not put our foot in it at all, and we told him the whole story. "Don't let us have a lawsuit, whatever you do," said Mr. X. "The magazine isn't worth it." We ridiculed the idea of a lawsuit, but we took away with us Messrs. Badger and Blister's letter and showed it to our legal adviser, Mr. Sharp. Mr. Sharp was of opinion that Badger and Blister meant fighting. When we pointed out to him the absolute absurdity of the whole thing, he merely informed us that we did not know Badger and Blister. "They'll take up any case," said he, "however hopeless, and work it with superhuman energy, on the mere chance of getting something out of the defendant. Whatever is got out of him becomes theirs. They never disgorge." We were quite confident that nothing could be got out of the magazine on behalf of Mrs. Brumby, and we left the case in Mr. Sharp's hands, thinking that our trouble in the matter was over.

A fortnight elapsed, and then we were called upon to meet Mr. Sharp in Paternoster Row. We found our friend Mr. X. with a somewhat unpleasant visage. Mr. X. was a thriving man, usually just, and sometimes generous; but he didn't like being "put upon." Mr. Sharp had actually recommended that some trifle should be paid to Mrs. Brumby, and Mr. X. seemed to think that this expense would, in case that advice were followed, have been incurred through fault on our part. "A ten-pound note will set it all right," said Mr. Sharp.

"Yes;—a ten-pound note,—just flung into the gutter. I wonder that you allowed yourself to have anything to do with such a woman." We protested against this injustice, giving Mr. X. to know that he didn't understand and couldn't understand our business. "I'm not so sure of that," said Mr. X. There was almost a quarrel, and we began to doubt whether Mrs. Brumby would not be the means of taking the very bread from out of our mouths. Mr. Sharp at last suggested that in spite of what he had seen from Mrs. Brumby, the lieutenant would probably be a gentleman. "Not a doubt about it," said Mr. X., who was always fond of officers and of the army, and at the moment seemed to think more of a paltry lieutenant than of his own Editor.

Mr. Sharp actually pressed upon us and upon Mr. X. that we should call upon the lieutenant and explain matters to him. Mrs. Brumby had always been with us at twelve o'clock. "Go at noon," said Mr. Sharp, "and you'll certainly find her out." He instructed us to tell the lieutenant "just the plain truth," as he called it, and to explain that in no way could the proprietors of a magazine be made liable to payment for an article because the Editor in discharge of his duty had consented to read it. "Perhaps the lieutenant doesn't know that his name has been used at all," said Mr. Sharp. "At any rate, it will be well to learn what sort of a man he is."

"A high-minded gentleman, no doubt," said Mr. X., the name of whose second boy was already down at the Horse Guards for a commission.

Though it was sorely against the grain, and in direct opposition to our own opinion, we were constrained to go to Harpur Street, Theobald's Road, and to call upon Lieutenant Brumby. We had not explained to Mr. X. or to Mr. Sharp what had passed between Mrs. Brumby and ourselves when she suggested such a visit, but the memory of the words which we and she had then spoken was on us as we endeavoured to dissuade our lawyer and our publisher. Nevertheless, at their instigation, we made the visit. The house in Harpur Street was small, and dingy, and old. The door was opened for us by the normal lodging-house maid-of-all-work, who, when we asked for the lieutenant, left us in the passage, that she might go and see. We sent up our name, and in a few minutes were ushered into a sitting-room up two flights of stairs. The room was not untidy, but it was as comfortless as any chamber we ever saw. The lieutenant was lying on an old horsehair sofa, but we had been so far lucky as to find him alone. Mr. Sharp had been correct in his prediction as to the customary absence of the lady at that hour in the morning. In one corner of the room we saw an old ram-shackle desk, at which, we did not doubt, were written those essays on Costume and other subjects, in the disposing of which the lady displayed so much energy. The lieutenant himself was a small grey man, dressed, or rather enveloped, in what I supposed to be an old wrapper of his wife's. He held in his hands a well-worn volume of a novel, and when he rose to greet us he almost trembled with dismay and bashfulness. His feet were thrust into slippers which were too old to stick on them, and round his throat he wore a dirty, once white, woollen comforter. We never learned what was the individual character of the corps which specially belonged to H.R.H. the Duke of Sussex; but if it was conspicuous for dash and gallantry, Lieutenant Brumby could hardly have held his own among his brother officers. We knew, however, from his wife, that he had been invalided, and as an invalid we respected him. We proceeded to inform him that we had been called upon to pay him a sum of twenty-five guineas, and to explain how entirely void of justice any such claim must be. We suggested to him that he might be made to pay some serious sum by the lawyers he employed, and that the matter to us was an annoyance and a trouble,—chiefly because we had no wish to be brought into conflict with any one so respectable as Lieutenant Brumby. He looked at us with imploring eyes, as though begging us not to be too hard upon him in the absence of his wife, trembled from head to foot, and muttered a few words which were nearly inaudible. We will not state as a fact that the lieutenant had taken to drinking spirits early in life, but that certainly was our impression during the only interview we ever had with him. When we pressed upon him as a question which he must answer whether he did not think that he had better withdraw his claim, he fell back upon his sofa, and began to sob. While he was thus weeping Mrs. Brumby entered the room. She had in her hand the card which we had given to the maid-of-all-work, and was therefore prepared for the interview. "Sir," she said, "I hope you have come to settle my husband's just demands."

Amidst the husband's wailings there had been one little sentence which reached our ears. "She does it all," he had said, throwing his eyes up piteously towards our face. At that moment the door had been opened, and Mrs. Brumby had entered the room. When she spoke of her husband's "just demands," we turned to the poor prostrate lieutenant, and were deterred from any severity towards him by the look of supplication in his eye. "The lieutenant is not well this morning," said Mrs. Brumby, "and you will therefore be pleased to address yourself to me." We explained that the absurd demand for payment had been made on the proprietors of the magazine in the name of Lieutenant Brumby, and that we had therefore been obliged, in the performance of a most unpleasant duty, to call upon that gentleman; but she laughed our argument to scorn. "You have driven me to take legal steps," she said, "and as I am only a woman I must take them in the name of my husband. But I am the person aggrieved, and if you have any excuse to make you can make it to me. Your safer course, sir, will be to pay me the money that you owe me."

I had come there on a fool's errand, and before I could get away was very angry both with Mr. Sharp and Mr. X. I could hardly get a word in amidst the storm of indignant reproaches which was bursting over my head during the whole of the visit. One would have thought from hearing her that she had half filled the pages of the magazine for the last six months, and that we, individually, had pocketed the proceeds of her labour. She laughed in our face when we suggested that she could not really intend to prosecute the suit, and told us to mind our own business when we hinted that the law was an expensive amusement. "We, sir," she said, "will have the amusement, and you will have to pay the bill." When we left her she was indignant, defiant, and self-confident.

And what will the reader suppose was the end of all this? The whole truth has been told as accurately as we can tell it. As far as we know our own business we were not wrong in any single step we took. Our treatment of Mrs. Brumby was courteous, customary, and conciliatory. We had treated her with more consideration than we had perhaps ever before shown to an unknown, would-be contributor. She had been admitted thrice to our presence. We had read at any rate enough of her trash to be sure of its nature. On the other hand, we had been insulted, and our clerk had had his ears boxed. What should have been the result? We will tell the reader what was the result. Mr. X. paid £10 to Messrs. Badger and Blister on behalf of the lieutenant; and we, under Mr. Sharp's advice, wrote a letter to Mrs. Brumby, in which we expressed deep sorrow for our clerk's misconduct, and our own regret that we should have delayed,—"the perusal of her manuscript." We could not bring ourselves to write the words ourselves with our own fingers, but signed the document which Mr. Sharp put before us. Mr. Sharp had declared to Messrs. X., Y., and Z., that unless some such arrangement were made, he thought that we should be cast for a much greater sum before a jury. For one whole morning in Paternoster Row we resisted this infamous tax, not only on our patience but,—as we then felt it,—on our honour. We thought that our very old friend Mr. X. should have stood to us more firmly, and not have demanded from us a task that was so peculiarly repugnant to our feelings. "And it is peculiarly repugnant to my feelings to pay £10 for nothing," said Mr. X., who was not, we think, without some little feeling of revenge against us; "but I prefer that to a lawsuit." And then he argued that the simple act on our part of signing such a letter as that presented to us could cost us no trouble, and ought to occasion us no sorrow. "What can come of it? Who'll know it?" said Mr. X. "We've got to pay £10, and that we shall feel." It came to that at last, that we were constrained to sign the letter,—and did sign it. It did us no harm, and can have done Mrs. Brumby no good; but the moment in which we signed it was perhaps the bitterest we ever knew.

That in such a transaction Mrs. Brumby should have been so thoroughly successful, and that we should have been so shamefully degraded, has always appeared to us to be an injury too deep to remain unredressed for ever. Can such wrongs be, and the heavens not fall! Our greatest comfort has been in the reflection that neither the lieutenant nor his wife ever saw a shilling of the £10. That, doubtless, never went beyond Badger and Blister.

Christmas Day at Kirkby Cottage

Originally appeared in *Routledge's Christmas Annual*, 1870. Never reprinted by Trollope. Probably written 3–10 June 1870, during the composition of *The Eustace Diamonds*. Edmund Routledge was keen to get a Christmas story out of Trollope: he had tried, unsuccessfully, the previous year, and was not put off when Trollope asked him for a steep fee (£100). Maurice Archer's contempt for the materialism of Christmas recalls the attitude of Lucius Mason in *Orley Farm* (1862).

Chapter I

What Maurice Archer said about Christmas

"AFTER ALL, Christmas is a bore!"

"Even though you should think so, Mr. Archer, pray do not say so here."

"But it is."

"I am very sorry that you should feel like that; but pray do not say anything so very horrible."

"Why not? and why is it horrible? You know very well what I mean."

"I do not want to know what you mean; and it would make papa very unhappy if he were to hear you."

"A great deal of beef is roasted, and a great deal of pudding is boiled, and then people try to be jolly by eating more than usual. The consequence is, they get very sleepy, and want to go to bed an hour before the proper time. That's Christmas."

He who made this speech was a young man about twenty-three years old, and the other personage in the dialogue was a young lady, who might be, perhaps, three years his junior. The "papa" to whom the lady had alluded was the Rev. John Lownd, parson of Kirkby Cliffe, in Craven, and the scene was the parsonage library, as pleasant a little room as you would wish to see, in which the young man who thought Christmas to be a bore was at present sitting over the fire, in the parson's armchair, with a novel in his hand, which he had been reading till he was interrupted by the parson's daughter. It was nearly time for him to dress for dinner, and the young lady was already dressed. She had entered the room on the pretext of looking for some book or paper, but perhaps her main object may have been to ask for some assistance from Maurice Archer in the work of decorating the parish church. The necessary ivy and holly branches had been collected, and the work was to be performed on the morrow. The day following would be Christmas Day. It must be acknowledged, that Mr. Archer had not accepted the proposition made to him very graciously.

Maurice Archer was a young man as to whose future career in life many of his elder friends shook their heads and expressed much fear. It was not that his conduct was dangerously bad, or that he spent his money too fast, but that he was abominably conceited, so said these elder friends; and then there was the unfortunate fact of his being altogether beyond control. He had neither father, nor mother, nor uncle, nor guardian. He was the owner of a small property not far from Kirkby Cliffe, which gave him an income of some six or seven hundred a year, and he had altogether declined any of the professions which had been suggested to him. He had, in the course of the year now coming to a close, taken his degree at Oxford, with some academical honours, which were not high enough to confer distinction, and had already positively refused to be ordained, although, would he do so, a small living would be at his disposal on the death of a septuagenarian cousin. He intended, he said, to farm a portion of his own land, and had already begun to make amicable arrangements for buying up the interest of one of his two tenants. The rector of Kirkby Cliffe, the Rev. John Lownd, had been among his father's dearest friends, and he was now the parson's guest for the Christmas.

There had been many doubts in the parsonage before the young man had been invited. Mrs. Lownd had considered that the visit would be dangerous. Their family consisted of two daughters, the youngest of whom was still a child; but Isabel was turned twenty, and if a young man were brought into the house, would it not follow, as a matter of course, that she should fall in love with him? That was the mother's first argument. "Young people don't always fall in love," said the father. "But people will say that he is brought here on purpose," said the mother, using her second argument. The parson, who in family matters generally had his own way, expressed an opinion that if they were to be governed by what other people might choose to say, their course of action would be very limited indeed. As for his girl, he did not think she would ever give her heart to any man before it had been asked; and as for the young man—whose father had been for over thirty years his dearest friend—if he chose to fall in love, he must run his chance, like other young men. Mr. Lownd declared he knew nothing against him, except that he was, perhaps, a little self-willed; and so Maurice Archer came to Kirkby Cliffe, intending to spend two months in the same house with Isabel Lownd.

Hitherto, as far as the parents or the neighbours saw—and in their endeavours to see, the neighbours were very diligent—there had been no love-making. Between Mabel, the young daughter, and Maurice, there had grown up a violent friendship—so much so, that Mabel, who was fourteen, declared that Maurice Archer was "the jolliest person" in the world. She called him Maurice, as did Mr. and Mrs. Lownd; and to Maurice, of course, she was Mabel. But between Isabel and Maurice it was always Miss Lownd and Mr. Archer, as was proper. It was so, at least, with this difference, that each of them had got into a way of dropping, when possible, the other's name.

It was acknowledged throughout Craven—which my readers of course know to be a district in the northern portion of the West Riding of Yorkshire, of which Skipton is the capital—that Isabel Lownd was a very pretty girl. There were those who thought that Mary Manniwick, of Barden, excelled her; and others, again, expressed a preference for Fanny Grange, the pink-cheeked daughter of the surgeon at Giggleswick. No attempt shall here be made to award the palm of superior merit; but it shall be asserted boldly, that no man need desire a prettier girl with whom to fall in love than was Isabel Lownd. She was tall, active, fair, the very picture of feminine health, with bright grey eyes, a perfectly beautiful nose—as is common to almost all girls belonging to Craven—a mouth by no means delicately small, but eager, eloquent, and full of spirit, a well-formed short chin, with a dimple, and light brown hair, which was worn plainly smoothed over her brows, and fell in short curls behind her head. Of Maurice Archer it cannot be said that he was handsome. He had a snub nose; and a man so visaged can hardly be good-looking, though a girl with a snub nose may be very pretty. But he was a well-made young fellow, having a look of power about him, with dark-brown hair, cut very short, close shorn, with clear but rather small blue eyes, and an expression of countenance which allowed no one for a moment to think that he was weak in character, or a fool. His own place, called Hundlewick Hall, was about five miles from the parsonage. He had been there four or five times a week since his arrival at Kirkby Cliffe, and had already made arrangements for his own entrance upon the land in the following September. If a marriage were to come of it, the arrangement would be one very comfortable for the father and mother at Kirkby Cliffe. Mrs. Lownd had already admitted as much as that to herself, though she still trembled for her girl. Girls are so prone to lose their hearts, whereas the young men of these days are so very cautious and hard! That, at least, was Mrs. Lownd's idea of girls and young men; and even at this present moment she was hardly happy about her child. Maurice, she was sure, had spoken never a word that might not have been proclaimed from the church tower; but her girl, she thought, was not quite the same as she had been before the young man had come among them. She was somewhat less easy in her manner, more preoccupied, and seemed to labour under a conviction that the presence in the house of Maurice Archer must alter the nature of her life. Of course it had altered the nature of her life, and of course she thought a great deal of Maurice Archer.

It had been chiefly at Mabel's instigation that Isabel had invited the co-operation of her father's visitor in the adornment of the church for Christmas Day. Isabel had expressed her opinion that Mr. Archer didn't care a bit about such things, but Mabel declared that she had already extracted a promise from him. "He'll do anything I ask him," said Mabel proudly. Isabel, however, had not cared to undertake the work in such company, simply under her sister's management, and had proffered the request herself. Maurice had not declined the task—had indeed promised his assistance in some indifferent fashion—but had accompanied his promise by a suggestion that Christmas was a bore! Isabel had rebuked him, and then he had explained. But his explanation, in Isabel's view of the case, only made the matter worse. Christmas to her was a very great affair indeed—a festival to which the roast beef and the plum pudding were, no doubt, very necessary; but not by any means the essence, as he had chosen to consider them. Christmas a bore! No; a man who thought Christmas to be a bore should never be more to her than a mere acquaintance. She listened to his explanation, and then left the room, almost indignantly. Maurice, when she had gone, looked after her, and then read a page of his novel; but he was thinking of Isabel, and not of the book. It was quite true that he had never said a word to her that might not have been declared from the church tower;

but, nevertheless, he had thought about her a good deal. Those were days on which he was sure that he was in love with her, and would make her his wife. Then there came days on which he ridiculed himself for the idea. And now and then there was a day on which he asked himself whether he was sure that she would take him were he to ask her. There was sometimes an air with her, some little trick of the body, a manner of carrying her head when in his presence, which he was not physiognomist enough to investigate, but which in some way suggested doubts to him. It was on such occasions as this that he was most in love with her; and now she had left the room with that particular motion of her head which seemed almost to betoken contempt.

"If you mean to do anything before dinner you'd better do it at once," said the parson, opening the door. Maurice jumped up, and in ten minutes was dressed and down in the dining-room. Isabel was there, but did not greet him.

"You'll come and help us to-morrow," said Mabel, taking him by the arm and whispering to him.

"Of course I will," said Maurice.

"And you won't go to Hundlewick again till after Christmas?"

"It won't take up the whole day to put up the holly."

"Yes, it will—to do it nicely—and nobody ever does any work the day before Christmas."

"Except the cook," suggested Maurice. Isabel, who heard the words, assumed that look of which he was already afraid, but said not a word. Then dinner was announced, and he gave his arm to the parson's wife.

Not a word was said about Christmas that evening. Isabel had threatened the young man with her father's displeasure on account of his expressed opinion as to the festival being a bore, but Mr. Lownd was not himself one who talked a great deal about any Church festival. Indeed, it may be doubted whether his more enthusiastic daughter did not in her heart think him almost too indifferent on the subject. In the decorations of the church he, being an elderly man, and one with other duties to perform, would of course take no part. When the day came he would preach, no doubt, an appropriate sermon, would then eat his own roast beef and pudding with his ordinary appetite, would afterwards, if allowed to do so, sink into his armchair behind his book—and then, for him, Christmas would be over. In all this there was no disrespect for the day, but it was hardly an enthusiastic observance. Isabel desired to greet the morning of her Saviour's birth with some special demonstration of joy. Perhaps from year to year she was somewhat disappointed—but never before had it been hinted to her that Christmas was a bore.

On the following morning the work was to be commenced immediately after breakfast. The same thing had been done so often at Kirkby Cliffe, that the rector was quite used to it. David Drum, the clerk, who was also schoolmaster, and Barty Crossgrain, the parsonage gardener, would devote their services to the work in hand throughout the whole day, under the direction of Isabel. Mabel would of course be there assisting, as would also two daughters of a neighbouring farmer. Mrs. Lownd would go down to the church about eleven, and stay till one, when the whole party would come up to the parsonage for refreshment. Mrs. Lownd would not return to the work, but the others would remain there till it was finished, which finishing was never accomplished till candles had been burned in the church for a couple of hours. Then there would be more refreshments; but on this special day the parsonage dinner was never comfortable and orderly. The rector bore it all with good humour, but no one could say that he was enthusiastic in the matter. Mabel, who delighted in going up ladders, and leaning over the pulpit, and finding herself in all those odd parts of the church to which her imagination would stray during her father's sermons, but which were ordinarily inaccessible to her, took great delight in the work. And perhaps Isabel's delight had commenced with similar feelings. Immediately after breakfast, which was much hurried on the occasion, she put on her hat and hurried down to the church, without a word to Maurice on the subject. There was another whisper from Mabel, which was answered also with a whisper, and then Mabel also went. Maurice took up his novel, and seated himself comfortably by the parlour fire.

But again he did not read a word. Why had Isabel made herself so disagreeable, and why had she perked up her head as she left the room in that self-sufficient way, as though she was determined to show him that she did not want his assistance? Of course, she had understood well enough that he had not intended to say that the ceremonial observance of the day was a bore. He had spoken of the beef and the pudding, and she had chosen to pretend to misunderstand him. He would not go near the church. And as for his love, and his half-formed resolution to make her his wife, he would get over it altogether. If there were one thing more fixed with him than another, it was that on no consideration would he marry a girl who should give herself airs. Among them they might decorate the church as they pleased, and when he should see their handywork—as he would do, of course, during the service of Christmas Day—he would pass it by without a remark. So resolving, he again turned over a page or two of his novel, and then remembered that he was bound, at any rate, to keep his promise to his friend Mabel. Assuring himself that it was on that plea that he went, and on no other, he sauntered down to the church.

Chapter II

Kirkby Cliffe Church

KIRKBY CLIFFE Church stands close upon the River Wharfe, about a quarter of a mile from the parsonage, which is on a steep hillside running down from the moors to the stream. A prettier little church or graveyard you shall hardly find in England. Here, no large influx of population has necessitated the removal of the last home of the parishioners from beneath the shelter of the parish church. Every inhabitant of Kirkby Cliffe has, when dead, the privilege of rest among those green hillocks. Within the building is still room for tablets commemorative of the rectors and their wives and families, for there are none others in the parish to whom such honour is accorded. Without the walls, here and there, stand the tombstones of the farmers; while the undistinguished graves of the peasants lie about in clusters which, solemn though they be, are still picturesque. The church itself is old, and may probably be doomed before long to that kind of destruction which is called restoration; but hitherto, it has been allowed to stand beneath all its weight of ivy, and has known but little change during the last two hundred years. Its old oak pews, and ancient exalted reading-desk and pulpit are offensive to many who come to see the spot; but Isabel Lownd is of opinion that neither the one nor the other could be touched, in the way of change, without profanation.

In the very porch Maurice Archer met Mabel, with her arms full of ivy branches, attended by David Drum. "So you have come at last, Master Maurice?" she said.

"Come at last! Is that all the thanks I get? Now let me see what it is you're going to do. Is your sister here?"

"Of course she is. Barty is up in the pulpit, sticking holly branches round the sounding-board, and she is with him."

"T' boorde's that rotten an' maaky, it'll be doon on Miss Is'bel's heede, an' Barty Crossgrain ain't more than or'nary saft-handed," said the clerk.

They entered the church, and there it was, just as Mabel had said. The old gardener was standing on the rail of the pulpit, and Isabel was beneath, handing up to him nails and boughs, and giving him directions as to their disposal. "Naa, miss, naa; it wonot do that a-way," said Barty. "Thou'll ha' me on to t' stanes—thou wilt, that a-gait. Lard-a-mussy, miss, thou munnot clim' up, or thou'lt be doon, and brek thee banes, thee ull!" So saying, Barty Crossgrain, who had contented himself with remonstrating when called upon by his young mistress to imperil his own neck, jumped on to the floor of the pulpit and took hold of the young lady by both her ankles. As he did so, he looked up at her with anxious eyes, and steadied himself on his own feet, as though it might become necessary for him to perform some great feat of activity. All this Maurice Archer saw, and Isabel saw that he saw it. She was not well pleased at knowing that he should see her in that position, held by the legs by the old gardener, and from which she could only extricate herself by putting her hand on the old man's neck as she jumped down from her perch. But she did jump down, and then began to scold Crossgrain, as though the awkwardness had come from fault of his.

"I've come to help, in spite of the hard words you said to me yesterday, Miss Lownd," said Maurice, standing on the lower steps of the pulpit. "Couldn't I get up and do the things at the top?" But

Isabel thought that Mr. Archer could not get up and "do the things at the top." The wood was so far decayed that they must abandon the idea of ornamenting the sounding-board, and so both Crossgrain and Isabel descended into the body of the church.

Things did not go comfortably with them for the next hour. Isabel had certainly invited his co-operation, and therefore could not tell him to go away; and yet, such was her present feeling towards him, she could not employ him profitably, and with ease to herself. She was somewhat angry with him, and more angry with herself. It was not only that she had spoken hard words to him, as he had accused her of doing, but that, after the speaking of the last words, she had been distant and cold in her manner to him. And yet he was so much to her! She liked him so well!—and though she had never dreamed of admitting to herself that she was in love with him, yet—yet it would be pleasant to have the opportunity of asking herself whether she could not love him, should he ever give her a fair and open opportunity of searching her own heart on the matter. There had now sprung up some half-quarrel between them, and it was impossible that it could be set aside by any action on her part. She could not be otherwise than cold and haughty in her demeanour to him. Any attempt at reconciliation must come from him, and the longer she continued to be cold and haughty, the less chance there was that it would come. And yet she knew that she had been right to rebuke him for what he had said. "Christmas a bore!" She would rather lose his friendship for ever than hear such words from his mouth, without letting him know what she thought of them. Now he was there with her, and his coming could not but be taken as a sign of repentance. Yet she could not soften her manners to him, and become intimate with him, and playful, as had been her wont. He was allowed to pull about the masses of ivy, and to stick up branches of holly here and there at discretion; but what he did was done under Mabel's direction, and not under hers—with the aid of one of the farmer's daughters, and not with her aid. In silence she continued to work round the chancel and communion-table, with Crossgrain, while Archer, Mabel, and David Drum used their taste and diligence in the nave and aisles of the little church. Then Mrs. Lownd came among them, and things went more easily; but hardly a word had been spoken between Isabel and Maurice when, after sundry hints from David Drum as to the lateness of the hour, they left the church and went up to the parsonage for their luncheon.

Isabel stoutly walked on first, as though determined to show that she had no other idea in her head but that of reaching the parsonage as quickly as possible. Perhaps Maurice Archer had the same idea, for he followed her. Then he soon found that he was so far in advance of Mrs. Lownd and the old gardener as to be sure of three minutes' uninterrupted conversation; for Mabel remained with her mother, making earnest supplication as to the expenditure of certain yards of green silk tape, which she declared to be necessary for the due performance of the work which they had in hand. "Miss Lownd," said Maurice, "I think you are a little hard upon me."

"In what way, Mr. Archer?"

"You asked me to come down to the church, and you haven't spoken to me all the time I was there."

"I asked you to come and work, not to talk," she said.

"You asked me to come and work with you."

"I don't think that I said any such thing; and you came at Mabel's request, and not at mine. When I asked you, you told me it was all—a bore. Indeed you said much worse than that. I certainly did not mean to ask you again. Mabel asked you, and you came to oblige her. She talked to you, for I heard her; and I was half disposed to tell her not to laugh so much, and to remember that she was in church."

"I did not laugh, Miss Lownd."

"I was not listening especially to you."

"Confess, now," he said, after a pause; "don't you know that you misinterpreted me yesterday, and that you took what I said in a different spirit from my own."

"No; I do not know it."

"But you did. I was speaking of the holiday part of Christmas, which consists of pudding and beef, and is surely subject to ridicule, if one chooses to ridicule pudding and beef. You answered me as though I had spoken slightingly of the religious feeling which belongs to the day."

"You said that the whole thing was—; I won't repeat the word. Why should pudding and beef be a bore to you, when it is prepared as a sign that there shall be plenty on that day for people who perhaps don't have plenty on any other day of the year? The meaning of it is, that you don't like it all, because that which gives unusual enjoyment to poor people, who very seldom have any pleasure, is tedious to you. I don't like you for feeling it to be tedious. There! that's the truth. I don't mean to be uncivil, but— "

"You are very uncivil."

"What am I to say, when you come and ask me?"

"I do not well know how you could be more uncivil, Miss Lownd. Of course it is the commonest thing in the world, that one person should dislike another. It occurs every day, and people know it of each other. I can perceive very well that you dislike me, and I have no reason to be angry with you for disliking me. You have a right to dislike me, if your mind runs that way. But it is very unusual for one person to tell another so to his face—and more unusual to say so to a guest." Maurice Archer, as he said this, spoke with a degree of solemnity to which she was not at all accustomed, so that she became frightened at what she had said. And not only was she frightened, but very unhappy also. She did not quite know whether she had or had not told him plainly that she disliked him, but she was quite sure that she had not intended to do so. She had been determined to scold him—to let him see that, however much of real friendship there might be between them, she would speak her mind plainly, if he offended her; but she certainly had no desire to give him cause for lasting wrath against her. "However," continued Maurice, "perhaps the truth is best after all, though it is so very unusual to hear such truths spoken."

"I didn't mean to be uncivil," stammered Isabel.

"But you meant to be true?"

"I meant to say what I felt about Christmas Day." Then she paused a moment. "If I have offended you, I beg your pardon."

He looked at her and saw that her eyes were full of tears, and his heart was at once softened towards her. Should he say a word to her, to let her know that there was—or, at any rate, that henceforth there should be no offence? But it occurred to him that if he did so, that word would mean so much, and would lead perhaps to the saying of other words, which ought not to be shown without forethought. And now, too, they were within the parsonage gate, and there was no time for speaking. "You will go down again after lunch?" he asked.

"I don't know;—not if I can help it. Here's papa." She had begged his pardon—had humbled herself before him. And he had not said a word in acknowledgment of the grace she had done him. She almost thought that she did dislike him—really dislike him. Of course he had known what she meant, and he had chosen to misunderstand her and to take her, as it were, at an advantage. In her difficulty she had abjectly apologized to him, and he had not even deigned to express himself as satisfied with what she had done. She had known him to be conceited and masterful; but that, she had thought, she could forgive, believing it to be the common way with men—imagining, perhaps, that a man was only the more worthy of love on account of such fault; but now she found that he was ungenerous also, and deficient in that chivalry without which a man can hardly appear at advantage in a woman's eyes. She went on into the house, merely touching her father's arm, as she passed him, and hurried up to her own room. "Is there anything wrong with Isabel?" asked Mr. Lownd.

"She has worked too hard, I think, and is tired," said Maurice.

Within ten minutes they were all assembled in the dining-room, and Mabel was loud in her narrative of the doings of the morning. Barty Crossgrain and David Drum had both declared the sounding-board to be so old that it mustn't even be touched, and she was greatly afraid that it would tumble down some day and "squash papa" in the pulpit. The rector ridiculed the idea of any such disaster; and then there came a full description of the morning's scene, and of Barty's fears lest Isabel should "brek her banes." "His own wig was almost off," said Mabel, "and he gave Isabel such a lug by the leg that she very nearly had to jump into his arms."

"I didn't do anything of the kind," said Isabel.

"You had better leave the sounding-board alone," said the parson.

"We have left it alone, papa," said Isabel, with great dignity. "There are some other things that can't be done this year." For Isabel was becoming tired of her task, and would not have returned to the church at all could she have avoided it.

"What other things?" demanded Mabel, who was as enthusiastic as ever. "We can finish all the rest. Why shouldn't we finish it? We are ever so much more forward than we were last year, when David and Barty went to dinner. We've finished the Granby-Moor pew, and we never used to get to that till after luncheon." But Mabel on this occasion had all the enthusiasm to herself. The two farmer's daughters, who had been brought up to the parsonage as usual, never on such occasions uttered a word. Mrs. Lownd had completed her part of the work; Maurice could not trust himself to speak on the subject; and Isabel was dumb. Luncheon, however, was soon over, and something must be done. The four girls of course returned to their labours, but Maurice did not go with them, nor did he make any excuse for not doing so.

"I shall walk over to Hundlewick before dinner," he said, as soon as they were all moving. The rector suggested that he would hardly be back in time. "Oh, yes; ten miles—two hours and a half; and I shall have two hours there besides. I must see what they are doing with our own church, and how they mean to keep Christmas there. I'm not quite sure that I shan't go over there again to-morrow." Even Mabel felt that there was something wrong, and said not a word in opposition to this wicked desertion.

He did walk to Hundlewick and back again, and when at Hundlewick he visited the church, though the church was a mile beyond his own farm. And he added something to the store provided for the beef and pudding of those who lived upon his own land; but of this he said nothing on his return to Kirkby Cliffe. He walked his dozen miles, and saw what was being done about the place, and visited the cottages of some who knew him, and yet was back at the parsonage in time for dinner. And during his walk he turned many things over in his thoughts, and endeavoured to make up his mind on one or two points. Isabel had never looked so pretty as when she jumped down into the pulpit, unless it was when she was begging his pardon for her want of courtesy to him. And though she had been, as he described it to himself, "rather down upon him," in regard to what he had said of Christmas, did he not like her the better for having an opinion of her own? And then, as he had stood for a few minutes leaning on his own gate, and looking at his own house at Hundlewick, it had occurred to him that he could hardly live there without a companion. After that he had walked back again, and was dressed for dinner, and in the drawing-room before any one of the family.

With poor Isabel the afternoon had gone much less satisfactorily. She found that she almost hated her work, that she really had a headache, and that she could put no heart into what she was doing. She was cross to Mabel, and almost surly to David Drum and Barty Crossgrain. The two farmer's daughters were allowed to do almost what they pleased with the holly branches—a state of things which was most unusual—and then Isabel, on her return to the parsonage, declared her intention of going to bed! Mrs. Lownd, who had never before known her to do such a thing, was perfectly shocked. Go to bed, and not come down the whole of Christmas Eve! But Isabel was resolute. With a bad headache she would be better in bed than up. Were she to attempt to shake it off, she would be ill the next day. She did not want anything to eat, and would not take anything. No; she would not have any tea, but would go to bed at once. And to bed she went.

She was thoroughly discontented with herself, and felt that Maurice had, as it were, made up his mind against her for ever. She hardly knew whether to be angry with herself or with him; but she did know very well that she had not intended really to quarrel with him. Of course she had been in earnest in what she had said; but he had taken her words as signifying so much more than she had intended! If he chose to quarrel with her, of course he must; but a friend could not, she was sure, care for her a great deal who would really be angry with her for such a trifle. Of course this friend did not care for her at all—not the least, or he would not treat her so savagely. He had been quite savage to her, and she hated him for it. And yet she hated herself almost more. What right could she have had first to scold him, and then to tell him to his face that she disliked him? Of course he had gone away to Hundlewick. She would not have been a bit surprised if he had stayed there and never come back again. But he did come back, and she hated herself as she heard their voices as they all went in to dinner without her. It seemed to her that his voice was more cheery than ever. Last night and all the morning he had been silent and almost sullen, but now, the moment that she was away, he could talk and be full of spirits. She heard Mabel's ringing laughter downstairs, and she almost hated Mabel. It seemed to her that everybody was gay and happy because she was upstairs in her bed, and ill. Then there came a peal of laughter. She was glad that she was upstairs in bed, and ill. Nobody would have laughed, nobody would have been gay, had she been there. Maurice Archer liked them all, except her—she was sure of that. And what could be more natural after her conduct to him? She had taken upon herself to lecture him, and of course he had not chosen to endure it. But of one thing she was quite sure, as she lay there, wretched in her solitude—that now she would never alter her demeanour to him. He had chosen to be cold to her, and she would be like frozen ice to him. Again and again she heard their voices, and then, sobbing on her pillow, she fell asleep.

Chapter III

Showing how Isabel Lownd told a Lie

On the following morning—Christmas morning—when she woke, her headache was gone, and she was able as she dressed, to make some stern resolutions. The ecstasy of her sorrow was over, and she could see how foolish she had been to grieve as she had grieved. After all, what had she lost, or what harm had she done? She had never fancied that the young man was her lover, and she had never wished—so she now told herself—that he should become her lover. If one thing was plainer to her than another, it was this—that they two were not fitted for each other. She had sometimes whispered to herself, that if she were to marry at all, she would fain marry a clergyman. Now, no man could be more unlike a clergyman than Maurice Archer. He was, she thought, irreverent, and at no pains to keep his want of reverence out of sight, even in that house. He had said that Christmas was a bore, which, to her thinking, was abominable. Was she so poor a creature as to go to bed and cry for a man who had given her no sign that he even liked her, and of whose ways she disapproved so greatly, that even were he to offer her his hand she would certainly refuse it? She consoled herself for the folly of the preceding evening by assuring herself that she had really worked in the church till she was ill, and that she would have gone to bed, and must have gone to bed, had Maurice Archer never been seen or heard of at the parsonage. Other people went to bed when they had headaches, and why should not she? Then she resolved, as she dressed, that there should be no sign of illness, no bit of ill-humour on her, on this sacred day. She would appear among them all full of mirth and happiness, and would laugh at the attack brought upon her by Barty Crossgrain's sudden fear in the pulpit; and she would greet Maurice Archer with all possible cordiality, wishing him a merry Christmas as she gave him her hand, and would make him understand in a moment that she had altogether forgotten their mutual bickerings. He should understand that, or should, at least, understand that she willed that it should all be regarded as forgotten. What was he to her, that any thought of him should be allowed to perplex her mind on such a day as this?

She went downstairs, knowing that she was the first up in the house—the first, excepting the servants. She went into Mabel's room, and kissing her sister, who was only half awake, wished her many, many, many happy Christmases.

"Oh, Bell," said Mabel, "I do so hope you are better!"

"Of course I am better. Of course I am well. There is nothing for a headache like having twelve hours round of sleep. I don't know what made me so tired and so bad."

"I thought it was something Maurice said," suggested Mabel.

"Oh, dear, no. I think Barty had more to do with it than Mr. Archer. The old fellow frightened me so when he made me think I was falling down. But get up, dear. Papa is in his room, and he'll be ready for prayers before you."

Then she descended to the kitchen, and offered her good wishes to all the servants. To Barty, who always breakfasted there on Christmas mornings, she was especially kind, and said something civil about his work in the church.

"She'll 'bout brek her little heart for t'young mon there, an' he's naa true t' her," said Barty, as soon as Miss Lownd had closed the kitchen door; showing, perhaps, that he knew more of the matter concerning herself than she did.

She then went into the parlour to prepare the breakfast, and to put a little present, which she had made for her father, on his plate;—when, whom should she see but Maurice Archer!

It was a fact known to all the household, and a fact that had not recommended him at all to Isabel, that Maurice never did come downstairs in time for morning prayers. He was always the last; and, though in most respects a very active man, seemed to be almost a sluggard in regard to lying in bed late. As far as she could remember at the moment, he had never been present at prayers a single morning since the first after his arrival at the parsonage, when shame, and a natural feeling of strangeness in the house, had brought him out of his bed. Now he was there half an hour before the appointed time, and during that half-hour she was doomed to be alone with him. But her courage did not for a moment desert her.

"This is a wonder!" she said, as she took his hand. "You will have a long Christmas Day, but I sincerely hope that it may be a happy one."

"That depends on you," said he.

"I'll do everything I can," she answered. "You shall only have a very little bit of roast beef, and the unfortunate pudding shan't be brought near you." Then she looked in his face, and saw that his manner was very serious—almost solemn—and quite unlike his usual ways. "Is anything wrong?" she asked.

"I don't know; I hope not. There are things which one has to say which seem to be so very difficult when the time comes. Miss Lownd, I want you to love me."

"What!" She started back as she made the exclamation, as though some terrible proposition had wounded her ears. She had ever dreamed of his asking for her love, she had dreamed of it as a thing that future days might possibly produce;—when he should be altogether settled at Hundlewick, and when they should have got to know each other intimately by the association of years.

"Yes, I want you to love me, and to be my wife. I don't know how to tell you; but I love you better than anything and everything in the world—better than all the world put together. I have done so from the first moment that I saw you; I have. I knew how it would be the very first instant I saw your dear face, and every word you have spoken, and every look out of your eyes, has made me love you more and more. If I offended you yesterday, I will beg your pardon."

"Oh, no," she said.

"I wish I had bitten my tongue out before I had said what I did about Christmas Day. I do, indeed. I only meant, in a half-joking way, to—to—to—. But I ought to have known you wouldn't like it, and I beg your pardon. Tell me, Isabel, do you think that you can love me?"

Not half an hour since she had made up her mind that, even were he to propose to her—which she then knew to be absolutely impossible—she would certainly refuse him. He was not the sort of man for whom she would be a fitting wife; and she had made up her mind also, at the same time, that she did not at all care for him, and that he certainly did not in the least care for her. And now the offer had absolutely been made to her! Then came across her mind an idea that he ought in the first place to have gone to her father; but as to that she was not quite sure. Be that as it might, there he was, and she must give him some answer. As for thinking about it, that was altogether beyond her. The shock to her was too great to allow of her thinking. After some fashion, which afterwards was quite unintelligible to herself, it seemed to her, at that moment, that duty, and maidenly reserve, and filial obedience, all required her to reject him instantly. Indeed, to have accepted him would have been quite beyond her power. "Dear Isabel," said he, "may I hope that some day you will love me?"

"Oh! Mr. Archer, don't," she said. "Do not ask me."

"Why should I not ask you?"

"It can never be." This she said quite plainly, and in a voice that seemed to him to settle his fate for ever; and yet at the moment her heart was full of love towards him. Though she could not think, she could feel. Of course she loved him. At the very moment in which she was telling him that it could never be, she was elated by an almost ecstatic triumph, as she remembered all her fears, and now knew that the man was at her feet.

When a girl first receives the homage of a man's love, and receives it from one whom, whether she loves him or not, she thoroughly respects, her earliest feeling is one of victory—such a feeling as warmed the heart of a conqueror in the Olympian games. He is the spoil of her spear, the fruit of her prowess, the quarry brought down by her own bow and arrow. She, too, by some power of her own which she is hitherto quite unable to analyse, has stricken a man to the very heart, so as to compel him for the moment to follow wherever she may lead him. So it was with Isabel Lownd as she stood there, conscious of the eager gaze which was fixed upon her face, and fully alive to the anxious tones of her lover's voice. And yet she could only deny him. Afterwards, when she thought of it, she could not imagine why it had been so with her; but, in spite of her great love, she continued to tell herself that there was some obstacle which could never be overcome—or was it that a certain maidenly reserve sat so strong within her bosom that she could not bring herself to own to him that he was dear to her?

"Never!" exclaimed Maurice, despondently.

"Oh, no!"

"But why not? I will be very frank with you, dear. I did think you liked me a little before that affair in the study." Like him a little! Oh, how she had loved him! She knew it now, and yet not for worlds could she tell him so. "You are not still angry with me, Isabel?"

"No; not angry."

"Why should you say never? Dear Isabel, cannot you try to love me?" Then he attempted to take her hand, but she recoiled at once from his touch, and did feel something of anger against him in that he should thus refuse to take her word. She knew not what it was that she desired of him, but certainly he should not attempt to take her hand, when she told him plainly that she could not love him. A red spot rose to each of her cheeks as again he pressed her. "Do you really mean that you can never, never love me?" She muttered some answer, she knew not what, and then he turned from her, and stood looking out upon the snow which had fallen during the night.

She kept her ground for a few seconds, and then escaped through the door, and up to her own bedroom. When once there, she burst out into tears. Could it be possible that she had thrown away for ever her own happiness, because she had been too silly to give a true answer to an honest question? And was this the enjoyment and content which she had promised herself for Christmas Day? But surely, surely he would come to her again. If he really loved her as he had declared, if it was true that ever since his arrival at Kirkby Cliffe he had thought of her as his wife, he would not abandon her because in the first tumult of her surprise she had lacked courage to own to him the truth; and then in the midst of her tears there came upon her that delicious recognition of a triumph which, whatever be the victory won, causes such elation to the heart! Nothing, at any rate, could rob her of this—that he had loved her. Then, as a thought suddenly struck her, she ran quickly across the passage, and in a moment was upstairs, telling her tale with her mother's arm close folded round her waist.

In the meantime Mr. Lownd had gone down to the parlour, and had found Maurice still looking out upon the snow. He, too, with some gentle sarcasm, had congratulated the young man on his early rising, as he expressed the ordinary wish of the day. "Yes," said Maurice, "I had something special to do. Many happy Christmases, sir! I don't know much about its being happy to me."

"Why, what ails you?"

"It's a nasty sort of day, isn't it?" said Maurice.

"Does that trouble you? I rather like a little snow on Christmas Day. It has a pleasant, old-fashioned look. And there isn't enough to keep even an old woman at home."

"I dare say not," said Maurice, who was still beating about the bush, having something to tell, but not knowing how to tell it. "Mr. Lownd, I should have come to you first, if it hadn't been for an accident."

"Come to me first! What accident?"

"Yes; only I found Miss Lownd down here this morning, and I asked her to be my wife. You needn't be unhappy about it, sir. She refused me point blank."

"You must have startled her, Maurice. You have startled me, at any rate."

"There was nothing of that sort, Mr. Lownd. She took it all very easily. I think she does take things easily." Poor Isabel! "She just told me plainly that it never could be so, and then she walked out of the room."

"I don't think she expected it, Maurice."

"Oh, dear no! I'm quite sure she didn't. She hadn't thought about me any more than if I were an old dog. I suppose men do make fools of themselves sometimes. I shall get over it, sir."

"Oh, I hope so."

"I shall give up the idea of living here. I couldn't do that. I shall probably sell out the property, and go to Africa."

"Go to Africa!"

"Well, yes. It's as good a place as any other, I suppose. It's wild, and a long way off, and all that kind of thing. As this is Christmas, I had better stay here to-day, I suppose."

"Of course you will."

"If you don't mind, I'll be off early to-morrow, sir. It's a kind of thing, you know, that does flurry a man. And then my being here may be disagreeable to her;—not that I suppose she thinks about me any more than if I were an old cow."

It need hardly be remarked that the rector was a much older man than Maurice Archer, and that he therefore knew the world much better. Nor was he in love. And he had, moreover, the advantage of a much closer knowledge of the young lady's character than could be possessed by the lover. And, as it happened, during the last week, he had been fretted by fears expressed by his wife—fears which were altogether opposed to Archer's present despondency and African resolutions. Mrs. Lownd had been uneasy—almost more than uneasy—lest poor dear Isabel should be stricken at her heart; whereas, in regard to that young man, she didn't believe that he cared a bit for her girl. He ought not to have been brought into the house. But he was there, and what could they do? The rector was of opinion that things would come straight—that they would be straightened not by any lover's propensities on the part of his guest, as to which he protested himself to be altogether indifferent, but by his girl's good sense. His Isabel would never allow herself to be seriously affected by a regard for a young man who had made no overtures to her. That was the rector's argument; and perhaps, within his own mind, it was backed by a feeling that, were she so weak, she must stand the consequence. To him it seemed to be an absurd degree of caution that two young people should not be brought together in the same house lest one should fall in love with the other. And he had seen no symptoms of such love. Nevertheless his wife had fretted him, and he had been uneasy. Now the shoe was altogether on the other foot. The young man was the despondent lover, and was asserting that he must go instantly to Africa, because the young lady treated him like an old dog, and thought no more about him than of an old cow.

A father in such a position can hardly venture to hold out hopes to a lover, even though he may approve of the man as a suitor for his daughter's hand. He cannot answer for his girl, nor can he very well urge upon a lover the expediency of renewing his suit. In this case Mr. Lownd did think, that in spite of the cruel, determined obduracy which his daughter was said to have displayed, she might probably be softened by constancy and perseverance. But he knew nothing of the circumstances, and could only suggest that Maurice should not take his place for the first stage on his way to Africa quite at once. "I do not think you need hurry away because of Isabel," he said, with a gentle smile.

"I couldn't stand it—I couldn't indeed," said Maurice, impetuously. "I hope I didn't do wrong in speaking to her when I found her here this morning. If you had come first I should have told you."

"I could only have referred you to her, my dear boy. Come—here they are; and now we will have prayers." As he spoke, Mrs. Lownd entered the room, followed closely by Mabel, and then at a little distance by Isabel. The three maid-servants were standing behind in a line, ready to come in for prayers. Maurice could not but feel that Mrs. Lownd's manner to him was especially affectionate; for, in truth, hitherto she had kept somewhat aloof from him, as though he had been a ravening wolf. Now she held him by the hand, and had a spark of motherly affection in her eyes, as she, too, repeated her Christmas greeting. It might well be so, thought Maurice. Of course she would be more kind to him than ordinary, if she knew that he was a poor blighted individual. It was a thing of course that Isabel should have told her mother; equally a thing of course that he should be pitied and treated tenderly. But on the next day he would be off. Such tenderness as that would kill him.

As they sat at breakfast, they all tried to be very gracious to each other. Mabel was sharp enough to know that something special had happened, but could not quite be sure what it was. Isabel struggled very hard to make little speeches about the day, but cannot be said to have succeeded well. Her mother, who had known at once how it was with her child, and had required no positive answers to direct questions to enable her to assume that Isabel was now devoted to her lover, had told her girl that if the man's love were worth having, he would surely ask her again. "I don't think he will, mamma," Isabel had whispered, with her face half-hidden on her mother's arm. "He must be very unlike other men if he does not," Mrs. Lownd had said, resolving that the opportunity should not be wanting. Now she was very gracious to Maurice, speaking before him as though he were quite one of the family. Her trembling maternal heart had feared him, while she thought that he might be a ravening wolf, who would steal away her daughter's heart, leaving nothing in return; but now that he had proved himself willing to enter the fold as a useful domestic sheep, nothing could be too good for him. The parson himself, seeing all this, understanding every turn in his wife's mind, and painfully anxious that no word might be spoken which should seem to entrap his guest, strove diligently to talk as though nothing was amiss. He spoke of his sermon, and of David Drum, and of the allowance of pudding that was to be given to the inmates of the neighbouring poorhouse. There had been a subscription, so as to relieve the rates from the burden of the plum-pudding, and Mr. Lownd thought that the farmers had not been sufficiently liberal.

"There's Furness, at Loversloup, gave us half a crown. I told him he ought to be ashamed of himself. He declared to me to my face that if he could find puddings for his own bairns, that was enough for him."

"The richest farmer in these parts, Maurice," said Mrs. Lownd.

"He holds above three hundred acres of land, and could stock double as many, if he had them," said the would-be indignant rector, who was thinking a great deal more of his daughter than of the poor-house festival. Maurice answered him with a word or two, but found it very hard to assume any interest in the question of the pudding. Isabel was more hard-hearted, he thought, than even Farmer Furness, of Loversloup. And why should he trouble himself about these people—he, who intended to sell his acres, and go away to Africa? But he smiled and made some reply, and buttered his toast, and struggled hard to seem as though nothing ailed him.

The parson went down to church before his wife, and Mabel went with him. "Is anything wrong with Maurice Archer?" she asked her father.

"Nothing, I hope," said he.

"Because he doesn't seem to be able to talk this morning."

"Everybody isn't a chatter-box like you, Mab."

"I don't think I chatter more than Mamma, or Bell. Do you know, Papa, I think Bell has quarrelled with Maurice Archer."

"I hope not. I should be very sorry that there should be any quarrelling at all—particularly on this day. Well, I think you've done it very nicely; and it is none the worse because you've left the sounding-board alone." Then Mabel went over to David Drum's cottage, and asked after the condition of Mrs. Drum's plum-pudding.

No one had ventured to ask Maurice Archer whether he would stay in church for the sacrament, but he did. Let us hope that no undue motive of pleasing Isabel Lownd had any effect upon him at such a time. But it did please her. Let us hope also that, as she knelt beside her lover at the low railing, her young heart was not too full of her love. That she had been thinking of him throughout her father's sermon—thinking of him, then resolving that she would think of him no more, and then thinking of him more than ever—must be admitted. When her mother had told her that he would come again to her, she had not attempted to assert that, were he to do so, she would again reject him. Her mother knew all her secret, and, should he not come again, her mother would know that she was heart-broken. She had told him positively that she would never love him. She had so told him, knowing well that at the very moment he was dearer to her than all the world beside. Why had she been so wicked as to lie to him? And if now she were punished for her lie by his silence, would she not be served properly? Her mind ran much more on the subject of this great sin which she had committed on that very morning—that sin against one who loved her so well, and who desired to do good to her—than on those general arguments in favour of Christian kindness and forbearance which the preacher drew from the texts applicable to Christmas Day. All her father's eloquence was nothing to her. On ordinary occasions he had no more devoted listener; but, on this morning, she could only exercise her spirit by repenting her own unchristian conduct. And then he came and knelt beside her at that sacred moment! It was impossible that he should forgive her, because he could not know that she had sinned against him.

There were certain visits to her poorer friends in the immediate village which, according to custom, she would make after church. When Maurice and Mrs. Lownd went up to the parsonage, she and Mabel made their usual round. They all welcomed her, but they felt that she was not quite herself with them, and even Mabel asked her what ailed her.

"Why should anything ail me?—only I don't like walking in the snow."

Then Mabel took courage. "If there is a secret, Bell, pray tell me. I would tell you any secret."

"I don't know what you mean," said Isabel, almost crossly.

"Is there a secret, Bell? I'm sure there is a secret about Maurice."

"Don't—don't," said Isabel.

"I do like Maurice so much. Don't you like him?"

"Pray do not talk about him, Mabel."

"I believe he is in love with you, Bell; and, if he is, I think you ought to be in love with him. I don't know how you could have anybody nicer. And he is going to live at Hundlewick, which would be such great fun. Would not Papa like it?"

"I don't know. Oh, dear!—oh, dear!" Then she burst out into tears, and, walking out of the village, told Mabel the whole truth. Mabel heard it with consternation, and expressed her opinion that, in these circumstances Maurice would never ask again to make her his wife.

"Then I shall die," said Isabel frankly.

Chapter IV

Showing bow Isabel Lownd repented her Fault

IN SPITE of her piteous condition and near prospect of death, Isabel Lownd completed her round of visits among her old friends. That Christmas should be kept in some way by every inhabitant of Kirkby Cliffe, was a thing of course. The district is not poor, and plenty on that day was rarely wanting. But Parson Lownd was not what we call a rich man; and there was no resident squire in the parish. The farmers, comprehending well their own privileges, and aware that the obligation of gentle living did not lie on them, were inclined to be close-fisted; and thus there was sometimes a difficulty in providing for the old and the infirm. There was a certain ancient widow in the village, of the name of Mucklewort, who was troubled with three orphan grandchildren and a lame daughter; and Isabel had, some days since, expressed a fear up at the parsonage that the good things of this world might be scarce in the old widow's cottage. Something had, of course, been done for the old woman, but not enough, as Isabel had thought. "My dear," her mother had said, "it is no use trying to make very poor people think that they are not poor."

"It is only one day in the year," Isabel had pleaded.

"What you give in excess to one, you take from another," replied Mrs. Lownd, with the stern wisdom which experience teaches. Poor Isabel could say nothing further, but had feared greatly that the rations in Mrs. Mucklewort's abode would be deficient. She now entered the cottage, and found the whole family at that moment preparing themselves for the consumption of a great Christmas banquet. Mrs. Mucklewort, whose temper was not always the best in the world, was radiant. The children were silent, open-eyed, expectant, and solemn. The lame aunt was in the act of transferring a large lump of beef, which seemed to be commingled in a most inartistic way with potatoes and cabbage, out of a pot on to the family dish. At any rate there was plenty; for no five appetites—had the five all been masculine, adult, and yet youthful—could, by any feats of strength, have emptied that dish at a sitting. And Isabel knew well that there had been pudding. She herself had sent the pudding; but that, as she was well aware, had not been allowed to abide its fate till this late hour of the day. "I'm glad you're all so well employed," said Isabel. "I thought you had done dinner long ago. I won't stop a minute now."

The old woman got up from her chair, and nodded her head, and held out her withered old hand to be shaken. The children opened their mouths wider than ever, and hoped there might be no great delay. The lame aunt curtseyed and explained the circumstances. "Beef, Miss Isabel, do take a mortal time t' boil; and it ain't no wise good for t' bairns to have it any ways raw." To this opinion Isabel gave her full assent, and expressed her gratification that the amount of beef should be sufficient to require so much cooking. Then the truth came out. "Muster Archer just sent us over from Rowdy's a meal's meat with a vengeance; God bless him!" crooned out the old woman, and the children muttered some unintelligible sound, as though aware that duty required them to express some Amen to the prayer of their elders. Now Rowdy was the butcher living at Grassington, some six miles away—for at Kirkby Cliffe there was no butcher. Isabel smiled all round upon them sweetly, with her eyes full of tears, and then left the cottage without a word.

He had done this because she had expressed a wish that these people should be kindly treated—had done it without a syllable spoken to her or to any one—had taken trouble, sending all the way to Grassington for Mrs. Mucklewort's beef! No doubt he had given other people beef, and had whispered no word of his kindness to any one at the rectory. And yet she had taken upon herself to rebuke him, because he had not cared for Christmas Day. As she walked along, silent, holding Mabel's hand, it seemed to her that of all men he was the most perfect. She had rebuked him, and had then told him—with incredible falseness—that she did not like him; and after that, when he had proposed to her in the kindest, noblest manner, she had rejected him—almost as though he had not been good enough for her! She felt now as though she would like to bite the tongue out of her head for such misbehaviour.

"Was not that nice of him?" said Mabel. But Isabel could not answer the question. "I always thought he was like that," continued the younger sister. "If he were my lover, I'd do anything he asked me, because he is so good-natured."

"Don't talk to me," said Isabel. And, Mabel, who comprehended something of the condition of her sister's mind, did not say another word on their way back to the parsonage.

It was the rule of the house that on Christmas Day they should dine at four o'clock;—a rule which almost justified the very strong expression with which Maurice first offended the young lady whom he loved. To dine at one or two o'clock is a practice which has its recommendations. It suits the appetite, is healthy, and divides the day into two equal halves, so that no man so dining fancies that his dinner should bring to him an end of his usual occupations. And to dine at six, seven, or eight is well adapted to serve several purposes of life. It is convenient, as inducing that gentle lethargy which will sometimes follow the pleasant act of eating at a time when the work of the day is done; and it is both fashionable and comfortable. But to dine at four is almost worse than not to dine at all. The rule, however, existed at Kirkby Cliffe parsonage in regard to this one special day in the year, and was always obeyed.

On this occasion Isabel did not see her lover from the moment in which he left her at the church door till they met at table. She had been with her mother, but her mother had not said a word to her about Maurice. Isabel knew very well that they two had walked home together from the church, and she had thought that her best chance lay in the possibility that he would have spoken of what had occurred during the walk. Had this been so, surely her mother would have told her; but not a word had been said; and even with her mother Isabel had been too shame-faced to ask a question. In truth, Isabel's name had not been mentioned between them, nor had any allusion been made to what had taken place during the morning. Mrs. Lownd had been too wise and too wary—too well aware of what was really due to her daughter—to bring up the subject herself; and he had been silent, subdued, and almost sullen. If he could not get an acknowledgment of affection from the girl herself, he certainly would not endeavour to extract a cold compliance by the mother's aid. Africa, and a disruption of all the plans of his life, would be better to him than that. But Mrs. Lownd knew very well how it was with him; knew how it was with them both; and was aware that in such a condition things should be allowed to arrange themselves. At dinner, both she and the rector were full of mirth and good humour, and Mabel, with great glee, told the story of Mrs. Mucklewort's dinner. "I don't want to destroy your pleasure," she said, bobbing her head at Maurice; "but it did look so nasty! Beef should always be roast beef on Christmas Day."

"I told the butcher it was to be roast beef," said Maurice, sadly.

"I dare say the little Muckleworts would just as soon have it boiled," said Mrs. Lownd. "Beef is beef to them, and a pot for boiling is an easy apparatus."

"If you had beef, Miss Mab, only once or twice a year," said her father, "you would not care whether it were roast or boiled." But Isabel spoke not a word. She was most anxious to join the conversation about Mrs. Mucklewort, and would have liked much to give testimony to the generosity displayed in regard to quantity; but she found that she could not do it. She was absolutely dumb. Maurice Archer did speak, making, every now and then, a terrible effort to be jocose; but Isabel from first to last was silent. Only by silence could she refrain from a renewed deluge of tears.

In the evening two or three girls came in with their younger brothers, the children of farmers of the better class in the neighbourhood, and the usual attempts were made at jollity. Games were set on foot, in which even the rector joined, instead of going to sleep behind his book, and Mabel, still conscious of her sister's wounds, did her very best to promote the sports. There was blindman's-buff, and hide and seek, and snapdragon, and forfeits, and a certain game with music and chairs—very prejudicial to the chairs—in which it was everybody's object to sit down as quickly as possible when the music stopped. In the game Isabel insisted on playing, because she could do that alone. But even to do this was too much for her. The sudden pause could hardly be made without a certain hilarity of spirit, and her spirits were unequal to any exertion. Maurice went through his work like a man, was blinded, did his forfeits, and jostled for the chairs with the greatest diligence; but in the midst of it all he, too, was as solemn as a judge, and never once spoke a single word to Isabel. Mrs. Lownd, who usually was not herself much given to the playing of games, did on this occasion make an effort, and absolutely consented to cry the forfeits; but Mabel was wonderfully quiet, so that the farmer's daughters hardly perceived that there was anything amiss.

It came to pass, after a while, that Isabel had retreated to her room—not for the night, as it was as yet hardly eight o'clock—and she certainly would not disappear till the visitors had taken their departure—a ceremony which was sure to take place with the greatest punctuality at ten, after an early supper. But she had escaped for a while, and in the meantime some frolic was going on which demanded the absence of one of the party from the room, in order that mysteries might be arranged of which the absent one should remain in ignorance. Maurice was thus banished, and desired to remain in desolation for the space of five minutes; but, just as he had taken up his position, Isabel descended with slow, solemn steps, and found him standing at her father's study door. She was passing on, and had almost entered the drawing-room, when he called her. "Miss Lownd," he said. Isabel stopped, but did not speak; she was absolutely beyond speaking. The excitement of the day had been so great, that she was almost overcome by it, and doubted, herself, whether she would be able to keep up appearances till the supper should be over, and she should be relieved for the night. "Would you let me say one word to you?" said Maurice. She bowed her head and went with him into the study.

Five minutes had been allowed for the arrangement of the mysteries, and at the end of the five minutes Maurice was authorized, by the rules of the game, to return to the room. But he did not come, and upon Mabel's suggesting that possibly he might not be able to see his watch in the dark, she was sent to fetch him. She burst into the study, and there she found the truant and her sister, very close, standing together on the hearthrug. "I didn't know you were here, Bell," she exclaimed. Whereupon Maurice, as she declared afterwards, jumped round the table after her, and took her in his arms and kissed her. "But you must come," said Mabel, who accepted the embrace with perfect goodwill.

"Of course you must. Do go, pray, and I'll follow—almost immediately." Mabel perceived at once that her sister had altogether recovered her voice.

"I'll tell 'em you're coming," said Mabel, vanishing.

"You must go now," said Isabel. "They'll all be away soon, and then you can talk about it." As she spoke, he was standing with his arm round her waist, and Isabel Lownd was the happiest girl in all Craven.

Mrs. Lownd knew all about it from the moment in which Maurice Archer's prolonged absence had become cause of complaint among the players. Her mind had been intent upon the matter, and she had become well aware that it was only necessary that the two young people should be alone together for a few moments. Mabel had entertained great hopes, thinking, however, that perhaps three or four years must be passed in melancholy gloomy doubts before the path of true love could be made to run smooth; but the light had shone upon her as soon as she saw them standing together. The parson knew nothing about it till the supper was over. Then, when the front door was open, and the farmers' daughters had been cautioned not to get themselves more wet than they could help in the falling snow, Maurice said a word to his future father-in-law. "She has consented at last, sir. I hope you have nothing to say against it."

"Not a word," said the parson, grasping the young man's hand, and remembering, as he did so, the extension of the time over which that phrase "at last" was supposed to spread itself.

Maurice had been promised some further opportunity of "talking about it," and of course claimed a fulfilment of the promise. There was a difficulty about it, as Isabel, having now been assured of her happiness, was anxious to talk about it all to her mother rather than to him; but he was imperative, and there came at last for him a quarter of an hour of delicious triumph in that very spot on which he had been so scolded for saying that Christmas was a bore. "You were so very sudden," said Isabel, excusing herself for her conduct in the morning.

"But you did love me?"

"If I do now, that ought to be enough for you. But I did, and I've been so unhappy since; and I thought that, perhaps, you would never speak to me again. But it was all your fault; you were so sudden. And then you ought to have asked Papa first—you know you ought. But, Maurice, you will promise me one thing. You won't ever again say that Christmas Day is a bore!"

Christmas at Thompson Hall

Originally appeared in *The Graphic*, Christmas Number, 1876. Reprinted in *Why Frau Frohmann Raised Her Prices and Other Stories* (1882). Written around April 1876. This is the story Trollope complains in *An Autobiography* he has been cudgelling his brain to write for the last month. The whole passage on the painful duty of supplying Christmas fiction is of interest. See *An Autobiography*, ch. 20.

Chapter I

Mrs. Brown's Success.

Everyone remembers the severity of the Christmas of 187—. I will not designate the year more closely, lest I should enable those who are too curious to investigate the circumstances of this story, and inquire into details which I do not intend to make known. That winter, however, was especially severe, and the cold of the last ten days of December was more felt, I think, in Paris than in any part of England. It may, indeed, be doubted whether there is any town in any country in which thoroughly bad weather is more afflicting than in the French capital. Snow and hail seem to be colder there, and fires certainly are less warm, than in London. And then there is a feeling among visitors to Paris that Paris ought to be gay; that gaicty, prettiness, and liveliness are its aims, as money, commerce, and general business are the aims of London,—which with its outside sombre darkness does often seem to want an excuse for its ugliness. But on this occasion, at this Christmas of 187—, Paris was neither gay nor pretty nor lively. You could not walk the streets without being ankle deep, not in snow, but in snow that had just become slush; and there was falling throughout the day and night of the 23rd of December a succession of damp half-frozen abominations from the sky which made it almost impossible for men and women to go about their business.

It was at ten o'clock on that evening that an English lady and gentleman arrived at the Grand Hotel on the Boulevard des Italiens. As I have reasons for concealing the names of this married couple I will call them Mr. and Mrs. Brown. Now I wish it to be understood that in all the general affairs of life this gentleman and this lady lived happily together, with all the amenities which should bind a husband and a wife. Mrs. Brown was one of a wealthy family, and Mr. Brown, when he married her, had been relieved from the necessity of earning his bread. Nevertheless she had at once yielded to him when he expressed a desire to spend the winters of their life in the south of France; and he, though he was by disposition somewhat idle, and but little prone to the energetic occupations of life, would generally allow himself, at other periods of the year, to be carried hither and thither by her, whose more robust nature delighted in the excitement of travelling. But on this occasion there had been a little difference between them.

Early in December an intimation had reached Mrs. Brown at Pau that on the coming Christmas there was to be a great gathering of all the Thompsons in the Thompson family hall at Stratford-le-Bow, and that she who had been a Thompson was desired to join the party with her husband. On this occasion her only sister was desirous of introducing to the family generally a most excellent young man to whom she had recently become engaged. The Thompsons,—the real name, however, is in fact concealed,—were a numerous and a thriving people. There were uncles and cousins and brothers who had all done well in the world, and who were all likely to do better still. One had lately been returned to Parliament for the Essex Flats, and was at the time of which I am writing a conspicuous member of the gallant Conservative majority. It was partly in triumph at this success that the great Christmas gathering of the Thompsons was to be held, and an opinion had been expressed by the legislator himself that should Mrs. Brown, with her husband, fail to join the family on this happy occasion she and he would be regarded as being but *fainéant* Thompsons.

Since her marriage, which was an affair now nearly eight years old, Mrs. Brown had never passed a Christmas in England. The desirability of doing so had often been mooted by her. Her very soul craved the festivities of holly and mince-pies. There had ever been meetings of the Thompsons at Thompson Hall, though meetings not so significant, not so important to the family, as this one which was now to be collected. More than once had she expressed a wish to see old Christmas again in the old house among the old faces. But her husband had always pleaded a certain weakness about his throat and chest as a reason for remaining among the delights of Pau. Year after year she had yielded, and now this loud summons had come.

It was not without considerable trouble that she had induced Mr. Brown to come as far as Paris. Most unwillingly had he left Pau; and then, twice on his journey,—both at Bordeaux and Tours,—he had made an attempt to return. From the first moment he had pleaded his throat, and when at last he had consented to make the journey he had stipulated for sleeping at those two towns and at Paris. Mrs. Brown, who, without the slightest feeling of fatigue, could have made the journey from Pau to Stratford without stopping, had assented to everything,—so that they might be at Thompson Hall on Christmas Eve. When Mr. Brown uttered his unavailing complaints at the two first towns at which they stayed, she did not perhaps quite believe all that he said of his own condition. We know how prone the strong are to suspect the weakness of the weak,—as the weak are to be disgusted by the strength of the strong. There were perhaps a few words between them on the journey, but the result had hitherto been in favour of the lady. She had succeeded in bringing Mr. Brown as far as Paris.

Had the occasion been less important, no doubt she would have yielded. The weather had been bad even when they left Pau, but as they had made their way northwards it had become worse and still worse. As they left Tours Mr. Brown, in a hoarse whisper, had declared his conviction that the journey would kill him. Mrs. Brown, however, had unfortunately noticed half an hour before that he had scolded the waiter on the score of an overcharged franc or two with a loud and clear voice. Had she really believed that there was danger, or even suffering, she would have yielded;—but no woman is satisfied in such a matter to be taken in by false pretences. She observed that he ate a good dinner on his way to Paris, and that he took a small glass of cognac with complete relish,—which a man really suffering from bronchitis surely would not do. So she persevered, and brought him into Paris, late in the evening, in the midst of all that slush and snow. Then, as they sat down to supper, she thought that he did speak hoarsely, and her loving feminine heart began to misgive her.

But this now was at any rate clear to her,—that he could not be worse off by going on to London than he would be should he remain in Paris. If a man is to be ill he had better be ill in the bosom of his family than at an hotel. What comfort could he have, what relief, in that huge barrack? As for the cruelty of the weather, London could not be worse than Paris, and then she thought she had heard that sea air is good for a sore throat. In that bedroom which had been alloted to them au quatrième, they could not even get a decent fire. It would in every way be wrong now to forego the great Christmas gathering when nothing could be gained by staying in Paris.

She had perceived that as her husband became really ill he became also more tractable and less disputatious. Immediately after that little glass of cognac he had declared that he would be——if he would go beyond Paris, and she began to fear that, after all, everything would have been done in vain. But as they went down to supper between ten and eleven he was more subdued, and merely remarked that this journey would, he was sure, be the death of him. It was half-past eleven when they got back to their bedroom, and then he seemed to speak with good sense,—and also with much real apprehension. "If I can't get something to relieve me I know I shall never make my way on," he said. It was intended that they should leave the hotel at half-past five the next morning, so as to arrive at Stratford, travelling by the tidal train, at half-past seven on Christmas Eve. The early hour, the long journey, the infamous weather, the prospect of that horrid gulf between Boulogne and Folkestone, would have been as nothing to Mrs. Brown, had it not been for that settled look of anguish which had now pervaded her husband's face. "If you don't find something to relieve me I shall never live through it," he said again, sinking back into the questionable comfort of a Parisian hotel arm-chair.

"But, my dear, what can I do?" she asked, almost in tears, standing over him and caressing him. He was a thin, genteel-looking man, with a fine long, soft brown beard, a little bald at the top of the head, but certainly a genteel-looking man. She loved him dearly, and in her softer moods was apt to spoil him with her caresses. "What can I do, my dearie? You know I would do anything if I could. Get into bed, my pet, and be warm, and then to-morrow morning you will be all right." At this moment he was preparing himself for his bed, and she was assisting him. Then she tied a piece of flannel round his throat, and kissed him, and put him in beneath the bed-clothes.

"I'll tell you what you can do," he said very hoarsely. His voice was so bad now that she could hardly hear him. So she crept close to him, and bent over him. She would do anything if he would only say what. Then he told her what was his plan. Down in the salon he had seen a large jar of mustard standing on a sideboard. As he left the room he had observed that this had not been withdrawn with the other appurtenances of the meal. If she could manage to find her way down there, taking with her a handkerchief folded for the purpose, and if she could then appropriate a part of the contents of that jar, and, returning with her prize, apply it to his throat, he thought that he could get some relief, so that he might be able to leave his bed the next morning at five. "But I am afraid it will be very disagreeable for you to go down all alone at this time of night," he croaked out in a piteous whisper.

"Of course I'll go," said she. "I don't mind going in the least. Nobody will bite me," and she at once began to fold a clean handkerchief. "I won't be two minutes, my darling, and if there is a grain of mustard in the house I'll have it on your chest immediately." She was a woman not easily cowed, and the journey down into the salon was nothing to her. Before she went she tucked the clothes carefully up to his ears, and then she started.

To run along the first corridor till she came to a flight of stairs was easy enough, and easy enough to descend them. Then there was another corridor, and another flight, and a third corridor, and a third flight, and she began to think that she was wrong. She found herself in a part of the hotel which she had not hitherto visited, and soon discovered by looking through an open door or two that she had found her way among a set of private sitting-rooms which she had not seen before. Then she tried to make her way back, up the same stairs and through the same passages, so that she might start again. She was beginning to think that she had lost herself altogether, and that she would be able to find neither the salon nor her bedroom, when she happily met the night-porter. She was dressed in a loose white dressing-gown, with a white net over her loose hair, and with white worsted slippers. I ought perhaps to have described her personal appearance sooner. She was a large woman, with a commanding bust, thought by some to be handsome, after the manner of Juno. But with strangers there was a certain severity of manner about her,—a fortification, as it were, of her virtue against all possible attacks,—a declared determination to maintain, at all points, the beautiful character of a British matron, which, much as it had been appreciated at Thompson Hall, had met with some ill-natured criticism among French men and women. At Pau she had been called La Fière Anglaise. The name had reached her own ears and those of her husband. He had been much annoyed, but she had taken it in good part,—had, indeed, been somewhat proud of the title,—and had endeavoured to live up to it. With her husband she could, on occasion, be soft, but she was of opinion that with other men a British matron should be stern. She was now greatly in want of assistance; but, nevertheless, when she met the porter she remembered her character. "I have lost my way wandering through these horrid passages," she said, in her severest tone. This was in answer to some question from him,—some question to which her reply was given very slowly. Then when he asked where Madame wished to go, she paused, again thinking what destination she would announce. No doubt the man could take her back to her bedroom, but if so, the mustard must be renounced, and with the mustard, as she now feared, all hope of reaching Thompson Hall on Christmas Eve. But she, though she was in many respects a brave woman, did not dare to tell the man that she was prowling about the hotel in order that she might make a midnight raid upon the mustard pot. She paused, therefore, for a moment, that she might collect her thoughts, erecting her head as she did so in her best Juno fashion, till the porter was lost in admiration. Thus she gained time to fabricate a tale. She had, she said, dropped her handkerchief under the supper-table; would he show her the way to the salon, in order that she might pick it up? But the porter did more than that, and accompanied her to the room in which she had supped.

Here, of course, there was a prolonged, and, it need hardly be said, a vain search. The good-natured man insisted on emptying an enormous receptacle of soiled table-napkins, and on turning them over one by one, in order that the lady's property might be found. The lady stood by unhappy, but still patient, and, as the man was stooping to his work, her eye was on the mustard pot. There it was, capable of containing enough to blister the throats of a score of sufferers. She edged off a little towards it while the man was busy, trying to persuade herself that he would surely forgive her if she took the mustard, and told him her whole story. But the descent from her Juno bearing would have been so great! She must have owned, not only to the quest for mustard, but also to a fib,—and she could not do it. The porter was at last of opinion that Madame must have made a mistake, and Madame acknowledged that she was afraid it was so.

With a longing, lingering eye, with an eye turned back, oh! so sadly, to the great jar, she left the room, the porter leading the way. She assured him that she could find it by herself, but he would not leave her till he had put her on to the proper passage. The journey seemed to be longer now even than before, but as she ascended the many stairs she swore to herself that she would not even yet be baulked of her object. Should her husband want comfort for his poor throat, and the comfort be there within her reach, and he not have it? She counted every stair as she went up, and marked every turn well. She was sure now that she would know the way, and that she could return to the room without fault. She would go back to the salon. Even though the man should encounter her again, she would go boldly forward and seize the remedy which her poor husband so grievously required.

"Ah, yes," she said, when the porter told her that her room, No. 333, was in the corridor which they had then reached, "I know it all now. I am so much obliged. Do not come a step further." He was anxious to accompany her up to the very door, but she stood in the passage and prevailed. He lingered awhile—naturally. Unluckily she had brought no money with her, and could not give him the two-franc piece which he had earned. Nor could she fetch it from her room, feeling that were she to return to her husband without the mustard no second attempt would be possible. The disappointed man turned on his heel at last, and made his way down the stairs and along the passage. It seemed to her to be almost an eternity while she listened to his still audible footsteps. She had gone on, creeping noiselessly up to the very door of her room, and there she stood, shading the candle in her hand, till she thought that the man must have wandered away into some furthest corner of that endless building. Then she turned once more and retraced her steps.

There was no difficulty now as to the way. She knew it, every stair. At the head of each flight she stood and listened, but not a sound was to be heard, and then she went on again. Her heart beat high with anxious desire to achieve her object, and at the same time with fear. What might have been explained so easily at first would now be as difficult of explanation. At last she was in the great public vestibule, which she was now visiting for the third time, and of which, at her last visit, she had taken the bearings accurately. The door was there—closed, indeed, but it opened easily to the hand. In the hall, and on the stairs, and along the passages, there had been gas, but here there was no light beyond that given by the little taper which she carried. When accompanied by the porter she had not feared the darkness, but now there was something in the obscurity which made her dread to walk the length of the room up to the mustard jar. She paused, and listened, and trembled. Then she thought of the glories of Thompson Hall, of the genial warmth of a British Christmas, of that proud legislator who was her first cousin, and with a rush she made good the distance, and laid her hand upon the copious delf. She looked round, but there was no one there; no sound was heard; not the distant creak of a shoe, not a rattle from one of those thousand doors. As she paused with her fair hand upon the top of the jar, while the other held the white cloth on which the medicinal compound was to be placed, she looked like Lady Macbeth as she listened at Duncan's chamber door.

There was no doubt as to the sufficiency of the contents. The jar was full nearly up to the lips. The mixture was, no doubt, very different from that good wholesome English mustard which your cook makes fresh for you, with a little water, in two minutes. It was impregnated with a sour odour, and was, to English eyes, unwholesome of colour. But still it was mustard. She seized the horn spoon, and without further delay spread an ample sufficiency on the folded square of the handkerchief. Then she commenced to hurry her return.

But still there was a difficulty, no thought of which had occurred to her before. The candle occupied one hand, so that she had but the other for the sustenance of her treasure. Had she brought a plate or saucer from the salon, it would have been all well. As it was she was obliged to keep her eye intent on her right hand, and to proceed very slowly on her return journey. She was surprised to find what an aptitude the thing had to slip from her grasp. But still she progressed slowly, and was careful not to miss a turning. At last she was safe at her chamber door. There it was, No. 333.

Chapter II

Mrs. Brown's Failure.

WITH HER eye still fixed upon her burden, she glanced up at the number of the door—333. She had been determined all through not to forget that. Then she turned the latch and crept in. The chamber also was dark after the gaslight on the stairs, but that was so much the better. She herself had put out the two candles on the dressing-table before she had left her husband. As she was closing the door behind her she paused, and could hear that he was sleeping. She was well aware that she had been long absent,—quite long enough for a man to fall into slumber who was given that way. She must have been gone, she thought, fully an hour. There had been no end to that turning over of napkins which she had so well known to be altogether vain. She paused at the centre table of the room, still looking at the mustard, which she now delicately dried from off her hand. She had had no idea that it would have been so difficult to carry so light and so small an affair. But there it was, and nothing had been lost. She took some small instrument from the washing-stand, and with the handle collected the flowing fragments into the centre. Then the question occurred to her whether, as her husband was sleeping so sweetly, it would be well to disturb him. She listened again, and felt that the slight murmur of a snore with which her ears were regaled was altogether free from any real malady in the throat. Then it occurred to her, that after all, fatigue perhaps had only made him cross. She bethought herself how, during the whole journey, she had failed to believe in his illness. What meals he had eaten! How thoroughly he had been able to enjoy his full complement of cigars! And then that glass of brandy, against which she had raised her voice slightly in feminine opposition. And now he was sleeping there like an infant, with full, round, perfected, almost sonorous workings of the throat. Who does not know that sound, almost of two rusty bits of iron scratching against each other, which comes from a suffering windpipe? There was no semblance of that here. Why disturb him when he was so thoroughly enjoying that rest which, more certainly than anything else, would fit him for the fatigue of the morrow's journey?

I think that, after all her labour, she would have left the pungent cataplasm on the table, and have crept gently into bed beside him, had not a thought suddenly struck her of the great injury he had been doing her if he were not really ill. To send her down there, in a strange hotel, wandering among the passages, in the middle of the night, subject to the contumely of anyone who might meet her, on a commission which, if it were not sanctified by absolute necessity, would be so thoroughly objectionable! At this moment she hardly did believe that he had ever really been ill. Let him have the cataplasm; if not as a remedy, then as a punishment. It could, at any rate, do him no harm. It was with an idea of avenging rather than of justifying the past labours of the night that she proceeded at once to quick action.

Leaving the candle on the table so that she might steady her right hand with the left, she hurried stealthily to the bedside. Even though he was behaving badly to her, she would not cause him discomfort by waking him roughly. She would do a wife's duty to him as a British matron should. She would not only put the warm mixture on his neck, but would sit carefully by him for twenty minutes, so that she might relieve him from it when the proper period should have come for removing the counter irritation from his throat. There would doubtless be some little difficulty in this,—in collecting the mustard after it had served her purpose. Had she been at home, surrounded by her own comforts, the application would have been made with some delicate linen bag, through which the pungency of the spice would have penetrated with strength sufficient for the purpose. But the circumstance of the occasion had not admitted this. She had, she felt, done wonders in achieving so much success as this which she had obtained. If there should be anything disagreeable in the operation he must submit to it. He had asked for mustard for his throat, and mustard he should have.

As these thoughts passed quickly through her mind, leaning over him in the dark, with her eye fixed on the mixture lest it should slip, she gently raised his flowing beard with her left hand, and with her other inverted rapidly, steadily but very softly fixed the handkerchief on his throat. From the bottom of his chin to the spot at which the collar bones meeting together form the orifice of the chest it covered the whole noble expanse. There was barely time for a glance, but never had she been more conscious of the grand proportions of that manly throat. A sweet feeling of pity came upon her, causing her to determine to relieve his sufferings in the shorter space of fifteen minutes. He had been lying on his back, with his lips apart, and, as she held back his beard, that and her hand nearly covered the features of his face. But he made no violent effort to free himself from the encounter. He did not even move an arm or a leg. He simply emitted a snore louder than any that had come before. She was aware that it was not his wont to be so loud—that there was generally something more delicate and perhaps more querulous in his nocturnal voice, but then the present circumstances were exceptional. She dropped the beard very softly—and there on the pillow before her lay the face of a stranger. She had put the mustard plaster on the wrong man.

Not Priam wakened in the dead of night, not Dido when first she learned that Æneas had fled, not Othello when he learned that Desdemona had been chaste, not Medea when she became conscious of her slaughtered children, could have been more struck with horror than was this British matron as she stood for a moment gazing with awe on that stranger's bed. One vain, half-completed, snatching grasp she made at the handkerchief, and then drew back her hand. If she were to touch him would he not wake at once, and find her standing there in his bedroom? And then how could she explain it? By what words could she so quickly make him know the circumstances of that strange occurrence that he should accept it all before he had said a word that might offend her? For a moment she stood all but paralyzed after that faint ineffectual movement of her arm. Then he stirred his head uneasily on the pillow, opened wider his lips, and twice in rapid succession snored louder than before. She started back a couple of paces, and with her body placed between him and the candle, with her face averted, but with her hand still resting on the foot of the bed, she endeavoured to think what duty required of her.

She had injured the man. Though she had done it most unwittingly, there could be no doubt but that she had injured him. If for a moment she could be brave, the injury might in truth be little; but how disastrous might be the consequences if she were now in her cowardice to leave him, who could tell? Applied for fifteen to twenty minutes a mustard plaster may be the salvation of a throat ill at ease, but if left there throughout the night upon the neck of a strong man, ailing nothing, only too prone in his strength to slumber soundly, how sad, how painful, for aught she knew how dangerous might be the effects! And surely it was an error which any man with a heart in his bosom would pardon! Judging from what little she had seen of him she thought that he must have a heart in his bosom. Was it not her duty to wake him, and then quietly to extricate him from the embarrassment which she had brought upon him?

But in doing this what words should she use? How should she wake him? How should she make him understand her goodness, her beneficence, her sense of duty, before he should have jumped from the bed and rushed to the bell, and have summoned all above and all below to the rescue? "Sir, sir, do not move, do not stir, do not scream. I have put a mustard plaster on your throat, thinking that you were my husband. As yet no harm has been done. Let me take it off, and then hold your peace for ever." Where is the man of such native constancy and grace of spirit that, at the first moment of waking with a shock, he could hear these words from the mouth of an unknown woman by his bedside, and at once obey them to the letter? Would he not surely jump from his bed, with that horrid compound falling about him,—from which there could be no complete relief unless he would keep his present attitude without a motion? The picture which presented itself to her mind as to his probable conduct was so terrible that she found herself unable to incur the risk.

Then an idea presented itself to her mind. We all know how in a moment quick thoughts will course through the subtle brain. She would find that porter and send him to explain it all. There should be no concealment now. She would tell the story and would bid him to find the necessary aid. Alas! as she told herself that she would do so, she knew well that she was only running from the danger which it was her duty to encounter. Once again she put out her hand as though to return along the bed. Then thrice he snorted louder than before, and moved up his knee uneasily beneath the clothes as though the sharpness of the mustard were already working upon his skin. She watched him for a moment longer, and then, with the candle in her hand, she fled.

Poor human nature! Had he been an old man, even a middle aged man, she would not have left him to his unmerited sufferings. As it was, though she completely recognised her duty, and knew what justice and goodness demanded of her, she could not do it. But there was still left to her that plan of sending the night-porter to him. It was not till she was out of the room and had gently closed the door behind her, that she began to bethink herself how she had made the mistake. With a glance of her eye she looked up, and then saw the number on the door: 353. Remarking to herself, with a Briton's natural criticism on things French, that those horrid foreigners do not know how to make their figures, she scudded rather than ran along the corridor, and then down some stairs and along another passage,—so that she might not be found in the neighbourhood should the poor man in his agony rush rapidly from his bed.

In the confusion of her first escape she hardly ventured to look for her own passage,—nor did she in the least know how she had lost her way when she came upstairs with the mustard in her hand. But at the present moment her chief object was the night-porter. She went on descending till she came again to that vestibule, and looking up at the clock saw that it was now past one. It was not yet midnight when she left her husband, but she was not at all astonished at the lapse of time. It seemed to her as though she had passed a night among these miseries. And, oh, what a night! But there was yet much to be done. She must find that porter, and then return to her own suffering husband. Ah,—what now should she say to him? If he should really be ill, how should she assuage him? And yet how more than ever necessary was it that they should leave that hotel early in the morning,—that they should leave Paris by the very earliest and quickest train that would take them as fugitives from their present dangers! The door of the salon was open, but she had no courage to go in search of a second supply. She would have lacked strength to carry it up the stairs. Where now, oh, where, was that man? From the vestibule she made her way into the hall, but everything seemed to be deserted. Through the glass she could see a light in the court beyond, but she could not bring herself to endeavour even to open the hall doors.

And now she was very cold,—chilled to her very bones. All this had been done at Christmas, and during such severity of weather as had never before been experienced by living Parisians. A feeling of great pity for herself gradually came upon her. What wrong had she done that she should be so grievously punished? Why should she be driven to wander about in this way till her limbs were failing her? And then, so absolutely important as it was that her strength should support her in the morning! The man would not die even though he were left there without aid, to rid himself of the cataplasm as best he might. Was it absolutely necessary that she should disgrace herself?

But she could not even procure the means of disgracing herself, if that telling her story to the night-porter would have been a disgrace.

She did not find him, and at last resolved to make her way back to her own room without further quest. She began to think that she had done all that she could do. No man was ever killed by a mustard plaster on his throat. His discomfort at the worst would not be worse than hers had been—or too probably than that of her poor husband. So she went back up the stairs and along the passages, and made her way on this occasion to the door of her room without any difficulty. The way was so well known to her that she could not but wonder that she had failed before. But now her hands had been empty, and her eyes had been at her full command. She looked up, and there was the number, very manifest on this occasion,—333. She opened the door most gently, thinking that her husband might be sleeping as soundly as that other man had slept, and she crept into the room.

Chapter III

Mrs. Brown Attempts To Escape.

But her husband was not sleeping. He was not even in bed, as she had left him. She found him sitting there before the fire-place, on which one half-burned log still retained a spark of what had once pretended to be a fire. Nothing more wretched than his appearance could be imagined. There was a single lighted candle on the table, on which he was leaning with his two elbows, while his head rested between his hands. He had on a dressing-gown over his night-shirt, but otherwise was not clothed. He shivered audibly, or rather shook himself with the cold, and made the table to chatter as she entered the room. Then he groaned, and let his head fall from his hands on to the table. It occurred to her at the moment as she recognised the tone of his querulous voice, and as she saw the form of his neck, that she must have been deaf and blind when she had mistaken that stalwart stranger for her husband. "Oh, my dear," she said, "why are you not in bed?" He answered nothing in words, but only groaned again. "Why did you get up? I left you warm and comfortable"

"Where have you been all night?" he half whispered, half croaked, with an agonising effort.

"I have been looking for the mustard."

"Have been looking all night and haven't found it? Where have you been?"

She refused to speak a word to him till she had got him into bed, and then she told her story! But, alas, that which she told was not the true story! As she was persuading him to go back to his rest, and while she arranged the clothes again around him, she with difficulty made up her mind as to what she would do and what she would say. Living or dying he must be made to start for Thompson Hall at half-past five on the next morning. It was no longer a question of the amenities of Christmas, no longer a mere desire to satisfy the family ambition of her own people, no longer an anxiety to see her new brother-in-law. She was conscious that there was in that house one whom she had deeply injured, and from whose vengeance, even from whose aspect, she must fly. How could she endure to see that face which she was so well sure that she would recognise, or to hear the slightest sound of that voice which would be quite familiar to her ears, though it had never spoken a word in her hearing? She must certainly fly on the wings of the earliest train which would carry her towards the old house; but in order that she might do so she must propitiate her husband.

So she told her story. She had gone forth, as he had bade her, in search of the mustard, and then had suddenly lost her way. Up and down the house she had wandered, perhaps nearly a dozen times. "Had she met no one?" he asked in that raspy, husky whisper. "Surely there must have been some one about the hotel! Nor was it possible that she could have been roaming about all those hours." "Only one hour, my dear," she said. Then there was a question about the duration of time, in which both of them waxed angry, and as she became angry her husband waxed stronger, and as he became violent beneath the clothes the comfortable idea returned to her that he was not perhaps so ill as he would seem to be. She found herself driven to tell him something about the porter, having to account for that lapse of time by explaining how she had driven the poor man to search for the handkerchief which she had never lost.

"Why did you not tell him you wanted the mustard?"

"My dear!"

"Why not? There is nothing to be ashamed of in wanting mustard."

"At one o'clock in the morning! I couldn't do it. To tell you the truth, he wasn't very civil, and I thought that he was,—perhaps a little tipsy. Now, my dear, do go to sleep."

"Why didn't you get the mustard?"

"There was none there,—nowhere at all about the room. I went down again and searched everywhere. That's what took me so long. They always lock up those kind of things at these French hotels. They are too close-fisted to leave anything out. When you first spoke of it I knew that it would be gone when I got there. Now, my dear, do go to sleep, because we positively must start in the morning."

"That is impossible," said he, jumping up in bed.

"We must go, my dear. I say that we must go. After all that has passed I wouldn't not be with Uncle John and my cousin Robert to-morrow evening for more,—more,—more than I would venture to say."

"Bother!" he exclaimed.

"It's all very well for you to say that, Charles, but you don't know. I say that we must go to-morrow, and we will."

"I do believe you want to kill me, Mary."

"That is very cruel, Charles, and most false, and most unjust. As for making you ill, nothing could be so bad for you as this wretched place, where nobody can get warm either day or night. If anything will cure your throat for you at once it will be the sea air. And only think how much more comfortable they can make you at Thompson Hall than anywhere in this country. I have so set my heart upon it, Charles, that I will do it. If we are not there to-morrow night Uncle John won't consider us as belonging to the family."

"I don't believe a word of it."

"Jane told me so in her letter. I wouldn't let you know before because I thought it so unjust. But that has been the reason why I've been so earnest about it all through."

It was a thousand pities that so good a woman should have been driven by the sad stress of circumstances to tell so many fibs. One after another she was compelled to invent them, that there might be a way open to her of escaping the horrors of a prolonged sojourn in that hotel. At length, after much grumbling, he became silent, and she trusted that he was sleeping. He had not as yet said that he would start at the required hour in the morning, but she was perfectly determined in her own mind that he should be made to do so. As he lay there motionless, and as she wandered about the room pretending to pack her things, she more than once almost resolved that she would tell him everything. Surely then he would be ready to make any effort. But there came upon her an idea that he might perhaps fail to see all the circumstances, and that, so failing, he would insist on remaining that he might tender some apology to the injured gentleman. An apology might have been very well had she not left him there in his misery—but what apology would be possible now? She would have to see him and speak to him, and everyone in the hotel would know every detail of the story. Everyone in France would know that it was she who had gone to the strange man's bedside, and put the mustard plaster on the strange man's throat in the dead of night! She could not tell the story even to her husband, lest even her husband should betray her.

Her own sufferings at the present moment were not light. In her perturbation of mind she had foolishly resolved that she would not herself go to bed. The tragedy of the night had seemed to her too deep for personal comfort. And then how would it be were she to sleep, and have no one to call her? It was imperative that she should have all her powers ready for thoroughly arousing him. It occurred to her that the servant of the hotel would certainly run her too short of time. She had to work for herself and for him too, and therefore she would not sleep. But she was very cold, and she put on first a shawl over her dressing-gown and then a cloak. She could not consume all the remaining hours of the night in packing one bag and one portmanteau, so that at last she sat down on the narrow red cotton velvet sofa, and looking at her watch, perceived that as yet it was not much past two o'clock. How was she to get through those other three long, tedious, chilly hours?

Then there came a voice from the bed—"Ain't you coming?"

"I hoped you were asleep, my dear."

"I haven't been asleep at all. You'd better come, if you don't mean to make yourself as ill as I am."

"You are not so very bad, are you, darling?"

"I don't know what you call bad. I never felt my throat so choked in my life before!" Still as she listened she thought that she remembered his throat to have been more choked. If the husband of her bosom could play with her feelings and deceive her on such an occasion as this,—then, then,—then she thought that she would rather not have any husband of her bosom at all. But she did creep into bed, and lay down beside him without saying another word.

Of course she slept, but her sleep was not the sleep of the blest. At every striking of the clock in the quadrangle she would start up in alarm, fearing that she had let the time go by. Though the night was so short it was very long to her. But he slept like an infant. She could hear from his breathing that he was not quite so well as she could wish him to be, but still he was resting in beautiful tranquillity. Not once did he move when she started up, as she did so frequently. Orders had been given and repeated over and over again that they should be called at five. The man in the office had almost been angry as he assured Mrs. Brown for the fourth time that Monsieur and Madame would most assuredly be wakened at the appointed time. But still she would trust to no one, and was up and about the room before the clock had struck half-past four.

In her heart of hearts she was very tender towards her husband. Now, in order that he might feel a gleam of warmth while he was dressing himself, she collected together the fragments of half-burned wood, and endeavoured to make a little fire. Then she took out from her bag a small pot, and a patent lamp, and some chocolate, and prepared for him a warm drink, so that he might have it instantly as he was awakened. She would do anything for him in the way of ministering to his comfort,—only he must go! Yes, he certainly must go!

And then she wondered how that strange man was bearing himself at the present moment. She would fain have ministered to him too had it been possible; but ah!—it was so impossible! Probably before this he would have been aroused from his troubled slumbers. But then—how aroused? At what time in the night would the burning heat upon his chest have awakened him to a sense of torture which must have been so altogether incomprehensible to him? Her strong imagination showed to her a clear picture of the scene,—clear, though it must have been done in the dark. How he must have tossed and hurled himself under the clothes; how those strong knees must have worked themselves up and down before the potent god of sleep would allow him to return to perfect consciousness; how his fingers, restrained by no reason, would have trampled over his feverish throat, scattering everywhere that unhappy poultice! Then when he should have sat up wide awake, but still in the dark—with her mind's eye she saw it all—feeling that some fire as from the infernal regions had fallen upon him, but whence he would know not, how fiercely wild would be the working of his spirit! Ah, now she knew, now she felt, now she acknowledged how bound she had been to awaken him at the moment, whatever might have been the personal inconvenience to herself! In such a position what would he do—or rather what had he done? She could follow much of it in her own thoughts;—how he would scramble madly from his bed, and, with one hand still on his throat, would snatch hurriedly at the matches with the other. How the light would come, and how then he would rush to the mirror. Ah, what a sight he would behold! She could see it all to the last widespread daub.

But she could not see, she could not tell herself, what in such a position a man would do;—at any rate, not what that man would do. Her husband, she thought, would tell his wife, and then the two of them, between them, would—put up with it. There are misfortunes which, if they be published, are simply aggravated by ridicule. But she remembered the features of the stranger as she had seen them at that instant in which she had dropped his beard, and she thought that there was a ferocity in them, a certain tenacity of self-importance, which would not permit their owner to endure such treatment in silence. Would he not storm and rage, and ring the bell, and call all Paris to witness his revenge?

But the storming and the raging had not reached her yet, and now it wanted but a quarter to five. In three-quarters of an hour they would be in that demi-omnibus which they had ordered for themselves, and in half an hour after that they would be flying towards Thompson Hall. Then she allowed herself to think of the coming comforts,—of those comforts so sweet, if only they would come! That very day now present to her was the 24th December, and on that very evening she would be sitting in Christmas joy among all her uncles and cousins, holding her new brother-in-law affectionately by the hand. Oh, what a change from Pandemonium to Paradise;—from that wretched room, from that miserable house in which there was such ample cause for fear, to all the domestic Christmas bliss of the home of the Thompsons! She resolved that she would not, at any rate, be deterred by any light opposition on the part of her husband. "It wants just a quarter to five," she said, putting her hand steadily upon his shoulder, "and I'll get a cup of chocolate for you, so that you may get up comfortably."

"I've been thinking about it," he said, rubbing his eyes with the back of his hands. "It will be so much better to go over by the mail train to-night. We should be in time for Christmas just the same."

"That will not do at all," she answered, energetically. "Come, Charles, after all the trouble do not disappoint me."

"It is such a horrid grind."

"Think what I have gone through,—what I have done for you! In twelve hours we shall be there, among them all. You won't be so little like a man as not to go on now." He threw himself back upon the bed, and tried to readjust the clothes round his neck. "No, Charles, no," she continued; "not if I know it. Take your chocolate and get up. There is not a moment to be lost." With that she laid her hand upon his shoulder, and made him clearly understand that he would not be allowed to take further rest in that bed.

Grumbling, sulky, coughing continually, and declaring that life under such circumstances was not worth having, he did at last get up and dress himself. When once she knew that he was obeying her she became again tender to him, and certainly took much more than her own share of the trouble of the proceedings. Long before the time was up she was ready, and the porter had been summoned to take the luggage downstairs. When the man came she was rejoiced to see that it was not he whom she had met among the passages during her nocturnal rambles. He shouldered the box, and told them that they would find coffee and bread and butter in the small salle-à-manger below.

"I told you that it would be so, when you would boil that stuff," said the ungrateful man, who had nevertheless swallowed the hot chocolate when it was given to him.

They followed their luggage down into the hall; but as she went, at every step, the lady looked around her. She dreaded the sight of that porter of the night; she feared lest some potential authority of the hotel should come to her and ask her some horrid question; but of all her fears her greatest fear was that there should arise before her an apparition of that face which she had seen recumbent on its pillow.

As they passed the door of the great salon, Mr. Brown looked in. "Why, there it is still!" said he.

"What?" said she, trembling in every limb.

"The mustard-pot!"

"They have put it in there since," she exclaimed energetically, in her despair. "But never mind. The omnibus is here. Come away." And she absolutely took him by the arm.

But at that moment a door behind them opened, and Mrs. Brown heard herself called by her name. And there was the night-porter,—with a handkerchief in his hand. But the further doings of that morning must be told in a further chapter.

Chapter IV

Mrs. Brown Does Escape.

It had been visible to Mrs. Brown from the first moment of her arrival on the ground floor that "something was the matter," if we may be allowed to use such a phrase; and she felt all but convinced that this something had reference to her. She fancied that the people of the hotel were looking at her as she swallowed, or tried to swallow, her coffee. When her husband was paying the bill there was something disagreeable in the eye of the man who was taking the money. Her sufferings were very great, and no one sympathised with her. Her husband was quite at his ease, except that he was complaining of the cold. When she was anxious to get him out into the carriage, he still stood there leisurely, arranging shawl after shawl around his throat. "You can do that quite as well in an omnibus," she had just said to him very crossly, when there appeared upon the scene through a side door that very night-porter whom she dreaded, with a soiled pocket-handkerchief in his hand.

Even before the sound of her own name met her ears Mrs. Brown knew it all. She understood the full horror of her position from that man's hostile face, and from the little article which he held in his hand. If during the watches of the night she had had money in her pocket, if she had made a friend of this greedy fellow by well-timed liberality, all might have been so different! But she reflected that she had allowed him to go unfee'd after all his trouble, and she knew that he was her enemy. It was the handkerchief that she feared. She thought that she might have brazened out anything but that. No one had seen her enter or leave that strange man's room. No one had seen her dip her hands in that jar. She had, no doubt, been found wandering about the house while the slumberer had been made to suffer so strangely, and there might have been suspicion, and perhaps accusation. But she would have been ready with frequent protestations to deny all charges made against her, and, though no one might have believed her, no one could have convicted her. Here, however, was evidence against which she would be unable to stand for a moment. At the first glance she acknowledged the potency of that damning morsel of linen.

During all the horrors of the night she had never given a thought to the handkerchief, and yet she ought to have known that the evidence it would bring against her was palpable and certain. Her name, "M.Brown," was plainly written on the corner. What a fool she had been not to have thought of this! Had she but remembered the plain marking which she, as a careful, well-conducted British matron, had put upon all her clothes, she would at any hazard have recovered the article. Oh that she had waked the man, or bribed the porter, or even told her husband! But now she was, as it were, friendless, without support, without a word that she could say in her own defence, convicted of having committed this assault upon a strange man in his own bedroom, and then of having left him! The thing must be explained by the truth; but how to satisfy injured folk, and she with only barely time sufficient to catch the train! Then it occurred to her that they could have no legal right to stop her because the pocket-handkerchief had been found in a strange gentleman's bedroom. "Yes, it is mine," she said, turning to her husband, as the porter, with a loud voice, asked if she were not Madame Brown. "Take it, Charles, and come on." Mr. Brown naturally stood still in astonishment. He did put out his hand, but the porter would not allow the evidence to pass so readily out of his custody.

"What does it all mean?" asked Mr. Brown.

"A gentleman has been—eh—eh—. Something has been done to a gentleman in his bedroom," said the clerk.

"Something done to a gentleman!" repeated Mr. Brown.

"Something very bad indeed," said the porter. "Look here," and he showed the condition of the handkerchief.

"Charles, we shall lose the train," said the affrighted wife.

"What the mischief does it all mean?" demanded the husband.

"Did Madame go into the gentleman's room?" asked the clerk. Then there was an awful silence, and all eyes were fixed upon the lady.

"What does it all mean?" demanded the husband. "Did you go into anybody's room?"

"I did," said Mrs. Brown with much dignity, looking round upon her enemies as a stag at bay will look upon the hounds which are attacking him. "Give me the handkerchief." But the night-porter quickly put it behind his back. "Charles, we cannot allow ourselves to be delayed. You shall write a letter to the keeper of the hotel, explaining it all." Then she essayed to swim out, through the front door, into the courtyard in which the vehicle was waiting for them. But three or four men and women interposed themselves, and even her husband did not seem quite ready to continue his journey. "To-night is Christmas Eve," said Mrs. Brown, "and we shall not be at Thompson Hall! Think of my sister!"

"Why did you go into the man's bedroom, my dear?" whispered Mr. Brown in English.

But the porter heard the whisper, and understood the language;—the porter who had not been "tipped." "Ye'es;—vy?" asked the porter.

"It was a mistake, Charles; there is not a moment to lose. I can explain it all to you in the carriage." Then the clerk suggested that Madame had better postpone her journey a little. The gentleman upstairs had certainly been very badly treated, and had demanded to know why so great an outrage had been perpetrated. The clerk said that he did not wish to send for the police—here Mrs. Brown gasped terribly and threw herself on her husband's shoulder,—but he did not think he could allow the party to go till the gentleman upstairs had received some satisfaction. It had now become clearly impossible that the journey could be made by the early train. Even Mrs. Brown gave it up herself, and demanded of her husband that she should be taken back to her own bedroom.

"But what is to be said to the gentleman?" asked the porter.

Of course it was impossible that Mrs. Brown should be made to tell her story there in the presence of them all. The clerk, when he found he had succeeded in preventing her from leaving the house, was satisfied with a promise from Mr. Brown that he would inquire from his wife what were these mysterious circumstances, and would then come down to the office and give some explanation. If it were necessary, he would see the strange gentleman,—whom he now ascertained to be a certain Mr. Jones returning from the east of Europe. He learned also that this Mr. Jones had been most anxious to travel by that very morning train which he and his wife had intended to use,—that Mr. Jones had been most particular in giving his orders accordingly, but that at the last moment he had declared himself to be unable even to dress himself, because of the injury which had been done him during the night. When Mr. Brown heard this from the clerk just before he was allowed to take his wife upstairs, while she was sitting on a sofa in a corner with her face hidden, a look of awful gloom came over his own countenance. What could it be that his wife had done to the man of so terrible a nature? "You had better come up with me," he said to her with marital severity, and the poor cowed woman went with him tamely as might have done some patient Grizel. Not a word was spoken till they were in the room and the door was locked. "Now," said he, "what does it all mean?"

It was not till nearly two hours had passed that Mr. Brown came down the stairs very slowly,—turning it all over in his mind. He had now gradually heard the absolute and exact truth, and had very gradually learned to believe it. It was first necessary that he should understand that his wife had told him many fibs during the night; but as she constantly alleged to him when he complained of her conduct in this respect, they had all been told on his behalf. Had she not struggled to get the mustard for his comfort, and when she had secured the prize had she not hurried to put it on,—as she had fondly thought,—his throat? And though she had fibbed to him afterwards, had she not done so in order that he might not be troubled? "You are not angry with me because I was in that man's room?" she asked, looking full into his eyes, but not quite without a sob. He paused a moment and then declared, with something of a true husband's confidence in his tone, that he was not in the least angry with her on that account. Then she kissed him, and bade him remember that after all no one could really injure them. "What harm has been done, Charles? The gentleman won't die because he has had a mustard plaster on his throat. The worst is about Uncle John and dear Jane. They do think so much of Christmas Eve at Thompson Hall!"

Mr. Brown, when he again found himself in the clerk's office, requested that his card might be taken up to Mr. Jones. Mr. Jones had sent down his own card, which was handed to Mr. Brown: "Mr. Barnaby Jones." "And how was it all, sir?" asked the clerk, in a whisper—a whisper which had at the same time something of authoritative demand and something also of submissive respect. The clerk of course was anxious to know the mystery. It is hardly too much to say that everyone in that vast hotel was by this time anxious to have the mystery unravelled. But Mr. Brown would tell nothing to anyone. "It is merely a matter to be explained between me and Mr. Jones," he said. The card was taken upstairs, and after awhile he was ushered into Mr. Jones' room. It was, of course, that very 353 with which the reader is already acquainted. There was a fire burning, and the remains of Mr. Jones' breakfast were on the table. He was sitting in his dressing-gown and slippers, with his shirt open in the front, and a silk handkerchief very loosely covering his throat. Mr. Brown, as he entered the room, of course looked with considerable anxiety at the gentleman of whose condition he had heard so sad an account; but he could only observe some considerable stiffness of movement and demeanour as Mr. Jones turned his head round to greet him.

"This has been a very disagreeable accident, Mr. Jones," said the husband of the lady.

"Accident! I don't know how it could have been an accident. It has been a most—most—most—a most monstrous,—er,—er,—I must say, interference with a gentleman's privacy, and personal comfort."

"Quite so, Mr. Jones, but,—on the part of the lady, who is my wife— "

"So I understand. I myself am about to become a married man, and I can understand what your feelings must be. I wish to say as little as possible to harrow them." Here Mr. Brown bowed. "But,—there's the fact. She did do it."

"She thought it was—me!"

"What!"

"I give you my word as a gentleman, Mr. Jones. When she was putting that mess upon you she thought it was me! She did, indeed."

Mr. Jones looked at his new acquaintance and shook his head. He did not think it possible that any woman would make such a mistake as that.

"I had a very bad sore throat," continued Mr. Brown, "and indeed you may perceive it still,"—in saying this, he perhaps aggravated a little the sign of his distemper, "and I asked Mrs. Brown to go down and get one,—just what she put on you."

"I wish you'd had it," said Mr. Jones, putting his hand up to his neck.

"I wish I had,—for your sake as well as mine,—and for hers, poor woman. I don't know when she will get over the shock."

"I don't know when I shall. And it has stopped me on my journey. I was to have been to-night, this very night, this Christmas Eve, with the young lady I am engaged to marry. Of course I couldn't travel. The extent of the injury done nobody can imagine at present."

"It has been just as bad to me, sir. We were to have been with our family this Christmas Eve. There were particular reasons,—most particular. We were only hindered from going by hearing of your condition."

"Why did she come into my room at all? I can't understand that. A lady always knows her own room at an hotel."

"353—that's yours; 333—that's ours. Don't you see how easy it was? She had lost her way, and she was a little afraid lest the thing should fall down."

"I wish it had, with all my heart."

"That's how it was. Now I'm sure, Mr. Jones, you'll take a lady's apology. It was a most unfortunate mistake,—most unfortunate; but what more can be said?"

Mr. Jones gave himself up to reflection for a few moments before he replied to this. He supposed that he was bound to believe the story as far as it went. At any rate, he did not know how he could say that he did not believe it. It seemed to him to be almost incredible,—especially incredible in regard to that personal mistake, for, except that they both had long beards and brown beards, Mr. Jones thought that there was no point of resemblance between himself and Mr. Brown. But still, even that, he felt, must be accepted. But then why had he been left, deserted, to undergo all those torments? "She found out her mistake at last, I suppose?"

"Oh, yes."

"Why didn't she wake a fellow and take it off again?"

"Ah!"

"She can't have cared very much for a man's comfort when she went away and left him like that."

"Ah! there was the difficulty, Mr. Jones."

"Difficulty! Who was it that had done it? To come to me, in my bedroom, in the middle of the night, and put that thing on me, and then leave it there and say nothing about it! It seems to me deuced like a practical joke."

"No, Mr. Jones!"

"That's the way I look at it," said Mr. Jones, plucking up his courage.

"There isn't a woman in all England, or in all France, less likely to do such a thing than my wife. She's as steady as a rock, Mr. Jones, and would no more go into another gentleman's bedroom in joke than—Oh dear no! You're going to be a married man yourself."

"Unless all this makes a difference," said Mr. Jones, almost in tears. "I had sworn that I would be with her this Christmas Eve."

"Oh, Mr. Jones, I cannot believe that will interfere with your happiness. How could you think that your wife, as is to be, would do such a thing as that in joke?"

"She wouldn't do it at all;—joke or anyway."

"How can you tell what accident might happen to anyone?"

"She'd have wakened the man then afterwards. I'm sure she would. She would never have left him to suffer in that way. Her heart is too soft. Why didn't she send you to wake me, and explain it all? That's what my Jane would have done; and I should have gone and wakened him. But the whole thing is impossible," he said, shaking his head as he remembered that he and his Jane were not in a condition as yet to undergo any such mutual trouble. At last Mr. Jones was brought to acknowledge that nothing more could be done. The lady had sent her apology, and told her story, and he must bear the trouble and inconvenience to which she had subjected him. He still, however, had his own opinion about her conduct generally, and could not be brought to give any sign of amity. He simply bowed when Mr. Brown was hoping to induce him to shake hands, and sent no word of pardon to the great offender.

The matter, however, was so far concluded that there was no further question of police interference, nor any doubt but that the lady with her husband was to be allowed to leave Paris by the night train. The nature of the accident probably became known to all. Mr. Brown was interrogated by many, and though he professed to declare that he would answer no question, nevertheless he found it better to tell the clerk something of the truth than to allow the matter to be shrouded in mystery. It is to be feared that Mr. Jones, who did not once show himself through the day, but who employed the hours in endeavouring to assuage the injury done him, still lived in the conviction that the lady had played a practical joke on him. But the subject of such a joke never talks about it, and Mr. Jones could not be induced to speak even by the friendly adherence of the night-porter.

Mrs. Brown also clung to the seclusion of her own bedroom, never once stirring from it till the time came in which she was to be taken down to the omnibus. Upstairs she ate her meals, and upstairs she passed her time in packing and unpacking, and in requesting that telegrams might be sent repeatedly to Thompson Hall. In the course of the day two such telegrams were sent, in the latter of which the Thompson family were assured that the Browns would arrive, probably in time for breakfast on Christmas Day, certainly in time for church. She asked more than once tenderly after Mr. Jones' welfare, but could obtain no information. "He was very cross, and that's all I know about it," said Mr. Brown. Then she made a remark as to the gentleman's Christian name, which appeared on the card as "Barnaby." "My sister's husband's name will be Burnaby," she said. "And this man's Christian name is Barnaby; that's all the difference," said her husband, with ill-timed jocularity.

We all know how people under a cloud are apt to fail in asserting their personal dignity. On the former day a separate vehicle had been ordered by Mr. Brown to take himself and his wife to the station, but now, after his misfortunes, he contented himself with such provision as the people at the hotel might make for him. At the appointed hour he brought his wife down, thickly veiled. There were many strangers as she passed through the hall, ready to look at the lady who had done that wonderful thing in the dead of night, but none could see a feature of her face as she stepped across the hall, and was hurried into the omnibus. And there were many eyes also on Mr. Jones, who followed very quickly, for he also, in spite of his sufferings, was leaving Paris on the evening in order that he might be with his English friends on Christmas Day. He, as he went through the crowd, assumed an air of great dignity, to which, perhaps, something was added by his endeavours, as he walked, to save his poor throat from irritation. He, too, got into the same omnibus, stumbling over the feet of his enemy in the dark. At the station they got their tickets, one close after the other, and then were brought into each other's presence in the waiting-room. I think it must be acknowledged that here Mr. Jones was conscious, not only of her presence, but of her consciousness of his presence, and that he assumed an attitude, as though he should have said, "Now do you think it possible for me to believe that you mistook me for your husband?" She was perfectly quiet, but sat through that quarter of an hour with her face continually veiled. Mr. Brown made some little overture of conversation to Mr. Jones, but Mr. Jones, though he did mutter some reply, showed plainly enough that he had no desire for further intercourse. Then came the accustomed stampede, the awful rush, the internecine struggle in which seats had to be found. Seats, I fancy, are regularly found, even by the most tardy, but it always appears that every British father and every British husband is actuated at these stormy moments by a conviction that unless he proves himself a very Hercules he and his daughters and his wife will be left desolate in Paris. Mr. Brown was quite Herculean, carrying two bags and a hat-box in his own hands, besides the cloaks, the coats, the rugs, the sticks, and the umbrellas. But when he had got himself and his wife well seated, with their faces to the engine, with a corner seat for her,—there was Mr. Jones immediately opposite to her. Mr. Jones, as soon as he perceived the inconvenience of his position, made a scramble for another place, but he was too late. In that contiguity the journey as far as Calais had to be made. She, poor woman, never once took up her veil. There he sat, without closing an eye, stiff as a ramrod, sometimes showing by little uneasy gestures that the trouble at his neck was still there, but never speaking a word, and hardly moving a limb.

Crossing from Calais to Dover the lady was, of course, separated from her victim. The passage was very bad, and she more than once reminded her husband how well it would have been with them now had they pursued their journey as she had intended,—as though they had been detained in Paris by his fault! Mr. Jones, as he laid himself down on his back, gave himself up to wondering whether any man before him had ever been made subject to such absolute injustice. Now and again he put his hand up to his own beard, and began to doubt whether it could have been moved, as it must have been moved, without waking him. What if chloroform had been used? Many such suspicions crossed his mind during the misery of that passage.

They were again together in the same railway carriage from Dover to London. They had now got used to the close neighbourhood, and knew how to endure each the presence of the other. But as yet Mr. Jones had never seen the lady's face. He longed to know what were the features of the woman who had been so blind—if indeed that story were true. Or if it were not true, of what like was the woman who would dare in the middle of the night to play such a trick as that? But still she kept her veil close over her face.

From Cannon Street the Browns took their departure in a cab for the Liverpool Street Station, whence they would be conveyed by the Eastern Counties Railway to Stratford. Now at any rate their troubles were over. They would be in ample time, not only for Christmas Day church, but for Christmas Day breakfast. "It will be just the same as getting in there last night," said Mr. Brown, as he walked across the platform to place his wife in the carriage for Stratford. She entered it the first, and as she did so there she saw Mr. Jones seated in the corner! Hitherto she had borne his presence well, but now she could not restrain herself from a little start and a little scream. He bowed his head very slightly, as though acknowledging the compliment, and then down she dropped her veil. When they arrived at Stratford, the journey being over in a quarter of an hour, Jones was out of the carriage even before the Browns.

"There is Uncle John's carriage," said Mrs. Brown, thinking that now, at any rate, she would be able to free herself from the presence of this terrible stranger. No doubt he was a handsome man to look at, but on no face so sternly hostile had she ever before fixed her eyes.

She did not, perhaps, reflect that the owner of no other face had ever been so deeply injured by herself.

Chapter V

Mrs. Brown At Thompson Hall.

"PLEASE, SIR, we were to ask for Mr. Jones," said the servant, putting his head into the carriage after both Mr. and Mrs. Brown had seated themselves.

"Mr. Jones!" exclaimed the husband.

"Why ask for Mr. Jones?" demanded the wife. The servant was about to tender some explanation when Mr. Jones stepped up and said that he was Mr. Jones. "We are going to Thompson Hall," said the lady with great vigour.

"So am I," said Mr. Jones, with much dignity. It was, however, arranged that he should sit with the coachman, as there was a rumble behind for the other servant. The luggage was put into a cart, and away all went for Thompson Hall.

"What do you think about it, Mary?" whispered Mr. Brown, after a pause. He was evidently awe-struck by the horror of the occasion.

"I cannot make it out at all. What do you think?"

"I don't know what to think. Jones going to Thompson Hall?"

"He's a very good-looking young man," said Mrs. Brown.

"Well;—that's as people think. A stiff, stuck-up fellow, I should say. Up to this moment he has never forgiven you for what you did to him."

"Would you have forgiven his wife, Charles, if she'd done it to you?"

"He hasn't got a wife,—yet."

"How do you know?"

"He is coming home now to be married," said Mr. Brown. "He expects to meet the young lady this very Christmas Day. He told me so. That was one of the reasons why he was so angry at being stopped by what you did last night."

"I suppose he knows Uncle John, or he wouldn't be going to the Hall," said Mrs. Brown.

"I can't make it out," said Mr. Brown, shaking his head.

"He looks quite like a gentleman," said Mrs. Brown, "though he has been so stiff. Jones! Barnaby Jones! You're sure it was Barnaby?"

"That was the name on the card."

"Not Burnaby?" asked Mrs. Brown.

"It was Barnaby Jones on the card,—just the same as 'Barnaby Rudge,' and as for looking like a gentleman, I'm by no means quite so sure. A gentleman takes an apology when it's offered."

"Perhaps, my dear, that depends on the condition of his throat. If you had had a mustard plaster on all night, you might not have liked it. But here we are at Thompson Hall at last."

Thompson Hall was an old brick mansion, standing within a huge iron gate, with a gravel sweep before it. It had stood there before Stratford was a town, or even a suburb, and had then been known by the name of Bow Place. But it had been in the hands of the present family for the last thirty years, and was now known far and wide as Thompson Hall,—a comfortable, roomy, old-fashioned place, perhaps a little dark and dull to look at, but much more substantially built than most of our modern villas. Mrs. Brown jumped with alacrity from the carriage, and with a quick step entered the home of her forefathers. Her husband followed her more leisurely, but he, too, felt that he was at home at Thompson Hall. Then Mr. Jones walked in also;—but he looked as though he were not at all at home. It was still very early, and no one of the family was as yet down. In these circumstances it was almost necessary that something should be said to Mr. Jones.

"Do you know Mr. Thompson?" asked Mr. Brown.

"I never had the pleasure of seeing him,—as yet," answered Mr. Jones, very stiffly.

"Oh,—I didn't know;—because you said you were coming here."

"And I have come here. Are you friends of Mr. Thompson?"

"Oh, dear, yes," said Mrs. Brown. "I was a Thompson myself before I married."

"Oh,—indeed!" said Mr. Jones. "How very odd,—very odd, indeed."

During this time the luggage was being brought into the house, and two old family servants were offering them assistance. Would the new comers like to go up to their bedrooms? Then the housekeeper, Mrs. Green, intimated with a wink that Miss Jane would, she was sure, be down quite immediately. The present moment, however, was still very unpleasant. The lady probably had made her guess as to the mystery; but the two gentlemen were still altogether in the dark. Mrs. Brown had no doubt declared her parentage, but Mr. Jones, with such a multitude of strange facts crowding on his mind, had been slow to understand her. Being somewhat suspicious by nature, he was beginning to think whether possibly the mustard had been put by this lady on his throat with some reference to his connexion with Thompson Hall. Could it be that she, for some reason of her own, had wished to prevent his coming, and had contrived this untoward stratagem out of her brain? or had she wished to make him ridiculous to the Thompson family,—to whom, as a family, he was at present unknown? It was becoming more and more improbable to him that the whole thing should have been an accident. When, after the first horrid torments of that morning in which he had in his agony invoked the assistance of the night-porter, he had begun to reflect on his situation, he had determined that it would be better that nothing further should be said about it. What would life be worth to him if he were to be known wherever he went as the man who had been mustard-plastered in the middle of the night by a strange lady? The worst of a practical joke is that the remembrance of the absurd condition sticks so long to the sufferer! At the hotel that night-porter, who had possessed himself of the handkerchief and had read the name, and had connected that name with the occupant of 333 whom he had found wandering about the house with some strange purpose, had not permitted the thing to sleep. The porter had pressed the matter home against the Browns, and had produced the interview which has been recorded. But during the whole of that day Mr. Jones had been resolving that he would never again either think of the Browns or speak of them. A great injury had been done to him,—a most outrageous injustice;—but it was a thing which had to be endured. A horrid woman had come across him like a nightmare. All he could do was to endeavour to forget the terrible visitation. Such had been his resolve,—in making which he had passed that long day in Paris. And now the Browns had stuck to him from the moment of his leaving his room! he had been forced to travel with them, but had travelled with them as a stranger. He had tried to comfort himself with the reflection that at every fresh stage he would shake them off. In one railway after another the vicinity had been bad,—but still they were strangers. Now he found himself in the same house with them,—where of course the story would be told. Had not the thing been done on purpose that the story might be told there at Thompson Hall?

Mrs. Brown had acceded to the proposition of the housekeeper, and was about to be taken to her room when there was heard a sound of footsteps along the passage above and on the stairs, and a young lady came bounding on to the scene. "You have all of you come a quarter of an hour earlier than we thought possible," said the young lady. "I did so mean to be up to receive you!" With that she passed her sister on the stairs,—for the young lady was Miss Jane Thompson, sister to our Mrs. Brown,—and hurried down into the hall. Here Mr. Brown, who had ever been on affectionate terms with his sister-in-law, put himself forward to receive her embraces; but she, apparently not noticing him in her ardour, rushed on and threw herself on to the breast of the other gentleman. "This is my Charles," she said. "Oh, Charles, I thought you never would be here."

Mr. Charles Burnaby Jones, for such was his name since he had inherited the Jones property in Pembrokeshire, received into his arms the ardent girl of his heart with all that love and devotion to which she was entitled, but could not do so without some external shrinking from her embrace. "Oh, Charles, what is it?" she said.

"Nothing, dearest—only—only—." Then he looked piteously up into Mrs. Brown's face, as though imploring her not to tell the story.

"Perhaps, Jane, you had better introduce us," said Mrs. Brown.

"Introduce you! I thought you had been travelling together, and staying at the same hotel—and all that."

"So we have; but people may be in the same hotel without knowing each other. And we have travelled all the way home with Mr. Jones without in the least knowing who he was."

"How very odd! Do you mean you have never spoken?"

"Not a word," said Mrs. Brown.

"I do so hope you'll love each other," said Jane.

"It shan't be my fault if we don't," said Mrs. Brown.

"I'm sure it shan't be mine," said Mr. Brown, tendering his hand to the other gentleman. The various feelings of the moment were too much for Mr. Jones, and he could not respond quite as he should have done. But as he was taken upstairs to his room he determined that he would make the best of it.

The owner of the house was old Uncle John. He was a bachelor, and with him lived various members of the family. There was the great Thompson of them all, Cousin Robert, who was now member of Parliament for the Essex Flats, and young John, as a certain enterprising Thompson of the age of forty was usually called, and then there was old Aunt Bess, and among other young branches there was Miss Jane Thompson, who was now engaged to marry Mr. Charles Burnaby Jones. As it happened, no other member of the family had as yet seen Mr. Burnaby Jones, and he, being by nature of a retiring disposition, felt himself to be ill at ease when he came into the breakfast parlour among all the Thompsons. He was known to be a gentleman of good family and ample means, and all the Thompsons had approved of the match, but during the first Christmas breakfast he did not seem to accept his condition jovially. His own Jane sat beside him, but then on the other side sat Mrs. Brown. She assumed an immediate intimacy,—as women know how to do on such occasions,—being determined from the very first to regard her sister's husband as a brother; but he still feared her. She was still to him the woman who had come to him in the dead of night with that horrid mixture,—and had then left him.

"It was so odd that both of you should have been detained on the very same day," said Jane.

"Yes, it was odd," said Mrs. Brown, with a smile looking round upon her neighbour.

"It was abominably bad weather you know," said Brown.

"But you were both so determined to come," said the old gentleman. "When we got the two telegrams at the same moment, we were sure that there had been some agreement between you."

"Not exactly an agreement," said Mrs. Brown; whereupon Mr. Jones looked as grim as death.

"I'm sure there is something more than we understand yet," said the Member of Parliament.

Then they all went to church, as a united family ought to do on Christmas Day, and came home to a fine old English early dinner at three o'clock,—a sirloin of beef a foot-and-a-half broad, a turkey as big as an ostrich, a plum-pudding bigger than the turkey, and two or three dozen mince-pies. "That's a very large bit of beef," said Mr. Jones, who had not lived much in England latterly. "It won't look so large," said the old gentleman, "when all our friends downstairs have had their say to it." "A plum-pudding on Christmas Day can't be too big," he said again, "if the cook will but take time enough over it. I never knew a bit go to waste yet."

By this time there had been some explanation as to past events between the two sisters. Mrs. Brown had indeed told Jane all about it, how ill her husband had been, how she had been forced to go down and look for the mustard, and then what she had done with the mustard. "I don't think they are a bit alike you know, Mary, if you mean that," said Jane.

"Well, no; perhaps not quite alike. I only saw his beard, you know. No doubt it was stupid, but I did it."

"Why didn't you take it off again?" asked the sister.

"Oh, Jane, if you'd only think of it! Could you?" Then of course all that occurred was explained, how they had been stopped on their journey, how Brown had made the best apology in his power, and how Jones had travelled with them and had never spoken a word. The gentleman had only taken his new name a week since, but of course had had his new card printed immediately. "I'm sure I should have thought of it if they hadn't made a mistake with the first name. Charles said it was like Barnaby Rudge."

"Not at all like Barnaby Rudge," said Jane; "Charles Burnaby Jones is a very good name."

"Very good indeed,—and I'm sure that after a little bit he won't be at all the worse for the accident."

Before dinner the secret had been told no further, but still there had crept about among the Thompsons, and, indeed, downstairs also, among the retainers, a feeling that there was a secret. The old housekeeper was sure that Miss Mary, as she still called Mrs. Brown, had something to tell if she could only be induced to tell it, and that this something had reference to Mr. Jones' personal comfort. The head of the family, who was a sharp old gentleman, felt this also, and the member of Parliament, who had an idea that he specially should never be kept in the dark, was almost angry. Mr. Jones, suffering from some kindred feeling throughout the dinner, remained silent and unhappy. When two or three toasts had been drunk,—the Queen's health, the old gentleman's health, the young couple's health, Brown's health, and the general health of all the Thompsons, then tongues were loosened and a question was asked, "I know that there has been something doing in Paris between these young people that we haven't heard as yet," said the uncle. Then Mrs. Brown laughed, and Jane, laughing too, gave Mr. Jones to understand that she at any rate knew all about it.

"If there is a mystery I hope it will be told at once," said the member of Parliament, angrily.

"Come, Brown, what is it?" asked another male cousin.

"Well, there was an accident. I'd rather Jones should tell," said he.

Jones' brow became blacker than thunder, but he did not say a word. "You mustn't be angry with Mary," Jane whispered into her lover's ear.

"Come, Mary, you never were slow at talking," said the uncle.

"I do hate this kind of thing," said the member of Parliament.

"I will tell it all," said Mrs. Brown, very nearly in tears, or else pretending to be very nearly in tears. "I know I was very wrong, and I do beg his pardon, and if he won't say that he forgives me I never shall be happy again." Then she clasped her hands, and turning round, looked him piteously in the face.

"Oh yes; I do forgive you," said Mr. Jones.

"My brother," said she, throwing her arms round him and kissing him. He recoiled from the embrace, but I think that he attempted to return the kiss. "And now I will tell the whole story," said Mrs. Brown. And she told it, acknowledging her fault with true contrition, and swearing that she would atone for it by life-long sisterly devotion.

"And you mustard-plastered the wrong man!" said the old gentleman, almost rolling off his chair with delight.

"I did," said Mrs. Brown, sobbing, "and I think that no woman ever suffered as I suffered."

"And Jones wouldn't let you leave the hotel?"

"It was the handkerchief stopped us," said Brown.

"If it had turned out to be anybody else," said the member of Parliament, "the results might have been most serious,—not to say discreditable."

"That's nonsense, Robert," said Mrs. Brown, who was disposed to resent the use of so severe a word, even from the legislator cousin.

"In a strange gentleman's bedroom!" he continued. "It only shows that what I have always said is quite true. You should never go to bed in a strange house without locking your door."

Nevertheless it was a very jovial meeting, and before the evening was over Mr. Jones was happy, and had been brought to acknowledge that the mustard-plaster would probably not do him any permanent injury.

Why Frau Frohmann Raised Her Prices

Originally appeared in *Good Words*, February–May 1877. Reprinted in *Why Frau Frohmann Raised Her Prices and Other Stories* (1882). In 1881 Trollope wrote to his published, Isbister: 'The Frau Frohmann is a good story, though I say it who ought not.'

Chapter I

The Brunnenthal Peacock.

IF EVER there was a Tory upon earth, the Frau Frohmann was a Tory; for I hold that landed possessions, gentle blood, a gray-haired butler behind one's chair, and adherence to the Church of England, are not necessarily the distinguishing marks of Toryism. The Frau Frohmann was a woman who loved power, but who loved to use it for the benefit of those around her,—or at any rate to think that she so used it. She believed in the principles of despotism and paternal government,—but always on the understanding that she was to be the despot. In her heart of hearts she disliked education, thinking that it unfitted the minds of her humbler brethren for the duties of their lives. She hated, indeed, all changes,—changes in costume, changes in hours, changes in cookery, and changes in furniture; but of all changes she perhaps hated changes in prices the most. Gradually there had come over her a melancholy conviction that the world cannot go on altogether unaltered. There was, she felt, a fate in things,—a necessity which, in some dark way within her own mind, she connected with the fall of Adam and the general imperfection of humanity,—which demanded changes, but they were always changes for the worse; and therefore, though to those around her she was mostly silent on this matter, she was afflicted by a general idea that the world was going on towards ruin. That all things throve with herself was not sufficient for her comfort; for, being a good woman with a large heart, she was anxious for the welfare not only of herself and of her children, but for that of all who might come after her, at any rate in her own locality. Thus, when she found that there was a tendency to dine at one instead of twelve, to wear the same clothes on week days as on Sundays, to desire easy chairs, and linen that should be bleached absolutely white, thoughts as to the failing condition of the world would get the better of her and make her melancholy.

These traits are perhaps the evidences of the weakness of Toryism;—but then Frau Frohmann also had all its strength. She was thoroughly pervaded by a determination that, in as far as in her lay, all that had aught to do with herself should be "well-to-do" in the world. It was a grand ambition in her mind that every creature connected with her establishment, from the oldest and most time-honoured guest down to the last stray cat that had taken refuge under her roof, should always have enough to eat. Hunger, unsatisfied hunger, disagreeable hunger, on the part of any dependent of hers, would have been a reproach to her. Her own eating troubled her little or not at all, but the cooking of the establishment generally was a great care to her mind. In bargaining she was perhaps hard, but hard only in getting what she believed to be her own right. Aristides was not more just. Of bonds, written bonds, her neighbours knew not much; but her word for twenty miles round was as good as any bond. And though she was perhaps a little apt to domineer in her bargains,—to expect that she should fix the prices and to resent opposition,—it was only to the strong that she was tyrannical. The poor sick widow and the little orphan could generally deal with her at their own rates; on which occasions she would endeavour to hide her dealings from her own people, and would give injunctions to the favoured ones that the details of the transaction should not be made public. And then, though the Frau was, I regret to say, no better than a Papist, she was a thoroughly religious woman, believing in real truth what she professed to believe, and complying, as far as she knew how, with the ordinances of her creed.

Therefore I say that if ever there was a Tory, the Frau Frohmann was one.

And now it will be well that the reader should see the residence of the Frau, and learn something of her condition in life. In one of the districts of the Tyrol, lying some miles south of Innsbruck, between that town and Brixen, there is a valley called the Brunnenthal, a most charming spot, in which all the delights of scenery may be found without the necessity of climbing up heart-rending mountains, or sitting in oily steamboats, or paying for greedy guides, or riding upon ill-conditioned ponies. In this valley Frau Frohmann kept an hotel called the Peacock, which, however, though it was known as an inn, and was called by that name, could hardly be regarded as a house of common public entertainment. Its purpose was to afford recreation and comfort to a certain class of customers during the summer months,—persons well enough to do in the world to escape from their town work and their town residences for a short holiday, and desirous during that time of enjoying picturesque scenery, good living, moderate comfort, and some amount of society. Such institutions have now become so common that there is hardly any one who has not visited or at any rate seen such a place. They are to be found in every country in Europe, and are very common in America. Our own Scotland is full of them. But when the Peacock was first opened in Brunnenthal they were not so general.

Of the husband of the Frau there are not many records in the neighbourhood. The widow has been a widow for the last twenty years at least, and her children,—for she has a son and daughter,—have no vivid memories of their father. The house and everything in it, and the adjacent farm, and the right of cutting timber in the forests, and the neighbouring quarry, are all the undoubted property of the Frau, who has a reputation for great wealth. Though her son is perhaps nearly thirty, and is very diligent in the affairs of the establishment, he has no real authority. He is only, as it were, the out-of-doors right hand of his mother, as his sister, who is perhaps five years younger, is an in-doors right hand. But they are only hands. The brain, the intelligence, the mind, the will by which the Brunnenthal Peacock is conducted and managed, come all from the Frau Frohmann herself. To this day she can hardly endure a suggestion either from Peter her son or from her daughter Amalia, who is known among her friends as Malchen, but is called "the fraulein" by the Brunnenthal world at large. A suggestion as to the purchase of things new in their nature she will not stand at all, though she is liberal enough in maintaining the appurtenances of the house generally.

But the Peacock is more than a house. It is almost a village; and yet every shed, cottage, or barn at or near the place forms a part of the Frau's establishment. The centre or main building is a large ordinary house of three stories,—to the lower of which there is an ascent by some half-dozen stone steps,—covered with red tiles, and with gable ends crowded with innumerable windows. The ground-floor is devoted to kitchens, offices, the Frau's own uses, and the needs of the servants. On the first-story are the two living rooms of the guests, the greater and by far the more important being devoted to eating and drinking. Here, at certain hours, are collected all the forces of the establishment,—and especially at one o'clock, when, with many ringing of bells and great struggles in the culinary department, the dinner is served. For to the adoption of this hour has the Frau at last been driven by the increasing infirmities of the world around her. The scenery of the locality is lovely; the air is considered to be peculiarly health-compelling; the gossipings during the untrammelled idleness of the day are very grateful to those whose lives are generally laborious; the love-makings are frequent, and no doubt sweet; skittles and bowls and draughts and dominoes have their devotees; and the smoking of many pipes fills up the vacant hours of the men.

But, at the Brunnenthal, dinner is the great glory of the day. It would be vain for any æsthetical guest, who might conceive himself to be superior to the allurements of the table, to make little of the Frau's dinner. Such a one had better seek other quarters for his summer's holiday. At the Brunnenthal Peacock it is necessary that you should believe in the paramount importance of dinner. Not to come to it at the appointed time would create, first marvel, in the Frau's mind, then pity,—as to the state of your health,—and at last hot anger should it be found that such neglect arose from contempt. What muse will assist me to describe these dinners in a few words? They were commenced of course by soup,—real soup, not barley broth with a strong prevalence of the barley. Then would follow the boiled meats, from which the soup was supposed to have been made,—but such boiled meat, so good, that the supposition must have contained a falsehood. With this there would be always potatoes and pickled cabbages and various relishes. Then there would be two other kinds of meat, generally with accompaniment of stewed fruit; after that fish,—trout from the neighbouring stream, for the preservation of which great tanks had been made. Vegetables with unknown sauces would follow,—and then would come the roast, which consisted always of poultry, and was accompanied of course by salad. But it was after this that were made the efforts on which the Frau's fame most depended. The puddings, I think, were the subject of her greatest struggles and most complete success. Two puddings daily were, by the rules of the house, required to be eaten; not two puddings brought together so that you might choose with careless haste either one or the other; but two separate courses of puddings, with an interval between for appreciation, for thought, and for digestion. Either one or both can, no doubt, be declined. No absolute punishment,—such as notice to leave the house,—follows such abstention. But the Frau is displeased, and when dressed in her best on Sundays does not smile on those who abstain. After the puddings there is dessert, and there are little cakes to nibble if you will. They are nibbled very freely. But the heat of the battle is over with the second pudding.

They have a great fame, these banquets; so that ladies and gentlemen from Innsbruck have themselves driven out here to enjoy them. The distance each way is from two to three hours, so that a pleasant holiday is made by a visit to the Frau's establishment. There is a ramble up to the waterfall and a smoking of pipes among the rocks, and pleasant opportunities for secret whispers among young people;—but the Frau would not be well pleased if it were presumed that the great inducement for the visit were not to be found in the dinner which she provides. In this way, though the guests at the house may not exceed perhaps thirty in number, it will sometimes be the case that nearly twice as many are seated at the board. That the Frau has an eye to profit cannot be doubted. Fond of money she is certainly;—fond of prosperity generally. But, judging merely from what comes beneath his eye, the observer will be led to suppose that her sole ambition on these occasions is to see the food which she has provided devoured by her guests. A weak stomach, a halting appetite, conscientious scruples as to the over-enjoyment of victuals, restraint in reference to subsequent excesses or subsequent eatings,—all these things are a scandal to her. If you can't, or won't, or don't eat your dinner when you get it, you ought not to go to the Brunnenthal Peacock.

This banqueting-hall, or Speise-Saal, occupies a great part of the first-floor; but here also is the drawing-room, or reading-room, as it is called, having over the door "Lese-Saal" painted, so that its purpose may not be doubted. But the reading-room is not much, and the guests generally spend their time chiefly out of doors or in their bedrooms when they are not banqueting. There are two other banquets, breakfast and supper, which need not be specially described;—but of the latter it may be said that it is a curtailed dinner, having limited courses of hot meat, and only one pudding.

On this floor there is a bedroom or two, and a nest of others above; but the accommodation is chiefly afforded in other buildings, of which the one opposite is longer, though not so high, as the central house; and there is another, a little down the road, near the mill, and another as far up the stream, where the baths have been built,—an innovation to which Frau Frohmann did not lend herself without much inward suffering. And there are huge barns and many stables; for the Frau keeps a posting establishment, and a diligence passes the door three times each way in the course of the day and night, and the horses are changed at the Peacock;—or it was so, at any rate, in the days of which I am speaking, not very long ago. And there is the blacksmith's forge, and the great carpenter's shed, in which not only are the carts and carriages mended, but very much of the house furniture is made.

And there is the mill, as has been said before, in which the corn is ground, and three or four cottages for married men, and a pretty little chapel, built by the Frau herself, in which mass is performed by her favourite priest once a month,—for the parish chapel is nearly three miles distant if you walk by the mountain path, but is fully five if you have yourself carried round by the coach road. It must, I think, be many years since the Frau can have walked there, for she is a dame of portly dimensions.

Whether the buildings are in themselves picturesque I will not pretend to say. I doubt whether there has been an attempt that way in regard to any one except the chapel. But chance has so grouped them, and nature has so surrounded them, that you can hardly find anywhere a prettier spot. Behind the house, so as to leave only space for a little meadow which is always as green as irrigation can make it, a hill rises, not high enough to be called a mountain, which is pine-clad from the foot to the summit. In front and around the ground is broken, but immediately before the door there is a way up to a lateral valley, down which comes a nameless stream which, just below the house, makes its way into the Ivil, the little river which runs from the mountain to the inn, taking its course through that meadow which lies between the hill and the house. It is here, a quarter of a mile perhaps up this little stream, at a spot which is hidden by many turnings from the road, that visitors come upon the waterfall,—the waterfall which at Innsbruck is so often made to be the excuse of these outings which are in truth performed in quest of Frau Frohmann's dinners. Below the Peacock, where the mill is placed, the valley is closely confined, as the sombre pine-forests rise abruptly on each side; and here, or very little lower, is that gloomy or ghost-like pass through the rocks, which is called the Höllenthor; a name which I will not translate. But it is a narrow ravine, very dark in dark weather, and at night as black as pitch. Among the superstitious people of the valley the spot is regarded with the awe which belonged to it in past ages. To visitors of the present day it is simply picturesque and sublime. Above the house the valley spreads itself, rising, however, rapidly; and here modern engineering has carried the road in various curves and turns round knolls of hills and spurs of mountains, till the traveller as he ascends hardly knows which way he is going. From one or two points among these curves the view down upon the Peacock with its various appendages, with its dark-red roofs, and many windows glittering in the sun, is so charming, that the tourist is almost led to think that they must all have been placed as they are with a view to effect.

The Frau herself is what used to be called a personable woman. To say that she is handsome would hardly convey a proper idea. Let the reader suppose a woman of about fifty, very tall and of large dimensions. It would be unjust to call her fat, because though very large she is still symmetrical. When she is dressed in her full Tyrolese costume,—which is always the case at a certain hour on Sunday, and on other stated and by no means unfrequent days as to which I was never quite able to learn the exact rule,—when she is so dressed her arms are bare down from her shoulders, and such arms I never saw on any human being. Her back is very broad and her bust expansive. But her head stands erect upon it as the head of some old Juno, and in all her motions,—though I doubt whether she could climb by the mountain path to her parish church,—she displays a certain stately alertness which forbids one to call her fat. Her smile,—when she really means to smile and to show thereby her good-will and to be gracious,—is as sweet as Hebe's. Then it is that you see that in her prime she must in truth have been a lovely woman. There is at these moments a kindness in her eyes and a playfulness about her mouth which is apt to make you think that you can do what you like with the Frau. Who has not at times been charmed by the frolic playfulness of the tiger? Not that Frau Frohmann has aught of the tiger in her nature but its power. But the power is all there, and not unfrequently the signs of power. If she be thwarted, contradicted, counselled by unauthorised counsellors,—above all if she be censured,—then the signs of power are shown. Then the Frau does not smile. At such times she is wont to speak her mind very plainly, and to make those who hear her understand that, within the precincts and purlieus of the Brunnenthal Peacock, she is an irresponsible despot. There have been guests there rash enough to find some trifling faults with the comforts provided for them,—whose beds perhaps have been too hard, or their towels too limited, or perhaps their hours not agreeably arranged for them. Few, however, have ever done so twice, and they who have so sinned,—and have then been told that the next diligence would take them quickly to Innsbruck if they were discontented,—have rarely stuck to their complaints and gone. The comforts of the house, and the prices charged, and the general charms of the place have generally prevailed,—so that the complainants, sometimes with spoken apologies, have in most cases sought permission to remain. In late years the Frau's certainty of victory has created a feeling that nothing is to be said against the arrangements of the Peacock. A displeased guest can exercise his displeasure best by taking himself away in silence.

The Frau of late years has had two counsellors; for though she is but ill inclined to admit advice from those who have received no authority to give it, she is not therefore so self-confident as to feel that she can live and thrive without listening to the wisdom of others. And those two counsellors may be regarded as representing—the first or elder her conscience, and the second and younger her worldly prudence. And in the matter of her conscience very much more is concerned than simple honesty. It is not against cheating or extortion that her counsellor is sharp to her; but rather in regard to those innovations which he and she think to be prejudicial to the manner and life of Brunnenthal, of Innsbruck, of the Tyrol, of the Austrian empire generally, and, indeed, of the world at large. To be as her father had been before her,—for her father, too, had kept the Peacock; to let life be cheap and simple, but yet very plentiful as it had been in his days, this was the counsel given by Father Conolin the old priest, who always spent two nights in each month at the establishment, and was not unfrequently to be seen there on other occasions. He had been opposed to many things which had been effected,—that alteration of the hour of dinner, the erection of the bath-house, the changing of plates at each course, and especially certain notifications and advertisements by which foreigners may have been induced to come to the Brunnenthal. The kaplan, or chaplain, as he was called, was particularly averse to strangers, seeming to think that the advantages of the place should be reserved, if not altogether for the Tyrolese, at any rate for the Germans of Southern Germany, and was probably of opinion that no real good could be obtained by harbouring Lutherans. But, of late, English also had come, to whom, though he was personally very courteous, he was much averse in his heart of hearts. Such had ever been the tendency of his advice, and it had always been received with willing, nay, with loving ears. But the fate of the kaplan had been as is the fate of all such counsellors. Let the toryism of the Tory be ever so strong, it is his destiny to carry out the purposes of his opponents. So it had been, and was, with the Frau. Though she was always in spirit antagonistic to the other counsellor, it was the other counsellor who prevailed with her.

At Innsbruck for many years there had lived a lawyer, or rather a family of lawyers, men always of good repute and moderate means, named Schlessen; and in their hands had been reposed by the Frau that confidence as to business matters which almost every one in business must have in some lawyer. The first Schlessen whom the Frau had known in her youth, and who was then a very old man, had been almost as Conservative as the priest. Then had come his son, who had been less so, but still lived and died without much either of the light of progress or contamination of revolutionary ideas from the outer world. But about three years before the date of our tale he also had passed away, and now young Fritz Schlessen sat in the chair of his forefathers. It was the opinion of Innsbruck generally that the young lawyer was certainly equal, probably superior, in attainments and intellect to any of his predecessors. He had learned his business both at Munich and Vienna, and though he was only twenty-six when he was left to manage his clients himself, most of them adhered to him. Among others so did our Frau, and this she did knowing the nature of the man and of the counsel she might expect to receive from him. For though she loved the priest, and loved her old ways, and loved to be told that she could live and thrive on the rules by which her father had lived and thriven before her,—still, there was always present to her mind the fact that she was engaged in trade, and that the first object of a tradesman must be to make money. No shoemaker can set himself to work to make shoes having as his first intention an ambition to make the feet of his customers comfortable. That may come second, and to him, as a conscientious man, may be essentially necessary. But he sets himself to work to make shoes in order that he may earn a living. That law,—almost of nature we may say,—had become so recognised by the Frau that she felt that it must be followed, even in spite of the priest if need were, and that, in order that it might be followed, it would be well that she should listen to the advice of Herr Schlessen. She heard, therefore, all that her kaplan would say to her with gracious smiles, and something of what her lawyer would say to her, not always very graciously; but in the long-run she would take her lawyer's advice.

It will have to be told in a following chapter how it was that Fritz Schlessen had a preponderating influence in the Brunnenthal, arising from other causes than his professional soundness and general prudence. It may, however, be as well to explain here that Peter Frohmann the son sided always with the priest, and attached himself altogether to the conservative interest. But he, though he was honest, diligent, and dutiful to his mother, was lumpy, uncouth, and slow both of speech and action. He understood the cutting of timber and the making of hay,—something perhaps of the care of horses and of the nourishment of pigs; but in money matters he was not efficient. Amalia, or Malchen, the daughter, who was four or five years her brother's junior, was much brighter, and she was strong on the reforming side. British money was to her thinking as good as Austrian, or even Tyrolese. To thrive even better than her forefathers had thriven seemed to her to be desirable. She therefore, though by her brightness and feminine ways she was very dear to the priest, was generally opposed to him in the family conclaves. It was chiefly in consequence of her persistency that the table napkins at the Peacock were now changed twice a week.

Chapter II

The Beginning Of Troubles.

Of late days, and up to the time of which we are speaking, the chief contest between the Frau, with the kaplan and Peter on one side, and Malchen with Fritz Schlessen on the other, was on that most important question whether the whole rate of charges should not be raised at the establishment. The prices had been raised, no doubt, within the last twenty years, or the Frau could not have kept her house open;—but this had been done indirectly. That the matter may not be complicated for our readers, we will assume that all charges are made at the Peacock in zwansigers and kreutzers, and that the zwansiger, containing twenty kreutzers, is worth eightpence of English money. Now it must be understood that the guests at the Peacock were entertained at the rate of six zwansigers, or four shillings, a day, and that this included everything necessary,—a bed, breakfast, dinner, a cup of coffee after dinner, supper, as much fresh milk as anybody chose to drink when the cows were milked, and the use of everything in and about the establishment. Guests who required wine or beer, of course, were charged for what they had. Those who were rich enough to be taken about in carriages paid so much per job,—each separate jaunt having been inserted in a tariff. No doubt there were other possible and probable extras; but an ordinary guest might live for his six zwansigers a day;—and the bulk of them did so live, with the addition of whatever allowance of beer each might think appropriate. From time to time a little had been added to the cost of luxuries. Wine had become dearer, and perhaps the carriages. A bath was an addition to the bill, and certain larger and more commodious rooms were supposed to be entitled to an extra zwansiger per week;—but the main charge had always remained fixed. In the time of the Frau's father guests had been entertained at, let us say, four shillings a head, and guests were so entertained now. All the world,—at any rate all the Tyrolese world south of Innsbruck,—knew that six zwansigers was the charge in the Brunnenthal. It would be like adding a new difficulty to the path of life to make a change. The Frau had always held her head high,—had never been ashamed of looking her neighbour in the face, but when she was advised to rush at once up to seven zwansigers and a half (or five shillings a day), she felt that, should she do so, she would be overwhelmed with shame. Would not her customers then have cause of complaint? Would not they have such cause that they would in truth desert her? Did she not know that Herr Weiss, the magistrate from Brixen, with his wife, and his wife's sister, and the children, who came yearly to the Peacock, could not afford to bring his family at this increased rate of expense? And the Fraulein Tendel with her sister would never come from Innsbruck if such an announcement was made to her. It was the pride of this woman's heart to give all that was necessary for good living, to those who would come and submit themselves to her, for four shillings a day. Among the "extras" she could endure some alteration. She did not like extras, and if people would have luxuries they must be made to pay for them. But the Peacock had always been kept open for six zwansigers, and though Fritz Schlessen was very eloquent, she would not give way to him.

Fritz Schlessen simply told her that the good things which she provided for her guests cost at present more than six zwansigers, and could not therefore be sold by her at that price without a loss. She was rich, Fritz remarked, shrugging his shoulders, and having amassed property could if she pleased dispose of it gradually by entertaining her guests at a loss to herself;—only let her know what she was doing. That might be charity, might be generosity, might be friendliness; but it was not trade. Everything else in the world had become dearer, and therefore living at the Peacock should be dearer. As to the Weisses and the Tendels, no doubt they might be shocked, and perhaps hindered from coming. But their places would surely be filled by others. Was not the house always full from the 1st of June till the end of September? Were not strangers refused admittance week after week from want of accommodation? If the new prices were found to be too high for the Tyrolese and Bavarians, they would not offend the Germans from the Rhine, or the Belgians, or the English. Was it not plain to every one that people now came from greater distances than heretofore?

These were the arguments which Herr Schlessen used; and, though they were very disagreeable, they were not easily answered. The Frau repudiated altogether the idea of keeping open her house on other than true trade principles. When the young lawyer talked to her about generosity she waxed angry, and accused him of laughing at her. "Dearest Frau Frohmann," he said, "it is so necessary you should know the truth! Of course you intend to make a profit;—but if you cannot do so at your present prices, and yet will not raise them, at any rate understand what it is that you are doing." Now the last year had been a bad year, and she knew that she had not increased her store. This all took place in the month of April, when a proposition was being made as to the prices for the coming season. The lawyer had suggested that a circular should be issued, giving notice of an altered tariff.

Malchen was clearly in favour of the new idea. She could not see that the Weisses and Tendels, and other neighbours, should be entertained at a manifest loss; and, indeed, she had prepossessions in favour of foreigners, especially of the English, which, when expressed, brought down upon her head sundry hard words from her mother, who called her a "pert hussey," and implied that if Fritz Schlessen wanted to pull the house down she, Malchen, would be willing that it should be done. "Better do that, mother, than keep the roof on at a loss," said Malchen; who upon that was turned at once out of the little inner room in which the conference was being held.

Peter, who was present on the occasion, was decidedly opposed to all innovations, partly because his conservative nature so prompted him, and partly because he did not regard Herr Schlessen with a friendship so warm as that entertained by his sister. He was, perhaps, a little jealous of the lawyer. And then he had an idea that as things were prosperous to the eye, they would certainly come right at last. The fortunes of the house had been made at the rate of six zwansigers a day, and there was, he thought, no wisdom more clear than that of adhering to a line of conduct which had proved itself to be advantageous.

The kaplan was clear against any change of prices; but then he burdened his advice on the question with a suggestion which was peculiarly disagreeable to the Frau. He acknowledged the truth of much that the lawyer had said. It appeared to him that the good things provided could not in truth be sold at the terms as they were now fixed. He was quite alive to the fact that it behoved the Frau as a wise woman to make a profit. Charity is one thing, and business is another. The Frau did her charities like a Christian, generally using Father Conolin as her almoner in such matters. But, as a keeper of a house of public entertainment, it was necessary that she should live. The kaplan was as wide awake to this as was the Frau herself, or the lawyer. But he thought that the changes should not be in the direction indicated by Schlessen. The condition of the Weisses and of the Tendels should be considered. How would it be if one of the "meats" and one of the puddings were discontinued, and if the cup of coffee after dinner were made an extra? Would not that so reduce the expenditure as to leave a profit? And in that case the Weisses and the Tendels need not necessarily incur any increased charges.

When the kaplan had spoken the lawyer looked closely into the Frau's face. The proposition might no doubt for the present meet the difficulty, but he knew that it would be disagreeable. There came a cloud upon the old woman's brow, and she frowned even upon the priest.

"They'd want to be helped twice out of the one pudding, and you'd gain nothing," said Peter.

"According to that," said the lawyer, "if there were only one course the dinner would cost the same. The fewer the dishes, the less the cost, no doubt."

"I don't believe you know anything about it," said the Frau.

"Perhaps not," said the lawyer. "On those little details no doubt you are the best judge. But I think I have shown that something should be done."

"You might try the coffee, Frau Frohmann," said the priest.

"They would not take any. You'd only save the coffee," said the lawyer.

"And the sugar," said the priest.

"But then they'd never ask for brandy," suggested Peter.

The Frau on that occasion said not a word further, but after a little while got up from her chair and stood silent among them; which was known to be a sign that the conference was dismissed.

All this had taken place immediately after dinner, which at this period of the year was eaten at noon. It had simply been a family meal, at which the Frau had sat with her two children and her two friends. The kaplan on such occasions was always free. Nothing that he had in that house ever cost him a kreutzer. But the attorney paid his way like any one else. When called on for absolute work done,—not exactly for advice given in conference,—he made his charges. It might be that a time was coming in which no money would pass on either side, but that time had not arrived as yet. As soon as the Frau was left alone, she reseated herself in her accustomed arm-chair, and set herself to work in sober and almost solemn sadness to think over it all. It was a most perplexing question. There could be no doubt that all the wealth which she at present owned had been made by a business carried on at the present prices and after the existing fashion. Why should there be any change? She was told that she must make her customers pay more because she herself was made to pay more. But why should she pay more? She could understand that in the general prosperity of the Brunnenthal those about her should have somewhat higher wages. As she had prospered, why should not they also prosper? The servants of the poor must, she thought, be poorer than the servants of the rich. But why should poultry be dearer, and meat? Some things she knew were cheaper, as tea and sugar and coffee. She had bought three horses during the winter, and they certainly had been costly. Her father had not given such prices, nor, before this, had she. But that probably had been Peter's fault, who had too rashly acceded to the demands made upon him. And now she remembered with regret that, on the 1st of January, she had acceded to a petition from the carpenter for an addition of six zwansigers to his monthly wages. He had made the request on the plea of a sixth child, adding also, that journeymen carpenters both at Brixen and at Innsbruck were getting what he asked. She had granted to the coming of the additional baby that which she would probably have denied to the other argument; but it had never occurred to her that she was really paying the additional four shillings a month because carpenters were becoming dearer throughout the world. Malchen's clothes were certainly much more costly than her own had been, when she was young; but then Malchen was a foolish girl, fond of fashion from Munich, and just at this moment was in love. It could hardly be right that those poor Tendel females, with their small and fixed means, should be made to pay more for their necessary summer excursions because Malchen would dress herself in so-called French finery, instead of adhering, as she ought, to Tyrolese customs.

The Frau on this occasion spent an hour in solitude, thinking over it all. She had dismissed the conference, but that could not be regarded as an end to the matter. Herr Schlessen had come out from Innsbruck with a written document in his pocket, which he was proposing to have printed and circulated, and which, if printed and circulated, would intimate to the world at large that the Frau Frohmann had raised her prices. Therein the new rates, seven zwansigers and a half a head, were inserted unblushingly at full length, as though such a disruption of old laws was the most natural thing in the world. There was a flippancy about it which disgusted the old woman. Malchen seemed to regard an act which would banish from the Peacock the old friends and well-known customers of the house as though it were an easy trifle; and almost desirable with that very object. The Frau's heart warmed to the well-known faces as she thought of this. Would she not have infinitely greater satisfaction in cooking good dinners for her simple Tyrolese neighbours, than for rich foreigners who, after all, were too often indifferent to what was done for them? By those Tendel ladies her puddings were recognised as real works of art. They thought of them, talked of them, ate them, and no doubt dreamed of them. And Herr Weiss—how he enjoyed her dinners, and how proud he always was as he encouraged his children around him to help themselves to every dish in succession! And the Frau Weiss—with all her cares and her narrow means—was she to be deprived of that cheap month's holiday which was so necessary for her, in order that the Peacock and the charms of the Brunnenthal generally might be devoted to Jews from Frankfort, or rich shopkeepers from Hamburg, or, worse still, to proud and thankless Englishmen? At the end of the hour the Frau had determined that she would not raise her prices.

But yet something must be done. Had she resolved, even silently resolved, that she would carry on her business at a loss, she would have felt that she was worthy of restraint as a lunatic. To keep a house of public entertainment and to lose by it was, to her mind, a very sad idea! To work and be out of pocket by working! To her who knew little or nothing of modern speculation, such a catastrophe was most melancholy. But to work with the intention of losing could be the condition only of a lunatic. And Schlessen had made good his point as to the last season. The money spent had been absolutely more than the money received. Something must be done. And yet she would not raise her prices.

Then she considered the priest's proposition. Peter, she knew, had shown himself to be a fool. Though his feelings were good, he always was a fool. The expenses of the house no doubt might be much diminished in the manner suggested by Herr Conolin. Salt butter could be given instead of fresh at breakfast. Cheaper coffee could be procured. The courses at dinner might be reduced. The second pudding might be discontinued with economical results. But had not her success in these things been the pride of her life; and of what good would her life be to her if its pride were crushed? The Weisses no doubt would come all the same, but how would they whisper and talk of her among themselves when they found these parsimonious changes! The Tendel ladies would not complain. It was not likely that a breath of complaint would ever pass their humble lips; but she herself, she, Frau Frohmann, who was perhaps somewhat unduly proud of her character for wealth, would have to explain to them why it was that that second pudding had been abolished. She would be forced to declare that she could no longer afford to supply it, a declaration which to her would have in it something of meanness, something of degradation. No! she could not abandon the glory of her dinner. It was as though you should ask a Royal Academician to cease to exhibit his pictures, or an actor to consent to have his name withdrawn from the bills. Thus at last she came to that further resolve. The kaplan's advice must be rejected, as must that of the lawyer.

But something must be done. For a moment there came upon her a sad idea that she would leave the whole thing to others, and retire into obscurity at Schwatz, the village from whence the Frohmanns had originally come. There would be ample means for private comfort. But then who would carry on the Peacock, who would look after the farm, and the timber, and the posting, and the mill? Peter was certainly not efficient for all that. And Malchen's ambition lay elsewhere. There was, too, a cowardice in this idea of running away which was very displeasing to her.

Why need there be any raising of prices at all,—either in one direction or in the other?—Had she herself never been persuaded into paying more to others, then she would not have been driven to demand more from others. And those higher payments on her part had, she thought, not been obligatory on her. She had been soft and good-natured, and therefore it was that she was now called upon to be exorbitant. There was something abominable to her in this general greed of the world for more money. At the moment she felt almost a hatred for poor Seppel the carpenter, and regarded that new baby of his as an impertinent intrusion. She would fall back upon the old wages, the old prices for everything. There would be a difficulty with that Innsbruck butcher; but unless he would give way she would try the man at Brixen. In that matter of fowls she would not yield a kreutzer to the entreaties of her poor neighbours who brought them to her for sale.

Then she walked forth from the house to a little arbour or summer-house which was close to the chapel opposite, in which she found Schlessen smoking his pipe with a cup of coffee before him, and Malchen by his side. "I have made up my mind. Herr Schlessen," she said. It was only when she was very angry with him that she called him Herr Schlessen.

"And what shall I do?" asked the lawyer.

"Do nothing at all; but just destroy that bit of paper." So saying, the Frau walked back to the house, and Fritz Schlessen, looking round at Malchen, did destroy that bit of paper.

Chapter III

The Question Of The Mitgift.

ABOUT TWO months after the events described in the last chapter, Malchen and Fritz Schlessen were sitting in the same little arbour, and he was again smoking his pipe, and again drinking his coffee. And they were again alone. When these two were seated together in the arbour, at this early period of the season, they were usually left alone, as they were known to be lovers by the guests who would then be assembled at the Peacock. When the summer had grown into autumn, and the strangers from a distance had come, and the place was crowded, then the ordinary coffee-drinkers and smokers would crowd round the arbour, regardless of the loves of Amalia and Fritz.

The whole family of the Weisses were now at the Peacock, and the two Tendel ladies and three or four others, men with their wives and daughters, from Botzen, Brunecken, and places around at no great distance. It was now the end of June; but it is not till July that the house becomes full, and it is in August that the real crowd is gathered at Frau Frohmann's board. It is then that folk from a distance cannot find beds, and the whole culinary resources of the establishment are put to their greatest stress. It was now Monday, and the lawyer had been making a holiday, having come to the Brunnenthal on the previous Saturday. On the Sunday there had been perhaps a dozen visitors from Innsbruck who had been driven out after early mass for their dinner and Sunday holiday. Everything had been done at the Peacock on the old style. There had been no diminution either in the number or in the excellence of the dishes, nor had there been any increase in the tariff. It had been the first day of the season at which there had been a full table, and the Frau had done her best. Everybody had known that the sojourners in the house were to be entertained at the old rates; but it had been hoped by the lawyer and the priest, and by Malchen,—even by Peter himself—that a zwansiger would be added to the charge for dinner demanded from the townspeople. But at the last moment word had gone forth that there should be no increase. All the morning the old lady had been very gloomy. She had heard mass in her own chapel, and had then made herself very busy in the kitchen. She had spoken no word to any one till, at the moment before dinner, she gave her instructions to Malchen, who always made out the bills, and saw that the money was duly received. There was to be no increase. Then, when the last pudding had been sent in, she went, according to her custom, to her room and decorated herself in her grand costume. When the guests had left the dining-room and were clustering about in the passages and on the seats in front of the house, waiting for their coffee, she had come forth, very fine, with her grand cap on her head, with her gold and silver ornaments, with her arms bare, and radiant with smiles. She shook Madame Weiss very graciously by the hand and stooped down and kissed the youngest child. To one fraulein after another she said a civil word. And when, as it happened, Seppel the carpenter went by, dressed in his Sunday best, with a child in each hand, she stopped him and asked kindly after the baby. She had made up her mind that, at any rate for a time, she would not submit to the humiliation of acknowledging that she was driven to the necessity of asking increased prices.

That had taken place on the Sunday, and it was on the following day that the two lovers were in the arbour together. Now it must be understood that all the world knew that these lovers were lovers, and that all the world presumed that they were to become husband and wife. There was not and never had been the least secrecy about it. Malchen was four or five and twenty, and he was perhaps thirty. They knew their own minds, and were, neither of them, likely to be persuaded by others either to marry or not to marry. The Frau had given her consent,—not with that ecstacy of joy with which sons-in-law are sometimes welcomed,—but still without reserve. The kaplan had given in his adhesion. The young lawyer was not quite the man he liked,—entertained some of the new ideas about religion, and was given to innovations; but he was respectable and well-to-do. He was a lover against whom he, as a friend of the family, could not lift up his voice. Peter did not like the man, and Peter, in his way, was fond of his sister. But he had not objected. Had he done so, it would not have mattered much. Malchen was stronger at the Brunnenthal than Peter. Thus it may be said that things generally smiled upon the lovers. But yet no one had ever heard that a day was fixed for their marriage. Madame Weiss had once asked Malchen, and Malchen had told her—not exactly to mind her own business; but that had been very nearly the meaning of what she had said.

There was, indeed, a difficulty; and this was the difficulty. The Frau had assented—in a gradual fashion, rather by not dissenting as the thing had gone on, so that it had come to be understood that the thing was to be. But she had never said a word as to the young lady's fortune—as to that "mitgift" which in such a case would certainly be necessary. Such a woman as the Frau in giving her daughter would surely have to give something with her. But the Frau was a woman who did not like parting with her money; and was such a woman that even the lawyer did not like asking the question. The fraulein had once inquired, but the mother had merely raised her eyebrows and remained silent. Then the lawyer had told the priest that in the performance of her moral duties the Frau ought to settle something in her own mind. The priest had assented, but had seemed to imply that in the performance of such a duty an old lady ought not to be hurried. A year or two, he seemed to think, would not be too much for consideration. And so the matter stood at the present moment.

Perhaps it is that the Germans are a slow people. It may be that the Tyrolese are especially so. Be that as it may, Herr Schlessen did not seem to be driven into any agony of despair by these delays. He was fondly attached to his Malchen; but as to offering to take her without any mitgift,—quite empty-handed, just as she stood,—that was out of the question. No young man who had anything, ever among his acquaintances, did that kind of thing. Scales should be somewhat equally balanced. He had a good income, and was entitled to some substantial mitgift. He was quite ready to marry her to-morrow, if only this important question could get itself settled.

Malchen was quite as well aware as was he that her mother should be brought to do her duty in this matter; but, perhaps of the two, she was a little the more impatient. If there should at last be a slip between the cup and the lip, the effect to her would be so much more disastrous than to him! He could very easily get another wife. Young women were as plenty as blackberries. So the fraulein told herself. But she might find it difficult to suit herself, if at last this affair were to be broken off. She knew herself to be a fair, upstanding, good-looking lass, with personal attractions sufficient to make such a young man as Fritz Schlessen like her society; but she knew also that her good looks, such as they were, would not be improved by fretting. It might be possible that Fritz should change his mind some day, if he were kept waiting till he saw her becoming day by day more commonplace under his eyes. Malchen had good sense enough not to overrate her own charms, and she knew the world well enough to be aware that she would be wise to secure, if possible, a comfortable home while she was at her best. It was not that she suspected Fritz; but she did not think that she would be justified in supposing him to be more angelic than other young men simply because he was her lover. Therefore, Malchen was impatient, and for the last month or two had been making up her mind to be very "round" with her mother on the subject.

At the present moment, however, the lovers, as they were sitting in the arbour, were discussing rather the Frau's affairs in regard to the establishment than their own. Schlessen had, in truth, come to the Brunnenthal on this present occasion to see what would be done, thinking that if the thin edge of the wedge could have been got in,—if those people from the town could have been made to pay an extra zwansiger each for their Sunday dinner,—then, even yet, the old lady might be induced to raise her prices in regard to the autumn and more fashionable visitors. But she had been obstinate, and had gloried in her obstinacy, dressing herself up in her grandest ornaments and smiling her best smiles, as in triumph at her own victory.

"The fact is, you know, it won't do," said the lawyer to his love. "I don't know how I am to say any more, but anybody can see with half an eye that she will simply go on losing money year after year. It is all very fine for the Weisses and Tendels, and very fine for old Trauss,"—old Trauss was a retired linen-draper from Vienna, who lived at Innsbruck, and was accustomed to eat many dinners at the Peacock; a man who could afford to pay a proper price, but who was well pleased to get a good dinner at a cheap rate,—"and very well for old Trauss," continued the lawyer, becoming more energetic as he went on, "to regale themselves at your mother's expense;—but that's what it comes to. Everybody knows that everybody has raised the price of everything. Look at the Golden Lion." The Golden Lion was the grand hotel in the town. "Do you think they haven't raised their prices during the last twenty years?"

"Why is it, Fritz?"

"Everything goes up together, of course. If you'll look into old accounts you'll see that three hundred years ago you could buy a sheep at Salzburg for two florins and a half. I saw it somewhere in a book. If a lawyer's clerk then had eighty florins a year he was well off. That would not surprise her. She can understand that there should be an enormous change in three hundred years; but she can't make out why there should be a little change in thirty years."

"But many things have got cheaper, Fritz."

"Living altogether hasn't got cheaper. Look at wages!"

"I don't know why we should pay more. Everybody says that bread is lower than it used to be."

"What sort of bread do the people eat now? Look at that man." The man was Seppel, who was dragging a cart which he had just mended out of the shed which was close by,—in which cart were seated his three eldest children, so that he might help their mother as assistant nurse even while he was at his work. "Don't you think he gets more wheaten flour into his house in a week than his grandfather did in a year? His grandfather never saw white bread."

"Why should he have it?"

"Because he likes it, and because he can get it. Do you think he'd have stayed here if his wages had not been raised?"

"I don't think Seppel ever would have moved out of the Brunnenthal, Fritz."

"Then Seppel would have been more stupid than the cow, which knows very well on which side of the field it can find the best grass. Everything gets dearer;—and if one wants to live one has to swim with the stream. You might as well try to fight with bows and arrows, or with the old-fashioned flint rifles, as to live at the same rate as your grandfather." The young lawyer, as he said this, rapped his pipe on the table to knock out the ashes, and threw himself back on his seat with a full conviction that he had spoken words of wisdom.

"What will it all come to, Fritz?" This Malchen asked with real anxiety in her voice. She was not slow to join two things together. It might well be that her mother should be induced by her pride to carry on the business for a while, so as to lose some of her money, but that she should, at last, be induced to see the error of her ways before serious damage had been done. Her financial position was too good to be brought to ruin by small losses. But during the period of her discomfiture she certainly would not be got to open her hand in that matter of the mitgift. Malchen's own little affair would never get itself settled till this other question should have arranged itself satisfactorily. There could be no mitgift from a failing business. And if the business were to continue to fail for the next year or two, where would Malchen be then? It was not, therefore, wonderful that she should be in earnest.

"Your mother is a very clever woman," said the lover.

"It seems to me that she is very foolish about this," said Malchen, whose feeling of filial reverence was not at the moment very strong.

"She is a clever woman, and has done uncommonly well in the world. The place is worth double as much as when she married your father. But it is that very success which makes her obstinate. She thinks that she can see her way. She fancies that she can compel people to work for her and deal with her at the old prices. It will take her, perhaps, a couple of years to find out that this is wrong. When she has lost three or four thousand florins she'll come round."

Fritz, as he said this, seemed to be almost contented with this view of the case,—as though it made no difference to him. But with the fraulein the matter was so essentially personal that she could not allow it to rest there. She had made up her mind to be round with her mother; but it seemed to her to be necessary, also, that something should be said to her lover. "Won't all that be very bad for you, Fritz?"

"Her business with me will go on just the same."

This was felt to be unkind and very unloverlike. But she could not afford at the present moment to quarrel with him. "I mean about our settling," she said.

"It ought not to make a difference."

"I don't know about ought;—but won't it? You don't see her as I do, but, of course, it puts her into a bad temper."

"I suppose she means to give you some fixed sum. I don't doubt but she has it all arranged in her own mind."

"Why doesn't she name it, then?"

"Ah, my dear,—mein schatz,—there is nobody who likes too well to part with his money."

"But when is there to be an end of it?"

"You should find that out. You are her child, and she has only two. That she should hang back is a matter of course. When one has the money of his own one can do anything. It is all in her own hand. See what I bear. When I tell her this or that she turns upon me as if I were nobody. Do you think I should suffer it if she were only just a client? You must persuade her, and be gentle with her; but if she would name the sum it would be a comfort, of course."

The fraulein herself did not in the least know what the sum ought to be; but she thought she did know that it was a matter which should be arranged between her lover and her parent. What she would have liked to have told him was this,—that as there were only two children, and as her mother was at any rate an honest woman, he might be sure that a proper dowry would come at last. But she was well aware that he would think that a mitgift should be a mitgift. The bride should come with it in her hand, so that she might be a comfort to her husband's household. Schlessen would not be at all willing to wait patiently for the Frau's death, or even for some final settlement of her affairs when she might make up her mind to leave the Peacock and betake herself to Schwatz. "You would not like to ask her yourself?" she said.

He was silent for a while, and then he answered her by another question. "Are you afraid of her?"

"Not afraid. But she would just tell me I was impertinent. I am not a bit afraid, but it would do no good. It would be so reasonable for you to do it."

"There is just the difference, Malchen. I am afraid of her."

"She could not bite you."

"No;—but she might say something sharp, and then I might answer her sharply. And then there might be a quarrel. If she were to tell me that she did not want to see me any more in the Brunnenthal, where should we be then? Mein schatz, if you will take my advice, you will just say a word yourself, in your softest, sweetest way." Then he got up and made his way across to the stable, where was the horse which was to take him back to Innsbruck. Malchen was not altogether well pleased with her lover, but she perceived that on the present occasion she must, perforce, follow his advice.

Chapter IV

The Frau Returns To The Simplicity Of The Old Days.

Two or three weeks went by in the Brunnenthal without any special occurrence, and Malchen had not as yet spoken to her mother about her fortune. The Frau had during this time been in more than ordinary good humour with her own household. July had opened with lovely weather, and the house had become full earlier than usual. The Frau liked to have the house full, even though there might be no profit, and therefore she was in a good humour. But she had been exceptionally busy, and was trying experiments in her housekeeping, as to which she was still in hope that they would carry her through all her difficulties. She had been both to Brixen on one side of the mountain and to Innsbruck on the other, and had changed her butcher. Her old friend Hoff, at the latter place, had altogether declined to make any reduction in his prices. Of course they had been raised within the last five or six years. Who did not know that that had been the case with butchers' meat all the world over? As it was, he charged the Frau less than he charged the people at the Golden Lion.

So at least he swore; and when she told him that unless an alteration was made she must take her custom elsewhere—he bade her go elsewhere. Therefore she did make a contract with the butcher at Brixen on lower terms, and seemed to think that she had got over her difficulty. But Brixen was further than Innsbruck, and the carriage was more costly. It was whispered also about the house that the meat was not equally good. Nobody, however, had as yet dared to say a word on that subject to the Frau. And she, though in the midst of her new efforts she was good-humoured herself,—as is the case with many people while they have faith in the efforts they are making,—had become the cause of much unhappiness among others. Butter, eggs, poultry, honey, fruit, and vegetables, she was in the habit of buying from her neighbours, and had been so excellent a customer that she was as good as a market to the valley in general. There had usually been some haggling; but that, I think, by such vendors is considered a necessary and almost an agreeable part of the operation. The produce had been bought and sold, and the Frau had, upon the whole, been regarded as a kind of providence to the Brunnenthal. But now there were sad tales told at many a cottage and small farmstead around. The Frau had declared that she would give no more than three zwansigers a pair for chickens, and had insisted on having both butter and eggs at a lower price than she had paid last year. And she had succeeded, after infinite clamours. She had been their one market, their providence, and they had no other immediate customers to whom to betake themselves. The eggs and the butter, the raspberries and the currants, must be sold. She had been imperious and had succeeded, for a while. But there were deep murmurs, and already a feeling was growing up in favour of Innsbruck and a market cart. It was very dreadful. How were they to pay their taxes, how were they to pay anything, if they were to be crimped and curtailed in this way? One poor woman had already walked to Innsbruck with three dozen eggs, and had got nearly twice the money which the Frau had offered. The labour of the walk had been very hard upon her, and the economy of the proceeding generally may have been doubtful; but it had been proved that the thing could be done.

Early in July there had come a letter, addressed to Peter, from an English gentleman who, with his wife and daughter, had been at the Brunnenthal on the preceding year. Mr. Cartwright had now written to say, that the same party would be glad to come again early in August, and had asked what were the present prices. Now the very question seemed to imply a conviction on the gentleman's mind that the prices would be raised. Even Peter, when he took the letter to his mother, thought that this would be a good opportunity for taking a step in advance. These were English people, and entitled to no loving forbearance. The Cartwrights need know nothing as to the demands made on the Weisses and Tendels. Peter who had always been on his mother's side, Peter who hated changes, even he suggested that he might write back word that seven zwansigers and a half was now the tariff. "Don't you know I have settled all that?" said the old woman, turning upon him fiercely. Then he wrote to Mr. Cartwright to say that the charge would be six zwansigers a day, as heretofore. It was certainly a throwing away of money. Mr. Cartwright was a Briton, and would, therefore, almost have preferred to pay another zwansiger or two. So at least Peter thought. And he, even an Englishman, with his wife and daughter, was to be taken in and entertained at a loss! At a loss!—unless, indeed, the Frau could be successful in her new mode of keeping her house. Father Conolin in these days kept away. The complaints made by the neighbours around reached his ears,—very sad complaints,—and he hardly knew how to speak of them to the Frau. It was becoming very serious with him. He had counselled her against any rise in her own prices, but had certainly not intended that she should make others lower. That had not been his plan; and now he did not know what advice to give.

But the Frau, resolute in her attempt, and proud of her success as far as it had gone, constantly adducing the conduct of these two rival butchers as evidence of her own wisdom, kept her ground like a Trojan. All the old courses were served, and the puddings and the fruit were at first as copious as ever. If the meat was inferior in quality,—and it could not be so without her knowledge, for she had not reigned so long in the kitchen of the Peacock without having become a judge in such matters,—she was willing to pass the fault over for a time. She tried to think that there was not much difference. She almost tried to believe that second-rate meat would do as well as first-rate. There should at least be no lack of anything in the cookery. And so she toiled and struggled, and was hopeful that she might have her own way and prove to all her advisers that she knew how to manage the house better than any of them.

There was great apparent good humour. Though she had frowned upon Peter when he had shown a disposition to spoil those Egyptians the Cartwrights, she had only done so in defence of her own resolute purpose, and soon returned to her kind looks. She was, too, very civil to Malchen, omitting for the time her usual gibes and jeers as to her daughter's taste for French finery and general rejection of Tyrolese customs. And she said nothing of the prolonged absence of her two counsellors, the priest and the lawyer. A great struggle was going on within her own bosom, as to which she in these days said not a word to anybody. One counsellor had told her to raise her prices; another had advised her to lessen the luxuries supplied. As both the one proposition and the other had gone against her spirit, she had looked about her to find some third way out of her embarrassments. She had found it, and the way was one which recommended itself to her own sense of abstract justice. The old prices should prevail in the valley everywhere. She would extort nothing from Mr. Cartwright, but then neither should her neighbours extort anything from her. Seppel's wife was ill, and she had told him that in consequence of that misfortune the increased wages should be continued for three months, but that after that she must return to the old rate. In the softness of her heart she would have preferred to say six months, but that in doing so she would have seemed to herself to have departed from the necessary rigour of her new doctrine. But when Seppel stood before her, scratching his head, a picture of wretchedness and doubt, she was not comfortable in her mind. Seppel had a dim idea of his own rights, and did not like to be told that his extra zwansigers came to him from the Frau's charity. To go away from the Brunnenthal at the end of the summer, to go away at all, would be terrible to him; but to work for less than fair wages, would that not be more terrible? Of all which the Frau, as she looked at him, understood much.

And she understood much also of the discontent and almost despair which was filling the minds of the poor women all around her. All those poor women were dear to her. It was in her nature to love those around her, and especially those who were dependent on her. She knew the story of every household,—what children each mother had reared and what she had lost, when each had been brought to affliction by a husband's illness or a son's misconduct. She had never been deaf to their troubles; and though she might have been heard in violent discussions, now with one and now with another, as to the selling value of this or that article, she had always been held by them to be a just woman and a constant friend. Now they were up in arms against her, to the extreme grief of her heart.

Nevertheless it was necessary that she should support herself by an outward appearance of tranquillity, so that the world around her might know that she was not troubled by doubts as to her own conduct. She had heard somewhere that no return can be made from evil to good courses without temporary disruptions, and that all lovers of justice are subject to unreasonable odium. Things had gone astray because there had been unintentional lapses from justice. She herself had been the delinquent when she had allowed herself to be talked into higher payments than those which had been common in the valley in her young days. She had not understood, when she made these lapses gradually, how fatal would be their result. Now she understood, and was determined to plant her foot firmly down on the old figures. All this evil had come from a departure from the old ways. There must be sorrow and trouble, and perhaps some ill blood, in this return. That going back to simplicity is always so difficult! But it should be done. So she smiled, and refused to give more than three zwansigers a pair for her chickens.

One old woman came to her with the express purpose of arguing it all out. Suse Krapp was the wife of an old woodman who lived high up above the Peacock, among the pines, in a spot which could only be reached by a long and very steep ascent, and who being old, and having a daughter and granddaughters whom she could send down with her eggs and wild fruit, did not very often make her appearance in the valley. But she had known the Frau well for many years, having been one of those to welcome her when she had arrived there as a bride, and had always been treated with exceptional courtesy. Suse Krapp was a woman who had brought up a large family, and had known troubles; but she had always been able to speak her own mind; and when she arrived at the house, empty-handed, with nothing to sell, declaring at once her purpose of remonstrating with the Frau, the Frau regarded her as a delegate from the commercial females of the valley generally; and she took the coming in good part, asking Suse into her own inner room.

After sundry inquiries on each side, respecting the children and the guests, and the state of things in the world at large, the real question was asked, "Ah, meine liebe Frau Frohmann,—my very dear Mrs. Frohmann, as one might say here,—why are you dealing with us all in the Brunnenthal after this hard fashion?"

"What do you call a hard fashion, Suse?"

"Only giving half price for everything that you buy. Why should anything be cheaper this year than it was last? Ah, alas! does not everybody know that everything is dearer?"

"Why should anything be dearer, Suse? The people who come here are not charged more than they were twenty years ago."

"Who can tell? How can an old woman say? It is all very bad. The world, I suppose, is getting worse. But it is so. Look at the taxes."

The taxes, whether imperial or municipal, was a matter on which Frau did not want to speak. She felt that they were altogether beyond her reach. No doubt there had been a very great increase in such demands during her time, and it was an increase against which nobody could make any stand at all. But, if that was all, there had been a rise in prices quite sufficient to answer that. She was willing to pay three zwansigers a pair for chickens, and yet she could remember when they were to be bought for a zwansiger each.

"Yes, taxes," she said; "they are an evil which we must all endure. It is no good grumbling at them. But we have had the roads made for us."

This was an unfortunate admission, for it immediately gave Suse Krapp an easy way to her great argument. "Roads, yes! and they are all saying that they must make use of them to send the things into market. Josephine Bull took her eggs into the city and got two kreutzers apiece for them."

The Frau had already heard of that journey, and had also heard that poor Josephine Bull had been very much fatigued by her labours. It had afflicted her much, both that the poor woman should have been driven to such a task, and that such an innovation should have been attempted. She had never loved Innsbruck dearly, and now she was beginning to hate the place. "What good did she get by that, Suse? None, I fear. She had better have given her eggs away in the valley."

"But they will have a cart."

"Do you think a cart won't cost money? There must be somebody to drive the cart, I suppose." On this point the Frau spoke feelingly, as she was beginning to appreciate the inconvenience of sending twice a week all the way to Brixen for her meat. There was a diligence, but though the horses were kept in her own stables, she had not as yet been able to come to terms with the proprietor.

"There is all that to think of certainly," said Suse. "But—. Wouldn't you come back, meine liebe Frau, to the prices you were paying last year? Do you not know that they would sooner sell to you than to any other human being in all the world, and they must live by their little earnings?"

But the Frau could not be persuaded. Indeed had she allowed herself to be persuaded, all her purpose would have been brought to an end. Of course there must be trouble, and her refusal of such a prayer as this was a part of her trouble. She sent for a glass of kirsch-wasser to mitigate the rigour of her denial, and as Suse drank the cordial she endeavoured to explain her system. There could be no happiness, no real prosperity in the valley, till they had returned to their old ways. "It makes me unhappy," said the Frau, shaking her head, "when I see the girls making for themselves long petticoats." Suse quite agreed with the Frau as to the long petticoats; but, as she went, she declared that the butter and eggs must be taken into Innsbruck, and another allusion to the cart was the last word upon her tongue.

It was on the evening of that same day that Malchen, unaware that her mother's feelings had just then been peculiarly stirred up by an appeal from the women of the valley, came at last to the determination of asking that something might be settled as to the "mitgift." "Mother," she said, "Fritz Schlessen thinks that something should be arranged."

"Arranged as how?"

"I suppose he wants—to be married."

"If he don't, I suppose somebody else does," said the mother smiling.

"Well, mother! Of course it is not pleasant to be as we are now. You must feel that yourself. Fritz is a good young man, and there is nothing about him that I have a right to complain of. But of course, like all the rest of 'em, he expects some money when he takes a wife. Couldn't you tell him what you mean to give?"

"Not at present, Malchen."

"And why not now? It has been going on two years."

"Nina Cobard at Schwatz was ten years before her people would let it come off. Just at present I am trying a great experiment, and I can say nothing about money till the season is over." With this answer Malchen was obliged to be content, and was not slow in perceiving that it almost contained a promise that the affairs should be settled when the season was over.

Chapter V

A Zwansiger Is A Zwansiger.

In the beginning of August, the Weisses and the Tendels and Herr Trauss had all left the Brunnenthal, and our friend Frau Frohmann was left with a house full of guests who were less intimately known to her, but who not the less demanded and received all her care.

But, as those departed whom she had taught herself to regard as neighbours and who were therefore entitled to something warmer and more generous than mere tavern hospitality, she began to feel the hardness of her case in having to provide so sumptuously for all these strangers at a loss. There was a party of Americans in the house who had absolutely made no inquiry whatsoever as to prices till they had shown themselves at her door. Peter had been very urgent with her to mulct the Americans, who were likely, he thought, to despise the house merely because it was cheap. But she would not give way. If the American gentleman should find out the fact and turn upon her, and ask her why he was charged more than others, how would she be able to answer him? She had never yet been so placed as not to be able to answer any complaints, boldly and even indignantly. It was hard upon her; but if the prices were to be raised to any, they must be raised to all.

The whole valley now was in a hubbub. In the matter of butter there had been so great a commotion that the Frau had absolutely gone back to the making of her own, a system which had been abandoned at the Peacock a few years since, with the express object of befriending the neighbours. There had been a dairy with all its appurtenances; but it had come to pass that the women around had got cows, and that the Frau had found that without damage to herself she could buy their supplies. And in this way her own dairy had gone out of use. She had kept her cows because there had grown into use a great drinking of milk at the Peacock, and as the establishment had gradually increased, the demand for cream, custards, and such luxuries had of course increased also. Now, when, remembering this, she conceived that she had a peculiar right to receive submission as to the price of butter, and yet found more strong rebellion here than on any other point, she at once took the bull by the horns, and threw not only her energies, but herself bodily into the dairy. It was repaired and whitewashed, and scoured and supplied with all necessary furniture in so marvellously short a time, that the owners of cows around could hardly believe their ears and their eyes. Of course there was a spending of money, but there had never been any slackness as to capital at the Peacock when good results might be expected from its expenditure. So the dairy was set agoing.

But there was annoyance, even shame, and to the old woman's feeling almost disgrace, arising from this. As you cannot eat your cake and have it, so neither can you make your butter and have your cream. The supply of new milk to the milk-drinkers was at first curtailed, and then altogether stopped. The guests were not entitled to the luxury by any contract, and were simply told that as the butter was now made at home, the milk was wanted for that purpose. And then there certainly was a deterioration in the puddings. There had hitherto been a rich plenty which was now wanting. No one complained; but the Frau herself felt the falling off. The puddings now were such as might be seen at other places,—at the Golden Lion for instance. Hitherto her puddings had been unrivalled in the Tyrol.

Then there had suddenly appeared a huckster, a pedlar, an itinerant dealer in the valley who absolutely went round to the old women's houses and bought the butter at the prices which she had refused to give. And this was a man who had been in her own employment, had been brought to the valley by herself, and had once driven her own horses! And it was reported to her that this man was simply an agent for a certain tradesman in Innsbruck. There was an ingratitude in all this which nearly broke her heart. It seemed to her that those to whom in their difficulties she had been most kind were now turning upon her in her difficulty. And she thought that there was no longer left among the people any faith, any feeling of decent economy, any principle. Disregarding right or wrong, they would all go where they could get half a zwansiger more! They knew what it was she was attempting to do; for had she not explained it all to Suse Krapp? And yet they turned against her.

The poor Frau knew nothing of that great principle of selling in the dearest market, however much the other lesson as to buying in the cheapest had been brought home to her. When a fixed price had become fixed, that, she thought, should not be altered. She was demanding no more than she had been used to demand, though to do so would have been so easy! But her neighbours, those to whom she had even been most friendly, refused to assist her in her efforts to re-establish the old and salutary simplicity. Of course when the butter was taken into Innsbruck, the chickens and the eggs went with the butter. When she learned how all this was she sent for Suse Krapp, and Suse Krapp again came down to her.

"They mean then to quarrel with me utterly?" said the Frau with her sternest frown.

"Meine liebe Frau Frohmann!" said the old woman, embracing the arm of her ancient friend.

"But they do mean it?"

"What can we do, poor wretches? We must live."

"You lived well enough before," said the Frau, raising her fist in the unpremeditated eloquence of her indignation. "Will it be better for you now to deal with strangers who will rob you at every turn? Will Karl Muntz, the blackguard that he is, advance money to any of you at your need? Well; let it be so. I too can deal with strangers. But when once I have made arrangements in the town, I will not come back to the people of the valley. If we are to be severed, we will be severed. It goes sadly against the grain with me, as I have a heart in my bosom."

"You have, you have, my dearest Frau Frohmann."

"As for the cranberries, we can do without them." Now it had been the case that Suse Krapp with her grandchildren had supplied the Peacock with wild fruits in plentiful abundance, which wild fruits, stewed as the Frau knew how to stew them, had been in great request among the guests at the Brunnenthal. Great bowls of cranberries and bilberries had always at this period of the year turned the Frau's modest suppers into luxurious banquets. But there must be an end to that now; not in any way because the price paid for the fruit was grudged, but because the quarrel, if quarrel there must be, should be internecine at all points. She had loved them all; but, if they turned against her, not the less because of her love would she punish them. Poor old Suse wiped her eyes and took her departure, without any kirsch-wasser on this occasion.

It all went on from bad to worse. Seppel the carpenter gave her notice that he would leave her service at the end of August. "Why at the end of August?" she asked, remembering that she had promised to give him the higher rate of wages up to a later date than that. Then Seppel explained, that as he must do something for himself,—that is, find another place,—the sooner he did that the better. Now Seppel the carpenter was brother to that Anton who had most wickedly undertaken the huckstering business, on the part of Karl Muntz the dealer in Innsbruck, and it turned out that Seppel was to join him. There was an ingratitude in this which almost drove the old woman frantic. If any one in the valley was more bound to her by kindly ties than another, it was Seppel, with his wife and six children. Wages! There had been no question of wages when Babette, Seppel's wife, had been ill; and Babette had always been ill. And when he had chopped his own foot with his own axe, and had gone into the hospital for six weeks, they had wanted nothing! That he should leave her for a matter of six zwansigers a month, and not only leave her, but become her active enemy, was dreadful to her. Nor was her anger at all modified when he explained it all to her. As a man, and as a carpenter who was bound to keep up his own respect among carpenters, he could not allow himself to work for less than the ordinary wages. The Frau had been very kind to him, and he and his wife and children were all grateful. But she would not therefore wish him,—this was his argument,—she would not on that account require him to work for less than his due. Seppel put his hand on his heart, and declared that his honour was concerned. As for his brother's cart and his huckstery trade and Karl Muntz, he was simply lending a hand to that till he could get a settled place as carpenter. He was doing the Frau no harm. If he did not look after the cart, somebody else would. He was very submissive and most anxious to avoid her anger; but yet would not admit that he was doing wrong. But she towered in her wrath, and would listen to no reason. It was to her all wrong. It was innovation, a spirit of change coming from the source of all evil, bringing with it unkindness, absence of charity, ingratitude! It was flat mutiny, and rebellion against their betters. For some weeks it seemed to the Frau that all the world was going to pieces.

Her position was the more painful because at the time she was without counsellors. The kaplan came indeed as usual, and was as attentive and flattering to her as of yore; but he said nothing to her about her own affairs unless he was asked; and she did not ask him, knowing that he would not give her palatable counsel. The kaplan himself was not well versed in political economy or questions of money generally; but he had a vague idea that the price of a chicken ought to be higher now than it was thirty years ago. Then why not also the price of living to the guests at the Peacock? On that matter he argued with himself that the higher prices for the chickens had prevailed for some time, and that it was at any rate impossible to go back. And perhaps the lawyer had been right in recommending the Frau to rush at once to seven zwansigers and a half. His mind was vacillating and his ideas misty; but he did agree with Suse Krapp when she declared that the poor people must live. He could not, therefore, do the Frau any good by his advice.

As for Schlessen he had not been at the Brunnenthal for a month, and had told Malchen in Innsbruck that unless he were specially wanted, he would not go to the Peacock until something had been settled as to the mitgift. "Of course she is going to lose a lot of money," said Schlessen. "Anybody can see that with half an eye. Everybody in the town is talking about it. But when I tell her so, she is only angry with me."

Malchen of course could give no advice. Every step which her mother took seemed to her to be unwise. Of course the old women would do the best they could with their eggs. The idea that any one out of gratitude should sell cheaper to a friend than to an enemy was to her monstrous. But when she found that her mother was determined to swim against the stream, to wound herself by kicking against the pricks, to set at defiance all the common laws of trade, and that in this way money was to be lost, just at that very epoch of her own life in which it was so necessary that money should be forthcoming for her own advantage,—then she became moody, unhappy, and silent. What a pity it was that all this power should be vested in her mother's hands.

As for Peter, he had been altogether converted. When he found that a cart had to be sent twice a week to Brixen, and that the very poultry which had been carried from the valley to the town had to be brought back from the town to the valley, then his spirit of conservatism deserted him. He went so far as to advise his mother to give way. "I don't see that you do any good by ruining yourself," he said.

But she turned at him very fiercely. "I suppose I may do as I like with my own," she replied.

Yes; she could do what she liked with her own. But now it was declared by all those around her, by her neighbours in the valley, and by those in Innsbruck who knew anything about her, that it was a sad thing and a bad thing that an old woman should be left with the power of ruining all those who belonged to her, and that there should be none to restrain her! And yet for the last twenty-five years previous to this it had been the general opinion in these parts that nobody had ever managed such a house as well as the Frau Frohmann. As for being ruined,—Schlessen, who was really acquainted with her affairs, knew better than that. She might lose a large sum of money, but there was no fear of ruin. Schlessen was inclined to think that all this trouble would end in the Frau retiring to Schwatz, and that the settlement of the mitgift might thus be accelerated. Perhaps he and the Frau herself were the only two persons who really knew how well she had thriven. He was not afraid, and, being naturally patient, was quite willing to let things take their course.

The worst of it to the Frau herself was that she knew so well what people were saying of her. She had enjoyed for many years all that delight which comes from success and domination. It had not been merely, not even chiefly, the feeling that money was being made. It is not that which mainly produces the comfortable condition of mind which attends success. It is the sense of respect which it engenders. The Frau had held her head high, and felt herself inferior to none, because she had enjoyed to the full this conviction. Things had gone pleasantly with her. Nothing is so enfeebling as failure; but she, hitherto, had never failed. Now a new sensation had fallen upon her, by which at certain periods she was almost prostrated. The woman was so brave that at her worst moments she would betake herself to solitude and shed her tears where no one could see her. Then she would come out and so carry herself that none should guess how she suffered. To no ears did she utter a word of complaint, unless her indignation to Seppel, to Suse, and the others might be called complaining. She asked for no sympathy. Even to the kaplan she was silent, feeling that the kaplan, too, was against her. It was natural that he should take part with the poor. She was now, for the first time in her life, driven, alas, to feel that the poor were against her.

The house was still full, but there had of late been a great falling off in the midday visitors. It had, indeed, almost come to pass that that custom had died away. She told herself, with bitter regret, that this was the natural consequence of her deteriorated dinners. The Brixen meat was not good. Sometimes she was absolutely without poultry. And in those matters of puddings, cream, and custards, we know what a falling off there had been. I doubt, however, whether her old friends had been stopped by that cause. It may have been so with Herr Trauss, who in going to Brunnenthal, or elsewhere, cared for little else but what he might get to eat and drink. But with most of those concerned the feeling had been that things were generally going wrong in the valley, and that in existing circumstances the Peacock could not be pleasant. She at any rate felt herself to be deserted, and this feeling greatly aggravated her trouble.

"You are having beautiful weather," Mr. Cartwright said to her one day when in her full costume she came out among the coffee-drinkers in the front of the house. Mr. Cartwright spoke German, and was on friendly terms with the old lady. She was perhaps a little in awe of him as being a rich man, an Englishman, and one with a white beard and a general deportment of dignity.

"The weather is well enough, sir," she said.

"I never saw the place all round look more lovely. I was up at Sustermann's saw-mills this morning, and I and my daughter agreed that it is the most lovely spot we know."

"The saw-mill is a pretty spot, sir, no doubt."

"It seems to me that the house becomes fuller and fuller every year, Frau Frohmann."

"The house is full enough, sir; perhaps too full." Then she hesitated as though she would say something further. But the words were wanting to her in which to explain her difficulties with sufficient clearness for the foreigner, and she retreated, therefore, back into her own domains. He, of course, had heard something of the Frau's troubles, and had been willing enough to say a word to her about things in general if the occasion arose. But he had felt that the subject must be introduced by herself. She was too great a potentate to have advice thrust upon her uninvited.

A few days after this she asked Malchen whether Schlessen was ever coming out to the Brunnenthal again. This was almost tantamount to an order for his presence. "He will come directly, mother, if you want to see him," said Malchen. The Frau would do no more than grunt in answer to this. It was too much to expect that she should say positively that he must come. But Malchen understood her, and sent the necessary word to Innsbruck.

On the following day Schlessen was at the Peacock and took a walk up to the waterfall with Malchen before he saw the Frau. "She won't ruin herself," said Fritz. "It would take a great deal to ruin her. What she is losing in the house she is making up in the forests and in the land."

"Then it won't matter if it does go on like this?"

"It does matter because it makes her so fierce and unhappy, and because the more she is knocked about the more obstinate she will get. She has only to say the word, and all would be right to-morrow."

"What word?" asked Malchen.

"Just to acknowledge that everything has got to be twenty-five per cent. dearer than it was twenty-five years ago."

"But she does not like paying more, Fritz. That's just the thing."

"What does it matter what she pays?"

"I should think it mattered a great deal."

"Not in the least. What does matter is whether she makes a profit out of the money she spends. Florins and zwansigers are but names. What you can manage to eat, and drink, and wear, and what sort of a house you can live in and whether you can get other people to do for you what you don't like to do yourself,—that is what you have got to look after."

"But, Fritz;—money is money."

"Just so; but it is no more than money. If she could find out suddenly that what she has been thinking was a zwansiger was in truth only half a zwansiger, then she would not mind paying two where she had hitherto paid one, and would charge two where she now charges one,—as a matter of course. That's about the truth."

"But a zwansiger is a zwansiger."

"No;—not in her sense. A zwansiger now is not much more than half what it used to be. If the change had come all at once she could have understood it better."

"But why is it changed?"

Here Schlessen scratched his head. He was not quite sure that he knew, and felt himself unable to explain clearly what he himself only conjectured dimly. "At any rate it is so. That's what she has got to be made to understand, or else she must give it up and go and live quietly in private. It'll come to that, that she won't have a servant about the place if she goes on like this. Her own grandfather and grandmother were very good sort of people, but it is useless to try and live like them. You might just as well go back further, and give up knives and forks and cups and saucers."

Such was the wisdom of Herr Schlessen; and when he had spoken it he was ready to go back from the waterfall, near which they were seated, to the house. But Malchen thought that there was another subject as to which he ought to have something to say to her. "It is all very bad for us;—isn't it, Fritz?"

"It will come right in time, my darling."

"Your darling! I don't think you care for me a bit." As she spoke she moved herself a little further away from him. "If you did, you would not take it all so easily."

"What can I do, Malchen?" She did not quite know what he could do, but she was sure that when her lover, after a month's absence, got an opportunity of sitting with her by a waterfall, he should not confine his conversation to a discussion on the valuc of zwansigers.

"You never seem to think about anything except money now."

"That is very unfair, Malchen. It was you asked me, and so I endeavoured to explain it."

"If you have said all that you've got to say, I suppose we may go back again."

"Of course, Malchen, I wish she'd settle what she means to do about you. We have been engaged long enough."

"Perhaps you'd like to break it off."

"You never knew me break off anything yet." That was true. She did know him to be a man of a constant, if not of an enthusiastic temperament. And now, as he helped her up from off the rock, and contrived to snatch a kiss in the process, she was restored to her good humour.

"What's the good of that?" she said, thumping him, but not with much violence. "I did speak to mother a little while ago, and asked her what she meant to do."

"Was she angry?"

"No;—not angry; but she said that everything must remain as it is till after the season. Oh, Fritz! I hope it won't go on for another winter. I suppose she has got the money."

"Oh, yes; she has got it; but, as I've told you before, people who have got money do not like to part with it." Then they returned to the house; and Malchen, thinking of it all, felt reassured as to her lover's constancy, but was more than ever certain that, though it might be for five years, he would never marry her till the mitgift had been arranged.

Shortly afterwards he was summoned into the Frau's private room, and there had an interview with her alone. But it was very short; and, as he afterwards explained to Malchen, she gave him no opportunity of proffering any advice. She had asked him nothing about prices, and had made no allusion whatever to her troubles with her neighbours. She said not a word about the butcher, either at Innsbruck or at Brixen, although they were both at this moment very much on her mind. Nor did she tell him anything of the wickedness of Anton, nor of the ingratitude of Seppel. She had simply wanted so many hundred florins,—for a purpose, as she said,—and had asked him how she might get them with the least inconvenience. Hitherto the money coming in, which had always gone into her own hands, had sufficed for her expenditure, unless when some new building was required. But now a considerable sum was necessary. She simply communicated her desire, and said nothing of the purpose for which it was wanted. The lawyer told her that she could have the money very easily,—at a day's notice, and without any peculiar damage to her circumstances. With that the interview was over, and Schlessen was allowed to return to his lady love,—or to the amusements of the Peacock generally.

"What did she want of you?" asked Peter.

"Only a question about business."

"I suppose it was about business. But what is she going to do?"

"You ought to know that, I should think. At any rate, she told me nothing."

"It is getting very bad here," said Peter, with a peculiarly gloomy countenance. "I don't know where we are to get anything soon. We have not milk enough, and half the time the visitors can't have eggs if they want them. And as for fowls, they have to be bought for double what we used to give. I wonder the folk here put up with it without grumbling."

"It'll come right after this season."

"Such a name as the place is getting!" said Peter. "And then I sometimes think it will drive her distracted. I told her yesterday we must buy more cows,—and, oh, she did look at me!"

Chapter VI

Hoff The Butcher.

THE LAWYER returned to town, and on the next day the money was sent out to the Brunnenthal. Frau Frohmann had not winced when she demanded the sum needed, nor had she shown by any contorted line in her countenance that she was suffering when she asked for it; but, in truth, the thing had not been done without great pain. Year by year she had always added something to her store, either by investing money, or by increasing her property in the valley, and it would generally be at this time of the year that some deposit was made; but now the stream, which had always run so easily and so prosperously in one direction, had begun to flow backwards. It was to her as though she were shedding her blood. But, as other heroes have shed their blood in causes that have been dear to them, so would she shed hers in this. If it were necessary that these veins of her heart should be opened, she would give them to the knife. She had scowled when Peter had told her that more cows must be bought; but before the week was over the cows were there. And she had given a large order at Innsbruck for poultry to be sent out to her, almost irrespective of price. All idea of profit was gone. It was pride now for which she was fighting. She would not give way, at any rate till the end of this season. Then—then—then! There had come upon her mind an idea that some deluge was about to flow over her; but also an idea that even among the roar of the waters she would hold her head high, and carry herself with dignity.

But there had come to her now a very trouble of troubles, a crushing blow, a misfortune which could not be got over, which could not even be endured, without the knowledge of all those around her. It was not only that she must suffer, but that her sufferings must be exposed to all the valley,—to all Innsbruck. When Schlessen was closeted with her, at that very moment, she had in her pocket a letter from that traitorous butcher at Brixen, saying that after such and such a date he could not continue to supply her with meat at the prices fixed. And this was the answer which the man had sent to a remonstrance from her as to the quality of the article! After submitting for weeks to inferior meat she had told him that there must be some improvement, and he had replied by throwing her over altogether!

What was she to do? Of all the blows which had come to her this was the worst. She must have meat. She could, when driven to it by necessity, make her own butter; but she could not kill her own beef and mutton. She could send into the town for ducks and chickens, and feel that in doing so she was carrying out her own project,—that, at any rate, she was encountering no public disgrace. But now she must own herself beaten, and must go back to Innsbruck.

And there came upon her dimly a conviction that she was bound, both by prudence and justice, to go back to her old friend Hoff. She had clearly been wrong in this matter of meat. Hoff had plainly told her that she was wrong, explaining to her that he had to give much more for his beasts and sheep than he did twenty years ago, to pay more wages to the men who killed them and cut them up, and also to make a greater profit himself, so as to satisfy the increased needs of his wife and daughters. Hoff had been outspoken, and had never wavered for a moment. But he had seemed to the Frau to be almost insolent; she would have said, too independent. When she had threatened to take away her custom he had shrugged his shoulders, and had simply remarked that he would endeavour to live without it. The words had been spoken with, perhaps, something of a jeer, and the Frau had left the shop in wrath. She had since repented herself of this, because Hoff had been an old friend, and had attended to all her wishes with friendly care. But there had been the quarrel, and her custom had been transferred to that wretch at Brixen. If it had been simply a matter of forgiving and forgetting she could have made it up with Hoff, easily enough, an hour after her anger had shown itself. But now she must own herself to have been beaten. She must confess that she had been wrong. It was in that matter of meat, from that fallacious undertaking made by the traitor at Brixen, that she, in the first instance, had been led to think that she could triumph. Had she not been convinced of the truth of her own theory by that success, she would not have been led on to quarrel with all her neighbours, and to attempt to reduce Seppel's wages. But now, when this, her great foundation, was taken away from her, she had no ground on which to stand. She had the misery of failure all around her, and, added to that, the growing feeling that, in some step of her argument, she must have been wrong. One should be very sure of all the steps before one allows oneself to be guided in important matters by one's own theories!

But after some ten days' time the supply of meat from Brixen would cease, and something therefore must be done. The Brixen traitor demanded now exactly the price which Hoff had heretofore charged. And then there was the carriage! That was not to be thought of. She would not conceal her failure from the world by submission so disgraceful as that. With the Brixen man she certainly would deal no more. She took twenty-four hours to think of it, and then she made up her mind that she would herself go into the town and acknowledge her mistake to Hoff. As to the actual difference of price, she did not now care very much about it. When a deluge is coming, one does not fret oneself as to small details of cost; but even when a deluge is coming one's heart and pride, and perhaps one's courage, may remain unchanged.

On a certain morning it was known throughout the Peacock at an early hour that the Frau was going into town that day. But breakfast was over before any one was told when and how she was to go. Such journeyings, which were not made very often, had always about them something of ceremony. On such occasions her dress would be, not magnificent as when she was arrayed for festive occasions at home, but yet very carefully arranged and equally unlike her ordinary habiliments. When she was first seen on this day,—after her early visit to the kitchen, which was not a full-dress affair,—she was clad in what may be called the beginnings or substratum of her travelling gear. She wore a very full, rich-looking, dark-coloured merino gown, which came much lower to the ground than her usual dress, and which covered her up high round the throat. Whenever this was seen it was known as a certainty that the Frau was going to travel. Then there was the question of the carriage and the horses. It was generally Peter's duty and high privilege to drive her in to town; and as Peter seldom allowed himself a holiday, the occasion was to him always a welcome one. It was her custom to let him know what was to befall him at any rate the night before; but now not a word had been said. After breakfast, however, a message went out that the carriage and horses would be needed, and Peter prepared himself accordingly. "I don't think I need take you," said the Frau.

"Why not me? There is no one else to drive them. The men are all employed." Then she remembered that when last she had dispensed with Peter's services Anton had driven her,—that Anton who was now carrying the butter and eggs into market. She shook her head, and was silent for a while in her misery. Then she asked whether the boy, Jacob, could not take her. "He would not be safe with those horses down the mountains," said Peter. At last it was decided that Peter should go;—but she yielded unwillingly, being very anxious that no one in the valley should be informed that she was about to visit Hoff. Of course it would be known at last. Everybody about the place would learn whence the meat came. But she could not bear to think that those around her should talk of her as having been beaten in the matter.

About ten they started, and on the whole road to Innsbruck hardly a word was spoken between the mother and son. She was quite resolved that she would not tell him whither she was going, and resolved also that she would pay the visit alone. But, of course, his curiosity would be excited. If he chose to follow her about and watch her, there could be no help for that. Only he had better not speak to her on the subject, or she would pour out upon him all the vials of her wrath! In the town there was a little hostel called the Black Eagle, kept by a cousin of her late husband, which on these journeys she always frequented: there she and Peter ate their dinner. At table they sat, of course, close to each other; but still not a word was spoken as to her business. He made no inquiry, and when she rose from the table simply asked her whether there was anything for him to do. "I am going—alone—to see a friend," she said. No doubt he was curious, probably suspecting that Hoff the butcher might be the friend; but he asked no further question. She declared that she would be ready to start on the return journey at four, and then she went forth alone.

So great was her perturbation of spirit that she did not take the directest way to the butcher's house, which was not, indeed, above two hundred yards from the Black Eagle, but walked round slowly by the river, studying as she went the words with which she would announce her purpose to the man,—studying, also, by what wiles and subtlety she might get the man all to herself,—so that no other ears should hear her disgrace. When she entered the shop Hoff himself was there, conspicuous with the huge sharpening-steel which hung from his capacious girdle, as though it were the sword of his knighthood. But with him there was a crowd either of loungers or customers, in the midst of whom he stood, tall above all the others, laughing and talking. To our poor Frau it was terrible to be seen by so many eyes in that shop;—for had not her quarrel with Hoff and her dealings at Brixen been so public that all would know why she had come? "Ah, my friend, Frau Frohmann," said the butcher, coming up to her with hand extended, "this is good for sore eyes. I am delighted to see thee in the old town." This was all very well, and she gave him her hand. As long as no public reference was made to that last visit of hers, she would still hold up her head. But she said nothing. She did not know how to speak as long as all those eyes were looking at her.

The butcher understood it all, being a tender-hearted man, and intelligent also. From the first moment of her entrance he knew that there was something to be said intended only for his own ears. "Come in, come in, Frau Frohmann," he said; "we will sit down within, out of the noise of the street and the smell of the carcases." With that he led the way into an inner room, and the Frau followed him. There were congregated three or four of his children, but he sent them away, bidding them join their mother in the kitchen. "And now, my friend," he said, again taking her hand, "I am glad to see thee. Thirty years of good fellowship is not to be broken by a word." By this time the Frau was endeavouring to hide with her handkerchief the tears which were running down her face. "I was thinking I would go out to the valley one of these days, because my heart misgave me that there should be anything like a quarrel between me and thee. I should have gone, but that, day after day, there comes always something to be done. And now thou art come thyself. What, shall the price of a side of beef stand betwixt thee and me?"

Then she told her tale,—quite otherwise than as she had intended to tell it. She had meant to be dignified and very short. She had meant to confess that the Brixen arrangement had broken down, and that she would resort to the old plan and the old prices. To the saying of this she had looked forward with an agony of apprehension, fearing that the man would be unable to abstain from some killing expression of triumph,—fearing that, perhaps, he might decline her offer. For the butcher was a wealthy man, who could afford himself the luxury of nursing his enmity. But his manner with her had been so gracious that she was altogether unable to be either dignified or reticent. Before half an hour was over she had poured out to him, with many tears, all her troubles;—how she had refused to raise her rate of charges, first out of consideration for her poorer customers, and then because she did not like to demand from one class more than from another. And she explained how she had endeavoured to reduce her expenditure, and how she had failed. She told him of Seppel and Anton, of Suse Krapp and Josephine Bull,—and, above all, of that traitor at Brixen. With respect to the valley folk Hoff expressed himself with magnanimity and kindness; but in regard to the rival tradesman at Brixen his scorn was so great that he could not restrain himself from expressing wonder that a woman of such experience should have trusted to so poor a reed for support. In all other respects he heard her with excellent patience, putting in a little word here and there to encourage her, running his great steel all the while through his fingers, as he sat opposite to her on a side of the table.

"Thou must pay them for their ducks and chickens as before," he said.

"And you?"

"I will make all that straight. Do not trouble thyself about me. Thy guests at the Peacock shall once again have a joint of meat fit for the stomach of a Christian. But, my friend—!"

"My friend!" echoed the Frau, waiting to hear what further the butcher would say to her.

"Let a man who has brought up five sons and five daughters, and who has never owed a florin which he could not pay, tell thee something that shall be useful. Swim with the stream." She looked up into his face, feeling rather than understanding the truth of what he was saying. "Swim with the stream. It is the easiest and the most useful."

"You think I should raise my prices."

"Is not everybody doing so? The Tendel ladies are very good, but I cannot sell them meat at a loss. That is not selling; it is giving. Swim with the stream. When other things are dearer, let the Peacock be dearer also."

"But why are other things dearer?"

"Nay;—who shall say that? Young Schlessen is a clear-headed lad, and he was right when he told thee of the price of sheep in the old days. But why—? There I can say nothing. Nor is there reason why I should trouble my head about it. There is a man who has brought me sheep from the Achensee these thirty years,—he and his father before him. I have to pay him now,—ay, more than a third above his first prices."

"Do you give always what he asks?"

"Certainly not that, or there would be no end to his asking. But we can generally come to terms without hard words. When I pay him more for sheep, then I charge more for mutton; and if people will not pay it, then they must go without. But I do sell my meat, and I live at any rate as well now as I did when the prices were lower." Then he repeated his great advice, "Swim with the stream, my friend; swim with the stream. If you turn your head the other way, the chances are you will go backwards. At any rate you will make no progress."

Exactly at four o'clock she started on her return with her son, who, with admirable discretion, asked no question as to her employment during the day. The journey back took much longer than that coming, as the road was up hill all the way, so that she had ample time to think over the advice which had been given her as she leaned back in the carriage. She certainly was happier in her mind than she had been in the morning. She had made no step towards success in her system,—had rather been made to feel that no such step was possible. But, nevertheless, she had been comforted. The immediate trouble as to the meat had been got over without offence to her feelings. Of course she must pay the old prices,—but she had come to understand that the world around her was, in that matter, too strong for her. She knew now that she must give up the business, or else raise her own terms at the end of the season. She almost thought that she would retire to Schwatz and devote the remainder of her days to tranquillity and religion. But her immediate anxiety had reference to the next six weeks, so that when she should have gone to Schwatz it might be said of her that the house had not lost its reputation for good living up to the very last. At any rate, within a very few days, she would again have the pleasure of seeing good meat roasting in her oven.

Peter, as was his custom, had walked half the hill, and then, while the horses were slowly advancing, climbed up to his seat on the box. "Peter," she said, calling to him from the open carriage behind. Then Peter looked back. "Peter, the meat is to come from Hoff again after next Thursday."

He turned round quick on hearing the words. "That's a good thing, mother."

"It is a good thing. We were nearly poisoned by that scoundrel at Brixen."

"Hoff is a good butcher," said Peter.

"Hoff is a good man," said the Frau. Then Peter pricked up, because he knew that his mother was happy in her mind, and became eloquent about the woods, and the quarry, and the farm.

Chapter VII

And Gold Becomes Cheap.

"But if there is more money, sir, that ought to make us all more comfortable." This was said by the Frau to Mr. Cartwright a few days after her return from Innsbruck, and was a reply to a statement made by him. She had listened to advice from Hoff the butcher, and now she was listening to advice from her guest. He had told her that these troubles of hers had come from the fact that gold had become more plentiful in the world than heretofore, or rather from that other fact that she had refused to accommodate herself to this increased plenty of gold. Then had come her very natural suggestion, "If there is more money that ought to make us all more comfortable."

"Not at all, Frau Frohmann."

"Well, sir!" Then she paused, not wishing to express an unrestrained praise of wealth, and so to appear too worldly-minded, but yet feeling that he certainly was wrong according to the clearly expressed opinion of the world.

"Not at all. Though you had your barn and your stores filled with gold, you could not make your guests comfortable with that. They could not eat it, nor drink it, nor sleep upon it, nor delight themselves with looking at it as we do at the waterfall, or at the mill up yonder."

"But I could buy all those things for them."

"Ah, if you could buy them! That's just the question. But if everybody had gold so common, if all the barns were full of it, then people would not care to take it for their meat and wine."

"It never can be like that, surely."

"There is no knowing; probably not. But it is a question of degree. When you have your hay-crop here very plentiful, don't you find that hay becomes cheap?"

"That's of course."

"And gold becomes cheap. You just think it over, and you'll find how it is. When hay is plentiful, you can't get so much for a load because it becomes cheap. But you can feed more cows, and altogether you know that such plenty is a blessing. So it is with gold. When it is plentiful, you can't get so much meat for it as you used to do; but, as you can get the gold much easier, it will come to the same thing,—if you will swim with the stream, as your friend in Innsbruck counselled you."

Then the Frau again considered, and again found that she could not accept this doctrine as bearing upon her own case. "I don't think it can be like that here, sir," she said.

"Why not here as well as elsewhere?"

"Because we never see a bit of gold from one year's end to the other. Barns full of it! Why, it's so precious that you English people, and the French, and the Americans always change it for paper before you come here. If you mean that it is because bank-notes are so common— "

Then Mr. Cartwright scratched his head, feeling that there would be a difficulty in making the Frau understand the increased use of an article which, common as it had become in the great marts of the world, had not as yet made its way into her valley. "It is because bank-notes are less common." The Frau gazed at him steadfastly, trying to understand something about it. "You still use bank-notes at Innsbruck?"

"Nothing else," she said. "There is a little silver among the shops, but you never see a bit of gold."

"And at Munich?"

"At Munich they tell me the French pieces have become—well, not common, but not so very scarce."

"And at Dresden?"

"I do not know. Perhaps Dresden is the same."

"And at Paris?"

"Ah, Paris! Do they have gold there?"

"When I was young it was all silver at Paris. Gold is now as plentiful as blackberries. And at Berlin it is nearly the same. Just here in Austria, you have not quite got through your difficulties."

"I think we are doing very well in Austria;—at any rate, in the Tyrol."

"Very well, Frau Frohmann; very well indeed. Pray do not suppose that I mean anything to the contrary. But though you haven't got into the way of using gold money yourself, the world all around you has done so; and, of course, if meat is dear at Munich because gold won't buy so much there as it used to do, meat will be dearer also at Innsbruck, even though you continue to pay for it with bank-notes."

"It is dearer, sir, no doubt," said the Frau, shaking her head. She had endeavoured to contest that point gallantly, but had been beaten by the conduct of the two butchers. The higher prices of Hoff at Innsbruck had become at any rate better than the lower prices of that deceitful enemy at Brixen.

"It is dearer. For the world generally that may suffice. Your friend's doctrine is quite enough for the world at large. Swim with the stream. In buying and selling,—what we call trade,—things arrange themselves so subtly, that we are often driven to accept them without quite knowing why they are so. Then we can only swim with the stream. But, in this matter, if you want to find out the cause, if you cannot satisfy your mind without knowing why it is that you must pay more for everything, and must, therefore, charge more to other people, it is because the gold which your notes represent has become more common in the world during the last thirty years."

She did want to know. She was not satisfied to swim with the stream as Hoff had done, not caring to inquire, but simply feeling sure that as things were so, so they must be. That such changes should take place had gone much against the grain of her conservative nature. She, in her own mind, had attributed these pestilently increased expenses to elongated petticoats, French bonnets, swallow-tailed coats, and a taste for sour wine. She had imagined that Josephine Bull might have been contented with the old price for her eggs if she would also be contented with the old raiment and the old food. Grounding her resolutions on that belief, she had endeavoured not only to resist further changes, but even to go back to the good old times. But she now was quite aware that in doing so she had endeavoured to swim against the stream. Whether it ought to be so or not, she was not as yet quite sure, but she was becoming sure that such was the fact, and that the fact was too strong for her to combat.

She did not at all like swimming with the stream. There was something conveyed by the idea which was repugnant to her sense of honour. Did it not mean that she was to increase her prices because other people increased theirs, whether it was wrong or right? She hated the doing of anything because other people did it. Was not that base propensity to imitation the cause of the long petticoats which all the girls were wearing? Was it not thus that all those vile changes were effected which she saw around her on every side? Had it not been her glory, her great resolve, to stand as fast as possible on the old ways? And now in her great attempt to do so, was she to be foiled thus easily?

It was clear to her that she must be foiled, if not in one way, then in another. She must either raise her prices, or else retire to Schwatz. She had been thoroughly beaten in her endeavour to make others carry on their trade in accordance with her theories. On every side she had been beaten. There was not a poor woman in the valley, not one of those who had wont to be so submissive and gracious to her, who had not deserted her. A proposed reduction of two kreutzers on a dozen of eggs had changed the most constant of humble friends into the bitterest foes. Seppel would have gone through fire and water for her. Anything that a man's strength or courage could do, he would have done. But a threat of going back to the old wages had conquered even Seppel's gratitude. Concurrent testimony had convinced her that she must either yield—or go. But, when she came to think of it in her solitude, she did not wish to go. Schwatz! oh yes; it would be very well to have a quiet place ready chosen for retirement when retirement should be necessary. But what did retirement mean? Would it not be to her simply a beginning of dying? A man, or a woman, should retire when no longer able to do the work of the world. But who in all the world could keep the Brunnenthal Peacock as well as she? Was she fatigued with her kitchen, or worn out with the charge of her guests, or worried inwardly by the anxieties of her position? Not in the least, not at all, but for this later misfortune which had come upon her, a misfortune which she knew how to remedy at once if only she could bring herself to apply the remedy. The kaplan had indiscreetly suggested to her that as Malchen was about to marry and be taken away into the town, it would be a good thing that Peter should take a wife, so that there might be a future mistress of the establishment in readiness. The idea caused her to arm herself instantly with renewed self-assertion. So;—they were already preparing for her departure to Schwatz! It was thus she communed with herself. They had already made up their minds that she must succumb to these difficulties and go! The idea had come simply from the kaplan without consultation with any one, but to the Frau it seemed as though the whole valley were already preparing for her departure. No, she would not go! With her strength and her energy, why should she shut herself up as ready for death? She would not go to Schwatz yet awhile.

But if not, then she must raise her prices. To waste her substance, to expend the success of her life in entertaining folk gratis who, after all, would believe that they were paying for their entertainment, would be worse even than going to Schwatz. "I have been thinking over what you were telling me," she said to Mr. Cartwright about a week after their last interview, on the day before his departure from the valley.

"I hope you do not find I was wrong, Frau Frohmann."

"As for wrong and right, that is very difficult to get at in this wicked world."

"But one can acknowledge a necessity."

"That is where it is, sir. One can see what is necessary; but if one could only see that it were right also, one would be so much more comfortable."

"There are things so hard to be seen, my friend, that let us do what we will we cannot see clearly into the middle of them. Perhaps I could have explained to you better all this about the depreciation of money, and the nominal rise in the value of everything else, if I had understood it better myself."

"I am sure you understand all about it,—which a poor woman can't ever do."

"But this at any rate ought to give you confidence, that that which you purpose to do is being done by everybody around you. You were talking to me about the Weisses. Herr Weiss, I hear, had his salary raised last spring."

"Had he?" asked the Frau with energy and a little start. For this piece of news had not reached her before.

"Somebody was saying so the other day. No doubt it was found that he must be paid more because he had to pay more for everything he wanted. Therefore he ought to expect to have to pay you more."

This piece of information gave the Frau more comfort than anything she had yet heard. That gold should be common, what people call a drug in the market, did not come quite within the scope of her comprehension. Gold to her was gold, and a zwansiger a zwansiger. But if Herr Weiss got more for his services from the community, she ought to get more from him for her services. That did seem plain to her. But then her triumph in that direction was immediately diminished by a tender feeling as to other customers. "But what of those poor Fraulein Tendels?" she said.

"Ah, yes," said Mr. Cartwright. "There you come to fixed incomes."

"To what?"

"To people with fixed incomes. They must suffer, Frau Frohmann. There is an old saying that in making laws you cannot look after all the little things. The people who work and earn their living are the multitude, and to them these matters adjust themselves. The few who live upon what they have saved or others have saved for them must go to the wall." Neither did the Frau understand this; but she at once made up her mind that, however necessary it might be to raise her prices against the Weisses and the rest of the world, she would never raise them against those two poor desolate frauleins.

So Herr Weiss had had his salary raised, and had said nothing to her about it, no doubt prudently wishing to conceal the matter! He had said nothing to her about it, although he had talked to her about her own affairs, and had applauded her courage and her old conservatism in that she would not demand that extra zwansiger and a half! This hardened her heart so much that she felt she would have a pleasure in sending a circular to him as to the new tariff. He might come or let it alone, as he pleased,—certainly he ought to have told her that his own salary had been increased!

But there was more to do than sending out the new circular to her customers. How was she to send a circular round the valley to the old women and the others concerned? How was she to make Seppel, and Anton, and Josephine Bull understand that they should be forgiven, and have their old prices and their increased wages if they would come back to their allegiance, and never say a word again as to the sad affairs of the past summer? This circular must be of a nature very different from that which would serve for her customers. Thinking over it, she came to the opinion that Suse Krapp would be the best circular. A day or two after the Cartwrights were gone, she sent for Suse.

Suse was by no means a bad diplomate. When gaining her point she had no desire to triumph outwardly. When feeling herself a conqueror, she was quite ready to flatter the conquered one. She had never been more gracious, more submissive, or more ready to declare that in all matters the Frau's will was the law of the valley than now, when she was given to understand that everything should be bought on the same terms as heretofore, that the dairy should be discontinued during the next season, and that the wild fruits of the woods and mountains should be made welcome at the Peacock as had heretofore always been the case.

"To-morrow will be the happiest day that ever was in the valley," said Suse in her enthusiasm. "And as for Seppel, he was telling me only yesterday that he would never be a happy man again till he could find himself once more at work in the old shed behind the chapel."

Then Suse was told that Seppel might come as soon as he pleased.

"He'll be there the morning after next if I'm a living woman," continued Suse energetically; and then she said another word, "Oh, meine liebe Frau Frohmann, it broke my heart when they told me you were going away."

"Going away!" said the Frau, as though she had been stung. "Who said that I was going away?"

"I did hear it."

"Psha! it was that stupid priest." She had never before been heard to say a word against the kaplan; but now she could hardly restrain herself. "Why should I go away?"

"No, indeed!"

"I am not thinking of going away. It would be a bad thing if I were to be driven out of my house by a little trouble as to the price of eggs and butter! No, Suse Krapp, I am not going away."

"It will be the best word we have all of us heard this many a day, Frau Frohmann. When it came to that, we were all as though we would have broken our hearts." Then she was sent away upon her mission, not, upon this occasion, without a full glass of kirsch-wasser.

On the very day following Seppel was back. There was nothing said between him and his mistress, but he waited about the front of the house till he had an opportunity of putting his hand up to his cap and smiling at her as she stood upon the doorstep. And then, before the week was over, all the old women and all the young girls were crowding round the place with little presents which, on this their first return to their allegiance, they brought to the Frau as peace-offerings.

The season was nearly over when she signified to Malchen her desire that Fritz Schlessen should come out to the valley. This she did with much good humour, explaining frankly that Fritz would have to prepare the new circulars, and that she must discuss with him the nature of the altered propositions which were to be made to the public. Fritz of course came, and was closeted with her for a full hour, during which he absolutely prepared the document for the Innsbruck printer. It was a simple announcement that for the future the charge made at the Brunnenthal Peacock would be seven and a half zwansigers per head per day. It then went on to declare that, as heretofore, the Frau Frohmann would endeavour to give satisfaction to all those who would do her the honour of visiting her establishment. And instructions were given to Schlessen as to sending the circulars out to the public. "But whatever you do," said the Frau, "don't send one to those Tendel ladies."

And something else was settled at this conference. As soon as it was over Fritz Schlessen was encountered by Malchen, who on such occasions would never be far away. Though the spot on which they met was one which might not have been altogether secure from intrusive eyes, he took her fondly by the waist and whispered a word in her ear.

"And will that do?" asked Malchen anxiously; to which question his reply was made by a kiss. In that whisper he had conveyed to her the amount now fixed for the mitgift.

Chapter VIII

It Doesn't Make Any Difference To Any Of Them.

And so Frau Frohmann had raised her prices, and had acknowledged herself to all the world to have been beaten in her enterprise. There are, however, certain misfortunes which are infinitely worse in their anticipation than in their reality; and this, which had been looked forward to as a terrible humiliation, was soon found to be one of them. No note of triumph was sounded; none at least reached her ear. Indeed, it so fell out that those with whom she had quarrelled for awhile seemed now to be more friendly with her than ever. Between her and Hoff things were so sweet that no mention was ever made of money. The meat was sent and the bills were paid with a reticence which almost implied that it was not trade, but an amiable giving and taking of the good things of the world. There had never been a word of explanation with Seppel; but he was late and early about the carts and the furniture, and innumerable little acts of kindnesses made their way up to the mother and her many children. Suse and Josephine had never been so brisk, and the eggs had never been so fresh or the vegetables so good. Except from the working of her own mind, she received no wounds.

But the real commencement of the matter did not take place till the following summer,—the commencement as regarded the public. The circulars were sent out, but to such letters no answers are returned; and up to the following June the Frau was ignorant what effect the charge would have upon the coming of her customers. There were times at which she thought that her house would be left desolate, that the extra charge would turn away from her the hearts of her visitors, and that in this way she would be compelled to retire to Schwatz.

"Suppose they don't come at all," she said to Peter one day.

"That would be very bad," said Peter, who also had his fears in the same direction.

"Fritz Schlessen thinks it won't make any difference," said the Frau.

"A zwansiger and a half a day does make a difference to most men," replied Peter uncomfortably.

This was uncomfortable; but when Schlessen came out he raised her spirits.

"Perhaps old Weiss won't come," he said, "but then there will be plenty in his place. There are houses like the Peacock all over the country now, in the Engadine, and the Bregenz, and the Salzkammergut; and it seems to me the more they charge the fuller they are."

"But they are for the grand folk."

"For anybody that chooses. It has come to that, that the more money people are charged the better they like it. Money has become so plentiful with the rich, that they don't know what to do with it."

This was a repetition of Mr. Cartwright's barn full of gold. There was something in the assertion that money could be plentiful, in the idea that gold could be a drug, which savoured to her of innovation, and was therefore unpleasant. She still felt that the old times were good, and that no other times could be so good as the old times. But if the people would come and fill her house, and pay her the zwansiger and a half extra without grumbling, there would be some consolation in it.

Early in June Malchen made a call at the house of the Frauleins Tendel. Malchen at this time was known to all Innsbruck as the handsome Frau Schlessen who had been brought home in the winter to her husband's house with so very comfortable a mitgift in her hand. That was now quite an old story, and there were people in the town who said that the young wife already knew quite as much about her husband's business as she had ever done about her mother's. But at this moment she was obeying one of her mother's commands.

"Mother hopes you are both coming out to the Brunnenthal this year," said Malchen. The elder fraulein shook her head sadly. "Because— " Then Malchen paused, and the younger of the two ladies shook her head. "Because you always have been there."

"Yes, we have."

"Mother means this. The change in the price won't have anything to do with you if you will come."

"We couldn't think of that, Malchen."

"Then mother will be very unhappy;—that's all. The new circular was not sent to you."

"Of course we heard of it."

"If you don't come mother will take it very bad." Then of course the ladies said they would come, and so that little difficulty was overcome.

This took place in June. But at that time the young wife was staying out in the valley with her mother, and had only gone into Innsbruck on a visit. She was with her mother preparing for the guests; but perhaps, as the Frau too often thought, preparing for guests who would never arrive. From day to day, however, there came letters bespeaking rooms as usual, and when the 21st of June came there was Herr Weiss with all his family.

She had taught herself to regard the coming of the Weisses as a kind of touchstone by which she might judge of the success of what she had done. If he remained away it would be because, in spite of the increase in his salary, he could not encounter the higher cost of this recreation for his wife and family. He was himself too fond of the good living of the Peacock not to come if he could afford it. But if he could not pay so much, then neither could others in his rank of life; and it would be sad indeed to the Frau if her house were to be closed to her neighbour Germans, even though she might succeed in filling it with foreigners from a distance. But now the Weisses had come, not having given their usual notice, but having sent a message for rooms only two days before their arrival. And at once there was a little sparring match between Herr Weiss and the Frau.

"I didn't suppose that there would be much trouble as to finding rooms," said Herr Weiss.

"Why shouldn't there be as much trouble as usual?" asked the Frau in return. She had felt that there was some slight in this arrival of the whole family without the usual preliminary inquiries,—as though there would never again be competition for rooms at the Peacock.

"Well, my friend, I suppose that that little letter which was sent about the country will make a difference."

"That's as people like to take it. It hasn't made any difference with you, it seems."

"I had to think a good deal about it, Frau Frohmann; and I suppose we shall have to make our stay shorter. I own I am a little surprised to see the Tendel women here. A zwansiger and a half a day comes to a deal of money at the end of a month, when there are two or three."

"I am happy to think it won't hurt you, Herr Weiss, as you have had your salary raised."

"That is neither here nor there, Frau Frohmann," said the magistrate, almost with a touch of anger. All the world knew, or ought to know, how very insufficient was his stipend when compared with the invaluable public services which he rendered. Such at least was the light in which he looked at the question.

"At any rate," said the Frau as he stalked away, "the house is like to be as full as ever."

"I am glad to hear it. I am glad to hear it." These were his last words on the occasion. But before the day was over he told his wife that he thought the place was not as comfortable as usual, and that the Frau with her high prices was more upsetting than ever.

His wife, who took delight in being called Madame Weiss at Brixen, and who considered herself to be in some degree a lady of fashion, had nevertheless been very much disturbed in her mind by the increased prices, and had suggested that the place should be abandoned. A raising of prices was in her eyes extortion;—though a small raising of salary was simply justice, and, as she thought, inadequate justice. But the living at the Peacock was good. Nobody could deny that. And when a middle-aged man is taken away from the comforts of his home, how is he to console himself in the midst of his idleness unless he has a good dinner? Herr Weiss had therefore determined to endure the injury, and as usual to pass his holiday in the Brunnenthal. But when Madame Weiss saw those two frauleins from Innsbruck in the house, whose means she knew down to the last kreutzer, and who certainly could not afford the increased demand, she thought that there must be something not apparent to view. Could it be possible that the Frau should be so unjust, so dishonest, so extortious as to have different prices for different neighbours! That an Englishman, or even a German from Berlin, should be charged something extra, might not perhaps be unjust or extortious. But among friends of the same district, to put a zwansiger and a half on to one and not to another seemed to Madame Weiss to be a sin for which there should be no pardon. "I am so glad to see you here," she said to the younger fraulein.

"That is so kind of you. But we always are here, you know."

"Yes;—yes. But I feared that perhaps—. I know that with us we had to think more than once about it before we could make up our minds to pay the increased charges. The 'Magistrat' felt a little hurt about it." To this the fraulein at first answered nothing, thinking that perhaps she ought not to make public the special benevolence shown by the Frau to herself and her sister. "A zwansiger and a half each is a great deal of money to add on," said Madame Weiss.

"It is, indeed."

"We might have got it cheaper elsewhere. And then I thought that perhaps you might have done so too."

"She has made no increase to us," said the poor lady, who at last was forced to tell the truth, as by not doing so she would have been guilty of a direct falsehood in allowing it to be supposed that she and her sister paid the increased price.

"Soh—oh—oh!" exclaimed Madame Weiss, clasping her hands together and bobbing her head up and down. "Soh—oh—oh!" She had found it all out.

Then, shortly after that,—the next day,—there was an uncomfortable perturbation of affairs at the Peacock, which was not indeed known to all the guests, but which to those who heard it, or heard of it, seemed for the time to be very terrible. Madame Weiss and the Frau had,—what is commonly called,—a few words together.

"Frau Frohmann," said Madame Weiss, "I was quite astonished to hear from Agatha Tendel that you were only charging them the old prices."

"Why shouldn't I charge them just what I please,—or nothing at all, if I pleased?" asked the Frau sharply.

"Of course you can. But I do think, among neighbours, there shouldn't be one price to one and one to another."

"Would it do you any good, Frau Weiss, if I were to charge those ladies more than they can pay? Does it do you any harm if they live here at a cheap rate?"

"Surely there should be one price—among neighbours!"

"Herr Weiss got my circular, no doubt. He knew. I don't suppose he wants to live here at a rate less than it costs me to keep him. You and he can do what you like about coming. And you and he can do what you like about staying away. You knew my prices. I have not made any secret about the change. But as for interference between me and my other customers, it is what I won't put up with. So now you know all about it."

By the end of her speech the Frau had worked herself up into a grand passion, and spoke aloud, so that all near her heard her. Then there was a great commotion in the Peacock, and it was thought that the Weisses would go away. But they remained for their allotted time.

This was the only disturbance which took place, and it passed off altogether to the credit of the Frau. Something in a vague way came to be understood about fixed incomes;—so that Peter and Malchen, with the kaplan, even down to Seppel and Suse Krapp, were aware that the two frauleins ought not to be made to pay as much as the prosperous magistrate who had had his salary raised. And then it was quite understood that the difference made in favour of those two poor ladies was a kindness shown to them, and could not therefore be an injury to any one else.

Later in the year, when the establishment was full and everything was going on briskly, when the two puddings were at the very height of their glory, and the wild fruits were brought up on the supper-table in huge bowls, when the Brunnenthal was at its loveliest, and the Frau was appearing on holidays in her gayest costume, the Cartwrights returned to the valley. Of course they had ordered their rooms much beforehand; and the Frau, trusting altogether to the wisdom of those counsels which she did not even yet quite understand, had kept her very best apartments for them. The greeting between them was most friendly,—the Frau condescending to put on something of her holiday costume to add honour to their arrival;—a thing which she had never been known to do before on behalf of any guests. Of course there was not then time for conversation; but a day or two had not passed before she made known to Mr. Cartwright her later experience. "The people have come, sir, just the same," she said.

"So I perceive."

"It don't seem to make any difference to any of them."

"I didn't think it would. And I don't suppose anybody has complained."

"Well;—there was a little said by one lady, Mr. Cartwright. But that was not because I charged her more, but because another old friend was allowed to pay less."

"She didn't do you any harm, I dare say."

"Harm;—oh dear no! She couldn't do me any harm if she tried. But I thought I'd tell you, sir, because you said it would be so. The people don't seem to think any more of seven zwansigers and a half than they do of six! It's very odd,—very odd, indeed. I suppose it's all right, sir?" This she asked, still thinking that there must be something wrong in the world when so monstrous a condition of things seemed to prevail.

"They'd think a great deal of it if you charged them more than they believed sufficient to give you a fair profit for your outlay and trouble."

"How can they know anything about it, Mr. Cartwright?"

"Ah,—indeed. How do they? But they do. You and I, Frau Frohmann, must study these matters very closely before we can find out how they adjust themselves. But we may be sure of this, that the world will never complain of fair prices, will never long endure unfair prices, and will give no thanks at all to those who sell their goods at a loss."

The Frau curtseyed and retired,—quite satisfied that she had done the right thing in raising her prices; but still feeling that she had many a struggle to make before she could understand the matter.

The Telegraph Girl

Originally appeared in *Good Cheer*, the Christmas number of *Good Words*, December 1877. Reprinted in *Why Frau Frohmann Raised Her Prices and Other Stories* (1882). Trollope was much impressed with the efficiency and modesty of the 'young women in the London Central Telegraph Office' and 'gratified at the success of this branch of female employment'.

Chapter I

Lucy Wilson and Sophy Wilson.

THREE SHILLINGS a day to cover all expenses of life, food, raiment, shelter, a room in which to eat and sleep, and fire and light,—and recreation if recreation there might be,—is not much; but when Lucy Graham, the heroine of this tale, found herself alone in the world, she was glad to think that she was able to earn so much by her work, and that thus she possessed the means of independence if she chose to be independent. Her story up to the date with which we are dealing shall be very shortly told. She had lived for many years with a married brother, who was a bookseller in Holborn,—in a small way of business, and burdened with a large family, but still living in decent comfort. In order, however, that she might earn her own bread she had gone into the service of the Crown as a "Telegraph Girl" in the Telegraph Office.* And there she had remained till the present time, and there she was earning eighteen shillings a week by eight hours' continual work daily. Her life had been full of occupation, as in her spare hours she had been her brother's assistant in his shop, and had made herself familiar with the details of his trade. But the brother had suddenly died, and it had been quickly decided that the widow and the children should take themselves off to some provincial refuge.

Then it was that Lucy Graham had to think of her independence and her eighteen shillings a week on the one side, and of her desolation and feminine necessities on the other. To run backwards and forwards from High Holborn to St. Martin's-le-Grand had been very well as long as she could comfort herself with the companionship of her sister-in-law and defend herself with her brother's arm;—but how would it be with her if she were called upon to live all alone in London? She was driven to consider what else she could do to earn her bread. She might become a nursemaid, or perhaps a nursery governess. Though she had been well and in some respects carefully educated, she knew that she could not soar above that. Of music she did not know a note. She could draw a little and understood enough French,—not to read it, but to teach herself to read it. With English literature she was better acquainted than is usual with young women of her age and class; and, as her only personal treasures, she had managed to save a few books which had become hers through her brother's kindness. To be a servant was distasteful to her, not through any idea that service was disreputable, but from a dislike to be subject at all hours to the will of others. To

* I presume my readers to be generally aware that the headquarters of the National Telegraph Department are held at the top of one of the great buildings belonging to the General Post Office, in St. Martin's-le-Grand.

work and work hard she was quite willing, so that there might be some hours of her life in which she might not be called upon to obey.

When, therefore, it was suggested to her that she had better abandon the Telegraph Office and seek the security of some household, her spirit rebelled against the counsel. Why should she not be independent, and respectable, and safe? But then the solitude! Solitude would certainly be hard, but absolute solitude might not perhaps be necessary. She was fond too of the idea of being a government servant, with a sure and fixed salary,—bound of course to her work at certain hours, but so bound only for certain hours. During a third of the day she was, as she proudly told herself, a servant of the Crown. During the other two-thirds she was lord,—or lady,—of herself.

But there was a quaintness, a mystery, even an awe, about her independence which almost terrified her. During her labours she had eight hundred female companions, all congregated together in one vast room, but as soon as she left the Post Office she was to be all alone! For a few months after her brother's death she continued to live with her sister-in-law, during which time this great question was being discussed. But then the sister-in-law and the children disappeared, and it was incumbent on Lucy to fix herself somewhere. She must begin life after what seemed to her to be a most unfeminine fashion,—"just as though she were a young man,"—for it was thus that she described to herself her own position over and over again.

At this time Lucy Graham was twenty-six years old. She had hitherto regarded herself as being stronger and more steadfast than are women generally of that age. She had taught herself to despise feminine weaknesses, and had learned to be almost her brother's equal in managing the affairs of his shop in his absence. She had declared to herself, looking forward then to some future necessity which had become present to her with terrible quickness, that she would not be feckless, helpless, and insufficient for herself as are so many females. She had girded herself up for a work-a-day life,—looking forward to a time when she might leave the telegraphs and become a partner with her brother. A sudden disruption had broken up all that.

She was twenty-six, well made, cheery, healthy, and to some eyes singularly good-looking, though no one probably would have called her either pretty or handsome. In the first place her complexion was—brown. It was impossible to deny that her whole face was brown, as also was her hair, and generally her dress. There was a pervading brownness about her which left upon those who met her a lasting connection between Lucy Graham and that serviceable, long-enduring colour. But there was nobody so convinced that she was brown from head to foot as was she herself. A good lasting colour she would call it,—one that did not require to be washed every half-hour in order that it might be decent, but could bear real washing when it was wanted; for it was a point of her inner creed, of her very faith of faith, that she was not to depend upon feminine good looks, or any of the adventitious charms of dress for her advance in the world. "A good strong binding," she would say of certain dark-visaged books, "that will stand the gas, and not look disfigured even though a blot of ink should come in its way." And so it was that she regarded her own personal binding.

But for all that she was to some observers very attractive. There was not a mean feature in her face. Her forehead was spacious and well formed. Her eyes, which were brown also, were very bright, and could sparkle with anger or solicitude, or perhaps with love. Her nose was well formed, and delicately shaped enough. Her mouth was large, but full of expression, and seemed to declare without speech that she could be eloquent. The form of her face was oval, and complete, not as though it had been moulded by an inartistic thumb, a bit added on here and a bit there. She was somewhat above the average height of women, and stood upon her legs,—or walked upon them,—as though she understood that they had been given to her for real use.

Two years before her brother's death there had been a suitor for her hand,—as to whose suit she had in truth doubted much. He also had been a bookseller, a man in a larger way of business than her brother, some fifteen years older than herself,—a widower, with a family. She knew him to be a good man, with a comfortable house, an adequate income, and a kind heart. Had she gone to him she would not have been required then to live among the bookshelves or the telegraphs. She had doubted much whether she would not go to him. She knew she could love the children. She thought that she could buckle herself to that new work with a will. But she feared,—she feared that she could not love him.

Perhaps there had come across her heart some idea of what might be the joy of real, downright, hearty love. If so it was only an idea. No personage had come across her path thus to disturb her. But the idea, or the fear, had been so strong with her that she had never been able to induce herself to become the wife of this man; and when he had come to her after her brother's death, in her worst desolation,—when the prospect of service in some other nursery had been strongest before her eyes,—she had still refused him. Perhaps there had been a pride in this,—a feeling that as she had rejected him in her comparative prosperity, she should not take him now when the renewal of his offer might probably be the effect of generosity. But she did refuse him; and the widowed bookseller had to look elsewhere for a second mother for his children.

Then there arose the question, how and where she should live? When it came to the point of settling herself, that idea of starting in life like a young man became very awful indeed. How was she to do it? Would any respectable keeper of lodgings take her in upon that principle? And if so, in what way should she plan out her life? Sixteen hours a day were to be her own. What should she do with them? Was she or was she not to contemplate the enjoyment of any social pleasures; and if so, how were they to be found of such a nature as not to be discreditable? On rare occasions she had gone to the play with her brother, and had then enjoyed the treat thoroughly. Whether it had been *Hamlet* at the Lyceum, or *Lord Dundreary* at the Haymarket, she had found herself equally able to be happy. But there could not be for her now even such rare occasions as these. She thought that she knew that a young woman all alone could not go to the theatre with propriety, let her be ever so brave. And then those three shillings a day, though sufficient for life, would hardly be more than sufficient.

But how should she begin? At last chance assisted her. Another girl, also employed in the Telegraph Office, with whom there had been some family acquaintance over and beyond that formed in the office, happened at this time to be thrown upon the world in some such fashion as herself, and the two agreed to join their forces.

She was one Sophy Wilson by name,—and it was agreed between them that they should club their means together and hire a room for their joint use. Here would be a companionship,—and possibly, after awhile, sweet friendship. Sophy was younger than herself, and might probably need, perhaps be willing to accept, assistance. To be able to do something that should be of use to somebody would, she felt, go far towards giving her life that interest which it would otherwise lack.

When Lucy examined her friend, thinking of the closeness of their future connection, she was startled by the girl's prettiness and youth, and thorough unlikeness to herself. Sophy had long, black, glossy curls, large eyes, a pink complexion, and was very short. She seemed to have no inclination for that strong, serviceable brown binding which was so valuable in Lucy's eyes; but rather to be wedded to bright colours and soft materials. And it soon became evident to the elder young woman that the younger looked upon her employment simply as a stepping-stone to a husband. To get herself married as soon as possible was unblushingly declared by Sophy Wilson to be the one object of her ambition,—and as she supposed that of every other girl in the telegraph department. But she seemed to be friendly and at first docile, to have been brought up with aptitudes for decent life, and to be imbued with the necessity of not spending more than her three shillings a day. And she was quick enough at her work in the office,—quicker even than Lucy herself,—which was taken by Lucy as evidence that her new friend was clever, and would therefore probably be an agreeable companion.

They took together a bedroom in a very quiet street in Clerkenwell,—a street which might be described as genteel because it contained no shops; and here they began to keep house, as they called it. Now the nature of their work was such that they were not called upon to be in their office till noon, but that then they were required to remain there till eight in the evening. At two a short space was allowed them for dinner, which was furnished to them at a cheap rate in a room adjacent to that in which they worked. Here for eightpence each they could get a good meal, or if they preferred it they could bring their food with them, and even have it cooked upon the premises. In the evening tea and bread and butter were provided for them by the officials; and then at eight or a few minutes after they left the building and walked home. The keeping of house was restricted in fact to providing tea and bread and butter for the morning meal, and perhaps when they could afford it for the repetition of such comfort later in the evening. There was the Sunday to be considered,—as to which day they made a contract with the keeper of the lodging-house to sit at her table and partake of her dishes. And so they were established.

From the first Lucy Graham made up her mind that it was her duty to be a very friend of friends to this new companion. It was as though she had consented to marry that widowed bookseller. She would then have considered herself bound to devote herself to his welfare. It was not that she could as yet say that she loved Sophy Wilson. Love with her could not be so immediate as that. But the nature of the bond between them was such, that each might possibly do so much either for the happiness, or the unhappiness of the other! And then, though Sophy was clever,—for as to this Lucy did not doubt,—still she was too evidently in many things inferior to herself, and much in want of such assistance as a stronger nature could give her. Lucy in acknowledging this put down her own greater strength to the score of her years and the nature of the life which she had been called upon to lead. She had early in her days been required to help herself, to hold her own, and to be as it were a woman of business. But the weakness of the other was very apparent to her. That doctrine as to the necessity of a husband, which had been very soon declared, had,—well,—almost disgusted Lucy. And then she found cause to lament the peculiar arrangement which the requirements of the office had made as to their hours. At first it had seemed to her to be very pleasant that they should have their morning hours for needlework, and perhaps for a little reading; but when she found that Sophy would lie in bed till ten because early rising was not obligatory, then she wished that they had been classed among those whose presence was demanded at eight.

After awhile, there was a little difference between them as to what might or what might not be done with propriety after their office hours were over. It must be explained that in that huge room in which eight hundred girls were at work together, there was also a sprinkling of boys and young men. As no girls were employed there after eight there would always be on duty in the afternoon an increasing number of the other sex, some of whom remained there till late at night,—some indeed all night. Now, whether by chance,—or as Lucy feared by management,—Sophy Wilson had her usual seat next to a young lad with whom she soon contracted a certain amount of intimacy. And from this intimacy arose a proposition that they two should go with Mr. Murray,—he was at first called Mister, but the formal appellation soon degenerated into a familiar Alec,—to a Music Hall! Lucy Graham at once set her face against the Music Hall.

"But why?" asked the other girl. "You don't mean to say that decent people don't go to Music Halls?"

"I don't mean to say anything of the kind, but then they go decently attended."

"How decently? We should be decent."

"With their brothers," said Lucy;—"or something of that kind."

"Brothers!" ejaculated the other girl with a tone of thorough contempt. A visit to a Music Hall with her brother was not at all the sort of pleasure to which Sophy was looking forward. She did her best to get over objections which to her seemed to be fastidious and absurd, observing, "that if people were to feel like that there would be no coming together of people at all." But when she found that Lucy could not be instigated to go to the Music Hall, and that the idea of Alec Murray and herself going to such a place unattended by others was regarded as a proposition too monstrous to be discussed, Sophy for a while gave way. But she returned again and again to the subject, thinking to prevail by asserting that Alec had a friend, a most excellent young man, who would go with them,—and bring his sister. Alec was almost sure that the sister would come. Lucy, however, would have nothing to do with it. Lucy thought that there should be very great intimacy indeed before anything of that kind should be permitted.

And so there was something of a quarrel. Sophy declared that such a life as theirs was too hard for her, and that some kind of amusement was necessary. Unless she were allowed some delight she must go mad, she must die, she must throw herself off Waterloo Bridge. Lucy, remembering her duty, remembering how imperative it was that she should endeavour to do good to the one human being with whom she was closely concerned, forgave her, and tried to comfort her;—forgave her even though at last she refused to be guided by her monitress. For Sophy did go to the Music Hall with Alec Murray,—reporting, but reporting falsely, that they were accompanied by the friend and the friend's sister. Lucy, poor Lucy, was constrained by certain circumstances to disbelieve this false assertion. She feared that Sophy had gone with Alec alone,—as was the fact. But yet she forgave her friend. How are we to live together at all if we cannot forgive each other's offences?

Chapter II

Abraham Hall.

AS THERE was no immediate repetition of the offence the forgiveness soon became complete, and Lucy found the interest of her life in her endeavours to be good to this weak child whom chance had thrown in her way. For Sophy Wilson was but a weak child. She was full of Alec Murray for awhile, and induced Lucy to make the young man's acquaintance. The lad was earning twelve shillings a week, and if these two poor young creatures chose to love each other and get themselves married, it would be respectable, though it might be unfortunate. It would at any rate be the way of the world, and was a natural combination with which she would have no right to interfere. But she found that Alec was a mere boy, and with no idea beyond the enjoyment of a bright scarf and a penny cigar, with a girl by his side at a Music Hall. "I don't think it can be worth your while to go much out of your way for his sake," said Lucy.

"Who is going out of her way? Not I. He's as good as anybody else, I suppose. And one must have somebody to talk to sometimes." These last words she uttered so plaintively, showing so plainly that she was unable to endure the simple unchanging dulness of a life of labour, that Lucy's heart was thoroughly softened towards her. She had the great gift of being not the less able to sympathize with the weakness of the weak because of her own abnormal strength. And so it came to pass that she worked for her friend,—stitching and mending when the girl ought to have stitched and mended for herself,—reading to her, even though but little of what was read might be understood,—yielding to her and assisting her in all things, till at last it came to pass that in truth she loved her. And such love and care were much wanted, for the elder girl soon found that the younger was weak in health as well as weak in spirit. There were days on which she could not,—or at any rate did not go to her office. When six months had passed by Lucy had not once been absent since she had begun her new life.

"Have you seen that man who has come to look at our house?" asked Sophy one day as they were walking down to the office. Lucy had seen a strange man, having met him on the stairs. "Isn't he a fine fellow?"

"For anything that I know. Let us hope that he is very fine," said Lucy laughing.

"He's about as handsome a chap as I think I ever saw."

"As for being a chap the man I saw must be near forty."

"He is a little old I should say, but not near that. I don't think he can have a wife or he wouldn't come here. He's an engineer, and he has the care of a steam-engine in the City Road,—that great printing place. His name is Abraham Hall, and he's earning three or four pounds a week. A man like that ought to have a wife."

"How did you learn all about him?"

"It's all true. Sally heard it from Mrs. Green." Mrs. Green was the keeper of the lodging-house and Sally was the maid. "I couldn't help speaking to him yesterday because we were both at the door together. He talked just like a gentleman although he was all smutty and greasy."

"I am glad he talked like a gentleman."

"I told him we lodged here and that we were telegraph girls, and that we never got home till half-past eight. He would be just the beau for you because he is such a big steady-looking fellow."

"I don't want a beau," said Lucy angrily.

"Then I shall take him myself," said Sophy as she entered the office.

Soon after that it came to pass that there did arise a slight acquaintance between both the girls and Abraham Hall, partly from the fact of their near neighbourhood, partly perhaps from some little tricks on Sophy's part. But the man seemed to be so steady, so solid, so little given to lightnesses of flirtation or to dangerous delights, that

Lucy was inclined to welcome the accident. When she saw him on a Sunday morning free from the soil of his work, she could perceive that he was still a young man, probably not much over thirty;—but there was a look about him as though he were well inured to the cares of the world, such as is often produced by the possession of a wife and family,—not a look of depression by any means, but seeming to betoken an appreciation of the seriousness of life. From all this Lucy unconsciously accepted an idea of security in the man, feeling that it might be pleasant to have some strong one near her, from whom in case of need assistance might be asked without fear. For this man was tall and broad and powerful, and seemed to Lucy's eyes to be a very pillar of strength when he would stand still for a moment to greet her in the streets.

But poor Sophy, who had so graciously offered the man to her friend at the beginning of their intercourse, seemed soon to change her mind and to desire his attention for herself. He was certainly much more worthy than Alec Murray. But to Lucy, to whom it was a rule of life as strong as any in the commandments that a girl should not throw herself at a man, but should be sought by him, it was a painful thing to see how many of poor Sophy's much-needed sixpences were now spent in little articles of finery by which it was hoped that Mr. Hall's eyes might be gratified, and how those glossy ringlets were brushed and made to shine with pomatum, and how the little collars were washed and re-washed and starched and re-starched, in order that she might be smart for him. Lucy, who was always neat, endeavoured to become browner and browner. This she did by way of reproach and condemnation, not at all surmising that Mr. Hall might possibly prefer a good solid wearing colour to glittering blue and pink gewgaws.

At this time Sophy was always full of what Mr. Hall had last said to her; and after awhile broached an idea that he was some gentleman in disguise. "Why in disguise? Why not a gentleman not in disguise?" asked Lucy, who had her own ideas, perhaps a little exaggerated, as to Nature's gentlemen. Then Sophy explained herself. A gentleman, a real gentleman, in disguise would be very interesting;—one who had quarrelled with his father, perhaps, because he would not endure paternal tyranny, and had then determined to earn his own bread till he might happily come into the family honours and property in a year or two. Perhaps instead of being Abraham Hall he was in reality the Right Honourable Russell Howard Cavendish; and if, during his temporary abeyance, he should prove his thorough emancipation from the thraldom of his aristocracy by falling in love with a telegraph girl, how fine it would be! When Lucy expressed an opinion that Mr. Hall might be a very fine fellow though he were fulfilling no more than the normal condition of his life at the present moment, Sophy would not be contented, declaring that her friend, with all her reading, knew nothing of poetry. In this way they talked very frequently about Abraham Hall, till Lucy would often feel that such talking was indecorous. Then she would be silent for awhile herself, and rebuke the other girl for her constant mention of the man's name. Then again she would be brought back to the subject;—for in all the little intercourse which took place between them and the man, his conduct was so simple and yet so civil, that she could not really feel him to be unworthy of a place in her thoughts. But Sophy soon declared frankly to her friend that she was absolutely in love with the man. "You wouldn't have him, you know," she said when Lucy scolded her for the avowal.

"Have him! How can you bring yourself to talk in such a way about a man? What does he want of either of us?"

"Men do marry you know,—sometimes," said Lucy; "and I don't know how a young man is to get a wife unless some girl will show that she is fond of him."

"He should show first that he is fond of her."

"That's all very well for talkee-talkee," said Sophy; "but it doesn't do for practice. Men are awfully shy. And then though they do marry sometimes, they don't want to get married particularly,—not as we do. It comes like an accident. But how is a man to fall into a pit if there's no pit open?"

In answer to this Lucy used many arguments and much scolding. But to very little effect. That the other girl should have thought so much about it and be so ready with her arguments was horrid to her. "A pit open!" ejaculated Lucy; "I would rather never speak to a man again than regard myself in such a light." Sophy said that all that might be very well, but declared that it "would not wash."

The elder girl was so much shocked by all this that there came upon her gradually a feeling of doubt whether their joint life could be continued. Sophy declared her purpose openly of entrapping Abraham Hall into a marriage, and had absolutely induced him to take her to the theatre. He had asked Lucy to join them; but she had sternly refused, basing her refusal on her inability to bear the expense. When he offered to give her the treat, she told him with simple gravity that nothing would induce her to accept such a favour from any man who was not either a very old friend or a near relation. When she said this he so looked at her that she was sure that he approved of her resolve. He did not say a word to press her;—but he took Sophy Wilson, and, as Lucy knew, paid for Sophy's ticket.

All this displeased Lucy so much that she began to think whether there must not be a separation. She could not continue to live on terms of affectionate friendship with a girl whose conduct she so strongly disapproved. But then again, though she could not restrain the poor light thing altogether, she did restrain her in some degree. She was doing some good by her companionship. And then, if it really was in the man's mind to marry the girl, that certainly would be a good thing,—for the girl. With such a husband she would be steady enough. She was quite sure that the idea of preparing a pit for such a one as Abraham Hall must be absurd. But Sophy was pretty and clever, and if married would at any rate love her husband. Lucy thought she had heard that steady, severe, thoughtful men were apt to attach themselves to women of the butterfly order. She did not like the way in which Sophy was doing this; but then, who was she that she should be a judge? If Abraham Hall liked it, would not that be much more to the purpose? Therefore she resolved that there should be no separation at present;—and, if possible, no quarrelling.

But soon it came to pass that there was another very solid reason against separation. Sophy, who was often unwell, and would sometimes stay away from the office for a day or two on the score of ill-health, though by doing so she lost one of her three shillings on each such day, gradually became worse. The superintendent at her department had declared that in case of further absence a medical certificate must be sent, and the doctor attached to the office had called upon her. He had looked grave, had declared that she wanted considerable care, had then gone so far as to recommend rest,—which meant absence from work,—for at least a fortnight, and ordered her medicine. This of course meant the loss of a third of her wages. In such circumstances and at such a time it was not likely that Lucy should think of separation.

While Sophy was ill Abraham Hall often came to the door to inquire after her health;—so often that Lucy almost thought that her friend had succeeded. The man seemed to be sympathetic and anxious, and would hardly have inquired with so much solicitude had he not really been anxious as to poor Sophy's health. Then, when Sophy was better, he would come in to see her, and the girl would deck herself out with some little ribbon and would have her collar always starched and ironed, ready for his reception. It certainly did seem to Lucy that the man was becoming fond of her foolish little friend.

During this period Lucy of course had to go to the office alone, leaving Sophy to the care of the lodging-house keeper. And, in her solitude, troubles were heavy on her. In the first place Sophy's illness had created certain necessarily increased expenses; and at the same time their joint incomes had been diminished by one shilling a week out of six. Lucy was in general matters allowed to be the dispenser of the money; but on occasions the other girl would assert her rights,—which always meant her right to some indulgence out of their joint incomes which would be an indulgence to her and her alone. Even those bright ribbons could not be had for nothing. Lucy wanted no bright ribbons. When they were fairly prosperous she had not grudged some little expenditure in this direction. She had told herself that young girls like to be bright in the eyes of men, and that she had no right even to endeavour to make her friend look at all these things with her eyes. She even confessed to herself some deficiency on her own part, some want of womanliness in that she did not aspire to be attractive,—still owning to herself, vehemently declaring to herself, that to be attractive in the eyes of a man whom she could love would of all delights be the most delightful. Thinking of all this she had endeavoured not to be angry with poor Sophy; but when she became pinched for shillings and sixpences and to feel doubtful whether at the end of each fortnight there would be money to pay Mrs. Green for lodgings and coal, then her heart became sad within her, and she told herself that Sophy, though she was ill, ought to be more careful.

And there was another trouble which for awhile was very grievous.

Telegraphy is an art not yet perfected among us and is still subject to many changes. Now it was the case at this time that the pundits of the office were in favour of a system of communicating messages by ear instead of by eye. The little dots and pricks which even in Lucy's time had been changed more than once, had quickly become familiar to her. No one could read and use her telegraphic literature more rapidly or correctly than Lucy Graham. But now that this system of little tinkling sounds was coming up,—a system which seemed to be very pleasant to those females who were gifted with musical aptitudes,—she found herself to be less quick, less expert, less useful than her neighbours. This was very sad, for she had always been buoyed up by an unconscious conviction of her own superior intelligence. And then, though there had been neither promises nor threats, she had become aware,—that those girls who could catch and use the tinkling sounds would rise more quickly to higher pay than the less gifted ones. She had struggled therefore to overcome the difficulty. She had endeavoured to force her ears to do that which her ears were not capable of accomplishing. She had failed, and to-day had owned to herself that she must fail. But Sophy had been one of the first to catch the tinkling sounds. Lucy came back to her room sad and down at heart and full of troubles. She had a long task of needlework before her, which had been put by for awhile through causes consequent on Sophy's illness. "Now she is better perhaps he will marry her and take her away, and I shall be alone again," she said to herself, as though declaring that such a state of things would be a relief to her, and almost a happiness.

"He has just been here," said Sophy to her as soon as she entered the room. Sophy was painfully, cruelly smart, clean and starched, and shining about her locks,—so prepared that, as Lucy thought, she must have evidently expected him.

"Well;—and what did he say?"

"He has not said much yet, but it was very good of him to come and see me,—and he was looking so handsome. He is going out somewhere this evening to some political meeting with two or three other men, and he was got up quite like a gentleman. I do like to see him look like that."

"I always think a working man looks best in his working clothes," said Lucy. "There's some truth about him then. When he gets into a black coat he is pretending to be something else, but everybody can see the difference."

There was a severity, almost a savageness in this, which surprised Sophy so much that at first she hardly knew how to answer it. "He is going to speak at the meeting," she said after a pause. "And of course he had to make himself tidy. He told me all that he is going to say. Should you not like to hear him speak?"

"No," said Lucy very sharply, setting to work instantly upon her labours, not giving herself a moment for preparation or a moment for rest. Why should she like to hear a man speak who could condescend to love so empty and so vain a thing as that? Then she became gradually ashamed of her own feelings. "Yes," she said; "I think I should like to hear him speak;—only if I were not quite so tired. Mr. Hall is a man of good sense, and well educated, and I think I should like to hear him speak."

"I should like to hear him say one thing I know," said Sophy. Then Lucy in her rage tore asunder some fragment of a garment on which she was working.

Chapter III

Sophy Wilson Goes To Hastings.

SOPHY WENT back to her work, and in a very few days was permanently moved from the seat which she had hitherto occupied next to Alec Murray and near to Lucy, to a distant part of the chamber in which the tinkling instruments were used. And as a part of the arrangement consequent on this she was called on to attend from ten till six instead of from noon till eight. And her hour for dining was changed also. In this way a great separation between the girls was made, for neither could they walk to the office together, nor walk from it. To Lucy, though she was sometimes inclined to be angry with her friend, this was very painful. But Sophy triumphed in it greatly. "I think we are to have a step up to 21*s.* in the musical box," she said laughing. For it was so that she called the part of the room in which the little bells were always ringing. "Won't it be nice to have 3*s.* 6*d.* instead of 3*s*?" Lucy said solemnly that any increase of income was always nice, and that when such income was earned by superiority of acquirement it was a matter of just pride. This she enunciated with something of a dogmatic air; having schooled herself to give all due praise to Sophy, although it had to be given at the expense of her own feelings. But when Sophy said in reply that that was just what she had been thinking herself, and that as she could do her work by ear she was of course worth more than those who could not, then the other could only with difficulty repress the soreness of her heart.

But to Sophy I think the new arrangements were most pleasant because it enabled her to reach the street in which she lived just when Abraham Hall was accustomed to return from his work. He would generally come home,—to clean himself as she called it,—and would then again go out for his employment or amusement for the evening; and now, by a proper system of lying in wait, by creeping slow or walking quick, and by watching well, she was generally able to have a word or two with him. But he was so very bashful! He would always call her Miss Wilson; and she of course was obliged to call him Mr. Hall. "How is Miss Graham?" he asked one evening.

"She is very well. I think Lucy is always well. I never knew anybody so strong as she is."

"It is a great blessing. And how are you yourself?"

"I do get so tired at that nasty office. Though of course I like what

I am doing now better than the other. It was that rolling up the bands that used to kill me. But I don't think I shall ever really be strong till I get away from the telegraphs. I suppose you have no young ladies where you are?"

"There are I believe a lot of them in the building, stitching bindings; but I never see them."

"I don't think you care much for young ladies, Mr. Hall."

"Not much—now."

"Why not now? What does that mean?"

"I dare say I never told you or Miss Graham before. But I had a wife of my own for a time."

"A wife! You!"

"Yes indeed. But she did not stay with me long. She left me before we had been a year married."

"Left you!"

"She died," he said, correcting very quickly the false impression which his words had been calculated to make.

"Dear me! Died before a year was out. How sad!"

"It was very sad."

"And you had no,—no,—no baby, Mr. Hall?"

"I wish she had had none, because then she would have been still living. Yes, I have a boy. Poor little mortal! It is two years old I think to-day."

"I should so like to see him. A little boy! Do bring him some day, Mr. Hall." Then the father explained that the child was in the country, down in Hertfordshire; but nevertheless he promised that he would some day bring him up to town and show him to his new friends.

Surely having once been married and having a child he must want another wife! And yet how little apt he was to say or do any of those things by saying and doing which men are supposed to express their desire in that direction! He was very slow at making love;—so slow that Sophy hardly found herself able to make use of her own little experiences with him. Alec Murray, who, however, in the way of a husband was not worth thinking of, had a great deal more to say for himself. She could put on her ribbons for Mr. Hall, and wait for him in the street, and look up into his face, and call him Mr. Hall;—but she could not tell him how dearly she would love that little boy and what an excellent mother she would be to him, unless he gave her some encouragement.

When Lucy heard that he had been a married man and that he had a child she was gratified, though she knew not why. "Yes, I should like to see him of course," she said, speaking of the boy. "A child, if you have not the responsibility of taking care of it, is always nice."

"I should so like to take care of it."

"I should not like to ask him to bring the boy up out of the country." She paused a moment, and then added, "He is just the man whom I should have thought would have married, and just the man to be made very serious by the grief of such a loss. I am coming to think it does a person good to have to bear troubles."

"You would not say that if you always felt as sick as I do after your day's work."

About a week after that Sophy was so weak in the middle of the day that she was obliged to leave the office and go home. "I know it will kill me," she said that evening, "if I go on with it. The place is so stuffy and nasty, and then those terrible stairs. If I could get out of it and settle down, then I should be quite well. I am not made for that kind of work;—not like you are."

"I think I was made for it certainly."

"It is such a blessing to be strong," said poor Sophy.

"Yes; it is a blessing. And I do bless God that he has made me so. It is the one good thing that has been given to me, and it is better, I think, than all the others." As she said this she looked at Sophy and thought that she was very pretty; but she thought also that prettiness had its dangers and its temptations; and that good strong serviceable health might perhaps be better for one who had to earn her bread.

But through all these thoughts there was a great struggle going on within her. To be able to earn one's bread without personal suffering is very good. To be tempted by prettiness to ribbons, pomatum, and vanities which one cannot afford is very bad. To do as Sophy was doing in regard to this young man, setting her cap at him and resolving to make prey of him as a fowler does of a bird, was, to her way of thinking, most unseemly. But to be loved by such a man as Abraham Hall, to be chosen by him as his companion, to be removed from the hard, outside, unwomanly work of the world to the indoor occupations which a husband would require from her; how much better a life according to her real tastes would that be, than anything which she now saw before her! It was all very well to be brown and strong while the exigencies of her position were those which now surrounded her; but she could not keep herself from dreaming of something which would have been much better than that.

A month or two passed away during which the child had on one occasion been brought up to town on a Saturday evening, and had been petted and washed and fed and generally cared for by the two girls during the Sunday,—all which greatly increased their intimacy with the father. And now, as Lucy quickly observed, Abraham Hall called Sophy by her christian name. When the word was first pronounced in Lucy's presence Sophy blushed and looked round at her friend. But she never said that the change had been made at her own request. "I do so hate to be called Miss Wilson," she had said. "It seems among friends as though I were a hundred years old." Then he had called her Sophy. But she did not dare,—not as yet,—to call him Abraham. All which the other girl watched very closely, saying nothing.

But during these two months Sophy had been away from her office more than half the time. Then the doctor said she had better leave town for awhile. It was September, and it was desired that she should pass that month at Hastings. Now it should be explained that in such emergencies as this the department has provided a most kindly aid for young women. Some five or six at a time are sent out for a month to

Hastings or to Brighton, and are employed in the telegraph offices in those towns. Their railway fares are paid for them, and a small extra allowance is made to them to enable them to live away from their homes. The privilege is too generally sought to be always at the command of her who wants it; nor is it accorded except on the doctor's certificate. But in the September Sophy Wilson was sent down to Hastings.

In spite, however, of the official benevolence which greatly lightened the special burden which illness must always bring on those who have to earn their bread, and which in Sophy Wilson's case had done so much for her, nevertheless the weight of the misfortune fell heavily on poor Lucy. Some little struggle had to be made as to clothes before the girl could be sent away from her home; and, though the sick one was enabled to support herself at Hastings, the cost of the London lodgings which should have been divided fell entirely upon Lucy. Then at the end of the month there came worse tidings. The doctor at Hastings declared that the girl was unfit to go back to her work,—was, indeed, altogether unfit for such effort as eight hours' continued attendance required from her. She wanted at any rate some period of perfect rest, and therefore she remained down at the seaside without the extra allowance which was so much needed for her maintenance.

Then the struggle became very severe with Lucy,—so severe that she began to doubt whether she could long endure it. Sophy had her two shillings a day, the two-thirds of her wages, but she could not subsist on that. Something had to be sent to her in addition, and this something could only come from Lucy's wages. So at least it was at first. In order to avoid debt she gave up her more comfortable room and went upstairs into a little garret. And she denied herself her accustomed dinner at the office, contenting herself with bread and cheese,—or often simply with bread,—which she could take in her pocket. And she washed her own clothes and mended even her own boots, so that still she might send a part of her earnings to the sick one.

"Is she better?" Abraham asked her one day.

"It is hard to know, Mr. Hall. She writes just as she feels at the moment. I am afraid she fears to return to the office."

"Perhaps it does not suit her."

"I suppose not. She thinks some other kind of life would be better for her. I dare say it would."

"Could I do anything?" asked the man very slowly.

Could he do anything? well; yes. Lucy at least thought that he could do a great deal. There was one thing which, if he would do it, would make Sophy at any rate believe herself to be well. And this sickness was not organic,—was not, as it appeared, due to any cause which could be specified. It had not as yet been called by any name,—such as consumption. General debility had been spoken of both by the office doctor and by him at Hastings. Now Lucy certainly thought that a few words from Mr. Hall would do more than all the doctors in the way of doing that which was distasteful to her. And that idea of a husband had taken such hold of her, that nothing else seemed to her to give a prospect of contentment. "Why don't you go down and see her, Mr. Hall?" she said.

Then he was silent for awhile before he answered,—silent and very thoughtful. And Lucy as the sound of her own words rested on her ears felt she had done wrong in asking such a question. Why should he go down, unless indeed he were in love with the girl and prepared to ask her to be his wife? If he were to go down expressly to visit her at Hastings unless he were so prepared, what false hopes he would raise; what damage he would do instead of good! How indeed could he possibly go down on such a mission without declaring to all the world that he intended to make the girl his wife? But it was necessary that the question should be answered. "I could do no good by that," he said.

"No; perhaps not. Only I thought— "

"What did you think?" Now he asked a question and showed plainly by his manner that he expected an answer.

"I don't know," said Lucy blushing. "I suppose I ought not to have thought anything. But you seemed to be so fond of her."

"Fond of her! Well; one does get fond of kind neighbours. I suppose you would think me impertinent, Miss Lucy,"—he had never made even this approach to familiarity before,—"if I were to say that I am fond of both of you."

"No indeed," she replied, thinking that as a fondness declared by a young man for two girls at one and the same moment could not be interesting, so neither could it be impertinent.

"I don't think I should do any good by going down. All that kind of thing costs so much money."

"Of course it does, and I was very wrong."

"But I should like to do something, Miss Lucy." And then he put his hand into his trousers pocket, and Lucy knew that he was going to bring forth money.

She was very poor; but the idea of taking money from him was shocking to her. According to her theory of life, even though Sophy had been engaged to the man as his promised wife, she should not consent to accept maintenance from him or pecuniary aid till she had been made, in very truth, flesh of his flesh, and bone of his bone. Presents an engaged girl might take of course, but hardly even presents of simple utility. A shawl might be given, so that it was a pretty thing and not a shawl merely for warmth. An engaged girl should rather live on bread and water up to her marriage, than take the means of living from the man she loved, till she could take it by right of having become his wife. Such were her feelings, and now she knew that this man was about to offer her money. "We shall do very well," she said, "Sophy and I together."

"You are very hard pinched," he replied. "You have given up your room."

"Yes, I have done that. When I was alone I did not want so big a place."

"I suppose I understand all about it," he said somewhat roughly, or, perhaps, gruffly would be the better word. "I think there is one thing poor people ought never to do. They ought never to be ashamed of being poor among themselves."

Then she looked up into his face, and as she did so a tear formed itself in each of her eyes. "Am I ashamed of anything before you?" she asked.

"You are afraid of telling the truth lest I should offer to help you. I know you don't have your dinner regular as you used."

"Who has dared to tell you that, Mr. Hall? What is my dinner to anybody?"

"Well. It is something to me. If we are to be friends of course I don't like seeing you go without your meals. You'll be ill next yourself."

"I am very strong."

"It isn't the way to keep so, to work without the victuals you're used to." He was talking to her now in such a tone as to make her almost feel that he was scolding her. "No good can come of that. You are sending your money down to Hastings to her."

"Of course we share everything."

"You wouldn't take anything from me for yourself I dare say. Anybody can see how proud you are. But if I leave it for her I don't think you have a right to refuse it. Of course she wants it if you don't." With that he brought out a sovereign and put it down on the table.

"Indeed I couldn't, Mr. Hall," she said.

"I may give it to her if I please."

"You can send it her yourself," said Lucy, not knowing how else to answer him.

"No, I couldn't. I don't know her address." Then without waiting for another word he walked out of the room, leaving the sovereign on the table. This occurred in a small back parlour on the ground floor, which was in the occupation of the landlady, but was used sometimes by the lodgers for such occasional meetings.

What was she to do with the sovereign? She would be very angry if any man were to send her a sovereign; but it was not right that she should measure Sophy's feelings by her own. And then it might still be that the man was sending the present to the girl whom he intended to make his wife. But why—why—why, had he asked about her dinner? What were her affairs to him? Would she not have gone without her dinner for ever rather than have taken it at his hands? And yet, who was there in all the world of whom she thought so well as of him? And so she took the sovereign upstairs with her into her garret.

Chapter IV

Mr. Brown The Hairdresser.

Lucy, when she got up to her own little room with the sovereign, sat for a while on the bed, crying. But she could not in the least explain to herself why it was that she was shedding tears at this moment. It was not because Sophy was ill, though that was cause to her of great grief; nor because she herself was so hard put to it for money to meet her wants. It may be doubted whether grief or pain ever does of itself produce tears, which are rather the outcome of some emotional feeling. She was not thinking much of Sophy as she cried, nor certainly were her own wants present to her mind. The sovereign was between her fingers, but she did not at first even turn her mind to that, or consider what had best be done with it. But what right had he to make inquiry as to her poverty? It was that, she told herself, which now provoked her to anger so that she wept from sheer vexation. Why should he have searched into her wants and spoken to her of her need of victuals? What had there been between them to justify him in tearing away that veil of custom which is always supposed to hide our private necessities from our acquaintances till we ourselves feel called upon to declare them? He had talked to her about her meals. He ought to know that she would starve rather than accept one from him. Yes;—she was very angry with him, and would henceforth keep herself aloof from him.

But still, as she sat, there were present to her eyes and ears the form and words of an heroic man. He had seemed to scold her; but there are female hearts which can be better reached and more surely touched by the truth of anger than by the patent falseness of flattery. Had he paid her compliments she would not now have been crying, nor would she have complained to herself of his usage; but she certainly would not have sat thinking of him, wondering what sort of woman had been that young wife to whom he had first given himself, wondering whether it was possible that Sophy should be good enough for him.

Then she got up, and looking down upon her own hand gazed at the sovereign till she had made up her mind what she would do with it. She at once sat down and wrote to Sophy. She had made up her mind. There should be no diminution in the contribution made from her own wages. In no way should any portion of that sovereign administer to her own comfort. Though she might want her accustomed victuals ever so badly, they should not come to her from his earnings. So she told Sophy in the letter that Mr. Hall had expressed great anxiety for her welfare, and had begged that she would accept a present from him. She was to get anything with the sovereign that might best tend to her happiness. But the shilling a day which Lucy contributed out of her own wages was sent with the sovereign.

For an entire month she did not see Abraham Hall again so as to do more than just speak to him on the stairs. She was almost inclined to think that he was cold and unkind in not seeking her;—and yet she wilfully kept out of his way. On each Sunday it would at any rate have been easy for her to meet him; but with a stubborn purpose which she did not herself understand she kept herself apart, and when she met him on the stairs, which she would do occasionally when she returned from her work, she would hardly stand till she had answered his inquiries after Sophy. But at the end of the month one evening he came up and knocked at her door. "I am sorry to intrude, Miss Lucy."

"It is no intrusion, Mr. Hall. I wish I had a place to ask you to sit down in."

"I have come to bring another trifle for Miss Sophy."

"Pray do not do it. I cannot send it her. She ought not to take it. I am sure you know that she ought not to take it."

"I know nothing of the kind. If I know anything, it is that the strong should help the weak, and the healthy the sick. Why should she not take it from me as well as from you?"

It was necessary that Lucy should think a little before she could answer this;—but, when she had thought, her answer was ready. "We are both girls."

"Is there anything which ought to confine kindness to this or the other sex? If you were knocked down in the street would you let no one but a woman pick you up?"

"It is not the same. I know you understand it, Mr. Hall. I am sure you do."

Then he also paused to think what he would say, for he was conscious that he did "understand it." For a young woman to accept money from a man seemed to imply that some return of favours would be due. But,—he said to himself,—that feeling came from what was dirty and not from what was noble in the world. "You ought to lift yourself above all that," he said at last. "Yes; you ought. You are very good, but you would be better if you would do so. You say that I understand, and I think that you, too, understand."

This again was said in that voice which seemed to scold, and again her eyes became full of tears. Then he was softer on a sudden. "Good night, Miss Lucy. You will shake hands with me;—will you not?" She put her hand in his, being perfectly conscious at the moment that it was the first time that she had ever done so. What a mighty hand it seemed to be as it held hers for a moment! "I will put the sovereign on the table," he said, again leaving the room and giving her no option as to its acceptance.

But she made up her mind at once that she would not be the means of sending his money to Sophy Wilson. She was sure that she would take nothing from him for her own relief, and therefore sure that neither ought Sophy to do so,—at any rate unless there had been more between them than either of them had told to her. But Sophy must judge for herself. She sent, therefore, the sovereign back to Hall with a little note as follows:—

"Dear Mr. Hall,—Sophy's address is at
"Mrs. Pike's,
"19, Paradise Row,
"Fairlight, near Hastings.

"You can do as you like as to writing to her. I am obliged to send back the money which you have so *very generously* left for her, because I do not think she ought to accept it. If she were quite in want it might be different, but we have still five shillings a day between us. If a young woman were starving perhaps it ought to be the same as though she were being run over in the street, but it is not like that. In my next letter I shall tell Sophy all about it.

"Yours truly,
"LUCY GRAHAM."

The following evening, when she came home, he was standing at the house door evidently waiting for her. She had never seen him loitering in that way before, and she was sure that he was there in order that he might speak to her.

"I thought I would let you know that I got the sovereign safely," he said. "I am so sorry that you should have returned it."

"I am sure that I was right, Mr. Hall."

"There are cases in which it is very hard to say what is right and what is wrong. Some things seem right because people have been wrong so long. To give and take among friends ought to be right."

"We can only do what we think right," she said, as she passed in through the passage upstairs.

She felt sure from what had passed that he had not sent the money to Sophy. But why not? Sophy had said that he was bashful. Was he so far bashful that he did not dare himself to send the money to the girl he loved, though he had no scruple as to giving it to her through another person? And, as for bashfulness, it seemed to her that the man spoke out his mind clearly enough. He could scold her, she thought, without any difficulty, for it still seemed that his voice and manner were rough to her. He was never rough to Sophy; but then she had heard so often that love will alter a man amazingly!

Then she wrote her letter to Sophy, and explained as well as she could the whole affair. She was quite sure that Sophy would regret the loss of the money. Sophy, she knew, would have accepted it without scruple. People, she said to herself, will be different. But she endeavoured to make her friend understand that she, with her feelings, could not be the medium of sending on presents of which she disapproved. "I have given him your address," she said, "and he can suit himself as to writing to you." In this letter she enclosed a money order for the contribution made to Sophy's comfort out of her own wages.

Sophy's answer, which came in a day or two, surprised her very much. "As to Mr. Hall's money," she began, "as things stand at present perhaps it is as well that you didn't take it." As Lucy had expected that grievous fault would be found with her, this was comfortable. But it was after that, that the real news came. Sophy was a great deal better; that was also good tidings;—but she did not want to leave Hastings just at present. Indeed she thought that she did not want to leave it at all. A very gentlemanlike young man, who was just going to be taken into partnership in a hairdressing establishment, had proposed to her;—and she had accepted him. Then there were two wishes expressed;—the first was that Lucy would go on a little longer with her kind generosity, and the second,—that Mr. Hall would not feel it very much.

As regarded the first wish, Lucy resolved that she would go on at least for the present. Sophy was still on sick leave from the office, and, even though she might be engaged to a hairdresser, was still to be regarded as an invalid. But as to Mr. Hall, she thought that she could do nothing. She could not even tell him,—at any rate till that marriage at Hastings was quite a settled thing. But she thought that Mr. Hall's future happiness would not be lessened by the event. Though she had taught herself to love Sophy, she had been unable not to think that her friend was not a fitting wife for such a man. But in telling herself that he would have an escape, she put it to herself as though the fault lay chiefly in him. "He is so stern and so hard that he would have crushed her, and she never would have understood his justness and honesty." In her letter of congratulation, which was very kind, she said not a word of Abraham Hall, but she promised to go on with her own contribution till things were a little more settled.

In the meantime she was very poor. Even brown dresses won't wear for ever, let them be ever so brown, and in the first flurry of sending Sophy off to Hastings,—with that decent apparel which had perhaps been the means of winning the hairdresser's heart,—she had got somewhat into debt with her landlady. This she was gradually paying off, even on her reduced wages, but the effort pinched her closely. Day by day, in spite of all her efforts with her needle, she became sensible of a deterioration in her outward appearance which was painful to her at the office, and which made her most careful to avoid any meeting with Abraham Hall. Her boots were very bad, and she had now for some time given up even the pretence of gloves as she went backwards and forwards to the office. But perhaps it was her hat that was most vexatious. The brown straw hat which had lasted her all the summer and autumn could hardly be induced to keep its shape now when November was come.

One day, about three o'clock in the afternoon, Abraham Hall went to the Post Office, and, having inquired among the messengers, made his way up to the telegraph department at the top of the building. There he asked for Miss Graham, and was told by the doorkeeper that the young ladies were not allowed to receive visitors during office hours. He persisted, however, explaining that he had no wish to go into the room, but that it was a matter of importance, and that he was very anxious that Miss Graham should be asked to come out to him. Now it is a rule that the staff of the department who are engaged in sending and receiving messages, the privacy of which may be of vital importance, should be kept during the hours of work as free as possible from communication with the public. It is not that either the girls or the young men would be prone to tell the words which they had been the means of passing on to their destination, but that it might be worth the while of some sinner to offer great temptation, and that the power of offering it should be lessened as much as possible. Therefore, when Abraham Hall pressed his request the door-keeper told him that it was quite impossible.

"Do you mean to say that if it were an affair of life and death she could not be called out?" Abraham asked in that voice which had sometimes seemed to Lucy to be so impressive. "She is not a prisoner!"

"I don't know as to that," replied the man; "you would have to see the superintendent, I suppose."

"Then let me see the superintendent." And at last he did succeed in seeing some one whom he so convinced of the importance of his message as to bring Lucy to the door.

"Miss Graham," he said, when they were at the top of the stairs, and so far alone that no one else could hear him, "I want you to come out with me for half an hour."

"I don't think I can. They won't let me."

"Yes they will. I have to say something which I must say now."

"Will not the evening do, Mr. Hall?"

"No; I must go out of town by the mail train from Paddington, and it will be too late. Get your hat and come with me for half an hour."

Then she remembered her hat, and she snatched a glance at her poor stained dress, and she looked up at him. He was not dressed in his working clothes, and his face and hands were clean, and altogether there was a look about him of well-to-do manly tidiness which added to her feeling of shame.

"If you will go on to the house I will follow you," she said.

"Are you ashamed to walk with me?"

"I am, because— "

He had not understood her at first, but now he understood it all. "Get your hat," he said, "and come with a friend who is really a friend. You must come; you must, indeed." Then she felt herself compelled to obey, and went back and got her old hat and followed him down the stairs into the street. "And so Miss Wilson is going to be married," were the first words he said in the street.

"Has she written to you?"

"Yes; she has told me all about it. I am so glad that she should be settled to her liking, out of town. She says that she is nearly well now. I hope that Mr. Brown is a good sort of man, and that he will be kind to her."

It could hardly be possible, Lucy thought, that he should have taken her away from the office merely to talk to her of Sophy's prospects. It was evident that he was strong enough to conceal any chagrin which might have been caused by Sophy's apostacy. Could it, however, be the case that he was going to leave London because his feelings had been too much disturbed to allow of his remaining quiet? "And so you are going away? Is it for long?" "Well, yes; I suppose it is for always." Then there came upon her a sense of increased desolation. Was he not her only friend? And then, though she had refused all pecuniary assistance, there had been present to her a feeling that there was near to her a strong human being whom she could trust, and who in any last extremity could be kind to her.

"For always! And you go to-night!" Then she thought that he had been right to insist on seeing her. It would certainly have been a great blow to her if he had gone without a word of farewell.

"There is a man wanted immediately to look after the engines at a great establishment on the Wye, in the Forest of Dean. They have offered me four pounds a week."

"Four pounds a week!"

"But I must go at once. It has been talked about for some time, and now it has come all in a clap. I have to be off without a day's notice, almost before I know where I am. As for leaving London, it is just what I like. I love the country."

"Oh, yes," said Lucy, "that will be nice;—and about your little boy?" Could it be that she was to be asked to do something for the child?

They were now at the door of their house.

"Here we are," he said, "and perhaps I can say better inside what I have got to say." Then she followed him into the back sitting-room on the ground floor.

Chapter V

Abraham Hall Married.

"YES;" he said;—"about my little boy. I could not say what I had to say in the street, though I had thought to do so." Then he paused, and she sat herself down, feeling, she did not know why, as though she would lack strength to hear him if she stood. It was then the case that some particular service was to be demanded from her,—something that would show his confidence in her. The very idea of this seemed at once to add a grace to her life. She would have the child to love. There would be something for her to do. And there must be letters between her and him. It would certainly add a grace to her life. But how odd that he should not take his child with him! He had paused a moment while she thought of all this, and she was aware that he was looking at her. But she did not dare to return his gaze, or even to glance up at his face. And then gradually she felt that she was shivering and trembling. What was it that ailed her,—just now when it would be so necessary that she should speak out with some strength? She had eaten nothing since her breakfast when he had come to her, and she was afraid that she would show herself to be weak. "Will you be his mother?" he said.

What did it mean? How was she to answer him? She knew that his eyes were on her, but hers were more than ever firmly fixed upon the floor. And she was aware that she ought briskly to have acceded to his request,—so as to have shown by her ready alacrity that she had attributed no other meaning to the words than they had been intended to convey,—that she had not for a moment been guilty of rash folly. But though it was so imperative upon her to say a word, yet she could not speak. Everything was swimming round her. She was not even sure that she could sit upon her chair. "Lucy," he said;—then she thought she would have fallen;—"Lucy, will you be my wife?"

There was no doubt about the word. Her sense of hearing was at any rate not deficient. And there came upon her at once a thorough conviction that all her troubles had been changed for ever and a day into joys and blessings. The word had been spoken from which he certainly would never go back, and which of course,—of course,—must be a commandment to her. But yet there was an unfitness about it which disturbed her, and she was still powerless to speak. The remembrance of the meanness of her clothes and poorness of her position came upon her,—so that it would be her duty to tell him that she was not fit for him; and yet she could not speak.

"If you will say that you want time to think about it, I shall be contented," he said. But she did not want a moment to think about it. She could not have confessed to herself that she had learned to love him,—oh, so much too dearly,—if it were not for this most unexpected, most unthought of, almost impossible revelation. But she did not want a moment to make herself sure that she did love him. Yet she could not speak. "Will you say that you will think of it for a month?"

Then there came upon her an idea that he was not asking this because he loved her, but in order that he might have a mother whom he could trust for his child. Even that would have been flattering, but that would not have sufficed. Then when she told herself what she was, or rather what she thought herself to be, she felt sure that he could not really love her. Why should such a man as he love such a woman? Then her mouth was opened. "You cannot want me for myself," she said.

"Not for yourself! Then why? I am not the man to seek any girl for her fortune, and you have none." Then again she was dumfounded. She could not explain what she meant. She could not say,—because I am brown, and because I am plain, and because I have become thin and worn from want, and because my clothes are old and shabby. "I ask you," he said, "because with all my heart I love you."

It was as though the heavens had been opened to her. That he should speak a word that was not true was to her impossible. And, as it was so, she would not coy her love to him for a moment. If only she could have found words with which to speak to him! She could not even look up at him, but she put out her hand so as to touch him. "Lucy," he said, "stand up and come to me." Then she stood up and with one little step crept close to his side. "Lucy, can you love me?" And as he asked the question his arm was pressed round her waist, and as she put up her hand to welcome rather than to restrain his embrace, she again felt the strength, the support, and the warmth of his grasp. "Will you not say that you love me?"

"I am such a poor thing," she replied.

"A poor thing, are you? Well, yes; there are different ways of being poor. I have been poor enough in my time, but I never thought myself a poor thing. And you must not say it ever of yourself again."

"No?"

"My girl must not think herself a poor thing. May I not say, my girl?" Then there was just a little murmur, a sound which would have been "yes" but for the inability of her lips to open themselves. "And if my girl, then my wife. And shall my wife be called a poor thing? No, Lucy. I have seen it all. I don't think I like poor things;—but I like you."

"Do you?"

"I do. And now I must go back to the City Road and give up charge and take my money. And I must leave this at seven—after a cup of tea. Shall I see you again?"

"See me again! Oh, to-day, you mean. Indeed you shall. Not see you off? My own, own, own man?"

"What will they say at the office?"

"I don't care what they say. Let them say what they like. I have never been absent a day yet without leave. What time shall I be here?" Then he named an hour. "Of course I will have your last words. Perhaps you will tell me something that I must do."

"I must leave some money with you."

"No; no; no; not yet. That shall come after." This she said smiling up at him, with a sparkle of a tear in each eye, but with such a smile! Then he caught her in his arms and kissed her. "That may come at present at any rate," he said. To this, though it was repeated once and again, there was no opposition. Then in his own masterful manner he put on his hat and stalked out of the room without any more words.

She must return to the office that afternoon, of course, if only for the sake of explaining her wish to absent herself the rest of the day. But she could not go forth into the streets just yet. Though she had been able to smile at him and to return his caress, and for a moment so to stand by him that she might have something of the delight of his love, still she was too much flurried, too weak from the excitement of the last half-hour, to walk back to the Post Office without allowing herself some minutes to recruit her strength and collect her thoughts. She went at once up to her own room and cut for herself a bit of bread which she began to eat,—just as one would trim one's lamp carefully for some night work, even though oppressed by heaviest sorrow, or put fuel on the fire that would be needed. Then having fed herself, she leaned back in her chair, throwing her handkerchief over her face, in order that she might think of it.

Oh,—how much there was to fill her mind with many thoughts! Looking back to what she had been even an hour ago, and then assuring herself with infinite delight of the certain happiness of her present position, she told herself that all the world had been altered to her within that short space. As for loving him;—there was no doubt about that! Now she could own to herself that she had long since loved him, even when she thought that he might probably take that other girl as his wife. That she should love him,—was it not a matter of course, he being what he was? But that he should love her,—that, that was the marvel! But he did. She need not doubt that. She could remember distinctly each word of assurance that he had spoken to her. "I ask you, because with all my heart I love you." "May I not say my girl;—and, if my girl, then my wife?" "I do not think that I like poor things; but

I like you." No. If she were regarded by him as good enough to be his wife then she would certainly never call herself a poor thing again.

In her troubles and her poverty,—especially in her solitude, she had often thought of that other older man who had wanted to make her his wife,—sometimes almost with regret. There would have been duties for her and a home, and a mode of life more fitting to her feminine nature than this solitary tedious existence. And there would have been something for her to love, some human being on whom to spend her human solicitude and sympathies. She had leagued herself with Sophy Wilson, and she had been true to the bond; but it had had in it but little satisfaction. The other life, she had sometimes thought, would have been better. But she had never loved the man, and could not have loved him as a husband should, she thought, be loved by his wife. She had done what was right in refusing the good things which he had offered her,—and now she was rewarded! Now had come to her the bliss of which she had dreamed, that of belonging to a man to whom she felt that she was bound by all the chords of her heart. Then she repeated his name to herself,—Abraham Hall, and tried in a lowest whisper the sound of that other name,—Lucy Hall. And she opened her arms wide as she sat upon the chair as though in that way she could take his child to her bosom.

She had been sitting so nearly an hour when she started up suddenly and again put on her old hat and hurried off towards her office. She felt now that as regarded her clothes she did not care about herself. There was a paradise prepared for her so dear and so near that the present was made quite bright by merely being the short path to such a future. But for his sake she cared. As belonging to him she would fain, had it been possible, not have shown herself in a garb unfitting for his wife. Everything about him had always been decent, fitting, and serviceable! Well! It was his own doing. He had chosen her as she was. She would not run in debt to make herself fit for his notice, because such debts would have been debts to be paid by him. But if she could squeeze from her food what should supply her with garments fit at any rate to stand with him at the altar it should be done.

Then, as she hurried on to the office, she remembered what he had said about money. No! She would not have his money till it was hers of right. Then with what perfect satisfaction would she take from him whatever he pleased to give her, and how hard would she work for him in order that he might never feel that he had given her his good things for nothing!

It was five o'clock before she was at the office, and she had promised to be back in the lodgings at six, to get for him his tea. It was quite out of the question that she should work to-day. "The truth is, ma'am," she said to the female superintendent, "I have received and accepted an offer of marriage this afternoon. He is going out of town to-night, and I want to be with him before he goes." This is a plea against which official rigour cannot prevail. I remember once when a young man applied to a saturnine pundit who ruled matters in a certain office for leave of absence for a month to get married. "To get married!" said the saturnine pundit. "Poor fellow! But you must have the leave." The lady at the telegraph office was no doubt less caustic, and dismissed our Lucy for the day with congratulations rather than pity.

She was back at the lodging before her lover, and had borrowed the little back parlour from Mrs. Green, and had spread the tea-things, and herself made the toast in the kitchen before he came. "There's something I suppose more nor friendship betwixt you and Mr. Hall, and better," said the landlady smiling. "A great deal better, Mrs. Green," Lucy had replied, with her face intent upon the toast. "I thought it never could have been that other young lady," said Mrs. Green.

"And now, my dear, about money," said Abraham as he rose to prepare himself for the journey. Many things had been settled over that meal,—how he was to get a house ready, and was then to say when she should come to him, and how she should bring the boy with her, and how he would have the banns called in the church, and how they would be married as soon as possible after her arrival in the new country. "And now, my dear, about money?"

She had to take it at last. "Yes," she said, "it is right that I should have things fit to come to you in. It is right that you shouldn't be disgraced."

"I'd marry you in a sack from the poor-house, if it were necessary," he said with vehemence.

"As it is not necessary, it shall not be so. I will get things;—but they shall belong to you always; and I will not wear them till the day that I also shall belong to you."

She went with him that night to the station, and kissed him openly as she parted from him on the platform. There was nothing in her love now of which she was ashamed. How, after some necessary interval, she followed him down into Gloucestershire, and how she became his wife standing opposite to him in the bright raiment which his liberality had supplied, and how she became as good a wife as ever blessed a man's household, need hardly here be told.

That Miss Wilson recovered her health and married the hairdresser may be accepted by all anxious readers as an undoubted fact.

The Lady of Launay

Originally appeared in *Light* (Belles Lettres Section), weekly from 6 April 1878 to 11 May 1878. The story was the lead item in the first number of a short-lived periodical conducted by Robert Buchanan. Trollope supplied the story at very short notice on 18 March 1878. In a letter preserved among Trollope's working-papers Buchanan stipulates: 'we strongly desire a story with great sexual interest'. 'The Lady of Launay' was reprinted in *Why Frau Frohmann Raised Her Prices and Other Stories* (1882). There are parallels between the situation of orphaned Bessy Pryor, farmed out to the unbending Mrs. Miles, and that of the orphaned Ayala Dormer, farmed out to the dutiful Dossetts in the novel Trollope was about to begin, *Ayala's Angel* (1881).

Chapter I

How Bessy Pryor Became A Young Lady Of Importance.

HOW GREAT is the difference between doing our duty and desiring to do it; between doing our duty and a conscientious struggle to do it; between duty really done and that satisfactory state of mind which comes from a conviction that it has been performed. Mrs. Miles was a lady who through her whole life had thought of little else than duty. Though she was possessed of wealth and social position, though she had been a beautiful woman, though all phases of self-indulgent life had been open to her, she had always adhered to her own idea of duty. Many delights had tempted her. She would fain have travelled, so as to see the loveliness of the world; but she had always remained at home. She could have enjoyed the society of intelligent sojourners in capitals; but she had confined herself to that of her country neighbours. In early youth she had felt herself to be influenced by a taste for dress; she had consequently compelled herself to use raiment of extreme simplicity. She would buy no pictures, no gems, no china, because when young she found that she liked such things too well. She would not leave the parish church to hear a good sermon elsewhere, because even a sermon might be a snare. In the early days of her widowed life it became, she thought, her duty to adopt one of two little motherless, fatherless girls, who had been left altogether unprovided for in the world; and having the choice between the two, she took the plain one, who had weak eyes and a downcast, unhappy look, because it was her duty to deny herself. It was not her fault that the child, who was so unattractive at six, had become beautiful at sixteen, with sweet soft eyes, still downcast occasionally, as though ashamed of their own loveliness; nor was it her fault that Bessy Pryor had so ministered to her in her advancing years as almost to force upon her the delights of self-indulgence. Mrs. Miles had struggled manfully against these wiles, and, in the performance of her duty, had fought with them, even to an attempt to make herself generally disagreeable to the young child. The child, however, had conquered, having wound herself into the old woman's heart of hearts. When Bessy at fifteen was like to die, Mrs. Miles for awhile broke down altogether. She lingered by the bedside, caressed the thin hands, stroked the soft locks, and prayed to the Lord to stay his hand, and to alter his purpose. But when Bessy was strong again she strove to return to her wonted duties. But Bessy, through it all, was quite aware that she was loved.

Looking back at her own past life, and looking also at her days as they were passing, Mrs. Miles thought that she did her duty as well as it is given to frail man or frail woman to perform it. There had been lapses, but still she was conscious of great strength. She did believe of herself that should a great temptation come in her way she would stand strong against it. A great temptation did come in her way, and it is the purport of this little story to tell how far she stood and how far she fell.

Something must be communicated to the reader of her condition in life, and of Bessy's; something, but not much. Mrs. Miles had been a Miss Launay, and, by the death of four brothers almost in their infancy, had become heiress to a large property in Somersetshire. At twenty-five she was married to Mr. Miles, who had a property of his own in the next county, and who at the time of their marriage represented that county in Parliament. When she had been married a dozen years she was left a widow, with two sons, the younger of whom was then about three years old. Her own property, which was much the larger of the two, was absolutely her own; but was intended for Philip, who was her younger boy. Frank Miles, who was eight years older, inherited the other. Circumstances took him much away from his mother's wings. There were troubles among trustees and executors; and the father's heir, after he came of age, saw but little of his mother. She did her duty, but what she suffered in doing it may be imagined.

Philip was brought up by his mother, who, perhaps, had some consolation in remembering that the younger boy, who was always good to her, would become a man of higher standing in the world than his brother. He was called Philip Launay, the family name having passed on through the mother to the intended heir of the Launay property. He was thirteen when Bessy Pryor was brought home to Launay Park, and, as a school-boy, had been good to the poor little creature, who for the first year or two had hardly dared to think her life her own amidst the strange huge spaces of the great house. He had despised her, of course; but had not been boyishly cruel to her, and had given her his old playthings. Everybody at Launay had at first despised Bessy Pryor; though the mistress of the house had been thoroughly good to her. There was no real link between her and Launay. Mrs. Pryor had, as a humble friend, been under great obligations to Mrs. Launay, and these obligations, as is their wont, had produced deep love in the heart of the person conferring them. Then both Mr. and Mrs. Pryor had died, and Mrs. Miles had declared that she would take one of the children. She fully intended to bring the girl up sternly and well, with hard belongings, such as might suit her condition. But there had been lapses, occasioned by those unfortunate female prettinesses, and by that equally unfortunate sickness. Bessy never rebelled, and gave, therefore, no scope to an exhibition of extreme duty; and she had a way of kissing her adopted mamma which Mrs. Miles knew to be dangerous. She struggled not to be kissed, but ineffectually. She preached to herself, in the solitude of her own room, sharp sermons against the sweet softness of the girl's caresses; but she could not put a stop to them. "Yes; I will," the girl would say, so softly, but so persistently! Then there would be a great embrace, which Mrs. Miles felt to be as dangerous as a diamond, as bad as a box at the opera.

Bessy had been despised at first all around Launay. Unattractive children are despised, especially when, as in this case, they are nobodies. Bessy Pryor was quite nobody. And certainly there had never been a child more powerless to assert herself. She was for a year or two inferior to the parson's children, and was not thought much of by the farmers' wives. The servants called her Miss Bessy, of course; but it was not till after that illness that there existed among them any of that reverence which is generally felt in the servants' hall for the young ladies of the house. It was then, too, that the parson's daughters found that Bessy was nice to walk with, and that the tenants began to make much of her when she called. The old lady's secret manifestations in the sick bedroom had, perhaps, been seen. The respect paid to Mrs. Miles in that and the next parish was of the most reverential kind. Had she chosen that a dog should be treated as one of the Launays, the dog would have received all the family honours. It must be acknowledged of her that in the performance of her duty she had become a rural tyrant. She gave away many petticoats; but they all had to be stitched according to her idea of stitching a petticoat. She administered physic gratis to the entire estate; but the estate had to take the doses as she chose to have them mixed. It was because she had fallen something short of her acknowledged duty in regard to Bessy Pryor that the parson's daughters were soon even proud of an intimacy with the girl, and that the old butler, when she once went away for a week in the winter, was so careful to wrap her feet up warm in the carriage.

In this way, during the two years subsequent to Bessy's illness, there had gradually come up an altered condition of life at Launay. It could not have been said before that Bessy, though she had been Miss Bessy, was as a daughter in the house. But now a daughter's privileges were accorded to her. When the old squiress was driven out about the county, Bessy was expected, but was asked rather than ordered to accompany her. She always went; but went because she decided on going, not because she was told. And she had a horse to ride; and she was allowed to arrange flowers for the drawing-room; and the gardener did what she told him. What daughter could have more extensive privileges? But poor Mrs. Miles had her misgivings, often asking herself what would come of it all.

When Bessy had been recovering from her illness, Philip, who was seven years her senior, was making a grand tour about the world. He had determined to see, not Paris, Vienna, and Rome, which used to make a grand tour, but Japan, Patagonia, and the South Sea Islands. He had gone in such a way as to ensure the consent of his mother. Two other well-minded young men of fortune had accompanied him, and they had been intent on botany, the social condition of natives, and the progress of the world generally. There had been no harum-scarum rushing about without an object. Philip had been away for more than two years, and had seen all there was to be seen in Japan, Patagonia, and the South Sea Islands. Between them, the young men had written a book, and the critics had been unanimous in observing how improved in those days were the aspirations of young men. On his return he came to Launay for a week or two, and then went up to London. When, after four months, he returned to his mother's house, he was twenty seven years of age; and Bessy was just twenty. Mrs. Miles knew that there was cause for fear; but she had already taken steps to prevent the danger which she had foreseen.

Chapter II

How Bessy Pryor Wouldn't Marry The Parson.

OF COURSE there would be danger. Mrs. Miles had been aware of that from the commencement of things. There had been to her a sort of pleasure in feeling that she had undertaken a duty which might possibly lead to circumstances which would be altogether heartbreaking. The duty of mothering Bessy was so much more a duty because, even when the little girl was blear-eyed and thin, there was present to her mind all the horror of a love affair between her son and the little girl. The Mileses had always been much, and the Launays very much in the west of England. Bessy had not a single belonging that was anything. Then she had become beautiful and attractive, and worse than that, so much of a person about the house that Philip himself might be tempted to think that she was fit to be his wife!

Among the duties prescribed to herself by Mrs. Miles was none stronger than that of maintaining the family position of the Launays. She was one of those who not only think that blue blood should remain blue, but that blood not blue should be allowed no azure mixture. The proper severance of classes was a religion to her. Bessy was a gentlewoman, so much had been admitted, and therefore she had been brought into the drawing-room instead of being relegated among the servants, and had thus grown up to be, oh, so dangerous! She was a gentlewoman, and fit to be a gentleman's wife, but not fit to be the wife of the heir of the Launays. The reader will understand, perhaps, that I, the writer of this little history, think her to have been fit to become the wife of any man who might have been happy enough to win her young heart, however blue his blood. But Mrs. Miles had felt that precautions and remedies and arrangements were necessary.

Mrs. Miles had altogether approved of the journey to Japan. That had been a preventive, and might probably afford time for an arrangement. She had even used her influence to prolong the travelling till the arrangements should be complete; but in this she had failed. She had written to her son, saying that, as his sojourn in strange lands would so certainly tend to the amelioration of the human races generally—for she had heard of the philanthropic inquiries, of the book, and the botany—she would by no means press upon him her own natural longings. If another year was required, the necessary remittances should be made with a liberal hand. But Philip, who had chosen to go because he liked it, came back when he liked it, and there he was at Launay before a certain portion of the arrangements had been completed, as to which Mrs. Miles had been urgent during the last six months of his absence.

A good-looking young clergyman in the neighbourhood, with a living of £400 a year, and a fortune of £6,000 of his own, had during the time been proposed to Bessy by Mrs. Miles. Mr. Morrison, the Rev. Alexander Morrison, was an excellent young man; but it may be doubted whether the patronage by which he was put into the living of Budcombe at an early age, over the head of many senior curates, had been exercised with sound clerical motives. Mrs. Miles was herself the patroness, and, having for the last six years felt the necessity of providing a husband for Bessy, had looked about for a young man who should have good gifts and might probably make her happy. A couple of thousand pounds added had at first suggested itself to Mrs. Miles. Then love had ensnared her, and Bessy had become dear to every one, and money was plenty. The thing should be made so beautiful to all concerned that there should be no doubt of its acceptance. The young parson didn't doubt. Why should he? The living had been a wonderful stroke of luck for him! The portion proposed would put him at once among the easy-living gentlemen of the county; and then the girl herself! Bessy had loomed upon him as feminine perfection from the first moment he had seen her. It was to him as though the heavens were raining their choicest blessings on his head.

Nor had Mrs. Miles any reason to find fault with Bessy. Had Bessy jumped into the man's arms directly he had been offered to her as a lover, Mrs. Miles would herself have been shocked. She knew enough of Bessy to be sure that there would be no such jumping. Bessy had at first been startled, and, throwing herself into her old friend's arms, had pleaded her youth. Mrs. Miles had accepted the embrace, had acknowledged the plea, and had expressed herself quite satisfied, simply saying that Mr. Morrison would be allowed to come about the house, and use his own efforts to make himself agreeable. The young parson had come about the house, and had shown himself to be good-humoured and pleasant. Bessy never said a word against him; did in truth try to persuade herself that it would be nice to have him as a lover; but she failed. "I think he is very good," she said one day, when she was pressed by Mrs. Miles.

"And he is a gentleman."

"Oh, yes," said Bessy.

"And good-looking."

"I don't know that that matters."

"No, my dear, no; only he is handsome. And then he is very fond of you." But Bessy would not commit herself, and certainly had never given any encouragement to the gentleman himself.

This had taken place just before Philip's return. At that time his stay at Launay was to be short; and during his sojourn his hands were to be very full. There would not be much danger during that fortnight, as Bessy was not prone to put herself forward in any man's way. She met him as his little pet of former days, and treated him quite as though he were a superior being. She ran about for him as he arranged his botanical treasures, and took in all that he said about the races. Mrs. Miles, as she watched them, still trusted that there might be no danger. But she went on with her safeguards. "I hope you like Mr. Morrison," she said to her son.

"Very much indeed, mother; but why do you ask?"

"It is a secret; but I'll tell you. I think he will become the husband of our dear Bessy."

"Marry Bessy!"

"Why not?" Then there was a pause. "You know how dearly I love Bessy. I hope you will not think me wrong when I tell you that I propose to give what will be for her a large fortune, considering all things."

"You should treat her just as though she were a daughter and a sister," said Philip.

"Not quite that! But you will not begrudge her six thousand pounds?"

"It is not half enough."

"Well, well. Six thousand pounds is a large sum of money to give away. However, I am sure we shall not differ about Bessy. Don't you think Mr. Morrison would make her a good husband?" Philip looked very serious, knitted his brows, and left the room, saying that he would think about it.

To make him think that the marriage was all but arranged would be a great protection. There was a protection to his mother also in hearing him speak of Bessy as being almost a sister. But there was still a further protection. Down away in Cornwall there was another Launay heiress coming up, some third or fourth cousin, and it had long since been settled among certain elders that the Launay properties should be combined. To this Philip had given no absolute assent; had even run away to Japan just when it had been intended that he should go to Cornwall. The Launay heiress had then only been seventeen, and it had been felt to be almost as well that there should be delay, so that the time was not passed by the young man in dangerous neighbourhoods. The South Sea Island and Patagonia had been safe. And now when the idea of combining the properties was again mooted, he at first said nothing against it. Surely such precautions as these would suffice, especially as Bessy's retiring nature would not allow her to fall in love with any man within the short compass of a fortnight.

Not a word more was said between Mrs. Miles and her son as to the prospects of Mr. Morrison; not a word more then. She was intelligent enough to perceive that the match was not agreeable to him; but she attributed this feeling on his part to an idea that Bessy ought to be treated in all respects as though she were a daughter of the house of Launay. The idea was absurd, but safe. The match, if it could be managed, would of course go on, but should not be mentioned to him again till it could be named as a thing absolutely arranged. But there was no present danger. Mrs. Miles felt sure that there was no present danger. Mrs. Miles had seen Bessy grow out of meagre thinness and early want of ruddy health, into gradual proportions of perfect feminine loveliness; but, having seen the gradual growth, she did not know how lovely the girl was. A woman hardly ever does know how omnipotent may be the attraction which some feminine natures, and some feminine forms, diffuse unconsciously on the young men around them.

But Philip knew, or rather felt. As he walked about the park he declared to himself that Alexander Morrison was an insufferably impudent clerical prig; for which assertion there was, in truth, no ground whatsoever. Then he accused his mother of a sordid love of money and property, and swore to himself that he would never stir a step towards Cornwall. If they chose to have that red-haired Launay girl up from the far west, he would go away to London, or perhaps back to Japan. But what shocked him most was that such a girl as Bessy, a girl whom he treated always just like his own sister, should give herself to such a man as that young parson at the very first asking! He struck the trees among which he was walking with his stick as he thought of the meanness of feminine nature. And then such a greasy, ugly brute! But Mr. Morrison was not at all greasy, and would have been acknowledged by the world at large to be much better looking than Philip Launay.

Then came the day of his departure. He was going up to London in March to see his book through the press, make himself intimate at his club, and introduce himself generally to the ways of that life which was to be his hereafter. It had been understood that he was to pass the season in London, and that then the combined-property question should come on in earnest. Such was his mother's understanding; but by this time, by the day of his departure, he was quite determined that the combined-property question should never receive any consideration at his hands.

Early on that day he met Bessy somewhere about the house. She was very sweet to him on this occasion, partly because she loved him dearly,—as her adopted brother; partly because he was going; partly because it was her nature to be sweet! "There is one question I want to ask you," he said suddenly, turning round upon her with a frown. He had not meant to frown, but it was his nature to do so when his heart frowned within him.

"What is it, Philip?" She turned pale as she spoke, but looked him full in the face.

"Are you engaged to that parson?" She went on looking at him, but did not answer a word. "Are you going to marry him? I have a right to ask." Then she shook her head. "You certainly are not?" Now as he spoke his voice was changed, and the frown had vanished. Again she shook her head. Then he got hold of her hand, and she left her hand with him, not thinking of him as other than a brother. "I am so glad. I detest that man."

"Oh, Philip; he is very good!"

"I do not care two-pence for his goodness. You are quite sure?" Now she nodded her head. "It would have been most awful, and would have made me miserable; miserable. Of course, my mother is the best woman in the world; but why can't she let people alone to find husbands and wives for themselves?" There was a slight frown, and then with a visible effort he completed his speech. "Bessy, you have grown to be the loveliest woman that ever I looked upon."

She withdrew her hand very suddenly. "Philip, you should not say such a thing as that."

"Why not, if I think it?"

"People should never say anything to anybody about themselves."

"Shouldn't they?"

"You know what I mean. It is not nice. It's the sort of stuff which people who ain't ladies and gentlemen put into books."

"I should have thought I might say anything."

"So you may; and of course you are different. But there are things that are so disagreeable!"

"And I am one of them?"

"No, Philip, you are the truest and best of brothers."

"At any rate you won't— " Then he paused.

"No, I won't."

"That's a promise to your best and dearest brother?" She nodded her head again, and he was satisfied.

He went away, and when he returned to Launay at the end of four months he found that things were not going on pleasantly at the Park. Mr. Morrison had been refused, with a positive assurance from the young lady that she would never change her mind, and Mrs. Miles had become more stern than ever in the performance of her duty to her family.

Chapter III

How Bessy Pryor Came To Love The Heir Of Launay.

Matters became very unpleasant at the Park soon after Philip went away. There had been something in his manner as he left, and a silence in regard to him on Bessy's part, which created, not at first surprise, but uneasiness in the mind of Mrs. Miles. Bessy hardly mentioned his name, and Mrs. Miles knew enough of the world to feel that such restraint must have a cause. It would have been natural for a girl so circumstanced to have been full of Philip and his botany. Feeling this she instigated the parson to renewed attempts; but the parson had to tell her that there was no chance for him. "What has she said?" asked Mrs. Miles.

"That it can never be."

"But it shall be," said Mrs. Miles, stirred on this occasion to an assertion of the obstinacy which was in her nature. Then there was a most unpleasant scene between the old lady and her dependent. "What is it that you expect?" she asked.

"Expect, aunt!" Bessy had been instructed to call Mrs. Miles her aunt.

"What do you think is to be done for you?"

"Done for me! You have done everything. May I not stay with you?" Then Mrs. Miles gave utterance to a very long lecture, in which many things were explained to Bessy. Bessy's position was said to be one very peculiar in its nature. Were Mrs. Miles to die there would be no home for her. She could not hope to find a home in Philip's house as a real sister might have done. Everybody loved her because she had been good and gracious, but it was her duty to marry—especially her duty—so that there might be no future difficulty. Mr. Morrison was exactly the man that such a girl as Bessy ought to want as a husband. Bessy through her tears declared that she didn't want any husband, and that she certainly did not want Mr. Morrison.

"Has Philip said anything?" asked the imprudent old woman. Then Bessy was silent. "What has Philip said to you?"

"I told him, when he asked, that I should never marry Mr. Morrison." Then it was—in that very moment—that Mrs. Miles in truth suspected the blow that was to fall upon her; and in that same moment she resolved that, let the pain be what it might to any or all of them, she would do her duty by her family.

"Yes," she said to herself, as she sat alone in the unadorned, unattractive sanctity of her own bedroom, "I will do my duty at any rate now." With deep remorse she acknowledged to herself that she had been remiss. For a moment her anger was very bitter. She had warmed a reptile in her bosom. The very words came to her thoughts, though they were not pronounced. But the words were at once rejected. The girl had been no reptile. The girl had been true. The girl had been as sweet a girl as had ever brightened the hearth of an old woman. She acknowledged so much to herself even in this moment of her agony. But not the less would she do her duty by the family of the Launays. Let the girl do what she might, she must be sent away—got rid of—sacrificed in any way rather than that Philip should be allowed to make himself a fool.

When for a couple of days she had turned it all in her mind she did not believe that there was as yet any understanding between the girl and Philip. But still she was sure that the danger existed. Not only had the girl refused her destined husband—just such a man as such a girl as Bessy ought to have loved—but she had communicated her purpose in that respect to Philip. There had been more of confidence between them than between her and the girl. How could they two have talked on such a subject unless there had been between them something of stricter, closer friendship even than that of brother and sister? There had been something of a conspiracy between them against her—her who at Launay was held to be omnipotent, against her who had in her hands all the income, all the power, all the ownership—the mother of one of them, and the protectress and only friend of the other! She would do her duty, let Bessy be ever so sweet. The girl must be made to marry Mr. Morrison—or must be made to go.

But whither should she go, and if that "whither" should be found, how should Philip be prevented from following her? Mrs. Miles, in her agony, conceived an idea that it would be easier to deal with the girl herself than with Philip. A woman, if she thinks it to be a duty, will more readily sacrifice herself in the performance of it than will a man. So at least thought Mrs. Miles, judging from her own feelings; and Bessy was very good, very affectionate, very grateful, had always been obedient. If possible she should be driven into the arms of Mr. Morrison. Should she stand firm against such efforts as could be made in that direction, then an appeal should be made to herself. After all that had been done for her, would she ruin the family of the Launays for the mere whim of her own heart?

During the process of driving her into Mr. Morrison's arms—a process which from first to last was altogether hopeless—not a word had been said about Philip. But Bessy understood the reticence. She had been asked as to her promise to Philip, and never forgot that she had been asked. Nor did she ever forget those words which at the moment so displeased her—"You have grown to be the loveliest woman that I have ever looked upon." She remembered now that he had held her hand tightly while he had spoken them, and that an effort had been necessary as she withdrew it. She had been perfectly serious in decrying the personal compliment; but still, still, there had been a flavour of love in the words which now remained among her heartstrings. Of course he was not her brother—not even her cousin. There was not a touch of blood between them to warrant such a compliment as a joke. He, as a young man, had told her that he thought her, as a young woman, to be lovely above all others. She was quite sure of this—that no possible amount of driving should drive her into the arms of Mr. Morrison.

The old woman became more and more stern. "Dear aunt," Bessy said to her one day, with an air of firmness which had evidently been assumed purposely for the occasion, "indeed, indeed, I cannot love Mr. Morrison." Then Mrs. Miles had resolved that she must resort to the other alternative. Bessy must go. She did believe that when everything should be explained Bessy herself would raise no difficulty as to her own going. Bessy had no more right to live at Launay than had any other fatherless, motherless, penniless living creature. But how to explain it? What reason should be given? And whither should the girl be sent?

Then there came delay, caused by another great trouble. On a sudden Mrs. Miles was very ill. This began about the end of May, when Philip was still up in London inhaling the incense which came up from the success of his book. At first she was very eager that her son should not be recalled to Launay. "Why should a young man be brought into the house with a sick old woman? Of course she was eager. What evils might not happen if they two were brought together during her illness? At the end of three weeks, however, she was worse—so much worse that the people around her were afraid; and it became manifest to all of them that the truth must be told to Philip in spite of her injunctions. Bessy's position became one of great difficulty, because words fell from

Mrs. Miles which explained to her almost with accuracy the condition of her aunt's mind. "You should not be here," she said over and over again. Now, it had been the case, as a matter of course, that Bessy, during the old lady's illness, had never left her bedside day or night. Of course she had been the nurse, of course she had tended the invalid in everything. It had been so much a matter of course that the poor lady had been impotent to prevent it, in her ineffectual efforts to put an end to Bessy's influence. The servants, even the doctors, obeyed Bessy in regard to the household matters. Mrs. Miles found herself quite unable to repel Bessy from her bedside. And then, with her mind always intent on the necessity of keeping the young people apart, and when it was all but settled that Philip should be summoned, she said again and again, "You should not be here, Bessy. You must not be here, Bessy."

But whither should she go? No place was even suggested to her. And were she herself to consult some other friend as to a place—the clergyman of their own parish for instance, who out of that house was her most intimate friend—she would have to tell the whole story, a story which could not be told by her lips. Philip had never said a word to her, except that one word: "You have grown to be the loveliest woman that ever I looked upon." The word was very frequent in her thoughts, but she could tell no one of that!

If he did think her lovely, if he did love her, why should not things run smoothly? She had found it to be quite out of the question that she should be driven into the arms of Mr. Morrison, but she soon came to own to herself that she might easily be enticed into those other arms. But then perhaps he had meant nothing—so probably had meant nothing! But if not, why should she be driven away from Launay? As her aunt became worse and worse, and when Philip came down from London, and with Philip a London physician, nothing was settled about poor Bessy, and nothing was done. When Philip and Bessy stood together at the sick woman's bedside she was nearly insensible, wandering in her mind, but still with that care heavy at her heart. "No, Philip; no, no, no," she said. "What is it, mother?" asked Philip. Then Bessy escaped from the room and resolved that she would always be absent when Philip was by his mother's bedside.

There was a week in which the case was almost hopeless; and then a week during which the mistress of Launay crept slowly back to life. It could not but be that they two should see much of each other during such weeks. At every meal they sat together. Bessy was still constant at the bedside of her aunt, but now and again she was alone with Philip. At first she struggled to avoid him, but she struggled altogether in vain. He would not be avoided. And then of course he spoke. "Bessy, I am sure you know that I love you."

"I am sure I hope you do," she replied, purposely misinterpreting him.

Then he frowned at her. "I am sure, Bessy, you are above all subterfuges."

"What subterfuges? Why do you say that?"

"You are no sister of mine; no cousin even. You know what I mean when I say that I love you. Will you be my wife?"

Oh! if she might only have knelt at his feet and hidden her face among her hands, and have gladly answered him with a little "Yes," extracted from amidst her happy blushes! But, in every way, there was no time for such joys. "Philip, think how ill your mother is," she said.

"That cannot change it. I have to ask you whether you can love me. I am bound to ask you whether you will love me." She would not answer him then; but during that second week in which Mrs. Miles was creeping back to life she swore that she did love him, and would love him, and would be true to him for ever and ever.

Chapter IV

How Bessy Pryor Owned That She Was Engaged.

When these pretty oaths had been sworn, and while Mrs. Miles was too ill to keep her eyes upon them or to separate them, of course the two lovers were much together. For whispering words of love, for swearing oaths, for sweet kisses and looking into each other's eyes, a few minutes now and again will give ample opportunities. The long hours of the day and night were passed by Bessy with her aunt; but there were short moments, heavenly moments, which sufficed to lift her off the earth into an Elysium of joy. His love for her was so perfect, so assured! "In a matter such as this," he said in his fondly serious air, "my mother can have no right to interfere with me."

"But with me she may," said Bessy, foreseeing in the midst of her Paradise the storm which would surely come.

"Why should she wish to do so? Why should she not allow me to make myself happy in the only way in which it is possible?" There was such an ecstacy of bliss coming from such words as these, such a perfection of the feeling of mutual love, that she could not but be exalted to the heavens, although she knew that the storm would surely come. If her love would make him happy, then, then, surely he should be happy. "Of course she has given up her idea about that parson," he said.

"I fear she has not, Philip."

"It seems to me too monstrous that any human being should go to work and settle whom two other human beings are to marry."

"There was never a possibility of that."

"She told me it was to be so."

"It never could have been," said Bessy with great emphasis. "Not even for her, much as I love her—not even for her to whom I owe everything—could I consent to marry a man I did not love. But— "

"But what?"

"I do not know how I shall answer her when she bids me give you up. Oh, my love, how shall I answer her?"

Then he told her at considerable length what was the answer which he thought should in such circumstances be made to his mother. Bessy was to declare that nothing could alter her intentions, that her own happiness and that of her lover depended on her firmness, and that they two did, in fact, intend to have their own way in this matter sooner or later. Bessy, as she heard the lesson, made no direct reply, but she knew too well that it could be of no service to her. All that it would be possible for her to say, when the resolute old woman should declare her purpose, would be that come what might she must always love Philip Launay; that she never, never, never could become the wife of any other man. So much she thought she would say. But as to asserting her right to her lover, that she was sure would be beyond her.

Everyone in the house except Mrs. Miles was aware that Philip and Bessy were lovers, and from the dependents of the house the tidings spread through the parish. There had been no special secrecy. A lover does not usually pronounce his vows in public. Little half-lighted corners and twilight hours are chosen, or banks beneath the trees supposed to be safe from vulgar eyes, or lonely wanderings. Philip had followed the usual way of the world in his love-making, but had sought his secret moments with no special secrecy. Before the servants he would whisper to Bessy with that look of thorough confidence in his eyes which servants completely understand; and thus while the poor old woman was still in her bed, while she was unaware both of the danger and of her own immediate impotence, the secret—as far as it was a secret—became known to all Launay. Mr. Morrison heard it over at Budcombe, and, with his heart down in his boots, told himself that now certainly there could be no chance for him. At Launay Mr. Gregory was the rector, and it was with his daughters that Bessy had become intimate. Knowing much of the mind of the first lady of the parish, he took upon himself to say a word or two to Philip. "I am so glad to hear that your mother is much better this morning."

"Very much better."

"It has been a most serious illness."

"Terribly serious, Mr. Gregory."

Then there was a pause, and sundry other faltering allusions were made to the condition of things up at the house, from which Philip was aware that words of counsel or perhaps reproach were coming. "I hope you will excuse me, Philip, if I tell you something."

"I think I shall excuse anything from you."

"People are saying about the place that during your mother's illness you have engaged yourself to Bessy Pryor."

"That's very odd," said Philip.

"Odd!" repeated the parson.

"Very odd indeed, because what the people about the place say is always supposed to be untrue. But this report is true."

"It is true?"

"Quite true, and I am proud to be in a position to assure you that I have been accepted. I am really sorry for Mr. Morrison, you know."

"But what will your mother say?"

"I do not think that she or anyone can say that Bessy is not fit to be the wife of the finest gentleman in the land." This he said with an air of pride which showed plainly enough that he did not intend to be talked out of his purpose.

"I should not have spoken, but that your dear mother is so ill," rejoined the parson.

"I understand that. I must fight my own battle and Bessy's as best I may. But you may be quite sure, Mr. Gregory, that I mean to fight it."

Nor did Bessy deny the fact when her friend Mary Gregory interrogated her. The question of Bessy's marriage with Mr. Morrison had, somewhat cruelly in regard to her and more cruelly still in regard to the gentleman, become public property in the neighbourhood. Everybody had known that Mrs. Miles intended to marry Bessy to the parson of Budcombe, and everybody had thought that Bessy would, as a matter of course, accept her destiny. Everybody now knew that Bessy had rebelled; and, as Mrs. Miles's autocratic disposition was well understood, everybody was waiting to see what would come of it. The neighbourhood generally thought that Bessy was unreasonable and ungrateful. Mr. Morrison was a very nice man, and nothing could have been more appropriate. Now, when the truth came out, everybody was very much interested indeed. That Mrs. Miles should assent to a marriage between the heir and Bessy Pryor was quite out of the question. She was too well known to leave a doubt on the mind of anyone either in Launay or Budcombe on that matter. Men and women drew their breath and looked at each other. It was just when the parishes thought that she was going to die that the parishioners first heard that Bessy would not marry Mr. Morrison because of the young squire. And now, when it was known that Mrs. Miles was not going to die, it was known that the young squire was absolutely engaged to Bessy Pryor. "There'll be a deal o' vat in the voir," said the old head ploughman of Launay, talking over the matter with the wife of Mr. Gregory's gardener. There was going to be "a deal of fat in the fire."

Mrs. Miles was not like other mothers. Everything in respect to present income was in her hands. And Bessy was not like other girls. She had absolutely no "locus standi" in the world, except what came to her from the bounty of the old lady. By favour of the Lady of Launay she held her head among the girls of that part of the country as high as any girl there. She was only Bessy Pryor; but, from love and kindness, she was the recognised daughter of the house of Launay. Everybody knew it all. Everybody was aware that she had done much towards reaching her present position by her own special sweetness. But should Mrs. Miles once frown, Bessy would be nobody. "Oh, Bessy, how is this all to be?" asked Mary Gregory.

"As God pleases," said Bessy, very solemnly.

"What does Mrs. Miles say?"

"I don't want anybody to ask me about it," said Bessy. "Of course I love him. What is the good of denying it? But I cannot talk about it."

Then Mary Gregory looked as though some terrible secret had been revealed to her—some secret of which the burden might probably be too much for her to bear.

The first storm arose from an interview which took place between the mother and son as soon as the mother found herself able to speak on a subject which was near her heart. She sent for him and once again besought him to take steps towards that combining of the properties which was so essential to the Launay interests generally. Then he declared his purpose very plainly. He did not intend to combine the properties. He did not care for the red-haired Launay cousin. It was his intention to marry—Bessy Pryor; yes—he had proposed to her and she had accepted him. The poor sick mother was at first almost overwhelmed with despair. "What can I do but tell you the truth when you ask me?" he said.

"Do!" she screamed. "What could you do? You could have remembered your honour! You could have remembered your blood! You could have remembered your duty!" Then she bade him leave her, and after an hour passed in thought she sent for Bessy. "I have had my son with me," she said, sitting bolt upright in her bed, looking awful in her wanness, speaking with low, studied, harsh voice, with her two hands before her on the counterpane. "I have had my son with me and he has told me." Bessy felt that she was trembling. She was hardly able to support herself. She had not a word to say. The sick old woman was terrible in her severity. "Is it true?"

"Yes, it is true," whispered Bessy.

"And this is to be my return?"

"Oh, my dearest, my darling, oh, my aunt, dear, dearest, dearest aunt! Do not speak like that! Do not look at me like that! You know I love you. Don't you know I love you?" Then Bessy prostrated herself on the bed, and getting hold of the old woman's hand covered it with kisses. Yes, her aunt did know that the girl loved her, and she knew that she loved the girl perhaps better than any other human being in the world. The eldest son had become estranged from her. Even Philip had not been half so much to her as this girl. Bessy had wound herself round her very heartstrings. It made her happy even to sit and look at Bessy. She had denied herself all pretty things; but this prettiest of all things had grown up beneath her eyes. She did not draw away her hand; but, while her hand was being kissed, she made up her mind that she would do her duty.

"Of what service will be your love," she said, "if this is to be my return?" Bessy could only lie and sob and hide her face. "Say that you will give it up." Not to say that, not to give him up, was the only resolution at which Bessy had arrived. "If you will not say so, you must leave me, and I shall send you word what you are to do. If you are my enemy you shall not remain here."

"Pray—pray do not call me an enemy."

"You had better go." The woman's voice as she said this was dreadful in its harshness. Then Bessy, slowly creeping down from the bed, slowly slunk out of the room.

Chapter V

How Bessy Pryor Ceased To Be A Young Lady Of Importance.

WHEN THE old woman was alone she at once went to work in her own mind resolving what should be her course of proceeding. To yield in the matter, and to confirm the happiness of the young people, never occurred to her. Again and again she repeated to herself that she would do her duty; and again and again she repeated to herself that in allowing Philip and Bessy to come together she had neglected her duty. That her duty required her to separate them, in spite of their love, in spite of their engagement, though all the happiness of their lives might depend upon it, she did not in the least doubt. Duty is duty. And it was her duty to aggrandise the house of Launay, so that the old autocracy of the land might, so far as in her lay, be preserved. That it would be a good and pious thing to do,—to keep them apart, to force Philip to marry the girl in Cornwall, to drive Bessy into Mr. Morrison's arms, was to her so certain that it required no further thought. She had never indulged herself. Her life had been so led as to maintain the power of her own order, and relieve the wants of those below her. She had done nothing for her own pleasure. How should it occur to her that it would be well for her to change the whole course of her life in order that she might administer to the joys of a young man and a young woman?

It did not occur to her to do so. Lying thus all alone, white, sick, and feeble, but very strong of heart, she made her resolutions. As Bessy could not well be sent out of the house till a home should be provided for her elsewhere, Philip should be made to go. As that was to be the first step, she again sent for Philip that day. "No, mother; not while you are so ill." This he said in answer to her first command that he should leave Launay at once. It had not occurred to him that the house in which he had been born and bred, the house of his ancestors, the house which he had always supposed was at some future day to be his own, was not free to him. But, feeble as she was, she soon made him understand her purpose. He must go,—because she ordered him, because the house was hers and not his, because he was no longer welcome there as a guest unless he would promise to abandon Bessy. "This is tyranny, mother," he said.

"I do not mean to argue the question," said Mrs. Miles, leaning back among the pillows, gaunt, with hollow cheeks, yellow with her long sickness, seeming to be all eyes as she looked at him. "I tell you that you must go."

"Mother!"

Then, at considerable length, she explained her intended arrangements. He must go, and live upon the very modest income which she proposed. At any rate he must go, and go at once. The house was hers, and she would not have him there. She would have no one in the house who disputed her will. She had been an over-indulgent mother to him, and this had been the return made to her! She had condescended to explain to him her intention in regard to Bessy, and he had immediately resolved to thwart her. When she was dead and gone it might perhaps be in his power to ruin the family if he chose. As to that she would take further thought. But she, as long as she lived, would do her duty. "I suppose I may understand," she said, "that you will leave Launay early after breakfast to-morrow."

"Do you mean to turn me out of the house?"

"I do," she said, looking full at him, all eyes, with her grey hair coming dishevelled from under the large frill of her nightcap, with cheeks gaunt and yellow. Her extended hands were very thin. She had been very near death, and seemed, as he gazed at her, to be very near it now. If he went it might be her fate never to see him again.

"I cannot leave you like this," he said.

"Then obey me."

"Why should we not be married, mother?"

"I will not argue. You know as well as I do. Will you obey me?"

"Not in this, mother. I could not do so without perjuring myself."

"Then go you out of this house at once." She was sitting now bolt upright on her bed, supporting herself on her hands behind her. The whole thing was so dreadful that he could not endure to prolong the interview, and he left the room.

Then there came a message from the old housekeeper to Bessy, forbidding her to leave her own room. It was thus that Bessy first understood that her great sin was to be made public to all the household. Mrs. Knowl, who was the head of the domestics, had been told, and now felt that a sort of authority over Bessy had been confided to her. "No, Miss Bessy; you are not to go into her room at all. She says that she will not see you till you promise to be said by her."

"But why, Mrs. Knowl?"

"Well, miss; I suppose it's along of Mr. Philip. But you know that better than me. Mr. Philip is to go to-morrow morning and never come back any more."

"Never come back to Launay?"

"Not while things is as they is, miss. But you are to stay here and not go out at all. That's what Madam says." The servants about the place all called Mrs. Miles Madam.

There was a potency about Mrs. Miles which enabled her to have her will carried out, although she was lying ill in bed,—to have her will carried out as far as the immediate severance of the lovers was concerned. When the command had been brought by the mouth of a servant, Bessy determined that she would not see Philip again before he went. She understood that she was bound by her position, bound by gratitude, bound by a sense of propriety, to so much obedience as that. No earthly authority could be sufficient to make her abandon her troth. In that she could not allow even her aunt to sway her,—her aunt though she were sick and suffering, even though she were dying! Both her love and her vow were sacred to her. But obedience at the moment she did owe, and she kept her room. Philip came to the door, but she sat mute and would not speak to him. Mrs. Knowl, when she brought her some food, asked her whether she intended to obey the order. "Your aunt wants a promise from you, Miss Bessy?"

"I am sure my aunt knows that I shall obey her," said Bessy.

On the following morning Philip left the house. He sent a message to his mother, asking whether she would see him; but she refused. "I think you had better not disturb her, Mr. Philip," said Mrs. Knowl. Then he went, and as the waggonette took him away from the door, Bessy sat and listened to the sound of the wheels on the gravel.

All that day and all the next passed on and she was not allowed to see her aunt. Mrs. Knowl repeated that she could not take upon herself to say that Madam was better. No doubt the worry of the last day or two had been a great trouble to her. Mrs. Knowl grew much in self-importance at the time, and felt that she was overtopping Miss Bessy in the affairs of Launay.

It was no less true than singular that all the sympathies of the place should be on the side of the old woman. Her illness probably had something to do with it. And then she had been so autocratic, all Launay and Budcombe had been so accustomed to bow down to her, that rebellion on the part of anyone seemed to be shocking. And who was Bessy Pryor that she should dare to think of marrying the heir? Who, even, was the supposed heir that he should dare to think of marrying anyone in opposition to the actual owner of the acres? Heir though he was called, he was not necessarily the heir. She might do as she pleased with all Launay and all Budcombe, and there were those who thought that if Philip was still obstinate she would leave everything to her elder son. She did not love her elder son. In these days she never saw him. He was a gay man of the world, who had never been dutiful to her. But he might take the name of Launay, and the family would be perpetuated as well that way as the other. Philip was very foolish. And as for Bessy; Bessy was worse than foolish. That was the verdict of the place generally.

I think Launay liked it. The troubles of our neighbours are generally endurable, and any subject for conversation is a blessing. Launay liked the excitement; but, nevertheless, felt itself to be compressed into whispers and a solemn demeanour. The Gregory girls were solemn, conscious of the iniquity of their friend, and deeply sensitive of the danger to which poor Philip was exposed. When a rumour came to the vicarage that a fly had been up at the great house, it was immediately conceived that Mr. Jones, the lawyer from Taunton, had been sent for, with a view to an alteration of the will. This suddenness, this anger, this disruption of all things was dreadful! But when it was discovered that the fly contained no one but the doctor there was disappointment.

On the third day there came a message from Mrs. Miles to the rector. Would Mr. Gregory step up and see Mrs. Miles? Then it was thought at the rectory that the dear old lady was again worse, and that she had sent for her clergyman that she might receive the last comforts of religion. But this again was wrong. "Mr. Gregory," she said very suddenly, "I want to consult you as to a future home for Bessy Pryor."

"Must she go from this?"

"Yes; she must go from this. You have heard, perhaps, about her and my son." Mr. Gregory acknowledged that he had heard. "Of course she must go. I cannot have Philip banished from the house which is to be his own. In this matter he probably has been the most to blame."

"They have both, perhaps, been foolish."

"It is wickedness rather than folly. But he has been the wickeder. It should have been a duty to him, a great duty, and he should have been the stronger. But he is my son, and I cannot banish him."

"Oh, no!"

"But they must not be brought together. I love Bessy Pryor dearly, Mr. Gregory; oh, so dearly! Since she came to me, now so many years ago, she has been like a gleam of sunlight in the house. She has always been gentle with me. The very touch of her hand is sweet to me. But I must not on that account sacrifice the honour of the family. I have a duty to do; and I must do it, though I tear my heart in pieces. Where can I send her?"

"Permanently?"

"Well, yes; permanently. If Philip were married, of course she might come back. But I will still trust that she herself may be married first. I do not mean to cast her off;—only she must go. Anything that may be wanting in money shall be paid for her. She shall be provided for comfortably. You know what I had hoped about Mr. Morrison. Perhaps he may even yet be able to persuade her; but it must be away from here. Where can I send her?"

This was a question not very easy to answer, and Mr. Gregory said that he must take time to think of it. Mrs. Miles, when she asked the question, was aware that Mr. Gregory had a maiden sister, living at Avranches in Normandy, who was not in opulent circumstances.

Chapter VI

How Bessy Pryor Was To Be Banished.

When a man is asked by his friend if he knows of a horse to be sold he does not like immediately to suggest a transfer of the animal which he has in his own stable, though he may at the moment be in want of money and anxious to sell his steed. So it was with Mr. Gregory. His sister would be delighted to take as a boarder a young lady for whom liberal payment would be made; but at the first moment he had hesitated to make an offer by which his own sister would be benefited. On the next morning, however, he wrote as follows:—

> "DEAR MRS. MILES,—My sister Amelia is living at Avranches, where she has a pleasant little house on the outskirts of the town, with a garden. An old friend was living with her, but she died last year, and my sister is now alone. If you think that Bessy would like to sojourn for awhile in Normandy, I will write to Amelia and make the proposition. Bessy will find my sister good-tempered and kind-hearted.—Faithfully yours,
> JOSHUA GREGORY."

Mrs. Miles did not care much for the good temper and the kind heart. Had she asked herself whether she wished Bessy to be happy she would no doubt have answered herself in the affirmative. She would probably have done so in regard to any human being or animal in the world. Of course, she wanted them all to be happy. But happiness was to her thinking of much less importance than duty; and at the present moment her duty and Bessy's duty and Philip's duty were so momentous that no idea of happiness ought to be considered in the matter at all. Had Mr. Gregory written to say that his sister was a woman of severe morals, of stern aspect, prone to repress all youthful ebullitions, and supposed to be disagreeable because of her temper, all that would have been no obstacle. In the present condition of things suffering would be better than happiness; more in accord with the feelings and position of the person concerned. It was quite intelligible to Mrs. Miles that Bessy should really love Philip almost to the breaking of her heart, quite intelligible that Philip should have set his mind upon the untoward marriage with all the obstinacy of a proud man. When young men and young women neglect their duty, hearts have to be broken. But it is not a soft and silken operation, which can be made pleasant by good temper and social kindness. It was necessary, for certain quite adequate reasons, that Bessy should be put on the wheel, and be racked and tormented. To talk to her of the good temper of the old woman who would have to turn the wheel would be to lie to her. Mrs. Miles did not want her to think that things could be made pleasant for her.

Soon after the receipt of Mr. Gregory's letter she sent for Bessy, who was then brought into the room under the guard, as it were, of Mrs. Knowl. Mrs. Knowl accompanied her along the corridor, which was surely unnecessary, as Bessy's door had not been locked upon her. Her imprisonment had only come from obedience. But Mrs. Knowl felt that a great trust had been confided to her, and was anxious to omit none of her duties. She opened the door so that the invalid on the bed could see that this duty had been done, and then Bessy crept into the room. She crept in, but very quickly, and in a moment had her arms round the old woman's back and her lips pressed to the old woman's forehead. "Why may not I come and be with you?" she said.

"Because you are disobedient."

"No, no; I do all that you tell me. I have not stirred from my room, though it was hard to think you were ill so near me, and that I could do nothing. I did not try to say a word to him, or even to look at him; and now that he has gone, why should I not be with you?"

"It cannot be."

"But why not, aunt? Even though you would not speak to me I could be with you. Who is there to read to you?"

"There is no one. Of course it is dreary. But there are worse things than dreariness."

"Why should not I come back, now that he has gone?" She still had her arm round the old woman's back, and had now succeeded in dragging herself on to the bed and in crouching down by her aunt's side. It was her perseverance in this fashion that had so often forced Mrs. Miles out of her own ordained method of life, and compelled her to leave for a moment the strictness which was congenial to her. It was this that had made her declare to Mr. Gregory, in the midst of her severity, that Bessy had been like a gleam of sunshine in the house. Even now she knew not how to escape from the softness of an embrace which was in truth so grateful to her. It was a consciousness of this,—of the potency of Bessy's charm even over herself,—which had made her hasten to send her away from her. Bessy would read to her all the day, would hold her hand when she was half dozing, would assist in every movement with all the patience and much more than the tenderness of a waiting-maid. There was no voice so sweet, no hand so cool, no memory so mindful, no step so soft as Bessy's. And now Bessy was there, lying on her bed, caressing her, more closely bound to her than had ever been any other being in the world, and yet Bessy was an enemy from whom it was imperatively necessary that she should be divided.

"Get down, Bessy," she said; "go off from me."

"No, no, no," said Bessy, still clinging to her and kissing her.

"I have that to say to you which must be said calmly."

"I am calm,—quite calm. I will do whatever you tell me; only pray, pray, do not send me away from you."

"You say that you will obey me."

"I will; I have. I always have obeyed you."

"Will you give up your love for Philip?"

"Could I give up my love for you, if anybody told me? How can I do it? Love comes of itself. I did not try to love him. Oh, if you could know how I tried not to love him! If somebody came and said I was not to love you, would it be possible?"

"I am speaking of another love."

"Yes; I know. One is a kind of love that is always welcome. The other comes first as a shock, and one struggles to avoid it. But when it has come, how can it be helped? I do love him, better than all the world." As she said this she raised herself upon the bed, so as to look round upon her aunt's face; but still she kept her arm upon the old woman's shoulder. "Is it not natural? How could I have helped it?"

"You must have known that it was wrong."

"No!"

"You did not know that it would displease me?"

"I knew that it was unfortunate,—not wrong. What did I do that was wrong? When he asked me, could I tell him anything but the truth?"

"You should have told him nothing." At this reply Bessy shook her head. "It cannot be that you should think that in such a matter there should be no restraint. Did you expect that I should give my consent to such a marriage? I want to hear from yourself what you thought of my feelings."

"I knew you would be angry."

"Well?"

"I knew you must think me unfit to be Philip's wife."

"Well?"

"I knew that you wanted something else for him, and something else also for me."

"And did such knowledge go for nothing?"

"It made me feel that my love was unfortunate,—but not that it was wrong. I could not help it. He had come to me, and I loved him. The other man came, and I could not love him. Why should I be shut up for this in my own room? Why should I be sent away from you, to be miserable because I know that you want things done? He is not here. If he were here and you bade me not to go near him, I would not go. Though he were in the next room I would not see him. I would obey you altogether, but I must love him. And as I love him I cannot love another. You would not wish me to marry a man when my heart has been given to another."

The old woman had not at all intended that there should be such arguments as these. It had been her purpose simply to communicate her plan, to tell Bessy that she would have to live probably for a few years at Avranches, and then to send her back to her prison. But Bessy had again got the best of her, and then had come caressing, talking, and excuses. Bessy had been nearly an hour in her room before Mrs. Miles had disclosed her purpose, and had hovered round her aunt, doing as had been her wont when she was recognised as having all the powers of head nurse in her hands. Then at last, in a manner very different from that which had been planned, Mrs. Miles proposed the Normandy scheme. She had been, involuntarily, so much softened that she condescended even to repeat what Mr. Gregory had said as to the good temper and general kindness of his maiden sister. "But why should I go?" asked Bessy, almost sobbing.

"I wonder that you should ask."

"He is not here."

"But he may come."

"If he came ever so I would not see him if you bade me not. I think you hardly understand me, aunt. I will obey you in everything. I am sure you will not now ask me to marry Mr. Morrison."

She could not say that Philip would be more likely to become amenable and marry the Cornish heiress if Bessy were away at Avranches than if she still remained shut up at Launay. But that was her feeling. Philip, she knew, would be less obedient than Bessy. But then, too, Philip might be less obstinate of purpose. "You cannot live here, Bessy, unless you will say that you will never become the wife of my son."

"Never?"

"Never!"

"I cannot say that." There was a long pause before she found the courage to pronounce these words, but she did pronounce them at last.

"Then you must go."

"I may stay and nurse you till you are well. Let me do that. I will go whenever you may bid me."

"No. There shall be no terms between us. We must be friends, Bessy, or we must be enemies. We cannot be friends as long as you hold yourself to be engaged to Philip Launay. While that is so I will not take a cup of water from your hands. No, no," for the girl was again trying to embrace her. "I will not have your love, nor shall you have mine."

"My heart would break were I to say it."

"Then let it break! Is my heart not broken? What is it though our hearts do break,—what is it though we die,—if we do our duty? You owe this for what I have done for you."

"I owe you everything."

"Then say that you will give him up."

"I owe you everything, except this. I will not speak to him, I will not write to him, I will not even look at him, but I will not give him up. When one loves, one cannot give it up." Then she was ordered to go back to her room, and back to her room she went.

Chapter VII

How Bessy Pryor Was Banished To Normandy.

THERE WAS nothing for it but to go, after the interview described in the last chapter. Mrs. Miles sent a message to the obstinate girl, informing her that she need not any longer consider herself as a prisoner, but that she had better prepare her clothes so as to be ready to start within a week. The necessary correspondence had taken place between Launay and Avranches, and within ten days from the time at which Mr. Gregory had made the proposition,—in less than a fortnight from the departure of her lover,—Bessy came down from her room all equipped, and took her place in the same waggonette which so short a time before had taken her lover away from her. During the week she had had liberty to go where she pleased, except into her aunt's room. But she had, in truth, been almost as much a prisoner as before. She did for a few minutes each day go out into the garden, but she would not go beyond the garden into the park, nor did she accept an invitation from the Gregory girls to spend an evening at the rectory. It would be so necessary, one of them wrote, that everything should be told to her as to the disposition and ways of life of Aunt Amelia! But Bessy would not see the Gregory girls. She was being sent away from home because of the wickedness of her love, and all Launay knew it. In such a condition of things she could not go out to eat sally-lunn and pound-cake, and to be told of the delights of a small Norman town. She would not even see the Gregory girls when they came up to the house, but wrote an affectionate note to the elder of them explaining that her misery was too great to allow her to see any friend.

She was in truth very miserable. It was not only because of her love, from which she had from the first been aware that misery must come,—undoubted misery, if not misery that would last through her whole life. But now there was added to this the sorrow of absolute banishment from her aunt. Mrs. Miles would not see her again before she started. Bessy was well aware of all that she owed to the mistress of Launay; and, being intelligent in the reading of character, was aware also that through many years she had succeeded in obtaining from the old woman more than the intended performance of an undertaken duty. She had forced the old woman to love her, and was aware that by means of that love the old woman's life had been brightened. She had not only received, but had conferred kindness,—and it is by conferring kindness that love is created. It was an agony to her that she should be compelled to leave this dearest friend, who was still sick and infirm, without seeing her. But Mrs. Miles was inexorable. These four words written on a scrap of paper were brought to her on that morning:—"Pray, pray, see me!" She was still inexorable. There had been long pencil-written notes between them on the previous day. If Bessy would pledge herself to give up her lover all might yet be changed. The old woman at Avranches should be compensated for her disappointment. Bessy should be restored to all her privileges at Launay. "You shall be my own, own child," said Mrs. Miles. She condescended even to promise that not a word more should be said about Mr. Morrison. But Bessy also could be inexorable. "I cannot say that I will give him up," she wrote. Thus it came to pass that she had to get into the waggonette without seeing her old friend. Mrs. Knowl went with her, having received instructions to wait upon Miss Bessy all the way to Avranches. Mrs. Knowl felt that she was sent as a guard against the lover. Mrs. Miles had known Bessy too well to have fear of that kind, and had sent Mrs. Knowl as general guardian against the wild beasts which are supposed to be roaming about the world in quest of unprotected young females.

In the distribution of her anger Mrs. Miles had for the moment been very severe towards Philip as to pecuniary matters. He had chosen to be rebellious, and therefore he was not only turned out of the house, but told that he must live on an uncomfortably small income. But to Bessy Mrs. Miles was liberal. She had astounded Miss Gregory by the nobility of the terms she had proposed, and on the evening before the journey had sent ten five-pound notes in a blank envelope to Bessy.

Then in a subsequent note she had said that a similar sum would be paid to her every half-year. In none of these notes was there any expression of endearment. To none of them was there even a signature. But they all conveyed evidence of the amount of thought which Mrs. Miles was giving to Bessy and her affairs.

Bessy's journey was very comfortless. She had learned to hate Mrs. Knowl, who assumed all the airs of a duenna. She would not leave Bessy out of sight for a moment, as though Philip might have been hidden behind every curtain or under every table. Once or twice the duenna made a little attempt at persuasion herself: "It ain't no good, miss, and it had better be give up." Then Bessy looked at her, and desired that she might be left alone. This had been at the hotel at Dover. Then again Mrs. Knowl spoke as the carriage was approaching Avranches: "If you wish to come back, Miss Bessy, the way is open." "Never mind my wishes, Mrs. Knowl," said Bessy. When, on her return to Launay, Mrs. Knowl once attempted to intimate to her mistress that Miss Bessy was very obstinate, she was silenced so sternly, so shortly, that the housekeeper began to doubt whether she might not have made a mistake and whether Bessy would not at last prevail. It was evident that Mrs. Miles would not hear a word against Bessy.

On her arrival at Avranches Miss Gregory was very kind to her. She found that she was received not at all as a naughty girl who had been sent away from home in order that she might be subjected to severe treatment. Miss Gregory fulfilled all the promises which her brother had made on her behalf, and was thoroughly kind and good-tempered. For nearly a month not a word was said about Philip or the love affairs. It seemed to be understood that Bessy had come to Avranches quite at her own desire. She was introduced to the genteel society with which that place abounds, and was conscious that a much freer life was vouchsafed to her than she had ever known before. At Launay she had of course been subject to Mrs. Miles. Now she was subject to no one. Miss Gregory exercised no authority over her,—was indeed rather subject to Bessy, as being recipient of the money paid for Bessy's board and lodging.

But by the end of the month there had grown up so much of friendship between the elder and the younger lady, that something came to be said about Philip. It was impossible that Bessy should be silent as to her past life. By degrees she told all that Mrs. Miles had done for her; how she herself had been a penniless orphan; how Mrs. Miles had taken her in from simple charity; how love had grown up between them two,—the warmest, truest love; and then how that other love had grown! The telling of secrets begets the telling of secrets. Miss Gregory, though she was now old, with the marks of little feeble crow's-feet round her gentle eyes, though she wore a false front and was much withered, had also had her love affair. She took delight in pouring forth her little tale; how she had loved an officer and had been beloved; how there had been no money; how the officer's parents had besought her to set the officer free, so that he might marry money; how she had set the officer free, and how, in consequence, the officer had married money and was now a major-general, with a large family, a comfortable house, and the gout. "And I have always thought it was right," said the excellent spinster. "What could I have done for him?"

"It couldn't be right if he loved you best," said Bessy.

"Why not, my dear? He has made an excellent husband. Perhaps he didn't love me best when he stood at the altar."

"I think love should be more holy."

"Mine has been very holy,—to me, myself. For a time I wept; but now I think I am happier than if I had never seen him. It adds something to one's life to have been loved once."

Bessy, who was of a stronger temperament, told herself that happiness such as that would not suffice for her. She wanted not only to be happy herself, but also to make him so. In the simplicity of her heart she wondered whether Philip would be different from that easy-changing major-general; but in the strength of her heart she was sure he would be very different. She would certainly not release him at the request of any parent;—but he should be free as air at the slightest hint of a request from himself. She did not believe for a moment that such a request would come; but, if it did,—if it did,—then there should be no difficulty. Then would she submit to banishment,—at Avranches or elsewhere as it might be decided for her,—till it might please the Lord to release her from her troubles.

At the end of six weeks Miss Gregory knew the whole secret of Philip and Bessy's love, and knew also that Bessy was quite resolved to persevere. There were many discussions about love, in which Bessy always clung to the opinion that when it was once offered and taken, given and received, it ought to be held as more sacred than any other bond. She owed much to Mrs. Miles;—she acknowledged that;—but she thought that she owed more to Philip. Miss Gregory would never quite agree with her;—was strong in her own opinion that women are born to yield and suffer and live mutilated lives, like herself; but not the less did they become fast friends. At the end of six weeks it was determined between them that Bessy should write to Mrs. Miles. Mrs. Miles had signified her wish not to be written to, and had not herself written. Messages as to the improving state of her health had come from the Gregory girls, but no letter had as yet passed. Then Bessy wrote as follows, in direct disobedience to her aunt's orders:

> "Dearest Aunt,—I cannot help writing a line because I am so anxious about you. Mary Gregory says you have been up and out on the lawn in the sunshine, but it would make me so happy if I could see the words in your own dear handwriting. Do send me one little word. And though I know what you told me, still I think you will be glad to hear that your poor affectionate loving Bessy is well. I will not say that I am quite happy. I cannot be quite happy away from Launay and you. But Miss Gregory has been very, very kind to me, and there are nice people here. We live almost as quietly as at Launay, but sometimes we see the people. I am reading German and making lace, and I try not to be idle.

'Good-bye, dear, dearest aunt. Try to think kindly of me. I pray for you every morning and night. If you will send me a little note from yourself it will fill me with joy.'—Your most affectionate and devoted niece,

Bessy Pryor."

This was brought up to Mrs. Miles when she was still in bed, for as yet she had not returned to the early hours of her healthy life. When she had read it she at first held it apart from her. Then she put it close to her bosom, and wept bitterly as she thought how void of sunshine the house had been since that gleam had been turned away from it.

Chapter VIII

How Bessy Pryor Received Two Letters From Launay.

The same post brought Bessy two letters from England about the middle of August, both of which the reader shall see;—but first shall be given that which Bessy read the last. It was from Mrs. Miles, and had been sent when she was beginning to think that her aunt was still resolved not to write to her. The letter was as follows, and was written on square paper, which in these days is only used even by the old-fashioned when the letter to be sent is supposed to be one of great importance.

"My dear Bessy,—Though I had told you not to write to me, still I am glad to hear that you are well, and that your new home has been made as comfortable for you as circumstances will permit. Launay has not been comfortable since you went. I miss you very much. You have become so dear to me that my life is sad without you. My days have never been bright, but now they are less so than ever. I should scruple to admit so much as this to you, were it not that I intend it as a prelude to that which will follow.

"We have been sent into this world, my child, that we may do our duties, independent of that fleeting feeling which we call happiness. In the smaller affairs of life I am sure you would never seek a pleasure at the cost of your conscience. If not in the smaller things, then certainly should you not do so in the greater. To deny yourself, to remember the welfare of others, when temptation is urging you to do wrong, then do that which you know to be right,—that is your duty as a Christian, and especially your duty as a woman. To sacrifice herself is the special heroism which a woman can achieve. Men who are called upon to work may gratify their passions and still be heroes. A woman can soar only by suffering.

"You will understand why I tell you this. I and my son have been born into a special degree of life which I think it to be my duty and his to maintain. It is not that I or that he may enjoy any special delights that I hold fast to this opinion, but that I may do my part towards maintaining that order of things which has made my country more blessed than others. It would take me long to explain all this, but I know you will believe me when I say that an imperative sense of duty is my guide. You have not been born into that degree. That this does not affect my own personal feeling to you, you must know. You have had many signs how dear you are to me. At this moment my days are heavy to bear because I have not my Bessy with me,—my Bessy who has been so good to me, so loving, such an infinite blessing that to see the hem of her garments, to hear the sound of her foot, has made things bright around me. Now, there is nothing to see, nothing to hear, that is not unsightly and harsh of sound. Oh, Bessy, if you could come back to me!

"But I have to do that duty of which I have spoken, and I shall do it. Though I were never to see you again I shall do it. I am used to suffering, and sometimes think it wrong even to wish that you were back with me. But I write to you thus that you may understand everything. If you will say that you will give him up, you shall return to me and be my own, own beloved child. I tell you that you are not of the same degree. I am bound to tell you so. But you shall be so near my heart that nothing shall separate us.

"You two cannot marry while I am living. I do not think it possible that you should be longing to be made happy by my death. And you should remember that he cannot be the first to break away from this foolish engagement without dishonour. As he is the wealthy one, and the higher born, and as he is the man, he ought not to be the first to say the word. You may say it without falsehood and without disgrace. You may say it, and all the world will know that you have been actuated only by a sense of duty. It will be acknowledged that you have sacrificed yourself,—as it becomes a woman to do.

"One word from you will be enough to assure me. Since you came to me you have never been false. One word, and you shall come back to me and to Launay, my friend and my treasure! If it be that there must be suffering, we will suffer together. If tears are necessary there shall be joint tears. Though I am old still I can understand. I will acknowledge the sacrifice. But, Bessy, my Bessy, dearest Bessy, the sacrifice must be made.

"Of course he must live away from Launay for awhile. The fault will have been his, and what of inconvenience there may be he must undergo. He shall not come here till you yourself shall say that you can bear his presence without an added sorrow.

"I know you will not let this letter be in vain. I know you will think it over deeply, and that you will not keep me too long waiting for an answer. I need hardly tell you that I am

"Your most loving friend,
"M. Miles."

When Bessy was reading this, when the strong words with which her aunt had pleaded her cause were harrowing her heart, she had clasped in her hand this other letter from her lover. This too was written from Launay.

"My own dearest Bessy,—It is absolutely only now that I have found out where you are, and have done so simply because the people at the rectory could not keep the secret. Can anything be more absurd than supposing that my mother can have her way by whisking you away, and shutting you up in Normandy? It is too foolish! She has sent for me, and I have come like a dutiful son. I have, indeed, been rejoiced to see her looking again so much like herself. But I have not extended my duty to obeying her in a matter in which my own future happiness is altogether bound up; and in which, perhaps, the happiness of another person may be slightly concerned. I have told her that I would venture to say nothing of the happiness of the other person. The other person might be indifferent, though I did not believe it was so; but I was quite sure of my own. I have assured her that I know what I want myself, and that I do not mean to abandon my hope of achieving it. I know that she is writing to you. She can of course say what she pleases.

"The idea of separating two people who are as old as you and I, and who completely know our own minds,—you see that I do not really doubt as to yours,—is about as foolish as anything well can be. It is as though we were going back half a dozen centuries into the tyrannies of the middle ages. My object shall be to induce her to let you come home and be married properly from Launay. If she will not consent by the end of this month I shall go over to you, and we must contrive to be married at Avranches. When the thing has been once done all this rubbish will be swept away. I do not believe for a moment that my mother will punish us by any injustice as to money.

"Write and tell me that you agree with me, and be sure that I shall remain, as I am, always altogether your own,

"Truly and affectionately,

"PHILIP MILES."

When Bessy Pryor began to consider these two letters together, she felt that the task was almost too much for her. Her lover's letter had been the first read. She had known his handwriting, and of course had read his the first. And as she had read it everything seemed to be of rose colour. Of course she had been filled with joy. Something had been done by the warnings of Miss Gregory, something, but not much, to weaken her strong faith in her lover. The major-general had been worldly and untrue, and it had been possible that her Philip should be as had been the major-general. There had been moments of doubt in which her heart had fainted a little; but as she read her lover's words she acknowledged to herself how wrong she had been to faint at all. He declared it to be "a matter in which his own future happiness was altogether bound up." And then there had been his playful allusion to her happiness, which was not the less pleasant to her because he had pretended to think that the "other person might be indifferent." She pouted her lips at him, as though he were present while she was reading, with a joyous affectation of disdain. No, no; she could not consent to an immediate marriage at Avranches. There must be some delay. But she would write to him and explain all that. Then she read her aunt's letter.

It moved her very much. She had read it all twice before there came upon her a feeling of doubt, an acknowledgment to herself that she must reconsider the matter. But even when she was only reading it, before she had begun to consider, her former joy was repressed and almost quenched. So much of it was too true, terribly true. Of course her duty should be paramount. If she could persuade herself that duty required her to abandon Philip, she must abandon him, let the suffering to herself or to others be what it might. But then, what was it that duty required of her? "To sacrifice herself is the special heroism which a woman can achieve." Yes, she believed that. But then, how about sacrificing Philip, who, no doubt, was telling the truth when he said that his own happiness was altogether bound up in his love?

She was moved too by all that which Mrs. Miles said as to the grandeur of the Launay family. She had learned enough of the manners of Launay to be quite alive to the aristocratic idiosyncrasies of the old woman. She, Bessy Pryor, was nobody. It would have been well that Philip Launay should have founded his happiness on some girl of higher birth. But he had not done so. King Cophetua's marriage had been recognised by the world at large. Philip was no more than King Cophetua, nor was she less than the beggar-girl. Like to like in marriages was no doubt expedient,—but not indispensable. And though she was not Philip's equal, yet she was a lady. She would not disgrace him at his table, or among his friends. She was sure that she could be a comfort to him in his work.

But the parts of the old woman's letter which moved her most were those in which she gave full play to her own heart, and spoke, without reserve, of her own love for her dearest Bessy. "My days are heavy to bear because I have not my Bessy with me." It was impossible to read this and not to have some desire to yield. How good this lady had been to her! Was it not through her that she had known Philip? But for Mrs. Miles, what would her own life have been? She thought that had she been sure of Philip's happiness, could she have satisfied herself that he would bear the blow, she would have done as she was asked. She would have achieved her heroism, and shown the strength of her gratitude, and would have taken her delight in administering to the comforts of her old friend,—only that Philip had her promise. All that she could possibly owe to all the world beside must be less, so infinitely less, than what she owed to him.

She would have consulted Miss Gregory, but she knew so well what Miss Gregory would have advised. Miss Gregory would only have mentioned the major-general and her own experiences. Bessy determined, therefore, to lie awake and think of it, and to take no other counsellor beyond her own heart.

Chapter IX

How Bessy Pryor Answered The Two Letters, And What Came Of It.

THE LETTERS were read very often, and that from Mrs. Miles I think the oftener. Philip's love was plainly expressed, and what more is expected from a lover's letter than a strong, manly expression of love? It was quite satisfactory, declaring the one important fact that his happiness was bound up in hers. But Mrs. Miles' was the stronger letter, and by far the more suggestive. She had so mingled hardness and softness, had enveloped her stern lesson of feminine duty in so sweet a frame of personal love, that it was hardly possible that such a girl as Bessy Pryor should not be shaken by her arguments. There were moments during the night in which she had almost resolved to yield. "A woman can soar only by suffering." She was not sure that she wanted to soar, but she certainly did want to do her duty, even though suffering should come of it. But there was one word in her aunt's letter which militated against the writer's purpose rather than assisted it. "Since you first came to me, you have never been false." False! no; she hoped she had not been false. Whatever might be the duty of a man or a woman, that duty should be founded on truth. Was it not her special duty at this moment to be true to Philip? I do not know that she was altogether logical. I do not know but that in so supporting herself in her love there may have been a bias of personal inclination. Bessy perhaps was a little prone to think that her delight and her duty went together. But that flattering assurance, that she had never yet been false, strengthened her resolution to be true, now, to Philip.

She took the whole of the next day to think, abstaining during the whole day from a word of confidential conversation with Miss Gregory. Then on the following morning she wrote her letters. That to Philip would be easily written. Words come readily when one has to give a hearty assent to an eager and welcome proposition. But to deny, to make denial to one loved and respected, to make denial of that which the loved one has a right to ask, must be difficult. Bessy, like a brave girl, went to the hard task first, and she rushed instantly at her subject, as a brave horseman rides at his fence without craning.

"Dearest Aunt,—I cannot do as you bid me. My word to him is so sacred to me that I do not dare to break it. I cannot say that I won't be his when I feel that I have already given myself to him.

"Dear, dearest aunt, my heart is very sad as I write this, because I feel that I am separating myself from you almost for ever. You know that I love you. You know that I am miserable because you have banished me from your side. All the sweet kind words of your love to me are like daggers to me, because I cannot show my gratitude by doing as you would have me. It seems so hard! I know it is probable that I may never see him again, and yet I am to be separated from you, and you will be my enemy. In all the world there are but two that I really love. Though I cannot and will not give him up, I desire to be back at Launay now only that I might be with you. My love for him would be contented with a simple permission that it should exist. My love for you cannot be satisfied unless I am allowed to be close to you once again. You say that a woman's duty consists in suffering. I am striving to do my duty, but I know how great is my suffering in doing it. However angry you may be with your Bessy, you will not think that she can appear even to be ungrateful without a pang.

"Though I will not give him up, you need not fear that I shall do anything. Should he come here I could not, I suppose, avoid seeing him, but I should ask him to go at once; and I should beg Miss Gregory to tell him that she could not make him welcome to her house. In all things I will do as though I were your daughter—though I know so well how far I am from any right to make use of so dear a name!

"But dear, dear aunt, no daughter could love you better, nor strive more faithfully to be obedient.

"I shall always be, even when you are most angry with me, your own, poor, loving, most affectionate

"BESSY."

The other letter need perhaps be not given in its entirety. Even in such a chronicle as this there seems to be something of treachery, something of a want of that forbearance to which young ladies are entitled, in making public the words of love which such a one may write to her lover. Bessy's letter was no doubt full of love, but it was full of prudence also. She begged him not to come to Avranches. As to such a marriage as that of which he had spoken, it was, she assured him, quite impossible. She would never give him up, and so she had told Mrs. Miles. In that respect her duty to him was above her duty to her aunt. But she was so subject to her aunt that she would not in any other matter disobey her. For his sake—for Philip's sake—only for Philip's sake, she grieved that there should be more delay. Of course she was aware that it might possibly be a trouble in life too many for him to bear. In that case he might make himself free from it without a word of reproach from her. Of that he alone must be the judge. But, for the present, she could be no partner to any plans for the future. Her aunt had desired her to stay at Avranches, and at Avranches she must remain. There were words of love, no doubt; but the letter, taken altogether, was much sterner and less demonstrative of affection than that written to her aunt.

There very soon came a rejoinder from Mrs. Miles, but it was so curt and harsh as almost to crush Bessy by its laconic severity. "You are separated from me, and I am your enemy." That was all. Beneath that one line the old woman had signed her name, M. Miles, in large, plain angry letters. Bessy, who knew every turn of the woman's mind, understood exactly how it had been with her when she wrote those few words, and when, with care, she had traced that indignant signature. "Then everything shall be broken, and though there was but one gleam of sunshine left to me, that gleam shall be extinguished. No one shall say that I, as Lady of Launay, did not do my duty." It was thus the Lady of Launay had communed with herself when she penned that dreadful line. Bessy understood it all, and could almost see the woman as she wrote it.

Then in her desolation she told everything to Miss Gregory—-showed the two former letters, showed that dreadful denunciation of lasting wrath, and described exactly what had been her own letter, both to Mrs. Miles and to her lover. Miss Gregory had but one recipe to offer in such a malady; that, namely, which she had taken herself in a somewhat similar sickness. The gentleman should be allowed to go forth into the world and seek a fitter wife, whereas Bessy should content herself, for the remainder of her life, with the pleasures of memory. Miss Gregory thought that it was much even to have been once loved by the major-general. When Bessy almost angrily declared that this would not be enough for her, Miss Gregory very meekly suggested that possibly affection might change in the lapse of years, and that some other suitor—perhaps Mr. Morrison—might in course of time suffice. But at the idea Bessy became indignant, and Miss Gregory was glad to confine herself to the remedy pure and simple which she acknowledged to have been good for herself.

Then there passed a month—a month without a line from Launay or from Philip. That Mrs. Miles should not write again was to be expected. She had declared her enmity, and there was an end of everything. During the month there had come a cheque to Miss Gregory from some man of business, and with the cheque there had been no intimation that the present arrangement was to be brought to a close. It appeared therefore that Mrs. Miles, in spite of her enmity, intended to provide for the mutinuous girl a continuation of the comforts which she now enjoyed. Certainly nothing more than this could have been expected from her. But, in regard to Philip, though Bessy had assured herself, and had assured Miss Gregory also, that she did not at all desire a correspondence in the present condition of affairs, still she felt so total a cessation of all tidings to be hard to bear. Mary Gregory, when writing to her aunt, said nothing of Philip—merely remarked that Bessy Pryor would be glad to know that her aunt had nearly recovered her health, and was again able to go out among the poor. Then Bessy began to think—not that Philip was like the major-general, for to that idea she would not give way at all—but that higher and nobler motives had induced him to yield to his mother. If so she would never reproach him. If so she would forgive him in her heart of hearts. If so she would accept her destiny and entreat her old friend to allow her to return once more to Launay, and thenceforth to endure the evil thing which fate would have done to her in patient submission. If once the word should have come to her from Philip, then would she freely declare that everything should be over, then and for always, between her and her lover. After such suffering as that, while she was undergoing agony so severe, surely her friend would forgive her. That terrible word, "I am your enemy," would surely then be withdrawn.

But if it were to be so, if this was to be the end of her love, Philip, at least, would write. He would not leave her in doubt, after such a decision on his own part. That thought ought to have sustained her; but it was explained to her by Miss Gregory that the major-general had taken three months before he had been inspirited to send the fatal letter, and to declare his purpose of marrying money. There could be but little doubt, according to Miss Gregory, that Philip was undergoing the same process. It was, she thought, the natural end to such an affair. This was the kind of thing which young ladies without dowry, but with hearts to love, are doomed to suffer. There could be no doubt that Miss Gregory regarded the termination of the affair with a certain amount of sympathetic satisfaction. Could she have given Bessy all Launay, and her lover, she would have done so. But sadness and disappointment were congenial to her, and a heart broken, but still constant, was, to her thinking, a pretty feminine acquisition. She was to herself the heroine of her own romance, and she thought it good to be a heroine. But Bessy was indignant; not that Philip should be false, but that he should not dare to write and say so. "I think he ought to write," was on her lips, when the door was opened, and, lo, all of a sudden, Philip Miles was in the room.

Chapter X

How Bessy Pryor's Lover Argued His Case.

WE MUST now go back to Launay. It will be remembered that Bessy received both her letters on the same day—those namely from Mrs. Miles and from Philip—and that they both came from Launay. Philip had been sent away from the place when the fact of his declared love was first made known to the old lady, as though into a banishment which was to be perpetual till he should have repented of his sin. Such certainly had been his mother's intention. He was to be sent one way, and the girl another, and everyone concerned was to be made to feel the terrible weight of her displeasure, till repentance and retractation should come. He was to be starved into obedience by a minimised allowance, and she by the weariness of her life at Avranches. But the person most grievously punished by these arrangements was herself. She had declared to herself that she would endure anything, everything, in the performance of her duty. But the desolation of her life was so extreme that it was very hard to bear. She did not shrink and tell herself that it was unendurable, but after awhile she persuaded herself that now that Bessy was gone there could be no reason why Philip also should be exiled. Would not her influence be more potent over Philip if he were at Launay? She therefore sent for him, and he came. Thus it was that the two letters were written from the same house.

Philip obeyed his mother's behest in coming as he had obeyed it in going; but he did not hesitate to show her that he felt himself to be aggrieved. Launay of course belonged to her. She could leave it and all the property to some hospital if she chose. He was well aware of that. But he had been brought up as the heir, and he could not believe that there should come such a ruin of heaven and earth as would be produced by any change in his mother's intentions as to the Launay property. Touching his marriage, he felt that he had a right to marry whom he pleased, as long as she was a lady, and that any dictation from his mother in such a matter was a tyranny not to be endured. He had talked it all over with the rector before he went. Of course it was possible that his mother should commit such an injustice as that at which the rector hinted. "There are," said Philip, "no bounds to possibilities." It was, however, he thought, all but impossible; and whether probable or improbable, no fear of such tyranny should drive him from his purpose. He was a little magniloquent, perhaps, in what he said, but he was very resolved.

It was, therefore, with some feeling of an injury inflicted upon him that he first greeted his mother on his return to the house. For a day or two not a word passed about Bessy. "Of course, I am delighted to be with you, and glad enough to have the shooting," he said, in answer to some word of hers. "I shouldn't have gone, as you know, unless you had driven me away." This was hard on the old woman; but she bore it, and, for some days, was simply affectionate and gentle to her son—more gentle than was her wont. Then she wrote to Bessy, and told her son that she was writing. "It is so impossible," she said, "that I cannot conceive that Bessy should not obey me when she comes to regard it at a distance."

"I see no impossibility; but Bessy can, of course, do as she pleases," replied Philip, almost jauntily. Then he determined that he also would write.

There were no further disputes on the matter till Bessy's answer came, and then Mrs. Miles was very angry indeed. She had done her best so to write her letter that Bessy should be conquered both by the weight of her arguments and by the warmth of her love. If reason would not prevail, surely gratitude would compel her to do as she was bidden. But the very first words of Bessy's letter contained a flat refusal. "I cannot do as you bid me." Who was this girl, that had been picked out of a gutter, that she should persist in the right of becoming the mistress of Launay? In a moment the old woman's love was turned into a feeling of condemnation, nearly akin to hatred. Then she sent off her short rejoinder, declaring herself to be Bessy's enemy.

On the following morning regret had come, and perhaps remorse. She was a woman of strong passion, subject to impulses which were, at the time, uncontrollable; but she was one who was always compelled by her conscience to quick repentance, and sometimes to an agonising feeling of wrong done by herself. To declare that Bessy was her enemy—Bessy, who for so many years had prevented all her wishes, who had never been weary of well-doing to her, who had been patient in all things, who had been her gleam of sunshine, of whom she had sometimes said to herself in her closet that the child was certainly nearer to perfection than any other human being that she had known! True, it was not fit that the girl should become mistress of Launay! A misfortune had happened which must be cured—if even by the severance of persons so dear to each other as she and her Bessy. But she knew that she had sinned in declaring one so good, and one so dear, to be her enemy.

But what should she do next? Days went on and she did nothing. She simply suffered. There was no pretext on which she could frame an affectionate letter to her child. She could not write and ask to be forgiven for the harshness of her letter. She could not simply revoke the sentence she had pronounced without any reference to Philip and his love. In great misery, with a strong feeling of self-degradation because she had allowed herself to be violent in her wrath, she went on, repentant but still obstinate, till Philip himself forced the subject upon her.

"Mother," he said one day, "is it not time that things should be settled?"

"What things, Philip?"

"You know my intention."

"What intention?"

"As to making Bessy my wife."

"That can never be."

"But it will be. It has to be. If as regards my own feelings I could bring myself to yield to you, how could I do so with honour in regard to her? But, for myself, nothing on earth would induce me to change my mind. It is a matter on which a man has to judge for himself, and I have not heard a word from you or from anyone to make me think that I have judged wrongly."

"Do birth and rank go for nothing?"

He paused a moment, and then he answered her very seriously, standing up and looking down upon her as he did so. "For very much—with me. I do not think that I could have brought myself to choose a wife, whatever might have been a woman's charms, except among ladies. I found this one to be the chosen companion and dearest friend of the finest lady I know." At this the old woman, old as she was, first blushed, and then, finding herself to be sobbing, turned her face away from him. "I came across a girl of whose antecedents I could be quite sure, of whose bringing up I knew all the particulars, as to whom I could be certain that every hour of her life had been passed among the best possible associations. I heard testimony as to her worth and her temper which I could not but believe. As to her outward belongings, I had eyes of my own to judge. Could I be wrong in asking such a one to be my wife? Can I be regarded as unhappy in having succeeded with her? Could I be acquitted of dishonour if I were to desert her? Shall I be held to be contemptible if I am true to her?"

At every word he spoke he grew in her esteem. At this present crisis of her life she did not wish to think specially well of him, though he was her son, but she could not help herself. He became bigger before her than he had ever been before, and more of a man. It was, she felt, almost vain for a woman to lay her commands, either this way or that, upon a man who could speak to her as Philip had spoken.

But not the less was the power in her hands. She could bid him go and marry—and be a beggar. She could tell him that all Launay should go to his brother, and she could instantly make a will to that effect. So strong was the desire for masterdom upon her that she longed to do it. In the very teeth of her honest wish to do what was right, there was another wish—a longing to do what she knew to be wrong. There was a struggle within, during which she strove to strengthen herself for evil. But it was vain. She knew of herself that were she to swear today to him that he was disinherited, were she to make a will before nightfall carrying out her threat, the pangs of conscience would be so heavy during the night that she would certainly change it all on the next morning. Of what use is a sword in your hand if you have not the heart to use it? Why seek to be turbulent with a pistol if your bosom be of such a nature that your finger cannot be forced to pull the trigger? Power was in her possession—but she could not use it. The power rather was in her hands. She could not punish her boy, even though he had deserved it. She had punished her girl, and from that moment she had been crushed by torments, because of the thing that she had done. Others besides Mrs. Miles have felt, with something of regret, that they have lacked the hardness necessary for cruelty and the courage necessary for its doing.

"How shall it be, mother?" asked Philip. As she knew not what to answer she rose slowly from her chair, and leaving the room went to the seclusion of her own chamber.

Days again passed before Philip renewed his question, and repeated it in the same words: "How shall it be, mother?" Wistfully she looked up at him, as though even yet something might be accorded by him to pity; as though the son might even yet be induced to accede to his mother's prayers. It was not that she thought so. No. She had thought much, and was aware that it could not be so. But as a dog will ask with its eyes when it knows that asking is in vain, so did she ask. "One word from you, mother, will make us all happy."

"No; not all of us."

"Will not my happiness make you happy?" Then he stooped over her and kissed her forehead. "Could you be happy if you knew that I were wretched?"

"I do not want to be happy. It should be enough that one does one's duty."

"And what is my duty? Can it be my duty to betray the girl I love in order that I may increase an estate which is already large enough?"

"It is for the family."

"What is a family but you, or I, or whoever for the moment may be its representative? Say that it shall be as I would have it, and then I will go to her and let her know that she may come back to your arms."

Not then, or on the next day, or on the next, did she yield; though she knew well during all these hours that it was her fate to yield. She had indeed yielded. She had confessed to herself that it must be so, and as she did so she felt once more the soft pressure of Bessy's arms as they would cling round her neck, and she could see once more the brightness of Bessy's eyes as the girl would hang over her bed early in the morning. "I do not want to be happy," she had said; but she did want, sorely want, to see her girl. "You may go and tell her," she said one night as she was preparing to go to her chamber. Then she turned quickly away, and was out of the room before he could answer her with a word.

Chapter XI

How Bessy Pryor Received Her Lover.

Miss Gregory was certainly surprised when, on the entrance of the young man, Bessy jumped from her chair and rushed into his arms. She knew that Bessy had no brother, and her instinct rather than her experience told her that the greeting which she saw was more than fraternal,—more than cousinly. She did not doubt but that the young man was Philip Launay, and knowing what she knew she was not disposed to make spoken complaints. But when Bessy lifted her face to be kissed, Miss Gregory became red and very uneasy. It is probable that she herself had never progressed as far as this with the young man who afterwards became the major-general.

Bessy herself, had a minute been allowed to her for reflection, would have been less affectionate. She knew nothing of the cause which had brought Philip to Avranches. She only knew that her dear friend at Launay had declared her to be an enemy, and that she had determined that she could not, for years, become the wife of Philip Launay, without the consent of her who had used that cruel word. And at the moment of Philip's entering the room her heart had been sore with reproaches against him. "He ought at any rate to write." The words had been on her lips as the door had been opened, and the words had been spoken in the soreness of heart coming from a fear that she was to be abandoned.

Then he was there. In the moment that sufficed for the glance of his eye to meet hers she knew that she was not abandoned. With whatever tidings he had come that was not to be the burden of his news. No man desirous of being released from his vows ever looked like that. So up she jumped and flew to him, not quite knowing what she intended, but filled with delight when she found herself pressed to his bosom. Then she had to remember herself, and to escape from his arms. "Philip," she said, "this is Miss Gregory. Miss Gregory, I do not think you ever met Mr. Launay."

Then Miss Gregory had to endeavour to look as though nothing particular had taken place,—which was a trial. But Bessy bore her part, if not without a struggle, at least without showing it. "And now, Philip," she said, "how is my aunt?"

"A great deal stronger than when you left her."

"Quite well?"

"Yes; for her, I think I may say quite well."

"She goes out every day?"

"Every day,—after the old plan. The carriage toddles round to the door at three, and then toddles about the parish at the rate of four miles an hour, and toddles home exactly at five. The people at Launay, Miss Gregory, don't want clocks to tell them the hour in the afternoon."

"I do love punctuality," said Miss Gregory.

"I wish I were with her," said Bessy.

"I have come to take you," said Philip.

"Have you?" Then Bessy blushed,—for the first time. She blushed as a hundred various thoughts rushed across her mind. If he had been sent to take her back, sent by her aunt, instead of Mrs. Knowl, what a revulsion of circumstances must there not have been at Launay! How could it all have come to pass? Even to have been sent for at all, to be allowed to go back even in disgrace, would have been an inexpressible joy. Had Knowl come for her, with a grim look and an assurance that she was to be brought back because a prison at Launay was thought to be more secure than a prison at Avranches, the prospect of a return would have been hailed with joy. But now,—to be taken back by Philip to Launay! There was a whole heaven of delight in the thought of the very journey.

Miss Gregory endeavoured to look pleased, but in truth the prospect to her was not so pleasant as to Bessy. She was to be left alone again. She was to lose her pensioner. After so short a fruition of the double bliss of society and pay, she was to be deserted without a thought. But to be deserted without many thoughts had been her lot in life, and now she bore her misfortune like a heroine. "You will be glad to go back to your aunt, Bessy; will you not?"

"Glad!" The ecstasy was almost unkind, but poor Miss Gregory bore it, and maintained that pretty smile of gratified serenity as though everything were well with all of them.

But Bessy felt that she had as yet heard nothing of the real news, and that the real news could not be told in the presence of Miss Gregory. It had not even yet occurred to her that Mrs. Miles had actually given her sanction to the marriage. "This is a very pretty place," said Philip.

"What, Avranches?" said Miss Gregory, mindful of future possible pensioners. "Oh, delightful. It is the prettiest place in Normandy, and I think the most healthy town in all France."

"It seemed nice as I came up from the hotel. Suppose we go out for a walk, Bessy. We have to start back to-morrow."

"To-morrow!" ejaculated Bessy. She would have been ready to go in half an hour had he demanded it.

"If you can manage it. I promised my mother to be as quick as I could; and, when I arranged to come, I had ever so many engagements."

"If she must go to-morrow, she won't have much time for walking," said Miss Gregory, with almost a touch of anger in her voice. But Bessy was determined to have her walk. All her fate in life was to be disclosed to her within the next few minutes. She was already exultant, but she was beginning to think that there was a heaven, indeed, opening for her. So she ran away for her hat and gloves, leaving her lover and Miss Gregory together.

"It is very sudden," said the poor old lady with a gasp.

"My mother felt that, and bade me tell you that, of course, the full twelvemonth— "

"I was not thinking about that," said Miss Gregory. "I did not mean to allude to such a thing. Mrs. Miles has always been so kind to my brother, and anything I could have done I should have been so happy, without thinking of money. But— " Philip sat with the air of an attentive listener, so that Miss Gregory could get no answer to her question without absolutely asking it. "But there seems to be a change."

"Yes, there is a change, Miss Gregory."

"We were afraid that Mrs. Miles had been offended."

"It is the old story, Miss Gregory. Young people and old people very often will not think alike: but it is the young people who generally have their way."

She had not had her way. She remembered that at the moment. But then, perhaps, the major-general had had his. When a period of life has come too late for success, when all has been failure, the expanding triumphs of the glorious young, grate upon the feelings even of those who are generous and self-denying. Miss Gregory was generous by nature and self-denying by practice, but Philip's pæan and Bessy's wondrous prosperity were for a moment a little hard upon her. There had been a comfort to her in the conviction that Philip was no better than the major-general. "I suppose it is so," she said. "That is, if one of them has means."

"Exactly."

"But if they are both poor, I don't see how their being young can enable them to live upon nothing." She intended to imply that Philip probably would have been another major-general, but that he was heir to Launay.

Philip, who had never heard of the major-general, was a little puzzled; nevertheless, he acceded to the proposition, not caring, however, to say anything as to his own circumstances on so very short an acquaintance.

Then Bessy came down with her hat, and they started for their walk. "Now tell me all about it," she said, in a fever of expectation, as soon as the front door was closed behind them.

"There is nothing more to tell," said he.

"Nothing more?"

"Unless you want me to say that I love you."

"Of course I do."

"Well, then,—I love you. There!"

"Philip, you are not half nice to me."

"Not after coming all the way from Launay to say that?"

"There must be so much to tell me? Why has my aunt sent for me?"

"Because she wants you."

"And why has she sent you?"

"Because I want you too."

"But does she want me?"

"Certainly she does."

"For you?" If he could say this, then everything would have been said. If he could say this truly, then everything would have been done necessary for the perfection of her happiness. "Oh, Philip, do tell me. It is so strange that she should send for me! Do you know what she said to me in her last letter? It was not a letter. It was only a word. She said that I was her enemy."

"All that is changed."

"She will be glad to have me again?"

"Very glad. I fancy that she has been miserable without you."

"I shall be as glad to be with her again, Philip. You do not know how I love her. Think of all she has done for me!"

"She has done something now that I hope will beat everything else."

"What has she done?"

"She has consented that you and I shall be man and wife. Isn't that more than all the rest?"

"But has she? Oh, Philip, has she really done that?"

Then at last he told his whole story. Yes; his mother had yielded. From the moment in which she had walked out of the room, having said that he might "go and tell her," she had never endeavoured to renew the fight. When he had spoken to her, endeavouring to draw from her some warmth of assent, she had generally been very silent. She had never brought herself absolutely to wish him joy. She had not as yet so crucified her own spirit in the matter as to be able to tell him that he had chosen his wife well; but she had shown him in a hundred ways that her anger was at an end, and that if any feeling was left opposed to his own happiness, it was simply one of sorrow. And there were signs which made him think that even that was not deep-seated. She would pat him, stroking his hair, and leaning on his shoulder, administering to his comforts with a nervous accuracy as to little things which was peculiar to her. And then she gave him an infinity of directions as to the way in which it would be proper that Bessy should travel, being anxious at first to send over a maid for her behoof,—not Mrs. Knowl, but a younger woman, who would have been at Bessy's command. Philip, however, objected to the maid. And when Mrs. Miles remarked that if it was Bessy's fate to become mistress of Launay, Bessy ought to have a maid to attend her, Philip said that that would be very well a month or two hence, when Bessy would have become,—not mistress of Launay, which was a place which he trusted might not be vacant for many a long day,—but first lieutenant to the mistress, by right of marriage. He refused altogether to take the maid with him, as he explained to Bessy with much laughter. And so they came to understand each other thoroughly, and Bessy knew that the great trouble of her life, which had been as a mountain in her way, had disappeared suddenly, as might some visionary mountain. And then, when they thoroughly understood each other, they started back to England and to Launay together.

Chapter XII

How Bessy Pryor Was Brought Back, And What Then Became Of Her.

BESSY UNDERSTOOD the condition of the old woman much better than did her son. "I am sad a little," she said, on her way home, "because of her disappointment."

"Sad, because she is to have you,—you yourself,—for her daughter-in-law?"

"Yes, indeed, Philip; because I know that she has not wanted me. She will be kind because I shall belong to you, and perhaps partly because she loves me; but she will always regret that that young lady down in Cornwall has not been allowed to add to the honour and greatness of the family. The Launays are everything to her, and what can I do for the Launays?" Of course he said many pretty things to her in answer to this, but he could not eradicate from her mind the feeling that, in regard to the old friend who had been so kind to her, she was returning evil for good.

But even Bessy did not quite understand the old woman. When she found that she had yielded, there was disappointment in the old woman's heart. Who can have indulged in a certain longing for a lifetime, in a special ambition, and seen that ambition and that longing crushed and trampled on, without such a feeling? And she had brought this failure on herself,—by her own weakness, as she told herself. Why had she given way to Bessy and to Bessy's blandishments? It was because she had not been strong to do her duty that this ruin had fallen upon her hopes. The power in her own hands had been sufficient. But for her Philip need never have seen Bessy Pryor. Might not Bessy Pryor have been sent somewhere out of the way when it became evident that she had charms of her own with which to be dangerous? And even after the first evil had been done her power had been sufficient. She need have written no letter to Bessy. She might have been calm and steady in her purpose, so that there should have been no violent ebullition of anger,—so violent as to induce repentance, and with repentance renewed softness and all the pangs of renewed repentance.

When Philip had left her on his mission to Normandy her heart was heavy with regret, and heavy also with anger. But it was with herself that she was angry. She had known her duty and she had not done it. She had known her duty, and had neglected it,—because Bessy had been soft to her, and dear, and pleasant. It was here that Bessy did not quite understand her friend. Bessy reproached herself because she had made to her friend a bad return to all the kindness she had received. The old woman would not allow herself to entertain any such a thought. Once she had spoken to herself of having warmed a serpent in her bosom; but instantly, with infinite self-scorn, she had declared to herself that Bessy was no serpent. For all that she had done for Bessy,

Bessy had made ample return, the only possible return that could be full enough. Bessy had loved her. She too had loved Bessy, but that should have had no weight. Though they two had been linked together by their very heartstrings, it had been her duty to make a severance because their joint affection had been dangerous. She had allowed her own heart to over-ride her own sense of duty, and therefore she was angry,—not with Bessy, but with herself.

But the thing was done. To quarrel with Philip had been impossible to her. One feeling coming upon another, her own repentance, her own weakness, her acknowledgment of a certain man's strength on the part of her son, had brought her to such a condition that she had yielded. Then it was natural that she should endeavour to make the best of it. But even the doing of that was a trial to her. When she told herself that as far as the woman went, the mere woman, Philip could not have found a better wife had he searched the world all round, she found that she was being tempted from her proper path even in that. What right could she have to look for consolation there? For other reasons, which she still felt to be adequate, she had resolved that something else should be done. That something else had not been done, because she had failed in her duty. And now she was trying to salve the sore by the very poison which had created the wound. Bessy's sweet temper, and Bessy's soft voice, and Bessy's bright eye, and Bessy's devotion to the delight of others, were all so many temptations. Grovelling as she was in sackcloth and ashes because she had yielded to them, how could she console herself by a prospect of these future enjoyments either for herself or her son?

But there were various duties to which she could attend, grievously afflicted as she was by her want of attention to that great duty. As Fate had determined that Bessy Pryor was to become mistress of Launay, it was proper that all Launay should know and recognise its future mistress. Bessy certainly should not be punished by any want of earnestness in this respect. No one should be punished but herself. The new mistress should be made as welcome as though she had been the red-haired girl from Cornwall. Knowl was a good deal put about because Mrs. Miles, remembering a few hard words which Knowl had allowed herself to use in the days of the imprisonment, became very stern. "It is settled that Miss Pryor is to become Mrs. Philip Launay, and you will obey her just as myself." Mrs. Knowl, who had saved a little money, began to consider whether it would not be as well to retire into private life.

When the day came on which the two travellers were to reach Launay Mrs. Miles was very much disturbed in her mind. In what way should she receive the girl? In her last communication,—her very last,—she had called Bessy her enemy; and now Bessy was being brought home to be made her daughter-in-law under her own roof. How sweet it would be to stand at the door and welcome her in the hall, among all the smiling servants, to make a tender fuss and hovering over her, as would be so natural with a mother-in-law who loved an adopted daughter as tenderly as Mrs. Miles loved Bessy! How pleasant to take her by the hand and lead her away into some inner sanctum where warm kisses as between mother and child would be given and taken; to hear her praises of Philip, and then to answer again with other praises; to tell her with words half serious and half drollery that she must now buckle on her armour and do her work, and take upon herself the task of managing the household! There was quite enough of softness in the old woman to make all this delightful. Her imagination revelled in thinking of it even at the moment in which she was telling herself that it was impossible. But it was impossible. Were she to force such a change upon herself Bessy would not believe in the sincerity of the change. She had told Bessy that she was her enemy!

At last the carriage which had gone to the station was here; not the waggonette on this occasion, but the real carriage itself, the carriage which was wont to toddle four miles an hour about the parish. "This is an honour meant for the prodigal daughter," said Philip, as he took his seat. "If you had never been naughty, we should only have had the waggonette, and we then should have been there in half the time." Mrs. Miles, when she heard the wheels on the gravel, was even yet uncertain where she would place herself. She was fluttered, moving about from the room into the hall and back, when the old butler spoke a careful word: "Go into the library, madam, and Mr. Philip will bring her to you there." Then she obeyed the butler,—as she had probably never done in her life before.

Bessy, as soon as her step was off the carriage, ran very quickly into the house. "Where is my aunt?" she said. The butler was there showing the way, and in a moment she had thrown her arms round the old woman. Bessy had a way of making her kisses obligatory, from which Mrs. Miles had never been able to escape. Then, when the old woman was seated, Bessy was at once upon her knees before her. "Say that you love me, aunt. Say that at once! Say that first of all!"

"You know I love you."

"I know I love you. Oh, I am so glad to have you again. It was so hard not to be with you when I thought that you were ill. I did not know how sick it would make me to be away from you." Neither then nor at any time afterwards was there a word spoken on the one side or the other as to that declaration of enmity.

There was nothing then said in way of explanation. There was nothing perhaps necessary. It was clear to Bessy that she was received at Launay as Philip's future wife,—not only by Mrs. Miles herself, but by the whole household,—and that all the honours of the place were to be awarded to her without stint. For herself that would have sufficed. To her any explanation of the circumstances which had led to a change so violent was quite unnecessary. But it was not so with Mrs. Miles herself. She could not but say some word in justification of herself,—in excuse rather than justification. She had Bessy into her bedroom that night, and said the word, holding between her two thin hands the hand of the girl she addressed. "You have known, Bessy, that I did not wish this." Bessy muttered that she did know it. "And I think you knew why."

"How could I help it, aunt?"

Upon this the old woman patted the hand. "I suppose he could not help it. And, if I had been a young man, I could not have helped it. I could not help it as I was, though I am an old woman. I think I am as foolish as he is."

"Perhaps he is foolish, but you are not."

"Well; I do not know. I have my misgivings about that, my dear. I had objects which I thought were sacred and holy, to which I had been wedded through many years. They have had to be thrust aside."

"Then you will hate me!"

"No, my child; I will love you with all my heart. You will be my son's wife now, and, as such, you will be dear to me, almost as he is dear. And you will still be my own Bessy, my gleam of sunlight, without whom the house is so gloomy that it is like a prison to me. For myself, do you think I could want any other young woman about the house than my own dear Bessy;—that any other wife for Philip could come as near my heart as you do?"

"But if I have stood in the way?"

"We will not think of it any more. You, at any rate, need not think of it," added the old woman, as she remembered all the circumstances. "You shall be made welcome with all the honours and all the privileges due to Philip's wife; and if there be a regret, it shall never trouble your path. It may be a comfort to you to hear me say that you, at least, in all things have done your duty." Then, at last, there were more tears, more embracings, and, before either of them went to their rest, a perfect ecstacy of love.

Little or nothing more is necessary for the telling of the story of the Lady of Launay. Before the autumn had quite gone, and the last tint had left the trees, Bessy Pryor became Bessy Launay, under the hand of Mr. Gregory, in the Launay parish church. Everyone in the neighbourhood around was there, except Mr. Morrison, who had taken this opportunity of having a holiday and visiting Switzerland. But even he, when he returned, soon became reconciled to the arrangement, and again became a guest in the dining-room of the mansion. I hope I shall have no reader who will not think that Philip Launay did well in not following the example of the major-general.

Alice Dugdale

Originally appeared in *Good Cheer*, the Christmas number of *Good Words*, December 1878. Reprinted in *Why Frau Frohmann Raised Her Prices and Other Stories* (1882). Trollope promised to write the story on 12 May 1878, and sent it in on 10 June.

Chapter I

The Doctor's Family.

IT USED to be said in the village of Beetham that nothing ever went wrong with Alice Dugdale,—the meaning of which, perhaps, lay in the fact that she was determined that things should be made to go right. Things as they came were received by her with a gracious welcome, and "things," whatever they were, seemed to be so well pleased with the treatment afforded to them, that they too for most part made themselves gracious in return.

Nevertheless she had had sorrows, as who has not? But she had kept her tears for herself, and had shown her smiles for the comfort, of those around her. In this little story it shall be told how in a certain period of her life she had suffered much;—how she still smiled, and how at last she got the better of her sorrow.

Her father was the country doctor in the populous and straggling parish of Beetham. Beetham is one of those places so often found in the south of England, half village, half town, for the existence of which there seems to be no special reason. It had no mayor, no municipality, no market, no pavements, and no gas. It was therefore no more than a village;—but it had a doctor, and Alice's father, Dr. Dugdale, was the man. He had been established at Beetham for more than thirty years, and knew every pulse and every tongue for ten miles round. I do not know that he was very great as a doctor;—but he was a kind-hearted, liberal man, and he enjoyed the confidence of the Beethamites, which is everything. For thirty years he had worked hard and had brought up a large family without want. He was still working hard, though turned sixty, at the time of which we are speaking. He had even in his old age many children dependent on him, and though he had fairly prospered, he had not become a rich man.

He had been married twice, and Alice was the only child left at home by his first wife. Two elder sisters were married, and an elder brother was away in the world. Alice had been much younger than they, and had been the only child living with him when he had brought to his house a second mother for her. She was then fifteen. Eight or nine years had since gone, and almost every year had brought an increase to the doctor's family. There were now seven little Dugdales in and about the nursery; and what the seven would do when Alice should go away the folk of Beetham always declared that they were quite at a loss even to guess. For Mrs. Dugdale was one of those women who succumb to difficulties,—who seem originally to have been made of soft material and to have become warped, out of joint, tattered, and almost useless under the wear of the world. But Alice had been constructed of thoroughly seasoned timber, so that, let her be knocked about as she might, she was never out of repair. Now the doctor, excellent as he was at doctoring, was not very good at household matters,—so that the folk at Beetham had reason to be at a loss when they bethought themselves as to what would happen when Alice should "go away."

Of course there is always that prospect of a girl's "going away." Girls not unfrequently intend to go away. Sometimes they "go away" very suddenly, without any previous intention. At any rate such a girl as Alice cannot be regarded as a fixture in a house. Binding as may be her duties at home, it is quite understood that should any adequate provocation to "go away" be brought within her reach, she will go, let the duties be what they may. Alice was a thoroughly good girl,—good to her father, good to her little brothers and sisters, unutterably good to that poor foolish stepmother;—but, no doubt she would "go away" if duly asked.

When the vista of future discomfort in the doctor's house first made itself clearly apparent to the Beethamites, an idea that Alice might perhaps go very soon had begun to prevail in the village. The eldest son of the vicar, Parson Rossiter, had come back from India as Major Rossiter, with an appointment, as some said, of £2,000 a year;—let us put it down as £1,500;—and had renewed his acquaintance with his old play-fellow. Others, more than one or two, had endeavoured before this to entice Alice to "go away," but it was said that the dark-visaged warrior, with his swarthy face and black beard, and bright eyes,—probably, too, something in him nobler than those outward bearings,—had whispered words which had prevailed. It was supposed that Alice now had a fitting lover, and that therefore she would "go away."

There was no doubt in the mind of any single inhabitant of Beetham as to the quality of the lover. It was considered on all sides that he was fitting,—so fitting that Alice would of course go when asked. John Rossiter was such a man that every Beethamite looked upon him as a hero,—so that Beetham was proud to have produced him. In small communities a man will come up now and then as to whom it is surmised that any young lady would of course accept him. This man, who was now about ten years older than Alice, had everything to recommend him. He was made up of all good gifts of beauty, conduct, dignity, good heart,—and fifteen hundred a year at the very least. His official duties required him to live in London, from which Beetham was seventy miles distant; but those duties allowed him ample time for visiting the parsonage. So very fitting he was to take any girl away upon whom he might fix an eye of approbation, that there were others, higher than Alice in the world's standing, who were said to grudge the young lady of the village so great a prize. For Alice Dugdale was a young lady of the village and no more; whereas there were county families around, with daughters, among whom the Rossiters had been in the habit of mixing. Now that such a Rossiter had come to the fore, the parsonage family was held to be almost equal to county people.

To whatever extent Alice's love affairs had gone, she herself had been very silent about them; nor had her lover as yet taken the final step of being closeted for ten minutes with her father. Nevertheless everybody had been convinced in Beetham that it would be so,—unless it might be Mrs. Rossiter. Mrs. Rossiter was ambitious for her son, and in this matter sympathised with the county people. The county people certainly were of opinion that John Rossiter might do better, and did not altogether see what there was in Alice Dugdale to make such a fuss about. Of course she had a sweet countenance, rather brown, with good eyes. She had not, they said, another feature in her face which could be called handsome. Her nose was broad. Her mouth was large. They did not like that perpetual dimpling of the cheek which, if natural, looked as if it were practised. She was stout, almost stumpy, they thought. No doubt she danced well, having a good ear and being active and healthy; but with such a waist no girl could really be graceful. They acknowledged her to be the best nursemaid that ever a mother had in her family; but they thought it a pity that she should be taken away from duties for which her presence was so much desired, at any rate by such a one as John Rossiter. I, who knew Beetham well, and who though turned the hill of middle life had still an eye for female charms, used to declare to myself that Alice, though she was decidedly village and not county, was far, far away the prettiest girl in that part of the world.

The old parson loved her, and so did Miss Rossiter,—Miss Janet Rossiter,—who was four or five years older than her brother, and therefore quite an old maid. But John was so great a man that neither of them dared to say much to encourage him,—as neither did Mrs. Rossiter to use her eloquence on the other side. It was felt by all of them that any persuasion might have on John anything but the intended effect. When a man at the age of thirty-three is Deputy Assistant Inspector-General of Cavalry, it is not easy to talk him this way or that in a matter of love. And John Rossiter, though the best fellow in the world, was apt to be taciturn on such a subject. Men frequently marry almost without thinking about it at all. "Well; perhaps I might as well. At any rate I cannot very well help it." That too often is the frame of mind. Rossiter's discussion to himself was of a higher nature than that, but perhaps not quite what it should have been. "This is a thing of such moment that it requires to be pondered again and again. A man has to think of himself, and of her, and of the children which have to come after him;—of the total good or total bad which may come of such a decision." As in the one manner there is too much of negligence, so in the other there may be too much of care. The "perhaps I might as wells,"—so good is Providence,—are sometimes more successful than those careful, long-pondering heroes. The old parson was very sweet to Alice, believing that she would be his daughter-in-law, and so was Miss Rossiter, thoroughly approving of such a sister. But Mrs. Rossiter was a little cold;—all of which Alice could read plainly and digest, without saying a word. If it was to be, she would welcome her happy lot with heart-felt acknowledgment of the happiness provided for her; but if it was not to be, no human being should know that she had sorrowed. There should be nothing lack-a-daisical in her life or conduct. She had her work to do, and she knew that as long as she did that, grief would not overpower her

In her own house it was taken for granted that she was to "go," in a manner that distressed her. "You'll never be here to lengthen 'em," said her stepmother to her, almost whining, when there was a question as to flounces in certain juvenile petticoats which might require to be longer than they were first made before they should be finally abandoned.

"That I certainly shall if Tiny grows as she does now."

"I suppose he'll pop regularly when he next comes down," said Mrs. Dugdale.

There was ever so much in this which annoyed Alice. In the first place, the word "pop" was to her abominable. Then she was almost called upon to deny that he would "pop," when in her heart she thought it very probable that he might. And the word, she knew, had become intelligible to the eldest of her little sisters who was present. Moreover, she was most unwilling to discuss the subject at all, and could hardly leave it undiscussed when such direct questions were asked. "Mamma," she said, "don't let us think about anything of the kind." This did not at all satisfy herself. She ought to have repudiated the lover altogether; and yet she could not bring herself to tell the necessary lie.

"I suppose he will come—some day," said Minnie, the child old enough to understand the meaning of such coming.

> "For men may come and men may go,
> But I go on for ever,—for ever,"

said or sang Alice, with a pretence of drollery, as she turned herself to her little sister. But even in her little song there was a purpose. Let any man come or let any man go, she would go on, at any rate apparently untroubled, in her walk of life.

"Of course he'll take you away, and then what am I to do?" said Mrs. Dugdale moaning. It is sad enough for a girl thus to have her lover thrown in her face when she is by no means sure of her lover.

A day or two afterwards another word, much more painful, was said to her up at the parsonage. Into the parsonage she went frequently to show that there was nothing in her heart to prevent her visiting her old friends as had been her wont.

"John will be down here next week," said the parson, whom she met on the gravel drive just at the hall door.

"How often he comes! What do they do at the Horse Guards, or wherever it is that he goes to?"

"He'll be more steady when he has taken a wife," said the old man.

"In the meantime what becomes of the cavalry?"

"I dare say you'll know all about that before long," said the parson laughing.

"Now, my dear, how can you be so foolish as to fill the girl's head with nonsense of that kind?" said Mrs. Rossiter, who at that moment came out from the front door. "And you're doing John an injustice. You are making people believe that he has said that which he has not said."

Alice at the moment was very angry,—as angry as she well could be. It was certain that Mrs. Rossiter did not know what her son had said or had not said. But it was cruel that she who had put forward no claim, who had never been forward in seeking her lover, should be thus almost publicly rebuked. Quiet as she wished to be, it was necessary that she should say one word in her own defence. "I don't think Mr. Rossiter's little joke will do John any injustice or me any harm," she said. "But, as it may be taken seriously, I hope he will not repeat it."

"He could not do better for himself. That's my opinion," said the old man, turning back into the house. There had been words before on the subject between him and his wife, and he was not well pleased with her at this moment.

"My dear Alice, I am sure you know that I mean everything the best for you," said Mrs. Rossiter.

"If nobody would mean anything, but just let me alone, that would be best. And as for nonsense, Mrs. Rossiter, don't you know of me that I'm not likely to be carried away by foolish ideas of that kind?"

"I do know that you are very good."

"Then why should you talk at me as though I were very bad?" Mrs. Rossiter felt that she had been reprimanded, and was less inclined than ever to accept Alice as a daughter-in-law.

Alice, as she walked home, was low in spirits, and angry with herself because it was so. People would be fools. Of course that was to be expected. She had known all along that Mrs. Rossiter wanted a grander wife for her son, whereas the parson was anxious to have her for his daughter-in-law. Of course she loved the parson better than his wife. But why was it that she felt at this moment that Mrs. Rossiter would prevail?

"Of course it will be so," she said to herself. "I see it now. And I suppose he is right. But then certainly he ought not to have come here. But perhaps he comes because he wishes to—see Miss Wanless." She went a little out of her road home, not only to dry a tear, but to rid herself of the effect of it, and then spent the remainder of the afternoon swinging her brothers and sisters in the garden.

Chapter II

Major Rossiter.

"PERHAPS HE is coming here to see Miss Wanless," Alice had said to herself. And in the course of that week she found that her surmise was correct. John Rossiter stayed only one night at the parsonage, and then went over to Brook Park where lived Sir Walter Wanless and all the Wanlesses. The parson had not so declared when he told Alice that his son was coming, but John himself said on his arrival that this was a special visit made to Brook Park, and not to Beetham. It had been promised for the last three months, though only fixed lately. He took the trouble to come across to the doctor's house with the express purpose of explaining the fact. "I suppose you have always been intimate with them," said Mrs. Dugdale, who was sitting with Alice and a little crowd of the children round them. There was a tone of sarcasm in the words not at all hidden. "We all know that you are a great deal finer than we mere village folk. We don't know the Wanlesses, but of course you do. You'll find yourself much more at home at Brook Park than you can in such a place as this." All that, though not spoken, was contained in the tone of the lady's speech.

"We have always been neighbours," said John Rossiter.

"Neighbours ten miles off!" said Mrs. Dugdale.

"I dare say the Good Samaritan lived thirty miles off," said Alice.

"I don't think distance has much to do with it," said the Major.

"I like my neighbours to be neighbourly. I like Beetham neighbours," said Mrs. Dugdale. There was a reproach in every word of it. Mrs. Dugdale had heard of Miss Georgiana Wanless, and Major Rossiter knew that she had done so. After her fashion the lady was accusing him for deserting Alice.

Alice understood it also, and yet it behoved her to hold herself well up and be cheerful. "I like Beetham people best myself," she said, "but then it is because I don't know any other. I remember going to Brook Park once, when there was a party of children, a hundred years ago, and I thought it quite a paradise. There was a profusion of strawberries by which my imagination has been troubled ever since. You'll just be in time for the strawberries, Major Rossiter." He had always been John till quite lately,—John with the memories of childhood; but now he had become Major Rossiter.

She went out into the garden with him for a moment as he took his leave,—not quite alone, as a little boy of two years old was clinging to her hand. "If I had my way," she said, "I'd have my neighbours everywhere,—at any distance. I envy a man chiefly for that."

"Those one loves best should be very near, I think."

"Those one loves best of all? Oh yes, so that one may do something. It wouldn't do not to have you every day, would it, Bobby?" Then she allowed the willing little urchin to struggle up into her arms and to kiss her, all smeared as was his face with bread-and-butter.

"Your mother meant to say that I was running away from my old friends."

"Of course she did. You see, you loom so very large to us here. You are—such a swell, as Dick says, that we are a little sore when you pass us by. Everybody likes to be bowed to by royalty. Don't you know that? Brook Park is, of course, the proper place for you; but you don't expect but what we are going to express our little disgusts and little prides when we find ourselves left behind!" No words could have less declared her own feelings on the matter than those she was uttering; but she found herself compelled to laugh at him, lest, in the other direction, something of tenderness might escape her, whereby he might be injured worse than by her raillery. In nothing that she might say could there be less of real reproach to him than in this.

"I hate that word 'swell,'" he said.

"So do I."

"Then why do you use it?"

"To show you how much better Brook Park is than Beetham. I am sure they don't talk about swells at Brook Park."

"Why do you throw Brook Park in my teeth?"

"I feel an inclination to make myself disagreeable to-day. Are you never like that?"

"I hope not."

"And then I am bound to follow up what poor dear mamma began. But I won't throw Brook Park in your teeth. The ladies I know are very nice. Sir Walter Wanless is a little grand;—isn't he?"

"You know," said he, "that I should be much happier here than there."

"Because Sir Walter is so grand?"

"Because my friends here are dearer friends. But still it is right that I should go. One cannot always be where one would be happiest."

"I am happiest with Bobby," said she; "and I can always have Bobby." Then she gave him her hand at the gate, and he went down to the parsonage.

That night Mrs. Rossiter was closeted for awhile with her son before they both went to bed. She was supposed, in Beetham, to be of a higher order of intellect,—of a higher stamp generally,—than her husband or daughter, and to be in that respect nearly on a par with her son. She had not travelled as he had done, but she was of an ambitious mind and had thoughts beyond Beetham. The poor dear parson cared for little outside the bounds of his parish. "I am so glad you are going to stay for awhile over at Brook Park," she said.

"Only for three days."

"In the intimacy of a house three days is a lifetime. Of course I do not like to interfere." When this was said the Major frowned, knowing well that his mother was going to interfere. "But I cannot help thinking how much a connection with the Wanlesses would do for you."

"I don't want anything from any connection."

"That is all very well, John, for a man to say; but in truth we all depend on connections one with another. You are beginning the world."

"I don't know about that, mother."

"To my eyes you are. Of course, you look upwards."

"I take all that as it comes."

"No doubt; but still you must have it in your mind to rise. A man is assisted very much by the kind of wife he marries. Much would be done for a son-in-law of Sir Walter Wanless."

"Nothing, I hope, ever for me on that score. To succeed by favour is odious."

"But even to rise by merit, so much outside assistance is often necessary! Though you will assuredly deserve all that you will ever get, yet you may be more likely to get it as a son-in-law to Sir Walter Wanless than if you were married to some obscure girl. Men who make the most of themselves in the world do think of these things. I am the last woman in the world to recommend my boy to look after money in marriage."

"The Miss Wanlesses will have none."

"And therefore I can speak the more freely. They will have very little,—as coming from such a family. But he has great influence. He has contested the county five times. And then—where is there a handsomer girl than Georgiana Wanless?" The Major thought that he knew one, but did not answer the question. "And she is all that such a girl ought to be. Her manners are perfect,—and her conduct. A constant performance of domestic duties is of course admirable. If it comes to one to have to wash linen, she who washes her linen well is a good woman. But among mean things high spirits are not to be found."

"I am not so sure of that."

"It must be so. How can the employment of every hour in the day on menial work leave time for the mind to fill itself? Making children's frocks may be a duty, but it must also be an impediment."

"You are speaking of Alice."

"Of course I am speaking of Alice."

"I would wager my head that she has read twice more in the last two years than Georgiana Wanless. But, mother, I am not disposed to discuss either the one young lady or the other. I am not going to Brook Park to look for a wife; and if ever I take one, it will be simply because I like her best, and not because I wish to use her as a rung of a ladder by which to climb upwards into the world." That all this and just this would be said to her Mrs. Rossiter had been aware; but still she had thought that a word in season might have its effect.

And it did have its effect. John Rossiter, as he was driven over to Brook Park on the following morning, was unconsciously mindful of that allusion to the washerwoman. He had seen that Alice's cheek had been smirched by the greasy crumbs from her little brother's mouth, he had seen that the tips of her fingers showed the mark of the needle; he had seen fragments of thread about her dress, and the mud even from the children's boots on her skirts. He had seen this, and had been aware that Georgiana Wanless was free from all such soil on her outward raiment. He liked the perfect grace of unspotted feminine apparel, and he had, too, thought of the hours in which Alice might probably be employed amidst the multifarious needs of a nursery, and had argued to himself much as his mother had argued. It was good and homely,—worthy of a thousand praises; but was it exactly that which he wanted in a wife? He had repudiated with scorn his mother's cold, worldly doctrine; but yet he had felt that it would be a pleasant thing to have it known in London that his wife was the daughter of Sir Walter Wanless. It was true that she was wonderfully handsome,—a complexion perfectly clear, a nose cut as out of marble, a mouth delicate as of a goddess, with a waist quite to match it. Her shoulders were white as alabaster. Her dress was at all times perfect. Her fingers were without mark or stain. There might perhaps be a want of expression; but faces so symmetrical are seldom expressive. And then, to crown all this, he was justified in believing that she was attached to himself. Almost as much had been said to him by Lady Wanless herself,—a word which would amount to as much, coupled as it was with an immediate invitation to Brook Park. Of this he had given no hint to any human being; but he had been at Brook Park once before, and some rumour of something between him and Miss Georgiana Wanless had reached the people at Beetham,—had reached, as we have seen, not only Mrs. Rossiter, but also Alice Dugdale.

There had been moments up in London when his mind had veered round towards Miss Wanless. But there was one little trifle which opposed the action of his mind, and that was his heart. He had begun to think that it might be his duty to marry Georgiana;—but the more he thought so the more clearly would the figure of Alice stand before him, so that no veil could be thrown over it. When he tried to summon to his imagination the statuesque beauty of the one girl, the bright eyes of the other would look at him, and the words from her speaking mouth would be in his ears. He had once kissed Alice, immediately on his return, in the presence of her father, and the memory of the halcyon moment was always present to him. When he thought most of Miss Wanless he did not think much of her kisses. How grand she would be at his dining-table, how glorious in his drawing-room! But with Alice how sweet would it be to sit by some brook side and listen to the waters!

And now since he had been at Beetham, from the nature of things which sometimes make events to come from exactly contrary causes, a new charm had been added to Alice, simply by the little effort she had made to annoy him. She had talked to him of "swells," and had pretended to be jealous of the Wanlesses, just because she had known that he would hate to hear such a word from her lips, and that he would be vexed by exhibition of such a feeling on her part! He was quite sure that she had not committed these sins because they belonged to her as a matter of course. Nothing could be more simple than her natural language or her natural feelings. But she had chosen to show him that she was ready to run into little faults which might offend him. The reverse of her ideas came upon him. She had said, as it were,—"See how little anxious I must be to dress myself in your mirror when I put myself in the same category with my poor stepmother." Then he said to himself that he could see her as he was fain to see her, in her own mirror, and he loved her the better because she had dared to run the risk of offending him.

As he was driven up to the house at Brook Park he knew that it was his destiny to marry either the one girl or the other; and he was afraid of himself,—that before he left the house he might be engaged to the one he did not love. There was a moment in which he thought he would turn round and go back. "Major Rossiter," Lady Wanless had said, "you know how glad we are to see you here. There is no young man of the day of whom Sir Walter thinks so much." Then he had thanked her. "But—may I say a word in warning?"

"Certainly."

"And I may trust to your honour?"

"I think so, Lady Wanless."

"Do not be much with that sweet darling of mine,—unless indeed— " And then she had stopped. Major Rossiter, though he was a major and had served some years in India, blushed up to his eyebrows and was unable to answer a word. But he knew that Georgiana Wanless had been offered to him, and was entitled to believe that the young lady was prone to fall in love with him. Lady Wanless, had she been asked for an excuse for such conduct, would have said that the young men of the present day were slow in managing their own affairs, unless a little help were given to them.

When the Major was almost immediately invited to return to Brook Park, he could not but feel that, if he were so to make his choice, he would be received there as a son-in-law. It may be that unless he intended so to be received, he should not have gone. This he felt as he was driven across the park, and was almost minded to return to Beetham.

Chapter III

Lady Wanless.

SIR WALTER Wanless was one of those great men who never do anything great, but achieve their greatness partly by their tailors, partly by a breadth of eyebrow and carriage of the body,—what we may call deportment,—and partly by the outside gifts of fortune. Taking his career altogether we must say that he had been unfortunate. He was a baronet with a fine house and park,—and with an income hardly sufficient for the place. He had contested the county four times on old Whig principles, and had once been in Parliament for two years. There he had never opened his mouth; but in his struggle to get there had greatly embarrassed his finances. His tailor had been well chosen, and had always turned him out as the best dressed old baronet in England. His eyebrow was all his own, and certainly commanded respect from those with whom eyebrows are efficacious. He never read; he eschewed farming, by which he had lost money in early life; and had, so to say, no visible occupation at all. But he was Sir Walter Wanless, and what with his tailor and what with his eyebrow he did command a great deal of respect in the country round Beetham. He had, too, certain good gifts for which people were thankful as coming from so great a man. He paid his bills, he went to church, he was well behaved, and still maintained certain old-fashioned family charities, though money was not plentiful with him.

He had two sons and five daughters. The sons were in the army, and were beyond his control. The daughters were all at home, and were altogether under the control of their mother. Indeed everything at Brook Park was under the control of Lady Wanless,—though no man alive gave himself airs more autocratic than Sir Walter. It was on her shoulders that fell the burden of the five daughters, and of maintaining with straitened means the hospitality of Brook Park on their behoof. A hard-worked woman was Lady Wanless, in doing her duty,—with imperfect lights no doubt, but to the best of her abilities with such lights as she possessed. She was somewhat fine in her dress, not for any comfort that might accrue to herself, but from a feeling that an alliance with the Wanlesses would not be valued by the proper sort of young men unless she were grand herself. The girls were beautifully dressed; but oh, with such care and economy and daily labour among them, herself, and the two lady's-maids upstairs! The father, what with his election and his farming, and a period of costly living early in his life, had not done well for the family. That she knew, and never rebuked him. But it was for her to set matters right, which she could only do by getting husbands for the daughters. That this might be achieved the Wanless prestige must be maintained; and with crippled means it is so hard to maintain a family prestige! A poor duke may do it, or perhaps an earl; but a baronet is not high enough to give bad wines to his guests without serious detriment to his unmarried daughters.

A beginning to what might be hoped to be a long line of successes had already been made. The eldest girl, Sophia, was engaged. Lady Wanless did not look very high, knowing that failure in such operations will bring with it such unutterable misfortune. Sophia was engaged to the eldest son of a neighbouring Squire,—whose property indeed was not large, nor was the squire likely to die very soon; but there were the means of present living and a future rental of £4,000 a year. Young Mr. Cobble was now staying at the house, and had been duly accepted by Sir Walter himself. The youngest girl, who was only nineteen, had fallen in love with a young clergyman in the neighbourhood. That would not do at all, and the young clergyman was not allowed withing the Park. Georgiana was the beauty; and for her, if for any, some great destiny might have been hoped. But it was her turn, a matter of which Lady Wanless thought a great deal, and the Major was too good to be allowed to escape. Georgiana, in her cold, impassive way, seemed to like the Major, and therefore Lady Wanless paired them off instantly with that decision which was necessary amidst the labours of her life. She had no scruples in what she did, feeling sure that her daughters would make honest, good wives, and that the blood of the Wanlesses was a dowry in itself.

The Major had been told to come early, because a party was made to visit certain ruins about eight miles off,—Castle Owless, as it was called,—to which Lady Wanless was accustomed to take her guests, because the family history declared that the Wanlesses had lived there at some very remote period. It still belonged to Sir Walter, though unfortunately the intervening lands had for the most part fallen into other hands. Owless and Wanless were supposed to be the same, and thus there was room for a good deal of family tattle.

"I am delighted to see you at Brook Park," said Sir Walter as they met at the luncheon table. "When I was at Christchurch your father was at Wadham, and I remember him well." Exactly the same words had been spoken when the Major, on a former occasion, had been made welcome at the house, and clearly implied a feeling that Christchurch, though much superior, may condescend to know Wadham—under certain circumstances. Of the Baronet nothing further was heard or seen till dinner.

Lady Wanless went in the open carriage with three daughters, Sophie being one of them. As her affair was settled it was not necessary that one of the two side-saddles should be allotted to her use. Young Cobble, who had been asked to send two horses over from Cobble Hall so that Rossiter might ride one, felt this very hard. But there was no appeal from Lady Wanless. "You'll have plenty enough of her all the evening." said the mother, patting him affectionately, "and it is so necessary just at present that Georgiana and Edith should have horse exercise." In this way it was arranged that Georgiana should ride with the Major, and Edith, the third daughter, with young Burmeston, the son of Cox and Burmeston, brewers at the neighbouring town of Slowbridge. A country brewer is not quite what Lady Wanless would have liked; but with difficulties such as hers a rich young brewer might be worth having. All this was hard upon Mr. Cobble, who would not have sent his horses over had he known it.

Our Major saw at a glance that Georgiana rode well. He liked ladies to ride, and doubted whether Alice had ever been on horseback in her life. After all, how many advantages does a girl lose by having to pass her days in a nursery! For a moment some such idea crossed his mind. Then he asked Georgiana some question as to the scenery through which they were passing. "Very fine, indeed," said Georgiana. She looked square before her, and sat with her back square to the horse's tail. There was no hanging in the saddle, no shifting about in uneasiness. She could rise and fall easily, even gracefully, when the horse trotted. "You are fond of riding I can see," said the Major. "I do like riding," answered Georgiana. The tone in which she spoke of her present occupation was much more lively than that in which she had expressed her approbation of scenery.

At the ruin they all got down, and Lady Wanless told them the entire story of the Owlesses and the Wanlesses, and filled the brewer's mind with wonder as to the antiquity and dignity of the family. But the Major was the fish just at this moment in hand. "The Rossiters are very old, too," she said smiling; "but perhaps that is a kind of thing you don't care for."

"Very much indeed," said he. Which was true,—for he was proud of knowing that he had come from the Rossiters who had been over four hundred years in Herefordshire. "A remembrance of old merit will always be an incitement to new."

"It is just that, Major Rossiter. It is strange how very nearly in the same words Georgiana said the same thing to me yesterday." Georgiana happened to overhear this, but did not contradict her mother, though she made a grimace to her sister which was seen by no one else. Then Lady Wanless slipped aside to assist the brewer and Edith, leaving the Major and her second daughter together. The two younger girls, of whom the youngest was the wicked one with the penchant for the curate, were wandering among the ruins by themselves.

"I wonder whether there ever were any people called Owless," said Rossiter, not quite knowing what subject of conversation to choose.

"Of course there were. Mamma always says so."

"That settles the question;—does it not?"

"I don't see why there shouldn't be Owlesses. No; I won't sit on the wall, thank you, because I should stain my habit."

"But you'll be tired."

"Not particularly tired. It is not so very far. I'd go back in the carriage, only of course we can't because of the habits. Oh, yes; I'm very fond of dancing,—very fond indeed. We always have two balls every year at Slowbridge. And there are some others about the county. I don't think you ever have balls at Beetham."

"There is no one to give them."

"Does Miss Dugdale ever dance?"

The Major had to think for a moment before he could answer the question. Why should Miss Wanless ask as to Alice's dancing? "I am sure she does. Now I think of it I have heard her talk of dancing. You don't know Alice Dugdale?" Miss Wanless shook her head. "She is worth knowing."

"I am quite sure she is. I have always heard that you thought so. She is very good to all those children; isn't she?"

"Very good indeed."

"She would be almost pretty if she wasn't so,—so, so dumpy I should say." Then they got on their horses again and rode back to Brook Park. Let Georgiana be ever so tired she did not show it, but rode in under the portico with perfect equestrian grace.

"I'm afraid you took too much out of her," said Lady Wanless to the Major that evening. Georgiana had gone to bed a little earlier than the others.

This was in some degree hard upon him, as he had not proposed the ride,—and he excused himself. "It was you arranged it all, Lady Wanless."

"Yes indeed," said she, smiling. "I did arrange the little excursion, but it was not I who kept her talking the whole day." Now this again was felt to be unfair, as nearly every word of conversation between the young people has been given in this little chronicle.

On the following day the young people were again thrust together, and before they parted for the night another little word was spoken by Lady Wanless which indicated very clearly that there was some special bond of friendship between the Major and her second daughter. "You are quite right," she had said in answer to some extracted compliment; "she does ride very well. When I was up in town in May I thought I saw no one with such a seat in the row. Miss Green, who taught the Duchess of Ditchwater's daughters, declared that she knew nothing like it."

On the third morning he returned to Beetham early, as he intended to go up to town the same afternoon. Then there was prepared for him a little valedictory opportunity in which he could not but press the young lady's fingers for a moment. As he did so no one was looking at him, but then he knew that it was so much the more dangerous because no one was looking. Nothing could be more knowing than the conduct of the young lady, who was not in any way too forward. If she admitted that slight pressure, it was done with a retiring rather than obtrusive favour. It was not by her own doing that she was alone with him for a moment. There was no casting down or casting up of her eyes. And yet it seemed to him as he left her and went out into the hall that there had been so much between them that he was almost bound to propose to her. In the hall there was the Baronet to bid him farewell,—an honour which he did to his guests only when he was minded to treat them with great distinction. "Lady Wanless and I are delighted to have had you here," he said. "Remember me to your father, and tell him that I remember him very well when I was at Christchurch and he was at Wadham." It was something to have had one's hand taken in so paternal a manner by a baronet with such an eyebrow, and such a coat.

And yet when he returned to Beetham he was not in a good-humour with himself. It seemed to him that he had been almost absorbed among the Wanlesses without any action or will of his own. He tried to comfort himself by declaring that Georgiana was, without doubt, a remarkably handsome young woman, and that she was a perfect horsewoman,—as though all that were a matter to him of any moment! Then he went across to the doctor's house to say a word of farewell to Alice.

"Have you had a pleasant visit?" she asked.

"Oh, yes; all very well."

"That second Miss Wanless is quite beautiful; is she not?"

"She is handsome certainly."

"I call her lovely," said Alice. "You rode with her the other day over to that old castle."

Who could have told this of him already? "Yes; there was a party of us went over."

"When are you going there again?" Now something had been said of a further visit, and Rossiter had almost promised that he would return. It is impossible not to promise when undefined invitations are given. A man cannot declare that he is engaged for ever and ever. But how was it that Alice knew all that had been said and done? "I cannot say that I have fixed any exact day," he replied almost angrily.

"I've heard all about you, you know. That young Mr. Burmeston was at Mrs. Tweed's and told them what a favourite you are. If it be true I will congratulate you, because I do really think that the young lady is the most beautiful that I ever saw in my life." This she said with a smile and a good-humoured little shake of the head. If it was to be that her heart must be broken he at least should not know it. And she still hoped, she still thought, that by being very constant at her work she might get over it.

Chapter IV

The Beethamites.

IT WAS told all through Beetham before a week was over that Major Rossiter was to marry the second Miss Wanless, and Beetham liked the news. Beetham was proud that one of her sons should be introduced into the great neighbouring family, and especially that he should be honoured by the hand of the acknowledged beauty. Beetham, a month ago, had declared that Alice Dugdale, a Beethamite herself from her babyhood,—who had been born and bred at Beetham and had ever lived there,—was to be honoured by the hand of the young hero. But it may be doubted whether Beetham had been altogether satisfied with the arrangement. We are apt to envy the good luck of those who have always been familiar with us. Why should it have been Alice Dugdale any more than one of the Tweed girls, or Miss Simkins, the daughter of the attorney, who would certainly have a snug little fortune of her own,—which unfortunately would not be the case with Alice Dugdale? It had been felt that Alice was hardly good enough for their hero,—Alice who had been seen about with all the Dugdale children, pushing them in perambulators almost every day since the eldest was born! We prefer the authority of a stranger to that of one chosen from among ourselves. As the two Miss Tweeds, and Miss Simkins, with Alice and three or four others, could not divide the hero among them, it was better then that the hero should go from among them, and choose a fitting mate in a higher realm. They all felt the greatness of the Wanlesses, and argued with Mrs. Rossiter that the rising star of the village should obtain such assistance in rising as would come to him from an almost noble marriage.

There had been certainly a decided opinion that Alice was to be the happy woman. Mrs. Dugdale, the stepmother, had boasted of the promotion; and old Mr. Rossiter had whispered his secret conviction into the ear of every favoured parishioner. The doctor himself had allowed his patients to ask questions about it. This had become so common that Alice herself had been inwardly indignant,—would have been outwardly indignant but that she could not allow herself to discuss the matter. That having been so, Beetham ought to have been scandalised by the fickleness of her hero. Beetham ought to have felt that her hero was most unheroic. But, at any rate among the ladies, there was no shadow of such a feeling. Of course such a man as the Major was bound to do the best for himself. The giving away of his hand in marriage was a very serious thing, and was not to be obligatory on a young hero because he had been carried away by the fervour of old friendship to kiss a young lady immediately on his return home. The history of the kiss was known all over Beetham, and was declared by competent authorities to have amounted to nothing. It was a last lingering touch of childhood's happy embracings, and if Alice was such a fool as to take it for more, she must pay the penalty of her folly. "It was in her father's presence," said Mrs. Rossiter, defending her son to Mrs. Tweed, and Mrs. Tweed had expressed her opinion that the kiss ought to go for nothing. The Major was to be acquitted,—and the fact of the acquittal made its way even to the doctor's nursery; so that Alice knew that the man might marry that girl at Brook Park with clean hands. That, as she declared to herself, did not increase her sorrow. If the man were minded to marry the girl he was welcome for her. And she apologised for him to her own heart. What a man generally wants, she said, is a beautiful wife; and of the beauty of Miss Georgiana Wanless there could be no doubt. Only,—only—only, there had been a dozen words which he should have left unspoken!

That which riveted the news on the minds of the Beethamites was the stopping of the Brook Park carriage at the door of the parsonage one day about a week after the Major's visit. It was not altogether an unprecedented occurrence. Had there been no precedent it could hardly have been justified on the present occasion. Perhaps once in two years Lady Wanless would call at the parsonage, and then there would be a return visit during which a reference would always be made to Wadham and Christchurch. The visit was now out of its order, only nine months having elapsed,—of which irregularity Beetham took due notice. On this occasion Miss Wanless and the third young lady accompanied their mother, leaving Georgiana at home. What was whispered between the two old ladies Beetham did not quite know,—but made its surmises. It was in this wise. "We were so glad to have the Major over with us," said her ladyship.

"It was so good of you," said Mrs. Rossiter.

"He is a great favourite with Sir Walter."

"That is so good of Sir Walter."

"And we are quite pleased to have him among our young people." That was all, but it was quite sufficient to tell Mrs. Rossiter that John might have Georgiana Wanless for the asking, and that Lady Wanless expected him to ask. Then the parting was much more affectionate than it had ever been before, and there was a squeezing of the hand and a nodding of the head which meant a great deal.

Alice held her tongue, and did her work and attempted to be cheery through it all. Again and again she asked herself,—what did it matter? Even though she were unhappy, even though she felt a keen, palpable, perpetual aching at her heart, what would it matter so long as she could go about and do her business? Some people in this world had to be unhappy;—perhaps most people. And this was a sorrow which, though it might not wear off, would by wearing become dull enough to be bearable. She distressed herself in that there was any sorrow. Providence had given to her a certain condition of life to which many charms were attached. She thoroughly loved the people about her,—her father, her little brothers and sisters, even her overworn and somewhat idle step-mother. She was a queen in the house, a queen among her busy toils; and she liked being a queen, and liked being busy. No one ever scolded her or crossed her or contradicted her. She had the essential satisfaction of the consciousness of usefulness. Why should not that suffice to her? She despised herself because there was a hole in her heart,—because she felt herself to shrink all over when the name of Georgiana Wanless was mentioned in her hearing. Yet she would mention the name herself, and speak with something akin to admiration of the Wanless family. And she would say how well it was that men should strive to rise in the world, and how that the world progressed through such individual efforts. But she would not mention the name of John Rossiter, nor would she endure that it should be mentioned in her hearing with any special reference to herself.

Mrs. Dugdale, though she was overworn and idle,—a warped and almost useless piece of furniture, made, as was said before, of bad timber,—yet saw more of this than anyone else, and was indignant. To lose Alice, to have no one to let down those tucks and take up those stitches, would be to her the loss of all her comforts. But, though she was feckless, she was true-hearted, and she knew that Alice was being wronged. It was Alice that had a right to the hero, and not that stuck-up young woman at Brook Park. It was thus she spoke of the affair to the doctor, and after awhile found herself unable to be silent on the subject to Alice herself. "If what they say does take place I shall think worse of John Rossiter than I ever did of any man I ever knew." This she said in the presence both of her husband and her step-daughter.

"John Rossiter will not be very much the worse for that," said Alice without relaxing a moment from her work. There was a sound of drolling in her voice, as though she were quizzing her stepmother for her folly.

"It seems to me that men may do anything now," continued Mrs. Dugdale.

"I suppose they are the same now as they always were," said the doctor. "If a man chose to be false he could always be false."

"I call it unmanly," said Mrs. Dugdale. "If I were a man I would beat him."

"What would you beat him for?" said Alice, getting up, and as she did so throwing down on the table before her the little frock she was making. "If you had the power of beating him, why would you beat him?"

"Because he is ill-using you."

"How do you know that? Did I ever tell you so? Have you ever heard a word that he has said to me, either direct from himself, or second-hand, that justifies you in saying that he has ill-used me? You ill-use me when you speak like that."

"Alice, do not be so violent," said the doctor.

"Father, I will speak of this once, and once for all;—and then pray, pray, let there be no further mention of it. I have no right to complain of anything in Major Rossiter. He has done me no wrong. Those who love me should not mention his name in reference to me."

"He is a villain," said Mrs. Dugdale.

"He is no villain. He is a gentleman, as far as I know, from the crown of his head to the sole of his foot. Does it ever occur to you how little you make of me when you talk of him in this way? Dismiss it all from your mind, father, and let things be as they were. Do you think that I am pining for any man's love? I say that Major Rossiter is a true man and a gentleman;—but I would not give my Bobby's little finger for all his whole body." Then there was silence, and afterwards the doctor told his wife that the Major's name had better not be mentioned again among them. Alice on this occasion was, or appeared to be, very angry with Mrs. Dugdale; but on that evening and the next morning there was an accession of tenderness in her usually sweet manner to her stepmother. The expression of her mother's anger against the Major had been wrong;—but the feeling of anger was not the less endearing.

Some time after that, one evening, the parson came upon Alice as she was picking flowers in one of the Beetham lanes. She had all the children with her, and was filling Minnie's apron with roses from the hedge. Old Mr. Rossiter stopped and talked to them, and after awhile succeeded in getting Alice to walk on with him. "You haven't heard from John?" he said.

"Oh, no," replied Alice, almost with a start. And then she added quickly, "There is no one at our house likely to hear from him. He does not write to anyone there."

"I did not know whether any message might have reached you."

"I think not."

"He is to be here again before long," said the parson.

"Oh, indeed." She had but a moment to think of it all; but, after thinking, she continued, "I suppose he will be going over to Brook Park."

"I fear he will."

"Fear;—why should you fear, Mr. Rossiter? If that is true, it is the place where he ought to be."

"But I doubt its truth, my dear."

"Ah! I know nothing about that. If so he had better stay up in London, I suppose."

"I don't think John can care much for Miss Wanless."

"Why not? She is the most thoroughly beautiful young woman I ever saw."

"I don't think he does, because I believe his heart is elsewhere. Alice, you have his heart."

"No."

"I think so, Alice."

"No, Mr. Rossiter. I have not. It is not so. I know nothing of Miss Wanless, but I can speak of myself."

"It seems to me that you are speaking of him now."

"Then why does he go there?"

"That is just what I cannot answer. Why does he go there?

Why do we do the worst thing so often, when we see the better?"

"But we don't leave undone the thing which we wish to do, Mr. Rossiter."

"That is just what we do do,—under constraint. Alice, I hope, I hope that you may become his wife." She endeavoured to deny that it could ever be so;—she strove to declare that she herself was much too heart-free for that; but the words would not come to her lips, and she could only sob while she struggled to retain her tears. "If he does come to you give him a chance again, even though he may have been untrue to you for a moment."

Then she was left alone among the children. She could dry her tears and suppress her sobs, because Minnie was old enough to know the meaning of them if she saw them; but she could not for awhile go back into the house. She left them in the passage and then went out again, and walked up and down a little pathway that ran through the shrubs at the bottom of the garden. "I believe his heart is elsewhere." Could it be that it was so? And if so, of what nature can be a man's love, if when it be given in one direction, he can go in another with his hand? She could understand that there had not been much heart in it;—that he, being a man and not a woman, could have made this turning point of his life an affair of calculation, and had taken himself here or there without much love at all; that as he would seek a commodious house, so would he also a convenient wife. Resting on that suggestion to herself, she had dared to declare to her father and mother that Major Rossiter was, not a villain, but a perfect gentleman. But all that was not compatible with his father's story. "Alice, you have his heart," the old man had said. How had it come to pass that the old man had known it? And yet the assurance was so sweet, so heavenly, so laden to her ears with divine music, that at this moment she would not even ask herself to disbelieve it. "If he does come to you, give him a chance again." Why;—yes! Though she never spoke a word of Miss Wanless without praise, though she had tutored herself to swear that Miss Wanless was the very wife for him, yet she knew herself too well not to know that she was better than Miss Wanless. For his sake, she could with a clear conscience—give him a chance again. The dear old parson! He had seen it all. He had known. He had appreciated. If it should ever come to pass that she was to be his daughter-in-law, he should have his reward. She would not tell herself that she expected him to come again; but, if he did come, she would give the parson his chance. Such was her idea at that moment. But she was forced to change it before long.

Chapter V

The Invitation.

When Major Rossiter discussed his own conduct with himself as men are so often compelled to do by their own conscience, in opposition to their own wishes, he was not well pleased with himself. On his return home from India he had found himself possessed of a liberal income, and had begun to enjoy himself without thinking much about marrying. It is not often that a man looks for a wife because he has made up his mind that he wants the article. He roams about unshackled, till something, which at the time seems to be altogether desirable, presents itself to him; and then he meditates marriage. So it had been with our Major. Alice had presented herself to him as something altogether desirable,—a something which, when it was touched and looked at, seemed to be so full of sweetnesses, that to him it was for the moment of all things the most charming. He was not a forward man,—one of those who can see a girl for the first time on a Monday, and propose to her on the Tuesday. When the idea first suggested itself to him of making Alice his wife he became reticent and undemonstrative. The kiss had in truth meant no more than Mrs. Tweed had said. When he began to feel that he loved her, then he hardly dared to dream of kissing her.

But though he felt that he loved her,—liked perhaps it would be fairer to say in that early stage of his feelings,—better than any other woman, yet when he came to think of marriage, the importance of it all made him hesitate; and he was reminded, by little hints from others, and by words plain enough from one person, that Alice Dugdale was after all a common thing. There is a fitness in such matters,—so said Mrs. Rossiter,—and a propriety in like being married to like. Had it been his lot to be a village doctor, Alice would have suited him well. Destiny, however, had carried him,—the Major,—higher up, and would require him to live in London, among ornate people, with polished habits, and peculiar manners of their own. Would not Alice be out of her element in London? See the things among which she passed her life! Not a morsel of soap or a pound of sugar was used in the house, but what she gave it out. Her hours were passed in washing, teaching, and sewing for the children. In her very walks she was always pushing a perambulator. She was, no doubt, the doctor's daughter; but, in fact, she was the second Mrs. Dugdale's nursemaid. Nothing could be more praiseworthy. But there is a fitness in things; and he, the hero of Beetham, the Assistant Deputy Inspector-General of the British Cavalry, might surely do better than marry a praiseworthy nursery girl. It was thus that Mrs. Rossiter argued with her son, and her arguments were not without avail.

Then Georgiana Wanless had been, as it were, thrown at his head. When one is pelted with sugar-plums one can hardly resent the attack. He was clever enough to feel that he was pelted, but at first he liked the sweetmeats. A girl riding on horseback, with her back square to the horse's tail, with her reins well held, and a chimney-pot hat on her head, is an object, unfortunately, more attractive to the eyes of ordinary men, than a young woman pushing a perambulator with two babies. Unfortunately, I say, because in either case the young woman should be judged by her personal merits and not by externals. But the Major declared to himself that the personal merits would be affected by the externals. A girl who had pushed a perambulator for many years, would hardly have a soul above perambulators. There would be wanting the flavour of the aroma of romance, that something of poetic vagueness without which a girl can hardly be altogether charming to the senses of an appreciative lover. Then, a little later on, he asked himself whether Georgiana Wanless was romantic and poetic,—whether there was much of true aroma there.

But yet he thought that fate would require him to marry Georgiana Wanless, whom he certainly did not love, and to leave Alice to her perambulator,—Alice, whom he certainly did love. And as he thought of this, he was ill at ease with himself. It might be well that he should give up his Assistant Deputy Inspector-Generalship, go back to India, and so get rid of his two troubles together. Fate, as he personified fate to himself in this matter,—took the form of Lady Wanless. It made him sad to think that he was but a weak creature in the hands of an old woman, who wanted to use him for a certain purpose;—but he did not see his way of escaping. When he began to console himself by reflecting that he would have one of the handsomest women in London at his dinner-table he knew that he would be unable to escape.

About the middle of July he received the following letter from Lady Wanless:—

"Dear Major Rossiter,—The girls have been at their father for the last ten days to have an archery meeting on the lawn, and have at last prevailed, though Sir Walter has all a father's abhorrence to have the lawn knocked about. Now it is settled. 'I'll see about it,' Sir Walter said at last, and when so much as that had been obtained, they all knew that the archery meeting was to be. Sir Walter likes his own way, and is not always to be persuaded. But when he has made the slightest show of concession, he never goes back from it. Then comes the question as to the day, which is now in course of discussion in full committee. In that matter Sir Walter is supposed to be excluded from any voice. 'It cannot matter to him what day of the week or what day of the month,' said Georgiana very irreverently. It will not, however, much matter to him so long as it is all over before St. Partridge comes round.

"The girls one and all declared that you must be here,—as one of the guests in the house. Our rooms will be mostly full of young ladies, but there will be one at any rate for you. Now, what day will suit you,—or rather what day will suit the Cavalry generally? Everything must of course depend on the Cavalry. The girls say that the Cavalry is sure to go out of town after the tenth of August. But they would put it off for a week longer rather than not have the Inspector-General. Would Wednesday 14th suit the Cavalry? They are all reading every word of my letter as it is written, and bid me say that if Thursday or Friday in that week, or Wednesday or Thursday in the next, will do better, the accommodation of the Cavalry shall be consulted. It cannot be on a Monday or Saturday because there would be some Sunday encroachment. On Tuesday we cannot get the band from Slowbridge.

"Now you know our great purpose and our little difficulties. One thing you cannot know,—how determined we are to accommodate ourselves to the Cavalry. *The meeting is not to take place without the Inspector-General.* So let us have an early answer from that august functionary. The girls think that the Inspector had better come down before the day, so as to make himself useful in preparing.

"Pray believe me, with Sir Walter's kind regards,
yours most sincerely,
"MARGARET WANLESS."

The Major felt that the letter was very flattering, but that it was false and written for a certain purpose. He could read between the lines at every sentence of it. The festival was to be got up, not at the instance of the girls but of Lady Wanless herself, as a final trap for the catching of himself,—and perhaps for Mr. Burmeston. Those irreverent words had never come from Georgiana, who was too placid to have said them. He did not believe a word of the girls looking over the writing of the letter. In all such matters Lady Wanless had more life, more energy than her daughters. All that little fun about the Cavalry came from Lady Wanless herself. The girls were too like their father for such ebullitions. The little sparks of joke with which the names of the girls were connected,—with which in his hearing the name of Georgiana had been specially connected,—had, he was aware, their origin always with Lady Wanless. Georgiana had said this funny thing and that,—but Georgiana never spoke after that fashion in his hearing. The traps were plain to his eyes, and yet he knew that he would sooner or later be caught in the traps.

He took a day to think of it before he answered the letter, and meditated a military tour to Berlin just about the time. If so, he must be absent during the whole of August, so as to make his presence at the toxopholite meeting an impossibility. And yet at last he wrote and said that he would be there. There would be something mean in flight. After all, he need not ask the girl to be his wife unless he chose to do so. He wrote a very pretty note to Lady Wanless saying that he would be at Brook Park on the 14th, as she had suggested.

Then he made a great resolution and swore an oath to himself,—that he would not be caught on that occasion, and that after this meeting he would go no more either to Brook Park or to Beetham for awhile. He would not marry the girl to whom he was quite indifferent, nor her who from her position was hardly qualified to be his wife. Then he went about his duties with a quieted conscience, and wedded himself for once and for always to the Cavalry.

Some tidings of the doings proposed by the Wanlesses had reached the parson's ears when he told Alice in the lane that his son was soon coming down to Beetham again, and that he was again going to Brook Park. Before July was over the tidings of the coming festivity had been spread over all that side of the county. Such a thing had not been done for many years,—not since Lady Wanless had been herself a young wife, with two sisters for whom husbands had to be,—and were provided. There were those who could still remember how well Lady Wanless had behaved on that occasion. Since those days hospitality on a large scale had not been rife at Brook Park—and the reason why it was so was well known. Sir Walter was determined not to embarrass himself further, and would do nothing that was expensive. It could not be but that there was great cause for such a deviation as this. Then the ladies of the neighbourhood put their heads together,—and some of the gentlemen,—and declared that a double stroke of business was to be done in regard to Major Rossiter and Mr. Burmeston. How great a relief that would be to the mother's anxiety if the three eldest girls could be married and got rid of all on the same day!

Beetham, which was ten miles from Brook Park, had a station of its own, whereas Slowbridge with its own station was only six miles from the house. The Major would fain have reached his destination by Slowbridge, so as to have avoided the chance of seeing Alice, were it not that his father and mother would have felt themselves aggrieved by such desertion. On this occasion his mother begged him to give them one night. She had much that she wished to say to him, and then of course he could have the parsonage horse and the parsonage phaeton to take him over to Brook Park free of expense. He did go down to Beetham, did spend an evening there, and did go on to the Park without having spoken to Alice Dugdale.

"Everybody says you are to marry Georgiana Wanless," said Mrs. Rossiter.

"If there were no other reason why I should not, the saying of everybody would be sufficient against it."

"That is unreasonable, John. The thing should be looked at itself, whether it is good or bad. It may be the case that Lady Wanless talks more than she ought to do. It may be the case that, as people say, she is looking out for husbands for her daughters. I don't know but that I should do the same if I had five of them on my hands and very little means for them. And if I did, how could I get a better husband for one of them than—such a one as Major John Rossiter?" Then she kissed his forehead.

"I hate the kind of thing altogether," said he. He pretended to be stern, but yet he showed that he was flattered by his mother's softness.

"It may well be, John, that such a match shall be desirable to them and to you too. If so, why should there not be a fair bargain between the two of you? You know that you admire the girl." He would not deny this, lest it should come to pass hereafter that she should become his wife. "And everybody knows that as far as birth goes there is not a family in the county stands higher. I am so proud of my boy that I wish to see him mated with the best."

He reached the parsonage that evening only just before dinner, and on the next morning he did not go out of the house till the phaeton came round to take him to Brook Park. "Are you not going up to see the old doctor?" said the parson after breakfast.

"No;—I think not. He is never at home, and the ladies are always surrounded by the children."

"She will take it amiss," said the father almost in a whisper.

"I will go as I come back," said he, blushing as he spoke at his own falsehood. For, if he held to his present purpose, he would return by Slowbridge. If Fate intended that there should be nothing further between him and Alice, it would certainly be much better that they should not be brought together any more. He knew too what his father meant, and was more unwilling to take counsel from his father even than his mother. Yet he blushed because he knew that he was false.

"Do not seem to slight her," said the old man. "She is too good for that."

Then he drove himself over to Brook Park, and, as he made his way by one of the innumerable turnings out of Beetham, he saw at one of the corners Alice, still with the children and still with the perambulator. He merely lifted his hat as he passed, but did not stop to speak to her.

Chapter VI

The Archery Meeting.

THE ASSISTANT Deputy Inspector-General, when he reached Brook Park, found that things were to be done on a great scale. The two drawing-rooms were filled with flowers, and the big dining-room was laid out for to-morrow's lunch, in preparation for those who would prefer the dining-room to the tent. Rossiter was first taken into the Baronet's own room, where Sir Walter kept his guns and administered justice. "This is a terrible bore, Rossiter," he said.

"It must disturb you a great deal, Sir Walter."

"Oh, dear—dreadfully! What would my old friend, your father, think of having to do this kind of thing? Though, when I was at Christchurch and he at Wadham, we used to be gay enough. I'm not quite sure that I don't owe it to you."

"To me, Sir Walter!"

"I rather think you put the girls up to it." Then he laughed as though it were a very good joke and told the Major where he would find the ladies. He had been expressly desired by his wife to be genial to the Major, and had been as genial as he knew how.

Rossiter, as he went out on to the lawn, saw Mr. Burmeston, the brewer, walking with Edith, the third daughter. He could not but admire the strategy of Lady Wanless when he acknowledged to himself how well she managed all these things. The brewer would not have been allowed to walk with Gertrude, the fourth daughter, nor even with Maria, the naughty girl who liked the curate,—because it was Edith's turn. Edith was certainly the plainest of the family, and yet she had her turn. Lady Wanless was by far too good a mother to have favourites among her own children.

He then found the mother, the eldest daughter, and Gertrude overseeing the decoration of a tent, which had been put up as an addition to the dining-room. He expected to find Mr. Cobble, to whom he had taken a liking, a nice, pleasant, frank young country gentleman; but Mr. Cobble was not wanted for any express purpose, and might have been in the way. Mr. Cobble was landed and safe. Before long he found himself walking round the garden with Lady Wanless herself. The other girls, though they were to be his sisters, were never thrown into any special intimacy with him. "She will be down before long now that she knows you are here," said Lady Wanless. "She was fatigued a little, and I thought it better that she should lie down. She is so impressionable, you know." "She" was Georgiana. He knew that very well. But why should Georgiana be called "She" to him, by her mother? Had "She" been in truth engaged to him it would have been intelligible enough. But there had been nothing of the kind. As "She" was thus dinned into his ears, he thought of the very small amount of conversation which had ever taken place between himself and the young lady.

Then there occurred to him an idea that he would tell Lady Wanless in so many words that there was a mistake. The doing so would require some courage, but he thought that he could summon up manliness for the purpose,—if only he could find the words and occasion. But though "She" were so frequently spoken of, still nothing was said which seemed to give him the opportunity required. It is hard for a man to have to reject a girl when she has been offered,—but harder to do so before the offer has in truth been made. "I am afraid there is a little mistake in your ideas as to me and your daughter." It was thus that he would have had to speak, and then to have endured the outpouring of her wrath, when she would have declared that the ideas were only in his own arrogant brain. He let it pass by and said nothing, and before long he was playing lawn-tennis with Georgiana, who did not seem to have been in the least fatigued.

"My dear, I will not have it," said Lady Wanless about an hour afterwards, coming up and disturbing the game. "Major Rossiter, you ought to know better." Whereupon she playfully took the racket out of the Major's hand. "Mamma is such an old bother," said Georgiana as she walked back to the house with her Major. The Major had on a previous occasion perceived that the second Miss Wanless rode very well, and now he saw that she was very stout at lawn-tennis; but he observed none of that peculiarity of mental or physical development which her mother had described as "impressionable." Nevertheless she was a handsome girl, and if to play at lawn-tennis would help to make a husband happy, so much at any rate she could do.

This took place on the day before the meeting,—before the great day. When the morning came the girls did not come down early to breakfast, and our hero found himself left alone with Mr. Burmeston. "You have known the family a long time," said the Major as they were sauntering about the gravel paths together, smoking their cigars.

"No, indeed," said Mr. Burmeston. "They only took me up about three months ago,—just before we went over to Owless. Very nice people;—don't you think so?"

"Very nice," said the Major.

"They stand so high in the county, and all that sort of thing. Birth does go a long way, you know."

"So it ought," said the Major.

"And though the Baronet does not do much in the world, he has been in the House, you know. All those things help." Then the Major understood that Mr. Burmeston had looked the thing in the face, and had determined that for certain considerations it was worth his while to lead one of the Miss Wanlesses to the hymeneal altar. In this Mr. Burmeston was behaving with more manliness than he,—who had almost made up his mind half-a-dozen times, and had never been satisfied with the way he had done it.

About twelve the visitors had begun to come, and Sophia with Mr. Cobble were very soon trying their arrows together. Sophia had not been allowed to have her lover on the previous day, but was now making up for it. That was all very well, but Lady Wanless was a little angry with her eldest daughter. Her success was insured for her. Her business was done. Seeing how many sacrifices had been made to her during the last twelvemonths, surely now she might have been active in aiding her sisters, instead of merely amusing herself.

The Major was not good at archery. He was no doubt an excellent Deputy Inspector–General of Cavalry; but if bows and arrows had still been the weapons used in any part of the British army, he would not, without further instruction, have been qualified to inspect that branch. Georgiana Wanless, on the other hand, was a proficient. Such shooting as she made was marvellous to look at. And she was a very image of Diana, as with her beautiful figure and regular features, dressed up to the work, she stood with her bow raised in her hand and let twang the arrows. The circle immediately outside the bull's-eye was the farthest from the mark she ever touched. But good as she was and bad as was the Major, nevertheless they were appointed always to shoot together. After a world of failures the Major would shoot no more,—but not the less did he go backwards and forwards with Georgiana when she changed from one end to the other, and found himself absolutely appointed to that task. It grew upon him during the whole day that this second Miss Wanless was supposed to be his own,—almost as much as was the elder the property of Mr. Cobble. Other young men would do no more than speak to her. And when once, after the great lunch in the tent, Lady Wanless came and put her hand affectionately upon his arm, and whispered some word into his ear in the presence of all the assembled guests, he knew that the entire county had recognised him as caught.

There was old Lady Deepbell there. How it was that towards the end of the day's delights Lady Deepbell got hold of him he never knew. Lady Deepbell had not been introduced to him, and yet she got hold of him. "Major Rossiter, you are the luckiest man of the day," she said to him.

"Pretty well," said he, affecting to laugh; "but why so?"

"She is the handsomest young woman out. There hasn't been one in London this season with such a figure."

"You are altogether wrong in your surmise, Lady Deepbell."

"No, no; I am right enough. I see it all. Of course the poor girl won't have any money; but then how nice it is when a gentleman like you is able to dispense with that. Perhaps they do take after their father a little, and he certainly is not bright; but upon my word, I think a girl is all the better for that. What's the good of having such a lot of talkee-talkee?"

"Lady Deepbell, you are alluding to a young lady without the slightest warrant," said the Major.

"Warrant enough;—warrant enough," said the old woman, toddling off.

Then young Cobble came to him, and talked to him as though he were a brother of the house. Young Cobble was an honest fellow, and quite in earnest in his matrimonial intentions. "We shall be delighted if you'll come to us on the first," said Cobble. The first of course meant the first of September. "We ain't so badly off just for a week's shooting. Sophia is to be there, and we'll get Georgiana too."

The Major was fond of shooting, and would have been glad to accept the offer; but it was out of the question that he should allow himself to be taken in at Cobble Hall under a false pretext. And was it not incumbent on him to make this young man understand that he had no pretensions whatever to the hand of the second Miss Wanless? "You are very good," said he.

"We should be delighted," said young Cobble.

"But I fear there is a mistake. I can't say anything more about it now because it doesn't do to name people;—but there is a mistake. Only for that I should have been delighted. Good-bye." Then he took his departure, leaving young Cobble in a state of mystified suspense.

The day lingered on to a great length. The archery and the lawn-tennis were continued till late after the so-called lunch, and towards the evening a few couples stood up to dance. It was evident to the Major that Burmeston and Edith were thoroughly comfortable together. Gertrude amused herself well, and even Maria was contented, though the curate as a matter of course was not there. Sophia with her legitimate lover was as happy as the day and evening were long. But there came a frown upon Georgiana's brow, and when at last the Major, as though forced by destiny, asked her to dance, she refused. It had seemed to her a matter of course that he should ask her, and at last he did;—but she refused. The evening with him was very long, and just as he thought that he would escape to bed, and was meditating how early he would be off on the morrow, Lady Wanless took possession of him and carried him off alone into one of the desolate chambers. "Is she very tired?" asked the anxious mother.

"Is who tired?" The Major at that moment would have given twenty guineas to have been in his lodgings near St. James's Street.

"My poor girl," said Lady Wanless, assuming a look of great solicitude.

It was vain for him to pretend not to know who was the "she" intended. "Oh, ah, yes; Miss Wanless."

"Georgiana."

"I think she is tired. She was shooting a great deal. Then there was a quadrille;—but she didn't dance. There has been a great deal to tire young ladies."

"You shouldn't have let her do so much."

How was he to get out of it? What was he to say? If a man is clearly asked his intentions he can say that he has not got any. That used to be the old fashion when a gentleman was supposed to be dilatory in declaring his purpose. But it gave the oscillating lover so easy an escape! It was like the sudden jerk of the hand of the unpractised fisherman: if the fish does not succumb at once it goes away down the stream and is no more heard of. But from this new process there is no mode of immediate escape. "I couldn't prevent her because she is nothing to me." That would have been the straightforward answer;—but one most difficult to make. "I hope she will be none the worse to-morrow morning," said the Major.

"I hope not, indeed. Oh, Major Rossiter!" The mother's position was also difficult, as it is of no use to play with a fish too long without making an attempt to stick the hook into his gills.

"Lady Wanless!"

"What am I to say to you? I am sure you know my feelings. You know how sincere is Sir Walter's regard."

"I am very much flattered, Lady Wanless."

"That means nothing." This was true, but the Major did not mean to intend anything. "Of all my flock she is the fairest." That was true also. The Major would have been delighted to accede to the assertion of the young lady's beauty, if this might have been the end of it. "I had thought— "

"Had thought what, Lady Wanless?"

"If I am deceived in you, Major Rossiter, I never will believe in a man again. I have looked upon you as the very soul of honour."

"I trust that I have done nothing to lessen your good opinion."

"I do not know. I cannot say. Why do you answer me in this way about my child?" Then she held her hands together and looked up into his face imploringly. He owned to himself that she was a good actress. He was almost inclined to submit and to declare his passion for Georgiana. For the present that way out of the difficulty would have been so easy!

"You shall hear from me to-morrow morning," he said, almost solemnly.

"Shall I?" she asked, grasping his hand. "Oh, my friend, let it be as I desire. My whole life shall be devoted to making you happy,—you and her." Then he was allowed to escape.

Lady Wanless, before she went to bed, was closeted for awhile with the eldest daughter. As Sophia was now almost as good as a married woman, she was received into closer counsel than the others. "Burmeston will do," she said; "but, as for that Cavalry man, he means it no more than the chair." The pity was that Burmeston might have been secured without the archery meeting, and that all the money, spent on behalf of the Major, should have been thrown away.

Chapter VII

After The Party.

When The Major left Brook Park on the morning after the archery amusements he was quite sure of this,—that under no circumstances whatever would he be induced to ask Miss Georgiana Wanless to be his wife. He had promised to write a letter,—and he would write one instantly. He did not conceive it possible but that Lady Wanless should understand what would be the purport of that letter, although as she left him on the previous night she had pretended to hope otherwise. That her hopes had not been very high we know from the words which she spoke to Sophia in the privacy of her own room.

He had intended to return by Slowbridge, but when the morning came he changed his mind and went to Beetham. His reason for doing so was hardly plain, even to himself. He tried to make himself believe that the letter had better be written from Beetham,—hot, as it were, from the immediate neighbourhood,—than from London; but, as he thought of this, his mind was crowded with ideas of Alice Dugdale. He would not propose to Alice. At this moment, indeed, he was averse to matrimony, having been altogether disgusted with female society at Brook Park; but he had to acknowledge a sterling worth about Alice, and the existence of a genuine friendship between her and himself, which made it painful to him to leave the country without other recognition than that raising of his hat when he saw her at the corner of the lane. He had behaved badly in this Brook Park affair,—in having been tempted thither in opposition to those better instincts which had made Alice so pleasant a companion to him,—and was ashamed of himself. He did not think that he could go back to his former ideas. He was aware that Alice must think ill of him,—would not believe him to be now such as she had once thought him. England and London were distasteful to him. He would go abroad on that foreign service which he had proposed to himself. There was an opening for him to do so if he liked, and he could return to his present duties after a year or two. But he would see Alice again before he went. Thinking of all this, he drove himself back to Beetham.

On that morning tidings of the successful festivities at Brook Park reached the doctor's house. Tidings of the coming festivities, then of the preparations, and at last of the festal day itself, had reached Alice, so that it seemed to her that all Beetham talked of nothing else. Old Lady Deepbell had caught a cold, walking about on the lawn with hardly anything on her old shoulders,—stupid old woman,—and had sent for the doctor the first thing in the morning. "Positively settled," she had said to the doctor, "absolutely arranged, Dr. Dugdale. Lady Wanless told me so herself, and I congratulated the gentleman." She did not go on to say that the gentleman had denied the accusation,—but then she had not believed the denial. The doctor, coming home, had thought it his duty to tell Alice, and Alice had received the news with a smile. "I knew it would be so, father."

"And you?" This he said, holding her hand and looking tenderly into her eyes.

"Me! It will not hurt me. Not that I mean to tell a lie to you, father," she added after a moment. "A woman isn't hurt because she doesn't get a prize in the lottery. Had it ever come about, I dare say I should have liked him well enough."

"No more than that?"

"And why should it have come about?" she went on saying, avoiding her father's last question, determined not to lie if she could help it, but determined, also, to show no wound. "I think my position in life very happy, but it isn't one from which he would choose a wife."

"Why not, my dear?"

"A thousand reasons; I am always busy, and he would naturally like a young lady who had nothing to do." She understood the effect of the perambulator and the constant needle and thread. "Besides, though he might be all very well, he could never, I think, be as dear to me as the bairns. I should feel that I lost more than I got by going." This she knew to be a lie, but it was so important that her father should believe her to be contented with her home duties! And she was contented, though very unhappy. When her father kissed her, she smiled into his face,—oh, so sweetly, so pleasantly! And the old man thought that she could not have loved very deeply. Then she took herself to her own room, and sat awhile alone with a countenance much changed. The lines of sorrow about her brow were terrible. There was not a tear; but her mouth was close pressed, and her hand was working constantly by her side. She gazed at nothing, but sat with her eyes wide open, staring straight before her. Then she jumped up quickly, and striking her hand upon her heart, she spoke aloud to herself. "I will cure it," she said. "He is not worthy, and it should therefore be easier. Though he were worthy, I would cure it. Yes, Bobby, I am coming." Then she went about her work.

That might have been about noon. It was after their early dinner with the children that the Major came up to the doctor's house. He had reached the parsonage in time for a late breakfast, and had then written his letter. After that he had sat idling about on the lawn,—not on the best terms with his mother, to whom he had sworn that, under no circumstances, would he make Georgiana Wanless his wife. "I would sooner marry a girl from a troop of tight-rope dancers," he had said in his anger. Mrs. Rossiter knew that he intended to go up to the doctor's house, and therefore the immediate feeling between the mother and son was not pleasant. My readers, if they please, shall see the letter to Lady Wanless.

"My Dear Lady Wanless,—It is a great grief to me to say that there has been, I fear, a misconception between you and me on a certain matter. This is the more a trouble to me because you and Sir Walter have been so very kind to me. From a word or two which fell from you last night I was led to fear that you suspected feelings on my part which I have never entertained, and aspirations to which I have never pretended. No man can be more alive than I am to the honour which has been suggested, but I feel bound to say that I am not in a condition to accept it.

"Pray believe me to be,
"Dear Lady Wanless,
"Yours always very faithfully,
"John Rossiter."

The letter, when it was written, was, to himself, very unsatisfactory. It was full of ambiguous words and namby-pamby phraseology which disgusted him. But he did not know how to alter it for the better. It is hard to say an uncivil thing civilly without ambiguous namby-pamby language. He could not bring it out in straight-forward stout English: "You want me to marry your daughter, but I won't do anything of the kind." So the letter was sent. The conduct of which he was really ashamed did not regard Miss Wanless, but Alice Dugdale.

At last, very slowly, he took himself up to the doctor's house. He hardly knew what it was that he meant to say when he found himself there, but he was sure that he did not mean to make an offer. Even had other things suited, there would have been something distasteful to him in doing this so quickly after the affair of Miss Wanless. He was in no frame now for making love; but yet it would be ungracious in him, he thought, to leave Beetham without seeing his old friend. He found the two ladies together, with the children still around them, sitting near a window which opened down to the ground. Mrs. Dugdale had a novel in hand, and, as usual, was leaning back in a rocking-chair. Alice had also a book open on the table before her, but she was bending over a sewing-machine. They had latterly divided the cares of the family between them. Mrs. Dugdale had brought the children into the world, and Alice had washed, clothed, and fed them when they were there. When the Major entered the room, Alice's mind was, of course, full of the tidings she had heard from her father,—which tidings, however, had not been communicated to Mrs. Dugdale.

Alice at first was very silent while Mrs. Dugdale asked as to the festivities. "It has been the grandest thing anywhere about here for a long time."

"And, like other grand things, a great bore," said the Major.

"I don't suppose you found it so, Major Rossiter," said the lady.

Then the conversation ran away into a description of what had been done during the day. He wished to make it understood that there was no permanent link binding him to Brook Park, but he hardly knew how to say it without going beyond the lines of ordinary conversation. At last there seemed to be an opening,—not exactly what he wished, but still an opening. "Brook Park is not exactly the place," said he, "at which I should ever feel myself quite at home." This was in answer to some chance word which had fallen from Mrs. Dugdale.

"I am sorry for that," said Alice. She would have given a guinea to bring the word back after it had been spoken. But spoken words cannot be brought back.

"Why sorry?" he asked, smiling.

"Because—Oh, because it is so likely that you may be there often."

"I don't know that at all."

"You have become so intimate with them!" said Alice. "We are told in Beetham that the party was got up all for your honour."

So Sir Walter had told him, and so Maria, the naughty girl, had said also—"Only for your beaux yeux, Major Rossiter, we shouldn't have had any party at all." This had been said by Maria when she was laughing at him about her sister Georgiana. "I don't know how that may be," said the Major; "but all the same I shall never be at home at Brook Park."

"Don't you like the young ladies?" asked Mrs. Dugdale.

"Oh, yes; very much; and Lady Wanless; and Sir Walter. I like them all, in a way. But yet I shall never find myself at home at Brook Park."

Alice was very angry with him. He ought not to have gone there at all. He must have known that he could not be there without paining her. She thoroughly believed that he was engaged to marry the girl of whose family he spoke in this way. He had thought,—so it seemed to her,—that he might lessen the blow to her by making little of the great folk among whom his future lot was to be cast. But what could be more mean? He was not the John Rossiter to whom she had given her heart. There had been no such man. She had been mistaken. "I am afraid you are one of those," she said, "who, wherever they find themselves, at once begin to wish for something better."

"That is meant to be severe."

"My severity won't go for much."

"I am sure you have deserved it," said Mrs. Dugdale, most indiscreetly.

"Is this intended for an attack?" he asked, looking from one to the other.

"Not at all," said Alice, affecting to laugh. "I should have said nothing if I thought mamma would take it up so seriously. I was only sorry to hear you speak of your new friends so slightingly."

After that the conversation between them was very difficult, and he soon got up to go away. As he did so, he asked Alice to say a word to him out in the garden, having already explained to them both that it might be some time before he would be again down at Beetham. Alice rose slowly from her sewing-machine, and, putting on her hat, led the way with a composed and almost dignified step out through the window. Her heart was beating within her, but she looked as though she were mistress of every pulse.

"Why did you say that to me?" he asked.

"Say what?"

"That I always wished for better things and better people than I found."

"Because I think you ambitious,—and discontented. There is nothing disgraceful in that, though it is not the character which I myself like the best."

"You meant to allude specially to the Wanlesses?"

"Because you have just come from there, and were speaking of them."

"And to one of that family specially?"

"No, Major Rossiter. There you are wrong. I alluded to no one in particular. They are nothing to me. I do not know them; but I hear that they are kind and friendly people, with good manners and very handsome. Of course I know, as we all know everything of each other in this little place, that you have of late become very intimate with them. Then when I hear you aver that you are already discontented with them, I cannot help thinking that you are hard to please. I am sorry that mamma spoke of deserving. I did not intend to say anything so seriously."

"Alice!"

"Well, Major Rossiter."

"I wish I could make you understand me."

"I do not know that that would do any good. We have been old friends, and of course I hope that you may be happy. I must say good-bye now. I cannot go beyond the gate, because I am wanted to take the children out."

"Good-bye then. I hope you will not think ill of me."

"Why should I think ill of you? I think very well,—only that you are ambitious." As she said this, she laughed again, and then she left him.

He had been most anxious to tell her that he was not going to marry that girl, but he had not known how to do it. He could not bring himself to declare that he would not marry a girl when by such declaration he would have been forced to assume that he might marry her if he pleased. So he left Alice at the gate, and she went back to the house still convinced that he was betrothed to Georgiana Wanless.

Chapter VIII

Sir Walter Up In London.

THE MAJOR, when he left the doctor's house, was more thoroughly in love with Alice than ever. There had been something in her gait as she led the way out through the window, and again, as with determined purpose she bade him speedily farewell at the gate, which forced him to acknowledge that the dragging of perambulators and the making of petticoats had not detracted from her feminine charm or from her feminine dignity. She had been dressed in her ordinary morning frock,—the very frock on which he had more than once seen the marks of Bobby's dirty heels; but she had pleased his eye better than Georgiana, clad in all the glory of her toxopholite array. The toxopholite feather had been very knowing, the tight leathern belt round her waist had been bright in colour and pretty in design. The looped-up dress, fit for the work in hand, had been gratifying. But with it all there had been the show of a thing got up for ornament and not for use. She was like a box of painted sugar-plums, very pretty to the eye, but of which no one wants to extract any for the purpose of eating them. Alice was like a housewife's store, kept beautifully in order, but intended chiefly for comfortable use. As he went up to London he began to doubt whether he would go abroad. Were he to let a few months pass by would not Alice be still there, and willing perhaps to receive him with more kindness when she should have heard that his follies at Brook Park were at an end?

Three days after his return, when he was sitting in his offices thinking perhaps more of Alice Dugdale than of the whole British Cavalry, a soldier who was in waiting brought a card to him. Sir Walter Wanless had come to call upon him. If he were disengaged Sir Walter would be glad to see him. He was not at all anxious to see Sir Walter; but there was no alternative, and Sir Walter was shown into the room.

In explaining the purport of Sir Walter's visit we must go back for a few minutes to Brook Park. When Sir Walter came down to breakfast on the morning after the festivities he was surprised to hear that Major Rossiter had taken his departure. There sat young Burmeston. He at any rate was safe. And there sat young Cobble, who by Sophia's aid had managed to get himself accommodated for the night, and all the other young people, including the five Wanless girls. The father, though not observant, could see that Georgiana was very glum. Lady Wanless herself affected a good-humour which hardly deceived him, and certainly did not deceive anyone else. "He was obliged to be off this morning, because of his duties," said Lady Wanless. "He told me that it was to be so, but I did not like to say anything about it yesterday." Georgiana turned up her nose, as much as to say that the going and coming of Major Rossiter was not a matter of much importance to any one there, and, least of all, to her. Except the father, there was not a person in the room who was not aware that Lady Wanless had missed her fish.

But she herself was not quite sure even yet that she had failed altogether. She was a woman who hated failure, and who seldom failed. She was brave of heart too, and able to fight a losing battle to the last. She was very angry with the Major, who she well knew was endeavouring to escape from her toils. But he would not on that account be the less useful as a son-in-law;—nor on that account was she the more willing to allow him to escape. With five daughters without fortunes it behoved her as a mother to be persistent. She would not give it up, but must turn the matter well in her mind before she took further steps. She feared that a simple invitation could hardly bring the

Major back to Brook Park. Then there came the letter from the Major which did not make the matter easier.

"My dear," she said to her husband, sitting down opposite to him in his room, "that Major Rossiter isn't behaving quite as he ought to do."

"I'm not a bit surprised," said the Baronet angrily. "I never knew anybody from Wadham behave well."

"He's quite a gentleman, if you mean that," said Lady Wanless; "and he's sure to do very well in the world; and poor Georgiana is really fond of him,—which doesn't surprise me in the least."

"Has he said anything to make her fond of him? I suppose she has gone and made a fool of herself,—like Maria."

"Not at all. He has said a great deal to her;—much more than he ought to have done, if he meant nothing. But the truth is, young men nowadays never know their own minds unless there is somebody to keep them up to the mark. You must go and see him."

"I!" said the afflicted father.

"Of course, my dear. A few judicious words in such a case may do so much. I would not ask Walter to go,"—Walter was the eldest son, who was with his regiment,—"because it might lead to quarrelling. I would not have anything of that kind, if only for the dear girl's sake. But what you would say would be known to nobody; and it might have the desired effect. Of course you will be very quiet,—and very serious also. Nobody could do it better than you will. There can be no doubt that he has trifled with the dear girl's affections. Why else has he been with her whenever he has been here? It was so visible on Wednesday that everybody was congratulating me. Old Lady Deepbell asked whether the day was fixed. I treated him quite as though it were settled. Young men do so often get these sudden starts of doubt. Then, sometimes, just a word afterwards will put it all right." In this way the Baronet was made to understand that he must go and see the Major.

He postponed the unwelcome task till his wife at last drove him out of the house. "My dear," she said, "will you let your child die broken-hearted for want of a word?" When it was put to him in that way he found himself obliged to go, though, to tell the truth, he could not find any sign of heart-breaking sorrow about his child. He was not allowed to speak to Georgiana herself, his wife telling him that the poor child would be unable to bear it.

Sir Walter, when he was shown into the Major's room, felt himself to be very ill able to conduct the business in hand, and to the Major himself the moment was one of considerable trouble. He had thought it possible that he might receive an answer to his letter, a reply that might be indignant, or piteous, admonitory, or simply abusive, as the case might be,—one which might too probably require a further correspondence; but it had never occurred to him that Sir Walter would come in person. But here he was,—in the room,—by no means with that pretended air of geniality with which he had last received the Major down at Brook Park. The greeting, however, between the gentlemen was courteous if not cordial, and then Sir Walter began his task. "We were quite surprised you should have left us so early that morning."

"I had told Lady Wanless."

"Yes; I know. Nevertheless we were surprised. Now, Major Rossiter, what do you mean to do about,—about,—about this young lady?" The Major sat silent. He could not pretend to be ignorant what young lady was intended after the letter which he had himself written to Lady Wanless. "This, you know, is a very painful kind of thing, Major Rossiter."

"Very painful indeed, Sir Walter."

"When I remembered that I had been at Christchurch and your excellent father at Wadham both at the same time, I thought that I might trust you in my house without the slightest fear."

"I make bold to say, Sir Walter, that you were quite justified in that expectation, whether it was founded on your having been at Christchurch or on my position and character in the world." He knew that the scene would be easier to him if he could work himself up to a little indignation on his own part.

"And yet I am told,—I am told— "

"What are you told, Sir Walter?"

"There can, I think, be no doubt that you have—in point of fact, paid attention to my daughter." Sir Walter was a gentleman, and felt that the task imposed upon him grated against his better feelings.

"If you mean that I have taken steps to win her affections, you have been wrongly informed."

"That's what I do mean. Were you not received just now at Brook Park as,—as paying attention to her?"

"I hope not."

"You hope not, Major Rossiter?"

"I hope no such mistake was made. It certainly was not made by me. I felt myself much flattered by being received at your house. I wrote the other day a line or two to Lady Wanless and thought I had explained all this."

Sir Walter opened his eyes when he heard, for the first time, of the letter, but was sharp enough not to exhibit his ignorance at the moment. "I don't know about explaining," he said. "There are some things which can't be so very well explained. My wife assures me that that poor girl has been deceived,—cruelly deceived. Now I put it to you, Major Rossiter, what ought you as a gentleman to do?"

"Really, Sir Walter, you are not entitled to ask me any such question."

"Not on behalf of my own child?"

"I cannot go into the matter from that view of the case. I can only declare that I have said nothing and done nothing for which I can blame myself. I cannot understand how there should have been such a mistake; but it did not, at any rate, arise with me."

Then the Baronet sat dumb. He had been specially instructed not to give up the interview till he had obtained some sign of weakness from the enemy. If he could only induce the enemy to promise another visit to Brook Park that would be much. If he could obtain some expression of liking or admiration for the young lady that would be something. If he could induce the Major to allude to delay as being necessary, farther operations would be founded on that base. But nothing had been obtained. "It's the most,—the most,—the most astonishing thing I ever heard," he said at last.

"I do not know that I can say anything further."

"I'll tell you what," said the Baronet. "Come down and see Lady Wanless. The women understand these things much better than we do. Come down and talk it over with Lady Wanless. She won't propose anything that isn't proper." In answer to this the Major shook his head. "You won't?"

"It would do no good, Sir Walter. It would be painful to me, and must, I should say, be distressing to the young lady."

"Then you won't do anything!"

"There is nothing to be done."

"Upon my word, I never heard such a thing in all my life, Major Rossiter. You come down to my house; and then,—then,—then you won't,—you won't come again! To be sure he was at Wadham; but I did think your father's son would have behaved better." Then he picked up his hat from the floor and shuffled out of the room without another word.

Tidings that Sir Walter had been up to London and had called upon Major Rossiter made their way into Beetham and reached the ears of the Dugdales,—but not correct tidings as to the nature of the conversation. "I wonder when it will be," said Mrs. Dugdale to Alice. "As he has been up to town I suppose it'll be settled soon."

"The sooner the better for all parties," said Alice cheerily. "When a man and a woman have agreed together, I can't see why they shouldn't at once walk off to the church arm in arm."

"The lawyers have so much to do."

"Bother the lawyers! The parson ought to do all that is necessary, and the sooner the better. Then there would not be such paraphernalia of presents and gowns and eatings and drinkings, all of which is got up for the good of the tradesmen. If I were to be married, I should like to slip out round the corner, just as though I were going to get an extra loaf of bread from Mrs. Bakewell."

"That wouldn't do for my lady at Brook Park."

"I suppose not."

"Nor yet for the Major."

Then Alice shook her head and sighed, and took herself out to walk alone for a few minutes among the lanes. How could it be that he should be so different from that which she had taken him to be! It was now September, and she could remember an early evening in May, when the leaves were beginning to be full, and they were walking together with the spring air fresh around them, just where she was now creeping alone with the more perfect and less fresh beauty of the autumn around her. How different a person he seemed to her to be now from that which he had seemed to be then;—not different because he did not love her, but different because he was not fit to be loved! "Alice," he had then said, "you and I are alike in this, that simple, serviceable things are dear to both of us." The words had meant so much to her that she had never forgotten them. Was she simple and serviceable, so that she might be dear to him? She had been sure then that he was simple, and that he was serviceable, so that she could love him. It was thus that she had spoken of him to herself, thinking herself to be sure of his character. And now, before the summer was over, he was engaged to marry such a one as Georgiana Wanless and to become the hero of a fashionable wedding!

But she took pride to herself as she walked alone that she had already overcome the bitterness of the malady which, for a day or two, had been so heavy that she had feared for herself that it would oppress her. For a day or two after that farewell at the gate she had with a rigid purpose tied herself to every duty,—even to the duty of looking pleasant in her father's eyes, of joining in the children's games, of sharing the gossip of her stepmother. But this she had done with an agony that nearly crushed her. Now she had won her way through it, and could see her path before her. She had not cured altogether that wound in her heart; but she had assured herself that she could live on without further interference from the wound.

Chapter IX

Lady Deepbell.

THEN BY degrees it began to be rumoured about the country, and at last through the lanes of Beetham itself, that the alliance between Major Rossiter and Miss Georgiana Wanless was not quite a settled thing. Mr. Burmeston had whispered in Slowbridge that there was a screw loose, perhaps thinking that if another could escape, why not he also? Cobble, who had no idea of escaping, declared his conviction that Major Rossiter ought to be horsewhipped; but Lady Deepbell was the real town-crier who carried the news far and wide. But all of them heard it before Alice, and when others believed it Alice did not believe it,—or, indeed, care to believe or not to believe.

Lady Deepbell filled a middle situation, half way between the established superiority of Brook Park and the recognised humility of Beetham. Her title went for something; but her husband had been only a Civil Service Knight, who had deserved well of his country by a meritorious longevity. She lived in a pretty little cottage half way between Brook Park and Beetham, which was just large enough to enable her to talk of her grounds. She loved Brook Park dearly, and all the country people; but in her love for social intercourse generally she was unable to eschew the more frequent gatherings of the village. She was intimate not only with Mrs. Rossiter, but with the Tweeds and Dugdales and Simkinses, and, while she could enjoy greatly the grandeur of the Wanless aristocracy, so could she accommodate herself comfortably to the cosy gossip of the Beethamites. It was she who first spread the report in Beetham that Major Rossiter was,—as she called it,—"off."

She first mentioned the matter to Mrs. Rossiter herself; but this she did in a manner more subdued than usual. The "alliance" had been high, and she was inclined to think that Mrs. Rossiter would be disappointed. "We did think, Mrs. Rossiter, that these young people at Brook Park had meant something the other day."

Mrs. Rossiter did not stand in awe of Lady Deepbell, and was not pleased at the allusion. "It would be much better if young people could be allowed to arrange their own affairs without so much tattling about it," she said angrily.

"That's all very well, but tongues will talk, you know, Mrs. Rossiter. I am sorry for both their sakes, because I thought that it would do very well."

"Very well indeed, if the young people, as you call them, liked each other."

"But I suppose it's over now, Mrs. Rossiter?"

"I really know nothing about it, Lady Deepbell." Then the old woman, quite satisfied after this that the "alliance" had fallen to the ground, went on to the Tweeds.

"I never thought it would come to much," said Mrs. Tweed.

"I don't see why it shouldn't," said Matilda Tweed. "Georgiana Wanless is good-looking in a certain way; but they none of them have a penny, and Major Rossiter is quite a fashionable man." The Tweeds were quite outside the Wanless pale; and it was the feeling of this that made Matilda love to talk about the second Miss Wanless by her Christian name.

"I suppose he will go back to Alice now," said Clara, the younger Tweed girl.

"I don't see that at all," said Mrs. Tweed.

"I never believed much in that story," said Lady Deepbell.

"Nor I either," said Matilda. "He used to walk about with her, but what does that come to? The children were always with them. I never would believe that he was going to make so little of himself."

"But is it quite sure that all the affair at Brook Park will come to nothing, after the party and everything?" asked Mrs. Tweed.

"Quite positive," said Lady Deepbell authoritatively. "I am able to say certainly that that is all over." Then she toddled off and went to the Simkinses.

The rumour did not reach the doctor's house on that day. The conviction that Major Rossiter had behaved badly to Alice,—that Alice had been utterly thrown over by the Wanless "alliance," had been so strong, that even Lady Deepbell had not dared to go and probe wilfully that wound. The feeling in this respect had been so general that no one in Beetham had been hard-hearted enough to speak to Alice either of the triumph of Miss Wanless, or of the misconduct of the Major; and now Lady Deepbell was afraid to carry her story thither.

It was the doctor himself who first brought the tidings to the house, and did not do this till some days after Lady Deepbell had been in the village. "You had better not say anything to Alice about it." Such at first had been the doctor's injunction to his wife. "One way or the other, it will only be a trouble to her." Mrs. Dugdale, full of her secret, anxious to be obedient, thinking that the gentleman relieved from his second love, would be ready at once to be on again with his first, was so fluttered and fussy that Alice knew that there was something to be told. "You have got some great secret, mamma," she said.

"What secret, Alice?"

"I know you have. Don't wait for me to ask you to tell it. If it is to come, let it come."

"I'm not going to say anything."

"Very well, mamma. Then nothing shall be said."

"Alice, you are the most provoking young woman I ever had to deal with in my life. If I had twenty secrets I would not tell you one of them."

On the next morning Alice heard it all from her father. "I knew there was something by mamma's manner," she said.

"I told her not to say anything."

"So I suppose. But what does it matter to me, papa, whether Major Rossiter does or does not marry Miss Wanless? If he has given her his word, I am sure I hope that he will keep it."

"I don't suppose he ever did."

"Even then it doesn't matter. Papa, do not trouble yourself about him."

"But you?"

"I have gone through the fire, and have come out without being much scorched. Dear papa, I do so wish that you should understand it all. It is so nice to have some one to whom everything can be told. I did like him."

"And he?"

"I have nothing to say about that;—not a word. Girls, I suppose, are often foolish, and take things for more than they are intended to mean. I have no accusation to make against him. But I did,—I did allow myself to be weak. Then came this about Miss Wanless, and I was unhappy. I woke from a dream, and the waking was painful. But I have got over it. I do not think that you will ever know from your girl's manner that anything has been the matter with her."

"My brave girl!"

"But don't let mamma talk to me as though he could come back because the other girl has not suited him. He is welcome to the other girl,—welcome to do without her,—welcome to do with himself as it may best please him; but he shall not trouble me again." There was a stern strength in her voice as she said this, which forced her father to look at her almost with amazement. "Do not think that I am fierce, papa."

"Fierce, my darling!"

"But that I am in earnest. Of course, if he comes to Beetham we shall see him. But let him be like anybody else. Don't let it be supposed that because he flitted here once, and was made welcome, like a bird that comes in at the window, and then flitted away again, that he can be received in at the window just as before, should he fly this way any more. That's all, papa." Then, as before, she went off by herself,—to give herself renewed strength by her solitary thinkings. She had so healed the flesh round that wound that there was no longer danger of mortification. She must now take care that there should be no further wound. The people around her would be sure to tell her of this breach between her late lover and the Wanless young lady. The Tweeds and the Simkinses, and old Lady Deepbell would be full of it. She must take care so to answer them at the first word that they should not dare to talk to her of Major Rossiter. She had cured herself so that she no longer staggered under the effects of the blow. Having done that, she would not allow herself to be subject to the little stings of the little creatures around her. She had had enough of love,—of a man's love, and would make herself happy now with Bobby and the other bairns.

"He'll be sure to come back," said Mrs Dugdale to her husband.

"We shall do no good by talking about it," said the doctor. "If you will take my advice, you will not mention his name to her. I fear that he is worthless and unworthy of mention." That might be very well, thought Mrs. Dugdale; but no one in the village doubted that he had at the very least £1,500 a year, and that he was a handsome man, and such a one as is not to be picked up under every hedge. The very men who go about the world most like butterflies before marriage "steady down the best" afterwards. These were her words as she discussed the matter with Mrs. Tweed, and they both agreed that if the hero showed himself again at the doctor's house "bygones ought to be bygones."

Lady Wanless, even after her husband's return from London, declared to herself that even yet the game had not been altogether played out. Sir Walter, who had been her only possible direct messenger to the man himself, had been, she was aware, as bad a messenger as could have been selected. He could be neither authoritative nor persuasive. Therefore when he told her, on coming home, that it was easy to perceive that Major Rossiter's father could not have been educated at Christchurch, she did not feel very much disappointed. As her next step she determined to call on Mrs. Rossiter. If that should fail she must beard the lion in his den, and go herself to Major Rossiter at the Horse Guards. She did not doubt but that she would at least be able to say more than Sir Walter. Mrs. Rossiter, she was aware, was herself favourable to the match.

"My dear Mrs. Rossiter," she said in her most confidential manner, "there is a little something wrong among these young people, which I think you and I can put right if we put our heads together."

"If I know one of the young people," said Mrs. Rossiter, "it will be very hard to make him change his mind."

"He has been very attentive to the young lady."

"Of course I know nothing about it, Lady Wanless. I never saw them together."

"Dear Georgiana is so very quiet that she said nothing even to me, but I really thought that he had proposed to her. She won't say a word against him, but I believe he did. Now, Mrs. Rossiter, what has been the meaning of it?"

"How is a mother to answer for her son, Lady Wanless?"

"No;—of course not. I know that. Girls, of course, are different. But I thought that perhaps you might know something about it, for I did imagine you would like the connection."

"So I should. Why not? Nobody thinks more of birth than I do, and nothing in my opinion could have been nicer for John. But he does not see with my eyes. If I were to talk to him for a week it would have no effect."

"Is it that girl of the doctor's, Mrs. Rossiter?"

"I think not. My idea is that when he has turned it all over in his mind he has come to the conclusion that he will be better without a wife than with one."

"We might cure him of that, Mrs. Rossiter. If I could only have him down there at Brook Park for another week, I am sure he would come to." Mrs. Rossiter, however, could not say that she thought it probable that her son would be induced soon to pay another visit to Brook Park.

A week after this Lady Wanless absolutely did find her way into the Major's presence at the Horse Guards,—but without much success. The last words at that interview only shall be given to the reader,—the last words as they were spoken both by the lady and by the gentleman. "Then I am to see my girl die of a broken heart?" said Lady Wanless, with her handkerchief up to her eyes.

"I hope not, Lady Wanless; but in whatever way she might die, the fault would not be mine." There was a frown on the gentleman's brow as he said this which cowed even the lady.

As she went back to Slowbridge that afternoon, and then home to Brook Park, she determined at last that the game must be looked upon as played out. There was no longer any ground on which to stand and fight. Before she went to bed that night she sent for Georgiana. "My darling child," she said, "that man is unworthy of you."

"I always thought he was," said Georgiana. And so there was an end to that little episode in the family of the Wanlesses.

Chapter X

The Bird That Pecked At The Window.

THE BIRD that had flown in at the window and had been made welcome, had flown away ungratefully. Let him come again pecking as he might at the window, no more crumbs of love should be thrown to him. Alice, with a steady purpose, had resolved on that. With all her humble ways, her continual darning of stockings, her cutting of bread and butter for the children, her pushing of the perambulator in the lanes, there was a pride about her, a knowledge of her own dignity as a woman, which could have been stronger in the bosom of no woman of title, of wealth, or of fashion. She claimed nothing. She had expected no admiration. She had been contented to take the world as it came to her, without thinking much of love or romance. When John Rossiter had first shown himself at Beetham, after his return from India, and when he had welcomed her so warmly,—too warmly,—as his old playfellow, no idea had occurred to her that he would ever be more to her than her old playfellow. Her own heart was too precious to herself to be given away idly to the first comer. Then the bird had flown in at the window, and it had been that the coming of the stranger had been very sweet to her. But, even for the stranger, she would not change her ways,—unless, perchance, some day she might appertain to the stranger. Then it would be her duty to fit herself entirely to him. In the meantime, when he gave her little hints that something of her domestic slavery might be discontinued, she would not abate a jot from her duties. If he liked to come with her when she pushed the children, let him come. If he cared to see her when she was darning a stocking or cutting bread and butter, let him pay his visits. If he thought those things derogatory, certainly let him stay away. So the thing had grown till she had found herself surprised, and taken, as it were, into a net,—caught in a pitfall of love. But she held her peace, stuck manfully to the perambulator, and was a little colder in her demeanour than heretofore. Whereupon Major Rossiter, as the reader is aware, made two visits to Brook Park. The bird might peck at the window, but he should never again be taken into the room.

But the bird, from the moment in which he had packed up his portmanteau at Brook Park, had determined that he would be taken in at the window again,—that he would at any rate return to the window, and peck at the glass with constancy, soliciting that it might be opened. As he now thought of the two girls, the womanliness of the one, as compared with the worldliness of the other, conquered him completely. There had never been a moment in which his heart had in truth inclined itself towards the young athlete of Brook Park,—never a moment, hardly a moment, in which his heart had been untrue to Alice. But glitter had for awhile prevailed with him, and he had, just for a moment, allowed himself to be discontented with the homely colour of unalloyed gold. He was thoroughly ashamed of himself, knowing well that he had given pain. He had learned, clearly enough, from what her father, mother, and others had said to him, that there were those who expected him to marry Alice Dugdale, and others who hoped that he would marry Georgiana Wanless. Now, at last, he could declare that no other love than that which was warm within his heart at present could ever have been possible to him. But he was aware that he had much to do to recover his footing. Alice's face and her manner as she bade him good-bye at the gate were very clear before his eyes.

Two months passed by before he was again seen at Beetham. It had happened that he was, in truth, required elsewhere, on duty, during the period, and he took care to let it be known at Beetham that such was the case. Information to this effect was in some shape sent to Alice. Openly, she took no notice of it; but, inwardly, she said to herself that they who troubled themselves by sending her such tidings, troubled themselves in vain. "Men may come and men may go," she sang to herself, in a low voice. How little they knew her, to come to her with news as to Major Rossiter's coming and going!

Then one day he came. One morning early in December the absolute fact was told at the dinner table. "The Major is at the parsonage," said the maid-servant. Mrs. Dugdale looked at Alice, who continued, however, to distribute hashed mutton with an equanimity which betrayed no flaw.

After that not a word was said about him. The doctor had warned his wife to be silent; and though she would fain have spoken, she restrained herself. After dinner the usual work went on, and then the usual playing in the garden. The weather was dry and mild for the time of year, so that Alice was swinging two of the children when Major Rossiter came up through the gate. Minnie, who had been a favourite, ran to him, and he came slowly across the lawn to the tree on which the swing was hung. For a moment Alice stopped her work that she might shake hands with him, and then at once went back to her place. "If I were to stop a moment before Bobby has had his turn," she said, "he would feel the injustice."

"No, I isn't," said Bobby. "Oo may go 'is time."

"But I don't want to go, Bobby, and Major Rossiter will find mamma in the drawing-room;" and Alice for a moment thought of getting her hat and going off from the place. Then she reflected that to run away would be cowardly. She did not mean to run away always because the man came. Had she not settled it with herself that the man should be nothing to her? Then she went on swinging the children,—very deliberately, in order that she might be sure of herself, that the man's coming had not even flurried her.

In ten minutes the Major was there again. It had been natural to suppose that he should not be detained long in conversation by Mrs. Dugdale. "May I swing one of them for a time?" he asked.

"Well, no; I think not. It is my allotted exercise, and I never give it up." But Minnie, who knew what a strong arm could do, was imperious, and the Major got possession of the swing.

Then of a sudden he stopped. "Alice," he said, "I want you to take a turn with me up the road."

"I am not going out at all to-day," she said. Her voice was steady and well preserved; but there was a slight rising of colour on her cheeks.

"But I wish it expressly. You must come to-day."

She could consider only for a moment,—but for a moment she did think the matter over. If the man chose to speak to her seriously, she must listen to him,—once, and once only. So much he had a right to demand. When a bird of that kind pecks in that manner some attention must be paid to him. So she got her hat, and leading the way down the road, opened the gate and turned up the lane away from the street of the village. For some yards he did not speak. She, indeed, was the first to do so. "I cannot stay out very long, Major Rossiter; so, if there is anything— ?

"There is a something, Alice." Of course she knew, but she was quite resolved. Resolved! Had not every moment of her life since last she had parted with him been given up to the strengthening of this resolution? Not a stitch had gone through the calico which had not been pulled the tighter by the tightening of her purpose! And now he was there. Oh, how more than earthly sweet it had been to have him there, when her resolutions had been of another kind! But she had been punished for that, and was strong against such future ills. "Alice, it had better come out simply. I love you, and have ever loved you with all my heart." Then there was a frown and a little trampling of the ground beneath her feet, but she said not a word. Oh, if it only could have come sooner,—a few weeks sooner! "I know what you would say to me, if possible, before you say it. I have given you cause to be angry with me."

"Oh no!" she cried, interrupting him.

"But I have never been untrue to you for a moment. You seemed to slight me."

"And if I did?"

"That may pass. If you should slight me now, I must bear it. Even though you should deliberately tell me that you cannot love me, I must bear that. But with such a load of love as I have at my heart, it must be told to you. Day and night it covers me from head to foot. I can think of nothing else. I dream that I have your hand in mine, but when I wake I think it can never be so."

There was an instinct with her at the moment to let her fingers glide into his; but it was shown only by the gathering together of her two hands, so that no rebellious fingers straying from her in that direction might betray her. "If you have never loved me, never can love me, say so, and I will go away." She should have spoken now, upon the instant; but she simply moved her foot upon the gravel and was silent. "That I should be punished might be right. If it could be possible that the punishment should extend to two, that could not be right."

She did not want to punish him,—only to be brave herself. If to be obdurate would in truth make him unhappy, then would it be right that she should still be firm? It would be bad enough, after so many self-assurances, to succumb at the first word; but for his sake,—for his sake,—would it not be possible to bear even that? "If you never have loved me, and never can love me, say so, and I will go." Even to herself, she had not pledged herself to lie. If he asked her to be his wife in the plain way, she could say that she would not. Then the way would be plain before her. But what reply was she to make in answer to such a question as this? Could she say that she had not loved him,—or did not love him? "Alice," he said, putting his hand up to her arm.

"No!"

"Alice, can you not forgive me?"

"I have forgiven."

"And will you not love me?"

She turned her face upon him with a purpose to frown, but the fulness of his eyes upon her was too much, and the frown gave way, and a tear came into her eye, and her lips trembled; and then she acknowledged to herself that her resolution had not been worth a straw to her.

It should be added that considerably before Alice's wedding, both Sophia and Georgiana Wanless were married,—Sophia, in due order, as of course, to young Cobble, and Georgiana to Mr. Burmeston, the brewer. This, as the reader will remember, was altogether unexpected; but it was a great and guiding principle with Lady Wanless that the girls should not be taken out of their turns.

Catherine Carmichael; or Three Years Running

Originally appeared in *Masonic Magazine*, Christmas Number, 1878. It was not reprinted in Trollope's lifetime. Trollope delivered the completed manuscript on 14 October 1878, a mere eleven days after he had agreed to write it. Trollope visited New Zealand in August and September 1872, and wrote up his trip in *Australia and New Zealand* (1874).

Christmas Day. No. 1

CATHERINE CARMICHAEL, whose name is prefixed to this story, was very early in her life made acquainted with trouble. That name became hers when she was married, but the reader must first know her as Catherine Baird. Her father was a Scotchman of good birth, and had once been possessed of fair means. But the world had gone against him, and he had taken his family out to New Zealand when Catherine was yet but ten years old. Of Mr. Baird and his misfortunes little need be said, except that for nearly a dozen years he followed the precarious and demoralizing trade of a gold-digger at Hokitika. Sometimes there was money in plenty, sometimes there was none. Food there was, always plenty, though food of the roughest. Drink there was, generally, much more than plenty. Everything around the young Bairds was rough. Frequently changing their residence from one shanty to another, the last shanty inhabited by them would always be the roughest. As for the common decencies of life, they seemed to become ever scarcer and more scarce with them, although the females among them had a taste for decency, and although they lived in a region which then seemed to be running over with gold. The mother was ever decent in language, in manners, and in morals, and strove gallantly for her children. That they could read and write, and had some taste for such pursuits, was due to her; for the father, as years passed over him, and as he became more and more hardened to the rough usages of a digger's life, fell gradually into the habits of a mere miner. A year before his death no one would have thought he had been the son of Fergus Baird, Esq., of Killach, and that when he had married the daughter of a neighbouring laird, things had smiled pleasantly on him and his young wife.

Then his wife died, and he followed her within one year. Of the horrors of that twelve months it is useless now to tell. A man's passion for drink, if he be not wholly bad, may be moderated by a wife, and then pass all bounds when she is no longer there to restrain him. So it was with him; and for a while there was danger that it should be so with his boys also. Catherine was the eldest daughter, and was then twenty-two. There was a brother older, then four younger, and after them three other girls. That year to Catherine was very hard,—too hard, almost, for endurance. But there came among them at the diggings, where they were still dwelling, a young man whose name was John Carmichael, whose presence there gave something of grace to her days. He, too, had come for gold and had joined himself to the Bairds in consequence of some distant family friendship.

Within twelve months the father of the family had followed the mother, and the eight children were left without protection and without anything in the world worthy of the name of property. The sons could fight for themselves, and were left to do so. The three younger children were carried back to Scotland, a sister of their mother's having undertaken to maintain them; but Catherine was left. When the time came in which the three younger sisters were sent, it was found that a home presented itself for Catherine; and as the burden of providing for even the younger orphans was very great, it was thought proper that Catherine should avail herself of the home which was offered her.

John Carmichael, when he came among the diggers at Hokitika,—on the western coast of the southern of the two New Zealand islands,—-had done so chiefly because he had quarrelled with his cousin, Peter Carmichael, a squatter settled across the mountains in the Canterbury Province, with whom he had been living for the last three or four years. This Peter Carmichael, who was now nearly fifty, had for many years been closely connected with Baird, and at one period had been in partnership with him at the diggings. John had heard of Baird and Hokitika, and when the quarrel had become, as he thought, unbearable, he had left the Canterbury sheep-farm, and had tried his fortune in a gold-gully.

Then Baird died, and what friends there were laid their heads together to see how best the family should be maintained. The boys and John Carmichael with them, would stick to the gold. Word came out from the aunt in Scotland that she would do what was needed. Let the burden not be made too heavy for her. If it were found necessary to send children home, let them, if possible, be young. Peter Carmichael himself came across the mountains to Hokitika and arranged things for the journey;—and before he left, he had arranged things also for Catherine. Catherine should go with him across the mountains, and live with him at Mount Warriwa,—as his home was called,—and be his wife.

Catherine found everything to be settled for her almost before she was able to say a word as to her own desire in the matter. It was so evident that she could not be allowed to increase the weight of the burden which was to be imposed upon the aunt at home! It was so evident that her brothers were not able to find a home for her! It was so evident that she could not live alone in that wild country! And it seemed also to be quite evident that John Carmichael had no proposition of his own to make to her! Peter Carmichael was odious to her, but the time was such that she could not allow herself to think of her own dislikings.

There had never been a word of overt outspoken love between John Carmichael and Catherine Baird. The two were nearly of an age, and, as such, the girl had seemed to be the elder. They had come to be friends more loving than any other that either had. Catherine, in those gloomy days, in which she had seen her father perishing and her brothers too often straying in the wrong path, had had much need of a friend. And he had been good to her, keeping himself to sober, hard-working ways, because he might so best assist her in her difficulties. And she had trusted him, begging him to watch over the boys, and to help her with the girls. Her conduct had been beyond all praise; and he also,—for her sake following her example,—had been good. Of course she had loved him, but of course she had not said so, as he had not chosen to speak first.

Then had come the second death and the disruption. The elder Carmichael had come over, and had taken things into his own hands. He was known to be a very hard man, but nevertheless he spent some small sums of money for them, eking out what could be collected from the sale of their few goods. He settled this, and he settled that, as men do settle things when they have money to spend. By degrees,—not very slowly, but still gradually,—it was notified to Catherine that she might go across the mountains, and become mistress of Warriwa. It was very little that he said to her in the way of love-making.

"You might as well come home with me, Kate, and I'll send word on, and we'll get ourselves spliced as we go through Christchurch."

When he put it thus clearly to her, she certainly already knew what was intended. Her elder brother had spoken of it. It did not surprise her, nor did she start back and say at once that it should not be so.

From the moment in which Peter Carmichael had appeared upon the scene all Kate's intimacy with John seemed to come to an end. The two men, whose relationship was distant, did not renew their quarrel. The elder, indeed, was gracious, and said something to his younger kinsman as to the expediency of his returning to Warriwa. But John seemed to be oppressed by the other's presence, and certainly offered no advice as to Kate's future life. Nor did Kate say a word to him. When first an allusion to the suggested marriage was made in her presence she did not dare, indeed, to look at him, but she could perceive that neither did he look at her. She did not look, but yet she could see. There was not a start, not a change of colour, not a motion even of her foot. He expressed no consent, but she told herself that, by his silence, he gave it. There was no need for a question, even had it been possible that she could ask one.

And so it was settled. Peter Carmichael was a just man, in his way, but coarse, and altogether without sentiment. He spoke of the arrangement that had been made as he might have done of the purchase of a lot of sheep, not, however, omitting to point out that in this bargain he was giving everything and getting almost nothing. As a wife, Catherine might, perhaps, be of some service about the house; but he did not think that he should have cared to take a wife really for the sake of the wife. But it would do. They could get themselves married as they went through Christchurch, and then settle down comfortably. The brothers had nothing to say against it, and to John it seemed to be a matter of indifference. So it was settled. What did it signify to Catherine, as no one else cared for her?

Peter Carmichael was a hard-working man, who had the name of considerable wealth. But he was said to be hard of hand and hard of heart,—a stern, stubborn man, who was fond only of his money. There had been much said about him between John and Catherine before he had come to Hokitika,—when there had been no probability of his coming. "He is just," John had said, "but so ungenial that it seems to me impossible that a human being should stay with him." And yet this young man, of whose love she had dreamt, had not had a word to say when it was being arranged that she should be taken off to live all her future life with this companionship and no other! She would not condescend to ask even a question about her future home. What did it matter? She must be somewhere, because she could not be got rid of and buried at once beneath the sod. Nobody wanted her. She was only a burden. She might as well be taken to Warriwa and die there as elsewhere,—and so she went.

They travelled for two days and two nights across the mountains to Christchurch, and there they were married, as it happened, on Christmas Day,—on Christmas Day, because they passed that day and no other in the town as they went on. There was a further journey, two other days and two other nights, down nearly to the southern boundary of the Canterbury Province; and thither they went on with no great change between them, having become merely man and wife during that day they had remained at Christchurch. As they passed one great river after another on their passage down Kate felt how well it would be that the waters should pass over her head. But the waters refused to relieve her of the burden of her life. So she went on and reached her new home at Warriwa.

Catherine Carmichael, as she must now be called, was a well-grown, handsome young woman, who, through all the hardships of her young life, still showed traces of the gentle blood from which she had sprung. And ideas had come to her from her mother of things better than those around her. To do something for others, and then something, if possible, for herself,—these had been the objects nearest to her. Of the amusements, of the lightness and pleasures of life, she had never known anything. To sit vacant for an hour dreaming over a book had never come to her; nor had it been for her to make the time run softly with some apology for women's work in her hands. The hard garments, fit for a miner's work, passed through her hands. The care of the children, the preparation of their food, the doing the best she could for the rough household,—these things had kept her busy from her early rising till she would go late to her bed. But she had loved her work because it had been done for her father and her mother, for her brothers and her sisters. And she had respected herself, never despising the work she did; no man had ever dared to say an uncivil word to Kate Baird among all those rough miners with whom her father associated. Something had come to her from her mother which, while her mother lived,—even while her father lived,—had made her feel herself to be mistress of herself. But all that independence had passed away from her,—all that consciousness of doing the best she could,—as soon as Peter Carmichael had crossed her path.

It was not till the hard, dry, middle-aged man had taken possession of her that she acknowledged to herself that she had really loved John Carmichael. When Peter had come among them, he had seemed to dominate her as well as the others. He and he only had money. He and he only could cause aught to be done. And then it had seemed that for all the others there was a way of escape open, but none for her. No one wanted her, unless it was this dry old man. The young man certainly did not want her. Then in her sorrow she allowed herself to be crushed, in spite of the strength for which she had given herself credit. She was astounded, almost stupefied, so that she had no words with which to assert herself. When she was told that the hard, dry man would find a home for her, she had no reason to give why it should not be so. When she did not at first refuse to be taken away across the mountains, she had failed to realize what it all meant. When she reached Warriwa, and the waters in the pathless, unbridged rivers had not closed over her head,—then she realized it.

She was the man's wife, and she hated him. She had never known before what it was to hate a human being. She had always been helpful, and it is our nature to love those we help. Even the rough men who would lure her father away to drink had been her friends. "Oh, Dick," she would say, to the roughest of the rough, putting her hand prayerfully on the man's sleeve, "do not ask him to-night;" and the rough man would go from the shanty for the time. She would have mended his jacket for him willingly, or washed his shirt. Though the world had been very hard to her, she had hated no one. Now, she hated a man with all the strength of her heart, and he was her husband.

It was good for the man, though whether good for herself or not she could never tell, that he did not know that he was hated. "Now, old woman; here you'll have a real home," he said, as he allowed her to jump out of the buggy in which he had driven her all the way from Christchurch; "you'll find things tidier than you ever had 'em away at Hokitika." She jumped down on the yard into which he had driven, with a bandbox in her hand, and passed into the house by a back door. As she did so a very dirty old woman,—fouler looking, certainly, than any she had ever seen away among the gold-diggings,—followed her from the kitchen, which was built apart, a little to the rear of the house. "So you be the new wife, be ye?" said the old woman.

"Yes; I am Mr. Carmichael's wife. Are you the servant?"

"I don't know nothing about servants. I does for 'un,—what he can't do for 'unself. You'll be doing for 'un all now, I guess." Then her husband followed her in and desired her to come and help to unload the buggy. Anything to be done was a relief to her. If she could load and unload the buggy night and day it would be better than anything else she could see in prospect before her. Then there came a Maori in a blanket, to assist in carrying the things. The man was soft and very silent,—softly and silently civil, so that he seemed to be a protection to her against the foul old woman, and that lord of hers, who was so much fouler to her imagination.

Then her home life began. A woman can generally take an interest in the little surroundings of her being, feeling that the tables and the chairs, the beds and the linen are her own. Being her own, they are dear to her and will give a constancy of employment which a man cannot understand. She tried her hand at this, though the things were not her own,—were only his. But he told her so often that they were his that she could not take them to her heart. There was not much there for a woman to love; but little as there was, she could have loved it for the man's sake, had the man been lovable. The house consisted of three rooms, in the centre of which they lived, sleeping in one of the others. The third was unfurnished and unoccupied, except by sheepskins, which, as they were taken by the shepherds from the carcases of sheep that had died about the run, were kept there till they could be sent to the market. A table or two, with a few chairs; a bedstead with an old feather bed upon it; a washing-basin with a broken jug, with four or five large boxes in lieu of presses, made up nearly all the furniture. An iron pot or two and a frying-pan, with some ill-matched broken crockery, completed the list of domestic goods. How was she to love such as these with such an owner for them?

He had boasted that things were tidier there than she had known them at the diggings. The outside of the house was so, for the three rooms fronting on to the wide prairie-land of the sheep-run had a verandah before them, and the place was not ruinous. But there had been more of comfort in the shanty which her father and brothers had built for their home down in the gold-gully. As to food, to which she was indifferent, there was no question but that it had been better and more plentiful at the diggings. For the food she would not have cared at all,—but she did care for the way in which it was doled out to her hands, so that at every dole she came to hate him more. The meat was plentiful enough. The men who took their rations from the station came there and cut it from the sheep as they were slaughtered, almost as they would. Peter would count the sheep's heads every week, and would then know that, within a certain wide margin, he had not been robbed. Could she have made herself happy with mutton she might have lived a blessed life. But of other provisions every ounce was weighed to her, as it was to the station hands. So much tea for the week, so much sugar, so much flour, and so much salt. That was all,—unless when he was tempted to buy a sack of potatoes by some itinerant vendor, when he would count them out almost one by one. There was a storeroom attached to the kitchen, double-locked, the strongest of all the buildings about the place. Of this, for some month or two, he never allowed her to see the inside. She became aware that there were other delicacies there besides the tea and sugar,—jam and pickles, and boxes of sardines. The station-hands about the place, as the shepherds were called, would come and take the pots and bottles away with them, and Peter would score them down in his book and charge them in his account of wages against the men, with a broad profit to himself. But there could be no profit in sending such luxuries into the house. And then, as the ways of these people became gradually known to her, she learned that the rations which had been originally allowed for Peter himself and the old woman and the Maori had never been increased at her coming. Rations for three were made to do as rations for four. "It's along of you that he's a-starving of us," said the old woman. Why on earth should he have married her and brought her there, seeing that there was so little need for her!

But he had known what he was about. Little though she found for her to do, there was something which added to his comfort. She could cook,—an art which the old woman did not possess. She could mend his clothes, and it was something for him to have some one to speak to him. Perhaps in this way he liked her, though it was as a man may like a dog whom he licks into obedience. Though he would tell her that she was sulky, and treat her with rough violence if she answered him, yet he never repented him of his bargain. If there was work which she could do, he took care not to spare her,—as when the man came for the sheepskins, and she had to hand them out across the verandah, counting them as she did so. But there was, in truth, little for her to do.

There was so little to do that the hours and days crept by with feet so slow that they never seemed to pass away. And was it to be thus with her for always,—for her, with her young life, and her strong hands, and her thoughts always full? Could there be no other life than this? And if not, could there be no death? And then she came to hate him worse and worse,—to hate him and despise him, telling herself that of all human beings he was the meanest. Those miners who would work for weeks among the clay,—working almost day and night,—with no thought but of gold, and who then, when gold had been found, would make beasts of themselves till the gold was gone, were so much better than him! Better! why, they were human; while this wretch, this husband of hers, was meaner than a crawling worm! When she had been married to him about eight months, it was with difficulty that she could prevail upon herself not to tell him that she hated him.

The only creature about the place that she could like was the Maori. He was silent, docile, and uncomplaining. His chief occupation was that of drawing water and hewing wood. If there was aught else to do, he would be called upon to do it, and in his slow manner he would set about the task. About twice a month he would go to the nearest post-office, which was twenty miles off, and take a letter, or, perhaps, fetch one. The old woman and the squatter would abuse him for everything or nothing; and the Maori, to speak the truth, seemed to care little for what they said. But Catherine was kind to him, and he liked her kindness. Then there fell upon the squatter a sense of jealousy,—or feeling, probably, that his wife's words were softer to the Maori than to himself,—and the Maori was dismissed. "What's that for?" asked Catherine sulkily.

"He is a lazy skunk."

"Who is to get the wood?"

"What's that to you? When you were down at Hokitika you could get wood for yourself." Not another word was said, and for a week she did cut the wood. After that, there came a lad who had been shepherding, and was now well-nigh idiotic; but with such assistance as Catherine could give him, he did manage to hew the wood and draw the water.

Then one day a great announcement was made to her. "Next week John Carmichael will be here."

"John!"

"Yes; why not John? He will have that room. If he wants a bed, he must bring it with him." When this was said November had come round again, and it wanted about six weeks to Christmas.

Christmas Day. No. 2

John Carmichael was to come! And she understood that he was to come there as a resident;—for Peter had spoken of the use of that bedroom as though it were to be permanent. With no direct telling, but by degrees, something of the circumstances of the run at Warriwa had become known to her. There were on it 15,000 sheep, and these, with the lease of the run, were supposed to be worth £15,000. The sheep and all were the property of her husband. Some years ago he had taken John, when he was a boy, to act with him as his foreman or assistant, and the arrangement had been continued till the quarrel had sprung up. Peter had more than once declared his purpose of leaving all that he possessed to the young man, and John had never doubted his word. But, in return for all this future wealth, it was expected, not only that the lad should be his slave, but that the lad, grown into a man should remain so as long as Peter might live. As Peter was likely to live for the next twenty years, and as the slavery was hard to bear, John had quarrelled with his kinsman, and had gone away to the diggings. Now, it seemed, the quarrel had been arranged, and John was to come back to Warriwa. That someone was needed to ride round among the four or five shepherds,—someone beyond Peter himself,—someone to overlook the shearing, someone to attend to the young lambs, someone to see that the water-holes did not run dry, had become manifest even to Kate herself. It had leaked out from Peter's dry mouth that someone must come, and now she was told that John Carmichael would return to his old home.

Though she hated her husband, Kate knew what was due to him. Hating him as she had learned to do, hating him as she acknowledged to herself that she did, still she had endeavoured to do her duty by him. She could not smile upon him, she could not even speak to him with a kind voice; but she could make his bed, and iron his shirts, and cook his dinner, and see that the things confided to her charge were not destroyed by the old woman or the idiot boy. Perhaps he got from her all that he wanted to get. He did not complain that her voice was not loving. He was harsh, odious in his ways with her, sometimes almost violent; but it may be doubted whether he would have been less so had she attempted to turn him by any show of false affection. She had learned to feel that if she served him she did for him all that he required, and that duty demanded no more. But now! would not duty demand more from her now?

Since she had been brought home to Warriwa, she had given herself up freely to her thoughts, telling herself boldly that she hated her husband, and that she loved that other man. She told herself, also, that there was no breach of duty in this. She would never again see that other man. He had crossed her path and had gone. There was nothing for her left in the world, except her husband Peter and Warriwa. As for her hating the one man, not to do that would be impossible. As for loving the other man, there was nothing in it but a dream. Her thoughts were her own, and therefore she went on loving him. She had no other food for her thoughts, except the hope that death might come to her, and some vague idea that that last black fast-running river, over which she had been ferried in the dark, might perhaps be within her reach, should death be too long in coming of its own accord. With such thoughts running across her brain, there was, she thought, no harm in loving John Carmichael,—till now, when she was told that John was to be brought here to live under the same roof with her.

Now there must be harm in it! Now there would be crime in loving him! And yet she knew that she could not cease to love him because he should be there, meeting her eye every day. How comely he was, with that soft brown hair of his, and the broad, open brow, and the smile that would curl round his lips! How near they had once been to swearing that they would be each, all things to the other! "Kate!" he had said, "Kate!" as she had stood close to him, fastening a button to his shirt. Her finger had trembled against his neck, and she knew that he had felt the quiver. The children had come upon them at the moment, and no other word had been said. Then Peter had come there,—Peter who was to be her husband,—and after that John Carmichael had spoken no word at all to her. Though he had been so near to loving her while her finger had touched him in its trembling, all that had passed away when Peter came. But it had not passed away from her heart, nor would she be able to stifle it when he should be there, sitting daily at the same board with her. Though the man himself was so odious, there was something sacred to her in the name of husband,—something very sacred to her in the name of wife. "Why should he be coming?" she said to her husband the day after the announcement had been made to her, when twenty-four hours for thinking had been allowed to her.

"Because it suits," he said, looking up at her from the columns of a dirty account-book, in which he was slowly entering figures.

What could she say to him that might be of avail? How much could she say to him? Should she tell him everything, and then let him do as he pleased? It was in her mind to do so, but she could not bring herself to speak the words. He would have thought—! Oh! what might he not have thought! There was no dealing in fair words with one so suspicious, so unmanly, so inhuman.

"It won't suit," she said, sullenly.

"Why not? what have you got to do with it?"

"It won't suit; he and I will be sure to,—sure to,—sure to have words."

"Then you must have 'em. Ain't he my cousin? Do you expect me to be riding round among them lying, lazy varmint every day of my life, while you sit at home twiddling your thumbs?" Here she knew that allusion was made both to the sheep and to the shepherds. "If anything happens to me, who do you think is to have it all after me?" One day at Hokitika he had told her coarsely that it was a good thing for a young woman to marry an old man, because she would be sure to get everything when he was dead. "I suppose that's why you don't like John," he added, with a sneer.

"I do like him," she said, with a clear, loud voice; "I do like him." Then he leered round at her, shaking his head at her, as though declaring that he was not to be taken in by her devices, and after that he went on with his figures.

Before the end of November John arrived. Something, at any rate, she could do for his comfort. Wherever she got them, there, when he came, were the bed and bedstead for his use. At first she asked simply after her brothers. They had been tempted to go off to other diggings in New South Wales, and he had not thought well to follow them. "Sheep is better nor gold, Jack," said Peter, shaking his head and leering.

She tried to be very silent with him;—but she succeeded so far that her very silence made him communicative. In her former intercourse she had always talked the most,—a lass of that age having always more to say for herself than a lad. But now he seemed to struggle to find chance opportunities. As a rule he was always out early in the morning on horseback, and never home till Peter was there also. But opportunities would, of course, be forthcoming. Nor would it be wise that she should let him feel that she avoided them. It was not only necessary that Peter should not suspect, but that John, too, should be kept in the dark. Indeed, it might be well that Peter should suspect a little. But if he were to suspect,—that other he,—and then he were to speak out, how should she answer him?

"Kate," he said to her one day, "do you ever think of Hokitika?"

"Think, indeed!—of the place where father and mother lie."

"But of the time when you and I used to fight it out for them? I used not to think in those days, Kate, that you would ever be over here,—mistress of Warriwa."

"No, indeed, nobody would have thought it."

"But Kate— "

It was clearly necessary that she should put an end to these reminiscences, difficult as it might be to do so. "John," she said, "I think you'd better make a change."

"What change?"

She struggled not to blush as she answered him, and she succeeded. "I was a girl in those days, but now I'm a married woman. You had better not call me Kate any more."

"Why? what's the harm?"

"Harm! no, there's no harm; but it isn't the proper thing when a young woman's married, unless he be her brother, or her cousin at furthest; you don't call me by my name before him."

"Didn't I?"

"No, you call me nothing at all. What you do before him, you must do behind his back."

"And we were such friends!" But as she could not stand this, she left the room, and did not come back from the kitchen till Peter had returned.

So a month went on, and still there was the word Kate sounding in her ears whenever the old man's back was turned. And it sounded now as it sounded on that one day when her finger was trembling at his throat. Why not give way to the sound! Why not ill-treat the man who had so foully ill-treated her? What did she owe to him but her misery? What had he done for her but make a slave of her? And why should she, living there in the wild prairie, beyond the ken of other women, allow herself to be trammelled by the laws which the world had laid down for her sex? To other women the world made some return for true obedience. The love of one man, the strong protecting arm of one true friend, the consciousness of having one to buckler her against the world, one on whom she might hang with trust! This was what other women have in return for truth;—but was any of this given to her when he would turn round and leer at her, reminding her by his leer that he had caught her and made a slave of her? And then there was this young man, sweeter to her now than ever, and dearer!

As she thought of all this she came suddenly,—in a moment,—to a resolution, striking her hand violently on the table as she did so. She must tell her husband everything. She must do that, or else she must become a false wife. As she thought of that possibility of being false, an ecstasy of sweetness for a moment pervaded her senses. To throw herself on his bosom and tell him that she loved him would be compensation almost sufficient to the misery of the last twelve months. Then the word wife crept into her ears, and she remembered words that she had read as to woman's virtue. She thought of her father and her mother! And how would it be with her when, after a while, she would awake from her dream? She had sat silent for an hour alone, now melting into softness, and then rousing herself to all the strength of womanhood. At last a frown came across her brow, very dark; and then, dashing her clenched hand down upon the table, she expressed her purpose in spoken words: "I will tell it him all!"

Then she told him all, after her fashion. It was the custom of the two men to go forth together almost at dawn, and it was her business to prepare their meal for them before they went. On the first morning after her resolution had been formed, she bade her husband to stay awhile. She had thought to say it in the seclusion of their own room; but she had felt that it would be better that John should not be in the house when it was spoken. Peter stayed at her bidding, looking eagerly into her face, as she stood at the back door watching till the young man had started on his horse. Then she turned round to her husband. "He must go away from this," she said, pointing over her shoulder to the retreating figure of the horseman.

"Why is he to go? What has he been and done?" This last question he asked, lowering his voice to a whisper, as though thinking that she had detected his cousin in some delinquency.

There was a savage purpose in her heart to make the revelation as bitter to him as it might be. He must know her own purity, but he must know also her thorough contempt for himself. There was no further punishment that he could inflict upon her, save that of thinking her to be false. Though he were to starve her, beat her, murder her, she would care for that not at all. He had carried her away helpless to his foul home, and all that was left her was to preserve herself strong against disgrace.

"He is a man, a young man, and I am a woman. You had better let him go." Then he stood for a while with his mouth open, holding her by the arm, not looking at her, but with his eyes fixed on the spot whence his cousin was disappearing. After a moment or two, his lips came together and produced a long low whistle. He still clutched her, and still looked out upon the far-retreating figure; but he was for a while as though he had been stricken dumb. "You had better let him go," she repeated. Then he whispered some word into her ear. She threw up the arm that he was holding so violently that he was forced to start back from her, and to feel how much stronger she was than he, should she choose to put out her strength. "I tell you all," she said, "that you have to know. Little as you deserve, you have fallen into honest hands. Let him go."

"And he hasn't said a word?"

"I have told you all that you are to hear."

"I would kill him."

"If you are beast enough to accuse him, he will kill you;—or I will do it, if you ever tell him what I have said to you. Bid him go; and let that be all." Then she turned away from him, and passing through the house, crossed the verandah, and went out upon the open space on the other side. He lingered about the place for half an hour, but did not follow her. Then he mounted his old horse, and rode away across the prairie after his sheep.

"Have you told him?" she said, that night when they were alone.

"Told him what?"

"That he must go." He shook his head, not angrily, but in despair. Since that morning he had learned to be afraid of her. "If you do not," she said very slowly, looking him full in the face—"if you do not—I will. He shall be told to-night, before he goes to his bed."

"Am I to say that he—that he—?" As he endeavoured to ask the question, he was white with despair.

"You are to say nothing to him but that he must quit Warriwa at once. If you will say that, he will understand you."

What took place between the two men on the next day she did not know. It may be doubted whether she would ever know it. Peter said not a word further to her on the matter. But on the morning of the second day there was the buggy ready, and Peter with it, prepared to drive his cousin away. It was apparent to her that her husband had not dared to say an evil word of her, nor did she believe that he suspected her. She felt that, poor a creature as he was, she had driven him to respect her. But the thing was settled as she would have it, and the young man was to go.

During those last two days there was not a word spoken between her and John unless when she handed him his food. When he was away across the land she took care that not a stitch should be wanting to his garments. She washed his things and laid them smooth for him in his box,—oh, with such loving hands! As she kneeled down to her work, she looked round to the door of the room to see that it was closed, and to the window, lest the eyes of that old woman should be prying in; and then she stooped low, and burying her face beneath the lid, kissed the linen which her hands had smoothed. This she could do, and not feel herself disgraced;—but when the morning came she could let him go and not speak a word. She came out before he was up and prepared the breakfast, and then went back to her own room, so that they two might eat it together and then start. But he could not bring himself to go without one word of farewell. "Say good-bye, at any rate," he sobbed, standing at her door, which opened out upon the verandah. Peter the while was looking on with a lighted pipe in his mouth.

"Good-bye, John." The words were heard, but the sobs were almost hidden.

"Give me your hand," said he. Then there came forth a hand,—nothing but a hand. He took it in his, and for a moment thought that he would touch it with his lips. But he felt,—feeling like a man,—that it behoved him to spare her all he could. He pressed it in his grasp for a moment, and then the hand disappeared.

"If we are to go, we might as well be off," said Peter. So they mounted the buggy and went away.

The nearest town to Warriwa was a place called Timaru, through which a coach, running from Dunedin to Christchurch, passed three times a week. This was forty miles off, and here was transacted what business was necessary for the carrying on of the sheep-station. Stores were bought at Timaru, such as sugar, tea, and flour, and here Peter Carmichael generally sold his wool. Here was the bank at which he kept his money, and in which his credit always stood high. There were not many journeys made from Warriwa to Timaru; but when one became necessary it was always a service of pleasure to Peter. He could, as it were, finger his money by looking at the bank which contained it, and he could learn what might probably be the price which the merchants would give him for his next clip. On this occasion he seemed to be quite glad of an excuse for driving into Timaru, though it can hardly be imagined that he and his companion were pleasant to each other in the buggy. From Warriwa the road, or track rather, was flat the whole way to Timaru. There was nothing to be seen on either way but a long everlasting plain of grey, stunted, stony grass. At Warriwa the outlines of the distant mountains were just visible in the west, but the traveller, as he went eastward towards the town and the road, soon lost sight of the hills, and could see nothing but the grey plain. There were, however, three rivers to be passed, the Warriwa, and two others, which, coming down from the northwest, ran into the Warriwa. Of these the Warriwa itself was the widest, and the deepest, and the fastest. It was in crossing this, within ten miles of her home,—crossing it after dark,—that Catherine had thought how well it would be that the waters should pass over her head, so that she might never see that home. Often, since that, she had thought how well it would have been for her had she been saved from the horrors of her home by the waters of the river.

We may suppose that very little was said by the two men as they made their way into Timaru. Peter was one who cared little for conversation, and could be quite content to sit for hours together in his buggy, calculating the weight of his wool, and the money which would come from it. At Timaru they dined together, still, we may say, without many words. Then the coach came, and John Carmichael was carried away,—whither his cousin did not even inquire. There was some small money transaction between them, and John was carried away to follow out his own fortune.

Had it been possible Peter would have returned at once, so as to save expense, but the horses made it necessary that he should remain that night in town. And, having done so, he stayed the greater part of the following day, looking after his money and his wool, and gathering his news. At about two he started, and made his way back over the two smaller rivers in safety. At the Warriwa there was but one ferryman, and in carrying a vehicle with horses over it was necessary that the man in charge of them should work also. On the former day, though the rivers had been very high, there had been daylight, and John Carmichael had been there. Now it was pitch dark, though it was in the middle of summer, and the waters were running very strong. The ferryman refused at first to put the buggy on the raft, bidding old Carmichael wait till the next morning. It was Christmas Eve, he said, and he did not care to be drowned on Christmas Eve.

Nor was such to be his destiny. But it was the destiny of Peter Carmichael. The waters went over him and one of his horses. At three o'clock in the morning his body was brought home to Warriwa, lying across the back of the other. The ferryman had been unable to save the man's life, but had got the body, and had brought it home to the young widow just twelve months after the day on which she had become a wife.

Christmas Day. No. 3

There she was, on the morning of that Christmas Day, with the ferryman and that old woman, with the half-idiot boy, and the body of her dead husband! She was so stunned that she sat motionless for hours, with the corpse close to her, lying stretched out on the verandah, with a sheet over it. It is a part of the cruelty of the life which is lived in desolate places, far away, that when death comes, the small incidents of death are not mitigated to the sufferer by the hands of strangers.

If the poorest wife here at home becomes a widow, some attendant hands will close the glazed eye and cover up the limbs, and close the coffin which is there at hand; and then it will be taken away and hidden forever. There is an appropriate spot, though it be but under the poorhouse wall. Here there was no appropriate spot, no ready hand, no coffin, no coroner with his authority, no parish officer ready with his directions. She sat there numb, motionless, voiceless, thinking where John Carmichael might be. Could it be that he would come back to her, and take from her that ghastly duty of getting rid of the object that was lying within a yard or two of her arm?

She tried to weep, telling herself that, as a wife now widowed, she was bound to weep for her husband. But there was not a tear, nor a sob, nor a moan. She argued it with herself, saying that she would grieve for him now that he was dead. But she could not grieve,—not for that; only for her own wretchedness and desolation. If the waters had gone over her instead of him, then how merciful would heaven have been to her! The misery of her condition came home to her with its full weight,—her desolation, her powerlessness, her friendlessness, the absence of all interest in life, of all reason for living; but she could not induce herself to say, even to herself, that she was struck with anguish on account of him. That voice, that touch, the cunning leer of that eye, would never trouble her again. She had been freed from something. She became angry with herself because it was in this way that she regarded it; but it was thus that she continued to regard it. She had threatened once to kill him,—to kill him should he speak a word as to which she bade him to be silent. Now he was dead,—whether he had spoken that word or not. Then she wondered whether he had spoken it, and she wondered, also, what John Carmichael would say or do when he should hear that his kinsman was no more. So she sat motionless for hours within her room, but with the door open on to the verandah, and the feet of the corpse within a few yards of her chair.

The old ferryman took the horse, and went out under the boy's guidance in quest of the shepherds. Distances are large on these sheepruns, and a shepherd with his flock is not always easily found. It was nearly evening before he returned with two of these men, and then they dug the grave,—not very far away, as the body must be carried in their arms; and then they buried him, putting up a rough palisade around the spot to guard it, if it might be so guarded for a while, from the rats. She walked with them as they carried it, and stood there as they did their work; and the old woman went with them, helping a little. But the widow spoke not a word, and when returning, seated herself again in the same chair. Not once did there come to her the relief of a tear, or even a sob.

The ferryman went back to his river, and the shepherds to their sheep, and the old woman and the boy remained with her, preparing what food was eaten. The key of the store-room was now in her possession, having been taken out of his pocket before they laid him in his grave, and they could do what they pleased with what it contained. So she remained for a fortnight, altogether inactive, having as yet resolved upon nothing. Thoughts no doubt there were running through her mind. What was now to become of her? To whom did the place belong, and the sheep, and the money, which, as she knew, was lying in the bank? It had all been promised to John, before her marriage. Then the old man had hinted to her, in his coarse way, that it would be hers. Then he had hinted again that John was to be brought back, and to live here. How would it be? Without the speaking of words, even to herself, it was settled in her heart that John

Carmichael should be, ought to be, must be, the owner of Warriwa. Then how different would Warriwa become? But she strove gallantly against feeling that, for herself, there would be any personal interest in such a settlement. She would have kept her thoughts away from that if it had been possible;—if it had been possible.

At the end of a fortnight there came out to her from Timaru a young man, who declared himself to be the clerk of a solicitor established there, and this young man brought with him a letter from the manager of the bank. The purport of the letter was this: Mr. Carmichael, as he had passed through Timaru on his way home from Christchurch after his marriage, had then executed a will, which he had deposited at the bank. In this he had named the manager as his sole executor, and had left everything of which he was possessed to his wife. The writer of the letter then went on to explain that there might have been a subsequent will made. He was aware that John Carmichael had been again at Warriwa, and it was possible that Peter Carmichael might have reverted to his old intention of making his kinsman his heir. There had been a former will to that effect, which had been destroyed in the presence of the banker. There was no such document at Timaru. If anywhere, it must be at Warriwa. Would Mrs. Carmichael allow the young man to search? If no such document could be found, the money and the property would be hers. It would be well that she should return with the young man to the town, and take up her abode there in lodgings for a few weeks till things should have settled themselves.

And thus she found herself mistress of Warriwa, owner of the sheep, and possessor of all the money. Of course, she obeyed the counsel given her, and went into the town. No other will was found; no other claimant came forward. Week after week went by, and month after month, very slowly, and at the end of six months she found that everything was undoubtedly hers. An agent had been hired to live at Warriwa, and her signature was recognized at the bank as commanding all that money. The sum seemed so large that it was a wonder to her that the old man should have lived in such misery at home. Then two of her brothers came to her, across from New South Wales. They had come to her because she was alone. No, they said; they did not want her help, though a little money would go a long way with them. They had come because she was alone.

Then she laid a task upon them, and told them her plans. Yes; she had been very much alone;—altogether without counsel in this particular matter; but she had formed her plans. If they would assist her, no doubt they would be compensated for their time. Where was John Carmichael? They had not heard of John Carmichael since they had left him when they went away from Hokitika.

Thereupon she explained to them that none of all that property was hers;—that none of it all should ever be hers; that, to her view of the matter, the station, with the run, and the sheep, and the money, all belonged to John Carmichael. When they told her that she had been the man's wife, and, therefore, much nearer than John Carmichael, she only shook her head. She could not explain to them her thoughts and feelings. She could not say to them that she would not admit herself to have been the wife of a man whom she had ever hated,—for whom, not for a single moment, had she ever entertained anything of wifely feeling. "I am here," she said, "only as his care-taker;—only as such will I ever spend a farthing of the money." Then she showed them a letter, of which she had sent copies addressed to him at the post-offices of various towns in New Zealand, having spent many of her hours in making the copies, and the letter was as follows;—

> "If you will return to Warriwa, you will find that everything has been kept for you as well as I have known how to keep it. The sheep are nearly up to the number. The money is at the bank at Timaru, except a very little which I have taken to pay the wages and just to support myself,—till I can go away and leave it all. You should hurry to Warriwa, because I cannot go away till you come.
>
> CATHERINE."

It was not, perhaps, a very wise letter. An advertisement in the New Zealand papers would have done better, and have cost less trouble. But that was her way of setting about her work,—till her brothers had come to her, and then she sent them forth upon her errand. It was in vain that they argued with her. They were to go and find him, and send him,—not to her,—but to Warriwa. On his arrival he should find that everything was ready for him. There would be some small thing for the lawyer to arrange, but that could be arranged at once. When the elder brother asked at the bank about his sister, the manager told him that all Timaru had failed to understand the purposes of the heiress. That old Peter Carmichael had been a miser, everybody had known, and that a large sum was lying in the bank, and that the sheep were out on the run at Warriwa. They knew, too, that the widow had inherited it all. But they could not understand why she should be careful with the money as old Peter had been; why she should live there in lodgings, seeing no one; why she should be taken out to Warriwa once a month; and why on these occasions she should remain there a day or two, going through every figure, as it was said that she did do. If she liked the life of a squatter, why did she not live there and make the place comfortable? If, as was more probable, the place could hardly be delightful to her, why not sell it, and go away among her friends? There would be friends enough now to make her welcome. For, though she had written the letters, and sent them out, one or two at a time, she had told no one of her purpose till her brothers came to her. Then the banker understood it all, and the brothers probably understood something also.

They got upon his traces at last, and found him in Queensland, up to his throat in mud, looking for gold in a gully. "Luck? Yes; he had got a little, and spent the most of it. There was gold, no doubt, but he was not much in love with the spot." 'Tis always thus the wandering gold-digger speaks of his last adventure. When they told him that Peter Carmichael was dead, he jumped out of the gully, leaving the cradle behind him in which he had been washing the dirt, searching for specks of gold. "And Warriwa?" he said. Then they explained the nature of the will. "And the money, too?" Yes; the money also had been left to the widow. "It would have been hers any way," he said, "whether he left a will or not. Well, well! So Kate is a rich woman." Then he jumped into the gully again, and went to work at his cradle. By degrees they explained it all to him,—as much, at least, as they could explain. He must go to Warriwa. She would do nothing till he had been there.

"She says it is to be all yours," said the younger brother.

"Don't you say no more than you know," said the elder. "Let him go and find it out for himself."

"But Kate said so."

"Kate is a woman, and may change her mind as well as another. Let him go and find it out for himself." So he sold his claim at the gully for what little it would fetch, and started off once again for New Zealand and Warriwa.

He had himself landed at Dunedin in order that he might not be seen and questioned in passing through Timaru, and from Dunedin he made his way across the country direct to Warriwa. I need not trouble my readers with New Zealand geography, but at a little place called Oamaru he hired a buggy and a pair of horses, and had himself driven across the country to the place. He knew that Catherine was living in the town, and not at the station; but even though the distance were forty miles, he thought that it would be better to send for her than to discuss such things as would have to be discussed before the bankers and the attorney, and all the eager eyes and ears of Timaru. What it was that he would have to discuss he hardly yet knew; but he did know, or thought that he knew, that he had been banished from Warriwa because old Peter Carmichael had not chosen to have "a young fellow like that hopping about round his wife." It was thus that Peter had explained his desire in that matter of John's departure. Now he had been sent for, because of the property. The property was the property of the widow. He did not in the least doubt that. Christmas had again come around, and it was just a year,—a year and a day,—since she had put her hand out to him through the closed door and had bade him good-bye.

There she was, when he entered the house, sitting at that little side-table, with the very books before her at which Peter had spent so many of his hours. "Kate," he said, as he entered, "I have come, you see,—because you sent for me."

She jumped up, rushing at him, as though to throw her arms round him, forgetting,—forgetting that there had been no love spoken between them. Then she stopped herself, and stood a moment looking at him. "John," she said, "John Carmichael, I am so glad you have come at last. I am tired minding it,—very tired, and I know that I do not do it as it should be."

"Do what, Kate?"

"Mind it all,—for you. No one else could do it, because I had to sign the papers. Now you have come, and may do as you please with it. Now you have come,—and I may go."

"He left it to you; all of it,—the money, and the sheep, and the station."

Then there came a frown across her brow,—not of anger, but of perplexity. How should she explain it? How should she let him know that it must be as she would have it,—that he must have it all; and have it not from her, but as heir to his kinsman? How could she do all this and teach him at the same time that there need be nothing of gratitude in it all,—nothing certainly of love?

"John," she said, "I will not take it from him as his widow. I never loved him. I never had a kindly feeling towards him. It would kill me to take it. I will not have it. It must be yours."

"And you?"

"I will go away."

"Whither will you go? Where will you live?" Then she stood there dumb before him, frowning at him. What was it to him where she might go? She thought of the day when she had sewn the button on his shirt, when he might have spoken to her. And she remembered, too, how she had prepared his things for him, when he had been sent away, at her bidding, from Warriwa. What was it to him what might become of her?

"I am tired of this," she said. "You must come to Timaru, so that the lawyer may do what is necessary. There must be papers prepared. Then I will go away."

"Kate!" She only stamped her foot. "Kate,—why was it that he made me go?"

"He could not bear to have people about the place, eating and drinking."

"Was it that?"

"Or perhaps he hated you. It is easy, I think, to hate in a place so foul as this."

"And not easy to love?"

"I have had no chance of loving. But what is the use of all that? Will you do as I bid you?"

"What!—take it all from your hands?"

"No; not from mine,—from his. I will not take it, coming to me from him. It is not mine, and I cannot give it; but it is yours. You need not argue, for it must be so." Then she turned away, as though going;—but she knew not whither to go, and stopped at the end of the verandah, looking towards the spot at which the grave was marked by the low railings.

There she stood for some minutes before she stirred. Then he followed her, and, laying his hand upon her shoulder, spoke the one word which was necessary. "Kate, will you take it, if not from him, then from me?" She did not answer him at once, and then his arm was passed round her waist. "If not from him, then from me?"

"Yes; from you," she said. "Anything from you." And so it was.

The Two Heroines of Plumplington

Originally appeared in *Good Cheer*, the Christmas number of *Good Words*, December 1882. Written by 28 June 1882. Although Trollope told the American politician Henry Howard in 1881 there could be no more Chronicles of Barset, he unbent sufficiently to make Plumplington a small Barsetshire town. The story has a few cross-references with the major Barset novels, including a memory of Mr Harding's crisis of conscience over the Wardenship of Hiram's Hospital. The full story will be found in *The Warden* (1855).

Chapter I

The Two Girls.

IN THE little town of Plumplington last year, just about this time of the year,—it was in November,—the ladies and gentlemen forming the Plumplington Society were much exercised as to the affairs of two young ladies. They were both the only daughters of two elderly gentlemen, well known and greatly respected in Plumplington. All the world may not know that Plumplington is the second town in Barsetshire, and though it sends no member to Parliament, as does Silverbridge, it has a population of over 20,000 souls, and three separate banks. Of one of these Mr. Greenmantle is the manager, and is reputed to have shares in the bank. At any rate he is known to be a warm man. His daughter Emily is supposed to be the heiress of all he possesses, and has been regarded as a fitting match by many of the sons of the country gentlemen around. It was rumoured a short time since that young Harry Gresham was likely to ask her hand in marriage, and Mr. Greenmantle was supposed at the time to have been very willing to entertain the idea. Whether Mr. Gresham has ever asked or not, Emily Greenmantle did not incline her ear that way, and it came out while the affair was being discussed in Plumplington circles that the young lady much preferred one Mr. Philip Hughes. Now Philip Hughes was a very promising young man, but was at the time no more than a cashier in her father's bank. It became known at once that Mr. Greenmantle was very angry. Mr. Greenmantle was a man who carried himself with a dignified and handsome demeanour, but he was one of whom those who knew him used to declare that it would be found very difficult to turn him from his purpose. It might not be possible that he should succeed with Harry Gresham, but it was considered out of the question that he should give his girl and his money to such a man as Philip Hughes.

The other of these elderly gentlemen is Mr. Hickory Peppercorn. It cannot be said that Mr. Hickory Peppercorn had ever been put on a par with Mr. Greenmantle. No one could suppose that Mr. Peppercorn had ever sat down to dinner in company with Mr. and Miss Greenmantle. Neither did Mr. or Miss Peppercorn expect to be asked on the festive occasion of one of Mr. Greenmantle's dinners. But Miss Peppercorn was not unfrequently made welcome to Miss Greenmantle's five o'clock tea-table; and in many of the affairs of the town the two young ladies were seen associated together. They were both very active in the schools, and stood nearly equal in the good graces of old Dr. Freeborn. There was, perhaps, a little jealousy on this account in the bosom of Mr. Greenmantle, who was pervaded perhaps by an idea that Dr. Freeborn thought too much of himself. There never was a quarrel, as Mr. Greenmantle was a good churchman; but there was a jealousy. Mr. Greenmantle's family sank into insignificance if you looked beyond his grandfather; but Dr. Freeborn could talk glibly of his ancestors in the time of Charles I. And it certainly was the fact that Dr. Freeborn would speak of the two young ladies in one and the same breath.

Now Mr. Hickory Peppercorn was in truth nearly as warm a man as his neighbour, and he was one who was specially proud of being warm. He was a foreman,—or rather more than foreman,—a kind of top sawyer in the brewery establishment of Messrs. Du Boung and Co., a firm which has an establishment also in the town of Silverbridge. His position in the world may be described by declaring that he always wears a dark-coloured tweed coat and trousers, and a chimney-pot hat. It is almost impossible to say too much that is good of Mr. Peppercorn. His one great fault has been already designated. He was and still is very fond of his money. He does not talk much about it; but it is to be feared that it dwells too constantly on his mind. As a servant to the firm he is honesty and constancy itself. He is a man of such a nature that by means of his very presence all the partners can be allowed to go to bed if they wish it. And there is not a man in the establishment who does not know him to be good and true. He understands all the systems of brewing, and his very existence in the brewery is a proof that Messrs. Du Boung and Co. are prosperous.

He has one daughter, Polly, to whom he is so thoroughly devoted that all the other girls in Plumplington envy her. If anything is to be done Polly is asked to go to her father, and if Polly does go to her father the thing is done. As far as money is concerned it is not known that Mr. Peppercorn ever refused Polly anything. It is the pride of his heart that Polly shall be, at any rate, as well dressed as Emily Greenmantle. In truth nearly double as much is spent on her clothes, all of which Polly accepts without a word to show her pride. Her father does not say much, but now and again a sigh does escape him. Then it came out, as a blow to Plumplington, that Polly too had a lover. And the last person in Plumplington who heard the news was Mr. Peppercorn. It seemed from his demeanour, when he first heard the tidings, that he had not expected that any such accident would ever happen. And yet Polly Peppercorn was a very pretty, bright girl of one-and-twenty of whom the wonder was,—if it was true,—that she had never already had a lover. She looked to be the very girl for lovers, and she looked also to be one quite able to keep a lover in his place.

Emily Greenmantle's lover was a two-months'-old story when Polly's lover became known to the public. There was a young man in Barchester who came over on Thursdays dealing with Mr. Peppercorn for malt. He was a fine stalwart young fellow, six-feet-one, with bright eyes and very light hair and whiskers, with a pair of shoulders which would think nothing of a sack of wheat, a hot temper, and a thoroughly good heart. It was known to all Plumplington that he had not a shilling in the world, and that he earned forty shillings a week from Messrs. Mealing's establishment at Barchester. Men said of him that he was likely to do well in the world, but nobody thought that he would have the impudence to make up to Polly Peppercorn.

But all the girls saw it and many of the old women, and some even of the men. And at last Polly told him that if he had anything to say to her he must say it to her father. "And you mean to have him, then?" said Bessy Rolt in surprise. Her lover was by at the moment, though not exactly within hearing of Bessy's question. But Polly when she was alone with Bessy spoke up her mind freely. "Of course I mean to have him, if he pleases. What else? You don't suppose I would go on with a young man like that and mean nothing. I hate such ways."

"But what will your father say?"

"Why shouldn't he like it? I heard papa say that he had but 7s. 6d. a week when he first came to Du Boungs. He got poor mamma to marry him, and he never was a good-looking man."

"But he had made some money."

"Jack had made no money as yet, but he is a good-looking fellow. So they're quits. I believe that father would do anything for me, and when he knows that I mean it he won't let me break my heart."

But a week after that a change had come over the scene. Jack had gone to Mr. Hickory Peppercorn, and Mr. Peppercorn had given him a rough word or two. Jack had not borne the rough word well, and old Hickory, as he was called, had said in his wrath, "Impudent cub! you've got nothing. Do you know what my girl will have?"

"I've never asked."

"I know nothing about it. I'm ready to take the rough and the smooth together. I'll marry the young lady and wait till you give her something." Hickory couldn't turn him out on the spur of the moment because there was business to be done, but warned him not to go into his private house. "If you speak another word to Polly, old as I am, I'll measure you across the back with my stick." But Polly, who knew her father's temper, took care to keep out of her father's sight on that occasion.

Polly after that began the battle in a fashion that had been invented by herself. No one heard the words that were spoken between her and her father,—her father who had so idolized her; but it appeared to the people of Plumplington that Polly was holding her own. No disrespect was shown to her father, not a word was heard from her mouth that was not affectionate or at least decorous. But she took upon herself at once a certain lowering of her own social standing. She never drank tea with Emily Greenmantle, or accosted her in the street with her old friendly manner. She was terribly humble to Dr. Freeborn, who however would not acknowledge her humility on any account. "What's come over you?" said the Doctor. "Let me have none of your stage plays or I shall take you and shake you."

"You can shake me if you like it, Dr. Freeborn," said Polly, "but I know who I am and what my position is."

"You are a determined young puss," said the Doctor, "but I am not going to help you in opposing your own father." Polly said not a word further, but looked very demure as the Doctor took his departure.

But Polly performed her greatest stroke in reference to a change in her dress. All her new silks, that had been the pride of her father's heart, were made to give way to old stuff gowns. People wondered where the old gowns, which had not been seen for years, had been stowed away. It was the same on Sundays as on Mondays and Tuesdays. But the due gradation was kept between Sundays and week-days. She was quite well enough dressed for a brewer's foreman's daughter on one day as on the other, but neither on one day or on the other was she at all the Polly Peppercorn that Plumplington had known for the last couple of years. And there was not a word said about it. But all Plumplington knew that Polly was fitting herself, as regarded her outside garniture, to be the wife of Jack Hollycombe with 40s. a week. And all Plumplington said that she would carry her purpose, and that Hickory Peppercorn would break down under stress of the artillery brought to bear against him. He could not put out her clothes for her, or force her into wearing them as her mother might have done, had her mother been living. He could only tear his hair and greet, and swear to himself that under no such artillery as this would he give way. His girl should never marry Jack Hollycombe. He thought he knew his girl well enough to be sure that she would not marry without his consent. She might make him very unhappy by wearing dowdy clothes, but she would not quite break his heart. In the meantime Polly took care that her father should have no opportunity of measuring Jack's back.

With the affairs of Miss Greenmantle much more ceremony was observed, though I doubt whether there was more earnestness felt in the matter. Mr. Peppercorn was very much in earnest, as was Polly,—and Jack Hollycombe. But Peppercorn talked about it publicly, and Polly showed her purpose, and Jack exhibited the triumphant lover to all eyes. Mr. Greenmantle was silent as death in respect to the great trouble that had come upon him. He had spoken to no one on the subject except to the peccant lover, and just a word or two to old Dr. Freeborn. There was no trouble in the town that did not reach Dr. Freeborn's ears; and Mr. Greenmantle, in spite of his little jealousy, was no exception. To the Doctor he had said a word or two as to Emily's bad behaviour. But in the stiffness of his back, and the length of his face, and the continual frown which was gathered on his brows, he was eloquent to all the town. Peppercorn had no powers of looking as he looked. The gloom of the bank was awful. It was felt to be so by the two junior clerks, who hardly knew whether to hate or to pity most Mr. Philip Hughes. And if Mr. Greenmantle's demeanour was hard to bear down below, within the bank, what must it have been up-stairs in the family sitting-room? It was now, at this time, about the middle of November; and with Emily everything had been black and clouded for the last two months past. Polly's misfortune had only begun about the first of November. The two young ladies had had their own ideas about their own young men from nearly the same date. Philip Hughes and Jack Hollycombe had pushed themselves into prominence about the same time. But Emily's trouble had declared itself six weeks before Polly had sent her young man to her father. The first scene which took place with Emily and

Mr. Greenmantle, after young Hughes had declared himself, was very impressive. "What is this, Emily?"

"What is what, papa?" A poor girl when she is thus cross-questioned hardly knows what to say.

"One of the young men in the bank has been to me." There was in this a great slur intended. It was acknowledged by all Plumplington that Mr. Hughes was the cashier, and was hardly more fairly designated as one of the young men than would have been Mr. Greenmantle himself,—unless in regard to age.

"Philip, I suppose," said Emily. Now Mr. Greenmantle had certainly led the way into this difficulty himself. He had been allured by some modesty in the young man's demeanour,—or more probably by something pleasant in his manner which had struck Emily also,—to call him Philip. He had, as it were, shown a parental regard for him, and those who had best known Mr. Greenmantle had been sure that he would not forget his manifest good intentions towards the young man. As coming from Mr. Greenmantle the use of the christian name had been made. But certainly he had not intended that it should be taken up in this manner. There had been an ingratitude in it, which Mr. Greenmantle had felt very keenly.

"I would rather that you should call the young man Mr. Hughes in anything that you may have to say about him."

"I thought you called him Philip, papa."

"I shall never do so again,—never. What is this that he has said to me? Can it be true?"

"I suppose it is true, papa."

"You mean that you want to marry him?"

"Yes, papa."

"Goodness gracious me!" After this Emily remained silent for a while. "Can you have realised the fact that the young man has—-nothing; literally nothing!" What is a young lady to say when she is thus appealed to? She knew that though the young man had nothing, she would have a considerable portion of her own. She was her father's only child. She had not "cared for" young Gresham, whereas she had "cared for" young Hughes. What would be all the world to her if she must marry a man she did not care for? That, she was resolved, she would not do. But what would all the world be to her if she were not allowed to marry the man she did love? And what good would it be to her to be the only daughter of a rich man if she were to be baulked in this manner? She had thought it all over, assuming to herself perhaps greater privileges than she was entitled to expect.

But Emily Greenmantle was somewhat differently circumstanced from Polly Peppercorn. Emily was afraid of her father's sternness, whereas Polly was not in the least afraid of her governor, as she was wont to call him. Old Hickory was, in a good-humoured way, afraid of Polly. Polly could order the things, in and about the house, very much after her own fashion. To tell the truth Polly had but slight fear but that she would have her own way, and when she laid by her best silks she did not do it as a person does bid farewell to those treasures which are not to be seen again. They could be made to do very well for the future Mrs. Hollycombe. At any rate, like a Marlborough or a Wellington, she went into the battle thinking of victory and not of defeat. But Wellington was a long time before he had beaten the French, and Polly thought that there might be some trouble also for her. With Emily there was no prospect of ultimate victory.

Mr. Greenmantle was a very stern man, who could look at his daughter as though he never meant to give way. And, without saying a word, he could make all Plumplington understand that such was to be the case. "Poor Emmy," said the old Doctor to his old wife; "I'm afraid there's a bad time coming for her." "He's a nasty cross old man," said the old woman. "It always does take three generations to make a 'gentleman.'" For Mrs. Freeborn's ancestors had come from the time of James I.

"You and I had better understand each other," said Mr. Greenmantle, standing up with his back to the fireplace, and looking as though he were all poker from the top of his head to the heels of his boots. "You cannot marry Mr. Philip Hughes." Emily said nothing but turned her eyes down upon the ground. "I don't suppose he thinks of doing so without money."

"He has never thought about money at all."

"Then what are you to live upon? Can you tell me that? He has £220 from the bank. Can you live upon that? Can you bring up a family?" Emily blushed as she still looked upon the ground. "I tell you fairly that he shall never have the spending of my money. If you mean to desert me in my old age,—go."

"Papa, you shouldn't say that."

"You shouldn't think it." Then Mr. Greenmantle looked as though he had uttered a clenching argument. "You shouldn't think it. Now go away, Emily, and turn in your mind what I have said to you."

Chapter II

"Down I Shall Go."

THEN THERE came about a conversation between the two young ladies which was in itself very interesting. They had not met each other for about a fortnight when Emily Greenmantle came to Mr. Peppercorn's house. She had been thoroughly unhappy, and among her causes for sorrow had been the severance which seemed to have taken place between her and her friend. She had discussed all her troubles with Dr. Freeborn, and Dr. Freeborn had advised her to see Polly. "Here's Christmas-time coming on and you are all going to quarrel among yourselves. I won't have any such nonsense. Go and see her."

"It's not me, Dr. Freeborn," said Emily. "I don't want to quarrel with anybody; and there is nobody I like better than Polly." Thereupon Emily went to Mr. Peppercorn's house when Peppercorn would be certainly at the brewery, and there she found Polly at home.

Polly was dressed very plainly. It was manifest to all eyes that the Polly Peppercorn of to-day was not the same Polly Peppercorn that had been seen about Plumplington for the last twelve months. It was equally manifest that Polly intended that everybody should see the difference. She had not meekly put on her poorer dress so that people should see that she was no more than her father's child; but it was done with some ostentation. "If father says that Jack and I are not to have his money I must begin to reduce myself by times." That was what Polly intended to say to all Plumplington. She was sure that her father would have to give way under such shots as she could fire at him.

"Polly, I have not seen you, oh, for such a long time."

Polly did not look like quarrelling at all. Nothing could be more pleasant than the tone of her voice. But yet there was something in her mode of address which at once excited Emily Greenmantle's attention. In bidding her visitor welcome she called her Miss Greenmantle. Now on that matter there had been some little trouble heretofore, in which the banker's daughter had succeeded in getting the better of the banker. He had suggested that Miss Peppercorn was safer than Polly; but Emily had replied that Polly was a nice dear girl, very much in Dr. Freeborn's good favours, and in point of fact that Dr. Freeborn wouldn't allow it. Mr. Greenmantle had frowned, but had felt himself unable to stand against Dr. Freeborn in such a matter. "What's the meaning of the Miss Greenmantle?" said Emily sorrowfully.

"It's what I'm come to," said Polly, without any show of sorrow, "and it's what I mean to stick to as being my proper place. You have heard all about Jack Hollycombe. I suppose I ought to call him John as I'm speaking to you."

"I don't see what difference it will make."

"Not much in the long run; but yet it will make a difference. It isn't that I should not like to be just the same to you as I have been, but father means to put me down in the world, and I don't mean to quarrel with him about that. Down I shall go."

"And therefore I'm to be called Miss Greenmantle."

"Exactly. Perhaps it ought to have been always so as I'm so poorly minded as to go back to such a one as Jack Hollycombe. Of course it is going back. Of course Jack is as good as father was at his age. But father has put himself up since that and has put me up. I'm such poor stuff that I wouldn't stay up. A girl has to begin where her husband begins; and as I mean to be Jack's wife I have to fit myself for the place."

"I suppose it's the same with me, Polly."

"Not quite. You're a lady bred and born, and Mr. Hughes is a gentleman. Father tells me that a man who goes about the country selling malt isn't a gentleman. I suppose father is right. But Jack is a good enough gentleman to my thinking. If he had a share of father's money he would break out in quite a new place."

"Mr. Peppercorn won't give it to him?"

"Well! That's what I don't know. I do think the governor loves me. He is the best fellow anywhere for downright kindness. I mean to try him. And if he won't help me I shall go down as I say. You may be sure of this,—that I shall not give up Jack."

"You wouldn't marry him against your father's wishes?"

Here Polly wasn't quite ready with her answer. "I don't know that father has a right to destroy all my happiness," she said at last. "I shall wait a long time first at any rate. Then if I find that Jack can remain constant,—I don't know what I shall do."

"What does he say?"

"Jack? He's all sugar and promises. They always are for a time. It takes a deal of learning to know whether a young man can be true. There is not above one in twenty that do come out true when they are tried."

"I suppose not," said Emily sorrowfully.

"I shall tell Mr. Jack that he's got to go through the ordeal. Of course he wants me to say that I'll marry him right off the reel and that he'll earn money enough for both of us. I told him only this morning— "

"Did you see him?"

"I wrote him,—out quite plainly. And I told him that there were other people had hearts in their bodies besides him and me. I'm not going to break father's heart,—not if I can help it. It would go very hard with him if I were to walk out of this house and marry Jack Hollycombe, quite plain like."

"I would never do it," said Emily with energy.

"You are a little different from me, Miss Greenmantle. I suppose my mother didn't think much about such things, and as long as she got herself married decent, didn't trouble herself much what her people said."

"Didn't she?"

"I fancy not. Those sort of cares and bothers always come with money. Look at the two girls in this house. I take it they only act just like their mothers, and if they're good girls, which they are, they get their mother's consent. But the marriage goes on as a matter of course. It's where money is wanted that parents become stern and their children become dutiful. I mean to be dutiful for a time. But I'd rather have Jack than father's money."

"Dr. Freeborn says that you and I are not to quarrel. I am sure I don't see why we should."

"What Dr. Freeborn says is very well." It was thus that Polly carried on the conversation after thinking over the matter for a moment or two. "Dr. Freeborn is a great man in Plumplington, and has his own way in everything. I'm not saying a word against Dr. Freeborn, and goodness knows I don't want to quarrel with you, Miss Greenmantle."

"I hope not."

"But I do mean to go down if father makes me, and if Jack proves himself a true man."

"I suppose he'll do that," said Miss Greenmantle. "Of course you think he will."

"Well, upon the whole I do," said Polly. "And though I think father will have to give up, he won't do it just at present, and I shall have to remain just as I am for a time."

"And wear— " Miss Greenmantle had intended to inquire whether it was Polly's purpose to go about in her second-rate clothes, but had hesitated, not quite liking to ask the question.

"Just that," said Polly. "I mean to wear such clothes as shall be suitable for Jack's wife. And I mean to give up all my airs. I've been thinking a deal about it, and they're wrong. Your papa and my father are not the same."

"They are not the same, of course," said Emily.

"One is a gentleman, and the other isn't. That's the long and the short of it. I oughtn't to have gone to your house drinking tea and the rest of it; and I oughtn't to have called you Emily. That's the long and the short of that," said she, repeating herself.

"Dr. Freeborn thinks— "

"Dr. Freeborn mustn't quite have it all his own way. Of course Dr. Freeborn is everything in Plumplington; and when I'm Jack's wife I'll do what he tells me again."

"I suppose you'll do what Jack tells you then."

"Well, yes; not exactly. If Jack were to tell me not to go to church,—which he won't,—I shouldn't do what he told me. If he said he'd like to have a leg of mutton boiled, I should boil it. Only legs of mutton wouldn't be very common with us, unless father comes round."

"I don't see why all that should make a difference between you and me."

"It will have to do so," said Polly with perfect self-assurance. "Father has told me that he doesn't mean to find money to buy legs of mutton for Jack Hollycombe. Those were his very words. I'm determined I'll never ask him. And he said he wasn't going to find clothes for Jack Hollycombe's brats. I'll never go to him to find a pair of shoes for Jack Hollycombe or one of his brats. I've told Jack as much, and Jack says that I'm right. But there's no knowing what's inside a young man till you've tried him. Jack may fall off, and if so there's an end of him. I shall come round in time, and wear my fine clothes again when I settle down as an old maid. But father will never make me wear them, and I shall never call you anything but Miss Greenmantle, unless he consents to my marrying Jack."

Such was the eloquence of Polly Peppercorn as spoken on that occasion. And she certainly did fill Miss Greenmantle's mind with a strong idea of her persistency. When Polly's last speech was finished the banker's daughter got up, and kissed her friend, and took her leave. "You shouldn't do that," said Polly with a smile. But on this one occasion she returned the caress; and then Miss Greenmantle went her way thinking over all that had been said to her.

"I'll do it too, let him persuade me ever so." This was Polly's soliloquy to herself when she was left alone, and the "him" spoken of on this occasion was her father. She had made up her own mind as to the line of action she would follow, and she was quite resolved never again to ask her father's permission for her marriage. Her father and Jack might fight that out among themselves, as best they could. There had already been one scene on the subject between herself and her father in which the brewer's foreman had acted the part of stern parent with considerable violence. He had not beaten his girl, nor used bad words to her, nor, to tell the truth, had he threatened her with any deprivation of those luxuries to which she had become accustomed; but he had sworn by all the oaths which he knew by heart that if she chose to marry Jack Hollycombe she should go "bare as a tinker's brat." "I don't want anything better," Polly had said. "He'll want something else though," Peppercorn had replied, and had bounced out of the room and banged the door.

Miss Greenmantle, in whose nature there was perhaps something of the lugubrious tendencies which her father exhibited, walked away home from Mr. Peppercorn's house with a sad heart. She was very sorry for Polly Peppercorn's grief, and she was very sorry also for her own. But she had not that amount of high spirits which sustained Polly in her troubles. To tell the truth Polly had some hope that she might get the better of her father, and thereby do a good turn both to him and to herself. But Emily Greenmantle had but little hope. Her father had not sworn at her, nor had he banged the door, but he had pressed his lips together till there was no lip really visible. And he had raised his forehead on high till it looked as though one continuous poker descended from the crown of his head passing down through his entire body. "Emily, it is out of the question. You had better leave me." From that day to this not a word had been spoken on the "subject." Young Gresham had been once asked to dine at the bank, but that had been the only effort made by Mr. Greenmantle in the matter.

Emily had felt as she walked home that she had not at her command weapons so powerful as those which Polly intended to use against her father. No change in her dress would be suitable to her, and were she to make any it would be altogether inefficacious. Nor would her father be tempted by his passion to throw in her teeth the lack of either boots or legs of mutton which might be the consequence of her marriage with a poor man. There was something almost vulgar in these allusions which made Emily feel that there had been some reason for her papa's exclusiveness,—but she let that go by. Polly was a dear girl, though she had found herself able to speak of the brats' feet without even a blush. "I suppose there will be brats, and why shouldn't she,—when she's talking only to me. It must be so I suppose." So Emily had argued to herself, making the excuse altogether on behalf of her friend. But she was sure that if her father had heard Polly he would have been offended.

But what was Emily to do on her own behalf? Harry Gresham had come to dinner, but his coming had been altogether without effect. She was quite sure that she could never care for Harry Gresham, and she did not quite believe that Harry Gresham cared very much for her. There was a rumour about in the country that Harry Gresham wanted money, and she knew well that Harry Gresham's father and her own papa had been closeted together. She did not care to be married after such a fashion as that. In truth Philip Hughes was the only young man for whom she did care.

She had always felt her father to be the most impregnable of men,— but now on this subject of her marriage he was more impregnable than ever. He had never yet entirely digested that poker which he had swallowed when he had gone so far as to tell his daughter that it was "entirely out of the question." From that hour her home had been terrible to her as a home, and had not been in the least enlivened by the presence of Harry Gresham. And now how was she to carry on the battle? Polly had her plans all drawn out, and was preparing herself for the combat seriously. But for Emily, there was no means left for fighting.

And she felt that though a battle with her father might be very proper for Polly, it would be highly unbecoming for herself. There was a difference in rank between herself and Polly of which Polly clearly understood the strength. Polly would put on her poor clothes, and go into the kitchen, and break her father's heart by preparing for a descent into regions which would be fitting for her were she to marry her young man without a fortune. But to Miss Greenmantle this would be impossible. Any marriage, made now or later, without her father's leave, seemed to her out of the question. She would only ruin her "young man" were she to attempt it, and the attempt would be altogether inefficacious. She could only be unhappy, melancholy,—and perhaps morose; but she could not be so unhappy and melancholy,—or morose, as was her father. At such weapons he could certainly beat her. Since that unhappy word had been spoken, the poker within him had not been for a moment lessened in vigour. And she feared even to appeal to Dr. Freeborn. Dr. Freeborn could do much,—almost everything in Plumplington,—but there was a point at which her father would turn even against Dr. Freeborn. She did not think that the Doctor would ever dare to take up the cudgels against her father on behalf of Philip Hughes. She felt that it would be more becoming for her to abstain and to suffer in silence than to apply to any human being for assistance. But she could be miserable;—outwardly miserable as well as inwardly;—and very miserable she was determined that she would be! Her father no doubt would be miserable too; but she was sad at heart as she bethought herself that her father would rather like it. Though he could not easily digest a poker when he had swallowed it, it never seemed to disagree with him. A state of misery in which he would speak to no one seemed to be almost to his taste. In this way poor Emily Greenmantle did not see her way to the enjoyment of a happy Christmas.

Chapter III

Mr. Greenmantle Is Much Perplexed.

THAT EVENING Mr. Greenmantle and his daughter sat down to dinner together in a very unhappy humour. They always dined at half-past seven; not that Mr. Greenmantle liked to have his dinner at that hour better than any other, but because it was considered to be fashionable. Old Mr. Gresham, Harry's father, always dined at half-past seven, and Mr. Greenmantle rather followed the habits of a county gentleman's life. He used to dine at this hour when there was a dinner-party, but of late he had adopted it for the family meal. To tell the truth there had been a few words between him and Dr. Freeborn while Emily had been talking over matters with Polly Peppercorn. Dr. Freeborn had not ventured to say a word as to Emily's love affairs; but had so discussed those of Jack Hollycombe and Polly as to leave a strong impression on the mind of Mr. Greenmantle. He had quite understood that the Doctor had been talking at himself, and that when Jack's name had been mentioned, or Polly's, the Doctor had intended that the wisdom spoken should be intended to apply to Emily and to Philip Hughes. "It's only because he can give her a lot of money," the Doctor had said. "The young man is a good young man, and steady. What is Peppercorn that he should want anything better for his child? Young Hollycombe has taken her fancy, and why shouldn't she have him?"

"I suppose Mr. Peppercorn may have his own views," Mr. Greenmantle had answered.

"Bother his views," the Doctor had said. "He has no one else to think of but the girl and his views should be confined to making her happy. Of course he'll have to give way at last, and will only make himself ridiculous. I shouldn't say a word about it only that the young man is all that he ought to be."

Now in this there was not a word which did not apply to Mr. Greenmantle himself. And the worst of it was the fact that Mr. Greenmantle felt that the Doctor intended it.

But as he had taken his constitutional walk before dinner, a walk which he took every day of his life after bank hours, he had sworn to himself that he would not be guided, or in the least affected, by Dr. Freeborn's opinion in the matter. There had been an underlying bitterness in the Doctor's words which had much aggravated the banker's ill-humour. The Doctor would not so have spoken of the marriage of one of his own daughters,—before they had all been married. Birth would have been considered by him almost before anything. The Peppercorns and the Greenmantles were looked down upon almost from an equal height. Now Mr. Greenmantle considered himself to be infinitely superior to Mr. Peppercorn, and to be almost, if not altogether, equal to Dr. Freeborn. He was much the richer man of the two, and his money was quite sufficient to outweigh a century or two of blood.

Peppercorn might do as he pleased. What became of Peppercorn's money was an affair of no matter. The Doctor's argument was no doubt good as far as Peppercorn was concerned. Peppercorn was not a gentleman. It was that which Mr. Greenmantle felt so acutely. The one great line of demarcation in the world was that which separated gentlemen from non-gentlemen. Mr. Greenmantle assured himself that he was a gentleman, acknowledged to be so by all the county. The old Duke of Omnium had customarily asked him to dine at his annual dinner at Gatherum Castle. He had been in the habit of staying occasionally at Greshambury, Mr. Gresham's county seat, and Mr. Gresham had been quite willing to forward the match between Emily and his younger son. There could be no doubt that he was on the right side of the line of demarcation. He was therefore quite determined that his daughter should not marry the Cashier in his own bank.

As he sat down to dinner he looked sternly at his daughter, and thought with wonder at the viciousness of her taste. She looked at him almost as sternly as she thought with awe of his cruelty. In her eyes Philip Hughes was quite as good a gentleman as her father. He was the son of a clergyman who was now dead, but had been intimate with Dr. Freeborn. And in the natural course of events might succeed her father as manager of the Bank. To be manager of the Bank at Plumplington was not very much in the eyes of the world; but it was the position which her father filled. Emily vowed to herself as she looked across the table into her father's face, that she would be Mrs. Philip Hughes,—or remain unmarried all her life. "Emily, shall I help you to a mutton cutlet?" said her father with solemnity.

"No thank you, papa," she replied with equal gravity.

"On what then do you intend to dine?" There had been a sole of which she had also declined to partake. "There is nothing else, unless you will dine off rice pudding."

"I am not hungry, papa." She could not decline to wear her customary clothes as did her friend Polly, but she could at any rate go without her dinner. Even a father so stern as was Mr. Greenmantle could not make her eat. Then there came a vision across her eyes of a long sickness, produced chiefly by inanition, in which she might wear her father's heart out. And then she felt that she might too probably lack the courage. She did not care much for her dinner; but she feared that she could not persevere to the breaking of her father's heart. She and her father were alone together in the world, and he in other respects had always been good to her. And now a tear trickled from her eye down her nose as she gazed upon the empty plate. He ate his two cutlets one after another in solemn silence and so the dinner was ended.

He, too, had felt uneasy qualms during the meal. "What shall I do if she takes to starving herself and going to bed, all along of that young rascal in the outer bank?" It was thus that he had thought of it, and he too for a moment had begun to tell himself that were she to be perverse she must win the battle. He knew himself to be strong in purpose, but he doubted whether he would be strong enough to stand by and see his daughter starve herself. A week's starvation or a fortnight's he might bear, and it was possible that she might give way before that time had come.

Then he retired to a little room inside the bank, a room that was half private and half official, to which he would betake himself to spend his evening whenever some especially gloomy fit would fall upon him. Here, within his own bosom, he turned over all the circumstances of the case. No doubt he had with him all the laws of God and man. He was not bound to give his money to any such interloper as was Philip Hughes. On that point he was quite clear. But what step had he better take to prevent the evil? Should he resign his position at the bank, and take his daughter away to live in the south of France? It would be a terrible step to which to be driven by his own Cashier. He was as efficacious to do the work of the bank as ever he had been, and he would leave this enemy to occupy his place. The enemy would then be in a condition to marry a wife without a fortune; and who could tell whether he might not show his power in such a crisis by marrying Emily! How terrible in such a case would be his defeat! At any rate he might go for three months, on sick leave. He had been for nearly forty years in the bank, and had never yet been absent for a day on sick leave. Thinking of all this he remained alone till it was time for him to go to bed.

On the next morning he was dumb and stiff as ever, and after breakfast sat dumb and stiff, in his official room behind the bank counter, thinking over his great trouble. He had not spoken a word to Emily since yesterday's dinner beyond asking her whether she would take a bit of fried bacon. "No thank you, papa," she had said; and then Mr. Greenmantle had made up his mind that he must take her away somewhere at once, lest she should be starved to death. Then he went into the bank and sat there signing his name, and meditating the terrible catastrophe which was to fall upon him. Hughes, the Cashier, had become Mr. Hughes, and if any young man could be frightened out of his love by the stern look and sterner voice of a parent, Mr. Hughes would have been so frightened.

Then there came a knock at the door, and Mr. Peppercorn having been summoned to come in, entered the room. He had expressed a desire to see Mr. Greenmantle personally, and having proved his eagerness by a double request, had been allowed to have his way. It was quite a common affair for him to visit the bank on matters referring to the brewery; but now it was evident to any one with half an eye that such at present was not Mr. Peppercorn's business. He had on the clothes in which he habitually went to church instead of the light-coloured pepper and salt tweed jacket in which he was accustomed to go about among the malt and barrels. "What can I do for you, Mr. Peppercorn?" said the banker. But the aspect was the aspect of a man who had a poker still fixed within his head and gullet.

"'Tis nothing about the brewery, sir, or I shouldn't have troubled you. Mr. Hughes is very good at all that kind of thing." A further frown came over Mr. Greenmantle's face, but he said nothing. "You know my daughter Polly, Mr. Greenmantle?"

"I am aware that there is a Miss Peppercorn," said the other. Peppercorn felt that an offence was intended. Mr. Greenmantle was of course aware. "What can I do on behalf of Miss Peppercorn?"

"She's as good a girl as ever lived."

"I do not in the least doubt it. If it be necessary that you should speak to me respecting Miss Peppercorn, will it not be well that you should take a chair?"

Then Mr. Peppercorn sat down, feeling that he had been snubbed. "I may say that my only object in life is to do every mortal thing to make my girl happy." Here Mr. Greenmantle simply bowed. "We sit close to you in church, where, however, she comes much more reg'lar than me, and you must have observed her scores of times."

"I am not in the habit of looking about among young ladies at church time, but I have occasionally been aware that Miss Peppercorn has been there."

"Of course you have. You couldn't help it. Well, now, you know the sort of appearance she has made."

"I can assure you, Mr. Peppercorn, that I have not observed Miss Peppercorn's dress in particular. I do not look much at the raiment worn by young ladies even in the outer world,—much less in church. I have a daughter of my own— "

"It's her as I'm coming to." Then Mr. Greenmantle frowned more severely than ever. But the brewer did not at the moment say a word about the banker's daughter, but reverted to his own. "You'll see next Sunday that my girl won't look at all like herself."

"I really cannot promise— "

"You cannot help yourself, Mr. Greenmantle. I'll go bail that every one in church will see it. Polly is not to be passed over in a crowd;—at least she didn't used to be. Now it all comes of her wanting to get herself married to a young man who is altogether beneath her. Not as I mean to say anything against John Hollycombe as regards his walk of life. He is an industrious young man, as can earn forty shillings a week, and he comes over here from Barchester selling malt and such like. He may rise himself to £3 some of these days if he looks sharp about it. But I can give my girl—; well; what is quite unfit that he should think of looking for with a wife. And it's monstrous of Polly wanting to throw herself away in such a fashion. I don't believe in a young man being so covetous."

"But what can I do, Mr. Peppercorn?"

"I'm coming to that. If you'll see her next Sunday you'll think of what my feelings must be. She's a doing of it all just because she wants to show me that she thinks herself fit for nothing better than to be John Hollycombe's wife. When I tell her that I won't have it,—this sudden changing of her toggery, she says it's only fitting. It ain't fitting at all. I've got the money to buy things for her, and I'm willing to pay for it. Is she to go poor just to break her father's heart?"

"But what can I do, Mr. Peppercorn?"

"I'm coming to that. The world does say, Mr. Greenmantle, that your young lady means to serve you in the same fashion."

Hereupon Mr. Greenmantle waxed very wroth. It was terrible to his ideas that his daughter's affairs should be talked of at all by the people at Plumplington at large. It was worse again that his daughter and the brewer's girl should be lumped together in the scandal of the town. But it was worse, much worse, that this man Peppercorn should have dared to come to him, and tell him all about it. Did the man really expect that he, Mr. Greenmantle, should talk unreservedly as to the love affairs of his Emily? "The world, Mr. Peppercorn, is very impertinent in its usual scandalous conversations as to its betters. You must forgive me if I do not intend on this occasion to follow the example of the world. Good morning, Mr. Peppercorn."

"It's Dr. Freeborn as has coupled the two girls together."

"I cannot believe it."

"You ask him. It's he who has said that you and I are in a boat together."

"I'm not in a boat with any man."

"Well;—in a difficulty. It's the same thing. The Doctor seems to think that young ladies are to have their way in everything. I don't see it. When a man has made a tidy bit of money, as have you and I, he has a right to have a word to say as to who shall have the spending of it. A girl hasn't the right to say that she'll give it all to this man or to that. Of course, it's natural that my money should go to Polly. I'm not saying anything against it. But I don't mean that John Hollycombe shall have it. Now if you and I can put our heads together, I think we may be able to see our way out of the wood."

"Mr. Peppercorn, I cannot consent to discuss with you the affairs of Miss Greenmantle."

"But they're both alike. You must admit that."

"I will admit nothing, Mr. Peppercorn."

"I do think, you know, that we oughtn't to be done by our own daughters."

"Really, Mr. Peppercorn— "

"Dr. Freeborn was saying that you and I would have to give way at last."

"Dr. Freeborn knows nothing about it. If Dr. Freeborn coupled the two young ladies together he was I must say very impertinent; but I don't think he ever did so. Good morning, Mr. Peppercorn. I am fully engaged at present and cannot spare time for a longer interview." Then he rose up from his chair, and leant upon the table with his hands by way of giving a certain signal that he was to be left alone. Mr. Peppercorn, after pausing a moment, searching for an opportunity for another word, was overcome at last by the rigid erectness of Mr. Greenmantle and withdrew.

Chapter IV

Jack Hollycombe.

MR. PEPPERCORN's visit to the bank had been no doubt inspired by Dr. Freeborn. The Doctor had not actually sent him to the bank, but had filled his mind with the idea that such a visit might be made with good effect. "There are you two fathers going to make two fools of yourselves," the Doctor had said. "You have each of you got a daughter as good as gold, and are determined to break their hearts because you won't give your money to a young man who happens to want it."

"Now, Doctor, do you mean to tell me that you would have married your young ladies to the first young man that came and asked for them?"

"I never had much money to give my girls, and the men who came happened to have means of their own."

"But if you'd had it, and if they hadn't, do you mean to tell me you'd never have asked a question?"

"A man should never boast that in any circumstances of his life he would have done just what he ought to do,—much less when he has never been tried. But if the lover be what he ought to be in morals and all that kind of thing, the girl's father ought not to refuse to help them. You may be sure of this,—that Polly means to have her own way. Providence has blessed you with a girl that knows her own mind." On receipt of this compliment Mr. Peppercorn scratched his head. "I wish I could say as much for my friend Greenmantle. You two are in a boat together, and ought to make up your mind as to what you should do." Peppercorn resolved that he would remember the phrase about the boat, and began to think that it might be good that he should see Mr. Greenmantle. "What on earth is it you two want? It is not as though you were dukes, and looking for proper alliances for two ducal spinsters."

Now there had no doubt been a certain amount of intended venom in this. Dr. Freeborn knew well the weak points in Mr. Greenmantle's character, and was determined to hit him where he was weakest. He did not see the difference between the banker and the brewer nearly so clearly as did Mr. Greenmantle. He would probably have said that the line of demarcation came just below himself. At any rate, he thought that he would be doing best for Emily's interest if he made her father feel that all the world was on her side. Therefore it was that he so contrived that Mr. Peppercorn should pay his visit to the bank.

On his return to the brewery the first person that Peppercorn saw standing in the doorway of his own little sanctum was Jack Hollycombe. "What is it you're wanting?" he asked gruffly.

"I was just desirous of saying a few words to yourself, Mr. Peppercorn."

"Well, here I am!" There were two or three brewers and porters about the place and Jack did not feel that he could plead his cause well in their presence. "What is it you've got to say,—because I'm busy? There ain't no malt wanted for the next week; but you know that, and as we stand at present you can send it in without any more words, as it's needed."

"It ain't about malt or anything of that kind."

"Then I don't know what you've got to say. I'm very busy just at present, as I told you."

"You can spare me five minutes inside."

"No I can't." But then Peppercorn resolved that neither would it suit him to carry on the conversation respecting his daughter in the presence of the workmen, and he thought that he perceived that Jack Hollycombe would be prepared to do so if he were driven. "Come in if you will," he said; "we might as well have it out." Then he led the way into the room, and shut the door as soon as Jack had followed him. "Now what is it you have got to say? I suppose it's about that young woman down at my house."

"It is, Mr. Peppercorn."

"Then let me tell you that the least said will be soonest mended. She's not for you,—with my consent. And to tell you the truth I think that you have a mortal deal of brass coming to ask for her. You've no edication suited to her edication,—and what's wus, no money." Jack had shown symptoms of anger when his deficient education had been thrown in his teeth, but had cheered up somewhat when the lack of money had been insisted upon. "Them two things are so against you that you haven't a leg to stand on. My word! what do you expect that I should say when such a one as you comes a-courting to a girl like that?"

"I did, perhaps, think more of what she might say."

"I daresay;—because you knew her to be a fool like yourself. I suppose you think yourself to be a very handsome young man."

"I think she's a very handsome young woman. As to myself I never asked the question."

"That's all very well. A man can always say as much as that for himself. The fact is you're not going to have her."

"That's just what I want to speak to you about, Mr. Peppercorn."

"You're not going to have her. Now I've spoken my intentions, and you may as well take one word as a thousand. I'm not a man as was ever known to change my mind when I'd made it up in such a matter as this."

"She's got a mind too, Mr. Peppercorn."

"She have, no doubt. She have a mind and so have you. But you haven't either of you got the money. The money is here," and Mr. Peppercorn slapped his breeches pocket. "I've had to do with earning it, and I mean to have to do with giving it away. To me there is no idea of honesty at all in a chap like you coming and asking a girl to marry you just because you know that she's to have a fortune."

"That's not my reason."

"It's uncommon like it. Now you see there's somebody else that's got to be asked. You think I'm a good-natured fellow. So I am, but I'm not soft like that."

"I never thought anything of the kind, Mr. Peppercorn."

"Polly told you so, I don't doubt. She's right in thinking so, because I'd give Polly anything in reason. Or out of reason for the matter of that, because she is the apple of my eye." This was indiscreet on the part of Mr. Peppercorn, as it taught the young man to think that he himself must be in reason or out of reason, and that in either case Polly ought to be allowed to have him. "But there's one thing I stop at; and that is a young man who hasn't got either edication, or money,—nor yet manners."

"There's nothing against my manner, I hope, Mr. Peppercorn."

"Yes; there is. You come a-interfering with me in the most delicate affair in the world. You come into my family, and want to take away my girl. That I take it is the worst of manners."

"How is any young lady to get married unless some young fellow comes after her?"

"There'll be plenty to come after Polly. You leave Polly alone, and you'll find that she'll get a young man suited to her. It's like your impudence to suppose that there's no other young man in the world so good as you. Why;—dash my wig; who are you? What are you? You're merely acting for them corn-factors over at Barsester."

"And you're acting for them brewers here at Plumplington. What's the difference?"

"But I've got the money in my pocket, and you've got none. That's the difference. Put that in your pipe and smoke it. Now if you'll please to remember that I'm very busy, you'll walk yourself off. You've had it out with me, which I didn't intend; and I've explained my mind very fully. She's not for you;—at any rate my money's not."

"Look here, Mr. Peppercorn."

"Well?"

"I don't care a farthing for your money."

"Don't you, now?"

"Not in the way of comparing it with Polly herself. Of course money is a very comfortable thing. If Polly's to be my wife— "

"Which she ain't."

"I should like her to have everything that a lady can desire."

"How kind you are."

"But in regard to money for myself I don't value it that." Here Jack Hollycombe snapped his fingers. "My meaning is to get the girl I love."

"Then you won't."

"And if she's satisfied to come to me without a shilling, I'm satisfied to take her in the same fashion. I don't know how much you've got, Mr. Peppercorn, but you can go and found a Hiram's Hospital with every penny of it." At this moment a discussion was going on respecting a certain charitable institution in Barchester,—and had been going on for the last forty years,—as to which Mr. Hollycombe was here expressing the popular opinion of the day. "That's the kind of thing a man should do who don't choose to leave his money to his own child." Jack was now angry, having had his deficient education twice thrown in his teeth by one whom he conceived to be so much less educated than himself. "What I've got to say to you, Mr. Peppercorn, is that Polly means to have me, and if she's got to wait—why, I'm so minded that I'll wait for her as long as ever she'll wait for me." So saying Jack Hollycombe left the room.

Mr. Peppercorn thrust his hat back upon his head, and stood with his back to the fire, with the tails of his coat appearing over his hands in his breeches pockets, glaring out of his eyes with anger which he did not care to suppress. This man had presented to him a picture of his future life which was most unalluring. There was nothing he desired less than to give his money to such an abominable institution as Hiram's Hospital. Polly, his own dear daughter Polly, was intended to be the recipient of all his savings. As he went about among the beer barrels, he had been a happy man as he thought of Polly bright with the sheen which his money had provided for her. But it was of Polly married to some gentleman that he thought at these moments;—of Polly surrounded by a large family of little gentlemen and little ladies. They would all call him grandpapa; and in the evenings of his days he would sit by the fire in that gentleman's parlour, a welcome guest, because of the means which he had provided; and the little gentlemen and the little ladies would surround him with their prattle and their noises and caresses. He was not a man whom his intimates would have supposed to be gifted with a strong imagination, but there was the picture firmly set before his mind's eye. "Edication," however, in the intended son-in-law was essential. And the son-in-law must be a gentleman. Now Jack Hollycombe was not a gentleman, and was not educated up to that pitch which was necessary for Polly's husband.

But Mr. Peppercorn, as he thought of it all, was well aware that Polly had a decided will of her own. And he knew of himself that his own will was less strong than his daughter's. In spite of all the severe things which he had just said to Jack Hollycombe, there was present to him a dreadful weight upon his heart, as he thought that Polly would certainly get the better of him. At this moment he hated Jack Hollycombe with most un-Christian rancour. No misfortune that could happen to Jack, either sudden death, or forgery with flight to the antipodes, or loss of his good looks,—which Mr. Peppercorn most unjustly thought would be equally efficacious with Polly,—would at the present moment of his wrath be received otherwise than as a special mark of good-fortune. And yet he was well aware that if Polly were to come and tell him that she had by some secret means turned herself into Mrs. Jack Hollycombe, he knew very well that for Polly's sake he would have to take Jack with all his faults, and turn him into the dearest son-in-law that the world could have provided for him. This was a very trying position, and justified him in standing there for a quarter of an hour with his back to the fire, and his coat-tails over his arms, as they were thrust into his trousers pockets.

In the meantime Jack had succeeded in obtaining a few minutes' talk with Polly,—or rather the success had been on Polly's side, for she had managed the business. On coming out from the brewery Jack had met her in the street, and had been taken home by her. "You might as well come in, Jack," she had said, "and have a few words with me. You have been talking to father about it, I suppose."

"Well; I have. He says I am not sufficiently educated. I suppose he wants to get some young man from the colleges."

"Don't you be stupid, Jack. You want to have your own way, I suppose."

"I don't want him to tell me I'm uneducated. Other men that I've heard of ain't any better off than I am."

"You mean himself,—which isn't respectful."

"I'm educated up to doing what I've got to do. If you don't want more, I don't see what he's got to do with it."

"As the times go of course a man should learn more and more. You are not to compare him to yourself; and it isn't respectful. If you want to say sharp things against him, Jack, you had better give it all up;—for I won't bear it."

"I don't want to say anything sharp."

"Why can't you put up with him? He's not going to have his own way. And he is older than you. And it is he that has got the money. If you care about it— "

"You know I care."

"Very well. Suppose I do know, and suppose I don't. I hear you say you do, and that's all I've got to act upon. Do you bide your time if you've got the patience, and all will come right. I shan't at all think so much of you if you can't bear a few sharp words from him."

"He may say whatever he pleases."

"You ain't educated,—not like Dr. Freeborn, and men of that class."

"What do I want with it?" said he.

"I don't know that you do want it. At any rate I don't want it; and that's what you've got to think about at present. You just go on, and let things be as they are. You don't want to be married in a week's time."

"Why not?" he asked.

"At any rate I don't; and I don't mean to. This time five years will do very well."

"Five years! You'll be an old woman."

"The fitter for you, who'll still be three years older. If you've patience to wait leave it to me."

"I haven't over much patience."

"Then go your own way and suit yourself elsewhere."

"Polly, you're enough to break a man's heart. You know that I can't go and suit myself elsewhere. You are all the world to me, Polly."

"Not half so much as a quarter of malt if you could get your own price for it. A young woman is all very well just as a plaything; but business is business;—isn't it, Jack?"

"Five years! Fancy telling a fellow that he must wait five years."

"That'll do for the present, Jack. I'm not going to keep you here idle all the day. Father will be angry when I tell him that you've been here at all."

"It was you that brought me."

"Yes, I did. But you're not to take advantage of that. Now I say, Jack, hands off. I tell you I won't. I'm not going to be kissed once a week for five years. Well. Mark my words, this is the last time I ever ask you in here. No; I won't have it. Go away." Then she succeeded in turning him out of the room and closing the house door behind his back. "I think he's the best young man I see about anywhere. Father twits him about his education. It's my belief there's nothing he can't do that he's wanted for. That's the kind of education a man ought to have. Father says it's because he's handsome I like him. It does go a long way, and he is handsome. Father has got ideas of fashion into his head which will send him crazy before he has done with them." Such was the soliloquy in which Miss Peppercorn indulged as soon as she had been left by her lover.

"Educated! Of course I'm not educated. I can't talk Latin and Greek as some of those fellows pretend to,—though for the matter of that I never heard it. But two and two make four, and ten and ten make twenty. And if a fellow says that it don't he is trying on some dishonest game. If a fellow understands that, and sticks to it, he has education enough for my business,—or for Peppercorn's either." Then he walked back to the inn yard where he had left his horse and trap.

As he drove back to Barchester he made up his mind that Polly Peppercorn would be worth waiting for. There was the memory of that kiss upon his lips which had not been made less sweet by the severity of the words which had accompanied it. The words indeed had been severe; but there had been an intention and a purpose about the kiss which had altogether redeemed the words. "She is just one in a thousand, that's about the truth. And as for waiting for her;—I'll wait like grim death, only I hope it won't be necessary!" It was thus he spoke of the lady of his love as he drove himself into the town under Barchester Towers.

Chapter V

Dr. Freeborn And Philip Hughes.

THINGS WENT on at Plumplington without any change for a fortnight,—that is without any change for the better. But in truth the ill-humour both of Mr. Greenmantle and of Mr. Peppercorn had increased to such a pitch as to add an additional blackness to the general haziness and drizzle and gloom of the November weather. It was now the end of November, and Dr. Freeborn was becoming a little uneasy because the Christmas attributes for which he was desirous were still altogether out of sight. He was a man specially anxious for the mundane happiness of his parishioners and who would take any amount of personal trouble to insure it; but he was in fault perhaps in this, that he considered that everybody ought to be happy just because he told them to be so. He belonged to the Church of England certainly, but he had no dislike to Papists or Presbyterians, or dissenters in general, as long as they would arrange themselves under his banner as "Freebornites." And he had such force of character that in Plumplington,—beyond which he was not ambitious that his influence should extend,—he did in general prevail. But at the present moment he was aware that Mr. Greenmantle was in open mutiny. That Peppercorn would yield he had strong hope. Peppercorn he knew to be a weak, good fellow, whose affection for his daughter would keep him right at last. But until he could extract that poker from Mr. Greenmantle's throat, he knew that nothing could be done with him.

At the end of the fortnight Mr. Greenmantle called at the Rectory about half an hour before dinner time, when he knew that the Doctor would be found in his study before going up to dress for dinner. "I hope I am not intruding, Dr. Freeborn," he said. But the rust of the poker was audible in every syllable as it fell from his mouth.

"Not in the least. I've a quarter of an hour before I go and wash my hands."

"It will be ample. In a quarter of an hour I shall be able sufficiently to explain my plans." Then there was a pause, as though Mr. Greenmantle had expected that the explanation was to begin with the Doctor. "I am thinking," the banker continued after a while, "of taking my family abroad to some foreign residence." Now it was well known to Dr. Freeborn that Mr. Greenmantle's family consisted exclusively of Emily.

"Going to take Emily away?" he said.

"Such is my purpose,—and myself also."

"What are they to do at the bank?"

"That will be the worst of it, Dr. Freeborn. The bank will be the great difficulty."

"But you don't mean that you are going for good?"

"Only for a prolonged foreign residence;—that is to say for six months. For forty years I have given but very little trouble to the Directors. For forty years I have been at my post and have never suggested any prolonged absence. If the Directors cannot bear with me after forty years I shall think them unreasonable men." Now in truth Mr. Greenmantle knew that the Directors would make no opposition to anything that he might propose; but he always thought it well to be armed with some premonitory grievance. "In fact my pecuniary matters are so arranged that should the Directors refuse I shall go all the same."

"You mean that you don't care a straw for the Directors."

"I do not mean to postpone my comfort to their views,—or my daughter's."

"But why does your daughter's comfort depend on your going away?

I should have thought that she would have preferred Plumplington at present."

That was true, no doubt. And Mr. Greenmantle felt;—well; that he was not exactly telling the truth in putting the burden of his departure upon Emily's comfort. If Emily, at the present crisis of affairs, were carried away from Plumplington for six months, her comfort would certainly not be increased. She had already been told that she was to go, and she had clearly understood why. "I mean as to her future welfare," said Mr. Greenmantle very solemnly.

Dr. Freeborn did not care to hear about the future welfare of young people. What had to be said as to their eternal welfare he thought himself quite able to say. After all there was something of benevolent paganism in his disposition. He liked better to deal with their present happiness,—so that there was nothing immoral in it. As to the world to come he thought that the fathers and mothers of his younger flock might safely leave that consideration to him. "Emily is a remarkably good girl. That's my idea of her."

Mr. Greenmantle was offended even at this. Dr. Freeborn had no right, just at present, to tell him that his daughter was a good girl. Her goodness had been greatly lessened by the fact that in regard to her marriage she was anxious to run counter to her father. "She is a good girl. At least I hope so."

"Do you doubt it?"

"Well, no;—or rather yes. Perhaps I ought to say no as to her life in general."

"I should think so. I don't know what a father may want,—but I should think so. I never knew her miss church yet,—either morning or evening."

"As far as that goes she does not neglect her duties."

"What is the matter with her that she is to be taken off to some foreign climate for prolonged residence?" The Doctor among his other idiosyncrasies entertained an idea that England was the proper place for all Englishmen and Englishwomen who were not driven out of it by stress of pecuniary circumstances. "Has she got a bad throat or a weak chest?"

"It is not on the score of her own health that I propose to move her," said Mr. Greenmantle.

"You did say her comfort. Of course that may mean that she likes the French way of living. I did hear that we were to lose your services for a time, because you could not trust your own health."

"It is failing me a little, Dr. Freeborn. I am already very near sixty."

"Ten years my junior," said the Doctor.

"We cannot all hope to have such perfect health as you possess."

"I have never frittered it away," said the Doctor, "by prolonged residence in foreign parts." This quotation of his own words was most harassing to Mr. Greenmantle, and made him more than once inclined to bounce in anger out of the Doctor's study. "I suppose the truth is that Miss Emily is disposed to run counter to your wishes in regard to her marriage, and that she is to be taken away not from consumption or a weak throat, but from a dangerous lover." Here Mr. Greenmantle's face became black as thunder. "You see, Greenmantle, there is no good in our talking about this matter unless we understand each other."

"I do not intend to give my girl to the young man upon whom she thinks that her affections rest."

"I suppose she knows."

"No, Dr. Freeborn. It is often the case that a young lady does not know; she only fancies, and where that is the case absence is the best remedy. You have said that Emily is a good girl."

"A very good girl."

"I am delighted to hear you so express yourself. But obedience to parents is a trait in character which is generally much thought of. I have put by a little money, Dr. Freeborn."

"All Plumplington knows that."

"And I shall choose that it shall go somewhat in accordance with my wishes. The young man of whom she is thinking— "

"Philip Hughes, an excellent fellow. I've known him all my life. He doesn't come to church quite so regularly as he ought, but that will be mended when he's married."

"Hasn't got a shilling in the world," continued Mr. Greenmantle, finishing his sentence. "Nor is he—just,—just—just what I should choose for the husband of my daughter. I think that when I have said so he should take my word for it."

"That's not the way of the world, you know."

"It's the way of my world, Dr. Freeborn. It isn't often that I speak out, but when I do it's about something that I've a right to speak of. I've heard this affair of my daughter talked about all over the town. There was one Mr. Peppercorn came to me— "

"One Mr. Peppercorn? Why, Hickory Peppercorn is as well known in Plumplington as the church-steeple."

"I beg your pardon, Dr. Freeborn; but I don't find any reason in that for his interfering about my daughter. I must say that I took it as a great piece of impertinence. Goodness gracious me! If a man's own daughter isn't to be considered peculiar to himself I don't know what is. If he'd asked you about your daughters,—before they were married?" Dr. Freeborn did not answer this, but declared to himself that neither Mr. Peppercorn nor Mr. Greenmantle could have taken such a liberty. Mr. Greenmantle evidently was not aware of it, but in truth Dr. Freeborn and his family belonged altogether to another set. So at least Dr. Freeborn told himself. "I've come to you now, Dr. Freeborn, because I have not liked to leave Plumplington for a prolonged residence in foreign parts without acquainting you."

"I should have thought that unkind."

"You are very good. And as my daughter will of course go with me, and as this idea of a marriage on her part must be entirely given up;— " the emphasis was here placed with much weight on the word entirely;—"I should take it as a great kindness if you would let my feelings on the subject be generally known. I will own that I should not have cared to have my daughter talked about, only that the mischief has been done."

"In a little place like this," said the Doctor, "a young lady's marriage will always be talked about."

"But the young lady in this case isn't going to be married."

"What does she say about it herself?"

"I haven't asked her, Dr. Freeborn. I don't mean to ask her. I shan't ask her."

"If I understand her feelings, Greenmantle, she is very much set upon it."

"I cannot help it."

"You mean to say then that you intend to condemn her to unhappiness merely because this young man hasn't got as much money at the beginning of his life as you have at the end of yours?"

"He hasn't got a shilling," said Mr. Greenmantle.

"Then why can't you give him a shilling? What do you mean to do with your money?" Here Mr. Greenmantle again looked offended. "You come and ask me, and I am bound to give you my opinion for what it's worth. What do you mean to do with your money? You're not the man to found a Hiram's Hospital with it. As sure as you are sitting there your girl will have it when you're dead. Don't you know that she will have it?"

"I hope so."

"And because she's to have it, she's to be made wretched about it all her life. She's to remain an old maid, or else to be married to some well-born pauper, in order that you may talk about your son-in-law. Don't get into a passion, Greenmantle, but only think whether I'm not telling you the truth. Hughes isn't a spendthrift."

"I have made no accusation against him."

"Nor a gambler, nor a drunkard, nor is he the sort of man to treat a wife badly. He's there at the bank so that you may keep him under your own eye. What more on earth can a man want in a son-in-law?"

Blood, thought Mr. Greenmantle to himself; an old family name; county associations, and a certain something which he felt quite sure that Philip Hughes did not possess. And he knew well enough that Dr. Freeborn had married his own daughters to husbands who possessed these gifts; but he could not throw the fact back into the Rector's teeth. He was in some way conscious that the Rector had been entitled to expect so much for his girls, and that he, the banker, was not so entitled. The same idea passed through the Rector's mind. But the Rector knew how far the banker's courage would carry him. "Good night, Dr. Freeborn," said Mr. Greenmantle suddenly.

"Good night, Greenmantle. Shan't I see you again before you go?" To this the banker made no direct answer, but at once took his leave.

"That man is the greatest ass in all Plumplington," the Doctor said to his wife within five minutes of the time of which the hall door was closed behind the banker's back. "He's got an idea into his head about having some young county swell for his son-in-law."

"Harry Gresham. Harry is too idle to earn money by a profession, and therefore wants Greenmantle's money to live upon. There's Peppercorn wants something of the same kind for Polly. People are such fools." But Mrs. Freeborn's two daughters had been married much after the same fashion. They had taken husbands nearly as old as their father, because Dr. Freeborn and his wife had thought much of "blood."

On the next morning Philip Hughes was summoned by the banker into the more official of the two back parlours. Since he had presumed to signify his love for Emily, he had never been asked to enjoy the familiarity of the other chamber. "Mr. Hughes, you may probably have heard it asserted that I am about to leave Plumplington for a prolonged residence in foreign parts." Mr. Hughes had heard it and so declared. "Yes, Mr. Hughes, I am about to proceed to the south of France. My daughter's health requires attention,—and indeed on my own behalf I am in need of some change as well. I have not as yet officially made known my views to the Directors."

"There will be, I should think, no impediment with them."

"I cannot say. But at any rate I shall go. After forty years of service in the Bank I cannot think of allowing the peculiar views of men who are all younger than myself to interfere with my comfort. I shall go."

"I suppose so, Mr. Greenmantle."

"I shall go. I say it without the slightest disrespect for the Board. But I shall go."

"Will it be permanent, Mr. Greenmantle?"

"That is a question which I am not prepared to answer at a moment's notice. I do not propose to move my furniture for six months. It would not, I believe, be within the legal power of the Directors to take possession of the Bank house for that period."

"I am quite sure they would not wish it."

"Perhaps my assurance on that subject may be of more avail. At any rate they will not remove me. I should not have troubled you on this subject were it not that your position in the Bank must be affected more or less."

"I suppose that I could do the work for six months," said Philip Hughes.

But this was a view of the case which did not at all suit Mr. Greenmantle's mind. His own duties at Plumplington had been, to his thinking, the most important ever confided to a Bank Manager. There was a peculiarity about Plumplington of which no one knew the intricate details but himself. The man did not exist who could do the work as he had done it. But still he had determined to go, and the work must be intrusted to some man of lesser competence. "I should think it probable," he said, "that some confidential clerk will be sent over from Barchester. Your youth, Mr. Hughes, is against you. It is not for me to say what line the Directors may determine to take."

"I know the people better than any one can do in Barchester."

"Just so. But you will excuse me if I say you may for that reason be the less efficient. I have thought it expedient, however, to tell you of my views. If you have any steps that you wish to take you can now take them."

Then Mr. Greenmantle paused, and had apparently brought the meeting to an end. But there was still something which he wished to say. He did think that by a word spoken in due season,—by a strong determined word, he might succeed in putting an end to this young man's vain and ambitious hopes. He did not wish to talk to the young man about his daughter; but, if the strong word might avail here was the opportunity. "Mr. Hughes," he began.

"Yes, sir."

"There is a subject on which perhaps it would be well that I should be silent." Philip, who knew the manager thoroughly, was now aware of what was coming, and thought it wise that he should say nothing at the moment. "I do not know that any good can be done by speaking of it." Philip still held his tongue. "It is a matter no doubt of extreme delicacy,—of the most extreme delicacy I may say. If I go abroad as I intend, I shall as a matter of course take with me—Miss Greenmantle."

"I suppose so."

"I shall take with me—Miss Greenmantle. It is not to be supposed that when I go abroad for a prolonged sojourn in foreign parts, that I should leave—Miss Greenmantle behind me."

"No doubt she will accompany you."

"Miss Greenmantle will accompany me. And it is not improbable that my prolonged residence may in her case be—still further prolonged. It may be possible that she should link her lot in life to some gentleman whom she may meet in those realms."

"I hope not," said Philip.

"I do not think that you are justified, Mr. Hughes, in hoping anything in reference to my daughter's fate in life."

"All the same, I do."

"It is very,—very,—! I do not wish to use strong language, and therefore I will not say impertinent."

"What am I to do when you tell me that she is to marry a foreigner?"

"I never said so. I never thought so. A foreigner! Good heavens! I spoke of a gentleman whom she might chance to meet in those realms. Of course I meant an English gentleman."

The truth is, Mr. Greenmantle, I don't want your daughter to marry anyone unless she can marry me."

"A most selfish proposition."

"It's a sort of matter in which a man is apt to be selfish, and it's my belief that if she were asked she'd say the same thing. Of course you can take her abroad and you can keep her there as long as you please."

"I can;—and I mean to do it."

"I am utterly powerless to prevent you, and so is she. In this contention between us I have only one point in my favour."

"You have no point in your favour, sir."

"The young lady's good wishes. If she be not on my side,—why then I am nowhere. In that case you needn't trouble yourself to take her out of Plumplington. But if— "

"You may withdraw, Mr. Hughes," said the banker. "The interview is over." Then Philip Hughes withdrew, but as he went he shut the door after him in a very confident manner.

Chapter VI

The Young Ladies Are To Be Taken Abroad.

How should Philip Hughes see Emily before she had been carried away to "foreign parts" by her stern father? As he regarded the matter it was absolutely imperative that he should do so. If she should be made to go, in her father's present state of mind, without having reiterated her vows, she might be persuaded by that foreign-living English gentleman whom she would find abroad, to give him her hand. Emily had no doubt confessed her love to Philip, but she had not done so in that bold unshrinking manner which had been natural to Polly Peppercorn. And her lover felt it to be incumbent upon him to receive some renewal of her assurance before she was taken away for a prolonged residence abroad. But there was a difficulty as to this. If he were to knock at the door of the private house and ask for Miss Greenmantle, the servant, though she was in truth Philip's friend in the matter, would not dare to show him up. The whole household was afraid of Mr. Greenmantle, and would receive any hint that his will was to be set aside with absolute dismay. So Philip at last determined to take the bull by the horns and force his way into the drawing-room. Mr. Greenmantle could not be made more hostile than he was; and then it was quite on the cards, that he might be kept in ignorance of the intrusion. When therefore the banker was sitting in his own more private room, Philip passed through from the bank into the house, and made his way up-stairs with no one to announce him.

With no one to announce him he passed straight through into the drawing-room, and found Emily sitting very melancholy over a half-knitted stocking. It had been commenced with an idea that it might perhaps be given to Philip, but as her father's stern severity had been announced, she had given up that fond idea, and had increased the size, so as to fit them for the paternal feet. "Good gracious, Philip," she exclaimed, "how on earth did you get here?"

"I came up-stairs from the bank."

"Oh, yes; of course. But did you not tell Mary that you were coming?"

"I should never have been let up had I done so. Mary has orders not to let me put my foot within the house."

"You ought not to have come; indeed you ought not."

"And I was to let you go abroad without seeing you! Was that what

I ought to have done? It might be that I should never see you again. Only think of what my condition must be."

"Is not mine twice worse?"

"I do not know. If it be twice worse than mine then I am the happiest man in all the world."

"Oh, Philip, what do you mean?"

"If you will assure me of your love— "

"I have assured you."

"Give me another assurance, Emily," he said, sitting down beside her on the sofa. But she started up quickly to her feet. "When you gave me the assurance before, then—then— "

"One assurance such as that ought to be quite enough."

"But you are going abroad."

"That can make no difference."

"Your father says, that you will meet there some Englishman who will— "

"My father knows nothing about it. I shall meet no Englishman, and no foreigner; at least none that I shall care about. You oughtn't to get such an idea into your head."

"That's all very well, but how am I to keep such ideas out? Of course there will be men over there; and if you come across some idle young fellow who has not his bread to earn as I do, won't it be natural that you should listen to him?"

"No; it won't be natural."

"It seems to me to be so. What have I got that you should continue to care for me?"

"You have my word, Philip. Is that nothing?" She had now seated herself on a chair away from the sofa, and he, feeling at the time some special anxiety to get her into his arms, threw himself down on his knees before her, and seized her by both her hands. At that moment the door of the drawing-room was opened, and Mr. Greenmantle appeared within the room. Philip Hughes could not get upon his feet quick enough to return the furious anger of the look which was thrown on him. There was a difficulty even in disembarrassing himself of poor Emily's hands; so that she, to her father, seemed to be almost equally a culprit with the young man. She uttered a slight scream, and then he very gradually rose to his legs.

"Emily," said the angry father, "retire at once to your chamber."

"But, papa, I must explain."

"Retire at once to your chamber, miss. As for this young man, I do not know whether the laws of his country will not punish him for this intrusion."

Emily was terribly frightened by this allusion to her country's laws. "He has done nothing, papa; indeed he has done nothing."

"His very presence here, and on his knees! Is that nothing? Mr. Hughes, I desire that you will retire. Your presence in the bank is required. I lay upon you my strict order never again to presume to come through that door. Where is the servant who announced you?"

"No servant announced me."

"And did you dare to force your way into my private house, and into my daughter's presence unannounced? It is indeed time that I should take her abroad to undergo a prolonged residence in some foreign parts. But the laws of the country which you have outraged will punish you. In the meantime why do you not withdraw? Am I to be obeyed?"

"I have just one word which I wish to say to Miss Greenmantle."

"Not a word. Withdraw! I tell you, sir, withdraw to the bank. There your presence is required. Here it will never be needed."

"Good-bye, Emily," he said, putting out his hand in his vain attempt to take hers.

"Withdraw, I tell you." And Mr. Greenmantle, with all the stiffness of the poker apparent about him, backed poor young Philip Hughes through the doorway on to the staircase, and then banged the door behind him. Having done this, he threw himself on to the sofa, and hid his face with his hands. He wished it to be understood that the honour of his family had been altogether disgraced by the lightness of his daughter's conduct.

But his daughter did not see the matter quite in the same light. Though she lacked something of that firmness of manner which Polly Peppercorn was prepared to exhibit, she did not intend to be altogether trodden on. "Papa," she said, "why do you do that?"

"Good heavens!"

"Why do you cover up your face?"

"That a daughter of mine should have behaved so disgracefully!"

"I haven't behaved disgracefully, papa."

"Admitting a young man surreptitiously to my drawing-room!"

"I didn't admit him; he walked in."

"And on his knees! I found him on his knees."

"I didn't put him there. Of course he came,—because,—because— "

"Because what?" he demanded.

"Because he is my lover. I didn't tell him to come; but of course he wanted to see me before we went away."

"He shall see you no more."

"Why shouldn't he see me? He's a very good young man, and I am very fond of him. That's just the truth."

"You shall be taken away for a prolonged residence in foreign parts before another week has passed over your head."

"Dr. Freeborn quite approves of Mr. Hughes," pleaded Emily. But the plea at the present moment was of no avail. Mr. Greenmantle in his present frame of mind was almost as angry with Dr. Freeborn as with Emily or Philip Hughes. Dr. Freeborn was joined in this frightful conspiracy against him.

"I do not know," said he grandiloquently, "that Dr. Freeborn has any right to interfere with the private affairs of my family. Dr. Freeborn is simply the Rector of Plumplington,—nothing more."

"He wants to see the people around him all happy," said Emily.

"He won't see me happy," said Mr. Greenmantle with awful pride.

"He always wishes to have family quarrels settled before Christmas."

"He shan't settle anything for me." Mr. Greenmantle, as he so expressed himself, determined to maintain his own independence. "Why is he to interfere with my family quarrels because he's the Rector of Plumplington? I never heard of such a thing. When I shall have taken up my residence in foreign parts he will have no right to interfere with me."

"But, papa, he will be my clergyman all the same."

"He won't be mine, I can tell him that. And as for settling things by Christmas, it is all nonsense. Christmas, except for going to church and taking the Sacrament, is no more than any other day."

"Oh, papa!"

"Well, my dear, I don't quite mean that. What I do mean is that Dr. Freeborn has no more right to interfere with my family at this time of the year than at any other. And when you're abroad, which you will be before Christmas, you'll find that Dr. Freeborn will have nothing to say to you there."

"You had better begin to pack up at once," he said on the following day.

"Pack up?"

"Yes, pack up. I shall take you first to London, where you will stay for a day or two. You will go by the afternoon train to-morrow."

"To-morrow!"

"I will write and order beds to-day."

"But where are we to go?"

"That will be made known to you in due time," said Mr. Greenmantle.

"But I've got no clothes," said Emily.

"France is a land in which ladies delight to buy their dresses."

"But I shall want all manner of things,—boots and underclothing,—and—and linen, papa."

"They have all those things in France."

"But they won't fit me. I always have my things made to fit me. And I haven't got any boxes."

"Boxes! what boxes? work-boxes?"

"To put my things in. I can't pack up unless I've got something to pack them in. As to going to-morrow, papa, it's quite impossible. Of course there are people I must say good-bye to. The Freeborns— "

"Not the slightest necessity," said Mr. Greenmantle. "Dr. Freeborn will quite understand the reason. As to boxes, you won't want the boxes till you've bought the things to put in them."

"But, papa, I can't go without taking a quantity of things with me. I can't get everything new; and then I must have my dresses made to fit me." She was very lachrymose, very piteous, and full of entreaties; but still she knew what she was about. As the result of the interview, Mr. Greenmantle did almost acknowledge that they could not depart for a prolonged residence abroad on the morrow.

Early on the following morning Polly Peppercorn came to call. For the last month she had stuck to her resolution,—that she and Miss Greenmantle belonged to different sets in society, and could not be brought together, as Polly had determined to wear her second-rate dresses in preparation for a second-rate marriage,—and this visit was supposed to be something altogether out of the way. It was clearly a visit with a cause, as it was made at eleven o'clock in the morning. "Oh, Miss Greenmantle," she said, "I hear that you're going away to France,—you and your papa, quite at once."

"Who has told you?"

"Well, I can't quite say; but it has come round through Dr. Freeborn." Dr. Freeborn had in truth told Mr. Peppercorn, with the express view of exercising what influence he possessed so as to prevent the rapid emigration of Mr. Greenmantle. And Mr. Peppercorn had told his daughter, threatening her that something of the same kind would have to happen in his own family if she proved obstinate about her lover. "It's the best thing going," said Mr. Peppercorn, "when a girl is upsetting and determined to have her own way." To this Polly made no reply, but came away early on the following morning, so as to converse with her late friend, Miss Greenmantle.

"Papa says so; but you know it's quite impossible."

"What is Mr. Hughes to do?" asked Polly in a whisper.

"I don't know what anybody is to do. It's dreadful, the idea of going away from home in this sudden manner."

"Indeed it is."

"I can't do it. Only think, Polly, when I talk to him about clothes he tells me I'm to buy dresses in some foreign town. He knows nothing about a woman's clothes;—nor yet a man's for the matter of that. Fancy starting to-morrow for six months. It's the sort of thing that Ida Pfeiffer used to do."

"I didn't know her," said Polly.

"She was a great traveller, and went about everywhere almost without anything. I don't know how she managed it, but I'm sure that I can't."

"Dr. Freeborn says that he thinks it's all nonsense." As Polly said this she shook her head and looked uncommonly wise. Emily, however, made no immediate answer. Could it be true that Dr. Freeborn had thus spoken of her father? Emily did think that it was all nonsense, but she had not yet brought herself to express her thoughts openly. "To tell the truth, Miss Greenmantle," continued Polly, "Dr. Freeborn thinks that Mr. Hughes ought to be allowed to have his own way." In answer to this Emily could bring herself to say nothing; but she declared to herself that since the beginning of things Dr. Freeborn had always been as near an angel as any old gentleman could be. "And he says that it's quite out of the question that you should be carried off in this way."

"I suppose I must do what papa tells me."

"Well; yes. I don't know quite about that. I'm all for doing everything that papa likes, but when he talks of taking me to France, I know I'm not going. Lord love you, he couldn't talk to anybody there." Emily began to remember that her father's proficiency in the French language was not very great. "Neither could I for the matter of that," continued Polly. "Of course, I learned it at school, but when one can only read words very slowly one can't talk them at all. I've tried it, and I know it. A precious figure father and I would make finding our way about France."

"Does Mr. Peppercorn think of going?" asked Emily.

"He says so;—if I won't drop Jack Hollycombe. Now I don't mean to drop Jack Hollycombe; not for father nor for anyone. It's only Jack himself can make me do that."

"He won't, I suppose."

"I don't think he will. Now it's absurd, you know, the idea of our papas both carrying us off to France because we've got lovers in Plumplington. How all the world would laugh at them! You tell your papa what my papa is saying, and Dr. Freeborn thinks that that will prevent him. At any rate, if I were you, I wouldn't go and buy anything in a hurry. Of course, you've got to think of what would do for married life."

"Oh, dear, no!" exclaimed Emily.

"At any rate I should keep my mind fixed upon it. Dr. Freeborn says that there's no knowing how things may turn out." Having finished the purport of her embassy, Polly took her leave without even having offered one kiss to her friend.

Dr. Freeborn had certainly been very sly in instigating Mr. Peppercorn to proclaim his intention of following the example of his neighbour the banker. "Papa," said Emily when her father came in to luncheon, "Mr. Peppercorn is going to take his daughter to foreign parts."

"What for?"

"I believe he means to reside there for a time."

"What nonsense! He reside in France! He wouldn't know what to do with himself for an hour. I never heard anything like it. Because I am going to France is all Plumplington to follow me? What is Mr. Peppercorn's reason for going to France?" Emily hesitated; but Mr. Greenmantle pressed the question, "What object can such a man have?"

"I suppose it's about his daughter," said Emily. Then the truth flashed upon Mr. Greenmantle's mind, and he became aware that he must at any rate for the present abandon the idea. Then, too, there came across him some vague notion that Dr. Freeborn had instigated Mr. Peppercorn and an idea of the object with which he had done so.

"Papa," said Emily that afternoon, "am I to get the trunks I spoke about?"

"What trunks?"

"To put my things in, papa. I must have trunks if I am to go abroad for any length of time. And you will want a large portmanteau. You would get it much better in London than you would at Plumplington." But here Mr. Greenmantle told his daughter that she need not at present trouble her mind about either his travelling gear or her own.

A few days afterwards Dr. Freeborn sauntered into the bank, and spoke a few words to the cashier across the counter. "So Mr. Greenmantle, I'm told, is not going abroad," said the Rector.

"I've heard nothing more about it," said Philip Hughes.

"I think he has abandoned the idea. There was Hickory Peppercorn thinking of going, too, but he has abandoned it. What do they want to go travelling about France for?"

"What indeed, Dr. Freeborn;—unless the two young ladies have something to say to it."

"I don't think they wish it, if you mean that."

"I think their fathers thought of taking them out of harm's way."

"No doubt. But when the harm's way consists of a lover it's very hard to tear a young lady away from it." This was said so that Philip only could hear it. The two lads who attended the bank were away at their desks in distant parts of the office. "Do you keep your eyes open, Philip," said the Rector, "and things will run smoother yet than you expected."

"He is frightfully angry with me, Dr. Freeborn. I made my way up into the drawing-room the other day, and he found me there."

"What business had you to do that?"

"Well, I was wrong, I suppose. But if Emily was to be taken away suddenly I had to see her before she went. Think, Doctor, what a prolonged residence in a foreign country means. I mightn't see her again for years."

"And so he found you up in the drawing-room. It was very improper; that's all I can say. Nevertheless, if you'll behave yourself, I shouldn't be surprised if things were to run smoother before Christmas." Then the Doctor took his leave.

"Now, father," said Polly, "you're not going to carry me off to foreign parts."

"Yes, I am. As you're so wilful it's the only thing for you."

"What's to become of the brewery?"

"The brewery may take care of itself. As you won't want the money for your husband there'll be plenty for me. I'll give it up. I ain't going to slave and slave all my life and nothing come of it. If you won't oblige me in this the brewery may go and take care of itself."

"If you're like that, father, I must take care of myself. Mr. Greenmantle isn't going to take his daughter over."

"Yes; he is."

"Not a bit of it. He's as much as told Emily that she's not to get her things ready." Then there was a pause, during which Mr. Peppercorn showed that he was much disturbed. "Now, father, why don't you give way, and show yourself what you always were,—the kindest father that ever a girl had."

"There's no kindness in you, Polly. Kindness ought to be reciprocal."

"Isn't it natural that a girl should like her young man?"

"He's not your young man."

"He's going to be. What have you got to say against him? You ask Dr. Freeborn."

"Dr. Freeborn, indeed! He isn't your father!"

"He's not my father, but he's my friend. And he's yours, if you only knew it. You think of it, just for another day, and then say that you'll be good to your girl." Then she kissed him, and as she left him she felt that she was about to prevail.

Chapter VII

The Young Ladies Are To Remain At Home.

MISS EMILY Greenmantle had always possessed a certain character for delicacy. We do not mean delicacy of sentiment. That of course belonged to her as a young lady,—but delicacy of health. She was not strong and robust, as her friend Polly Peppercorn. When we say that she possessed that character, we intend to imply that she perhaps made a little use of it. There had never been much the matter with her, but she had always been a little delicate. It seemed to suit her, and prevented the necessity of over-exertion. Whereas Polly, who had never been delicate, felt herself always called upon to "run round," as the Americans say. "Running round" on the part of a young lady implies a readiness and a willingness to do everything that has to be done in domestic life. If a father wants his slippers or a mother her thimble, or the cook a further supply of sauces, the active young lady has to "run round." Polly did run round; but Emily was delicate and did not. Therefore when she did not get up one morning, and complained of a headache, the doctor was sent for. "She's not very strong, you know," the doctor said to her father. "Miss Emily always was delicate."

"I hope it isn't much," said Mr. Greenmantle.

"There is something I fear disturbing the even tenor of her thoughts," said the doctor, who had probably heard of the hopes entertained by Mr. Philip Hughes and favoured them. "She should be kept quite quiet. I wouldn't prescribe much medicine, but I'll tell Mixet to send her in a little draught. As for diet she can have pretty nearly what she pleases. She never had a great appetite." And so the doctor went his way. The reader is not to suppose that Emily Greenmantle intended to deceive her father, and play the old soldier. Such an idea would have been repugnant to her nature. But when her father told her that she was to be taken abroad for a prolonged residence, and when it of course followed that her lover was to be left behind, there came upon her a natural feeling that the best thing for her would be to lie in bed, and so to avoid all the troubles of life for the present moment.

"I am very sorry to hear that Emily is so ill," said Dr. Freeborn, calling on the banker further on in the day.

"I don't think it's much, Dr. Freeborn."

"I hope not; but I just saw Miller, who shook his head. Miller never shakes his head quite for nothing."

In the evening Mr. Greenmantle got a little note from Mrs. Freeborn. "I am *so unhappy* to hear about *dear* Emily. The poor child always is *delicate*. *Pray* take care of her. She must see Dr. Miller twice every day. Changes do take place so *frequently*. If you think she would be better here, we would be *delighted* to have her. There is so much in having the attention of a *lady*."

"Of course I am nervous," said Mr. Philip Hughes next morning to the banker. "I hope you will excuse me, if I venture to ask for one word as to Miss Greenmantle's health."

"I am very sorry to hear that Miss Greenmantle has been taken so poorly," said Mr. Peppercorn, who met Mr. Greenmantle in the street. "It is not very much, I have reason to hope," said the father, with a look of anger. Why should Mr. Peppercorn be solicitous as to his daughter?

"I am told that Dr. Miller is rather alarmed." Then Polly called at the front door to make special inquiry after Miss Greenmantle's health.

Mr. Greenmantle wrote to Mrs. Freeborn thanking her for the offer, and expressing a hope that it might not be necessary to move Emily from her own bed. And he thanked all his other neighbours for the pertinacity of their inquiries,—feeling however all the while that there was something of a conspiracy being hatched against him. He did not quite think his daughter guilty, but in his answer made to the inquiry of Philip Hughes, he spoke as though he believed that the young man had been the instigator of it. When on the third day his daughter could not get up, and Mr. Miller had ordered a more potent draught, Mr. Greenmantle almost owned to himself that he had been beaten. He took a walk by himself and meditated on it. It was a cruel case. The money was his money, and the girl was his girl, and the young man was his clerk. He ought according to the rules of justice in the world to have had plenary power over them all. But it had come to pass that his power was nothing. What is a father to do when a young lady goes to bed and remains there? And how is a soft-hearted father to make any use of his own money when all his neighbours turn against him?

"Miss Greenmantle is to have her own way, father," Polly said to Mr. Peppercorn on one of these days. It was now the second week in December, and the whole ground was hard with frost. "Dr. Freeborn will be right after all. He never is much wrong. He declared that Emily would be given to Philip Hughes as a Christmas-box."

"I don't believe it a bit," said Mr. Peppercorn.

"It is so all the same. I knew that when she became ill her father wouldn't be able to stand his ground. There is no knowing what these delicate young ladies can do in that way. I wish I were delicate."

"You don't wish anything of the kind. It would be very wicked to wish yourself to be sickly. What should I do if you were running up a doctor's bill?"

"Pay it,—as Mr. Greenmantle does. You've never had to pay half-a-crown for a doctor for me, I don't know when."

"And now you want to be poorly."

"I don't think you ought to have it both ways, you know. How am I to frighten you into letting me have my own lover? Do you think that I am not as unhappy about him as Emily Greenmantle? There he is now going down to the brewery. You go after him and tell him that he shall have what he wants."

Mr. Peppercorn turned round and looked at her. "Not if I know," he said.

"Then I shall go to bed," said Polly, "and send for Dr. Miller to-morrow. I don't see why I'm not to have the same advantage as other girls. But, father, I wouldn't make you unhappy, and I wouldn't cost you a shilling I could help, and I wouldn't not wait upon you for anything. I wouldn't pretend to be ill,—not for Jack Hollycombe."

"I should find you out if you did."

"I wouldn't fight my battle except on the square for any earthly consideration. But, father— "

"What do you want of me?"

"I am broken-hearted about him. Though I look red in the face, and fat, and all that, I suffer quite as much as Emily Greenmantle. When I tell him to wait perhaps for years, I know I'm unreasonable. When a young man wants a wife, he wants one. He has made up his mind to settle down, and he doesn't expect a girl to bid him remain as he is for another four or five years."

"You've no business to tell him anything of the kind."

"When he asks me I have a business,—if it's true. Father!"

"Well!"

"It is true. I don't know whether it ought to be so, but it is true. I'm very fond of you."

"You don't show it."

"Yes, I am. And I think I do show it, for I do whatever you tell me. But I like him the best."

"What has he done for you?"

"Nothing;—not half so much as I have done for him. But I do like him the best. It's human nature. I don't take on to tell him so;—only once. Once I told him that I loved him better than all the rest,—and that if he chose to take my word for it, once spoken, he might have it. He did choose, and I'm not going to repeat it, till I tell him when I can be his own."

"He'll have to take you just as you stand."

"May be; but it will be worth while for him to wait just a little, till he shall see what you mean to do. What do you mean to do with it, father? We don't want it at once."

"He's not edicated as a gentleman should be."

"Are you?"

"No; but I didn't try to get a young woman with money. I made the money, and I've a right to choose the sort of son-in-law my daughter shall marry."

"No; never!" she said.

"Then he must take you just as you are; and I'll make ducks and drakes of the money after my own fashion. If you were married to-morrow what do you mean to live upon?"

"Forty shillings a week. I've got it all down in black and white."

"And when children come;—one after another, year by year."

"Do as others do. I'll go bail my children won't starve;—or his. I'd work for them down to my bare bones. But would you look on the while, making ducks and drakes of your money, or spending it at the pot-house, just to break the heart of your own child? It's not in you to do it. You'd have to alter your nature first. You speak of yourself as though you were strong as iron. There isn't a bit of iron about you;—but there's something a deal better. You are one of those men, father, who are troubled with a heart."

"You're one of those women," said he, "who trouble the world by their tongues." Then he bounced out of the house and banged the door.

He had seen Jack Hollycombe through the window going down to the brewery, and he now slowly followed the young man's steps. He went very slowly as he got to the entrance to the brewery yard, and there he paused for a while thinking over the condition of things. "Hang the fellow," he said to himself; "what on earth has he done that he should have it all his own way? I never had it all my way. I had to work for it;—and precious hard too. My wife had to cook the dinner with only just a slip of a girl to help her make the bed. If he'd been a gentleman there'd have been something in it. A gentleman expects to have things ready to his hand. But he's to walk into all my money just because he's good-looking. And then Polly tells me, that I can't help myself because I'm good-natured. I'll let her know whether I'm good-natured! If he wants a wife he must support a wife;—and he shall." But though Mr. Peppercorn stood in the doorway murmuring after his fashion he knew very well that he was about to lose the battle. He had come down the street on purpose to signify to Jack Hollycombe that he might go up and settle the day with Polly; and he himself in the midst of all his objurgations was picturing to himself the delight with which he would see Polly restored to her former mode of dressing. "Well, Mr. Hollycombe, are you here?"

"Yes, Mr. Peppercorn, I am here."

"So I perceive,—as large as life. I don't know what on earth you're doing over here so often. You're wasting your employers' time, I believe."

"I came over to see Messrs. Grist and Grindall's young man."

"I don't believe you came to see any young man at all."

"It wasn't any young woman, as I haven't been to your house, Mr. Peppercorn."

"What's the good of going to my house? There isn't any young woman there can do you any good." Then Mr. Peppercorn looked round and saw that there were others within hearing to whom the conversation might be attractive. "Do you come in here. I've got something to say to you." Then he led the way into his own little parlour, and shut the door. "Now, Mr. Hollycombe, I've got something to communicate."

"Out with it, Mr. Peppercorn."

"There's that girl of mine up there is the biggest fool that ever was since the world began."

"It's astonishing," said Jack, "what different opinions different people have about the same thing."

"I daresay. That's all very well for you; but I say she's a fool. What on earth can she see in you to make her want to give you all my money?"

"She can't do that unless you're so pleased."

"And she won't neither. If you like to take her, there she is."

"Mr. Peppercorn, you make me the happiest man in the world."

"I don't make you the richest;—and you're going to make yourself about the poorest. To marry a wife upon forty shillings a week! I did it myself, however,—upon thirty-five, and I hadn't any stupid old father-in-law to help me out. I'm not going to see her break her heart; and so you may go and tell her. But you needn't tell her as I'm going to make her any regular allowance. Only tell her to put on some decent kind of gown, before I come home to tea. Since all this came up the slut has worn the same dress she bought three winters ago. She thinks I didn't know it."

And so Mr. Peppercorn had given way; and Polly was to be allowed to flaunt it again this Christmas in silks and satins. "Now you'll give me a kiss," said Jack when he had told his tale.

"I've only got it on your bare word," she answered, turning away from him.

"Why; he sent me here himself; and says you're to put on a proper frock to give him his tea in."

"No."

"But he did."

"Then, Jack, you shall have a kiss. I am sure the message about the frock must have come from himself. Jack, are you not the happiest young man in all Plumplington?"

"How about the happiest young woman," said Jack.

"Well; I don't mind owning up. I am. But it's for your sake. I could have waited, and not have been a bit impatient. But it's so different with a man. Did he say, Jack, what he meant to do for you?"

"He swore that he would not give us a penny."

"But that's rubbish. I am not going to let you marry till I know what's fixed. Nor yet will I put on my silk frock."

"You must. He'll be sure to go back if you don't do that. I should risk it all now, if I were you."

"And so make a beggar of you. My husband shall not be dependent on any man,—not even on father. I shall keep my clothes on as I've got 'em till something is settled."

"I wouldn't anger him if I were you," said Jack cautiously.

"One has got to anger him sometimes, and all for his own good. There's the frock hanging up-stairs, and I'm as fond of a bit of finery as any girl. Well;—I'll put it on tonight because he has made something of a promise; but I'll not continue it till I know what he means to do for you. When I'm married my husband will have to pay for my clothes, and not father."

"I guess you'll pay for them yourself."

"No, I shan't. It's not the way of the world in this part of England. One of you must do it, and I won't have it done by father,—not regular. As I begin so I must go on. Let him tell me what he means to do and then we shall know how we're to live. I'm not a bit afraid of you and your forty shillings."

"My girl!" Here was some little attempt at embracing, which, however, Polly checked.

"There's no good in all that when we're talking business. I look upon it now that we're to be married as soon as I please. Father has given way as to that, and I don't want to put you off."

"Why no! You ought not to do that when you think what I have had to endure."

"If you had known the picture which father drew just now of what we should have to suffer on your forty shillings a week!"

"What did he say, Polly?"

"Never mind what he said. Dry bread would be the best of it. I don't care about the dry bread;—but if there is to be anything better it must be all fixed. You must have the money for your own."

"I don't suppose he'll do that."

"Then you must take me without the money. I'm not going to have him giving you a five-pound note at the time and your having to ask for it. Nor yet am I going to ask for it. I don't mind it now. And to give him his due, I never asked him for a sovereign but what he gave me two. He's very generous."

"Is he now?"

"But he likes to have the opportunity. I won't live in the want of any man's generosity,—only my husband's. If he chooses to do anything extra that'll be as he likes it. But what we have to live upon,—to pay for meat and coals and such like,—that must be your own. I'll put on the dress to-night because I won't vex him. But before he goes to bed he must be made to understand all that. And you must understand it too, Jack. As we mean to go on so must we begin!" The interview ended, however, in an invitation given to Jack to stay in Plumplington and eat his supper. He knew the road so well that he could drive himself home in the dark.

"I suppose I'd better let them have two hundred a year to begin with," said Peppercorn to himself, sitting alone in his little parlour. "But I'll keep it in my own hands. I'm not going to trust that fellow further than I can see him."

But on this point he had to change his mind before he went to bed. He was gracious enough to Jack as they were eating their supper, and insisted on having a hot glass of brandy and water afterwards,—all in honour of Polly's altered dress. But as soon as Jack was gone Polly explained her views of the case, and spoke such undoubted wisdom as she sat on her father's knee, that he was forced to yield. "I'll speak to Mr. Scribble about having it all properly settled." Now Mr. Scribble was the Plumplington attorney.

"Two hundred a year, father, which is to be Jack's own,—for ever. I won't marry him for less,—not to live as you propose."

"When I say a thing I mean it," said Peppercorn. Then Polly retired, having given him a final kiss.

About a fortnight after this Mr. Greenmantle came to the Rectory and desired to see Dr. Freeborn. Since Emily had been taken ill there had not been many signs of friendship between the Greenmantle and the Freeborn houses. But now there he was in the Rectory hall, and within five minutes had followed the Rectory footman into Dr. Freeborn's study. "Well, Greenmantle, I'm delighted to see you. How's Emily?"

Mr. Greenmantle might have been delighted to see the Doctor but he didn't look it. "I trust that she is somewhat better. She has risen from her bed to-day."

"I'm glad to hear that," said the Doctor.

"Yes; she got up yesterday, and to-day she seems to be restored to her usual health."

"That's good news. You should be careful with her and not let her trust too much to her strength. Miller said that she was very weak, you know."

"Yes; Miller has said so all through," said the father; "but I'm not quite sure that Miller has understood the case."

"He hasn't known all the ins and outs you mean,—about Philip Hughes." Here the Doctor smiled, but Mr. Greenmantle moved about uneasily as though the poker were at work. "I suppose Philip Hughes had something to do with her malady."

"The truth is—," began Mr. Greenmantle.

"What's the truth?" asked the Doctor. But Mr. Greenmantle looked as though he could not tell his tale without many efforts. "You heard what old Peppercorn has done with his daughter?—Settled £250 a year on her for ever, and has come to me asking me whether I can't marry them on Christmas Day. Why if they were to be married by banns there would not be time."

"I don't see why they shouldn't be married by banns," said Mr. Greenmantle, who amidst all these difficulties disliked nothing so much as that he should be put into the category with Mr. Peppercorn, or Emily with Polly Peppercorn.

"I say nothing about that. I wish everybody was married by banns. Why shouldn't they? But that's not to be. Polly came to me the next day, and said that her father didn't know what he was talking about."

"I suppose she expects a special licence like the rest of them," said Mr. Greenmantle.

"What the girls think mostly of is their clothes. Polly wouldn't mind the banns the least in the world; but she says she can't have her things ready. When a young lady talks about her things a man has to give up. Polly says that February is a very good month to be married in."

Mr. Greenmantle was again annoyed, and showed it by the knitting of his brow, and the increased stiffness of his head and shoulders. The truth may as well be told. Emily's illness had prevailed with him and he too had yielded. When she had absolutely refused to look at her chicken-broth for three consecutive days her father's heart had been stirred. For Mr. Greenmantle's character will not have been adequately described unless it be explained that the stiffness lay rather in the neck and shoulders than in the organism by which his feelings were conducted. He was in truth very like Mr. Peppercorn, though he would have been infuriated had he been told so. When he found himself alone after his defeat,—which took place at once when the chicken-broth had gone down untasted for the third time,—he was ungainly and ill-natured to look at. But he went to work at once to make excuses for Philip Hughes, and ended by assuring himself that he was a manly honest sort of fellow, who was sure to do well in his profession; and ended by assuring himself that it would be very comfortable to have his married daughter and her husband living with him. He at once saw Philip, and explained to him that he had certainly done very wrong in coming up to his drawing-room without leave. "There is an etiquette in those things which no doubt you will learn as you grow older." Philip thought that the etiquette wouldn't much matter as soon as he had married his wife. And he was wise enough to do no more than beg Mr. Greenmantle's pardon for the fault which he had committed. "But as I am informed by my daughter," continued Mr. Greenmantle, "that her affections are irrevocably settled upon you,"—here Philip could only bow,—"I am prepared to withdraw my opposition, which has only been entertained as long as I thought it necessary for my daughter's happiness. There need be no words now," he continued, seeing that Philip was about to speak, "but when I shall have made up my mind as to what it may be fitting that I shall do in regard to money, then I will see you again. In the meantime you're welcome to come into my drawing-room when it may suit you to pay your respects to Miss Greenmantle." It was speedily settled that the marriage should take place in February, and Mr. Greenmantle was now informed that Polly Peppercorn and Mr. Hollycombe were to be married in the same month!

He had resolved, however, after much consideration, that he would himself inform Dr. Freeborn that he had given way, and had now come for this purpose. There would be less of triumph to the enemy, and less of disgrace to himself, if he were to declare the truth. And there no longer existed any possibility of a permanent quarrel with the Doctor. The prolonged residence abroad had altogether gone to the winds. "I think I will just step over and tell the Doctor of this alteration in our plans." This he had said to Emily, and Emily had thanked him and kissed him, and once again had called him "her own dear papa." He had suffered greatly during the period of his embittered feelings, and now had his reward. For it is not to be supposed that when a man has swallowed a poker the evil results will fall only upon his companions. The process is painful also to himself. He cannot breathe in comfort so long as the poker is there.

"And so Emily too is to have her lover. I am delighted to hear it. Believe me she hasn't chosen badly. Philip Hughes is an excellent young fellow. And so we shall have the double marriage coming after all." Here the poker was very visible. "My wife will go and see her at once, and congratulate her; and so will I as soon as I have heard that she's got herself properly dressed for drawing-room visitors. Of course I may congratulate Philip."

"Yes, you may do that," said Mr. Greenmantle very stiffly.

"All the town will know all about it before it goes to bed to-night. It is better so. There should never be a mystery about such matters. Good-bye, Greenmantle, I congratulate you with all my heart."

Chapter VIII

Christmas-Day.

"Now I'll tell you what we'll do," said the Doctor to his wife a few days after the two marriages had been arranged in the manner thus described. It yet wanted ten days to Christmas, and it was known to all Plumplington that the Doctor intended to be more than ordinarily blithe during the present Christmas holidays. "We'll have these young people to dinner on Christmas-day, and their fathers shall come with them."

"Will that do, Doctor?" said his wife.

"Why should it not do?"

"I don't think that Mr. Greenmantle will care about meeting Mr. Peppercorn."

"If Mr. Peppercorn dines at my table," said the Doctor with a certain amount of arrogance, "any gentleman in England may meet him. What! not meet a fellow towns-man on Christmas-day and on such an occasion as this!"

"I don't think he'll like it," said Mrs. Freeborn.

"Then he may lump it. You'll see he'll come. He'll not like to refuse to bring Emily here especially, as she is to meet her betrothed. And the Peppercorns and Jack Hollycombe will be sure to come. Those sort of vagaries as to meeting this man and not that, in sitting next to one woman and objecting to another, don't prevail on Christmas-day, thank God. They've met already at the Lord's Supper, or ought to have met; and they surely can meet afterwards at the parson's table. And we'll have Harry Gresham to show that there is no ill-will. I hear that Harry is already making up to the Dean's daughter at Barchester."

"He won't care whom he meets," said Mrs. Freeborn. "He has got a position of his own and can afford to meet anybody. It isn't quite so with Mr. Greenmantle. But of course you can have it as you please. I shall be delighted to have Polly and her husband at dinner with us."

So it was settled and the invitations were sent out. That to the Peppercorns was despatched first, so that Mr. Greenmantle might be informed whom he would have to meet. It was conveyed in a note from Mrs. Freeborn to Polly, and came in the shape of an order rather than of a request. "Dr. Freeborn hopes that your papa and Mr. Hollycombe will bring you to dine with us on Christmas-day at six o'clock. We'll try and get Emily Greenmantle and her lover to meet you. You must come because the Doctor has set his heart upon it."

"That's very civil," said Mr. Peppercorn. "Shan't I get any dinner till six o'clock?"

"You can have lunch, father, of course. You must go."

"A bit of bread and cheese when I come out of church—just when I'm most famished! Of course I'll go. I never dined with the Doctor before."

"Nor did I; but I've drunk tea there. You'll find he'll make himself very pleasant. But what are we to do about Jack?"

"He'll come, of course."

"But what are we to do about his clothes?" said Polly. "I don't think he's got a dress coat; and I'm sure he hasn't a white tie. Let him come just as he pleases, they won't mind on Christmas-day as long as he's clean. He'd better come over and go to church with us; and then I'll see as to making him up tidy." Word was sent to say that Polly and her father and her lover would come, and the necessary order was at once despatched to Barchester.

"I really do not know what to say about it," said Mr. Greenmantle when the invitation was read to him. "You will meet Polly Peppercorn and her husband as is to be," Mrs. Freeborn had written in her note; "for we look on you and Polly as the two heroines of Plumplington for this occasion." Mr. Greenmantle had been struck with dismay as he read the words. Could he bring himself to sit down to dinner with Hickory Peppercorn and Jack Hollycombe; and ought he to do so? Or could he refuse the Doctor's invitation on such an occasion? He suggested at first that a letter should be prepared declaring that he did not like to take his Christmas dinner away from his own house. But to this Emily would by no means consent. She had plucked up her spirits greatly since the days of the chicken-broth, and was determined at the present moment to rule both her future husband and her father. "You must go, papa. I wouldn't not go for all the world."

"I don't see it, my dear; indeed I don't."

"The Doctor had been so kind. What's your objection, papa?"

"There are differences, my dear."

"But Dr. Freeborn likes to have them."

"A clergyman is very peculiar. The rector of a parish can always meet his own flock. But rank is rank you know, and it behoves me to be careful with whom I shall associate. I shall have Mr. Peppercorn slapping my back and poking me in the ribs some of these days. And moreover they have joined your name with that of the young lady in a manner that I do not quite approve. Though you each of you may be a heroine in your own way, you are not the two heroines of Plumplington. I do not choose that you shall appear together in that light."

"That is only his joke," said Emily.

"It is a joke to which I do not wish to be a party. The two heroines of Plumplington! It sounds like a vulgar farce."

Then there was a pause, during which Mr. Greenmantle was thinking how to frame the letter of excuse by which he would avoid the difficulty. But at last Emily said a word which settled him. "Oh, papa, they'll say that you were too proud, and then they'll laugh at you." Mr. Greenmantle looked very angry at this, and was preparing himself to use some severe language to his daughter. But he remembered how recently she had become engaged to be married, and he abstained. "As you wish it, we will go," he said. "At the present crisis of your life I would not desire to disappoint you in anything." So it happened that the Doctor's proposed guests all accepted; for Harry Gresham too expressed himself as quite delighted to meet Emily Greenmantle on the auspicious occasion.

"I shall be delighted also to meet Jack Hollycombe," Harry had said. "I have known him ever so long and have just given him an order for twenty quarters of oats."

They were all to be seen at the Parish Church of Plumplington on that Christmas morning;—except Harry Gresham, who, if he did so at all, went to church at Greshamsbury,—and the Plumplington world all looked at them with admiring eyes. As it happened the Peppercorns sat just behind the Greenmantles, and on this occasion Jack Hollycombe and Polly were exactly in the rear of Philip Hughes and Emily. Mr. Greenmantle as he took his seat observed that it was so, and his devotions were, we fear, disturbed by the fact. He walked up proudly to the altar among the earliest and most aristocratic recipients, and as he did so could not keep himself from turning round to see whether Hickory Peppercorn was treading on his kibes. But on the present occasion Hickory Peppercorn was very modest and remained with his future son-in-law nearly to the last.

At six o'clock they all met in the Rectory drawing-room. "Our two heroines," said the Doctor as they walked in, one just after the other, each leaning on her lover's arm. Mr. Greenmantle looked as though he did not like it. In truth he was displeased, but he could not help himself. Of the two young ladies Polly was by far the most self-possessed. As long as she had got the husband of her choice she did not care whether she were or were not called a heroine. And her father had behaved very well on that morning as to money. "If you come out like that, father," she had said, "I shall have to wear a silk dress every day." "So you ought," he said with true Christmas generosity. But the income then promised had been a solid assurance, and Polly was the best contented young woman in all Plumplington.

They all sat down to dinner, the Doctor with a bride on each side of him, the place of honour to his right having been of course accorded to Emily Greenmantle; and next to each young lady was her lover. Miss Greenmantle as was her nature was very quiet, but Philip Hughes made an effort and carried on, as best he could, a conversation with the Doctor. Jack Hollycombe till after pudding-time said not a word, and Polly tried to console herself through his silence by remembering that the happiness of the world did not depend upon loquacity. She herself said a little word now and again, always with a slight effort to bring

Jack into notice. But the Doctor with his keen power of observation understood them all, and told himself that Jack was to be a happy man. At the other end of the table Mr. Greenmantle and Mr. Peppercorn sat opposite to each other, and they too, till after pudding-time, were very quiet. Mr. Peppercorn felt himself to be placed a little above his proper position, and could not at once throw off the burden. And Mr. Greenmantle would not make the attempt. He felt that an injury had been done him in that he had been made to sit opposite to Hickory Peppercorn. And in truth the dinner party as a dinner party would have been a failure, had it not been for Harry Gresham, who, seated in the middle between Philip and Mr. Peppercorn, felt it incumbent upon him in his present position to keep up the rattle of the conversation. He said a good deal about the "two heroines," and the two heroes, till Polly felt herself bound to quiet him by saying that it was a pity that there was not another heroine also for him.

"I'm an unfortunate fellow," said Harry, "and am always left out in the cold. But perhaps I may be a hero too some of these days."

Then when the cloth had been removed,—for the Doctor always had the cloth taken off his table,—the jollity of the evening really began. The Doctor delighted to be on his legs on such an occasion and to make a little speech. He said that he had on his right and on his left two young ladies both of whom he had known and had loved throughout their entire lives, and now they were to be delivered over by their fathers, whom he delighted to welcome this Christmas-day at his modest board, each to the man who for the future was to be her lord and her husband. He did not know any occasion on which he, as a pastor of the church, could take greater delight, seeing that in both cases he had ample reason to be satisfied with the choice which the young ladies had made. The bridegrooms were in both instances of such a nature and had made for themselves such characters in the estimation of their friends and neighbours as to give all assurance of the happiness prepared for their wives. There was much more of it, but this was the gist of the Doctor's eloquence. And then he ended by saying that he would ask the two fathers to say a word in acknowledgment of the toast.

This he had done out of affection to Polly, whom he did not wish to distress by calling upon Jack Hollycombe to take a share in the speech-making of the evening. He felt that Jack would require a little practice before he could achieve comfort during such an operation; but the immediate effect was to plunge Mr. Greenmantle into a cold bath. What was he to say on such an opportunity? But he did blunder through, and gave occasion to none of that sorrow which Polly would have felt had Jack Hollycombe got upon his legs, and then been reduced to silence. Mr. Peppercorn in his turn made a better speech than could have been expected from him. He said that he was very proud of his position that day, which was due to his girl's manner and education. He was not entitled to be there by anything that he had done himself. Here the Doctor cried, "Yes, yes, yes, certainly." But Peppercorn shook his head. He wasn't specially proud of himself, he said, but he was awfully proud of his girl. And he thought that Jack Hollycombe was about the most fortunate young man of whom he had ever heard. Here Jack declared that he was quite aware of it.

After that the jollity of the evening commenced; and they were very jolly till the Doctor began to feel that it might be difficult to restrain the spirits which he had raised. But they were broken up before a very late hour by the necessity that Harry Gresham should return to Greshamsbury. Here we must bid farewell to the "two heroines of Plumplington," and to their young men, wishing them many joys in their new capacities. One little scene however must be described, which took place as the brides were putting on their hats in the Doctor's study. "Now I can call you Emily again," said Polly, "and now I can kiss you; though I know I ought to do neither the one nor the other."

"Yes, both, both, always do both," said Emily. Then Polly walked home with her father, who, however well satisfied he might have been in his heart, had not many words to say on that evening.

Not If I Know It

Originally appeared in *Life*, Christmas number, 1882. The publisher's agreement for this story is dated 9 August 1882, making it Trollope's last completed work of fiction.

NOT IF I know it." It was an ill-natured answer to give, made in the tone that was used, by a brother-in-law to a brother-in-law, in the hearing of the sister of the one and wife of the other,—made, too, on Christmas Eve, when the married couple had come as visitors to the house of him who made it! There was no joke in the words, and the man who had uttered them had gone for the night. There was to be no other farewell spoken indicative of the brightness of the coming day. "Not if I know it!" and the door was slammed behind him. The words were very harsh in the ears even of a loving sister.

"He was always a cur," said the husband.

"No; not so. George has his ill-humours and his little periods of bad temper; but he was not always a cur. Don't say so of him, Wilfred."

"He always was so to me. He wanted you to marry that fellow Cross because he had a lot of money."

"But I didn't," said the wife, who now had been three years married to Wilfred Horton.

"I cannot understand that you and he should have been children of the same parents. Just the use of his name, and there would be no risk."

"I suppose he thinks that there might have been risk," said the wife. "He cannot know you as I do."

"Had he asked me I would have given him mine without thinking of it. Though he knows that I am a busy man, I have never asked him to lend me a shilling. I never will."

"Wilfred!"

"All right, old girl—I am going to bed; and you will see that I shall treat him to-morrow just as though he had refused me nothing. But I shall think that he is a cur." And Wilfred Horton prepared to leave the room.

"Wilfred!"

"Well, Mary, out with it."

"Curs are curs— "

"Because other curs make them so; that is what you are going to say."

"No, dear, no; I will never call you a cur, because I know well that you are not one. There is nothing like a cur about you." Then she took him in her arms and kissed him. "But if there be any signs of ill-humour in a man, the way to increase it is to think much of it. Men are curs because other men think them so; women are angels sometimes, just because some loving husband like you tells them that they are. How can a woman not have something good about her when everything she does is taken to be good? I could be as cross as George is if only I were called cross. I don't suppose you want the use of his name so very badly."

"But I have condescended to ask for it. And then to be answered with that jeering pride! I wouldn't have his name to a paper now, though you and I were starving for the want of it. As it is, it doesn't much signify. I suppose you won't be long before you come." So saying, he took his departure.

She followed him, and went away through the house till she came to her brother's apartments. He was a bachelor, and was living all alone when he was in the country at Hallam Hall. It was a large, rambling house, in which there had been of custom many visitors at Christmas time. But Mrs. Wade, the widow, had died during the past year, and there was nobody there now but the owner of the house, and his sister, and his sister's husband. She followed him to his rooms, and found him sitting alone, with a pipe in his mouth, and as she entered she saw that preparations had been made for the comfort of more than one person. "If there be anything that I hate," said George Wade, "it is to be asked for the use of my name. I would sooner lend money to a fellow at once,—or give it to him."

"There is no question about money, George."

"Oh, isn't there? I never knew a man's name wanted when there was no question about money."

"I suppose there is a question—in some remote degree." Here George Wade shook his head. "In some remote degree," she went on repeating her words. "Surely you know him well enough not to be afraid of him."

"I know no man well enough not to be afraid of him where my name is concerned."

"You need not have refused him so crossly, just on Christmas Eve."

"I don't know much about Christmas where money is wanted."

"'Not if I know it!' you said."

"I simply meant that I did not wish to do it. Wilfred expects that everybody should answer him with such constrained courtesy! What I said was as good a way of answering him as any other; and if he didn't like it—he must lump it."

"Is that the message that you send him?" she asked.

"I don't send it as a message at all. If he wants a message you may tell him that I'm extremely sorry, but that it's against my principles. You are not going to quarrel with me as well as he?"

"Indeed, no," said she, as she prepared to leave him for the night. "I should be very unhappy to quarrel with either of you." Then she went.

"He is the most punctilious fellow living at this moment, I believe," said George Wade, as he walked alone up and down the room. There were certain regrets which did make the moment bitter to him. His brother-in-law had on the whole treated him well,—had been liberal to him in all those matters in which one brother comes in contact with another. He had never asked him for a shilling, or even for the use of his name. His sister was passionately devoted to her husband. In fact, he knew Wilfred Horton to be a fine fellow. He told himself that he had not meant to be especially uncourteous, but that he had been at the moment startled by the expression of Horton's wishes. But looking back over his own conduct, he could remember that in the course of their intimacy he himself had been occasionally rough to his brother-in-law, and he could remember that his brother-in-law had not liked it. "After all what does it mean, 'Not if I know it?' It is just a form of saying that I had rather not." Nevertheless, Wilfred Horton could not persuade himself to go to bed in a good humour with George Wade.

"I think I shall get back to London to-morrow," said Mr. Horton, speaking to his wife from beneath the bedclothes, as soon as she had entered the room.

"To-morrow?"

"It is not that I cannot bear his insolence, but that I should have to show by my face that I had made a request, and had been refused. You need not come."

"On Christmas Day?"

"Well, yes. You cannot understand the sort of flutter I am in. 'Not if I know it!' The insolence of the phrase in answering such a request! The suspicion that it showed! If he had told me that he had any feeling about it, I would have deposited the money in his hands. There is a train in the morning. You can stay here and go to church with him, while I run up to town."

"That you two should part like that on Christmas Day; you two dear ones! Wilfred, it will break my heart." Then he turned round and endeavoured to make himself comfortable among the bedclothes. "Wilfred, say that you will not go out of this to-morrow."

"Oh, very well! You have only to speak and I obey. If you could only manage to make your brother more civil for the one day it would be an improvement."

"I think he will be civil. I have been speaking to him, and he seems to be sorry that he should have annoyed you."

"Well, yes; he did annoy me. 'Not if I know it!' in answer to such a request! As if I had asked him for five thousand pounds! I wouldn't have asked him or any man alive for five thousand pence. Coming down to his house at Christmas-time, and to be suspected of such a thing!" Then he prepared himself steadily to sleep, and she, before she stretched herself by his side, prayed that God's mercy might obliterate the wrath between these men, whom she loved so well, before the morrow's sun should have come and gone.

The bells sounded merry from Hallam Church tower on the following morning, and told to each of the inhabitants of the old hall a tale that was varied according to the minds of the three inhabitants whom we know. With her it was all hope, but hope accompanied by that despondency which is apt to afflict the weak in the presence of those that are stronger. With her husband it was anger,—but mitigated anger. He seemed, as he came into his wife's room while dressing, to be aware that there was something which should be abandoned, but which still it did his heart some good to nourish. With George Wade there was more of Christian feeling, but of Christian feeling which it was disagreeable to entertain. "How on earth is a man to get on with his relatives, if he cannot speak a word above his breath?" But still he would have been very willing that those words should have been left unsaid.

Any observer might have seen that the three persons as they sat down to breakfast were each under some little constraint. The lady was more than ordinarily courteous, or even affectionate, in her manner. This was natural on Christmas Day, but her too apparent anxiety was hardly natural. Her husband accosted his brother-in-law with almost loud good humour. "Well, George, a merry Christmas, and many of them. My word;—how hard it froze last night! You won't get any hunting for the next fortnight. I hope old Burnaby won't spin us a long yarn."

George Wade simply kissed his sister, and shook hands with his brother-in-law. But he shook hands with more apparent zeal than he would have done but for the quarrel, and when he pressed Wilfred Horton to eat some devilled turkey, he did it with more ardour than was usual with him. "Mrs. Jones is generally very successful with devilled turkey." Then, as he passed round the table behind his sister's back, she put out her hand to touch him, and as though to thank him for his goodness. But any one could see that it was not quite natural.

The two men as they left the house for church, were thinking of the request that had been made yesterday, and which had been refused. "Not if I know it!" said George Wade to himself. "There is nothing so unnatural in that, that a fellow should think so much of it. I didn't mean to do it. Of course, if he had said that he wanted it particularly I should have done it."

"Not if I know it!" said Wilfred Horton. "There was an insolence about it. I only came to him just because he was my brother-in-law. Jones, or Smith, or Walker would have done it without a word." Then the three walked into church, and took their places in the front seat, just under Dr. Burnaby's reading-desk.

We will not attempt to describe the minds of the three as the Psalms were sung, and as the prayers were said. A twinge did cross the minds of the two men as the coming of the Prince of Peace was foretold to them; and a stronger hope did sink into the heart of her whose happiness depended so much on the manner in which they two stood with one another. And when Dr. Burnaby found time, in the fifteen minutes which he gave to his sermon, to tell his hearers why the Prophet had specially spoken of Christ as the Prince of Peace, and to describe what the blessings were, hitherto unknown, which had come upon the world since a desire for peace had filled the minds of men, a feeling did come on the hearts of both of them,—to one that the words had better not have been spoken, and to the other that they had better have been forgiven. Then came the Sacrament, more powerful with its thoughts than its words, and the two men as they left the church were ready in truth to forgive each other—if they only knew how.

There was something a little sheep-faced about the two men as they walked up together across the grounds to the old hall,—something sheep-faced which Mrs. Horton fully understood, and which made her feel for the moment triumphant over them. It is always so with a woman when she knows that she has for the moment got the better of a man. How much more so when she has conquered two? She hovered about among them as though they were dear human beings subject to the power of some beneficent angel. The three sat down to lunch, and Dr. Burnaby could not but have been gratified had he heard the things that were said of him. "I tell you, you know," said George, "that Burnaby is a right good fellow, and awfully clever. There isn't a man or woman in the parish that he doesn't know how to get to the inside of."

"And he knows what to do when he gets there," said Mrs. Horton, who remembered with affection the gracious old parson as he had blessed her at her wedding.

"No; I couldn't let him do it for me." It was thus Horton spoke to his wife as they were walking together about the gardens.

"Dear Wilfred, you ought to forgive him."

"I have forgiven him. There!" And he made a sign as of blowing his anger away to the winds. "I do forgive him. I will think no more about it. It is as though the words had never been spoken,—though they were very unkind. 'Not if I know it!' All the same, they don't leave a sting behind."

"But they do."

"Nothing of the kind. I shall drink prosperity to the old house and a loving wife to the master just as cheerily by and by as though the words had never been spoken."

"But there will not be peace,—not the peace of which Dr. Burnaby told us. It must be as though it had really—really never been uttered. George has not spoken to me about it, not to-day, but if he asks, you will let him do it?"

"He will never ask—unless at your instigation."

"I will not speak to him," she answered,—"not without telling you. I would never go behind your back. But whether he does it or not, I feel that it is in his heart to do it." Then the brother came up and joined them in their walk, and told them of all the little plans he had in hand in reference to the garden. "You must wait till *she* comes, for that, George," said his sister.

"Oh, yes; there must always be a she when another she is talking. But what will you say if I tell you there is to be a she?"

"Oh, George!"

"Your nose is going to be put out of joint, as far as Hallam Hall is concerned." Then he told them all his love story, and so the afternoon was allowed to wear itself away till the dinner hour had nearly come.

"Just come in here, Wilfred," he said to his brother-in-law when his sister had gone up to dress. "I have something I want to say to you before dinner."

"All right," said Wilfred. And as he got up to follow the master of the house, he told himself that after all his wife would prove herself too many for him.

"I don't know the least in the world what it was you were asking me to do yesterday."

"It was a matter of no consequence," said Wilfred, not able to avoid assuming an air of renewed injury.

"But I do know that I was cross," said George Wade.

"After that," said Wilfred, "everything is smooth between us. No man can expect anything more straightforward. I was a little hurt, but I know that I was a fool. Every man has a right to have his own ideas as to the use of his name."

"But that will not suffice," said George.

"Oh! yes it will."

"Not for me," repeated George. "I have brought myself to ask your pardon for refusing, and you should bring yourself to accept my offer to do it."

"It was nothing. It was only because you were my brother-in-law, and therefore the nearest to me. The Turco-Egyptian New Water-works Company simply requires somebody to assert that I am worth ten thousand pounds."

"Let me do it, Wilfred," said George Wade. "Nobody can know your circumstances better than I do. I have begged your pardon, and I think that you ought now in return to accept this at my hand."

"All right," said Wilfred Horton. "I will accept it at your hand." And then he went away to dress. What took place up in the dressing-room need not here be told. But when Mrs. Horton came down to dinner the smile upon her face was a truer index of her heart than it had been in the morning.

"I have been very sorry for what took place last night," said George afterwards in the drawing-room, feeling himself obliged, as it were, to make full confession and restitution before the assembled multitude,—which consisted, however, of his brother-in-law and his sister. "I have asked pardon, and have begged Wilfred to show his grace by accepting from me what I had before declined. I hope that he will not refuse me."

"Not if I know it," said Wilfred Horton.